MW00444619

HOLT

CALL TO FREEDOM

Beginnings to 1914

Sterling Stuckey ■ **Linda Kerrigan Salvucci**
Reading Consultant • Judith Irvin

Lincoln Charter School

Lincoln Charter School

HOLT, RINEHART AND WINSTON

A Harcourt Education Company

Austin • New York • Orlando • Atlanta • San Francisco • Boston • Dallas • Toronto • London

About the Authors

Sterling Stuckey is Professor of History and holds the Presidential Chair at the University of California, Riverside. Dr. Stuckey is the author of *Slave Culture: Nationalist Theory and the Foundations of Black America* and *Going Through the Storm: The Influence of African American Art in History*.

Linda Kerrigan Salvucci is Associate Professor of History at Trinity University, San Antonio, Texas. Dr. Salvucci is currently working on a book entitled *Ironies of Empire: The United States–Cuba Trade Under Spanish Rule*.

Editorial
Sue Miller, *Director*
Steven L. Hayes,
Executive Editor
Robert Wehnke,
Managing Editor
Rhonda Haynes,
Senior Editor

Pupil's Edition
Doug Sims,
Project Editor
Laura M. Shankland,
Associate Editor

Teacher's Edition
Kristie L. Kelly,
Associate Editor

Ancillaries
Jeffrey C. Herndon,
Associate Editor

Technology Resources
Rob Hrechko,
Internet Editor

Fact Checking
Bob Fullilove,
Editor
Jenny Rose,
Assistant Editor

Copy Editing
Julie Beckman,
Senior Copy Editor
Katelijne A. Lefevere,
Copy Editor

Support
Gina Tasby-Rogers,
Administrative Assistant
Sue Minkler,
Assistant Editorial Coordinator

Editorial Permissions
Ann B. Farrar,
Senior Permissions Editor

Art, Design, and Photo
Book Design
Diane Motz,
Senior Design Director
Christine Stanford,
Design Manager
Candace Moore,
Senior Designer
Lori Male,
Senior Designer
Cathy Jenevein,
Designer
Bob Prestwood,
Designer

Ed Diaz,
Design Associate

Image Acquisitions
Joe London, *Director*
Tim Taylor, *Photo Research Supervisor*
Andy Christiansen,
Photo Researcher
Stephanie Morris,
Photo Researcher
Michelle Rumpf,
Art Buyer Supervisor
Julie Kelly, *Art Buyer*

Technology Design
Susan Michael, *Design Director*
Kimberly Cammerata,
Design Manager
Grant Davidson, *Designer*

Media Design
Curtis Riker, *Design Director*
Richard Chavez, *Designer*

Graphic Services
Kristen Darby, *Manager*
Cathy Murphy,
Senior Image Designer
Linda Wilbourn,
Image Designer

Jane Dixon,
Image Designer
Jeff Robinson,
Senior Ancillary Designer

Design and Production
DECODE, Inc.

Prepress and Manufacturing
Gene Rumann,
Production Manager
Nancy Hargis,
Production Supervisor
Leanna Ford,
Production Coordinator
Cynthia Munoz,
Production Coordinator
Antonella Posterino,
Coordinator
Jevara Jackson,
Manufacturing Coordinator, Book
Rhonda Farris,
Inventory Planner
Kim Harrison,
Manufacturing Coordinator, Media

Cover photo: Wells Fargo Bank Historical Services

Copyright © 2003 by Holt, Rinehart and Winston

All rights reserved. No part of this publication may be reproduced or transmitted in any form or by any means, electronic or mechanical, including photocopy, recording, or any information storage and retrieval system, without permission in writing from the publisher.

Requests for permission to make copies of any part of the work should be mailed to the following address: Permissions Department, Holt, Rinehart and Winston, 10801 N. Mopac Expressway, Building 3, Austin, Texas 78759.

For acknowledgments, see page R76, which is an extension of the copyright page.

Copyright © 2000 **CNN** and **CNNfyi.com** are trademarks of Cable News Network LP, LLLP, a Time Warner Company. All rights reserved. Copyright © 2000 Turner Learning logos are trademarks of Turner Learning, Inc., a Time Warner Company. All rights reserved.

Printed in the United States of America

ISBN 0-03-065487-4

3 4 5 6 7 8 9 48 05 04 03

COVER: *The Concord Stagecoach, elegant but rugged, was built for Wells, Fargo & Co. by Abott-Downing Co. of Concord, New Hampshire. By 1866, Wells Fargo had the largest staging operation in the world.*

Content Reviewers

Dr. Richard Abbott
Eastern Michigan University
Reconstruction

Dr. Larry Conyers
University of Denver
Anthropology

Dr. R. Douglas Cope
Brown University
Colonial Latin America

Dr. Paul A. Gilje
University of Oklahoma
U.S., 1492–1865

Dr. Christopher Hendricks
Armstrong Atlantic State University
Early U.S.

Dr. Melvin Holli
University of Illinois at Chicago
U.S. urban and ethnic

Dr. Raymond Hyser
James Madison University
Gilded Age and Progressive Era

Dr. Elizabeth Jameson
University of New Mexico
American West and U.S. social

Dr. Beverly Jones
North Carolina Central University
Reconstruction

Dr. Yasuhide Kawashima
University of Texas at El Paso
Colonial and revolutionary America, American legal

Dr. F. Daniel Larkin
State University of New York-Oneonta
19th-century U.S.

Dr. Helen Nader
University of Arizona
Renaissance, Spain

Dr. Edward Peters
University of Pennsylvania
Medieval European

Dr. Jack Rakove
Stanford University
American Revolution, early American political

Dr. Leonard Richards
University of Massachusetts
Jacksonian America

Dr. Joel Silbey
Cornell University
19th-century U.S.

Dr. David Switzer
Plymouth State College
Civil War and Reconstruction

Dr. Jesús F. de la Teja
Southwest Texas State University
Spanish Borderlands

Dr. Patricia Tracy
Williams College
Colonial America

Dr. Clarence E. Walker
University of California at Davis
African American 1450–present

Dr. John R. Wunder
University of Nebraska
American West

Educational Reviewers

Anistacio Asuncion
Piedmont Middle School
San Jose, California

Michelle Bohanek
Orozco Academy
Chicago, Illinois

Jeri Goodspeed-Gross
Minnetonka Middle School West
Chaska, Minnesota

Cynthia Gore
Castillero Middle School
San Jose, California

Tom Harris
Oak Park Middle School
Leesburg, Florida

Valerie Hill
Gaston Middle School
Dallas, Texas

Robert Jones
Perry Junior High School
New Hartford, New York

Marilyn Kretzer
Johnston Middle School
Houston, Texas

Janie Maldanado
Lanier High School
Austin, Texas

Barbara Mayo
Program Facilitator
Austin Independent School District
Austin, Texas

Steve Munzel
Jane Lathrop Stanford Middle School
Palo Alto, California

Milt Perlman
Junior High School 185
Flushing, New York

Pat Tobbe
Newburg Middle School
Louisville, Kentucky

Helen Webb
Wynn Seale Middle School
Corpus Christi, Texas

George Wood
Gregory-Portland Junior High School
Portland, Texas

Field Test Teachers
Sandra Poe Borowiecki
New Hartford Perry Junior High School
New Hartford, New York

Mary Beth Breshears
Wood Middle School
Fort Leonard Wood, Missouri

Richard J. Giannicchi
West Seneca Junior High School
West Seneca, New York

Kim Gravell
Dripping Springs Middle School
Dripping Springs, Texas

Deborah K. Lofton
Charles F. Blackstock Junior High School
Port Hueneme, California

Stan Mendenhall
Broadmoor Junior High School
Pekin, Illinois

Daniel Murray
Hackett Middle School
Albany, New York

Martha Potter
John Jay Middle School
Katonah, New York

Linda B. Rothrock
Harlandale Middle School
San Antonio, Texas

Amy Thompson
Union Middle School
San Jose, California

Call to Freedom
Beginnings to 1914

CONTENTS

UNIT 1 American Beginnings

CHAPTER 1
The World before the Opening of the Atlantic

CHAPTER 2
The Age of Exploration

*Pottery made by
Native Americans*

Colonists build their first settlement in New England.

Benjamin Franklin

A cannon from the American Revolution

Washington's cabinet

*Images from Andrew Jackson's
campaign (right) and presidency (left)*

Sequoya

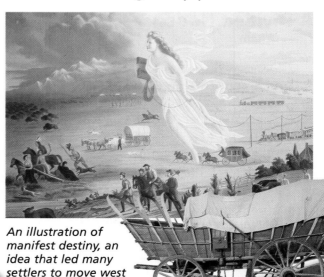

An illustration of
manifest destiny, an
idea that led many
settlers to move west

Abraham Lincoln

A fur-trading post built in 1834 and a pair of Sioux moccasins

Primary Sources

History Makers Speak

The bald eagle

Abigail Adams

Primary Sources, continued

Frederick Douglass

Primary Sources

Historical Documents

The Emancipation Proclamation

Political Cartoons

History and Your World

National Guard members helping a community

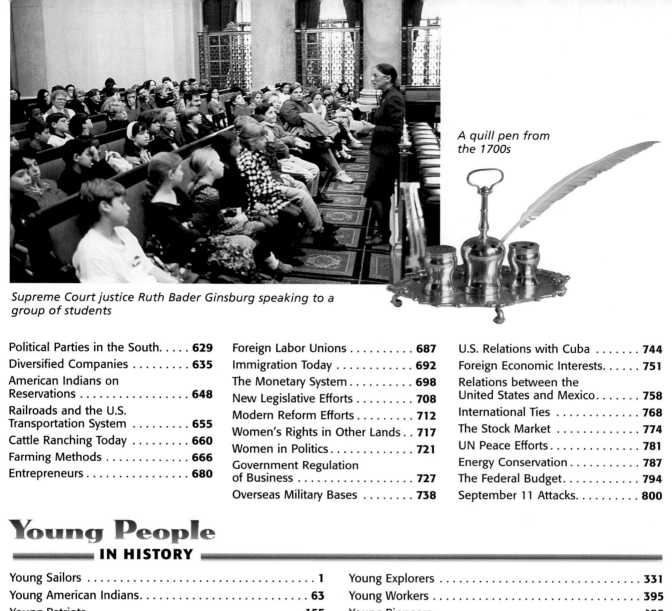

A quill pen from the 1700s

Supreme Court justice Ruth Bader Ginsburg speaking to a group of students

Young People
IN HISTORY

LINKING
PAST to ★ PRESENT ★

Citizenship ★★★★★
★★★★★ and You

Interdisciplinary Activities

CONNECTING TO Geography

CONNECTING TO THE ARTS

CONNECTING TO Literature

CONNECTING TO SCIENCE AND TECHNOLOGY

CONNECTING TO MATH

Historical Highlights

Early pioneers used wagons such as this one to settle the frontier.

THE GRANGER COLLECTION, NEW YORK

★★★★★★★★★★★★★ That's Interesting! ★★★★★★★★★★★★★

Daily Life

BIOGRAPHIES and PRESIDENTIAL PROFILES

GLOBAL CONNECTIONS

Technology Activities

Research on the R⊙M

internet connect go.hrw.com

Skill-Building Activities

Social Studies Skills WORKSHOPS

History in Action UNIT SIMULATIONS

Skill-Building Activities, continued

MAPS

An astrolabe

THE GRANGER COLLECTION, NEW YORK

GRAPHS AND CHARTS

TIME LINES ➡

VISUALIZING HISTORY

How to Use Your Textbook

Use the chapter opener to get an overview of the time period.

The Chapter Time Line shows you a comparison of U.S. and global events.

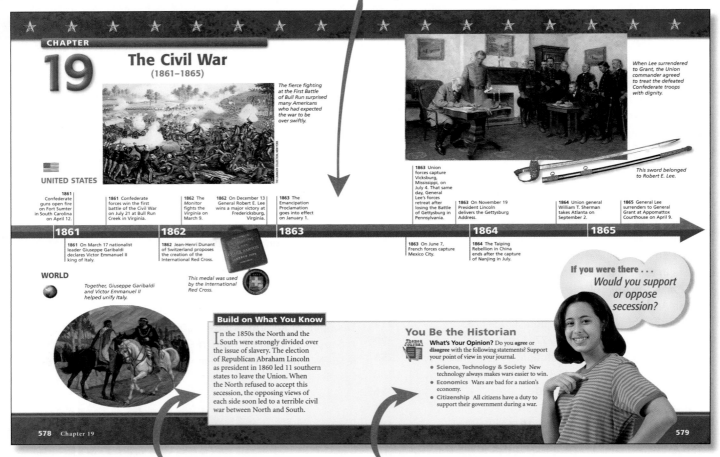

Build on What You Know bridges the material you have studied in previous chapters with the material you are about to begin. As you read the Build on What You Know feature, take a few minutes to think about the topics that might apply to the chapter you are starting.

You Be the Historian puts you in the place of a historian looking at the past. In this feature you will be asked to respond to three general statements about the chapter. Each statement is tied to one of the key themes of the program. You should respond based on your own knowledge and then record your responses in your journal. There are no right or wrong answers, just your informed opinion.

Use these built-in tools to read for ▦ understanding.

Read to Discover questions begin each section of *Call to Freedom.* These questions serve as your guide as you read through the section. Keep them in mind as you explore the section content.

Why It Matters Today is an exciting way for you to make connections between what you are reading in your history book and the world around you. In each section you will be invited to explore a topic that is relevant to our lives today by using **CNNfyi.com** connections.

Define and Identify terms are introduced at the beginning of each section. The terms will be defined in context.

The Story Continues features an interesting episode from American history that shows you that history is not just a collection of facts but a blend of many individual stories and adventures.

History Makers Speak quotations appear frequently throughout the book. These exciting primary source quotations give you a glimpse into the lives of actual people who made history. Many of these quotations are accompanied by an Analyzing Primary Sources question to help you better interpret the sources and draw inferences about their importance.

Interpreting the Visual Record features accompany many of the book's rich images. Pictures are one of the most important primary sources historians can use to help analyze the past. These features invite you to examine the images and to interpret their content.

Section 1

Europeans Set Sail

Read to Discover
1. How did the Commercial Revolution and the Renaissance change Europe?
2. Why did western Europeans want to find a new sea route for trade with Africa and Asia?
3. How did Portugal's early explorations affect Africans?

WHY IT MATTERS TODAY

Scientific and technological changes continue to affect our world. Use **CNNfyi.com** or other current events sources to find out about important scientific and technological changes taking place today. Record your findings in your journal.

Define
• capital
• joint-stock companies
• astrolabe
• monopoly
• caravel

Identify
• Black Death
• Commercial Revolution
• Renaissance
• Prince Henry
• Bartolomeu Dias

A trade union in the Netherlands used this seal.

The Story Continues

In 1299 the city of Arras in present-day France was famous for its wealthy merchants. The powerful Crespin family was so rich that it loaned money to cities, bishops, and even monarchs. Some people worried about this new interest in money. "Money is too much worshipped here," wrote poet Adam de la Halle about Arras. Others welcomed the changing economy. They thought it provided ways for workers to make money and improve their social status. When Baude Crespin died in 1316 his tombstone read, "Pray for his immortal spirit then, Laborers and working men."

★ The European Economy Grows

Europe's wealth and population grew steadily during the late Middle Ages. Then, in the mid-1300s Europe suffered a terrible blow. Some ships belonging to Italian merchants returned from Asia carrying rats infected with bubonic plague, a deadly disease. The plague led to an epidemic called the **Black Death**, which swept through Europe from about 1348 to 1350. The epidemic killed as many as 30 million people, about

32 Chapter 2

These leaders had not signed any treaties with Britain and would not give up their land because of an agreement between Britain and France. Chippewa leader Minavavana expressed this view to a trader in 1761. "Englishman, although you have conquered the French, you have not yet conquered us!"

In the 1760s American Indian tribes began to join together to resist the British. Chief Pontiac of the Ottawa led forces that included the Delaware, Huron, Miami, Ottawa, and Shawnee peoples. Pontiac followed the teachings of the so-called Delaware Prophet. This leader called on Indians to drive out the white settlers and give up all European practices. In 1763 Pontiac shared these ideas with a gathering of American Indians.

Interpreting the Visual Record

Fort Detroit *Pontiac's forces tried for months to capture Fort Detroit from the British.* **What in the image suggests the difficulties of attacking the fort?**

> **History Makers Speak**
> "How comes it that you suffer the whites on your lands? Can't you do without them? You might live wholly [completely] as you did before you knew them. . . . Those who come to trouble your country, drive them out, make war [on] them! . . . They are my enemies and the enemies of your brothers!"
>
> —Pontiac, quoted in *The World Turned Upside Down,* edited by Colin G. Calloway

Analyzing Primary Sources
Identifying Points of View How does Pontiac describe white settlers?

Pontiac's Rebellion began in May 1763 when American Indians attacked British forts on the frontier. Within a month Pontiac's forces had destroyed or captured seven forts. Pontiac then led the attack on Fort Detroit, Britain's political and trading center in the Great Lakes area. Despite the best efforts of Pontiac and his allies, the British held out for months. The American Indians following Pontiac grew tired of attacking the fort and returned to their villages. An Indian attack on the important British position at Fort Pitt also failed. Both sides suffered many casualties. As more Indians left Pontiac, he surrendered in 1766.

✔ **Reading Check: Identifying Cause and Effect** Why did Pontiac and his followers fight the British, and what happened as a result?

Conflicts in the Colonies **165**

Reading Check questions appear throughout the book to allow you to check your comprehension while you are reading. As you read each section, pause for a moment to consider each Reading Check. If you have trouble answering the question, go back and examine the material you just read.

Use these review tools to pull together all the information you have learned.

Graphic Organizers will help you review important information from the section. You can complete the graphic organizer as a study tool to prepare for a test or writing assignment.

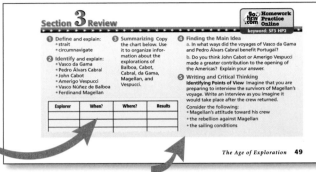

Homework Practice Online lets you log on to the go.hrw.com Web site to complete an interactive self-check of the material covered in the section.

Writing and Critical Thinking activities allow you to explore a section topic in greater depth and to build your skills.

The Chapter at a Glance is an interesting visual summary of the main ideas of the chapter.

Social Studies Skills Workshop is a way for you to build your skills at analyzing information and to practice answering standardized-test questions.

Thinking Critically questions ask you to use the information you have learned in the chapter to extend your knowledge. You will be asked to analyze information by using your critical thinking skills.

Building Your Portfolio is an exciting and creative way to demonstrate your understanding of history.

Use these online tools to review and complete online activities.

Homework Practice Online
lets you log on for review anytime.

Internet Connect
activities are just one part of the world of online learning experiences that awaits you on the go.hrw.com Web site. By exploring these online activities, you will take a journey through some of the richest American history materials available on the World Wide Web. You can then use these resources to create real-world projects, such as newspapers, brochures, reports, and even your own Web site!

Why History Matters Today

> "**H**istory and destiny have made America the leader of the world that would be free. And the world that would be free is looking to us for inspiration."
>
> —Colin Powell

Right now at this very second, somewhere in the United States, someone is making history. It is impossible to know whom or in what way, but the actions of people today may become the history of tomorrow.

JANA JACOBS
CNN STUDENT BUREAU

Blind children share with sighted
CNN Student Bureau's Jana Jacobs reports on a program in Alanta that brings sighted and blind children together (August 7)

History and Your World

All you need to do is watch or read the news to see history unfolding. How many news stories do you see or hear about ordinary people doing extraordinary things? The Why It Matters Today feature beginning every section of *Call to Freedom* invites you to use the vast resources of **CNNfyi.com** or other current events sources to examine the links between past and present. Through this feature you will be able to draw connections between what you are studying in your history book and the events that are taking place today.

Anyone Can Be a History Maker

When you think of the word *history,* what comes to mind? Do you picture politicians sitting around a table deciding the future of the nation? Or do you see a long list of dates and boring facts to be memorized? Of course, politicians, dates, and facts are part of history, but there is actually much more to understanding and exploring our past. Our nation has developed through the efforts of many different people, from all backgrounds and walks of life. Many of them were teenagers like yourself. Did you know that teenagers helped settle the West? It's true. For example, teenager Nancy Kelsey was among the first pioneers to arrive in California in 1841.

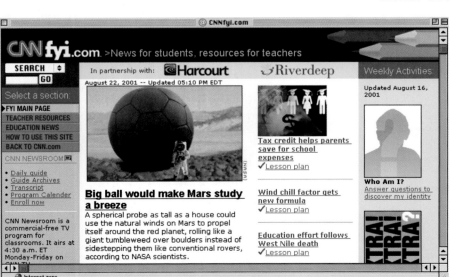

Student reporters contribute to CNNfyi.com.

*Student visiting the
Vietnam Veterans Memorial*

History Makes Us Who We Are

There is no one single "story" in history. Instead, the combined experiences of millions of people across time have come together to form the foundation of American society today.

"So when someone asks you 'Why does history matter today?' you might answer, 'Because in our past, we see a reflection of ourselves.'"

Teenagers also played a role in the Civil War. Thousands of soldiers, like 15-year-old Thomas Galway, fought in this bloody conflict, which shaped the nation's future. You might also be interested to know that young Americans in the Civilian Conservation Corps played a key role in keeping the nation going during the darkest hours of the Great Depression. These are just a few of the many examples of how people about the same age as yourself have helped shape our nation's past. What contributions do you think your generation will make to our national history?

These young people are participating in a reenactment to celebrate the unveiling of the African American Civil War Memorial at Arlington National Cemetery.

Themes in American History

Call to Freedom begins every chapter with a set of theme statements under the heading "You Be the Historian." These statements are drawn from several broad themes central to American history: Geography; Economics; Government; Citizenship; Culture; Science, Technology & Society; Constitutional Heritage; and Global Relations. As you begin each chapter of *Call to Freedom*, you will be asked to respond to the theme statements in a general way, based on your own knowledge. At the end of the chapter, you will be asked to respond to more specific questions about the themes, based on the chapter content.

Geography

The Geography theme explores ways in which the nation's vast and diverse geography has played an important role in American history. The theme examines how the development of the nation's resources has helped shape its economy, society, and politics. In addition, the Geography theme traces how public and government attitudes about resources and the environment have changed over time.

Economics

President Calvin Coolidge once said that "the business of America is business." The Economics theme asks you to explore the relationship between history and economics in the United States. The theme traces the changing relationship between government, business, and labor in America. It examines how the growth of a strong national free-enterprise economic system has influenced the country's domestic and global politics as well as individual lives and American society.

Catalogs display hundreds of goods for consumers.

Government

Even before the nation had won its independence from Great Britain in the Revolution, the Founding Fathers saw the need to establish a national government. The Government theme asks you to explore the workings of the American system of government—from the Articles of Confederation up to the present. This theme also examines the relationships between federal, state and local governments and how the system is designed to serve the people.

The American West

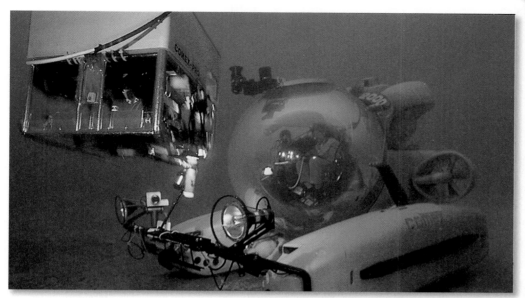

Scientists such as these underwater archaeologists search for clues about the distant past.

Citizenship

Throughout our history, Americans have struggled to define, possess, and protect individual rights and personal freedoms, such as the freedoms of speech and of religion, the right to vote, and the right to privacy. Americans have also worked to uphold the responsibilities of citizenship that accompany participation in our democracy. The Citizenship theme explores how changing social, economic, and political conditions have influenced the theory and practices of these rights, freedoms, and responsibilities. This theme also examines the many conflicts that have arisen over these democratic values as well as Americans' attempts to resolve these conflicts.

Science, Technology & Society

From the building of the transcontinental railroad and the construction of skyscrapers during the Second Industrial Revolution, to the computers that help you with your school assignments and personal projects today, science and technology have influenced every aspect of our culture and society. The Science, Technology & Society theme explores scientific and technological developments and their influence on the U.S. economy and life.

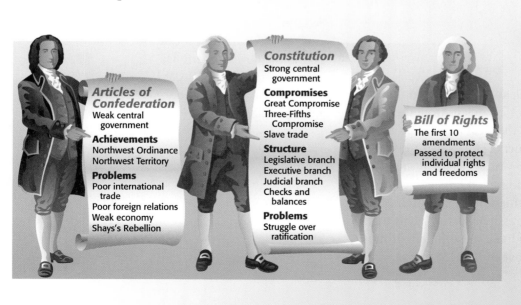

Articles of Confederation
Weak central government

Achievements
Northwest Ordinance
Northwest Territory

Problems
Poor international trade
Poor foreign relations
Weak economy
Shays's Rebellion

Constitution
Strong central government

Compromises
Great Compromise
Three-Fifths Compromise
Slave trade

Structure
Legislative branch
Executive branch
Judicial branch
Checks and balances

Problems
Struggle over ratification

Bill of Rights
The first 10 amendments
Passed to protect individual rights and freedoms

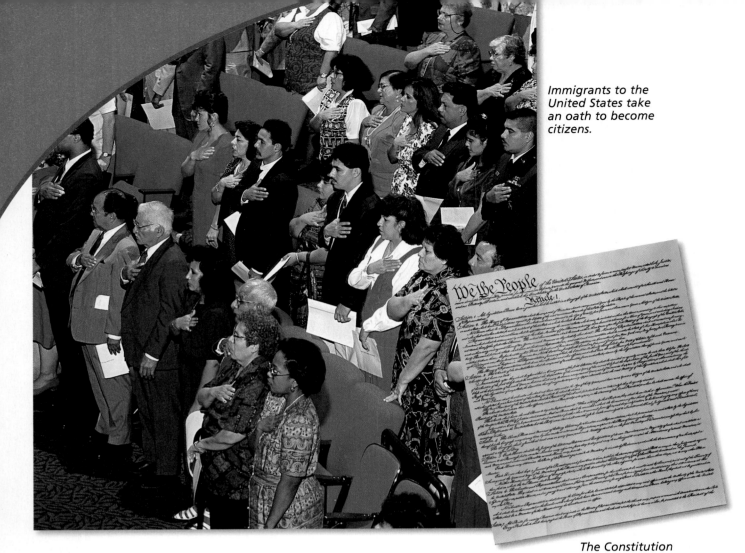

Immigrants to the United States take an oath to become citizens.

The Constitution

Culture

Our nation's rich and unique cultural heritage comes from its many ethnic, racial, and religious groups. The Culture theme examines the influences of diverse culture groups, from before the time of the European explorers to recent immigrants from around the world.

Constitutional Heritage

No study of American history would be complete without examining the U.S. Constitution, the document that provides the legal framework for our democratic government. The Constitutional Heritage theme will help you understand the Constitution's origins and how it has evolved through constitutional amendments, Supreme Court rulings, and congressional action. This theme also explores how individuals and different groups in the nation's history have influenced the Constitution.

Global Relations

Since the first Asian nomads crossed a land bridge to this continent thousands of years ago, America has been involved in global events. The Global Relations theme invites you to trace ways in which our nation's political, social, and economic development has affected—and been affected by—other countries and their people.

International Red Cross medal

Essential Elements of Geography

History and geography share many elements. History describes important events that have taken place from ancient times until the present day. Geography describes how physical environments affect human events. It also examines how people's actions influence the environment around them. One way to look at geography is to identify essential elements of its study. The following six essential elements, developed from the National Geography Standards, will be used throughout Call to Freedom.

The World in Spatial Terms

This essential element refers to the way geographers view the world. They look at where things are and how they are arranged on Earth's surface. For example, geographers might be interested to learn why certain cities developed where they did.

Places and Regions

Geographers often focus on the physical and human characteristics that make particular parts of Earth special. A region is an area with common characteristics that make it different from surrounding areas. People create regions as a convenient way to study the world. Regions can be large, like North America, or small like a neighborhood.

Physical Systems

Geographers study the physical processes and interactions between four physical systems—Earth's atmosphere, land, water, and life. Physical processes shape and change Earth's physical features and environments.

Human Systems

As with physical systems, studying human systems can tell geographers much about the world around us. For example, studying population growth, distribution, and movement helps in understanding human events and their effects on the environment.

Environment and Society

One of the most important topics in geography is how people interact with the environment. People depend on the environment's natural resources for survival. However, human activities can have both positive and negative effects on Earth's environment.

The Uses of Geography

Historians use geography to understand the past. They look not only at when things happened but where and why they happened. But geography is important to the present as well as the past. People use geography every day to explore how to use Earth's limited resources, such as water and minerals, more effectively and in a way that ensures the success of future generations.

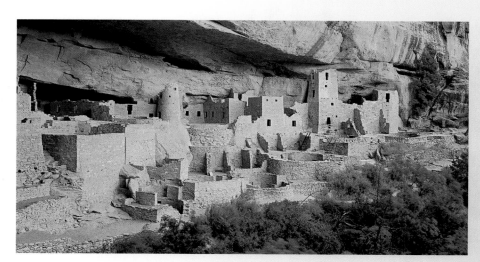

Anasazi homes were built of stone and sun-dried clay bricks. Some were built in openings in high cliffs.

Skills Handbook

The first battle of the American Revolution took place in Lexington.

Critical Thinking

Throughout *Call to Freedom,* you will be asked to think critically about the events and issues that have shaped U.S. history. Critical thinking is the reasoned judgment of information and ideas. The development of critical thinking skills is essential to effective citizenship. Such skills empower you to exercise your civic rights and responsibilities. Helping you develop critical thinking skills is an important goal of *Call to Freedom.* The following critical thinking skills appear in the section reviews and chapter reviews of the book.

1 **Analyzing Information** is the process of breaking something down and examining the relationships between its parts. Analyzing enables you to better understand the whole. For example, to analyze the outcome of the 1876 presidential election, you might study how, since the election results were disputed, both sides had to come to an agreement before Rutherford B. Hayes could become president.

2 **Sequencing** is the process of placing events in correct chronological order to better understand the historical relationships be-tween the events. You can sequence events in two basic ways: according to absolute or relative chronology. Absolute chronology means that you pay close attention to the exact dates on which events took place. Placing events on a time line would be an example of absolute chronology. Relative chronology refers to the way events relate to one another. To put events in relative order, you need to know which one happened first, which came next, and so forth.

Coat of arms granted to Christopher Columbus

3 **Categorizing** is the process by which you group things together by the characteristics they have in common. By putting things or events into categories, it is easier to make comparisons and see differences among them.

4 **Identifying Cause and Effect** is a part of interpreting the relationships between historical events. A *cause* is an action that leads to an event. The outcome of the action is an *effect.* To explain historical events, historians often point out multiple causes and effects. For example, economic and politi-cal differences between the North and South, as well as the issue of slavery, brought about the Civil War—which in turn had many far-reaching effects.

Emancipation Proclamation

5 **Comparing and Contrasting** is examining events, situations, or points of view for their similarities and differences. *Comparing* focuses on both the similari-ties and the differences. *Contrasting* focuses only on the differences. For example, a comparison of early Irish and Chinese immigrants to the United States shows that both groups were recruited to help build railroads and that both groups faced discrimination. In contrast, language and racial barriers generally proved more of a problem for Chinese immigrants.

6 **Finding the Main Idea** is combining and sifting through information to determine what is most important. Historical writing often uses many examples and details to support the author's main ideas. Throughout *Call to Freedom,* you will find numerous Reading Checks and questions in section reviews to help you focus on the main ideas in the text.

7 **Summarizing** is the process of taking a large amount of information and boiling it down into a short and clear statement. Summarizing is particularly useful when you need to give a brief account of a longer story or event. For example, the story of the Battle of Gettysburg during the Civil War is an exciting but detailed one. Many different events came together to make up this story. You could summarize these events by saying something like, "In 1863 General Lee led his army north into Pennsylvania where he met the Union forces under General Meade at Gettysburg. After several days of bloody fighting, Lee was forced to retreat. Lee's defeat at Gettysburg was a major turning point in the war."

Lee's surrender at Appomattox Courthouse

8 **Making Generalizations and Predictions** is the process of interpreting information to form more general statements and to guess about what will happen next. A *generalization* is a broad statement that holds true for a variety of historical events or situations. Making generalizations can help you see the "big picture" of historical events, rather than just focusing on details. It is very

important, however, that when making generalizations you try not to include situations that do not fit the statement. When this occurs, you run the risk of creating a stereotype, or overgeneralization. A *prediction* is an educated guess about an outcome. When you read history, you should always be asking yourself questions like, "What will happen next? If this person does this, what will that mean for . . . ?", and so on. These types of questions help you draw on information you already know to see patterns throughout history.

9 **Drawing Inferences and Conclusions** is forming possible explanations for an event, a situation, or a problem. When you make an *inference,* you take the information you know to be true and come up with an educated guess about what else you think is true about that situation. A *conclusion* is a prediction about the outcome

Women's suffrage supporter

of a situation based on what you already know. Often, you must be prepared to test your inferences and conclusions against new evidence or arguments. For example, a historian might conclude that women's leadership roles in the abolition movement led to the development of the early women's movement. The historian would then organize the evidence needed to support this conclusion and challenge other arguments.

10 **Identifying Points of View** is the process of identifying factors that influence the outlook of an individual or group. A person's point of view includes beliefs and attitudes that are shaped by factors such as age, gender, religion, race, and economic status. This critical thinking skill helps you examine why people see things as they do, and it reinforces the realization that people's views may change over time or with a change in circumstances.

11 **Supporting a Point of View** involves choosing a viewpoint on a particular event or issue and arguing persuasively for that position. Your argument should be well organized and based on specific evidence that supports the point of view you have chosen. Supporting a point of view often involves working with controversial or emotional issues. For example, you might consider the points of view involved in the struggles between labor unions and businesses in the late 1800s. Whether you choose a position in favor of unions or in favor of businesses, you should state your opinion clearly and give reasons to defend it.

Labor union booklet

12 **Identifying Bias** is the process of evaluating the opinions of others about events or situations. Bias is an opinion based on prejudice or strong emotions, rather than on fact. It is important to identify bias when looking at historical sources, because biased sources often give you a false sense of what really happened. When looking at both primary and secondary sources, it is always important to keep the author's or speaker's point of view in mind and to adjust your interpretation of the source when you detect any bias.

13 **Evaluating** is assessing the significance or overall importance of something, such as the success of a reform movement, the actions of a president, or the results of a major conflict. You should base your judgment on standards that others will understand and are likely to share. For example, you might consider the outcome of the Mexican War and evaluate its importance to U.S. politics and expansion. You could also evaluate the effect of the war on the peoples already living in the West.

14 **Problem Solving** is the process by which you pose workable solutions to difficult situations. The first step in the process is to identify a problem. Next you will need to gather information about the problem, such as its history and the various factors that contribute to the problem. Once you have gathered information, you should list and consider the options for solving the problem. For each of the possible solutions, weigh their advantages and disadvantages and, based on your evaluation, choose and implement a solution. Once the solution has been tried, go back and evaluate the effectiveness of the solution you selected.

15 **Decision Making** is the process of reviewing a situation and then making decisions or recommendations for the best possible outcome. To complete the process, first identify a situation that requires a solution. Next, gather information that will help you reach a decision. You may need to do some background research to study the history of the situation. Once you have done your research, identify options that might resolve the situation. For each option, predict what the possible consequences might be if that option were followed. Once you have identified the best option, take action by making a recommendation and following through on any tasks that option requires.

Becoming a Strategic Reader

by Dr. Judith Irvin

Everywhere you look, print is all around us. In fact, you would have a hard time stopping yourself from reading. In a normal day, you might read cereal boxes, movie posters, notes from friends, T-shirts, instructions for video games, song lyrics, catalogs, billboards, information on the Internet, magazines, the newspaper, and much, much more. Each form of print is read differently depending on your purpose for reading. You read a menu differently from the way you read poetry, and a motorcycle magazine is read differently than a letter from a friend. Good readers switch easily from one type of text to another. In fact, they probably do not even think about it, they just do it.

When you read, it is helpful to use a strategy to remember the most important ideas. You can use a strategy before you read to help connect information you already know to the new information you will encounter. Before you read, you can also predict what a text will be about by using a previewing strategy. During the reading you can use a strategy to help you focus on main ideas, and after reading you can use a strategy to help you organize what you learned so that you can remember it later. *Call to Freedom* was designed to help you more easily understand the ideas you read. Important reading strategies employed in *Call to Freedom* include the following:

1 Methods to help you **anticipate** what is to come

2 Tools to help you **preview and predict** what the text will be about

3 Ways to help you **use and analyze visual information**

4 Ideas to help you **organize the information** you have learned

1. Anticipate Information

How Can I Use Information I Already Know to Help Me Understand What a New Chapter Will Be About?

Anticipating what a new chapter will be about helps you connect the upcoming information to what you already know. By drawing on your background knowledge, you can build a bridge to the new material.

1 Each chapter of *Call to Freedom* asks you to explore the main themes of the chapter before you start reading by forming opinions based on your current knowledge.

You Be the Historian

Themes Journal

What's Your Opinion? Do you **agree** or **disagree** with the following statements? Support your point of view in your journal.

- **Science, Technology & Society** New technology always makes wars easier to win.
- **Economics** Wars are bad for a nation's economy.
- **Citizenship** All citizens have a duty to support their government during a war.

Create a chart like this one to help you analyze the statements.

A Before Reading Agree/Disagree		B After Reading Agree/Disagree
2	*New technology always makes wars easier to win.*	**4**
	Wars are bad for a nation's economy.	
	All citizens have a duty to support their government during a war.	

Anticipating Information

▶ **Step 1** Identify the major concepts of the chapter. In *Call to Freedom*, these are presented in the **You Be the Historian** feature at the beginning of each chapter.

▼

Step 2 Agree or disagree with each of the statements and record your opinions in your journal.

▼

Step 3 Read the text and discuss your responses with your classmates.

▼

Step 4 After reading the chapter, revisit the statements and respond to them again based on what you have learned.

▼

Step 5 Go back and check your knowledge by answering the You Be the Historian—Reviewing Themes questions in the chapter review.

3 Read the text and discuss your answers with classmates.

5 You can also refine your knowledge by answering the You Be the Historian—Reviewing Themes questions in the chapter review.

You Be the Historian—Reviewing Themes

1. **Science, Technology & Society** How did ironclads reflect the changes that new technology brought to the war?
2. **Economics** What effect did the war have on the South's economy?
3. **Citizenship** How did northerners and southerners oppose the war, and how did the Union and Confederate governments respond?

2. Preview and Predict

How Can I Figure out What the Text Is about before I Even Start Reading a Section?

Previewing and **predicting** are good methods to help you understand the text. If you take the time to preview and predict before you read, the text will make more sense to you during your reading.

1 Usually, your teacher will set the purpose for reading. After reading some new information, you may be asked to write a summary, take a test, or complete some other type of activity.

"After reading about the Civil War, you will work with a partner to create a historical museum exhibit describing…"

2 As you preview the text, use *graphic signals* such as headings, subheadings, and boldfaced type to help you determine what is important in the text. Each section of *Call to Freedom* opens by giving you important clues to help you preview the material.

Previewing and Predicting

Step 1 Identify your purpose for reading. Ask yourself what will you do with this information once you have finished reading.

▼

Step 2 Ask yourself what the main idea of the text is and what key vocabulary words you need to know.

▼

Step 3 Use signal words to help identify the structure of the text.

▼

Step 4 Connect the information to what you already know.

Looking at the section's **main heading** and **subheadings** can give you an idea of what is to come.

Read to Discover questions give you clues as to the section's main ideas.

Define and Identify terms let you know the key vocabulary you will encounter in the section.

The War in the East

Read to Discover

1. What battles did the Confederates win in Virginia, and why were they important?
2. What stopped the northward advance of the Confederate army?
3. What was the significance of the *Monitor* and the *Virginia*?

WHY IT MATTERS TODAY

During the Civil War, powerful new types of warships were developed. Use CNN **fyi**.com or other **current events** sources to find out about the types of ships used by the U.S. Navy today. Record your findings in your journal.

Define
- ironclad

Identify
- Thomas "Stonewall" Jackson
- First Battle of Bull Run
- George B. McClellan
- Robert E. Lee
- Seven Days' Battles
- Second Battle of Bull Run
- Battle of Antietam

3 Other tools that can help you in previewing are **signal words**. These words prepare you to think in a certain way. For example, when you see words such as *similar to, same as,* or *different from,* you know that the text will probably compare and contrast two or more ideas. Signal words indicate how the ideas in the text relate to each other. Look at the list below of some of the most common signal words grouped by the type of text structures they indicate.

Signal Words

Cause and Effect	Compare and Contrast	Description	Problem and Solution	Sequence or Chronological Order
• because • since • consequently • this led to…so • if…then • nevertheless • accordingly • because of • as a result of • in order to • may be due to • for this reason	• different from • same as • similar to • as opposed to • instead of • although • however • compared with • as well as • either…or • but • on the other hand • unless	• for instance • for example • such as • to illustrate • in addition • most importantly • another • furthermore • first, second…	• the question is • a solution • one answer is	• not long after • next • then • initially • before • after • finally • preceding • following • on (date) • over time • today • when

4 Learning something new requires that you connect it in some way with something you already know. This means you have to think before you read and while you read. You may want to use a chart like this one to remind yourself of the information already familiar to you and to come up with questions you want answered in your reading. The chart will also help you organize your ideas after you have finished reading.

What I know	What I want to know	What I learned

3. Use and Analyze Visual Information

How Can All the Pictures, Maps, Graphs, and Time Lines with the Text Help Me Be a Stronger Reader?

Analyzing Visual Information

▶ **Step ➊** As you preview the text, ask yourself how the visual information relates to the text.

▼

Step ➋ Generate questions based on the visual information.

▼

Step ➌ After reading the text, go back and review the visual information again.

▼

Step ➍ Make connections to what you already know.

Using visual information can help you understand and remember the information presented in *Call to Freedom*. Good readers form a picture in their minds when they read. The pictures, charts, graphs, cartoons, time lines, and diagrams that occur throughout *Call to Freedom* are placed strategically to increase your understanding.

➊ You might ask yourself questions like:

> Why did the author include this information with the text? What details about this visual are mentioned in the text?

After you have read the text, see if you can answer your own questions.

➋

Why is the train important?
Are those people going to get on the train?
Why is the town right beside the railroad tracks?

➌ After reading, take another look at the visual information.

➍ Try to make connections to what you already know.

4. Organize Information
Once I Learn New Information, How Do I Keep It All Straight So That I Will Remember It?

To help you remember what you have read, you need to find a way of **organizing information**. Two good ways of doing this are by using graphic organizers and concept maps. **Graphic organizers** help you understand important relationships—such as cause-and-effect, compare/contrast, sequence of events, and problem/solution—within the text. **Concept maps** provide a useful tool to help you focus on the text's main ideas and organize supporting details.

Identifying Relationships

Using graphic organizers will help you recall important ideas from the section. They are also study tools you can use to prepare for a quiz or test or to help with a writing assignment. Some of the most common types of graphic organizers are shown below.

▶ Cause and Effect

Events in history cause people to react in certain ways. Cause-and-effect patterns show the relationship between results and the ideas or events that made the results occur. You may want to represent cause-and-effect relationships as one cause leading to multiple effects,

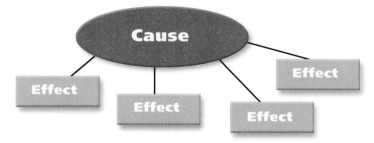

or as a chain of cause-and-effect relationships.

Constructing Graphic Organizers

▶ **Step ❶** Preview the text, looking for signal words and main ideas.

▼

Step ❷ Form a hypothesis as to which type of graphic organizer would work best to display the information presented.

▼

Step ❸ Work individually or with your classmates to create a visual representation of what you read.

Comparing and Contrasting

Graphic organizers are often useful when you are comparing or contrasting information. Compare-and-contrast diagrams point out similarities and differences between two concepts or ideas.

Sequencing

Keeping track of dates and the order in which events took place is essential to understanding history. Sequence or chronological-order diagrams show events or ideas in the order in which they happened.

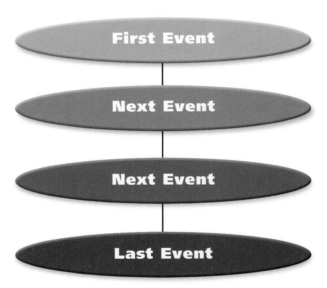

Problem and Solution

Problem/solution patterns identify at least one problem, offer one or more solutions to the problem, and explain or predict outcomes of the solutions.

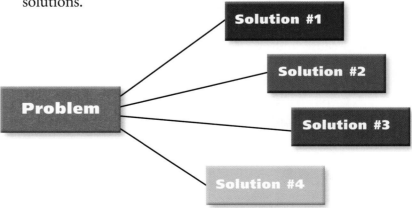

Identifying Main Ideas and Supporting Details

One special type of graphic organizer is the concept map. A concept map, sometimes called a semantic map, allows you to zero in on the most important points of the text. The map is made up of lines, boxes, circles, and/or arrows. It can be as simple or as complex as you need it to be to accurately represent the text.

Here are a few examples of concept maps you might use.

Constructing Concept Maps

▶ **Step 1** Preview the text, looking for what type of structure might be appropriate to display a concept map.

▼

Step 2 Taking note of the headings, boldfaced type, and text structure, sketch a concept map you think could best illustrate the text.

▼

Step 3 Using boxes, lines, arrows, circles, or any shapes you like, display the ideas of the text in the concept map.

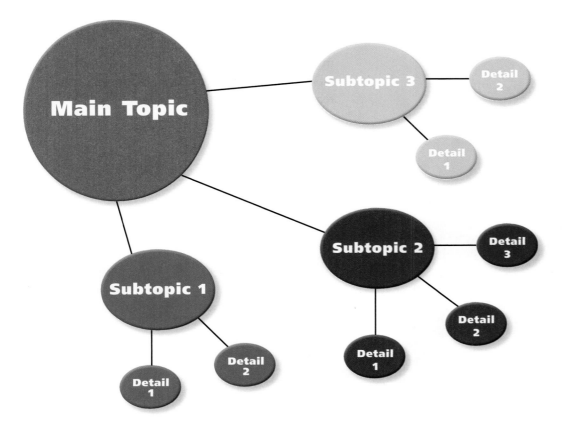

Standardized Test–Taking Strategies

A number of times throughout your school career, you may be asked to take standardized tests. These tests are designed to demonstrate the content and skills you have learned. It is important to keep in mind that in most cases the best way to prepare for these tests is to pay close attention in class and to take every opportunity to improve your general social studies, reading, writing, and mathematical skills.

Tips for Taking the Test

1. Be sure that you are well rested.
2. Be on time and be sure that you have the necessary materials.
3. Listen to the instructions of the teacher.
4. Read directions and questions carefully.
5. **DON'T STRESS!** Just remember what you have learned in class, and you should do well.

▶ **Practice the strategies at go.hrw.com.**

go.hrw.com
Standardized Test-Prep Online
keyword: SB SF3 STP

Tackling Social Studies

The social studies portions of many standardized tests are designed to test your knowledge of the content and skills that you have been studying in one or more of your social studies classes. Specific objectives for the test vary, but some of the most common include the following:

1. Demonstrate an understanding of issues and events in history.
2. Demonstrate an understanding of geographic influences on historical issues and events.
3. Demonstrate an understanding of economic and social influences on historical issues and events.
4. Demonstrate an understanding of political influences on historical issues and events.
5. Use critical thinking skills to analyze social studies information.

Standardized tests usually contain multiple-choice and, sometimes, open-ended questions. The multiple-choice items will often be based on maps, tables, charts, graphs, pictures, cartoons, and/or reading passages and documents.

Tips for Answering Multiple-Choice Questions

1. If there is a written or visual piece accompanying the multiple-choice question, pay careful attention to the title, author, and date.
2. Then read through or glance over the content of the piece accompanying the question.
3. Next, read the multiple-choice question for its general intent. Then reread it carefully, looking for words that give clues. For example, words such as *most* or *best* tell you that there may be several correct answers, but you should look for the most appropriate answer.

4. Always read all of the possible answer choices, even if the first one seems like the correct answer. There may be a better choice farther down in the list.

5. Reread the accompanying information (if any is included) carefully to determine the answer to the question. Again, note the title, author, and date of primary-source selections. The answer will rarely be stated exactly as it appears in the primary source, so you will need to use your critical thinking skills to read between the lines.

6. Use your knowledge of the time in history or person involved to help limit the answer choices.

7. Finally, reread the question and selected answer to be sure that you made the best choice and that you marked it correctly on the answer sheet.

Strategies for Success

There are many strategies you can use to help you feel more confident about answering questions on social studies standardized tests. Here are a few suggestions:

1. Adopt an acronym—a word formed from the first letters of other words—that you will always use for analyzing a document or visual that might accompany a question.

Helpful Acronyms

For a document, use **SOAPS**, which stands for

S	Subject
O	Occasion
A	Audience
P	Purpose
S	Speaker/author

For a picture, cartoon, map, or other visual piece of information, use **OPTIC**, which stands for

O	Overview
P	Parts (labels or details of the visual)
T	Title
I	Interrelations (how the different parts of the visual work together)
C	Conclusion (what the visual means)

2. Form visual images of maps and try to draw them from memory. The standardized test will most likely include important maps from the time period and subjects you have been studying. For example, in early U.S. history, be able to see in your mind's eye such things as where the New England, middle, and southern colonies were located, what land the Louisiana Purchase and Mexican Cession covered, and the dividing line for slave and free states. Know major physical features, such as the Mississippi River, the Appalachian and Rocky Mountains, the Great Plains, and the various regions of the United States, and be able to place them on a map.

3. When you have finished studying any historical era, try to think of who or what might be important enough for the test. You may want to keep your ideas in a notebook to refer to when it is almost time for the test.

4. Pay particular attention to the Constitution and its development. Many standardized tests contain questions about this all-important document and the period during which it was written. Questions may include Magna Carta, the English Bill of Rights, the Declaration of Independence, and *Common Sense,* as well as many other important historical documents.

5. For the skills area of the tests, practice putting major events and personalities in order in your mind. Sequencing people and events by dates can become a game you play with a friend who also has to take the test. Always ask yourself why this event is important.

6. Follow the tips under "Ready for Reading" on the next page when you encounter a reading passage in social studies, but remember that what you have learned about history can help you in answering reading-comprehension questions.

Ready for Reading

The main goal of the reading sections of most standardized tests is to determine your understanding of different aspects of a reading passage. Basically, if you can grasp the main idea and the author's purpose, then pay attention to the details and vocabulary so that you are able to draw inferences and conclusions, you will do well on the test.

Tips for Answering Multiple-Choice Questions

1. Read the passage as if you were not taking a test.
2. Look at the big picture. Ask yourself questions like, "What is the title?", "What do the illustrations or pictures tell me?", and "What is the author's purpose?"
3. Read the questions. This will help you know what information to look for.
4. Reread the passage, underlining information related to the questions.

Types of Multiple-Choice Questions

1. **Main Idea** This is the most important point of the passage. After reading the passage, locate and underline the main idea.
2. **Significant Details** You will often be asked to recall details from the passage. Read the question and underline the details as you read. But remember that the correct answers do not always match the wording of the passage precisely.
3. **Vocabulary** You will often need to define a word within the context of the passage. Read the answer choices and plug them into the sentence to see what fits best.
4. **Conclusion and Inference** There are often important ideas in the passage that the author does not state directly. Sometimes you must consider multiple parts of the passage to answer the question. If answers refer to only one or two sentences or details in the passage, they are probably incorrect.

5. Go back to the questions and try to answer each one in your mind before looking at the answers.
6. Read all the answer choices and eliminate the ones that are obviously incorrect.

Tips for Answering Short-Answer Questions

1. Read the passage in its entirety, paying close attention to the main events and characters. Jot down information you think is important.
2. If you cannot answer a question, skip it and come back later.
3. Words such as *compare, contrast, interpret, discuss,* and *summarize* appear often in short-answer questions. Be sure you have a complete understanding of each of these words.
4. To help support your answer, return to the passage and skim the parts you underlined.
5. Organize your thoughts on a separate sheet of paper. Write a general statement with which to begin. This will be your topic statement.
6. When writing your answer, be precise but brief. Be sure to refer to details in the passage in your answer.

Targeting Writing

On many standardized tests, you will occasionally be asked to write an essay. In order to write a concise essay, you must learn to organize your thoughts before you begin writing the actual composition. This keeps you from straying too far from the essay's topic.

Tips for Answering Composition Questions

1. Read the question carefully.

2. Decide what kind of essay you are being asked to write. Essays usually fall into one of the following types: persuasive, classificatory, compare/contrast, or "how to." To determine the type of essay, ask yourself questions like, "Am I trying to persuade my audience?", "Am I comparing or contrasting ideas?", or "Am I trying to show the reader how to do something?"

3. Pay attention to key words, such as *compare, contrast, describe, advantages, disadvantages, classify,* or *speculate*. They will give you clues as to the structure that your essay should follow.

4. Organize your thoughts on a separate sheet of paper. You will want to come up with a general topic sentence that expresses your main idea. Make sure this sentence addresses the question. You should then create an outline or some type of graphic organizer to help you organize the points that support your topic sentence.

5. Write your composition using complete sentences. Also, be sure to use correct grammar, spelling, punctuation, and sentence structure.

6. Be sure to proofread your essay once you have finished writing.

Gearing up for Math

On most standardized tests you will be asked to solve a variety of mathematical problems that draw on the skills and information you have learned in class. If math problems sometimes give you difficulty, use the tips below to help yourself work through the problems.

Tips for Solving Math Problems

1. Decide what the goal of the question is. Read or study the problem carefully and determine what information must be found.

2. Locate the factual information. Decide what information represents key facts—the ones you must use to solve the problem. You may also find facts you do not need to reach your solution. In some cases, you may determine that more information is needed to solve the problem. If so, ask yourself, "What assumptions can I make about this problem?" or "Do I need a formula to help solve this problem?"

3. Decide what strategies you might use to solve the problem, how you might use them, and what form your solution will be in. For example, will you need to create a graph or chart? Will you need to solve an equation? Will your answer be in words or numbers? By knowing what type of solution you should reach, you may be able to eliminate some of the choices.

4. Apply your strategy to solve the problem and compare your answer to the choices.

5. If the answer is still not clear, read the problem again. If you had to make calculations to reach your answer, use estimation to see if your answer makes sense.

The Geographer's Tool Kit

A map is an illustration drawn to scale of all or part of Earth's surface. Knowing how to read and interpret maps is one of the most valuable tools you can use to study history.

Types of Maps

Types of maps include physical maps, political maps, and thematic (special-purpose) maps.

▶ **Physical maps** illustrate the natural landscape of an area—the landforms that mark Earth's surface. Physical maps often use shading to show relief—the existence of mountains, hills, and valleys—and colors to show elevation, or height above sea level. The map of the United States on pages A2–A3 is strictly a physical map.

▶ **Political maps** illustrate political units, such as states and nations, and use color variations and lines to mark boundaries, dots for major cities, and stars or stars within circles for capitals. Political maps show information such as territorial changes or military alliances. The map of the United States on page A1 is a political map.

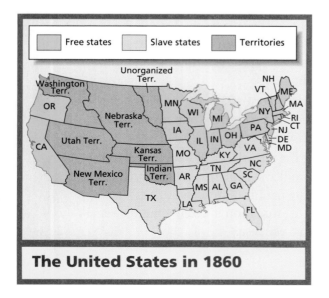

The United States in 1860

▶ **Thematic (special-purpose) maps** present specific information, such as the routes of explorers or the outcome of an election. Both the maps shown on these two pages are thematic maps.

Map Features

Most maps have some features in common. Familiarity with these elements makes reading maps easier.

▶ **Titles, legends, and labels** A map's title tells you what the map is about, what areas are shown, and usually what time period is represented. The legend, or key, explains any special symbols, colors, or shadings used on the map. Labels designate political and geographic place-names as well as physical features like mountain ranges and rivers.

▶ **The global grid** The absolute location of any place on Earth is given in terms of latitude (degrees north or south of the equator) and longitude (degrees east or west of the prime meridian). The symbol for a degree is °. Degrees are divided into 60 equal parts called minutes, which are represented by the symbol ´. The global grid is created by the intersecting lines of latitude (parallels) and lines of longitude (meridians). Lines of latitude and longitude may sometimes be indicated by tick marks near the edge of a map or by lines across an entire map.

▶ **Directions and distance** Most maps in *Call to Freedom* have a compass rose, or directional indicator. The compass rose indicates the four cardinal points—*N* for north, *S* for south, *E* for east, and *W* for west. You can also find intermediate directions—northeast, southeast, southwest, and northwest—using the compass rose. This helps in describing the relative location of a place. (If a map has no compass rose, assume that north is at the top, east is to the right, and so on.) Many maps in this textbook include a scale, showing both miles and kilometers, to help you relate distances on the map to actual distances on Earth's surface.

▶ **Map projections** Because Earth is a sphere, it is best represented by a three-dimensional globe. Although a flat map is an imperfect representation of Earth's surface, mapmakers have devised various ways of showing Earth two dimensionally. These different flat views of Earth's surface are called projections.

Every map projection, and therefore every map, distorts to some extent at least one of the following aspects: (1) the shape of land areas, (2) their relative sizes, (3) directions, or (4) distances. Mapmakers choose the projection that least distorts what they wish to show. For example, an equal-area projection shows the relative sizes of different countries or continents quite accurately but distorts shapes somewhat.

How to Read a Map

1. **Determine the focus of the map.** Read the map's title and labels to determine the map's focus—its subject and the geographic area it covers.

2. **Study the map legend.** Read the legend and become familiar with any special symbols, lines, colors, and shadings used on the map.

3. **Check directions and distance.** Use the directional indicator and scale as needed to determine direction, location, and distance between various points on the map.

4. **Check the grid lines.** Refer to lines of longitude and latitude or to a locator map to place the area on the map in a larger context.

5. **Study the map.** Study the map's basic features and details, keeping its purpose in mind. If it is a special-purpose map, study the specific information being presented.

PENNSYLVANIA

Susquehanna River

Potomac River

WEST VIRGINIA

Antietam
Sept. 1862

McCLELLAN

MARYLAND

Washington

Shenandoah Valley

Shenandoah River

Bull Run
July 1861 &
Aug. 1862

Chesapeake Bay

LEE

Rappahannock River

James River

Richmond
Fair Oaks
May–June 1862

Chickahominy River

Seven Days
June–July 1862

York River

McCLELLAN

ATLANTIC
OCEAN

VIRGINIA

76°W

37°N

	Union state
	Confederate state
	West Virginia (Separated from Virginia in 1861 and joined the Union in 1863)
→	Union forces
→	Confederate forces
✸	Union victory
✸	Confederate victory
✸	No victor

0   25   50 Miles
0   25   50 Kilometers
Albers Equal-Area Projection

N W E S

78°W

The War in the East, 1861–1862

Interpreting Maps One Union objective was to capture the Confederate capital of Richmond.

Skills Assessment Locate What battle took place in Maryland? What was the outcome?

United States of America: Political

WASHINGTON
Strait of Juan de Fuca
Puget Sound
Seattle
Olympia ★
Tacoma
Spokane ●
Portland ●
Columbia River
★ Salem
● Eugene
OREGON
Franklin D. Roosevelt Lake
Pend Oreille
Flathead Lake
Great Falls ●
Helena ★
MONTANA
Fort Peck Lake
Missouri River
Yellowstone River
Billings ●
Lake Sakakawea
Grand Forks ●
NORTH DAKOTA
★ Bismarck
Fargo ●

IDAHO
★ Boise
Sun Valley ●
Yellowstone Lake
Snake River
Pocatello ●

WYOMING
Cheyenne ★

Lake Oahe
SOUTH DAKOTA
Pierre ★
Rapid City ●
Minnesota
Sioux Falls ●
Missouri River
Sioux City

PACIFIC OCEAN
Cape Mendocino
Goose Lake
Shasta Lake
Pyramid Lake
Sacramento River
● Reno
★ Carson City
Lake Tahoe
NEVADA
Great Salt Lake
Ogden ●
★ Salt Lake City
Utah Lake
Provo ●
UTAH
Green River
Aspen ●
● Boulder
● Vail
● Denver
COLORADO
Colorado Springs ●
Pueblo ●
NEBRASKA
Platte River
Omaha ●
Lincoln ★

Berkeley ●
Oakland ●
San Francisco ●
● Sacramento
San Joaquin River
San Francisco Bay
● San Jose
Monterey Bay
● Fresno
CALIFORNIA
Las Vegas ●
Lake Mead
Lake Powell
Topeka ★
KANSAS
Wichita ●

Santa Barbara ●
Ventura ●
Channel
Los Angeles ●
Long Beach ●
Anaheim ●
Santa Ana ●
Riverside ●
Palm Springs ●
San Diego ●
Channel Islands
Salton Sea
Colorado River
Flagstaff ●
ARIZONA
Phoenix ★
Gila River
Casa Grande ●
Tucson ●
Taos ●
Santa Fe ★
Albuquerque ●
NEW MEXICO
Canadian River
Amarillo ●
OKLAHOMA
Oklahoma City ★
Keystone Lake
Tulsa ●
Arkansas River
Eufaula Lake
Lawton ●
Lake Texoma

Lubbock ●
Abilene ●
Fort Worth ●
Dallas ●
Midland ●
Odessa ●
TEXAS
Brazos River
Waco ●
Colorado River
Austin ★
Pecos River
Rio Grande
Amistad Reservoir
San Antonio ●
Las Cruces ●
El Paso ●
Houston ●
Laredo ●
Corpus Christi ●
PADRE ISLAND
GULF OF CALIFORNIA

GULF OF CALIFORNIA

To understand the relative locations of Alaska and Hawaii, as well as the vast distances separating them from the rest of the United States, see the world map.

HAWAII
KAUAI
NIIHAU
OAHU
Honolulu ★
MOLOKAI
LANAI
MAUI
KAHOOLAWE
PACIFIC OCEAN
Hilo ●
HAWAII
0   75   150 Miles
0   75   150 Kilometers

ARCTIC OCEAN
Arctic Circle
RUSSIA
Bering Strait
Nome ●
Yukon River
ST. LAWRENCE ISLAND
ST. MATTHEW ISLAND
NUNIVAK ISLAND
BERING SEA
Fairbanks ●
ALASKA
CANADA
Anchorage ●
Valdez ●
Skagway ●
Juneau ★
ATTU ISLAND
ALEUTIAN ISLANDS
PACIFIC OCEAN
KODIAK ISLAND
Gulf of Alaska
ALEXANDER ARCHIPELAGO
0   250   500 Miles
0   250   500 Kilometers
Projection: Albers Equal Area

MEXICO

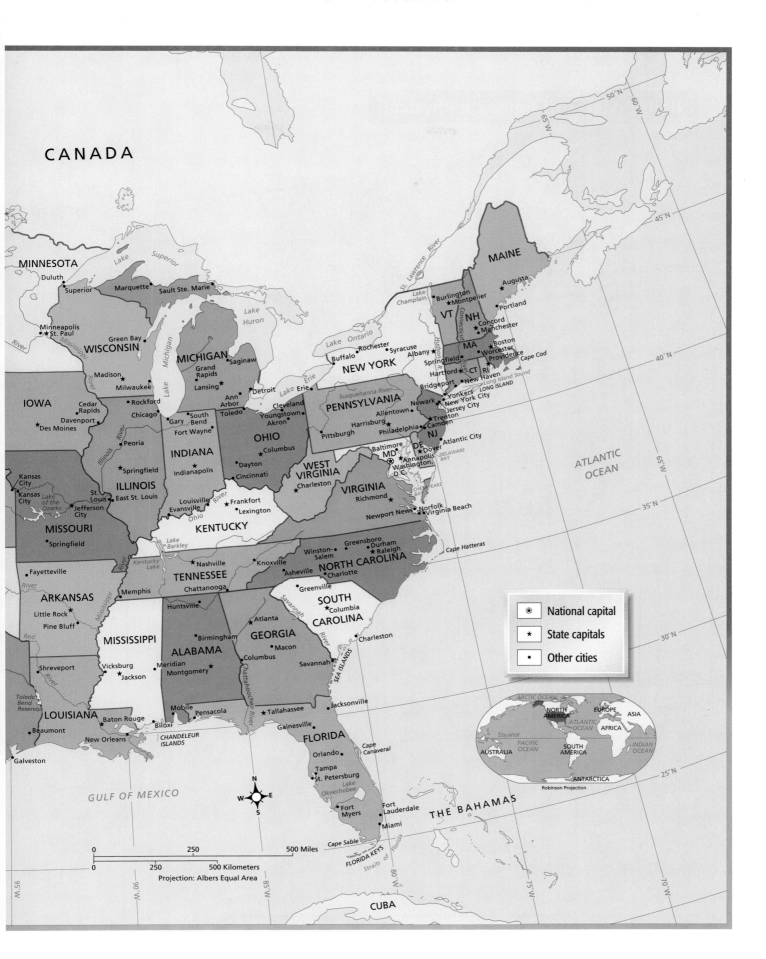

CANADA

MINNESOTA
Duluth
Superior
Marquette
Sault Ste. Marie

Lake Superior

Minneapolis
St. Paul
WISCONSIN
Green Bay
Madison
Milwaukee
Rockford

Lake Huron

MICHIGAN
Grand Rapids
Saginaw
Lansing
Ann Arbor
Detroit

Lake Michigan

IOWA
Cedar Rapids
Davenport
Des Moines
Chicago
Gary
South Bend
Fort Wayne
Peoria

Lake Ontario
Buffalo
Rochester
Syracuse

Lake Erie
Cleveland
Toledo
Youngstown
Akron

NEW YORK

St. Lawrence River

MAINE
Augusta
Portland

Lake Champlain
Burlington
Montpelier
VT
NH
Concord
Manchester
MA
Boston
Worcester
Springfield
Providence
Cape Cod
Albany
Hartford
CT
RI
New Haven
Bridgeport
Long Island Sound
Yonkers
LONG ISLAND
New York City
Jersey City
Newark
Trenton
Allentown
NJ
Harrisburg
Atlantic City

Hudson River

PENNSYLVANIA
Pittsburgh
Philadelphia
Camden
Susquehanna River

KANSAS
Kansas City
Kansas City

ILLINOIS
Springfield
East St. Louis
St. Louis

INDIANA
Indianapolis
Dayton
Cincinnati

OHIO
Columbus

WEST VIRGINIA
Charleston

Baltimore
MD
Annapolis
Washington, D.C.
DE
Dover
DELAWARE BAY

Illinois River

MISSOURI
Springfield
Fayetteville

Lake of the Ozarks
Jefferson City

Louisville
Evansville
Frankfort
Lexington
KENTUCKY

Ohio River

Lake Barkley
Kentucky Lake

VIRGINIA
Richmond

CHESAPEAKE BAY

Newport News
Norfolk
Virginia Beach

ARKANSAS
Little Rock
Pine Bluff

Red River

Nashville
Knoxville
Chattanooga
Memphis
Huntsville
TENNESSEE

Asheville
Winston-Salem
Greensboro
Durham
Raleigh
Charlotte
NORTH CAROLINA

Cape Hatteras

Greenville

SOUTH CAROLINA
Columbia
Charleston

ATLANTIC OCEAN

MISSISSIPPI
Vicksburg
Jackson
Meridian

Birmingham
ALABAMA
Montgomery
Columbus

GEORGIA
Atlanta
Macon
Savannah

Savannah River

Chattahoochee River

SEA ISLANDS

Shreveport
LOUISIANA
Beaumont
Baton Rouge
New Orleans
Galveston

Toledo Bend Reservoir

Mobile
Pensacola
Biloxi
CHANDELEUR ISLANDS

Tallahassee
Gainesville
Jacksonville

FLORIDA
Orlando
Cape Canaveral

GULF OF MEXICO

Tampa
St. Petersburg
Lake Okeechobee
Fort Myers
Fort Lauderdale
Miami

Cape Sable
FLORIDA KEYS
Straits of Florida

THE BAHAMAS

CUBA

National capital
State capitals
Other cities

ARCTIC OCEAN
NORTH AMERICA
EUROPE
ASIA
ATLANTIC OCEAN
AFRICA
Equator
PACIFIC OCEAN
SOUTH AMERICA
INDIAN OCEAN
AUSTRALIA
ANTARCTICA
Robinson Projection

N
W
E
S

0   250   500 Miles
0   250   500 Kilometers
Projection: Albers Equal Area

50° N
60° W
65° W
45° N
40° N
65° W
35° N
30° N
25° N
95° W
90° W
85° W
80° W
75° W
70° W

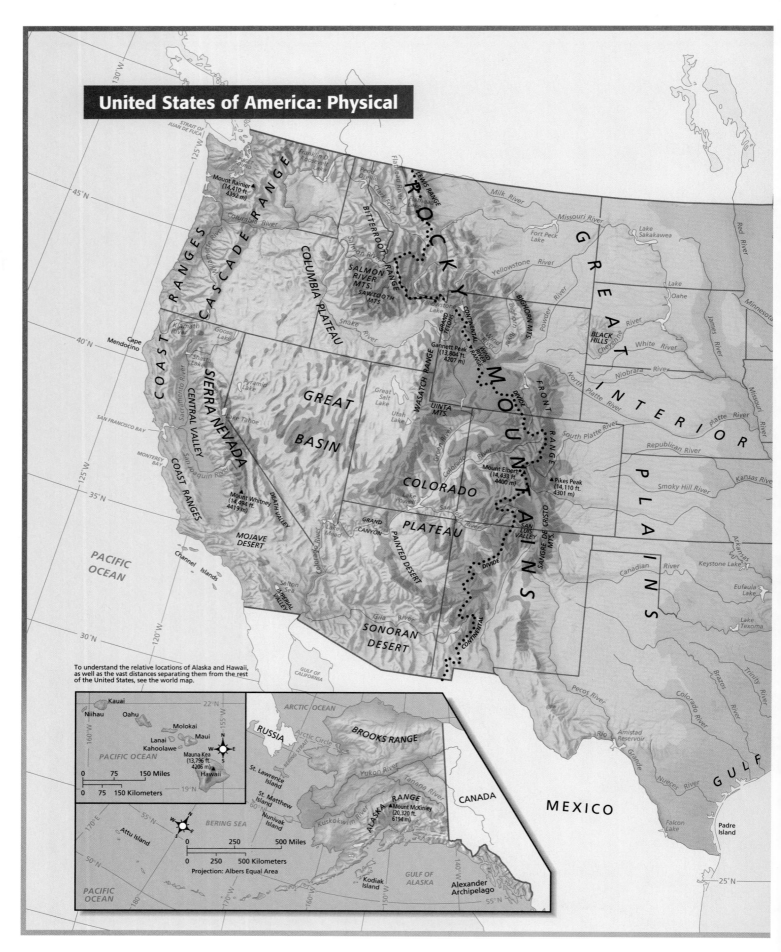

United States of America: Physical

STRAIT OF JUAN DE FUCA

PUGET SOUND

▲ Mount Rainier (14,410 ft. 4392 m)

Columbia River

Willamette River

COAST RANGES

CASCADE RANGE

Franklin D. Roosevelt Lake

Pend Oreille

Clark Fork

Flathead Lake

Flathead River

LEWIS RANGE

R O C K Y

Milk River

Missouri River

G R E A T

Fort Peck Lake

Lake Sakakawea

Red River

BITTERROOT RANGE

Salmon River

SALMON RIVER MTS.

SAWTOOTH MTS.

COLUMBIA PLATEAU

Snake River

Yellowstone Lake

Yellowstone River

GRAND TETONS

CONTINENTAL DIVIDE

WIND RIVER RANGE

Wind River

BIGHORN MTS.

Bighorn River

Powder River

Yellowstone River

BLACK HILLS

I N T E R I O R

Lake Oahe

Minnesota

James River

Klamath River

Shasta Lake

Goose Lake

Pyramid Lake

Great Salt Lake

WASATCH RANGE

UINTA MTS.

Gannett Peak (13,804 ft. 4207 m)

M O U N T A I N S

DIVIDE

FRONT RANGE

Cheyenne River

White River

Niobrara River

North Platte River

South Platte River

Platte River

Republican River

SIERRA NEVADA

CENTRAL VALLEY

Sacramento River

San Joaquin River

Lake Tahoe

G R E A T

B A S I N

Green River

Colorado River

COLORADO

Mount Elbert (14,433 ft. 4400 m)

▲ Pikes Peak (14,110 ft. 4301 m)

P L A I N S

Smoky Hill River

Kansas River

SAN FRANCISCO BAY

MONTEREY BAY

COAST RANGES

▲ Mount Whitney (14,494 ft. 4419 m)

DEATH VALLEY

MOJAVE DESERT

Lake Powell

GRAND CANYON

Lake Mead

PLATEAU

PAINTED DESERT

San Juan River

SAN LUIS VALLEY

SANGRE DE CRISTO MTS.

DIVIDE

Keystone Lake

Eufaula Lake

Arkansas River

PACIFIC OCEAN

Channel Islands

Colorado River

Salton Sea

IMPERIAL VALLEY

SONORAN DESERT

Gila River

CONTINENTAL

Lake Texoma

Canadian River

Pecos River

Colorado River

Brazos River

Trinity River

To understand the relative locations of Alaska and Hawaii, as well as the vast distances separating them from the rest of the United States, see the world map.

GULF OF CALIFORNIA

MEXICO

Rio Grande

Amistad Reservoir

Nueces River

Falcon Lake

Padre Island

GULF

Kauai

Niihau

Oahu

Molokai

Lanai

Kahoolawe

Maui

PACIFIC OCEAN

Mauna Kea (13,796 ft. 4206 m)

Hawaii

0   75   150 Miles

0   75   150 Kilometers

ARCTIC OCEAN

RUSSIA

Arctic Circle

BROOKS RANGE

BERING STRAIT

St. Lawrence Island

St. Matthew Island

Nunivak Island

Yukon River

Tanana River

Kuskokwim River

ALASKA RANGE

▲ Mount McKinley (20,320 ft. 6194 m)

CANADA

Attu Island

BERING SEA

Kodiak Island

GULF OF ALASKA

Alexander Archipelago

0   250   500 Miles

0   250   500 Kilometers

Projection: Albers Equal Area

PACIFIC OCEAN

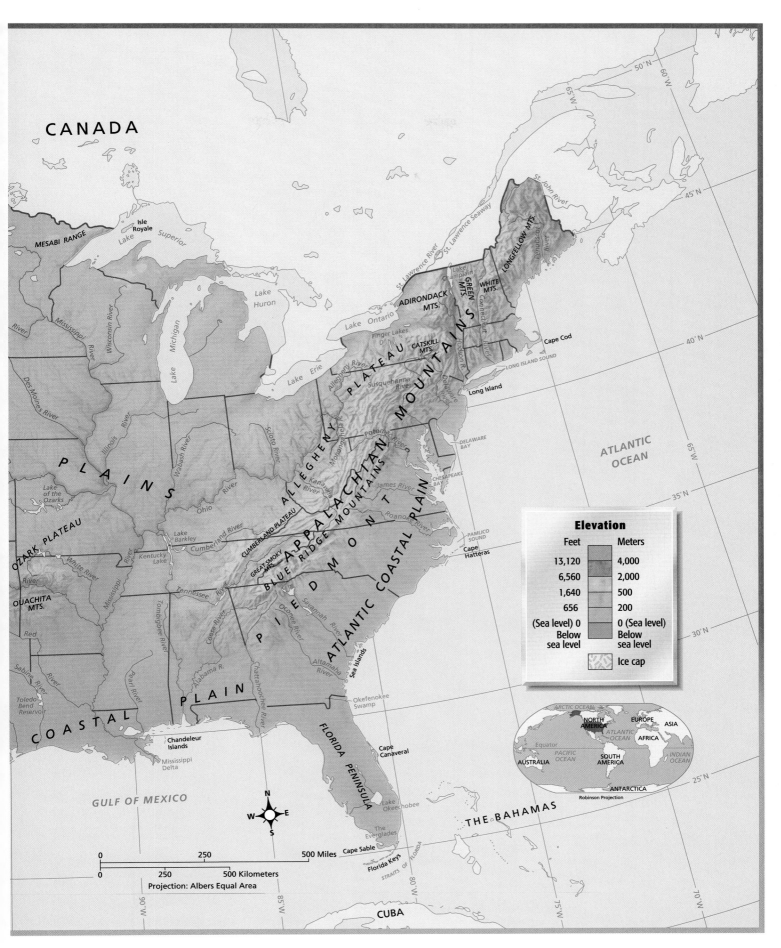

CANADA

MESABI RANGE
Isle
Royale
Lake Superior

Lake Huron

Lake Michigan

Lake Erie

Lake Ontario

St. Lawrence River
St. Lawrence Seaway
Lake Champlain

LONGFELLOW MTS.
St. John River
Penobscot River

WHITE MTS.
GREEN MTS.
ADIRONDACK MTS.

Finger Lakes

Connecticut River
Hudson R.

Cape Cod

CATSKILL MTS.

A L L E G H E N Y   P L A T E A U

Susquehanna River
Delaware River

LONG ISLAND SOUND
Long Island

P L A I N S

Mississippi River
Wisconsin River

Des Moines River

Illinois River

Wabash River

Scioto River

Ohio River

Allegheny River

Monongahela R.

Potomac River

Kanawha River

A P P A L A C H I A N   M O U N T A I N S

DELAWARE BAY

CHESAPEAKE BAY

Lake of the Ozarks

OZARK PLATEAU

Lake Barkley

Cumberland River

Kentucky Lake

CUMBERLAND PLATEAU

GREAT SMOKY MTS.

BLUE RIDGE MOUNTAINS

James River

Roanoke River

P I E D M O N T

A T L A N T I C   C O A S T A L   P L A I N

PAMLICO SOUND

Cape Hatteras

OUACHITA MTS.

White River

Red River

Tennessee River

Tombigbee River

Coosa River

Oconee River

Savannah River

Altamaha River

Sea Islands

ATLANTIC OCEAN

Sabine River

Toledo Bend Reservoir

Pearl River

Alabama R.

Chattahoochee River

Okefenokee Swamp

C O A S T A L   P L A I N

Chandeleur Islands

Mississippi Delta

FLORIDA PENINSULA

Cape Canaveral

GULF OF MEXICO

Lake Okeechobee

The Everglades

Cape Sable

Florida Keys

STRAITS OF FLORIDA

THE BAHAMAS

CUBA

N
W E
S

| 0 | 250 | 500 Miles |
| 0 | 250 | 500 Kilometers |

Projection: Albers Equal Area

Elevation

Feet		Meters
13,120		4,000
6,560		2,000
1,640		500
656		200
(Sea level) 0		0 (Sea level)
Below sea level		Below sea level
	Ice cap	

ARCTIC OCEAN
NORTH AMERICA
EUROPE
ASIA
ATLANTIC OCEAN
AFRICA
Equator
PACIFIC OCEAN
SOUTH AMERICA
INDIAN OCEAN
AUSTRALIA
ANTARCTICA
Robinson Projection

45° N
50° N
60° W
65° W
40° N
65° W
35° N
30° N
25° N
90° W
85° W
80° W
75° W
70° W

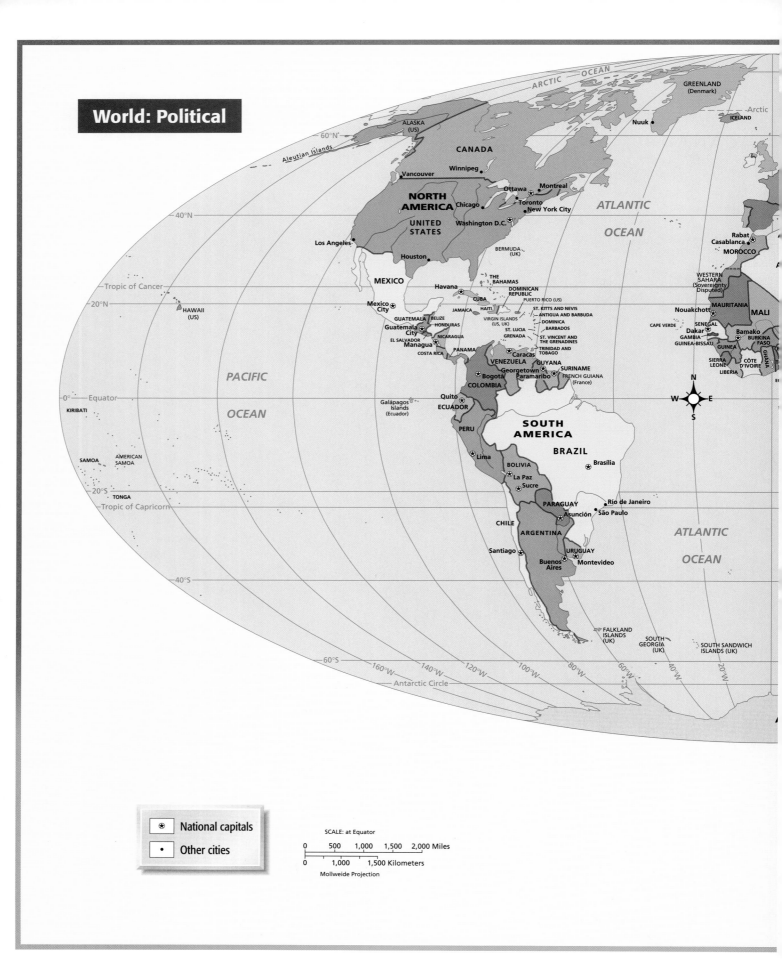

World: Political

ARCTIC OCEAN

GREENLAND (Denmark)

Arctic

Nuuk

ICELAND

ALASKA (US)

60°N

Aleutian Islands

CANADA

Vancouver   Winnipeg

NORTH   Ottawa   Montreal
AMERICA   Chicago   Toronto
                              New York City

40°N

UNITED   Washington D.C.
STATES

ATLANTIC

OCEAN

Los Angeles

BERMUDA (UK)

Rabat
Casablanca
MOROCCO

Houston

WESTERN SAHARA (Sovereignty Disputed)

MEXICO

Tropic of Cancer

20°N

THE BAHAMAS
Havana   DOMINICAN REPUBLIC
CUBA   PUERTO RICO (US)

Nouakchott   MAURITANIA   MALI

HAWAII (US)

Mexico City

JAMAICA   HAITI   VIRGIN ISLANDS (US, UK)

ST. KITTS AND NEVIS
ANTIGUA AND BARBUDA

CAPE VERDE

SENEGAL
Dakar
GAMBIA   Bamako   BURKINA FASO
GUINEA-BISSAU   GUINEA

GUATEMALA   BELIZE
Guatemala   HONDURAS
City   NICARAGUA
EL SALVADOR   Managua
         COSTA RICA

DOMINICA
ST. LUCIA
BARBADOS
GRENADA
ST. VINCENT AND THE GRENADINES

PANAMA

TRINIDAD AND TOBAGO

SIERRA LEONE   CÔTE D'IVOIRE   GHANA
LIBERIA

PACIFIC

Caracas
VENEZUELA   GUYANA
Bogotá   Georgetown   SURINAME
COLOMBIA   Paramaribo   FRENCH GUIANA (France)

N
W   E
S

KIRIBATI

0°   Equator

Galápagos Islands (Ecuador)

Quito
ECUADOR

OCEAN

PERU

SOUTH
AMERICA

BRAZIL

SAMOA   AMERICAN SAMOA

Lima

Brasília

BOLIVIA
La Paz
Sucre

20°S

TONGA

Tropic of Capricorn

PARAGUAY   Rio de Janeiro

CHILE   Asunción   São Paulo

ARGENTINA

ATLANTIC

URUGUAY

Santiago

Buenos   Montevideo
Aires

OCEAN

40°S

FALKLAND
ISLANDS (UK)

SOUTH
GEORGIA (UK)

SOUTH SANDWICH
ISLANDS (UK)

60°S

160°W   140°W   120°W   100°W   80°W   60°W   40°W   20°W

Antarctic Circle

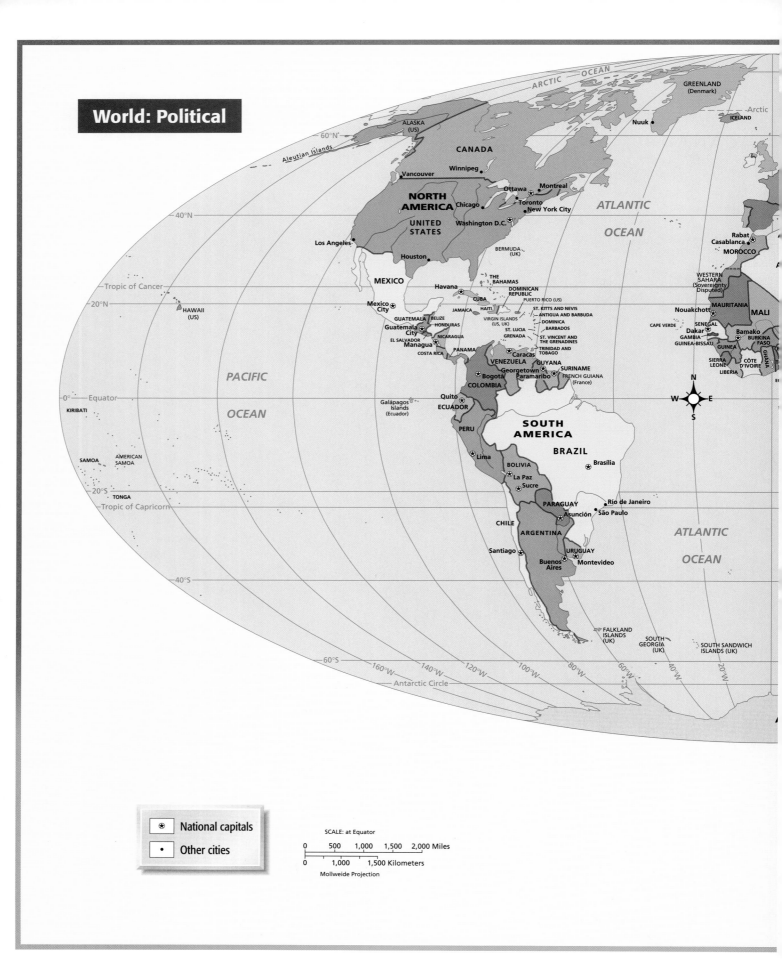

⊛   National capitals

•   Other cities

SCALE: at Equator

0   500   1,000   1,500   2,000 Miles

0   1,000   1,500 Kilometers

Mollweide Projection

A4   *Atlas*

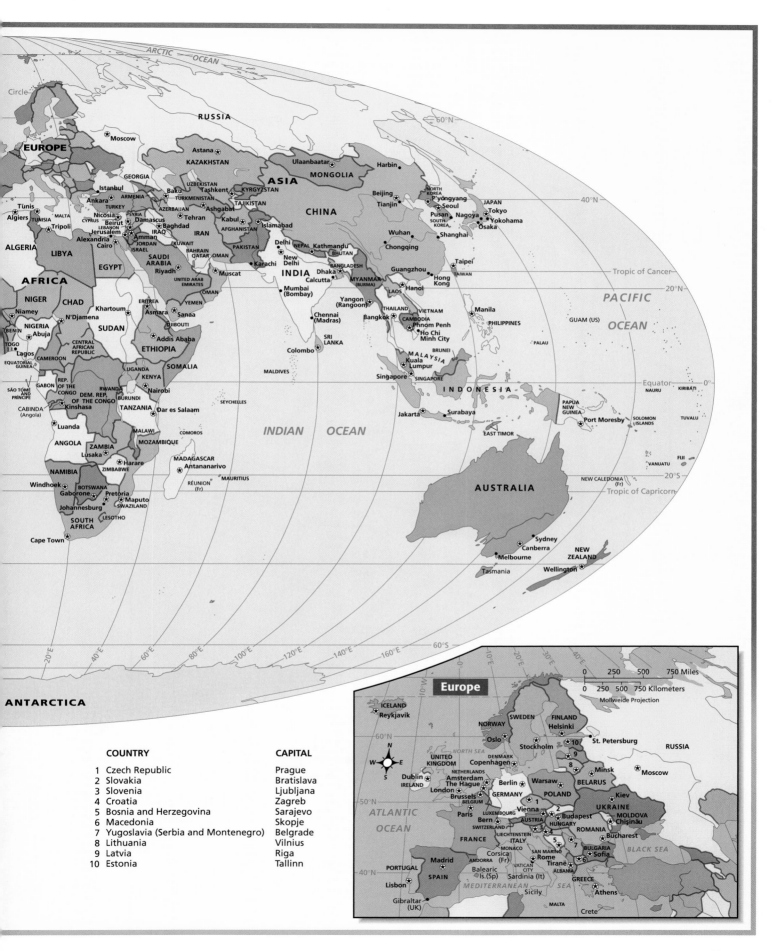

ARCTIC OCEAN

Circle

RUSSIA

EUROPE

Moscow

60°N

Astana
KAZAKHSTAN
Ulaanbaatar
ASIA
MONGOLIA
Harbin

GEORGIA
Istanbul
UZBEKISTAN
Tashkent
KYRGYZSTAN
Beijing
NORTH KOREA
P'yŏngyang
JAPAN
40°N
Ankara
ARMENIA
Baku
TURKMENISTAN
Ashgabat
TAJIKISTAN
Tianjin
Seoul
Tokyo
TURKEY
AZERBAIJAN
CHINA
SOUTH KOREA
Pusan
Nagoya
Yokohama
Tunis
MALTA
Nicosia
SYRIA
Tehran
Kabul
Osaka
Algiers
TUNISIA
CYPRUS
Beirut
Damascus
Baghdad
AFGHANISTAN
Islamabad
Wuhan
Shanghai
Tripoli
LEBANON
Jerusalem
IRAQ
IRAN
Chongqing
Alexandria
ISRAEL
Amman
JORDAN
KUWAIT
PAKISTAN
Delhi
NEPAL
Kathmandu
BHUTAN
Taipei
ALGERIA
Cairo
SAUDI
BAHRAIN
New Delhi
BANGLADESH
Guangzhou
TAIWAN
Tropic of Cancer
LIBYA
EGYPT
ARABIA
QATAR OMAN
Karachi
Dhaka
Hong Kong
Riyadh
UNITED ARAB EMIRATES
INDIA
Calcutta
MYANMAR (BURMA)
Hanoi
20°N
AFRICA
Muscat
Mumbai (Bombay)
LAOS
PACIFIC
OMAN
Yangon (Rangoon)
VIETNAM
Manila
NIGER CHAD
ERITREA
Khartoum
YEMEN
Sanaa
Chennai (Madras)
Bangkok
THAILAND
CAMBODIA
Phnom Penh
PHILIPPINES
GUAM (US)
OCEAN
Niamey
N'Djamena
Asmara
DJIBOUTI
SRI LANKA
Ho Chi Minh City
NIGERIA
SUDAN
Addis Ababa
Colombo
PALAU
Abuja
CENTRAL AFRICAN REPUBLIC
ETHIOPIA
BRUNEI
TOGO
Lagos
SOMALIA
MALAYSIA
Kuala Lumpur
EQUATORIAL GUINEA
CAMEROON
UGANDA
KENYA
MALDIVES
Singapore SINGAPORE
INDONESIA
Equator 0°
SÃO TOMÉ AND PRÍNCIPE
GABON
REP. OF THE CONGO
RWANDA
Nairobi
NAURU
KIRIBATI
CABINDA (Angola)
DEM. REP. OF THE CONGO
BURUNDI
TANZANIA
Dar es Salaam
SEYCHELLES
Jakarta
Surabaya
PAPUA NEW GUINEA
Port Moresby
SOLOMON ISLANDS
TUVALU
Kinshasa
Luanda
INDIAN OCEAN
EAST TIMOR
ANGOLA
MALAWI
COMOROS
FIJI
ZAMBIA
MOZAMBIQUE
MADAGASCAR
Antananarivo
20°S
Lusaka
Harare
NEW CALEDONIA (Fr)
NAMIBIA
ZIMBABWE
RÉUNION (Fr)
MAURITIUS
Tropic of Capricorn
Windhoek
BOTSWANA
AUSTRALIA
Gaborone
Pretoria
Maputo
SWAZILAND
Johannesburg
LESOTHO
SOUTH AFRICA
Sydney
Canberra
NEW ZEALAND
Cape Town
Melbourne
Wellington
Tasmania

ANTARCTICA

20°E 40°E 60°E 80°E 100°E 120°E 140°E 160°E 60°S

COUNTRY	CAPITAL
1 Czech Republic	Prague
2 Slovakia	Bratislava
3 Slovenia	Ljubljana
4 Croatia	Zagreb
5 Bosnia and Herzegovina	Sarajevo
6 Macedonia	Skopje
7 Yugoslavia (Serbia and Montenegro)	Belgrade
8 Lithuania	Vilnius
9 Latvia	Riga
10 Estonia	Tallinn

Europe

0 250 500 750 Miles
0 250 500 750 Kilometers
Mollweide Projection

ICELAND
Reykjavik

NORWAY
SWEDEN
FINLAND
Helsinki
10
St. Petersburg
RUSSIA
60°N
NORTH SEA
Oslo
Stockholm
9
Minsk
Moscow
UNITED KINGDOM
DENMARK
Copenhagen
8
Dublin
NETHERLANDS
Amsterdam
The Hague
Berlin
Warsaw
BELARUS
IRELAND
London
Brussels
GERMANY
1
POLAND
Kiev
50°N
BELGIUM
Paris
Vienna
2
UKRAINE
ATLANTIC
LUXEMBOURG
Bern
AUSTRIA
Budapest
MOLDOVA
Chișinău
OCEAN
FRANCE
SWITZERLAND
LIECHTENSTEIN
3
4
HUNGARY
ROMANIA
MONACO
5
Bucharest
ITALY
7
SAN MARINO
Rome
6
BULGARIA
Sofia
BLACK SEA
Corsica (Fr)
Madrid
ANDORRA
VATICAN CITY
Tiranë
PORTUGAL
40°N
SPAIN
Balearic Is. (Sp)
Sardinia (It)
ALBANIA
GREECE
Lisbon
MEDITERRANEAN SEA
Sicily
Athens
Gibraltar (UK)
MALTA
Crete

N W E S

North America: Political

ASIA

EUROPE

NORTH POLE

ARCTIC OCEAN

BERING SEA
BERING STRAIT
St. Lawrence Island
Nunivak Island

Point Barrow

Queen Elizabeth Islands
Ellesmere Island

GREENLAND (Denmark)

ICELAND

DENMARK STRAIT

Arctic Circle

Banks Island

Victoria Island

BAFFIN BAY

Nuuk

Cape Farewell

BEAUFORT SEA

ALASKA (US)
Anchorage

GULF OF ALASKA
Kodiak Island

Juneau
Alexander Archipelago

Queen Charlotte Islands

PACIFIC OCEAN

Vancouver Island
Vancouver

Seattle
Portland

San Francisco

Los Angeles
San Diego
Tijuana

Edmonton

Calgary

CANADA

Great Bear Lake

Great Slave Lake

Southampton Island
Coats Island
Mansel Island

HUDSON STRAIT

HUDSON BAY

DAVIS STRAIT

LABRADOR SEA

Anticosti Island
Newfoundland

ST. PIERRE AND MIQUELON (Fr)

Lake Winnipeg

Winnipeg

Prince Edward Island
GULF OF ST. LAWRENCE
Quebec

Cape Breton Island

ATLANTIC OCEAN

Salt Lake City
Great Salt Lake

Denver

Minneapolis
Milwaukee
Chicago
Indianapolis

Kansas City
St. Louis

Lake Superior
Lake Michigan
Lake Huron
Detroit
Lake Erie
Cleveland
Columbus
Lake Ontario
Toronto
Ottawa
Montreal

Boston
Cape Cod
New York City
Philadelphia
Baltimore
Washington, D.C.
Norfolk

UNITED STATES

Memphis

Phoenix

Dallas

Austin
San Antonio
Houston

New Orleans

Atlanta
Birmingham

Jacksonville

Cape Hatteras

BERMUDA (UK)

Cape Canaveral

GULF OF CALIFORNIA

Monterrey

MEXICO

Guadalajara

Mexico City
Puebla

Mérida

GULF OF MEXICO

Havana

Florida Keys
Miami

THE BAHAMAS

Nassau

STRAITS OF FLORIDA

CUBA

CAYMAN IS. (U.K.)

Kingston

JAMAICA

TURKS AND CAICOS ISLANDS (UK)

DOMINICAN REPUBLIC

HAITI
Port-au-Prince

Santo Domingo

PUERTO RICO (US)
San Juan

VIRGIN IS. (US, UK)
ST. KITTS & NEVIS
MARTINIQUE (Fr)
ST. VINCENT AND THE GRENADINES

NETHERLANDS ANTILLES (Neth)
ARUBA (Neth)

ANTIGUA & BARBUDA
GUADELOUPE (Fr)
DOMINICA
ST. LUCIA
BARBADOS
GRENADA
TRINIDAD AND TOBAGO

CARIBBEAN SEA

Belmopan
BELIZE

GUATEMALA
Guatemala City

San Salvador
EL SALVADOR

HONDURAS
Tegucigalpa

NICARAGUA
Managua

San José

COSTA RICA

Panama Canal

PANAMA

Panama City

Tropic of Cancer

SOUTH AMERICA

Legend
- ⊛ National capital
- • Other cities

Inset globe
ARCTIC OCEAN
NORTH AMERICA
EUROPE
ASIA
ATLANTIC OCEAN
AFRICA
Equator
PACIFIC OCEAN
SOUTH AMERICA
INDIAN OCEAN
AUSTRALIA
ANTARCTICA
Robinson Projection

Equator 0°

N W E S

| 0 | 250 | 500 | 750 | 1,000 Miles |
| 0 | 250 | 500 | 750 | 1,000 Kilometers |

Azimuthal Equal-Area Projection

South America: Political

CENTRAL AMERICA

CARIBBEAN SEA

Barranquilla
Cartagena
Caracas
Lake Maracaibo
VENEZUELA
Georgetown
Paramaribo
GUYANA
Cayenne
SURINAME
FRENCH GUIANA (Fr)
Medellín
Orinoco River
Bogotá
COLOMBIA
Cali

Malpelo Island (Colombia)

Quito
ECUADOR
Equator 0°
Río Negro
Amazon River
Belém
Guayaquil

Galápagos Islands (Ecuador)

Amazon River

BRAZIL

PERU
Marañón River
Ucayali River

Trujillo

Recife

Callao
Lima

Lake Titicaca
Arequipa
La Paz
BOLIVIA
São Francisco River
Brasília
Salvador

PACIFIC OCEAN

Lake Poopó
Sucre

Belo Horizonte

PARAGUAY
Paraguay River
Asunción
Campinas
São Paulo
Rio de Janeiro
Tropic of Capricorn
Curitiba

San Ambrosio Island (Chile)
San Félix Island (Chile)

Paraná River
CHILE
Uruguay River
Pôrto Alegre

Juan Fernández Islands (Chile)

Córdoba
Valparaíso
Santiago
Rosario
Buenos Aires
Morón
San Justo
Lomas de Zamora
URUGUAY
Montevideo
RIO DE LA PLATA

ATLANTIC OCEAN

ARGENTINA

⊛ National capital
• Other cities

0   250   500   750   1,000 Miles
0   250   500   750   1,000 Kilometers
Azimuthal Equal-Area Projection

STRAIT OF MAGELLAN
FALKLAND ISLANDS (UK)
Tierra del Fuego

SOUTH GEORGIA ISLAND (UK)

ARCTIC OCEAN
NORTH AMERICA
EUROPE
ASIA
ATLANTIC OCEAN
AFRICA
Equator
PACIFIC OCEAN
SOUTH AMERICA
INDIAN OCEAN
AUSTRALIA
ANTARCTICA
Robinson Projection

Europe: Political

ASIA

URAL MOUNTAINS

Ural River

RUSSIA

Volga River

CASPIAN SEA

50°E

40°E

SOUTHWEST ASIA

Nizhniy Novgorod

Moscow ⊕

Don River

BARENTS SEA

WHITE SEA

St. Petersburg •

Dnieper River

Kiev ⊕

UKRAINE

MOLDOVA

Chişinău ⊕

Odesa •

30°E

BLACK SEA

40°E

GULF OF FINLAND

Helsinki ⊕

Tallinn ⊕

ESTONIA

Riga ⊕

LATVIA

LITHUANIA

Vilnius ⊕

Minsk ⊕

BELARUS

Warsaw ⊕

Bucharest ⊕

ROMANIA

Danube River

BULGARIA

Sofia ⊕

AEGEAN SEA

Rhodes

FINLAND

SWEDEN

Stockholm ⊕

BALTIC SEA

RUSSIA

POLAND

Kraków •

Belgrade ⊕

SERBIA

YUGOSLAVIA

Skopje ⊕

MACEDONIA

Thessaloníki •

GREECE

Athens ⊕

Crete

30°E

North Cape

Göteborg •

Łódź •

SLOVAKIA

Bratislava ⊕

HUNGARY

Budapest ⊕

Zagreb ⊕

CROATIA

BOSNIA & HERZEGOVINA

Sarajevo ⊕

MONTENEGRO

ALBANIA

Tiranë ⊕

ADRIATIC SEA

MALTA

Valletta ⊕

SEA

20°E

ARCTIC OCEAN

GULF OF BOTHNIA

NORWAY

Oslo ⊕

Bergen •

DENMARK

Copenhagen ⊕

Hamburg •

Berlin ⊕

Leipzig •

Dresden •

Prague ⊕

CZECH REPUBLIC

Vienna ⊕

AUSTRIA

SLOVENIA

Ljubljana ⊕

SAN MARINO

San Marino ⊕

VATICAN CITY

Rome ⊕

ITALY

Naples •

Palermo •

Sicily

Elbe River

GERMANY

Cologne •

Bonn •

Munich •

LIECHTENSTEIN

Vaduz ⊕

SWITZERLAND

Bern ⊕

Milan •

Turin •

Po River

MONACO

Monaco ⊕

Corsica (France)

Sardinia (Italy)

MEDITERRANEAN

AFRICA

0°

NORTH SEA

THE NETHERLANDS

Amsterdam ⊕

The Hague •

Rotterdam •

Antwerp •

BELGIUM

Brussels ⊕

LUXEMBOURG

Luxembourg ⊕

Paris ⊕

FRANCE

Danube River

Rhine River

Lake Geneva

Lyon •

Rhône River

Marseille •

10°E

10°W

N E W S

ARCTIC OCEAN

Arctic Circle

Shetland Islands

FAEROE ISLANDS (Denmark)

ICELAND

Reykjavik ⊕

Scotland

Glasgow •

Edinburgh •

NORTHERN IRELAND

Belfast •

UNITED KINGDOM

Leeds •

Sheffield •

Manchester •

Liverpool •

Birmingham •

WALES

ENGLAND

London ⊕

Dublin ⊕

IRELAND

British Isles

Channel Islands (UK)

ENGLISH CHANNEL

Seine River

Loire River

BAY OF BISCAY

PYRENEES

ANDORRA

Andorra la Vella ⊕

Barcelona •

Balearic Islands (Spain)

Valencia •

SPAIN

Madrid ⊕

Seville •

Gibraltar (UK)

STRAIT OF GIBRALTAR

PORTUGAL

Lisbon ⊕

Tagus River

20°W

30°W

70°N

60°N

ATLANTIC OCEAN

ASIA

EUROPE

AFRICA

PACIFIC OCEAN

ATLANTIC OCEAN

INDIAN OCEAN

AUSTRALIA

ANTARCTICA

NORTH AMERICA

SOUTH AMERICA

PACIFIC OCEAN

Equator

Robinson Projection

National capital ⊕

Other cities •

500 Miles

500 Kilometers

250

250

500 Miles

Azimuthal Equal-Area Projection

0

0

40°N

30°N

30°W

20°W

10°W

0°

10°W

20°W

70°N

60°N

80°N

Asia: Political

National capital ⊛
Other cities •

PACIFIC OCEAN

NORTH AMERICA

BERING SEA

Aleutian Islands

SEA OF OKHOTSK

Sakhalin Island

Kuril Islands

JAPAN
Sapporo
Sendai
Tokyo
Yokohama
Kawasaki
Nagoya
Kyoto
Kobe
Osaka
Hiroshima
Fukuoka
Nagasaki

RUSSIA

Yakutsk

Lena River

Vladivostok

NORTH KOREA
Pyongyang
SOUTH KOREA
Seoul
Inchon
Pusan
Taegu

Harbin
Changchun
Shenyang
Anshan
Fushun
Dalian
Beijing
Tianjin
Jinan
Qingdao
Taiyuan
Shanghai
Nanjing

YELLOW SEA

EAST CHINA SEA

Ryukyu Islands

TAIWAN
Taipei

Amur River

MONGOLIA
Ulaanbaatar

CHINA
Lanzhou
Xi'an
GREAT WALL
Huang He
Chengdu
Chongqing
Wuhan

Hong Kong
Guangzhou
Macao (Port.)

Irkutsk
Lake Baykal

Angara River

Yenisey River

Novosibirsk
Omsk
Irtysh River

Chang River

Hanoi

SOUTH CHINA SEA

PHILIPPINES
Manila

CELEBES SEA

AUSTRALIA

IRIAN JAYA

EAST TIMOR

ARAFURA SEA

VIETNAM
LAOS
Vientiane
Mekong River
THAILAND
Bangkok
CAMBODIA
Phnom Penh
Ho Chi Minh City
GULF OF THAILAND

BRUNEI
Bandar Seri Begawan

MALAYSIA
Kuala Lumpur
SINGAPORE
Singapore

INDONESIA
Medan
JAVA SEA
Jakarta
Bandung
Semarang
Surabaya
Ujung Pandang

KAZAKHSTAN
Astana
Almaty
Lake Balqash

Yekaterinburg
Chelyabinsk
URAL MOUNTAINS

Ob River

MYANMAR (BURMA)
Mandalay
Yangon (Rangoon)
Irrawaddy River

ANDAMAN SEA

Andaman Islands (India)

Nicobar Islands (India)

BISHKEK
KYRGYZSTAN
Bishkek
TAJIKISTAN
Dushanbe
Tashkent
UZBEKISTAN

ARAL SEA

TURKMENISTAN
Ashgabat

Mashhad

AFGHANISTAN
Kabul

PAKISTAN
Islamabad
Lahore
Faisalabad
Karachi

Indus River

Delhi
New Delhi
Jaipur
Kanpur
Ahmadabad

INDIA
Nagpur
Hyderabad
Mumbai (Bombay)
Pune
Bangalore

NEPAL
Kathmandu
BHUTAN
Thimphu
BANGLADESH
Dhaka
Chittagong

Brahmaputra River
Ganges River

Calcutta

BAY OF BENGAL

SRI LANKA
Colombo

Chennai (Madras)

Lakshadweep Islands (India)

MALDIVES
Male

INDIAN OCEAN

CASPIAN SEA

Baku
AZERBAIJAN
GEORGIA
Tbilisi
ARMENIA
Yerevan
Tabriz

IRAN
Tehran
Esfahan
Shiraz
Mashhad

Salween River

KUWAIT
Kuwait City
BAHRAIN
Manama
QATAR
Doha
UNITED ARAB EMIRATES
Abu Dhabi
Muscat
OMAN

PERSIAN GULF

SOCOTRA (Yemen)

BLACK SEA

Istanbul
TURKEY
Ankara
Izmir
CYPRUS
Nicosia
LEBANON
Beirut
SYRIA
Aleppo
Damascus
ISRAEL
Tel Aviv
Jerusalem
JORDAN
Amman

Mosul
Baghdad
Basra
IRAQ
Tigris River
Euphrates River

SAUDI ARABIA
Riyadh
Jidda
Mecca

YEMEN
Sanaa

RED SEA

GULF OF ADEN

AFRICA

MADAGASCAR

Ural River

Moscow

RUSSIA

EUROPE

MEDITERRANEAN SEA

BARENTS SEA

KARA SEA

LAPTEV SEA

NORTH POLE

Arctic Circle

Tropic of Cancer

ARABIAN SEA

Equator

1,000 Miles
1,000 Kilometers
500
500

Modified Oblique Conic Projection

Robinson Projection

ASIA
EUROPE
AFRICA
AUSTRALIA
ANTARCTICA
NORTH AMERICA
SOUTH AMERICA
PACIFIC OCEAN
ATLANTIC OCEAN
INDIAN OCEAN

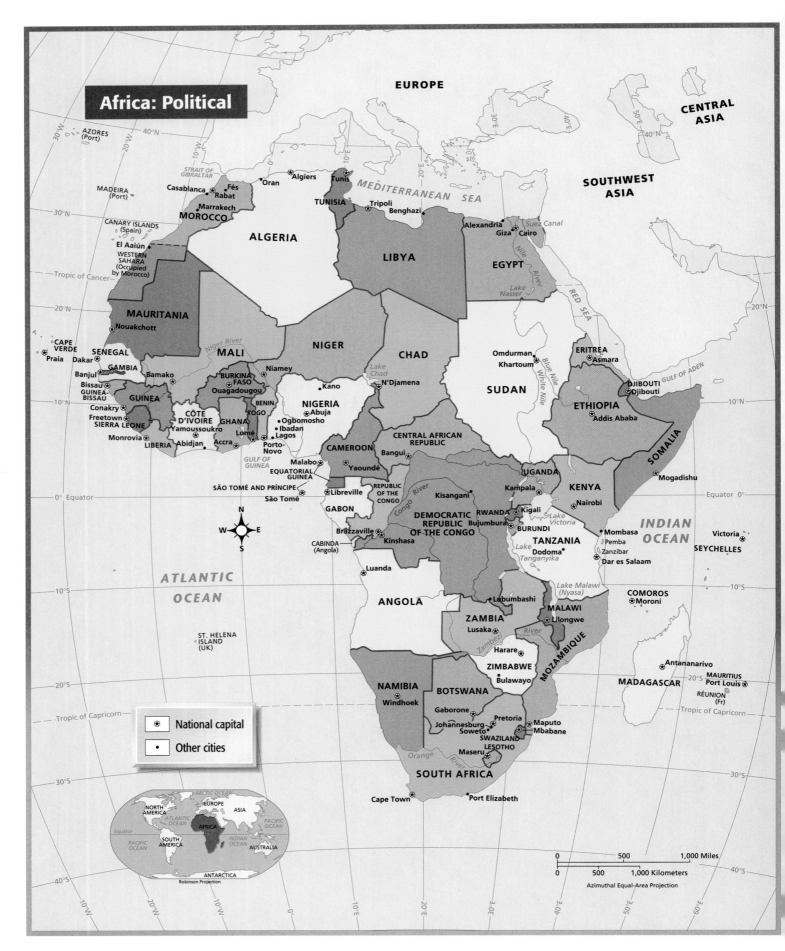

Africa: Political

EUROPE

CENTRAL ASIA

SOUTHWEST ASIA

AZORES (Port)

MEDITERRANEAN SEA

STRAIT OF GIBRALTAR

•Oran   •Algiers   Tunis•

Casablanca•   Fés
•Rabat

MADEIRA (Port)

Marrakech

MOROCCO

TUNISIA   Tripoli•   Benghazi•

CANARY ISLANDS (Spain)

El Aaiún•

WESTERN SAHARA (Occupied by Morocco)

ALGERIA

LIBYA

EGYPT

Alexandria•
Giza• •Cairo

Suez Canal

Tropic of Cancer

Lake Nasser

RED SEA

MAURITANIA

Nouakchott⊛

NIGER

CHAD

Omdurman•
Khartoum⊛

ERITREA
Asmara⊛

GULF OF ADEN

CAPE VERDE
Praia⊛

SENEGAL
Dakar⊛

Niger River

MALI

Lake Chad

SUDAN

Blue Nile
White Nile

DJIBOUTI
DJIBOUTI⊛

Banjul⊛
GAMBIA

Bamako⊛

Niamey⊛

•Kano

N'Djamena•

ETHIOPIA
Addis Ababa•

Bissau⊛
GUINEA-BISSAU

GUINEA

BURKINA FASO
Ouagadougou⊛

NIGERIA
Abuja⊛

Conakry⊛

BENIN
TOGO

Freetown⊛
SIERRA LEONE

CÔTE D'IVOIRE

GHANA

Ogbomosho•
•Ibadan
Lagos•

CENTRAL AFRICAN REPUBLIC

SOMALIA

Mogadishu⊛

Yamoussoukro⊛

Lomé⊛

UGANDA

Monrovia⊛
LIBERIA

Abidjan•

Accra⊛

Porto-Novo⊛

CAMEROON

Bangui⊛

Kampala⊛

KENYA

Nairobi⊛

Malabo⊛

Yaoundé⊛

EQUATORIAL GUINEA

SÃO TOMÉ AND PRÍNCIPE

Congo River

REPUBLIC OF THE CONGO

Kisangani•

RWANDA
Kigali⊛

Lake Victoria

Equator

São Tomé•

Libreville⊛

GABON

DEMOCRATIC REPUBLIC OF THE CONGO

Bujumbura⊛

BURUNDI

Mombasa•
Pemba

INDIAN OCEAN

Victoria⊛

SEYCHELLES

Equator 0°

TANZANIA
Dodoma⊛

Zanzibar
Dar es Salaam•

Brazzaville⊛

Kinshasa⊛

Lake Tanganyika

CABINDA (Angola)

Luanda⊛

ATLANTIC OCEAN

ST. HELENA ISLAND (UK)

ANGOLA

Lubumbashi•

Lake Malawi (Nyasa)

COMOROS
Moroni⊛

ZAMBIA
Lusaka⊛

MALAWI
Lilongwe⊛

Zambezi River

MOZAMBIQUE

Antananarivo⊛

MAURITIUS
Port Louis⊛

Harare⊛

ZIMBABWE

NAMIBIA

Windhoek⊛

BOTSWANA

Bulawayo•

MADAGASCAR

RÉUNION (Fr)

Tropic of Capricorn

Gaborone⊛

Pretoria⊛
Johannesburg• •Maputo
Soweto•   Mbabane⊛
SWAZILAND
LESOTHO

Orange River

Maseru⊛

SOUTH AFRICA

Cape Town⊛   •Port Elizabeth

Legend

⊛ National capital

• Other cities

N
W   E
S

NORTH AMERICA   EUROPE   ASIA
ATLANTIC OCEAN
Equator
PACIFIC OCEAN   AFRICA   PACIFIC OCEAN
SOUTH AMERICA   INDIAN OCEAN   AUSTRALIA
ANTARCTICA
Robinson Projection

0   500   1,000 Miles
0   500   1,000 Kilometers
Azimuthal Equal-Area Projection

Pacific Islands: Political

ASIA

NORTH AMERICA

NORTH PACIFIC OCEAN

SOUTH PACIFIC OCEAN

PHILIPPINE SEA

SOUTH CHINA SEA

INDONESIA

AUSTRALIA

INDIAN OCEAN

TASMAN SEA

CORAL SEA

ARAFURA SEA

TIMOR SEA

BONIN ISLANDS (Japan)

VOLCANO ISLANDS (Japan)

NORTHERN MARIANAS (US)

GUAM (US) • Agaña

MICRONESIA

Koror ⊛ PALAU

FEDERATED STATES OF MICRONESIA

⊛ Palikir

Chuuk Islands

New Guinea

Bismarck Archipelago

PAPUA NEW GUINEA ⊛ Port Moresby

SOLOMON ISLANDS

Honiara ⊛

Guadalcanal Island

M E L A N E S I A

WAKE ISLAND (US)

Eniwetok I.

MARSHALL ISLANDS

Kwajalein Island

⊛ Majuro

Gilbert Islands

Tarawa ⊛

NAURU

Yaren ⊛

TUVALU
Funafuti ⊛

Espíritu Santo I.

VANUATU

Malekula I.

Port-
Vila ⊛

NEW CALEDONIA (Fr)

Nouméa •

Loyalty Islands (Fr)

MIDWAY ISLAND (US)

JOHNSTON ISLAND (US)

International Date Line

KINGMAN REEF (US)

PALMYRA ISLAND (US)

Teraina

HOWLAND ISLAND (US)

BAKER ISLAND (US)

JARVIS I. (US)

Tabuaeran

McKean I.

Gardner

Phoenix Islands

KIRIBATI

Starbuck Island

TOKELAU (NZ)

Manihiki Island

AMERICAN SAMOA

Pago Pago ⊛

SAMOA
Apia ⊛

WALLIS & FUTUNA (Fr)

NIUE (NZ)

TONGA
⊛ Nuku'alofa

FIJI
• Suva ⊛

Hawaiian Islands

HAWAII (US)

P O L Y N E S I A

Society Islands (Fr)

COOK ISLANDS (NZ)

Rarotonga Island

Marquesas Islands (Fr)

Tuamotu Archipelago (Fr)

FRENCH POLYNESIA

Papeete ⊛
Tahiti (Fr)

Austral Islands (Fr)

Rapa Island (Fr)

PITCAIRN (UK)

Pitcairn Island

Ducie Island

Easter Island (Chile)

NORFOLK ISLAND (Aust)

NEW ZEALAND

Kermadec Islands (NZ)

Chatham Islands 9. (NZ)

Bounty Islands (NZ)

Auckland Islands (NZ)

Equator 0°

Tropic of Cancer

Tropic of Cancer

15°N

30°N

15°S

30°S

45°S

15°N

30°N

15°S

30°S

45°S

120°E

135°E

150°E

165°E

180°

165°W

150°W

135°W

120°W

Scale: At Equator

0   500   1,000 Miles

0   500   1,000 Kilometers

Miller Cylindrical Projection

National capital ⊛

Other cities •

N   E   S   W

ARCTIC OCEAN

PACIFIC OCEAN

ATLANTIC OCEAN

INDIAN OCEAN

NORTH AMERICA

SOUTH AMERICA

EUROPE

ASIA

AFRICA

AUSTRALIA

ANTARCTICA

Equator

Robinson Projection

UNIT 1

American Beginnings

(Beginnings–1550)

Young People

IN HISTORY

Young Sailors

During the early days of European exploration, sailors kept track of time with sand-filled hourglasses. They turned them over every half hour. On Spanish ships, some crew members would stand watch, or serve as lookouts. As they did, a young boy would announce that watch's eighth turning of the glass.

*"Good is that which passeth,
better that which cometh,
seven is past and eight floweth,
more shall flow if God willith."*

The boys who sang these verses were sailors-in-training called *gromets*. These boys often served as cabin boys and pages on their first voyages. The youngest ones helped with the ship's religious ceremonies. They sang the blessing every morning and led the hymns.

Gromets also helped take care of the ship. They maintained the ship's compass and made materials to help keep water out of the ship. *Gromets* also swept the decks and served as lookouts. Late at night, when the sea was calm and there was little danger, *gromets* could take the ship's steering wheel. Although some *gromets* were too small to see over the ship's railing, they learned to keep a steady course for the ship.

On his first voyage to the Americas, Christopher Columbus gave orders not to allow *gromets* to steer. He believed that it was too risky. The ships, he felt, were too far from home and in unknown waters. Not all the sailors followed these orders. Columbus reported in his log on December 25, 1492, that there had been an accident involving the *Santa María*, his flagship. "The sailor who was steering the ship decided to go away to sleep and left the [steering] to a ship's boy. . . . The currents of water carried the ship upon one of those banks [coral reefs]." Soon after that collision, the *Santa María* sank.

After a crew mutiny in 1611, explorer Henry Hudson, his young son, and seven others were set adrift in a small boat.

If You Were There *How would you contribute as a crew member on a sailing ship?*

LEFT PAGE: *The Spanish fleet arrives in the English Channel in the late 1500s.*

1 The World before the Opening of the Atlantic
(Beginnings–1500)

The Maya created many complex wall carvings.

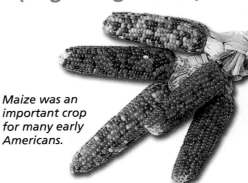

Maize was an important crop for many early Americans.

UNITED STATES

c. 38,000–10,000 B.C. Paleo-Indians migrate to the Americas.

c. 5000 B.C. Communities in Mexico cultivate corn.

c. 1200 B.C. The Olmec civilization appears in Mesoamerica.

c. A.D. 300 The Maya civilization begins a period of great development in Mesoamerica.

10,000 B.C.   5000 B.C.   1 B.C. / A.D. 1

WORLD

c. 8000 B.C. The Ice Age ends.

c. 2600 B.C. The Great Pyramid is built at Giza, Egypt, as the tomb for the pharaoh Cheops.

509 B.C. The Roman Republic is established.

A.D. 800s Vikings invade England, France, Iceland, and Ireland.

The Egyptian pyramids were considered wonders of the ancient world.

The Romans built aqueducts like this one to carry water to their towns.

Build on What You Know

Native Americans lived in the Americas for thousands of years before the first Europeans arrived after A.D. 1000. During this time, merchants and adventurers around the world traveled great distances in search of land and riches. Trade brought many different cultures into contact with one another.

This Inca knife is made of gold.

Tenochtitlán was the capital of the mighty Aztec Empire.

A.D. 1100 The Anasazi people begin moving into protected cliff dwellings.

c. A.D. 1250 The ceremonial center of the Mississippi culture in North America begins to decline.

c. A.D. 1325 The Aztec build the great city of Tenochtitlán in Mesoamerica.

c. A.D. 1400 The Inca begin expanding in South America.

A.D. 1000   **A.D. 1100**   **A.D. 1200**   **A.D. 1300**   **A.D. 1400**

A.D. 1066 William the Conqueror wins the Battle of Hastings.

A.D. 1099 The crusaders capture Jerusalem.

A.D. 1215 England's King John agrees to Magna Carta—one of the first documents to protect individuals' rights.

A.D. 1368 The Ming dynasty begins in China.

c. A.D. 1400 The African kingdom of Mali breaks apart.

If you were there . . .
What part of the world would you choose to visit in the early 1000s?

You Be the Historian

Themes Journal

What's Your Opinion? Do you **agree** or **disagree** with the following statements? Support your point of view in your journal.

- **Culture** A group's culture is heavily influenced by its environment.
- **Geography** A group's survival depends on its ability to adjust to its environment.
- **Global Relations** Trade is the cause of most contact between cultures.

3

The Earliest Americans

Read to Discover

1. How did the first people arrive in the Americas?
2. Why was the development of agriculture important?
3. What were some aspects of early Mesoamerican cultures?
4. What early societies existed in North America, and what were their accomplishments?

WHY IT MATTERS TODAY

People continue to move to new places in search of better living conditions. Use **CNNfyi.com** or other **current events** sources to identify a group that is currently migrating to a new home. Record your findings in your journal.

Define

- archaeology
- artifacts
- migration
- hunter-gatherers
- environments
- societies
- culture
- domestication
- maize
- glyphs

Identify

- Paleo-Indians

The Story Begins

When the world was young, there were only "the trees, the moon, the sun, water, and a few animals." So begins the creation story told by some northwestern Native Americans. In this emptiness, the Raven walked along the beach. The lonely bird wished for company. To Raven's surprise, a clam rose up from the sand. The clam opened and out came a crowd of tiny people. Raven "sang a beautiful song of great joy." He was happy because "he had brought the first people to the world." This story is just one of many different ways that Native Americans explain their origins.

The Raven was an important figure in some Native American myths.

⭐ The First Migration to the Americas

Many scientists believe that people first arrived in North America during the last Ice Age. At the start of the Ice Age, the world grew colder. Water froze into huge moving ice sheets called glaciers, which locked up large amounts of water. As a result, ocean levels dropped more than 300 feet lower than they are today. When the water level fell, a land bridge appeared between northeastern Asia and present-day Alaska. Geographers call this landmass Beringia.

No one knows exactly when people crossed into North America. The travelers from Asia left no written records. Instead, historians rely on **archaeology**—the study of the unwritten past. Archaeologists look at **artifacts**, or remains of objects made by humans. Artifacts suggest that **Paleo-Indians**, or the first Americans, crossed into Alaska sometime between 38,000 and 10,000 B.C.

This **migration**—a movement of people from one region to another—took place over a long period of time. Most archaeologists believe the Paleo-Indians first crossed over the land bridge in search of animals to hunt. One archaeologist described what the land crossing might have looked like.

 History Makers Speak

"The low lying land bridge was no landscape of gently waving grass. . . .[it] was a treeless, arctic land, covered with a patchwork of very different types of vegetation."

—Brian M. Fagan, *Ancient North America*

Analyzing Primary Sources

Drawing Inferences and Conclusions What does this quote suggest about the harshness of the journey across the Beringia land bridge?

Most Paleo-Indians and their descendants traveled into present-day Canada, the United States, and Mexico. Eventually their descendants reached as far as the tip of South America. The Paleo-Indians were **hunter-gatherers**. They lived by hunting animals and gathering wild plants. They also made stone tools to hunt large animals such as mammoths.

✔ **Reading Check: Finding the Main Idea** When and how did the first people come to the Americas?

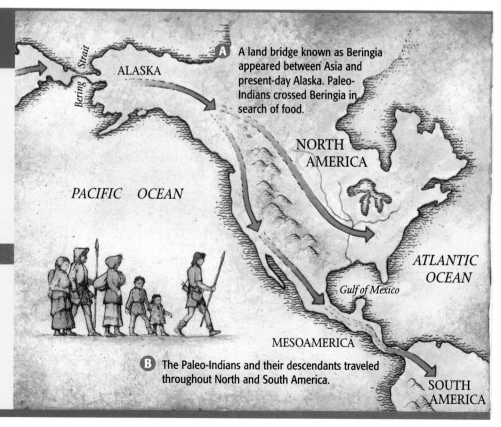

Migration to the Americas

During the Ice Age much of the world grew very cold. Water froze into huge moving ice sheets called glaciers. Ocean levels dropped more than 300 feet lower than they are today.

Visualizing History

1. **Geography** Where did the Paleo-Indians come from?
2. **Connecting to Today** What methods do people use to come to the Americas today?

A land bridge known as Beringia appeared between Asia and present-day Alaska. Paleo-Indians crossed Beringia in search of food.

B The Paleo-Indians and their descendants traveled throughout North and South America.

ALASKA
Bering Strait
PACIFIC OCEAN
NORTH AMERICA
ATLANTIC OCEAN
Gulf of Mexico
MESOAMERICA
SOUTH AMERICA

Adapting to a New Climate

When the Ice Age ended about 8000 B.C., the world's climate changed. Rising temperatures melted glaciers. The oceans rose, covering Beringia with water. As late as 1000 B.C. people continued to come to North America using small boats.

The warmer weather at the end of the Ice Age created many new **environments**—climates and landscapes that surround living things. Short grasses replaced the taller grasses that had fed giant animals such as the mammoth. These animals either died out naturally or were hunted to extinction by Native Americans. However, large herds of smaller animals such as buffalo and deer ate the new short grasses. Paleo-Indians adapted to the changes by hunting these animals. People also ate more berries, roots, and seeds.

Different environments influenced the development of Native American **societies**. A society is a group that shares a common **culture**—a set of common values and traditions. These traits include language, government, and family relationships. Like all societies, Native American groups changed over time.

The earliest farming societies in the Americas began in Mesoamerica, or Middle America, and South America. Mesoamerica includes southern Mexico and northern Central America. People in this region learned to breed and grow wild plants to create food crops. This process of breeding plants or animals to meet human needs is called **domestication**.

Archaeologists in Mexico have found signs of the first **maize**, or corn, grown by people. People in Mesoamerica also grew beans and peppers. In eastern North America, Native Americans domesticated plants by about 2000 B.C. In the Southwest, agricultural methods were introduced from Mesoamerica between 1000 and 750 B.C. Agriculture allowed many Native American groups to settle in villages. It thus led to the rise of larger and more complex societies.

✔ **Reading Check: Analyzing Information** How did the end of the Ice Age help make the rise of civilizations in North America possible?

Mesoamerica and South America

Some of the earliest American civilizations developed in Mesoamerica. The Olmec society was one of the first. It has been called the "mother culture" because it highly influenced most later civilizations in Mesoamerica. The Olmec developed along the Mexican Gulf Coast between about 1200 and 400 B.C. During that time Olmec priests created number and calendar systems. They invented a method of writing that used **glyphs,** or symbols that represent ideas.

The Maya civilization thrived in southeastern Mesoamerica from about A.D 300 to 900. The Maya built many large stone temples, palaces,

CONNECTING TO

SCIENCE AND TECHNOLOGY

Discovering the Distant Past

Archaeologists use scientific tests to determine the age of artifacts. In 1949 Willard Libby developed carbon-14 dating. This highly accurate test measures the amount of carbon 14—a form of carbon atom—that exists in an artifact. Before the use of carbon-14 dating, archaeologists used unreliable methods to guess the age of artifacts.

Scientists know that half the carbon 14 in a dead plant or animal decays about every 5,000 years. After 50,000 years almost all the carbon 14 is gone. Knowing this, archaeologists measure the amount of carbon 14 in a fossil or artifact. This measurement is then used to figure out its age. Today scientists can also use other advanced methods to date objects older than 50,000 years. How do scientists use carbon 14 to determine the age of artifacts?

and bridges. The city of Tikal was an important Maya center. The Maya created several calendars. They also studied mathematics and astronomy. By about A.D. 900 the Maya civilization started to decline. Historians are not sure why this took place.

About A.D. 1200, Aztec invaders came south and occupied the central valley of Mexico. The center of Aztec civilization was Tenochtitlán (tay-nawch-teet-LAHN). Present-day Mexico City was built on the site of this ancient city. Tenochtitlán stood in the middle of a huge lake, with raised highways connecting the city to the shore. It is thought that as many as 300,000 people may have lived in this great capital.

The Aztec created a large empire by conquering most of their neighbors. The empire had a vast trading network involving goods such as cocoa, gold, and jade. However, the Aztec knew that their success might not last. They expressed this idea in their poetry.

The Aztec used tax records like this one to keep track of their wealth.

Primary Sources

**"Truly do we live on earth?
Not forever on earth; only a little
    while here.
Although it be jade, it will be
    broken,
Although it be gold, it is
    crushed. . . .
Not forever on earth; only a little
    while here."**

—King Nezahualcóyotl, quoted in
Aztec Thought and Culture by Miguel León-Portilla

While the Aztec were thriving in Mexico, the Inca created their own civilization in South America. The Inca civilization began high in the Andes. In the A.D. 1400s they started to conquer surrounding lands. Eventually, the Inca ruled an area stretching from present-day Ecuador to central Chile. Across this empire the Inca built a network of roads some 25,000 miles long. These roads let armies and messengers move quickly. The Inca built palaces and temples in their capital city of Cuzco (KOO-skoh). Decorated with gold and silver, the palaces had beautiful gardens and bathrooms with running water. Most Inca subjects lived in villages. They were allowed to keep their own land and many of their customs. But families did have to dig canals and grow crops to help feed the Inca Empire.

Interpreting the Visual Record

Machu Picchu *The Inca built the great city of Machu Picchu high in the Andes of present-day Peru.* **What would be the advantages and disadvantages of building in such a location?**

✔ **Reading Check: Comparing** List some cultural developments of the Mesoamerican and South American civilizations.

⭐ Early North American Societies

Although less populated than South America and Mesoamerica, North America had several farming cultures. These cultures had to adapt to very different environments. For example, in the southwestern region of the present-day United States there was little rainfall for farming. As a result, Native Americans created irrigation systems to bring water to crops, allowing groups to build permanent settlements.

The Anasazi (ah-nuh-SAH-zee) lived in the Four Corners region, where present-day Arizona, Colorado, New Mexico, and Utah meet. They built their pueblos, or villages, among high hills and deep canyons. Anasazi pueblos were made mostly of cut stone or adobe—sun-baked clay and straw. Many pueblos were multistory buildings with ladders connecting the different levels. Pueblo Bonito in New Mexico's Chaco Canyon has five stories and 800 rooms.

The Anasazi built their early pueblos on mesas, or flat-topped hills. Later, about A.D. 1100, they began building their homes into cliffsides for defense. By A.D. 1300, some Anasazi began to leave the larger pueblos. Drought or war may have driven them away.

In eastern and midwestern North America, advanced cultures developed between 1000 B.C. and A.D. 1250. The Hopewell culture arose between 300 and 200 B.C. The Hopewell lived along the Mississippi,

Interpreting the Visual Record

Mesa Verde *Southwestern Indians built cliff dwellings, like this one in Mesa Verde, to protect themselves from harsh weather and enemy attacks.* **Why would the location of these buildings have offered protection?**

Interpreting the Visual Record

Burial mounds *The ancient mound builders constructed the Great Serpent Mound near what is now Hillsboro, Ohio.* **How do you think this mound got its present name?**

Ohio, and lower Missouri River valleys. They built large burial mounds, some 30 feet tall, to honor their dead. The Hopewell supported their large populations with agriculture and trade. However, by about A.D. 400, the Hopewell no longer dominated the region. Archaeologists have yet to discover why the Hopewell culture declined.

The Mississippians were another widespread farming culture that relied on trade. Like the Hopewell, the Mississippians also had religious practices honoring the dead. From about A.D. 700 to the early 1500s, the Mississippian people lived along the Ohio and Mississippi Rivers. Mississippians built pyramid mounds out of solid earth. Religious ceremonies were held on top of these pyramids. The largest of these is Monks Mound, near Cahokia (kuh-HOH-kee-uh), Illinois. Monks Mound covers 16 acres and stands 98 feet tall.

✔ **Reading Check: Summarizing** What were some features of early North American cultures?

Section 1 Review

go.hrw.com **Homework Practice Online** keyword: SF3 HP1

1 **Define** and explain:
• archaeology
• artifacts
• migration
• hunter-gatherers
• environments
• societies
• culture
• domestication
• maize
• glyphs

2 **Identify** and explain:
• Paleo-Indians

3 **Summarizing** Copy the chart below. Use it to identify the early societies in the Americas, where they were located, and one major accomplishment of each society.

Early American Societies	Location	Accomplishments

4 **Finding the Main Idea**
a. What events made it possible for Paleo-Indians to migrate to North America?

b. Why do you think that growing crops such as maize was important to many early Native American civilizations?

5 **Writing and Critical Thinking**
Analyzing Information Imagine that you are a visitor to one of the early Mesoamerican cultures. Write a letter to a friend describing the society you encounter.

Consider the following:
• the time period of the culture
• the location and physical environment of the society
• the society's cultural accomplishments

The World before the Opening of the Atlantic **9**

Cultural Areas in North America

Read to Discover

1. How did the environment influence Native American cultures in North America?
2. What types of housing did Native Americans build?
3. What were various traits of Native Americans in different culture areas?

WHY IT MATTERS TODAY

Many Native Americans still practice ancient cultural traditions. Use CNN fyi.com or other **current events** sources to find out about a Native American tradition being followed today. Examples might include story-telling, art, or dance. Record your findings in your journal.

Define

- kayaks
- igloos
- totems
- potlatches
- kivas
- wigwams
- longhouses

Identify

- Iroquois League

Southwestern Native Americans often decorated their pottery with animal symbols.

The Story Continues

Native Americans developed customs based on their close ties to the land. Many tribes in the American Southwest held dances that celebrated the importance of the Sun and rain. One Native American song called the Southwest "a House Made of Dawn . . . made of pollen and of rain." The Inuit of the Far North lived on land too cold to grow crops. They held ceremonies to help them hunt wild game. Native Americans across the continent adapted their lifestyles to their surroundings.

⭐ The Far North

Researchers use culture areas—the geographic locations that influenced societies—to help them describe ancient Native American peoples. The Far North of North America is divided into the Arctic and Subarctic culture areas. Few plants grow in the Arctic because the ground is always frozen. The Aleut and the Inuit adapted to these harsh conditions. The Inuit lived in present-day northern Alaska and Canada, and the Aleut lived in western Alaska. The two groups shared many cultural traits,

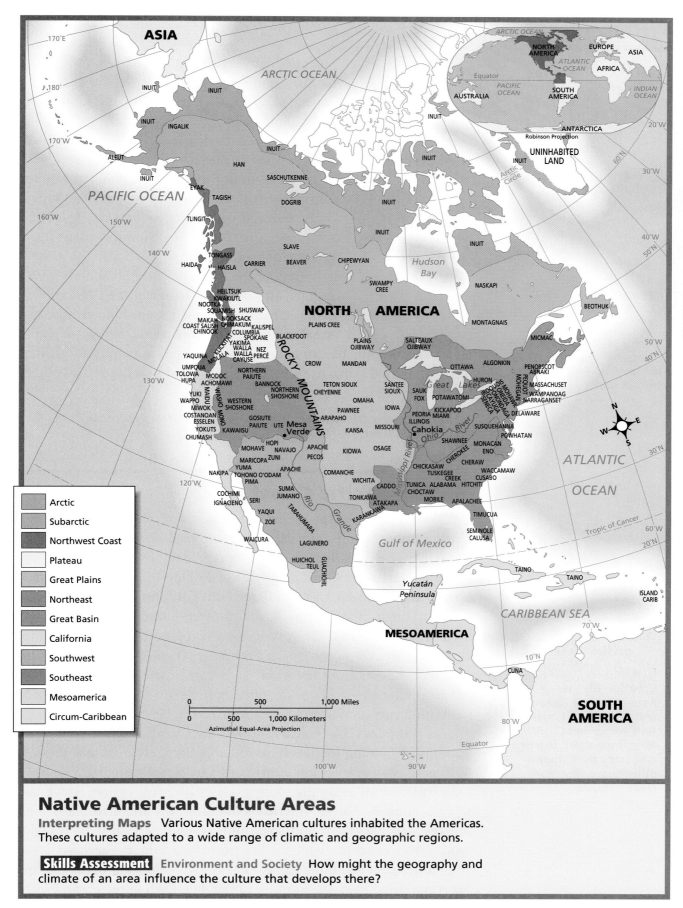

Map Legend:
- Arctic
- Subarctic
- Northwest Coast
- Plateau
- Great Plains
- Northeast
- Great Basin
- California
- Southwest
- Southeast
- Mesoamerica
- Circum-Caribbean

Native American Culture Areas

Interpreting Maps Various Native American cultures inhabited the Americas. These cultures adapted to a wide range of climatic and geographic regions.

Skills Assessment Environment and Society How might the geography and climate of an area influence the culture that develops there?

The Inuit used kayaks to cross icy waters in the Arctic. They also made carvings from walrus bones.

including language. Both survived by fishing and by hunting large mammals. They also both depended on dogs for many tasks, such as hunting and pulling sleds.

In addition to dogsleds, the Inuit and Aleut used **kayaks**, or one-person canoes covered with skins. Some Inuit built earthen, stone, or wooden houses partly underground. Other Inuit and Aleut built aboveground wooden houses. The Inuit sometimes used blocks of ice or other materials to build **igloos** for housing.

South of the Arctic lies the Subarctic, home to groups such as the Athabascan and Algonquian peoples. Each year these groups followed the seasonal migrations of the caribou. When they went on a hunt, the Athabascan and Algonquian lived in temporary shelters made of animal skins. At other times they lived in villages made up of log houses.

✔ **Reading Check: Summarizing** How did the Native Americans of the Far North get their food?

⭐ The Pacific Coast

Unlike the Far North, the Pacific Coast had a mild climate. The area had a rich supply of game animals, sea life, and wild plants. These resources allowed large populations to develop that did not need to rely on farming. The Northwest Coast area stretched along the shoreline between present-day southern Alaska and northern California.

The Tlingit, Nootka, and Skokomish were some of the peoples who lived in the Northwest. Their most important food was salmon, but they also hunted sea otters and whales from large canoes. People in the Northwest built houses from the wood of evergreen trees. They also carved images of **totems**—ancestor or animal spirits—on tall wooden poles.

With plenty of food and building materials, Northwest Coast culture groups prospered. Individuals showed their wealth and earned social standing by holding special events called **potlatches**. At these gatherings hosts gave away many belongings in order to gain respect.

Farther south along the coast was the California region, which had several climates. Native Americans living in this area had many food sources available year-round, so farming was not necessary. Their major food plant was acorns, which they ground into a flour. They also fished and hunted deer and other game. Most Native Americans in the California region lived in isolated groups of families. Each of these groups had

Research on the ROM

Free Find:
Creation Myths
Read about the Tuskegee and Caddo myths on the **Holt Researcher CD–ROM**. Then draw a picture based on a scene from these or other Native American creation myths.

a small population of only 50 to 300. Among these Native Americans—which included the Pomo, Hupa, and Yurok—more than 100 different languages were spoken.

✔ **Reading Check: Finding the Main Idea** How did the environment influence the food sources for Native Americans in the California and Northwest Coast regions?

★ The West and Southwest

The West and Southwest of the present-day United States received less rain than the Far West. As a result, the people had fewer resources than their neighbors on the Pacific Coast. Although they did not practice agriculture, groups in the dry Columbia Plateau region lived in permanent villages. Native Americans living near rivers fished for salmon, hunted small game, and gathered plants. These groups included the Flathead, Modoc, and Nez Percé.

Native Americans faced more difficulties surviving in the much drier Great Basin region. They adapted to the dry climate by gathering seeds, digging roots, and trapping small animals for food. They also ate ants, crickets, lizards, and rabbits. Rabbits were highly valued because they provided meat as well as fur and skins for blankets and clothing. Most Native Americans of the Great Basin lived in small family groups that moved often in search of food. Most groups in this region spoke variations of the same language. These groups included the Paiute, Shoshone, and Ute.

Native Americans of the Southwest also had to adapt to a dry climate. This region's landscape varied from deserts to evergreen forests. Southwestern culture groups included the Apache, Navajo, and Pueblo. The

CONNECTING TO

THE ARTS

Totems In parts of Alaska and British Columbia, Native Americans practice a unique and striking ancient tradition. Artists carve images of ravens, bears, fish, and human beings into towering totem poles. The Tlingit, Nootka, and other groups have long used these poles to tell important stories.

To create the poles, the artist first listens to the story that the purchaser wants to have shown. These tales can be personal, family, or tribal stories. Then the artist designs and carves the work. After the totem pole's completion, the buyer hosts a potlatch to dedicate it and raise it into place. During the potlatch, singers and actors often perform the pole's story. **How do totem poles reflect the relationship between people in the Northwest Coast culture area and their environment?**

Interpreting the Visual Record

Kachinas *Southwestern Native Americans such as the Zuni believed in ancestral spirits called kachinas, who were often represented in ceremonies by costumed dancers. This wooden doll is a model of a kachina dancer. Sandpaintings also had important ceremonial uses. This Navajo blanket was based on a sandpainting design.* **What is similar and different about the figures shown in these two images?**

Pueblo were farmers who irrigated their land to grow crops. Other tribes, such as the Apache, hunted game and gathered plants for food. These groups also raided the villages of farming groups such as the Pueblo.

The Pueblo people had many religious festivals. These rituals focused on the two key areas of Pueblo life—rain and maize. Pueblo religious activities were held in **kivas**—round ceremonial rooms.

✔ **Reading Check: Finding the Main Idea** How did Native Americans adapt to the dry environment of the West and Southwest?

⭐ The Great Plains

The huge Great Plains region stretches south from Canada into Texas. This culture area is bounded by the Mississippi Valley on the east and the Rocky Mountains on the west. The Plains were mainly grassland, on which millions of buffalo and other game grazed in herds. The Mandan lived in the northern Plains, while the Pawnee lived on the central Plains. Both groups grew crops such as beans, maize, and squash. Like some other Native American groups, the Pawnee society was matrilineal. This means that people traced their ancestry through their mothers, rather than through their fathers. In addition, when a couple married, the husband moved into the wife's home.

Several Native American groups, such as the Apache, lived in the southern Plains. People in this area hunted buffalo on foot and gathered berries, nuts, and vegetables. Some groups grew to depend largely on the buffalo for clothing, food, and shelter.

Many other Native Americans lived on the eastern or western borders of the Plains. These groups included the Arapaho, Blackfoot, Comanche, and Teton Sioux. Hunters among the Blackfoot sometimes killed huge numbers of buffalo by chasing the animals over steep cliffs.

The East

Unlike the Great Plains, eastern North America was rich in sources for food and shelter. The East was mainly forest. The Mississippi River and the Everglades—a huge swamp in what is now Florida—also provided many resources.

Native Americans of the Southeast included the Cherokee, Creek, Natchez, and Seminole. The Natchez were direct descendants of the ancient Mississippian people. Most southeastern groups lived in villages along river valleys. They relied mainly on farming but also hunted game, gathered plants, fished, and traded. Each of these groups was led by a village council.

Northeastern tribes lived in a broad area stretching west from the Atlantic Ocean to the Mississippi Valley. This area extended north to the Great Lakes region and south into present-day Virginia and North Carolina. The Algonquian and Iroquois peoples were the two main groups of the Northeast. Some Algonquian peoples lived north of the Great Lakes. These groups could not farm all year-round because the climate in this northern region was too cold. They survived by hunting and by gathering edible plants.

Other Algonquian peoples, including the Wampanoag and Pequot, lived farther south. In the warmer areas they farmed, hunted, gathered plants, and fished in rivers and the ocean. These groups lived in

Daily Life

Hunting buffalo Buffalo are large, powerful animals that once roamed the Great Plains in huge herds. Hunting these creatures was not an easy task for early Native Americans. But the buffalo could provide for so many needs, including food and clothing, that it was worth the risk to hunt them. Here two Native American hunters wearing wolf skins try to get close enough to bring down a buffalo. **Why do you think these hunters are wearing wolf skins?**

Iroquois warriors such as the one shown here had great success in warfare.

permanent villages. Some built large multifamily lodges, while others lived in small **wigwams**, or round huts.

To the east of the Algonquian lived the Iroquois. Unlike other Native American women, Iroquois women controlled the material goods of their people. They also oversaw most parts of community life. The Iroquois relied mostly on farming for food, although they also hunted and traded with other tribes. Men were responsible for hunting and trading. Women grew and harvested crops.

The Iroquois lived in **longhouses**, or rectangular homes made from logs and bark. Longhouses ranged from 50 to 100 feet long and housed 8 to 10 families each. Fences of pointed stakes surrounded longhouses for defense. Neighboring tribes feared the military skills of the Iroquois.

The Iroquois also developed the **Iroquois League**. This political confederation was made up of the Cayuga, Mohawk, Oneida, Onondaga, and Seneca. The League was responsible for waging war and making peace with non-Iroquois peoples. Women selected the male members of the League council. Women could overrule decisions made by the council and could remove its members. The League helped the Iroquois become one of the most powerful peoples in North America.

✔ **Reading Check: Comparing and Contrasting** What were some of the similarities and differences between the cultures of Native Americans in the Great Plains and the East?

Section 2 Review

go.hrw.com **Homework Practice Online** keyword: SF3 HP1

1 Define and explain:
• kayaks
• igloos
• totems
• potlatches
• kivas
• wigwams
• longhouses

2 Identify and explain:
• Iroquois League

3 Identifying Cause and Effect Copy the graphic organizer below. Use it to show how the environments of the Far North, the Southwest, and the East affected the cultures of the Native Americans who lived in each area.

4 Finding the Main Idea
a. Compare and contrast the major cultural traits of the Far North and the Southwest culture groups.

b. Why do you think that Native Americans who practiced agriculture were more likely than hunter-gatherers to establish permanent homes?

5 Writing and Critical Thinking
Summarizing Imagine that you are living in an early Native American society. Write a paragraph describing your life as a member of this group.

Consider the following:
• how you obtain your food
• the type of shelter in which you live
• other cultural traits your group shares

Far North
Environment
Food   Homes

Southwest
Environment
Food   Homes

East
Environment
Food   Homes

Europe during the Middle Ages

Read to Discover

1. What new lands did the Vikings explore?
2. What were society and daily life like during the Middle Ages?
3. How did the Catholic Church affect people's lives during the Middle Ages?
4. What events brought about major change in the late Middle Ages?

WHY IT MATTERS TODAY

A person who rules over a kingdom or empire is known as a monarch. Use **CNNfyi.com** or other **current events** sources to find information about a country that has a monarch today. Record your findings in your journal.

Define

- feudalism
- manors

Identify

- Leif Eriksson
- Middle Ages
- Eleanor of Aquitaine
- William of Normandy
- King John
- Magna Carta

The Story Continues

The bold Vikings described their adventures in sagas—long, heroic stories that mixed myth and fact. "Erik's Saga" tells how Leif Eriksson heard tales of a land across the sea. Seeking fame and fortune, he went in search of the mysterious land. Eriksson and his crew were tossed by the seas as they set sail from his home in Iceland. According to the saga, the Vikings eventually "came upon lands whose existence he [Eriksson] had never suspected." They saw "fields of flowing wheat there, and vines" with wild grapes. Eriksson, who had landed on the shore of North America, called this place Vinland.

This replica of a Viking ship shows the unique design used.

⭐ The Viking Explorations

The Vikings were from Scandinavia, which includes the present-day countries of Denmark, Norway, and Sweden. The Vikings were skilled sailors who developed a new style of ship that curved up at both ends. These ships traveled on the rough North Atlantic seas better than

Vikings led by Leif Eriksson attack a Native American camp in Vinland.

★ ★ ★ ★ ★ ★ ★ ★ ★ ★ ★ ★
That's Interesting!
★ ★ ★ ★ ★ ★ ★ ★ ★ ★ ★ ★

Fire and Ice Did you know that Iceland has more than 200 volcanoes? That's right! While icy glaciers cover one tenth of the island, large numbers of volcanoes erupt from the island's surface. There are also many geysers and hot springs, which supply energy used today to heat homes. And despite being located just south of the Arctic Circle, Iceland's average daily temperatures are only slightly below freezing in the winter. Iceland's unusually fair weather made it an inviting spot for the Vikings to start a settlement.

earlier designs. The Vikings raided and traded throughout Europe. Evidence shows that the Vikings reached the British Isles, the northern European coast, and as far away as the Mediterranean and the Black Sea. In many places their raids caused great fear. "Never before had such a terror appeared in Britain," noted Anglo-Saxon scholar Alcuin in A.D. 793.

Eventually the Vikings sailed west into the North Atlantic. Much of what historians know about these explorations comes from Viking stories called sagas. According to the sagas, the Vikings founded a settlement on the island of Iceland about A.D. 874. More than 100 years later, the Viking Erik the Red left Iceland to settle Greenland.

Leif Eriksson, son of Erik the Red, shared his father's love of adventure. About A.D. 1000 he gathered a crew and launched his own expedition, sailing west from Greenland. After a difficult journey, they reached North America, landing on Labrador Peninsula and the island of Newfoundland in present-day Canada. This landing represented the first time Europeans made contact with the North American continent. The Vikings then sailed farther south, perhaps as far as what is now New England. According to the sagas, they saw forests, meadows, and rivers that held "larger salmon than they had ever seen."

Eriksson settled in a coastal area he called Vinland. The Vikings left Vinland after only a few years, however. As one Viking reported, "they would always live in dread" of attacks by Native Americans. Vinland may also have simply been too far from other Viking settlements to be supported. In the 1400s the Vikings left Greenland as well. The settlers remained in Iceland, however.

✔ **Reading Check:** **Sequencing** What were the stages of Viking exploration that led to their landing in North America, and when did the landing take place?

The Middle Ages

While the Vikings were exploring, Europe was struggling through a difficult period. Beginning in the late A.D. 300s, the Roman Empire had suffered serious political and economic problems. The vast empire soon crumbled under continued invasion by groups such as the Huns. The fall of the Roman Empire marked the beginning of Europe's **Middle Ages**. This historical period lasted roughly from A.D. 500 to 1500. During the Middle Ages, trade and communication were limited. City populations also dropped as people moved into the countryside.

During the Middle Ages a new system of government called **feudalism** emerged. Under this system people known as vassals pledged their loyalty to a lord in exchange for land. Acquiring land was an important step to achieving power and wealth in the Middle Ages. The lord benefited by gaining the military services of his vassals. These vassals often included mounted warriors called knights. Feeding knights and their horses and equipping them with weapons and armor was expensive. However, nobles needed knights to defend their **manors**, or large estates, against attack. The feudal system relied on the loyalty of vassals.

Unlike the nobility, peasants—free tenants and serfs—farmed the land. Tenants rented land from lords and could leave when their rental agreements were over. In contrast, serfs lived on one manor for life, farming the lord's land or performing other services. In return they received the protection of the lord. The degree of personal freedom enjoyed by serfs varied in different parts of Europe. In addition to peasants, there were a small number of slaves in Europe.

Interpreting the Visual Record

Society in the Middle Ages
While peasants such as those shown here working in the fields had few belongings, wealthy nobles might own fine goods such as this beautifully decorated suit of armor. **What types of buildings can be seen behind the peasants?**

★ Life on a Manor

Manors provided most of what their inhabitants needed to live. Lords ruled their manors with little interference. Lords and their families lived in large wooden or stone houses or castles. These were often surrounded by water-filled trenches—called moats—and high walls for defense. Noblemen spent their time ruling, fighting in battles, and managing their farmland. Noblewomen usually ran the home and raised children. Noblemen and noblewomen also spent a large amount of time carrying out their duties as Christians. For example, women often prayed daily for the well-being of the household. In 1190 Richard of Devizes listed some of the qualities of **Eleanor of Aquitaine**, whom he considered an ideal noblewoman. He described her as "beautiful yet virtuous [moral], powerful yet gentle, humble yet keenwitted [intelligent]."

Life for peasants was very different. Whole families often slept and ate in a single room. Women and men worked in the fields from before sunrise until after sunset. From an early age, children were also expected to work. Children grew up knowing that they would have little chance to move ahead in life. Under feudalism, a person's birth usually determined his or her place in society.

✔ **Reading Check: Contrasting** How did daily life differ for nobles and peasants during the Middle Ages?

★ The Catholic Church

The Catholic Church was the center of religious and social life in the Middle Ages. Both peasants and nobles attended church services led by the local priest. Priests also cared for the sick and poor, counseled the rich, and taught the young. Frequent religious festivals offered everyone a chance to celebrate.

Many religious groups existed during the Middle Ages, but most Europeans were Roman Catholic. Christianity influenced culture and politics across Europe. By the late 800s, the Church owned large amounts of land. In addition, church leaders often advised rulers on important matters. The Catholic Church paid for many art and architecture projects. One example is the Notre Dame cathedral in Paris, France.

Monasteries were important during the early Middle Ages. These were religious communities in which men called monks devoted their lives to practicing Christianity. Monks gave up all personal possessions, but monasteries themselves often owned large estates. Monasteries became centers of learning, and some produced books.

Similar religious centers for women were called convents. The women who lived in these convents were known as nuns. Nuns spent most of their time running convent lands, reading religious texts, and writing. They also created works of art and earned money selling crafts

Interpreting the Visual Record

Medieval architecture *This French cathedral built in the 1200s reflects the beauty of medieval architecture.* **How might the design of such a building have affected those who worshiped there?**

such as woven goods. Many women joined convents because they wanted to devote their lives to learning and prayer. Convents gave women an alternative to getting married and having children. In other cases, families encouraged elderly or unmarried women to become nuns.

Convents offered women a rare chance to pursue an education. Some nuns wrote history, poetry, and plays. Others even advised leaders. Saint Hilda, who founded a religious community, received praise from an early historian of England.

 History Makers Speak ❝So great was her prudence [good judgment] that not only ordinary folk, but kings and princes used to come and ask her advice in their difficulties and take it.❞

Bede, *A History of the English Church and People*

✔ **Reading Check: Analyzing Information** What role did the Catholic Church play in people's lives during the Middle Ages?

⭐ The Rise of Nations

During the mid- and late Middle Ages, some nobles began losing power to growing kingdoms. These kingdoms, including England and France, became some of the first nations in the world. In 1066 **William of Normandy** conquered England. (Normandy is an area in present-day France.) He later ordered a survey of the entire kingdom. The result was the enormous Domesday Book, or Day of Judgment Book. A writer recorded the process used to collect the information.

 History Makers Speak ❝William, king of the English, sent [his men] through all the provinces of England and caused it to be inquired [asked] . . . how much the king had in lands and cattle and livestock in each province. . . . And so thoroughly was all this carried out that there did not remain in the whole of England . . . an ox or cow or a pig which was not written in that return [document]. And all the writings of all these things were brought back to the king.❞

—Anonymous, quoted in *English Historical Documents, 1042–1189*, edited by David C. Douglas and George W. Greenaway

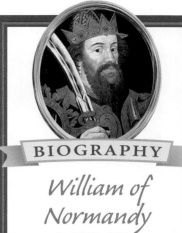

BIOGRAPHY

William of Normandy
(c. 1028–1087)

William of Normandy, also known as William the Conqueror, was born in what is now France. When the English king Edward the Confessor died in 1066, Duke William invaded England. He fought and defeated the new English king, Harold, at the Battle of Hastings.

William brought many changes to English society. He and his nobles established the feudal system in England and built the first English castles. William's court also introduced the English to French customs, laws, and language. **What were some of the ways that William changed English society?**

Analyzing Primary Sources

Making Generalizations and Predictions Why would the information from this survey have been important to the king?

The Bayeux Tapestry shows the Norman invasion of England.

As trade brought greater riches to Europe, wealthy couples could enjoy fine weddings such as the one shown here.

During the rule of William's great-great-grandson **King John**, the nobles rebelled against his misuse of royal power. In 1215 they forced John to agree to **Magna Carta**, or the Great Charter. The charter addressed the land rights of nobles. It also required the king to gain the agreement of the nobility before raising new taxes. In addition, Magna Carta was one of the first documents to protect some of the rights of free people.

The early 1200s brought other major changes to Europe. Trade greatly increased. One major cause for this was that Italian cities began expanding their trade connections. Eventually Italian merchants were trading regularly with nations around the Mediterranean Sea and northern Europe.

Across Europe, advances in farming led to increased food production and rising populations. Farmers began using horses instead of oxen to pull plows. They also learned to fertilize soil and to rotate crops. As the population grew, landowners cleared more land for farming. Many people began using new technology, such as windmills and watermills. These devices provided power for grinding grain, working with metals, and pumping water.

More people and more trade meant new towns and larger cities. With the growth of technology, trade, and kingdoms, by 1500 Europe's Middle Ages were drawing to a close.

✔ **Reading Check: Summarizing** How did countries change in the late Middle Ages?

Section 3 Review

go.hrw.com **Homework Practice Online** keyword: SF3 HP1

1. **Define** and explain:
   - feudalism
   - manors

2. **Identify** and explain:
   - Leif Eriksson
   - Middle Ages
   - Eleanor of Aquitaine
   - William of Normandy
   - King John
   - Magna Carta

3. **Comparing and Contrasting** Copy the diagram below. Use it to explain the similarities and differences between peasants' and nobles' daily lives under feudalism.

Peasants   Similarities   Nobles

4. **Finding the Main Idea**
   a. What technology enabled the Vikings to explore new lands, and what were the results of their explorations?

   b. How did the Catholic Church influence daily life and culture during the Middle Ages?

5. **Writing and Critical Thinking**
   Identifying Cause and Effect Imagine that you are a monk or a nun during the Middle Ages and you are recording the history of your time. Write a paragraph explaining the major changes of the late Middle Ages and their effects.

   Consider the following:
   - the significance of Magna Carta
   - the expansion of trade
   - advances in agricultural technology

Trade across Continents

Read to Discover

1. How did Islam affect the Mediterrean region?
2. What led the Chinese to join in and then withdraw from international trade?
3. How did trade influence African kingdoms?

Why it Matters Today

Trade remains an important way for cultures around the world to interact with one another. Use CNNfyi.com or other **current events** sources to find information about some of the products that the United States trades with other countries. Record your findings in your journal.

Identify

- Muhammad
- Islam
- Crusades
- Kublai Khan
- Silk Road
- Zheng He
- Mansa Musa

The Story Continues

The city of Mecca, in what is now Saudi Arabia, was a thriving trade center. One of its residents was Muhammad, a successful Arab merchant. In A.D. 610 Muhammad's life changed dramatically. That year he recorded having a vision of an angel, who ordered him to teach the word of God, or Allah. Muhammad dedicated his life to this task, spreading his faith first in Mecca and later in other communities. He overcame many obstacles and founded the religion known as Islam.

This Turkish miniature shows an Islamic scene.

⭐ The Spread of Islam

Muhammad devoted his life to preaching the messages of Allah. After his death, Muhammad's followers wrote these messages in the Qur'an (kuh-RAN), the holy book of **Islam**. Islam gained many followers, called Muslims, who swiftly spread their faith. Muslims took Jerusalem, Syria, the Persian Empire, and Egypt. Once they held the seaports of Syria and Egypt, Muslims built a powerful navy. By the late 600s they dominated the eastern Mediterranean Sea. Before long, North Africa, Sicily, and much of present-day Spain had come under Muslim control.

Muslim traders helped spread Islam. Trade also allowed people to exchange new ideas. Muslims valued learning highly. Muslim mathematicians adopted a numeral system from India, including the concept of zero. Using this system, they developed algebra. Muslim scholars also studied medicine, philosophy, astronomy, and physics. Some of this they learned from ancient Greek writings. Muslim doctors improved surgical methods and the understanding of diseases. One teacher gave the following advice to young students. "He who has not endured the stress of study will not taste the joy of knowledge."

✔ **Reading Check: Drawing Inferences and Conclusions** Besides the spread of knowledge, in what other ways do you think the Muslim empire benefited from trade?

★ The Crusades

Like Jews and Christians, Muslims showed their faith by visiting the Holy Land. This area included the city of Jerusalem and the land surrounding it. Muslims conquered Jerusalem in 637 but continued to let people of other religions visit. However, about 1077 the Seljuk Turks, who were also Muslims, took over the city and began to prevent Christians from visiting holy places. In 1095 Pope Urban II called on all Christians to start a holy war to seize control of Jerusalem.

History Makers Speak

❝Jerusalem is the center of the earth; the land is fruitful above all others, like another paradise of delights. . . . This royal city . . . is now held captive by the enemies of Christ. . . . When an armed attack is made upon the enemy, let this one cry be raised by all the soldiers of God: it is the will of God! It is the will of God!❞

Pope Urban II, quoted in *The Medieval Reader,* edited by Norman Cantor

Interpreting the Visual Record

Crusaders *A group of crusaders is preparing to travel to the Holy Land. The banners of different noble families fly above the ships.* **What does this image suggest about the difficulty of reaching the Holy Land?**

With these words, the pope asked Christians across Europe to take back the Holy Land. The resulting military expeditions to the Holy Land, which continued off and on for more than 150 years, were called the **Crusades**. Many knights, soldiers, and nobles joined the holy wars. According to William of Malmesbury, the Crusades greatly changed the European population. The "lands were deserted of their husbands-men, houses of their inhabitants, even whole cities migrated."

The crusaders captured Jerusalem in 1099 and controlled it for nearly 90 years. However, in 1187 Saladin, a Muslim sultan, arrived with a massive army. At the end of the battle that followed, the city was back in Muslim hands. Future Crusades were unable to recapture Jerusalem.

✔ **Reading Check: Finding the Main Idea** Why did the Crusades take place?

★ Empires in Asia

While fighting continued in the Holy Land, China faced an invasion by the Mongols of Central Asia. Chinese emperors had built the Great Wall—which stretched some 4,500 miles—to defend against such attacks. But Mongol leader Genghis Khan could not be stopped. By 1279 his grandson **Kublai Khan** (koo-bluh-KAHN) ruled an Asian empire that stretched to the Black Sea from China's southern coast. Kublai Khan used his large navy to expand trade. In addition, merchants used the **Silk Road**, an overland trade route running from China to the Black Sea.

In 1368 the Ming dynasty overthrew the Mongol Empire in China. Zhu Di seized the Ming throne in 1402. He soon built a large fleet of ships. This fleet allowed China to exchange silk and porcelain for spices and other goods. China established new trade with India and Arabia. Admiral **Zheng He** commanded the fleet's 317 brightly painted ships and more than 27,000 men. His expeditions brought wealth and knowledge of other cultures to China.

After Zheng He's death, the Ming dynasty reduced its long-distance ocean trade. By the mid-1400s, China had abandoned its command of the seas. Political conflicts, piracy, a lack of tax money, and other events led the country to refocus on internal affairs.

✔ **Reading Check Summarizing** What role did China play in international trade between the 1200s and 1400s?

★ African Trading Kingdoms

Well before Chinese merchants established trade contacts with East Africa, several African kingdoms had grown wealthy from long-distance trade. The Aksum kingdom began in present-day Ethiopia. Aksum gained much of its wealth by trading with Egypt and ports in the Indian Ocean.

GLOBAL CONNECTIONS

The Silk Road

In the 100s B.C. Chinese emperor Wu Di opened up China's western trade routes. Chinese merchants began sending goods to Central Asia along a great highway known as the Silk Road. It eventually stretched about 5,000 miles from eastern China to the Black Sea. Harsh weather and bandits made the Silk Road dangerous.

The promise of wealth kept traders on the Silk Road. By A.D. 100, large caravans made regular journeys from western China. Chinese merchants carried furs, ceramics, jade, cinnamon, and silk. Caravans returning to China carried valuables like gold, glass, and linen fabrics.

Trade along the Silk Road slowed in the 800s, renewed in the 1300s, and then ended. Today, adventurers explore parts of what was once the Silk Road. **Why was the Silk Road important?**

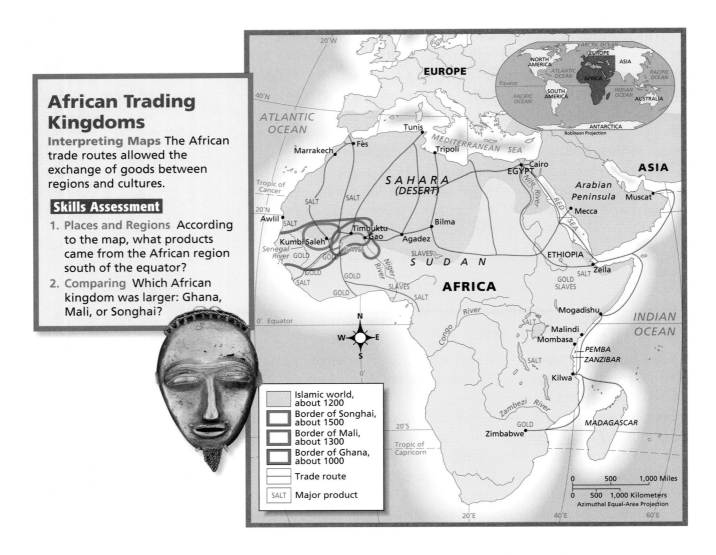

African Trading Kingdoms

Interpreting Maps The African trade routes allowed the exchange of goods between regions and cultures.

Skills Assessment

1. **Places and Regions** According to the map, what products came from the African region south of the equator?
2. **Comparing** Which African kingdom was larger: Ghana, Mali, or Songhai?

Map legend:
- Islamic world, about 1200
- Border of Songhai, about 1500
- Border of Mali, about 1300
- Border of Ghana, about 1000
- Trade route
- SALT — Major product

Research on the ROM

Free Find:
Two Views of Africa
After reading al-Mas'udi's and Ibn Battuta's accounts of traveling in Africa on the **Holt Researcher CD–ROM**, create a travel guide to these areas during the times the authors were there.

Important port cities were built along the Red Sea, which separates Africa from Southwest Asia. Aksum's most valuable trade good was ivory. Many Aksumites converted to Christianity after North African and Middle Eastern Christians introduced the religion.

Farther down the East African coast, Arab traders came into contact with Bantu-speaking peoples. They traded in market centers that grew into about 30 separate city-states. Each competed for control of the trade in gold, ivory, and slaves in southern Africa. Among the most important city-states were Mogadishu (moh-guh-DEE-shoo), Mombasa (mohm-BAH-sah), and Kilwa. Bantu and Arab influences in the region combined to create a unique culture. The people shared a common religion, Islam, and a new language, Swahili (swah-HEE-lee).

Long-distance trading networks also developed in West Africa. Traders eventually used camels to carry goods across the desert. These nomads from North Africa and the northern Sahara—called Berbers—brought salt south and gold north. Several kingdoms and empires grew wealthy and powerful from this trade. Ghana (GAH-nuh) ruled an area between the Niger (NY-juhr) and Senegal Rivers to the south and the

Sahara to the north. Most of Ghana's wealth came from trading gold. Berber merchants carried the gold north to the Mediterranean.

Mali emerged in the early 1200s, long after Ghana had collapsed. Mali stretched more than 1,000 miles inland from Africa's west coast. The empire of Mali included the important trading city of Timbuktu (tim-buhk-TOO). The Muslim traveler Ibn Battuta described the empire.

This mosque in Timbuktu, Mali, dates from the early 1300s.

 History Makers Speak **"**[The Malians] are seldom unjust, and have a greater horror of injustice than other people. Their [ruler] shows no mercy to anyone who is guilty of the least act of it. There is complete security in their country. Neither traveler nor inhabitant in it has anything to fear from robbers or men of violence.**"**

Ibn Battuta, quoted in *A Short History of Africa*, by Roland Oliver and J. D. Fage

In the mid-1200s North African traders brought Islam to Mali. Traders also introduced Islam to the large eastern region of the Sudan. Mali's emperors became Muslim, and Timbuktu became a center of Islamic culture and learning. **Mansa Musa** was one of the greatest Malian leaders. He made a pilgrimage to the Islamic holy city of Mecca in 1324. Arabs in Mecca were impressed with the African emperor's wealth and power.

The large Songhai (SAWNG-hy) Empire also had great influence in the region. Songhai's Muslim rulers encouraged the spread of Islamic culture throughout their vast territory. The Songhai Empire remained powerful until the late 1500s.

✔ **Reading Check: Summarizing** What effect did trade have on different empires in Africa?

Section 4 Review

go.hrw.com **Homework Practice Online**

keyword: SF3 HP1

1 Identify and explain:
• Muhammad
• Islam
• Crusades
• Kublai Khan
• Silk Road
• Zheng He
• Mansa Musa

2 Summarizing Copy the chart below. Use it to list the benefits of global trade for Africa, China, and the Muslim empire.

	Traded with	Benefits
Africa		
China		
Muslim empire		

3 Finding the Main Idea
a. How was Islam spread through much of the Mediterranean region?

b. When did China reopen trading networks with other countries, and what led to the decline of Chinese participation in international trade?

4 Writing and Critical Thinking
Supporting a Point of View Imagine that you are a noble lord in Europe at the time of the first Crusades. Write a speech to give to your vassals explaining why you think joining the Crusade is or is not a good idea.

Consider the following:
• Pope Urban's call to protect Jerusalem
• the risks of war so far from home
• the potential benefits of occupying the Holy Land

Chapter 1 Review

The Chapter at a Glance

Examine the visual summary of the chapter below. Then use it to create a graphic organizer covering the chapter's main ideas that you might give to a classmate.

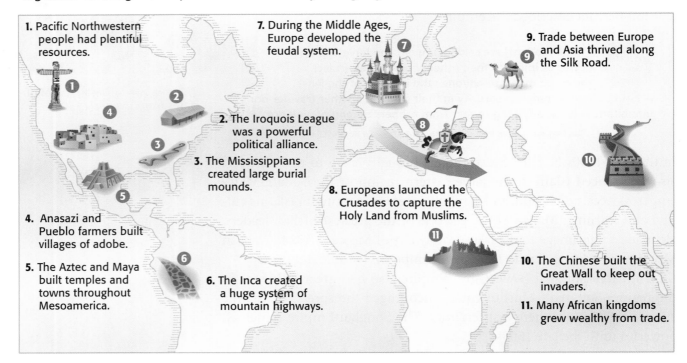

1. Pacific Northwestern people had plentiful resources.
2. The Iroquois League was a powerful political alliance.
3. The Mississippians created large burial mounds.
4. Anasazi and Pueblo farmers built villages of adobe.
5. The Aztec and Maya built temples and towns throughout Mesoamerica.
6. The Inca created a huge system of mountain highways.
7. During the Middle Ages, Europe developed the feudal system.
8. Europeans launched the Crusades to capture the Holy Land from Muslims.
9. Trade between Europe and Asia thrived along the Silk Road.
10. The Chinese built the Great Wall to keep out invaders.
11. Many African kingdoms grew wealthy from trade.

Identifying People and Ideas

Use the following terms and people in historically significant sentences.

1. archaeology
2. domestication
3. totems
4. Leif Eriksson
5. feudalism
6. Eleanor of Aquitaine
7. Magna Carta
8. Crusades
9. Silk Road
10. Zheng He

Understanding Main Ideas

Section 1 (Pages 4–9)

1. How did Paleo-Indians adapt to the widespread environmental changes caused by the end of the Ice Age?
2. What were some of the major achievements of Mesoamerican civilizations?

Section 2 (Pages 10–16)

3. How did the different environments in North America affect the ways that Native Americans gained food?
4. What was the Iroquois League?

Section 3 (Pages 17–22)

5. What role did the Catholic Church play in the Middle Ages?

Section 4 (Pages 23–27)

6. What were the Crusades, and why did they take place?
7. What were some of Africa's major kingdoms?

You Be the Historian— Reviewing Themes

1. **Culture** In what ways were Native American societies in the same region often similar?
2. **Geography** What types of housing did Native Americans build and why?
3. **Global Relations** How did trade networks benefit civilizations in Africa, Asia, and Europe?

Thinking Critically

1. **Comparing and Contrasting** How were the early Native American groups in the Northwest and Northeast culture areas similar and different?
2. **Finding the Main Idea** How did the development of agriculture change the way Native Americans lived?
3. **Supporting a Point of View** Do you think that all members of European society benefited from the feudal system during the Middle Ages? Explain your answer.

Interpreting Maps

Study the map below. Then use the information on the map to help you answer the questions that follow.

1. Which of the following is a fair statement based on the information provided on the map?
   a. The Maya Empire developed along the Pacific Coast.
   b. The Inca Empire developed along the Amazon River.
   c. Tenochtitlán was the capital of the Maya Empire.
   d. The Inca Empire controlled more land than the Aztec or Maya Empires.

2. Using the map, locate and identify the major geographic features within the Aztec and Inca Empires. How might these different environments have led to differences between the two civilizations?

Analyzing Primary Sources

Read the following pledge of loyalty by the knight Bernard Atton, then answer the questions.

> **❝I swear upon these four gospels of God that I will always be a faithful vassal to thee and to thy successors . . . in all things in which a vassal is required to be faithful to his lord; and I will defend thee, my lord, and all thy successors . . . and the castles and manors and all your men and their possessions against all malefactors [criminals] and invaders, of my own free will.❞**

3. Which of the following best sums up what Bernard Atton is promising?
   a. to provide land and money to his lord
   b. to protect the lord and his possessions
   c. to be faithful to the Church
   d. to capture criminals

4. Whom does Atton promise to serve?
   a. only his lord
   b. his lord and the king
   c. his lord and the Catholic Church
   d. his lord and all his lord's successors

5. Historians carefully examine the historical context in which a source was written. Why might a ruler during Europe's Middle Ages have needed the services of a knight like Bernard Atton?

Alternative Assessment

Building Your Portfolio

American History

Cooperative Learning

Complete the following activity in small groups. Your group is responsible for creating a detailed map of a manor during the Middle Ages. Assign each group member the role of one of the following members of feudal society: lord, vassal, peasant, or church official. Each member should study his or her role and make suggestions for how it should be represented on the map. Your map should show where different groups lived, public buildings such as a church, and images of daily activity.

▣ internet connect ▤▤▤▤▤

Internet Activity: go.hrw.com
keyword: SF3 CF1

Choose a topic about the World before the Opening of the Atlantic:
- Model Maya mathematics by solving a math problem.
- Learn about Paleolithic culture at the Clovis site.
- Research modern Africa and Asia.

2 The Age of Exploration
(1350–1550)

Columbus encountered the Taino Indians when he reached the Americas.

This ancient manuscript shows the Aztec people and their gods.

UNITED STATES

1428 The Aztec Empire is founded.

1492 Christopher Columbus and his crew reach the Americas on October 12.

1497 John Cabot reaches the coast of North America.

1350	1400	1450	1490

c. 1350 The Black Death ends in Europe.

1440s Johannes Gutenberg invents a printing press that uses movable type, making it much easier to print books.

1492 The *Reconquista* ends when the Muslim kingdom of Granada surrenders to Ferdinand and Isabella.

1495 Leonardo da Vinci begins painting his masterpiece *The Last Supper*.

WORLD

The invention of the printing press aided the spread of ideas during the Renaissance.

Build on What You Know

During the Middle Ages communication and trade between Europe and other areas slowed. By the 1300s, however, Europeans had formed trading relationships with merchants from Africa and Asia. During the Renaissance, Europeans began to explore and seek out new sea routes to Asia. While trying to find a new route, Christopher Columbus reached the Americas in 1492.

This map from the 1540s shows French explorations and settlements in North America. The map shows Canada at the bottom and Florida in the upper-right corner.

1500 Columbus is removed as governor of Spanish territories in the Americas.

1513 Vasco Núñez de Balboa is the first European to see the Pacific Ocean.

1535 Jacques Cartier sails up the St. Lawrence River to the site of present-day Montreal.

1500 | **1510** | **1520** | **1530** | **1540**

1500 Portuguese explorer Pedro Álvars Cabral lands in South America.

1522 Survivors of Ferdinand Magellan's expedition complete the first voyage around the world.

If you were there . . .

Would you be interested in exploration?

You Be the Historian

Themes Journal

What's Your Opinion? Do you **agree** or **disagree** with the following statements? Support your point of view in your journal.

- **Global Relations** Exploration is good for all peoples involved.
- **Economics** Global trade makes a nation stronger.
- **Science, Technology & Society** New inventions usually take much of the risk out of exploration.

Europeans Set Sail

Read to Discover

1. How did the Commercial Revolution and the Renaissance change Europe?
2. Why did western Europeans want to find a new sea route for trade with Africa and Asia?
3. How did Portugal's early explorations affect Africans?

WHY IT MATTERS TODAY

Scientific and technological changes continue to affect our world. Use CNNfyi.com or other **current events** sources to find out about important scientific and technological changes taking place today. Record your findings in your journal.

Define

- capital
- joint-stock companies
- astrolabe
- monopoly
- caravel

Identify

- Black Death
- Commercial Revolution
- Renaissance
- Prince Henry
- Bartolomeu Dias

A trade union in the Netherlands used this seal.

The Story Continues

In 1299 the city of Arras in present-day France was famous for its wealthy merchants. The powerful Crespin family was so rich that it loaned money to cities, bishops, and even monarchs. Some people worried about this new interest in money. "Money is too much worshipped here," wrote poet Adam de la Halle about Arras. Others welcomed the changing economy. They thought it provided ways for workers to make money and improve their social status. When Baude Crespin died in 1316 his tombstone read, "Pray for his immortal spirit then, Laborers and working men."

⭐ The European Economy Grows

Europe's wealth and population grew steadily during the late Middle Ages. Then, in the mid-1300s Europe suffered a terrible blow. Some ships belonging to Italian merchants returned from Asia carrying rats infected with bubonic plague, a deadly disease. The plague led to an epidemic called the **Black Death**, which swept through Europe from about 1348 to 1350. The epidemic killed as many as 30 million people, about one third of Europe's population. One Italian man described the horror of the scene. "Great pits were dug and piled deep with the multitude [large numbers] of dead." The man continued, "I . . . buried my five children with my own hands."

Eventually Europe recovered from the Black Death and the shortage of workers it created. In the 1200s Europe had begun to experience the **Commercial Revolution**, a period of great change in the European economy. During this time, the way people did business changed dramatically. Throughout most of the Middle Ages, merchants had set their prices based on what the local community agreed was fair. During the Commercial Revolution, however, merchants and craftspeople became more aggressive about making a profit. Landlords encouraged farmers on rented lands to grow crops that could be sold at market for profit. Many cities grew rich, often from specializing in certain crafts. For example, the Italian city of Florence became famous for dyeing cloth. Venice, on the other hand, was known for its glassmaking. Venice and many other cities also began dealing in rare goods brought from faraway lands. In this way they became rich trading centers.

Wealthy people in European society began to gain greater status and power. Spanish poet Juan Ruiz described this trend in the mid-1300s.

This French tombstone showed the effect of the Black Death.

History Makers Speak

“**Money can do much; it should be held in high esteem [regard]. It turns a tramp into a respected and honorable man. . . . The more money a man has, the more worthy he becomes, while the man who is penniless cannot call himself his own master. . . . Money makes hard things easy.**”

—Juan Ruiz, quoted in *The Medieval Reader,* edited by Norman Cantor

Merchant families in Europe wanted to get **capital**—money or property that is used to earn more money. The Medici (MED-ee-chee) family of Florence opened banks that made loans to monarchs, nobles, and other merchants. The borrowers repaid these loans with interest, which earned more money for the bankers. As a result of their wealth, the Medici and other bankers gained increasing influence in Europe. Merchants also created **joint-stock companies.** These are businesses in which a group of people invest together. The investors then share in the companies' profits and losses. Forming joint-stock companies helped merchants raise money while reducing the individual risk of starting a business for each investor.

Interpreting the Visual Record

Trade and finance *European moneylenders gained more influence as monarchs, nobles, and merchants sought loans.* **How does this image depict the demand for moneylenders?**

✔ Reading Check: **Analyzing Information** What effect did the Commercial Revolution have on Europe's economy?

★ ★ ★ ★ ★ ★ ★ ★ ★ ★ ★ ★
That's Interesting!
★ ★ ★ ★ ★ ★ ★ ★ ★ ★ ★ ★

The Genius of Leonardo
Did you know that Leonardo da Vinci had ideas for several inventions that would not appear for hundreds of years? It's true! Leonardo designed flying machines, parachutes, military devices, diving suits, and more. However, he actually built few of these "inventions." He drew detailed pictures of an armored military vehicle that moved about on wheels. The modern tank, however, was not used for the first time until World War I. Leonardo also drew flying machines with landing gear that pulled back into the machine. Not until 1933 was the first airplane with similar landing gear built.

★ The Renaissance

Some Europeans used their new wealth to support education and the arts. This change helped start the **Renaissance**, a rebirth of the arts and learning of ancient Greece and Rome. The Renaissance began in the 1300s in Italy and spread across Europe. It lasted into the 1600s.

During the Renaissance the interest in ancient Greek and Roman works mixed with new ideas about art, society, science, and technology. The translation of Arabic writings into Latin also shaped the Renaissance. Teachers taught students both the ideas of classical scholars and good morals. In his *Book of the Courtier,* Baldassare Castiglione (kahs-teel-YOH-nay) wrote that an ideal gentleman should know Greek and Latin. He should also "be very well acquainted with the poets . . . and also skilled at writing both verse and prose."

Wealthy merchants and public officials supported artists, writers, musicians, and poets. Italian artist Leonardo da Vinci (lay-oh-NAHR-doh dah VEEN-chee), who painted the *Mona Lisa,* had many talents. He studied architecture, astronomy, biology, geology, and machinery. "A painter is not admirable unless he is universal," he wrote. Michelangelo Buonarroti (mee-kay-LAHN-jay-loh bwaw-nahr-RAW-tee) was another gifted Italian artist. He carved the sculpture *David* and also painted the ceiling of the Sistine Chapel at the Vatican in Rome.

Johannes Gutenberg made a major contribution to the Renaissance in the 1440s. He invented movable type for printing presses. The printing press made it much easier and less expensive to make many copies of a book. By 1500, European printers had printed between 15 and 20 million books. As one Italian writer said, "What did the Greeks and Romans ever invent that could be compared to the printing press?" Access to books helped spread the science and literature of the Renaissance across Europe.

Interpreting the Visual Record

Raphael *The Renaissance artist Raphael painted the fresco* School of Athens *for Pope Julius II. The philosophers Aristotle and Plato stand at the center of the painting.* **How does this painting suggest the value that the Renaissance placed on Greek and Roman learning?**

During the Renaissance many people believed that human beings were superior to all living creatures. "To you is given a body more graceful than other animals . . . to you wit, reason, [and] memory," wrote one teacher. Some people believed that human beings could achieve anything, which encouraged Europeans to explore the rest of the world.

Technological advances also led to exploration. Sailors began to make use of important developments. They used ancient astronomical knowledge and tools such as the magnetic compass and the **astrolabe**. The astrolabe allowed navigators to learn their ship's location by charting the position of the stars. Better charts and instruments let sailors travel the sea without needing landmarks to guide them.

✔ **Reading Check: Finding the Main Idea** What were the major achievements of the Renaissance?

The Portuguese used astrolabes like this one to navigate at sea.

★ Trade with Africa and Asia

Much of the wealth of the Commercial Revolution was created through trade. The greatest profits came from trading with distant lands such as Africa and Asia. From Africa came gold, ivory, salt, and slaves. Salt was used to preserve foods. From Asia came silk and spices. Skilled European tailors used silk fabric to sew fancy clothing, and cooks used expensive spices to flavor food. An old English recipe for fruit pie used "powdered pepper, cinnamon, cloves, mace, powdered ginger, pines, raisins or currants, saffron, and salt." Most of these spices grew only in Asia.

Goods usually traveled long overland routes to reach Europe. The Silk Road, for example, stretched several thousand miles westward from China. These journeys were very dangerous for traders because of possible attacks from bandits. Still, many merchants risked the trip because they could earn huge profits. Along the way, each merchant raised the price of the goods when selling to the next trader. By the time the goods arrived in Europe, their prices had risen greatly.

Some countries in western Europe wanted to find a new sea route to Africa and Asia. English, French, Portuguese, and Spanish merchants had many reasons for wanting such a route. First, they did not want to depend on others for the goods they needed. Merchants in Venice had a **monopoly** on the Asian products that reached the Mediterranean. This meant they had sole economic control of these goods. Instead of paying third parties, merchants wanted to make their own money from trade. In addition, by 1400 overland trade routes had become less reliable. Political changes in Asia and a growing threat of bandit raids made it more difficult to use the Black Sea route to bring goods from Asia to Europe. At the same time, ship designs had improved.

Meanwhile, many educated Europeans had become interested in Asian cultures. Marco Polo's book about his travels in Asia remained

THE GRANGER COLLECTION, NEW YORK

LINKING
PAST to PRESENT ★ ★

From Printing Press to Desktop

The printing press was a remarkable invention. The mass production of books spread new ideas across Europe. In the late 1800s inventors made an exciting new advance. They invented machines that made it easier for printers to set type.

In the mid-1980s printing and publishing again went through important changes. Desktop publishing became possible for anyone with access to a computer, a laser printer, and the right software. Today people print newsletters, magazines, and even books in their own homes or offices. One reporter for the *New York Times* described the change. "Armed with a few articles [and] a desktop publishing program . . . almost anyone can become a publisher." **What benefits and drawbacks does desktop publishing have for us today?**

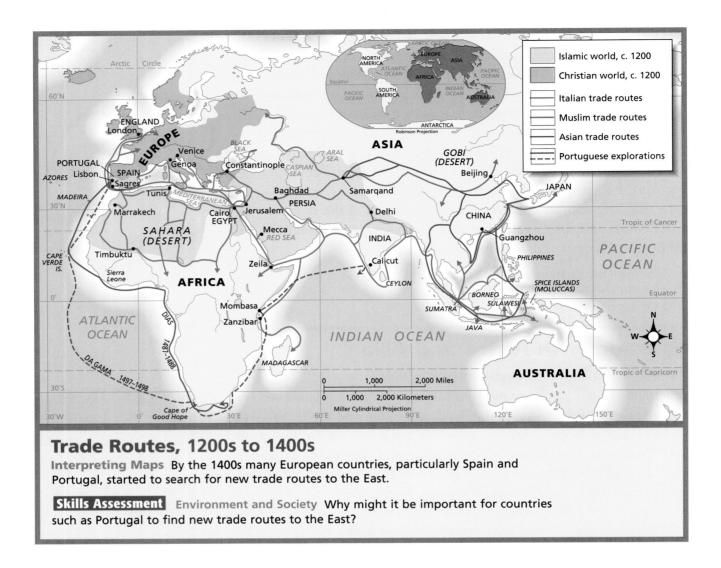

Trade Routes, 1200s to 1400s

Interpreting Maps By the 1400s many European countries, particularly Spain and Portugal, started to search for new trade routes to the East.

Skills Assessment Environment and Society Why might it be important for countries such as Portugal to find new trade routes to the East?

popular in Europe long after his death in 1324. Many Europeans hoped to learn more about these wondrous lands. Other Europeans hoped to spread Christianity. All of these factors encouraged Europeans to explore the Atlantic Ocean in search of new trade routes to Asia and Africa.

✔ **Reading Check: Summarizing** Why did Europeans want to trade directly with Asian and African merchants?

Research on the ROM

Free Find:
Henry the Navigator
After reading information about Prince Henry on the **Holt Researcher CD–ROM,** imagine what he studied. Make a list of classes that students hoping to become explorers would need to take.

⭐ The Portuguese Explore Africa

Portugal became one of the leaders in exploration in the early 1400s. **Prince Henry**, known as the Navigator, greatly aided Portugal's efforts. Henry gathered together the finest mapmakers, sailors, and shipbuilders in the town of Sagres (SAH-greesh). He helped improve navigational instruments, such as the compass. His designers developed the **caravel**, a small ship built to move quickly and handle well. One Italian called caravels "the best ships that sailed the seas." Henry also paid for expeditions to explore the west coast of Africa. One observer wrote that Prince

Henry believed if he did not send explorers to this area, "no mariners [sailors] or merchants would ever dare to attempt it."

In 1487–88 Portuguese navigator **Bartolomeu Dias** led an expedition southward along the African coast. A storm blew the ships out to sea. When Dias sighted land again, he discovered that his ships had safely passed the southern tip of Africa! This point became known as the Cape of Good Hope. Dias wanted to continue the voyage, but his crew did not. According to Dias, his men were "terrified by the great seas through which they had passed . . . [and demanded] that they proceed no farther." They also were running low on supplies, so Dias returned to Portugal.

The Portuguese explored all along the west coast of Africa and established small trading posts to supply their ships. They also bargained with local rulers and merchants for gold, ivory, and slaves. The slave trade that developed had a terrible effect on African communities. It led to more warfare among the kingdoms of West Africa and broke up many families. In 1444 a Portuguese record keeper reported what he saw in Africa.

This bronze statue of a flute player came from what is now Benin, in West Africa.

History Makers Speak

"Mothers would clasp [hold] their infants in their arms, and throw themselves on the ground to cover them with their bodies . . . so that they could prevent their children from being separated from them."

—Gomes Eanes de Zurara, from *The Chronicles of the Discovery and Conquest of Guinea*

Analyzing Primary Sources
Identifying Points of View How do you think the speaker feels about what he sees? Explain your answer.

The Portuguese sent many enslaved Africans to other Portuguese colonies. The Africans were forced to work hard and endured terrible living conditions.

✔ **Reading Check: Identifying Cause and Effect** Why did the Portuguese explore Africa, and how did they affect many African people?

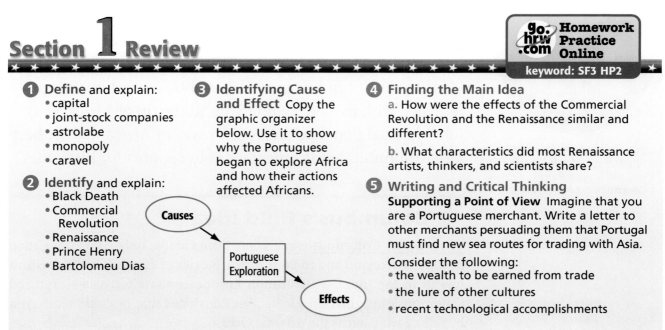

Section 1 Review

go.hrw.com **Homework Practice Online** keyword: SF3 HP2

1 **Define** and explain:
• capital
• joint-stock companies
• astrolabe
• monopoly
• caravel

2 **Identify** and explain:
• Black Death
• Commercial Revolution
• Renaissance
• Prince Henry
• Bartolomeu Dias

3 **Identifying Cause and Effect** Copy the graphic organizer below. Use it to show why the Portuguese began to explore Africa and how their actions affected Africans.

Causes → Portuguese Exploration → Effects

4 **Finding the Main Idea**
a. How were the effects of the Commercial Revolution and the Renaissance similar and different?
b. What characteristics did most Renaissance artists, thinkers, and scientists share?

5 **Writing and Critical Thinking**
Supporting a Point of View Imagine that you are a Portuguese merchant. Write a letter to other merchants persuading them that Portugal must find new sea routes for trading with Asia.

Consider the following:
• the wealth to be earned from trade
• the lure of other cultures
• recent technological accomplishments

Voyages to the Americas

Read to Discover

1. What was Christopher Columbus's goal?
2. What did Columbus do on his explorations in the Americas?
3. How did Portugal react to news of Columbus's discoveries?

WHY IT MATTERS TODAY

Christopher Columbus was the first European to explore the Caribbean. Today many Caribbean nations have a mix of European, Native American, and African cultures. Use **CNNfyi.com** or other **current events** sources to learn about some of the food, languages, music, or sports that are common in the Caribbean today. Record your findings in your journal.

Define

- viceroy
- convert

Identify

- Christopher Columbus
- King Ferdinand
- Queen Isabella
- *Reconquista*
- Line of Demarcation
- Treaty of Tordesillas

The Story Continues

THE METROPOLITAN MUSEUM OF ART

Columbus was inspired by travelers' tales, such as Marco Polo's Description of the World.

In 1488 Christopher Columbus traveled to Portugal to meet with King John II. The Italian explorer hoped to reach Asia by sailing across the Atlantic Ocean. He hoped that the king would give him money and ships to achieve his dream. King John had called Columbus "a big talker . . . full of fancy and imagination." However, he was still interested in Columbus's idea. Just as Columbus arrived in Lisbon, Bartolomeu Dias returned with news of sailing around the tip of Africa. King John decided that reaching Asia by way of Africa was the best idea. Columbus left Portugal without support for his plan.

⭐ Columbus's Bold Idea

Christopher Columbus was a sailor from Genoa, Italy. As a young man he sailed to Iceland and to West Africa. Stories of fabulous kingdoms and wealth in the Indies—a common European name for Asia—captured Columbus's imagination. He became convinced that he could reach Asia by sailing west across the Atlantic Ocean.

Columbus's plan was very risky at the time. No one knew the size of the great ocean to the west of Europe. Some people claimed that more than 10,000 miles separated Europe from the Indies. Traveling such a long distance seemed impossible. Navigating the open sea was hard, and crews would need enough food and water to last for months. Columbus believed such a voyage was possible. He was convinced that the Atlantic Ocean was much smaller than commonly thought.

Columbus went to Spain to ask **King Ferdinand** and **Queen Isabella** for help. Spain was fighting the kingdom of Granada, which was held by the Moors. These North African Muslims had conquered the area in the early Middle Ages. Ferdinand and Isabella did not answer Columbus for six years because they were trying to capture Granada. In the meantime, he failed to get support from other European leaders.

Finally, in January 1492 Spain won Granada, and the _Reconquista_ (re-kawng-KEE-stah)—the ongoing struggle to drive the Moors from Spain—ended. Ferdinand and Isabella agreed to pay for Columbus's trip. They hoped that Columbus would find a new sea route to the Indies so that Spain could better compete with Portugal.

Ferdinand and Isabella ordered Columbus to bring back any "Pearls, Precious Stones, Gold, Silver, Spiceries, and other Things and Merchandise of whatever kind, name or description that may be." They told him to claim for Spain any lands he explored. They promised to reward Columbus with some of the gold he sent back to Spain and with profits from any trading. In addition, he would become **viceroy**, or royal governor, of the lands he explored.

✔ **Reading Check: Summarizing** What did King Ferdinand and Queen Isabella hope to gain from Columbus's trip?

★ Crossing the Ocean

On August 3, 1492, just before sunrise, Columbus's three ships set sail. The _Niña_ and the _Pinta_ were caravels. Columbus sailed in the larger _Santa María_. The cramped ships were crewed by some 90 sailors in all and carried a year's worth of supplies.

Columbus sailed for the Canary Islands off the west coast of Africa. From there he caught a wind that blew his ships west across the Atlantic Ocean. The tiny fleet made good progress. Soon, the ships passed the limits of Columbus's maps. They were sailing into unknown waters. The crew grew more and more worried after a month passed with no sight of land. "Here the people could stand it no longer, and complained of the long voyage," wrote Columbus in his journal.

Just a few days later, the crew began to see signs that land was near. Columbus promised a reward "to him who first sang out that he saw land." On October 12, 1492, a lookout cried "Land! Land!" The journey from the Canary Islands had taken 33 days.

BIOGRAPHY

Queen Isabella

1451–1504

Queen Isabella was the daughter of the ruler of the powerful kingdom of Castile (ka-STEEL). At the age of 18, she married Ferdinand. He was the heir to the throne of Aragon, which was another powerful Spanish kingdom. Their marriage united the houses of Aragon and Castile. Isabella became queen of Castile in 1474.

During her reign, Isabella financed and helped direct Castile's military operations. When Christopher Columbus came to the royal court, Isabella's support proved essential to his cause. When she died in 1504, Spain was about to become one of the most powerful nations on Earth. **How did Queen Isabella strengthen Spain's power?**

⭐ Columbus's First Explorations

The ships landed on an island in the Bahamas. Columbus called the island San Salvador, which means "Holy Savior." Columbus thought that he was near the coast of China or the islands of Japan. He did not realize that he had reached a different continent entirely.

Columbus searched for riches on other islands, including one he called Hispaniola. There he met the Taino (TY-noh). He called these people Indians because he believed that he had landed in the fabled Indies. The Taino lived in small, peaceful farming villages. Columbus described them as "very well built, with very handsome bodies and very good faces." He also noted that the Taino were "so generous . . . that no one would believe it who has not seen it. They never refuse [to give] anything which they possess, if it be asked of them."

Columbus had little desire to learn about the Taino's culture. He and his crew were more interested in discovering gold. "There may be many things that I don't know," he wrote in his journal. "But I do not wish to delay but to discover and go to many islands to find gold." Columbus and his search parties explored several islands. They asked the Taino if they knew of any wealthy rulers, gold mines, or great palaces. They collected little gold but saw many natural wonders. Columbus described these sights in a letter.

Research on the ROM

Free Find:
Columbus and the Taino
After reading the letter in which Columbus describes his contact with the Taino on the **Holt Researcher CD–ROM**, imagine that you are a Taino. Create a story describing your thoughts when you saw Columbus for the first time.

 History Makers Speak
❝All [these islands] are beautiful, of a thousand shapes, and all are accessible [reachable] and filled with trees of a thousand kinds and tall, and they seem to touch the sky.❞

—Christopher Columbus, from *The Four Voyages of Columbus,*
edited by Cecil Jane

Columbus spent more than two months exploring. Then he decided that he had found enough gold and local treasures to return to Spain. Before he and his men left, however, the *Santa María* struck a coral reef and sank. There was not enough room for all of the sailors on the *Niña* and *Pinta*. Instead, Columbus and his men built a small colony on the north coast of Hispaniola. They called it La Navidad, the Spanish word for Christmas. Columbus left about 40 of his men at La Navidad and promised to return for them soon. He then boarded the *Niña* and set sail for Spain in January of 1493.

✔**Reading Check: Finding the Main Idea** What interested Columbus most on his first voyage to the Americas?

Columbus's small fleet faced great risks on its voyage across the Atlantic Ocean.

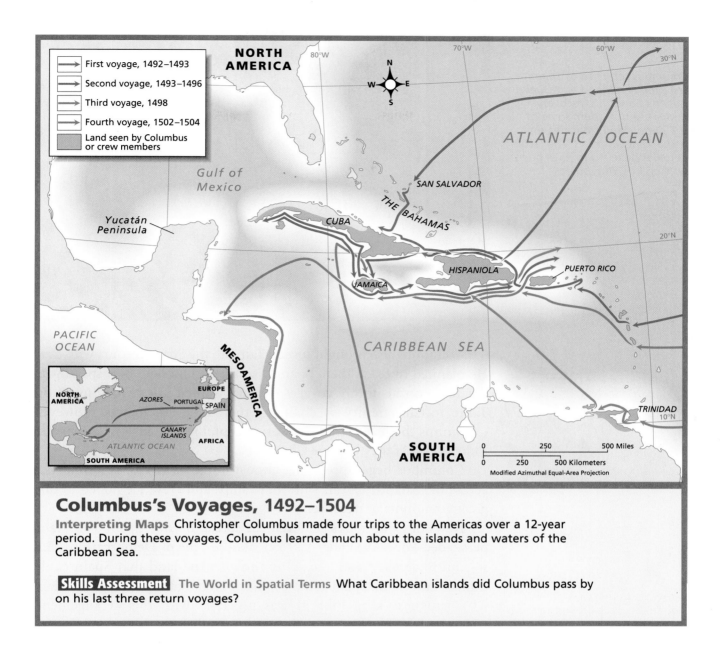

Columbus's Voyages, 1492–1504

Interpreting Maps Christopher Columbus made four trips to the Americas over a 12-year period. During these voyages, Columbus learned much about the islands and waters of the Caribbean Sea.

Skills Assessment The World in Spatial Terms What Caribbean islands did Columbus pass by on his last three return voyages?

⭐ Europe Learns of Columbus's Voyage

After a stormy return trip, Columbus finally reached Spain. He wrote a letter to King Ferdinand and Queen Isabella boasting of the wealth that lay across the ocean. The king and queen were excited by Columbus's news. They were even more pleased when he brought them gold nuggets and rare treasures. As a reward for his discoveries, Ferdinand and Isabella made Columbus an admiral and a governor.

History Makers Speak

❝We, considering the risk and danger to which you have exposed yourself for our service . . . [award you] the said offices of Admiral of the said Ocean Sea, . . . and of viceroy and governor of the said islands and mainland.❞

—King Ferdinand and Queen Isabella, quoted in *The Conquest of Paradise,* by Kirkpatrick Sale

Analyzing Primary Sources
Identifying Points of View
Why did Ferdinand and Isabella believe that Columbus deserved a reward?

THE GRANGER COLLECTION

Columbus returned to Spain to tell King Ferdinand and Queen Isabella about his discovery and present to them some of the people and treasures that he had encountered. The letter below is believed to have been written by Columbus.

Columbus also brought several Taino to the Spanish court with him. He planned to teach them Spanish so they could help him speak with the Taino on his future voyages. Isabella wanted priests to **convert** the Taino to Christianity by changing their religious beliefs. However, Columbus believed that it was acceptable to enslave American Indians even if they became Christians.

Columbus began preparing almost immediately for a second trip across the Atlantic Ocean with more ships and crew. He hoped to find greater amounts of treasure.

News of Columbus's achievement spread beyond Spain. Ferdinand persuaded Pope Alexander VI to create the **Line of Demarcation.** This was an imaginary boundary line showing the land that Spain could explore and claim. Spain could claim the land that was west of this line.

Portuguese king John II was unhappy with this arrangement, which he felt favored Spain. To prevent conflict, the leaders of the two nations chose to compromise. Spain and Portugal signed the **Treaty of Tordesillas** (tawr-day-SEEL-yahs) in June 1494, which moved the Line of Demarcation some 800 miles farther west. This gave Portugal more opportunity to claim lands unexplored by other Europeans.

✔ **Reading Check: Analyzing Information** What was done in response to Portugal's unhappiness with the Line of Demarcation?

★ Columbus's Later Voyages

Columbus returned to La Navidad in 1493 on his second voyage. He found that the colony had been destroyed and that all the sailors had been killed. Columbus was disappointed but began building new settlements on the islands. In 1498 Columbus became the first European explorer to see South America. He then returned to Hispaniola.

Although Columbus was the governor of these new Spanish territories, he spent his time exploring. The living conditions in the colonies grew poor, partly because the Spaniards had difficulty growing crops in the tropical climate. Columbus fought many small battles with the Taino. He enslaved the Taino he defeated despite Isabella's instructions not to do so.

These problems made Ferdinand and Isabella unhappy with Columbus. In 1500 they removed him from his post as governor. When he returned to Spain, Columbus pleaded to make one last voyage to the Americas. They agreed, and he set sail in 1502. The ships ran into bad weather off the coast of Central America and they wrecked on the Caribbean island of Jamaica. There Columbus wrote in his journal that the sailors had "nothing to look forward to but death." They spent a year on Jamaica before being rescued by Spanish colonists from Hispaniola. In 1504 Columbus returned to Spain a broken man.

Columbus lived for two more years in very poor health. His share of the royal income from the Caribbean had made him wealthy. However, he was too sick to participate in the royal court. Columbus often complained to family and friends that those he had served had forgotten him. In 1506 he died "unnoticed and unsung," according to one modern historian. It would be years before Europeans realized the impact of Columbus on their world.

✔ **Reading Check: Drawing Inferences and Conclusions** Why were the later voyages of Columbus less successful than his first?

THE GRANGER COLLECTION

Interpreting the Visual Record

A royal gift *Columbus was granted this coat of arms for his achievements.* **What do you think the different images on the coat of arms represent?**

Section 2 Review

go.hrw.com **Homework Practice Online**
keyword: SF3 HP2

① **Define** and explain:
- viceroy
- convert

② **Identify** and explain:
- Christopher Columbus
- King Ferdinand
- Queen Isabella
- *Reconquista*
- Line of Demarcation
- Treaty of Tordesillas

③ **Sequencing** Copy the graphic organizer below. Use it to organize the information you have learned about Columbus's four voyages.

Date	Results
1492	
1493	
1498	
1502	

④ **Finding the Main Idea**
a. Do you think Columbus's voyages succeeded or failed? Explain your answer.

b. What do you think would have happened in the Spanish settlements if Isabella and Ferdinand had not removed Columbus from his post as viceroy?

⑤ **Writing and Critical Thinking**
Identifying Cause and Effect Imagine that you are an adviser to the Portuguese king in 1493. Prepare a short report describing the reasons for and effects of the voyage Columbus has just made.

Consider the following:
- Europeans' goal of finding a new sea route to Asia
- the people and gold Columbus encountered in the Americas
- the Line of Demarcation

The Race for Trade Routes

Read to Discover

1. Where did Vasco da Gama and Pedro Álvars Cabral explore, and what was the result of these voyages for Portugal?
2. What did John Cabot and Amerigo Vespucci achieve?
3. Why was Ferdinand Magellan's voyage important?

WHY IT MATTERS TODAY

Instead of sea exploration, today some countries are interested in exploring space. Use **CNNfyi.com** or other **current events** sources to find stories related to recent space explorations and the people involved in these projects. Record your findings in your journal.

Define
- strait
- circumnavigate

Identify
- Vasco da Gama
- Pedro Álvars Cabral
- John Cabot
- Amerigo Vespucci
- Vasco Núñez de Balboa
- Ferdinand Magellan

Chinese porcelain was a highly valued trade item in Europe.

The Story Continues

Christopher Columbus always believed that he had landed just off the coast of China. He knew, however, that many people did not believe his claims. "Because everything [the wealth of the Indies] did not appear immediately, I was held up to abuse," he wrote. King Manuel had become ruler of Portugal in 1495. Manuel was one of those who thought that an eastern sea route to Asia, not Columbus's proposed western route, made more sense.

⭐ Portugal's Great Discoveries

King Manuel believed that the best route to Asia was around the southern tip of Africa. He sent **Vasco da Gama** on an expedition around the Cape of Good Hope. Da Gama, a minor noble and skilled sailor, spent two years preparing his fleet. He left Lisbon in July 1497 and arrived in southwestern India in May 1498. Two Muslim traders greeted da Gama when he sailed into the port of Calicut. They cried out in Portuguese, "A lucky venture, a lucky venture! Plenty of rubies, plenty of emeralds!

You owe great thanks to God, for having brought you to a country holding such riches!" The king of Calicut even became angry with da Gama for not bringing the traditional gifts. One of da Gama's crew members wrote, "We never expected to hear our language spoken so far away from Portugal."

The Portuguese soon realized that the Indians had been trading with Muslim and Italian merchants for many years. Da Gama made two more trips back to India. He governed a small Portuguese colony there. As a result of his efforts, Portugal had won the European race for a new sea route to the wealth of Asia.

Another Portuguese explorer, **Pedro Álvars Cabral**, made his discovery by accident. He was leading a fleet along da Gama's route down the west coast of Africa. A terrible storm blew the ships far off course. Cabral's ships drifted westward for weeks. In 1500 Cabral finally reached South America. He landed somewhere along the coast of what is now Brazil. He claimed the land for Portugal, not knowing at the time that he had landed on the coast of a continent rather than a large island. Brazil's eastern shore was on Portugal's side of the Line of Demarcation, so Cabral was able to claim this land for his country. Portugal eventually founded forts, trading posts, and settlements in Brazil.

✔ **Reading Check: Summarizing** Explain da Gama's and Cabral's important accomplishments.

Interpreting the Visual Record

India *Vasco da Gama and his crew arrived on the southwest coast of India in 1498. **What parts of this image suggest that da Gama had encountered a powerful kingdom?***

⭐ Cabot and Vespucci Explore

Like Christopher Columbus, other Italian explorers sailed for other nations, looking for wealth, knowledge, and adventure. Giovanni Caboto, called **John Cabot** by the English, also wanted to find a sea route to Asia. He knew that King Henry VII of England was interested in controlling such a route. Cabot offered to pay for his own expedition. He asked only that the king grant him a royal charter to any lands he found. The king agreed, and Cabot made voyages in 1497 and 1498.

King Henry told Cabot "to seeke out, discover, and finde . . . countreyes, regions or provinces . . . whiche before this time have beene unknowen to all Christians." Cabot hoped to sail farther north than Columbus and continue on to Asia. Instead, Cabot found North America. Cabot left very few records of his journey, but it is believed that he traveled along the coast of present-day Newfoundland in Canada. Although Cabot did not find a passage to the Indies, his voyages were successful. They became the basis of England's claim to land in North America. Henry VII rewarded Cabot and then sent him out again to find a way to Asia. Cabot and his fleet disappeared mysteriously on this expedition. Historian Polydore Vergil wrote at the time of Cabot's journey. "[Cabot] found his new lands only in the ocean's bottom, to which he and his ship are thought to have sunk."

CONNECTING TO
THE ARTS

Images of the Americas In the 1500s few Europeans had the chance to visit the Americas. Instead they relied on illustrated maps. Such maps often recorded where explorers went and what they found. The map of North and South America shown here is surrounded by pictures of explorers such as Columbus. As well as land masses and names of places, the map includes decorations such as a sea monster. These early maps were often not very accurate, but they helped feed people's curiosity about new lands. **What major geographic errors can you find on this early map of the Americas?**

The Italian explorer **Amerigo Vespucci** (ve-SPOO-chee) led Spanish ships on a westward voyage. Vespucci had worked as a business agent for the powerful Medici family. When the Medici were forced to leave Florence in 1494, Vespucci went to Spain. In 1501 he sailed with a fleet that reached the coast of present-day South America. Vespucci was amazed by the animals he saw. They were quite different from those in Europe.

History Makers Speak

❝**What should I tell of the multitude of wild animals, the abundance of pumas, of panthers, of wild cats not like those of Spain . . .; of so many wolves, red deer, monkeys . . . and many large snakes?**❞

—Amerigo Vespucci, quoted in *The Discoverers,* by Daniel J. Boorstin

Vespucci and his crew also met American Indians. He wrote many exaggerated letters about them, which captured the imaginations of European readers.

Martin Waldseemüller (VAHLT-zay-mool-uhr), a German mapmaker, published some of Vespucci's letters in a book and printed a large map. He labeled the continents across the Atlantic Ocean "America" in honor of Vespucci. The book and map became popular throughout Europe. As a result, Europeans soon began using the names North America and South America for the new lands.

✔ **Reading Check: Contrasting** Contrast Cabot's and Vespucci's voyages to the Americas.

★ Balboa Reaches the Pacific

Europeans came to understand that the Americas were a pair of continents. They realized that Columbus had not found a sea route to Asia after all. Some Spanish explorers began to search for a water passage around or through the American lands.

One of these explorers was **Vasco Núñez de Balboa** (NOON-yays day bahl-BOH-uh). Balboa had failed as a farmer in a Spanish colony in the Caribbean. After arriving at a new settlement in present-day Panama, he took control. Balboa improved the living conditions of the colonists. Using a combination of force and trade, he also made alliances with local American Indians. Peter Martyr was a historian from the time. He wrote that the son of an American Indian leader shared with the Spaniards some fascinating news.

 History Makers Speak

❝I will shewe [show] you a region flowing with golde, where you may satisfie your ravening [hungry] appetites. . . . When you are passing over [the] mountains . . . you shall see another sea, where they sayle [sail] with shippes as bigge as yours.❞

—Anonymous, quoted in *The Discoverers*, by Daniel J. Boorstin

Analyzing Primary Sources

Identifying Points of View What does this statement show about the American Indians' knowledge of the Europeans?

Balboa wanted to know if such stories were true. He went with about 200 of his men and some American Indian guides to search for this ocean. The men traveled for weeks through thick jungle and across deadly swamps. The journey was tiring and dangerous. The group fought with Indians along the way. In 1513 Balboa finally reached the top of a mountain near the coast. From there he saw a great blue sea stretching out as far as his eyes could see. "Behold the much-desired ocean!" he exclaimed. Balboa named these waters the South Sea.

There was no way for ships to cross Panama to reach these waters. However, Balboa's report offered hope that Spain might find a way into the South Sea. Balboa decided to build a fleet to explore the area around the coast. His ships had to be transported piece by piece across the mountains to the South Sea. However, Balboa's success threatened some Spanish authorities, including the governor of Panama. Balboa's enemies charged him with treason and executed him in 1519.

Interpreting the Visual Record

The South Sea *This detail from an early map shows Balboa claiming the South Sea for Spain.* **What does this illustration suggest about how Balboa's group was equipped and the terrain it had to cross?**

✔ **Reading Check: Finding the Main Idea** Why was Balboa's discovery of the South Sea important to Spain?

★ Sailing around the Globe

Ferdinand Magellan

News of Balboa's discovery interested other European explorers who were looking for a sea route to the Indies. **Ferdinand Magellan** (muh-JEL-uhn) was one sailor who believed he could sail to Asia through this South Sea.

Magellan was a Portuguese captain who had spent many years sailing to Africa and India. Antonio Pigafetta was an Italian adventurer who sailed along with Magellan. Pigafetta later wrote that Magellan "was always the most constant [dependable] in greatest adversity [danger]."

Magellan believed there was a sea passage through South America. Magellan had been accused of treason in Portugal, so he took his idea to Spain. At first, the Spanish did not trust the Portuguese sailor. Magellan's experience and confidence convinced the royal advisers to send him, however. Spain provided him with five ships for the trip.

Magellan set sail in September 1519. From the start he had many problems. Several of his captains did not trust or respect him. Magellan also made his officers angry by refusing to tell them where they were headed. When asked, he shouted, "Follow me and don't ask questions!" Magellan did not find the sea passage where he expected it. He traveled south, searching desperately for a channel through the continent. The weather grew colder, and supplies began to run low. At the same time, Magellan and his supporters had to put down a rebellion led by the Spanish officers.

Then the fleet of ships found a **strait**—a narrow, winding sea passage—between the coastal cliffs. It took them more than a month to pass through the strait. Along the way they battled fierce winds and avoided jagged rocks. Finally, as Pigafetta wrote, "The men . . . reported that they had seen the cape and the open sea. The captain-general [Magellan] wept for joy." The passageway at the southern tip of South America became known as the Strait of Magellan. By then Magellan had lost two of his five ships. He and the other captains thought that they could reach Asia in a few weeks. Instead, the journey took another 100 days. The ships quickly ran out of supplies. The conditions were terrible.

The Voyage of Magellan and Elcano, 1519–1522

Interpreting Maps After Ferdinand Magellan died, Juan Sebastián de Elcano became the fleet's leader.

Skills Assessment The World in Spatial Terms
What is the last ocean Magellan crossed?

Analyzing Primary Sources
Making Generalizations and Predictions How do you think sailors would react to such conditions?

"We were three months and twenty days without getting any kind of fresh food. We ate . . . powder of biscuit swarming with worms. We drank yellow water that had been putrid [spoiled] for many days. . . . Often we ate sawdust."

—Antonio Pigafetta, from *Magellan's Voyage, a Narrative Account of the First Circumnavigation*, edited by R. A. Skelton

The weather, however, was calm during the entire trip. The crew decided to rename the South Sea, calling it the Pacific, or peaceful, Ocean.

Magellan navigated the unknown waters using instinct and skill. His ships crossed the world's largest ocean and reached the Indies. Then he searched for islands that Portugal had not claimed. While doing so, Magellan landed in the present-day Philippines. There he was killed in a battle with a Philippine kingdom.

Magellan's crew wanted to return to Spain. Led by officer Juan Sebastián de Elcano (el-KAHN-oh), they decided to continue sailing west through unfamiliar waters. Along the way they had to avoid Portuguese seaports and pirate ships. In September 1522 one of the three remaining ships arrived in Spain, carrying a cargo of cloves. The sale of the cloves paid for the cost of the entire voyage and even earned a profit. However, only 18 of the fleet's approximately 250 original crew members and one of the fleet's five ships survived the long journey. These 18 sailors were the first people to **circumnavigate**, or sail completely around, the world. Their 40,000-mile voyage had taken them across three oceans. They had finally found the western route to Asia for which Columbus and others had been searching since 1492.

One member of Magellan's crew sketched this scene of two crew members sailing a boat, off the present-day island of Guam, in March 1521.

✔ **Reading Check: Sequencing** Describe the important events that took place on the first sea voyage around the world in their proper order.

Section 3 Review

go.hrw.com **Homework Practice Online**

keyword: SF3 HP2

1 **Define** and explain:
- strait
- circumnavigate

2 **Identify** and explain:
- Vasco da Gama
- Pedro Álvars Cabral
- John Cabot
- Amerigo Vespucci
- Vasco Núñez de Balboa
- Ferdinand Magellan

3 **Summarizing** Copy the chart below. Use it to organize information about the explorations of Balboa, Cabot, Cabral, da Gama, Magellan, and Vespucci.

Explorer	When?	Where?	Results

4 **Finding the Main Idea**
a. In what ways did the voyages of Vasco da Gama and Pedro Álvars Cabral benefit Portugal?

b. Do you think John Cabot or Amerigo Vespucci made a greater contribution to the opening of the Americas? Explain your answer.

5 **Writing and Critical Thinking**
Identifying Points of View Imagine that you are preparing to interview the survivors of Magellan's voyage. Write an interview as you imagine it would take place after the crew returned.

Consider the following:
- Magellan's attitude toward his crew
- the rebellion against Magellan
- the sailing conditions

The Opening of the Atlantic

Read to Discover

1. How did new trade routes affect Portugal and Spain?
2. How did the Columbian Exchange affect Europeans and American Indians?
3. Why were some countries searching for a Northwest Passage?

Identify

- Columbian Exchange
- Northwest Passage
- Jacques Cartier
- Samuel de Champlain
- Henry Hudson

WHY IT MATTERS TODAY

The opening of the Atlantic allowed goods and crops to be traded between Europe and the Americas. Today, countries around the world trade with each other. Use CNNfyi.com or other **current events** sources to learn about some of the items from faraway places that you use every day. Record your findings in your journal.

At different periods in history, saffron—a spice made from flowers such as these—has been worth much more than its weight in gold.

The Story Continues

The voyages of Christopher Columbus, Vasco da Gama, Ferdinand Magellan, and others changed the way Europeans looked at the world. The Atlantic Ocean was transformed into the gateway to Africa, India, and the Americas. Exploration changed world trade patterns. It also greatly changed the nations of western and northern Europe. One Spaniard explained the change. "Formerly we were at the end of the world; now we are in the middle of it, with an unprecedented [never-before-experienced] change in our fortunes."

⭐ A Shift in Trade

In the 1500s Europe turned to the Atlantic Ocean for trading routes. Portuguese ships traveled to India, around Africa, and across the Atlantic. Spanish ships went to Asia across the Atlantic and Pacific Oceans. These new routes made traditional overland trade routes less important. Venice lost its monopoly on trade with Asia and grew weaker.

Spanish and Portuguese traders made greater profits because they no longer dealt with third parties such as Muslim traders. Portugal came to control as much as 75 percent of the spice trade between Europe and Asia. Investors made great profits of nearly 90 percent on each voyage. Spain established an outpost in the Philippines to trade with China. As a result of their explorations, Portugal and Spain gained influence in European affairs. Other European nations also wanted to profit from this rich trade. Countries such as England, France, and the Netherlands began to explore the Atlantic. Each hoped to find its own sea route to Asia.

Around this time Europeans also began to see the Atlantic Ocean as more than just a path to Africa and Asia. The Americas promised to be full of wealth. Christopher Columbus and Amerigo Vespucci had said that the Americas were full of lush forests, clear streams, and many natural resources. In the 1500s some Europeans already were using some of these resources. For example, Spanish, Portuguese, English, and French fishermen traveled across the Atlantic to catch cod near present-day Canada.

✔ **Reading Check: Finding the Main Idea** Why did Spain and Portugal become stronger in the 1500s?

★ The Columbian Exchange

Explorers carried plants, animals, and diseases to the "New World" of the Americas. They also brought back plants and animals to the "Old World"—Asia, Africa, and Europe. This transfer became known as the **Columbian Exchange** because it resulted from Columbus's explorations. The Columbian Exchange dramatically changed the world.

European explorers in the Americas found many plants and animals that were unlike any seen back home. "All the trees were as different from ours as day from night," Columbus noted in his journal. These American plants proved valuable and useful. Explorers introduced corn to Europe for use as animal food. Many Europeans began to cook with tomatoes, particularly in Mediterranean countries. In the late 1600s some Europeans began to grow potatoes, which were from South America. Later, European settlers brought potatoes to North America. Europeans also saw American Indians using tobacco and cocoa, which became luxury items in Europe.

Settlers and explorers also brought plants and animals to the American continents. European horses, cattle, and pigs soon ran wild there. American Indians came to use these animals for transportation and to improve their diet. They also started to farm European grains, such as wheat and barley. These grains grew well in cool climates. Rice and bananas grew well in warmer parts of the Americas.

The explorers also unintentionally introduced deadly diseases. Measles, smallpox, and typhus were common in Europe. As a result, most adult Europeans had developed some degree of immunity, or natural resistance, to them. American Indians, however, had never been

★★★★★★★★★★★★
That's Interesting!
★★★★★★★★★★★★

"Golden Apples" Did you know that for many years some Europeans thought tomatoes were poisonous? It's true! Tomatoes originated in South America and later spread to Mesoamerica. The word *tomato* comes from the Aztec word *tomatl*. Tomatoes were first brought back to Europe by Spanish explorers. Northern Europeans grew tomato plants for decoration but were not sure that eating them was safe. In Italy and Spain, however, people soon began cooking with the new fruits. The Italians called tomatoes "golden apples," perhaps because some of the early varieties were yellow. Many years later European settlers brought tomatoes back across the Atlantic Ocean to North America.

AMERICAN MUSEUM OF NATURAL HISTORY

Interpreting the Visual Record

Deadly diseases *This illustration from a history of Spanish settlement in the Americas written in the 1500s shows the effects of smallpox on the Aztec of Mexico.* **What happened to many of the American Indians who came into contact with European explorers?**

exposed to such diseases. They had no immunity to them. As a result, many American Indians became terribly sick after the first encounters with Europeans took place. Hundreds of thousands of American Indians died.

No one knows how many American Indians died from European diseases, but the loss of life was staggering. Spanish author Fernández de Oviedo reported in 1548 about the destruction of the American Indians of Hispaniola. He reported that of the estimated 1 million American Indians who had lived on the island in 1492, "there are not now believed to be at the present time . . . five hundred persons [left]."

✔ **Reading Check: Drawing Inferences and Conclusions** What were some of the long-term benefits and drawbacks of the Columbian Exchange?

★ The Search for a Northwest Passage

Spain and Portugal were busy exploring Central and South America. Therefore, other European nations turned to North America. They hoped to find a path around or through the continent. A **Northwest Passage** through North America would allow ships to sail from the Atlantic to the Pacific.

In 1524 France sent Italian captain Giovanni da Verrazano (vayr-raht-SAHN-oh) to find the Northwest Passage. Verrazano sailed along the coast of North America from present-day North Carolina to Maine. **Jacques Cartier** (kahr-TYAY), a French sailor, led France's next major exploration of North America. He made two trips to what is now Canada in 1534 and 1535. He sailed into the St. Lawrence River and traveled all the way to present-day Montreal. Cartier's crew spent the winter near what is now Quebec. On these journeys, Cartier encountered the Huron Indians and strange animals such as polar bears.

Nearly 70 years later French sailor **Samuel de Champlain** began exploring North America. Champlain recorded his ideas about European exploration in his journal.

Analyzing Primary Sources

Identifying Points of View
Why does Champlain support European exploration?

History Makers Speak

❝Through [exploration] we gain knowledge of different countries, regions and kingdoms; through it we attract and bring into our countries all kinds of riches; through it . . . Christianity [is spread] in all parts of the earth.❞

—Samuel de Champlain, quoted in *The Canadian Frontier, 1534–1760,* by W. J. Eccles

Champlain followed Cartier's old paths. Over the years he made many journeys along the St. Lawrence River. He also visited the Great Lakes in 1615, led by Huron guides. Champlain founded a small colony on the St. Lawrence River that he named Quebec. His explorations became the basis of France's claim to much of Canada.

The Dutch hired English captain **Henry Hudson** to enter the race to find a Northwest Passage. Hudson first sailed to present-day New York in 1609. The following year Hudson returned to North America. This time he sailed under the English flag. He traveled far to the north. Eventually he reached a strait that he hoped would lead to the Pacific Ocean. Instead, it led into a huge bay, later named Hudson Bay.

Hudson and his crew spent a hungry, freezing winter there. "The cold was so extreme that it lamed [crippled] most of our company," wrote a member of Hudson's crew. Hudson wanted to continue exploring in the spring, but some of his crew rebelled. They put Hudson and his followers into a small boat and set it adrift. Some of his crew remained in the area for a day or so, "in all which time we saw not the [boat]," said one crewman, "nor ever saw her after." Hudson did not return.

Neither Verrazano, Cartier, Champlain, nor Hudson ever found a Northwest Passage. Their explorations, however, increased European interest in North America.

In 1609 Henry Hudson sailed the ship Half Moon *to present-day New York.*

✔ **Reading Check: Finding the Main Idea** Why did European explorers seek a Northwest Passage, and how successful were their efforts?

Section 4 Review

go.hrw.com **Homework Practice Online**
keyword: SF3 HP2

❶ Identify and explain:
- Columbian Exchange
- Northwest Passage
- Jacques Cartier
- Samuel de Champlain
- Henry Hudson

❷ Comparing Copy the web diagram below. Use it to show how explorations benefited Europe. In the smaller circles, list the key benefits of exploration to Spain, Portugal, and France. In the center circle, list the general benefits to Europe.

France

Spain

Europe

Portugal

❸ Finding the Main Idea
a. Do you think that the Columbian Exchange helped or harmed Europeans? American Indians? Explain your answers.

b. What problems did Spain's and Portugal's discoveries cause for other western European nations?

❹ Writing and Critical Thinking
Supporting a Point of View Imagine that you are asking the king of England to finance a journey to find the Northwest Passage. Write a petition asking for the money you need.

Consider the following:
- the benefits of a sea route to Asia
- the failures of Verrazano, Cartier, Champlain, and Hudson
- France's claim to land in North America

Chapter 2 Review

The Chapter at a Glance

Examine the visual summary of the chapter below. Use the summary to create a five-question quiz covering the chapter's main ideas that you might give to a classmate.

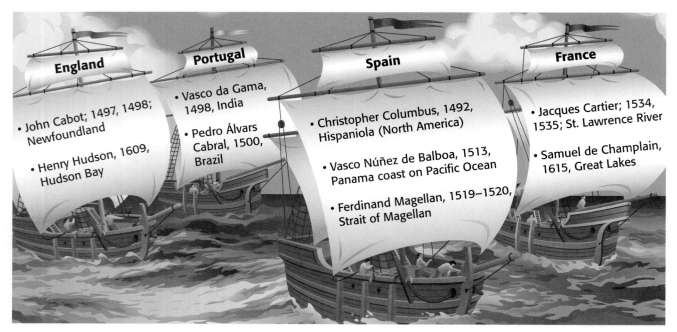

England
- John Cabot; 1497, 1498; Newfoundland
- Henry Hudson, 1609, Hudson Bay

Portugal
- Vasco da Gama, 1498, India
- Pedro Álvars Cabral, 1500, Brazil

Spain
- Christopher Columbus, 1492, Hispaniola (North America)
- Vasco Núñez de Balboa, 1513, Panama coast on Pacific Ocean
- Ferdinand Magellan, 1519–1520, Strait of Magellan

France
- Jacques Cartier; 1534, 1535; St. Lawrence River
- Samuel de Champlain, 1615, Great Lakes

Identifying People and Ideas

Use the following terms or people in historically significant sentences.

1. astrolabe
2. Prince Henry
3. Christopher Columbus
4. Treaty of Tordesillas
5. Vasco da Gama
6. Ferdinand Magellan
7. strait
8. Columbian Exchange
9. Northwest Passage
10. Samuel de Champlain

Understanding Main Ideas

Section 1 *(Pages 32–37)*
1. What effects did the Commercial Revolution and the Renaissance have on Europe?
2. Why did Portugal search for a new sea route to Asia?

Section 2 *(Pages 38–43)*
3. What did Christopher Columbus hope to achieve when he set out on his first journey in 1492, and how successful were his four voyages?

Section 3 *(Pages 44–49)*
4. How did Vasco da Gama's and Pedro Álvars Cabral's discoveries help Portugal?

Section 4 *(Pages 50–53)*
5. What types of goods were exchanged between Europe and the Americas?

6. Why were England, France, and the Netherlands interested in finding a Northwest Passage?

You Be the Historian— Reviewing Themes

1. **Global Relations** What were the positive and negative effects of the Columbian Exchange?
2. **Economics** What effect did their increased global trade have on the economic development of Spain and Portugal?
3. **Science, Technology & Society** How did technological developments help make it possible for Europeans to explore new lands?

Thinking Critically

1. **Summarizing** Why did John Cabot, Amerigo Vespucci, and Ferdinand Magellan set out on explorations across the Atlantic Ocean?
2. **Evaluating** Select the explorer that you think made the greatest contribution to European exploration in the Americas. Using specific examples from the chapter, explain why you have chosen this explorer.
3. **Drawing Inferences and Conclusions** Do you think the Renaissance would have taken place without the Commercial Revolution? Explain your answer.

Analyzing Primary Sources

Read the following quote from Bartolomé de Las Casas, a Spanish priest who wrote about Columbus's journey to the Americas, and then answer the following questions.

> **"The Admiral [Columbus] cheered them [his crew] as best he could, holding out good hope of the benefits they would have. And he added that it was useless to complain since he had come to find the Indies, and so had to continue until he found them."**

1. Which of the following statements best describes Columbus's point of view?
   a. He was worried about where he was going.
   b. He was willing to give up if difficulties arose.
   c. He did not care how his crew felt.
   d. He was determined to find the Indies.

2. What sort of benefits might Columbus have promised his crew if their journey was successful?

Interpreting Charts

Study the chart below. Then use the information on the chart to help you answer the following questions.

3. Which of the following inventions were important to sea travel?
   a. the astrolabe and the compass
   b. the heavy plow and the horse collar
   c. paper and the printing press
   d. none of the above

4. Using the information from the chart and your knowledge of the time period, create a list of changes made possible by the introduction of paper and the printing press.

Technology of the Middle Ages

	INVENTION	PLACE OF ORIGIN	BENEFIT TO EUROPE
	Astrolabe	Europe	Enabled sailors to determine their north-south position on Earth—that is, their degree of latitude—by using the location of the stars
	Compass	China	Enabled people to determine their direction of travel even when the stars were hidden
	Heavy plow	Europe	Enabled farming in the hard soils of northern Europe
	Horse collar	Central Asia	Enabled horses to pull the heavy plow
	Paper	China	Served as a cheap replacement for parchment
	Printing	China	Johannes Gutenberg later developed his own printing techniques in Europe, which allowed the quick and cheap printing of large quantities of material.

Alternative Assessment

American History

Building Your Portfolio

Linking to Community

Trading was one way that businesspeople in the 1300s through the 1500s earned money. Use your local library and primary and secondary sources or interview several people to find out the three most important economic activities in your community. Create a chart listing these three activities and explaining why they are important to your community.

internet connect

Internet Activity: go.hrw.com
keyword: SF3 CF2

Choose a topic about the Age of Exploration:
- Trace the history and impact of the printing press.
- Commemorate the life and work of Leonardo da Vinci.
- Follow Columbus's explorations of the Americas.

The Columbian Exchange

 On the morning of October 12, 1492, a lookout aboard the Pinta, one of three ships in Christopher Columbus's fleet, sighted land. That day Columbus and his crew landed on an island in the Bahamas, starting the European settlement of the Americas. Columbus's landing also started a long process known today as the Columbian Exchange.

In this process, explorers brought plants and animals from Europe, Africa, and Asia to the Americas. They often returned home with American plants and animals. These plants and animals were later spread throughout the Eastern Hemisphere.

Origins of Food Crops

When Columbus returned to the Americas in 1493, he brought with him a number of plants, including wheat. European explorers also took home some plants raised by American Indians, such as corn, potatoes, and tomatoes.

Origins and Production Areas of Food Crops

Modern Centers of Production
- Corn
- Rice
- Wheat
- Potatoes
- Cassava
- Soybeans
- Sugarcane

Centers of Plant Origins
- Cassava
- Cocoa
- Corn
- Peanuts
- Peppers
- Potatoes
- Sweet Potatoes
- Tomatoes
- Yams

NORTH AMERICA

SOUTH AMERICA

ATLANTIC OCEAN

PACIFIC OCEAN

Origins and Production Areas of Food Crops

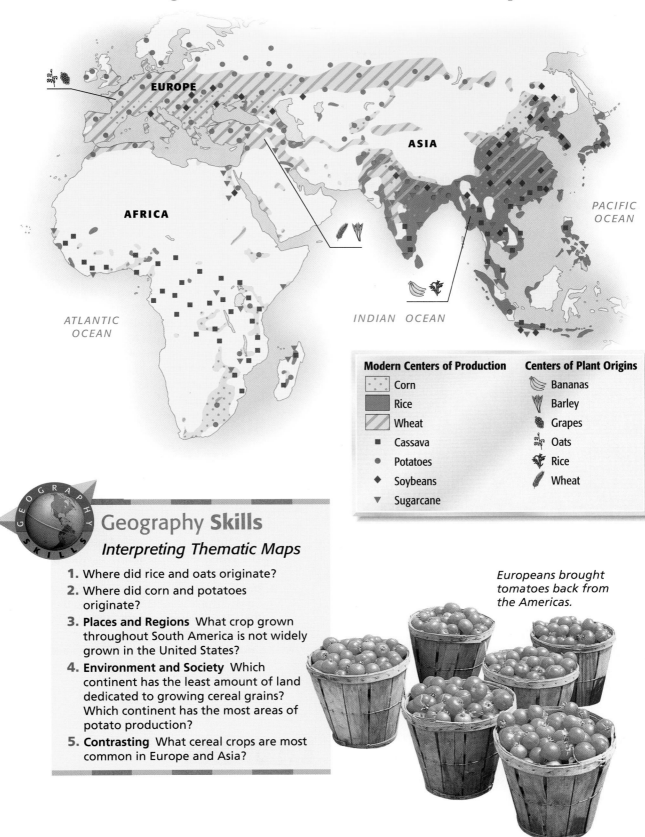

Modern Centers of Production

- Corn
- Rice
- Wheat
- ■ Cassava
- ● Potatoes
- ◆ Soybeans
- ▼ Sugarcane

Centers of Plant Origins

- Bananas
- Barley
- Grapes
- Oats
- Rice
- Wheat

Geography Skills
Interpreting Thematic Maps

1. Where did rice and oats originate?
2. Where did corn and potatoes originate?
3. **Places and Regions** What crop grown throughout South America is not widely grown in the United States?
4. **Environment and Society** Which continent has the least amount of land dedicated to growing cereal grains? Which continent has the most areas of potato production?
5. **Contrasting** What cereal crops are most common in Europe and Asia?

Europeans brought tomatoes back from the Americas.

Origins of Animals

On his second voyage to the Americas in 1493, Columbus brought many kinds of domesticated animals. Among these animals were dogs, horses, pigs, cattle, chickens, sheep, and goats. North and South America offered Europe, Africa, and Asia fewer types of animals. The animals that these areas offered included the turkey and the llama. Such animals had less economic importance.

Origins of Various Animals and Livestock Production Areas

NORTH AMERICA

ATLANTIC OCEAN

PACIFIC OCEAN

SOUTH AMERICA

Modern Centers of Livestock Production

- Cattle
- Pigs
- Sheep
- Poultry

Centers of Animal Origins

- Guinea pig
- Llama
- Turkey

History Note 1

During the 1500s and 1600s, Spanish colonists raised horses throughout the Americas. Runaway horses multiplied and formed wild herds. Gradually, horse herds spread throughout the grasslands of central and northern South America. Eventually they roamed from the plains of Mexico all the way north to Canada. By the early 1700s American Indians of the western Great Plains had learned to train and ride these horses. They made horses an important part of their culture.

Geography **Skills**
Interpreting Thematic Maps

1. Which types of animals are most common to the southern tip of South America?
2. **The World in Spatial Terms** In what part of the world did turkeys originate?
3. **Drawing Inferences and Conclusions** Why do you think settlers from Europe brought their own livestock, seeds, and plant clippings to the Americas?

History Note 2

Pigs had the easiest time adapting to the hot wet climate of the Caribbean and present-day southeastern United States. It even became common practice for explorers to leave pigs behind on islands as food for future expeditions.

Origins of Various Animals and Livestock Production Areas

Modern Centers of Livestock Production

- Cattle
- Sheep
- Pigs
- ◆ Poultry

Centers of Animal Origins

- Cow
- Horse
- Chicken
- Pig
- Goat
- Sheep
- Goose

EUROPE
ASIA
AFRICA
PACIFIC OCEAN
ATLANTIC OCEAN
INDIAN OCEAN

Geography Skills

Interpreting Thematic Maps

1. Which animals originated in Europe?
2. **Physical Systems** Which animal originated in both Europe and Asia?
3. **Summarizing** What are the geographic origins of the plants and animals involved in the Columbian Exchange? Create a chart or table that will help a fellow student organize this information. Then exchange charts with a partner and fill them in using the information in your textbook and notes.

History Note 3

The Africanized, or "killer," bee is an example of how intercontinental exchanges continue in modern times. In the 1950s research scientists brought African honeybees to Brazil. African bees accidentally escaped from Brazilian laboratories and mixed with South American bees to produce the so-called killer bee. These bees then began to spread north. Today swarms of killer bees live in both Texas and California.

Social Studies Skills
WORKSHOP

Decision-Making and Problem-Solving Skills

Like you, many figures in American history have faced difficult problems and decisions. By using appropriate skills such as problem solving and decision making, you will be better able to choose a solution or make a decision on important issues. The following activities will help you develop and practice these skills.

Decision Making

Decision making involves choosing between two or more options. Listed below are guidelines to help you with making decisions.

1. **Identify a situation that requires a decision.** Think about your current situation. What issue are you faced with that requires you to take some sort of action?

2. **Gather information.** Think about the issue. Examine the causes of the issue or problem and consider how it affects you and others.

3. **Identify your options.** Consider the actions that you could take to address the issue. List these options so that you can compare them.

4. **Make predictions about consequences.** Predict the consequences of taking the actions listed for each of your options. Compare these possible consequences. Be sure the option you choose produces the results you want.

5. **Take action to implement a decision.** Choose a course of action from your available options, and put it into effect.

Problem Solving

Problem solving involves many of the steps of decision making. Listed below are guidelines to help you solve problems.

1. **Identify the problem.** Identify just what the problem or difficulty is that you are facing. Sometimes you face a difficult situation made up of several different problems. Each problem may require its own solution.

2. **Gather information.** Conduct research on any important issues related to the problem. Try to find the answers to questions like the following: What caused this problem? Who or what does it affect? When did it start?

3. **List and consider options.** Look at the problem and the answers to the questions you asked in Step 2. List and then think about all the possible ways in which the problem could be solved. These are your options—possible solutions to the problem.

4. **Examine advantages and disadvantages.** Consider the advantages and disadvantages of all the options that you have listed. Make sure that you consider the possible long-term effects of each possible solution. You should also determine what steps you will need to take to achieve each possible solution. Some suggestions may sound good at first but may turn out to be impractical or hard to achieve.

5. **Choose and implement a solution.** Select the best solution from your list and take the steps to achieve it.

6. **Evaluate the effectiveness of the solution.** When you have completed the steps needed to put your plan into action, evaluate its effectiveness. Is the problem solved? Were the results worth the effort required? Has the solution itself created any other problems?

Practicing the Skill

1. Chapter 2, Section 4: The Opening of the Atlantic, describes the search for a Northwest Passage to Asia. Imagine that you are an explorer who is aware of the failed attempts to find this passage. Use the decision-making guidelines to help you decide whether to continue searching for such a passage. Be prepared to defend your decision.

2. Identify a similar problem discussed in Chapters 1 or 2 and apply the problem-solving process to come up with a solution.

History in Action

UNIT 1 SIMULATION

You Solve the Problem . . .

How Do You Convince a Monarch to Finance Your Expedition?

Complete the following activity in small cooperative groups. It is the era of exploration, 1492–1534. You and your crew wish to petition your country's monarch for more funds to further explore distant lands. Your group is not the only one that would like more money. The monarch does not want only personal presentations. He or she has requested that a brochure be submitted also. The ship that will transport the brochure to the monarch leaves with the next tide. Follow these steps to solve your problem.

1. Gather Information. Use your textbook and other resources to find information that might influence your plan of action for developing a brochure. Be sure to use what you learned from this unit's Skills Workshop on Decision Making and Problem Solving to help you find an effective solution to this problem. You may want to divide different parts of the research among group members.

2. List and Consider Options. After reviewing the information you have gathered, list and consider the options you might use as justifications for your request that the monarch fund further explorations. Your final solution to the problem may be easier to reach if you consider as many options as possible. Be sure to record your possible options for the preparation of your brochure.

3. Consider Advantages and Disadvantages. Now consider the advantages and disadvantages of taking each option. Ask yourselves questions like: "Will this information convince the monarch that my expedition will benefit his or her country?" Once you have considered the advantages and disadvantages, record them as notes for use in preparing your brochure.

4. Choose, Implement, and Evaluate a Solution. After considering the advantages and disadvantages, you should plan and create your brochure. Be sure to make your proposal very clear. You will need to support your reasons for exploration by including information you gathered and by explaining why you rejected other options or reasons for exploration. Your brochure needs to be visually appealing to attract the attention of the monarch. When you are ready, decide which group members will present the brochure, and then take your brochure to the monarch (the rest of the class). Good luck!

UNIT 2 Colonies in the Americas

(1500–1760)

Young People

IN HISTORY

Young American Indians

Many different American Indian peoples lived in the eastern woodlands region of North America. Teenagers from the various peoples shared similar responsibilities and experiences. Girls learned how to grow and harvest beans, corn, and squash in their own gardens and also in larger community fields. Girls also collected wild plants for food and medicine. They took care of household chores, such as collecting firewood and making clothes. Boys learned how to hunt and fish for survival. The Delaware people, who lived in what is now New York, required their teenage boys to stay alone in the woods for several days. These boys depended on their hunting and woodcraft skills to find food and build shelters.

Life for young American Indians was not all about work, however. Many peoples in eastern North America played ball games similar to lacrosse and soccer. The Cherokee of the Southeast liked to play a game called *anetsa*. In this rough physical game, players used netted sticks to carry a ball and throw it toward a goal. Only the most athletic young men played *anetsa,* and many suffered broken bones. Every Cherokee village had a team. The Cherokee believed that great honor and good fortune would come to the winner.

By their early teenage years most American Indians were considered adults. Among the Powhatan, who lived around Chesapeake Bay, boys took part in a special coming-of-age ritual. This ceremony required boys between the ages of about 10 and 15 to live in the woods for several months. They were tested with hardships and fasting. Those boys who proved their strength and bravery were declared worthy as future leaders. Virginia colonist Robert Beverly explained that the intention of the ritual was educational. The ritual encouraged the boys' progress into adulthood. Beverly observed, "Thus they unlive their former lives, and [become] men, by forgetting that they ever have been boys."

Young American Indians, like this boy, often played sports similar to some of those played today, such as lacrosse.

If You Were There *How would you survive on your own in the woods?*

LEFT PAGE: *In October 1764, British colonists met with American Indian leaders in what is now Ohio.*

3 New Empires in the Americas

(1500–1700)

Spanish explorer Juan Ponce de León was unable to found a settlement in Florida.

Spain built the fort of St. Augustine to protect its treasure fleets.

UNITED STATES

1513 Juan Ponce de León lands in Florida.

1542 Spanish explorer Álvar Núñez Cabeza de Vaca publishes an account of his travels in North America.

1565 Spain founds the first permanent European settlement in the present-day United States, at St. Augustine, Florida.

1585 Sir Walter Raleigh sends an expedition to found an English colony on Roanoke Island in North America.

1500	1520	1540	1560	1580

1517 Reformer Martin Luther posts his 95 Theses criticizing the Catholic Church.

1521 Hernán Cortés captures the Aztec capital of Tenochtitlán in present-day Mexico.

1531 Francisco Pizarro invades the Inca Empire in the Andes of South America.

1558 Elizabeth I becomes queen of England.

1571 A European fleet defeats the Ottoman navy at the Battle of Lepanto.

1588 The English navy defeats the Spanish Armada.

WORLD

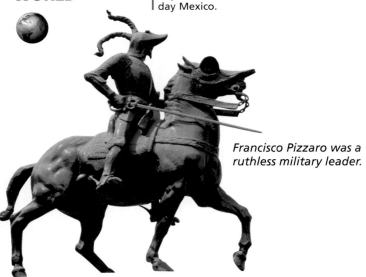

Francisco Pizzaro was a ruthless military leader.

Build on What You Know

By 1500, Europeans had begun crossing the Atlantic Ocean in search of wealth, glory, and converts to the Christian faith. Spain established a large colonial empire in North and South America. The Spanish were soon followed by explorers seeking to establish colonies for other European nations.

Explorer Samuel de Champlain allied with some American Indians against their enemies. This illustration shows him leading an attack on an Indian fort in what is now western New York.

THE GRANGER COLLECTION, NEW YORK

Canoes were a common method of travel in the rugged lands around the Great Lakes.

1615 French explorer Samuel de Champlain reaches the Great Lakes.

1626 The Dutch found New Amsterdam on the site of present-day New York City.

1655 The Dutch take control of New Sweden in North America.

1680 Pueblo Indians revolt in New Mexico.

1600 1620 1640 1660 1680

1611 William Shakespeare's play *The Tempest* is first performed.

1636 The Manchu establish the Qing Dynasty in Manchuria, later extending it into China.

1652 The Dutch establish a colony near the Cape of Good Hope in southern Africa.

If you were there . . .
How would you react to the arrival of strangers in your land?

You Be the Historian

Themes Journal

What's Your Opinion? Do you **agree** or **disagree** with the following statements? Support your point of view in your journal.

- **Global Relations** A large population defending its homeland will always defeat a smaller invading army.

- **Geography** Nations establish settlements in other lands in order to take advantage of their natural resources.

- **Economics** Establishing colonies always benefits a nation economically.

The Conquistadores

Read to Discover

1. How was Hernán Cortés's conquest of the Aztec similar to Francisco Pizarro's conquest of the Inca in Peru?
2. Why did the Spanish explore Florida and the American Southwest?

WHY IT MATTERS TODAY

People from different cultures sometimes fight against each other because their beliefs are different. Use **CNNfyi.com** or other **current events** sources to learn about a world conflict involving cultures with different beliefs. Record your findings in your journal.

Define
• conquistadores

Identify
• Hernán Cortés
• Moctezuma II
• Malintzin
• Francisco Pizarro
• Atahualpa
• Juan Ponce de León
• Álvar Núñez Cabeza de Vaca
• Hernando de Soto
• Francisco Vásquez de Coronado
• Juan Rodríguez Cabrillo

Hernán Cortés came to the Americas as a young man hoping to gain wealth and power.

The Story Continues

During the *Reconquista* there was constant warfare in Spain, creating a class of Spanish warriors that had little land or money. After the *Reconquista* these soldiers lacked work. Military leader Hernán Cortés explained the problem. "Since this harsh land will yield us no living, we must rely on our swords and lances. For the same reason, we must move on." In the 1500s many Spanish soldiers chose to "move on" to the Americas to seek their fortunes.

⭐ Cortés and the Aztec

Conquistadores (kahn-kees-tuh-DAWR-eez) were Spanish soldiers who led military expeditions in the Americas. The governor of Cuba sent conquistador **Hernán Cortés** to present-day Mexico in 1519. Cortés heard stories of a wealthy land to the west ruled by a king named **Moctezuma II** (mawk-tay-SOO-mah). "I decided to go and see him [Moctezuma] wherever he might be," wrote Cortés. "I would take him alive in chains or make him subject to [the King of Spain]." To prevent his soldiers from turning back, Cortés ordered their ships sunk. He then marched inland in search of Moctezuma and riches.

Moctezuma's kingdom was the Aztec Empire. The Aztec ruled several million people and had a rich civilization. They had thousands of warriors. In contrast, Cortés had only about 600 soldiers, 16 horses, and some guns. Cortés hoped that his superior weapons would bring him victory. In addition, the Aztec had never before seen horses and found them frightening. "These 'horses' . . . make a loud noise when they run . . . as if stones were raining on the earth," Aztec messengers told Moctezuma. Cortés received help from an American Indian woman named **Malintzin** (mah-LINT-suhn), also known as Malinche. She acted as an interpreter and advised him about the Aztec and their many enemies. These enemies allied with Cortés against the Aztec.

Moctezuma sent Cortés gifts of gold and other valuables, hoping to keep him away from the Aztec capital, Tenochtitlán. These signs of great wealth only encouraged Cortés. He and his men arrived in the capital in November 1519. Conquistador Bernal Díaz recorded his first impressions of the city, which sat in the middle of a great lake.

History Makers Speak

❝We were astounded [amazed]. These great towns and temples and buildings rising from the water, all made of stone, seemed like an enchanted vision.❞

—Bernal Díaz, quoted in *Cortés and the Downfall of the Aztec Empire,* by Jon Manchip White

Moctezuma was friendly to the Spanish, but Cortés was suspicious and took him prisoner. While Cortés was away, the Aztec rebelled and took back their city. The outnumbered Spanish who remained in the city fought their way out with heavy losses. Moctezuma was wounded during the battle and died soon after. Refusing to accept defeat, Cortés returned and fought the Aztec for several months. He then gathered thousands of soldiers from other American Indian groups and built a small fleet armed with cannons. This army attacked Tenochtitlán again. After three weeks of fighting, the city lay in ruins.

★★★★★★★★★★★★
That's Interesting!
★★★★★★★★★★★★

Mistaken Identity Can you imagine arriving in a new land and having strangers treat you like a legendary king? Indeed, some of the Aztec treated Cortés this way. Their reaction was based on Aztec legends about Quetzalcoatl (kwet-suhl-kuh-WAH-tuhl). In some Aztec historians' accounts, this being was a god who would return from beyond the sea. In other stories he was a powerful king. Images of him showed a man with pale skin and dark hair. Aztec historians wrote that when Moctezuma first heard of Cortés, "it was as if he thought the new arrival was our prince Quetzalcoatl."

Moctezuma II

The battle for Tenochtitlán destroyed much of the city. After Cortés and his forces won, an Aztec poet wrote, "The houses are roofless now, and the walls are red with blood."

Other Aztec towns soon fell to Cortés as well. The Aztec also suffered terribly from diseases that the Spanish introduced to Mexico. Illnesses such as smallpox caused hundreds of thousands of deaths in a very short time, hastening the fall of the Aztec Empire.

✔ **Reading Check: Identifying Cause and Effect** How was Cortés able to conquer the Aztec at Tenochtitlán, and how did this defeat affect the Aztec Empire?

Spanish Exploration and Conquests, 1513–1542

Interpreting Maps Spanish explorers claimed a tremendous amount of land in the Americas.

Skills Assessment The World in Spatial Terms Which of the explorers shown traveled the shortest distance?

★ Pizarro's Conquest of the Inca

Cortés had conquered a territory larger than Spain. His success brought him fame back home and inspired other conquistadores. Among these was **Francisco Pizarro** (pee-SAHR-roh), who had traveled with the explorer Nuñez de Balboa. Pizarro heard rumors of golden cities in the mountains of South America. In late 1531 Pizarro landed with a small army on the coast of what is now Peru. After marching for several weeks, he reached the Inca Empire.

The Inca ruled a huge region that stretched from Ecuador to central Chile. The Inca ruler, **Atahualpa** (ah-tah-WAHL-pah), heard about the Spanish invaders, but he was not worried. Fewer than 200 strangers did not seem much of a threat. Like the Aztec, however, the Inca had no weapons to match the conquistadores' swords and guns. The Inca had also been weakened by smallpox, which had killed tens of thousands of people. In addition, Atahualpa faced an ongoing civil war with his half-brother.

After reaching the Andes, Pizarro arranged a meeting with Atahualpa. He then kidnapped the Inca ruler. Atahualpa promised to fill a large room with gold and silver in return for his freedom. The Inca delivered 24 tons of gold and silver. Pizarro killed Atahualpa instead of freeing him, however. The Spaniard then joined with several powerful Inca rebel leaders. By 1534 he and his local American Indian allies had conquered the Inca Empire. The second great empire of the Americas had fallen.

✔ **Reading Check: Summarizing** Explain how Pizarro was able to defeat the Inca.

★ Conquistadores in Florida

The hope of finding another rich empire lured many other conquistadores to the Americas. One of these was **Juan Ponce de León** (PAWN-say day lay-AWN). King Ferdinand of Spain had given Ponce de León the right to settle the mainland of North America. According to legend, Ponce de León heard American Indian stories about a magic spring that "makes old men young again." This mythical spring became known as the Fountain of Youth.

Interpreting the Visual Record

The Fountain of Youth *Legends of a Fountain of Youth may have drawn Ponce de León and other explorers to Florida. This illustration shows a group of happy conquistadores supposedly finding the miraculous fountain.* **In what ways do you think the actual experiences of conquistadores would have differed from the scene shown here?**

In 1513 Ponce de León reached a land that he called Florida after the Spanish name for the Easter season, *Pascua florida,* or the season of flowers. There his forces soon fought with American Indians. Finding neither gold nor the Fountain of Youth, he gave up and sailed home. In 1521 Ponce de León returned to found a settlement in Florida, but was wounded in another battle with American Indians. His crew sailed to Cuba, where Ponce de León died.

Despite Ponce de León's failure, the Spanish remained interested in Florida. In 1528 Pánfilo de Narváez (PAHM-fee-loh day nahr-BAH-ays) arrived from Spain to explore Florida's western coast. Narváez split his forces. He sent the ships ahead to explore and led about 300 soldiers north through the inland swamps. This move proved to be a mistake. The ships lost contact with Narváez and had to return home.

Narváez and his conquistadores faced illness, hostile American Indians, and bad weather. They were starving and desperate. Finally they built simple boats and tried to sail west across the Gulf of Mexico. Most of the boats sank or wrecked, and Narváez died.

Among the few survivors were **Álvar Núñez Cabeza de Vaca** (kay-BAY-sah day BAH-kah) and a Moor named Estevanico (e-stay-bah-NEE-koh). In 1528 the survivors reached the coast of what is now Texas. They were captured by local American Indians but managed to escape. The group began a journey across Texas to what is now New Mexico. Cabeza de Vaca recalled this time as "years during which I wandered lost and naked through many and very strange lands." He and his companions survived by their wits and luck.

For eight years Cabeza de Vaca lived with various American Indian tribes while searching for a Spanish settlement. He worked as a servant, trader, and healer. During this time he gained fame and respect from the Pueblo Indians. Finally, in 1536 Cabeza de Vaca met a group of Spanish

Research on the ROM

Free Find:
El Dorado
After reading about El Dorado on the **Holt Researcher CD–ROM**, draw a picture of the ceremony described by the Spanish author.

soldiers "who were thunderstruck to see me so strangely dressed and in the company of Indians." Cabeza de Vaca traveled on with the soldiers to Mexico. In 1542 after returning to Spain, he published the story of his travels as *The Narrative of Álvar Núñez Cabeza de Vaca.*

✔ **Reading Check: Comparing and Contrasting** What were the similarities and differences between the explorations of Ponce de León and Cabeza de Vaca?

★ The Quest for Gold

While in Spain, Cabeza de Vaca described his adventures to **Hernando de Soto**. De Soto, who had fought for Pizarro in Peru, became convinced that Florida held a kingdom as rich as the Inca Empire. Arriving in Florida in 1539, de Soto led some 600 conquistadores north in search of gold. Once he reached what is now North Carolina, de Soto traveled west to present-day Arkansas. He became the first European to cross the Mississippi River. An expedition member described the river as "half a league [more than a mile] wide . . . of great depth and of very strong current."

De Soto encountered American Indian cultures that had rich farms and large populations. Ignoring chances for trade or settlement, de Soto kept moving. He stole food and fought American Indians as he went. One conquistador wrote about de Soto.

> **History Makers Speak**
> "His object [being] to find another treasure like that of [Atahualpa], . . . [he] would not be content with good lands nor pearls, even though many of them were worth their weight in gold."
>
> —The Gentleman of Elvas, "The Narrative of the Expedition of Hernando de Soto"

De Soto was worn down from battle and upset at his failure to find riches. At last, in 1542 he decided to return home. De Soto fell ill on the way, however, and died near the mouth of the Mississippi River. The other conquistadores reached Spanish settlements in Mexico the next year.

Meanwhile, Cabeza de Vaca's fellow adventurer, Estevanico, returned to New Mexico in 1539. He was part of a group led by Fray Marcos de Niza. The conquistadores' goal was to find the legendary Seven Cities of Cíbola, which were said to hold great wealth. After Estevanico was killed by Zuni Indians, the expedition returned to Mexico. There Fray Marcos claimed that he had seen the Seven Cities of Cíbola. He said that they were full of gold and gems.

These reports brought the conquistador **Francisco Vásquez de Coronado** to New

Interpreting the Visual Record

In search of gold *Coronado and his conquistadores traveled throughout the Southwest but never found the treasure they sought.* **What does this image suggest about the size and power of Coronado's expedition?**

Mexico in 1540. Coronado captured a Zuni town called Cíbola. Zuni legends later described the Spanish. "They wore coats of iron . . . and carried for weapons short canes that spit fire and made thunder." Instead of gold, Coronado found only adobe buildings and bushels of corn. However, he continued to search for the Seven Cities. One of his scouting groups even reached the Grand Canyon.

Traveling northeast, Coronado met Zuni and other Pueblo Indians, such as the Hopi. His demands for food and clothing angered the Pueblo, who drove him away. Coronado traveled all the way to present-day Kansas. There he discovered that his American Indian guide had tricked him. "[The guide took] us to a place where we and our horses would starve to death." But, Coronado and his conquistadores survived, only to return home in 1542 without any treasure.

That same year, Portuguese explorer **Juan Rodríguez Cabrillo** (kah-BRE-yoh) set sail under the Spanish flag. He sailed 1,200 miles along the coast of present-day California. Cabrillo was looking for gold and a new sea route to China. Bartolomé Ferrer, a crew member, described the northern coast. "There are mountains which seem to reach the heavens. . . . It appears as though they would fall on the ships." Cabrillo heard strange stories from American Indians. "Men like us [other Europeans] were traveling about, bearded, clothed, and armed." Cabrillo never returned from his voyage. He died during the winter in 1543, having failed to find wealth. However, his journey gave Spain a claim to the Pacific coast of North America.

After his travels with Cabeza de Vaca, Estevanico returned to the Southwest.

✔ **Reading Check: Sequencing** Create a time line listing the explorations of de Soto, Estevanico, Coronado, and Cabrillo. Note when they began and ended their journeys and what happened to them.

Section 1 Review

go.hrw.com **Homework Practice Online** keyword: SF3 HP3

1 **Define** and explain:
• conquistadores

2 **Identify** and explain:
• Hernán Cortés
• Moctezuma II
• Malintzin
• Francisco Pizarro
• Atahualpa
• Juan Ponce de León
• Álvar Núñez Cabeza de Vaca
• Hernando de Soto
• Francisco Vásquez de Coronado
• Juan Rodríguez Cabrillo

3 **Summarizing** Copy the chart below. Use it to link the conquistadores described in this section to the places they explored or to the people they conquered.

Conquistador	Place Explored or People Conquered

4 **Finding the Main Idea**
a. Compare Cortés's conquest of the Aztec Empire with Pizarro's conquest of the Inca Empire.

b. Why did conquistadores such as Ponce de León, de Soto, and Coronado explore the Americas, and what did they achieve?

5 **Writing and Critical Thinking**
Analyzing Information Imagine that you are an adviser to Atahualpa. Prepare a report that suggests how to deal with Pizarro's Spanish forces, which have just entered the Inca Empire.

Consider the following:
• the advantages and disadvantages the Inca have in comparison to the Spanish
• Pizarro's motives for coming to the Inca Empire
• civil conflict in the Inca Empire

New Empires in the Americas **71**

Spanish America

Read to Discover

1. How did Spain organize and govern its empire in the Americas?
2. How were the economy and society of New Spain structured?
3. Why did the Spanish settle in the borderlands?

WHY IT MATTERS TODAY

Women in many countries must often still fight for equal rights. Use **CNN fyi.com** or other **current events** sources to identify women in some part of the world who are struggling for equality. Record your findings in your journal.

Define

- pueblos
- missions
- presidios
- *encomienda* system
- plantations
- borderlands

Identify

- Council of the Indies
- Bartolomé de Las Casas
- Juan de Oñate
- Popé
- El Camino Real

Matias de Gálvez, was one of many viceroys of New Spain during Spanish rule.

The Story Continues

Conquistadores such as Hernán Cortés and Francisco Pizarro conquered a huge territory for Spain. By the mid-1500s Spain's American empire was larger than that of any other European nation. However, the challenge for Spain had changed. A Spanish official described the problem. "Without settlement there is no good conquest." Spain had to somehow settle and control an empire many times its size from across the ocean.

⭐ The Spanish Empire

Spain ruled its large American empire through a system of royal officials. At the top was the **Council of the Indies**, formed in 1524 to govern the Americas from Spain. The Council wrote laws, selected officials, and judged legal cases. The Council appointed two viceroys, or royal governors. One governor oversaw the Viceroyalty of Peru, which included most of South America. The other ruled the Viceroyalty of New Spain. This area included Central America, Mexico, and the southern part of what is now the United States. Each governor chose his local officials.

All officials in Spanish America had a great deal of independence. The empire was too large for the governors to know everything that was going on. Spain was so far away that the governors themselves could often ignore royal laws without being caught. One worried Spaniard wrote about this issue.

 History Makers Speak

❝Our people, transported across an ocean . . . leave [Spain] meeker than lambs, [but] change as soon as they arrive there [America] into wild wolves, forgetting all the royal commands.❞

—Angeleria, quoted in *A Violent Evangelism,* by Luis N. Rivera

Most people in Spanish America lived in the former Aztec and Inca Empires. These lands were rich with gold and silver mines. From 1503 to 1660, Spanish treasure fleets carried 200 tons of gold and 18,600 tons of silver to Spain. Thus Spain's American colonies helped make the country very wealthy. The people of Mexico and Peru also grew food to help support Spain's growing empire.

✔ **Reading Check: Summarizing** Explain the system of royal officials that Spain used to control its growing empire in the Americas.

⭐ Ruling New Spain

The Spanish established three kinds of settlements in New Spain. These settlements filled economic, religious, or military roles. **Pueblos** served as trading posts and sometimes as centers of government. Many pueblos were formed on the sites of American Indian villages. Priests started **missions** to convert local American Indians to Catholicism. Each mission community was built around a church. The Spanish built **presidios,** or military forts, to protect towns and missions. Many of these forts were built in frontier areas, such as present-day Florida and Texas.

The Catholic Church played an important part in ruling New Spain. King Philip II issued the Royal Orders for New Discoveries in 1573. In them he declared that spreading Christianity was the main reason for founding new settlements. The Royal Orders commanded priests to teach American Indians about Christianity. Missions were also to teach

CONNECTING TO MATH

Just the Facts

Imported Treasure from the Americas to Spain, 1506–1645

(in pesos)

20-Year Period	Total Treasure
1506–1525	3,139,158
1526–1545	11,580,568
1546–1565	34,580,779
1566–1585	72,668,380
1586–1605	117,849,324
1606–1625	113,056,467
1626–1645	72,143,787

Using Mathematical Skills

1. What was the value of treasure imported from 1506 to 1545?

2. Create a graph that shows the value of total treasure in 20-year periods from 1506 to 1645.

3. Imagine that you are an adviser to the Spanish government in 1645. Prepare a report that describes the trends in treasures imported from the Americas to Spain.

San José Mission was established in 1720 in present-day Texas.

American Indians "the use of . . . bread, silk, linen, horses, cattle, tools, and weapons, and all the rest that Spain has had." Some American Indians accepted this new way of life, combining Spanish customs with their own. Others rejected Spanish ideas completely.

✔ **Reading Check: Categorizing** What types of communities did the Spanish establish in New Spain?

The priest Bartolomé de Las Casas tried to get the Spanish government to treat American Indians more fairly.

Analyzing Primary Sources

Drawing Inferences and Conclusions Why do you think Las Casas criticized the treatment of American Indians under the *encomienda* system?

⭐ The Economy of New Spain

Many settlers in New Spain depended on the labor of American Indians. One viceroy complained that "no one comes to the Indies to plow and sow, but only to eat and loaf." To reward settlers for their service to the Crown, Spain established the **encomienda** (en-koh-mee-EN-duh) **system**. It gave Spanish settlers known as *encomenderos* (en-koh-muhn-DE-rohs) the right to tax local American Indians or to make them work. In exchange, these settlers were supposed to protect and teach local American Indians. *Encomenderos* were also expected to convert the Indians to Christianity. Most Spanish treated the Indians like slaves, forcing them to grow crops, to work in mines, and to herd cattle. The working conditions were very hard. Many American Indians died of disease and exhaustion.

Some settlers spoke out against this unjust treatment. **Bartolomé de Las Casas** was an *encomendero* who later became a priest. He protested the *encomienda* system and defended American Indians' rights.

 History Makers Speak ❝The natural laws and rules and rights of men are common to all nations . . . whatever their sect [religious faith], law, state, color, and condition, without any difference.❞

—Bartolomé de Las Casas, quoted in *The Conquest of America,* by Tzvetan Todorov

Las Casas wrote books and letters calling for an end to the *encomienda* system. He was not able to change the laws, however. Many settlers continued to force Indians to work for them.

In the Caribbean, American Indians resisted the *encomienda* system. In addition, many American Indians died from European diseases. These factors led the Spanish to start bringing enslaved Africans to New Spain in 1501. Thousands of these slaves worked on **plantations**—large farms that grew just one kind of crop. For example, sugar plantations were very common on the Caribbean islands. These plantations could make huge profits for their owners. At first, even Las Casas favored using enslaved Africans rather than American Indians for plantation labor. After watching the slave trade grow and seeing its harsh conditions, he changed his mind. Las Casas wrote in his *History of the Indies* that Africans were "unjustly and tyrannically [ruthlessly] reduced to slavery." The African slave trade continued despite the protests.

✔ **Reading Check: Finding the Main Idea** Why did the Spanish establish plantations and the *encomienda* system?

⭐ Expanding into the Borderlands

Most colonists in New Spain settled where they could gain the most wealth. Few lived in the **borderlands** on the outer reaches of the empire. This region included northern Mexico, Florida, and parts of present-day Arizona, California, New Mexico, and Texas. Spanish settlement of the borderlands took place over several hundred years.

Several explorers had died in Florida, and none had found great wealth. The Spanish government began to wonder if Florida was worth the risk. This view changed when the French settled on Florida's east coast. Spain's King Philip II sent Pedro Menéndez de Avilés (may NAYN-days day ah-bee-LAYS) to "cast them out by the best means . . . possible." In 1565 Menéndez de Avilés destroyed a French town. He then founded the fort of St. Augustine. From this base, the Spanish hoped to protect their treasure fleets.

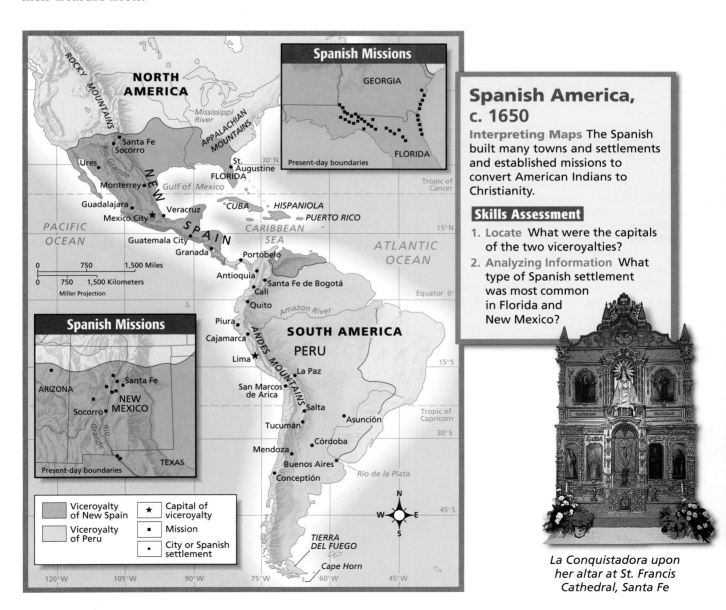

Spanish America, c. 1650

Interpreting Maps The Spanish built many towns and settlements and established missions to convert American Indians to Christianity.

Skills Assessment

1. **Locate** What were the capitals of the two viceroyalties?

2. **Analyzing Information** What type of Spanish settlement was most common in Florida and New Mexico?

La Conquistadora upon her altar at St. Francis Cathedral, Santa Fe

"World, in Hounding Me"

Sor Juana Inés de la Cruz

The nun Sor Juana Inés de la Cruz spoke out on a woman's right to education and independence. In the following poem she defends her choice to defy the traditional role of women in New Spain.

> World, in hounding me, what do you gain?
> How can it harm you if I choose, **astutely**[1],
> rather to stock my mind with things of beauty,
> than waste its stock on every beauty's claim?
>
> Costliness and wealth bring me no
>   pleasure;
> the only happiness I care to find
> derives from setting treasure in my mind,
> and not from mind that's set on winning
>   treasure.
>
> I prize no **comeliness**[2].
> All fair things pay to time, the victor, their
>   appointed fee and
> treasure cheats even the practiced eye.
> Mine is the better and truer way:
> to leave vanities of life aside,
> not to throw my life away on vanity.

---

[1] **astutely:** wisely [2] **comeliness:** beauty

Understanding What You Read

Literature and History What choices has the poet made in her life that were unusual for her time?

The first effort to settle New Mexico came in 1598. **Juan de Oñate** (ohn-YAH-tay) set out from Mexico City to explore and to start a colony. After fighting the Pueblo Indians, Oñate helped found the town of Santa Fe about 1609–10. Santa Fe soon became a trade center and the most important Spanish settlement in New Mexico. Other Spanish settlements in the area included missions founded by priests.

Spanish settlements depended on food and labor provided by the Pueblo Indians. Beginning in 1660 the Pueblo experienced crop failures and raids by other American Indians. Spanish abuses finally pushed the Pueblo to revolt in 1680. Led by Pueblo medicine man **Popé** (poh-PAY), some Pueblo came together and drove the Spanish out of New Mexico. Popé could not keep the Pueblo united, however. In 1692 the Spanish regained control.

Many Spanish survivors of the Pueblo Revolt had fled to what is now Texas. The first major Spanish settlement in Texas was founded in 1682 near the site of present-day El Paso. In the 1700s the Spanish learned that the French were building forts in Louisiana. Official Francisco Hidalgo warned the viceroy of New Spain. "[The French] are slipping behind our backs in silence, but God sees their intentions." The Spanish responded by building more missions and forts of their own. Father Eusebio Kino (yoo-SAYB-yoh KEE-noh) helped establish many missions in present-day Arizona.

To connect the scattered communities of New Spain, Spanish settlers built **El Camino Real**, or "the Royal Road." This network of trails ran for hundreds of miles. It eventually reached settlements in California, one of the last borderland areas settled by the Spanish. In the late 1760s missionary Junípero Serra (hoo-NEE-pay-roh SER-rah) traveled to California. Serra wanted to spread Christianity to the Indians in the area. He helped persuade the viceroy of New Spain to support further expansion. Serra led his friars and local Indians in founding San Francisco and eight other missions along the Pacific coast. Most Spanish settlers saw better opportunities in Mexico and Peru, however. Fewer than 1,000 Spanish had settled in California by 1790.

✔ **Reading Check: Identifying Cause and Effect** What factors led to Popé's revolt against the Spanish in New Mexico, and what was the result?

⭐ Colonial Society

By 1650 the Spanish Empire in the Americas had between 3 and 4 million people. American Indians made up about 80 percent of the population. The rest were whites, Africans, and people of mixed racial background. Spanish law divided society into classes based on birthplace and race. The *peninsulares* (pay-neen-soo-LAHR-ays) were white Spaniards born in Spain. They usually held the highest government offices in Spanish America. Just below them in status were the criollos (kree-OH-yohs), people born in the Americas to Spanish parents. Next came the mestizos (me-STEE-zohs), who had both Spanish and American Indian parents. Mestizos made up the largest part-European group in Spanish America. They often worked for criollos as laborers or craftspeople. American Indians had only limited rights. Enslaved Africans had little or no legal protection.

Women from all the social classes typically had fewer rights than men. In New Spain the high death rates for men often left female family members with added work. Married women in New Spain could own property and pass it on to their children. This was not the case in most European countries. Neither men nor women received much education. However, upper-class children were given some education.

Skilled artisans among the Pueblo Indians made beautifully decorated blankets and pottery.

✔ **Reading Check: Categorizing** Describe the major social classes that existed in Spanish America.

Section 2 Review

go.hrw.com
Homework Practice Online
keyword: SF3 HP3

1 **Define and explain:**
- pueblos
- missions
- presidios
- *encomienda* system
- plantations
- borderlands

2 **Identify and explain:**
- Council of the Indies
- Bartolomé de Las Casas
- Juan de Oñate
- Popé
- El Camino Real

3 **Categorizing** Copy the graphic organizer below. Use it to identify and describe the major institutions created by the Spanish to govern New Spain and Peru. Include a sentence describing each institution.

Council of the Indies

4 **Finding the Main Idea**
a. What were the advantages and disadvantages for Spain of having such a large empire in the Americas?

b. Why did the Spanish establish settlements in the borderlands?

5 **Writing and Critical Thinking**
Evaluating Imagine that you are an adviser to the Council of the Indies. Prepare an official report that describes the *encomienda* system and the Spanish colonial class structure.

Consider the following:
- the benefits of the *encomienda* system
- the drawbacks of the system
- the social structure of New Spain

Religious and Political Changes in Europe

Read to Discover

1. What was the Protestant Reformation, and how did it change Europe?
2. Why did Spain and England go to war in the late 1500s?
3. What led to the end of Spain's Golden Age?

WHY IT MATTERS TODAY

In many countries today, religion plays a key role in political issues and events. Use CNN**fyi**.com or other **current events** sources to learn about the influence of religion on a key present-day political issue or event. Record your findings in your journal.

Define

- sea dogs
- inflation

Identify

- Martin Luther
- Protestant Reformation
- Protestants
- Henry VIII
- Philip II
- Elizabeth I
- Francis Drake
- Spanish Armada

Martin Luther helped begin a major change in European religion.

The Story Continues

On October 31, 1517, a priest named Martin Luther nailed an important paper to the door of Castle Church in Wittenberg, Germany. The paper listed 95 theses about the Catholic Church. Luther charged that the church was too wealthy. He also thought the church abused its power. Charles V, emperor of the Holy Roman Empire, asked Luther to give up his views. Luther replied, "I cannot and will not." He added, "On this I take my stand. I can do no other."

⭐ The Protestant Reformation

Martin Luther was a Catholic priest in Germany. He became well known for protesting the policies of the Catholic Church. In 1517 Luther started the **Protestant Reformation**. This was a religious movement that began as an effort to reform the church. It spread through German towns in the 1520s and then to other parts of Europe. The reformers became known as **Protestants** because they protested the Catholic Church's practices. Many Protestants believed that the Bible intended for religion to be simple. They

A religious war *Spain sent the Duke of Alba to take control of the Netherlands, where he was soon feared for his cruel punishments of Dutch Protestants.* ***How do the people shown here appear to be treating the Duke?***

THE GRANGER COLLECTION, NEW YORK

thought the Catholic Church had too many rules. Protestants also objected to the great power held by the pope.

The printing press helped spread the ideas of the Reformation. Protestants printed large numbers of Bibles as well as short essays explaining their ideas. This let more people read and think about the Bible on their own, rather than relying on the teachings of a priest.

Confrontations between Catholics and Protestants took place throughout Europe, often leading to violence. During the late 1500s French Catholics fought French Protestants, known as Huguenots (HYOO-guh-nahts). Other parts of Europe also suffered violence and destruction. Political issues mixed with religious struggles. In 1534 King **Henry VIII** founded the Church of England, or the Anglican Church. This was a Protestant church that observed many Catholic ceremonies, such as mass. By making himself the head of the Anglican Church, Henry defied the authority of the pope. His actions angered English Catholics.

✔ **Reading Check: Identifying Cause and Effect** What issues led to the Protestant Reformation, and what effect did it have on Europe?

⭐ Conflict between Spain and England

In the late 1500s King **Philip II** used Spain's great wealth to lead a Catholic Reformation against the Protestant movement. Philip sent troops to fight Protestants in the Netherlands. He also hoped to drive the Protestants out of England, just as Ferdinand and Isabella had driven the Moors out of Spain. Standing in his way was Queen **Elizabeth I**, the daughter of Henry VIII. A Protestant, Elizabeth wanted peace between England's Protestants and Catholics. She opposed Spain's treatment of Protestants in the Netherlands, but feared supporting them openly because of Spain's power.

GLOBAL
CONNECTIONS

War in the Netherlands

In the mid-1500s fighting broke out in the Netherlands between Protestants and Catholics. At the time Spain, a Catholic nation, ruled the Netherlands. Some Dutch people became Calvinists— followers of Protestant leader and writer John Calvin. Spain responded by persecuting Protestants and trying to enforce Catholic beliefs. The Spanish also passed strict new laws and raised taxes. Protestants soon rebelled. In 1609 the civil war finally ended. The Dutch Protestants had won, but thousands of lives had been lost. **How did Philip II try to maintain control of the Netherlands?**

To fight Spain without going to war, Elizabeth made use of the **sea dogs.** These were veteran English sailors whom she encouraged to raid Spanish treasure ships. The raids hurt Spain's economy, and the sea dogs gained treasure for themselves. When Philip protested, Elizabeth pretended that her government had nothing to do with the raids.

The most successful sea dog was the daring Sir **Francis Drake**. In 1578 he sailed through the Strait of Magellan and attacked the west coast of Peru and New Spain. The Spanish were caught off guard by Drake's daring raids. They had not expected any English ships to pass through the strait. In addition to his raids, Drake sailed north and explored part of California's coast. He landed near present-day San Francisco. Turning west, he sailed back to England. Drake and his crew thus became the first English people to sail around the world.

✔ **Reading Check: Drawing Inferences and Conclusions** Why might Elizabeth have pretended that she did not ask sea dogs to attack Spanish treasure ships?

⭐ The Spanish Armada

King Philip was angered by the English attacks. He also feared England's ability to help the Protestants in the Netherlands. He decided to solve both problems by gathering a huge fleet known as the **Spanish Armada**. The Armada had about 130 ships and some 27,000 sailors and soldiers. This mighty fleet was sent to invade England. Philip hoped to overthrow both Queen Elizabeth and the Anglican Church.

From the beginning the Spanish had problems. The Armada's leader, the Duke of Medina-Sidonia, was a poor sailor who did not know how to run the fleet. Then, while the ships were in the Spanish port of Cádiz (KAH-dees), Drake raided their supplies. The attack delayed the Armada for several months.

Despite delays and poor leadership, the Armada was a strong fighting force. In contrast, England's navy had fewer than 40 ships. To try to even the odds, sea dogs, merchants, and fishermen added their ships to England's defense. The English ships had the advantages of speed, greater mobility, and better cannons. They could outmaneuver the larger Spanish vessels while firing on them from a distance. The Spanish, on the other hand, had to attempt to sail close to English ships and then board them with soldiers.

In late July 1588 the Armada and the English fleet finally met off the coast of England, in the English Channel. In a series of battles, the quicker English ships damaged but could not destroy the Armada. Then the English surprised the Spanish at night by sending ships loaded with explosives into the Spanish fleet. These fire ships exploded in the middle of the Armada, causing the Spanish to scatter. The next day the English fleet defeated the Armada in a huge battle.

BIOGRAPHY

Elizabeth I

(1533–1603)

Elizabeth was an intelligent and well-educated leader. She could read Greek and speak French, Italian, and Latin. Elizabeth was just 25 years old when she became queen of England in 1558. Many people did not want a woman to rule England, no matter how gifted she was. Despite such prejudices, Elizabeth became one of England's most popular rulers. After gaining the throne, Elizabeth led her country through many troubled years. By the time her long reign ended in 1603, England had become a world power. **What did Elizabeth I accomplish as queen?**

The defeat of the Armada was a disaster for Spain.

News of the Armada's defeat did not reach England immediately. Queen Elizabeth gave a stirring speech to an army of English soldiers preparing to face the Spanish.

History Makers Speak

❝I know I have but the body of a weak and feeble woman; but I have the heart and stomach of a King, and a King of England, too; and I think it foul scorn [pride] that . . . Spain . . . should dare to invade the borders of my realm.❞

—Queen Elizabeth I, quoted in *Armada*, by Duff Hart-Davis

Analyzing Primary Sources
Drawing Inferences and Conclusions What do you think was the purpose of Elizabeth's speech?

While the soldiers cheered for their queen, the Armada struggled home to Spain. Storms sank many of the surviving ships. Only about half made it back safely to Spain. Philip's attempt to conquer England had failed.

✔ **Reading Check: Summarizing** Explain why England was able to defeat the larger Spanish Armada.

⭐ The Decline of the Spanish Empire

The Armada's defeat shocked Spain. As Spain's power and wealth had grown, the country had enjoyed a Golden Age. Spain made great strides in the arts. King Philip oversaw the building of the Escorial, a huge palace that included its own monastery. Religious art was particularly valued in Spain. El Greco, a Greek artist living in Spain, became famous for his religious paintings in the late 1500s.

Causes and Effects of Spain's Golden Age

Long-Term Causes

Columbus's landing in the Caribbean

Spanish exploration and conquest

Founding of colonies in North and South America

Immediate Causes

Conquest of the Aztec by Cortés, 1521

Conquest of the Inca by Pizarro, 1534

Spanish treasure fleets from the Americas

Spain's Golden Age 1492 to mid-1600s

Effects

Rise in Spanish wealth and influence

Increase in the prices of Spanish goods because of high inflation caused in part by American silver and gold

Spain's dependence on imported goods

Spain also had many poets and playwrights. One was Lope de Vega, who had sailed with the Armada. Many Spanish authors wrote romantic novels about the courage of Spanish nobles and conquistadores. Author Miguel de Cervantes made fun of such stories in his novel *Don Quixote*. In this novel the aging knight Don Quixote and his companion Sancho Panza have many comical adventures.

Economic problems helped bring Spain's Golden Age to an end. The large amounts of gold and silver that Spain took from the Americas contributed to high **inflation**. Inflation is a rise in the amount of money in use and thus in the price of goods. Rather than buying local items made expensive by inflation, Spaniards bought cheaper goods from other countries. This further weakened Spain's economy.

England's defeat of the Spanish Armada showed that Spain's navy could be beaten. The weakened navy could no longer protect Spain's distant empire in the Americas. This led countries such as England, France, and the Netherlands to challenge Spanish power overseas.

✔ **Reading Check: Evaluating** What led to the decline of the Spanish Empire?

Section 3 Review

go.hrw.com

Homework Practice Online

keyword: SF3 HP3

1 **Define** and explain:
- sea dogs
- inflation

2 **Identify** and explain:
- Martin Luther
- Protestant Reformation
- Protestants
- Henry VIII
- Philip II
- Elizabeth I
- Francis Drake
- Spanish Armada

3 **Sequencing** Copy the graphic organizer below. Use it to show religious and political events leading to the defeat of the Spanish Armada and to show how the defeat affected Spain.

Defeat of the Spanish Armada

4 **Finding the Main Idea**
a. Why did the Protestant Reformation take place, and how did it influence Europe?

b. Why did Philip II of Spain want to drive Protestants out of England, and how did Elizabeth I respond to Spain's aggression?

5 **Writing and Critical Thinking**
Sequencing Imagine that you are a poet in Spain in 1700. Write a poem of 6 to 10 lines about the events that led to the end of Spain's Golden Age.

Consider the following:
- the defeat of the Spanish Armada
- economic problems in Spain

The Race for Empires

Read to Discover

1. Why were the French, Dutch, and English interested in colonizing North America?
2. What common problems did the French, Dutch, and Swedish colonies face?
3. What happened to the first English settlements in North America?

Define

• charter

Identify

• René-Robert de La Salle
• Peter Minuit
• Walter Raleigh

WHY IT MATTERS TODAY

The urge to explore remains strong today. Use **CNNfyi.com** or other **current events** sources to learn how people continue to explore our world. Record your findings in your journal.

The Story Continues

When French explorer Jacques Cartier sailed to North America in 1534, he witnessed many strange sights. He saw walruses and thousands of seabirds. He said these birds covered islands "as a field is covered with grass." However, one of the most unexpected sights was a French fishing boat! French fishermen had begun traveling to the north coast of North America in the early 1500s. Cartier soon saw why. There were so many fish that he and his crew could catch about 100 cod in an hour. Some of the fishermen had built temporary settlements to trade with local American Indians.

French explorer Jacques Cartier

Early French Settlement

France built its first North American settlement in Florida. French Huguenots started a few small colonies there in 1564. The Spanish soon destroyed these settlements and drove out the French. Religious wars in France slowed further French efforts to colonize North America. When the fighting ended, the French renewed efforts to settle present-day eastern Canada. The explorations of Jacques Cartier and Samuel de Champlain had given France a claim to this region.

American Indians in cold northern regions taught Europeans how to make and use snowshoes to travel in the winter.

AMERICAN MUSEUM OF NATURAL HISTORY

Analyzing Primary Sources
Identifying a Point of View
How do you think this observer viewed the French traders he describes?

In 1604 the French settled in a region they called Acadia. This area included what is now Nova Scotia, New Brunswick, and parts of Maine. There they formed small trading communities and fishing villages. Champlain founded Port Royal on the coast of Nova Scotia, then headed west. He reached the St. Lawrence River and the Great Lakes. He founded the town of Quebec on the St. Lawrence in 1608. He also explored areas in present-day New York and Vermont, where Lake Champlain was named after him.

The Great Lakes region proved valuable to France because of the fur trade. Europeans used animal furs, particularly beaver pelts, to make expensive hats. The French traded tools, jewelry, and cloth with American Indians in exchange for furs. Merchants then shipped the furs back to France. Founded in 1642, Montreal became a center for the fur trade.

Fur traders often had to travel deep into the wilderness to meet with their American Indian trading partners. The traders usually traveled by river, braving the dangers of white-water rapids. French traders used Indian birch-bark canoes, which were light enough to carry. Fur traders lived far from French settlements for long periods of time. Many of them adopted local American Indians' clothing and customs to survive. One observer in the mid-1700s described the life of a fur trader.

 History Makers Speak ❝It is inconceivable [unbelievable] what hardships the people of Canada must undergo on their hunting journeys. . . . They often suffer hunger, thirst, heat, and cold, and are bitten by . . . dangerous animals and insects. . . . None of them fears danger or hardships. Many of them settle among the Indians far from Canada, marry Indian women, and never come back again.❞

—Peter Kalm, quoted in *The Canadian Frontier, 1534–1760*, by W. J. Eccles

✔ **Reading Check: Finding the Main Idea** Why did the French move inland from the coast of North America?

★ The Expansion of the French Empire

In the late 1600s the French began spreading out from the Great Lakes region. Fur traders, explorers, and missionaries were all on the move. Many headed south, toward New Spain. In the 1650s French missionaries heard stories about "a beautiful river, large, broad, and deep." In 1673 the explorer Louis Jolliet (jahl-ee-et) and the missionary Jacques Marquette set out to find this great river, the Mississippi. They reached the river and traveled down it as far as present-day Arkansas. Finally they turned back to avoid encountering the Spanish. Nine years later, <u>René-Robert de La Salle</u> followed the Mississippi River to the Gulf of Mexico. He claimed the Mississippi Valley for King Louis XIV of France. To honor the king, La Salle named the region Louisiana.

The French called their North American territory New France. France had trouble building up the number of settlers in this territory, which had

THE GRANGER COLLECTION, NEW YORK

Daily Life

Louisiana Robert de La Salle claims Louisiana for France in this painting. The French did not begin settling Louisiana until the early 1700s. The city of New Orleans was founded in 1718, and Louisiana became a royal colony of France in 1731. At that time the colony's population of settlers and slaves was still fairly small, numbering some 8,000 people. **Why would a city with access to the Mississippi River be valuable to France?**

only about 12,000 French settlers by 1688. In the late 1600s and early 1700s the French built new outposts, including Detroit on the Great Lakes and New Orleans along the Mississippi River. For a time the French government also helped pay the travel costs for interested colonists.

New France's small population and the value of the fur trade led French settlers to ally with the Algonquian and Huron Indians. As a result, they became enemies of the Iroquois. In general, the French treated American Indians with more respect than did other Europeans.

★ New Netherland and New Sweden

Europeans were drawn to America by the promise of good farmland and the fur trade. The Dutch, who had merchant fleets around the world, came to America in search of trade. Explorer Henry Hudson's first voyage to North America gave the Dutch a claim to the land between the Delaware and Hudson Rivers. The Dutch called this area New Netherland. This region included parts of what are now New Jersey, New York, Connecticut, and Delaware. In 1624 the newly formed Dutch West India Company sent about 30 families to settle in New Netherland. Two years later **Peter Minuit** bought Manhattan Island from local American Indians. There he founded the town of New Amsterdam.

To bring more settlers to America, the Dutch West India Company decided to let other Europeans settle in New Netherland. To attract colonists, the Dutch practiced religious toleration. In 1646 missionary Isaac Jogues (zhawg) described the people of New Amsterdam. "There may well be four or five hundred men of different sects [religious groups] and nations."

Minuit left the Dutch West India Company and helped Swedish settlers found New Sweden along the Delaware River. He also helped them choose the site for Fort Christina, which was built in 1638. There the Swedish farmed and traded with local American Indians for furs. Swedish settlers were among the first in North America to build log cabins. The Swedish settlement was small, but the Dutch felt that it threatened Dutch lands and fur trading. The two sides fought a series of battles. Finally the governor of New Netherland, Peter Stuyvesant (STY-vi-suhnt), conquered New Sweden in 1655.

✔ **Reading Check: Comparing** How were French, Dutch, and Swedish settlements similar?

Dutch, English, and French Exploration of North America

Interpreting Maps Spain's rivals sent their own explorers to claim lands in the Americas and the riches those lands might hold.

Skills Assessment Places and Regions What country explored the Great Lakes region?

★ English Settlements

In the late 1500s England decided to start its own North American colony. In 1578 Sir Humphrey Gilbert received a patent, or **charter**, a document giving him royal permission to start a colony. Gilbert sent an expedition to Newfoundland, which England claimed as a result of John Cabot's explorations. Gilbert's efforts to found a colony failed, and he drowned at sea in 1583. His half-brother, Sir **Walter Raleigh**, soon led a new effort.

Raleigh paid for an expedition that landed in present-day Virginia and North Carolina. He named the entire area Virginia. In 1585 he sent another group to found a colony on Roanoke Island. The English colonists found life hard. They fought with local American Indians and had trouble finding and growing food. In 1586 Sir Francis Drake stopped at Roanoke after a raid on New Spain. He offered to take the remaining settlers home to England.

John White resettled the Roanoke colony in the spring of 1587. White's granddaughter, Virginia Dare, was the first English child born in the present-day United States. White returned to England at the end of the summer and did not come back until 1590. He found the colony's buildings still standing but deserted. Carved into a post was the word *CROATOAN*. This may have been the name of a nearby island inhabited by American Indians. White searched for the settlers and his granddaughter. Years later he recalled his efforts. "And thus we [stopped] seeking our Colony, that was never any of them found, nor seen to this day." Historians are not certain just what happened to the colony.

John White painted many American plants and animals. His works are among the earliest known European pictures of North American wildlife.

✔ **Reading Check: Summarizing** Explain the reasons for and the results of England's first attempts to colonize North America.

Section 4 Review

go.hrw.com **Homework Practice Online**
keyword: SF3 HP3

1 **Define** and explain:
• charter

2 **Identify** and explain:
• René-Robert de La Salle
• Peter Minuit
• Walter Raleigh

3 **Summarizing** Copy the graphic organizer below. Use it to list the European nations that established colonies in North America during the 1500s and 1600s. Include the location of these colonies.

North America

4 **Finding the Main Idea**
a. What motivated France, England, and the Netherlands to establish settlements in North America?

b. What problems did the French, Dutch, and Swedish settlements face?

5 **Writing and Critical Thinking**
Drawing Inferences and Conclusions Imagine that you are a sailor on John White's resupply expedition to Roanoke. Prepare a brief report to Queen Elizabeth explaining what might have happened to the missing settlers.

Consider the following:
• relations between American Indians and Europeans
• the word carved into the post at Roanoke

Chapter 3 Review

The Chapter at a Glance

Examine the visual summary of the chapter below. Prepare a poster that illustrates each of the main ideas contained in the boxes representing each section. Use facts and ideas from the chapter to prepare your poster. Present your poster to the class.

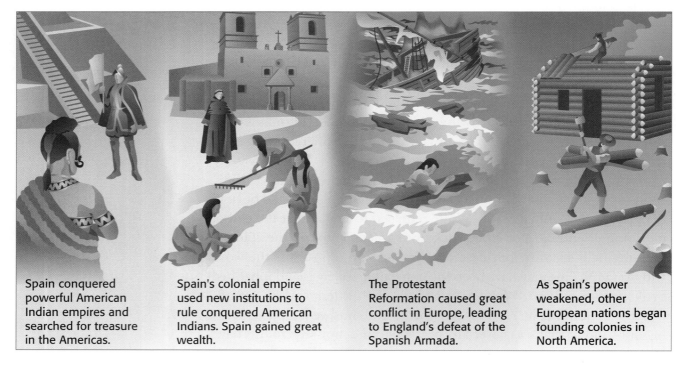

Spain conquered powerful American Indian empires and searched for treasure in the Americas.

Spain's colonial empire used new institutions to rule conquered American Indians. Spain gained great wealth.

The Protestant Reformation caused great conflict in Europe, leading to England's defeat of the Spanish Armada.

As Spain's power weakened, other European nations began founding colonies in North America.

Identifying People and Ideas

Use the following terms or people in historically significant sentences.

1. conquistadores
2. Council of the Indies
3. *encomienda* system
4. Bartolomé de Las Casas
5. plantations
6. Protestant Reformation
7. Elizabeth I
8. Spanish Armada
9. inflation
10. Walter Raleigh

Understanding Main Ideas

Section 1 *(Pages 66–71)*
1. How was Cortés's conquest of the Aztec Empire similar to Pizarro's conquest of the Inca Empire?

Section 2 *(Pages 72–77)*
2. What institutions did the Spanish establish in order to govern the vast territories under their control?

Section 3 *(Pages 78–82)*
3. What led to conflict between Spain and England?

Section 4 *(Pages 83–87)*
4. How were the French, Dutch, and English settlements different from and similar to each other?

5. What motivated other European nations to challenge Spain and to establish settlements of their own in North America?

You Be the Historian— Reviewing Themes

1. **Global Relations** Why were the Aztec and Inca unable to defeat the smaller invading armies led by conquistadores?
2. **Geography** Why did the Spanish and the French establish settlements in the Americas?
3. **Economics** How did having colonies in the Americas affect Spain's economy?

Thinking Critically

1. **Finding the Main Idea** What effect did its colonies in the Americas have on Spain?
2. **Identifying Cause and Effect** What led to the establishment of the *encomienda* system, and how did this system affect the daily lives of American Indians?
3. **Analyzing Information** How did the Protestant Reformation affect European colonization of the Americas in the 1600s?

Interpreting Maps

Study the map below. Then use the information on the map to help you answer the questions that follow.

Early European Settlements

1. What is the earliest settlement shown on the map?
   a. Quebec
   b. New Amsterdam
   c. Roanoke
   d. Fort Christina

2. Using the map and your knowledge of the period, what European nations appear to have the most powerful settlements?

Analyzing Primary Sources

Read the following quote by Bartolomé de Las Casas, a Spanish priest commenting on the conquest of the lands that became New Spain, then answer the questions.

"Any reasonable person who knows something . . . of rights and of civil law can imagine for himself what the likely reaction would be of any people living peaceably within their own frontiers, unaware that they owe allegiance to anyone save their natural lords, were a stranger suddenly to issue a demand along the following lines: 'You shall henceforth obey a foreign king, whom you have never seen nor ever heard of and, if you do not, we will cut you to pieces'—Especially when they discover that these strangers are indeed quite prepared to carry out this threat to the letter."

3. Which of the following statements best describes the author's point of view?
   a. Europeans had a legal right to conquer American Indians.
   b. American Indians were probably happy to become subjects of European empires.
   c. American Indians had a right to resist when Europeans took their lands.
   d. Nobody can guess how American Indians felt when they first met Europeans.

4. Based on your knowledge of the period, how did American Indians in different parts of the Americas respond to European settlers?

Alternative Assessment

Building Your Portfolio

Cooperative Learning

Complete the following activity in small groups. Create a newspaper titled *Settling the Americas*. Devote one page each to the colonies of Spain, France, Sweden, and the Netherlands. Your newspaper should have thematic maps, a chart listing each of the colonies, a feature story, a biography of an important person, and quotations from people who were involved in the establishment of the colonies. Each group should present its newspaper to the class.

internet connect

Internet Activity: go.hrw.com
keyword: SF3 CF3

Choose a topic about new empires in the Americas to:
- Learn about the settlement of St. Augustine.
- Research the role of Spanish missions in the New World.
- Follow the French explorers of the New World.

4 The English Colonies
(1605–1735)

THE GRANGER COLLECTION, NEW YORK

John Smith was an early leader at Jamestown.

THE GRANGER COLLECTION, NEW YORK

Puritan colonists built their first settlement in New England.

UNITED STATES

1607 English colonists found the Jamestown settlement in present-day Virginia.

1619 The first representative assembly in North America is formed in Virginia.

1620 The Pilgrims sign the Mayflower Compact.

1630 Puritans found the Massachusetts Bay Colony.

1639 Thomas Hooker helps draft the Fundamental Orders of Connecticut.

| 1610 | 1620 | 1630 | 1640 |

1611 The first edition of the King James Version of the Bible is published.

1630s The Great Migration begins as thousands of people leave England to settle in colonies or other European countries.

The King James Version of the Bible was produced by dozens of scholars over a period of seven years.

Build on What You Know

By the early 1600s, European exploration of the Americas had led to great interest in colonization. At first, the English wanted to colonize North America because they hoped to have a better quality of life there. However, many English colonists quickly found that merely surviving in their harsh new environment took most of their efforts.

COURTESY OF THE PENNSYLVANIA ACADEMY OF THE FINE ARTS, PHILADELPHIA. GIFT OF MRS. SARAH HARRISON (THE JOSEPH HARRISON, JR. COLLECTION)

The Puritans placed people's head and arms in stocks such as these as a form of punishment.

Pennsylvania proprietor William Penn signs a peace treaty with local Indians on one of his trips to America.

1649 Maryland passes the Toleration Act, which promotes religious freedom.

1676 Bacon's Rebellion begins in Virginia.

1692 The Salem witch trials take place in Massachusetts.

1702 East and West Jersey are united into the single royal colony of New Jersey.

1733 James Oglethorpe founds Savannah, Georgia.

1650 // 1675 1700 1725

1649 King Charles I of England is overthrown and executed.

1670 The Hudson Bay Company is formed to trade in the Hudson Bay region of North America.

1682 Peter the Great becomes czar of Russia.

If you were there . . .
What factors would lead you to settle in a new country?

You Be the Historian

Themes Journal

What's Your Opinion? Do you **agree** or **disagree** with the following statements? Support your point of view in your journal.

- **Geography** Weather and geography determine a people's way of life—how they work, where they live, and how wealthy they can become.

- **Economics** A colony cannot survive unless the colonists find a way to make money.

- **Culture** Religious freedom is a basic right of all people.

The Virginia Colony

Read to Discover

1. Why were people in England interested in founding Jamestown, and when was the colony established?
2. How did the Jamestown colonists interact with local American Indians?
3. How did the English plantation system begin?
4. What role did indentured servants and enslaved Africans have in Virginia's economy?

WHY IT MATTERS TODAY

Many important historical places in the United States have been protected and preserved. Use CNNfyi.com or other **current events** sources to find out about a historical site in the United States today. Record your findings in your journal.

Define

- headright
- indentured servants
- planters

Identify

- John Smith
- Powhatan Confederacy
- John Rolfe
- Pocahontas
- Nathaniel Bacon
- Bacon's Rebellion

THE GRANGER COLLECTION, NEW YORK

Posters like this one promoted the opportunities that were to be found in the colonies.

The Story Continues

In 1605 a company of English merchants asked the Crown for the right to found a new settlement in North America. They asked to settle in a region called Virginia. At the time, Virginia extended from present-day Maine to South Carolina. In 1606 King James I granted the request. He promised the London Company the rights to "all the lands ... rivers ... [and] commodities [goods]" along part of the Virginia coast. The company's efforts, wrote King James, "may in time bring ... a settled and quiet government."

★ Settlement in Jamestown

The members of the London Company knew about the Roanoke colony's failure. They wanted to start a settlement without depending on the wealth of just one person. Instead, investors formed a joint-stock company, which allowed a group to share the cost and risk of founding a colony. Colonies formed in this way were called company colonies. To attract investors and settlers, the London Company printed advertisements praising Virginia.

"The land yields . . . [an] abundance of fish, infinite store [endless supply] of deer, and hares, with many fruits and roots. . . . There are hills and mountains making a sensible proffer [offer] of hidden treasure, never yet searched."

—The Virginia Company of London, quoted in *Ordinary Americans,* edited by Linda R. Monk

Analyzing Primary Sources
Identifying Bias What might this report have left out of its description of Virginia?

The promise of such wealth attracted adventurers and people who were suffering economic hardship in England.

On April 26, 1607, the first three ships sent by the London Company arrived off the Virginia coast. The fleet brought 105 male colonists to found a settlement. The ships sailed into Chesapeake Bay and up the James River. About 40 miles upstream, the colonists founded their first settlement, named Jamestown after the English king.

The men who came to Jamestown were poorly prepared to start a settlement. Most were adventurers interested in making their fortune and returning to England. One of the colonists, Captain **John Smith**, complained that "ten good workmen would have done more substantial work in a day than ten of these [colonists] in a week." In fact, very few colonists had farming experience or useful skills such as carpentry. Jamestown was also a poor site for a settlement. The settlement was surrounded by marshes full of disease-carrying mosquitoes. In addition, the river water was too salty to drink safely. These conditions proved deadly. By the time winter arrived, two thirds of the original colonists had died. The few survivors were hungry and sick. The situation temporarily improved after Smith took control of the colony in September 1608. He forced the settlers to work and to build better housing. This reduced the number of deaths from starvation and exposure.

April 26, 1607
The London Company founds Jamestown.

Interpreting the Visual Record

Jamestown *The settlers at Jamestown settled close by the James River.* **Why do you think the colonists built their settlement in the manner shown here?**

COLONIAL WILLIAMSBURG FOUNDATION

The Powhatan Confederacy

The colonists also received help from the powerful **Powhatan Confederacy**. Wahunsonacock (wah-hoohn-SUH-nuh-kahk) led this alliance of Algonquian Indians. At times, the Powhatan brought food to aid the colonists. The Powhatan also taught them how to grow corn.

The relationship between the Powhatan and the Virginia colonists was not entirely peaceful, however. The colonists at times took food from the Powhatan by force. These actions led Wahunsonacock to say:

 "Why will you take by force what you may obtain by love? Why will you destroy us who supply you with food? What can you get by war? . . . We are unarmed, and willing to give you what you ask, if you come in a friendly manner."

—Wahunsonacock, quoted in *The Portable North American Indian Reader*, edited by Frederick W. Turner III

Analyzing Primary Sources

Identifying Points of View
How does Wahunsonacock describe his people's view of the colonists?

In 1609 some 400 more settlers arrived in Jamestown. An injury from an accident forced John Smith to return to England, leaving the settlers without a strong leader. That winter, disease and famine once again hit the colony. The colonists called this period the "starving time." By the spring of 1610, only 60 colonists were still alive.

Because the colony struggled to survive, Jamestown failed to make a profit for the London Company. Colonist **John Rolfe** helped solve this problem in 1612. Smoking tobacco had been a favorite pastime in England since the 1560s. Tobacco grew well in Virginia. However, the local variety grown by the Powhatan was too bitter for European tastes, so Rolfe introduced a sweeter West Indian variety. Soon the colonists were able to export tobacco to England successfully. As Virginia colonist John Pory wrote in 1619, "All our riches for the present doe consiste in [come from] Tobacco." Another important change in the colony was a shift in land ownership from the London Company to individual colonists. The possibility of owning land attracted new settlers and thus helped the colony survive.

✔ **Reading Check: Finding the Main Idea** When did English settlers arrive in Virginia, and what challenges did they face?

Research on the

Free Find:
Pocahontas
After reading about Pocahontas on the **Holt Researcher CD–ROM,** write a short essay describing the way the Powhatan treated the English settlers of Jamestown.

★ War in Virginia

John Rolfe married **Pocahontas**, Wahunsonacock's daughter, in 1614. Their marriage helped the Jamestown colony form more peaceful relations with the Powhatan. However, in 1617 Pocahontas died while visiting England, and Wahunsonacock died the next year. By that time, the colonists no longer depended on the Powhatan for food. They lost interest in allying with their American Indian neighbors. Many colonists also wanted to grow tobacco on American Indian lands. As the colony grew, the Powhatan and the Virginia colonists came into greater conflict.

In 1622, colonists killed a Powhatan leader. Opechancanough (OH-puh-chan-kuh-noh), the brother of Wahunsonacock, responded by attacking the Virginia settlers later that year. The Powhatan killed about 350 men, women, and children. Among the dead was John Rolfe. Angry survivors then burned American Indian villages. Fighting between the colonists and the Powhatan continued for the next 20 years.

The war in Virginia showed that the London Company could not help its colonists. Settlers were running short of supplies and were angry that the Company failed to send them any military support. These problems persuaded the English Crown to cancel the London Company's charter in 1624. Virginia became a royal colony under the authority of a governor chosen by the king.

✔ **Reading Check: Sequencing** List the events that marked the Jamestown colonists' changing relationship with American Indians in the proper sequence.

Pocahontas had this portrait painted when she visited England with John Rolfe in 1616.

⭐ Daily Life in Virginia

In early Virginia, people lived on scattered farms rather than in towns. Tobacco farmers soon began founding large farms called plantations. These plantations were made possible in part by use of the **headright** system. Under this system, colonists who paid their own way to Virginia received 50 acres of land. A colonist could earn 50 acres more for every

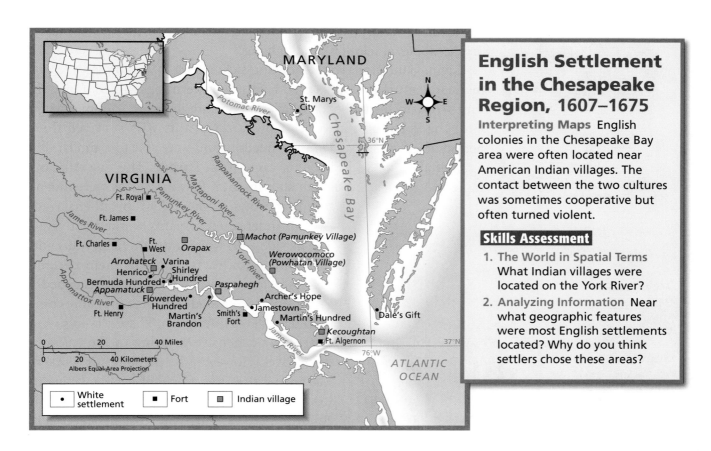

English Settlement in the Chesapeake Region, 1607–1675

Interpreting Maps English colonies in the Chesapeake Bay area were often located near American Indian villages. The contact between the two cultures was sometimes cooperative but often turned violent.

Skills Assessment

1. **The World in Spatial Terms** What Indian villages were located on the York River?

2. **Analyzing Information** Near what geographic features were most English settlements located? Why do you think settlers chose these areas?

additional person brought from England. Rich colonists brought servants or relatives to Virginia and gained large amounts of land.

Those who brought relatives to Virginia found that raising a family was difficult. Loved ones often died of deadly diseases, such as malaria. The London Company tried to bring women to the colony by offering promises of marriage. However, during the early years of the settlement men outnumbered women seven to one. Colonial families in Virginia focused on providing the basic necessities for themselves. Most colonists provided their own food and shelter. They also made eating utensils, tools, furniture, and clothing by hand. Parents gave lessons in reading and religion at home because there were no schools and few churches.

✔ **Reading Check** **Summarizing** How and why did the plantation system develop in the South?

⭐ Labor in Virginia

Colonists in Virginia faced a hard life. They suffered very high death rates, which led to labor shortages in the colony. More laborers were needed to work on plantations and farms. The majority of these workers were **indentured servants.** These colonists signed a contract to work from four to seven years for those who paid their ship fare to America. Of the early Virginia colonists, some 75 percent arrived as indentured servants. In one such contract, Margarett Williams promised to work for plantation owner Richard Smyth for four years. Smyth agreed "to pay for her [ocean] passing, and to find and allow [provide] her meate, drinke, apparrel [clothes] and lodging."

Living conditions were poor, and sickness was common. As a result, many indentured servants died before their term had ended. One servant wrote to his parents: "I have eaten more in a day at home than I have [had] here for a week." However, servants who survived their period of indenture gained their freedom and were able to claim land.

Not all laborers in Virginia came from Europe. The first Africans came to Virginia on a Dutch ship in 1619. Some Africans were indentured servants. Others had been enslaved. African indentured servants worked and lived side by side with white indentured servants and had similar contracts. Some of them became successful farmers when their contracts ended.

At first, indentured servants were more common than slaves in Virginia. These servants were clearly less expensive to bring to the colonies than slaves. However, the demand for workers was greater than the supply of people willing to work as indentured servants under the harsh conditions. Over time the cost of slaves fell.

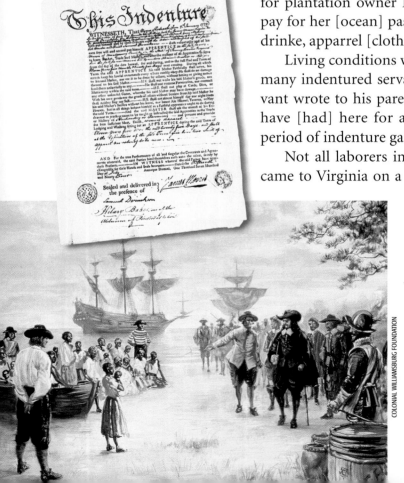

The first enslaved Africans to arrive in the English colonies were brought in the early 1600s.

COLONIAL WILLIAMSBURG FOUNDATION

These factors led some colonists, particularly **planters**—wealthy farmers with large plantations—to turn to slave labor. By the late 1600s most Africans in Virginia were being kept in lifelong slavery. The widespread use of slave labor helped some tobacco plantation owners become rich. However, this wealth came at a great cost in human life and liberty.

★ Bacon's Rebellion

During the mid-1600s many colonists grew increasingly unhappy with conditions in the colony. They were angered by the governor's tight control over the colony and his refusal to call elections. Poor colonists also believed that members of Virginia's assembly were ignoring their concerns. They complained about higher taxes and the lack of available farmland. Many of them began farming on land belonging to American Indians. In doing so, they ignored treaties between the government and local American Indians.

In 1676 a group of former indentured servants attacked some peaceful American Indians. These angry colonists were led by **Nathaniel Bacon**, a wealthy frontier planter and a relative of the governor. When the governor tried to stop Bacon, he and his followers attacked and burned Jamestown. The uprising was known as **Bacon's Rebellion**. At one point Bacon controlled much of the colony. After he died of fever, however, the rebellion soon ended, and 23 of the remaining rebels were eventually hanged. Following the rebellion, the Virginia colonists found it difficult to make peace with American Indians. In addition, fears of future uprisings by former indentured servants led some planters in Virginia to depend more on slavery.

✔ **Reading Check: Analyzing Information** What factors led to the increased use of slave labor in Virginia?

Interpreting the Visual Record

Bacon's Rebellion *This scene shows a confrontation between Nathaniel Bacon at the right and Governor William Berkeley on the left.* **What is threatening about Bacon's appearance in this image?**

Section 1 Review

go.
hrw
.com
Homework Practice Online
keyword: SF3 HP4

1 **Define** and explain:
- headright
- indentured servants
- planters

2 **Identify** and explain:
- John Smith
- Powhatan Confederacy
- John Rolfe
- Pocahontas
- Nathaniel Bacon
- Bacon's Rebellion

3 **Summarizing** Copy the graphic organizer below. Use it to explain the reasons people from England decided to establish the Jamestown colony in 1607.

Problems in England → Jamestown Colony, 1607 ← Advantages of America

4 **Finding the Main Idea**
a. Provide examples of the cooperation and conflict between American Indians and Virginia colonists.

b. Why did the plantation system develop in Virginia, and what economic role did tobacco play?

5 **Writing and Critical Thinking**
Supporting a Point of View Imagine that you are a wealthy planter in colonial Virginia. Create a pamphlet for investors in England explaining why indentured servants and enslaved Africans are important for the colonial economy.

Consider the following:
- the headright system
- the development of tobacco plantations
- high death rates in the colony

The English Colonies **97**

The Pilgrims' Experience

Read to Discover

1. Why did the Pilgrims come to America?
2. What was the Mayflower Compact, and why was it important?
3. What was life like in the Plymouth colony?

WHY IT MATTERS TODAY

Religious intolerance is still present in many parts of the world. Use CNNfyi.com or other **current events** sources to identify a religious group that recently faced intolerance. Record your findings in your journal.

Define

- sect
- immigrants

Identify

- Puritans
- Separatists
- Pilgrims
- William Bradford
- Mayflower Compact
- Squanto

The Story Continues

England's King James I held a conference in 1604 to meet with Protestant leaders. They wanted to reform the Church of England, also known as the Anglican Church. The leaders criticized the power held by Anglican bishops. As they talked, the king grew restless. Finally, he interrupted one of the reformers and began shouting furiously. "While I am in England I will have bishops to govern the Church." The king had plans for those who asked for reform, too. James stated, "I will make them conform themselves [become Anglicans] or I will harry [drive] them out of this land."

King James I disagreed with many proposed Puritan religious reforms.

★ Puritans and Pilgrims

Religious tension in England remained high after the Protestant Reformation. A Protestant group called the **Puritans** wanted to reform, or purify, the Church of England. The Puritans thought that bishops and priests had too much power over church members. They believed that the Bible was the most reliable source of authority. The most extreme **sect**, or religious group, of Puritans wanted to separate from the Church of England. These **Separatists** formed their own churches and cut all ties with the Church of England. In response, English leaders began to punish Separatists.

One group of Separatists who faced such treatment became known as the **Pilgrims**. In 1608 the Pilgrims left England to escape this persecution and moved to the Netherlands. The Pilgrims were **immigrants**—people who came to a new country after leaving the land of their birth. Dutch officials welcomed the Pilgrims and allowed them to practice their religion freely.

DETAIL, COURTESY OF THE PILGRIM SOCIETY, PLYMOUTH, MASSACHUSETTS

The Pilgrims were glad to be able to practice their faith. They were not happy, however, that their children were learning the Dutch language and culture. The Pilgrims feared that their children would forget their English traditions. They were also disappointed by the types of jobs available to them. These concerns led the Pilgrims to leave the Netherlands. First, they formed a joint-stock company with some merchants. Then, they returned to England to apply for permission to settle in Virginia.

✔ **Reading Check: Summarizing** What factors led the Pilgrims to leave England and come to America?

Interpreting the Visual Record

Plymouth Rock *After the Pilgrims arrived at Plymouth Rock, their ship, the* Mayflower, *stayed with them as they struggled through the winter to build their settlement.* **What does this image suggest about the condition of the Pilgrims when they arrived in America?**

★ The Founding of Plymouth

On September 16, 1620, a ship called the *Mayflower* left England with more than 100 men, women, and children aboard. Not all of these colonists were Pilgrims. However, Pilgrim leaders such as **William Bradford** were in charge. The Pilgrims also hired Captain Myles Standish to help organize the defense of their colony.

After two months of rough ocean travel, the Pilgrims sighted land. Soon they realized that they were far north of present-day Virginia. The Pilgrims realized that they were outside the boundaries of their English charter. They decided to establish basic laws and social rules to govern their colony. On November 21, 1620, 41 of the male passengers on board the *Mayflower* signed a legal contract. They called this contract the **Mayflower Compact**. In it they agreed to have fair laws to protect the general good. This was one of the first attempts at self-government in the English colonies.

In late 1620 the Pilgrims landed at Plymouth Rock in present-day Massachusetts. Bradford described the scene. "They [the Pilgrims] fell upon their knees and blessed the God of Heaven who had brought them over the vast and furious ocean." As they struggled to build the Plymouth settlement, nearly half the tired Pilgrims died from cold and sickness during the first winter.

✔ **Reading Check: Finding the Main Idea** Why was the Mayflower Compact created, and why is it significant?

THE MAYFLOWER COMPACT

In November 1620, the Pilgrim leaders aboard the *Mayflower* drafted the Mayflower Compact. This was the first document in the English colonies to establish guidelines for self-government. This excerpt from the Mayflower Compact describes the principles of the Pilgrim colony's government.

We whose names are underwritten, . . . having undertaken, for the glory of God, and advancement of the Christian faith, and the honour of our King and country, a voyage to plant the first colony in the northern parts of Virginia, do by these **presents**[1] solemnly and mutually in the presence of God, and one of another, **covenant**[2] and combine ourselves together into a civil body **politic**[3] for our better ordering and preservation and furtherance of the ends **aforesaid**[4]; and by **virtue**[5] hereof, to enact, constitute, and frame such just and equal laws, **ordinances**[6], acts, constitutions, and offices . . . as shall be thought most **meet**[7] and convenient for the general good of the colony unto which we promise all due . . . obedience. In witness whereof, we have . . . subscribed our names at Cape Cod, the eleventh of November, 1620.

Analyzing Primary Sources

1. Why do you think the colonists felt the need to establish a government for themselves?
2. How do you think the Mayflower Compact influenced later governments in America?

[1] **by these presents:** by this document
[2] **covenant:** promise
[3] **civil body politic:** group organized for government
[4] **aforesaid:** mentioned above
[5] **virtue:** authority
[6] **ordinances:** regulations
[7] **meet:** fitting

THE GRANGER COLLECTION, NEW YORK

The Pilgrims arrived in the Mayflower.

⭐ Pilgrims and American Indians

European fishing boats had already visited the Plymouth area before the Pilgrims' arrival. These European fishermen brought new diseases to the region. These sicknesses killed most of the local American Indians, such as the Patuxet. For some time the Pilgrims met no American Indians. Occasionally they came across deserted American Indian villages and empty cornfields. The Pilgrims used these empty fields in the spring to plant their crops.

Then, according to Bradford, in March 1621 an American Indian walked boldly into the settlement. He "spoke to them in broken English, which they could well understand, but marveled at it." The man's name was Samoset. He came from a Pemaquid tribe that lived in the area. Samoset had learned some English from the crews of fishing boats. He gave the Pilgrims useful information about the peoples and places surrounding Plymouth. Later he introduced them to a Patuxet Indian named **Squanto**.

"such just and equal laws . . . as shall be thought most . . . convenient for the general good of the colony . . ."

Squanto had lived in Europe and spoke English. He was a great help to the colonists. Bradford described Squanto's contributions.

 History Makers Speak

❝Squanto continued with them and was their interpreter. . . . He directed them how to set [plant] corn, where to take [catch] fish, and procure [get] other commodities [goods], and was also their pilot [guide] to bring them to unknown places.❞

—William Bradford, *History of Plymouth Plantation*

Analyzing Primary Sources

Identifying Points of View
How did Bradford regard Squanto?

From Squanto the Pilgrims learned to fertilize the soil on their farms with fish remains. Squanto also helped the Pilgrims establish relations with Massasoit, the chief of the local Wampanoag Indians.

Conditions in the Plymouth colony began to improve. William Bradford described the Pilgrims' first harvest.

 History Makers Speak

❝They began now to gather in the small harvest that they had, and to fit up their houses and dwellings against winter, being all well recovered in health and strength and had all things in good plenty.❞

—William Bradford, *History of Plymouth Plantation*

The Pilgrims invited Chief Massasoit and 90 other Wampanoag guests to celebrate their harvest. This feast, held to thank God, became known as the first Thanksgiving. For the event, the Pilgrims killed wild turkeys. For three days the two groups feasted with each other. This event marked the survival of the Pilgrims in the new colony.

✔ **Reading Check: Summarizing** What was the relationship like between Pilgrims and American Indians, and what did this mean for the colony?

⭐ The Pilgrim Community

Although the Pilgrims overcame many problems, their small settlement still struggled. Most Pilgrims tried farming, but the farmland around their settlement was poor. They had hoped to prosper by trading furs and by fishing. Unfortunately, fishing and hunting conditions were not good in their area. Some colonists traded corn with American Indians for beaver furs. The Pilgrims were not wealthy but were able to form a strong community. The colony began to grow stronger in the mid-1620s after new settlers arrived and, as in Jamestown, colonists began to have more rights to farm their own land.

The Pilgrim settlement was different from Virginia in that families were common there. Most people hoped to have many children, who were needed to help with the work. If parents died, Pilgrim families quickly adopted children left behind. They raised them as their own. The Pilgrims taught their children to read and offered some education to their indentured servants. The family served as the center of religious life, health care, and community well-being. All family members worked together to survive during the early years of the colony. Women generally cooked, spun

★ ★ ★ ★ ★ ★ ★ ★ ★ ★ ★
That's Interesting!
★ ★ ★ ★ ★ ★ ★ ★ ★ ★ ★

Squanto's Journey Did you know that Squanto had traveled even farther than the Pilgrims when they first met in America? It's true! Squanto had been kidnapped by English explorers in 1605. He lived in England until 1614, when he returned to New England. Squanto was captured once again in 1615 and sold into slavery in Spain. He managed to escape the Spanish and make his way to England, returning to New England in 1619. When Squanto finally reached his home, however, he discovered that his tribe had been wiped out by disease. He then lived with the Wampanoag until Samoset introduced him to the Pilgrims.

THE GRANGER COLLECTION, NEW YORK

Interpreting the Visual Record

Homework *This woman works a spinning wheel in her kitchen. Colonial women made the family's clothing, often including shoes.* **What can you learn from the image about the different jobs that women had to do?**

and wove wool, and sewed clothing. They also made soap and butter, carried water, dried fruit, and cared for livestock. Men spent most of their time repairing tools and working in the fields. They also chopped wood and built shelters.

In Plymouth, women had more legal rights than they did in England. In England women were not allowed to make contracts, to sue, or to own property. In America, Pilgrim women had the right to sign contracts and to bring certain cases before local courts. Widows could also own property. A widow often received one third of her husband's land and belongings. In addition, married and widowed women could get licenses to run inns and to sell liquor.

From time to time, local courts recognized the ways women helped the business community. Widow Naomi Silvester received a large share of her husband's estate. The court called her "a frugal [thrifty] and laborious [hardworking] woman in the providing of the said estate." Widow Elizabeth Warren's business ability convinced colonial leaders to make her a purchaser for the colony. She took the place of her late husband. The hard work of such women helped the Plymouth colony to survive.

✔ **Reading Check: Analyzing Information** How did the Pilgrims view the importance of women and children to the colony?

Section 2 Review

go.hrw.com

Homework Practice Online

keyword: SF3 HP4

1. **Define** and explain:
   • sect
   • immigrants

2. **Identify** and explain:
   • Puritans
   • Separatists
   • Pilgrims
   • William Bradford
   • Mayflower Compact
   • Squanto

3. **Identifying Cause and Effect** Copy the web diagram below. Use it to describe the problems that the Pilgrims faced in Europe, and explain how they responded to these problems.

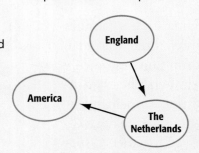

England → The Netherlands → America

4. **Finding the Main Idea**
   a. How were family relations and religion important to the Plymouth colony?

   b. How did American Indians help the Plymouth colonists survive the early years?

5. **Writing and Critical Thinking**
   Summarizing Imagine that you are Pilgrim leader William Bradford. Write an essay describing the Mayflower Compact to place in the official records of the Plymouth colony.

   Consider the following:
   • why the Compact was necessary
   • who signed the document
   • the influence of the document on government

The New England Colonies

Read to Discover

1. What was the Great Migration, and why did it occur?
2. What role did religion and the Church play in the Massachusetts Bay Colony?
3. How did the Puritans respond to dissenters?

WHY IT MATTERS TODAY

The Puritans made education an important part of their community. Many colleges founded in colonial times still operate today. Use **CNNfyi.com** or other **current events** sources to identify ways in which colleges and universities affect our lives today. Record your findings in your journal.

Define

* dissenters
* covenant

Identify

* Great Migration
* John Winthrop
* Thomas Hooker
* Fundamental Orders of Connecticut
* Roger Williams
* Anne Hutchinson

The Story Continues

In the early 1600s John Winthrop wrote to his wife, Margaret. He worried that "this land [England] grows weary of her inhabitants." As an Englishman, John Winthrop was fond of his country. As a Puritan, however, he believed that the members of his church were no longer welcome in England. Winthrop believed that the time was coming when they would have to leave their comfortable life behind. He later wrote that the Puritans would have to seek a new home to "be better preserved from the common corruptions [sins] of this evil world."

John Winthrop was one of many Puritans who left England in search of religious freedom.

★ The Massachusetts Bay Colony

Beginning about 1620, England experienced an economic downturn, costing many people their jobs. Charles I, who became king in 1625, made the situation worse by raising taxes. This unpopular act led to a political crisis. At the same time, the Church of England began to punish Puritans because they were **dissenters**—people who disagree with official opinions. Charles I refused to allow Puritans to criticize Church actions.

These economic, political, and religious problems in England led to the **Great Migration**. Between 1630 and 1640 tens of thousands of English men, women, and children left England. More than 40,000 English emigrants moved to colonies in the Caribbean and New England. In 1629 a group of Puritans and merchants began planning a Puritan colony in North America. King Charles I granted the group a charter, allowing its members to establish a colony in the area known as New England. They formed the Massachusetts Bay Company.

In 1630 a fleet of ships carrying Puritan colonists left England for Massachusetts. There they hoped to have the freedom to practice their religion freely. While on board the flagship, *Arbella*, the colony's governor, **John Winthrop**, wrote about the Puritans' goals.

 History Makers Speak 66We must delight in each other, make others' conditions our own and rejoice together, mourn together, labor and suffer together, always having before our eyes . . . our community . . . . For we must consider that we shall be like a City upon a Hill; the eyes of all people are on us.99

—John Winthrop, quoted in *The Annals of America*

Analyzing Primary Sources
Identifying Points of View What did Winthrop believe should be the focus of the Puritan colony?

Winthrop's speech reflected the Puritans' belief that they had made a **covenant** with God. Under this covenant, or sacred agreement, Puritans agreed to build an ideal Christian community.

The Puritans arrived in New England well prepared to start their colony. They brought large numbers of tools and livestock. Trade with the colony of Plymouth helped them too. Like the Pilgrims, the Puritans faced little resistance at first from local American Indians. In addition, the Massachusetts region, unlike coastal Virginia, had a healthy climate. Thus, few Puritans died from sickness. All of these factors helped the Puritan colony do well.

Religious services were a key part of community life for both the Pilgrim and Puritan colonies in New England.

THE GRANGER COLLECTION, NEW YORK

By the end of 1630, about 1,000 more men, women, and children had joined the first settlers. These immigrants established the towns of Salem, Mystic, Newton, Watertown, and Dorchester. In addition, they built Boston, which became the colony's chief city and capital. Colonists also settled to the north, in present-day New Hampshire. In 1679 New Hampshire became a royal colony.

✔ **Reading Check: Summarizing** In what ways was religion an important factor in the establishment of the Massachusetts Bay Colony?

⭐ Church and State in New England

According to its company charter, Massachusetts was subject to English laws. However, the company charter provided more independence than did the royal charter of Virginia. The company charter created a General Court to help run the colony. The Puritan colonists turned this court into a type of self-government that tried to represent the needs of the people. Each town sent two or three delegates to the Court. After John Winthrop served as the first governor of Massachusetts, the General Court elected the governor and his assistants. In 1644 the General Court became a two-house legislature. This meant that the lawmaking body had two groups, and all decisions required a majority in each house.

Politics and religion were closely linked in Puritan New England. Government leaders were also church members. Although ministers were not political officials, they often had a great deal of power in Puritan communities. Male church members were the only colonists who could vote. Colonists became full members in the church by becoming what the Puritans called God's "elect," or chosen. Reaching this status was a difficult process. Individuals had to pass a public test to prove that their faith was strong.

In 1636 minister **Thomas Hooker** and his followers decided to leave Massachusetts to help found Connecticut, another New England colony. In 1639 Hooker helped draft the **Fundamental Orders of Connecticut**, a set of principles that made Connecticut's government more democratic. For example, the Orders allowed men who were not church members to vote. As a result of his role, some historians have called Hooker "the father of American democracy." The Fundamental Orders of Connecticut also outlined the powers of the general courts.

 History Makers Speak ❝General courts . . . shall have power to make laws or repeal them, to grant levies, to admit . . . freemen, dispose of [distribute] lands undisposed of to several towns or persons.❞

—The Fundamental Orders of Connecticut

✔ **Reading Check: Finding the Main Idea** What was distinctive about Connecticut's government?

Historical Document

FUNDAMENTAL ORDERS OF CONNECTICUT

This excerpt describes the structure of the government adopted by the citizens of Connecticut in 1639. The Fundamental Orders are an example of the development of representative democracy in the colonies.

It is ordered . . . that there shall be yearly two general assemblies or courts: . . . The first shall be called the Court of Election, wherein shall be yearly chosen . . . public officers . . . which choice shall be made by all that are admitted freemen and have taken the oath of **fidelity**[1]. . . . It is ordered . . . that . . . [each town] shall have power . . . to send four of their freemen as their deputies to every general court; . . . which deputies shall have the power . . . to give their votes . . . as may be for the public good, and unto which the said towns are to be bound.

[1] **fidelity:** faithfulness

Analyzing Primary Sources

1. Who elected the public officials in Connecticut?
2. How are the people represented in the General Court?

⭐ Daily Life and Customs

New England colonists' lives centered around religion, family duties, and public work. Puritan religion strongly shaped everyday life in colonial New England. On Sundays, Puritans often heard two sermons. These weekly church meetings brought all members of the community together. In general, community life was more stable than in Virginia. Colonists in Virginia tended to be either wealthy or poor. Most colonists who immigrated to New England, however, were somewhere in between. Many New England colonists were skilled workers, and some were experienced farmers. Others had success with fishing enterprises or fur trading.

New England farmers grew food mainly for their own use rather than crops like tobacco for sale. Most New England farms were owned and run entirely by families. These small farms did not bring great wealth to their owners but also did not need as many laborers as did southern plantations. New England thus had little need for indentured servants or slaves.

Most colonists came to New England in family groups. As the colony grew, couples often had many children, who helped run the family farm. Parents helped choose their children's marriage partners in colonial New England in part because marriage involved a transfer of property from one family to another. Puritans believed that women had three main duties to fulfill in marriage. They had to obey their husbands, have children, and run the household. Husbands were expected in turn to treat their wives "with the greatest love, gentleness, kindness, [and] tenderness."

Education was an important part of New England society, largely because mothers and fathers wanted their children to be able to read the Bible. The Massachusetts Bay Colony passed some of the first laws requiring parents to provide instruction for their children. In 1636 John Harvard and the General Court founded Harvard College. Harvard taught ministers and met the colony's need for higher education. By 1700 about 70 percent of the men and 45 percent of the women in New England could read and write. Figures for literacy were much lower in Virginia.

✔ **Reading Check: Contrasting** In what ways were the Massachusetts Bay Colony and the Virginia colony different?

This is how a Puritan couple might be dressed for walking to church.

NEW FRANCE

Land claimed by New York and New Hampshire.

MASSACHUSETTS

St. Lawrence River

Lake Champlain

Penobscot River

Connecticut River

Lake Ontario

Annexed by Massachusetts in 1652.

44°N

NEW HAMPSHIRE
Portsmouth 1623

Salem 1626

NEW YORK   MASSACHUSETTS
Boston 1630

Massachusetts Bay

42°N

Hudson River

Hartford 1636
CONNECTICUT

Plymouth 1620

Providence 1636

ATLANTIC OCEAN

PENNSYLVANIA

New Haven 1638   RHODE ISLAND

NEW JERSEY

LONG ISLAND   72°W   70°W   68°W

0   100   200 Miles
0   100   200 Kilometers
Albers Equal-Area Projection

N W E S

The New England Colonies

Intrepreting Maps Many groups seeking religious freedom settled in New England.

Skills Assessment Human Systems What New England settlement was founded in 1630?

"To My Dear and Loving Husband"

Anne Bradstreet

In 1650 Puritan Anne Bradstreet published her poetry collection The Tenth Muse Lately Sprung Up in America. *She was the first published American poet. She wrote the following poem to her husband, Simon Bradstreet.*

THE TENTH MUSE Lately sprung up in AMERICA. OR Severall Poems, compiled with great variety of VVit and Learning, full of delight.

The Granger Collection, New York

> If ever two were one, then surely we.
> If ever man were loved by wife, then thee;
> If ever wife was happy in a man,
> Compare with me, ye women, if you can.
> I prize thy love more than whole mines of gold
> Or all the riches the East doth hold.
> My love is such that rivers cannot quench,
> Nor ought but love from thee, give **recompense**[1].
> Thy love is such I can no way repay,
> The heavens reward thee **manifold**[2] I pray.
> Then while we live, in love let's so **persevere**[3]
> That when we live no more, we may live ever.

[1] **recompense:** pay or satisfy
[2] **manifold:** many times
[3] **persevere:** continue on

Understanding What You Read

1. **Literature and History** How did Anne Bradstreet feel about her marriage?
2. **Literature and You** Do you think most colonial women would share Bradstreet's view of marriage? Explain your answer.

Dissent in Massachusetts

Not all Puritans shared the same religious views. Minister **Roger Williams** did not agree with the leadership of Massachusetts. He called for his church to separate completely from the other New England congregations. Williams also criticized the General Court for taking land from American Indians without paying them.

Puritan leaders worried that Williams's ideas might hurt the colony and made him leave Massachusetts forever. Williams took his supporters to southern New England where they formed a new settlement called Providence. This settlement later became the colony of Rhode Island. Williams received a charter for his small settlement in 1644. In Providence, Williams supported the separation of the church from politics and promoted religious tolerance for all members of the community. In addition, he wanted to deal with American Indians fairly.

In Boston, **Anne Hutchinson** angered Puritan church leaders by publicly discussing religious ideas that some leaders thought radical. For example, Hutchinson believed that God speaks directly to people, apart from the Bible. A group of important community members often met at her home for religious discussions.

Anne Hutchinson's beliefs led to her exile from Massachusetts.

Hutchinson's views alarmed Puritan leaders such as John Winthrop. Puritan officials therefore put Hutchinson on trial for her ideas. The court decided to force Hutchinson out of the colony. With a group of followers, Hutchinson helped found the new colony of Portsmouth on Aquidneck Island (Rhode Island).

✔ **Reading Check: Identifying Cause and Effect** What led to religious disagreements among the Puritans, and what was the result?

⭐ The Salem Witch Trials

Perhaps the worst community conflicts in New England involved the witchcraft trials of the early 1690s. The largest number of trials were held in Salem, Massachusetts. In Salem a group of girls had accused people of casting spells on them. Most of the accused were women. The community formed a special court to judge the witchcraft cases. During the trials the young girls often screamed and fainted when someone accused of witchcraft entered the room. Witnesses reported they had seen witches speaking with the devil. The court often pressured the suspected witches to confess. One woman accused of witchcraft protested, "There was no other way to save our lives . . . but by our confessing."

The Salem witch trials led to 19 people being put to death. By the next year, many of the local officials and clergymen involved regretted their acts. Judge Samuel Sewall became one of the first to apologize publicly for his role in the wrongs committed by the Salem court.

✔ **Reading Check: Drawing Inferences and Conclusions** What effect do you think the witch trials had on Puritan communities?

Research on the ROM

Free Find:
Anne Hutchinson
After reading about Anne Hutchinson on the **Holt Researcher CD–ROM,** create a news report that explains both sides of her conflict with religious leaders.

Section 3 Review

go.hrw.com **Homework Practice Online**
keyword: SF3 HP4

1 **Define** and explain:
• dissenters
• covenant

2 **Identify** and explain:
• Great Migration
• John Winthrop
• Thomas Hooker
• Fundamental Orders of Connecticut
• Roger Williams
• Anne Hutchinson

3 **Summarizing** Copy the chart below. Use it to show how religious beliefs influenced the founding of various New England colonies and their systems of government.

Colony	Founded By	Reason for Founding	Form of Government

4 **Finding the Main Idea**
a. How did religion and the Church influence the government and daily life of the Massachusetts Bay Colony?

b. How did Puritan leaders treat dissenters such as Roger Williams and Anne Hutchinson?

5 **Writing and Critical Thinking**
Analyzing Information Imagine that you are a Dutch citizen living in London during the time of the Great Migration. Write a letter to your friends in the Netherlands describing the Great Migration and why it is taking place.

Consider the following:
• freedom of religion
• economic and political unrest in England
• the number of English citizens leaving for the Americas

The Southern and Middle Colonies

Read to Discover

1. What role did religion play in the founding and development of Maryland?
2. How were the Carolinas established, and how did their economies develop?
3. How were the middle colonies founded?

WHY IT MATTERS TODAY

The United States continues to receive thousands of immigrants each year. Use CNNfyi.com or other **current events** sources to find information on one or more groups of immigrants coming to the United States today. Record your findings in your journal.

Define
- proprietors

Identify
- Cecilius Calvert
- Toleration Act of 1649
- Peter Stuyvesant
- Quakers
- William Penn
- James Oglethorpe

The Story Continues

The English ship the *Ark* sailed into Chesapeake Bay. As it did, one passenger, Father Andrew White, looked out in wonder. He called the Potomac the "greatest river I have seene, so that the Thames is but a little finger to it." The *Ark* and its sister ship, the *Dove,* landed along the banks of the Potomac in March 1634. Most of the colonists on board were Catholic. On the riverbank, the colonists made a cross out of a large tree to celebrate their first Catholic mass in the new colony.

Maryland's St. Ignatius Church was established in 1641.

⭐ Tolerant Maryland

Many English Catholics came to America for the same reason that many Puritans did. They wanted to escape religious persecution. English Catholics had long been against England's separation from the Roman Catholic Church. For this reason, they were not allowed by the Church of England to worship freely. England's leaders also feared that English

Cecilius Calvert never visited the colony that he founded.

Analyzing Primary Sources

Drawing Inferences and Conclusions What historical events in Europe might have caused Lord Baltimore to introduce the Toleration Act?

Catholics would aid Catholic countries, such as France and Spain. In 1632 King Charles I gave **Cecilius Calvert** a charter to found a new colony. Also known as Lord Baltimore, Calvert intended the colony to be a refuge for English Catholics. He named the southern colony Maryland in honor of England's queen, Henrietta Maria.

Maryland was a proprietary colony. This meant that **proprietors**, or owners, controlled the government. Maryland was located just north of Virginia in the Chesapeake Bay area. In 1634 about 200 colonists arrived in Maryland to start a settlement.

Settlers in Maryland benefited from the lessons learned by the Jamestown colonists. They spent their time raising corn, cattle, and hogs. This way they would have enough to eat. Before long, however, many colonists turned their energies to growing tobacco for profit. Most of the colonists were men, and there were few families in Maryland at first.

Although Catholics founded Maryland, a growing number of Protestants began moving there in the 1640s. Soon religious conflicts between the two groups arose. To reduce tensions, Lord Baltimore presented a bill to the colonial assembly that became known as the **Toleration Act of 1649**. It made restricting the religious rights of Christians a crime. This act was one of the first laws supporting religious tolerance passed in the English colonies.

 ❝No person or persons whatsoever within this province . . . professing [claiming] to believe in Jesus Christ shall . . . be any way troubled, molested [persecuted], or . . . any way compelled [forced] to the belief or exercise of any other religion against his or her consent.**❞**

—Lord Baltimore, quoted in *Colonial America*, by Richard Middleton

The Toleration Act did not put an end to all religious conflict. However, it did show that the government wanted to offer some religious freedom and to protect the rights of minority groups.

✔ **Reading Check: Finding the Main Idea** How did religion shape the Maryland colony?

The Carolinas

In 1663 Charles II gave much of the land between Virginia and Spanish Florida to eight of his supporters. These colonial proprietors named the new southern colony Carolina, which is a Latin form of the name *Charles.* For many years Carolina was a single colony. However, the settlements within the colony were widely divided, making it hard for leaders to govern them all. Finally, in 1712 North and South Carolina became separate colonies. Most of the colonists in North Carolina were farmers who had moved south from Virginia. Unlike Virginia, North Carolina had few plantations. The colony had no towns and few churches until the early 1700s.

Colonial settlement in South Carolina began in 1670. That year three ships arrived from London with about 100 settlers. The colonists founded the port of Charles Town, which later became Charleston. Colonists who paid their own way to South Carolina received large grants of land. South Carolina drew many settlers from other English colonies, particularly from the British West Indies. These Caribbean colonists brought enslaved Africans with them. Because of this, South Carolina became one of the first colonies to depend mainly on the work of slaves.

Some colonists thought that rice might grow well in South Carolina's lowland swamps. However, they had little experience growing the crop. Many historians believe that African laborers taught the colonists how to raise rice in the 1690s. By the mid-1700s South Carolina's royal governor James Glen saw a change. He reported that "the only Commodity of Consequence [importance] produced in South Carolina is Rice."

Rice production required many workers, and plantation owners chose to meet their growing labor needs by using slaves. By 1730 about 20,000 enslaved Africans were living in the colony, compared to half as many white settlers. South Carolina was the only mainland colony with a higher population of enslaved Africans than free whites.

The proprietors' poor management of the Carolinas displeased the colonists. In 1719 the British government bought South Carolina from the original proprietors. The Crown then bought North Carolina in 1729, making it a royal colony as well.

✔ **Reading Check: Analyzing Information** How was South Carolina different from the other colonies, and why was this the case?

Daily Life

Charleston Charleston was the commercial, political, and social center of South Carolina. Because of the city's climate and location, many planters and officials chose to make it home. Soon, the wealth of merchants and planters helped build Charleston's cultural life. Cultural attractions included the city's library society and one of two newspapers published in the southern colonies. Over the years, Charleston's architecture has become another famous feature. Instead of using official buildings, government officials met in the large private homes of political leaders. **What features do you see in the image that might have drawn people to Charleston?**

THE GRANGER COLLECTION, NEW YORK

⭐ Diversity in New York and New Jersey

The Dutch founded New Netherland on the Hudson River in 1613 as a trading post for exchanging furs with the Iroquois. The town of New Amsterdam became the center of the fur trade in New Netherland. This settlement was founded on Manhattan Island. Most colonists in New Amsterdam were fur traders and farmers. Generous land grants and religious tolerance soon brought Jews, French Huguenots, Puritans, and others to the colony. Director General **Peter Stuyvesant** took control of the colony beginning in 1647. Stuyvesant was an experienced soldier with a wooden leg who ruled the colony as a dictator.

In 1664 the English took control of New Netherland when an English fleet captured New Amsterdam without a shot. New Netherland became an English colony and was renamed New York, the first of the middle colonies. Many Dutch settlers remained in the colony, shaping colonial life in different ways. For example, the Dutch contributed words such as *boss, cookie,* and *stoop* to the English language.

Soon after the conquest in 1664, the Duke of York made Sir George Carteret and John Lord Berkeley proprietors of New Jersey. This colony occupied lands between the Hudson and Delaware Rivers. It had a diverse population, including Dutch, Swedes, Finns, and Scots.

The fur trade remained important to New York's economy, and overseas trade grew over time. Both New York and New Jersey also produced large amounts of wheat.

✔ **Reading Check: Sequencing** List in their proper order the steps that established the colonies of New York and New Jersey.

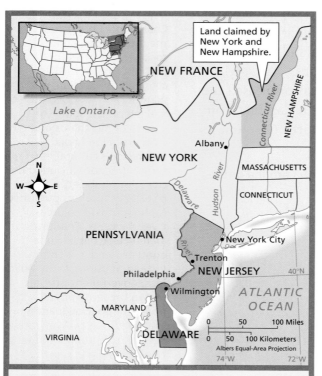

Land claimed by New York and New Hampshire.

The Middle Colonies

Interpreting Maps The middle colonies were formed from land grants given by King Charles II.

Skills Assessment The World in Spatial Terms What river connects major cities in Delaware, New Jersey, and Pennsylvania?

After the English captured New Amsterdam, they renamed it New York, in honor of the Duke of York.

THE GRANGER COLLECTION, NEW YORK

THE GRANGER COLLECTION, NEW YORK

⭐ The Pennsylvania Experiment

The Society of Friends, or the **Quakers**, made up one of the largest religious groups in New Jersey. The Quakers were a Protestant sect founded by George Fox in the mid-1600s in England. Quakers believed that all people had an "inner light" that could help them experience God. They rejected formal religious practices and dressed plainly. The Quakers supported nonviolence as well as religious tolerance for all peoples. Such views differed from those of many Christians. As a result, Quakers were persecuted in both England and the American colonies.

One proprietor of the New Jersey colony was a Quaker named **William Penn**. Penn wished to found a larger colony under his own control that would provide a safe home for Quakers. In 1681 King Charles II agreed to grant Penn a charter to begin a colony west of New Jersey.

Known as Pennsylvania, this middle colony grew rapidly. Penn tried to create a government that was fair to all its people. He limited his own powers so that "the will of one man may not hinder [harm] the good of a whole country." He also provided a means of changing the colony's laws to reflect the will of the people. Penn sold land to colonists at low prices, and he also promised religious freedom to all Christians. In addition, Penn said that the government would care for the poor. His work

Interpreting the Visual Record

Quaker meeting *Many of the colonists in Pennsylvania were farmers and helped create a peaceful and stable society there.* **What does this image suggest about life in Pennsylvania?**

BIOGRAPHY

William Penn

(1644–1718)

William Penn was born in London, the son of a wealthy admiral. Penn joined the Quakers in 1666 and became an active preacher and writer of religious works. He supported toleration for dissenters. In 1681 he received a charter to establish a new colony called Pennsylvania. There Penn put his beliefs into practice. He insisted on fair dealings with local American Indians, welcomed immigrants, and promised religious toleration. Because he believed in nonviolence, he did not require settlers to serve in a colonial militia.

Although Penn played a major role in establishing Pennsylvania, he lived there only a few years.

How did William Penn put his Quaker beliefs into practice when he founded Pennsylvania?

made Pennsylvania a key example of representative self-government in the colonies. Some of the largest groups to arrive in the colony were Welsh and Irish Quakers, and Germans. After arriving, many became farmers. These groups helped create a peaceful and stable society in Pennsylvania. Penn described one type of colonist he was seeking.

 History Makers Speak

❝Another sort of person [who is] . . . necessary in the colonies is the person of universal spirits. These people are concerned about the future. They both understand and promote good discipline and just government. Such persons . . . may find a place in the colonies for their good advice. These people deserve our esteem and should be encouraged to settle here.❞

—William Penn, "Some Account of the Province of Pennsylvania in America"

Penn named the capital of his colony Philadelphia, or the City of Brotherly Love. Penn designed the city himself. He laid it out in a checkerboard pattern that became a model for city planners in other colonies. Pennsylvania grew a great deal in 1682. That year the Duke of York sold Penn a region to the south of Pennsylvania. This area, called Delaware, remained part of Pennsylvania until 1776.

✔ **Reading Check: Finding the Main Idea** Why did William Penn establish Pennsylvania, and how did he influence its government?

⭐ The Ideal of Georgia

The English also founded the southern colony of Georgia. In 1732 King George II granted a charter to **James Oglethorpe** and other trustees. They received permission to start a colony for poor English citizens. Among the group were people who had been jailed for unpaid debts. The king hoped that Georgia would also serve as a shield between South Carolina and Spanish Florida.

In 1733 Oglethorpe and 120 other English colonists founded the city of Savannah on the coast of Georgia. Many of the early colonists were German, Swiss, and Welsh Protestants. Jewish settlers also moved to Savannah. Oglethorpe had high hopes for the Georgia settlement.

 History Makers Speak

❝The examples of other colonies suggest that the new colony will succeed. . . . Georgia is even more likely to succeed than either Virginia or Pennsylvania were.❞

James Oglethorpe, quoted in *Voices of America*, edited by Thomas R. Frazier

Oglethorpe wanted his colony to be different from the other southern colonies. He did not want Georgia to have large plantations ruled by a few wealthy individuals. He hoped that the colony would draw small farmers and avoid the rise of a class of wealthy planters. To reach this goal, Oglethorpe outlawed slavery and limited the size of land grants. He also gave poor colonists free passage to Georgia. Colonists received cattle, land, and food until they could provide their own. Soon, however,

THE GRANGER COLLECTION, NEW YORK

Interpreting the Visual Record

An orderly community *James Oglethorpe carefully planned the town of Savannah, Georgia.* **What suggests that this town has been planned?**

the settlers grew unhappy with Oglethorpe's strict rules. For example, many settlers wanted to allow slavery. They also wanted to have larger farms.

Finally, in 1752 the trustees of Georgia gave up their charter. The English government then made Georgia a royal colony with new laws. Coastal Georgia was soon filled with large rice plantations worked by thousands of slaves.

✔ **Reading Check: Analyzing Information** How did James Oglethorpe hope to make Georgia's population different from the other colonies?

Section 4 Review

go.hrw.com **Homework Practice Online**
keyword: SF3 HP4

1 **Define** and explain:
  • proprietors

2 **Identify** and explain:
  • Cecilius Calvert
  • Toleration Act of 1649
  • Peter Stuyvesant
  • Quakers
  • William Penn
  • James Oglethorpe

3 **Comparing and Contrasting** Copy the chart below. Use it to compare and contrast the reasons why each of the colonies discussed in this section was founded. Include the type of charter given to each colony and its main economic pursuit.

Colony	Reason for Founding	Type of Charter	Economic Pursuit
MD			
NC			
SC			
NY			
NJ			
PA			
GA			

4 **Finding the Main Idea**
  a. In what ways did religion affect settlement and law in the Maryland colony?

  b. When were the Carolinas founded, and how were their economies different from each other?

5 **Writing and Critical Thinking**
  Summarizing Imagine that you are a colonial historian. Create a pamphlet describing the founding and development of the middle colonies.

  Consider the following:
  • the capture of New Netherland
  • the role of William Penn
  • the economies of the middle colonies

Chapter 4 Review

The Chapter at a Glance

Examine the visual summary of the chapter below. Use the visual summary to create a chart comparing the thirteen colonies that shows which were founded for economic, political, or social reasons. If a colony was founded for more than one reason, list it in all appropriate columns on the chart.

New England Colonies

Massachusetts: Founded for religious freedom; Plymouth, 1620; Massachusetts Bay, 1630
New Hampshire: Founded for farming in 1623
Connecticut: Founded for political and religious freedom in 1635
Rhode Island: Founded for religious freedom in 1636

Middle Colonies

New York: Originally New Netherland; captured by England in 1664
New Jersey: Founded for farming and trade in 1664
Pennsylvania: Founded for religious freedom in 1682
Delaware: Established in 1776

Southern Colonies

Virginia: Jamestown founded in 1607 to find wealth
Maryland: Founded in 1634 for religious freedom
North and South Carolina: Founded in 1670 for farming and trade; divided into two colonies in the 1700s
Georgia: Founded in 1733 to provide relief for poor and protection from Spanish Florida

Identifying People and Ideas

Use the following terms or people in historically significant sentences.
1. Bacon's Rebellion
2. Pilgrims
3. Mayflower Compact
4. Squanto
5. John Winthrop
6. covenant
7. Fundamental Orders of Connecticut
8. Anne Hutchinson
9. Toleration Act of 1649
10. William Penn

Understanding Main Ideas

Section 1 *(Pages 92–97)*
1. What factors made it difficult for the Jamestown settlement to survive?

Section 2 *(Pages 98–102)*
2. In what ways did American Indians help the Pilgrims survive in Plymouth?

Section 3 *(Pages 103–108)*
3. How did Puritan dissenters such as Roger Williams contribute to the development of self-government in the colonies?

Section 4 *(Pages 109–115)*
4. Contrast the founding and settlement of the Carolinas, Georgia, and Maryland.

You Be the Historian— Reviewing Themes

1. **Geography** How did climate and geography affect the colonies' development?
2. **Economics** Why were indentured servants and enslaved Africans more important to the southern colonies' economies than to New England's?
3. **Culture** Why did Catholics, Puritans, and Quakers immigrate to America, and what colonies did they establish?

Thinking Critically

1. **Evaluating** Why was it important for members of colonial families to support each other?
2. **Comparing and Contrasting** Compare and contrast the economic reasons for founding each of the thirteen colonies.
3. **Categorizing** What were the social differences between the colonies at Jamestown and Plymouth, and what caused those differences?

Interpreting Maps

Study the map below. Then use the information on the map to help you answer the questions that follow.

The Thirteen Colonies

British Colonies
- New England colonies
- Middle colonies
- Southern colonies

1. Using your knowledge of the period, explain why it would have been important for major towns to be located along rivers or along the coast.

2. Which colonies were known as the middle colonies?
   a. Georgia, Maryland, North Carolina, South Carolina, and Virginia
   b. Connecticut, Massachusetts, New Hampshire, and Rhode Island
   c. Delaware, New Jersey, New York, and Pennsylvania
   d. New Hampshire and New York

Analyzing Primary Sources

Read the following quotation by a woman accused of witchcraft in Massachusetts, and then answer the questions that follow.

> "There was no other way to save our lives, . . . but by our confessing. . . . Indeed, that confession, that it is said we made, was no other than what was suggested to us by some gentlemen, they telling us that we were witches, and they knew it and we knew it, which made us thinking that it was so. . . . Some time after, when we were better composed, they telling us what we had confessed, we did profess that we were innocent and ignorant of such things."

3. Which of the following statements best describes the claim being made by the accused woman?
   a. She and her friends are now convinced that they are witches.
   b. She and her friends confessed out of confusion and to save their lives.
   c. The confessions were given freely and fairly.
   d. There was a lot of evidence to back up the confessions.

4. Based on the information in this quote, do you think the woman and her friends received a fair trial? Explain your answer.

Alternative Assessment

Building Your Portfolio

Interdisciplinary Connection to Geography

Imagine that you are an English merchant traveling through the thirteen colonies to find new trade goods. Create a travel journal of your trip through the colonies. Include a map showing your route and descriptions of the people, places, and types of goods you encounter. Your journal should have at least one entry for each of the thirteen colonies.

internet connect

Internet Activity: go.hrw.com
keyword: SF3 CF4

Choose a topic about the English colonies to:
- Research settlement in Jamestown and create a graph to illustrate your information.
- Construct a scale model of a colonial home.
- Learn about colonial cuisine.

5 Life in the English Colonies
(1630–1770)

This scene shows Harvard College in Cambridge, Massachusetts, some 100 years after it was founded.

Puritan leaders of the Massachusetts Bay Colony had the Bay Psalm Book *printed.*

UNITED STATES

1636 Harvard College, located in Massachusetts, is the first college in the colonies.

1640 The *Bay Psalm Book* is the first book published in the English colonies.

1661 Virginia passes an act recognizing African slavery.

1686 The Dominion of New England is founded.

1630   1650   1670   1690

1648 Work is finished on India's Taj Mahal.

1653 Oliver Cromwell becomes Lord Protector of England.

1660 King Charles II is crowned as ruler of England.

1687 Sir Isaac Newton publishes the first volume of *Principia*, a new theory of physics.

WORLD

The crowning of Charles II was known as the Restoration because it returned the English monarchy to power.

Build on What You Know

English colonists began settling in North America in the 1600s. Some people came to America hoping to make their fortunes. Others came to escape religious persecution. Each region of the colonies developed its own economy. All of the colonies were still closely tied to England, but a unique colonial culture also began to develop.

Benjamin Franklin flew a kite in a thunderstorm during one of his experiments with electricity.

These bifocals are based on Benjamin Franklin's design.

1730 John Smibert holds the first art exhibition in America.

1734 John Peter Zenger is arrested for publishing criticisms of the governor of New York.

1752 Benjamin Franklin proves that lightning is a form of electricity.

1710　　　　　**1730**　　　　　**1750**　　　　　**1770**

1721 Regular postal service begins between London and New England.

1727 Coffee is first planted in Brazil.

1748 The Treaty of Aix-la-Chapelle ends the War of the Austrian Succession in Europe.

If you were there . . .
What occupation would you choose as a colonist?

You Be the Historian

Themes Journal

What's Your Opinion? Do you **agree** or **disagree** with the following statements? Support your point of view in your journal.

- **Economics** Colonies should trade only with their home country.

- **Geography** A colony must have good weather and many natural resources to be successful.

- **Science, Technology & Society** Scientific discoveries are always good for everyone.

Forms of Government

Read to Discover

1. How did representative government develop in the colonies?
2. How did colonists influence the rulings of colonial courts?
3. How did the Dominion of New England affect the New England colonies?
4. How did the English Bill of Rights influence colonists?

WHY IT MATTERS TODAY

Many citizens participate in their local governments today. Use CNNfyi.com or other current events sources to find examples of ways citizens voice their opinions to their local governments. Record your findings in your journal.

Define

- bicameral legislature
- town meeting
- libel

Identify

- Privy Council
- Parliament
- House of Burgesses
- John Peter Zenger
- Dominion of New England
- Edmund Andros
- Glorious Revolution
- English Bill of Rights

The Story Continues

One September morning, William Byrd II rose at 5 A.M. to begin the business of running his Virginia plantation. After a few hours, he met Colonel Bassett, and the two men rode into Williamsburg. In the busy colonial capital, Byrd met with several members of the Council of State. These men were an important part of the colony's government. That day he was sworn in as a member of the Council—a major step in his political career. He wrote in his diary, "God grant I may distinguish myself with honor and good conscience."

The colonial Capitol Building in Williamsburg, Virginia, still stands.

★ Colonial Governments

The English colonies in America all had their own governments when they were first founded. Each government was given power by a charter. The three charter types were proprietary—meaning that one or more individuals had authority over the colony—company, and royal. The English monarch owned all of the colonies and had the sole power to grant charters. A group of royal advisers called the **Privy Council** set English policies in the colonies. However, the Privy Council allowed most colonies to run their own affairs. For example, Rhode Island's 1644 charter stated that all of the colony's laws should agree with those of England. At the same time, the charter stated that the colonists had "full Power and Authority to rule themselves."

Each colony had a governor who served as head of the government. Most governors were assisted by an advisory council. In royal colonies the English king or queen selected the governor and the council members. In proprietary colonies the proprietors chose all of these officials. In a few colonies, such as Connecticut, the people elected the governor. No matter who chose them, governors often possessed significant powers. It was their job to carry out the policies set by England.

✔ **Reading Check: Summarizing** What were the three types of colonial charters?

★ Colonial Assemblies

In the colonies the people also elected representatives to help make laws and set policy. These officials served in assemblies. Colonists based their assemblies on **Parliament**, England's national legislature, or lawmaking body. Parliament is a **bicameral legislature**—a lawmaking body made up of two houses, or groups. Colonial assemblies worked like the lower house of Parliament. They had the power to raise taxes and organize local governments. They also shared control of the military with the governor. The laws passed by each assembly had to be approved first by the advisory council and then by the governor. Then the Privy Council reviewed the colonial laws to make sure that they followed English laws.

Interpreting the Visual Record

Virginia's assembly *This scene shows an early meeting of Virginia's legislature.* **What does this image suggest about the wealth and social status of these representatives? Explain your answer.**

Virginia's assembly, founded in Jamestown in 1619, was the first colonial legislature in North America. At first it met as a single body, but it was later split into two houses. The first house was known as the Council of State. The governor's advisory council and the Virginia Company selected its members. The **House of Burgesses** was the assembly's second house. The members of this house were elected by colonists to represent Virginia's plantations and towns.

Sometimes assemblies and governors disagreed. In such cases the governor had the final say on whether a law was passed. But assemblies could influence governors' actions by refusing to pay their salaries. William Byrd II described the relationship between the House of Burgesses and the royal governor of Virginia.

History Makers Speak

❝Our government . . . is so happily constituted [designed] that a governor must first outwit us before he can oppress [subdue] us. And if he ever squeezes money out of us he must first take care to deserve it.❞

—William Byrd II, quoted in *Albion's Seed,* by David Hackett Fischer

Legislatures were not the only important political bodies in the colonies. The center of New England politics was the **town meeting**. In town meetings people talked about and decided issues of local interest, such as paying for schools. They also regulated other important issues, including the ownership and use of unsettled lands. The men in the community met one or more times every year. They would also select the group of officials who would carry out the town's decisions.

In the southern colonies people typically lived farther away from one another. Therefore, many decisions were made at the county level. The middle colonies used a combination of county meetings and town meetings in their local governments.

✔ **Reading Check: Analyzing Information** Why were colonial assemblies and town meetings created, and what did they do?

★ Colonial Courts

Colonial courts made up another important part of colonial governments. Royal officials could have a strong influence on the courts. Whenever possible, however, colonists used the courts to control local affairs. In general, the courts supported the interests and ideas of their communities. For example, many laws in Massachusetts enforced the Puritans' religious views.

Sometimes colonial courts also protected individual freedoms. For example, the court case of **John Peter Zenger** dealt with the issue of freedom of the press. In 1733 Zenger began criticizing the royal governor of New York in his newspaper. Officials charged him with committing **libel** against a public official. They accused him of printing a false

Citizenship and You

Town Meetings

Watertown, Massachusetts, is known as the "cradle of the town meeting." It held its first town meeting in the 1630s. In colonial times, the town meeting was the preferred form of local government in New England. Today any gathering open to the public to discuss community issues may be called a town meeting. The U.S. government has held such meetings so that citizens can discuss issues ranging from nuclear science to ways to improve neighborhoods.

Presidential candidates also have held town meetings to let voters ask questions and make their views known. Historian John Hope Franklin declared, "The town meeting movement seems to me a magnificent opportunity to catch the whole country up in a common effort." Do you think town meetings are a good way for people to participate in government? Explain your answer.

A town meeting in Hebron, Massachusetts

THE GRANGER COLLECTION, NEW YORK

written statement that damaged the governor's reputation. Zenger was arrested in 1734.

Andrew Hamilton served as Zenger's attorney at the trial. He said that Zenger could publish whatever he wished as long as it was true. Even damaging facts could be printed, Hamilton said. The chief justice of the court did not agree with this view. He explained his opinion to the jury. "Nothing can be worse to any government than to have people attempt to create distrust and dislike of the management of it." The jury, however, found Zenger not guilty. The jury's decision showed its dislike of the royal governor. The jury's agreement with Hamilton's argument also reflected their support for the idea that colonists had a right to express their views openly.

✔ **Reading Check: Finding the Main Idea** Why might colonists support freedom of the press?

Interpreting the Visual Record

Freedom of the Press *Attorney Andrew Hamilton argued that John Peter Zenger could publish the truth even if it offended people.* **In what ways does this courtroom scene look different from the trial system used in the United States today?**

⭐ The Dominion of New England

In 1685 James II became king of England. He was determined to take more control over the English government, both in England and in the colonies. James believed that the northern colonies were too independent. He wanted them to be more connected to each other and to England. In 1686 James united the northern colonies under one government called the **Dominion of New England**. The Dominion eventually included the colonies of Connecticut, Maine, Massachusetts, New Hampshire, New Jersey, New York, and Rhode Island. James appointed Sir **Edmund Andros** as royal governor of the Dominion. James also chose a royal council for the Dominion.

The Dominion government took the place of the northern colonies' original charters. The king's actions greatly upset many of the colonists. As one colonist grumbled, the Dominion was "without any liberty for an Assembly."

In December 1686 Sir Edmund Andros arrived in Boston. Andros was a former governor of New York. The colonists disliked him, as one pamphlet writer explained.

History Makers Speak

❝Sir Edmund Andros arrived as our governor; who besides his power, with the advice and consent of his Council, to make laws and raise taxes as he pleased, had also authority by himself to muster [gather for military duty] and employ all persons residing in the territory. . . . And several companies of soldiers were now brought from Europe to support what was to be imposed upon us.❞

—"A. B.," quoted in *The Annals of America*

Analyzing Primary Sources

Identifying Points of View
Why does the speaker think the colonists dislike Andros?

In 1687 many residents of Ipswich, Massachusetts, protested Andros's taxation policy. Five were arrested and jailed. To prevent further protests, Andros used his royal authority to limit the powers of town meetings in 1688.

✔ **Reading Check: Summarizing** How did James II and Governor Andros limit New England colonists' participation in government?

★ The Glorious Revolution

The new policies of James II were unpopular in England as well as in the colonies. Parliament felt threatened when he tried to change England from a Protestant country back to a Catholic one. To stop the king, leaders of Parliament asked James's Protestant daughter, Mary, and her husband, William of Orange, to rule England. William, the leader of the Netherlands, landed in England with his army in the fall of 1688. James left the country. The overthrow of James II became known as the **Glorious Revolution**.

Protestant colonists celebrated the crowning of King William and Queen Mary with songs and pictures.

THE GRANGER COLLECTION, NEW YORK

When residents of the Dominion first learned about the Glorious Revolution in 1689, they removed Andros as governor. The delighted colonists sent Andros to England to answer for his actions. The individual colonies left the Dominion and quickly formed new assemblies. They then sent declarations of support for William and Mary. In time, William and Mary replaced the canceled colonial charters. The new charters were like the original ones, except in Massachusetts. The colonists there had originally elected the governor. However, the Crown now chose this person. In addition, men no longer had to be full church members to vote. Instead, they had to own a certain amount of property. Massachusetts also grew in size with the addition of Plymouth and Maine to its territory.

The political ideas of the Glorious Revolution led Parliament to pass the **English Bill of Rights** in 1689. Under this act, the powers of the English monarchy were reduced. At the same time, Parliament gained power. American colonists were greatly interested in this shift in power from the monarch to a representative governing body. As time went on, the colonists valued their own right to elect the representatives that governed them. (See pages 228–29.)

THE GRANGER COLLECTION, NEW YORK

The English Bill of Rights gave greater powers to Parliament, shown here meeting in London's Westminster Hall about 1700.

✔ **Reading Check: Finding the Main Idea** How did the Glorious Revolution and the English Bill of Rights affect the political views of colonists?

Section 1 Review

go.hrw.com **Homework Practice Online** keyword: SF3 HP5

1 **Define** and explain:
- bicameral legislature
- town meeting
- libel

2 **Identify** and explain:
- Privy Council
- Parliament
- House of Burgesses
- John Peter Zenger
- Dominion of New England
- Edmund Andros
- Glorious Revolution
- English Bill of Rights

3 **Contrasting** Copy the chart below. Use it to compare and contrast the powers that different institutions of colonial government held.

Privy Council	
Governors	
Assemblies	
Town Meetings	
Courts	

4 **Finding the Main Idea**
a. Provide at least two examples of how colonists began to develop representative governments.

b. Make a time line that describes the creation of the Dominion of New England, its actions and their effects on the colonies, and the Dominion's end.

5 **Writing and Critical Thinking**
Making Generalizations and Predictions
Imagine that you publish a colonial newspaper. Write an editorial announcing the passage of the English Bill of Rights and predicting its effect on the colonies.

Consider the following:
- reaction to the Glorious Revolution
- the shift toward representative government in England
- the document's guarantee of rights

The Growth of Trade

Read to Discover

1. What effects did the Navigation Acts have on colonial economies?
2. What types of trade took place in the colonies during the 1700s?
3. Why did the colonies participate in the slave trade?

WHY IT MATTERS TODAY

Many countries around the world have formed trading networks. Use CNNfyi.com or other **current events** sources to identify a trading network involving the United States. Record your findings in your journal.

Define

- mercantilism
- balance of trade
- imports
- exports
- duties
- free enterprise
- triangular trade

Identify

- Navigation Acts
- Middle Passage
- Olaudah Equiano

After gaining his freedom, Olaudah Equiano spoke out against slavery and published an account of his life.

The Story Continues

The beat of a drum began trade at the slave market. African slaves stood terrified as buyers rushed in to make their choices. Cries were heard from people who were separated from their family and friends. Such scenes led Olaudah Equiano (oh-LOW-duh ek-wee-AHN-oh), once a slave himself, to ask, "Why are parents to lose their children, brothers their sisters, or husbands their wives?" The answer was money and greed. The slave trade had become an important part of the colonial economy.

★ English Trade Laws

Trade was one of England's main reasons for founding its American colonies. In 1689 an English official pointed out that the colonies made up "a full third part of the whole Trade and Navigation of England." In the late 1600s England, like most western European nations, practiced **mercantilism**. Using this economic system, nations created and maintained wealth by carefully controlling trade. A nation could be self-sufficient if it had a good **balance of trade**. This meant a country had fewer **imports**—goods bought from other countries—than **exports**—goods sold to other countries. Between 1650 and 1696 Parliament passed a series of **Navigation Acts**. These acts required colonists to do the bulk of their trading with England. The Navigation Acts also set **duties**, or import taxes, on some trade products.

England claimed that the Navigation Acts were good for the colonies. After all, the colonies had a steady market in England for their goods. But not everyone agreed. Many colonists wanted more freedom to buy or sell goods in whatever markets offered the best prices. Within the colonies many merchants practiced **free enterprise**—economic competition with little government control. But local demand for colonial goods was small compared to foreign demand for colonial products. English laws limited free enterprise by preventing colonists from selling or buying goods directly to or from many foreign countries. This led to an unfavorable balance of trade for the colonies.

✔ **Reading Check: Analyzing Information** In what ways did mercantilism and the Navigation Acts limit free enterprise in the colonies?

Mercantilism and the Colonies

Under the system of mercantilism, nations such as England tried to control what goods were traded to and from their colonies.

The colonies sold raw materials to England.

Timber

Fur

Tobacco

Furniture

Hardware

Machines

England sold manufactured goods to the colonies.

Colonists were not allowed to trade many of these goods with other countries. They had to buy from and sell only to England.

The colonies

Tobacco

Cotton

Navigation Acts

Fabric

France

Visualizing History

1. **Economics** What were some of the disadvantages that colonists experienced under mercantilism?

2. **Connecting to Today** Do you think American businesses would support such a system today? Why or why not?

⭐ Colonial Trade

Despite colonial complaints, trade restrictions continued into the 1700s. In 1733 Parliament passed the Molasses Act, which placed duties on sugar, molasses, and rum. In response, some colonists began to bring these goods into the colonies illegally, a practice known as smuggling. However, British officials rarely punished these smugglers. One colonial official in Massachusetts complained that he could only enforce the law "with great delay and too many difficulties."

Legal trade was much more significant than smuggling. By the early 1700s the newly unified kingdom of Great Britain was trading around the world. Most American merchants traded directly with Britain or with its colonies in the West Indies. The West Indies produced large amounts of sugar. Writer and economist Adam Smith commented on the wealth that the sugar trade brought to the British West Indies.

Analyzing Primary Sources

Supporting a Point of View
Why does Smith suggest that sugar plantations are particularly important?

History Makers Speak ❝The profits of a [sugar] plantation in any of our West Indian colonies are generally much greater than those of any other cultivation [crop] that is known either in Europe or America.❞

—Adam Smith, *The Wealth of Nations*

Some merchants also took part in the **triangular trade**, which could follow several different routes. In one route the colonies sold goods like fish, grain, beef, and horses to plantation owners in the West Indies. In exchange, merchants received sugar and molasses. Some of these goods were then shipped to Britain. This was just one example of how colonial merchants sought the best markets for their products. This colonial participation in trade all across the Atlantic Ocean was an early form of free enterprise.

✔ **Reading Check: Finding the Main Idea** In what ways were colonists beginning to practice free enterprise?

Interpreting the Visual Record

Sugar refining *Slaves in the West Indies refined sugar by boiling sugarcane and drying the sugar in bins.* **What do you think working conditions in such a refinery would be like?**

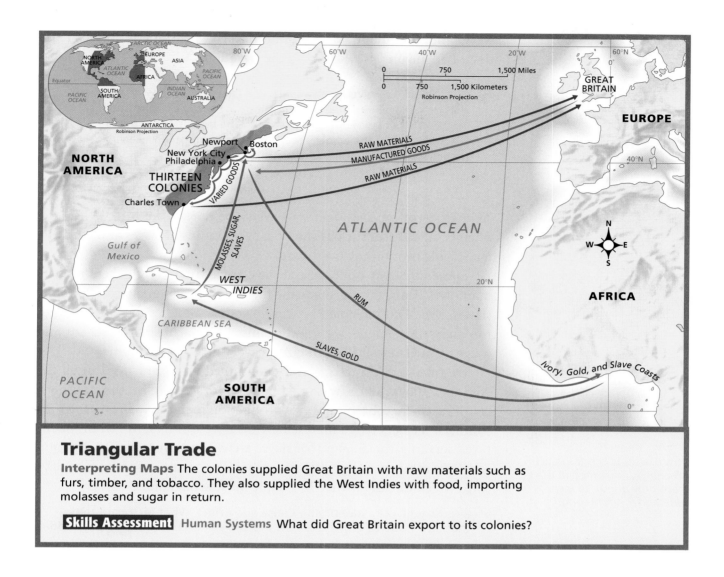

Triangular Trade

Interpreting Maps The colonies supplied Great Britain with raw materials such as furs, timber, and tobacco. They also supplied the West Indies with food, importing molasses and sugar in return.

Skills Assessment Human Systems What did Great Britain export to its colonies?

⭐ The Middle Passage

One version of the triangular trade had a much greater cost in human suffering. It began with New England traders exchanging rum for slaves on the West African coast. The traders then sold the enslaved Africans in the West Indies for molasses or brought them back to sell in the mainland American colonies.

The slave trade brought around 10 million Africans across the Atlantic Ocean. This terrifying and often deadly voyage was called the **Middle Passage**. The journey could last as long as three months. Enslaved Africans were chained by the neck and legs. They lived between the upper and lower decks of the ship, in spaces just a few feet high. Even the sailors remarked on the terrible conditions enslaved Africans faced on the voyage. "They [the Africans] had not so much room as a man in his coffin," wrote one slave ship captain. Slave traders carried as many slaves as possible so they could earn greater profits when they sold their human cargo in North or South America.

Research on the ROM

Free Find:
Olaudah Equiano
After reading about Olaudah Equiano on the **Holt Researcher CD–ROM**, create a brochure for a museum exhibition on Equiano that shows the different stages of his life.

On slave ships like this, each African was confined in a space only about 16 inches wide and 5 ½ feet long.

Olaudah Equiano was sold into slavery when he was about 11. He described life under the decks of the slave ships.

History Makers Speak

❝I received such a salutation [smell] in my nostrils, as I had never experienced in my life; . . . I became so sick and low that I was not able to eat. . . . The groans of the dying rendered [made] the whole a scene of horror almost inconceivable [unbelievable].❞

—Olaudah Equiano, *The Interesting Narrative of the Life of Olaudah Equiano, or Gustavus Vassa, the African*

Thousands of captives died on slave ships during the Middle Passage, often from diseases such as smallpox. Thousands of slaves also committed suicide by jumping overboard.

Some colonists opposed the slave trade. In 1688 Quakers in Germantown, Pennsylvania, made the first recorded colonial protest against slavery. One Quaker stated his view: "To bring men hither [here], or to rob and sell them . . . we stand against." Massachusetts merchant and judge Samuel Sewall also criticized slavery in a 1700 pamphlet.

Despite such protests, slavery continued to be practiced in all the colonies. Slave labor was particularly important in the southern colonies, where tobacco and rice production required many workers. As southern farmers relied increasingly on slave workers instead of indentured servants, the demand for slaves grew. The slave trade also brought wealth to areas that used little slave labor. For example, some of the slave ships were built and owned by people in New England.

✔ **Reading Check: Identifying Cause and Effect** What factors caused the slave trade to grow, and how did this affect conditions on the Middle Passage?

Section 2 Review

go.hrw.com **Homework Practice Online**
keyword: SF3 HP5

1 Define and explain:
• mercantilism
• balance of trade
• imports
• exports
• duties
• free enterprise
• triangular trade

2 Identify and explain:
• Navigation Acts
• Middle Passage
• Olaudah Equiano

3 Summarizing Copy the web diagram below. Fill in each circle with goods and people that came from that region. Use arrows to show what goods were exchanged between the four regions.

The Colonies — Atlantic Ocean — Great Britain

West Indies

West Africa

4 Finding the Main Idea
a. Why did colonists participate in the slave trade?

b. Imagine that you are a British official. How would you address the problem of colonial smuggling?

5 Writing and Critical Thinking
Supporting a Point of View Imagine that you are a New England merchant who supports a freer market in the colonies. Create a handbill that explains the Navigation Acts and mercantilism and that calls for an end to both.

Consider the following:
• the economic effects of the Navigation Acts
• the overseas demand for colonial products
• the benefits of free enterprise

The Colonial Economy

Read to Discover

1. Why were enslaved Africans the main workforce in the southern colonies?
2. How were New England's economic activities different from those of the southern colonies?
3. How did the middle colonies combine economic aspects of the southern and New England colonies?

WHY IT MATTERS TODAY

The different parts of the United States still have different economies. Use **CNN fyi**.com or other **current events** sources to find out about the major economic activities of a region of the United States. Record your findings in your journal.

Define
- cash crops
- slave codes
- apprentices
- staple crops

Identify
- Eliza Lucas Pinckney

The Story Continues

In 1647 Leonard Calvert, the governor of Maryland, lay dying. He asked that Margaret Brent be brought to his bedside. Brent had left England in 1638 to escape religious persecution. She now owned a Maryland plantation. Before witnesses, Governor Calvert said to Brent, "I make you my sole executrix [woman who carries out a will]. Take all and pay all." Brent was well known for her business skills and the management of her plantation. Calvert trusted her to handle his estate wisely.

Leonard Calvert was sent by his older brother, Cecilius Calvert, to rule the Maryland colony.

⭐ Agriculture in the Southern Colonies

The economies of the southern colonies depended on agriculture. They also exported materials for building ships, such as wood and tar. Some colonies also traded with local American Indians for deerskins to sell.

The colonies had many small farms and some large plantations. Farms did well because the South enjoyed a warm climate and long growing season. Many farms grew **cash crops** that were sold for profit. Tobacco, rice, and indigo—a plant used to make blue dye—were the

THE GRANGER COLLECTION, NEW YORK

Charleston, July 24th, 1769.

TO BE SOLD,
On Thursday the third Day
of August next,

A CARGO
OF
NINETY-FOUR
PRIME, HEALTHY

NEGROES,
CONSISTING OF
Thirty-nine MEN, Fifteen BOYS,
Twenty-four WOMEN, and
Sixteen GIRLS.
JUST ARRIVED,
In the Brigantine DEMBIA, Francis Bare, Master, from SIERRA-LEON, by
DAVID & JOHN DEAS.

Daily Life

Tobacco Industry Many of the slaves in the Chesapeake Bay area worked on tobacco plantantions, as shown in this 1670 painting. The tremendous demand for tobacco led planters to increase greatly their production. By the early 1700s the American colonies were exporting millions of pounds of tobacco to Europe. The demand for slave labor also increased. The growing slave trade led to more slave auctions such as the one listed on the poster above. **What does this image suggest about the effort it took to produce tobacco?**

most important cash crops. Virginia specialized in tobacco, and South Carolina specialized in rice and indigo. Eliza Lucas (later **Eliza Lucas Pinckney**) introduced indigo to the colony after she learned how to grow it on her family's plantation.

Crops such as indigo and rice required many workers to grow and harvest. By the 1700s the indentured servants who had first done this labor had been largely replaced by enslaved Africans. Unlike indentured servants, slaves and their children had to work for life.

Slaves performed most of the plantation labor. In his diary, William Byrd II described his daily life as a plantation owner.

 History Makers Speak
“I said my prayers and ate milk for breakfast. I walked out to see my people [slaves] at work at the ditch. I read a little geometry. I ate mutton [sheep] for dinner. I walked to the ditch again. In the evening I said my prayers.”

—William Byrd II, *The Secret Diary of William Byrd of Westover, 1709–1712*

When a job was finished, slaves might be allowed to do their own work. A few slaves were able to earn enough money to buy their freedom.

Most of the southern colonies passed **slave codes**, or laws to control slaves. Colonies with large numbers of slaves had the most extensive slave codes. South Carolina's slaveholders feared that slaves would revolt. As a result, South Carolina's code said slaves could not hold meetings or own weapons. Some colonies did not allow slaveholders to free their slaves. The Virginia Assembly claimed that runaway slaves committed "injuries to the inhabitants of this dominion [colony]." Assembly members passed a law allowing people to kill a runaway slave who resisted capture.

✔ **Reading Check: Summarizing** What role did slavery play in the southern plantation economy, and how was slavery regulated?

★ Industry and Trade in New England

Connecticut, Massachusetts, New Hampshire, and Rhode Island were very different from the southern colonies. The often harsh climate and rocky soil meant that few New England farms grew cash crops. They had little demand for large numbers of farm laborers. Although some people held slaves, slavery did not become as important to this region.

Trade was vital to New England's economy. New England entrepeneurs—people who undertake new businesses to make a profit—traded goods locally, with other colonies, and overseas. Many entrepeneurs traded local products such as furs, pickled beef, and pork.

Fishing and shipbuilding became two of the region's leading industries. One of the earliest settlers in Massachusetts exclaimed, "Here is a good store of fish, if we had boats to go 8 or 10 leagues [about 25 to 30 miles] to sea to fish in." Merchants exported dried fish. Whaling provided valuable oil for lighting. In addition, whale meat became an important part of the colonial diet.

The shipbuilding industry prospered in New England for several reasons. The region had plenty of forests and the local fishing industry needed ships. In addition, as trade in the New England seaports grew, more merchant ships were built. Shipyards throughout New England towns made high-quality, valuable vessels. Shipowners sometimes even told their captains to sell the ship along with the cargo when they reached their destination.

The diverse economy of New England needed skilled craftspeople. Families often sent younger sons off to learn skilled trades such as blacksmithing, weaving, shipbuilding, and printing. The young boys who learned skilled trades were known as **apprentices**. They lived with a master craftsman and learned from him. In exchange, the boys performed simple tasks. Gabriel Ginings was an apprentice in Portsmouth, Rhode Island. He received "sufficient food and raiment [clothing] suitable for such an apprentice," as his 1663 contract stated.

✔ **Reading Check: Contrasting** How were New England's economic activities different from those in the southern colonies, and why was this the case?

CONNECTING TO
SCIENCE AND TECHNOLOGY

Indigo Dye

During colonial times, the finest blue dyes came from an Asian plant called indigo. Indigo was not grown in the American colonies, however, until the mid-1700s. In 1740 Eliza Lucas (later Eliza Lucas Pinckney) began growing indigo on her family's plantation in South Carolina.

Removing the blue compounds from indigo was hard work. Skilled workers—usually slaves—had to soak, whip, and strain the plants for many hours. It took around 100 pounds of indigo plants to make a single four-ounce indigo bar!

By 1747 South Carolina was exporting more than 135,000 pounds of indigo each year. Today artificial indigo dye is used to color clothes such as blue jeans. **How did Eliza Lucas Pinckney contribute to indigo production?**

THE GRANGER COLLECTION, NEW YORK

Tremendous labor went into building sailing ships such as these three vessels in a New England shipyard.

133

⭐ The Middle Colonies

The middle colonies—Delaware, Pennsylvania, New Jersey, and New York—combined qualities of the New England and southern colonies. With a good growing season and rich land, farmers there could grow large amounts of food. The middle colonies grew **staple crops**, or crops that are always needed. Some of these crops were wheat, barley, and oats. Farmers also raised and sold livestock.

Slaves were more important to the middle colonies than they were to New England. They worked in cities as skilled laborers, such as black-smiths and carpenters. Other slaves also worked on farms, in dockyards, on board ships, and in the growing shipbuilding industry. However, indentured servants largely filled the middle colonies' growing labor needs. Between 1700 and 1775 about 135,000 indentured servants came to the middle colonies from Britain and Germany. About half of them moved to Pennsylvania. By the mid-1700s Philadelphia had become one of the largest British colonial cities. Other cities in the middle colonies, such as New York City, also grew quickly.

Trade and free enterprise were important to the economy of the middle colonies. Merchants in Philadelphia and New York City exported colonial goods to markets in Britain and the West Indies. These products included wheat from New York. Colonial merchants also sold wheat and flour from Pennsylvania and New Jersey. Through hard work, they could make a comfortable living. A Philadelphia merchant noted this in a letter he wrote in 1768. He said that he was able "to live well, but [I] have not been able to lay up such a Stock, as would maintain me without daily labor."

✔ **Reading Check: Comparing** How did geography factors affect agriculture in each colonial region?

CONNECTING TO MATH

Just the Facts

African American Population in the American Colonies

Year	Population of African Ancestry	Total Population
1660	2,920	75,058
1680	6,971	151,507
1700	27,817	250,888
1720	68,839	466,185
1740	150,024	905,563
1760	325,806	1,593,625
1780	575,420	2,780,369

Using Mathematical Skills

1. About what percent of the colonial population in 1660 were people of African ancestry? About what percent were they in 1760?

2. Create a line graph showing these population figures.

3. Imagine that you are a colonial Quaker who opposes slavery. Prepare a pamphlet attacking the rise of slavery in the colonies, using these statistics to support your argument.

Philadelphia was a major center of colonial trade.

RARE BOOK DEPARTMENT, THE FREE LIBRARY OF PHILADELPHIA

⭐ Women and the Economy

Throughout the colonies, women made important contributions to the economy. They ran farms and businesses, such as clothing and grocery stores, bakeries, and drugstores. A few female shopkeepers used their business success to call for a voice in colonial politics. One group of women wrote to a New York newspaper in 1733.

History Makers Speak ❝We are House keepers, Pay our taxes, carry on Trade, and most of us are the Merchants, and as we in some measure contribute to the Support of Government, we ought to be Intitled to some of the Sweets of it.❞

—New York shopkeepers, quoted in *Colonial Women of Affairs*, by Elisabeth Anthony Dexter

Plantation manager Margaret Brent—shown here speaking to colonial officials—was respected for her business skills.

Some women also practiced medicine, often as nurses and midwives. However, colonial laws and customs limited women's economic activities. Typically, a married woman could not work outside the home without her husband's permission. A husband also had the right to keep the money his wife earned.

Most colonial women worked in the home. Married women managed households and raised children. Sometimes they earned money for their families by washing clothes or selling products such as butter. Many women made items that their family needed, such as clothing.

✔ **Reading Check: Finding the Main Idea** How did women play important roles in the colonial economy?

Section 3 Review

go.hrw.com **Homework Practice Online**

keyword: SF3 HP5

1 **Define** and explain:
- cash crops
- slave codes
- apprentices
- staple crops

2 **Identify** and explain:
- Eliza Lucas Pinckney

3 **Comparing and Contrasting** Copy the graphic organizer below. Use it to compare and contrast the characteristics of the economies of the three major colonial regions.

4 **Finding the Main Idea**
a. Why was slavery common on southern plantations, and how did it affect laws in the southern colonies?

b. What types of contributions did women make to the colonial economy?

5 **Writing and Critical Thinking**
Summarizing Imagine that you are going to participate in a debate about the different colonial economic regions. Write a speech explaining how and why the middle colonies are similar to and different from the southern and New England colonies.

Consider the following:
- the economic activities of each region
- the labor required by each region
- the physical features of each region

The Great Awakening

Read to Discover

1. What was the message of the Great Awakening?
2. How did the Great Awakening change colonial religious organizations and leaders?
3. How did the Great Awakening change colonial society?

WHY IT MATTERS TODAY

In some countries religious differences have led to conflict. Use CNN fyi.com or other **current events** sources to find out about a country where groups with different religious beliefs are either involved in or resolving a conflict. Record your findings in your journal.

Define

- revivals

Identify

- Great Awakening
- Jonathan Edwards
- George Whitefield
- Gilbert Tennent

The Story Continues

One morning a Connecticut farmer and his wife heard that George Whitefield would be preaching in a nearby town. They quickly dropped their work. As fast as they could, they rushed to make the 12-mile journey. Still several miles from the meeting site, the couple met a line of horses carrying fellow travelers. To the farmer, each horse appeared "to go with all his might to carry his rider to hear news from heaven for the saving of souls." After hearing Whitefield's message, the inspired farmer joined others who had religious conversions. "I was born on Feb 15th 1711 and born again Octo 1741," he later wrote in the first line of his autobiography.

★ Words of the Great Awakening

In the early 1700s many church leaders worried that colonists were losing their religious faith. These leaders wanted to bring back the sense of religious duty held by previous generations. Some believed that emotional and inspiring sermons would revive interest in religion. Several ministers in the middle colonies began holding **revivals**, emotional gatherings where people came together to hear sermons and declare their faith.

Because of these ministers' work, many colonists experienced "a great awakening" in their religious lives. This **Great Awakening** reached its height in the 1730s and 1740s. It was a widespread Christian movement involving sermons and revivals that emphasized faith in God. The Great Awakening changed not only colonial religion but also social and political life. **Jonathan Edwards** was one of the most important leaders of the Great Awakening. He was a pastor of the Congregational Church in Northampton, Massachusetts. Edwards's dramatic sermons urged sinners to seek forgiveness for their sins or face punishment in Hell forever.

In 1739 British minister **George Whitefield** made the second of his seven trips to America. On this visit he held revivals from Georgia to New England. Whitefield became one of the most popular ministers of the Great Awakening. Because of Whitefield, thousands of colonists found new faith in Christianity. New England farmer Nathan Cole was one of many people who found Whitefield's message inspiring.

Interpreting the Visual Record

Revival *The Great Awakening preacher George Whitefield could draw crowds of thousands to his outdoor revival meetings.* **How does this image suggest the power of Whitefield's preaching?**

 History Makers Speak ❝When I saw Mr. Whitefield come upon the scaffold [platform], he looked almost angelical [like an angel]. . . . And my hearing how God was with him everywhere as he came along, it solemnized [made serious] my mind and put me into a trembling fear before he began to preach; for he looked as if he was clothed with authority from the Great God . . . and my hearing him preach gave me a heart wound.❞

—Nathan Cole, quoted in *The Great Awakening*, edited by Alan Heimert and Perry Miller

Analyzing Primary Sources
Identifying Points of View Why does Cole feel that Mr. Whitefield's words are important?

The ministers of the Great Awakening preached that all people were born sinners who could only be saved by the will of God. However, the opportunity to be saved was available to all—rich and poor alike—who confessed their sins and accepted God's grace. This message brought hope to many people. However, the ministers of the Great Awakening could use a threatening tone. Jonathan Edwards's 1741 sermon *Sinners in the Hands of an Angry God* called up frightening images. "God . . . holds you over the pit of hell, much as one holds a spider, or some loathsome [disgusting] insect over the fire."

✔ **Reading Check: Finding the Main Idea** What did preachers of the Great Awakening and their followers believe?

Minister Jonathan Edwards was known for sermons such as Sinners in the Hands of an Angry God.

THE GRANGER COLLECTION, NEW YORK

Not all colonists believed in these new religious ideas. Eventually, some church congregations divided because of disagreements. There were traditionalists and those who followed the new ministers. In New England the traditionalists were called the "Old Lights." The followers of the Great Awakening were called the "New Lights."

Old Light ministers did not believe that the enthusiasm of the Great Awakening could truly awaken one's spirituality. Charles Chauncy of Boston's First Church agreed with this view. He stated that anyone who took part in such revivals was "under no other influence than that of an over-heated imagination." Chauncy thought that this excited form of religion was not a proper way to try to save one's soul.

The Great Awakening also changed the Presbyterian Church in the middle colonies. Presbyterian minister **Gilbert Tennent** was a leader of the new movement. His sermons attacked the traditionalists. As a result of Tennent's efforts, the Presbyterian Church split into two groups with opposing views on the revival movement. These became known as the "Old Side" and the "New Side."

In the middle and southern colonies, particularly Virginia, the Great Awakening greatly increased church membership. Much of this growth took place among the Baptists and Methodists. The Great Awakening was also influential on the frontier, where traveling preachers held revivals in small towns. There were few churches on the frontier. Therefore, these ministers were important to settlers.

Traditional and new ideas were in conflict even in these distant areas, however. Frontier missionary Charles Woodmason tried to oppose the changes brought about by the Great Awakening. He expressed his frustration.

> **History Makers Speak**
>
> ❝If I give out [announce] to be at such a Place at such a Time, three or four of these fellows [Great Awakening ministers] are constantly at my Heels—They either get there before me, and hold forth—or after I have finish'd, or the next Day, or for days together. Had I a hundred Tongues, or as many Pairs of Legs, I could not singly [alone] oppose such a Numerous Crew.❞
>
> —Charles Woodmason, quoted in *The Power of Words*, edited by T. H. Breen

✔ **Reading Check: Identifying Cause and Effect** What conflicts did the Great Awakening cause, and what were some of the effects of these conflicts?

Research on the R⊙M

Free Find:
Jonathan Edwards
After reading about Jonathan Edwards on the **Holt Researcher CD–ROM**, imagine that you had attended one of his sermons. Write a letter to a friend. In the letter, explain how Edwards's ideas were different from what other Protestants of the time believed.

Analyzing Primary Sources

Drawing Inferences and Conclusions Why might ministers of the Great Awakening want to follow Woodmason to places he was going to deliver sermons?

★ The Great Awakening and Society

The Great Awakening attracted people of different classes and races. Women, members of minority groups, and poor people often took part in services. Women in particular welcomed the message of the Great Awakening. Many women sought spiritual renewal around the time of childbirth. They were interested in part because their lives were at risk during this time. One woman explained that her faith "would wear off again 'till the time of my first Lying in [labor]; and then I was . . . brought to the very brink of eternity." Both free and enslaved African Americans were drawn to the Great Awakening's message of acceptance and spiritual equality. Despite the stated belief in equality, however, some revivals were separated by race.

Before the Great Awakening, there was little communication between people living in different colonies. This changed as ministers began moving about and exchanging ideas. Educational opportunities also improved as many colleges were founded to provide religious instruction. Such efforts helped bring together the different colonial regions.

The Great Awakening promoted ideals that may also have affected colonial politics. Sermons about the spiritual equality of all people led some colonists to begin demanding more political equality. Revivals became popular places to talk about political and social issues. As a result of sharing new ideas, some colonists began to question the authority of existing institutions.

This illustration shows the First Baptist Church of Providence, Rhode Island. Baptist congregations were among those that grew rapidly during the Great Awakening.

✔ **Reading Check: Summarizing** How did the Great Awakening change colonial communities and society?

Section 4 Review

go.hrw.com
Homework Practice Online
keyword: SF3 HP5

1 **Define** and explain:
• revivals

2 **Identify** and explain:
• Great Awakening
• Jonathan Edwards
• George Whitefield
• Gilbert Tennent

3 **Identifying Cause and Effect** Copy the cause-and-effect chart below. Fill in at least three causes and effects relating to why the Great Awakening came about and how it affected society.

Great Awakening

Cause		Effect
	→	
	→	
	→	

4 **Finding the Main Idea**
a. What message did preachers of the Great Awakening tell their followers?

b. Why might the teachings of the Great Awakening have led to a movement for greater democracy?

5 **Writing and Critical Thinking**
Analyzing Information Imagine that you are a leader of a church that has become divided between New Lights and Old Lights. Write a story to share with church members that describes the problems faced by churches such as yours.

Consider the following:
• the beliefs of the Old Lights and New Lights
• religion on the frontier
• the splitting of some religious groups

American Culture

Read to Discover

1. How did both the Scientific Revolution and the Enlightenment reflect new ways of thinking?
2. What was education like during colonial times?
3. What were Benjamin Franklin's key achievements?
4. What contributions were made to American culture in the 1700s?

WHY IT MATTERS TODAY

Scientists are always making new, important discoveries. Use **CNNfyi.com** or other **current events** sources to learn more about a new scientific discovery. Think about fields such as medicine or computer science. Record your findings in your journal.

Define

• scientific method

Identify

• Scientific Revolution
• Galileo Galilei
• Isaac Newton
• Enlightenment
• David Rittenhouse
• Benjamin Banneker
• Benjamin Franklin
• Anne Bradstreet
• Phillis Wheatley

Galileo built and decorated his first telescope by hand.

The Story Continues

Night after night in 1610 Italian scientist Galileo Galilei looked up at the sky. People had long believed that Earth was the center of the universe. Galileo, however, began to doubt this idea. He used his newly built telescope to view Jupiter and observed small moons around this planet. This discovery told him that not everything in the universe moved around Earth. Other scientists began to share Galileo's views. They thought that many other ideas about the natural world also needed to be reconsidered.

⭐ New Ideas in Europe

During the 1600s Western Europeans began to re-examine their world. As scientists performed more experiments, they made exciting discoveries. Scientists began to better understand the basic laws that govern nature. Their new ideas about the universe began what is known as the **Scientific Revolution**. This revolution began in mathematics and astronomy, but it later changed all areas of natural science.

Galileo Galilei was one of the leading figures in the Scientific Revolution. He demonstrated that the planets revolve around the Sun. In the late 1600s Sir **Isaac Newton** explained how objects on Earth and in the sky behaved. His theories proved that the same laws of physics govern both. He also developed much of the scientific method used today. The scientific method requires that scientists carefully study natural events. Scientists then form theories based on their observations and experiments. These ideas can be used to predict other behaviors or events. Scientists then test their theories as they learn new facts.

The Scientific Revolution also began changing the way people viewed human actions. This change in thought is often called the Age of Reason, or the **Enlightenment**. The Enlightenment took place during the 1700s. Enlightenment philosophers used reason and logic, much as scientists were doing. These thinkers, however, studied human nature and suggested ways to improve their world. Jean-Jacques Rousseau (roo-SOH), Voltaire, and Baron de Montesquieu (mohn-tes-kyoo) all formed ideas about how government should work to best serve the people.

Some Enlightenment thinkers believed that there was a social contract between government and citizens. With this contract, rulers needed the consent of the governed. Philosophers such as John Locke believed that people had natural rights such as equality and liberty. Locke stated that people should obey their rulers only if the state protected their life, liberty, and property. Eventually the ideas of the Scientific Revolution and the Enlightenment began to influence some colonial leaders.

✔ **Reading Check: Summarizing** What changes in ways of thinking took place in the 1600s and 1700s in Europe?

LINKING
PAST *to* PRESENT

Public Schools

Today most Americans consider public education to be a basic right. This was not the case in colonial America. In many places children received little or no formal education. Pennsylvania and most New England colonies were exceptions to this rule. In 1642 Massachusetts passed one of the first public education laws in Europe or the Americas. In 1683, Quaker officials passed laws requiring all children in Pennsylvania to learn how to read and write. Quaker leaders also decided to offer free schooling for poor children. In both Massachusetts and Pennsylvania male and female children received instruction. **How does current education compare with colonial public education? Use examples to support your answer.**

N   NOAH did view
     The old world & new

O   Young OBADIAS,
     DAVID, JOSIAS
     All were pious.

P   PETER deny'd
     His Lord and cry'd.

A page from the *New England Primer*, a colonial schoolbook

⭐ Colonial Education

In the colonies few people could afford a formal education. The availability of schooling also varied widely in the colonies. For example, there were more schools in New England than in the southern and middle colonies. New England colonists particularly valued the ability to read the Bible. They also wanted to make sure future generations had educated ministers. Therefore, communities founded and paid for town schools. Schoolchildren often used the *New England Primer*, which had characters and stories from the Bible. They learned to read at the same time that they learned about the community's religious values. In the middle and southern colonies, most children lived far from towns. They had to be taught by their parents or private tutors.

Most colonial children stopped their education after the elementary grades. Many went to work, either on the family farm or away from home. Some boys became apprentices. In New England and in the middle colonies, some girls became servants for other families.

Yale College, in New Haven, Connecticut, was founded in 1701.

A growing number of young men did attend universities. In 1636 colonists in Massachusetts founded Harvard College. Colonists went on to establish nine colleges, most of which were in the middle colonies and in New England. The classes at many of these colleges focused on religion. Some young men also went to English universities to study the sciences or law. Others studied at a colonial college and then trained with a professional in their field.

✔ **Reading Check: Contrasting** How did education in the New England colonies compare to schooling in the middle and southern colonies?

THE GRANGER COLLECTION, NEW YORK

THE GRANGER COLLECTION, NEW YORK

★★★★★★★★★★★★
That's Interesting!
★★★★★★★★★★★★

Banneker's Clock Did you know that Benjamin Banneker was the first colonist to build a clock? It's true! He did this even though he had never seen one before. In his early twenties, Banneker, who only had a few years of formal education, designed and built a clock. He used only a picture of a clock from an English journal and a geometry book for help. The clock kept time with great accuracy. His clock is said to have run for over 40 years.

★ Colonial Scientists

Although few schools taught science, there were several talented scientists in the colonies. These scientists taught themselves by observing the world around them. In 1743 the American Philosophical Society was founded in Philadelphia for the study of science. Its members also wanted to improve communication among colonial scientists. **David Rittenhouse**, the society's second president, designed mathematical and astronomical instruments. Thomas Jefferson thought Rittenhouse was "second to no astronomer living."

Rittenhouse admired the astronomer and surveyor **Benjamin Banneker**, a free African American who lived in Maryland. In 1789 Banneker predicted a solar eclipse—when the Moon passes in front of the Sun. Banneker published his work in an almanac.

Botanist John Bartram was also self-taught. He traveled throughout the colonies studying plants and founded a botanical garden. Bartram also exchanged plants and information with scientists in Britain.

★ Benjamin Franklin

Perhaps the most famous colonial scientist was **Benjamin Franklin**. A man with many interests, Franklin was one of the most important thinkers of his time. He was born in Boston in 1706 and worked first in his father's candle and soap shop. Later he became an apprentice in his brother's printing shop. In 1723 Franklin moved to Philadelphia. In his mid-20s, he started a newspaper, which quickly became the most successful paper in the colonies. Franklin published *Poor Richard's Almanack* between 1732 and 1757. He wrote the almanac under the made-up name of Richard Saunders. Franklin came up with sayings that are still used today, including "Early to Bed, and early to rise, makes a Man healthy, wealthy and wise." Poor Richard offered much additional advice.

> **❝If you would be wealthy, think of Saving as well as of Getting: The Indies have not made Spain rich, because her Outgoes [expenses] are greater than her Incomes.❞**
>
> —Poor Richard (Benjamin Franklin), quoted in *Anthology of American Literature, Volume I,* 2nd edition

Analyzing Primary Sources
Identifying Points of View
What does Franklin advise a person to do in order to get rich?

Franklin believed that reason could be used to make life better for people. During his life, he invented many useful devices. The lightning rod reduced the risk of fire started by electrical storms. The Franklin stove heated homes better than previous stoves had. Franklin also invented bifocals, eyeglasses with lenses that correct for both far- and nearsightedness. Franklin once said he was "glad of an opportunity to serve others" through his inventions. He did not take out patents on his work because he wanted all people to benefit from his good ideas.

Franklin also conducted many scientific experiments. He flew a kite during a thunderstorm in 1752 as an experiment to prove lightning is a form of electricity. He also found the positive and negative charges in electricity. These discoveries made him well known in the colonies and in Europe. Thomas Jefferson even boasted:

> **❝We [Americans] have produced a Franklin, than whom no one of the present age has made more important discoveries, nor has enriched philosophy [improved scientific knowledge] with more, or more ingenious [clever] solutions of the phaenomena [events] of nature.❞**
>
> —Thomas Jefferson, quoted in *The Americans: The Colonial Experience,* by Daniel J. Boorstin

Franklin helped people in other ways as well. He started the first subscription library in the colonies, and opened an academy that later became the University of Pennsylvania. In addition, Franklin founded the American Philosophical Society.

✔ **Reading Check: Drawing Inferences and Conclusions** How are Franklin's many accomplishments alike?

Benjamin Franklin served as the first president of the American Philosophical Society, which he helped found.

BIOGRAPHY

Phillis Wheatley

c. 1753–1784

Phillis Wheatley was one of the first African Americans to be published. She was educated by the Boston family that bought her as a slave in 1761. Wheatley began writing poetry while still a teenager. Her first poem was published in 1770. In 1773 the Wheatleys freed Phillis so that she could go to England. While there she published a book of poetry. After both of the Wheatleys died, Phillis married John Peters. **What is remarkable about Phillis Wheatley's career?**

★ Colonial Writers and Artists

Self-taught writers and artists also contributed to colonial American culture. Religious speech and writing changed the colonies in many ways. Ministers such as John Cotton, Jonathan Edwards, and Cotton Mather developed a new American way of preaching, revealed in their dramatic sermons.

New England poet **Anne Bradstreet** wrote about her love for her family and her faith. Her poetry was published in *The Tenth Muse* in London in 1650. **Phillis Wheatley** also used religious language and imagery in her poetry. In "On Being Brought from Africa to America," Wheatley described how Christianity changed her life.

In the early 1700s the fine arts began to grow in the colonies. A few European artists came to America to paint and teach. British-born painter John Smibert held the first art exhibition in the English colonies in Boston in 1730. His pupil, American-born portrait artist Robert Feke, became a widely admired painter. Most colonial artists painted portraits because they were popular with colonists.

Colonial architecture and household furniture also improved in style and quality. The houses of the richest colonists were often made of brick, not wood, and were often built in fancy British styles. Inside these homes beautiful furniture showed the talents of highly skilled local carpenters and cabinetmakers. These changes reflected the general improvement in the colonists' lives.

✔ **Reading Check: Analyzing Information** What areas of the arts did colonists begin to pursue, and how did interest in the arts change over time in the colonies?

Section 5 Review

go.hrw.com **Homework Practice Online**
keyword: SF3 HP5

★ ★

1 **Define** and explain:
• scientific method

2 **Identify** and explain:
• Scientific Revolution
• Galileo Galilei
• Sir Isaac Newton
• Enlightenment
• David Rittenhouse
• Benjamin Banneker
• Benjamin Franklin
• Anne Bradstreet
• Phillis Wheatley

3 **Summarizing** Copy the table below. Use it to list three important achievements made during colonial times for each category.

Science			
Writing			
Art			

4 **Finding the Main Idea**
a. What new ways of thinking resulted from the Scientific Revolution and the Enlightenment?

b. How does education in colonial times compare with modern schooling?

5 **Writing and Critical Thinking**
Supporting a Point of View Imagine that you are a teenager living in colonial Philadelphia. You would like to serve as an apprentice to Benjamin Franklin. Write a letter to Franklin explaining why you would like to study with him and what you hope to learn.

Consider the following:
• Franklin's inventions and scientific experiments

• Franklin's writings

• Franklin's contributions to his community

Benjamin Franklin's *Autobiography*

Benjamin Franklin's Autobiography *was not published until the year after his death. Many people believe Franklin's* Autobiography *to be a classic of American literature. Franklin's simple, clear writing influenced and inspired many American readers. The success of the* Autobiography *popularized the autobiography as a literary form.*

The Autobiography *also emphasized one of the values closely associated with the American character—self-reliance. In the following passage, Franklin shares his strategy for leading a successful life.*

Benajmin Franklin's Autobiography *was full of advice for readers.*

It was about this time that I **conceiv'd**[1] the bold and **arduous**[2] Project of arriving at moral Perfection. . . . As I knew, or thought I knew, what was right and wrong, I did not see why I might not always do the one and avoid the other. But I soon found I had undertaken a Task of more Difficulty than I have imagined. . . . I therefore **contriv'd**[3] the following Method. . . . I proposed to myself, for the sake of clearness, to use rather more names with fewer ideas **annexed**[4] to each than a few names with more ideas, and I included after . . . Names of Virtues all that at that time occurr'd to me as necessary or desirable, and annex'd to each a short **Precept**[5] . . . .

1. **Temperance** Eat not to Dulness. Drink not to Elevation.
2. **Silence** Speak not but what may benefit others or yourself. Avoiding **trifling**[6] Conversation.
3. **Order** Let all your Things have their Places. Let each Part of your Business have its Time.
4. **Resolution** Resolve to perform what you ought. Perform without fail what you resolve.
5. **Frugality** Make no Expense but to do good to others or yourself: **i.e.**[7], Waste nothing.
6. **Industry** Lose no Time. Be always employ'd in something useful. Cut off all unnecessary Actions.
7. **Sincerity** Use no hurtful Deceit. Think innocently and justly; and, if you speak, speak accordingly.
8. **Justice** Wrong none by doing Injuries or omitting the Benefits that are your Duty.
9. **Moderation** Avoid extremes. **Forbear**[8] resenting Injuries so much as you think they deserve.
10. **Cleanliness** Tolerate no Uncleanness in Body, Clothes or **Habitation**.[9]
11. **Tranquility** Be not disturbed at trifles or at accidents common or unavoidable.

Understanding What You Read

1. **Literature and History** What similarities exist among the virtues that Franklin lists?
2. **Literature and You** Do you think the virtues described by Franklin represent universal themes that still matter today? Explain your answer.

---

[1] **conceiv'd:** thought up
[2] **arduous:** difficult
[3] **contriv'd:** developed

[4] **annexed:** attached
[5] **precept:** rule
[6] **trifling:** unimportant

[7] **i.e.:** that is
[8] **forbear:** keep from
[9] **habitation:** home

Chapter 5 Review

The Chapter at a Glance

Examine the visual summary of the chapter below. Create a written summary of colonial events and achievements based on the drawing.

Government

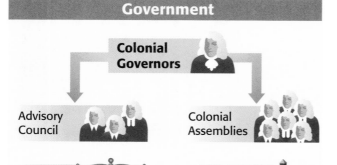

Colonial Governors

Advisory Council

Colonial Assemblies

Colonial Courts

Town Meetings

Economy

New England
Fishing, Manufacturing, Small Farms, Trade

Middle Colonies
Large Farms, Staple Crops, Trade

Southern Colonies
Cash Crops, Plantations, Slave System

Society

The Great Awakening

Colonial Culture

Identifying People and Ideas

Use the following terms or people in historically significant sentences.

1. House of Burgesses
2. English Bill of Rights
3. mercantilism
4. Middle Passage
5. cash crops
6. slave codes
7. Eliza Lucas Pinckney
8. Great Awakening
9. Benjamin Franklin
10. Anne Bradstreet

Understanding Main Ideas

Section 1 *(Pages 120–125)*

1. What roles did governors, assemblies, courts, and town meetings play in local governments?
2. Why were colonists interested in the Glorious Revolution and the English Bill of Rights?

Section 2 *(Pages 126–130)*

3. Why did mercantilism and English trade laws upset colonial merchants and farmers?
4. What items were part of the triangular trade?

Section 3 *(Pages 131–135)*

5. How did the economies of the New England, middle, and southern colonies differ?

Section 4 *(Pages 136–139)*

6. How did the Great Awakening change colonial society?

Section 5 *(Pages 140–144)*

7. Who were the most important writers and artists of the colonial period, and what were some of their accomplishments?

You Be the Historian— Reviewing Themes

1. **Economics** Why did England pass the Navigation Acts?
2. **Geography** How was the economy of each colonial region affected by its geography?
3. **Science, Technology & Society** In what ways did Benjamin Franklin's scientific discoveries and inventions benefit the colonies?

Thinking Critically

1. **Analyzing Information** Why did colonists begin thinking about representative government and political equality?
2. **Drawing Inferences and Conclusions** Why did much of the slave trade take place in northern ports?
3. **Evaluating** In what ways did the colonists practice free enterprise, and how did this benefit the colonies?

Interpreting Graphs

Study the graph below. Then use the information in the graph to help you answer the following questions.

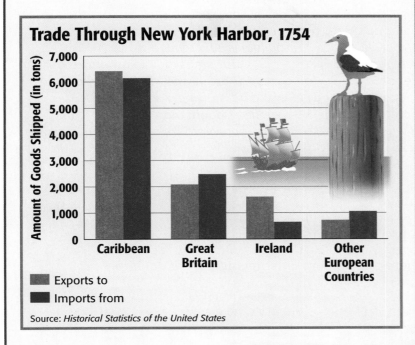

Trade Through New York Harbor, 1754

Amount of Goods Shipped (in tons)

- Exports to
- Imports from

Source: *Historical Statistics of the United States*

1. About how many tons of goods did the American colonies export to Great Britain through New York Harbor?
   a. less than 1,000
   b. more than 6,000
   c. about 4,400
   d. about 2,000

2. Based on your knowledge of the period, why do you think the amount of trade with the Caribbean was so much higher than with other areas?

Analyzing Primary Sources

Read the following quote about the rules of Harvard College written by the clergymen Hugh Peter and Thomas Weld. Then answer the questions that follow.

66 Studiously redeem [make use of] the time, observe the general hours appointed for all the students, and the special hours for their own classes, and then diligently attend the lectures without any disturbance by word or gesture. . . . Every scholar shall be present in his tutor's chamber at the seventh hour in the morning, immediately after the sound of the bell . . . so also at the fifth hour at night, and then give account of his own private reading . . . and constantly attend lectures in the hall at the hours appointed. 99

3. Which of the following statements best describes the schedule of the Harvard students?
   a. They could attend classes whenever they pleased and study on their own time.
   b. They had to report to tutors in the morning and evening and also go to other classes.
   c. They had to go to class from seven in the morning till five at night.
   d. Students had to attend classes regularly and were expected to ask many questions during lectures.

4. How do these requirements compare to a typical day at your school?

Alternative Assessment

Building Your Portfolio

American History

Linking to Community
Private citizens still play an important part in local government. Using newspapers and other resources, find out about an issue in your community that has been raised at a town meeting or a council meeting. Learn about different opinions on the issue as well as what actions were taken. Then write a dramatization of the meeting showing the views of all the participants. Perform the dramatization with some of your classmates.

internet connect

Internet Activity: go.hrw.com
keyword: SF3 CF5

Choose a topic about life in the English colonies to:

- Analyze the impact of the Zenger case on the concept of freedom of the press.
- Create a model of a concept or theory from the Scientific Revolution.
- Explore modern trade in the original thirteen colonies and create a map.

go. hrw .com

Colonial Economies

Many settlers came to the American colonies for economic opportunities. For example, there was a great demand in Europe for furs from North America. Europeans explored north and west looking for new sources of furs.

As the colonies grew, they also became a rich source of farm products. The colonies exported tobacco, rice, and wheat to Great Britain. Plantation owners expanded agri-cultural production in the southern colonies. As they did so, they imported many enslaved Africans to work their plantations. Slaves cleared land, put up buildings, and tended crops.

As a result of their many efforts, many colonists often were able to improve their standard of living. As settlements grew and colonists sought more land, they came increasingly into conflict with American Indians.

Colonial Trade and Industry

The British colonies produced a variety of goods for sale around the world. Most exports went to Britain, but markets in the West Indies and Europe were also important shipping destinations.

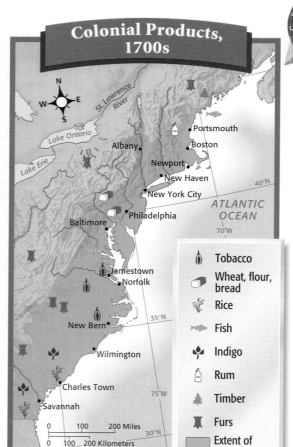

Colonial Products, 1700s

Portsmouth
Albany
Boston
Newport
New Haven
New York City
Philadelphia
Baltimore
Jamestown
Norfolk
New Bern
Wilmington
Charles Town
Savannah

ATLANTIC OCEAN

St. Lawrence River
Lake Ontario
Lake Erie

40°N
70°W
35°N
75°W
30°N

0   100   200 Miles
0 100 200 Kilometers
Albers Equal-Area Projection

Tobacco
Wheat, flour, bread
Rice
Fish
Indigo
Rum
Timber
Furs
Extent of settlement

Geography **Skills**

Interpreting Thematic Maps

1. Where was fish an important colonial product?
2. **Places and Regions** In what area of the colonies was tobacco an important product?
3. **Drawing Inferences and Conclusions** Why do you think the towns shown on the map were important to colonial trade?

Colonial Boston Harbor

British Colonial Exports, 1770

Percentage of total value of exports from the British colonies by destination*

51%

24.7%

20.1%

3.5%

less than 1%

- Great Britain
- West Indies
- Southern Europe
- Ireland
- Africa

*Includes Bahamas, Bermuda, and Newfoundland

Source: *Historical Statistics of the United States*

History Note 1

In the 1700s, most exports from the thirteen colonies went to Great Britain. In recent years, however, most U.S. trade has stayed closer to home. Canada and Mexico are now major markets for U.S. exports. The United States also imports many goods from these two neighboring nations.

Many colonial goods were shipped in barrels.

Geography **Skills**
Interpreting Pie Graphs

1. What percentage of the total value of British exports from colonies in North America went to Britain in 1770?

2. Human Systems Which destination received the smallest percentage of the value of colonial exports?

3. Analyzing Information Rank each of the destinations shown on the pie graph in order of their importance to the colonial economy. Show your list to a fellow student. Ask him or her to explain why the colonists traded the most with the top two destinations on the list.

History Note 2

Which colony's settlers were the wealthiest? One way to address this question is to compare the average net worth per person in each area. Net worth equals the total value of a person's property, cash, and all other possessions of value minus the debts that they owe. In 1774 a free settler in the southern colonies had more than twice the net worth of a free settler in the middle colonies. A southern settler's net worth was about four times that of a free settler in New England.

The Growth of the Fur Trade in North America

Legend:
- British
- Spanish
- French
- Claimed by Britain and France
- Claimed by Britain and Spain
- HURON Indian group
- → French inland trading route, 1680s
- → French inland trading route, 1750s
- → Major shipping route
- ⬠ French fort or trading post, 1680s
- ● French fort or trading post, 1750s
- ▲ British fort or trading post

Geography Skills

Interpreting Thematic Maps

1. Which nation's trading posts were located farthest north?

2. **Human Systems** What French town was located farthest south? What British town was located farthest south?

3. **Evaluating** How would the location of these two southern towns have made them important to the French and the British?

History Note 3

The fur trade was very important to French Canada. The French built trading forts along rivers west of the British colonies to protect the fur trade. The thirteen colonies concentrated more on agriculture, although some British colonists traded in furs.

The Slave Trade

Colonial settlers in the Americas imported many enslaved Africans to clear land and plant crops. Slaves were particularly important in the southern British colonies. In these colonies tobacco, rice, and indigo were often grown on large plantations.

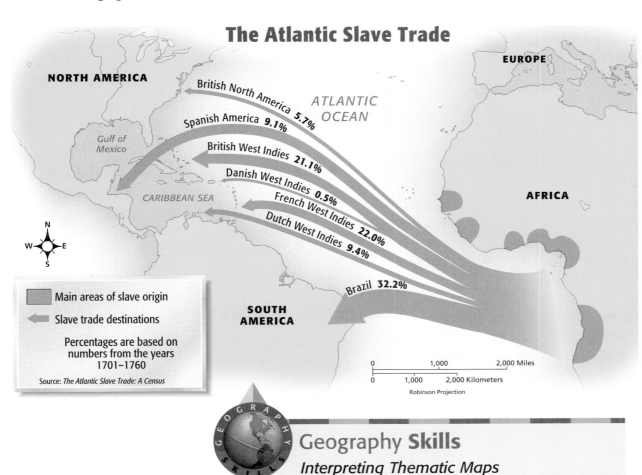

The Atlantic Slave Trade

British North America 5.7%
Spanish America 9.1%
British West Indies 21.1%
Danish West Indies 0.5%
French West Indies 22.0%
Dutch West Indies 9.4%
Brazil 32.2%

Main areas of slave origin

Slave trade destinations

Percentages are based on numbers from the years 1701–1760

Source: *The Atlantic Slave Trade: A Census*

0   1,000   2,000 Miles
0   1,000   2,000 Kilometers
Robinson Projection

Geography Skills
Interpreting Thematic Maps

1. In what part of Africa did most slave trading take place?
2. **Human Systems** What percentage of slaves went to British North America during this period?
3. **Summarizing** Which destination received the highest percentage of slaves? Create a pie graph showing how the percentage of slaves brought across the Atlantic Ocean was divided among the regions shown on the map.

African slave market

History Note 4

Millions of Africans were taken to the Americas as slaves between the 1500s and 1800s. Enslaved Africans were the main labor force for large plantations in North America, South America, and the West Indies. Opposition to slavery grew gradually in the mid-1700s. Great Britain, once one of the world's largest traders in slaves, abolished the slave trade in 1807.

Social Studies Skills
WORKSHOP

Interpreting Charts and Graphs

Charts and graphs categorize and display data in a variety of ways. How the data is displayed depends on the type of chart or graph used and the subject matter.

Charts There are various types of charts. *Flowcharts,* used to show cause-and-effect relationships, display a sequence of events or steps. *Organizational charts* show the structure of an organization. *Tables* are columned charts that present data in categories.

Graphs There are several different types of graphs. A *line graph* often plots changes in quantities over time and has a horizontal axis and a vertical axis. A *bar graph* can also be used to display changes in quantities over time. Most often, however, bar graphs compare quantities within categories. A *pie graph,* or *circle graph,* shows sections of a whole graph as if they were slices of a pie. Taken together, all the sections of this circular graph total 100 percent.

How to Read a Chart or Graph

1. **Read the title.** Read the title to identify the subject and purpose of the chart or graph.

2. **Study the key parts.** Read the headings, subheadings, and labels of the chart or graph to identify the categories used.

3. **Analyze the data.** When reading quantities, note any increases or decreases in amounts presented in the chart. When reading dates, note intervals of time. When viewing an organizational chart, follow the direction of the arrows or lines.

Trade through New York Harbor, 1754

Source: *Historical Statistics of the United States*

Practicing the Skills

Study the graph above. Then answer the following questions.

1. What labels are used for each axis?
2. What was the total amount of goods shipped through New York Harbor in 1754?
3. Using the information in this graph, what generalizations or conclusions can you draw about colonial trade in 1754?

History in Action

UNIT 2 SIMULATION

You Make the Decision . . .

Which Colonies Should Receive Financial Support from Great Britain?

Complete the following activity in small cooperative groups. It is 1755. George II is king of England. Britain and France are fighting each other for control of North American colonies and trade routes in the French and Indian War. In order to increase the cash flow for his country, King George II has to cut finances to the colonies. Your group has been asked to help the king decide which colonies Britain should not continue funding. Follow these steps to reach your decision.

1. Gather Information. Use your textbook and other resources to find information that might help you decide which colonies are least valuable to Great Britain. These colonies will not continue to receive financial assistance. Be sure to use what you learned from this unit's Skills Workshop on Interpreting Charts and Graphs to help you make an informed decision. For example, you might refer to charts on colonial exports. You may want to divide different parts of the research among group members.

2. Identify Options. After reviewing the information you have gathered, consider the options you might recommend to the king about which colonies should not get financial assistance. Your final decision may be easier to reach if you consider as many options as possible. Be sure to record your possible options for your presentation.

3. Predict Consequences. Now take each option you and the members of your group came up with and consider what might be the outcome of each course of action. Ask yourselves questions like: "How will not giving financial support to the colony affect Great Britain?" Once you have predicted the consequences, record them as notes for your presentation.

4. Take Action to Implement Your Decision. After you have considered your options, you should create your presentation. Be sure to make your decision on which colonies should receive financial aid very clear. You will need to support your decision by including information you gathered and by explaining why you rejected other options. Your presentation needs to be visually appealing to convince the king. When you are ready, decide which group members will make each part of the presentation, and then take your decision to the king (the rest of the class). Good luck!

VALUE OF COLONIAL GOODS
- PRODUCT 1
- PRODUCT 2
- PRODUCT 3
- PRODUCT 4
- PRODUCT 5

UNIT 3

The Colonies Break Free

(1675–1783)

CHAPTER 6 **Conflicts in the Colonies** (1675–1774)

CHAPTER 7 **The American Revolution** (1774–1783)

Young People

IN HISTORY

Young Patriots

Jonathan Nickerson had quite a story to tell. At age 14 he volunteered to join the Continental Army during the Revolutionary War. Years after serving his country, he told of an event that happened outside of White Plains, New York. The year was 1782. About 80 British cavalrymen rode up to a group of American soldiers, including Nickerson. The British demanded, "Surrender, you . . . rebels, surrender!" Outnumbered, Nickerson and several American Patriots laid down their muskets to surrender. However, the British wanted blood and attacked the unarmed men. Nickerson was knocked to the ground and trampled by a horse. Then the British struck him repeatedly in the head and body with a sword. He recalled a soldier asking, "Shall we kill him?" The British commander replied, "No, let him alone. He will die soon himself." Nickerson proved the British captain wrong. He recovered from his wounds and lived to tell about his dramatic brush with death.

Young battlefield drummers, like the boy shown on the left, helped boost soldiers' morale during the Revolutionary War.

Among those who bravely contributed to the revolutionary struggle was 16-year-old Sybil Ludington. In April 1777, Ludington rode some 40 miles through the night to warn American colonists that British forces had landed at Danbury, Connecticut.

Another teenager to fight for American independence was 16-year-old Michael Smith. Smith's regiment served on a gunboat on the Hudson River in New York. The gunboat crew was ordered to protect Americans living in the area from British raiding parties. When a British warship approached the shore to land its raiding party, the gunboat's crew opened fire. The cannon shots that Smith and two of his fellow crew members fired successfully turned the British away. Smith and his crewmates were declared heroes.

If You Were There *How would you help the Patriots?*

LEFT PAGE: *Patrick Henry spoke before the Virginia legislature in favor of American independence.*

CHAPTER

Conflicts in the Colonies
(1675–1774)

The Stamp Act required colonists to display stamps such as this one on nearly all paper documents.

George Washington served as a member of the Virginia militia.

THE GRANGER COLLECTION, NEW YORK

UNITED STATES

1676 King Philip's War ends.

1754 George Washington's surrender of Fort Necessity marks the beginning of the French and Indian War.

1763 Pontiac's Rebellion begins in March.

In October King George III issues the Proclamation of 1763, limiting western expansion.

1765 Parliament passes the Stamp Act to raise revenue in the colonies.

1767 Parliament passes the Townshend Acts, which place import duties on many every-day items.

1675 /   1760   1765

WORLD

1759 The British capture Quebec from the French.

1763 The Treaty of Paris ends the Seven Years' War.

1764 The British East India Company takes control of Bengal in India.

Colonial artist Benjamin West painted this scene of the Battle of Quebec entitled The Death of Wolfe.

Build on What You Know

A series of wars beginning in the late 1600s between France and Britain left the British as the major European power in eastern North America. As colonists began to move to the frontier, tensions rose between the settlers and American Indians. New British tax laws also upset the colonists.

On December 16, 1773, a group of colonists disguised as American Indians dumped British tea off of several ships while crowds watched from the shore.

This box contains the same brand of tea dumped by the colonists during the Boston Tea Party.

1773 Parliament passes the Tea Act in May, which allows the East India Company to sell tea cheaply in the colonies.

Patriots stage the Boston Tea Party in December.

1774 Parliament passes the Intolerable Acts, which restrict colonial power.

1768 British troops arrive in Boston.

1770 The Boston Massacre takes place.

1770

1775

1768 British explorer James Cook sets sail on his first trip to the South Pacific.

1771 The first edition of the *Encyclopaedia Britannica* is published.

1774 Louis XVI becomes king of France.

If you were there . . .
How would you respond to British efforts to increase control of the colonies?

You Be the Historian

Themes Journal

What's Your Opinion? Do you **agree** or **disagree** with the following statements? Support your point of view in your journal.

- **Global Relations** A nation's colonies should fight on its behalf.

- **Geography** The growth of one nation will cause conflict with other nations.

- **Economics** People who are not represented in government will gladly pay taxes if they are protected from their enemies.

Trouble on the Frontier

Read to Discover

1. How did English colonists and American Indians view each other?
2. What wars did the English colonists fight against other European colonists?
3. How did the French and Indian War affect the British colonies?

WHY IT MATTERS TODAY

Nations still struggle against each other to control areas of the world. Use CNN fyi.com or other **current events** sources to find out where modern nations are in conflict over land or resources. Record your findings in your journal.

Define
- militia
- casualties

Identify
- Metacomet
- Albany Plan of Union
- Edward Braddock
- Treaty of Paris

The Story Continues

Chief Massasoit of the Wampanoag made a peace agreement with the Pilgrims in 1621. The agreement lasted his entire life. However, by the 1670s, Massasoit's son Metacomet had begun to distrust and dislike the English colonists. He said that they treated their Wampanoag neighbors poorly and were greedy for more land. Metacomet wanted the colonial leaders to treat him with respect. He finally told the colonists, "Your governor is but a subject. I shall treat [negotiate] only with my brother [equal], King Charles of England."

Metacomet opposed further colonial expansion onto American Indian lands.

★ Colonists' Relations with American Indians

English settlers called **Metacomet** King Philip because he had compared himself to King Charles II. Metacomet opposed the colonists' efforts to take his people's land. At the same time, the colonists were afraid that Metacomet wanted to destroy them. In 1675 these tensions finally erupted into a conflict called King Philip's War. The colonial **militia**—civilians serving as soldiers—fought American Indian warriors.

Both sides also attacked each other's settlements, killing men, women, and children. The fighting finally ended in 1676, but only after about 600 colonists and some 3,000 Indians had been killed, including Metacomet.

Some American Indians allied with the colonists to fight against Metacomet's forces. This alliance was based on trade. Indian leaders wanted tools, weapons, and other goods that Europeans could provide. In exchange, the colonists wanted furs, which they sold for large profits in Europe. As a result, each side came to depend upon the other.

French colonists traded and allied with the Algonquian and Huron. English colonists traded and allied with the Iroquois League. This powerful group united American Indians from six different tribes. Many American Indians trusted the French more than they did the English. This was in part because the smaller French settlements were less threatening to Indians than the rapidly growing English colonies. No matter who their allies were, American Indian leaders took care to protect their people's independence.

History Makers Speak

❝We are born free. We neither depend upon [the governor of New France] nor [the governor of New York]. We may go where we please, and carry with us whom we please, and buy and sell what we please.❞

—Garangula, an Iroquois leader, quoted in *The World Turned Upside Down,* edited by Colin G. Calloway

✔ **Reading Check: Finding the Main Idea** Why did some American Indians join Europeans in wars against other Indians?

Interpreting the Visual Record

Raiding party *During King Philip's War, colonists and American Indians raided each other's towns and forts.* **Who are the defenders in this image, and what difficulties are the attackers facing?**

★★★★★★★★★★★★
That's Interesting!
★★★★★★★★★★★★

Following Orders Could you stand still while people shot at you? That's how the British and other Europeans fought during the 1600s and 1700s. Their old muskets were not very accurate. Soldiers were told to get close to the enemy, stand in one place, and shoot as quickly as possible. It could take dozens of shots to hit one enemy soldier! American colonists were not used to this style of fighting, and many had difficulty adjusting to it.

Research on the ROM

Free Find:
Iroquois Great Law of Peace
After reading about the Iroquois on the **Holt Researcher CD–ROM**, create a version of the Great Law of Peace for you and your classmates.

★ Conflicts with France

In the late 1600s France and England each wanted control over both Europe and North America. This conflict caused a series of wars between the two empires. The first, King William's War, lasted from 1689 to 1697 but did not change colonial boundaries in North America. Queen Anne's War began in 1702, with England fighting both France and Spain. In the colonies, English and French forces each had American Indian allies who raided the other side's frontier towns. English forces gained the upper hand in the war when they captured French Canada's Port Royal. Later they burned the Spanish settlement of St. Augustine in Florida. In 1713 a treaty ended Queen Anne's War. This time, Great Britain received what are now Hudson Bay, Newfoundland, and Nova Scotia from France. King George's War, fought against France in the 1740s, had little lasting effect on the colonies.

After King George's War, Great Britain and France were still competing for the Ohio Valley and the Great Lakes. British colonists wanted to settle the region. The French believed this settlement would harm their valuable fur trade with American Indians in the area. To protect their interests, the French built three forts in the Ohio Valley, on land claimed by the colony of Virginia. The British colonists felt that the French were keeping them from expanding west. In 1753 Virginia demanded that France give up its forts. When French officers refused, another war seemed likely.

British colonists knew that they were poorly organized and that fighting the French would be dangerous. In 1754 seven colonies sent delegates to Albany, New York. Colonial leaders wanted to make a treaty with the powerful Iroquois League. Soon the colonists were also talking about ways that the colonies could work together. Pennsylvania delegate Benjamin Franklin helped write the **Albany Plan of Union**, which called for all the colonies except Georgia to unite. Franklin based much of the proposal on the example of unified government that the Iroquois League represented.

History Makers Speak

❝It would be a strange thing if Six Nations [of American Indians] should be capable of such a scheme [plan] for such a union, and be able to execute it in such a manner as that it has subsisted [lasted] ages . . . and yet that a like union should be impracticable [not practical] for ten or a dozen English colonies.❞

—Benjamin Franklin, quoted in
From Colonies to Country, by Joy Hakim

However, the colonial governments did not want to give up their individual authority to form a union. They rejected the Albany Plan, as did Parliament.

✔ **Reading Check: Comparing and Contrasting** How were British and French goals for the Ohio Valley similar and different?

★ The French and Indian War

While the delegates were meeting in Albany, the British had begun building a fort along the Ohio River. However, the French drove them off and built Fort Duquesne (dooh-KAYN) on the site. A young Virginian named George Washington arrived with more soldiers and built a simple fort, which he named Fort Necessity. The French attacked, causing many **casualties**—killed, injured, or captured soldiers—and forcing Washington to surrender. Washington's defeat in 1754 was the start of the French and Indian War, between Britain and France. In 1756 fighting also began in Europe and elsewhere. This worldwide conflict was called the Seven Years' War.

King George II sent General **Edward Braddock** to command British forces in North America. Braddock knew little about frontier fighting, which led to disaster when he decided to attack Fort Duquesne in 1755. His forces marched straight into a forest ambush

This medallion commemorates the British victory at Quebec.

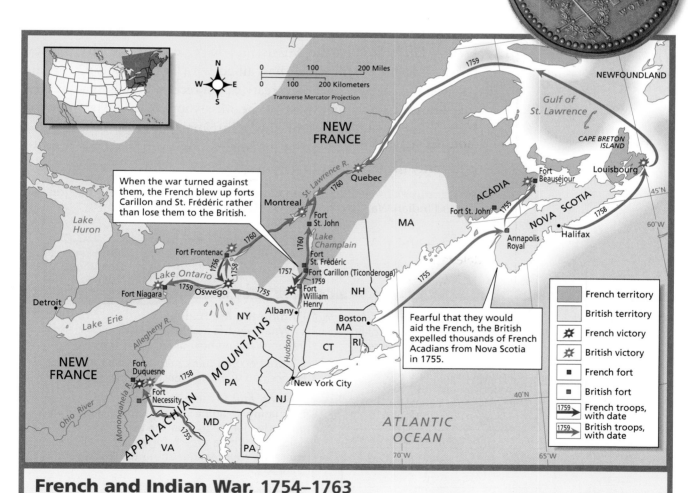

French and Indian War, 1754–1763

Interpreting Maps Great Britain gained most of France's North American lands at the end of the French and Indian War.

Skills Assessment The World in Spatial Terms Which French fort was located near Lake Erie?

GLOBAL CONNECTIONS

Spain and the Seven Years' War

During the 1700s, kings from the Bourbon family ruled both France and Spain. These nations signed the Family Compact of 1761, which stated that "whoever attacked one crown, attacked the other." This Family Compact drew Spain into the conflict between France and Great Britain. Spain paid a high price for joining the war. In the Treaty of Paris, Britain gained control of Florida. Britain had become Spain's main enemy in North America. **Why did Spain enter the Seven Years' War?**

by French and American Indian troops. As one survivor explained, "The Enemy kept behind Trees, and cut down our Troops." The surprised British soon retreated. The British suffered almost 500 casualties, including Braddock himself, but the French and American Indians lost just 50.

The turning point of the war came in 1759, when British general James Wolfe captured Quebec, the capital of New France. Both Wolfe and the French commander were killed in the battle. Although fighting continued until 1763, Britain won most of the important battles.

★ The Treaty of Paris

Finally, in 1763 Great Britain and France signed the **Treaty of Paris**, officially ending the war. The treaty stated that the war "had spread trouble in the four parts of the world." Now the two sides wanted peace. In the process of ending their conflict, Britain and France redrew the political map of North America.

The terms of the treaty gave Canada to Britain, which also gained all French lands east of the Mississippi River except the city of New Orleans. From Spain, which had allied with France in 1762, Britain received Florida. (In an earlier treaty, Spain received Louisiana, the land that France had claimed west of the Mississippi River.) The Treaty of Paris changed the balance of power in North America. Britain had a claim to almost all land east of the Mississippi River. Spain was now the only other major European nation with lands in North America.

✔ **Reading Check: Identifying Cause and Effect** What caused the French and Indian War, and how did it affect North America?

Section 1 Review

go.hrw.com Homework Practice Online

keyword: SF3 HP6

1 Define and explain:
• militia
• casualties

2 Identify and explain:
• Metacomet
• Albany Plan of Union
• Edward Braddock
• Treaty of Paris

3 Summarizing Copy the table below. Use it to explain how each of the five wars that British colonists fought against Europeans and American Indians affected the American colonies.

War	Opponent	Effect on Colonies

4 Finding the Main Idea
a. What was the main cause of the French and Indian War, and how did it affect the colonies?

b. What do you think might have happened if France had won the French and Indian War?

5 Writing and Critical Thinking
Evaluating Imagine that you are an American Indian leader living near the British and French colonies. Write a speech for your council that expresses your feelings about the British colonists.

Consider the following:
• worries about British expansion
• the value of trade with the British
• actions of the French compared to the British

Consequences of the French and Indian War

Read to Discover

1. Why did many colonists move to the frontier?
2. What factors led to Pontiac's Rebellion?
3. What was the Proclamation of 1763, and how effective was it?

WHY IT MATTERS TODAY

Great Britain tried to tell its colonists where they could and could not live. Use CNNfyi.com or other **current events** sources to find an area that a modern government has made off-limits to growth. Record your findings in your journal.

Define

- backcountry
- pioneers

Identify

- Pontiac's Rebellion
- King George III
- Proclamation of 1763

The Story Continues

In 1759 British minister Andrew Burnaby decided to visit the American colonies to learn about their culture. He found life on the frontier interesting and kept a journal of his travels. To Burnaby, Americans seemed to want more and more new land. He wrote that families "will gradually retire [move] westward and settle upon fresh land."

THE GRANGER COLLECTION, NEW YORK

Early pioneers used wagons such as this one to settle the frontier.

⭐ The Frontier

Colonists set up most of the early settlements along the eastern coast or by major rivers. To the west was a huge frontier. Fur traders and a few forts were often the only signs of Europeans in this area. Yet European settlers slowly moved into the Virginia and Carolina **backcountry**. The backcountry was a thinly populated frontier area between the coastal settlements and the Appalachian Mountains. The first Europeans to settle the frontier were called **pioneers**. They risked attacks from American Indians who resisted this settlement on their land. There was little colonial settlement in what is now Tennessee and Kentucky until the 1770s.

Some pioneers crossed the Appalachians farther to the north. They moved into the forested lands along the Ohio River in the 1750s. Pioneers found that the soil in the Ohio River valley was good for farming, and the valley was full of wild game such as turkey and deer. Although these were good conditions, fears of American Indian attacks kept British settlements small and isolated. However, this worry eased after the British won the French and Indian War. Then settlers began crossing the Appalachian Mountains in greater numbers.

✔ **Reading Check: Summarizing** When and why did pioneers begin settling in large numbers beyond the Appalachian Mountains?

Wild honeysuckle was one of the many colorful plants that pioneers encountered in the Ohio Valley.

⭐ Conflict in the Ohio River Valley

After the Treaty of Paris, Great Britain replaced France as the European power in the Ohio River valley. The British believed they were entitled to the land that France had controlled. This area included all of the American Indian lands in the Ohio River valley and the Great Lakes region. Unlike the French, the British wanted to build settlements in the area. This new policy led to problems between the British and American Indian leaders who opposed an increase in British settlements.

Pontiac's Rebellion

Interpreting Maps American Indians under the leadership of the Ottawa chief Pontiac won early battles, but their inability to capture key forts eventually doomed their rebellion.

Skills Assessment

1. **Locate** What British forts lay along Lake Erie?
2. **Analyzing Information** What British fort was not captured despite many nearby American Indian victories?

Chief Pontiac

THE GRANGER COLLECTION, NEW YORK

These leaders had not signed any treaties with Britain and would not give up their land because of an agreement between Britain and France. Chippewa leader Minavavana expressed this view to a trader in 1761. "Englishman, although you have conquered the French, you have not yet conquered us!"

In the 1760s American Indian tribes began to join together to resist the British. Chief Pontiac of the Ottawa led forces that included the Delaware, Huron, Miami, Ottawa, and Shawnee peoples. Pontiac followed the teachings of the so-called Delaware Prophet. This leader called on Indians to drive out the white settlers and give up all European practices. In 1763 Pontiac shared these ideas with a gathering of American Indians.

History Makers Speak "How comes it that you suffer the whites on your lands? Can't you do without them? You might live wholly [completely] as you did before you knew them. . . . Those who come to trouble your country, drive them out, make war [on] them! . . . They are my enemies and the enemies of your brothers!"

—Pontiac, quoted in *The World Turned Upside Down*, edited by Colin G. Calloway

Pontiac's Rebellion began in May 1763 when American Indians attacked British forts on the frontier. Within a month Pontiac's forces had destroyed or captured seven forts. Pontiac then led the attack on Fort Detroit, Britain's political and trading center in the Great Lakes area. Despite the best efforts of Pontiac and his allies, the British held out for months. The American Indians following Pontiac grew tired of attacking the fort and returned to their villages. An Indian attack on the important British position at Fort Pitt also failed. Both sides suffered many casualties. As more Indians left Pontiac, he surrendered in 1766.

✔ **Reading Check: Identifying Cause and Effect** Why did Pontiac and his followers fight the British, and what happened as a result?

Interpreting the Visual Record

Fort Detroit *Pontiac's forces tried for months to capture Fort Detroit from the British.* **What in the image suggests the difficulties of attacking the fort?**

Analyzing Primary Sources
Identifying Points of View How does Pontiac describe white settlers?

THE GRANGER COLLECTION, NEW YORK

BIOGRAPHY

King George III
(1738–1820)

George III became king of Great Britain in 1760. King George had many rigid views. He wanted to assert his royal power and keep a strict rule over the colonies. But the economic and political changes that took place during his rule were beyond his control, and his harsh measures could not keep the thirteen colonies loyal. In 1788 King George began to show signs of mental illness, and by 1811 his son had to rule as king until George's death in 1820. **What did King George III hope to achieve?**

⭐ The Proclamation of 1763

Tensions with American Indians worried officials in the British government. Leaders feared that more fighting would take place on the frontier if colonists kept moving onto American Indian lands. These conflicts would disrupt trade in the region and force Britain to spend more money on defense. To avoid these problems, Britain's **King George III** issued the **Proclamation of 1763**. This law banned the British from settling west of the Appalachian Mountains. The Proclamation created a border between colonial and American Indian lands. King George stated his position.

"It is just and reasonable and essential to our interest and the security of our colonies that the several nations or tribes of Indians with whom we are connected, and who live under our protection should not be . . . [attacked] or disturbed."

—Proclamation of 1763, from *The Annals of America*

The Proclamation also ordered colonists in the upper Ohio River valley "to remove themselves from such settlements." Many colonists defied the Proclamation. Some felt that Britain should allow the colonies to grow rapidly following France's defeat.

The Proclamation proved difficult to enforce. Most people who wanted to settle or trade in the Ohio River valley ignored it. As explorers like Daniel Boone led people west of the Appalachians, colonial settlement expanded. The colonists' disregard for the Proclamation showed their increasing unhappiness with British attempts to control them.

✔ **Reading Check: Summarizing** Why did King George III issue the Proclamation of 1763, and how did colonists respond to it?

Section 2 Review

go.hrw.com **Homework Practice Online**
keyword: SF3 HP6

1 **Define and explain:**
• backcountry
• pioneers

2 **Identify and explain:**
• Pontiac's Rebellion
• King George III
• Proclamation of 1763

3 **Identifying Cause and Effect**
Copy the diagram below. Use it to show the reasons that Great Britain issued the Proclamation of 1763 and how it affected the colonies.

4 **Finding the Main Idea**
a. Why did colonists move west of the Appalachians?

b. Why did American Indians in the Ohio River valley unite and join Pontiac to fight the British?

5 **Writing and Critical Thinking**
Supporting a Point of View Imagine that you are a settler on the frontier in the 1760s. Write a letter to relatives back East explaining what you do or do not like about living on the frontier.

Consider the following:
• relations between pioneers and American Indians
• the British victory in the French and Indian War
• the Proclamation of 1763

Trouble over Colonists' Rights

Read to Discover

1. Why did Great Britain create new taxes for the colonies?
2. Why did colonists dislike the new tax laws?
3. How did colonists challenge these new taxes?

WHY IT MATTERS TODAY

Colonists formed organizations to protest British abuses of colonial rights. Use CNNfyi.com or other **current events** sources to research a modern organization that protests violations of certain rights. Record your findings in your journal.

Define

- boycott
- repeal

Identify

- George Grenville
- Sugar Act
- James Otis
- Samuel Adams
- Committees of Correspondence
- Stamp Act
- Sons of Liberty
- Patrick Henry

The Story Continues

Great Britain had heavy debts from its recent war against France. Prime Minister and Lord of the Treasury George Grenville set out to pay these debts. After taking office in 1763, he spared no one in his search for money. Grenville turned his attention to the American colonists.

Eighteen PENCE. No. 3996
THIS Bill by LAW shall pass current in NEW-JERSEY, for Four Penny-weight, [¶] and Nine Grains of PLATE. December 31, 1763. § Eighteen Pence. §

The colonies used bills such as this New Jersey 18-pence note for currency.

⭐ Raising Taxes

Great Britain had won the French and Indian War, but Parliament still had to pay for it. In addition, Britain kept an army in North America to protect the colonists against American Indian attacks. To help pay for this standing army, Prime Minister **George Grenville** asked Parliament to tax the colonists. In 1764 Parliament passed the **Sugar Act**. This law set duties, or taxes, on molasses and sugar imported by colonists. This was the first act passed specifically to raise money in the colonies, rather than to regulate trade.

In addition to passing new taxes, the British would not let the colonies print their own money. Parliament also made life much harder for

Parliament made great efforts to force colonists to obey mercantile laws and pay the new taxes.

Colonial merchants had to give royal officials a list of all the trade goods on their ships. This made it hard for traders to avoid paying duties.

The British also began to stop and search ships for smuggled goods.

Traders caught smuggling could have their goods and ships taken from them.

Visualizing History

1. **Government** How did the British punish smugglers?

2. **Connecting to Today** Why is it important for a government to stop smugglers?

smugglers by giving the vice-admiralty courts greater powers. These courts had no juries, and their judges treated suspected smugglers as guilty until proven innocent. In regular British courts, accused persons were treated as innocent until proven guilty. In addition, trial by jury was a recognized right of British citizens.

✔ **Reading Check: Finding the Main Idea** In what ways did Parliament's new laws increase British control of the American colonies?

Samuel Adams encouraged colonists to protest the new British taxes.

★ Taxation without Representation

Parliament's actions upset many colonists who had grown used to being independent. Merchants thought the taxes were unfair and hurt business. **James Otis**, a lawyer from Boston, was one of the first colonists to protest taxation by Parliament. Otis argued that Parliament could not "take from any man any part of his property, without his consent in person or by representation." No one in Britain had asked the colonists if they wanted to be taxed. The colonists had no direct representatives in Parliament. In addition, colonial assemblies had little influence on Parliament's decisions. Therefore, Otis said, the tax was unfair and violated colonists' rights.

At a Boston town meeting in May 1764, leader **Samuel Adams** agreed with Otis. He believed that Parliament could not tax the colonists without their consent and said that agreeing to the tax would be dangerous.

DEPOSITED BY THE CITY OF BOSTON, COURTESY, MUSEUM OF FINE ARTS BOSTON

"For if our trade may be taxed, why not our lands? Why not the produce of our lands and, in short, everything we possess or make use of?"

—Samuel Adams, quoted in *Patriots*, by A. J. Langguth

The ideas of Otis and Adams helped spread the slogan "No Taxation without Representation" throughout the colonies.

Adams also helped found the **Committees of Correspondence**, groups that contacted other towns and colonies. They shared ideas and information about the new British laws and ways to challenge them. A popular protest method was the **boycott**, in which people refuse to buy certain goods. In many homes women made substitutes for British goods. The boycott began in Massachusetts and soon spread to other colonies. Colonists hoped such efforts would hurt the British economy, perhaps convincing Parliament to end the new taxes.

✔ **Reading Check: Analyzing Information** How did Samuel Adams and James Otis influence colonial protests against new taxes?

⭐ The Stamp Act

By early 1765 Prime Minister Grenville had heard the complaints about the Sugar Act. He asked the colonists if they had a better plan for paying their share of military costs. Some colonists suggested taxing themselves, but Grenville rejected the idea. Grenville then proposed the **Stamp Act**, which Parliament passed in March 1765. This act affected most colonists. It required them to pay for an official stamp, or seal, whenever they bought paper items. The tax had to be paid on legal documents, licenses, newspapers, pamphlets, and even playing cards. Colonists who refused to buy stamps could be fined or sent to jail.

Grenville thought this tax was fair. After all, in Britain people already paid similar taxes. But colonists saw it differently. The Stamp Act was Parliament's first effort to raise money by taxing them directly. Protests against the Stamp Act began almost immediately.

In places such as New York and Massachusetts, colonists formed secret societies called the **Sons of Liberty**. Samuel Adams helped organize the Sons of Liberty in Boston. These groups sometimes used violence to frighten tax collectors. They told tax collector Andrew Oliver that "his house would be destroyed and his life [would be] in continual danger" unless he quit his job. Oliver quit. Many colonial courts shut down because people refused to buy the stamps required for legal documents. Businesses openly ignored the law by refusing to buy stamps.

In May 1765 **Patrick Henry** presented a series of resolutions to the House of Burgesses in Virginia. These resolutions stated that the Stamp Act violated the rights of the colonists as British citizens. In addition to taxation without representation, the Stamp Act denied the accused trial

Analyzing Primary Sources

Identifying Points of View What did Adams fear would happen if Americans did not protest the new British taxes?

"No Taxation without Representation"

This teapot was one of many ways in which the colonists opposed the Stamp Act.

COLONIAL WILLIAMSBURG FOUNDATION

COURTESY OF THE JOHN CARTER BROWN LIBRARY AT BROWN UNIVERSITY

Interpreting the Visual Record

The end of the Stamp Act *This cartoon shows members of Parliament giving a funeral for the Stamp Act.* **Do you think the artist was pleased or upset at the repeal of the act? Explain your answer.**

by jury. The leader of the House, John Robinson, interrupted Henry's speech by crying, "Treason! Treason!" "If this be treason," replied Henry, "make the most of it!" Henry's speech convinced the assembly to support some of his ideas.

⭐ Repealing the Stamp Act

Word of Virginia's action reached Boston. There the members of the Massachusetts legislature called for a Stamp Act Congress. In October 1765, delegates from nine colonies met in New York. They issued a declaration that the Stamp Act violated their rights and liberties. They then asked Parliament to **repeal**, or end, the act.

Pressure to repeal the Stamp Act began to grow. A group of London merchants said that their trade suffered from the colonial boycott and asked Parliament to repeal the Stamp Act. Benjamin Franklin, serving as an official agent for Pennsylvania, spoke before Parliament. Repeal the stamp tax, he said, and colonists would buy British goods again. William Pitt, an important member of Parliament, also believed that the Stamp Act was unfair. Pitt led Parliament in repealing the act in 1766.

The members of Parliament were still upset that colonists had challenged their authority. Thus, Parliament issued the Declaratory Act, which stated that Parliament had the power to make laws for the colonies "in all cases whatsoever." In other words, Parliament made the rules, not the colonists.

✔ **Reading Check: Summarizing** What methods did the colonists use to protest the Sugar and Stamp Acts, and what were the results of their efforts?

Section 3 Review

Homework Practice Online
keyword: SF3 HP6

1 **Define** and explain:
• boycott
• repeal

2 **Identify** and explain:
• George Grenville
• Sugar Act
• James Otis
• Samuel Adams
• Committees of Correspondence
• Stamp Act
• Sons of Liberty
• Patrick Henry

3 **Summarizing** Copy the graphic organizer below. Use it to show why the British taxed the American colonists, what the British tax laws were, and how the colonists responded.

Reasons for Taxation → British Tax Laws 1._____ 2._____ → Colonial Response

4 **Finding the Main Idea**
a. Why did colonists dislike the Sugar Act, the vice-admiralty courts, and the Stamp Act?

b. Compare and contrast the ways in which colonists challenged new taxes.

5 **Writing and Critical Thinking**
Supporting a Point of View Imagine that you are a colonist upset by new taxes. Write a newspaper editorial persuading colonists to protest these new taxes.

Consider the following:
• reasons for British taxes
• ideas of James Otis and Samuel Adams
• Benjamin Franklin's testimony before Parliament

New Taxes and Tensions

Read to Discover

1. How did colonists respond to the Townshend Acts?
2. Why were the Boston Massacre and the Boston Tea Party significant events?
3. What was the purpose of the Intolerable Acts?

WHY IT MATTERS TODAY

The British government taxed the colonies to pay for the French and Indian War. Today our government uses taxes to pay for many services. Use **CNNfyi.com** or other **current events** sources to learn about a U.S. government program that uses tax dollars. Record your findings in your journal.

Define

- writs of assistance
- propaganda

Identify

- Townshend Acts
- Daughters of Liberty
- Boston Massacre
- Tea Act
- Boston Tea Party
- Intolerable Acts
- Mercy Otis Warren

The Story Continues

People in cities across the colonies celebrated the repeal of the Stamp Act with fireworks. In Boston the people built a giant pyramid lit by 280 lamps. The Massachusetts legislature thanked King George III and promised to be loyal to him. However, Parliament and the colonies still disagreed on many issues.

Colonial lanterns and lamps were often lit by candles or oil.

The Townshend Acts

In June 1767 Parliament passed the **Townshend Acts**, which placed duties on imported glass, lead, paint, paper, and tea. The money from these duties paid for military costs and the salaries of colonial governors. These payments violated the guarantee of having no standing army in peacetime without the colonists' consent. To enforce the Townshend Acts, British officials used **writs of assistance**. These special forms allowed tax collectors to search for smuggled goods. Colonists hated the new laws because they violated colonists' constitutional rights.

The colonists responded to the Townshend Acts by once again boycotting British goods. Women calling themselves the **Daughters of Liberty** supported the boycott. One leader explained their actions.

History Makers Speak

❝I hope [we] would sooner wrap ourselves in sheep and goatskin than buy English goods of a people who have insulted us in such a scandalous [shocking] way.❞

—Anonymous Daughter of Liberty, quoted in
A History of Women in America, by Carol Hymowitz and Michaele Weissman

Colonial legislatures also protested the Townshend Acts. In February 1768 Samuel Adams wrote a letter stating that the acts violated the legal rights of the colonists. The Massachusetts legislature sent this letter to other colonies, asking for their help. In a few months several legislatures voted to join the protest against the Townshend Acts.

At the same time, tax collectors in Massachusetts seized the ship *Liberty* on suspicion of smuggling. This action angered the ship's owner, Boston merchant John Hancock, who accused the tax collectors of punishing him because he opposed the Townshend Acts. The Sons of Liberty supported Hancock. They began to attack the houses of customs officials in protest. In response, Governor Francis Bernard broke up the Massachusetts legislature. He also asked troops to restore order. British soldiers arrived in Boston in October 1768.

✔ **Reading Check: Sequencing** What series of events led to the arrival of British troops in Boston in 1768?

The Sons of Liberty displayed posters like this one calling for a boycott against a Boston merchant.

WILLIAM JACKSON,
an *IMPORTER*; at the
BRAZEN HEAD,
North Side of the TOWN-HOUSE,
and *Oppofite the Town-Pump, in*
Corn-hill, BOSTON.

It is defired that the Sons and
DAUGHTERS of *LIBERTY,*
would not buy any one thing of
him, for in fo doing they will bring
Difgrace upon *themfelves,* and their
Pofterity, for *ever* and *ever,* AMEN
PROSCRIBING AN IMPORTER.

★ The Boston Massacre

Many Bostonians believed that the British government had sent the troops to silence its critics. Local leader Samuel Adams declared, "I look upon [British soldiers] as foreign enemies." Both sides disliked each other—name-calling and fights between locals and the soldiers were common.

The tension exploded on March 5, 1770, when a lone British soldier standing guard got into a fight with a colonist. A crowd gathered around the soldier, throwing snowballs and shouting insults. Soon a small group of troops arrived. The mob grew louder and angrier by the moment. Suddenly, the soldiers fired into the crowd killing several colonists.

Samuel Adams and others used the event as a form of **propaganda**—information giving only one side in an argument—against the British. Colonists called the shootings the **Boston Massacre**. The soldiers and their officer, Thomas Preston, were charged with murder. Two Boston lawyers, Josiah Quincy and John Adams—Samuel Adams's cousin—agreed to defend the soldiers. They argued that the troops had acted in self-defense. The Boston jury agreed. The jury found Preston and six soldiers not guilty. Two soldiers were convicted of killing people in the crowd by accident. These men were branded on the hand and then released. The trial helped calm people down, but many colonists were still angry at the British.

✔ **Reading Check: Contrasting** How did Samuel Adams and John Adams differ in their response to the Boston Massacre?

Research on the R⊙M

Free Find:
Samuel Adams
After reading about Samuel Adams on the **Holt Researcher CD–ROM,** imagine that you are a reporter for a Boston newspaper. Write a set of questions you might ask Adams about British treatment of the colonies. Include the answers you think Adams would give.

The BLOODY MASSACRE perpetrated in King — Street BOSTON on March 5 1770 by a party of the 29th REG.

Engrav'd Printed & Sold by PAUL REVERE BOSTON

CONNECTING TO

THE ARTS

Colonial Art Colonial artists often tried to show what daily life was like. Some used art to make a political point. Paul Revere's engraving of the Boston Massacre was one example. The picture shows British soldiers attacking unarmed colonists. The *Boston Gazette* advertised it as "A Print . . . of the late horrid [terrible] Massacre in King St." Revere's engraving sold many copies. It became a symbol of Great Britain's injustice toward the colonies. **How does Paul Revere's picture reveal changing colonial attitudes toward the British?**

★ A Tax on Tea

To reduce tensions in the colonies, Parliament repealed almost all of the Townshend Acts—but it kept the tax on tea. British officials knew that the colonial demand for tea was high despite the boycott. But the colonies were smuggling most of this imported tea and paying no duty on it. The British East India Company offered Parliament a solution. If allowed to sell its tea directly to the colonies, the company could charge low prices and still profit. Cheaper tea might lead to less smuggling and the collection of more money in taxes.

Parliament agreed and passed the **Tea Act** in 1773. Many colonial merchants and smugglers feared that cheap British tea would put them out of business. Other colonists worried that the British East India Company would monopolize—or gain complete control of—the tea trade. Other British companies might follow its example and threaten colonial businesses. As a result, colonists united against the Tea Act.

A ship carrying British tea arrived in Boston Harbor in November 1773. Two other tea ships soon joined it. The Sons of Liberty demanded that the ships leave immediately. But Thomas Hutchinson, governor of Massachusetts since 1771, would not let the ships leave without paying

Battling British Acts

ACT	COLONIAL RESPONSE	BRITISH REACTION
The **Sugar Act (1764)** replaced the Molasses Act and was aimed specifically at raising revenues from the colonies.	Colonists protested the act and called for a boycott on items with duties.	After asking colonists for a plan to pay military expenses and not receiving a satisfactory one, the prime minister proposed the Stamp Act.
The **Stamp Act (1765)** required colonists to purchase a stamp for newspapers, pamphlets, legal documents, and other items.	Colonists formed the Sons of Liberty, boycotted goods, and used violence to frighten tax collectors; Stamp Act Congress asked Parliament to repeal the act.	Parliament repealed the Stamp Act in March 1766, then issued the Declaratory Act.
The **Townshend Acts (1767)** placed duties on imported glass, lead, paint, paper, and tea and made it easier for tax collectors to get writs of assistance.	Colonists used boycotts, colonial legislatures circulated a letter protesting the acts, and the Sons of Liberty attacked homes of tax collectors.	Soldiers were sent to Boston in October 1768; colonists were killed in the Boston Massacre on March 5, 1770; most of the acts were repealed by Parliament; troops were removed from Boston.
The **Tea Act (1773)** kept in place duties on imported tea and allowed the British East India Company to export directly to the colonies.	Colonists used boycotts and propaganda, held the Boston Tea Party, and destroyed tea shipments in some colonies.	Parliament passed the Coercive Acts, also called the Intolerable Acts by colonists.
The **Intolerable Acts (1774)** closed Boston Harbor, canceled the Massachusetts charter, moved trials of colonial officials to Britain, allowed quartering of British troops in all colonies, and gave Canada control of the Ohio region.	Colonists called for large-scale boycotts, published propaganda, and convened the First Continental Congress.	King George III rejected the suggestions of the First Continental Congress.

the tea duty. On the night of December 16, colonists disguised as American Indians snuck onto the three tea-filled ships. One participant recalled his experience.

Analyzing Primary Sources

Drawing Inferences and Conclusions Based on George Hewes's statement, how organized does the Boston Tea Party seem? Explain your answer.

History Makers Speak

❝In about three hours from the time we went on board, we had thus broken and thrown overboard every tea chest to be found in the ship, while those in the other ships were disposing of the tea in the same way, at the same time. . . . No attempt was made to resist us.**❞**

—George Hewes, quoted in *The Spirit of 'Seventy-Six*, edited by Henry Steele Commager and Richard B. Morris

After dumping 342 tea chests into Boston Harbor, the colonists headed home to remove their disguises. Word of this **Boston Tea Party** spread. Soon the streets echoed with shouts of "Boston harbour [is] a teapot tonight!"

✔ **Reading Check: Finding the Main Idea** Why did colonists oppose the Tea Act?

★ The Intolerable Acts

Lord North, the new British prime minister, was furious when he heard about the Boston Tea Party. "Can we remain in this situation long?" he asked Parliament. Parliament decided to punish Massachusetts. In the spring of 1774 Britain passed the Coercive Acts, which colonists called the **Intolerable Acts**. The acts had several effects.

1. Boston Harbor was closed until Boston paid for the lost tea.
2. The Massachusetts charter was canceled. The governor decided if and when the legislature could meet.
3. Royal officials accused of crimes were sent to Britain for trial. This let them face a more friendly judge and jury.
4. The Quartering Act forced colonists to quarter, or house and supply, British soldiers.
5. General Thomas Gage became the new governor of Massachusetts.

Playwright Mercy Otis Warren was the daughter of James Otis and a friend of John Adams and Abigail Adams.

The British hoped that these steps would bring back order in the colonies by making an example of Massachusetts. But the acts simply made more people angry. The acts went against many of the traditional rights of British citizens, such as freedom of travel in peacetime and no quartering of troops in private homes. Some colonists wrote essays and poems critical of the British government's actions. **Mercy Otis Warren** wrote plays such as *The Group* and *The Blockheads*. In *The Group*, Warren gave British supporters names such as Hum Humbug to make them look foolish.

Colonial leaders in Boston proposed a boycott of all British goods in the colonies. They also tried to bring together leaders from each colony to decide the best way to respond to Britain's abuses of colonial rights.

✔ **Reading Check: Summarizing** What were the major effects of the Intolerable Acts, and what methods did colonists use to protest them?

Section 4 Review

go.hrw.com   Homework Practice Online

keyword: SF3 HP6

1 **Define** and explain:
• writs of assistance
• propaganda

2 **Identify** and explain:
• Townshend Acts
• Daughters of Liberty
• Boston Massacre
• Tea Act
• Boston Tea Party
• Intolerable Acts
• Mercy Otis Warren

3 **Sequencing** Copy the graphic organizer below. Use it to explain the sequence of major events that led to the Intolerable Acts of 1774.

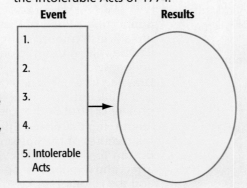

Event	Results
1.	
2.	
3.	
4.	
5. Intolerable Acts	

4 **Finding the Main Idea**
a. In what ways did colonists react to the Townshend Acts?

b. How did the Boston Massacre and the Boston Tea Party affect relations between Great Britain and the colonies?

5 **Writing and Critical Thinking**
Evaluating Imagine that you are a colonist. Write a brief pamphlet explaining what you think Parliament hopes to achieve with the Intolerable Acts.

Consider the following:
• the Boston Tea Party
• the writings of Mercy Otis Warren
• colonial boycott efforts

Chapter 6 Review

The Chapter at a Glance

Examine the visual summary of the chapter below. Write a one-paragraph summary of the main ideas covered in the chapter. Share your summary with a classmate to compare and contrast your ideas.

Colonists Support Great Britain

Colonists Oppose Great Britain

Proclamation of 1763
Sugar Act (1764)
Stamp Act (1765)
Townshend Acts (1767)
Boston Massacre (1770)
Tea Act (1773)
Intolerable Acts (1774)

King William's War (1689)*
Queen Anne's War (1702)
King George's War (1744)
French and Indian War (1754)
Pontiac's Rebellion (1763)
* dates indicate start of war

Loyalty in the Balance

Identifying People and Ideas

Use the following terms or people in historically significant sentences.

1. Albany Plan of Union
2. pioneers
3. King George III
4. Proclamation of 1763
5. Samuel Adams
6. Committees of Correspondence
7. Stamp Act
8. Patrick Henry
9. writs of assistance
10. Mercy Otis Warren

Understanding Main Ideas

Section 1 *(Pages 158–162)*

1. What events led to the French and Indian War?
2. What were the terms of the Treaty of Paris?

Section 2 *(Pages 163–166)*

3. Why and how did King George III and Parliament try to limit colonial expansion?

Section 3 *(Pages 167–170)*

4. Why did colonists oppose new taxes?
5. How did colonists try to change the new taxes?

Section 4 *(Pages 171–175)*

6. How did colonists view the Townshend Acts?
7. Why did Parliament pass the Intolerable Acts?

You Be the Historian—Reviewing Themes

1. **Global Relations** How did the wars between France and Great Britain affect the British colonists in North America?
2. **Geography** What region did American pioneers settle during the 1760s, and what happened as a result?
3. **Economics** How did Americans react when they were taxed by Parliament, in which they were not represented?

Thinking Critically

1. **Supporting a Point of View** Imagine that you are a British colonist during the 1760s. Would you be willing to settle on the frontier? Explain your answer.
2. **Drawing Inferences and Conclusions** Why do you think British leaders felt the need to take greater control of the colonies?
3. **Identifying Cause and Effect** What were the main causes of the Boston Massacre and the Boston Tea Party, and how did these two events affect the relationship between Great Britain and the colonies?

Interpreting Graphs

Study the graph below. Then use the information on the graph to help you answer the questions that follow.

Declining Imports from Britain, 1764–1776

Value of British imports (in millions of pounds sterling*)

Sugar Act 1764

Intolerable Acts 1774

Townshend Acts (except for tea tax) repealed 1770

Year

*British currency   Source: *Historical Statistics of the United States*

1. What happened to the value of British imports in the colonies between 1770 and 1771, and 1774 and 1775?
   a. Imports increased during both periods.
   b. Imports decreased during both periods.
   c. Imports fell in 1770 and rose in 1774.
   d. Imports rose in 1770 and fell in 1774.

2. Based on the graph and your knowledge of the period, do you think that the colonial boycotts against British goods were effective? Explain your answer.

Analyzing Primary Sources

Read the following quote by colonial militia member David Perry, and then answer the questions that follow.

"We had proceeded but a short distance into the woods before we were met by the enemy. . . . It was the first engagement I had ever seen, and the whistling of balls [bullets] and roar of musquetry [guns] terrified me not a little. At length our regiment formed among the trees, behind which the men kept stepping from their ranks for shelter. Colonel Preble, who, I well remember, was a harsh man, swore he would knock the first man down who should step out of his ranks, which greatly surprised me, to think that I must stand still to be shot at."

3. Which of the following statements best describes Perry's reaction to this style of fighting?
   a. He was pleased that the militia was allowed to take cover behind trees.
   b. He was frightened by the fighting and confused by his orders.
   c. He was eager to fight against the French and American Indians.
   d. He was angry that Colonel Preble knocked him down.

4. What would be some of the disadvantages of the style of fighting described by Perry?

Alternative Assessment

American History

Building Your Portfolio

Cooperative Learning

Complete this activity in small groups. Imagine that you are attending a meeting of the Sons of Liberty after the Stamp Act has been passed. Write a skit that explains why you are upset with the British government and what actions you might take. Have at least one character in the skit urge the group to proceed with caution. Perform your skit for the class.

🔲 internet connect

Internet Activity: go.hrw.com
keyword: **SF3 CF6**

Choose an activity on conflict in the colonies to:

● Research battles of the French and Indian War, and create a map of the major engagements.

● Examine the fur trade in New France, and create a pamphlet on settlements.

● Research the life of Daniel Boone, and write a biography.

A Shift in Power

The British colonies in North America grew rapidly in the late 1600s and 1700s. New France grew more slowly. Yet the French were still a significant threat to British expansion. This was particularly true in Canada and the area west of the thirteen colonies. The two colonial powers fought a number of wars during this period. Britain's victories gave the British control over much of North America by the late 1700s.

During this same time, another shift in power was taking place. American Indians were gradually losing their lands to European colonists. As more Europeans settled in North America, American Indians found themselves being pushed westward.

Conflict with American Indians

Like other parts of colonial America, the population of New England grew rapidly. Chief Metacomet of the Wampanoag Indians, called King Philip by the settlers, led a war against colonists in New England in 1675. Such conflicts slowed colonial growth, but did not stop it.

Rate of New England Population Growth, 1660–1750

Source: *Historical Statistics of the United States*

Geography **Skills**

Interpreting Bar Graphs

1. **Human Systems** During what 10-year period was New England's percentage of population growth the greatest?
2. **Drawing Inferences and Conclusions** What might have accounted for the drop in population growth from 1670 to 1680?

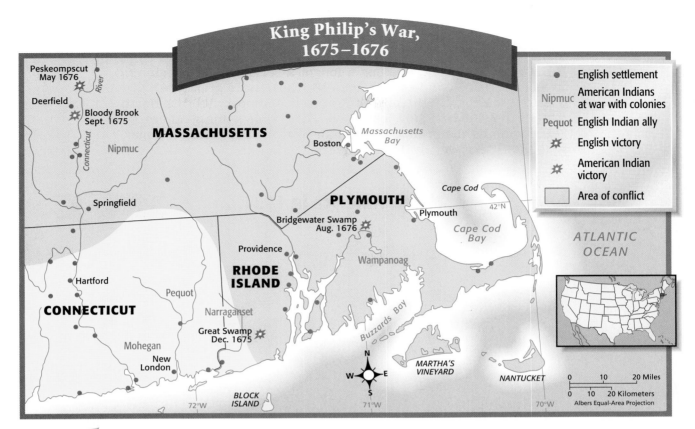

King Philip's War, 1675–1676

Legend:
- English settlement
- Nipmuc — American Indians at war with colonies
- Pequot — English Indian ally
- ✷ English victory
- ✷ American Indian victory
- Area of conflict

**Map labels:**

MASSACHUSETTS

Peskeompscut May 1676 ✷
Deerfield
Bloody Brook Sept. 1675 ✷
Nipmuc
Springfield
Boston
Massachusetts Bay
Connecticut River

PLYMOUTH
Bridgewater Swamp Aug. 1676 ✷
Cape Cod
Plymouth
42°N
Cape Cod Bay

Providence
Wampanoag
RHODE ISLAND
Hartford
Pequot
Narraganset
CONNECTICUT
Mohegan
Great Swamp Dec. 1675 ✷
New London

ATLANTIC OCEAN

Buzzards Bay
MARTHA'S VINEYARD
NANTUCKET
BLOCK ISLAND

72°W   71°W   70°W

0   10   20 Miles
0   10   20 Kilometers
Albers Equal-Area Projection

Geography Skills

Interpreting Thematic Maps

1. **The World in Spatial Terms** Locate the settlements of Boston and Plymouth. Which battle in the war was closest to these towns?
2. **Summarizing** Which colonies were involved in the conflict?

Metacomet, also known as King Philip

History Note 1

Historians have made widely varying estimates of the American Indian population in North America when the first Europeans arrived. Some researchers have put the number as low as 1 million. Others have placed the American Indian population as high as 18 million. Experts believe that both European diseases and wars with European settlers greatly reduced the American Indian population. By 1890 there were only some 250,000 American Indians.

History Note 2

In 1675, disagreements between the Wampanoag and the growing number of New England colonists led to war. Many people on both sides were killed in the conflict, known as King Philip's War. The defeated American Indians had to accept colonial authority and the loss of more of their land.

Changing Empires

France, Great Britain, and Spain fought a series of wars beginning in the late 1600s and ending in 1763. These wars greatly changed their colonial empires. France lost almost all of its North American colonies. Spain lost some lands while gaining others. After winning the French and Indian War, Britain gained a huge amount of territory in North America.

North America in 1754

Legend:
- British
- Spanish
- French
- Russian
- Disputed by Britain and France
- Disputed by Britain and Spain
- --- Boundary of the Iroquois League

0   500   1,000 Miles
0   500   1,000 Kilometers
Azimuthal Equal-Area Projection

Geography Skills

Interpreting Political Maps

1. Trace this map on a separate sheet of paper and ask a fellow student to fill in the general locations of each of the European colonial empires in North America in 1754.
2. **The Uses of Geography** Which European powers appeared to control the largest parts of the present-day United States in 1754?
3. **Analyzing Information** Over which areas of North America did European powers dispute control?

History Note 3

Many modern U.S. place-names reflect the colonial influence of France and Spain. The name of Terre Haute, Indiana, means "high land" in French. Des Moines, Iowa, comes from the French for "some monks." Louisiana was named after French king Louis XIV. Florida is Spanish for "flowered." Spanish names in the Southwest include Rio Grande, or "great river," and Las Cruces, New Mexico, which means "the crosses."

North America in 1763

ARCTIC OCEAN

UNCLAIMED

Disputed

PACIFIC OCEAN

Hudson Bay

NEWFOUNDLAND

CANADA

FRENCH

Great Lakes

St. Lawrence River

Mississippi River

Ohio River

APPALACHIAN MTS.

LOUISIANA

THIRTEEN COLONIES

ATLANTIC OCEAN

Rio Grande

FLORIDA

Gulf of Mexico

NEW SPAIN

WEST INDIES

CARIBBEAN SEA

0   500   1,000 Miles
0   500   1,000 Kilometers
Azimuthal Equal-Area Projection

British	Russian
Spanish	Disputed by Britain, Russia, and Spain
French	

ARCTIC OCEAN, NORTH AMERICA, EUROPE, ASIA, ATLANTIC OCEAN, AFRICA, Equator, PACIFIC OCEAN, AUSTRALIA, SOUTH AMERICA, INDIAN OCEAN, ANTARCTICA
Robinson Projection

History Note 5

By the late 1700s there were about 20,000 Spanish-speaking settlers living in New Mexico. Still, the population of the Spanish Southwest never approached the size of the growing British colonies in the East.

Geography Skills

Interpreting Political Maps

1. Which areas in North America did each European power hold in 1763?

2. **Places and Regions** What areas of North America were disputed or unclaimed?

3. **Contrasting** Compare the map of North America in 1754 with the map of North America in 1763. Then create a map of North America in 1763 that shows which parts of the territories controlled by Britain and Spain were once held by France.

History Note 4

France gave Louisiana to Spain in 1762. But the Spanish never really had full control over most of this huge territory. French influence remained strong in the area, and Louisiana was returned to French control in 1800.

Fort St. Marie de Gannentaha, Lake Onondaga, New York

NEW YO

7 The American Revolution
(1774–1783)

Colonial minutemen were outnumbered by British soldiers at the Battle of Lexington in Massachusetts.

Patriot Thomas Jefferson was the author of the Declaration of Independence.

UNITED STATES

1774 The First Continental Congress meets.

1775 On April 19 the Revolutionary War begins with the fighting at Lexington and Concord.

1776 On July 4 the thirteen colonies issue the Declaration of Independence and break away from Great Britain.

1776 On December 26 General George Washington wins the Battle of Trenton.

1777 On October 17 a British army surrenders to the Patriots after the Battle of Saratoga.

1778 The Continental Army suffers through the end of a harsh winter while stationed at Valley Forge, Pennsylvania.

1774	1775	1776	1777	1778

WORLD

1776 Scottish economist Adam Smith writes *The Wealth of Nations* about open economic markets and competition.

1778 France allies with the Americans and joins the war against Great Britain.

A gold British guinea coin

French allies supplied the Patriots with much-needed weapons such as this cannon.

Build on What You Know

By 1774 many colonists were angry with the British government. These colonists believed that Parliament had repeatedly violated their rights. Eventually their protests led to battles with British troops and a war for independence from Great Britain. The American Revolution marked the birth of the United States of America.

George Washington looks on as American forces accept the British surrender at Yorktown, Virginia.

The early U.S. flag had a star and a stripe for each state.

COLONIAL WILLIAMSBURG FOUNDATION

1779 Patriot George Rogers Clark and his forces recapture Vincennes.

1780 The British defeat the southern Patriot army at Camden, South Carolina.

1781 On October 19 the British surrender to George Washington at Yorktown, securing the American victory in the Revolutionary War.

1783 The Treaty of Paris is signed, ending the war.

1779   1780   1781   1782   1783

1779 Spain declares war on Britain.

1780 Great Britain declares war on the Netherlands.

1783 Great Britain agrees to return Florida to Spain.

If you were there . . .
Would you support the Revolution?

You Be the Historian

Themes Journal

What's Your Opinion? Do you **agree** or **disagree** with the following statements? Support your point of view in your journal.

- **Citizenship** Citizens have the right to rebel against an unjust government.

- **Constitutional Heritage** All human beings possess certain natural rights that should be protected.

- **Global Relations** A powerful nation will always defeat a weaker country in war.

The Revolution Begins

Read to Discover

1. What actions did the First Continental Congress take?
2. How did the fighting at Lexington and Concord affect the colonies' conflict with Great Britain?
3. What did the Second Continental Congress accomplish?
4. How did geography influence the early battles of the war?

WHY IT MATTERS TODAY

At times Americans still have to defend their liberties. Sometimes the United States also helps protect the freedoms of people in other countries. Use **CNNfyi.com** or other **current events** sources to find a country in which the United States is helping to protect basic human rights. Record your findings in your journal.

Define

• minutemen
• siege

Identify

• First Continental Congress
• Thomas Gage
• Redcoats
• Second Continental Congress
• Continental Army
• George Washington
• Olive Branch Petition
• Battle of Bunker Hill

THE GRANGER COLLECTION, NEW YORK

This is a collection of swords used during the Revolutionary War.

The Story Continues

By the fall of 1774 the colonists had to do something about their problems with Great Britain. Cousins John and Samuel Adams were part of the debate. Samuel Adams was the rebel who had organized the Boston Tea Party. John Adams had defended the British soldiers who took part in the Boston Massacre. Both cousins thought that colonial leaders needed to respond to British acts. They agreed to represent Massachusetts at a colonial assembly taking place in Philadelphia.

⭐ The First Continental Congress

In September 1774 the **First Continental Congress** met in Philadelphia. The Congress had 56 colonial delegates, including John and Samuel Adams. Georgia was the only colony that did not send representatives. The delegates at the meeting debated the best way to respond to the crisis taking place in Boston. Delegate John Dickinson thought that the colonists should make peace with Great Britain. Delegate Patrick Henry said that there was no way to avoid a fight. "Arms [weapons] are a resource to which we shall be forced," he declared.

In the end, the delegates reached a compromise. They recommended that colonists continue to boycott British goods but also warned colonial militias to be prepared to fight. Meanwhile, they assembled a list of 10 resolutions to present to King George III. This Declaration of Rights listed freedoms that the delegates believed colonists should possess, including the right to "life, liberty, and property." The delegates agreed to meet again in May 1775 if the king did not agree.

✔ **Reading Check: Summarizing** Describe the accomplishments of the First Continental Congress.

Paul Revere's heroic ride helped warn the Patriots of the British advance toward Concord.

⭐ The "Shot Heard round the World"

Tensions remained high in Boston. Local militia members began calling themselves **minutemen** because they were ready to fight on a minute's notice. In April 1775 British general **Thomas Gage** decided to take away the minutemen's weapons and ammunition. These weapons were stored in Concord, a town about 20 miles west of Boston.

The Sons of Liberty learned of the British plan. On the evening of April 18, 1775, spies brought serious news to Paul Revere and William Dawes. British troops were heading toward Concord. The two men raced on their horses through the countryside, warning minutemen that the British were coming! Isaac Davis was one of the minutemen who heard the warning. His wife later described his response to Revere's call.

History Makers Speak ❝The alarm was given early in the morning, and my husband lost no time in making ready to go to Concord with his company. . . . [he] said but little that morning. He seemed serious and thoughtful; but never seemed to hesitate. . . . He only said, 'Take good care of the children.'❞

—Mrs. Isaac Davis, quoted in *From Colonies to Country*, by Joy Hakim

On the morning of April 19, fewer than 70 minutemen gathered at the Lexington village green, near Concord. There they met a much larger force of British troops. The colonial commander shouted to his soldiers,

THE GRANGER COLLECTION, NEW YORK

Interpreting the Visual Record

The first battle *The fighting at Lexington was fierce but brief. The colonists suffered their first casualties of the war.* **What differences does this image show between the fighting style of the minutemen and that of the British regular troops?**

GIFT OF JOSEPH W. REVERE, WILLIAM B. REVERE, AND EDWARD H.R. REVERE, COURTESY, MUSEUM OF FINE ARTS, BOSTON

"Don't fire unless fired upon. But if they mean to have a war, let it begin here!" Suddenly a shot rang out. No one knows who fired this "shot heard round the world"—but once the soldiers heard it, the fight began. The battle ended in minutes. When the smoke cleared, the badly outnumbered colonists had suffered 8 dead and 10 wounded.

The British marched on to Concord, where they found few weapons because the colonists had already removed them. In anger, British troops set fire to a few buildings. One of the colonists shouted, "Will you let them burn the town down?" In response, the minutemen charged forward.

As the British retreated back to Boston, the minutemen fired upon them from behind trees and buildings. The British soldiers' bright red uniforms made easy targets. The colonists called the British soldiers **Redcoats** because of these uniforms. By the time the British reached Boston, they had suffered more than 250 casualties. Fewer than 100 colonists were killed or wounded. Isaac Davis was among those who died that day.

Word of the fighting at Lexington and Concord spread. Many people responded with shock and anger. Dr. James Thacher noted the effect on one Massachusetts town.

Analyzing Primary Sources

Identifying Bias Do you think Dr. Thacher supports the minutemen or the Redcoats? Why?

History Makers Speak

"This tragical event seems to have electrified all classes of people. . . . The sword is now unsheathed [drawn], and our friends are slaughtered by our cruel enemies. Expresses [messengers] are hastening from town to town, in all directions through the country . . . rousing the people To Arms! To Arms!"

—Dr. James Thacher, quoted in *Military Journal of the American Revolution*

✔ **Reading Check: Identifying Cause and Effect** What led to the fighting at Lexington and Concord, and how did it affect the colonies' conflict with Great Britain?

George Washington had fought in the French and Indian War.

⭐ The Second Continental Congress

In May 1775, representatives from 12 of the colonies met in the city of Philadelphia for the **Second Continental Congress**. The leaders of the Congress had to decide how to react to the fighting. They decided not to break away from Great Britain. The Congress did make plans to create a **Continental Army** to defend the colonies and chose Virginian **George Washington** to command this army.

As Washington began gathering his troops, the Congress tried one last time to keep the peace. On July 5 the delegates signed the **Olive Branch Petition**. This petition was so named because the olive branch is a symbol of peace. In November the colonists learned that King George III had angrily rejected the peace offer. By that time the fighting in the colonies had spread.

✔ **Reading Check: Drawing Inferences and Conclusions** Why do you think King George III rejected the Olive Branch Petition?

★ Early Battles

While the Second Continental Congress was meeting, some colonists were striking at the British. Their target was Fort Ticonderoga in northern New York. This fort guarded access to Lake Champlain, a key waterway. Colonel Benedict Arnold joined Ethan Allen, from present-day Vermont, to lead the effort. On May 10, 1775, the colonists surprised the British by attacking during an early morning storm. They quickly took the fort and its large supply of weapons, including cannons.

Back in Massachusetts, minutemen held Boston under **siege**—a situation in which soldiers surround a city or fort. In mid-June 1775 the British prepared to take Charlestown, an area that overlooks Boston from the north. Warned of the plan, colonial forces rushed to build defenses on nearby Bunker Hill and Breed's Hill. The British were surprised when they saw the colonial soldiers already on the hills. Still, the Redcoats tried to capture the colonists' positions. The colonial forces were well protected from attack, but they were low on gunpowder. The colonial commander ordered his troops not to fire on the Redcoats "until you see the whites of their eyes."

Research on the ROM

Free Find:
George Washington
After reading about George Washington on the **Holt Researcher CD–ROM**, list the information you think led the Second Continental Congress to select him to command the Continental Army.

The Siege of Boston, 1775–1776

Interpreting Maps After the fighting at Lexington and Concord, the British retreated to the safety of Boston. It was not long, however, before the American forces moved closer to threaten the British positions.

Skills Assessment

1. **Locate** Find the location of Boston, Breed's Hill, and Bunker Hill on the map.

2. **Drawing Inferences and Conclusions** Why do you think the British did not retreat by land?

As the British attacked Breed's Hill, Bostonians climbed onto city rooftops to watch the battle unfold.

THE GRANGER COLLECTION, NEW YORK

Most of the fighting took place on Breed's Hill. The outnumbered colonists turned back several assaults. Yet, they eventually ran out of ammunition and had to retreat. The British suffered more than 1,000 casualties, compared to about 400 for the colonists. The **Battle of Bunker Hill** showed the colonists that they could hold their own against the British.

General Washington soon arrived to command the siege of Boston. To drive out the British, Washington needed the cannons from Fort Ticonderoga. In November he gave the task of transporting these guns to officer Henry Knox. Knox managed to haul the guns 300 miles in the middle of winter.

In March 1776 Washington used the cannons to fire on the British from Dorchester Heights, a hill overlooking southern Boston. The British were in trouble. The situation astonished British general William Howe. "The rebels have done more in one night than my whole army could do in months," he declared. On March 7 Howe ordered a retreat from Boston. The birthplace of the rebellion was back in colonial hands.

✔ Reading Check: **Identifying Cause and Effect** How did geography influence the early battles in New York and around Boston?

Section 1 Review

go.hrw.com **Homework Practice Online**
keyword: SF3 HP7

1 Define and explain:
• minutemen
• siege

2 Identify and explain:
• First Continental Congress
• Thomas Gage
• Redcoats
• Second Continental Congress
• Continental Army
• George Washington
• Olive Branch Petition
• Battle of Bunker Hill

3 Analyzing Information Copy the graphic organizer below. Use it to describe some of the factors that led to the start of the American Revolution, including the battles of Lexington and Concord.

Causes

Revolution

4 Finding the Main Idea
a. How were the actions of the First and Second Continental Congresses similar and different?

b. How did the colonial forces use geography to their advantage at Bunker Hill and Dorchester Heights?

5 Writing and Critical Thinking
Supporting a Point of View Imagine that you are a supporter of either John Dickinson or Patrick Henry at the First Continental Congress. Write a speech persuading others to support your position.

Consider the following:
• the abuses committed by British authorities
• the colonies' economic and social ties to Great Britain
• the risks of fighting against the British

My Brother Sam Is Dead

James Collier and Christopher Collier

James and Christopher Collier describe the Revolutionary War in their book My Brother Sam Is Dead. *They write from the viewpoint of young Connecticut colonist Timmy Meeker. Tim's father is a Loyalist, or Tory, but his older brother Sam has joined the Patriots. In the following excerpt, Tim and Sam talk with Betsy Read about the possibility of war between the Americans and the British.*

Tim Meeker's family is divided by the Revolutionary War.

"Is your grandfather going to fight the Lobster-backs [Redcoats]?"

"I don't think so," Betsy said. "He's too old. He said he would probably resign his **commission**[1] to some younger man. Anyway he doesn't think we ought to fight unless we really have to. He says there ought to be some way of working it out with the King and Parliament without having to fight."

"There isn't any way to work it out," Sam said. "The British government is determined to keep us their slaves. We're going to fight."

"A lot of people aren't going to fight," I said.

"Around here they aren't. This is Tory country. Father, Mr. Beach, the Lyons, the Couches—most of them in our church are Tories. And they think it's the same everywhere, but it isn't. Down in New Haven they're ready to fight, and Windham's already marched their militia to Boston." He was being **scornful**.[2] Sam always got scornful when other people disagreed with him, because he always thought he was right, although to be honest, a lot of the time he was right, because of being so smart. But still it was hard for me to think that Father was wrong.

"Sam, Father says for most people it isn't being free, it's only a few **pence**[3] in taxes."

"That's Father for you, it's the money that counts. There are principles involved, Tim. Either you live up to your principles or you don't and maybe you have to take a chance on getting killed."

"Who wants to get killed?"

"Nobody *wants* to get killed," Sam said. "But you should be willing to die for your principles."

"That's right," Betsy said.

"But Betsy, you don't have to take a chance on getting killed," I said.

"I'd fight if I could," she said.

I hated arguing about it. "Well maybe the King will change his mind and get the Lobsterbacks out."

Sam shook his head. "He won't. He thinks he's going to teach us a lesson. But we're going to teach him one. We already taught him one at Lexington."

"That's what I mean," I said. "Maybe he'll give up now."

Betsy shook her head. "He won't. Not according to my father."

Everybody was quiet for a minute. Then Sam said, "There's going to be war. Which side are you going to be on?"

I couldn't answer. . . .

Understanding What You Read

1. **Literature and History** Why does Sam believe the colonists should fight the British?
2. **Literature and You** Why do you think Tim cannot say which side he will be on? Which side would you choose?

---

[1] **commission:** rank   [2] **scornful:** insulting   [3] **pence:** pennies

Declaring Independence

★ ★

Read to Discover

1. How did Thomas Paine's *Common Sense* influence the colonies?
2. What were the main ideas stated in the Declaration of Independence?
3. How did Americans react to the Declaration of Independence?

WHY IT MATTERS TODAY

The Declaration of Independence established the basic principles of our individual freedoms. Use CNNfyi.com or other **current events** sources to find an example of how we experience these freedoms today. Record your findings in your journal.

Define

- unalienable rights

Identify

- *Common Sense*
- Thomas Paine
- Thomas Jefferson
- Declaration of Independence
- Patriots
- Loyalists
- Abigail Adams

Thomas Paine became well known throughout the colonies for his political pamphlet Common Sense.

The Story Continues

On January 9, 1776, a 47-page pamphlet hit the streets of Philadelphia. The author was 38-year-old Thomas Paine, a self-educated British Quaker. About two years before, Paine had met Benjamin Franklin in London and impressed the colonist with his sharp mind. Franklin had helped Paine come to Philadelphia, where Paine became the editor of the *Pennsylvania Magazine*. Then in 1776 Paine produced a work that changed the course of American history.

★ Paine's *Common Sense*

In his pamphlet **Common Sense**, **Thomas Paine** argued for breaking away from Great Britain. News of the work spread through the thirteen colonies, and it eventually sold some 500,000 copies. *Common Sense* became popular because of its message and style. Most pamphlets of the time were written by lawyers in a style that only well-educated people could understand. Paine wrote as a common person speaking to common people, which allowed him to reach a wider audience.

Paine stated in *Common Sense* that the system of monarchy in countries such as Britain was not fair. He said that the people, not kings and queens, should make the laws. "A government of our own is our natural right," he wrote. At a time when monarchs ruled most countries of the world, this was a fairly new idea. Paine said that the colonies should demand their independence.

Paine's *Common Sense* helped change the way many colonists viewed Britain. With war now under way, the idea of independence gained more and more supporters.

✔ **Reading Check: Identifying Points of View** How did many colonists react to the ideas Thomas Paine expressed in *Common Sense*?

⭐ Declaring Independence

Many colonial leaders agreed with Paine that the colonies should be free. In June 1776 the Second Continental Congress created a committee to write a document declaring the colonies' independence. The committee members were John Adams, Benjamin Franklin, **Thomas Jefferson**, Robert R. Livingston, and Roger Sherman. Jefferson was the main author of the document.

The **Declaration of Independence** expresses three main ideas. First, Jefferson argued that all men possess **unalienable rights**. He stated that these basic rights include "life, liberty, and the pursuit of happiness." The writings of Enlightenment philosophers such as John Locke inspired the idea of unalienable rights.

Jefferson's second point was that King George III had violated the colonists' rights. Like Thomas Paine, he charged the king with passing unfair laws and interfering with colonial self-government. He also accused the king of taxing colonists without their consent. In addition, the presence of a large British army in the colonies upset Jefferson.

". . . life, liberty, and the pursuit of happiness."

Interpreting the Visual Record

Independence *Delegate Thomas Jefferson and the other members of his committee present the Declaration of Independence before the Second Continental Congress.* **Who are some of the colonial leaders shown in this image?**

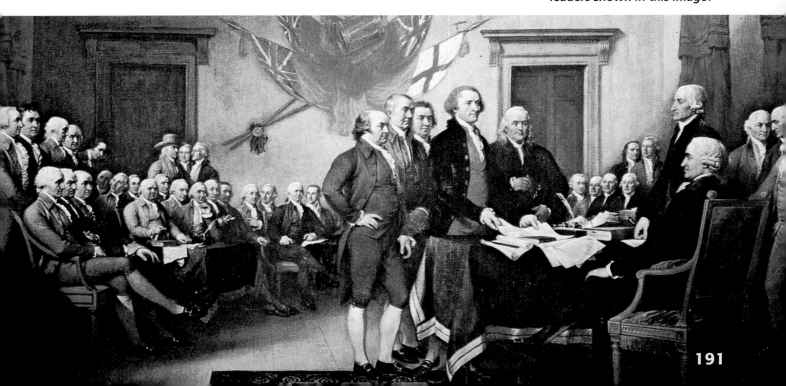

Third, Jefferson argued that the colonies had the right to break away from Great Britain. Jefferson was influenced by the Enlightenment idea of the social contract, which states that rulers should protect the rights of their citizens. In exchange, the people agree to be governed. Jefferson said that because King George III had broken the social contract, the colonists need no longer obey him.

On July 4, 1776, the Continental Congress approved the Declaration of Independence. This act broke all ties to the British Crown. The United States of America was born.

✔ **Reading Check: Finding the Main Idea** What are the key ideas stated by Jefferson in 1776 in the Declaration of Independence?

July 4, 1776
The United States of America is formed.

⭐ Choosing Sides

Colonists who chose to fight for independence became known as **Patriots**. Those who remained loyal to Great Britain were called **Loyalists** or Tories. Many other colonists remained neutral, choosing neither side. People on both sides often felt very strongly about their views. In March 1775, before the fighting had even started, Patriot Patrick Henry spoke before the Virginia House of Burgesses.

History Makers Speak

❝Is life so dear or peace so sweet as to be purchased at the price of chains and slavery? Forbid it, Almighty God! I know not what course others may take; but as for me, give me liberty, or give me death!❞

—Patrick Henry, quoted in *The Annals of America*

Interpreting the Visual Record

Rebellion *Patriots pull down a statue of King George III in New York.* **How do you think these colonists feel about King George and Great Britain?**

Once the Declaration of Independence was signed, Loyalists became targets of abuse by Patriots. It is estimated that more than 100,000 Loyalists fled the colonies during the Revolution. Most of them went to Canada.

Many Loyalists shared the feelings of Samuel Curwen of Massachusetts. He was a merchant who believed that the colonies did not need independence. To Curwen, British rule was the best way to maintain peace and prosperity in the colonies. He refused to blame the fighting at Lexington and Concord entirely on the British. Patriot neighbors called him a Tory. Curwen had to flee his home to escape "the looks, words, and actions of the mad rabble [masses]."

The divisions caused by the war also affected some key Patriot leaders. For example, Thomas Fairfax, one of George Washington's closest friends, fled to Britain because he was a Loyalist. Even the great Patriot Benjamin Franklin had a Loyalist son, William.

✔ **Reading Check: Identifying Points of View** Why did some colonists remain Loyalists?

★ Other Reactions to the Declaration

Some people pointed out that the Declaration ignored many colonists. Although many women were Patriots, the Declaration did not address their rights. The phrase "all men are created equal" failed to mention women at all. This issue worried **Abigail Adams**, the wife of John Adams. In a letter she asked her husband to protect the rights of women.

 History Makers Speak ❝In the new code of Laws which I suppose it will be necessary for you to make I desire you would Remember the Ladies. . . . If particular care and attention is not paid to the Ladies we . . . will not hold ourselves bound by any Laws in which we have no voice, or Representation.❞

—Abigail Adams, quoted in *Notable American Women*

In addition, the Declaration did not recognize the rights of enslaved African Americans. In July 1776 slavery was legal in all the colonies. In his first draft of the Declaration, Thomas Jefferson—a slaveholder himself—had included a passage that attacked the slave trade. However, southern delegates insisted that the passage be removed.

The Revolution raised questions about whether slavery should exist in a land that valued liberty. Some Patriots had compared living under British rule to living as slaves. These writers could not ignore the difference between the ideals of liberty and the practice of slavery. Some colonists wanted the principle "all men are created equal" to apply to all people. Massachusetts abolished slavery in 1783, and by 1784 the rest of New England also had taken steps to end slavery. Even so, the conflict over slavery continued long after the Revolutionary War had ended.

✔ **Reading Check: Finding the Main Idea** What groups felt ignored by the Declaration of Independence?

BIOGRAPHY

Abigail Adams
(1744–1818)

Abigail Adams was born in Massachusetts in 1744. Educated at home by her parents, she developed a great love of reading and writing. She married John Adams in 1764, and they raised five children. Abigail Adams ran most of the family's businesses and advised her husband on political issues. Many of her letters to family and friends were saved long after her death in 1818. Some historians have called her "one of the great letter writers of all time." **How have historians been able to learn about the life of Abigail Adams?**

Section 2 Review

 Homework Practice Online
keyword: SF3 HP7

1 **Define** and explain:
• unalienable rights

2 **Identify** and explain:
• *Common Sense*
• Thomas Paine
• Thomas Jefferson
• Declaration of Independence
• Patriots
• Loyalists
• Abigail Adams

3 **Comparing** Copy the graphic organizer below. Use it to compare the arguments that colonists offered for and against independence, including Thomas Jefferson's arguments in the Declaration of Independence.

Arguments for Independence		Arguments against Independence
	VS.	

4 **Finding the Main Idea**
a. Why did colonists find Thomas Paine's arguments in *Common Sense* so persuasive?

b. Why was 1776 significant for the colonies, and what major events took place that year?

5 **Writing and Critical Thinking**
Identifying Points of View Imagine that you are living in the colonies in 1776. Write an essay explaining how colonists reacted to the Declaration of Independence.

Consider the following:
• the views of Loyalists and Patriots
• the contributions of women to society
• the meaning of the phrase "all men are created equal"

THE
DECLARATION
of
INDEPENDENCE

Exploring the Document

Thomas Jefferson wrote the first draft of the Declaration in a little more than two weeks. **How is the Declaration's idea about why governments are formed still important to our country today?**

¹**impel:** force

²**endowed:** provided

³**usurpations:** wrongful seizures of power

⁴**evinces:** clearly displays

⁵**despotism:** unlimited power

In Congress, July 4, 1776
The unanimous Declaration of the thirteen
united States of America,

When in the Course of human events, it becomes necessary for one people to dissolve the political bands which have connected them with another, and to assume among the Powers of the earth, the separate and equal station to which the Laws of Nature and of Nature's God entitle them, a decent respect to the opinions of mankind requires that they should declare the causes which **impel**¹ them to the separation.

Natural Rights

We hold these truths to be self-evident, that all men are created equal, that they are **endowed**² by their Creator with certain unalienable Rights, that among these are Life, Liberty, and the pursuit of Happiness. That to secure these rights, Governments are instituted among Men, deriving their just powers from the consent of the governed,

That whenever any Form of Government becomes destructive of these ends, it is the Right of the People to alter or to abolish it, and to institute new Government, laying its foundation on such principles and organizing its powers in such form, as to them shall seem most likely to effect their Safety and Happiness. Prudence, indeed, will dictate that Governments long established should not be changed for light and transient causes; and accordingly all experience hath shown, that mankind are more disposed to suffer, while evils are sufferable, than to right themselves by abolishing the forms to which they are accustomed. But when a long train of abuses and **usurpations**,³ pursuing invariably the same Object **evinces**⁴ a design to reduce them under absolute **Despotism**,⁵ it is their right, it is their duty, to throw off such Government, and to provide new Guards for their future security.—

LEFT: *Thomas Jefferson*

Colonists' Complaints against the King

Such has been the patient sufferance of these Colonies; and such is now the necessity which constrains them to alter their former Systems of Government. The history of the present King of Great Britain is a history of repeated injuries and usurpations, all having in direct object the establishment of an absolute **Tyranny**[6] over these States. To prove this, let Facts be submitted to a **candid**[7] world.

He has refused his Assent to Laws, the most wholesome and necessary for the public good.

He has forbidden his Governors to pass Laws of immediate and pressing importance, unless suspended in their operation till his Assent should be obtained; and when so suspended, he has utterly neglected to attend to them.

He has refused to pass other Laws for the accommodation of large districts of people, unless those people would **relinquish**[8] the right of Representation in the Legislature, a right **inestimable**[9] to them and **formidable**[10] to tyrants only.

He has called together legislative bodies at places unusual, uncomfortable, and distant from the depository of their Public Records, for the sole purpose of fatiguing them into compliance with his measures.

He has dissolved Representative Houses repeatedly, for opposing with manly firmness his invasions on the rights of the people.

He has refused for a long time, after such dissolutions, to cause others to be elected; whereby the Legislative Powers, incapable of **Annihilation**,[11] have returned to the People at large for their exercise; the State remaining in the mean time exposed to all the dangers of invasion from without, and **convulsions**[12] within.

He has endeavored to prevent the population of these States; for that purpose obstructing the Laws of **Naturalization of Foreigners**;[13] refusing to pass others to encourage their migration hither, and raising the conditions of new **Appropriations of Lands**.[14]

He has obstructed the Administration of Justice, by refusing his Assent to Laws for establishing Judiciary Powers.

He has made Judges dependent on his Will alone, for the **tenure**[15] of their offices, and the amount and payment of their salaries.

He has erected **a multitude of**[16] New Offices, and sent hither swarms of Officers to harass our people, and eat out their substance.

He has kept among us, in times of peace, Standing Armies without the Consent of our legislature.

He has affected to render the Military independent of and superior to the Civil Power.

He has combined with others to subject us to a jurisdiction foreign to our constitution, and unacknowledged by our laws; giving his Assent to their Acts of pretended legislation:

[6]**tyranny:** oppressive power exerted by a government or ruler

[7]**candid:** fair

Exploring the Document

Here the Declaration lists the charges that the colonists had against King George III. How might the language and content of the list appeal to people's emotions?

[8]**relinquish:** release, yield

[9]**inestimable:** priceless

[10]**formidable:** causing dread

[11]**annihilation:** destruction

[12]**convulsions:** violent disturbances

[13]**naturalization of foreigners:** the process by which foreign-born persons become citizens

[14]**appropriations of land:** setting aside land for settlement

[15]**tenure:** term

[16]**a multitude of:** many

For **quartering**[17] large bodies of armed troops among us:

For protecting them, by a mock Trial, from Punishment for any Murders which they should commit on the Inhabitants of these States:

For cutting off our Trade with all parts of the world:

For imposing taxes on us without our Consent:

For depriving us in many cases, of the benefits of Trial by Jury:

For transporting us beyond Seas to be tried for pretended offences:

For abolishing the free System of English Laws in a neighboring Province, establishing therein an **Arbitrary**[18] government, and enlarging its Boundaries so as to **render**[19] it at once an example and fit instrument for introducing the same absolute rule into these Colonies:

For taking away our Charters, abolishing our most valuable Laws, and altering fundamentally the Forms of our Governments:

For suspending our own Legislature, and declaring themselves invested with Power to legislate for us in all cases whatsoever.

He has **abdicated**[20] Government here, by declaring us out of his Protection and waging War against us.

He has plundered our seas, ravaged our Coasts, burnt our towns, and destroyed the lives of our people.

He is at this time transporting large armies of **foreign mercenaries**[21] to complete the works of death, desolation and tyranny, already begun with circumstances of Cruelty & **perfidy**[22] scarcely paralleled in the most barbarous ages, and totally unworthy the Head of a civilized nation.

He has constrained our fellow Citizens taken Captive on the high Seas to bear Arms against their Country, to become the executioners of their friends and Brethren, or to fall themselves by their Hands.

He has excited domestic **insurrections**[23] amongst us, and has endeavored to bring on the inhabitants of our frontiers, the merciless Indian Savages, whose known rule of warfare, is an undistinguished destruction of all ages, sexes and conditions.

In every stage of these Oppressions We have **Petitioned for Redress**[24] in the most humble terms: Our repeated Petitions have been answered only by repeated injury. A Prince, whose character is thus marked by every act which may define a Tyrant, is unfit to be the ruler of a free People.

Nor have We been wanting in attention to our British brethren. We have warned them from time to time of attempts by their legislature to extend an **unwarrantable jurisdiction**[25] over us. We have reminded them of the circumstances of our emigration and settlement here. We have appealed to their native justice and **magnanimity**,[26] and we have **conjured**[27] them by the ties of our common kindred to disavow these usurpations, which, would inevitably interrupt our connections and correspondence. They too have been deaf to the voice of justice and of **consanguinity**.[28] We must, therefore, **acquiesce**[29] in the necessity, which denounces our Separation, and hold them, as we hold the rest of mankind, Enemies in War, in Peace Friends.

---

[17]**quartering:** lodging, housing

Exploring the Document

Colonists had been angry over British tax policies since just after the French and Indian War. **Why were the colonists protesting British tax policies?**

[18]**arbitrary:** not based on law

[19]**render:** make

[20]**abdicated:** given up

[21]**foreign mercenaries:** soldiers hired to fight for a country not their own

[22]**perfidy:** violation of trust

[23]**insurrections:** rebellions

[24]**petitioned for redress:** asked formally for a correction of wrongs

[25]**unwarrantable jurisdiction:** unjustified authority

[26]**magnanimity:** generous spirit

[27]**conjured:** urgently called upon

[28]**consanguinity:** common ancestry

[29]**acquiesce:** consent to

An Independent and United Nation

We, therefore, the Representatives of the united States of America, in General Congress, Assembled, appealing to the Supreme Judge of the world for the **rectitude**[30] of our intentions, do, in the Name, and by Authority of the good People of these Colonies, solemnly publish and declare, That these United Colonies are, and of Right ought to be Free and Independent States; that they are Absolved from all Allegiance to the British Crown, and that all political connection between them and the State of Great Britain, is and ought to be totally dissolved; and that as Free and Independent States, they have full Power to levy War, conclude Peace, contract Alliances, establish Commerce, and to do all other Acts and Things which Independent States may of right do. And for the support of this Declaration, with a firm reliance on the Protection of Divine Providence, we mutually pledge to each other our Lives, our Fortunes and our sacred Honor.

[30]**rectitude:** rightness

John Hancock
President of Massachusetts

GEORGIA
Button Gwinnett
Lyman Hall
George Walton

NORTH CAROLINA
William Hooper
Joseph Hewes
John Penn

SOUTH CAROLINA
Edward Rutledge
Thomas Heyward, Jr.
Thomas Lynch, Jr.
Arthur Middleton

MARYLAND
Samuel Chase
William Paca
Thomas Stone
Charles Carroll of
　Carrollton

VIRGINIA
George Wythe
Richard Henry Lee

Thomas Jefferson
Benjamin Harrison
Thomas Nelson, Jr.
Francis Lightfoot Lee
Carter Braxton

PENNSYLVANIA
Robert Morris
Benjamin Rush
Benjamin Franklin
John Morton
George Clymer
James Smith
George Taylor
James Wilson
George Ross

DELAWARE
Caesar Rodney
George Read
Thomas McKean

NEW YORK
William Floyd
Philip Livingston
Francis Lewis
Lewis Morris

NEW JERSEY
Richard Stockton
John Witherspoon
Francis Hopkinson
John Hart
Abraham Clark

NEW HAMPSHIRE
Josiah Bartlett
William Whipple
Matthew Thorton

MASSACHUSETTS
Samuel Adams
John Adams
Robert Treat Paine
Elbridge Gerry

RHODE ISLAND
Stephen Hopkins
William Ellery

CONNECTICUT
Roger Sherman
Samuel Huntington
William Williams
Oliver Wolcott

Exploring the Document

On July 4, 1776, Congress adopted the final draft of the Declaration of Independence. A formal copy written on parchment paper was signed on August 2, 1776. **From whom did the Declaration's signers receive their authority to declare independence in 1776?**

Exploring the Document

The following is part of a passage that the Congress removed from Jefferson's original draft: "He has waged cruel war against human nature itself, violating its most sacred rights of life and liberty in the persons of a distant people who never offended him, captivating and carrying them into slavery in another hemisphere, or to incur miserable death in their transportation thither." **Why do you think the Congress deleted this passage?**

Dark Hours for the Revolution

Read to Discover

1. What were the Patriots' advantages and disadvantages at the beginning of the Revolutionary War?
2. How did different groups contribute to the war effort?
3. What problems did the Patriots face in Canada and New York?

WHY IT MATTERS TODAY

When the colonies rebelled against Britain, they did not have a navy and a professional army. Today U.S. leaders consider it vital to have a well-equipped and prepared military. Use CNNfyi.com or other **current events** sources to learn where U.S. military forces are serving today. Record your findings in your journal.

Define

- mercenaries

Identify

- Lord Dunmore's Proclamation
- Thayendanegea
- Molly Pitcher
- William Howe

COURTESY OF MOUNT VERNON LADIES' ASSOCIATION

During the winters, Martha Washington joined her husband wherever his army was camped.

The Story Continues

General George Washington faced a challenging task when he took command of the Continental Army. The Patriots were up against a mighty enemy in Britain. Washington wrote to his wife, Martha, that he did not know if he could build a strong enough army. "I shall hope that my undertaking is designed to answer some good purpose," he said. He did not know what to expect when he led his men into the field.

⭐ Comparing Strengths and Weaknesses

At the beginning of the war, the British seemed much stronger than the Patriots. Great Britain had more money and resources than the colonies. Britain also had a powerful military. Its navy was the largest in the world. British soldiers were mostly well-trained professionals. In contrast, when the war began, the colonists had no navy at all. The colonial army was made up of poorly trained local militias. Few of these groups had ever fought together.

However, the colonists did have some advantages. Many Americans supported the Revolution. As a result, the British army often had to deal with hostile citizens. The British also had to ship their supplies across the Atlantic Ocean. This process slowed down their war effort. Finally, the Patriots were fighting for a cause in which they believed. On the other hand, some British soldiers were **mercenaries**, or hired foreign soldiers.

✔ **Reading Check: Categorizing** What advantages and disadvantages did the Patriots have when the war began?

Colonial soldiers often used horns such as this one to store their gunpowder.

⭐ A Call to Arms

General Washington's first task was to organize and raise more troops for the Continental Army. During the course of the war, more than 230,000 soldiers served in the Continental Army. Another 145,000 Americans joined local militias. These volunteers came from many backgrounds. Many were teenagers, such as 14-year-old James Forten, who served in the Continental Navy. Some officers had fought in the French and Indian War, but few of the volunteers had combat experience. General Charles Lee hoped that their courage would be enough.

History Makers Speak

❝They are admirable—young, stout, healthy, zealous [eager], good-humored and sober [serious]. . . . I really believe a very little time and pains would render [make] 'em the most invincible [unbeatable] army that have appeared.❞

—General Charles Lee, quoted in *Voices of 1776*, by Richard Wheeler

One question facing Washington was whether to recruit African Americans. Many African Americans, including some slaves, were already serving in local militias. African Americans like Peter Salem and Salem Poor had already fought in battles. But many southerners did not want the American forces to include black soldiers. Washington soon banned African Americans from serving in the army.

The British reacted quickly. Lord Dunmore, Virginia's governor, issued a proclamation on November 7, 1775. **Lord Dunmore's Proclamation** promised freedom to any slave who fought for the British. Thousands of slaves agreed. In response, the Continental Army began allowing free African Americans to enlist, and eventually some 5,000 joined.

⭐ Other Sources of Help

American Indian groups fought on both sides during the war. The British had many Indian allies. One of Great Britain's key allies was Mohawk leader **Thayendanegea** (thah-yuhn-dah-ne-GAY-uh), also known as Joseph Brant. He persuaded many of the Iroquois to support the British. However, the Patriots worked hard just to keep American Indians neutral. This effort was very important on the frontier.

CONNECTING TO

SCIENCE AND TECHNOLOGY

The Long Rifle

Many Patriots from the frontier used a gun known as the long rifle or Kentucky rifle. A rifle is a type of gun with a grooved barrel. The grooves spin the ball, or bullet, as it is shot. Compared to a musket, a long rifle can shoot a ball farther and with greater accuracy. However, soldiers could fire and reload muskets faster than rifles. Rifles also lacked bayonets for use in hand-to-hand combat.

General Washington used rifle units for special missions such as sharpshooting and scouting. These groups impressed the British with their accuracy at long range. By the end of the war, the long rifle was well known. Over time, it became one of the most common weapons in North America. **How were rifles different from muskets?**

This painting shows Molly Pitcher fighting alongside other Patriots at the Battle of Monmouth.

THE GRANGER COLLECTION, NEW YORK

Many women also helped the Patriot cause. Women often ran farms and businesses while men served as soldiers. Other women helped support the army by raising money for supplies or joining sewing groups to make uniforms.

Analyzing Primary Sources

Summarizing How are women supporting the war effort according to this speaker?

History Makers Speak

❝At every house Women and children [are] making Cartridges, running Bullets . . . and at the same time animating [encouraging] their Husbands and Sons to fight.❞

—Anonymous, quoted in *Born for Liberty,* by Sara M. Evans

Some women served as messengers, nurses, or spies. A few women, such as Deborah Sampson, even disguised themselves as men to fight in the war. The woman who perhaps became best known for her wartime service was Mary Ludwig Hays. She earned the nickname **Molly Pitcher** by bringing water to thirsty Patriot troops. When her husband was wounded in a 1778 battle, she quickly took his place loading cannons.

✔ **Reading Check: Summarizing** How did different groups living in the colonies contribute to the war effort?

★ British Victories

Many Patriot leaders favored fighting a defensive war. This would help the army's limited supplies last longer. However, other, more aggressive leaders wanted to make British-controlled Canada the "fourteenth colony." In November 1775, Patriot troops led by General Richard Montgomery took the town of St. John's, Canada. Shortly afterward Montgomery captured the nearby town of Montreal.

The next major target was the well-defended city of Quebec. General Benedict Arnold led his troops on a long march north through what is now Maine. When Arnold's forces reached Quebec, he waited for Montgomery's troops to arrive. Together, the commanders planned their attack. The American troops were cold and far from home. Many of the soldiers also had enlistments that would soon end. This meant that the Patriots had to act quickly, but the Americans had no cannons to knock down Quebec's walls. Arnold and Montgomery decided to wait for a snowstorm. They hoped the storm would provide cover while the Patriots got close to the city's defenses.

During a fierce blizzard on New Year's Eve, the Patriots attacked Quebec. The Americans suffered a crushing defeat. General Montgomery was killed early in the battle. More than half of the American troops were captured, killed, or wounded. Patriots' hopes of taking Canada soon faded.

Farther south, General Washington had moved his troops to New York. In early July 1776, Patriots spotted a large fleet of British ships nearing New York Bay. Led by General **William Howe**, the British drove the Continental Army off of Long Island. Washington's troops retreated to Manhattan Island. The British force was much larger and better equipped than that of the Patriots. Washington had to use all his leadership skills just to save his outnumbered army. In a series of battles, Howe forced the Continental Army to keep retreating. The Redcoats captured many Patriots as well as valuable supplies. After several months they pushed Washington out of New York. Howe's revenge for his defeat at Boston was complete.

Soldiers in the Continental Army (left) often wore the tricornered hat shown here.

British soldiers (below) were nicknamed Redcoats because of their uniforms.

COLLECTION OF THE NEW YORK HISTORICAL SOCIETY

✔ **Reading Check: Contrasting** Describe the different problems faced by the Continental Army in Canada and New York.

Section 3 Review

go.hrw.com **Homework Practice Online**

keyword: SF3 HP7

❶ **Define** and explain:
• mercenaries

❷ **Identify** and explain:
• Lord Dunmore's Proclamation
• Thayendanegea
• Molly Pitcher
• William Howe

❸ **Comparing** Copy the chart below. Use it to compare the military advantages of the British and the Patriots.

British Advantages	Patriots' Advantages

❹ **Finding the Main Idea**
a. Explain the roles that some young white men, African Americans, American Indians, and women played in supporting the Patriots during the American Revolution.
b. Why did the American invasion of Canada fail while the British attack on New York succeeded?

❺ **Writing and Critical Thinking**
Analyzing Information Imagine that you are a British officer on the frontier. Write a brief report to your commander explaining why you think that many American Indians will side with the British.

Consider the following:
• which side Indian leaders think will win the war
• conflicts on the frontier
• alliances between American Indians and the British

The Patriots Gain New Hope

Read to Discover

1. What were Washington's strategies at Trenton and Princeton?
2. Why was the Battle of Saratoga a turning point in the war?
3. How did foreign nations and individuals aid the Patriots?
4. How did the Patriots carry out the naval war?

WHY IT MATTERS TODAY

Foreign allies helped the Patriots fight the Revolutionary War. The United States still has close alliances with many countries. Use CNNfyi.com or other **current events** sources to learn more about a nation that is a U.S. ally today. Record your findings in your journal.

Identify

- Battle of Trenton
- Battle of Princeton
- John Burgoyne
- Battle of Brandywine Creek
- Battle of Saratoga
- Bernardo de Gálvez
- Marquis de Lafayette
- Friedrich von Steuben
- John Paul Jones

The Story Continues

General Howe was confident that the British would win the war quickly.

In November 1776 General Howe took the last Patriot fort on Manhattan Island. Patriot Alexander Graydon was among those captured. He later recalled a British officer warning the prisoners, "Young men, ye should never fight against your king!" Graydon and other Patriots like him survived their capture. But they began to fear that the British were getting close to complete victory in the war.

Victory in New Jersey

General Howe sent troops to take New Jersey in November 1776. After the British victories in Canada and New York, Howe thought the war would be over soon. So he gave his troops a rest and settled in New York City for the winter. Howe left New Jersey in the hands of Hessians. These were German mercenaries, many from the state of Hesse, hired to fight for the British.

Howe's delay allowed Washington to gather reinforcements. The Patriots were still in trouble, however. Writer Thomas Paine described the difficult situation in the first of his *Crisis* papers. "These are the times that try men's souls," he wrote. Paine urged the Patriots to stay loyal to their cause.

Washington decided to attack the Hessians at Trenton, New Jersey. He believed he could take them by surprise while they celebrated the holiday. On Christmas night in 1776, Washington and 2,400 soldiers silently crossed the icy Delaware River. The troops were short on supplies—many had no shoes. But, they were ready to fight. After landing early on the morning of December 26, the Patriots marched to Trenton. The **Battle of Trenton** lasted less than an hour. The Patriot forces captured more than 900 Hessians with just five American casualties. The impressive victory boosted the Patriots' spirits.

Washington was not satisfied with only one victory. As British general Charles Cornwallis rushed to stop him, Washington marched to the town of Princeton, northeast of Trenton. Washington planned another surprise for the enemy. On the night of January 2, the Patriots kept their campfires burning for the British to see. Most of the Patriots then left camp under cover of darkness and circled behind the British troops. The Patriots attacked the next morning. An 85-year-old civilian described the battle.

 History Makers Speak

"The battle was plainly seen from our door . . . and the guns went off so quick and many together that they could not be numbered. We presently went down into the cellar to keep out of the way of the shot. There was a neighbor woman down in the cellar with us that was so affrighted [frightened]. . . . Almost as soon as the firing was over, our house was filled and surrounded with General Washington's men."

—Anonymous, quoted in *Voices of 1776,* by Richard Wheeler

The hard-fought **Battle of Princeton** ended in another victory for the Patriots. As he watched the Redcoats flee, Washington cheered, "It is a fine fox chase, my boys!"

✔ **Reading Check: Summarizing** Explain General Washington's strategy at Trenton and Princeton.

CONNECTING TO
THE ARTS

Crossing the Delaware
George Washington and his troops crossed the partially frozen Delaware River on the night of December 25, 1776. This daring act led to a key Patriot victory. German-American artist Emanuel Leutze created this famous painting of the event in 1851. *Washington Crossing the Delaware* now hangs in the Metropolitan Museum of Art in New York City. In 1999 Leutze's painting was used as the basis for the image on the back of the New Jersey state quarter. What feelings do you think Leutze wanted to inspire with this painting?

THE GRANGER COLLECTION, NEW YORK

Interpreting the Visual Record

Patriot victory *British general John Burgoyne surrenders his army to American Patriot general Horatio Gates at Saratoga, New York, on October 17, 1777.* **What is Burgoyne handing over to the Americans?**

⭐ Turning Point at Saratoga

The defeats at Trenton and Princeton embarrassed the British. In the spring of 1777, they decided to strike back. They planned to cut New England off from the rest of the colonies. The plan called for British troops in Canada to take back Fort Ticonderoga. General **John Burgoyne** would lead this effort. He would then march south. Meanwhile, a second force would march east from Lake Ontario. Finally, General Howe's troops in New York City would move north. All three groups would come together at Albany, New York.

Burgoyne recaptured Fort Ticonderoga by early July. However, his route across New York cut through thick forests. Colonists chopped down large trees across his path to slow his progress. Another problem with the plan soon arose. General Howe decided to attack Philadelphia before marching to Albany. Washington raced to stop Howe, and the two sides met at the **Battle of Brandywine Creek**. On September 11, 1777, Howe's forces won a convincing victory. The Patriots suffered almost twice as many casualties as the British. Howe probably could have crushed the Continental Army completely, but he allowed many soldiers to escape.

Burgoyne did not know that Howe and the force from western Canada were both late. As a result, when Burgoyne neared Albany he found his army badly outnumbered by Patriot troops. At the **Battle of Saratoga** Burgoyne suffered a major defeat. Patriot troops led by General Horatio Gates drove back a British attack. American officer Benedict Arnold then led a bold charge that forced the British to retreat. Burgoyne soon found himself surrounded. On October 17, 1777, he surrendered to General Gates. The Patriots captured Burgoyne's entire army.

The victory at Saratoga was the greatest win yet for the American forces. It greatly boosted morale and led to increased foreign support for the Patriots. Patriot James Thacher wrote, "This event will make one of the most brilliant pages of American history."

✔ **Reading Check: Finding the Main Idea** Why was the Battle of Saratoga a turning point in the war for the Patriots?

Research on the R⊙M

Free Find:
Battle of Saratoga
After reading about the Battle of Saratoga on the **Holt Researcher CD–ROM**, create a fictional account of how the British might have won the battle.

Legend (battles):

- New York — August 1776
- Trenton — December 1776
- Princeton — January 1777
- Saratoga — September–October 1777
- Vincennes — February 1779
- Camden — August 1780
- Kings Mountain — October 1780
- Guilford Courthouse — March 1781
- Yorktown — October 1781

**Map labels:**

Lake Superior, Lake Michigan, Lake Huron, Lake Erie, Lake Ontario, CANADA, QUEBEC, Quebec, Montreal, St. Lawrence River, Fort Ticonderoga, Saratoga, Albany, NH, Boston, Dorchester Heights, MA, CT, RI, NOVA SCOTIA, Halifax, HOWE, 40° N, 70° W, ATLANTIC OCEAN, Fort Detroit, Fort Pitt, CLARK, Ohio River, Vincennes, Cahokia, Kaskaskia, SPANISH LOUISIANA, Mississippi River, NY, New York, Princeton, Trenton, Valley Forge, Philadelphia, PA, NJ, MD, DE, HOWE, BRITISH FLEET, WASHINGTON & ROCHAMBEAU, VA, James R., York R., Chesapeake Bay, Yorktown, DE GRASSE FROM WEST INDIES, Guilford Courthouse, CORNWALLIS, GREENE, GATES, NC, Kings Mountain, Camden, Wilmington, SC, Charleston, CLINTON & CORNWALLIS FROM NEW YORK, Savannah R., GA, Savannah, BRITISH EAST AND WEST FLORIDA, Natchez, Baton Rouge, Mobile, Pensacola, New Orleans, Gulf of Mexico, 30° N, 80° W, 90° W, 70° W

Map key:

- → American forces
- → British forces
- ✹ American victories
- ✹ British victories
- ■ Forts
- – – – Proclamation Line of 1763

Bernardo de Gálvez, the Spanish governor of Louisiana, defeated the British at Baton Rouge and Natchez in 1779, Mobile in 1780, and Pensacola in 1781.

Maj. Gen. Benedict Arnold fought at Saratoga, and later turned traitor.

0 — 125 — 250 Miles
0 — 125 — 250 Kilometers
Albers Equal-Area Projection

Battle of Saratoga

Albers Equal-Area Projection, QUEBEC, Montreal, St. Lawrence R., Lake Champlain, Lake Ontario, Lake George, Fort Ticonderoga, Fort Edward, BURGOYNE, NH, Connecticut R., Saratoga, GATES, ARNOLD, & MORGAN, Albany, NY, Boston, MA, CT, RI

0 — 50 — 100 Miles
0 — 50 — 100 Kilometers

The Fight for Independence, 1776–1781

Interpreting Maps During the Revolutionary War, battles took place throughout the thirteen colonies.

Skills Assessment Places and Regions Based on this map, where did the Patriot victories in the Revolutionary War take place?

The Marquis de Lafayette was an important ally of the Patriots.

THE HISTORIC NEW ORLEANS COLLECTION, COLOR ADDED

GLOBAL CONNECTIONS

Bernardo de Gálvez

Bernardo de Gálvez, the governor of Spanish Louisiana, was an important ally to the Patriots. Gálvez allowed the Americans to use the Spanish port of New Orleans. Gálvez also attacked British forts along the Mississippi River and in Florida. These actions helped Patriots in the West. His efforts also kept Spain in command of the Gulf of Mexico. The city of Galveston in present-day Texas was named in his honor. In what ways did Gálvez aid the Patriot cause?

★ Foreign Allies

France and Spain, who were enemies of Great Britain, had been secretly aiding the Patriots. In 1776 the Patriots had sent several delegates to France, including Benjamin Franklin. Franklin worked hard to increase French support for the Patriot cause. The victory at Saratoga convinced France that America could win the war. In May 1778 the Continental Congress approved an alliance with France that Franklin had helped arrange earlier in the year. Spain joined the war against Britain in 1779. The Spanish provided much of their help to the Patriots on the western frontier. **Bernardo de Gálvez**, the governor of Spanish Louisiana, was a key ally to the Patriots.

Individual foreigners also fought for the Patriots. One of the best-known was the **Marquis de Lafayette**. The wealthy, young Lafayette arrived in America from France in the summer of 1777. He spoke little English and lacked combat experience. However, his belief in the Patriot cause impressed General Washington. Lafayette said that "the welfare of America is closely bound up with the welfare of mankind." In his first battle, at Brandywine Creek, Lafayette was wounded in the leg. During the war he continued to aid the Patriots, even giving some $200,000 of his own money to support the Revolution.

Officers from countries not involved in the war also aided the Patriots. Tadeusz Kościuszko (kawsh-CHOOSH-kaw) and Kazimierz Pulaski came to America from Poland. Kościuszko brought army engineering skills to the war effort, and Pulaski helped train cavalry units.

✔ **Reading Check: Summarizing** Explain how foreign countries and individuals like the Marquis de Lafayette aided the Patriot war effort.

★ Winter at Valley Forge

The entry of France and Spain into the war came at a critical time for the Patriots because the Continental Army was running very low on supplies. In December 1777, Washington settled his troops at Valley Forge, Pennsylvania. There they suffered shortages of food and clothing. During the harsh winter of 1777–78, more than one fifth of the soldiers died of disease and malnutrition.

By the end of the winter, some of the troops were growing frustrated. They chanted "No pay, no clothes, no provisions [supplies]." In February 1778 a veteran Prussian army officer came to Washington's aid. Baron **Friedrich von Steuben** spoke no English. He led with a combination of respect and fear, teaching the American troops basic military skills. Von Steuben's drills worked. Soon he turned the Continental Army into a well-trained group of soldiers.

✔ **Reading Check: Finding the Main Idea** What challenges did the Continental Army face at Valley Forge?

⭐ The War at Sea

The Americans also faced difficult odds in the war at sea. The Continental Congress had created the Continental Navy and the marines in 1775. However, by February 1776, the navy had only eight fighting ships. This small fleet was no match for the much larger British one. The British navy could easily transport troops and attack American ports.

Instead of fighting large battles, the Patriots tried to attack individual British ships. The Patriots also attacked British supply ports and merchant ships. During the war the British lost hundreds of ships to small American raiding vessels. Many of these raiders were not officially part of the American navy. Their crews fought because they were allowed to sell any British cargo that they captured.

One of the most successful American captains was **John Paul Jones**. Jones was born John Paul in Scotland. He began working on ships at a young age. After accidentally killing the leader of a mutiny, he fled to America and added "Jones" to his name.

When the war broke out, Jones joined the newly created navy. He quickly established himself as a brave and clever sailor, capturing many British supply ships. The French greatly admired Jones. In 1779, French leaders gave him a small fleet of seven vessels to command. He named his flagship *Bonhomme Richard* ("Gentleman Richard") in honor of Benjamin Franklin's *Poor Richard's Almanack*.

One of Jones's most famous victories came against the British warship *Serapis* on September 23, 1779. Early in the battle, the British did heavy damage to the *Bonhomme Richard*. Captain Richard Pearson of the *Serapis* then called out to Jones, "Has your ship struck [surrendered]?" Jones replied, "I have not yet begun to fight!" More than two hours later, the British surrendered. Captain Pearson described the battle.

THE GRANGER COLLECTION, NEW YORK

Daily Life

Valley Forge Soldiers in the Continental Army had to deal with many shortages throughout the Revolutionary War. They went for long periods of time without pay and often lacked needed supplies. Some of the most difficult conditions they faced came during the harsh winter of 1777–78 at Valley Forge, Pennsylvania. Short on food, clothing, and shelter, about 2,500 of Washington's soldiers died in the camp. **How does this picture show the hardships faced by soldiers at Valley Forge?**

The Bonhomme Richard *defeated the* Serapis *in a long and bloody battle.*

THE GRANGER COLLECTION, NEW YORK

DONT TREAD ON ME

Ships of the Continental Navy flew this flag during the war.

Analyzing Primary Sources

Drawing Inferences and Conclusions According to the British captain, why did the Americans win the battle?

History Makers Speak

❝Long before the close of the action, it became clearly apparent that the American ship was dominated by a command will . . . and there could be no doubt that the intention of her commander was, if he could not conquer, to sink alongside.❞

—Captain Richard Pearson, quoted in *Voices of 1776*, by Richard Wheeler

The Continental Navy used fewer than 100 ships during the war. Yet the British navy lost almost 200 ships to the small but effective American naval forces.

✔ **Reading Check: Making Generalizations and Predictions** How did the achievements of John Paul Jones demonstrate the Patriots' naval strategy?

Section 4 Review

go.hrw.com
Homework Practice Online
keyword: SF3 HP7

★ ★

1 **Identify and explain:**
• Battle of Trenton
• Battle of Princeton
• John Burgoyne
• Battle of Brandywine Creek
• Battle of Saratoga
• Bernardo de Gálvez
• Marquis de Lafayette
• Friedrich von Steuben
• John Paul Jones

2 **Summarizing** Copy the graphic organizer below. Use it to explain why the battles at Trenton, Princeton, and Saratoga helped turn the tide for the Patriots in the Revolutionary War.

Morale

Allies

Battles

Victory

3 **Finding the Main Idea**
a. What was Washington's strategy for capturing Trenton and Princeton?
b. Explain how the achievements of John Paul Jones demonstrated the ways in which American captains fought the war at sea.

4 **Writing and Critical Thinking**
Supporting a Point of View Imagine that you are a foreign officer like the Marquis de Lafayette who has come to assist the Patriots against the British. Write a letter home explaining to a friend how and why you have chosen to help the Patriot cause.

Consider the following:
• your military experience
• your belief in the Patriot cause
• any economic help you might be able to provide

Independence!

Read to Discover

1. How did geography affect the Patriot strategy in the West?
2. How did the war take place in the southern colonies?
3. What events finally ended the war?

WHY IT MATTERS TODAY

The United States has grown from a small country to one of the most powerful nations in the world. Use CNNfyi.com or other **current events** sources to find an example that illustrates the strength of the United States today. Record your findings in your journal.

Define
- guerrilla warfare

Identify
- George Rogers Clark
- Battle of Vincennes
- Horatio Gates
- Francis Marion
- Comte de Rochambeau
- Battle of Yorktown
- Treaty of Paris of 1783

The Story Continues

Eventually the Revolutionary War reached the western frontier. Most of the fighting consisted of small battles between colonists and Britain's Indian allies. This situation changed when a young Virginian named George Rogers Clark stepped forward. Though only 24 years old at the time, Clark was a natural leader. His intelligence and forceful personality gained him the trust of men ranging from frontier fighters to Patriot Patrick Henry. Even the Indian leaders on the frontier viewed Clark with respect.

George Rogers Clark was a key American leader in the West.

★ The War in the West

<u>George Rogers Clark</u> had spent years exploring and mapping the frontier, and he had a plan for capturing some small forts and Indian villages. Clark's goal was to build an army while weakening the British. He traveled across the frontier, gathering soldiers from small towns. Clark's first target was the British trading village of Kaskaskia, located along the Mississippi River. Clark thought the small post had great strategic value, which he explained to his superiors.

★★★★★★★★★★★★

That's Interesting!

★★★★★★★★★★★★

Solar Eclipse Can a solar eclipse affect people's lives? You bet it can. George Rogers Clark was an experienced frontiersman. He knew that the route he had chosen to Kaskaskia would be difficult. But not even he expected the surprise his troops received on June 26, 1778. While crossing river rapids they viewed a total eclipse of the Sun! Clark guided his soldiers safely through the dangerous rapids and told them that the eclipse was a good sign. A week later his troops captured Kaskaskia without firing a shot.

History Makers Speak

❝The remote situation of this town . . . enables [the British] to . . . keep up a strict friendship with the Indians. . . . If it was in our possession it would distress the garrison [soldiers] at Detroit for provisions [supplies], it would fling [throw] the command of the two great rivers [Mississippi and Ohio] into our hands.❞

—George Rogers Clark, quoted in
Encyclopedia of the American Revolution, by Mark M. Boatner III

In June 1778 Clark and 175 soldiers set out toward Kaskaskia. To surprise the enemy, they took a difficult route. Clark's troops had to cross river rapids before marching more than 120 miles through thick forests and open prairies. The plan worked. On July 4, 1778, the surprised leaders of Kaskaskia surrendered to Clark without a fight.

News of Clark's achievement spread, and the town of Vincennes on the Wabash River also surrendered to the Patriots. Clark then organized meetings with American Indian leaders on the frontier. He persuaded some of them to be temporarily neutral in the war. During this period the British recaptured Vincennes. Clark's forces returned and took back the town at the **Battle of Vincennes** in late February 1779. Clark was never able to capture Fort Detroit, Britain's major base on the frontier, but his efforts greatly weakened the British army in the West.

✔ **Reading Check: Finding the Main Idea** Explain how geography affected Clark's campaign in the West.

⭐ The War in the South

After the American victory at Saratoga, the British focused more of their efforts on the southern colonies. General Henry Clinton led their campaign. The British strategy of freeing slaves who joined them worked well in the South. In Georgia a slave named Quamino Dolly showed the British a secret trail to the port city of Savannah. The British used the trail to surprise the Patriots and capture the city. The next major

Interpreting the Visual Record

Guerrilla war *A band of southern Patriots crosses a river in South Carolina.* **How does this image show the difficult conditions that Patriots fought under in the South?**

THE GRANGER COLLECTION, NEW YORK

southern city to fall to the British was the port of Charleston, South Carolina. Following months of hard-fought battles, the Patriots there surrendered on May 12, 1780. The British took more than 5,000 prisoners of war.

As the British marched through the South, they destroyed Patriot property. For example, in South Carolina they seized the plantation of indigo developer Eliza Lucas Pinckney. They stole her valuables, destroyed her crops, and killed her farm animals.

One of the most serious Patriot defeats was at Camden, South Carolina. In August 1780, Patriot forces led by **Horatio Gates** tried to drive out the British. The attack was poorly planned, however. Gates had only half as many soldiers as he first thought. In addition, most of his troops were hungry and tired from the march. In an attempt to raise their spirits, Gates fed the troops large amounts of molasses and cornmeal. This effort backfired, however, when the food made many of the troops sick.

When the weakened Patriots faced the British at Camden, a large group of Americans panicked and ran. The Patriot attack quickly fell apart. By the time the fighting ended, the British army had crushed Gates's forces. Only about 700 of approximately 4,000 American troops made it to safety. The Patriots had lost their southern army.

The southern Patriots did not stop fighting. Instead, they switched to **guerrilla warfare**—swift, hit-and-run attacks. No Patriot was better at this style of fighting than **Francis Marion**. He organized Marion's Brigade, a group of guerrilla soldiers that used surprise attacks to destroy British communications and supply lines. Despite great effort by the British, they could not catch Marion and his men. One frustrated British general claimed, "As for this . . . old fox, the devil himself could not catch him." From that point on, Marion was known as the Swamp Fox.

✔ **Reading Check: Sequencing** Describe the events of the war in the southern colonies in their proper order.

⭐ Victory at Yorktown

In early 1781 the war was going badly for the Patriots. They were low on money to pay soldiers and buy supplies. The entry of their foreign allies had not ended the war quickly. The army's morale took a blow when Benedict Arnold, one of America's most gifted officers, turned traitor. Arnold felt that the Continental Congress had treated him poorly and that Britain would reward his treachery. In addition to these problems, the British controlled most of the South.

British general Charles Cornwallis wanted to tighten his hold on the southern colonies. He therefore moved his forces into Yorktown, Virginia. Yorktown lies on a peninsula bounded by the Chesapeake Bay and the James and York Rivers. There Cornwallis prepared to attack a small Patriot force led by the Marquis de Lafayette.

CONNECTING TO

MATH

Just the Facts

American and British Troops in Battle

Year	American	British
1775	9,173	7,555
1776	47,993	78,918
1777	67,790	67,737
1778	19,922	21,159
1779	14,682	8,575
1780	16,652	27,089
1781	35,829	28,590
Total	212,041	239,623

Using Mathematical Skills

1. How many more British troops than American troops served in 1776?

2. Create a graph comparing the number of American and British forces during each year of the war.

3. Imagine that you are a Continental Army officer in 1776. Write a letter using these statistics to argue that the Continental Congress needs to raise a larger army.

During the siege at Yorktown, the Patriots made a daring attack that captured part of the British fortifications.

Meanwhile, General Washington was in New York. There he planned strategy with a French general, the **Comte de Rochambeau** (roh-shhn-boh). Rochambeau had recently arrived in New York with a large French army. A French fleet commanded by the naval officer Comte de Grasse was also sailing from the West Indies to aid the Patriots and challenge the mighty British navy. It could also prevent any British ships from entering Chesapeake Bay to bring reinforcements to Yorktown.

Washington saw a chance to trap Cornwallis. As the French fleet was taking control of Chesapeake Bay, Washington and Rochambeau moved their troops south. They surrounded Cornwallis with a Patriot army of some 16,000 soldiers. This was more than twice the size of Cornwallis's own forces. Suddenly the Patriots had the upper hand.

For weeks the Patriots held Yorktown under siege. During the **Battle of Yorktown** the Patriots steadily wore down the British defenses. The British navy tried to rescue Cornwallis's army, but the French fleet drove them away. In early October Washington prepared for a major attack on the weakened British troops. Fearing a defeat, Cornwallis surrendered. After negotiating for several days, the two sides agreed to terms of surrender for Cornwallis and his troops. The British marched out of Yorktown in defeat on October 20, 1781. Lord North, the British prime minister, received word of the Yorktown surrender in November. In shock he declared, "It is all over!"

✔ **Reading Check: Finding the Main Idea** How did Washington win the Battle of Yorktown?

North America in 1783

Interpreting Maps The Treaty of Paris officially marked the end of the Revolutionary War and granted the United States its independence as well as large areas of land to the West.

Skills Assessment

1. **Places and Regions** What nation controlled most of the present-day western United States in 1783?
2. **Analyzing Informaton** What three countries controlled most of the land shown on the map in 1783?

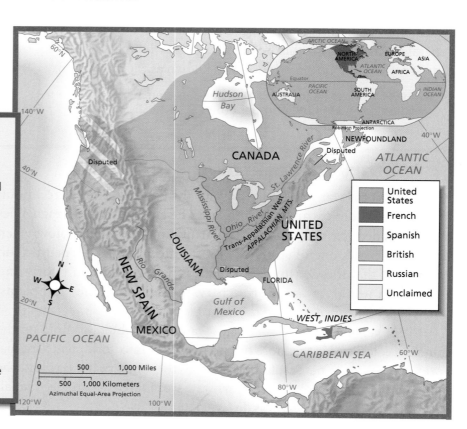

⭐ The Treaty of Paris

At Yorktown the Patriots captured the largest British army in America. Only a few small battles took place afterward. In June 1781 a committee from the Continental Congress began peace negotiations with the British. The American delegates were John Adams, Benjamin Franklin, John Jay, and Henry Laurens. Franklin had played a key role in gaining French aid during the war. He was also influential in the peace talks. He expressed his feelings in a letter to a British friend.

 History Makers Speak ❝Let us now forgive and forget. . . . America will, with God's blessing, become a great and happy Country; and England, if she has at length gained Wisdom, will have gained something.❞

—Benjamin Franklin, from *The Autobiography and Other Writings,* edited by L. Jesse Lemisch

The delegates took more than two years to come to an agreement, but in the **Treaty of Paris of 1783** Great Britain recognized the independent United States. The treaty also set the new nation's borders. The Great Lakes bounded the North. The Mississippi River served as the western border. A line at 31° north latitude formed the southern border. The British also accepted American rights to settle and trade west of the original thirteen colonies. With the war over, Patriot soldiers returned to their homes and families. The courage of soldiers and civilians had made America's victory possible. As the Continental Army's soldiers returned home, General Washington reflected on the triumph of his new country. "The citizens of America," he said, "are . . . acknowledged to be possessed of absolute freedom and independency."

✔ **Reading Check: Summarizing** Explain how the Revolutionary War finally ended.

This is a signed copy of the Treaty of Paris.

Analyzing Primary Sources
Identifying Points of View
How did Franklin think Great Britain and America should treat each other after the war?

Section 5 Review

go.hrw.com **Homework Practice Online**
keyword: SF3 HP7

❶ **Define** and explain:
- guerrilla warfare

❷ **Identify** and explain:
- George Rogers Clark
- Battle of Vincennes
- Horatio Gates
- Francis Marion
- Comte de Rochambeau
- Battle of Yorktown
- Treaty of Paris of 1783

❸ **Sequencing** Copy the graphic organizer below. Use it to list the major events that led to the end of the Revolutionary War.

1. _____
2. _____
3. _____

↓

Treaty of Paris

❹ **Finding the Main Idea**
a. How did geography affect the Patriot strategy on the western frontier?

b. How did the war progress in the southern colonies up to Washington's victory at Yorktown?

❺ **Writing and Critical Thinking**
Summarizing Imagine that you are a colonial diplomat. Create a pamphlet announcing the war's end. Your pamphlet should include a summary of the war's final events.

Consider the following:
- the Battle of Yorktown
- the terms of the Treaty of Paris of 1783
- how you think the United States will fare after the war

Chapter 7 Review

The Chapter at a Glance

Examine the visual summary of the chapter below. Use it to help you create a five-question quiz that you might give to a classmate.

Major Events of the Revolution

American Victories		British Victories
• Concord • Ticonderoga	**1775**	• Bunker Hill • Quebec
• Patriots take Boston • Trenton • Princeton • Declaration of Independence	**1776**	• British capture New York City
• Saratoga	**1777**	• Brandywine Creek
• Vincennes	**1779**	
	1780	• British capture Charleston • Camden
• Yorktown	**1781**	
	1783	

The Treaty of Paris
America wins its independence.

Identifying People and Ideas

Use the following terms or people in historically significant sentences.

1. minutemen
2. George Washington
3. *Common Sense*
4. Thomas Jefferson
5. Declaration of Independence
6. Abigail Adams
7. Marquis de Lafayette
8. John Paul Jones
9. Battle of Yorktown
10. Treaty of Paris of 1783

Understanding Main Ideas

Section 1 *(Pages 184–189)*

1. How did the fighting at Lexington and Concord affect the relationship between the colonies and Great Britain?
2. What did the First and Second Continental Congresses achieve?

Section 2 *(Pages 190–193)*

3. What effect did Thomas Paine's *Common Sense* have on colonial attitudes toward Britain?

Section 3 *(Pages 198–201)*

4. What advantages and disadvantages did the Patriots have when the Revolutionary War began?

Section 4 *(Pages 202–208)*

5. How did Washington defeat the British at Trenton and Princeton?
6. Why was the Battle of Saratoga important?

Section 5 *(Pages 209–213)*

7. How did the Patriots fight the war in the West and in the South?

You Be the Historian— Reviewing Themes

1. **Citizenship** Why did the colonies declare their independence from Britain?
2. **Constitutional Heritage** What are three rights that all men have according to the Declaration of Independence?
3. **Global Relations** Why did some foreign countries help the Patriots, and what role did Patriots such as Benjamin Franklin play in gaining this support?

Thinking Critically

1. **Supporting a Point of View** Did the Patriots' belief in their cause make up for their lack of supplies? Explain your answer.
2. **Summarizing** What key events occurred in 1776?
3. **Drawing Inferences and Conclusions** What do you think were the most significant causes of the American Revolution? Explain your answer.

Interpreting Charts

Study the chart below. Then use the information on the chart to help you answer the questions that follow.

Causes and Effects of the Revolution

Long-Term Causes

Proclamation of 1763

Increased taxation without representation

Increased British military presence and abuse of colonists' rights

Immediate Causes

Fighting at Lexington and Concord

Declaration of Independence

American Revolution
1775–1783

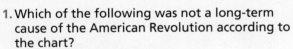

Effects

British recognition of U.S. independence

Boundaries of the United States extended west to the Mississippi River and south to Florida

1. Which of the following was not a long-term cause of the American Revolution according to the chart?
   a. the Proclamation of 1763
   b. taxation without representation
   c. abuse of colonial rights
   d. French attacks on the colonies

2. Based on the chart and your knowledge of the period, how do you think the long-term causes of the Revolution contributed to the immediate causes of the war?

Analyzing Primary Sources

Read the following excerpt from *Common Sense* by Thomas Paine, then answer the questions that follow.

❝A government of our own is our natural right; and when a man seriously reflects on the precariousness [uncertainness] of human affairs, he will become convinced that it is infinitely [completely] wiser and safer to form a constitution of our own in a cool deliberate manner, while we have it in our power, than to trust such an interesting event to time and chance.❞

3. Which of the following best describes Paine's viewpoint?
   a. Americans should rush to form a new nation.
   b. Americans would be better off independent.
   c. Americans should remain British citizens.
   d. It is best to take risks.

4. Why do you think that Paine's message was popular with many colonists?

Alternative Assessment

Building Your Portfolio

American History

Linking to Community

John Paul Jones was a hero of the American Revolution. Present an oral report on a war hero from your community. This hero can be someone living in your community today or someone who lived there in the past. If the person still lives in your community, you may want to interview the individual for your report.

internet connect

Internet Activity: go.hrw.com
keyword: SF3 CF7

Access the Internet through the HRW Go site to conduct research on the differing viewpoints of Loyalists and Patriots. Then create a newspaper that shows bias to the Loyalist or Patriot position on the Revolution. Make sure you use at least three examples of biased reporting in your newspaper. On a separate sheet of paper, explain where the bias occurs and why it is biased.

Social Studies Skills
WORKSHOP

Reading Skills

One of the biggest challenges you face in learning history is understanding what you read. By using appropriate Reading Skills, you will be able to understand more of what you read. Two important Reading Skills are Finding the Main Idea and Sequencing Information. The following activities will help you develop and practice these skills.

Finding the Main Idea

The main idea statement summarizes the most important point of a reading section. The main idea of a reading section is usually supported by sentences that provide details. Listed below are guidelines that will help you find the main idea of any reading assignment.

1. **Preview the material.** Read the title, introduction, and any other study clues that the assignment provides. These will often point to the main ideas being covered.

2. **Keep questions in mind.** Read the study questions that accompany the text. If the assignment does not provide study questions, create your own. Keeping these questions in mind will help you focus your reading.

3. **See how ideas are arranged.** Pay attention to the headings, subheadings, and opening paragraphs. Major ideas are often introduced in such material.

4. **Look for conclusions.** As you read, try to separate sentences that supply details from sentences that make general statements. Often a string of sentences providing detailed information leads to a conclusion that expresses a main idea.

Sequencing Information

Sequencing involves trying to determine the order in which certain events occurred. Specific dates and words related to time or time periods can provide clues for use in determining the proper sequence of certain events. For example, suppose you were asked to explain how the colonists declared their independence from Great Britain. You might come up with ideas that you place in the following order:

> Parliament taxed the colonists without their consent.
>
> Colonists held protests, such as the Boston Tea Party.
>
> British troops clashed with colonists at Lexington and Concord.
>
> The Second Continental Congress drafted the Declaration of Independence.

Practicing the Skills

1. In Chapter 7, The American Revolution, look at the section entitled The Patriots Gain New Hope. Read the Turning Point at Saratoga subsection. Write four sentences that summarize the material in that subsection. Then condense your sentences into a single sentence that states the main idea of the subsection.

2. Brainstorm some important events that took place in America from 1763 to 1783. Then place these events in their proper sequence from first to last.

History in Action

UNIT 3 SIMULATION

You Make the Decision . . .

Should France Help the Patriots Fight the British?

Complete the following activity in small cooperative groups. The year is 1778. You and your associates are a special committee of French government officials. Your assignment is to decide whether France should join the Patriots in their fight against Great Britain. Because your king has asked you to make a formal presentation of your answer to him very soon, you need to come to a decision quickly. Follow these steps to reach your decision.

1. Gather Information. Use your textbook and other resources to find information that might help you decide whether to support the Patriots. Be sure to use what you learned from this unit's Skills Workshop on Finding the Main Idea and Sequencing Information to help you focus on key points in your research. You may want to divide different parts of the research among group members.

2. Identify Options. After reviewing the information you have gathered, consider the options you might recommend to the king. Your final decision may be easier to reach if you consider as many options as possible. For example, you might think of ways to help the Patriots without joining the war against Britain directly. Be sure to record your possible options for your presentation.

3. Predict Consequences. Now take each option your associates came up with and consider what might be the outcome of each course of action. Ask yourselves questions like: "How might France benefit from doing this?" Once you have predicted the consequences, record them as notes for your presentation.

4. Take Action to Implement Your Decision. After you have considered your options, you should plan and create your presentation. Be sure to make your decision on whether to support the Patriots very clear. You will need to support your decision by including information you gathered and by explaining why you rejected other options. Your presentation needs to be visually appealing to convince the king. When you are ready, decide which group members will make each part of the presentation, and then take your decision to the king (the rest of the class). Good luck!

Young People

IN HISTORY

Young Americans

Several things shaped the lives of young citizens of the newly independent United States. Where these young people lived and what their parents did for a living often determined what they would do with their lives.

Young people growing up on the frontier could expect a life of hard work. This work included planting and harvesting crops, tending the farm animals, or helping to keep the house in order. Many young people on the frontier spent little or no time in school each year. In the early United States there were few free public schools. Most families could not afford to send their children to a private school. Most parents believed that the purpose of education was to teach young people how to work. This training helped young people support their families. Boys of six or seven worked with their fathers after they exchanged their infant clothes for breeches, or pants, like their fathers wore.

This illustration shows two girls from the early American republic studying geography.

Children from wealthy families could expect to receive a more formal education. Boys usually received more education than girls. A girl was expected to learn reading, writing, and some basic math. Any well-educated boy also learned Greek and Latin.

Most African American youths, particularly in the South, could expect to spend their lives working as slaves or house servants. Enslaved children also helped support their families. They tended the family garden and gathered berries, herbs, and nuts for cooking.

Almost all teenagers, from whatever region or social background, spent some time at play. Sometimes they flew kites, or played leapfrog and marbles. In some places, young people played tag—the same game played today. One teacher during this time period described how his students played. "They all find places of Rendesvous [meeting places] so soon as the Beell [bell] rings, and all seem to choose different sports!" In addition, many young Americans spent their time looking after their pets, which ranged from squirrels to dogs and cats.

If You Were There *How would you spend your time in the early United States?*

LEFT PAGE: *In September 1787, delegates at the Constitutional Convention signed the final draft of the Constitution.*

THE GRANGER COLLECTION, NEW YORK

Forming a Government
(1777–1791)

Members of the Second Continental Congress knew that the former colonies needed to create a central government.

States such as New York minted their own coins.

UNITED STATES

1777 The Continental Congress approves the Articles of Confederation on November 15.

1781 On March 1 the Articles of Confederation go into effect after being ratified by all 13 states.

1777	1779	1781	1783

WORLD

Early hot-air balloons, which were often decorated, delighted crowds in the late 1700s.

1781 German philosopher Immanuel Kant publishes his *Critique of Pure Reason,* a major theoretical work.

1782 Spain completes its conquest of British Florida.

1783 The Montgolfier brothers of France make the first flight in a hot-air balloon.

Build on What You Know

The United States declared its independence in 1776. But then Americans were faced with the difficult task of forming a new government. After a first attempt at national government failed to solve many of the nation's problems, many Americans wanted a change. In 1787, leaders from around the country came to Philadelphia to find a solution.

A signed copy of the Constitution

VIRGINIA MUSEUM OF FINE ARTS, RICHMOND, VA. DETAIL OF WASHINGTON ADDRESSING THE CONSTITUTIONAL CONVENTION BY JUNIUS BRUTUS STEARNS. GIFT OF EDGAR WILLIAM AND BERNICE CHRYSLER GARBISCH. PHOTO: RON JENNINGS ©2000 VIRGINIA MUSEUM OF FINE ARTS

George Washington served as president of the Constitutional Convention.

1785 The United States begins using the dollar currency.

1786 Shays's Rebellion breaks out in Massachusetts.

1787 On May 14, state delegates begin to arrive at the Constitutional Convention in Philadelphia.

Congress passes the Northwest Ordinance on July 13.

The final draft of the Constitution is signed on September 17.

1789 James Madison submits possible amendments to the Constitution.

1790 Rhode Island becomes the final state to ratify the Constitution.

1791 The Bill of Rights is ratified by the states in December.

1785 1787 1789 1791

1786 Mennonites from central Europe settle in Canada.

1787 The Ottoman Empire declares war on Russia.

1791 Austrian composer Wolfgang Amadeus Mozart dies.

If you were there . . .
How would you help create a new government?

You Be the Historian

Themes Journal

What's Your Opinion? Do you **agree** or **disagree** with the following statements? Support your point of view in your journal.

- **Global Relations** New nations will be taken advantage of by other countries.
- **Citizenship** Governments must protect certain rights of their citizens.
- **Constitutional Heritage** The power of the government must be limited.

The Articles of Confederation

Read to Discover

1. What ideas and documents shaped American beliefs about government?
2. How did state constitutions contribute to the development of representative government?
3. What powers did the central government have under the Articles of Confederation?
4. What did the Northwest Ordinance accomplish?

WHY IT MATTERS TODAY

Many countries have modeled their political systems on American and European ideas of representative government. Use **CNNfyi.com** or other **current events** sources to learn about how a foreign nation elects its leaders. Record your findings in your journal.

Define

- constitution
- republicanism
- limited government
- suffrage
- ratification

Identify

- Virginia Statute for Religious Freedom
- Articles of Confederation
- Land Ordinance of 1785
- Northwest Ordinance of 1787
- Northwest Territory

The Story Continues

The bald eagle is one of the symbols of the United States.

In 1776 a short essay by an unknown author appeared. The essay called for the newly independent states to take great care when building their new governments. "They [the people] are now planting a seed," it stated. The author predicted that the seed would grow into a tree, whose branches would "shelter the liberty of succeeding ages." Many Americans agreed with this idea. They hoped that a strong republic could be formed in America.

⭐ Ideas about Government

The American colonies had taken a bold step in declaring their independence from Great Britain in July 1776. Their next political goal was to form new governments. To do so, the American people drew from a wide range of political ideas.

Interpreting the Visual Record

The Enlightenment *During the Enlightenment, philosophers often discussed their ideas at elegant social gatherings. British philosopher John Locke was widely respected.* **How does the painting suggest the interest that the wealthy had in Enlightenment ideas?**

One source of inspiration was English law. England had limited the power of its kings and queens in two documents—Magna Carta and the English Bill of Rights. Magna Carta, signed by King John in 1215, required the king to follow the rule of law like other English people. The English Bill of Rights, passed in 1689, kept the king or queen from passing new taxes or changing laws without Parliament's approval. As a result, the people's representatives had a stronger voice in government.

Americans were also influenced by the Enlightenment. Writers of that period had called for the use of reason and expressed a belief in human goodness. Enlightenment philosopher John Locke believed that a social contract, or agreement, existed between political leaders and the people they ruled. One side of this contract was the government's duty to protect the people's unalienable rights. The rule of law, wrote Locke, was more important than the authority of any individual.

History Makers Speak

❝Whosoever in authority exceeds the power given him by the law . . . may be opposed as any other man who by force invades the right of another.❞

—John Locke, *Two Treatises on Government*

Analyzing Primary Sources

Identifying Points of View To whom does Locke compare a ruler who breaks the law?

Locke stated that leaders who broke the law or lost the approval of the people should be replaced.

Naturally American leaders looked to their own political traditions, such as the New England town meeting. At these meetings, townspeople addressed important issues in their community. Americans also looked to their own legislative assemblies, such as the Virginia House of Burgesses. These bodies offered models of representative governments. Christian traditions, such as the Great Awakening, may have also inspired colonists to question existing political institutions and look for more local control.

Americans also had written documents supporting the principles of self-government. In 1620 the Pilgrims had agreed to govern themselves at Plymouth colony by signing the Mayflower Compact. In 1639 the people of Connecticut had drawn up the Fundamental Orders of Connecticut. This plan was widely considered to be the first written **constitution** in the English colonies. A constitution is a set of basic principles and laws that state the powers and duties of the government. Finally, the Declaration of Independence clearly set forth the ideas on which Americans thought government should be based.

✔ **Reading Check: Summarizing** What influenced American ideas of government?

★ The State Constitutions

All of these political ideas were quickly put into practice after the United States declared independence. During the American Revolution nearly every colony wrote a new state constitution. These constitutions showed a belief in **republicanism**—that is, support for a system of government called a republic. In such a system, citizens elect representatives who are responsible to the people. Most Americans wanted to keep individual leaders from gaining too much power. Thus, each state constitution created a **limited government**. In a limited government all leaders have to obey the laws and no one has total power. For example, many states placed their courts outside of the governor's control.

Most state constitutions protected the individual rights of citizens. For example, George Mason wrote the Virginia Declaration of Rights. Some of the rights it defended were trial by jury, freedom of the press, and private ownership of property. In 1786 Thomas Jefferson's support for freedom of religion was included in the **Virginia Statute for Religious Freedom**. This law promoted the separation of church and state in Virginia. Other states soon followed, and by 1833 there were no state governments that supported an official church.

In addition, many state constitutions expanded **suffrage**, or voting rights. As one Virginian wrote, "The spirit of independence was converted into equality." Some states allowed any white man who was a taxpaying citizen to vote. Other states gave the vote only to white men who owned property. In most states people had to own property to hold an elected office. Seven of the first state constitutions gave voting rights to free African American men. However, by the 1860s these rights had been taken away or greatly limited by high property or residency requirements.

✔ **Reading Check: Analyzing Information** How did the first state constitutions promote the growth of democracy?

Interpreting the Visual Record

Female voters *The only state to give voting rights to women was New Jersey, though it took that right away in 1807. From the way these women voters are dressed, do you think that they are property owners? Why or why not?*

THE GRANGER COLLECTION, NEW YORK

Western Land Claims, 1781–1802

Interpreting Maps Many of the original 13 states had claims to western lands that dated back to their colonial charters. It took several years for all the states to cede these lands to the United States.

Skills Assessment

1. **Places and Regions** What states claimed land within the boundaries of what became the Northwest Territory?
2. **Summarizing** Which states had no land claims?

Map legend:
- Original 13 states
- Western lands claimed by states
- 1784 Date claims finally ceded to United States
- Boundary of Northwest Territory

☆ Forming a Union

To many members of the Second Continental Congress, it was not enough for each state to have its own government. They believed that a national government was necessary in order to hold the country together. Some leaders of the Revolution disagreed. They worried that a new central government would be too powerful. After all, they were rebelling against Great Britain in part because of Parliament's abuse of authority.

On June 12, 1776, the Congress appointed a Committee of Thirteen, made up of one member from each colony. This group was assigned to create a national constitution. Committee members met for a month to discuss and draft the new document, called the **Articles of Confederation**. Under the Articles of Confederation, a new Confederation Congress would become the central national government. Each state would have one vote in the Congress. The national government did not have a president or a court system.

The Confederation Congress had only limited powers. It could make coins and borrow money. It could negotiate and make treaties with other countries and with American Indians. Congress also could settle conflicts between the states and could ask states for money and soldiers. However, Congress could not force the states to provide money or troops, even in an emergency.

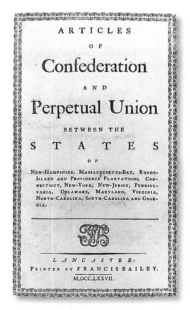

The Articles of Confederation created a central government with limited powers.

John Dickinson headed the Committee of Thirteen. He called the Articles "a firm league of friendship." But many people later criticized the Articles for having formed a weak central government.

History Makers Speak

❝Congress must have the same power to enact [pass] laws and compel [force] obedience throughout the continent, as the legislatures of the States have in their respective jurisdictions [areas of authority].❞

—Noah Webster, quoted in *The Growth of the American Republic*, by Samuel Eliot Morison, Henry Steele Commager, and William E. Leuchtenburg

Analyzing Primary Sources
Drawing Inferences and Conclusions Why might Webster have held this view?

The Second Continental Congress passed the Articles of Confederation on November 15, 1777. Then it sent them to each state legislature for **ratification**, or official approval. All 13 states had to ratify the Articles before the new national government could take effect. Conflicts over claims to western lands slowed the process. Many states claimed territory as far west as the Mississippi River. Virginia and New York had some of the largest land claims. States without land claims, such as Maryland, wanted these territories to belong to the new national government.

New York finally gave up its land claims in 1780. Virginia did the same the following year. This convinced Maryland to ratify the Articles of Confederation in March 1781, thus putting the first national government of the United States into effect.

✔ **Reading Check: Finding the Main Idea** What powers did the national government have under the Articles of Confederation?

Research on the ROM

Free Find:
Schooling
After reading about public schools on the **Holt Researcher CD–ROM**, imagine that you attend a public school in the late 1780s. Write a short account of your experiences.

⭐ The Northwest Territory

The new central government had to decide what to do with the western lands now under its control. It also had to raise money to pay war debts. The Confederation Congress hoped to solve both problems by selling western land to the public. It passed the **Land Ordinance of 1785**, which set up a system for surveying and dividing the public territory. First the land was split into townships of 36 square miles. Each township was divided into 36 lots of 640 acres each. One lot was set aside for a public school, with another 4 lots saved for Revolutionary War veterans. The remaining lots were for sale to the public.

To form a political system for the region north of the Ohio River, Congress passed the **Northwest Ordinance of 1787**. The ordinance created the **Northwest Territory**, which included the area that is now Illinois, Indiana, Michigan, Ohio, and Wisconsin.

The Northwest Ordinance also created a system for bringing new states into the Union. Congress agreed to divide the Northwest Territory into several smaller territories, each of which had a governor appointed by Congress. When the population of a territory reached 60,000, its settlers could draft their own constitution. The people could then ask Congress for permission to join the Union as a state.

Surveyors used tools like these to help them determine property boundaries.

Daily Life

Moving West After the Revolutionary War Americans began heading west in greater numbers. Thousands of people settled in the lands of the Northwest Territory. Many of these people were farmers from New England, where good farmland was scarce. As the population of the Northwest Territory grew and the region was divided into states, more settlers came from throughout the nation and from overseas. **Why do you think settlers would travel in a large group as shown here?**

In addition, the ordinance had a bill of rights. It also required that public education be provided for the citizens of the region. Finally, the Northwest Ordinance stated that "there shall be neither slavery nor involuntary servitude [forced labor] in the . . . territory." This last condition, based on a proposal by Thomas Jefferson, banned slavery in the Northwest Territory. However, the question of slavery would become more controversial as other new territories were formed.

✔ **Reading Check: Summarizing** How did the new Congress organize the nation's western lands?

Section 1 Review

Homework Practice Online
keyword: SF3 HP8

1 **Define** and explain:
- constitution
- republicanism
- limited government
- suffrage
- ratification

2 **Identify** and explain:
- Virginia Statute for Religious Freedom
- Articles of Confederation
- Land Ordinance of 1785
- Northwest Ordinance of 1787
- Northwest Territory

3 **Summarizing** Copy the graphic organizer below. Use it to identify the ideas and documents that influenced the U.S. state and national governments.

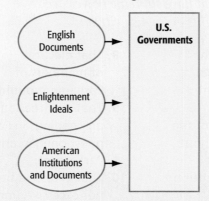

English Documents → U.S. Governments

Enlightenment Ideals →

American Institutions and Documents →

4 **Finding the Main Idea**
a. In what ways did the first state constitutions support the growth of representative government?

b. Why did Congress pass the Northwest Ordinance, and what did it achieve?

5 **Writing and Critical Thinking**
Analyzing Information Imagine that you are a member of the Committee of Thirteen. Write a brief report for the states describing the powers given to the central government under the Articles of Confederation.

Consider the following:
- the structure of the national government
- what the Confederation Congress could and could not do

Forming a Government **227**

MAGNA CARTA

A copy of Magna Carta

England's King John angered many people with high taxes. In 1215 a group of English nobles joined the archbishop of Canterbury to force the king to agree to sign Magna Carta. This document stated that the king was subject to the rule of law, just as other citizens of England were. It also presented the ideas of a fair and speedy trial and due process of law. These principles are still a part of the U.S. Bill of Rights.

1. That the English Church shall be free, and shall have her whole rights and her liberties **inviolable.**[1] . . .

12. No **scutage**[2] nor aid shall be imposed in our kingdom, unless by the common council of our kingdom. . . .

38. No **bailiff,**[3] for the future, shall put any man to his law upon his own simple **affirmation,**[4] without **credible**[5] witnesses **produced for that purpose.**[6] . . .

39. No freeman shall be seized, imprisoned, **dispossessed,**[7] outlawed, or **exiled,**[8] or in any way destroyed; nor will we proceed against or prosecute him except by the lawful judgment of his **peers,**[9] or by the law of the land.

40. To none will we sell, to none will we deny, to none will we delay right or justice. . . .

Analyzing Primary Sources

1. How does Magna Carta allow for fair taxation?

2. Which of these rights supports the ideas of a fair trial and due process of law?

---

[1] **inviolable:** safe from sudden change
[2] **scutage:** tax for military purposes
[3] **bailiff:** sheriff
[4] **affirmation:** testimony

[5] **credible:** believable
[6] **produced for that purpose:** brought forward to testify
[7] **dispossessed:** deprived of his land

[8] **exiled:** forced to leave the country
[9] **peers:** equals

THE ENGLISH BILL OF RIGHTS

The seal of the House of Commons in Parliament

After the Glorious Revolution, Parliament passed the English Bill of Rights, which ensured that Parliament would have supreme power over the monarchy. The bill also protected the rights of English citizens.

1. That the pretended power of suspending of laws or the execution of laws by **regal**[1] authority without consent of Parliament is illegal; . . .

4. That **levying money**[2] for or to the use of the crown by pretense of **prerogative**[3] without grant of Parliament . . . is illegal;

5. That it is the right of the subjects to petition the king, and all commitments and prosecutions for such petitioning are illegal.

8. That election of members of Parliament ought to be free;

9. That the freedom of speech and debates or proceedings in Parliament ought not to be . . . questioned in any court or place out of Parliament;

10. That excessive bail ought not to be required, nor excessive fines imposed, nor cruel and unusual punishments inflicted.

11. That jurors ought to be duly **impaneled**.[4] . . .

13. And that, for **redress of**[5] all grievances and for the amending, strengthening, and preserving of the laws, Parliaments ought to be held frequently.

---

[1] **regal:** royal
[2] **levying money:** raising taxes
[3] **prerogative:** right
[4] **impaneled:** selected
[5] **redress of:** to make up for

Analyzing Primary Sources

1. What parts of this document describe the rights and powers of Parliament, and what are those rights and powers?

2. What parts of this document do you think Americans would want to use in their government?

VIRGINIA STATUTE FOR RELIGIOUS FREEDOM

Thomas Jefferson wrote the Virginia Statute for Religious Freedom. Jefferson hoped that by separating church and state, Virginians could practice their religion—whatever it might be—freely.

I. Well aware that Almighty God has created the mind free; . . . that to **compel**[1] a man to **furnish contributions**[2] of money for the **propagation**[3] of opinions which he disbelieves is sinful and **tyrannical**;[4] that even . . . forcing him to support this or that teacher of his own religious **persuasion**[5] is depriving him of the comfortable liberty. . . . And, finally, that truth is great and will **prevail**[6] if left to herself . . . and has nothing to fear.

II. Be it **enacted**[7] by the General Assembly that no man shall be compelled to frequent or support any religious worship, place, or ministry whatsoever, nor shall be enforced, restrained, **molested**,[8] or burdened in his body or goods, nor shall otherwise suffer on account of his religious opinions or belief; but that all men shall be free to profess, and by argument to maintain, their opinion in matters of religion, and that the same shall in no wise **diminish**,[9] enlarge, or affect their civil capacities.

The Virginia Statute for Religious Freedom

III. And though we well know that this assembly . . . [has] no power to restrain the acts of succeeding assemblies . . . we are free to declare, and do declare, that the rights hereby **asserted**[10] are of the natural rights of mankind, and that if any act shall hereafter be passed to repeal the present or to narrow its operation, such act will be an **infringement**[11] of natural rights.

Analyzing Primary Sources

1. How does this document protect freedom of religion?

2. Why do you think section III was included?

---

[1] **compel:** force
[2] **furnish contributions:** pay
[3] **propagation:** spreading
[4] **tyrannical:** unjust
[5] **persuasion:** belief
[6] **prevail:** win
[7] **enacted:** decided
[8] **molested:** injured
[9] **diminish:** reduce
[10] **asserted:** stated
[11] **infringement:** violation

Problems in the New Nation

Read to Discover

1. How did other nations treat the new government of the United States?
2. What economic problems arose under the Articles of Confederation?
3. What were the causes and consequences of Shays's Rebellion?

WHY IT MATTERS TODAY

The United States today has a powerful central government. Use CNNfyi.com or other **current events** sources to learn about a way in which the U.S. government regulates business or trade. Record your findings in your journal.

Define

• tariffs
• interstate commerce
• inflation
• debtors
• creditors
• depression

Identify

• Shays's Rebellion
• Daniel Shays

The Story Continues

On June 7, 1786, Thomas Amis sailed his ship down the Mississippi River. He was carrying trade goods, as he had done many times before. This day was different, however. Amis's trip broke a new Spanish law, which greatly limited U.S. citizens' navigation rights along the lower part of the river. The Spanish troops at the town of Natchez—in present-day Mississippi—captured Amis. Then the Spanish stripped him of all his cargo, including 50 barrels of flour.

Merchants relied on barrels to ship many kinds of goods by land, river, and sea.

★ A Lack of Respect

Congress could do little to protect citizens like Thomas Amis against foreign threats. Under the Articles of Confederation, Congress could not force states to provide soldiers for an army. Without an army, the national government found it difficult to protect its citizens. It was also difficult to enforce the terms of international treaties. For example, Congress could do little to enforce the Treaty of Paris of 1783. The treaty called for the British to turn over "with all convenient speed" their forts on the U.S. side of the Great Lakes, but Great Britain was slow to leave these positions.

American Painters Artists John Singleton Copley, Gilbert Stuart, and Benjamin West all earned great success during the late 1700s. West was one of the most influential artists. Beginning his career as a portrait painter in America, West later moved to Britain and helped found the Royal Academy of Arts. West became known for his historical paintings, which showed people dressed in modern clothing instead of classical styles. West had to leave this painting of the signing of the Treaty of Paris unfinished when the British delegates refused to pose. **How is this unfinished painting symbolic of the relations between Britain and the United States?**

Spain also took advantage of the weakness of the United States. In 1784, Spanish officials closed the lower Mississippi River to U.S. shipping. Westerners who used the Mississippi to send goods to eastern markets were furious. But Spain refused to reopen the river to U.S. merchants.

Many state leaders began to criticize the weak Confederation Congress. Representatives from Rhode Island wrote to Congress. They said, "Our federal government is but a name; a mere shadow without substance [meaning]." Critics believed that a strong military would help the United States put pressure on Spain to open the Mississippi. For these political leaders, this failure showed that the national government needed to have more power.

✔ **Reading Check: Finding the Main Idea** How did the weaknesses of the Articles of Confederation affect U.S. relations with other countries?

★ Trouble with Trade

The United States also faced economic problems involving Great Britain. Before the Revolutionary War, colonial ships had traded a great deal with the British West Indies. But after the Treaty of Paris was signed, Britain closed many of its ports to American ships. In addition to shutting down this trade, Britain forced American merchants to pay high duties on U.S. exports. The tariffs applied to goods such as rice, tar, and tobacco, which colonial merchants wanted to sell in Britain.

The loss of trade with the British shook the U.S. economy. James Madison of Virginia wrote about the crisis.

Analyzing Primary Sources

Evaluating How did the end of the Revolutionary War affect the free enterprise system in the United States?

> **History Makers Speak**
>
> 66 The Revolution has robbed us of our trade with the West Indies . . . without opening any other channels to compensate [make up] for it. In every point of view, indeed, the trade of this country is in a deplorable [terrible] condition. 99
>
> —James Madison, quoted in *Independence on Trial*, by Frederick W. Marks III

Farmers could no longer export their goods to the British West Indies. They also had to hire British ships to carry their goods to British markets, which was very expensive. Samuel Adams wrote about this to his cousin John Adams, "Our merchants are complaining bitterly that Great Britain is ruining their trade and there is good reason to complain." American exports dropped. At the same time, British goods flowed freely into the United States. This unequal trade caused serious economic problems for the new nation. British merchants could sell manufactured products in the United States at much lower prices than locally made goods. This competition hurt American businesses.

The Confederation Congress could not fix the problem because it did not have the power to pass **tariffs**—taxes on imports or exports. The states could offer little help. If one state passed a tariff, the British could simply sell their goods in another state. Most states did not cooperate when passing tariffs. Instead, each looked only to improve its own trade. In 1785 the situation led a British magazine to call the new nation the "Dis-United States." As a result of the trade problems with Britain, American merchants began looking for other new markets. Such new markets included China, France, and the Netherlands. Despite these attempts, Britain remained the most important trading partner of the United States.

✔ **Reading Check: Summarizing** What trade problems did the United States face with Great Britain, and why did these occur?

⭐ Economic Problems at Home

In addition to international trade issues, trade among the states became a major problem. The Confederation Congress had no power to regulate **interstate commerce**—trade between two or more states. Without such regulation, states followed their own commercial interests. As a result, trade laws differed from state to state. This situation made trade difficult for merchants whose businesses crossed state lines.

The ability of the states to print their own money caused more problems. After the Revolutionary War, most states had a hard time paying off war debts. They also struggled to collect overdue taxes. To ease economic hardships, some states at times printed large amounts of paper money. The result was **inflation**—increased prices for goods and

★★★★★★★★★★★★
That's Interesting!
★★★★★★★★★★★★

Talking Turkey Did you know that Benjamin Franklin wanted the turkey, not the bald eagle, to be the national bird of the United States? It's true! He thought that the bald eagle was "a Bird of bad moral Character." He had more respect for the wild turkey. He lost his argument, and the bald eagle became an American symbol. But the turkey did not lose out completely. In the late 1900s Alabama, Massachusetts, Oklahoma, and South Carolina adopted the turkey as their official state game bird. Alabama recognized the turkey as "undoubtedly the most noble of all game birds upon the North American Continent."

services combined with the reduced value of money. Congress had no power to stop states from issuing more paper money. Thus, it could do little to stop inflation.

Inflation woes soon forced planters in North Carolina to sell tobacco to the state government in exchange for paper money. This money was worth almost nothing. In Rhode Island a similar problem arose. The state legislature printed large amounts of paper money worth very little. This made **debtors**—people who owe money—quite happy. They could pay back their debts with paper money worth less than the coins they had borrowed. However, **creditors**—people who lend money—were upset by the prospect of being paid back with worthless money. Similar situations took place in many states.

The rising inflation faced by the states combined with the loss of trade with Great Britain to cause a **depression**. A depression is a period of low economic activity combined with a rise in unemployment.

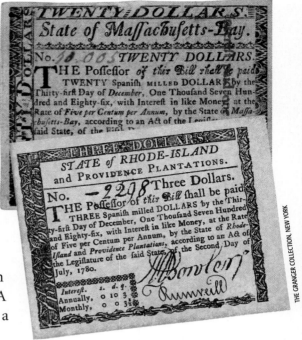

THE GRANGER COLLECTION, NEW YORK

The states of Massachusetts and Rhode Island both suffered economic problems related to their currency policies.

✔ **Reading Check: Identifying Cause and Effect** What led to the economic differences between the states, and how did this affect the national economy?

⭐ Debt in Massachusetts

Each state handled its economic problems differently. Massachusetts refused to print paper money and tried to pay its war debts by collecting taxes on land.

The state's economic policy hit farmers particularly hard. As landowners, they had to pay the new taxes. With little gold or silver and no paper money, however, farmers had trouble paying their debts. When people could not pay their debts, the Massachusetts courts began forcing them to sell their property. Some farmers also had to serve terms in debtors' prison. Some even had to sell themselves as indentured servants. People soon began calling for change.

 History Makers Speak 66We beg leave to inform your Honors that unless something takes place more favorable to the people, in a little time at least, one half of our inhabitants [people living in the state] in our opinion will become bankrupt [financially ruined] . . . . Sirs, in this situation what have we to live on—no money to be had; our estates [lands] daily posted and sold.99

—Petition from a rural town, quoted in *The Growth of the American Republic*, by Samuel Eliot Morison, Henry Steele Commager, and William E. Leuchtenburg

Analyzing Primary Sources
Identifying Points of View
What worries did farmers have?

However, many government leaders in Massachusetts had little sympathy for the problems of poor farmers. In some cases, farmers actually owed these politicians money.

THE GRANGER COLLECTION, NEW YORK

Interpreting the Visual Record

Shays's Rebellion *The follow-ers of Daniel Shays, shown above at left, took possession of a Massachusetts courthouse during their rebellion.* **Do you think this image portrays the rebels as dangerous? Why or why not?**

⭐ Shays's Rebellion

In September 1786, farmers in three western Massachusetts counties began a revolt. Bands of angry citizens armed with pitchforks and other farm tools closed down courts in the western part of the state. Their reasoning was simple—with the courts shut down, no one's property could be taken. This uprising became known as **Shays's Rebellion**. A poor farmer and Revolutionary War veteran named **Daniel Shays** was its main leader. The state government ordered the farmers to stop the revolt and threatened death to any captured rebel. However, these threats only made Shays and his followers more determined. Shays asked other citizens to join the rebellion. He signed a document stating, "The seeds of war are now sown. . . . Our cause is yours. Don't give yourself a rest and let us die here."

In September the rebels forced the state supreme court in the town of Springfield to close. Shays's forces returned to Springfield the next month, hoping to capture a federal weapons storehouse. This time, state troops defeated the rebels in a short battle in January 1787. By February many rebels had surrendered or been arrested. During their trials, 14 leaders were sentenced to death. However, the state soon freed most of the rebels, including Shays. State officials knew that many citizens in Massachusetts agreed with the rebels and their motives.

The rebellion greatly upset many political leaders. George Washington exclaimed, "I am mortified [embarrassed] beyond expression." He feared that the United States must look "ridiculous . . . in the eyes of all Europe." Not everyone saw the rebellion this way, however. Thomas Jefferson, serving as ambassador to France, also responded to the event. He said, "A little rebellion, now and then, is a good thing. . . . The tree of liberty must be refreshed from time to time with the blood of patriots and tyrants."

In the end, Shays's Rebellion helped reveal the weakness of the Confederation government. It led some Americans to admit that the Articles of Confederation were not working. When Massachusetts had asked the national government to help put down Shays's Rebellion, Congress could offer little help. More Americans began calling for a stronger central government. They wanted leaders who would be able to protect the nation in times of crisis.

✔ **Reading Check: Finding the Main Idea** What was Shays's Rebellion, and why was it important?

⭐ A Push for Change

In 1786 the Virginia legislature called for a national conference to talk about changing the Articles of Confederation. The meeting took place in Annapolis, Maryland, in September 1786. Only five states sent delegates to the Annapolis Convention, however. The New England states, the Carolinas, and Georgia were not represented. Even Maryland hesitated to send delegates.

Alexander Hamilton was a lawyer with considerable influence in New York politics.

James Madison and Alexander Hamilton attended the Annapolis Convention. At their urging, the Annapolis delegates called on all 13 states to send delegates to a Constitutional Convention at Philadelphia, in May 1787. They hoped this Convention would improve the national government. They wanted to make "the constitution of the Federal Government adequate to the exigencies [needs] of the Union."

✔ **Reading Check: Analyzing Information** How did the states address the problems of the central government?

Section 2 Review

go.hrw.com **Homework Practice Online**
keyword: SF3 HP8

1 **Define** and explain:
• tariffs
• interstate commerce
• inflation
• debtors
• creditors
• depression

2 **Identify** and explain:
• Shays's Rebellion
• Daniel Shays

3 **Categorizing** Copy the graphic organizer below. Use it to identify the domestic and international problems that arose under the Articles of Confederation.

Domestic Problems
International Problems
Articles of Confederation

4 **Finding the Main Idea**
a. In what ways did Great Britain and Spain take advantage of the weaknesses of the United States under its new government?
b. Why did Massachusetts's farmers take part in Shays's Rebellion, and what was the result of the rebellion?

5 **Writing and Critical Thinking**
Supporting a Point of View Imagine that you are a delegate to the Annapolis Convention. Write a letter to the states not attending the convention that explains why they should attend the next convention in Philadelphia.

Consider the following:
• economic problems under the Articles of Confederation
• problems with defining the authority of the central government
• social problems under the Articles of Confederation

The Constitution

Read to Discover

1. Why did the delegates meet for the Constitutional Convention?
2. What were some of the main issues debated and compromises reached at the Constitutional Convention?
3. How is the federal government balanced under the U.S. Constitution?

WHY IT MATTERS TODAY

Debate and compromise are still an important part of government in the United States. Use **CNNfyi.com** or other **current events** sources to learn about a recent political debate in the U.S. Congress. Record your findings in your journal.

Define

- popular sovereignty
- federalism
- legislative branch
- executive branch
- judicial branch
- checks and balances

Identify

- Constitutional Convention
- James Madison
- Virginia Plan
- William Paterson
- New Jersey Plan
- Great Compromise
- Three-Fifths Compromise

The Story Continues

In 1786 a Pennsylvania newspaper printed an article about the U.S. government stating that the government could not afford to pay ambassador John Adams. The newspaper's editors were shocked. "Ought we not to blush . . . that the ambassadors of the states are . . . depending on foreign charity for their support?" John Adams's wife, Abigail, agreed. She felt that this was an embarrassment. She noted that "with the present salary and the present temper of the English no one need envy the [American] embassy." Such problems led some Americans to seek a more powerful national government.

John Adams served as U.S. ambassador to Great Britain.

⭐ The Constitutional Convention

By the mid-1780s most political leaders agreed that it was time to change the Articles of Confederation. In February 1787 the Confederation Congress invited each state to send delegates to a convention in Philadelphia. The delegates planned to discuss ways to improve the

Articles of Confederation. The **Constitutional Convention** was held in May 1787 in Philadelphia's State House, now called Independence Hall. It was in this same building that Americans had officially declared their independence. Twelve states sent a total of 55 delegates to the Convention. Only Rhode Island refused to send a delegation.

The delegates were a remarkable group. Most were well educated, and many of them had served in state legislatures or the Confederation Congress. Benjamin Franklin of Pennsylvania was the oldest delegate. **James Madison** proved to be one of the most important delegates to the Convention. Madison took good notes and joined many talks during the Convention. Revolutionary War hero George Washington was part of the Virginia delegation and was soon elected president of the whole Convention.

Several important American political leaders did not attend the Convention. John Adams and Thomas Jefferson were serving as ambassadors. Others, like Revolutionary hero Patrick Henry, chose not to attend because they were against such a meeting. The states did not choose any women, African Americans, or American Indians as delegates to the Convention. Members of these groups did not yet have the rights of full citizens, including the right to represent other citizens in government.

✔ **Reading Check: Finding the Main Idea** Who were some of the delegates at the Constitutional Convention, and what did they hope to accomplish?

★★★★★★★★★★★★
That's Interesting!
★★★★★★★★★★★★

A "Heated" Debate Can you imagine sitting in a very hot room wearing a heavy suit and stockings? How about doing so in the middle of the summer with no air conditioning? That's what the framers of the Constitution did when they met in Philadelphia in 1787. Although it was hot, they kept the windows closed to keep out flies and so no one in the streets could hear their discussions. Despite the discomfort, the Founders were able to write a new Constitution for their country.

★ The Great Compromise

Several issues divided the delegates to the Constitutional Convention. Some members wanted only to make small changes to the Articles of Confederation, while others wanted to rewrite the Articles. But the delegates who wanted major changes in the Articles had different goals. For example, small and large states had different concerns about representation. States also had different views about regional issues such as slavery. Economic issues such as tariffs also divided northerners from southerners. In addition, there was disagreement over how strong to make the national government.

After the delegates had met for four days, Edmund Randolph of Virginia presented the **Virginia Plan**. James Madison wrote most of this plan, also called the large-state plan. It offered a new federal constitution that would give sovereignty, or supreme power, to the central government. The Virginia Plan divided the national government into three branches: executive, judicial, and legislative.

Delegates from 12 of the 13 states gathered at Philadelphia's Independence Hall to revise the Articles of Confederation.

THE GRANGER COLLECTION, NEW YORK

This engraving advised women that their proper place was in the home. Such attitudes were one reason that no female delegates were sent to the Constitutional Convention.

The legislature in this plan would be a bicameral, or two-house, legislature. This arrangement was similar to that used by several state assemblies. Representatives in the legislature would be chosen on the basis of state populations. Larger states would thus have more representatives than smaller states. Delegates from the smaller states did not like the Virginia Plan. They argued that it would give too much power to the larger states.

The delegates debated about the Virginia Plan for two weeks. New Jersey delegate **William Paterson** then presented the small-state or **New Jersey Plan**. This plan proposed keeping Congress's structure the same. It called for a unicameral, or one-house, legislature. In this case each state would have an equal number of votes, giving the smaller states an equal voice in the national government. The New Jersey Plan proposed that all acts passed by Congress "shall be the supreme law of the respective States." The plan gave the central government the power to tax citizens in all states. It also allowed the government to regulate commerce. Delegates from the large states were against the New Jersey Plan, which would give smaller states more influence.

After a month of debate, the delegates were still unable to agree. The Convention formed a committee to determine how states should be represented. The committee proposed a compromise—an agreement in which both sides give up some of their demands so that other demands can be met. Some historians call this agreement at the Convention the **Great Compromise**. Every state, regardless of its size, would have an equal vote in the upper house of the legislature. This would satisfy supporters of the New Jersey Plan. In the lower house, each state would have a number of representatives based on its population. This proposal would please those who liked the Virginia Plan. The delegates passed the Great Compromise, but there were still problems to settle.

✔ **Reading Check: Contrasting** What were the differences between the Virginia Plan and the New Jersey Plan, and how were these resolved?

Interpreting the Visual Record

Constitutional compromises The delegates at the Constitutional Convention had to compromise to make progress. *How does this sculpture show delegates working together to address issues?*

★ The Three-Fifths Compromise

The debate over representation also involved some regional differences. Southern delegates wanted slaves to be counted as part of their state populations. This way they would have more representatives in Congress. Northerners disagreed. They wanted the number of slaves to determine taxes but not representation.

To resolve this problem, some delegates proposed counting three fifths of the slaves in each state as part of its population. This number would then decide how many representatives a state would have in the lower house. New York delegate Gouverneur Morris spoke with much emotion against this idea.

THE LIBRARY COMPANY OF PHILADELPHIA

Interpreting the Visual Record

Liberty *This antislavery painting shows a woman representing Liberty offering to aid freed slaves. **What does Liberty offer to the freed slaves in the painting?***

History Makers Speak 66The admission of slaves into the Representation . . . comes to this: that the inhabitant of [a state] who goes to the coast of Africa and . . . tears away his fellow creatures from their dearest connections and damns them to the most cruel bondage [slavery], shall have more votes in a Government [established] for protection of the rights of mankind.99

—Gouverneur Morris, quoted in *Founding the Republic,* edited by John J. Patrick

However, the delegates voted to accept the so-called **Three-Fifths Compromise**. Under this agreement each slave would, in effect, be counted as three fifths of a person when determining representation.

Another major issue was the foreign slave trade. Some of the delegates wanted the federal government to end the slave trade. These people included George Mason of Virginia and John Dickinson of Delaware. Others said that the southern states' economies needed the slave trade. South Carolina delegate John Rutledge noted, "The people of these States will never be such fools as to give up so important an interest." Some of these southern delegates even threatened to leave the Union if the Constitution immediately ended the slave trade.

Worried delegates reached another compromise. Northern delegates agreed to wait 20 years before seeking to end the slave trade. Southern delegates agreed to stop insisting that laws in Congress be passed with a two-thirds majority vote. Oliver Ellsworth summed up the view of many delegates. He said, "The morality or wisdom of slavery . . . are considerations belonging to the states themselves."

✔ **Reading Check: Finding the Main Idea** What key compromises did delegates make about slavery at the Constitutional Convention?

Our Living Constitution

Most of the convention delegates wanted a strong national government to replace the Articles of Confederation. At the same time they wanted to protect **popular sovereignty**—the idea that political authority belongs to the people. They also wanted to balance the power of the national government with the powers of the states. Therefore, the delegates looked to **federalism**, or the sharing of power between a central government and the states that make up a country.

In this system, the federal government has power to enforce its laws in the states. This idea is stated in Article VI of the Constitution.

History Makers Speak

"This Constitution and the Laws of the United States which shall be made in Pursuance thereof; and all Treaties made, or which shall be made, under the Authority of the United States, shall be the supreme Law of the Land; and the Judges in every State shall be bound thereby, any Thing in the Constitution or Laws of any State to the Contrary notwithstanding."

—The Constitution of the United States

Each state must obey the authority of the federal government. Article VI also notes that all state officials are required "by Oath . . . to support this Constitution." The federal government has the power to use the military to enforce its laws. These troops are under the command of the president.

Under the Constitution, states have control over government functions not specifically assigned to the federal government. For example, the states control local government, education, and the chartering of corporations. States also create and oversee civil and criminal law. States must also protect the welfare of their citizens.

✔ **Reading Check: Summarizing** What are some of the powers that belong to the states under the Constitution?

 A Delicate Balance

The Constitution also balances the powers within the federal government. For this reason the federal government has three branches. Each is responsible for separate tasks. The first is the **legislative branch**, or Congress, which is responsible for proposing and passing laws. It is made up of two houses. The Senate, or upper house, has two members from each state, while in the House of Representatives, or lower house, each state is represented according to its population.

The second branch of the federal government is the **executive branch**. This branch includes the president and the departments that help run the government. The executive branch makes sure that laws are carried out. The third branch is the **judicial branch**, which is made up of all the national courts. This branch is responsible for interpreting laws,

Analyzing Primary Sources

Evaluating How does this quotation support the principle of federalism?

LINKING PAST to PRESENT

National Currency

The U.S. Constitution gives the federal government the sole power to issue legal currency, or money. Until the mid-1800s, however, many state banks could print banknotes. These notes could be exchanged at the bank that issued them for their value in gold or silver coins. However, banks often refused to accept notes from other banks, which interfered with trade. The federal government stopped the issuing of banknotes in the mid-1860s and created a national currency.

Recently, the Treasury has redesigned paper money to make it harder to copy. The U.S. Mint has also introduced new coins such as the state quarters and the Sacagawea gold dollar coin. How does our national currency demonstrate the system of federalism?

punishing criminals, and settling disputes between states. (*For the full text of the U.S. Constitution, see pages 264–83.*)

The framers of the Constitution created a system of **checks and balances** to keep any branch of government from becoming too powerful. For example, the framers gave Congress power to propose and pass legislation. The president has the power to veto, or reject, laws that Congress passes. However, Congress can override the president's veto with a two-thirds majority vote. Interpretation of the Constitution has provided the judicial branch with its own check. This check is the Supreme Court's power to review the laws passed by Congress. The Court may strike down a law that it finds unconstitutional—in violation of the Constitution.

The delegates knew that the Constitution was not a perfect document. They believed, however, that they had founded a strong government that still protected the ideas of republicanism. The long and difficult debates at the Constitutional Convention lasted 16 weeks. Finally, in September 1787 the delegates signed a final draft of the Constitution. Only three of the 42 delegates who remained refused to sign. These three were Elbridge Gerry of Massachusetts and Edmund Randolph and George Mason of Virginia. The delegates then sent the Constitution to Congress, which sent it to the states for ratification.

✔ **Reading Check: Summarizing** How was the government structured under the new Constitution, and how was power balanced?

This early draft of the Constitution shows corrections and comments by George Washington.

September 1787
The final draft of the Constitution is signed.

Section 3 Review

go.hrw.com
Homework Practice Online
keyword: SF3 HP8

① **Define** and explain:
• popular sovereignty
• federalism
• legislative branch
• executive branch
• judicial branch
• checks and balances

② **Identify** and explain:
• Constitutional Convention
• James Madison
• Virginia Plan
• William Paterson
• New Jersey Plan
• Great Compromise
• Three-Fifths Compromise

③ **Summarizing** Copy the graphic organizer below. Use it to explain the major compromises that took place at the Constitutional Convention.

Virginia Plan → New Jersey Plan →

Great Compromise

North → South →

Three-Fifths Compromise

④ **Finding the Main Idea**
a. What was the original purpose of the Constitutional Convention?

b. How does the Constitution reflect the ideas of republicanism and limited government?

⑤ **Writing and Critical Thinking**
Evaluating Imagine that you are a political scholar writing about the Constitutional Convention. Write an essay explaining how the actions of the Founding Fathers represented good citizenship.

Consider the following:
• the actions and beliefs of the Founding Fathers
• what it means to be a good citizen

Ratification of the Constitution

Read to Discover

1. Why were some people against the new Constitution?
2. What arguments for the Constitution did the *Federalist Papers* present?
3. When and how was the Constitution ratified?
4. Why did some people want a bill of rights, and how was it added to the Constitution?

WHY IT MATTERS TODAY

Debate still takes place over how much power the federal government has over the states. Use CNN**fyi**.com or other **current events** sources to study a recent dispute or legal case between a state and the federal government. Record your findings in your journal.

Define
- amendments

Identify
- Antifederalists
- George Mason
- Federalists
- *Federalist Papers*
- Bill of Rights

The Story Continues

John Dunlap and David Claypoole stayed up well into the night on September 17, 1787. They reset type and filled all four pages of their Philadelphia newspaper. Dunlap and Claypoole had begun their work only hours after the end of the Constitutional Convention. The next morning, they presented the first printed copy of the U.S. Constitution.

Newspapers supplied most Americans with their first look at the text of the Constitution.

★ Federalists and Antifederalists

When the Constitution was made public, a great debate began among Americans. People who opposed the Constitution were known as **Antifederalists**. Some Antifederalists thought that the Constitutional Convention had gone too far in creating a new government. Others thought the Constitution gave too much power to the central government. For some Antifederalists, the main problem was that the Constitution did not include a bill of rights. Constitutional Convention delegate **George Mason** became an Antifederalist for this reason.

CANADA

Disputed with Britain

NEW HAMPSHIRE
June 21, 1788

MASSACHUSETTS
Feb. 6, 1788

NEW YORK
July 26, 1788

RHODE ISLAND
May 29, 1790

CONNECTICUT
Jan. 9, 1788

PENNSYLVANIA
Dec. 12, 1787

NEW JERSEY
Dec. 18, 1787

DELAWARE
Dec. 7, 1787

MARYLAND
April 28, 1788

ATLANTIC OCEAN

VIRGINIA
June 25, 1788

KENTUCKY DISTRICT

TENNESSEE DISTRICT

NORTH CAROLINA
Nov. 21, 1789

SOUTH CAROLINA
May 23, 1788

GEORGIA
Jan. 2, 1788

0   100   200 Miles
0   100   200 Kilometers
Albers Equal-Area Projection

Federalist area

Antifederalist area

Evenly divided area

1784 Date indicates when Constitution was ratified

Federalists and Antifederalists

Interpreting Maps Federalists and Antifederalists often engaged in bitter debates over whether to ratify the new Constitution.

Skills Assessment

1. **Human Systems** According to the map, which states had the most complete Federalist support?

2. **Summarizing** In what month and year did the first states ratify the Constitution?

Many Antifederalists were small farmers and debtors, but some were wealthy. Some heroes of the American Revolution were also strong Antifederalists, such as Richard Henry Lee, Samuel Adams, and Patrick Henry. As the Constitution was debated in Virginia, George Mason warned against the power of a strong central government.

History Makers Speak

"The very idea of converting [changing] what was formerly a confederation to a consolidated [united] government, is totally subversive of [against] every principle which has hitherto [before] governed us. This power is calculated to annihilate [destroy] totally the state governments."

—George Mason, quoted in *Great Issues in American History*, edited by Richard Hofstadter

Antifederalists were challenged by many Americans who believed that the United States needed a stronger Constitution. Supporters of the Constitution called themselves **Federalists**. James Madison, George Washington, Benjamin Franklin, Alexander Hamilton, and John Jay were Federalists. Most Federalists believed that the Constitution offered a good balance of power. They thought it was a careful compromise between various political views.

✔ **Reading Check: Identifying Points of View** What were some of the Antifederalists' arguments against the Constitution?

Analyzing Primary Sources

Identifying Points of View What did George Mason believe a strong central government would do to the states?

Forming a Government **243**

THE GRANGER COLLECTION, NEW YORK

BIOGRAPHY

George Mason
(1725–1792)

George Mason was a Virginia planter who turned to politics. He became devoted to limited government and the protection of human rights. His many speeches and writings greatly influenced the development of the U.S. government. One of his most important works was the Virginia Declaration of Rights, which served as a model for the bills of rights of many states. Although Mason served as a delegate to the Constitutional Convention, he refused to sign the Constitution because it did not include a bill of rights. **What role did George Mason play in shaping American government?**

Analyzing Primary Sources
Identifying Points of View
What did Patrick Henry fear about the new form of government?

 # The *Federalist Papers*

The most important arguments in favor of the Constitution appeared in a series of widely read essays that became known as the **_Federalist Papers_**. The essays were written under the name Publius, but historians now know that of the 85 essays, Alexander Hamilton wrote about 50. James Madison wrote about 30 essays, and John Jay wrote the other 5.

The authors of the *Federalist Papers* told Americans that the new federal government would not overpower the states. In *Federalist Paper* "No. 10," Madison wrote about the many different groups of U.S. citizens. Their many points of view, Madison stated, would keep any single group from controlling the government. In *Federalist Paper* "No. 15," Hamilton discussed the need to fix the country's many problems under the Articles of Confederation. "Let us make a firm stand for our safety, our tranquillity [peace], our dignity, our reputation," he wrote. The *Federalist Papers* were widely reprinted and strongly influenced the debate over the Constitution.

✔ **Reading Check: Identifying Points of View** How did the *Federalist Papers* defend the Constitution?

 # The Ratification Fight

The true test of the Constitution's support came during the debate over state ratification, or approval. The Articles of Confederation had needed the approval of all 13 states to go into effect. However, the Constitution needed only 9 states to pass it. Each state except Rhode Island held special state conventions to give citizens the chance to discuss the Constitution. Then they could vote on whether the Constitution should be ratified.

Antifederalists also spoke out in state conventions. In New York one citizen said, "It appears that the government will fall into the hands of the few and the great." At the Virginia ratification convention, Patrick Henry spoke for many Antifederalists.

 History Makers Speak ❝If you make the citizens of this country agree to become the subjects of one great consolidated [united] empire of America, your government will not have sufficient energy to keep them together. . . . There will be no checks, no real balances, in this government.❞

—Patrick Henry, quoted in *Great Issues in American History*, edited by Richard Hofstadter

The Constitution had the support of heroes of the American Revolution such as Benjamin Franklin, Paul Revere, and George Washington. At the Massachusetts convention, Revere helped win the backing of other craftspeople.

On December 7, 1787, Delaware became the first state to ratify the Constitution. Throughout the rest of 1787 and the first half of 1788, eight other states ratified the Constitution. They did so in the following order: Pennsylvania, New Jersey, Georgia, Connecticut, Massachusetts, Maryland, South Carolina, and New Hampshire. The Constitution went into effect in June 1788 after New Hampshire became the ninth state to ratify it.

However, there was still debate in New York, North Carolina, Rhode Island, and Virginia. Political leaders across America knew the new government needed the support of Virginia and New York. Virginia had the largest population in the nation. New York was an important center for business and trade. Finally, James Madison and the other Virginia Federalists convinced Virginia to ratify the Constitution in late June 1788. In New York, Federalists John Jay and Alexander Hamilton said that New York City would break away and join the new government if the Constitution was not ratified. New York State finally ratified the Constitution in

June 1788
The Constitution goes into effect.

The Articles of Confederation and the Constitution

ARTICLES	CONSTITUTION
EXECUTIVE BRANCH	
No executive to administer and enforce legislation; Congress has sole authority to govern	President administers and enforces federal laws
Executive committee to oversee government when Congress is out of session	
LEGISLATIVE BRANCH	
A unicameral (one-house) legislature	A bicameral (two-house) legislature
Each state has one vote, regardless of population	Each state has equal representation in the Senate; each state is represented according to population in the House of Representatives
Nine votes (of the original 13) to enact major legislation	Simple majority to enact legislation
JUDICIAL BRANCH	
No national court system	National court system, headed by the Supreme Court
Congress to establish temporary courts to hear cases of piracy	Courts to hear cases involving national laws, treaties, and the Constitution as well as cases between states, between citizens of different states, or between a state and citizen of another state
OTHER MATTERS	
Admission to the Confederation by 9 votes (of 13)	Congress to admit new states; all must have a republican form of government
Amendment of the Articles by unanimous vote	Amendment of the Constitution by two-thirds vote of both houses of Congress or by national convention, followed by ratification by three fourths of the states
The states retain independence	The states accept the Constitution as the supreme law of the land

Interpreting the Visual Record

Political parade *Federalists held a parade to celebrate New York's ratification of the Constitution in July 1788.* **Whose name is on the float, and why do you think this person was chosen to represent the Federalist cause?**

July 1788. North Carolina ratified the Constitution in November 1789. Rhode Island was the last state to ratify the Constitution in May 1790.

✔ **Reading Check: Sequencing** In what order did the states ratify the Constitution, and which states ratified the Constitution after it went into effect?

Research on the ROM

Free Find:
James Madison
After reading about James Madison on the **Holt Researcher CD–ROM**, imagine that you are a newspaper editor. Write an obituary describing his political efforts to protect citizens' rights.

☆ Demanding a Bill of Rights

Several states ratified the Constitution only after they were promised that a bill of rights would be added to it. Many Antifederalists did not think that the Constitution would protect personal freedoms. The writer Mercy Otis Warren, an Antifederalist, expressed this concern in Boston's *Columbian Patriot.* "The whole constitution . . . appears a perversion [abuse] of the rights of particular states and of private citizens."

In the new Congress, some Federalists said that the nation did not need a federal bill of rights. They believed that state constitutions already promised these rights. Many Federalists also believed that the whole Constitution itself was a bill of rights. It was, they argued, written to protect the liberty of all U.S. citizens.

James Madison did not think that a bill of rights was necessary. However, he understood that the promise of such a bill had been key to ratification. He therefore wanted to make a bill of rights one of the new government's first priorities. Thomas Jefferson supported Madison's efforts. He wrote that "a bill of rights is what the people are entitled to against every government on earth, . . . and what no just government should refuse." In Congress's first session, Madison encouraged the legislators to put together a bill of rights. Then, the rights would be added to the Constitution as **amendments**—official changes, corrections, or additions. In Article V of the Constitution, the Founders had provided a way to change the document. They believed amendments would be necessary to reflect the will of the people. They designed the process to be difficult, however. Proposed amendments must be approved by a two-thirds majority of both houses of Congress. Then they must be ratified by three fourths of the states before taking effect.

To create a list of possible amendments, the legislators took ideas from the state ratifying conventions. They also consulted the Virginia Declaration of Rights and the Declaration of Independence. Members of Congress worked to make sure that the abuses listed in the Declaration would be illegal under the new government. Congress debated the amendments for three months. Finally, in September 1789, Congress proposed 12 amendments, which were then sent to the states for ratification. By December 1791, the required three fourths of the states had ratified 10 of these proposed amendments. These first 10 amendments to the U.S. Constitution are known as the **Bill of Rights**. *(For a full discussion of the Bill of Rights, see Chapter 9.)*

These 10 amendments added to the strength and flexibility of the Constitution. The Bill of Rights also set a clear example of how to amend the Constitution to address the needs of the nation.

The Constitution is a remarkable document. It has clear guidelines and principles, yet can be changed to meet new challenges. The flexibility of the U.S. Constitution has allowed it to survive for more than 200 years. It is the world's oldest written national constitution.

THE GRANGER COLLECTION, NEW YORK

The Bill of Rights assured many Americans that their new government would act to protect their liberties.

✔ **Reading Check: Analyzing Information** Why did some people feel a bill of rights was necessary, and how was it added to the Constitution?

Section 4 Review

go.hrw.com Homework Practice Online
keyword: SF3 HP8

1 **Define and explain:**
• amendments

2 **Identify and explain:**
• Antifederalists
• George Mason
• Federalists
• *Federalist Papers*
• Bill of Rights

3 **Contrasting** Copy the chart below. Use it to identify the arguments for and against the Constitution.

U.S. Constitution

Federalist Views	Antifederalist Views

4 **Finding the Main Idea**
a. Who wrote the *Federalist Papers*, and what were their arguments?

b. How was the Constitution ratified, and when did it take effect?

5 **Writing and Critical Thinking**
Summarizing Imagine that you are James Madison. Write an essay arguing why the Constitution should be amended with a bill of rights and explaining the amendment process.

Consider the following:
• the purpose of a Bill of Rights
• those who supported a Bill of Rights in the Constitution
• the process of amending the Constitution

Chapter 8 Review

The Chapter at a Glance

Examine the visual summary of the chapter below. Then create a poster illustrating the chapter's main ideas that you might present to the class.

Articles of Confederation
Weak central government

Achievements
Northwest Ordinance
Northwest Territory

Problems
Poor international trade
Poor foreign relations
Weak economy
Shays's Rebellion

Constitution
Strong central government

Compromises
Great Compromise
Three-Fifths Compromise
Slave trade

Structure
Legislative branch
Executive branch
Judicial branch
Checks and balances

Problems
Struggle over ratification

Bill of Rights
The first 10 amendments
Passed to protect individual rights and freedoms

Identifying People and Ideas

Use the following terms or people in historically significant sentences.

1. Virginia Statute for Religious Freedom
2. Articles of Confederation
3. Northwest Ordinance of 1787
4. James Madison
5. Great Compromise
6. Three-Fifths Compromise
7. federalism
8. George Mason
9. *Federalist Papers*
10. amendments

Understanding Main Ideas

Section 1 (Pages 222–227)

1. What English and colonial examples of political ideas did Americans draw from when creating their new government?
2. What did the Northwest Ordinance of 1787 accomplish?

Section 2 (Pages 230–235)

3. How did a weak central government affect the American economy?

Section 3 (Pages 236–241)

4. What were the terms of the Great Compromise?
5. How is the federal government organized under the Constitution?

Section 4 (Pages 242–247)

6. What arguments did the Federalists and Antifederalists make regarding the Constitution?

You Be the Historian— Reviewing Themes

1. **Global Relations** How did the Articles of Confederation affect the new national government's ability to conduct foreign policy?
2. **Citizenship** Why did many Americans want a federal bill of rights?
3. **Constitutional Heritage** How does the Constitution guard against the misuse of power?

Thinking Critically

1. **Making Generalizations and Predictions** Without compromises, how do you think the Constitutional Convention would have turned out?
2. **Supporting a Point of View** Imagine that you are a delegate at a state ratifying convention. You have read the arguments made by Alexander Hamilton and Patrick Henry. Explain whose point of view you support and how you will vote.
3. **Drawing Inferences and Conclusions** In what ways did the Founding Fathers serve as examples of civic virtue?

Interpreting Charts

Study the chart below. Then use the information from the chart to help you answer the questions that follow.

Ratifying the Constitution

STATE	RATIFICATION DATE
Delaware	December 7, 1787
Pennsylvania	December 12, 1787
New Jersey	December 18, 1787
Georgia	January 2, 1788
Connecticut	January 9, 1788
Massachusetts	February 6, 1788
Maryland	April 28, 1788
South Carolina	May 23, 1788
New Hampshire	June 21, 1788
Virginia	June 25, 1788
New York	July 26, 1788
North Carolina	November 21, 1789
Rhode Island	May 29, 1790

1. About how many months passed between the time that the first and last states ratified the Constitution?
   a. 31
   b. 33
   c. 6
   d. 3

2. During which year did the most states ratify the Constitution?
   a. 1787
   b. 1788
   c. 1789
   d. 1790

3. Based on your knowledge of the period and the information presented on the chart, when did the Constitution go into effect? Why was the support of New York and Virginia important?

Analyzing Primary Sources

Read the following quote by Benjamin Franklin, and then answer the questions that follow.

> **"Thus I consent, Sir, to this Constitution because I expect no better. . . . I hope therefore that for our own sakes as a part of the people, and for the sake of posterity [future generations], we shall act heartily and unanimously in recommending this constitution . . . wherever our influence may extend, and turn our future thoughts and endeavors to the means of having it well administered."**

4. Which of the following statements best describes Franklin's point of view?
   a. Future generations will like the Constitution more than the present one does.
   b. Americans should write a better constitution.
   c. The Constitution is as good as it can be, and the Founders should speak highly of it to Americans.
   d. The Constitution has broad influence.

5. Based on your knowledge of the period, do you think that Franklin's opinion would have been important to the other delegates at the Constitutional Convention? Explain your answer.

Alternative Assessment

Building Your Portfolio

American History

Interdisciplinary Connection to Drama

Imagine that you are attending the Constitutional Convention. Think of an issue that was not addressed in the original Constitution (for example, suffrage for all Americans or the ending of slavery). Write a one-act play about the discussion that takes place at the Convention surrounding your issue. If possible, perform your play for the class using actors and appropriate props.

☞ internet connect

Internet Activity: go.hrw.com
keyword: SF3 CF8

Choose an activity about forming a government to:

- Use graphic organizers to display global trade issues.
- Research a significant delegate to the Constitutional Convention and write a biography.
- Explore the political ideas of Federalists and Antifederalists.

The Living Constitution

The United States is governed by the Constitution, which was adopted by the original 13 states in 1789. The Constitution established a government in which the people choose their leaders. These officials make the nation's laws and run the government.

The framers of the Constitution created a federal system that is strong enough to enforce its authority. The principles and methods of governing that are outlined in the Constitution, however, are quite flexible. This flexibility has allowed the federal government to adjust to great change over more than 210 years. For example, the original nation of 13 states had a population of less than 4 million. Today the United States has 50 states and more than 280 million people.

The Union

The Northwest Ordinance was passed by the Confederation Congress in 1787, before the Constitution was written. The Ordinance established a method for admitting new states to the Union. The last states admitted to the Union were Alaska and Hawaii in 1959.

The Northwest Ordinance: Becoming a State

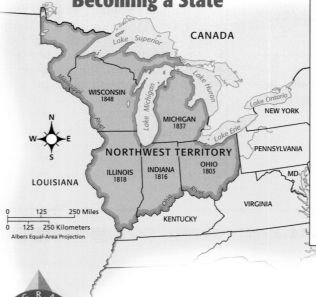

STEPS TO STATEHOOD

Congress specifies that three to five territories will be carved out of the Northwest Territory.

For each territory, Congress appoints a governor, a secretary, and three judges.

When a territory's population reaches 5,000 free male inhabitants of voting age, it elects a territorial legislature and sends a nonvoting delegate to Congress.

Once a territory's population increases to 60,000 free inhabitants, it becomes eligible for statehood and can draft a state constitution.

Congress approves the state constitution, and the territory becomes a state.

Sources: *Record of America; The Oxford Companion to American History*

Geography **Skills**

Interpreting Political Maps

1. When is a territory eligible for statehood?
2. **Human Systems** Under the Northwest Ordinance, who, or what, approves a territory's proposed constitution before the territory becomes a state?
3. **Sequencing** When did each state of the Northwest Territory join the Union?

Joining the Union

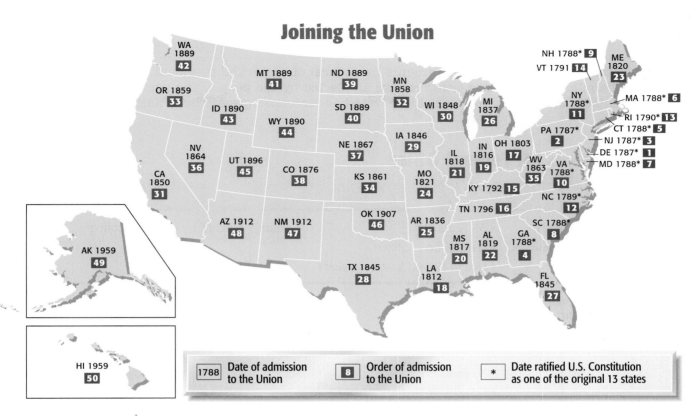

WA 1889 **42**
OR 1859 **33**
MT 1889 **41**
ID 1890 **43**
ND 1889 **39**
SD 1889 **40**
MN 1858 **32**
WI 1848 **30**
MI 1837 **26**
NH 1788* **9**
VT 1791 **14**
ME 1820 **23**
NY 1788* **11**
MA 1788* **6**
RI 1790* **13**
CT 1788* **5**
NV 1864 **36**
UT 1896 **45**
WY 1890 **44**
NE 1867 **37**
IA 1846 **29**
IL 1818 **21**
IN 1816 **19**
OH 1803 **17**
PA 1787* **2**
NJ 1787* **3**
DE 1787* **1**
MD 1788* **7**
CA 1850 **31**
CO 1876 **38**
KS 1861 **34**
MO 1821 **24**
KY 1792 **15**
WV 1863 **35**
VA 1788* **10**
NC 1789* **12**
AZ 1912 **48**
NM 1912 **47**
OK 1907 **46**
AR 1836 **25**
TN 1796 **16**
SC 1788* **8**
MS 1817 **20**
AL 1819 **22**
GA 1788* **4**
TX 1845 **28**
LA 1812 **18**
FL 1845 **27**
AK 1959 **49**
HI 1959 **50**

| 1788 | Date of admission to the Union | 8 | Order of admission to the Union | * | Date ratified U.S. Constitution as one of the original 13 states |

Geography **Skills**
Interpreting Thematic Maps

1. Which three states ratified the Constitution first?

2. Places and Regions What were the original 13 states of the Union?

3. Summarizing What states were admitted to the Union in the 1900s? In what years during this period were more than one state admitted?

History Note 1

Congress established the method for admitting new states to the Union in the Northwest Ordinance of 1787. Before that, however, some people in what is now the state of Tennessee made the first attempt to create a new state. In 1784 North Carolina turned over the Tennessee territory to the new government of the United States. Residents in northeastern Tennessee applied to Congress to form a new state named "Franklin" after Benjamin Franklin. However, North Carolina reclaimed the region before Congress could decide the issue. Finally, in 1790 North Carolina again gave the territory to the federal government. In 1796 the proposed state of Franklin became part of the new state of Tennessee.

Rocky Mount was the capital for the first territorial government of Tennessee.

Elected Officials and Voters

The Constitution sets the requirements for federal officials. The president, vice president, and members of Congress are all elected by the people. The percentage of the U.S. population that is eligible to vote has increased greatly over time.

Requirements for Federal Office

	OFFICE	REQUIREMENTS	TERM	SELECTION
	President **Vice President**	• 35 years old • Natural-born citizen • Live in United States 14 years	4 years	Elected by electoral college
	Supreme Court Justice	• None	Life	Appointed by president and approved by Senate
	Senator	• 30 years old • U.S. citizen 9 years • Live in state where elected	6 years	Originally chosen by state legislature (per Constitution); Currently elected by voters of state (per Seventeenth Amendment)
	Representative	• 25 years old • U.S. citizen 7 years • Live in state where elected	2 years	Elected by voters of district

Geography **Skills**

Interpreting Charts

1. What are the age requirements for federal officials?
2. What are the terms of the federal officials listed?
3. **Comparing and Contrasting** Which federal office has the fewest requirements listed? Which position listed is not an elected office?

History Note 2

Franklin D. Roosevelt was the only president elected to more than two terms. He was elected president four times. In 1951 the Twenty-second Amendment was adopted, stating that no president can be elected more than twice. In 1995 the Supreme Court ruled that neither the states nor Congress could pass laws limiting the terms of members of Congress. A constitutional amendment that would allow term limits has been proposed. However, such an amendment has failed to pass in Congress.

The inauguration of President George W. Bush

The Expanding Electorate

Estimated Percentage of Population Eligible to Vote

- 17.6%
- 18.4%
- 23.1%
- 25.0%
- 51.3%
- 64.1%
- 61.2%
- 72.7%
- 74.8%

Year: 1840, 1860, 1880, 1900, 1920, 1940, 1960, 1980, 1996

Sources: *Historical Statistics of the United States; Federal Election Commission; Congressional Quarterly's Guide to U.S. Elections; Datapedia of the United States, 1790–2000: America Year by Year*

Geography **Skills**

Interpreting Line Graphs

1. **Human Systems** What twenty-year interval on the graph shows the largest increase in the percentage of the U.S. population eligible to vote?
2. **Drawing Inferences and Conclusions** Show this graph to another student. Ask him or her to explain to you which amendments to the Constitution might account for the increases in voter eligibility seen in 1920 and 1980.

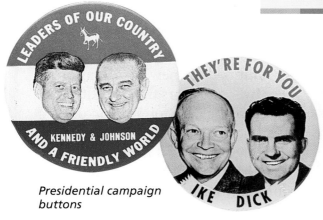

Presidential campaign buttons

History Note 3

The power to decide who is eligible to vote is reserved to the states under the Tenth Amendment. However, later constitutional amendments have extended the right to vote to more and more people. The Fifteenth Amendment, ratified in 1870, protects the right of people of any race to vote. In 1920 the Nineteenth Amendment gave women the right to vote in all states. The Twenty-sixth Amendment, ratified in 1971, lowered the legal voting age from 21 to 18.

9 Citizenship and the Constitution
(1787–Present)

Suffragists parade down a street in Washington, D.C.

THE GRANGER COLLECTION, NEW YORK

Congress sent the Constitution to the states for ratification in 1787.

THE GRANGER COLLECTION, NEW YORK

UNITED STATES

1791 The Bill of Rights becomes part of the Constitution on December 15.

1920 The Nineteenth Amendment gives women the right to vote.

1954 The Supreme Court rules that segregated public schools are unconstitutional.

1800 / **1920** **1930** **1940** **1950**

WORLD

1917 Mexico adopts a new constitution.

1930 Mohandas K. Gandhi leads acts of civil disobedience to protest British rule in India.

1945 Delegates from 50 nations meet in San Francisco to found the United Nations.

1948 The United Nations adopts the Universal Declaration of Human Rights.

Mohandas K. Gandhi (looking down at center) led many marches protesting British colonial rule in India.

The United Nations was formed to resolve international conflicts peacefully.

Build on What You Know

After much discussion, the states ratified the new Constitution. For over 200 years the Constitution has provided the foundation of American democracy and freedom. Throughout recent history this document has been an example for many nations and democratic movements around the world.

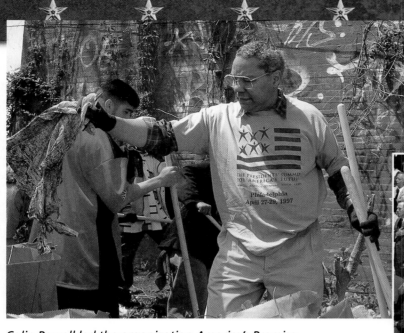

Colin Powell led the organization America's Promise— The Alliance for Youth to promote volunteerism.

Immigrants take an oath to become U.S. citizens.

1967 Thurgood Marshall becomes the first African American justice on the Supreme Court.

1971 The Twenty-sixth Amendment is passed, giving the right to vote to all U.S. citizens aged 18 years or older.

1981 Sandra Day O'Connor becomes the first woman justice on the Supreme Court.

1990 The Americans with Disabilities Act is passed.

1997 Colin Powell starts a campaign for volunteerism.

1960   1970   1980   1990   2000

1989 The East German government opens the Berlin Wall, allowing citizens of East Germany to travel to the West.

Demonstrators and celebrators gathered as the Berlin Wall was opened.

You Be the Historian

Themes Journal

What's Your Opinion? Do you **agree** or **disagree** with the following statements? Support your point of view in your journal.

● **Constitutional Heritage** The government should be set up to make sure that the president does not have too much power.

● **Citizenship** One person's vote is not important to the outcome of an election.

● **Culture** The government should protect the rights of minorities over the interests of the majority.

If you were there . . .
How would you educate Americans about their rights and responsibilities?

Understanding the Constitution

Read to Discover

1. How did the framers of the Constitution try to balance state and federal powers?
2. What are the three branches of the federal government, and what are the requirements for membership in each branch?
3. How is power divided between the three branches of government?

WHY IT MATTERS TODAY

The cabinet regularly advises the president on important issues. Use CNN fyi.com or other **current events** sources to identify a member of the presidential cabinet and read about some of the person's basic duties. Record your findings in your journal.

Define

- representative democracy
- delegated powers
- elastic clause
- reserved powers
- concurrent powers
- separation of powers
- apportionment
- impeach
- veto
- executive order
- pardon
- cabinet

Identify

- Thurgood Marshall
- Sandra Day O'Connor

The Story Continues

A sign on the Justice Department Building in Washington, D.C., describes the role of the Constitution. It reads, "No Free Government Can Survive That Is Not Based on the Supremacy of Law." This idea is central to the Constitution of the United States. The laws of our nation protect the freedom and the rights of our citizens.

The Department of Justice was established in 1870, with the attorney general as its head.

⭐ The Federal System

The United States is a **representative democracy**—a government led by officials who are chosen by the people. The Constitution created a federal system in which power is divided between the states and the federal government. The powers granted to the federal government are called **delegated powers**. Examples of these powers are coining money and regulating interstate and international trade. The federal government also runs the country's defense, declares war, and conducts diplomacy.

Federalism

POWERS DELEGATED TO THE NATIONAL GOVERNMENT	POWERS SHARED BY NATIONAL AND STATE GOVERNMENTS	POWERS RESERVED TO THE STATES
Declare war	Maintain law and order	Establish and maintain schools
Maintain armed forces	Levy taxes	Establish local governments
Regulate interstate and foreign trade	Borrow money	Regulate business within the state
Admit new states	Charter banks	Make marriage laws
Establish post offices	Establish courts	Provide for public safety
Set standard weights and measures	Provide for public welfare	Assume other powers not delegated to the national government or not prohibited to the states
Coin money		
Establish foreign policy		
Make all laws necessary and proper for carrying out delegated powers		

Sometimes, Congress has stretched its delegated powers to address new or unexpected issues. The "necessary and proper" clause of Article I, Section 8, of the Constitution makes this possible. The clause allows Congress to "make all Laws which shall be necessary and proper" for carrying out its duties. Because it provides flexibility for the government, this clause has become known as the **elastic clause**.

The powers kept by the state governments or by the citizens are **reserved powers**. These powers include creating local governments and holding elections. States also control education and trade within their borders. **Concurrent powers** are powers that the federal and state governments share. Taxing, borrowing money, enforcing laws, and providing for citizens' welfare are examples of these powers.

✔ **Reading Check: Categorizing** List at least two examples each of delegated, reserved, and concurrent powers.

⭐ The Legislative Branch

The federal government is divided into three separate branches, each with its own responsibilities and powers. This **separation of powers** is designed to balance each branch against the others. It keeps any single branch from becoming too powerful.

The legislative branch, or Congress, makes the nation's laws. "Members of Congress are the human connection between the citizen and . . . government," noted one member. Article I divides Congress into the House of Representatives and the Senate.

This is the seal of Congress, the lawmaking branch of the federal government.

Interpreting the Visual Record

Federal Hall *The first Congress under the Constitution met in Federal Hall in New York City.* **Why might the Congress later need a new building?**

With 435 members, the House of Representatives is the larger of the two houses of Congress. The U.S. census, a population count taken every 10 years, decides the number of representatives for each state. To keep each state's total current, Congress uses **apportionment**, or planned distribution, of representatives. Under this system, no state can gain a representative unless another state loses one. House members represent a particular district of voters in a state. House members must be at least 25 years old, have been U.S. citizens for seven or more years, and be residents of the state in which they are elected. House members serve two-year terms.

The Senate is made up of two representatives, called senators, from each state. Senators represent the interests of their entire state. They must be at least 30 years old and have been U.S. citizens for nine or more years. Senators serve six-year terms and must be residents of the state they represent. The senator who has served longer is the state's senior senator. No law limits the number of times someone may be elected to either house of Congress.

The political party that has the most members in each house of Congress is called the majority party. The party with fewer members is the minority party. The leader of the House of Representatives is the Speaker of the House. House members select the Speaker, who is usually from the majority party. The vice president of the United States serves as the president of the Senate. The vice president does not join in Senate debates but can cast a vote to break a tie. When the vice president is absent, the president *pro tempore* leads the Senate.

Congress begins its regular session, or meeting, each year in the first week of January. Each house of Congress carries out most of its work in committees that specialize in certain types of bills, or proposed laws. For example, all bills about taxes begin in the House Ways and Means Committee.

✔ **Reading Check: Summarizing** What are the requirements and terms of office for members of the House and the Senate?

⭐ The Executive Branch

Article II of the Constitution specifies the powers of the executive branch. This branch enforces the laws that Congress passes. The president, as head of the executive branch, is the most powerful elected leader in the country. To become president, one must be a native-born U.S. citizen, at least 35 years old, and have been a U.S. resident for at least 14 years. The requirements are the same for the vice president.

Thus far, all U.S. presidents have been white men. In more recent elections, candidates for the nation's highest offices have been more diverse. African Americans such as Jesse Jackson and Alan Keyes have campaigned for nomination. In 1984 Geraldine Ferraro ran as the Democratic nominee for vice president. She was the first female candidate for a major political party. In 2000 Democrat Joseph Lieberman became the first Jewish nominee for vice president.

Every four years Americans elect a president and vice president. Franklin D. Roosevelt, who won four presidential elections, was the only president to serve more than two terms. Later, the Twenty-second Amendment limited presidents to two terms. If the president dies, resigns, or is removed from office, the vice president becomes president.

The House of Representatives can **impeach,** or vote to bring charges of "treason, bribery, or other high crimes and misdemeanors" against, a president. The Senate tries all impeachment cases. If a president is found guilty, Congress can remove him or her from office. In 1868 Andrew Johnson became the first president to be impeached. President Bill Clinton was impeached in 1998. In each case the Senate tried the president and found him not guilty. In 1974 President Richard Nixon resigned to avoid possible impeachment.

⭐ Working with Congress

The system of checks and balances often places the president against Congress. This problem is quite challenging when the president's party is different from that of the majority party in Congress. Despite their differences, the executive and legislative branches must cooperate. President Lyndon Johnson described the role Congress played in his work.

> **History Makers Speak**
>
> ❝What a President says and thinks is not worth five cents unless he has the people and Congress behind him. Without the Congress I'm just a six-feet-four Texan. With Congress I'm President of the United States in the fullest sense.❞
>
> —President Lyndon Johnson, from *The Macmillan Dictionary of Political Quotations*

Although Congress passes laws, the president can ask members of Congress to pass or reject certain bills. The president also has the power to **veto,** or cancel, laws that Congress passes. Congress can override, or undo, a president's veto; however, doing so is very difficult. Overriding a veto requires a two-thirds majority vote. After Congress passes a law, federal agencies and departments often decide how to enforce it. In carrying out laws that affect parts of the Constitution, treaties, and statutes, the president may issue an **executive order,** a command that has the power of law. In an emergency the president might issue an executive order that stretches the definition of laws passed by Congress. The president also has the power to grant a **pardon,** or freedom from punishment. Pardons are sometimes given to persons convicted of federal crimes or who are facing criminal charges.

★★★★★★★★★★★★★
That's Interesting!
★★★★★★★★★★★★★

Electoral Oversights Did you know that the runner-up in a presidential election used to become vice president? It's true! Even if the top two finishers were from different policital parties, the candidate in second place served as vice president. To solve this problem, parties began choosing both a presidential and vice presidential candidate to run on the same ticket. But because electors cast only one ballot for both candidates, the two Democratic-Republican candidates in 1800 ended up tied with each other for president! In 1804, Congress passed the Twelfth Amendment, which directs electors to cast separate ballots for president and vice president.

THE GRANGER COLLECTION, NEW YORK

Aaron Burr tied with Thomas Jefferson in the 1800 electoral vote.

Analyzing Primary Sources

Drawing Inferences and Conclusions Why did President Johnson believe the support of Congress was important?

Research on the R©M

Free Find:
Pendleton Civil Service Act

After reading about the Pendleton Civil Service Act on the **Holt Researcher CD–ROM**, write an editorial describing why it is important to have civil service jobs that are not appointed positions.

BIOGRAPHY

Sandra Day O'Connor

1930–

Sandra Day O'Connor was born in El Paso, Texas, and attended law school at Stanford University in California. She served as Arizona's assistant attorney general and as a state legislator before becoming an Arizona state judge. In 1981 President Ronald Reagan chose O'Connor to serve on the Supreme Court. Although she was appointed by a conservative Republican president, at times O'Connor is often seen as a moderate justice. Her decisions show how Supreme Court justices can often be free from party politics. **What experience did O'Connor have before becoming a judge?**

The president is also commander in chief of the armed forces. In an emergency, the president can send in U.S. troops, but only Congress can declare war. Some other executive duties are foreign relations and arranging treaties. Currently, 14 executive departments do most of the executive branch's work. The president chooses the department heads, whom Congress must then approve. The **cabinet**, made up of these department secretaries, advises the president on important matters.

✔ **Reading Check: Comparing** What powers do the executive and legislative branches have over each other?

⭐ The Judicial Branch

The third branch of the government is the judicial branch. This branch is made up of a system of federal courts headed by the U.S. Supreme Court. Article III of the Constitution outlines the courts' duties. As an implied part of these duties, a federal court can strike down a state or federal law. However, a court can only do this if it finds a law unconstitutional. If Congress desires, it can propose an amendment to the Constitution that would make the law constitutional.

The president makes all appointments to federal courts. These judges receive the appointment for life to ensure that they will not be influenced by political parties. The lower courts in the federal system are divided according to the types of cases over which they have jurisdiction, or authority. Each state has at least one district court to handle federal cases. States with higher populations often have more than one district court. Today there are 94 U.S. district courts and 13 courts of appeals that review lower-court decisions.

At times, someone convicted of a crime believes that the original trial was unfair. That person can appeal his or her case to the higher court. Each of these courts of appeals has a panel of judges who decide whether the lower court tried the original case properly. If the judges uphold, or accept, the lower court's decision, then the case's original outcome stands. If not, the case may go back to the lower court for a new trial.

✔ **Reading Check: Analyzing Information** What check does the judicial branch have over the legislative branch?

⭐ The Supreme Court

After a case has been decided by the court of appeals, the losing side may appeal the decision to the Supreme Court. Thousands of cases are appealed to the Court each year. However, Supreme Court justices have time to review only about 100 of these cases. The justices carefully choose which cases to hear. Generally, cases that are chosen must involve an important constitutional or public interest issue. If the Court refuses to hear a case, the decision of the court of appeals is final. Most cases that are presented to the Supreme Court are review cases. However, some cases go directly to the Supreme Court. Some examples are cases that involve international diplomats or disputes between states.

Congress decides how many justices sit on the Court. Traditionally that number has been fixed at nine. The chief justice of the United States leads the Supreme Court. Unlike the president and members of Congress, Court justices do not have specific requirements set by the Constitution. So far, however, every justice has been an attorney.

In the past few decades the makeup of the Supreme Court has become more diverse. In 1967 **Thurgood Marshall** became the first African American justice, with Clarence Thomas becoming the second in 1991. Right now two women sit on the high court—Ruth Bader Ginsburg and **Sandra Day O'Connor**. O'Connor became the first female Court justice after her 1981 appointment by President Ronald Reagan.

Interpreting the Visual Record

The Supreme Court *Supreme Court justice Ruth Bader Ginsburg speaks to a group of students.* **What would you ask Justice Ginsburg if you were one of the students in the picture?**

✔ **Reading Check: Finding the Main Idea** What types of cases does the Supreme Court usually review?

Section 1 Review

go.hrw.com **Homework Practice Online** keyword: SF3 HP9

1 **Define** and explain:
• representative democracy
• delegated powers
• elastic clause
• reserved powers
• concurrent powers
• separation of powers
• apportionment
• impeach
• veto
• executive order
• pardon
• cabinet

2 **Identify** and explain:
• Thurgood Marshall
• Sandra Day O'Connor

3 **Categorizing** Copy the web diagram below. Use it to list the powers of the federal government's three branches.

4 **Finding the Main Idea**
a. What are the requirements for membership in the three branches of the federal government?

b. Do you think the three branches of government share power equally? Explain your answer.

5 **Writing and Critical Thinking**
Summarizing Imagine that you are one of the framers explaining the Constitution to U.S. citizens. Design a poster that explains how the Constitution balances state and federal powers. Your poster should define each power and provide examples.

Consider the following:
• delegated powers
• reserved powers
• concurrent powers

James Madison

FEDERALIST PAPER "NO. 51"

During the debates over the ratification of the Constitution, some New York newspapers printed essays favoring ratification. These essays answered Antifederalists' objections. The *Federalist Papers* were written by Alexander Hamilton, John Jay, and James Madison. In this excerpt from essay "No. 51," Madison describes the separation of powers. He also talks about how this separation would be preserved among the three branches of the government.

In order to lay a **due**[1] foundation for . . . the different powers of government, . . . it is evident that each department should have a will of its own; and consequently should be so **constituted**[2] that the members of each should have as little **agency**[3] as possible in the appointment of the members of the others. Were this principle **rigorously adhered to**,[4] it would require that all the appointments for the supreme executive, legislative, and judiciary **magistracies**[5] should be drawn from the same fountain of authority, the people, through channels having no communication whatever with one another. . . .

But the great security against a gradual concentration of the several powers in the same department [branch], consists in giving to those who administer each department the necessary constitutional means and personal motives to resist **encroachments**[6] of the others. The provision for defense must . . . be made **commensurate**[7] to the danger of attack. . . . It may be a reflection on human nature that such devices should be necessary to control the abuses of government. But what is government itself but the greatest of all reflections on human nature? If men were angels, no government would be necessary. If angels were to govern men, neither external nor internal controls on government would be necessary. In framing a government which is to be administered by men over men, the great difficulty lies in this: you must first enable the government to control the governed; and in the next place **oblige**[8] it to control itself.

THE GRANGER COLLECTION, NEW YORK

The essays supporting the Constitution appeared in a book called The Federalist *in 1788.*

---

[1] **due**: proper
[2] **constituted**: set up
[3] **agency**: power

[4] **rigorously adhered to**: strictly followed
[5] **magistracies**: offices

[6] **encroachments**: improper advances
[7] **commensurate**: equal
[8] **oblige**: force

George Mason

"THE OBJECTIONS OF THE HON. GEORGE MASON TO THE PROPOSED FEDERAL CONSTITUTION"

George Mason played a behind-the-scenes role in the Revolutionary War and wrote Virginia's Declaration of Rights. He attended the Constitutional Convention in 1787. Mason criticized the proposed Constitution for allowing slavery, creating a strong central government, and lacking a Bill of Rights. As a result, he refused to sign the Constitution. However, after the Constitution was ratified, the government soon added a Bill of Rights. In addition to addressing Mason's concerns, the government used Virginia's Declaration of Rights as a model. In the following excerpt, George Mason explains why he will not sign the Constitution.

There is no declaration of rights: and the laws of the general government being **paramount**[1] to the laws and constitutions of the several states, the declarations of rights, in the separate states, are no security. Nor are the people secured even in the enjoyment of the benefit of the common law, which stands here upon no other foundation than its having been adopted by the respective acts forming the constitutions of the several states.

In the House of Representatives there is not the substance, but the shadow only of representation; which can never produce proper information in the legislature, or inspire confidence in the people. The laws will, therefore, be generally made by men little concerned in, and unacquainted with their effects and consequences. . . .

The President of the United States has no constitutional council. . . . He will therefore be unsupported by proper information and advice; and will generally be directed by **minions**[2] and favorites— or he will become a tool to the Senate. . . .

George Mason wanted the Constitution to include a Bill of Rights similar to Virginia's Declaration of Rights.

. . . There is no declaration of any kind for preserving the liberty of the press, the trial by jury in civil cases, nor against the danger of standing armies in time of peace. . . .

. . . [T]he general legislature is restrained from prohibiting the further importation of slaves for twenty odd years, though such importations render the United States weaker, more vulnerable, and less capable of defense.

Analyzing Primary Sources

1. How does Madison plan to "control the abuses of government"?
2. According to Mason, what rights were not protected by the Constitution?
3. In what ways do Madison and Mason agree?

---

[1] **paramount:** superior   [2] **minions:** servants

THE CONSTITUTION

"**W**E THE PEOPLE OF THE UNITED STATES, IN ORDER TO FORM A MORE PERFECT UNION, ESTABLISH JUSTICE, INSURE DOMESTIC TRANQUILITY, PROVIDE FOR THE COMMON DEFENCE, PROMOTE THE GENERAL WELFARE, AND SECURE THE BLESSINGS OF LIBERTY TO OURSELVES AND OUR POSTERITY, DO ORDAIN AND ESTABLISH THIS CONSTITUTION FOR THE UNITED STATES OF AMERICA."

The parts of the Constitution that have been ruled through are no longer in force or no longer apply because of later amendments.

Preamble
The short and dignified Preamble explains the goals of the new government under the Constitution.

LEFT: Independence Hall, Philadelphia

ARTICLE I

Section 1. All legislative Powers herein granted shall be vested in a Congress of the United States, which shall consist of a Senate and House of Representatives.

Section 2. The House of Representatives shall be composed of Members chosen every second Year by the People of the several States, and the Electors in each State shall have the Qualifications requisite for Electors of the most numerous Branch of the State Legislature.

No Person shall be a Representative who shall not have attained to the Age of twenty five Years, and been seven Years a Citizen of the United States, and who shall not, when elected, be an Inhabitant of that State in which he shall be chosen.

Representatives and direct Taxes shall be apportioned among the several States which may be included within this Union, according to their respective Numbers, ~~which shall be determined by adding to the whole Number of free Persons, including~~ **those bound to Service**[1] ~~for a Term of Years, and excluding Indians not taxed, three fifths of~~ **all other Persons**.[2] The actual **Enumeration**[3] shall be made within three Years after the first Meeting of the Congress of the United States, and within every subsequent Term of ten Years, in such Manner as they shall by Law direct. The Number of Representatives shall not exceed one for every thirty Thousand, but each State shall have at Least one Representative; ~~and until such enumeration shall be made, the State of New Hampshire shall be entitled to chuse three; Massachusetts eight; Rhode Island and Providence Plantations one; Connecticut five; New York six; New Jersey four; Pennsylvania eight; Delaware one; Maryland six; Virginia ten; North Carolina five; South Carolina five; and Georgia three.~~

When vacancies happen in the Representation from any State, the Executive Authority thereof shall issue Writs of Election to fill such Vacancies.

The House of Representatives shall chuse their Speaker and other Officers; and shall have the sole Power of Impeachment.

Section 3. The Senate of the United States shall be composed of two Senators from each State, ~~chosen by the Legislature thereof,~~ for six Years; and each Senator shall have one Vote.

Immediately after they shall be assembled in Consequence of the first Election, they shall be divided as equally as may be into three Classes. The Seats of the Senators of the first Class shall be vacated at the Expiration of the second Year, of the second Class at the Expiration of the fourth Year, and of the third Class at the Expiration of the sixth Year, so that one third may be chosen every second Year; ~~and if Vacancies happen by~~

Legislative Branch
Article I explains how the legislative branch, called Congress, is organized. The chief purpose of the legislative branch is to make the laws. Congress is made up of the Senate and the House of Representatives.

The House of Representatives
The number of members each state has in the House is based on the population of the individual state. In 1929 Congress permanently fixed the size of the House at 435 members.

[1] **those bound to Service:** indentured servants
[2] **all other Persons:** slaves
[3] **Enumeration:** census or official population count

~~Resignation, or otherwise, during the Recess of the Legislature of any State, the Executive thereof may make temporary Appointments until the next Meeting of the Legislature, which shall then fill such Vacancies.~~

No Person shall be a Senator who shall not have attained to the Age of thirty Years, and been nine Years a Citizen of the United States, and who shall not, when elected, be an Inhabitant of that State for which he shall be chosen.

The Vice President of the United States shall be President of the Senate, but shall have no Vote, unless they be equally divided.

The Senate shall chuse their other Officers, and also a President **pro tempore**,[4] in the Absence of the Vice President, or when he shall exercise the Office of President of the United States.

The Senate shall have the sole Power to try all **Impeachments**.[5] When sitting for that Purpose, they shall be on Oath or Affirmation. When the President of the United States is tried, the Chief Justice shall preside: And no Person shall be convicted without the Concurrence of two thirds of the Members present.

Judgment in Cases of Impeachment shall not extend further than to removal from Office, and disqualification to hold and enjoy any Office of honor, Trust or Profit under the United States: but the Party convicted shall nevertheless be liable and subject to Indictment, Trial, Judgment and Punishment, according to Law.

Section 4. The Times, Places and Manner of holding Elections for Senators and Representatives, shall be prescribed in each State by the Legislature thereof; but the Congress may at any time by Law make or alter such Regulations, except as to the Places of chusing Senators.

~~The Congress shall assemble at least once in every Year, and such Meeting shall be on the first Monday in December, unless they shall by Law appoint a different Day.~~

Section 5. Each House shall be the Judge of the Elections, Returns and Qualifications of its own Members, and a Majority of each shall constitute a **Quorum**[6] to do Business; but a smaller Number may **adjourn**[7] from day to day, and may be authorized to compel the Attendance of absent Members, in such Manner, and under such Penalties as each House may provide.

Each House may determine the Rules of its Proceedings, punish its Members for disorderly Behaviour, and, with the Concurrence of two thirds, expel a Member.

Each House shall keep a Journal of its Proceedings, and from time to time publish the same, excepting such Parts as may in their Judgment require Secrecy; and the Yeas and Nays of the Members of either House on any question shall, at the Desire of one fifth of those Present, be entered on the Journal.

The Vice President
The only duty that the Constitution assigns to the vice president is to preside over meetings of the Senate. Modern presidents have usually given their vice presidents more responsibilities.

[4] **pro tempore:** temporarily
[5] **Impeachments:** official accusations of federal wrongdoing

Exploring the Document

If the House of Representatives charges a government official with wrongdoing, the Senate acts as a court to decide if the official is guilty. **How does the power of impeachment represent part of the system of checks and balances?**

[6] **Quorum:** the minimum number of people needed to conduct business
[7] **adjourn:** to stop indefinitely

Neither House, during the Session of Congress, shall, without the Consent of the other, adjourn for more than three days, nor to any other Place than that in which the two Houses shall be sitting.

Section 6. The Senators and Representatives shall receive a Compensation for their Services, to be ascertained by Law, and paid out of the Treasury of the United States. They shall in all Cases, except Treason, Felony and Breach of the Peace, be privileged from Arrest during their Attendance at the Session of their respective Houses, and in going to and returning from the same; and for any Speech or Debate in either House, they shall not be questioned in any other Place.

No Senator or Representative shall, during the Time for which he was elected, be appointed to any civil Office under the Authority of the United States, which shall have been created, or the **Emoluments**[8] whereof shall have been encreased during such time; and no Person holding any Office under the United States, shall be a Member of either House during his **Continuance**[9] in Office.

Section 7. All **Bills**[10] for raising Revenue shall originate in the House of Representatives; but the Senate may propose or concur with Amendments as on other Bills.

Every Bill which shall have passed the House of Representatives and the Senate, shall, before it become a Law, be presented to the President of the United States; If he approve he shall sign it, but if not he shall return it, with his Objections to that House in which it shall have originated, who shall enter the Objections at large on their Journal, and proceed to reconsider it. If after such Reconsideration two thirds of that House shall agree to pass the Bill, it shall be sent, together with the Objections, to the other House, by which it shall likewise be reconsidered, and if approved by two thirds of that House, it shall become a Law. But in all such Cases the Votes of both Houses shall be determined by yeas and Nays, and the Names of the Persons voting for and against the Bill shall be entered on the Journal of each House respectively. If any Bill shall not be returned by the President within ten Days (Sundays excepted) after it shall have been presented to him, the Same shall be a Law, in like Manner as if he had signed it, unless the Congress by their Adjournment prevent its Return, in which Case it shall not be a Law.

Every Order, Resolution, or Vote to which the Concurrence of the Senate and House of Representatives may be necessary (except on a question of Adjournment) shall be presented to the President of the United States; and before the Same shall take Effect, shall be approved by him, or being disapproved by him, shall be repassed by two thirds of the Senate and House of Representatives, according to the Rules and Limitations prescribed in the Case of a Bill.

[8] **Emoluments:** salary

[9] **Continuance:** term

[10] **Bills:** proposed laws

Exploring the Document

The framers felt that because members of the House are elected every two years, representatives would listen to the public and seek its approval before passing taxes. **How does Section 7 address the colonial demand of "no taxation without representation"?**

Exploring the Document

The veto power of the president is one of the important checks and balances in the Constitution. **Why do you think the Founding Fathers included the ability of Congress to override a veto?**

Section 8. The Congress shall have Power To lay and collect Taxes, **Duties**,[11] **Imposts**[12] and **Excises**,[13] to pay the Debts and provide for the common Defence and general Welfare of the United States; but all Duties, Imposts and Excises shall be uniform throughout the United States;

To borrow Money on the credit of the United States;

To regulate Commerce with foreign Nations, and among the several States, and with the Indian Tribes;

To establish an uniform **Rule of Naturalization**,[14] and uniform Laws on the subject of Bankruptcies throughout the United States;

To coin Money, regulate the Value thereof, and of foreign Coin, and fix the Standard of Weights and Measures;

To provide for the Punishment of counterfeiting the **Securities**[15] and current Coin of the United States;

To establish Post Offices and post Roads;

To promote the Progress of Science and useful Arts, by securing for limited Times to Authors and Inventors the exclusive Right to their respective Writings and Discoveries;

To constitute Tribunals inferior to the supreme Court;

To define and punish Piracies and Felonies committed on the high Seas, and Offences against the Law of Nations;

To declare War, grant **Letters of Marque and Reprisal**,[16] and make Rules concerning Captures on Land and Water;

To raise and support Armies, but no Appropriation of Money to that Use shall be for a longer Term than two Years;

To provide and maintain a Navy;

To make Rules for the Government and Regulation of the land and naval Forces;

To provide for calling forth the Militia to execute the Laws of the Union, suppress Insurrections and repel Invasions;

To provide for organizing, arming, and disciplining, the Militia, and for governing such Part of them as may be employed in the Service of the United States, reserving to the States respectively, the Appointment of the Officers, and the Authority of training the Militia according to the discipline prescribed by Congress;

To exercise exclusive Legislation in all Cases whatsoever, over such District (not exceeding ten Miles square) as may, by Cession of particular States, and the Acceptance of Congress, become the Seat of the Government of the United States, and to exercise like Authority over all Places purchased by the Consent of the Legislature of the State in which the Same shall be, for the Erection of Forts, Magazines, Arsenals, dock-Yards, and other needful Buildings;—And

To make all Laws which shall be necessary and proper for carrying into Execution the foregoing Powers, and all other Powers vested by this

[11] **Duties:** tariffs

[12] **Imposts:** taxes

[13] **Excises:** internal taxes on the manufacture, sale, or consumption of a commodity

[14] **Rule of Naturalization:** a law by which a foreign-born person becomes a citizen

[15] **Securities:** bonds

[16] **Letters of Marque and Reprisal:** documents issued by governments allowing merchant ships to arm themselves and attack ships of an enemy nation

The Elastic Clause
The framers of the Constitution wanted a national government that was strong enough to be effective. This section lists the powers given to Congress. The last sentence in Section 8 contains the so-called "elastic clause," which has been stretched (like elastic) to allow Congress to meet changing circumstances.

Constitution in the Government of the United States, or in any Department or Officer thereof.

Section 9. ~~The Migration or Importation of such Persons as any of the States now existing shall think proper to admit, shall not be prohibited by the Congress prior to the Year one thousand eight hundred and eight, but a Tax or duty may be imposed on such Importation, not exceeding ten dollars for each Person.~~

The Privilege of the **Writ of Habeas Corpus**[17] shall not be suspended, unless when in Cases of Rebellion or Invasion the public Safety may require it.

No **Bill of Attainder**[18] or **ex post facto Law**[19] shall be passed.

No **Capitation**,[20] or other direct, Tax shall be laid, unless in Proportion to the Census or Enumeration herein before directed to be taken.

No Tax or Duty shall be laid on Articles exported from any State.

No Preference shall be given by any Regulation of Commerce or Revenue to the Ports of one State over those of another: nor shall Vessels bound to, or from, one State, be obliged to enter, clear, or pay Duties in another.

No Money shall be drawn from the Treasury, but in Consequence of Appropriations made by Law; and a regular Statement and Account of the Receipts and Expenditures of all public Money shall be published from time to time.

No Title of Nobility shall be granted by the United States: And no Person holding any Office of Profit or Trust under them, shall, without the Consent of the Congress, accept of any present, Emolument, Office, or Title, of any kind whatever, from any King, Prince, or foreign State.

Section 10. No State shall enter into any Treaty, Alliance, or Confederation; grant Letters of Marque and Reprisal; coin Money; emit Bills of Credit; make any Thing but gold and silver Coin a Tender in Payment of Debts; pass any Bill of Attainder, ex post facto Law, or law impairing the Obligation of Contracts, or grant any Title of Nobility.

No State shall, without the Consent of the Congress, lay any Imposts or Duties on Imports or Exports, except what may be absolutely necessary for executing its inspection Laws: and the net Produce of all Duties and Imposts, laid by any State on Imports or Exports, shall be for the Use of the Treasury of the United States; and all such Laws shall be subject to the Revision and Controul of the Congress.

No State shall, without the Consent of Congress, lay any Duty of Tonnage, keep Troops, or Ships of War in time of Peace, enter into any Agreement or Compact with another State, or with a foreign Power, or engage in War, unless actually invaded, or in such imminent Danger as will not admit of delay.

[17] **Writ of Habeas Corpus:** a court order that requires the government to bring a prisoner to court and explain why he or she is being held

[18] **Bill of Attainder:** a law declaring that a person is guilty of a particular crime

[19] **ex post facto Law:** a law that is made effective prior to the date that it was passed and therefore punishes people for acts that were not illegal at the time

[20] **Capitation:** a direct uniform tax imposed on each head, or person

Exploring the Document

Although Congress has implied powers, there are also limits to its powers. Section 9 lists powers that are denied to the federal government. Several of the clauses protect the people of the United States from unjust treatment. **In what ways does the Constitution limit the powers of the federal government?**

Executive Branch
The president is the chief of the executive branch. It is the job of the president to enforce the laws. The framers wanted the president's and vice president's terms of office and manner of selection to be different from those of members of Congress. They decided on four-year terms, but they had a difficult time agreeing on how to select the president and vice president. The framers finally set up an electoral system, which varies greatly from our electoral process today.

Presidential Elections
In 1845 Congress set the Tuesday following the first Monday in November of every fourth year as the general election date for selecting presidential electors.

Exploring the Document

The youngest elected president was John F. Kennedy; he was 43 years old when he was inaugurated. (Theodore Roosevelt was 42 when he assumed office after the assassination of McKinley.) **What is the minimum required age for the office of president?**

ARTICLE II

Section 1. The executive Power shall be vested in a President of the United States of America. He shall hold his Office during the Term of four Years, and, together with the Vice President, chosen for the same Term, be elected, as follows.

Each State shall appoint, in such Manner as the Legislature thereof may direct, a Number of Electors, equal to the whole Number of Senators and Representatives to which the State may be entitled in the Congress: but no Senator or Representative, or Person holding an Office of Trust or Profit under the United States, shall be appointed an Elector.

~~The Electors shall meet in their respective States, and vote by Ballot for two Persons, of whom one at least shall not be an Inhabitant of the same State with themselves. And they shall make a List of all the Persons voted for, and of the Number of Votes for each; which List they shall sign and certify, and transmit sealed to the Seat of the Government of the United States, directed to the President of the Senate. The President of the Senate shall, in the Presence of the Senate and House of Representatives, open all the Certificates, and the Votes shall then be counted. The Person having the greatest Number of Votes shall be the President, if such Number be a Majority of the whole Number of Electors appointed; and if there be more than one who have such Majority, and have an equal Number of Votes, then the House of Representatives shall immediately chuse by Ballot one of them for President; and if no Person have a Majority, then from the five highest on the List the said House shall in like Manner chuse the President. But in chusing the President, the Votes shall be taken by States, the Representation from each State having one Vote; A quorum for this Purpose shall consist of a Member or Members from two-thirds of the States, and a Majority of all the States shall be necessary to a Choice. In every Case, after the Choice of the President, the Person having the greatest Number of Votes of the Electors shall be the Vice President. But if there should remain two or more who have equal Votes, the Senate shall chuse from them by Ballot the Vice President.~~

The Congress may determine the Time of chusing the Electors, and the Day on which they shall give their Votes; which Day shall be the same throughout the United States.

No Person except a natural born Citizen~~, or a Citizen of the United States, at the time of the Adoption of this Constitution~~, shall be eligible to the Office of President; neither shall any Person be eligible to that Office who shall not have attained to the Age of thirty five Years, and been fourteen Years a Resident within the United States.

In Case of the Removal of the President from Office, or of his Death, Resignation, or Inability to discharge the Powers and Duties of the said Office, the Same shall devolve on the Vice President, and the Congress may by Law provide for the Case of Removal, Death, Resignation or Inability, both of the President and Vice President, declaring what Officer shall then act as President, and such Officer shall act accordingly, until the Disability be removed, or a President shall be elected.

The President shall, at stated Times, receive for his Services, a Compensation, which shall neither be increased nor diminished during the period for which he shall have been elected, and he shall not receive within that Period any other Emolument from the United States, or any of them.

Before he enter on the Execution of his Office, he shall take the following Oath or Affirmation:—"I do solemnly swear (or affirm) that I will faithfully execute the Office of President of the United States, and will to the best of my Ability, preserve, protect and defend the Constitution of the United States."

Section 2. The President shall be Commander in Chief of the Army and Navy of the United States, and of the Militia of the several States, when called into the actual Service of the United States; he may require the Opinion, in writing, of the principal Officer in each of the executive Departments, upon any Subject relating to the Duties of their respective Offices, and he shall have Power to grant **Reprieves**[21] and **Pardons**[22] for Offenses against the United States, except in Cases of Impeachment.

He shall have Power, by and with the Advice and Consent of the Senate, to make Treaties, provided two thirds of the Senators present concur; and he shall nominate, and by and with the Advice and Consent of the Senate, shall appoint Ambassadors, other public Ministers and Consuls, Judges of the supreme Court, and all other Officers of the United States, whose Appointments are not herein otherwise provided for, and which shall be established by Law: but the Congress may by Law vest the Appointment of such inferior Officers, as they think proper, in the President alone, in the Courts of Law, or in the Heads of Departments.

The President shall have Power to fill up all Vacancies that may happen during the Recess of the Senate, by granting Commissions which shall expire at the End of their next Session.

Section 3. He shall from time to time give to the Congress Information of the State of the Union, and recommend to their Consideration such Measures as he shall judge necessary and expedient; he may, on extraordinary Occasions, convene both Houses, or either of them, and in Case of Disagreement between them, with Respect to the Time of Adjournment, he may adjourn them to such Time as he shall think proper; he shall receive Ambassadors and other public Ministers; he shall take Care that the Laws be faithfully executed, and shall Commission all the Officers of the United States.

Presidential Salary
In 1999 Congress voted to set future presidents' salaries at $400,000 per year. The president also receives an annual expense account. The president must pay taxes only on the salary.

Commander in Chief
Today, the president is in charge of the army, navy, air force, marines, and coast guard. Only Congress, however, can decide if the United States will declare war.

[21] **Reprieves:** delays of punishment
[22] **Pardons:** releases from the legal penalties associated with a crime

Appointments
Most of the president's appointments to office must be approved by the Senate.

The State of the Union
Every year the president presents to Congress a State of the Union message. In this message, the president introduces and explains a legislative plan for the coming year.

Section 4. The President, Vice President and all civil Officers of the United States, shall be removed from Office on Impeachment for, and Conviction of, Treason, Bribery, or other high Crimes and Misdemeanors.

ARTICLE III

Section 1. The judicial Power of the United States, shall be vested in one supreme Court, and in such inferior Courts as the Congress may from time to time ordain and establish. The Judges, both of the supreme and inferior Courts, shall hold their Offices during good Behaviour, and shall, at stated Times, receive for their Services, a Compensation, which shall not be diminished during their Continuance in Office.

Section 2. The judicial Power shall extend to all Cases, in Law and Equity, arising under this Constitution, the Laws of the United States, and Treaties made, or which shall be made, under their Authority;—to all Cases affecting Ambassadors, other public Ministers and Consuls;—to all Cases of admiralty and maritime Jurisdiction;—to Controversies to which the United States shall be a Party;—to Controversies between two or more States;— between a State and Citizens of another State;— between Citizens of different States;—between Citizens of the same State claiming Lands under Grants of different States, and between a State, or the Citizens thereof, and foreign States, Citizens or Subjects.

In all Cases affecting Ambassadors, other public Ministers and Consuls, and those in which a State shall be Party, the supreme Court shall have original Jurisdiction. In all the other Cases before mentioned, the supreme Court shall have appellate Jurisdiction, both as to Law and fact, with such Exceptions, and under such Regulations as the Congress shall make.

The Trial of all Crimes, except in Cases of Impeachment, shall be by Jury; and such Trial shall be held in the State where the said Crimes shall have been committed; but when not committed within any State, the Trial shall be at such Place or Places as the Congress may by Law have directed.

Section 3. Treason against the United States, shall consist only in levying War against them, or in adhering to their Enemies, giving them Aid and Comfort. No Person shall be convicted of Treason unless on the Testimony of two Witnesses to the same overt Act, or on Confession in open Court.

The Congress shall have Power to declare the Punishment of Treason, but no Attainder of Treason shall work **Corruption of Blood**,[23] or Forfeiture except during the Life of the Person attainted.

ARTICLE IV

Section 1. Full Faith and Credit shall be given in each State to the public Acts, Records, and judicial Proceedings of every other State. And the

---

Judicial Branch
The Articles of Confederation did not set up a federal court system. One of the first points that the framers of the Constitution agreed upon was to set up a national judiciary. In the Judiciary Act of 1789, Congress provided for the establishment of lower courts, such as district courts, circuit courts of appeals, and various other federal courts. The judicial system provides a check on the legislative branch: it can declare a law unconstitutional.

Exploring the Document

In the Declaration of Independence, the colonists accused the British king of not allowing them trial by jury. **How does trial by jury differ from the vice-admiralty courts that colonists had faced?**

[23] **Corruption of Blood:** punishing the family of a person convicted of treason

Congress may by general Laws prescribe the Manner in which such Acts, Records and Proceedings shall be proved, and the Effect thereof.

Section 2. The Citizens of each State shall be entitled to all Privileges and Immunities of Citizens in the several States.

A Person charged in any State with Treason, Felony, or other Crime, who shall flee from Justice, and be found in another State, shall on Demand of the executive Authority of the State from which he fled, be delivered up, to be removed to the State having Jurisdiction of the Crime.

~~No Person held to Service of Labour in one State, under the Laws thereof, escaping into another, shall, in Consequence of any Law or Regulation therein, be discharged from such Service or Labour, but shall be delivered up on Claim of the Party to whom such Service or Labour may be due~~.

Section 3. New States may be admitted by the Congress into this Union; but no new State shall be formed or erected within the Jurisdiction of any other State; nor any State be formed by the Junction of two or more States, or Parts of States, without the Consent of the Legislatures of the States concerned as well as of the Congress.

The Congress shall have Power to dispose of and make all needful Rules and Regulations respecting the Territory or other Property belonging to the United States; and nothing in this Constitution shall be so construed as to Prejudice any Claims of the United States, or of any particular State.

Section 4. The United States shall guarantee to every State in this Union a Republican Form of Government, and shall protect each of them against Invasion; and on Application of the Legislature, or of the Executive (when the Legislature cannot be convened) against domestic Violence.

ARTICLE V

The Congress, whenever two thirds of both Houses shall deem it necessary, shall propose Amendments to this Constitution, or, on the Application of the Legislatures of two thirds of the several States, shall call a Convention for proposing Amendments, which, in either Case, shall be valid to all Intents and Purposes, as Part of this Constitution, when ratified by the Legislatures of three fourths of the several States, or by Conventions in three fourths thereof, as the one or the other Mode of Ratification may be proposed by the Congress; Provided that ~~no Amendment which may be made prior to the Year One thousand eight hundred and eight shall in any Manner affect the first and fourth Clauses in the Ninth Section of the first Article; and that~~ no State, without its Consent, shall be deprived of its equal Suffrage in the Senate.

Exploring the Document

The framers wanted to ensure that the citizens could determine how the state governments would operate. **How does the need to respect the laws of each state support the principle of popular sovereignty?**

The States
States must honor the laws, records, and court decisions of other states. A person cannot escape a legal obligation by moving from one state to another.

Exploring the Document

In a republic, voters elect representatives to act in their best interest. **How does Article IV protect the practice of republicanism in the United States?**

Exploring the Document

America's founders may not have realized how long the Constitution would last, but they did set up a system for changing or adding to it. They did not want to make it easy to change the Constitution. **By what methods may the Constitution be amended? Under what sorts of circumstances do you think an amendment might be necessary?**

One of the biggest problems facing the delegates to the Constitutional Convention was the question of what would happen if a state law and a federal law conflicted. Which law would be followed? Who would decide? The second clause of Article VI answers those questions. When a federal law and a state law disagree, the federal law overrides the state law. The Constitution and other federal laws are the "supreme Law of the Land." This clause is often called the supremacy clause.

Ratification
The Articles of Confederation called for all 13 states to approve any revision to the Articles. The Constitution required that 9 out of the 13 states would be needed to ratify the Constitution. The first state to ratify was Delaware, on December 7, 1787. Almost two and a half years later, on May 29, 1790, Rhode Island became the last state to ratify the Constitution.

ARTICLE VI

All Debts contracted and Engagements entered into, before the Adoption of this Constitution, shall be as valid against the United States under this Constitution, as under the Confederation.

This Constitution, and the Laws of the United States which shall be made in Pursuance thereof; and all Treaties made, or which shall be made, under the Authority of the United States, shall be the supreme Law of the Land; and the Judges in every State shall be bound thereby, any Thing in the Constitution or Laws of any State to the Contrary notwithstanding.

The Senators and Representatives before mentioned, and the Members of the several State Legislatures, and all executive and judicial Officers, both of the United States and of the several States, shall be bound by Oath or Affirmation, to support this Constitution; but no religious Test shall ever be required as a Qualification to any Office or public Trust under the United States.

ARTICLE VII

The Ratification of the Conventions of nine States, shall be sufficient for the Establishment of this Constitution between the States so ratifying the Same.

Done in Convention by the Unanimous Consent of the States present the Seventeenth Day of September in the Year of our Lord one thousand seven hundred and Eighty seven and of the Independence of the United States of America the Twelfth. In witness whereof We have hereunto subscribed our Names,

George Washington—
President and deputy from Virginia

NEW HAMPSHIRE
John Langdon
Nicholas Gilman

DELAWARE
George Read
Gunning Bedford, Jr.
John Dickinson
Richard Bassett
Jacob Broom

MASSACHUSETTS
Nathaniel Gorham
Rufus King

MARYLAND
James McHenry
Daniel of St. Thomas Jenifer
Daniel Carroll

CONNECTICUT
William Samuel Johnson
Roger Sherman

NEW YORK
Alexander Hamilton

VIRGINIA
John Blair
James Madison, Jr.

NEW JERSEY
William Livingston
David Brearley
William Paterson
Jonathan Dayton

NORTH CAROLINA
William Blount
Richard Dobbs Spaight
Hugh Williamson

PENNSYLVANIA
Benjamin Franklin
Thomas Mifflin
Robert Morris
George Clymer

Thomas FitzSimons
Jared Ingersoll
James Wilson
Gouverneur Morris

SOUTH CAROLINA
John Rutledge
Charles Cotesworth
  Pinckney
Charles Pinckney
Pierce Butler

GEORGIA
William Few
Abraham Baldwin

Attest:
William Jackson, Secretary

THE AMENDMENTS

Articles in addition to, and Amendment of the Constitution of the United States of America, proposed by Congress, and ratified by the Legislatures of the several States, pursuant to the fifth Article of the original Constitution.

[The First through Tenth Amendments, now known as the Bill of Rights, were proposed to the states for ratification on September 25, 1789, and declared in force on December 15, 1791.]

First Amendment

Congress shall make no law respecting an establishment of religion, or prohibiting the free exercise thereof; or abridging the freedom of speech, or of the press; or the right of the people peaceably to assemble, and to petition the Government for a redress of grievances.

Second Amendment

A well regulated Militia, being necessary to the security of a free State, the right of the people to keep and bear Arms, shall not be infringed.

Third Amendment

No Soldier shall, in time of peace, be **quartered**[24] in any house, without the consent of the Owner, nor in time of war, but in a manner to be prescribed by law.

Fourth Amendment

The right of the people to be secure in their persons, houses, papers, and effects, against unreasonable searches and seizures, shall not be violated, and no **Warrants**[25] shall issue, but upon probable cause, supported by Oath or affirmation, and particularly describing the place to be searched, and the persons or things to be seized.

Fifth Amendment

No person shall be held to answer for a capital, or otherwise **infamous**[26] crime, unless on a presentment or **indictment**[27] of a Grand Jury, except in cases arising in the land or naval forces, or in the Militia, when in actual service in time of War or public danger; nor shall any person be subject for the same offence to be twice put in jeopardy of life or limb; nor shall be compelled in any criminal case to be a witness against himself, nor be deprived of life, liberty, or property, without due process of law; nor shall private property be taken for public use, without just compensation.

Sixth Amendment

In all criminal prosecutions, the accused shall enjoy the right to a speedy and public trial, by an impartial jury of the State and district wherein the

Bill of Rights
One of the conditions set by several states for ratifying the Constitution was the inclusion of a bill of rights. Many people feared that a stronger central government might take away basic rights of the people that had been guaranteed in state constitutions.

Exploring the Document

The First Amendment forbids Congress from making any "law respecting an establishment of religion" or restraining the freedom to practice religion as one chooses. Why is freedom of religion an important right?

[24] **quartered:** housed

[25] **Warrants:** written orders authorizing a person to make an arrest, a seizure, or search

[26] **infamous:** disgraceful

[27] **indictment:** the act of charging with a crime

Rights of the Accused
The Fifth, Sixth, and Seventh Amendments describe the procedures that courts must follow when trying people accused of crimes.

Trials
The Sixth Amendment makes several guarantees, including a prompt trial and a trial by a jury chosen from the state and district in which the crime was committed.

ously **ascertained**[28] by law, and to be informed of the nature and cause
of the accusation; to be confronted with the witnesses against him; to
have compulsory process for obtaining witnesses in his favor, and to have
the Assistance of Counsel for his defence.

Seventh Amendment

In Suits at common law, where the value in controversy shall exceed
twenty dollars, the right of trial by jury shall be preserved, and no fact
tried by a jury, shall be otherwise re-examined in any Court of the United
States, than according to the rules of the common law.

Eighth Amendment

Excessive bail shall not be required, nor excessive fines imposed, nor
cruel and unusual punishments inflicted.

Ninth Amendment

The enumeration in the Constitution, of certain rights, shall not be
construed to deny or disparage others retained by the people.

Tenth Amendment

The powers not delegated to the United States by the Constitution, nor
prohibited by it to the States, are reserved to the States respectively, or to
the people.

Eleventh Amendment

[Proposed March 4, 1794; declared ratified January 8, 1798]
The Judicial power of the United States shall not be **construed**[29] to
extend to any suit in law or equity, commenced or prosecuted against
one of the United States by Citizens of another State, or by Citizens or
Subjects of any Foreign State.

Twelfth Amendment

[Proposed December 9, 1803; declared ratified September 25, 1804]
The Electors shall meet in their respective states, and vote by ballot for
President and Vice-President, one of whom, at least, shall not be an inhabitant of the same state with themselves; they shall name in their ballots the
person voted for as President, and in distinct ballots the person voted for as
Vice-President, and they shall make distinct lists of all persons voted for as
President, and of all persons voted for as Vice-President, and of the number
of votes for each, which lists they shall sign and certify, and transmit sealed
to the seat of the government of the United States, directed to the President
of the Senate;—The President of the Senate shall, in the presence of the
Senate and House of Representatives, open all the certificates and the votes

28 ascertained: found out

Exploring the Document

The Ninth and Tenth Amendments were added because not every right of the people or of the states could be listed in the Constitution. **How do the Ninth and Tenth Amendments limit the power of the federal government?**

29 construed: explained or interpreted

President and Vice President
The Twelfth Amendment changed the election procedure for president and vice president.

shall then be counted;—The person having the greatest number of votes for President, shall be the President, if such number be a majority of the whole number of Electors appointed; and if no person have such majority, then from the persons having the highest numbers not exceeding three on the list of those voted for as President, the House of Representatives shall choose immediately, by ballot, the President. But in choosing the President, the votes shall be taken by states, the representation from each state having one vote; a quorum for this purpose shall consist of a member or members from two-thirds of the states, and a majority of all the states shall be necessary to a choice. ~~And if the House of Representatives shall not choose a President whenever the right of choice shall devolve upon them, before the fourth day of March next following, then the Vice-President shall act as President, as in the case of the death or other constitutional disability of the President.~~ — The person having the greatest number of votes as Vice-President, shall be the Vice-President, if such number be a majority of the whole number of Electors appointed, and if no person have a majority, then from the two highest numbers on the list, the Senate shall Choose the Vice-President; a quorum for the purpose shall consist of two-thirds of the whole number of Senators, and a majority of the whole number shall be necessary to a choice. But no person constitutionally ineligible to the office of President shall be eligible to that of Vice-President of the United States.

Thirteenth Amendment
[Proposed January 31, 1865; declared ratified December 18, 1865]

Section 1. Neither slavery nor **involuntary servitude**,[30] except as a punishment for crime whereof the party shall have been duly convicted, shall exist within the United States, or any place subject to their jurisdiction.

Section 2. Congress shall have power to enforce this article by appropriate legislation.

Fourteenth Amendment
[Proposed June 13, 1866; declared ratified July 28, 1868]

Section 1. All persons born or naturalized in the United States, and subject to the jurisdiction thereof, are citizens of the United States and of the State wherein they reside. No State shall make or enforce any law which shall abridge the privileges or immunities of citizens of the United States; nor shall any State deprive any person of life, liberty, or property, without due process of law; nor deny to any person within its jurisdiction the equal protection of the laws.

Section 2. Representatives shall be apportioned among the several States according to their respective numbers, counting the whole number of per-

Abolishing Slavery
Although some slaves had been freed during the Civil War, slavery was not abolished until the Thirteenth Amendment took effect.

[30] involuntary servitude: being forced to work against one's will

Protecting the Rights of Citizens
In 1833 the Supreme Court ruled that the Bill of Rights limited the federal government but not the state governments. This ruling was interpreted to mean that states were able to keep African Americans from becoming state citizens and keeping the Bill of Rights from protecting them. The Fourteenth Amendment defines citizenship and prevents states from interfering in the rights of citizens of the United States.

sons in each State, ~~excluding Indians not taxed~~. But when the right to vote at any election for the choice of electors for President and Vice President of the United States, Representatives in Congress, the Executive and Judicial officers of a State, or the members of the Legislature thereof, is denied to any of the ~~male~~ inhabitants of such State, ~~being twenty-one years of age,~~ and citizens of the United States, or in any way abridged, except for participation in rebellion, or other crime, the basis of representation therein shall be reduced in the proportion which the number of such ~~male~~ citizens shall bear to the whole number of ~~male~~ citizens ~~twenty-one years of age~~ in such State.

Section 3. No person shall be a Senator or Representative in Congress, or elector of President and Vice President, or hold any office, civil or military, under the United States, or under any State, who, having previously taken an oath, as a member of Congress, or as an officer of the United States, or as a member of any State legislature, or as an executive or judicial officer of any State, to support the Constitution of the United States, shall have engaged in insurrection or rebellion against the same, or given aid or comfort to the enemies thereof. But Congress may by a vote of two-thirds of each House, remove such disability.

Section 4. The validity of the public debt of the United States, authorized by law, including debts incurred for payment of pensions and bounties for services in suppressing insurrection or rebellion, shall not be questioned. But neither the United States nor any State shall assume or pay any debt or obligation incurred in aid of insurrection or rebellion against the United States, ~~or any claim for the loss of emancipation of any slave~~; but all such debts, obligations and claims shall be held illegal and void.

Section 5. The Congress shall have power to enforce, by appropriate legislation, the provisions of this article.

Fifteenth Amendment
[Proposed February 26, 1869; declared ratified March 30, 1870]

Section 1. The right of citizens of the United States to vote shall not be denied or abridged by the United States or by any State on account of race, color, or previous condition of servitude.

Section 2. The Congress shall have power to enforce this article by appropriate legislation.

Sixteenth Amendment
[Proposed July 12, 1909; declared ratified February 25, 1913]

The Congress shall have power to lay and collect taxes on incomes, from whatever source derived, without apportionment among the several States, and without regard to any census or enumeration.

Exploring the Document

The Fifteenth Amendment extended the vote to African American men. **Why is the right to vote guaranteed by the Fifteenth Amendment important?**

Seventeenth Amendment

[Proposed May 13, 1912; declared ratified May 31, 1913]

The Senate of the United States shall be composed of two Senators from each State, elected by the people thereof, for six years; and each Senator shall have one vote. The electors in each State shall have the qualifications requisite for electors of the most numerous branch of the State legislatures.

When vacancies happen in the representation of any State in the Senate, the executive authority of such State shall issue writs of election to fill such vacancies: *Provided*, That the legislature of any State may empower the executive thereof to make temporary appointments until the people fill the vacancies by election as the legislature may direct.

~~This amendment shall not be so construed as to affect the election or term of any Senator chosen before it becomes valid as part of the Constitution.~~

Eighteenth Amendment

[Proposed December 18, 1917; declared ratified January 29, 1919; repealed by the Twenty-first Amendment December 5, 1933]

~~Section 1. After one year from the ratification of this article the manufacture, sale, or transportation of intoxicating liquors within, the importation thereof into, or the exportation thereof from the United States and all territory subject to the jurisdiction thereof for beverage purposes is hereby prohibited.~~

~~Section 2. The Congress and the several States shall have concurrent power to enforce this article by appropriate legislation.~~

~~Section 3. This article shall be inoperative unless it shall have been ratified as an amendment to the Constitution by the legislatures of the several States, as provided in the Constitution, within seven years from the date of the submission hereof to the States by the Congress.~~

Nineteenth Amendment

[Proposed June 4, 1919; declared ratified August 26, 1920]

The right of citizens of the United States to vote shall not be denied or abridged by the United States or by any State on account of sex.

Congress shall have power to enforce this article by appropriate legislation.

Twentieth Amendment

[Proposed March 2, 1932; declared ratified February 6, 1933]

Section 1. The terms of the President and Vice-President shall end at noon on the 20th day of January, and the terms of Senators and Representatives

Exploring the Document

The Seventeenth Amendment requires that senators be elected directly by the people instead of by the state legislature. **What principle of our government does the Seventeenth Amendment protect?**

Prohibition
Although many people believed that the Eighteenth Amendment was good for the health and welfare of the American people, it was repealed 14 years later.

Women's Suffrage
Abigail Adams and others were disappointed that the Declaration of Independence and the Constitution did not specifically include women. It took almost 130 years and much campaigning by groups before suffrage for women was finally achieved.

Taking Office
In the original Constitution, a newly elected president and Congress did not take office until March 4, which was four months after the November election. The officials who were leaving office were called lame ducks because they had little influence during those four months. The Twentieth Amendment changed the date that the new president and Congress take office. Members of Congress now take office during the first week of January, and the president takes office on January 20.

at noon on the 3d day of January, of the years in which such terms would have ended if this article had not been ratified; and the terms of their successors shall then begin.

Section 2. The Congress shall assemble at least once in every year, and such meeting shall begin at noon on the 3d day of January, unless they shall by law appoint a different day.

Section 3. If, at the time fixed for the beginning of the term of the President, the President elect shall have died, the Vice-President elect shall become President. If a President shall not have been chosen before the time fixed for the beginning of his term, or if the President elect shall have failed to qualify, then the Vice-President elect shall act as President until a President shall have qualified; and the Congress may by law provide for the case wherein neither a President elect nor a Vice-President elect shall have qualified, declaring who shall then act as President, or the manner in which one who is to act shall be selected, and such person shall act accordingly until a President or Vice-President shall have qualified.

Section 4. The Congress may by law provide for the case of the death of any of the persons from whom the House of Representatives may choose a President whenever the right of choice shall have devolved upon them, and for the case of the death of any of the persons from whom the Senate may choose a Vice-President whenever the right of choice shall have devolved upon them.

~~**Section 5.** Sections 1 and 2 shall take effect on the 15th day of October following the ratification of this article.~~

~~**Section 6.** This article shall be inoperative unless it shall have been ratified as an amendment to the Constitution by the legislatures of three-fourths of the several States within seven years from the date of its submission.~~

Twenty-first Amendment
[Proposed February 20, 1933; declared ratified December 5, 1933]

Section 1. The eighteenth article of amendment to the Constitution of the United States is hereby repealed.

Section 2. The transportation or importation into any State, Territory, or possession of the United States for delivery or use therein of intoxicating liquors, in violation of the laws thereof, is hereby prohibited.

~~**Section 3.** This article shall be inoperative unless it shall have been ratified as an amendment to the Constitution by conventions in the several States, as provided in the Constitution, within seven years from the date of the submission hereof to the States by the Congress.~~

Exploring the Document

The Twenty-first Amendment was the first amendment not ratified by state legislatures. **According to the crossed-out text, what method was used to ratify the Twenty-first Amendment?**

Twenty-second Amendment

[Proposed March 21, 1947; declared ratified February 26, 1951]

Section 1. No person shall be elected to the office of the President more than twice, and no person who has held the office of President, or acted as President, for more than two years of a term to which some other person was elected President shall be elected to the office of the President more than once. ~~But this Article shall not apply to any person holding the office of President when this Article was proposed by the Congress, and shall not prevent any person who may be holding the office of President, or acting as President, during the term within which this Article becomes operative from holding the office of President or acting as President during the remainder of such term.~~

~~**Section 2.** This article shall be inoperative unless it shall have been ratified as an amendment to the Constitution by the legislatures of three-fourths of the several States within seven years from the date of its submission to the States by the Congress.~~

Twenty-third Amendment

[Proposed June 16, 1960; ratified March 29, 1961]

Section 1. The District constituting the seat of Government of the United States shall appoint in such manner as the Congress may direct:

A number of electors of President and Vice-President equal to the whole number of Senators and Representatives in Congress to which the District would be entitled if it were a State, but in no event more than the least populous state; they shall be in addition to those appointed by the States, but they shall be considered, for the purposes of the election of President and Vice-President, to be electors appointed by a State; and they shall meet in the District and perform such duties as provided by the twelfth article of amendment.

Section 2. The Congress shall have power to enforce this article by appropriate legislation.

Twenty-fourth Amendment

[Proposed August 27, 1962; ratified January 23, 1964]

Section 1. The right of citizens of the United States to vote in any primary or other election for President or Vice-President, for electors for President or Vice-President, or for Senator or Representative in Congress, shall not be denied or abridged by the United States or any State by reason of failure to pay any poll tax or other tax.

Exploring the Document

From the time of President George Washington's administration, it was a custom for presidents to serve no more than two terms in office. Franklin D. Roosevelt, however, was elected to four terms. The Twenty-second Amendment restricted presidents to no more than two terms in office. **Why do you think citizens chose to limit the power of the president in this way?**

Voting Rights
Until the ratification of the Twenty-third Amendment, the people of Washington, D.C., could not vote in presidential elections.

Section 2. The Congress shall have power to enforce this article by appropriate legislation.

Twenty-fifth Amendment
[Proposed July 6, 1965; ratified February 10, 1967]

Section 1. In case of the removal of the President from office or of his death or resignation, the Vice-President shall become President.

Section 2. Whenever there is a vacancy in the office of the Vice-President, the President shall nominate a Vice-President who shall take office upon confirmation by a majority vote of both Houses of Congress.

Section 3. Whenever the President transmits to the President pro tempore of the Senate and the Speaker of the House of Representatives his written declaration that he is unable to discharge the powers and duties of his office, and until he transmits to them a written declaration to the contrary, such powers and duties shall be discharged by the Vice-President as Acting President.

Section 4. Whenever the Vice-President and a majority of either the principal officers of the executive departments or of such other body as Congress may by law provide, transmit to the President pro tempore of the Senate and the Speaker of the House of Representatives their written declaration that the President is unable to discharge the powers and duties of his office, the Vice-President shall immediately assume the powers and duties of the office as Acting President.

Thereafter, when the President transmits to the President pro tempore of the Senate and the Speaker of the House of Representatives his written declaration that no inability exists, he shall resume the powers and duties of his office unless the Vice-President and a majority of either the principal officers of the executive department or of such other body as Congress may by law provide, transmit within four days to the President pro tempore of the Senate and the Speaker of the House of Representatives their written declaration that the President is unable to discharge the powers and duties of his office. Thereupon Congress shall decide the issue, assembling within forty-eight hours for that purpose if not in session. If the Congress, within twenty-one days after receipt of the latter written declaration, or, if Congress is not in session, within twenty-one days after Congress is required to assemble, determines by two-thirds vote of both Houses that the President is unable to discharge the powers and duties of his office, the Vice-President shall continue to discharge the same as Acting President; otherwise, the President shall resume the powers and duties of his office.

Presidential Disability
The illness of President Eisenhower in the 1950s and the assassination of President Kennedy in 1963 were the events behind the Twenty-fifth Amendment. The Constitution did not provide a clear-cut method for a vice president to take over for a disabled president or upon the death of a president. This amendment provides for filling the office of the vice president if a vacancy occurs, and it provides a way for the vice president—or someone else in the line of succession—to take over if the president is unable to perform the duties of that office.

Twenty-sixth Amendment

[Proposed March 23, 1971; ratified July 1, 1971]

Section 1. The right of citizens of the United States, who are eighteen years of age or older, to vote shall not be denied or abridged by the United States or by any State on account of age.

Section 2. The Congress shall have power to enforce this article by appropriate legislation.

Twenty-seventh Amendment

[Proposed September 25, 1789; ratified May 7, 1992]

No law, varying the compensation for the services of the Senators and Representatives, shall take effect, until an election of Representatives shall have intervened.

Expanded Suffrage
The Voting Act of 1970 tried to set the voting age at 18. However, the Supreme Court ruled that the act set the voting age for national elections only, not state or local elections. This ruling would make necessary several different ballots at elections. The Twenty-sixth Amendment gave 18-year-old citizens the right to vote in all elections.

Separation of Powers and Checks and Balances

LEGISLATIVE BRANCH (Congress)
- writes the laws
- confirms presidential appointments
- approves treaties
- grants money
- declares war

EXECUTIVE BRANCH (President)
- proposes laws
- administers the laws
- commands armed forces
- appoints ambassadors and other officials
- conducts foreign policy
- makes treaties

JUDICIAL BRANCH (Supreme Court)
- interprets the Constitution and other laws
- reviews lower-court decisions

may reject appointments

may reject treaties

may withhold funding for presidential initiatives

may impeach president

may override a veto

may adjourn Congress in certain situations

may veto bills

may propose constitutional amendments to overrule judicial decisions

may impeach Supreme Court justices

may reject appointments to the Supreme Court

may declare laws unconstitutional

may declare executive actions unconstitutional

appoints judges

The Bill of Rights

Read to Discover

1. What are the main freedoms outlined within the First Amendment, and why are they important?
2. How does the Bill of Rights address colonial grievances listed in the Declaration of Independence?
3. What protections does the Bill of Rights give to people accused of crimes?

WHY IT MATTERS TODAY

The Bill of Rights protects some of the basic rights that we enjoy in our daily lives. Not all countries let their citizens enjoy these same rights. Use CNNfyi.com or other **current events** sources to learn about people in another country who are trying to exercise some of the rights granted U.S. citizens in the Bill of Rights. Record your findings in your journal.

Define
- petition
- search warrant
- due process
- indict
- double jeopardy
- eminent domain

Identify
- James Madison

Quill pens like this one were used in the 1700s.

The Story Continues

James Madison was worried that the Constitution might not pass. The Antifederalists opposed it, and even Virginia, Madison's home state, was hesitating. Forceful speaker Patrick Henry wanted the Constitution to include a bill of rights before Virginia ratified it. The Virginia legislature rejected Henry's position and approved the Constitution on the condition that a bill of rights would be added later. At first, Madison had opposed amending the Constitution, but to satisfy the concerns of others, he put together a set of amendments.

⭐ The First Amendment

Federalist **James Madison** promised that a bill of rights would be added to the Constitution. With this promise, the Constitution was ratified. In 1789 Madison began narrowing down the huge list of proposed amendments. He then gave a shorter list of amendments to the House of Representatives. Of those, Congress approved 12 amendments. The states ratified 10. Those 10 amendments, called the Bill of Rights, protect U.S. citizens' individual liberties.

 "The safety and happiness of society are the objects at which all political institutions aim and to which all such institutions must be sacrificed.""

—James Madison, from *The Macmillan Dictionary of Political Quotations*

The ideas within the First Amendment form the most basic rights of all U.S. citizens. These rights include freedom of religion, the press, speech, assembly, and to **petition**—make a request of the government. The First Amendment begins by stating that "Congress shall make no law respecting an establishment of religion, or prohibiting the free exercise thereof." In other words, the government cannot support or interfere with the practice of a religion. This amendment keeps the government from favoring any religion over others. When the Constitution was written, many countries had an official state religion. However, some Americans wanted to keep the government from establishing an official religion.

The First Amendment also guarantees freedom of speech and of the press. Americans have the right to express their own ideas and views and to hear the ideas and views of others. John Peter Zenger, the publisher of the *New York Weekly Journal*, was an example of why freedom of the press is important. Zenger had gone on trial in 1735 for criticizing New York's royal governor. The jury found Zenger not guilty because the statements he printed were true.

Freedom of speech does not mean that people can say anything they want to, however. The Constitution does not protect slander—false statements meant to damage someone's reputation. Libel, or intentionally publishing a lie that harms another person, is not protected either. The Supreme Court has also ruled that the First Amendment does not protect speech that endangers public safety. For example, Justice Oliver Wendell Holmes explained that falsely shouting "Fire!" in a crowded theater is not protected as free speech.

 "The question in every case is whether the words used are used in such circumstances and are of such a nature to create a clear and present danger that . . . Congress has a right to prevent.""

—Oliver Wendell Holmes, quoted in *A March of Liberty,* by Melvin I. Urofsky

Americans also have freedom of assembly, or to hold meetings. Any group may gather to discuss issues or to conduct business. If those people gather peacefully and are not involved in any illegal activity, the government cannot interfere. Any American can present a petition to a government official. This right lets Americans show their dissatisfaction with a law, as well as suggest new laws.

✔ **Reading Check: Finding the Main Idea** What are the freedoms protected by the First Amendment?

THE GRANGER COLLECTION, NEW YORK

Analyzing Primary Sources

Identifying Points of View What does James Madison think the purpose of the government is?

BIOGRAPHY

James Madison

(1751–1836)

James Madison was born in Virginia in 1751. He attended the College of New Jersey, now Princeton University, before entering politics in Virginia. Early in his career, Madison became a strong supporter of religious freedom. Madison served in Congress until 1797. He later influenced politics from his family plantation. There he remained a slave-holder despite his stated belief in individual liberty. In 1801 Madison became secretary of state and went on to serve two terms as president. Madison played a central role in framing the Constitution and adding the Bill of Rights. For these reasons, he is often called the Father of the Constitution. **Why is Madison called the Father of the Constitution?**

Flood control *These members of the National Guard are helping local citizens prevent a river from flooding.* **Why do you think it is important for community members to join together in such efforts?**

Citizenship and You

Freedom of Assembly

When Congress first talked about what should be in the Bill of Rights, some members argued that people in power should not be able to stop rival groups from meeting. Thus, freedom of assembly became part of the First Amendment. Over the years Americans have gathered to privately and publicly express their views on issues ranging from civil rights to education.

Americans do not have an unlimited right of assembly, however. Citizens must follow rules that protect public safety. For example, parades usually require a local permit so that traffic flow can be managed during the parade time. Such restrictions cannot be used to keep people or groups with unpopular beliefs from publicly expressing their views. Should all groups have the same freedom of assembly? Explain your answer.

★ Protecting Citizens

The Second, Third, and Fourth Amendments all relate to colonial disputes with Great Britain before the Revolution. The Second Amendment deals with state militias. Colonial militias were vital to America's defense. The first battle of the Revolutionary War started when British troops tried to seize the Massachusetts militia's weapons. The framers believed that the states needed to keep their militias for emergencies. Today the National Guard has replaced state militias. National Guard members also serve in wars and help restore order during crises, such as natural disasters.

Some people believe that gun control laws violate the Second Amendment. This part of the Constitution states that "the right of the people to keep and bear arms shall not be infringed [violated]." In 1939 the Supreme Court passed rules for nonmilitary firearms. Years later, a U.S. court of appeals ruled that gun control laws do not violate the Second Amendment. The Supreme Court let that ruling stand in 1983.

The Third Amendment keeps the military from forcing citizens to give housing to soldiers. Before the Revolution, the British government pressured colonists to give food and shelter to its soldiers. British leaders also issued writs of assistance. These written orders let officials search any colonist's property for illegal goods. Anger over such actions led to the Fourth Amendment's rule against "unreasonable searches and seizures." Before authorities search someone's property, they must first get a **search warrant**, an order permitting them to look through someone's property. But authorities do not always need a warrant to conduct a search. Sometimes a suspect tries to destroy evidence or hide a weapon. When this happens, police can conduct an emergency search. This helps to protect both the officers and any evidence needed to prove criminal activity.

✔ **Reading Check: Contrasting** Contrast colonists' rights under British rule with the rights that Americans enjoy today under the Second, Third, and Fourth Amendments.

⭐ The Rights of the Accused

The Fifth, Sixth, Seventh, and Eighth Amendments provide guidelines for trying people accused of crimes. The framers designed these amendments to protect the rights of the accused. According to the Fifth Amendment, the government cannot punish anyone for a crime without **due process** of law. This means that the law should always be fairly applied. A grand jury decides if there is enough evidence to **indict**, or formally accuse, the person. Without an indictment, the court cannot try someone for a serious crime. The Fifth Amendment also protects people from being forced to testify in their own criminal trial. To keep from testifying, the defendant "takes the Fifth." Anyone found not guilty in a criminal trial cannot face **double jeopardy**. In other words, that person cannot be tried again for the same crime.

The final clause of the Fifth Amendment addresses property rights. It states that no one will have property taken "without due process of law." The one exception to this principle is the government's power of **eminent domain**—the power to take personal property to benefit the public. An example would be the taking of private lands to build a public road. The government must pay the owners a fair price for their property. However, if the property that is taken was gained through illegal activities, then the person is not paid.

The Sixth Amendment protects the rights of someone who is indicted for a crime. It states that the accused must have a quick public trial by a jury. The accused person has the right to know the charges against him or her. The accused can also hear and question the witnesses testifying against him or her. The accused has the right to an attorney. If the person cannot afford legal services, the government provides an attorney.

Sometimes the accused refuses his or her Sixth Amendment rights. For example, some defendants refuse the services of an attorney. Others choose to have a trial in front of a judge alone instead of before a jury. Defendants can bypass a trial by agreeing to a plea bargain. In these cases, the individual pleads guilty to a lesser charge. By plea bargaining, defendants avoid the risk of conviction of a crime that may carry a greater sentence.

The Seventh Amendment states that juries can decide civil cases. Sometimes an individual causes physical or financial harm to another person without committing a crime. In such cases the injured party may sue, or seek justice, in civil court. Civil cases usually involve disputes over money or property. For example, someone might bring a civil suit against an individual who refuses to pay back a debt.

A judge may issue a search warrant when it seems likely that someone's property contains evidence relating to a crime.

✔ **Reading Check: Summarizing** What rights do Americans have under the Fifth, Sixth, and Seventh Amendments?

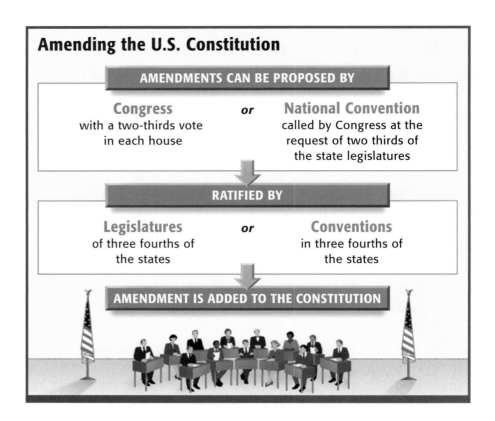

Amending the U.S. Constitution

AMENDMENTS CAN BE PROPOSED BY

Congress *or* **National Convention**
with a two-thirds vote | called by Congress at the
in each house | request of two thirds of
 | the state legislatures

RATIFIED BY

Legislatures *or* **Conventions**
of three fourths of | in three fourths of
the states | the states

AMENDMENT IS ADDED TO THE CONSTITUTION

★ Bail and Punishment

The Eighth Amendment allows for defendants to post bail. Bail is money that defendants promise to pay the court if they do not appear in court at the proper time. Bail ensures that defendants do not have to stay in jail during the trial. Sometimes, a defendant does not show up for trial. If this happens, the court demands the bail money and issues a warrant for the defendant's immediate arrest. The Eighth Amendment prevents courts from setting unfairly high bail. However, the judge may refuse to set bail for individuals accused of very serious crimes or who the court believes may flee before trial.

The Eighth Amendment also bans "cruel and unusual punishments" of individuals convicted of a crime. For many years, Americans have debated exactly what this wording means. For example, in the 1972 case *Furman* v. *Georgia* the Supreme Court ruled that the methods by which most states carried out the death penalty were cruel and unusual. The Court also found that the processes used by many states to sentence people to death were unfair to the accused. As a result, executions were temporarily halted in those states that allowed the death penalty. However, in 1976 the Court ruled that not all executions are cruel and unusual. Today all states that allow the death penalty must establish guidelines to ensure that their methods are constitutional.

✔ **Reading Check: Finding the Main Idea** What rights does the Eighth Amendment protect?

⭐ The Rights of States and Citizens

The final two amendments in the Bill of Rights provide general protections for individual rights not addressed by the first eight amendments. The Ninth and Tenth Amendments also reserve some governmental powers for the states and people. The Ninth Amendment states that the rights listed in the Constitution are not the only rights citizens have. This amendment allows the courts and Congress to recognize other basic rights of citizens. For example, the Constitution does not address education, however most Americans believe education is a basic right. "Education is not just another consumer item. It is the bedrock [foundation] of our democracy," explained educational leader Mary Hatwood Futrell. Today state governments offer free public education—from elementary to high school—to all citizens.

The Tenth Amendment recognizes that the states and the people have additional powers beyond those specifically mentioned in the Constitution. These include any powers that the Constitution does not specifically grant to Congress or deny to the states. Thus, the last amendment in the Bill of Rights protects citizens' rights in addition to helping keep the balance of power between the federal and state governments.

These students benefit from free public education, which many Americans now consider a right of citizenship.

✔ **Reading Check: Analyzing Information** How do the Ninth and Tenth Amendments balance individual rights and governmental powers?

Section 2 Review

go.hrw.com **Homework Practice Online** keyword: SF3 HP9

1 **Define** and explain:
• petition
• search warrant
• due process
• indict
• double jeopardy
• eminent domain

2 **Identify** and explain:
• James Madison

3 **Summarizing** Copy the chart below. Use it to list the rights guaranteed to citizens by the first 10 amendments.

Amendment	Right
1	
2	
3	
4	
5	
6	
7	
8	
9	
10	

4 **Finding the Main Idea**
a. Why are the rights protected by the First Amendment significant?

b. How are the Constitution and the Bill of Rights related to the complaints against Great Britain made in the Declaration of Independence?

5 **Writing and Critical Thinking**
Analyzing Information Imagine that you are a newspaper reporter covering a local trial. Write a brief article describing the rights of the accused as he or she faces trial.

Consider the following:
• due process
• trial by jury
• bail

Rights and Responsibilities of Citizenship

Read to Discover

1. How can a person become a U.S. citizen?
2. What are some of the most important responsibilities of citizenship?
3. Why should citizens be involved with their community and government?

Define

- naturalized citizen
- deport
- draft
- political action committees

WHY IT MATTERS TODAY

Taxes are the responsibility of all U.S. citizens. Taxes help pay for services like roads, salaries of government employees, and schools. Use **CNNfyi.com** or other **current events** sources to research a current or proposed use of tax dollars that affects your area. Record your findings in your journal.

The Statue of Liberty is a symbol of freedom for many immigrants.

The Story Continues

Patrick Henry argued that the United States should be open to all people who wanted to become citizens. "Let . . . Liberty stretch forth her fair hand toward the people of the old world," he said. "Tell them to come, and bid them welcome." Many people desiring liberty have become U.S. citizens. Jozef Patyna immigrated to the United States in the early 1980s. He wanted to leave an unjust government in Poland. "The idea of freedom and democracy is what the people have an instinctive need for," explained Patyna.

⭐ Becoming a U.S. Citizen

People can become U.S. citizens in several ways. Anyone born in the United States or a territory it controls is a citizen. For example, people born in Puerto Rico are citizens because that island is a commonwealth that is still a U.S. territory. When a person of foreign birth is granted full citizenship, he or she has become a **naturalized citizen**. People born in a foreign country can become U.S. citizens if one of their parents is a U.S. citizen. Foreign-born people whose parents are not U.S. citizens must move to the United States if they want to become citizens. After completing a long process, they can apply for citizenship. The rights and responsibilities that naturalized citizens take on help create the sense of what it means to be an American.

People who permanently move to a new country are called immigrants. In the United States, legal immigrants have many of the same rights and responsibilities as citizens. They cannot vote or hold public office, however. The U.S. government can **deport**, or return to their country of origin, any immigrant who breaks the law. Only two differences between naturalized and native-born citizens exist. Naturalized citizens can lose their citizenship, and they cannot become president or vice president. Many famous Americans have been naturalized citizens, including scientist Albert Einstein and former secretary of state Madeleine Albright.

Legal immigrants who are older than 18 may petition for naturalization. However, they may do this only after living in the United States for five years. All legal immigrants must be able to support themselves financially. If they cannot do this, someone must sponsor them and assume that financial responsibility. The U.S. Immigration and Naturalization Service (INS) oversees the process of becoming a citizen and sets a hearing to test the person's qualifications. The immigrants must prove that they are law-abiding and of good moral character. In addition, they must take a series of tests to show that they can read, write, and speak English. They must also have a basic understanding of U.S. history and government. The INS also conducts a background check to ensure that the candidates for naturalization have not hidden any information about themselves.

When all these steps are complete, the candidates appear before a naturalization court. There they take an oath of allegiance to the United States. Finally, they receive their certificate of naturalization. At that point all minors of the newly naturalized citizens also become citizens. Becoming a naturalized citizen takes dedication and effort. A Japanese immigrant wrote a poem to celebrate her naturalization.

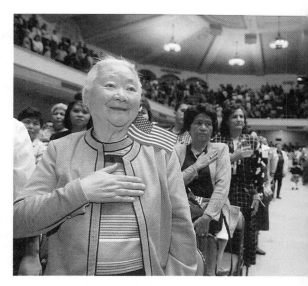

This immigrant and the people standing around her are taking the oath of allegiance to complete the process of becoming U.S. citizens.

History Makers Speak

**"Going steadily to study English,
Even through the rain at night,
I thus attain [acquire],
Late in life,
American citizenship."**

—Kiyoko Nieda, quoted in *Sounds from the Unknown*, edited by Lucille Nixon and Tomoe Tana

Analyzing Primary Sources

Identifying Points of View
How do you think the author of this poem valued U.S. citizenship?

✔ **Reading Check: Identifying Cause and Effect** How does someone become a naturalized citizen, and what rights do they gain when they do?

Upon turning 18, every male U.S. citizen must fill out a card like this one to register for a potential draft.

★ Duties of Citizens

In addition to having certain rights, U.S. citizens have responsibilities. These duties are to other citizens, their government, and themselves. For representative democracy to work, citizens must fulfill their civic responsibilities. Former Texas representative Barbara Jordan explained why these duties are important. "The stakes . . . are too high for government to be a spectator sport," she stated.

Citizens elect leaders to make laws for them. In turn, citizens must obey the laws those leaders pass. If citizens do not agree with a law, they can try to change it in several ways. They can speak with their local, state, or national representatives or petition elected leaders to change the law. Electing new leaders who might change the law is another option. Citizens can also challenge a law in court. Citizens have a duty to know what the laws are. Thus, citizens need to stay informed of changes to laws that affect them. Ignorance of a certain law will not keep a person from being punished for breaking it.

Citizens also have an obligation to respect people in authority and to respect the rights of others. People in authority include parents, police officers, and teachers. Such people have been trusted to protect the welfare of others. Parents have a responsibility to meet their children's basic needs for clothing, education, food, and shelter. In return, children have a responsibility to obey their parents. Government authorities may step in to protect any children whose parents do not take proper care of them.

Responsibilities of Citizenship

In addition to having rights protected by the Constitution, citizens of the United States have important responsibilities to uphold.

Visualizing History

1. **Citizenship** Which of the responsibilities of citizenship are related to the legal system?
2. **Connecting to Today** What responsibilities of citizenship can you fulfill?

Serving on juries

Protecting the nation in time of danger

Respecting authority figures

Voting

Responsibilities of Citizenship

Obeying the law

Helping your community

Good citizenship also includes paying taxes. The government relies on taxes to pay for public roads, police and fire departments, and public schools. If Americans did not pay taxes, the government might be unable to provide these services. People pay many kinds of taxes, such as property taxes, sales taxes, and tariffs. For example, consumers often pay sales taxes when buying items at a store. Sales tax rates vary from place to place because state and local governments set and collect most sales taxes. People also pay a certain percentage of the value of their property to the government, called a property tax. Most school funding comes from property taxes.

April 15 of every year is income tax day. By that day all Americans who earned money the year before must pay a certain percentage of their income to the federal government. Some must pay their state government too. Income taxes are progressive—that is, the rate of income tax that people pay increases as their income level rises. Regressive taxes, such as city or state sales taxes, are applied equally to people regardless of income. Property taxes are based on the value of a person's property and may vary from area to area. Local governments gain much of their revenues from property taxes.

Citizens also have the duty to protect and defend the nation from harm. If a war breaks out, citizens should try to help in the war effort. In some war situations the federal government has set up a **draft**, or requirement of military service. A draft helps raise the needed number of soldiers. The United States has had all-volunteer armed forces since 1973. However, young men must register for the draft when they turn 18. This process gives the government a list of people who could be draftees if war were to break out. Women do not have to register for the draft, but many women serve in the armed forces.

All citizens can be called to serve on a jury. Jury duty involves listening to a court case and reaching a verdict on it. By serving as jurors, citizens help fulfill each person's Sixth Amendment right to a trial by jury. Americans also have a duty to testify in court if needed. For example, someone who witnesses a crime may be called to testify about it. Judges may issue subpoenas, or orders to appear in court, to force individuals to testify.

✔ **Reading Check: Summarizing** What are some of the responsibilities of citizenship?

Daily Life

Political participation Even individuals who are not old enough to vote can find ways to join in the political process. These students are volunteering their time to help run a candidate's campaign in a local election. There are many ways in which students can assist public officials or express their own views on issues important to their community or nation. What do the students appear to be doing to participate in this local election?

Research on the ROM

Free Find:
Taxes
After examining the Federal Budget Net Receipts from 1940 to 1995 on the **Holt Researcher CD-ROM**, create a bar graph that shows how much the federal government collected in taxes in the following years: 1940, 1950, 1960, 1970, 1980, and 1990.

These members of Students Against Driving Drunk visited Washington, D.C., to speak out against drinking and driving.

⭐ Citizens and Elections

Elections form the basis of representative democracy in the United States. Through free elections, citizens choose who will lead their government. Citizens should learn as much as they can about the issues and candidates before voting. Information is available through the Internet, newspapers, television, and other forms of media. However, voters should be beware of propaganda, or material that is biased deliberately to help or harm a cause.

In addition to voting, many Americans choose to campaign for a certain candidate or issue. Anyone can help campaign, even if he or she is not eligible to vote. Citizens can also give money to a candidate directly or through **political action committees** (PACs). These groups collect money to give to candidates who support certain issues.

To vote in the United States, one must be at least 18 years old. People younger than 18 can help campaigns by handing out pamphlets, making signs, or encouraging other citizens to vote. Many other members of political clubs get to know political leaders well. Some members stay active in politics as adults.

⭐ Citizens and Government

When colonists protested British rule in the 1700s, they formed committees and presented their views to political leaders. Today, people can influence officials by letting them know what the citizens want done.

Some U.S. citizens join interest groups. These groups are formed to lobby, or try to influence, politicians on behalf of certain issues. Some groups hold demonstrations to show the government how they feel and to gather public support. In 2000, for example, mothers in favor of gun control gathered in Washington, D.C., on Mother's Day. They called this demonstration the Million Mom March. Donna Dees-Thomases planned the march. She explained that the movement "started in my family room and has grown . . . across the nation." Not everyone agreed with her group. On the day of the Million Mom March, the Second Amendment Sisters held their own demonstration calling for gun-safety and education programs instead of gun control.

Citizens do not have to join a group to influence political leaders. People can and should share their views with leaders by writing letters and attending public meetings. These activities are ways that Americans exercise their First Amendment rights. Political participation is an important duty for U.S. citizens and immigrants alike.

This woman is showing her support for the Americans with Disabilities Act.

✔ **Reading Check: Drawing Inferences and Conclusions** How do you think the shared rights and responsibilities of citizenship help unite Americans who hold different views?

☆ Community Service

Civic virtue, or the commitment to helping others, moves Americans to help their neighbors. Many of these Americans volunteer in community service groups. Some small communities rely on volunteers. These groups offer many public services, such as fire protection. Other volunteer groups help government-sponsored agencies, like police departments. For example, Citizens on Patrol and Neighborhood Watch are two groups that ask volunteers to walk their neighborhoods and report criminal activity. Neighborhoods with citizen patrols often have lower crime rates than other neighborhoods.

Other groups work along with the government. The American Red Cross aids citizens in times of natural disasters or other emergencies. Habitat for Humanity helps build houses for low-income families. The Boy Scouts and Girl Scouts plan many projects, such as planting trees to improve the environment.

Examples of community service could be found during the American Revolution, when patriotic women organized to make cloth and other goods for the colonists. Today the country's leaders want all citizens to serve others in their communities. Service projects can be simple acts like picking up trash or painting over graffiti.

Every day many Americans are in need. The nation is strengthened when all people do their part to help each other. Retired general Colin Powell, who was appointed secretary of state under President George W. Bush, launched a campaign in 1997 to promote volunteerism. He said, "This is the time for each and every one of us . . . to lift up a fellow American and put him on the road to success in this wonderful country of ours."

These volunteers are helping their neighbor by repainting a backyard fence.

✔ **Reading Check: Finding the Main Idea** What are some of the benefits of community service?

Section 3 Review

go.hrw.com

Homework Practice Online

keyword: SF3 HP9

① Define and explain:
- naturalized citizen
- deport
- draft
- political action committees

② Comparing and Contrasting Copy the graphic organizer below. Use it to contrast the different ways that a person can become a U.S. citizen and to compare the responsibilities that all U.S. citizens share.

[graphic organizer: three boxes pointing to "Citizenship" oval, pointing to "Responsibilities" box]

③ Finding the Main Idea
a. Describe the steps in the naturalization process.

b. How do responsibilities such as paying taxes, serving in the military, serving on juries, and voting help shape our national identity?

④ Writing and Critical Thinking
Supporting a Point of View Imagine that you will be making a presentation at an awards ceremony honoring volunteers in your community. Write a poem honoring the volunteers.

Consider the following:
- civic virtue and citizens' responsibilities
- how volunteerism benefits the community

Citizenship and the Constitution **295**

Chapter 9 Review

The Chapter at a Glance

Examine the visual summary of the chapter below. Using information in the chapter, create a five-question quiz for one of your classmates to complete.

Our Democratic System

The Constitution

Legislative, Executive, and Judicial Branches

Separation of Powers

Checks and Balances

Representative Democracy

Bill of Rights

Road to Citizenship: Be born in the United States or a U. S. territory, have a parent who is a U.S. citizen, or go through the naturalization process

Identifying People and Ideas

Use the following terms or people in historically significant sentences.

1. representative democracy
2. separation of powers
3. Sandra Day O'Connor
4. James Madison
5. search warrant
6. due process
7. double jeopardy
8. naturalized citizen
9. draft
10. political action committees

Understanding Main Ideas

Section 1 *(Pages 256–261)*

1. What are the three branches of the federal government, and what are their primary responsibilities?
2. What are delegated powers, reserved powers, and concurrent powers?

Section 2 *(Pages 284–289)*

3. How did complaints against Great Britain made in the Declaration of Independence shape the Constitution and the Bill of Rights?
4. Which amendments focus on the rights of people accused of crimes, and what rights do these amendments guarantee?

Section 3 *(Pages 290–295)*

5. How does someone become a naturalized citizen?

6. What are the duties and responsibilities of citizenship?

You Be the Historian— Reviewing Themes

1. **Constitutional Heritage** How does the Constitution prevent any one branch of government from becoming too powerful? Be sure to consider all three branches of government.
2. **Citizenship** Why is voting an important responsibility in a representative democracy?
3. **Culture** In what ways does the U.S. government protect the rights of all Americans?

Thinking Critically

1. **Evaluating** How do you think the rights and duties of U.S. citizens reflect our identity as a nation?
2. **Drawing Inferences and Conclusions** How have the first amendment guarantees of freedom of speech and religion impacted the American way of life?
3. **Making Generalizations and Predictions** Serving on juries is required by law and is an important responsibility of citizenship. What problems might arise if people were unwilling to fulfill this responsibility?

Interpreting Political Cartoons

Study the political cartoon below. Then use the information to help you answer the questions that follow.

FROM THE HERBLOCK GALLERY (SIMON & SCHUSTER, 1968)

1. What does the illustration suggest that President Johnson hopes to achieve by patting this Congressman on the back?
   a. Johnson wants the congressman to vote for his legislation.
   b. Johnson wants Congress to work harder.
   c. Johnson wants members of Congress to know how proud he is of their work.
   d. Johnson thinks Congress has too much power.

2. Based on your knowledge of the Constitution, why do you think President Johnson would find it necessary to encourage Congress to cooperate with him?

Analyzing Primary Sources

Read the following quote by President John F. Kennedy, and then answer the questions that follow.

> **The right to vote in a free American election is the most powerful and precious right in the world—and it must not be denied on the grounds of race or color. It is a potent [powerful] key to achieving other rights of citizenship. For American history—both recent and past—clearly reveals that the power of the ballot has enabled those who achieve it to win other achievements as well, gain a full voice in the affairs of their state and nation, and to see their interests represented in the governmental bodies which affect their future. In a free society, those with the power to govern are necessarily responsive to those with the right to vote.**

3. Which of the following statements best describes Kennedy's point of view?
   a. The only way that people can influence their government is by writing letters to elected officials.
   b. You are not a citizen if you do not vote.
   c. Voting affects everyone's future.
   d. Government officials are more likely to respond to citizens if they know that citizens can vote them out of office.

4. Based on what you know about the Constitution of the United States, what amendment is President Kennedy probably referring to when he says that people of any race or color should not be denied the right to vote?

Alternative Assessment

Building Your Portfolio

American History

Linking to Community

Think about something in your community that is important to you, such as the creation of crosswalks or parks. Write a letter to a local official about this element of your community. Make sure the letter explains to the official why you are writing and what you want to be done. Then organize a campaign to get others to sign your letter. Support your campaign by creating signs, flyers, and other items.

internet connect

Internet Activity: go.hrw.com
keyword: SF3 CF9

Access the Internet through the HRW Go site to research Supreme Court cases heard during the recent term. Then write a brief summary that describes the main issues in the case, the Constitutional questions raised in the case, the Supreme Court's decision, and whether you agree with the Court's decision. Make sure your summary includes standard grammar, spelling, and punctuation.

10 Launching the Nation
(1789–1800)

Angry farmers tar and feather a tax collector during the Whiskey Rebellion.

THE GRANGER COLLECTION, NEW YORK

President Washington with some members of his cabinet (left to right): Washington, Henry Knox, Alexander Hamilton, Thomas Jefferson, and Edmund Randolph

UNITED STATES

1789 George Washington is elected president on April 6.

1790 Washington is founded as the national capital.

1791 The Bank of the United States is formed.

1792 Kentucky becomes the 15th state.

1794 The Whiskey Rebellion begins in Pennsylvania.

1789   1791   1793

1789 The French Revolution begins.

1791 Thomas Paine defends the French Revolution in *Rights of Man*.

1792 Austrian and Prussian armies invade France to try to end the Revolution.

1793 French revolutionaries behead King Louis XVI.

WORLD

The citizens of Paris storm the prison known as the Bastille during the French Revolution.

Build on What You Know

The Constitution created a new system of government for the United States. This federal system divided power between the states and a strong central government. Yet there was still much work left for the nation's leaders to do. Americans chose George Washington and other Founding Fathers to lead the new nation.

Mount Vernon, Washington's Virginia home, has been preserved as a historical landmark.

As first lady, Martha Washington tried to bring a sense of dignity and grace to the new government.

1795 American Indian leaders sign the Treaty of Greenville with the United States.

1796 Washington publishes his Farewell Address on September 19.

John Adams is elected president on December 7.

1798 Congress passes the Sedition Act on July 14.

1799 George Washington dies at Mount Vernon, Virginia, on December 14.

1795   1797   1799

1798 Agents of French foreign minister Talleyrand demand a bribe from U.S. diplomats, leading to the XYZ affair.

1799 The Rosetta Stone is discovered in Egypt. Inscriptions on the stone make it possible for researchers to read Egyptian hieroglyphics.

If you were there . . .

What might your first actions be as part of this new government?

You Be the Historian

Themes Journal

What's Your Opinion? Do you **agree** or **disagree** with the following statements? Support your point of view in your journal.

- **Global Relations** A new country must stay away from conflicts and alliances.
- **Constitutional Heritage** There is one correct way to interpret the U.S. Constitution.
- **Economics** Countries should invest their money at home before paying their foreign debts.

Laying the Foundations of Government

Read to Discover

1. Why did Americans elect George Washington as their first president?
2. What did Americans expect of their new government?
3. What steps did Congress and the president take to organize the new government?

Define
- electoral college
- precedent

Identify
- George Washington
- Martha Washington
- Judiciary Act of 1789

WHY IT MATTERS TODAY

Every day, leaders around the world try to serve their countries. Use CNN **fyi**.com or other **current events** sources to learn more about the president or leader of a country. Record your findings in your journal.

The Story Continues

George Washington looked forward to retiring from public life once the states had ratified the Constitution. However, his friends had other plans for him. They soon drew him into politics as a presidential candidate. When Washington hesitated, politician Gouverneur Morris helped convince him. "Should the idea prevail [win] that you would not accept the presidency, it should prove fatal . . . to the new government." Morris ended confidently, "Of all men, you are the best fitted to fill that office."

COURTESY OF THE JOHN CARTER BROWN LIBRARY AT BROWN UNIVERSITY

This 1788 print shows George Washington surrounded by the seal of the United States and the seals of the 13 states.

⭐ The First President

<u>**George Washington**</u> was concerned that his age and lack of political experience might make him a poor president. He also knew that he would have to deal with many difficult issues. Yet many Americans saw Washington as a great leader and hero of the Revolution. They believed that his strong character, honesty, and patriotism would make him an excellent leader. They thought he would be a model for all citizens.

In January 1789 the 11 states that had passed the Constitution each sent electors to choose the first president. These delegates formed the **electoral college**. Each state legislature had chosen electors who would represent the popular vote in their states. However, electors could vote for different candidates if they felt the public had not chosen the right person. On April 6, 1789, Congress declared that the electoral college had selected Washington unanimously. John Adams became his vice president.

Washington accepted the presidency because he felt it was his duty "to render [give] service to my country in obedience to its call." He traveled to New York City to be sworn into office. Along the roads he traveled and in the city, Americans cheered him on and celebrated. Ships in New York Harbor flew colorful flags and fired their cannons.

The presidency brought many changes for the Washington family. <u>**Martha Washington**</u> had to entertain guests and attend social events with her husband. Two weeks after arriving in New York, Martha described the scene to her niece. "I have not had one half-hour to myself since the day of my arrival," she wrote. Martha Washington ran the presidential household with grace and style. Abigail Adams once wrote, "I found myself much more deeply impressed [by George and Martha Washington] than I ever did before their majesties of Britain."

Patriot and author Judith Sargent Murray hoped women would play a different role in the new nation. Murray declared in newspaper essays that young women needed to be educated. "I expect to see our young women forming a new era in female history," she wrote. Murray, Abigail Adams, and other women helped share the idea of Republican Motherhood. This was the idea that women played an important role because they taught their children to be good citizens. Still, most women lacked the opportunity to take part equally in society.

✔ **Reading Check: Analyzing Information** What qualities made George Washington a good candidate for president?

⭐ **Life in the New Republic**

Hard work lay ahead for the new government. Few Americans had ever thought of themselves as citizens of a united nation. They expected the federal government to protect their liberty and hoped it would improve the economy by providing stability. However, they did not want the government to restrict trade as the British Parliament had done.

In 1790 the United States was home to almost 4 million people. Most Americans lived in the countryside and worked on farms. Farmers wanted fair tax laws and the right to settle western lands. Other Americans worked in towns as craftspeople, laborers, or merchants. These people knew that Americans had begun buying and selling goods across the country and around the world. As a result, they became more interested in trade laws. Merchants wanted simpler trade laws

Cheering crowds greeted Washington as he traveled to his inauguration.

The Electoral College

Under the system established by the Constitution, American voters do not directly elect the president. Instead, each state is represented by a number of electors equal to the total number of representatives and senators it has in Congress.

Electors are sworn to represent the interests of the people of their state. In most cases the candidate who wins a state's popular vote receives all of that state's electoral votes. Electors meet in December in election years in the capital of their home state to cast their votes for president and vice president. If no candidate receives an electoral majority, the House of Representatives chooses the president and the Senate chooses the vice president. Why do you think that most states award all their electoral votes to the winner of the popular vote?

Like these women, many Americans worked on farms in the early republic.

established by a unified government. Manufacturers wanted laws to protect them from foreign competition.

Only New York City and Philadelphia had populations greater than 25,000. New York City was the first capital of the United States, and in many ways it represented the spirit of the new nation. Badly damaged during the Revolutionary War, the city had already begun recovering. Citizens got rid of the signs of British rule. They changed Crown Street to Liberty Street, for example. International trade became more active, and business activity increased. A French visitor noted the city's energy.

History Makers Speak

❝Everything in the city is in motion; everywhere the shops resound [ring out] with the noise of workers. . . . One sees vessels arriving from every part of the world.❞

—A French visitor to New York, quoted in *New York in the American Revolution,* by Wilbur Abbott

By 1790 the city's population had topped 33,000 and was growing rapidly. Many leaders thought this lively community showed the country's potential. They believed it was a fitting place for the new administration to plan the country's future.

 Reading Check: Finding the Main Idea How did Americans expect the new government to help free enterprise?

⭐ Setting Precedents

The new federal government had to make important decisions about policies and procedures. President Washington noted this fact in a letter to James Madison. "The first of everything in our situation will serve to establish a precedent," he wrote. A **precedent** is an action or a decision that serves as an example for later generations.

Planning the government's executive branch was one of Congress's first tasks. Congress created several executive departments. Each department specialized in a different area of national policy, such as military affairs. Washington nominated the department heads, who required approval by the Senate. He picked Alexander Hamilton as secretary of the treasury and Thomas Jefferson as secretary of state. Washington began meeting with the department heads as a group, which became known as

Analyzing Primary Sources

Drawing Inferences and Conclusions What does this quote tell you about New York City's economic activities?

the cabinet. The cabinet members advised the president and talked about important issues. By 1792, cabinet meetings were common practice.

The judicial branch also needed organizing. The Constitution did not state the number or location of federal courts. In September 1789 Congress passed the **Judiciary Act of 1789**, which created a federal court system with three levels. It also outlined the powers of the federal courts and their relationship to the state courts. District courts were at the lowest level. Then came the courts of appeals, which reviewed district court decisions. At the top level was the Supreme Court, which had six justices.

The president nominated the candidates for federal judgeships at each level, who then needed congressional approval. John Jay served as the Supreme Court's first chief justice. Washington selected Edmund Randolph as attorney general. Washington wrote to the justices to explain the importance of their duties.

THE GRANGER COLLECTION, NEW YORK

Washington's cabinet members advised him on issues of national defense, diplomacy, and finance.

 History Makers Speak

❝I have always been persuaded that the stability and success of the national government, and consequently the happiness of the people of the United States, would depend in a considerable degree on the interpretation and execution of its laws. In my opinion, therefore, it is important that the judiciary system should not only be independent in its operations, but as perfect as possible in its formation.❞

—George Washington, from *The Real George Washington, Part 2,* edited by Andrew M. Allison, Jay A. Parry, and W. Cleon Skousen

With the parts of the federal government in place, leaders began addressing the problems that faced the country.

✔ **Reading Check: Summarizing** How did Washington and Congress set up the executive and judicial branches?

Section 1 Review

go. hrw .com **Homework Practice Online** keyword: SF3 HP10

1 **Define and explain:**
- electoral college
- precedent

2 **Identify and explain:**
- George Washington
- Martha Washington
- Judiciary Act of 1789

3 **Summarizing** Copy the chart below. Use it to show how three important positions in the new U.S. government, such as the president or Supreme Court justices, were selected.

Position	How Selected
1.	
2.	
3.	

4 **Finding the Main Idea**
a. What did Americans want their government to do to help free enterprise?

b. What problems did Washington and Congress face in organizing the executive branch and the judicial branch, and how did they work together to solve these problems?

5 **Writing and Critical Thinking**
Supporting a Point of View Imagine that you are a member of the electoral college and that George Washington has not accepted his presidential nomination. Write a petition to persuade him to take office.

Consider the following:
- the needs of the nation
- the expectations Americans had of the new government
- Washington's civic and leadership qualities

Hamilton and National Finances

Read to Discover

1. What challenge did Alexander Hamilton face as secretary of the treasury, and what issues did his plans raise?
2. What issues did Hamilton and Thomas Jefferson disagree on, and what were their views?
3. What questions were raised when the Bank of the United States was founded, and what different views did Hamilton and Jefferson have concerning the Bank?

WHY IT MATTERS TODAY

The U.S. government still imposes tariffs on some foreign goods. Use CNN**fyi**.com or other **current events** sources to learn more about a tariff that is in place today. Record your findings in your journal.

Define

- national debt
- bonds
- speculators
- protective tariff
- loose construction
- strict construction

Identify

- Alexander Hamilton
- Thomas Jefferson
- Bank of the United States

Alexander Hamilton had served as an aide to George Washington during the Revolutionary War.

The Story Continues

President Washington was worried about how to solve the nation's money problems. "There is but one man in the United States who can tell you," his friend Robert Morris suggested. "That is Alexander Hamilton." Hamilton's impressive reputation helped him become secretary of the treasury. But his skills were quickly put to the test. Within days of his appointment, Congress directed him to prepare a plan to improve the national economy.

★ Settling the Debt

Alexander Hamilton had a strong interest in business matters. He grew up on the island of Nevis in the British West Indies. When he was just a teenager he had helped run a shipping company there. Because of his intelligence and hard work, family friends sent him to the American colonies for an education. Hamilton eventually married into a very wealthy New York family and began practicing law.

As secretary of the treasury, Hamilton's biggest challenge was paying off the **national debt**. This was the amount of money owed by the United States to its lenders. Hamilton figured that the United States owed about $11.7 million to foreign countries such as France.

The United States also owed about $40.4 million to U.S. citizens. Some of the debt was in the form of **bonds**, or certificates that represent money owed. During the Revolutionary War the government sold bonds to raise money. Officials promised to buy back these bonds with interest, thus allowing buyers to make a profit. But the government had trouble keeping this promise. Eventually, bondholders began to doubt that the government would ever repay them. Many people sold their bonds for less than their original value to **speculators**. Speculators are people who buy items at low prices in the hope that the value will rise.

Hamilton wanted to put the federal government on a solid financial footing. He feared that otherwise the government would lose the trust of the American people. He also wanted to pay the country's foreign debt immediately and repay the full value of all bonds over time. This caused great argument among politicians, because paying full value would allow speculators to make a profit. Hamilton believed this was only fair. As he saw it, speculators "paid what the commodity [bond] was worth in the market and took the risks." **Thomas Jefferson** opposed Hamilton's plan. He thought that the idea cheated the original bondholders who had sold their bonds at low prices. Jefferson wrote, "Immense sums were thus filched [stolen] from the poor and ignorant." A majority in Congress agreed with Hamilton. In early 1790 the government started exchanging the old bonds for new, more reliable ones whose value was guaranteed by the federal government.

✔ **Reading Check: Finding the Main Idea** What domestic problem did Alexander Hamilton face, and how did he plan to solve it?

⭐ The States' Debts

The states owed $25 million for Revolutionary War expenses. Hamilton wanted the federal government to pay for $21.5 million of this debt. Hamilton believed that this aid would increase support for the federal government. He also thought that paying the state debts would help the national economy. Debtor states would not have to spend so much on

U.S. Government Finances, 1789–1791

Total Money Owed ($81,497,000)

Federal and State Debts $77,228,000

Total Revenue ($4,418,000)

Government Operating Expenses $4,269,000

Revenue from Tariffs $4,399,000

Additional Revenue $19,000

Dollars (in millions)

Money Owed — Revenue

Source: *Historical Statistics of the United States*

Interpreting Graphs George Washington's administration had to deal with the federal government's financial problems.

Skills Assessment Analyzing Information What were the government's operating expenses from 1789 to 1791?

The value of government bonds such as this one varied greatly before Alexander Hamilton's efforts.

THE GRANGER COLLECTION, NEW YORK

Interpreting the Visual Record

Before and after *The future site of Washington, D.C., was a plot of land along the Potomac River. Today the city is a cultural center filled with treasured historical artifacts and monuments.* **Why do you think Congress chose to build a capital city rather than use an existing city for the national capital?**

Research on the R⊙M

Free Find:
Alexander Hamilton
After reading about Alexander Hamilton on the **Holt Researcher CD–ROM**, write a short essay explaining his contributions to the new government of the United States.

repayment. Therefore, Hamilton said, they would have resources to develop business and trade.

Not all states agreed. Southern states such as Virginia and North Carolina had few war debts. Their representatives did not want to help the federal government pay the debts of other states. Patrick Henry did not even believe that the Constitution gave Congress the power to pay state debts. Hamilton knew that he needed the help of southern representatives to get his plan approved.

He got this help because southern officials wanted a new national capital. Many southerners did not like having the capital in New York. They thought this gave the northern states too much influence over national policy. Hamilton, Jefferson, and Representative James Madison met in June 1790. Hamilton promised to convince northern members of Congress to move the capital. In exchange, Jefferson and Madison agreed to gather support in the South for Hamilton's debt payment plan.

The compromise worked. In July the House of Representatives approved the plan. They chose an area along the Potomac River for the new national capital. This site would become present-day Washington, D.C. Philadelphia served as the temporary capital while architects began designing the new capital city.

✔ **Reading Check: Summarizing** What compromise did Hamilton and Jefferson reach to allow Congress to repay the state debts?

★ Hamilton versus Jefferson

Hamilton and Jefferson did not cooperate for long. Instead, they began to disagree about how to define the authority of the central government. While Hamilton believed in a strong central government, Jefferson wanted to protect the powers of the states. Their conflict reflected basic differences in their opinions about democracy. Hamilton had little faith in the common person. He once said that "the people . . . seldom judge or determine [decide] right." He wanted a strong central government that balanced power between the "mass of the people" and wealthier citizens. He explained his beliefs.

 "We must take man as we find him, and if we expect him to serve the public, [we] must interest his passions in doing so. A reliance on pure patriotism has been the source of many of our errors."

—Alexander Hamilton, quoted in *Odd Destiny: The Life of Alexander Hamilton,* by Marie B. Hecht

Hamilton believed that his approach would protect everyone's liberties while keeping the people from having too much power.

Jefferson disagreed strongly with Hamilton's views of the average citizen's ability. He did admit that "the people can not be all, and always, well informed." However, Jefferson firmly defended the right of the people to rule the country.

 "It is my principle that the will of the Majority should always prevail [win]. . . . Above all things I hope the education of the common people will be attended to; [I am] convinced that on their good sense we may rely with the most security for the preservation of a due degree of liberty."

—Thomas Jefferson, quoted in *Thomas Jefferson,* edited by Joseph L. Gardner

Hamilton and Jefferson also argued over how the American economy should grow. Hamilton wanted new forms of economic growth. He also wanted to promote manufacturing and business. In a 1790 report he suggested that the government give prizes to certain American companies. These prizes would "reward some particular excellence or superiority" in the companies' products. In addition, Hamilton wanted to pass a higher tariff, or a tax on imported goods. Known as a **protective tariff**, this tax would raise the prices of foreign products. Hamilton hoped this would cause Americans to buy U.S. goods, which would protect American manufacturing from foreign competition.

Analyzing Primary Sources
Identifying Points of View
Does Hamilton believe that people are naturally good citizens? Explain your answer.

CONNECTING TO
THE ARTS

American Architecture and Classical Revival After the Revolution, American architects began to create buildings in the classical style of ancient Greece and Rome. Many Americans admired these civilizations because they had some of the same democratic ideals as the new American nation.

Thomas Jefferson started this trend in 1785 when he designed Virginia's capitol building. It was inspired by Roman architecture's use of columns, domes, and white stone. Architects designed banks, churches, colleges, and even the new U.S. Capitol Building in the same style. Shown here is William Thornton's winning design for the outside of the building. **What view is shown by Americans' new interest in classical architecture?**

PRESIDENTIAL PROFILES

George Washington

Many people consider George Washington to be the Father of Our Country. He entered the presidency as one of the great heroes of the American Revolution. He felt a great sense of responsibility to the nation. He wanted to be a dignified leader who also listened to the needs of the people. Yet the pressure of other people's expectations often made life difficult for him. Washington was very sensitive to attacks made against him in the press. Thomas Jefferson wrote, "I think he feels those things [criticisms] more than any person I ever met."

Washington left politics in 1797 and returned to his home in Mount Vernon. He died just two years later. His image is carved into the national monument at Mount Rushmore, South Dakota. Presidents' Day, a federal holiday, is held each year near his birthday, February 22. Why do you think George Washington has been called the "Father of Our Country"?

Jefferson, on the other hand, worried about depending too much on business and manufacturing. Jefferson believed that farmers were the most independent voters. They did not rely too much on other people's work to make a living. He wrote, "Our governments will remain virtuous [morally pure] for many centuries; as long as they are chiefly agricultural." Jefferson wanted lower tariffs, which would help farmers by keeping the price of imported goods low.

✔ **Reading Check: Comparing and Contrasting** Compare and contrast Hamilton's and Jefferson's ideas about government, the economy, and protective tariffs.

★ The Debate over the Bank

Hamilton's and Jefferson's differences came to the public's attention in early 1791. Hamilton wanted to start a national bank in which the government could safely deposit its money. The bank would also make loans to the government and businesses. Hamilton added that the United States should build a national mint—a place where coins are made. Then the country could begin issuing its own money. To limit the national bank's power, Hamilton asked for a 20-year charter. After this period of time, Congress could decide if it should extend the charter. Hamilton also asked each state to start its own bank so that the national bank would not have a monopoly.

The idea of establishing a national bank greatly worried both James Madison and Thomas Jefferson. They did not believe the U.S. Constitution gave Congress this power. In response, Hamilton and his supporters pointed to a clause in Article I, Section 8. This clause states that Congress has the power "to make all laws which shall be necessary and proper" for governing the nation. The passage later became known as the elastic clause because it has allowed the powers of the government to be stretched. Hamilton argued that this clause was meant to give the government the power to react to new situations. He saw the need for a national bank as an ideal example of such a situation. Hamilton's view became known as **loose construction** of the Constitution. According to loose construction, the federal government can take any reasonable actions that the Constitution does not specifically forbid it from taking.

Jefferson did not agree with Hamilton's argument. Jefferson believed that the "necessary and proper" clause should be used only in special cases. He wrote a letter explaining his view to President Washington. "The Constitution allows only the means which are 'necessary,' not those which are merely 'convenient.'" To Jefferson, the national bank was a convenience, not a necessity. Jefferson's view became known as **strict construction**. According to strict construction, the federal government should do only what the Constitution specifically says it can do.

THE GRANGER COLLECTION, NEW YORK

Interpreting the Visual Record

National finance *Both the Bank of the United States, shown at the left, and the U.S. Mint, which issued the coins shown below, were projects of Alexander Hamilton.* **How are these two institutions similar?**

President Washington and Congress agreed with Hamilton. They hoped a bank would offer more security for the national economy. As a result, in February 1791 Congress chartered the **Bank of the United States**. The Bank helped offer stability during the next 20 years and played an important role in improving the U.S. economy.

✔ **Reading Check:** **Identifying Points of View** How did Hamilton interpret the Constitution during the Bank debate, and what problems did he face with this argument?

Section 2 Review

go.hrw.com **Homework Practice Online** keyword: SF3 HP10

1 **Define** and explain:
• national debt
• bonds
• speculators
• protective tariff
• loose construction
• strict construction

2 **Identify** and explain:
• Alexander Hamilton
• Thomas Jefferson
• Bank of the United States

3 **Contrasting** Copy the graphic organizer below. Use it to contrast the ideas that Hamilton and Jefferson held about the topics listed.

Hamilton		Jefferson
	Bonds	
	Democracy	
	Economy	
	Tariffs	
	National Bank	
	Constitution	

4 **Finding the Main Idea**
a. What was Alexander Hamilton's biggest job, and what debate arose from his plans?

b. How did Hamilton win approval from Congress for the federal government to pay most of the states' war debts?

5 **Writing and Critical Thinking**
Summarizing Imagine that you are a member of Congress during Washington's administration. Write a speech to be delivered to the people of your home state that explains the conflict over the creation of a national bank.

Consider the following:
• different interpretations of the Constitution
• political differences between Hamilton and Jefferson
• the benefits of a national bank

Launching the Nation **309**

Troubles Abroad

Read to Discover

1. How did Americans and President Washington respond to events in France?
2. What policy did Washington follow toward foreign nations?
3. How did the United States settle its differences with Great Britain and Spain?

WHY IT MATTERS TODAY

The United States still signs treaties with other countries. Use CNNfyi.com or other current events sources to find out about an economic, military, or political treaty the United States has signed or considered signing in recent years. Record your findings in your journal.

Define

• privateers
• right of deposit

Identify

• French Revolution
• Neutrality Proclamation
• Edmond Genet
• John Jay
• Jay's Treaty
• Thomas Pinckney
• Pinckney's Treaty

The Story Continues

On July 14, 1789, the citizens of Paris, France, challenged their corrupt government. Masses of people attacked the Bastille, a hated fortress and prison that held the enemies of the French Crown. Soldiers defending the walls were shocked. One of them described "the people . . . in a crowd, armed with muskets . . . swords . . . and shouting, 'We want the Bastille! Down with the troops.'" After hours of fighting, the crowd captured the fortress. The fall of this mighty symbol of royal power stunned the country.

The fall of the Bastille is celebrated as a national holiday in France.

★ The French Revolution

The storming of the Bastille was one of the first acts of the **French Revolution**. During this rebellion the French people overthrew their monarchy and created a republican government. The Declaration of the Rights of Man stated the French Revolution's principles: "liberty, equality, and fraternity [brotherhood]." As U.S. minister to France, Thomas Jefferson witnessed the early days of the Revolution. He wrote to friends back in America that the changes in France were "the first chapter of European liberty."

In 1789 King Louis XVI addressed the members of the French Legislature. Four years later revolutionaries beheaded the king using a guillotine like the one below.

News of the French Revolution spread quickly, gaining the support of many Americans. They believed France was founding a democratic republic similar to the United States. These Americans celebrated French independence by burning huge bonfires and singing French songs. Jefferson wrote to a friend about the scene. He said that he was fortunate "to see in the course of fourteen years two such revolutions as were never before seen."

Some Americans were not as pleased. They were very worried about the French Revolution's violent riots. They also feared the many attacks on all forms of traditional authority. The revolutionaries shocked many Americans by beheading King Louis XVI in January 1793 and Queen Marie-Antoinette later that year.

✔ **Reading Check: Contrasting** What differing opinions did Americans hold about the French Revolution?

⭐ U.S. Neutrality

A few months after the French Revolution started, France and Great Britain went to war. Some Americans backed the French, while others backed the British. The debate over U.S. foreign policy soon divided Congress and split President Washington's cabinet. After considering different arguments on the issue, Washington presented his own views to Congress on April 22, 1793.

> **History Makers Speak**
>
> **"The duty and interest of the United States require that they should with sincerity and good faith adopt and pursue a conduct friendly and impartial [unbiased] towards the belligerent [fighting] powers."**
>
> —Proclamation of Neutrality

★ ★ ★ ★ ★ ★ ★ ★ ★ ★ ★ ★
That's Interesting!
★ ★ ★ ★ ★ ★ ★ ★ ★ ★ ★ ★

"Let them eat cake." Maybe you've heard the saying "Let them eat cake." Many people believe that the French queen Marie-Antoinette said this. As the story goes, this was her reply when a large mob of hungry women stormed the palace demanding bread. The story of the queen's heartless attitude became quite popular. The queen was probably out of touch with the needs of poor French citizens. But many historians believe that the French philosopher Jean-Jacques Rousseau actually made up the story to make the French monarchy look bad.

GLOBAL CONNECTIONS

Patriots in France

The democratic goals of the French Revolution encouraged some former Patriots to take part. Two of the more well-known examples were Thomas Paine and the Marquis de Lafayette. Paine is shown above holding a copy of *Rights of Man,* which he wrote in support of the Revolution and the creation of democracies in Europe. When Paine went to France, however, he was jailed for protesting the new government's violent acts. In prison he wrote *The Age of Reason,* which attacked organized religion and cost him many of his supporters. The Marquis de Lafayette helped write the Declaration of the Rights of Man and the French Constitution of 1791. Lafayette then fled the country and took little part in French politics once Napoléon came to power.
How did Paine and Lafayette contribute to the French Revolution?

This **Neutrality Proclamation** stated that the United States would not take sides with countries at war in Europe. Washington believed that this plan would be the safest and most reasonable. However, not everyone agreed. Some newspaper editors and members of Congress criticized him. James Madison questioned Washington's right to issue the proclamation without Congress's approval.

★ Citizen Genet

At this time **Edmond Genet** (zhuh-ne), France's new representative to the United States, arrived. Citizen Genet, as he was known, traveled across the country seeking American support for France. He found four sea captains who agreed to command **privateers**—private ships allowed by a country to attack its enemies. Washington warned Genet that recruiting privateers on American soil hurt U.S. neutrality. In response, Genet said he would ask the American people to overrule Washington. At that point, even pro-French Jefferson agreed that Genet should be sent back home.

Although he wanted Genet to be removed, Jefferson was still upset by the U.S. policy toward France. He also felt that pro-British Hamilton was influencing the president's foreign policy. Hamilton's influence interfered with Jefferson's duties as secretary of state. As a result, Jefferson eventually decided to leave Washington's cabinet. In December 1793 Jefferson resigned. This decision disappointed Washington, who had a high opinion of Jefferson's honesty and talent. Some 30 years after he resigned, Jefferson expressed his view of President Washington. Although he disagreed with some of Washington's policies, Jefferson had great respect for the president.

History Makers Speak

❝General Washington was himself sincerely a friend to the republican principles of our Constitution. . . . He repeatedly declared to me that he . . . would lose the last drop of his blood in its support.❞

—Thomas Jefferson, from *The Writings of Thomas Jefferson,* edited by Albert Ellery Bergh

 Reading Check: Identifying Cause and Effect What did President Washington do when France and Great Britain went to war, and how did Jefferson respond?

★ Jay's Treaty

Washington experienced other threats to U.S. neutrality. In late 1793 the British began seizing all ships carrying food to the French West Indies. In the process, the British captured hundreds of neutral American merchant ships. Rumors also flew that British officers on the western frontier were encouraging American Indian uprisings. The British had never abandoned these frontier forts, as the Treaty of Paris required. Now it looked as if the British might side with American Indians in a war against American settlers.

Even Alexander Hamilton recognized that the United States might be on the path to war. President Washington and Hamilton sent Chief Justice **John Jay** to London to work out a peaceful resolution. Jay's task was difficult. The British knew that the United States lacked a strong navy. Also, many American businesses relied on trade with Great Britain. However, the British did not want to fight another war in North America.

The two sides eventually reached an agreement in November 1794. **Jay's Treaty** was a compromise. The British agreed to pay damages for seized American ships. Small American merchant ships were allowed to continue trading certain items in the Caribbean. The British also said they would abandon their forts on the northwestern frontier. In exchange, the United States would pay the pre-Revolutionary debts it owed to British merchants.

Many congressional leaders argued that the treaty did not accomplish much. Critics pointed out that it ignored many important issues. The treaty did not prevent Britain from capturing large American ships or supporting American Indians on the frontier. It also did not make the British return slaves they had freed during the Revolutionary War. Although Washington disliked the treaty, he felt that it was the best that the United States could do. At his urging, the Senate approved the treaty.

THE GRANGER COLLECTION, NEW YORK

Interpreting the Visual Record

Protest *Some critics of Jay's Treaty were so angry that they protested in the streets.* **Whom does the figure being burned represent?**

✔ **Reading Check: Categorizing** Which aspects of Jay's Treaty benefited the United States, and which did not?

⭐ Pinckney's Treaty

Along the frontier with Spanish Florida and Louisiana, American settlers faced other problems. The Spanish disputed the border between the United States and Florida. As a result of this dispute, Spain closed the port of New Orleans to U.S. trade in 1784. New Orleans was an important port. All goods moving down the Mississippi to places in the East or overseas had to pass through the city. Closing the port separated settlers on the western frontier from their most important link with the outside world.

Washington asked U.S. ambassador **Thomas Pinckney** to help. Pinckney asked Spanish officials to reopen New Orleans to U.S. trade. Then he requested **right of deposit** at the port of New Orleans. This right would allow American boats to transfer their goods at New Orleans without paying fees on their cargo.

Western trade *The Mississippi River and the port of New Orleans were vital links to the wider world for settlers on the American frontier.* **What parts of this image show trade taking place?**

Spanish minister Manuel de Godoy (goh-DOY) tried to delay reaching an agreement. He hoped that Pinckney would grow desperate and sign a treaty favorable to the Spanish. But Pinckney was patient. Godoy became worried that the United States and Great Britain might join against Spain after signing Jay's Treaty. So he agreed to **Pinckney's Treaty**, which was signed in October 1795. Under the treaty, Spain agreed to change the Florida border. Spain's government also reopened the port at New Orleans to American ships and gave them right of deposit. Because it opened the frontier to further expansion, Washington and most other Americans considered Pinckney's Treaty a success.

✔ **Reading Check: Analyzing Information** Why did most Americans believe Pinckney's Treaty was more successful than Jay's Treaty?

Section 3 Review

go.hrw.com **Homework Practice Online** keyword: SF3 HP10

1 **Define** and explain:
- privateers
- right of deposit

2 **Identify** and explain:
- French Revolution
- Neutrality Proclamation
- Edmond Genet
- John Jay
- Jay's Treaty
- Thomas Pinckney
- Pinckney's Treaty

3 **Summarizing** Copy the web diagram below. Use it to show the dealings the United States had with each country, as well as any important politicians involved.

Spain

U.S. Policies Toward

France   Great Britain

4 **Finding the Main Idea**
a. Why did Washington want to pursue a policy of neutrality?

b. What problems led to Jay's Treaty and Pinckney's Treaty, and what were the results of these treaties?

5 **Writing and Critical Thinking**
Analyzing Information Imagine that news of the French Revolution has reached the U.S. capital. Write a script for a short skit that describes how the president and other individuals react to the news.

Consider the following:
- pro-French attitudes
- pro-British attitudes
- Washington's views on foreign policy

Challenges at Home

Read to Discover

1. What domestic problems did the United States face?
2. What advice did Washington give the nation in his Farewell Address?

WHY IT MATTERS TODAY

George Washington helped our country in many ways. Use CNNfyi.com or other **current events** sources to find out about another U.S. citizen who has made important contributions to the country. Record your findings in your journal.

Identify

- Little Turtle
- Anthony Wayne
- Battle of Fallen Timbers
- Treaty of Greenville
- Whiskey Rebellion

The Story Continues

In November 1786 Mohawk leader Joseph Brant, or Thayendanegea, addressed a council of American Indian nations from the Ohio Valley. "The interests of any one [Indian] nation should be the welfare of all the others," he said. By uniting their efforts, they hoped to stop settlers from taking their land. Thayendanegea said that Indians must take action if they were to keep from being pushed farther west. The councilmembers agreed and formed a confederation of American Indian nations. The members promised to stop selling land to settlers and agreed to seek a new treaty from the U.S. government.

Thayendanegea had fought with the British against the United States in the Revolutionary War.

⭐ Conflict in the Northwest Territory

Despite the protests of American Indians, Americans continued to settle the Northwest Territory. Meetings between U.S. officials and American Indian leaders achieved little. Supplied with guns and ammunition by British traders, American Indians went to war. In 1790 and 1791 an American Indian confederation under Miami chief **Little Turtle** defeated U.S. forces. Washington then sent General **Anthony Wayne** to the frontier to take charge of the army.

Little Turtle asked his British allies for support, but they refused. He then quit his command and warned other American Indian leaders not to fight.

Analyzing Primary Sources
Identifying Points of View
Why does Little Turtle give up the fight?

History Makers Speak

66 The trail has been long and bloody; it has no end. The [whites] come from where the sun rises, and they . . . are many. They are like the leaves of the trees. When the frost comes they fall and are blown away. But when the sunshine comes again they come back more plentiful than ever before. 99

—Little Turtle, quoted in *The Ohio Frontier,* by Douglas Hurt

American Indian forces and the U.S. Army fought the **Battle of Fallen Timbers** on August 20, 1794. The victory went to Wayne's troops, who then burned the American Indians' villages and fields. The frontier war soon ended. In August 1795, Indian leaders signed the **Treaty of Greenville**. This treaty gave the United States access to American Indian lands in the Northwest Territory and guaranteed the safety of U.S. citizens there. In exchange, Indians received $20,000 worth of goods and a formal acknowledgment of their claim to the lands they still held.

✔ **Reading Check:** **Sequencing** List the events in the Northwest Territory that affected U.S. national security in the order that they took place.

⭐ The Whiskey Rebellion

More conflicts arose on the frontier when Congress passed a tax on American-made whiskey in March 1791. Farmers who produced small amounts of whiskey for trade argued that they could not afford the tax. After being fined for not paying the tax, farmer William Smith wrote, "I felt my blood boil." What began as the complaints of a few turned into the **Whiskey Rebellion** in 1794. Protesters refused to pay the tax and even tarred and feathered tax collectors. Some called themselves the new Sons of Liberty.

President Washington saw the rebels as a threat to federal authority. Under the Constitution, Congress had the power to pass the tax. He assembled some 13,000 men from state militias. The army approached western Pennsylvania in November 1794. By this time, most of the rebels had fled, and the Whiskey Rebellion ended without a battle.

✔ **Reading Check:** **Finding the Main Idea** What did farmers say and do in response to the whiskey tax, and why did this response worry Washington?

Interpreting the Visual Record

Whiskey Rebellion
Washington led an army into western Pennsylvania to put down the Whiskey Rebellion. **Why do you think the government felt it was necessary to send such a large force for this task?**

THE METROPOLITAN MUSEUM OF ART, GIFT OF EDGAR WILLIAM AND BERNICE CHRYSLER GARBISCH, 1963 (63.201.2)

⭐ Washington's Farewell Address

In 1796 Washington decided not to run for a third presidential term. He wrote that he was "tired of public life" and "devoutly [strongly] wished for retirement." He also believed that by stepping down he would remind Americans that he was only a president, not a king. The people were the country's true leaders.

With the help of Alexander Hamilton and James Madison, the president wrote his Farewell Address. In it he spoke about what he believed were the greatest dangers to the American republic. Among these were the dangers of foreign ties and political divisions at home. Washington

Historical Document

WASHINGTON'S FAREWELL ADDRESS

On September 19, 1796, President George Washington's Farewell Address first appeared in a Philadelphia newspaper. In it, he wrote about the nation's economy, foreign policy, and political parties.

I have already **intimated**[1] to you the danger of [political] parties in the state, with particular reference to the founding of them on geographical discriminations. Let me now take a more **comprehensive**[2] view and warn you in the most solemn manner against the **baneful**[3] effects of the spirit of party generally. . . .

If, in the opinion of the people, the distribution or **modification**[4] of the constitutional powers be in any particular wrong, let it be corrected by an amendment. . . .

Promote, then, as an object of primary importance, institutions for the general **diffusion**[5] of knowledge. . . . As the structure of a government gives force to public opinion, it is essential that public opinion should be enlightened. . . .

[Avoid] likewise the accumulation of debt, . . . not ungenerously throwing upon **posterity**[6] the burden which we ourselves ought to bear. . . .

Observe good faith and justice toward all nations. **Cultivate**[7] peace and harmony with all. . . .

It is our true policy to steer clear of permanent alliances with any portion of the foreign world. . . . There can be no greater error than to expect, or **calculate**,[8] upon real favors from nation to nation. It is an illusion which experience must cure, which a just pride ought to discard.

George Washington

[1]**intimated:** told
[2]**comprehensive:** complete
[3]**baneful:** destructive
[4]**modification:** change
[5]**diffusion:** spreading
[6]**posterity:** future generations
[7]**cultivate:** seek
[8]**calculate:** plan

Analyzing Primary Sources

1. Under what circumstances does Washington propose changing the Constitution, and how should this be done?

2. Do you think Washington's advice on political parties and foreign policy is still appropriate today? Explain your answer.

Many Americans saw George Washington as a champion of liberty, represented by the woman standing by his statue.

also expressed his concerns about the public debt. He believed that the government should try not to borrow money. Such a policy would protect future generations from being saddled with debt.

Washington also wanted the country to be free from outside influences and to avoid diplomatic problems. He warned against forming permanent relationships, friendly or otherwise, with other countries.

History Makers Speak

❝The nation which indulges [allows] toward another an habitual [regular] hatred or an habitual fondness is in some degree a slave. It is a slave to its animosity [hate] or to its affection, either of which is sufficient [enough] to lead it astray from its duty and its interest.❞

—George Washington, quoted in *The Annals of America*

Washington believed that disagreements between political groups weaken government. He worried that regional differences could lead too easily to political conflict that would harm the nation. Political unity, he said, was key to national success. Thus, Washington left office telling the nation to work out its differences and protect its independence. He concluded his speech by looking forward to his retirement and praising his country. "I anticipate . . . the sweet enjoyment . . . of good laws under a free government, the ever favorite object of my heart."

✔ **Reading Check: Summarizing** What were the key points of Washington's Farewell Address?

Section 4 Review

go.hrw.com **Homework Practice Online** keyword: SF3 HP10

1 **Identify** and explain:
• Little Turtle
• Anthony Wayne
• Battle of Fallen Timbers
• Treaty of Greenville
• Whiskey Rebellion

2 **Sequencing** Copy the graphic organizer below. Use it to describe, in order, the major domestic problems leading up to Washington's Farewell Address. Include Washington's views on the greatest threats that faced the United States.

3 **Finding the Main Idea**
a. What challenge did the United States face on the frontier, and what was its outcome?

b. Do you think that the farmers in the Whiskey Rebellion were really like the Sons of Liberty? Why or why not?

4 **Writing and Critical Thinking**
Making Generalizations and Predictions Imagine that you are a historian reading George Washington's Farewell Address. Think about what the country would be like today if Washington's advice was followed strictly. Write a journal entry expressing your thoughts.

Consider the following:
• political divisions and parties
• the national debt
• alliances with foreign nations

John Adams's Presidency

Read to Discover

1. How did political parties form, and what role did they play in the presidential election of 1796?
2. What problems with foreign nations did John Adams face during his presidency?
3. What were the Alien and Sedition Acts, and how did Republicans respond to them?
4. What were the main issues in the election of 1800, and what were some of its outcomes?

WHY IT MATTERS TODAY

Today the United States has two main political parties. These are the Democratic Party and the Republican Party. Use CNNfyi.com and other **current events** sources to learn about how one party or the other has made the news recently. Record your findings in your journal.

Define

• political parties

Identify

• Federalist Party
• Democratic-Republican Party
• XYZ affair
• Alien and Sedition Acts
• Kentucky and Virginia Resolutions
• Twelfth Amendment

The Story Continues

When two-term vice president John Adams learned that President Washington was retiring, he thought about running for office. He asked his wife, Abigail, what she thought. She answered, "I would be second unto no Man but Washington." She thought that Adams should either run for president or quit politics. He considered her advice and chose to run for the presidency.

THE GRANGER COLLECTION, NEW YORK

Abigail Adams, a respected friend of several political figures, often gave her husband political advice.

⭐ The Election of 1796

The election of 1796 began a new era in U.S. politics. For the first time, more than one candidate was running for president. **Political parties**, groups that help elect government officials and shape government policies, also had an important role. Two political parties had begun to form during Washington's presidency. Despite the warnings about party conflict given in Washington's Farewell Address, the rivalry between these two parties dominated the 1796 election.

THE PRESENT State of our COUNTRY.

Parties *This political cartoon shows members of the Federalist and Democratic-Republican Parties threatening to pull down the foundations of the government with their arguing.* **Who is the person watching the party members and criticizing their actions?**

Supporters of John Adams created this campaign button.

The **Federalist Party** wanted to make the federal government stronger and to promote industry and trade. This party was most popular in New England. Alexander Hamilton helped found the Federalist Party. However, he chose not to run for president. The Federalists chose former vice president John Adams and South Carolinian Thomas Pinckney as their candidates. Adams was not popular in the South or the West. But he and his wife Abigail hoped that voters would support him "as soon as they have had time to . . . consider and reflect [think about]" his years of loyal service to the nation.

The **Democratic-Republican Party** was started by such leaders as Thomas Jefferson and James Madison. The party's members were called Republicans. (This party is not related to the modern Republican Party.) Republicans wanted to limit the power of the federal government. The party was most popular in the South and along the western frontier. The Republicans chose former secretary of state Thomas Jefferson and New York politician Aaron Burr as their candidates.

Both sides attacked each other during the election. Republicans called the Federalists the British party. Campaign posters for Jefferson called Adams a "Royalist." The Federalists answered that the Republicans were influenced too greatly by the French. They also questioned Jefferson's political skills. One Federalist wrote that Jefferson was "fit to be a professor in a College, [or] President of a Philosophical Society . . . but certainly not" president. Abigail Adams wrote to her son about the style of the campaign. "I fear America will never go through another Election without Blood Shed. We have had a paper War for six weeks past."

Hamilton, who did not like Adams, complicated matters by trying to get Pinckney elected instead. The plan failed, and Adams only narrowly defeated Jefferson. At the time, the person who took second place in a presidential election became vice president. This happened even if that person was not of the same political party as the president. So after months of running against each other, Adams and Jefferson took office together.

✔ **Reading Check: Summarizing** Explain how the Federalist and the Democratic-Republican Parties formed in the mid-1790s.

★ President Adams and the XYZ Affair

At first glance, John Adams did not appear well suited for the presidency. Adams had been a leading Patriot during the time of the American Revolution. He had later served as a foreign diplomat. Yet he lacked Washington's dignity, and most people saw him as a cold and distant person. Still, many people respected Adams—even his opponents. They recognized his hard work, honesty, and intelligence.

One of Adams's first goals as president was to improve relations between the United States and France. The French had been using privateers to attack American ships. In response, Adams sent U.S. diplomats Elbridge Gerry, John Marshall, and Charles C. Pinckney to Paris. Once in France, the diplomats learned that French foreign minister Charles-Maurice de Talleyrand-Périgord would not speak with them. Instead, three French agents paid them a secret visit. These agents said that Talleyrand would discuss a treaty only in exchange for a $250,000 bribe. The French government also wanted a loan of $12 million. The amazed diplomats refused this demand. In March 1798 President Adams told Congress that the peace-seeking mission had failed. He described the French terms, substituting the letters X, Y, and Z for the names of the French agents. Upon hearing the news, Federalists in Congress called for war with France.

Soon the story of the **XYZ affair**, as the requested bribe was called, spread across the country. "Millions for defense, but not one cent for tribute!" became the rallying cry of the American people. Fearing war, Adams asked Congress to expand the navy to a fleet of more than 30 ships. He also wanted to keep a peacetime army of several thousand troops. Congress approved both measures.

CONNECTING TO MATH

Just the Facts

Building the National Defense

Year	Total Federal Budget (in dollars)	Defense Spending (in dollars)
1792	5,080,000	1,101,000
1793	4,482,000	1,130,000
1794	6,991,000	2,700,000
1795	7,540,000	2,892,000
1796	5,727,000	1,535,000
1797	6,134,000	1,422,000
1798	7,677,000	3,391,000*
1799	9,666,000	5,325,000
1800	10,786,000	6,010,000

*The Department of the Navy was created in 1798.

Using Mathematical Skills

1. How much did military spending decrease from 1795 to 1796? How much did the total federal budget increase from 1796 to 1800? How much of this increase was military spending?

2. Create a line graph that compares the total federal budget from 1792 to 1800 with defense spending for those same years.

3. Imagine that you are a Federalist or Republican in 1800. Use these statistics to write a speech for your presidential candidate. Make your speech either in favor of or against President Adams's spending policies.

However, Adams did not ask Congress to declare war and instead tried to reopen peace talks. He believed that many people in the United States and France were against war. Adams was also worried about the cost of a war. Despite his efforts, American and French ships began fighting each other in the Caribbean.

Adams's opposition to a war stunned many Federalists. Some insulted him in speeches or essays. Hamilton even worked to weaken the president's power, but Adams refused to change his mind. In 1800 the United States and France finally signed a treaty that stopped fighting between American and French ships. Adams then forced two members of his cabinet to resign for trying to block his peace efforts.

✔ **Reading Check: Analyzing Information** What problems arose between France and the United States, and how did President Adams try to solve them?

★ The Alien and Sedition Acts

Republicans criticized Adams for making the military stronger. They also attacked the Federalists for supporting war with France. Many Federalists saw these attacks as disloyal. They said that the country needed to be protected from Republican traitors.

Federalists in Congress passed the **Alien and Sedition Acts** in the summer of 1798. The Alien Act allowed the president to have foreign residents removed from the country. They could be removed if the president believed they were involved "in any treasonable or secret machinations [plots] against the government." The Sedition Act stated that U.S. citizens could not join any plots against the government's policies. The act also made it illegal to "write, print, utter or publish" any false or hostile words against the government or its policies.

These laws were applied mostly against Republican newspapers. In some cases the editors of newspapers were arrested. Federalists even had Republican representative Matthew Lyon arrested for speaking out against the government. French citizens living in the United States also began to leave the country.

Jefferson and Madison decided to strike back with the **Kentucky and Virginia Resolutions**. The states' legislatures passed these resolutions in 1798 and 1799. Madison wrote the Virginia Resolutions, and Jefferson wrote the Kentucky Resolutions.

THE GRANGER COLLECTION, NEW YORK

Interpreting the Visual Record

Alien and Sedition Acts *In 1798 Federalist congressman Roger Griswald attacked Republican Matthew Lyon during an angry debate over the Alien and Sedition Acts.* **How are the other representatives responding to the fight?**

They stated that the Alien and Sedition Acts were unconstitutional. Madison and Jefferson claimed that the federal government did not have the power to pass such laws and that the acts interfered with the state government. Jefferson explained their views. "Whensoever the general government assumes undelegated [unassigned] powers, its acts are unauthoritative [without authority], void, and of no force."

Madison and Jefferson said that state governments could ignore any federal laws that they found to be unconstitutional. To avoid such a conflict, they asked Congress to repeal the Alien and Sedition Acts. Congress refused. The acts remained in effect until a later Congress decided not to renew them. However, the resolutions had an important impact on the idea of states' rights. They gave support to the idea that state governments could challenge the federal government. This precedent would help other politicians who wanted to declare laws or actions of the federal government to be illegal.

✔ **Reading Check: Drawing Inferences and Conclusions** How did the Alien and Sedition Acts pose a threat to freedom of speech and freedom of the press, and why was this important?

CONNECTING TO
SCIENCE AND TECHNOLOGY

The USS *Constitution*

To protect American merchant ships, in 1794 Congress decided to create a small navy. The USS *Constitution* became the most famous ship of this first fleet. The ship's toughness in battle gained it the popular nickname "Old Ironsides." When the *Constitution* became too old for active duty, the U.S. Navy preserved it for future generations. After 200 years it remains the world's oldest commissioned warship afloat. Tourists now visit Old Ironsides to touch a part of history. Why do you think Old Ironsides is respected today?

Gun deck: holds main guns used for long-range fighting

Spar deck: holds small cannons used for close-range fighting

Berthing deck: used as sailors' sleeping quarters

Hold: used to store supplies and ammunition

★ The Election Of 1800

Despite the problems his administration had faced, Adams decided to run for re-election. In the presidential election of 1800, Thomas Jefferson and Aaron Burr ran against Adams and Charles C. Pinckney. During the campaign the Republicans challenged the legality of the Alien and Sedition Acts. They criticized Adams's creation of a permanent army and the higher taxes needed to pay for it. In addition, Republicans said that Adams had hurt relations between France and the United States. The nation's leading Republican newspaper favored Jefferson.

 History Makers Speak

❝The friends of *peace will vote for Jefferson*— the friends of war will vote for *Adams* or for *Pinckney*.❞

—The *Philadelphia Aurora*, quoted in *In Pursuit of Reason*, by Noble E. Cunningham Jr.

The Federalists answered by calling Jefferson a pro-French revolutionary. If elected, they said, he would ruin the country. They also said that Jefferson, who was deeply interested in science and philosophy, was against organized religion. In response, Republicans reminded voters that Jefferson was the author of the Declaration of Independence. He could certainly be trusted to protect the liberties of all Americans.

Jefferson actively sought support, while Adams took little part in his own campaign. He believed that the people would judge him on his political record. Alexander Hamilton again worked against Adams, publishing a highly critical essay. By doing this, he caused further division among the Federalists.

★ A Narrow Republican Victory

Jefferson and Burr won 73 electoral votes each to 65 for Adams and 64 for Pinckney. The Republicans had won the election, but the tie caused a problem. At that time there were no votes for the vice president—the runner-up won this office. Both Jefferson and Burr were eligible for the presidency. The decision went to the House of Representatives.

The Federalists in the House refused to vote for Jefferson as president and tried to elect Burr. Meanwhile, the Republicans voted for Jefferson, resulting in another tie and another vote. This process was repeated more than 30 times. Finally, about half of the Federalists simply refused to vote for anybody. Because he trusted Jefferson more than Burr, Hamilton worked on Jefferson's behalf. The Republicans were thus able to elect Jefferson. The problems with the voting system led Congress to propose the **Twelfth Amendment** in 1803. This

Analyzing Primary Sources
Evaluating Sources Do you think the newspaper is making a fair statement? Explain your answer.

Bitterness between Hamilton and Burr over the 1800 election and other issues eventually led to this duel, in which Burr killed Hamilton.

THE GRANGER COLLECTION, NEW YORK

amendment created a separate ballot for president and vice president. The states passed it in September 1804 before the next election.

Their loss in the presidential election weakened the Federalists, and Adams retired from public life. For many years following the election, Adams and Jefferson did not speak to each other. However, their respect for one another finally led them to renew their friendship.

Jefferson believed the transfer of power between parties showed the strengths of the U.S. system of government. Later, he wrote to a friend about the achievement that some Americans called the Revolution of 1800.

This campaign banner was used by Jefferson's supporters in the election of 1800.

> **History Makers Speak** ❝[The election was] as real a revolution in the principles of our government as that of 1776 was in its form; not effected [caused] indeed by the sword, as that [was], but by the rational and peaceable instrument of reform, the suffrage [vote] of the people.❞
>
> —Thomas Jefferson, quoted in *In Pursuit of Reason,* by Noble E. Cunningham Jr.

Analyzing Primary Sources

Identifying Points of View Why did Jefferson think the election was revolutionary?

To Jefferson, his victory was the triumph of the people. In addition, it proved that his faith in the intelligence of the everyday citizen was justified.

✔ **Reading Check: Finding the Main Idea** How did Jefferson win the presidency?

Section 5 Review

go.hrw.com **Homework Practice Online** keyword: SF3 HP10

1 **Define** and explain:
• political parties

2 **Identify** and explain:
• Federalist Party
• Democratic-Republican Party
• XYZ affair
• Alien and Sedition Acts
• Kentucky and Virginia Resolutions
• Twelfth Amendment

3 **Identifying Cause and Effect** Use the diagram to explain why the Federalist and Republican Parties were formed and how they influenced the 1796 presidential election.

Reasons → Federalist Party → 1796 Election
Reasons → Republican Party → 1796 Election

4 **Finding the Main Idea**
a. How did John Adams address U.S. problems with France?

b. What were the key issues of the election of 1800, and how did the outcome affect the political process?

5 **Writing and Critical Thinking**
Supporting a Point of View Imagine that you are a newspaper editor who does not belong to either the Federalist or Republican Party. Write an editorial in response to the Alien and Sedition Acts and the Kentucky and Virginia Resolutions.

Consider the following:
• the extent of the powers of the federal government
• how the Alien and Sedition Acts were used
• the constitutional right to freedom of speech and freedom of the press

Chapter 10 Review

The Chapter at a Glance

Examine the visual summary of the chapter below. Write a paragraph describing the challenges that faced the new nation, leaving out the dates for key events. Have a classmate read the paragraph and fill in the missing dates.

Domestic Events

1789: Washington becomes president.

1790: The federal government assumes state debts. Washington, D. C., is declared the U.S. capital.

1791: The Bank of the United States is established.

1794: U.S. troops win the Battle of Fallen Timbers. The Whiskey Rebellion takes place.

1796: Washington gives his Farewell Address. John Adams is elected president.

1798: Congress passes the Alien and Sedition Acts.

1800: Thomas Jefferson is elected president.

International Events

1789: The French Revolution begins.

1794: Jay's Treaty is signed by Britain and the United States.

1795: Pinckney's Treaty with Spain reopens the port of New Orleans.

1798: The XYZ affair takes place in France.

Identifying People and Ideas

Use the following terms or people in historically significant sentences.

1. George Washington
2. Judiciary Act of 1789
3. protective tariff
4. Bank of the United States
5. Neutrality Proclamation
6. Jay's Treaty
7. Little Turtle
8. Whiskey Rebellion
9. political parties
10. XYZ affair

Understanding Main Ideas

Section 1 *(Pages 300–303)*

1. Describe how Washington and the first Congress organized the government.

Section 2 *(Pages 304–309)*

2. Why did Congress create a national bank, and what challenges did it face in doing this?

Section 3 *(Pages 310–314)*

3. What did Jay's Treaty and Pinckney's Treaty achieve?

Section 4 *(Pages 315–318)*

4. Why was the Whiskey Rebellion significant?
5. What issues concerned Washington when he retired?

Section 5 *(Pages 319–325)*

6. When were the Federalist Party and the Democratic-Republican Party formed, and what were their policies?
7. What effect did the Alien and Sedition Acts have on the Republicans?

You Be the Historian— Reviewing Themes

1. **Global Relations** How did Presidents Washington and Adams address foreign-policy issues?
2. **Constitutional Heritage** What constitutional issues did Alexander Hamilton confront when he proposed the creation of a national bank?
3. **Economics** How did Alexander Hamilton propose handling federal and state debts, and why?

Thinking Critically

1. **Supporting a Point of View** What qualities do you think made George Washington a good leader?
2. **Summarizing** What issues led to debates over the power of the federal government in the early republic, and how were these issues resolved?
3. **Drawing Inferences and Conclusions** Why do you think the Republican Party was more popular in the South and along the western frontier?

Interpreting Political Cartoons

Study the political cartoon of the XYZ affair below. Then answer the questions that follow.

THE GRANGER COLLECTION, NEW YORK

1. Which of the following statements best describes the main message of the cartoon?
   a. American diplomats are willing to take bribes and cannot be trusted.
   b. The Americans and the French were too different from each other to reach any kind of peace agreement.
   c. French officials are corrupt and dangerous but cannot frighten American officials.
   d. Americans should be willing to pay bribes to French agents if it will help achieve peace.

2. Why do you think the artist chose to portray the French agents as a many-headed monster? Do you think this cartoon supports going to war with France or not? Explain your answer.

Analyzing Primary Sources

Read the following quote by Secretary of the Treasury Alexander Hamilton, who argued that the Constitution allowed for the creation of a national bank. Then answer the questions that follow.

"A bank has a direct relation to the [constitutional] power of borrowing money. . . . The essentiality of such an institution . . . is exemplified at this very moment. An Indian expedition is to be prosecuted [performed]. The only fund out of which the money can arise . . . is a tax, which only begins to be collected in July next. The preparations, however, are instantly to be made. The money must, therefore, be borrowed—and of whom could it be borrowed if there were no public banks? It happens that there are institutions of this kind, but if there were none, it would be indispensable [necessary] to create one."

3. Which of the following statements best describes the author's point of view?
   a. The Constitution gives the federal government the power to borrow money to pay for Indian expeditions.
   b. It would be easier to defend the United States if there were a national bank.
   c. A national bank is necessary because Congress might need to borrow money to provide for an emergency or for national defense.
   d. Congress has the power to collect taxes in July.

4. Why does Hamilton think that banks are important for the economy?

5. Based on what you know about the time, why might Congress need to use its constitutional power to borrow money?

Alternative Assessment

American History

Building Your Portfolio

Interdisciplinary Connection to Geography
Learn more about the geographic history of present-day Washington, D.C. Discover what the area was like before the capital was founded and how the city has changed over time. Find the location of at least 10 major buildings or landmarks, such as the Capitol Building or the Washington Monument. Then create a city map that displays what you have learned.

internet connect

Internet Activity: go.hrw.com
keyword: SF3 CF10

Access the Internet through the HRW Go site to locate primary and secondary sources such as databases and media and news services. Use these resources to learn about the Alien and Sedition Acts of 1798 and the Pentagon Papers case during the Vietnam War. Then use a computer word-processing program to write a report outlining the connection between a free and a democratic society.

go.hrw.com

Social Studies Skills
WORKSHOP

Interpreting a Time Line

Time lines display events in chronological order—the sequence in which the events occurred. Knowing the proper sequence of historical events helps you understand their significance. Time lines allow you to see relationships between events and help you to remember the dates of important events.

Sequence in a Time Line Time lines are meant to be read from left to right, with the oldest dates on the left. The lines of the time line mark the time period between each event. For example, the lines might mark 10-, 5-, or 1-year periods. Each entry on the time line lists an important event and when it took place. These entries provide you with a sequence of events and may suggest a relationship to one another.

B.C. and A.D. Sometimes a time line will contain the abbreviations B.C. and A.D. The abbreviation B.C. stands for "before Christ." A.D. stands for "anno Domini," which means "in the year of

the Lord." The year 1 B.C. was followed by A.D. 1. There was no year "0." When you read dates marked B.C. or A.D., remember that the abbreviation B.C. appears after the year—for example, 100 B.C. The abbreviation A.D. appears before the year—for example, A.D. 100.

How to Read a Time Line

1. **Determine its framework.** Note the years covered and the intervals of time into which the time line is divided.

2. **Study the sequence of events.** Study the order of events on the time line and the length of time between events.

3. **Supply missing information.** Think about the people, places, and other events associated with each item on the time line.

4. **Note relationships.** Ask yourself how an event relates to earlier or later events. Look for cause-and-effect relationships and long-term developments.

1777 The Continental Congress approves the Articles of Confederation on November 15.	**1781** On March 1 the Articles of Confederation go into effect after being ratified by all 13 states.	**1787** On May 14, state delegates begin to arrive at the Constitutional Convention in Philadelphia. The final draft of the Constitution is signed on September 17.	**1788** On June 21 the Constitution is ratified by the required 9 out of 13 states.
1776	**1780**	**1784**	**1790**

Practicing the Skills

Study the time line above, which lists some important events in the history of the United States between 1776 and 1790. Then answer the following questions.

1. Into what periods is the time line divided?
2. How much time passed between the ratification of

the Articles of Confederation and the ratification of the Constitution?

3. Create your own time line, listing several significant events in U.S. history that occurred during a span of at least five years.

History in Action

UNIT 4 SIMULATION

You Solve the Problem . . .

How Should the President of the United States Be Selected?

Complete the following activity in small cooperative groups. It is early 1787. You are a delegate at the Constitutional Convention. The Convention has agreed upon the requirements for the candidates for the presidency: at least 35 years old, natural-born citizen, and a 14-year resident of the United States. Now you must give a presentation to the Constitutional Convention that suggests how the chief executive of the United States should be selected. Follow these steps to solve your problem.

1. Gather Information. Use your textbook and other resources to find information that might influence your plan of action for selecting a president. Be sure to use what you learned from this unit's Skills Workshop on Interpreting a Time Line to help you find an effective solution to the problem. For example, you might consider how often a new president should be selected. You may want to divide different parts of the research among group members.

2. List and Consider Options. Based on the information you have gathered, list and consider the options you might recommend for selecting a president. Your final solution to the problem may be easier to reach if you consider as many options as possible. Be sure to record your possible options for your presentation.

3. Consider Advantages and Disadvantages. Now consider the advantages and disadvantages of taking each option. Ask yourselves questions like: "Will all citizens be able to participate in the process?" Once you have considered the advantages and disadvantages, record them as notes for your presentation.

4. Choose, Implement, and Evaluate a Solution. After considering the advantages and disadvantages, you should plan and create a presentation. Be sure to make your proposal very clear. You will need to support your proposed method of selecting the president by including information you gathered and by explaining why you rejected other options. Your presentation needs to be visually appealing to the Constitutional Convention. When you are ready, decide which group members will make each part of the presentation, and then take your solution to Constitutional Convention (the rest of the class). Good luck!

Young People

IN HISTORY

Young Explorers

In 1804 Meriwether Lewis and William Clark set out on an expedition to the western lands of the Louisiana Purchase. At age 18 George Shannon was the youngest member of their Corps of Discovery. Lewis described this group as the "best young woodsmen & Hunters in this part of the Countery." Shannon excelled at his work and was put in charge of some expedition duties.

In late August 1804 Shannon failed to return after a day of hunting in Sioux Indian territory. Lewis and Clark sent out a search party, but it failed to find the young man, who had accidentally moved ahead of the group. Thinking he was actually behind the others, Shannon kept traveling westward as fast as he could.

Over time, he used all his bullets and was unable to hunt for food. He survived for a few weeks on plums and grapes. After becoming too weak to continue, Shannon sat down on a riverbank. He hoped that a trading boat might pass by. Instead, his friends rescued him! On September 11, 1804, the expedition rounded a bend in the Missouri River. To their surprise, they found an exhausted and hungry Shannon.

Shannon was one of many young adventurers who set their sights westward in the 1800s. William Swift and Titian Peale were two young men who accompanied Stephen Long on his expedition in 1819. Swift was 18 years old, and Peale was 19. They traveled along the Missouri River and into the western plains. Swift was hired to prepare a map of the territory, while Peale went along as an assistant naturalist.

Other teenagers explored the West as fur trappers. When he was about 18, Jim Bridger traveled to the upper Missouri River on a trapping expedition. Two years later, Bridger discovered what looked like a great shallow bay. Tasting the salty water, he reported he had found part of the Pacific Ocean. However, historians later determined that Bridger had actually seen the Great Salt Lake in what is now Utah.

Young frontiersmen, like those shown here, were an important part of the Lewis and Clark expedition.

If You Were There *What would you do if you got lost in the wilderness?*

LEFT PAGE: *Crossing the Rocky Mountains was one of the most difficult challenges facing western explorers.*

11 The Expanding Nation
(1800–1815)

Explorers Lewis and Clark kept several journals, including this one bound in elk skin.

Sacagawea helped Lewis and Clark travel through the Rockies and on to the Pacific Northwest.

THE GRANGER COLLECTION, NEW YORK

UNITED STATES

1801 Thomas Jefferson takes office as president.

1803 The U.S. Senate approves the Louisiana Purchase.

1804 Meriwether Lewis and William Clark set out to explore the Louisiana Territory.

1800	1802	1804	1806

WORLD

1803 France and Great Britain go to war.

1804 Napoléon becomes emperor of France.

1806 The Holy Roman Empire officially ends.

1807 The slave trade is abolished in the British Empire.

At the last minute, Napoléon took the crown from Pope Pius VII and placed it on his own head.

Build on What You Know

By 1800, Federalists knew they had lost control of both the presidency and Congress to their Republican rivals. During his presidency, Thomas Jefferson greatly expanded the size of the United States. The young nation also came into conflict with France and Great Britain.

Americans did not learn that the Treaty of Ghent had ended the War of 1812 until they had already fought the last battle.

British forces charged the walls built by General Andrew Jackson's troops in the Battle of New Orleans.

1809 President Jefferson signs the Non-Intercourse Act.

1811 William Henry Harrison's troops win the Battle of Tippecanoe against American Indian forces led by Tecumseh.

1812 Congress declares war on Great Britain.

1814 On August 24, British soldiers burn the city of Washington.

Federalist delegates from New England hold the Hartford Convention on December 15.

1815 Andrew Jackson leads U.S. soldiers to victory over the British in the Battle of New Orleans.

1808   **1810**   **1812**   **1814**

1808 Napoléon names his brother Joseph as king of Spain.

1811 Paraguay becomes the first Spanish colony in South America to gain independence.

1814 European nations meet at the Congress of Vienna to reorganize Europe after the fall of Napoléon.

If you were there . . .
How might you react to the election of Thomas Jefferson?

You Be the Historian

Themes Journal

What's Your Opinion? Do you **agree** or **disagree** with the following statements? Support your point of view in your journal.

- **Constitutional Heritage** The Supreme Court should have power equal to the president and Congress.

- **Geography** Nations do not need to explore new territories that they acquire.

- **Global Relations** Nations that share borders are likely to fight wars against each other.

Jefferson as President

Read to Discover

1. What views did Thomas Jefferson express about political parties in his first inaugural address?
2. What Republican policies did Jefferson introduce, and which Federalist policies did he accept?
3. Why was *Marbury* v. *Madison* an important court case?

WHY IT MATTERS TODAY

Americans go to the polls to elect their president as well as many other officials. Use **CNNfyi.com** or other **current events** sources to learn about the policies of an elected official. Record your findings in your journal.

Define

- judicial review

Identify

- Thomas Jefferson
- William Marbury
- John Marshall
- *Marbury* v. *Madison*

These coins celebrate Jefferson's inauguration.

The Story Continues

The day was March 4, 1801. Thomas Jefferson was about to become president of the United States. Washington and Adams had taken carriages to their inaugurations, or swearing-in ceremonies. Jefferson, however, chose to walk to the Capitol Building. Jefferson also decided not to wear fancy clothes. A reporter wrote, "His dress was, as usual, that of a plain citizen, without any distinctive badge of office."

☆ The Republican Victory

A large crowd attended the inauguration of **Thomas Jefferson**, yet former president John Adams was absent. He was so upset by his defeat that he left the city. One observer who attended the inauguration called it "one of the most interesting scenes a free people can ever witness." The crowd was celebrating more than Jefferson's election. Along with his victory, the Republican Party had also won control of both houses of Congress. As a result, Jefferson would have the support of Congress for many of his plans. The inauguration marked the first time that one political party had replaced another in power in the United States. Many Americans saw the election of Jefferson as proof that the country could change leaders peacefully. That was a rare achievement for a government at the time.

Interpreting the Visual Record

Monticello *Among his many talents, President Jefferson was a fine architect. He designed his magnificent home, Monticello.* **What does this image suggest about Jefferson's background?**

Jefferson read his carefully written speech in a quiet voice. He wanted to make it clear that he supported the will of the majority. However, he did not favor mob rule, as some Federalists had claimed. In his speech, Jefferson tried to comfort the Federalists still in the government by promising to run the government fairly.

History Makers Speak

66We are all Republicans, we are all Federalists. . . . Let us, then, with courage and confidence pursue our . . . attachment to union and representative government.99

—Thomas Jefferson, First Inaugural Address

Analyzing Primary Sources

Drawing Inferences and Conclusions Why do you think Jefferson said "We are all Republicans, we are all Federalists"?

After taking the oath of office, Jefferson walked back down New Jersey Avenue to his boardinghouse. There he met with supporters and friends.

✔ **Reading Check: Finding the Main Idea** What was significant about the Republican victory in 1800?

⭐ Jefferson in Office

President Jefferson faced the task of putting his Republican ideas into practice. First, he selected the members of his cabinet. He chose James Madison as secretary of state and Albert Gallatin as secretary of the treasury. Together they set new Republican policies. Jefferson lowered military spending, reducing the size of the army to about 3,200 troops. The navy was cut to seven active ships. Jefferson and Gallatin hoped that the money saved would allow the government to repay the national debt. Jefferson also asked Gallatin to find ways to get rid of domestic taxes, like the tax on whiskey. They even wanted to close down the government agency that collected such taxes. The Republican-led Congress passed the laws needed to carry out these policies.

Jefferson did keep some programs established by the Federalists. Even though he had opposed the Bank of the United States, he agreed to let the Bank continue as it had under the Federalists. Whatever its faults, the banking system created by Hamilton seemed practical to Jefferson.

★ ★ ★ ★ ★ ★ ★ ★ ★ ★ ★ ★
That's Interesting!
★ ★ ★ ★ ★ ★ ★ ★ ★ ★ ★ ★

Capital under Construction Did you know that when Jefferson became president, the city of Washington was not even finished? It's true! The streets of Washington were muddy and filled with tree stumps. Some people complained that the city had only "a few bad houses, [and] extensive swamps." The weather was also hot and humid. During the summers most people, including President Jefferson, left the capital to avoid the danger of disease. However, Washington went on to become a large and impressive city. Jefferson later said that he was proud to be a part of building the new U.S. capital.

PRESIDENTIAL PROFILES

Thomas Jefferson

Thomas Jefferson was born in 1743 to a family of Virginia plantation owners. He became a man of many talents. He attended private schools as a child and kept learning throughout his life. Jefferson loved architecture, art, farming, philosophy, and science. He put his studies to practical use. For example, he designed Monticello, his grand home on his Virginia plantation. Jefferson was a wealthy man who held more than 150 slaves. He became a member of the Virginia House of Burgesses in 1769. Jefferson was ambassador to France, secretary of state, and vice president before his two terms as president. Thomas Jefferson died on July 4, 1826, the 50th anniversary of the signing of the Declaration of Independence. **In what ways did Thomas Jefferson serve his country?**

This document presents the Supreme Court's decision in Marbury v. Madison.

The president faced a difficult challenge soon after he was sworn into office. Jefferson had planned to keep many Federalists in their government jobs. However, many from his party expected the president to replace all Federalists with Republicans. The New York *American Citizen*, a pro-Republican newspaper, expressed this view. "If this should not be the case, for what . . . have we been contending [struggling]?" Federalists were equally unhappy with Jefferson. They complained that his military spending cuts put the country in danger.

Under pressure from both parties, Jefferson finally agreed to replace a number of Federalist officials with Republicans. However, he refused to replace them all. He also stuck to his ideas on government spending.

✔ **Reading Check: Summarizing** What problems did Jefferson face when he took office, and what Republican policies did Jefferson introduce to solve them?

★ *Marbury v. Madison*

Early in 1801, before Jefferson took office, Federalists in Congress passed a new law that created many new judgeships and other court offices. Before his term ended, President John Adams had appointed dozens of Federalists to fill these positions. Jefferson accused Adams of filling these positions "till 9 o'clock of the night, at 12 o'clock of which he was to go out of office." Other Republicans called the people chosen by Adams "midnight judges."

When Jefferson entered office on March 4, 1801, some Federalists chosen by Adams had not yet received their special commissions. Without these forms they could not begin working as judges. Jefferson took advantage of this fact. He ordered Secretary of State James Madison not to give out the papers. **William Marbury** was one of the people affected by this decision. He demanded that the Supreme Court force the executive branch to hand over his commission. The Court had never done such a thing. However, Marbury claimed that the Judiciary Act of 1789 gave the Supreme Court the right to do so.

The chief justice of the United States was **John Marshall**, a Federalist appointed by Adams. Marshall and President Jefferson disagreed about many political issues. When Marshall agreed to hear Marbury's case, Jefferson protested, complaining that the Federalists "have retired into the judiciary as a stronghold." He was concerned that Marshall would make sure that "all the works of republicanism are to be beaten down and erased."

The Supreme Court's decision in ***Marbury v. Madison*** surprised many people, including Jefferson. All the justices agreed that Marbury had been treated unfairly. But did the Supreme Court have the power to force Madison to give Marbury his commission? The Judiciary Act of 1789 said the Court did. Chief Justice Marshall said the Court did not.

His reason was simple. He did not think that the Constitution allowed Congress to give the Supreme Court new powers. The Judiciary Act of 1789, he believed, had wrongly given the Court such a power. In other words, the act was unconstitutional—meaning it did something not allowed by the Constitution. Therefore, the Supreme Court did not have the power to force the federal government to give Marbury his commission.

Marshall seemed to be giving up a power of the Supreme Court. But he was really claiming a much greater power. Marshall's ruling established the power of **judicial review**. This power allows the Supreme Court to declare an act of Congress to be unconstitutional. Such a law is then no longer in force. Marshall strongly defended judicial review in his written decision.

 History Makers Speak "It is, emphatically [absolutely], the province and duty of the Judicial Department to say what the law is. . . . The Constitution is superior to any ordinary act of the legislature."

—John Marshall, *Marbury* v. *Madison*

Interpreting the Visual Record

Chief Justice *John Marshall served as the fourth chief justice of the Supreme Court.* **Why was Marshall's ruling in the** Marbury v. Madison *case so significant?*

Judicial review greatly increased the Supreme Court's legal authority. As a result, the Court became a much stronger branch within the national government.

✔ **Reading Check: Evaluating** What leadership qualities did Chief Justice John Marshall show in the *Marbury* v. *Madison* ruling?

Section 1 Review

go.hrw.com **Homework Practice Online**
keyword: SF3 HP11

1 **Define** and explain:
• judicial review

2 **Identify** and explain:
• Thomas Jefferson
• William Marbury
• John Marshall
• *Marbury* v. *Madison*

3 **Categorizing** Copy the chart below. Use it to show how President Jefferson continued some Federalist policies while introducing Republican policies.

Jefferson as President

Federalist Policies	Republican Policies

4 **Finding the Main Idea**
a. What were the major issues Thomas Jefferson discussed in his First Inaugural Address?

b. What did Jefferson hope to accomplish by changing Federalist policies on military spending and taxes?

5 **Writing and Critical Thinking**
Supporting a Point of View Imagine that you are a Supreme Court justice reviewing *Marbury* v. *Madison*. Write an opinion expressing your support for either Marbury or Madison.

Consider the following:
• "midnight judges"
• Judiciary Act of 1789
• judicial review

The Louisiana Purchase

Read to Discover

1. How and why did the Louisiana Purchase take place?
2. What did the Lewis and Clark expedition achieve?
3. What was the purpose of Pike's expedition?

WHY IT MATTERS TODAY

People continue to explore Earth and beyond. Use CNNfyi.com or other **current events** sources to learn about one area being explored today. Record your findings in your journal.

Identify

- Napoléon Bonaparte
- Toussaint-Louverture
- Louisiana Purchase
- Meriwether Lewis
- William Clark
- Lewis and Clark expedition
- Sacagawea
- Zebulon Pike

The Story Continues

As Spain's rivals grew stronger, it struggled to hold on to its American empire. Spanish foreign minister Manuel de Godoy worried about how to keep American settlers out of the Spanish territory of Louisiana. "You can't put doors on open country," he said in despair. Years of effort failed to improve Spain's position. Under a secret treaty, Spain traded Louisiana to France, passing the problem on to someone else. One Spanish officer expressed his relief at leaving. "I can hardly wait to leave them [the Americans] behind me," he said.

The Spanish flag flew over New Orleans after Spain took control of the city in 1762.

⭐ French Louisiana

In 1800 France was led by General **Napoléon Bonaparte** (nuh-POH-lee-uhn BOH-nuh-pahrt). His political ambition and military skill caused fear across Europe. As he conquered neighboring countries, Napoléon also dreamed of rebuilding France's empire in North America. First, he wanted to send troops to Louisiana. Then France would replace Spain as the key European power in western North America.

Standing in the way of this plan was the former French colony of St. Domingue (present-day Haiti). The colony was located on the Caribbean island of Hispaniola. Enslaved Africans had gained their freedom by taking over the colony in the 1790s, and former slave

Toussaint-Louverture (too-san-loo-ver-toohr) ruled the island. Before sending troops to Louisiana, Napoléon needed to take back the island to use as a supply base. However, Toussaint's troops defeated the French forces sent to recapture St. Domingue in 1802. This defeat kept Napoléon from sending troops to Louisiana.

U.S. leaders became suspicious of Napoléon when they learned France once again owned Louisiana. President Jefferson knew that France could block the westward growth of the United States. The French could also interfere with American trade. Jefferson worried that from New Orleans, France could control American trade along the Mississippi River.

New Orleans was founded by the French in 1718 and came under Spanish rule in 1762. The city remained Spanish for some 40 years before returning to French control. Its busy docks were filled with settlers' farm products and valuable furs bought from American Indians. Many of these cargoes were then sent to Europe. At the same time, manufactured goods passed through the port on their way upriver. The city was also home to many languages and cultures, such as African, English, French, and Spanish. New Orleans soon became the focus of Jefferson's foreign policy.

THE GRANGER COLLECTION, NEW YORK

Toussaint-Louverture played a key role in the founding of the nation of Haiti.

✔ **Reading Check: Making Generalizations and Predictions** How do you think Napoléon's failure to regain control of Haiti would affect his plans for North America?

⭐ The Louisiana Purchase

President Jefferson wanted to keep the French from controlling New Orleans, but he did not want to start a war. He hoped that the United States could find a peaceful answer.

Jefferson told the U.S. ambassador to France, Robert R. Livingston, to try to buy New Orleans and West Florida. Jefferson sent James Monroe to help Livingston. Livingston met with Talleyrand, the French foreign minister, to discuss the offer. Talleyrand said that without New Orleans "the rest [of Louisiana] would be of little value" to France. Then he asked what the United States would "give for the whole." The stunned Americans realized that France was offering to sell all of Louisiana.

Napoléon was willing to sell Louisiana for a number of reasons. France was about to go to war against Great Britain. Napoléon also did not want to fight the United States and Britain at once. In addition, the French still had no troops in Louisiana. Instead of more territory, Napoléon now wanted money to buy supplies for his armies in Europe. He also realized that if the United States owned Louisiana, it could challenge Britain's power in North America. "I have given England a rival who, sooner or later, will humble her pride," he boasted.

Livingston and Monroe were eager to take advantage of this sudden opportunity. Congress had only authorized them to offer $10 million. However, the ambassadors agreed to buy Louisiana from France for

October 20, 1803
The U.S. Senate approves the Louisiana Purchase.

Louisiana Purchase treaty and seals

about $15 million. They signed a treaty of purchase on May 2, 1803. Like Livingston and Monroe, Jefferson was pleased when he learned about the chance to buy all of Louisiana. But as a strict constructionist, Jefferson did not believe that the Constitution allowed him to buy the territory. However, Livingston and Monroe feared that the French might take back their offer, so they pushed the president to act quickly. Doing what he thought best for the country, Jefferson agreed to the purchase. On October 20, 1803, the Senate approved the treaty.

With the **Louisiana Purchase**, the size of the United States almost doubled. The Louisiana Territory was a huge region of land, stretching west from the Mississippi River all the way to the great Rocky Mountains. The exact boundaries of the territory were not yet clearly defined. President Jefferson was pleased that the land offered so much room for the United States to grow. He said proudly that the Louisiana Purchase expanded "the empire of liberty." He believed it would provide "a widespread field for the blessings of freedom."

✔ **Reading Check: Summarizing** What happened to U.S. territory in 1803, and why was this important to the future of the United States?

The Louisiana Purchase

Interpreting Maps Meriwether Lewis and William Clark, and later Zebulon Pike, led expeditions to explore the vast Louisiana Territory.

Skills Assessment The World in Spatial Terms From which city did both the Lewis and Clark and the Pike expeditions begin?

⭐ Mission of Discovery

Americans knew little about western American Indians or the lands they inhabited. Jefferson wanted to learn more about the people and land of the West. He also wanted to see if there was a river route that could be taken to the Pacific Ocean. In January 1803 the president asked Congress to fund a small western expedition. To lead it, he chose former army captain **Meriwether Lewis**. Lewis had served as his presidential assistant. Jefferson described Lewis as "brave, prudent [careful], habituated [used] to the woods, and familiar with Indian manners and character." Lewis chose Lieutenant **William Clark** to be the co-leader of the expedition. Jefferson told Lewis and Clark to explore the Missouri River. He wanted them to form peaceful relations with American Indians they met. Jefferson added a long list of other directions.

> **History Makers Speak** ❝The commerce which may be carried on with the people inhabiting the line you will pursue, renders [makes] a knowledge of these people important. . . . Other objects worthy of notice will be the soil and face of the country, its growth and vegetable productions . . . the animals of the country . . . mineral productions of every kind . . . [and the area's] climate.❞
>
> —Thomas Jefferson, quoted in *The Journals of Lewis and Clark*, edited by Frank Bergon

To prepare for the journey, Lewis spent weeks studying with experts about botany, surveying, and other subjects. This knowledge would allow him to take careful notes on what he saw. He also gathered supplies for the journey. With Clark, Lewis carefully selected skilled frontiersmen for their Corps of Discovery.

Interpreting the Visual Record

Lewis and Clark *Although Lewis and Clark tried to appear confident and powerful, they depended on the goodwill of American Indians they met.* **With what kinds of situations do you think the Indian guides in the picture might help Lewis and Clark?**

Analyzing Primary Sources

Summarizing What kind of information did Jefferson want Lewis and Clark to collect on their journey?

William Clark's journal contained illustrations and written descriptions of his travels.

Research on the ROM

Free Find:
From Lewis's Journal
After reading about Lewis's journal on the **Holt Researcher CD–ROM**, imagine that you are traveling with Lewis and Clark. Write your own journal entry for a typical day on the expedition.

⭐ The Lewis and Clark Expedition

In May 1804 the **Lewis and Clark expedition** began its long journey. The group set out from St. Louis, in present-day Missouri. The Corps of Discovery traveled up the Missouri River to the lands of the Mandan and the Sioux. Lewis used interpreters to talk to the leaders of each of the peoples they met. He told them that the United States now owned the land on which the American Indians lived. **Sacagawea** (sak-uh-juh-WEE-uh), a Shoshone from the Rocky Mountains, proved to be very helpful. Sacagawea's husband, a French fur trader who lived with the Mandan, offered to guide the expedition across the Great Plains.

Lewis and Clark kept journals describing the people, places, and animals that they encountered. Their journal entries are filled with wonder at things they saw for the first time. On the Great Plains, Lewis saw huge herds "of Buffaloe, Elk, deer, and Antelopes feeding in one common and boundless pasture." Their journals also revealed the many dangers of the journey. They told stories of sickness and conflicts with American Indians. They also described natural hazards, such as high mountains, raging rivers, and terrible storms.

After Lewis and Clark crossed the Plains, they came to the Rocky Mountains. The sight of this giant snowcapped mountain range amazed and worried Lewis. Fortunately for the explorers, the leader of the Shoshone who lived in the area was Sacagawea's brother. He provided horses and a guide to lead the expedition across the mountains. The journey was dangerous and difficult. An exhausted Lewis wrote, "We suffered everything Cold, Hunger, and Fatigue could impart [give]."

Leaving the mountains behind, Lewis and Clark followed the Columbia River, which forms the border between what are now Oregon and Washington. Along the way they met the powerful and friendly Nez Percé. Like the Shoshone, the Nez Percé provided the expedition with food. On November 7, 1805, Clark saw the Pacific Ocean. He wrote in his journal, "*Ocean in view! O! the joy.*" The expedition stayed in the Pacific Northwest during the rough winter. They traded with the Clatsop and explored the coast.

In March 1806 Lewis and Clark set out on the long trip home. The party arrived by canoe in St. Louis in late September 1806. Many people from the town lined up along the river to greet them. Clark happily wrote, "Every person . . . seemed to express great pleasure at our return."

Lewis and Clark had not found a river route across the West to the Pacific Ocean. Yet they learned much about western lands and paths across the Rockies. The explorers also established contact with many American Indian groups. They had also collected a great deal of valuable scientific information on western plants and animals.

✔ **Reading Check: Summarizing** What regions did Lewis and Clark cross, and why was their expedition important?

⭐ Pike's Exploration

The year that Lewis and Clark returned home, young army officer **Zebulon Pike** was sent on another mission to the West. He was ordered to find the starting point of the Red River. This river runs through Louisiana and along some of the northern border of present-day Texas. The United States considered the Red River to be part of the Louisiana Territory's southwestern border with New Spain. Pike may also have had instructions to spy on Spanish outposts in the Southwest.

Pike led his small expedition to the Rocky Mountains, in present-day Colorado. There he tried to climb the mountain known today as Pikes Peak. In 1807 he headed south with a few expedition members into present-day New Mexico. They struggled across mountains in the bitter winter before reaching a tributary of the Rio Grande.

Although he had passed into Spanish-held lands, Pike continued exploring. He followed the river until a group of Spanish cavalry arrested him. When stopped, Pike pointed to the Rio Grande. "What, is not this the Red River?" The Spanish were not fooled, however. They suspected Pike of being a spy and put him in jail. When he was finally released, he returned to the United States and reported on his trip. Despite his imprisonment, Pike thought there were good business opportunities for Americans in the Southwest.

THE GRANGER COLLECTION, NEW YORK

Interpreting the Visual Record

Zebulon Pike *Explorer Zebulon Pike's report on his journey offered many Americans their first description of the Southwest.* **What information do you think Pike's description contained?**

✔ **Reading Check: Supporting a Point of View** What would you do if you were Zebulon Pike and found yourself in Spanish territory?

Section 2 Review

go.hrw.com **Homework Practice Online**
keyword: SF3 HP11

★ ★

1 Identify and explain:
- Napoléon Bonaparte
- Toussaint-Louverture
- Louisiana Purchase
- Meriwether Lewis
- William Clark
- Lewis and Clark expedition
- Sacagawea
- Zebulon Pike

2 Sequencing Copy the graphic organizer below. Use it to show what events led to the Louisiana Purchase and what steps the United States took to learn about the Louisiana Territory afterward.

1.

2.

3. Louisiana Purchase

4.

5.

3 Finding the Main Idea

a. Why was France willing to sell Louisiana, and why did the United States purchase it?

b. What was the purpose of Pike's expedition, and where did he travel?

4 Writing and Critical Thinking
Summarizing Imagine that you are a soldier on the Lewis and Clark expedition. Write a diary entry describing a specific adventure on the trip.

Consider the following:
- the dangers faced on the journey
- the role of Sacagawea
- scientific knowledge gained on the expedition

The Coming of War

★★★

Read to Discover

1. Why did the United States place an embargo on France and Great Britain?
2. What did Tecumseh want to accomplish, and how successful was he?
3. Why did the United States declare war on Britain in 1812?

WHY IT MATTERS TODAY

Nations continue to use trade restrictions in their dealings with other countries. Use CNNfyi.com or other **current events** sources to learn more about an embargo—a government's refusal to buy another country's goods. Record your findings in your journal.

Define

- impressment
- embargo

Identify

- Embargo Act
- Non-Intercourse Act
- Tecumseh
- Battle of Tippecanoe
- War Hawks
- James Madison

The Barbary States were one of many threats to U.S. shipping in the late 1700s and early 1800s.

The Story Continues

In the fall of 1793 Samuel Calder wrote a desperate letter to the U.S. government. "I am very sorry to inform you of my present situation. . . . I was taken by an Algerian Cruzier [ship]." Calder went on to say that he and other Americans were being held prisoner by Algerian pirates. "We was immediately put into Chains and put to hard Labor," he wrote in despair. Calder begged for $100 so he could pay his ransom and be free again.

★ Danger on the High Seas

The state of Algiers was one of several North African lands known as the Barbary States. These countries practiced piracy and held foreign citizens captive for ransom. Many nations, including the United States, agreed to make payments to the Barbary States to protect their ships and citizens. However, U.S. officials eventually refused to pay any more and sent the U.S. Navy to end the pirate raids.

However, the United States faced greater threats on the high seas. When Great Britain and France went to war in 1803, the United States was drawn into the conflict. Each country wanted to stop the United States from supplying goods and war materials to the other. In the early 1800s Britain passed a series of acts allowing the British navy to search and seize ships carrying war supplies to France. The French quickly struck back, declaring that no country could ship goods to Britain.

Many American merchants ignored these foreign laws. As a result, the British and French navies captured many American merchant ships headed for Europe. The British also searched these ships for sailors who had run away from the British navy. The British then made these people return to British warships. This practice of pressing, or forcing, people to serve in the army or navy was called **impressment**. Sometimes U.S. citizens suffered impressment by accident.

One widely publicized example of impressment took place in June 1807. The British ship *Leopard* stopped the U.S. Navy ship *Chesapeake* and tried to remove four of its sailors. When the *Chesapeake*'s captain refused, the British opened fire and took the sailors by force. The *Chesapeake* incident angered many Americans. Attorney General Caesar A. Rodney declared that it "has excited the spirit of '76 and the whole country is literally in arms."

✔ **Reading Check: Finding the Main Idea** How did Great Britain's actions affect its relationship with the United States?

★ A Trade War

Debates raged about how the United States should respond to Great Britain's violations of U.S. neutrality. Some Americans wanted to go to war. Others favored an **embargo,** or the banning of trade, against Britain. A writer for the *Boston Chronicle* agreed. "Our trade is the most powerful weapon we can use in our defense."

Jefferson and the Republicans favored an embargo. In December 1807 Congress passed the **Embargo Act.** In effect, the law banned trade with foreign countries. Congress hoped to punish Britain and France and to protect American ships from capture. However, the act's main effect was to hurt American merchants. Without trade, they lost a great deal of money. The New England states and New York relied heavily on trade and were the most hard hit by the act.

The popularity of the Federalist Party rose, and Jefferson's support fell as the embargo continued. By December 1808 Jefferson had received 199 petitions asking him to repeal the Embargo Act. Meanwhile, the act had little effect on Britain or France. American merchants smuggled goods to Europe. The British also increased their trade with South America to replace lost U.S. trade. The U.S. minister in Paris noted that "here [the embargo] is not felt, and in England . . . it is forgotten."

GLOBAL CONNECTIONS

The Barbary Pirates

The small North African kingdoms of Algiers, Morocco, Tripoli, and Tunis—known as the Barbary States—operated pirate fleets. Like many European nations, the United States paid the Barbary States not to attack American ships. In 1801 Tripoli demanded a higher payment than normal. When the United States was slow to pay, Tripoli declared war. In response, Jefferson sent a small fleet to patrol the North African coast. Then in 1805, U.S. Marines and mercenaries marched across the desert to capture a Tripolitan town. Finally, the ruler of Tripoli signed a treaty and stopped attacks on American ships. The other Barbary States signed similar treaties in 1815. **How did the United States stop the Barbary pirates?**

Just the Facts

American Exports, 1800–1815
(in millions of dollars)

Year	Total Value All U.S. Exports	Total Value U.S. Exports to Great Britain
1800	71	19
1801	93	31
1802	72	16
1803	56	18
1804	78	13
1805	96	15
1806	102	16
1807	108	23
1808	22	3
1809	52	6
1810	67	12
1811	61	14
1812	39	6
1813	28	---
1814	7	---
1815	53	18

Using Mathematical Skills

1. What was the total value of U.S. exports to Great Britain from 1800 through 1815?
2. Create a graph that shows the value of all U.S. exports and the value of U.S. exports to Britain from 1800 through 1815.
3. Imagine that you are an economic adviser to President Madison in 1812. Prepare a presentation to show how the American economy has been affected by U.S. efforts to force Britain to respect American trade rights.

Congress replaced the unpopular law with the **Non-Intercourse Act** in 1809. This act banned trade only with Britain, France, and their colonies. It also stated that the United States would start trading with the first side that stopped violating U.S. neutrality. Congress wanted the new law to pressure Britain and France to stop taking American ships. In addition, Congress hoped that the Non-Intercourse Act would be less harmful to the nation's trade.

✔ **Reading Check: Comparing and Contrasting** How were the Embargo Act and the Non-Intercourse Act similar and different?

⭐ The Rise of Tecumseh

Disagreements between Great Britain and the United States went beyond the neutrality issue. In the West, the British, American Indians, and American settlers again clashed. In the early 1800s, thousands of American settlers were entering the Northwest Territory. They started farms and settlements on what had once been American Indian lands. The United States had gained control of much of this land through the Treaty of Greenville. The loss of this land had upset many Indians whose leaders had not agreed to the treaty.

Britain wanted to contain the rapid western growth of the United States and to protect its interests in Canada. British leaders did not want to fight the United States, however. Instead, the British government gave military aid to American Indian nations in the Northwest Territory.

One of the most influential and talented American Indian leaders of this period was **Tecumseh**. A Shawnee chief, Tecumseh was a skilled military leader and a brilliant speaker. He warned other American Indians about the dangers they faced from settlers.

History Makers Speak
❝Where [today are] the Narranganset, the Mohican, the Pokanoket and many other once powerful tribes of our people? They have vanished before the avarice [greed] and oppression [domination] of the white man, as snow before a summer sun.❞

—Tecumseh, quoted in *Indian Wars*, by Robert M. Utley and Wilcomb E. Washburn

Tecumseh hoped to unite the American Indians of the Northwest Territory, the South, and the eastern Mississippi Valley. Aided by his brother, a religious leader called the Prophet, Tecumseh founded a village for his followers near the Wabash and Tippecanoe Rivers.

✔ **Reading Check: Analyzing Information** What was Tecumseh's goal?

Tecumseh hoped his union of American Indians might stop American settlers.

THE GRANGER COLLECTION, NEW YORK

Interpreting the Visual Record

Fighting on the frontier *The Battle of Tippecanoe broke the power of Tecumseh's American Indian confederation.* **What advantages does each side have in the battle as shown in the image?**

★ War on the Frontier

William Henry Harrison, the governor of the Indiana Territory, believed that Tecumseh was a serious threat to American power. Tecumseh met Harrison face to face in 1810. The governor urged him to follow the treaties that had been signed. Tecumseh replied, "The white people have no right to take the land from the Indians, because the Indians had it first." No single chief, he insisted, could sell land belonging to all American Indians who used it. In response, Harrison warned Tecumseh not to resist the power of the United States.

Tecumseh then traveled south to ask the Creek nation to join his forces. Harrison decided to attack while Tecumseh was gone. Harrison raised an army and then marched his troops close to the village of Tecumseh's followers. The **Battle of Tippecanoe** began when the Prophet ordered an attack on Harrison's camp early on November 7. Indian forces broke through the camp lines. Yet Harrison remained "calm, cool, and collected," according to one observer. During the all-day battle, Harrison's soldiers forced the American Indian forces to retreat. Then they destroyed Tecumseh's village. Chief Shabonee said, "With the smoke of that town and the loss of the battle, I lost all hope." Although Tecumseh was safe, he had lost much of his support.

✔ **Reading Check: Finding the Main Idea** Why were U.S. officials worried by Tecumseh's actions?

347

Western politician Henry Clay was one of the leading War Hawks.

The War Debate

The frontier fighting angered many Americans. A Republican newspaper declared, "The war on the Wabash [River] is purely BRITISH." Many Americans believed that Britain had encouraged Tecumseh to attack settlers in the West.

The **War Hawks** were members of Congress who favored war against Great Britain. They saw war as the only answer to Britain's insults. Led by members of Congress such as Henry Clay of Kentucky and John C. Calhoun of South Carolina, the War Hawks were strongest in the West and the South. "If we submit," Calhoun warned, "the independence of this nation is lost." Philadelphia newspaper editor John Binns agreed with Calhoun. He insisted that "the honor of the Nation . . . will be sacrificed if war be not declared."

Some War Hawks believed that war would give the United States a chance to expand. Speaking to the House, Tennessee representative Felix Grundy explained his views. "I . . . feel anxious [eager] not only to add the Floridas to the South, but the Canadas to the North of this empire."

The strongest opponents of the War Hawks were New England Federalists. British trade restrictions and impressment were hurting New England's economy. But people there wanted to renew friendly business ties with Britain instead of fighting another war. Other politicians, such as John Randolph of Virginia, argued that war was foolish. Standing up in Congress, Randolph challenged the War Hawks.

Analyzing Primary Sources
Identifying Points of View
Why does Randolph oppose a war, and whom does he fear it would hurt?

 History Makers Speak

"But is war the true remedy? Who will profit by it? . . . A few lucky merchants . . . and contractors. Who must suffer by it? The people. It is their blood, their taxes, that must flow to support it."

—John Randolph, quoted in *Annals of America*

Other antiwar politicians feared that the United States was not yet ready to fight powerful Britain. Senator Obadiah German of New York observed that the U.S. Army and Navy were small and poorly equipped. German pleaded with Congress to be patient. "Prior to any declaration of war . . . my plan would be . . . to put the country in complete armor."

✔ **Reading Check: Contrasting** Contrast the arguments of the opposing sides in the war debate.

A Declaration of War

President **James Madison**, a Republican elected in 1808, faced the difficulty of carrying on the trade war. He also felt growing pressure from the War Hawks. Speaking to Congress on June 1, 1812, Madison described Great Britain's conduct. He complained of Britain's impressment of American sailors and criticized Britain's continuing violation of

In 1812 the United States had only a small standing army to face its enemies.

U.S. neutrality. He concluded that Britain was in "a state of war against the United States." The president called on Congress to decide what the nation should do about this situation.

A few days later, representatives of southern and western states voted for war. Representatives of Delaware, the New England states, New Jersey, New York, and Pennsylvania voted for peace. When the votes were counted, the War Hawks had won. For the first time in U.S. history, Congress declared war. Months later, Madison was reelected. He would serve as commander in chief during the War of 1812.

✔ **Reading Check: Summarizing** Why did the United States declare war against Great Britain in 1812?

Section 3 Review

go.hrw.com **Homework Practice Online**
keyword: SF3 HP11

① Define and explain:
- impressment
- embargo

② Identify and explain:
- Embargo Act
- Non-Intercourse Act
- Tecumseh
- Battle of Tippecanoe
- War Hawks
- James Madison

③ Identifying Cause and Effect Copy the graphic organizer below. Use it to explain the causes and effects of the Embargo and Non-Intercourse Acts.

British and French Actions → Embargo and Non-Intercourse Acts → Effects

④ Finding the Main Idea
a. What was Tecumseh's goal, and did he accomplish it?

b. What led the United States to declare war on Great Britain?

⑤ Writing and Critical Thinking
Analyzing Information Imagine that you are a reporter covering the War of 1812. Write an editorial on President Madison's foreign policy.

Consider the following:
- French and British interference with American ships
- fighting against American Indians on the frontier
- pressure from War Hawks

The Expanding Nation **349**

The War of 1812

Read to Discover

1. How did the war progress at sea and in the Great Lakes region?
2. How did actions by American Indians aid the British during the war?
3. What strategy did the British pursue in the East?
4. How did the war come to an end?

WHY IT MATTERS TODAY

The Federalists protested the War of 1812, even though Congress had the power to declare it. People today continue to disagree with actions of the government. Use CNN **fyi**.com or other **current events** sources to find a political issue over which people disagree. Record your findings in your journal.

Identify

- Oliver Hazard Perry
- Battle of Lake Erie
- Battle of the Thames
- Red Eagle
- Andrew Jackson
- Battle of Horseshoe Bend
- Battle of New Orleans
- Hartford Convention
- Treaty of Ghent

The Story Continues

On August 19, 1812, the USS *Constitution* met the British ship *Guerrière* off the coast of Nova Scotia. The crews on both ships scrambled across the decks as the vessels circled each other. An observer said the *Constitution*'s first cannon blast rocked the *Guerrière* like "the shock of an earthquake." When the British returned fire, a U.S. sailor saw a cannonball bounce off the side of the *Constitution*. "Huzza, her sides are made of iron!" he cried. Soon "Old Ironsides" won one of the first battles of the War of 1812.

This is the captain's wheel of the USS Constitution, *which fought one of the first battles of the War of 1812.*

The War at Sea

The *Constitution*'s triumph over the *Guerrière* shocked many observers who expected the British to sweep the U.S. Navy from the seas. When the War of 1812 began, the British navy had hundreds of ships stationed around the world. In contrast, the U.S. Navy had fewer than 20. Republican Adam Seybert declared, "We cannot contend [compete] with Great Britain on the ocean."

Although outnumbered, the United States did have some advantages. The U.S. government licensed privately owned ships to attack British merchant ships. Equipping and operating these privateers cost less than building more naval ships. One Republican leader called the privateers "our cheapest & best Navy." The privateers captured hundreds of British ships. A London newspaper complained, "On the ocean, and even on our own coasts, we have been insulted."

Most of the British navy's ships were scattered around the globe and could not be called away to fight the United States. The U.S. Navy had well-trained sailors and new warships such as the *Constitution*. These well-built vessels carried more cannons than most British ships of the same size. U.S. captains proved their skill and the power of their ships early in the war, several times defeating British ships in one-on-one duels. These victories embarrassed the British and raised American morale. Eventually, the British brought more ships to the American coast. They began patrolling in large groups that the smaller U.S. Navy could not fight. The British blockaded American seaports and captured many American merchant ships.

✔ **Reading Check: Contrasting** What advantages did Great Britain and the United States have at the start of the war?

The copper sheathing on the hull of the USS *Constitution* was made by Patriot Paul Revere.

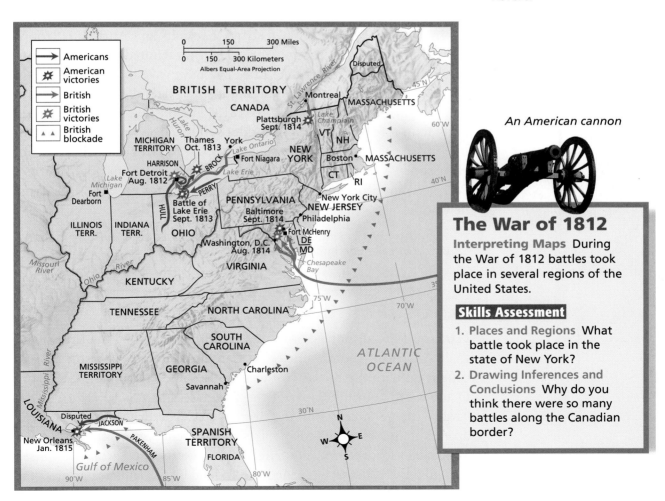

An American cannon

The War of 1812

Interpreting Maps During the War of 1812 battles took place in several regions of the United States.

Skills Assessment

1. **Places and Regions** What battle took place in the state of New York?

2. **Drawing Inferences and Conclusions** Why do you think there were so many battles along the Canadian border?

THE GRANGER COLLECTION, NEW YORK

Interpreting the Visual Record

The Battle of Lake Erie *Captain Oliver Hazard Perry was forced to abandon his damaged ship during the fighting and take command of a new one.* **How does this image display Captain Perry's determination to win the battle?**

★ The Canadian Border

Hoping to equal the early success of the U.S. Navy, American leaders planned to invade Canada with three separate armies. They expected French Canadians to welcome U.S. troops. Former president Thomas Jefferson thought that conquering Canada would be "a mere matter of marching [there]."

These hopes were soon dashed. In July 1812 the British joined with American Indians led by Tecumseh to defeat an American army and capture Fort Detroit. The other American forces had to retreat when militia members refused to cross the Canadian border. By the end of 1812, Britain controlled the strategic Great Lakes region. The situation worried Treasury Secretary Albert Gallatin.

 "The series of misfortunes exceeds [goes beyond] all anticipations made even by those who had least confidence in our inexperienced officers and undisciplined men.**"**

—Albert Gallatin, quoted in *The War of 1812*, by Donald R. Hickey

In 1813, the United States struck back. In late April U.S. troops burned the Canadian capital, York. Then the United States moved to break Britain's control of Lake Erie. The navy gave the task to Captain **Oliver Hazard Perry**. After building a small fleet, Perry sailed out to meet the British on September 10, 1813. The **Battle of Lake Erie** lasted more than three hours, and both sides suffered heavy casualties. Finally, the British surrendered. Perry sent a message to General William Henry Harrison. "We have met the enemy and they are ours," he reported. Perry's victory forced the British to withdraw and gave the U.S. Army new hope.

✔ **Reading Check: Finding the Main Idea** Why was Perry's victory in the Battle of Lake Erie important to the U.S. war effort?

★ The Frontier War

Harrison took advantage of Perry's victory by pursuing the British and their American Indian allies into Canada. General Harrison's forces caught up with the British by the Thames River in southern Canada in October 1813. In the **Battle of the Thames**, Harrison boldly ordered a cavalry charge directly into the British force. The British defenses broke apart, but the American Indian forces, led by Tecumseh, continued to fight. The Indian forces eventually retreated, but not before Tecumseh himself was killed. His death weakened the Indian-British alliance around the

Great Lakes. The U.S. victory in the Battle of the Thames broke British power on the Northwest frontier and secured the U.S. border with Canada.

Two years before his death, Tecumseh had tried to enlist the Creek Indians in his confederacy. In 1813 the Creek finally decided to take up arms against the United States. Led by Chief **Red Eagle**, Creek forces destroyed Fort Mims in present-day Alabama. Close to 250 of the fort's defenders were killed. **Andrew Jackson**, a general in the Tennessee militia, led his soldiers south to fight the Creek.

After several bloody battles, Jackson attacked the main Creek base in 1814. It was a small fort on the Tallapoosa River in what is now Alabama. The **Battle of Horseshoe Bend** was a convincing victory for Jackson and his troops. Days later, Red Eagle came into Jackson's camp and surrendered. Jackson's victory ended the Creek War and led to a treaty that forced the Creek to give up millions of acres of their land.

✔ **Reading Check: Summarizing** What major battles did the United States win in Canada and present-day Alabama?

⭐ The British on the Offensive

Despite U.S. success on the western and southern frontiers, the situation in the East grew worse. Having defeated France in April 1814, the British sent more troops to America. They also strengthened their blockade of Atlantic seaports. Now reinforced, the British moved to attack the U.S. capital. President Madison and most of his cabinet were forced to flee when the British broke through U.S. defenses. The British marched

Interpreting the Visual Record

Washington *First Lady Dolley Madison heard about the British advance on Washington. Despite the danger, she stayed and saved a famous portrait of George Washington before escaping.* **What threats would an American face trying to leave the capital?**

THE GRANGER COLLECTION, NEW YORK

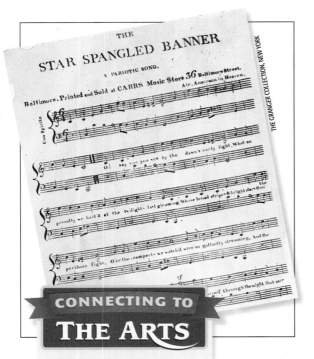

THE GRANGER COLLECTION, NEW YORK

CONNECTING TO
THE ARTS

The National Anthem In September 1814 American Francis Scott Key witnessed the British attack on Fort McHenry. Key could see the American flag flying over the fort as the battle began. He anxiously waited as the British fired their cannons throughout the night. At 7:00 A.M. the mist and smoke finally cleared. Key saw that the American flag still flew above the fort. The British had lost the battle. Key was so moved with joy that he wrote the words to "The Star-Spangled Banner," which became the national anthem in 1931. **Why do you think "The Star-Spangled Banner" became so popular?**

onward into the city setting fire to the White House and other government buildings.

This destruction was in response to the Americans' earlier burning of the British capital in Canada. After the British left the city, one observer surveyed the damage. All that was left of the president's home were "unroofed, marked walls, cracked, defaced [damaged], blackened with the smoke of fire." The British sailed on to Baltimore, Maryland, which was guarded by Fort McHenry. The British fleet shelled the fort and its defenders for 25 hours.

 History Makers Speak

❝The attack on Fort McHenry . . . was distinctly [clearly] seen from Federal Hill, and from the tops of houses which were covered with men, women, and children. The night . . . presented the whole awful spectacle [sight] of shot and shells, and rockets, shooting and bursting through the air.❞

—Reporter for the *Salem Gazette*, quoted in *The Rockets' Red Glare*, by Scott S. Sheads

The Americans refused to surrender Fort McHenry. The British chose to retreat instead of continuing to fight.

✔ **Reading Check: Sequencing** What did Great Britain's military forces do after destroying much of the nation's capital?

★ The Battle of New Orleans

After the attack on Washington, the British launched another offensive. From their Caribbean bases, they attacked New Orleans. They hoped to capture the city and thus take control of the Mississippi River. Andrew Jackson was in command of the U.S. forces around New Orleans. British troops advanced to within seven miles of the city. Startled, Jackson ordered his forces to make a stand. Jackson's troops were a mix of regular soldiers, state militia, and pirates led by Jean Laffite. They quickly constructed a wall of dirt and logs and waited for the attack.

The **Battle of New Orleans** began on the morning of January 8, 1815. Some 5,300 British troops attacked Jackson's force of 4,500. The British began marching toward the U.S. defenses under the cover of a thick morning fog. As they drew near, the air cleared. They were exposed to heavy fire from U.S. riflemen and artillery. Caught on an open field, the British were cut down with frightening speed. A militia member recalled the scene. "The field was entirely covered with . . . bodies. In some places they were lying in piles of several, one on top of the other." By the time the battle ended, more than 2,000 British soldiers had been killed or wounded. The Americans had suffered about 70 casualties.

✔ **Reading Check: Finding the Main Idea** What occurred at the Battle of New Orleans?

⭐ Ending the War

Before the battle at New Orleans, New England Federalists gathered at Hartford, Connecticut, to oppose the war. This gathering became known as the **Hartford Convention**. Some delegates to the convention wanted New England to withdraw from the United States. However, moderate members convinced the convention to send a delegation to meet with Congress to try to increase states' rights.

Before this delegation reached Washington, however, news reached North America that the war had ended. Some critics accused them of treason. The Federalists' attempt to challenge the power of the national government proved costly. Humiliated, the Federalists lost much of their political power.

The peace agreement that caught the Federalists by surprise was the **Treaty of Ghent**. It had been signed in Belgium on December 24, 1814, before the Battle of New Orleans took place. After months of frustrating negotiations, U.S. and British diplomats finally agreed to end the war. Each nation returned the territory it had conquered. However, the diplomats found no solutions to the problems of impressment or trade embargoes. Both sides agreed to address the remaining issues once there was peace. For the United States, the War of 1812 was a narrow escape from potential disaster. But Americans were proud that their young nation had stood up to the mighty British.

THE GRANGER COLLECTION, NEW YORK

Interpreting the Visual Record

Peace treaty *The signing of the Treaty of Ghent was a relief for two nations tired of war.* **How does this image contrast with the battle scenes from the War of 1812?**

✔ **Reading Check: Identifying Cause and Effect** What led to the Hartford Convention, and what effect did it have on the political future of the Federalist Party?

Section 4 Review

go.hrw.com **Homework Practice Online**

keyword: SF3 HP11

1 Identify and explain:
- Oliver Hazard Perry
- Battle of Lake Erie
- Battle of the Thames
- Red Eagle
- Andrew Jackson
- Battle of Horseshoe Bend
- Battle of New Orleans
- Hartford Convention
- Treaty of Ghent

2 Comparing and Contrasting Copy the chart below. Use it to compare and contrast the significant details of the major military battles fought on land and sea during the War of 1812.

Battle	Details (Winner, Location, Importance)

3 Finding the Main Idea
a. What role did American Indians play in the War of 1812?

b. How did the war progress in the East?

4 Writing and Critical Thinking
Evaluating Imagine that you are a member of President Madison's cabinet in 1815. Write a diary entry describing the events that took place at the end of the War of 1812 and their significance.

Consider the following:
- the Hartford Convention
- the Treaty of Ghent
- the Battle of New Orleans

Chapter 11 Review

The Chapter at a Glance

Examine the visual summary of the chapter below. Create a set of flash cards listing the chapter's main events and the dates on which they occurred. Use your flash cards with a classmate to review the chapter content.

The Nation at War and Peace

1801
Marbury v. *Madison* gives the Supreme Court the power of judicial review.

1803
The United States doubles its size by making the Louisiana Purchase.

1807–09
Congress passes the Embargo and Non-Intercourse Acts.

1811
William Henry Harrison defeats Tecumseh's forces at the Battle of Tippecanoe.

1812
The War of 1812 begins between Great Britain and the United States.

1814
Federalists hold the Hartford Convention to protest the War of 1812.

1814
The Treaty of Ghent ends the War of 1812.

1815
Andrew Jackson wins the Battle of New Orleans.

Identifying People and Ideas

Use the following terms or people in historically significant sentences.

1. John Marshall
2. judicial review
3. Louisiana Purchase
4. Lewis and Clark expedition
5. impressment
6. Tecumseh
7. War Hawks
8. Battle of New Orleans
9. Hartford Convention
10. Treaty of Ghent

Understanding Main Ideas

Section 1 *(Pages 334–37)*
1. What Federalist policy did President Jefferson leave in place?
2. Why did the Supreme Court review *Marbury* v. *Madison*?

Section 2 *(Pages 338–43)*
3. Why were New Orleans and the Mississippi River important to the United States?

Section 3 *(Pages 344–49)*
4. Starting with the war between Great Britain and France, list the series of events that led to the U.S. declaration of war on Britain in 1812.

Section 4 *(Pages 350–55)*
5. Was the War of 1812 a success from the American point of view? Explain your answer, considering the reasons why war was declared.

You Be the Historian— Reviewing Themes

1. **Constitutional Heritage** What was the significance of the *Marbury* v. *Madison* decision, and what issues did it resolve?
2. **Geography** Why did President Jefferson send Lewis and Clark to explore the West, and what important information did they bring back?
3. **Global Relations** What conflicts arose between the United States and American Indians along the western frontier?

Thinking Critically

1. **Evaluating** Do you think that Thomas Jefferson was right to purchase Louisiana despite his concerns that doing so was unconstitutional? Explain your answer.
2. **Supporting a Point of View** Write a speech arguing whether or not Congress should declare war on Great Britain in 1812.
3. **Drawing Inferences and Conclusions** What danger did the United States risk when it declared war on Britain in 1812?

Social Studies Skills Workshop

Interpreting Maps

Study the map below. Then use the information on the map to help you answer the questions that follow.

The Creek War

1. According to the map, where did the American victory in the Creek War take place?
   a. between the Alabama and Tallapoosa Rivers
   b. in Georgia near the border with the Mississippi Territory
   c. in Florida near the border with the Mississippi Territory
   d. in the Mississippi Territory near the border with Georgia

2. Based on your knowledge of the period, why was it significant that Jackson led his forces on to New Orleans after defeating the Creek?

Analyzing Primary Sources

Read the following quote from historian David Ramsay, who commented on the Louisiana Purchase in 1804, and then answer the questions that follow.

"History affords no example of the acquisition of such important benefits, at so moderate a price, and under such favorable circumstances. . . . [Aside from independence and the Constitution] the acquisition of Louisiana is the greatest political blessing ever conferred on these states."

3. Which of the following best describes Ramsay's view of the Louisiana Purchase?
   a. The purchase was very valuable to the nation but still too expensive.
   b. The purchase was one of the most impressive achievements of the United States.
   c. The price of the purchase was fair, but the United States had little to gain from the new territory.
   d. The purchase was even more important than the Constitution.

4. What do you think Ramsay means when he calls the Louisiana Purchase "the greatest political blessing ever conferred on these states"?

5. Based on your knowledge of the period, do you agree or disagree with Ramsay's viewpoint on the importance of the Louisiana Purchase? Explain your answer.

Alternative Assessment

Building Your Portfolio

Interdisciplinary Connection to the Arts
Using the library and other available sources, research the role of the USS *Constitution* ("Old Ironsides") in the War of 1812. Use this information to build a model or make a sketch of the warship. Then use your model or sketch as a visual aid for a short oral report that you present to the class. Have a classmate ask and answer questions related to your work on the model.

🖥 internet connect

Internet Activity: go.hrw.com
keyword: SF3 CF11

Choose a topic on the Expanding Nation to:
● Explore the American West with Lewis and Clark.
● Research the causes and effects of the War of 1812, and write an analysis of its impact.
● Review the outcome of the last general election and compare it to the election of 1800.

The Growing Republic

In 1790 the United States was a new nation. The 13 states were all located on the eastern coast of North America. But pioneers had already begun to head west beyond the Appalachian Mountains. In 1803 the United States bought Louisiana from France. This Louisiana Purchase nearly doubled the size of the country.

The United States remained mostly a nation of farmers. Much of the young country's wealth, however, was based on trade with foreign nations.

Population and Trade

In 1790 the United States had nearly 4 million people. It stretched from the Atlantic Ocean to the Mississippi River. As the nation grew, so did its trade with other countries. But international conflicts sometimes caused foreign trade to rise or fall dramatically.

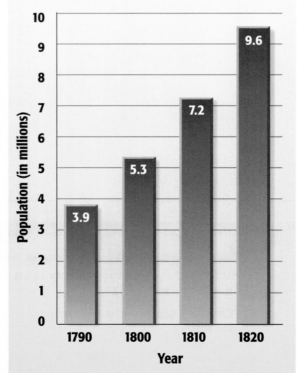

U.S. Population Growth, 1790–1820

Population (in millions)

- 1790: 3.9
- 1800: 5.3
- 1810: 7.2
- 1820: 9.6

Year

Source: *Historical Statistics of the United States*

Geography Skills
Interpreting Bar Graphs

1. **Human Systems** How much did the U.S. population increase between 1790 and 1820?
2. **Analyzing Information** During which ten-year periods did the U.S. population increase the most?

History Note 1

The U.S. population more than doubled between 1790 and 1820. The number of Americans in the West grew particularly fast. In 1790 about 4 percent of the U.S. population lived west of the Appalachian Mountains. By 1820 this figure had grown significantly.

Early American merchants sometimes listed their goods for sale in papers like this one. Decorated plates were one of many trade items.

U.S. Imports and Exports, 1790–1820

Source: *Historical Statistics of the United States*

Imports
Exports

History Note 2

Great Britain remained an important U.S. trading partner after the American Revolution. In 1790 more than a third of U.S. exports went to Britain. However, between 1790 and 1820 international conflicts sometimes made foreign trade difficult.

Geography Skills
Interpreting Line Graphs

1. Was the value of U.S. exports usually higher or lower than the value of imports from 1790 to 1820?

2. **Drawing Inferences and Conclusions** When were the values of U.S. exports and imports lowest? Why do you think trade was so low at those times?

ABBY ALDRICH ROCKEFELLER FOLK ART MUSEUM

This painting shows a scene of an ideal farm in the late 1700s.

The Expanding Nation

The territory of the United States expanded greatly between 1790 and 1820. But the United States still competed with American Indians and foreign nations for land.

The United States, 1790

Legend:
- U.S. territory
- Spanish territory
- British territory
- Disputed territory
- Northwest Territory
- Spanish settlements and missions
- UTE — Native American tribe

0   250   500 Miles
0   250   500 Kilometers
Albers Equal-Area Projection

History Note 3

The United States in 1790 was primarily a rural nation, with the vast majority of people living on farms. Only 24 U.S. cities had a population of more than 2,500.

Geography **Skills**
Interpreting Political Maps

1. What major American Indian peoples still populated U.S. territory in 1790?
2. **Physical Systems** In what ways was the physical geography of western North America different from the central and eastern parts of the continent?
3. **Summarizing** In what parts of the present-day United States were many Spanish settlements located?

History Note 4

Many American Indians in the West resisted the movement of settlers onto their lands. However, gradually most American Indian groups lost their lands to the expanding United States. By the 1790s treaties opened land to settlers throughout the Trans-Appalachian West. These areas included lands in Georgia, New York, North Carolina, and present-day Tennessee. A series of battles took place with American Indians in the Ohio Valley region. After a 1795 treaty, nearly two thirds of what is now the state of Ohio was opened for settlement.

The United States, 1820

Claimed by U.S., ceded to Great Britain in 1818

British Territory

49th Parallel

ROCKY MOUNTAINS

Oregon Country

42nd Parallel

Lake of the Woods

Great Lakes

Disputed

ME

VT

NH

MA

NY

CT

RI

Michigan Territory

Mississippi R.

Unorganized Territory

PA

NJ

IL

IN

OH

MD

DE

APPALACHIAN MOUNTAINS

VA

PACIFIC OCEAN

120° W

Spanish Territory

Missouri Territory

KY

Arkansas River

Arkansas Territory

Red River

TN

NC

SC

ATLANTIC OCEAN

MS

AL

GA

LA

Sabine R.

Unorganized Territory (Florida)

Gulf of Mexico

90° W

42° N

40° N

70° W

30° N

80° W

Legend
- Convention of 1818
- Adams-Onís Treaty of 1819
- Louisiana Purchase
- From Britain to United States, 1818
- From Spain to United States, 1819
- Claimed by United States and Great Britain, 1818

0   250   500 Miles
0   250   500 Kilometers
Albers Equal-Area Projection

Geography Skills
Interpreting Political Maps

1. Which two nations shared control of Oregon Country after 1818?
2. What state west of the Mississippi River had been admitted into the Union by 1820?
3. **Places and Regions** Create a blank map of the United States. Ask a fellow student to draw in the U.S. borders established by the Convention of 1818 and the Adams-Onís Treaty of 1819.
4. **Analyzing Information** What physical features helped form the western boundary of the Louisiana Purchase and the Adams–Onís Treaty?

History Note 5

Immigration has always been an important contributor to the U.S. population. The original thirteen colonies that became the United States were mostly populated by immigrants from Great Britain. There were also sizable numbers of immigrants from Germany. After the Revolutionary War, overall immigration slowed. By 1820 more people were coming to the United States from Ireland than from Great Britain.

History Note 6

As American settlers moved westward, the abundance of land and other resources helped support large families. In fact, the average American household was significantly larger than households in Europe. An average free household in the United States had 6 members, compared to an average of 4.5 persons in British homes. A higher birthrate and rising standard of living in the United States help explain this difference in size.

NEW YOR

12 A New National Identity
(1812–1840)

These five-dollar gold coins were issued by the U.S. Mint.

The Erie Canal was opened in 1825 and greatly reduced the cost of shipping goods from Buffalo to New York City.

(DETAIL) COLLECTION OF THE NEW YORK HISTORICAL SOCIETY

UNITED STATES

1816 James Monroe is elected president.

1817 Work on the Erie Canal begins.

1819 Spain and the United States sign the Adams-Onís Treaty in February, giving Florida to the United States.

In March the Supreme Court establishes the constitutionality of the Second Bank of the United States in *McCulloch v. Maryland*.

1824 John Quincy Adams is elected president.

1812	1815	1818	1821	1824

1815 Napoléon returns to power in France but is defeated at the Battle of Waterloo.

1819 Simon Bolívar becomes president of Gran Colombia.

1822 Brazil declares independence from Portugal.

1824 Simon Bolívar becomes president of Peru.

WORLD

The Brazilian Empire used this flag after it declared independence from Portugal.

The Duke of Wellington led an army of allied European nations to victory over Napoléon's French forces at the Battle of Waterloo.

Build on What You Know

The United States had survived a second war with Great Britain. Although the nation was at peace, there were still unresolved disputes with foreign powers. A rising sense of nationalism and an expansion of democracy played key roles in shaping American identity as the young nation began to assert itself.

This picture of Jackson was carried by supporters during one of his presidential campaigns.

THE GRANGER COLLECTION, NEW YORK

Andrew Jackson, shown standing before a crowd of well-wishers, received a record number of popular votes in 1828.

1828 Andrew Jackson is elected president.

1829 The Ottoman Empire recognizes the independence of Greece.

1830 Congress passes the Indian Removal Act.

1832 A British reform bill doubles the number of British men who can vote.

1834 Opponents of Andrew Jackson form the Whig Party.

1835 Dutch colonists in Africa, known as the Boers, begin their Great Trek into the African interior.

1836 Martin Van Buren is elected president.

1838 The Trail of Tears begins, as U.S. troops remove the Cherokee from Georgia.

1839 The Opium War breaks out between Britain and China.

1827   **1830**   **1833**   **1836**   **1839**

If you were there . . .
What would you do to help the country?

You Be the Historian

Themes Journal

What's Your Opinion? Do you **agree** or **disagree** with the following statements? Support your point of view in your journal.

- **Global Relations** Disputes over land can be resolved without armed force.

- **Citizenship** Voting rights make a democracy stronger.

- **Constitutional Heritage** States should have the right to ignore federal laws with which they disagree.

The Rise of Nationalism

Read to Discover

1. How did the United States settle its land disputes with Great Britain and Spain?
2. Why did President Monroe issue the Monroe Doctrine, and what were its most important points?

WHY IT MATTERS TODAY

Border disputes often lead to more serious international conflicts. Use **CNNfyi.com** or other **current events** sources to learn about a recent border dispute between countries. Record your findings in your journal.

Identify

- James Monroe
- Rush-Bagot Agreement
- Convention of 1818
- Adams-Onís Treaty
- Simon Bolívar
- Monroe Doctrine

The Story Continues

James Monroe greatly admired the French republic. Yet he believed that the United States could become the greatest republic ever. He shared these views with his daughter Eliza while they walked through the streets of Paris. When Eliza noted that the French had better roads, Monroe answered, "That's true, our country may be likened to a new house. We lack many things, but we possess the most precious of all—liberty!"

James Monroe was close friends with former presidents Thomas Jefferson and James Madison.

★ The Era of Good Feelings

After the War of 1812, the United States enjoyed a time of peace. National pride began to grow. By 1817, journalists had begun calling this time the Era of Good Feelings. The previous year **James Monroe**, a Republican, had easily won the presidency over Federalist Rufus King. Running unopposed, Monroe won re-election in 1820. During his presidency, the United States resolved several conflicts with foreign powers.

The Treaty of Ghent had ended the war with Britain. However, the United States and British Canada still disagreed about who controlled the waterways along their borders. Both countries wanted to keep their navies and fishing rights on the Great Lakes. In the spring of 1817, the two sides compromised by reaching the **Rush-Bagot Agreement**.

Secretary of State Richard Rush negotiated this treaty. It limited naval power on the Great Lakes for both the United States and British Canada. Another treaty, known as the **Convention of 1818**, gave the United States fishing rights off parts of the Newfoundland and Labrador coasts. It also set the border between the United States and Canada at the 49th parallel. This border extended as far west as the Rocky Mountains. In addition, both countries agreed to jointly occupy part of the Pacific Northwest.

✔ **Reading Check: Finding the Main Idea** How did the United States use compromise to settle its border disputes with British Canada?

⭐ The Issue of Florida

Another dispute involved the U.S. border with Spanish Florida. Some Americans wanted to settle in the area. Others were angered by raids on U.S. towns made by Seminole Indians from Florida. The Seminole also aided runaway slaves. In 1818 Secretary of State John Quincy Adams held talks with Spanish diplomat Luis de Onís about allowing American settlers into Florida. Meanwhile, President Monroe sent troops under the command of General Andrew Jackson to secure the border.

In April 1818 Jackson's troops invaded Florida to capture Seminole raiders, thus beginning the First Seminole War. During the war, Jackson fought the Spanish as well as the Seminole. He took over most of Spain's important military posts and overthrew the governor of Florida. He commited these acts against Spain without receiving direct orders from President Monroe.

Jackson's actions upset both British and Spanish leaders. "We can hardly believe that any thing so offensive to public decorum [proper behavior] could be admitted, *even in America!*" reported one London

★★★★★★★★★★★★
That's Interesting!
★★★★★★★★★★★★

Mistaken Identity Can you imagine the president of the United States being mistaken for a clerk? It happened to James Monroe. When a European diplomat paid a visit to the White House during Monroe's presidency, he came upon a man writing at a desk. The man had no wig and wore a dirty waistcoat spotted with ink. Ragged slippers hung on his feet. The diplomat was surprised that the president would hire such a messy assistant. Imagine his shock when he discovered this man was the president himself!

Interpreting the Visual Record

The Fourth of July *By 1819, when Joseph Krimmel painted* Fourth of July Celebration in Centre Square, *the Fourth of July had become a popular holiday celebrating the birth of the young United States.* **What parts of this picture suggest that a national holiday is being celebrated?**

journal. Most Americans, however, were in favor of Jackson. One U.S. newspaper of the time described Jackson's popularity and power.

Analyzing Primary Sources
Drawing Inferences and Conclusions How would the reader know that Jackson is a powerful leader?

History Makers Speak

❝Among the people of the West, his popularity is unbounded [unlimited]. . . . At his call, 50,000 of the most efficient warriors on this continent would rise, armed, and ready for any enemy.❞

—*Niles' Weekly Register*, quoted in *A Diplomatic History of the American People*, by Thomas A. Bailey

Jackson's presence in Florida helped convince Spanish leaders to settle all border disputes with the United States in the **Adams-Onís Treaty** of 1819. Under this treaty, Spain gave East Florida to the United States and gave up its claims to West Florida. In return, the United States gave up its claims to what is now Texas. The United States also agreed to take responsibility for up to $5 million of U.S. citizens' claims against Spain.

✔ **Reading Check: Summarizing** What disagreements did the United States have with Spain over Florida, and how were these settled?

⭐ The Monroe Doctrine

At the time of the Adams-Onís Treaty, Spain had other problems. The Spanish colonies of Central and South America began to challenge Spanish rule. By the early 1820s most of these Latin American countries had declared independence from Spain. Revolutionary fighter

Historical Document

THE MONROE DOCTRINE

On December 2, 1823, President James Monroe issued what became known as the Monroe Doctrine. The following is an excerpt from the doctrine, which has had a significant effect on U.S. foreign policy.

We . . . declare that we should consider any attempt on their [European powers'] part to extend their [political] system to any portion of this hemisphere as dangerous to our peace and safety.

With the existing colonies or dependencies of any European power we have not interfered and shall not interfere. But with the governments who have declared their independence and maintained it, and whose independence we have . . . acknowledged, we could not view any **interposition**[1] for the purpose of **oppressing**[2] them, or controlling in any other manner their destiny, by any European power in any other light than as the **manifestation**[3] of an unfriendly disposition toward the United States.

A replica of the Monroe Doctrine

[1] **interposition:** interference [2] **oppressing:** unjustly ruling [3] **manifestation:** evidence

Analyzing Primary Sources
1. What warning did President Monroe give to the European powers in the Monroe Doctrine?

2. What do you think is most important about this document?

Simon Bolívar, hailed as *the Liberator,* led many of these struggles. The revolutions in Latin America reminded most American leaders of the American Revolution. As a result, they supported the struggles for independence. In 1818 the *Nashville Whig* reported a toast given at a public dinner in Tennessee.

 History Makers Speak

❝*The patriots of South America:* **palsied [paralyzed] be the arm that would wrest [take] from them the standard of liberty for which they have so nobly struggled. Six cheers!**❞

—*Nashville Whig,* quoted in *Life of Andrew Jackson* by James Parton

Yet Latin American independence worried President Monroe. He thought that European powers might try to take control of the newly independent Latin American countries. Secretary of State Adams and President Monroe decided to warn European powers not to interfere with the Americas. Delivered on December 2, 1823, this warning became known as the **Monroe Doctrine**. It stated that foreign powers should not create new colonies in North and South America. The United States would view any European interference with Latin American governments as a hostile act.

Some Europeans strongly criticized the Monroe Doctrine. The French foreign minister said that the doctrine "ought to be resisted by all the powers having commercial or territorial interests in the hemisphere." Despite such threats, few European countries challenged the Monroe Doctrine, which has played a major role in shaping U.S.–Latin American relations.

Simon Bolívar led the revolutions against Spanish rule in what are now the nations of Bolivia, Columbia, Ecuador, and Peru.

✔ **Reading Check: Analyzing Information** What did the Monroe Doctrine accomplish?

Section 1 Review

go.hrw.com **Homework Practice Online**
keyword: SF3 HP12

1 Identify and explain:
- James Monroe
- Rush-Bagot Agreement
- Convention of 1818
- Adams-Onís Treaty
- Simon Bolívar
- Monroe Doctrine

2 Sequencing Copy the graphic organizer below. Use it to describe how the United States responded to foreign-policy problems during Monroe's presidency. List the date of each response.

Border Dispute with Great Britain →

Border Dispute with Spain →

Latin American Independence →

3 Finding the Main Idea

a. How did the United States settle its conflict with Great Britain over Canada, and why was resolving the conflict important to both nations?

b. What caused a dispute between the United States and Spain during Monroe's presidency, and how was this dispute settled?

4 Writing and Critical Thinking
Supporting a Point of View Imagine that you are a U.S. ambassador. Write a memo to the secretary of state explaining your opinion of the Monroe Doctrine.

Consider the following:
- the main points of the doctrine
- U.S. views on Latin American independence
- the potential dangers of European involvement in Latin America

Expansion and Improvements

Read to Discover

1. What issues was the Missouri Compromise supposed to address?
2. How did improvements in transportation affect the United States?
3. Why was the 1824 presidential election controversial?

WHY IT MATTERS TODAY

Transportation is still very important in our daily lives. Use **CNNfyi.com** or other **current events** sources to learn about transportation issues in the United States. Record your findings in your journal.

Identify

- Henry Clay
- Missouri Compromise
- American System
- Cumberland Road
- Erie Canal
- John Quincy Adams

Wagons were important for both settlement and trade on the western frontier.

The Story Continues

In the early 1800s, more Americans moved west. Most were looking for land and opportunity. An Ohio migrant described the scene in 1816. "The western country continues to rise in population and importance with unabated [unstoppable] rapidity." The writer mentioned the town of Mount Pleasant, Ohio. It grew from 7 families to about 90 families in just 10 years. As more Americans pushed west, debates arose over what laws would govern the newly settled lands.

★ The Missouri Compromise

A major regional conflict arose in 1819, when Congress considered the application of Missouri to enter the Union. Pro-slavery leaders in Missouri wanted to join the nation as a slave state. At the time, the Union included 11 free states and 11 slave states. Because free states in the North had a greater population, they controlled the House of Representatives. However, adding a new slave state would have tipped the balance in the Senate in favor of the South. Northern representatives in the House therefore passed a legislative amendment that would accept Missouri as a slave state with certain restrictions. Importing slaves into Missouri would become illegal. The amendment also required all children of Missouri slaves to be set free when they reached age 25. These proposed limits on slavery angered southern politicians.

Some senators, such as Rufus King of New York, opposed any expansion of slavery. "The existence of slavery impairs [harms] the industry and the power of a nation," he argued. North Carolina senator Nathaniel Macon wanted to continue adding slave states. "Why depart from the good old way, which has kept us in quiet, peace, and harmony?" he asked. Eventually, the Senate rejected the amendment. Missouri was still not a state.

To settle this dispute, Kentucky representative **Henry Clay** helped Congress reach the **Missouri Compromise**. This agreement had three main conditions.

Henry Clay had a long and distinguished political career and was noted for his efforts in Congress to achieve compromise between the North and the South.

1. Missouri would enter the Union as a slave state.
2. Maine would join the Union as a free state.
3. Slavery would be prohibited in any new territories or states formed north of 36°30' latitude—Missouri's southern border.

Another Kentucky representative, Benjamin Hardin, urged support for this compromise. He warned that regional differences over slavery threatened national unity.

History Makers Speak

"It is north and east against the south and the west. It is a great geographical line that separates the contending [competing] parties. And those parties, when so equally divided, shake mighty empires to their center, and break up the foundations of the great deep, that sooner or later, if not settled, will rend in twain [break in two] this temple of liberty."

—Benjamin Hardin, quoted in *Major Problems in the History of the American South, Volume I*, edited by Paul D. Escott and David R. Goldfield

Congress passed the Missouri Compromise in 1820. Maine became a state on March 15 of that year, and Missouri was admitted to the Union on August 10, 1821.

Clay earned the nickname the Great Pacificator, or peacemaker, for his efforts on behalf of the compromise. However, there were still strong disagreements between the North and the South over the expansion of slavery into the West. This controversial issue would continue to divide the nation.

✔ **Reading Check: Identifying Cause and Effect** Why did Henry Clay propose the Missouri Compromise, and what were its key points?

The Missouri Compromise
Interpreting Maps The Missouri Compromise allowed Maine to enter the Union as a free state and Missouri as a slave state.

Skills Assessment Places and Regions After the Missouri Compromise, how many slave states were there, and how many free states?

Research on the R⦿M

Free Find:
Henry Clay
After reading about Henry Clay on the **Holt Researcher CD–ROM**, create a poster in support of Clay for president. Be sure your poster shows his many accomplishments.

★ Internal Improvements

Henry Clay believed that a strong national economy would prevent regional conflicts. To strengthen the economy, he wanted a protective tariff. A tariff, Clay stated, would help domestic industries by keeping Americans from buying foreign goods. He wanted the tariff revenue to be used to improve roads and canals, or artificial waterways. These internal improvements would connect the regions of the country and make trade easier. Clay's plan became known as the **American System**.

Many people liked the idea of uniting the country through internal improvements. In 1816 a western citizen talked about these changes. "I believe the time [is] not very distant," he said, "when the wealth and resources of the western country will be brought almost to your doors." However, some members of Congress were against Clay's plan. They believed that the Constitution did not permit the federal government to spend money on internal improvements. Clay answered that the possible gains for the country justified federal action. Congress did pass a protective tariff, yet little of the money was used for internal improvements. Many state governments and private citizens continued to invest in improving the country's internal transportation systems.

✔ **Reading Check: Identifying Points of View** Why did some Americans believe the country needed internal improvements to build up the national economy?

The American System	The American System was Henry Clay's plan to strengthen the U.S. economy by protecting U.S. industries and improving national transportation.

An American-made fur hat might cost $1.50 to buy.

An imported British fur hat would be cheaper . . . but the tariff would raise the cost.

Clay hoped such protective tariffs would encourage Americans to buy domestic goods and also provide money to build roads and canals.

Visualizing History

1. **Economics** Why did Henry Clay want a tariff?

2. **Connecting to Today** Do you think that the American System would work in today's economy? Explain your answer.

Interpreting the Visual Record

The National Road *The Fairview Inn was a stopping place for merchants and settlers traveling the National Road.* **How busy does the road appear to be in this image?**

★ New Roads and Canals

In the early 1800s most roads in the United States were made of dirt, making land travel difficult. British actress Frances Kemble described one New York road on which she had struggled during a visit to the United States in the 1830s.

"The wickedest road, I do think, the cruellest, hard-heartedest road, that ever [a] wheel rumbled upon. Through bog [wet spongy ground] and marsh, and ruts [wheel tracks], wider and deeper than any . . . ruts I ever saw, with the roots of trees protruding [sticking out] across our path."

—Frances Anne (Kemble) Butler, *Journal*

Analyzing Primary Sources

Making Generalizations and Predictions How might travel over roads such as this one affect a nation?

The **Cumberland Road** was the first road built by the federal government. It ran from Cumberland, Maryland, to Wheeling, a town on the Ohio River in present-day West Virginia. Construction began in 1815, and by 1818 the road reached Wheeling. Then the Panic of 1819 hurt the economy, stopping further expansion. Construction on the road began again in the 1820s. In 1833 the National Road, as the extended road was called, stretched to Columbus, Ohio. It reached all the way to Illinois by 1850.

Water transportation was usually quicker, easier, and cheaper than overland travel. However, many areas of the country did not have rivers to connect them to other towns. Some Americans tried to make water transportation easier by building canals. During the early 1800s canal construction increased dramatically in the United States, particularly in the Northeast.

One of the largest projects was the **Erie Canal**, running from Albany to Buffalo, New York. Albany is located on the Hudson River, which feeds into New York Bay, and Buffalo is located on Lake Erie. Governor DeWitt Clinton of New York worked for many years to get approval for the project. Begun in 1817, it was completed in 1825. The Erie Canal

Building the Erie Canal

In 1817 New York began building the Erie Canal to connect Buffalo to Albany. One early difficulty was that much of the land between the two cities is hilly. Engineers solved this problem by using locks. A lock is a section of a canal with large gates at either end. Water inside the lock can be raised or lowered, allowing boats to move up and down hills. Today the Erie Canal is a tourist attraction and carries sightseers. The canal has also become part of American folklore, inspiring songs such as "Fifteen Miles on the Erie Canal." **What challenges did engineers overcome in building the Erie Canal?**

Towpaths: Animals such as horses and mules walked along the towpaths to pull barges through the canal.

14' towpath

Cement: The cement used in the Erie Canal was a special limestone and sand mixture that hardened underwater.

40'

3'

4'

28' cement

cost New York taxpayers millions of dollars, but it proved to be worth the expense. The canal allowed goods and people to move between all towns on Lake Erie and New York City. When the canal opened, a speaker at the opening ceremony called it a triumph of technology and praised its builders.

Analyzing Primary Sources

Identifying Points of View
What qualities of the Erie Canal most impressed this speaker?

History Makers Speak

❝They have built the longest canal in the world, in the least time, with the least experience, for the least money and to the greatest public benefit.❞

—Anonymous, quoted in *The Americans: The National Experience*, by Daniel Boorstin

The success of the Erie Canal helped start a canal-building boom across the country. South Carolina governor George McDuffie also sponsored a canal project. He hoped to make Charleston the center of southern Appalachian trade, wanting it to become "the New York of the South."

✔ **Reading Check: Summarizing** How did the creation of new roads and canals aid the economy?

★ The Election of 1824

Although Henry Clay had tried to build up a national economy, the country still faced many regional differences. The presidential election of 1824 showed these divisions. One of the two main candidates was Secretary of State **John Quincy Adams**. The other was Andrew Jackson, who had become a senator from Tennessee. Both men ran as Republicans. Jackson won the most popular votes, but he did not have enough electoral votes to win office. Under the rules set forth in the Constitution, the House of Representatives had to choose the winner. Speaker of the House Henry Clay influenced the vote by backing Adams. The House chose Adams as president. In response, Jackson's supporters claimed that Adams had made a "corrupt bargain" with Clay. These accusations only increased after Adams chose Clay to be his secretary of state.

The election controversy weakened President Adams's congressional and public support. He was already unpopular in the slaveholding South. He thus had little support when he asked for more federal money for canals, education, roads, and scientific research. Congress rejected most of these plans. However, it agreed to pay for some road and canal projects.

As president, John Quincy Adams supported higher education and tried unsuccessfully to establish a national university.

✔ **Reading Check: Finding the Main Idea** Why did John Quincy Adams have weak public and congressional support during his presidency?

Section 2 Review

go.
hrw
.com
Homework Practice Online
keyword: SF3 HP12

1 **Identify** and explain:
- Henry Clay
- Missouri Compromise
- American System
- Cumberland Road
- Erie Canal
- John Quincy Adams

2 **Summarizing** Copy the graphic organizer below. Use it to describe how the debate over slavery affected the growth of the North, South, and West in the 1820s.

3 **Finding the Main Idea**
a. How did new transportation systems affect the expansion and development of the nation?

b. What caused the controversy surrounding the 1824 presidential election?

4 **Writing and Critical Thinking**
Supporting a Point of View Imagine that you are Henry Clay. Write a letter to a friend in Missouri explaining your reasons for proposing the Missouri Compromise.

Consider the following:
- the balance of power between slave and free states in Congress
- the prohibition of slavery in territory north of latitude 36°30'
- the compromise's effect on national unity

The Age of Jackson

Read to Discover

1. How was Jacksonian Democracy a sign of change in American politics?
2. How did tariff disputes lead to the nullification crisis, and how did President Jackson respond?
3. Why was President Jackson against a national bank, and how did his opposition affect the economy?

WHY IT MATTERS TODAY

Voting is the foundation of our democracy. Use **CNNfyi.com** or other **current events** sources to learn about a recent local, state, or federal election. Record your findings in your journal.

Define

- nominating conventions
- spoils system
- kitchen cabinet
- states' rights
- nullification crisis

Identify

- Andrew Jackson
- Democratic Party
- John C. Calhoun
- Martin Van Buren
- Tariff of Abominations
- Daniel Webster
- *McCulloch v. Maryland*
- Whig Party
- Panic of 1837
- William Henry Harrison

This small figure of a frog was meant to encourage voters to "Croak for the Jackson Wagon."

The Story Continues

John Quincy Adams once described himself as "a man of reserved, cold . . . and forbidding [threatening] manners." Many citizens viewed Adams as part of an old, upper-class culture—wealthy people out of touch with the country's needs. Political rallies of the 1820s showed that the people wanted a more lively leader. The wild gatherings held by Andrew Jackson's supporters amazed politicians. One writer noted that Jackson's appeal proved there "must be a new order of things."

★ Jacksonian Democracy

Western lawmakers began expanding voting rights in the 1790s. These changes spread eastward in the early 1800s. Many more Americans gained the right to vote. Many states removed property requirements for voting, allowing more white men to vote. Some political parties began holding **nominating conventions**. These were public meetings to select the party's presidential and vice presidential candidates.

Expanded voting rights and conventions let more people become active in politics. Historians began calling this democratic expansion Jacksonian Democracy after popular politician **Andrew Jackson**.

Not everyone gained greater political power, however. In 1820 women were not allowed to vote in any state. In addition, free African Americans had no voting rights in most states. The supporters of Andrew Jackson were mostly farmers, frontier settlers, and southern slaveholders. They believed their leader would defend the rights of the common people and the slave states.

Many of these Americans believed that a "corrupt bargain" between Henry Clay and John Qunicy Adams had stolen the 1824 election from Jackson. These people got together to make sure that Jackson would become the next president. They began to call themselves Democrats and formed the **Democratic Party**. Many people who backed President Adams began calling themselves National Republicans. In the presidential election of 1828, Adams ran as a National Republican, while Jackson ran as a Democrat. Jackson chose Senator **John C. Calhoun** of South Carolina as his vice presidential running mate.

✔ **Reading Check: Finding the Main Idea** What led to the creation of the Democratic Party?

⭐ Jackson's Victory

The 1828 campaign focused a great deal on the candidates' personalities. Jackson's campaigners described him as a war hero. They said he had been born poor and rose to success through his own hard work. They contrasted this image with Adams, a Harvard-educated man whose father had been the second U.S. president. Some of Jackson's supporters also described Adams as being out of touch with everyday people. Even an ally of Adams said that he was as "cold as a lump of ice." In turn, Adams's supporters said Jackson was hot tempered, crude, and ill equipped to be president. Yet, when the election was over, Jackson and Calhoun had won with a record number of popular votes.

Jackson's supporters saw his victory as a win for the common people. One Kentucky newspaper editor described the feeling. "It was a proud day for the people. General Jackson is *their own* president." To show this, a crowd of Jackson voters celebrated his inauguration with a huge party on the White House lawn. The party caused a great deal of property damage. Some people feared that the mob at the White House was a sign of trouble. Margaret Bayard Smith recalled the inauguration party.

 "What a scene did we witness! . . . a rabble, a mob, of boys, . . . women, children, scrambling, fighting, romping. . . . But it was the people's day, and the people's President, and the people would rule."

—Margaret Bayard Smith, quoted in *Eyewitness to America*, edited by David Colbert

Andrew Jackson

Andrew Jackson's nickname was Old Hickory. The name reflected his reputation for being extremely tough, like the hard wood of a hickory tree. He was born in 1767 in South Carolina. By the time he was 13 years old both his parents had died. Jackson moved to North Carolina, where he became a lawyer, and then to Tennessee. He earned respect as a military leader during the War of 1812 and later represented Tennessee in the U.S. Senate. In 1828 he won the presidency in a landslide.

Jackson believed in being a take-charge president. He vetoed more bills during his presidency than all the previous presidents combined. He also had a quick temper with people who disagreed with his views. He was popular with the common people, however. They saw him as a simple man who had gained great influence and respect through hard work. Why was Andrew Jackson so popular?

Analyzing Primary Sources

Drawing Inferences and Conclusions How did this scene reflect Jacksonian Democracy?

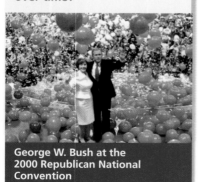

Citizenship
and You

Political Conventions

Before the 1830s U.S. presidential candidates were selected by members of Congress from each political party. In the election of 1832, however, the major parties began holding national conventions. There they chose their candidate for president. Each state held a convention to choose its delegates to the national meeting.

Many important changes have taken place over the years in party politics. For example, the number of delegates attending conventions has risen a great deal as the population has grown. In 1831 only 116 delegates attended the first convention. However, in 2000 the Democratic National Convention had 5,000 delegates. In addition, minorities, women, and young people have become an important influence on conventions. How have political nominating conventions changed over time?

George W. Bush at the 2000 Republican National Convention

Jackson rewarded some of his supporters with government jobs—a practice known as the **spoils system**. This term comes from the saying "to the victor belong the spoils [valued goods] of the enemy." However, Jackson changed few government positions, replacing less than one fifth of federal officeholders. Secretary of State <u>Martin Van Buren</u> was one of Jackson's strongest allies in his official cabinet. President Jackson also relied a great deal on an informal group of trusted advisers. This group was called the **kitchen cabinet** because its members sometimes met in the White House kitchen.

✔ **Reading Check: Analyzing Information** What effect did Jackson's election have on the government?

★ Conflict over Tariffs

One of the first challenges President Jackson faced was a growing regional conflict over tariffs. Northern manufacturers wanted high tariffs to protect their new industries from foreign competition, which came mostly from Great Britain. British companies could drive smaller American firms out of business by selling factory goods more cheaply than Americans could afford to make them. Protective tariffs blocked this practice.

However, the South had little industry to protect. The southern economy relied on agriculture, particularly cotton exports. Southerners imported most of their manufactured goods. High tariffs made these goods more expensive and also angered some of the South's European trading partners. Southerners thus wanted low tariffs. Westerners were divided on the tariff issue. Northern areas tended to support tariffs. For example, Kentucky wanted tariffs to protect its hemp industry, while further south, westerners tended to oppose tariffs.

In 1828, under strong pressure from northern manufacturers, Congress passed a tariff with very high rates. Angry southerners called the law the **Tariff of Abominations**. (An abomination is a hateful thing.) Some southern politicians saw the tariff as one way the federal government was abusing its power over the states.

✔ **Reading Check: Identifying Points of View** Why were the North, South, and West divided over the benefits of high tariffs?

★ The Nullification Crisis

Vice President John C. Calhoun, an experienced politician, helped lead opposition to the tariff. He wrote a statement in support of **states' rights**. People who favor states' rights believe that the federal government's authority is strictly limited by the Constitution. Calhoun's statement said that states had the right to nullify, or cancel, any federal law they considered unconstitutional. The dispute between the state and federal governments became known as the **nullification crisis**. Calhoun warned that states had the right to rebel if their rights were violated. Senator **Daniel Webster** of Massachusetts disagreed. He vowed, "Liberty and Union, now and forever, one and inseparable!"

South Carolina tested the nullification theory after Congress passed a new tariff in 1832. The South Carolina state legislature passed a resolution declaring that the 1828 and 1832 tariffs were "null, void . . . [and not] binding upon this State, its officers or citizens." Calhoun resigned from the vice presidency in support of his home state. Some thought the federal government would use force to collect the tariff duties. South Carolina officials said the state would withdraw from the Union if this happened.

Jackson was strongly against nullification. "I consider, then, the power to annul [cancel] a law of the United States . . . incompatible with [contrary to] the existence of the Union," he said. Jackson said he would send U.S. troops into South Carolina to enforce federal laws. However, he did not have to take this step, because the two sides reached a compromise. Congress agreed to lower the tariffs little by little over several years. South Carolina's leaders agreed to enforce the tariff law. However, they still believed that nullification was legal.

✔ **Reading Check: Summarizing** What led to the nullification crisis, and why was it significant?

★ The Second Bank of the United States

President Jackson upheld federal authority in the nullification crisis. However, he did not always support greater federal power. For example, he was against the Second Bank of the United States, which Congress had founded in 1816. Many states had also opposed the Bank and had taken action against it. For example, several states, including Maryland, passed laws that taxed branches of the national bank. James McCulloch, cashier of the Bank's branch in Maryland, refused to pay this tax. The state took him to court, and the resulting case, _**McCulloch v. Maryland**_, went all the way to the U.S. Supreme Court.

The Court, led by Chief Justice John Marshall, made two important rulings in the case. The Court supported the Bank's constitutionality. First, Marshall said that the elastic

Interpreting Political Cartoons

Jackson against the Bank *This political cartoon shows President Andrew Jackson, on the left, using his veto stick to fight against the Bank of the United States and its state branches.* **Why do you think the artist portrayed the Bank as a monster with many heads?**

COLLECTION OF THE NEW-YORK HISTORICAL SOCIETY

U.S. Debt from 1800 to 1840
(in thousands of dollars)

Year	Debt
1800	82,976
1805	82,312
1810	53,173
1815	99,834
1820	91,016
1825	83,788
1830	48,565
1835	38,000
1840	3,573

Using Mathematical Skills

1. What was the difference in the debt between 1800 and 1840?

2. Create a line graph that illustrates changes in the national debt between 1800 and 1840.

3. Imagine that you are a Democratic politician in 1836. Write a speech that summarizes the change in the national debt during Jackson's presidency.

clause of the Constitution allowed Congress to establish the Bank. This ruling was a broad interpretation of the implied powers of Congress. The Court also decided that federal law was superior to state law—an idea that challenged the principle of states' rights. This ruling meant that Maryland could not tax or interfere with the Bank.

This victory was not enough for Nicholas Biddle, the Bank's director, who decided to make the Bank a presidential issue. The Bank's charter was due to expire in 1836. Rather than wait, Biddle pushed for a bill to renew the Bank's charter in 1832. Jackson campaigned strongly for the defeat of this bill. "I will kill it," he promised. Jackson vetoed legislation to renew the charter. He then issued this strongly worded statement.

 History Makers Speak
❝It is to be regretted that the rich and powerful too often bend the acts of government to their selfish purposes. . . . By attempting to gratify their desires, we have in the results of our legislation arrayed [positioned] section against section, interest against interest.❞

—Andrew Jackson, quoted in *The Annals of America*

Congress could not gather the two-thirds majority needed to override Jackson's veto. Jackson also weakened the Bank's power by moving most of its funds to state banks, which his opponents called pet banks. In many cases, these state banks used the funds to offer credit to people buying land. While this practice helped promote expansion in the West, it also led to inflation.

In the summer of 1836, Jackson tried to slow this inflation. He did this by ordering Americans to use only gold or silver—instead of paper bank notes—to buy government-owned land. This policy did not help the national economy as Jackson had hoped. However, Jackson did improve the economy by lowering the national debt.

✔ **Reading Check: Contrasting** What positions did John Marshall and Andrew Jackson take on the Second Bank of the United States?

Martin Van Buren became the new vice president when Andrew Jackson won re-election in 1832.

★ Van Buren's Presidency

Jackson was still very popular with voters in 1836 at the end of his second term. However, his actions had angered members of Congress, many of whom believed he had abused his presidential powers. In 1834 a group of Jackson opponents had formed the **Whig Party**. Many Whigs supported the idea of a weak president and a strong legislature. In 1836 the Whigs nominated four candidates to run for president against Martin Van Buren, the Democratic candidate and former vice president under Jackson. Despite this opposition, with strong support from Jackson, Van Buren won the election.

The people never liked Van Buren the way they had liked Jackson, however. Shortly after Van Buren took office, the country experienced a financial crisis. Called the **Panic of 1837**, this crisis led to a severe economic depression. The policies of the pet banks and Jackson's plan to curb inflation had helped lead to the panic. Nevertheless, Van Buren received the blame for it. The financial crisis hurt President Van Buren's re-election campaign in 1840. The Whigs ran **William Henry Harrison**, a general from the Battle of Tippecanoe, as their candidate. He and John Tyler, his running mate, ran under the popular campaign slogan "Tippecanoe and Tyler too."

The Whigs called Van Buren a friend of the rich and claimed Harrison was the friend of the common people. Harrison had actually been born to a wealthy family. However, the Whigs' emphasis on his war record and log-cabin roots made Harrison seem like a rugged man from the frontier, similar to Jackson. More than 75 percent of the eligible voters turned out for this election. Although the popular vote was close, Harrison won the electoral college in a landslide, gaining 234 electoral votes to Van Buren's 60. The Whigs had achieved their goal of winning the presidency.

THE GRANGER COLLECTION, NEW YORK

Interpreting the Visual Record

Log cabin *This 1840 campaign illustration supposedly shows the log cabin where William Henry Harrison grew up.* **Why might showing Harrison in a setting like this have helped his popularity?**

✔ **Reading Check: Identifying Cause and Effect** How did Jackson's policies affect the economy, and what was the result for Van Buren?

Section 3 Review

Homework Practice Online
keyword: SF3 HP12

1 **Define** and explain:
- nominating conventions
- spoils system
- kitchen cabinet
- states' rights
- nullification crisis

2 **Identify** and explain:
- Andrew Jackson
- Democratic Party
- John C. Calhoun
- Martin Van Buren
- Tariff of Abominations
- Daniel Webster
- *McCulloch* v. *Maryland*
- Whig Party
- Panic of 1837
- William Henry Harrison

3 **Summarizing** Copy the graphic organizer below. Use it to describe the main events of Jackson's presidency and the major changes in politics that took place during that time.

Jacksonian Presidency

Jacksonian Era

Jacksonian Democracy

4 **Finding the Main Idea**
a. What caused the nullification crisis, and how did President Jackson deal with this issue?

b. Why did President Jackson veto the renewal of the Second Bank of the United States, and what effect did this have on the economy?

5 **Writing and Critical Thinking**
Analyzing Information Imagine that you are a reporter covering the effect of Jackson's election. Write a newspaper article describing the rise of Jacksonian Democracy.

Consider the following:
- expansion of voting rights and nominating conventions
- formation of the Democratic Party
- Jackson's appeal to the common people

Indian Removal

Read to Discover

1. Why did the federal and state governments begin an American Indian removal policy?
2. How did American Indians such as the Cherokee resist removal?
3. How were American Indians affected by the removal from their lands?

WHY IT MATTERS TODAY

Many American Indians were forced to leave their homes to live on reservations. Use CNNfyi.com or other **current events** sources to identify a group of people being forced to leave their homeland today. Record your findings in your journal.

Identify

- Black Hawk
- Indian Removal Act
- Indian Territory
- Bureau of Indian Affairs
- Treaty of Dancing Rabbit Creek
- Sequoya
- John Ross
- *Worcester* v. *Georgia*
- Trail of Tears
- Osceola

Black Hawk refused to leave his homeland.

The Story Continues

As American settlers moved west, American Indian leaders talked about the best way to deal with them. Keokuk, a Sauk leader from Illinois, wanted to compromise and avoid a war. Another Sauk leader named Black Hawk disagreed. He believed that U.S. officials had bribed Keokuk and other Indian leaders to gain their support. Black Hawk firmly resisted all attempts to take American Indian lands.

★ The Black Hawk War

In 1827 the federal government decided to end years of conflict between American Indians and U.S. settlers in Illinois. Officials ordered the removal of all Indians from the state. **Black Hawk** and his followers ignored the removal policy, rejecting the very idea of land ownership.

History Makers Speak

❝My reason teaches me that land cannot be sold. The Great Spirit gave it to his children to live upon. So long as they occupy and cultivate it they have the right to the soil. Nothing can be sold but such things as can be carried away.❞

—Black Hawk, quoted in *Atlas of the North American Indian,* by Carl Waldman

When the Sauk returned from their winter hunt in 1830, they found that white settlers had moved into their village. But Black Hawk and his followers refused to be pushed out. Although his forces were flying a white flag, U.S. troops fired on them. Black Hawk then decided to fight. Indian groups began to raid American settlements and attack U.S. troops. However, by August 1832 the Sauk forces were running out of food and supplies. Black Hawk surrendered and gave up leadership of the Sauk. By 1850 the U.S. Army had removed the American Indians living within the old Northwest Territory.

✔ **Reading Check: Finding the Main Idea** What was the outcome of the Black Hawk War?

★ The Indian Removal Act

Indian removal was also an issue in the Southeast. American Indians had long lived in settlements stretching from Georgia to Mississippi. However, President Jackson and other political leaders wanted to open this land to settlement by American farmers. They said that Indians in the Southeast should move to lands in the West. Under pressure from Jackson, Congress passed the **Indian Removal Act** in 1830. This act authorized the removal of American Indians who lived east of the Mississippi River.

Congress then established **Indian Territory** as a new Indian homeland. This area contained most of what is now Oklahoma.

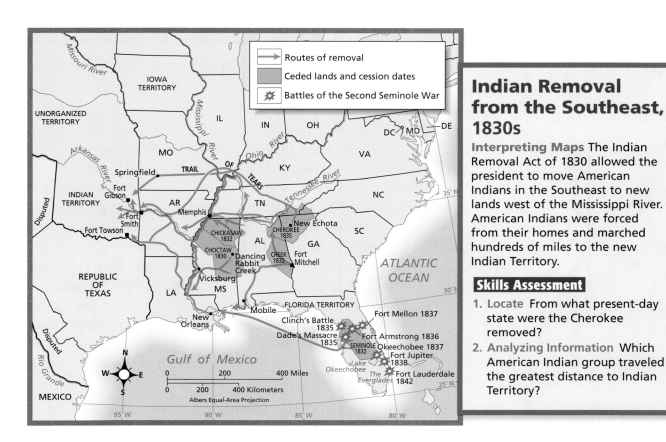

Indian Removal from the Southeast, 1830s

Interpreting Maps The Indian Removal Act of 1830 allowed the president to move American Indians in the Southeast to new lands west of the Mississippi River. American Indians were forced from their homes and marched hundreds of miles to the new Indian Territory.

Skills Assessment

1. **Locate** From what present-day state were the Cherokee removed?
2. **Analyzing Information** Which American Indian group traveled the greatest distance to Indian Territory?

Some supporters of this plan argued that it would protect American Indians. John C. Calhoun believed that removal would prevent more conflicts with American settlers. "One of the greatest evils to which they are subject is that incessant [constant] pressure of our population," he noted. Congress also approved the creation of the **Bureau of Indian Affairs** to oversee federal policy toward American Indians.

The Choctaw were the first American Indians sent to Indian Territory. After the Mississippi legislature abolished the government of the Choctaw, some Choctaw leaders signed the **Treaty of Dancing Rabbit Creek**. This treaty gave more than 7.5 million acres of their land to the state. The Choctaw journeyed from Mississippi to Indian Territory during the winter of 1831–32. The trip was disastrous. Federal officials in charge of the move did not provide enough food or supplies. As a result, about one fourth of the Choctaw died of cold, disease, and starvation. News of the U.S. treatment of the Choctaw caused other American Indians to resist removal. Some Creek decided to stay on their lands, located mainly in Alabama, but state officials ordered their forced removal. In 1836, federal troops led some 14,500 captured Creek, many in chains, to Indian Territory.

The Chickasaw, mostly from Mississippi, were moved west in the winter of 1837–38. They had been promised better supplies on their trip to Indian Territory. Yet, Chickasaw lives were also lost during removal.

✔ **Reading Check: Comparing** What was the Indian Removal Act, and how did it affect the Choctaw, Creek, and Chickasaw?

Interpreting the Visual Record

A new alphabet *Sequoya poses with the Cherokee alphabet he developed in the bottom image, while above him is a page from a Cherokee primer.* **Why would the creation of an alphabet be important?**

THE GRANGER COLLECTION, NEW YORK

⭐ The Cherokee Nation

American Indians resisted removal in various ways. Many Cherokee believed that they could prevent conflicts with settlers by adopting the culture of white people. For example, in the early 1800s the Cherokee invited missionary societies to found schools in their towns. In these schools Cherokee children learned how to read and write English.

American Indians used complex spoken languages, but none had a written language. In the early 1800s a Cherokee named **Sequoya** developed a writing system that used 86 characters to represent Cherokee syllables. In 1828 the Cherokee began publishing a newspaper, the *Cherokee Phoenix*. This paper was printed in both English and Cherokee. The Cherokee also created a government inspired by the U.S. Constitution with an election system, a bicameral council, and a court system. All of these were headed by a principal chief. Voters elected **John Ross**, a successful plantation owner, as the first principal chief.

✔ **Reading Check: Summarizing** What contributions did Sequoya make to Cherokee culture?

⭐ The Trail of Tears

However, the adoption of white culture did not protect the Cherokee. After gold was discovered on Cherokee land in Georgia, their treaty rights were ignored. When the Cherokee refused to move, the Georgia militia began attacking Cherokee towns. In response, the tribe sued the state. The Cherokee said that they were an independent nation, and that the government of Georgia had no legal power within their territory.

In 1832 the Supreme Court, under the leadership of Chief Justice John Marshall, agreed. In **_Worcester_ v. _Georgia_** the Court ruled that "[the Cherokee nation] is a distinct community, occupying its own territory, … in which the laws of Georgia can have no force." The Court stated that only the federal government, not the states, had authority over the Cherokee.

The Supreme Court decision declared Georgia's actions illegal. However, when Georgia ignored the Court's ruling, President Jackson took no action. "John Marshall has made his decision; now let him enforce it," Jackson said. Most Americans accepted Jackson's position.

With President Jackson refusing to enforce the Supreme Court's decision, many Cherokee saw removal as unavoidable. Elias Boudinot, editor of the _Cherokee Phoenix_, wrote that he had no hope "that we will be reinstated in [given back] our rights." To silence further criticism, the Georgia militia destroyed the _Phoenix_'s printing press.

In the spring of 1838, U.S. troops began to remove all Cherokee to Indian Territory. A few were able to escape and hide in the mountains of North Carolina. After the Cherokee were removed, Georgia took their businesses, farms, and property. The Cherokee's 800-mile forced march, which lasted from 1838 to 1839, became known as the **Trail of Tears**. Almost one fourth of the 18,000 Cherokee on the march died.

✔ **Reading Check: Summarizing** What did John Marshall decide in _Worcester_ v. _Georgia_, and how did Jackson's response affect the Cherokee?

Interpreting the Visual Record

The Trail of Tears _Disease and hunger were major causes of death for Cherokee on the Trail of Tears._ **What does the way that people are dressed in this painting suggest about the harshness of the weather on the march?**

At the end of the Second Seminole War, several hundred Seminole remained carefully hidden in the Florida everglades.

⭐ The Second Seminole War

Unlike the Cherokee, the Seminole of Florida fought removal with armed resistance. In 1832 some Seminole leaders were forced to sign a treaty promising to leave Florida within three years. They also agreed that any Seminole of African ancestry would be considered a runaway slave. This condition worried the Seminole, because many escaped slaves had become accepted as family members of the Seminole.

The Seminole ignored the treaty and refused to leave Florida or sign a new removal agreement. A Seminole leader named **Osceola** called upon the Seminole to resist removal by force.

 History Makers Speak ❝When the Great Spirit tells me to go with the white man, I go, but he tells me not to go. I have a rifle, and I have some powder and some lead. I say, we must not leave our homes and lands.❞

—Osceola, quoted in *Native American Testimony,* edited by Peter Nabakov

Osceola's followers agreed, and the Second Seminole War began. At first, the Seminole won many battles against U.S. forces. Then in 1837, U.S. forces captured Osceola, who soon died in prison. The Seminole continued to fight against the United States. By 1842 the U.S. Army had captured and removed some 4,000 Seminole and killed hundreds of others. In the process, some 1,500 U.S. soldiers lost their lives. After spending millions of dollars, U.S. officials decided to give up the fight. The Seminole had resisted removal, and many live in Florida today.

✔ **Reading Check: Identifying Cause and Effect** Why did the Second Seminole War begin, and what was the result of the war?

Section 4 Review

go.hrw.com Homework Practice Online
keyword: SF3 HP12

1 **Identify and explain:**
• Black Hawk
• Indian Removal Act
• Indian Territory
• Bureau of Indian Affairs
• Treaty of Dancing Rabbit Creek
• Sequoya
• John Ross
• *Worcester* v. *Georgia*
• Trail of Tears
• Osceola

2 **Comparing and Contrasting** Copy the chart below. Use it to identify American Indian groups removed during this period and their responses to removal.

American Indian Group	Response to Removal

3 **Finding the Main Idea**
a. Why did U.S. and state officials support an American Indian removal policy?

b. How did the Cherokee use the courts to resist removal from their lands, and what were the results of their actions?

4 **Writing and Critical Thinking**
Identifying Points of View Imagine that you are an American Indian forced to leave your home. Write a poem or song describing the effect of removal on American Indians in the East.

Consider the following:
• the American Indian policies of state and federal governments
• the groups forced to leave and the conditions they faced

Section

5

American Culture

Read to Discover

1. Who were the favorite writers of the early 1800s, and what did they write about?
2. What was the focus of the Hudson River school?

WHY IT MATTERS TODAY

Art and literature are important parts of a country's culture. Use CNN fyi.com and other **current events** sources to find an example of art or literature that reveals the culture of a country of your choice. Record your findings in your journal.

Identify

- Washington Irving
- James Fenimore Cooper
- Catharine Maria Sedgwick
- Hudson River school
- Thomas Cole
- George Caleb Bingham

The Story Continues

In 1817 Virginia politician William Wirt published a popular biography of Revolutionary leader Patrick Henry. Wirt spent years researching his book. Yet he found that Henry was not as exciting as he had hoped. "The incidents of Mr. Henry's life are extremely monotonous [boring]," Wirt told a friend. "It is all speaking, speaking, speaking." To make his book more exciting, Wirt exaggerated certain events. Some critics accused him of rewriting history. Despite these complaints, Wirt's book helped make Patrick Henry a hero for a whole generation of Americans.

Patrick Henry was seen as a hero of the American Revolution.

★ American Tales

Many developments in American life led to the success of William Wirt's biography of Patrick Henry. For example, much of the public was interested in the Revolutionary era. Wirt represented a growing number of writers who wrote about the heroes of the Revolution. These writers inspired pride in the United States. Unlike Wirt, however, most of these writers used fictional characters to represent American ideals.

One of the first American writers to gain international fame was **Washington Irving**. Born in 1783, he was named after George

A New National Identity **385**

CONNECTING TO

THE ARTS

The Legend of Sleepy Hollow The literature of the early 1800s often inspired artists. In his painting *The Headless Horseman Pursuing Ichabod Crane*, artist John Quidor captures one of the most frightening scenes in Washington Irving's story "The Legend of Sleepy Hollow." Here Crane, the local schoolmaster, flees a headless rider that he believes is an evil spirit. **How does the artist show the drama of this scene?**

Washington. Irving's writing often dealt with American history. He often wrote humorous stories, using a style of writing called satire. Through satire, Irving warned that Americans should learn from the past and be cautious about the future. He shared this idea in one of his best-known short stories, "Rip Van Winkle." Rip Van Winkle is a man who falls asleep during the time of the American Revolution. He wakes up 20 years later to a society he does not recognize. Irving published this and another well-known tale, "The Legend of Sleepy Hollow," in an 1819–20 collection.

Irving was one of the first American writers to gain respect in Europe. In fact, European writers helped shape his humorous style. Irving believed that the United States should not give up European traditions altogether. He said, "We are a young people . . . , and we must take our examples and models in a great degree, from the existing nations of Europe."

✔ **Reading Check: Finding the Main Idea** How did Washington Irving help make American writing more respected?

⭐ James Fenimore Cooper

In some of his most popular works, Irving combined European influences with American settings and characters. His work served as a bridge between European writing traditions and American writers exploring new styles. Perhaps the best known of these new writers was **James Fenimore Cooper**. Cooper was born to a wealthy New Jersey family in 1789. He never saw the American frontier, but stories about the West and the American Indians who lived there interested him. These topics became the focus of his best-known works.

In 1823 Cooper published *The Pioneers*. This novel was the first of five books that featured the heroic character Natty Bumppo. Together these books were called the Leatherstocking Tales. This series told of settling the western frontier. Cooper's hero, Bumppo, was a frontiersman who found truth in nature. Cooper's stories also included historical events. For example, *The Last of the Mohicans* takes place during the French and Indian War. By placing his fictional characters in the middle of a real historical event, Cooper popularized a type of writing called historical fiction.

Catharine Maria Sedgwick

Some critics, such as poet Russell Lowell, said that Cooper's characters were not interesting. They particularly criticized the women in his stories. Cooper's female characters seemed to have no purpose other than to be saved by the hero. Other authors of historical fiction, such as **Catharine Maria Sedgwick**, created more interesting heroines. In 1822 Sedgwick published her first novel, *A New England Tale*. This story describes the landscape and culture of New England life.

Another popular book by Sedgwick, *Hope Leslie*, was a historical novel set in Massachusetts in the 1600s. To make this 1827 novel realistic, Sedgwick did major research into the culture of the Mohawk who had lived in the area at the time. Some readers did not like Sedgwick's description of the Pilgrims. She included unpleasant parts of their lives, such as their superstitions and intolerance, in her novels. Sedgwick defended her work saying that it accurately showed both the strengths and weaknesses of early Americans in New England.

> **History Makers Speak**
>
> **❝These were the vices [bad habits] of their age. . . . They had a most generous and self-devoting zeal [energy] to the cause of liberty, so far as they understood it, but they were still in the thraldom [captivity] of . . . superstition.❞**
>
> —Catharine Maria Sedgwick, from *Life and Letters of Catharine M. Sedgwick*, edited by Mary E. Dewey

Sedgwick hoped that Americans could learn new ideas from reading about the lives of the Pilgrims.

Sedgwick was the most successful female author of her time, writing six books. Through her work, she also challenged commonly held ideas about women. For example, in *Married or Single?* Sedgwick, who never married, rejected the idea that all women had to marry. She hoped the novel would "lessen the stigma [disgrace] placed on the term, old maid."

✔ **Reading Check: Analyzing Information** How did American writers such as Cooper and Sedgwick describe the growth of a new cultural identity in the United States?

Catharine Maria Sedgwick hoped that her novels would teach people about America while entertaining them.

THE GRANGER COLLECTION, NEW YORK

Thomas Cole painted The Notch in the White Mountains *in 1839.*

⭐ A New Style of Art

The writings of Irving and Cooper also inspired painters. These artists began to paint landscapes that showed the history of America and the beauty of the land. Earlier American painters, such as John Singleton Copley, were portrait painters. By the 1830s a group of artists called the **Hudson River school** emerged. These artists primarily painted landscapes. Their name came from the subject of many of their paintings—the Hudson River valley.

Thomas Cole was the leader of the group. He had moved to the United States from Britain in 1819 and soon recognized the unique qualities of the American landscape. As his work gained fame, he encouraged other American artists to show the beauty of nature. Observer William Bryant praised Cole's painting.

Analyzing Primary Sources

Identifying Points of View According to Bryant, why was Cole's painting uniquely American?

History Makers Speak

❝[It] carried the eye over scenes of wild grandeur peculiar to our country, over our aerial mountain tops with their mighty growth of forests never touched by the axe, along the bank of streams never deformed by culture and into the depth of skies bright with the hues [colors] of our own climate.❞

—William Bryant, quoted in *Art and Life in America,* by Oliver W. Larkin

By the 1840s many American artists were combining rugged landscapes with scenes of frontier life. For example, **George Caleb Bingham** tried to show the ruggedness of the West. As the country grew, the new styles of art and literature helped form a new American national identity.

✔ **Reading Check: Finding the Main Idea** How did the style of American art change to reflect the American way of life in the early 1800s?

Section 5 Review

go.hrw.com
Homework Practice Online
keyword: SF3 HP12

❶ **Identify** and explain:
• Washington Irving
• James Fenimore Cooper
• Catharine Maria Sedgwick
• Hudson River school
• Thomas Cole
• George Caleb Bingham

❷ **Summarizing** Copy the graphic organizer below. Use it to identify the shared characteristics that made early American writers' and painters' work distinctly American.

| American Writers | + | American Painters | = | American Cultural Identity |

❸ **Finding the Main Idea**
a. Who were some major early American authors, and what did they write about?

b. What subjects did Thomas Cole and the other Hudson River school artists paint?

❹ **Writing and Critical Thinking**
Analyzing Information Imagine that you are an art student visiting America from Europe in the 1840s. Write a story to tell your classmates that describes how American culture reflects the American way of life.

Consider the following:
• the work of popular American writers
• the work of popular American painters

The Last of the Mohicans

James Fenimore Cooper

*James Fenimore Cooper was the first major American novelist.
His novels helped create the myth of the frontier and the
American frontier hero. Natty Bumppo, also called
Leatherstocking and Hawkeye, is the hero of the five novels
called the Leatherstocking Tales. Chingachgook, a Mohican, is also an
important character in the popular stories. Cooper did not have direct experience
with American Indians or the frontier. He simply read books and listened to the
stories his father told. Nevertheless, Cooper's novels brought the frontier to life for
many readers. Cooper had a wide audience in the United States and Europe. His
novels have remained popular since his death in 1851. The following excerpt is
from* The Last of the Mohicans, *set during the French and Indian War. In this
passage Chingachgook tells Hawkeye about the Mohicans' recent history.*

"The first pale-faces who came among us spoke no English. They came in a large canoe, when my fathers had **buried the tomahawk**[1] with the redmen around them. Then, Hawkeye," he continued, betraying his deep emotion . . . : "then, Hawkeye, we were one people, we were happy. The salt lake gave us its fish, the wood its deer, and the air its birds. We took wives who bore us children; we worshipped the Great Spirit; and we kept the **Maquas**[2] beyond the sound of our songs of triumph! . . .

"The Dutch landed, and gave my people the **fire-water**;[3] they drank until the heavens and the earth seemed to meet, and they foolishly thought they had found the Great Spirit. Then they parted with their land. Foot by foot, they were driven back from the shores, until I, that am a chief and a **sagamore**,[4] have never seen the sun shine but through the trees, and have never visited the graves of my fathers. . . .

"Where are the blossoms of those summers!— fallen, one by one: so all of my family departed, each in his turn, to the land of spirits. I am on the hill-top, and most go down into the valley; and when Uncas follows in my footsteps, there will no longer be any of the blood of the sagamores, for my boy is the last of the Mohicans."

Understanding What You Read

1. **Literature and History** According to the story told by Chingachgook, what has happened to the Mohicans?

2. **Literature and History** What does Chingachgook mean by going down into the valley, and how is this significant for the Mohicans?

3. **Literature and You** Why do you think that Cooper chose to portray the decline of the Mohicans in this way?

---

[1]**buried the tomahawk:** made peace
[2]**Maquas:** their enemy
[3]**fire-water:** alcoholic beverages
[4]**sagamore:** a lesser chief of the Algonquian

Chapter 12 Review

The Chapter at a Glance

Examine the visual summary of the chapter below. Use the chapter's main ideas to create a five-section outline that you might give to a classmate to study.

A Growing Nation

Identifying People and Ideas

Use the following terms or people in historically significant sentences.

1. Monroe Doctrine
2. Henry Clay
3. American System
4. Democratic Party
5. John C. Calhoun
6. nullification crisis
7. *McCulloch* v. *Maryland*
8. *Worcester* v. *Georgia*
9. Trail of Tears
10. Hudson River school

Understanding Main Ideas

Section 1 *(Pages 364–367)*

1. What effect did the revolutions in Latin America have on U.S. foreign policy, and what was the impact of the U.S. response?

Section 2 *(Pages 368–373)*

2. What led to the Missouri Compromise, and what did it achieve?

Section 3 *(Pages 374–379)*

3. How did the issue of protective tariffs divide northerners and southerners?
4. Why did President Jackson veto the rechartering of the Second Bank of the United States?

Section 4 *(Pages 380–384)*

5. How did American Indians resist removal to Indian Territory?

Section 5 *(Pages 385–388)*

6. What topics did early American authors write about?

You Be the Historian— Reviewing Themes

1. **Global Relations** How did the United States settle its border disputes with British Canada and Spanish Florida?
2. **Citizenship** How did U.S. political parties change between the elections of 1820 and 1828?
3. **Constitutional Heritage** What did Chief Justice John Marshall and the Supreme Court decide in *McCulloch* v. *Maryland* and *Worcester* v. *Georgia*, and how did these cases affect the power of state governments?

Thinking Critically

1. **Comparing** What was similar about the disputes that led to the Missouri Compromise and the nullification crisis?
2. **Contrasting** How did protective tariffs affect the economies of the North, the South, and the West?
3. **Analyzing Information** How did American culture develop in the 1820s?

Interpreting Political Cartoons

Study the editorial cartoon of Andrew Jackson below. Then answer the questions that follow.

BORN TO COMMAND.

OF VETO MEMORY.

HAD I BEEN CONSULTED.

THE GRANGER COLLECTION, NEW YORK

KING ANDREW THE FIRST.

1. Which of the following statements best describes the artist's attitude about Jackson?
   a. Jackson should be king.
   b. Jackson is a strong leader.
   c. Jackson has vetoed too many bills.
   d. Jackson is behaving more like a king than an elected leader.

2. Is the artist in favor of or opposed to Jackson's policies?

Analyzing Primary Sources

Read the following quote from Senator John C. Calhoun concerning tariffs and states' rights, then answer the questions that follow.

> **"The truth can no longer be disguised, that the peculiar domestick institutions of the Southern States [that is, slavery], and the consequent direction which that and her soil and climate have given to her industry, has placed them in regard to taxation . . . in opposite relation to [against] the majority of the Union; against the danger of which, if there be no protective power in the reserved rights of the states, they must in the end be forced to rebel."**

3. Why does Calhoun think that the South is opposed to the tariff that the other states support?
   a. The southern economy, based on agriculture and slavery, is very different from that of the North and other parts of the Union.
   b. Southern politicians believe that the tariff and other taxes like it are unconstitutional.
   c. The South fears that it might be attacked by other states in the Union.
   d. The true reasons why the South opposes the tariff are hidden.

4. Based on your knowledge of the period, do you think that President Jackson would have agreed or disagreed with Senator Calhoun's views?

Alternative Assessment

American History

Building Your Portfolio

Interdisciplinary Connection to Geography

Select a region of the country (either the South, the Northeast, or the Midwest). Then create a brochure that might be used to attract settlers or immigrants to that region in the 1830s. Your brochure should focus on the region's culture, economy, and historical points of interest.

internet connect

Internet Activity: go.hrw.com
keyword: SF3 CF12

Choose an activity about the New National Identity of America to:

- Learn about other wars of independence.
- Research the development of an American culture in art and literature.
- Create a newspaper about Andrew Jackson and the politics of the 1830s.

A New National Identity **391**

Social Studies Skills

WORKSHOP

Identifying Cause and Effect

Identifying and understanding cause-and-effect relationships is crucial to the study of history. To investigate why events happen and what else may have happened because of these events, historians often ask questions such as: What immediate activities may have triggered the event? What past activities may have led up to the event? Who was involved?

How to Identify Cause and Effect

1. Look for clues. Certain words and phrases are immediate clues. They reveal the existence of a cause-and-effect relationship in history. The following chart lists some examples of clue words and phrases.

Clue Words and Phrases	
Cause	**Effect**
because	as a consequence
brought about	as a result of
gave rise to	depended on
inspired	originating from
led to	outcome
produced	proceeded from
provoked	resulting in
the reason	this led to

2. Identify the relationship. Read carefully to identify how historical events may be connected. Writers do not always state the link between cause and effect. Therefore, you must read very carefully. You may have to draw your own conclusions about the cause or the effect of an event.

3. Check for complex connections. Beyond the immediate cause and effect, check for other more complex connections. For example, an event might have multiple causes or effects. Effects may also be the causes of further events.

The following diagram presents an important cause-and-effect relationship involving the *Marbury* v. *Madison* Supreme Court case. In 1801 President John Adams appointed William Marbury as a federal judge. The new secretary of state, James Madison, refused to give Marbury his commission. This led Marbury to take his case to the Supreme Court. Chief Justice John Marshall decided that the Court did not have the power to force the government to give Marbury his commission. This ruling produced the principle of judicial review, which allows the Supreme Court to decide whether an act of Congress is constitutional.

Practicing the Skills

1. Identify the clue words used in the example above.
2. Reread Chapter 11, Section 3, of your textbook, which discusses the causes of the War of 1812.

Draw a diagram like the one above, showing the relationships between the important events leading up to the War of 1812.

History in Action

UNIT 5 SIMULATION

You Solve the Problem . . .

How Do You Encourage Westward Expansion during the Early 1800s?

Complete the following activity in small cooperative groups. It is 1803. Thomas Jefferson has purchased the Louisiana Territory from France. The United States has expanded to the Mississippi River. You are a member of a congressional subcommittee that will propose a plan to Congress to encourage westward expansion. Follow these steps to solve your problem.

1. Gather Information. Use your textbook and other resources to find information that might influence your plan of action for encouraging westward expansion. Be sure to use what you learned from the unit's Skills Workshop on Identifying Cause and Effect to help you find an effective solution to this problem. For example, you might consider why people choose to settle new lands and what effects their settlements may have. You may want to divide different parts of the research among group members.

2. List and Consider Options. After reviewing the information you have gathered, list and consider the options you might recommend for encouraging westward expansion. Your final solution to the problem may be easier to reach if you consider as many options as possible. Be sure to record your possible options for your presentation.

3. Consider Advantages and Disadvantages. Now consider the advantages and disadvantages of taking each option. Ask yourselves questions like: "What are the main benefits of westward expansion for the nation and for individuals?" Once you have considered the advantages and disadvantages, record them as notes for your presentation.

4. Choose, Implement, and Evaluate a Solution. After considering the advantages and disadvantages, you should plan and create a presentation. Be sure to make your proposal very clear. You will need to support your proposed plans for encouraging westward expansion by including information you gathered and by explaining why you rejected other possible options or solutions. Your presentation needs to be visually appealing so that you can get Congress to support your proposal. When you are ready, decide which group members will make each part of the presentation, and then take your solution to Congress (the rest of the class). Good luck!

UNIT 6 A Changing Nation (1790–1860)

Young People

IN HISTORY

Young Workers

By the mid-1800s teenage girls throughout New England were working and earning money of their own. These teenagers included girls in the city and in the country. Girls in rural areas usually worked out of their homes. They wove cloth, braided hats, or stitched together shoes. Girls in the cities often did needlework or found work as housekeepers or cooks.

In Fitzwilliam, New Hampshire, many young women made hats to be sold at the local store. They were usually not paid in money, but in store credit. Martha Alexander was 18 years old when she began making hats. Over a period of nearly four years, she braided 341 hats. Her store credit allowed her to buy teacups, saucers, and plates for her upcoming marriage.

Other New England girls worked in textile mills. In Lowell, Massachusetts, about half of the young women working in the mills were between the ages of 15 and 19 when they first arrived. Despite the long hours, many girls enjoyed their work in the mills. It gave them independence and relieved the isolation of farm life. The girls used their hard-earned money in many ways. Many of them sent money home to help their families or saved it for their future. Some girls spent their money on clothes and recreation, such as plays and concerts.

Textile mills often employed young workers.

Some teenagers found that life at the mills opened up a bright, new future for them. Lucy Larcom worked in the Lowell mills while she was a teenager and wrote about her experiences.

> **"And I was everyday making discoveries about life, and about myself. . . . I found that the crowd was made up of single human lives, not one of them wholly uninteresting, when separately known. . . . I defied the machinery to make me its slave. Its incessant discords [constant noise] could not drown the music of my thoughts. . . . I know that I was glad to be alive, and to be just where I was."**

If You Were There *What sorts of jobs would you be interested in?*

LEFT PAGE: *These workers from a shoe factory in Lynn, Massachusetts, went on strike in 1860.*

13 Industrial Growth in the North
(1790–1860)

The invention of the steel plow increased farm productivity.

Ruggles, Nourse, Mason & Co.,
Boston,

Manufacture, and Offer for Sale, the most Complete and Extensive assortment of

PLOWS

TO BE FOUND IN THE UNITED STATES.

Also, Hay, Straw and Corn Stalk Cutters, Corn Shellers, Fanning Mills, Corn and Cob Crushers, Burr Stone Portable Grinding Mills, Seed Sowers, Corn Planters, Horse Powers, Threshers, Carts, Cart Harness, Ox Yokes, Hand Corn Mills, Store, Steamboat and Wharf Trucks, Sugar Mills, &c. &c.

SEEDS.

Steamboats made river travel easier.

UNITED STATES

1793 Samuel Slater helps build a mill in Rhode Island for spinning cotton thread.

1807 Robert Fulton's *Clermont* becomes the first commercially successful steamboat.

1818 Eli Whitney invents the milling machine, which can make complex parts for many kinds of equipment.

1824 *Gibbons v. Ogden*, a case dealing with the power of the federal government to regulate commerce, reaches the Supreme Court.

1790 | 1800 | 1810 | 1820

1790 The first steam-powered mill opens in Great Britain.

1796 British doctor Edward Jenner develops an inoculation to prevent people from getting smallpox.

1814 Sweden and Norway are united in the Treaty of Kiel.

1821 Greece starts fighting for its independence from the Ottoman Empire.

Dr. Edward Jenner

THE GRANGER COLLECTION, NEW YORK

WORLD

THE GRANGER COLLECTION, NEW YORK

The manufacture of cloth was one of the first breakthroughs in the Industrial Revolution.

Build on What You Know

In the early 1800s Americans began to feel an increased sense of national pride, which led to new styles of art and literature. The country was also beginning to experience revolutions in industry and transportation. Factories, railroads, and steamships were built throughout the nation, particularly in the Northeast. These helped the U.S. economy grow rapidly.

Sewing machines allowed many women to earn a living at home.

Railroads transported many of the goods that factories produced during the Industrial Revolution.

1831 Cyrus McCormick invents the mechanical reaper.

1837 John Deere invents the steel plow.

1840 Government employees receive a 10-hour workday.

1844 Samuel Morse uses his invention, the telegraph, to send campaign news from Baltimore, Maryland, to Washington, D.C.

1852 Elisha Graves Otis invents the safety elevator.

1856 Gail Borden patents a method of condensing milk so that it can be safely stored in cans.

1830   1840   1850   1860

1838 The *Sirius* becomes the first steamship to cross the Atlantic Ocean entirely under steam power.

1847 The British Factory Act limits the working day to 10 hours for women and children.

1851 The Great Exhibition in London displays inventions from around the world.

1859 Construction of the Suez Canal begins in Egypt.

If you were there . . .

What kind of invention would you try to develop?

You Be the Historian

Themes Journal

What's Your Opinion? Do you **agree** or **disagree** with the following statements? Support your point of view in your journal.

- **Government** Governments have the right to control new kinds of technology and transportation.

- **Science, Technology & Society** Technology changes the way people work whether they want it to or not.

- **Economics** Improved transportation leads to a stronger national economy.

The Industrial Revolution and America

Read to Discover

1. How did Samuel Slater contribute to the growth of the textile industry in the Northeast?
2. How did Eli Whitney's ideas benefit manufacturing?
3. How did events before and during the War of 1812 aid the growth of manufacturing and free enterprise in the United States?

WHY IT MATTERS TODAY

Each year inventors apply for patents and copyrights for their new inventions and products. Use **CNN fyi.com** or other **current events** sources to learn more about some of the different items that have been invented in recent years. Record your findings in your journal.

Define

- textiles
- technology
- interchangeable parts
- mass production

Identify

- Industrial Revolution
- Richard Arkwright
- Samuel Slater
- Eli Whitney

In the 1700s, women like the ones in this picture worked to prepare wool for spinning.

The Story Continues

In 1761 the British Society of Arts issued an advertisement. It asked for "the best invention of a machine that will spin six threads of wool . . . or cotton, at one time." The society also wanted this machine to "require but one person to work and attend it." The advertisement offered a cash reward for such an invention. The reward and the possibility that such a machine would increase profits attracted many entrepeneurs. The society's advertisement reflected a growing demand for new machinery to meet industrial needs.

★ The Industrial Revolution

At the beginning of the 1700s, most people in Europe and the United States were farmers. They made by hand much of what they needed at home. Some families sold extra cloth to merchants. In towns a few skilled workers—such as blacksmiths, carpenters, and shoemakers—made manufactured goods by hand in their own shops.

These ways of life had stayed the same for generations. However, by the mid-1700s changes in Great Britain were creating a greater demand for manufactured goods. As agriculture and roads improved, cities and populations grew. Overseas trade also expanded, and merchants found that traditional manufacturing methods could not produce enough goods to meet everyone's needs. People explored ways to use machines to make items quickly and efficiently. These changes led to the **Industrial Revolution**, a period of rapid growth in the use of machines in manufacturing and production.

The first important breakthrough of the Industrial Revolution took place in how **textiles**, or cloth items, were made. Before the Industrial Revolution, spinning thread took much more time than making cloth. Several workers were needed to spin enough thread to supply a single weaver. In 1770 Englishman James Hargreaves patented a small inexpensive machine called the spinning jenny. This new spinning wheel was powered by hand. Using it, a worker could produce many threads at the same time. Soon the spinning jenny was being used in homes across Britain.

A year earlier, Englishman **Richard Arkwright** had brought a more dramatic change to the textile industry. He patented a large spinning machine, called the water frame, that ran on waterpower. Arkwright's machine could create dozens of cotton threads at one time. Later versions could make even more threads. The machine lowered the cost of cotton cloth and increased the speed of production. In addition, Arkwright's invention was the first machine that could make high-quality thread. The water frame was too large to fit in people's homes and needed a source of power. These needs led merchants to build large textile mills, or factories, filled with spinning machines near streams. Merchants also began hiring people to come work in their mills.

✔ **Reading Check: Sequencing** List the steps in their proper order that led to the establishment of factories in Great Britain.

Daily Life

Factory Work Before the late 1700s, most people made cotton thread and cloth in their homes. Workers had much independence. In addition, they could set their own pace of work. This situation changed as factories were built. Many women and children joined the workforce. The woman shown here is using a spinning jenny to make many threads at once. In addition, many skilled weavers were forced to join unskilled factory workers and work for the same pay. Some weavers rioted and broke machines in protest. **Why might operating a machine like this one require careful attention?**

THE GRANGER COLLECTION, NEW YORK

399

Interpreting the Visual Record

Mills *The textile mill built by Samuel Slater used nearby waterfalls to turn waterwheels that powered the mill machinery.* **How do you think a textile mill might change a town like the one in the picture?**

★ Slater and His Secrets

The new textile machines allowed Great Britain to produce cloth faster and cheaper than other countries could. **Samuel Slater** was a skilled British mechanic who knew how to build these machines. Slater immigrated to the United States. Soon after arriving, he sent a letter to Moses Brown, who owned a textile business in New England. Slater claimed he could improve the way American textiles were manufactured.

Brown had one of his workers test Slater's knowledge of machinery, and Slater passed the test. Businessmen Smith Brown and William Almy formed a partnership with Slater. In 1790 they built their first mill, located in Pawtucket, Rhode Island. The production of cotton thread by machine had begun. Although mill workers made the thread, families wove it into cloth at home or in small shops. Slater ran the mill and the machinery. He was very confident that the new machines would be a success.

History Makers Speak

❝If I do not make as good yarn as they do in England, I will have nothing for my services, but will throw the whole of what I have attempted over the bridge.❞

—Samuel Slater, quoted in *The Ingenious Yankees*, by Joseph and Francis Gies

Slater's hopes came true. The Pawtucket mill became a success. Hannah Slater, Samuel's wife, even invented a type of cotton thread used for sewing. This thread became a popular item in the United States and Europe. Americans soon began building more textile mills, most of which were located in the Northeast. In New England in particular, investors saw the potential for making large profits and thus were willing to invest money in the mills. New England also had many fast-flowing rivers to supply power. Fewer mills were built in the South, partly because investors in the region concentrated on expanding agriculture.

✔ **Reading Check: Finding the Main Idea** What problem did American textile manufacturers face, and how did Samuel Slater help them solve it?

★★★★★★★★★★★
That's Interesting!
★★★★★★★★★★★

Slater's Secrets Can you imagine building a factory from memory? Well, that's what Samuel Slater had to do when he came to America. Parliament had passed a law to prevent British mill machines or their designs from leaving Great Britain. But American businesses were offering rewards to anyone who brought the secrets of mill machinery to America. In 1789 these offers convinced mechanic Samuel Slater to memorize the designs of several mill machines. Then posing as a farmworker, Slater boarded a ship. He wasn't carrying anything illegal—all the secrets were in his mind! Once he reached the United States, Slater built the first American mill machine from memory.

A Manufacturing Breakthrough

Despite these great changes, most manufacturing was still done by hand. For example, in the late 1790s the U.S. government worried about a possible war with France, and it wanted more muskets to equip the army. However, skilled workers made the parts for each weapon by hand. No two parts were exactly alike, and carefully fitting all the pieces together for each musket took much time and skill. As a result, U.S. gun makers could not produce the muskets quickly enough. Factories needed better **technology**—the tools used to produce items or to do work. In 1798 inventor **Eli Whitney** tried to address some of these problems. Whitney wanted to make guns for the U.S Army. He had new ideas about how this could be done using water-powered machinery. Whitney also came up with the idea of manufacturing using **interchangeable parts**. Products with interchangeable parts are made from pieces that are exactly the same. The products are thus easier to assemble and broken parts are easier to replace.

Whitney believed that this idea was a "new principle" in manufacturing, but his goal was difficult to achieve. To make his plans work he needed to invent new tools to do the job.

 "The tools which I contemplate [plan] are similar to an engraving [picture] on a copper plate from which may be taken a great number of impressions [copies] perceptibly alike [the same]."

—Eli Whitney, quoted in *Technology in America*, edited by Carroll W. Pursell Jr.

Analyzing Primary Sources
Identifying Points of View
What did Whitney hope his tools would let him do?

Early artisans had to create and fit together each part of a machine by hand, a time-consuming process that required great skill.

Whitney promised to build 10,000 muskets in two years. At the time, this was an incredible number. The federal government gave Whitney money to build his factory. However, designing the machines and training the workers took him longer than he expected. After two years he still had not produced a single musket. So in 1801 Whitney was called to Washington, D.C., to give a demonstration.

Whitney stood before President John Adams and Vice President Thomas Jefferson. He had brought an assortment of parts for 10 guns. He then randomly chose parts and quickly assembled them. To the amazement of his audience, Whitney repeated the process several times. Witness Elizur Goodrich recalled the event. "All Judges & Inspectors unite in a declaration that they [the muskets] are superior [better] to any [other muskets]."

Whitney proved that American inventors could keep up with and improve upon the new British technology. Other businesses did have success with **mass production**—making large numbers of goods that are exactly alike. For example, in the early 1800s Seth Thomas began mass-producing thousands of inexpensive clocks.

✔ **Reading Check: Summarizing** How did Eli Whitney influence American manufacturing?

LINKING
PAST to PRESENT
★ ★

Keeping Industrial Secrets

For hundreds of years, countries have spied on one anothers' businesses and industries. For example, more than 1,000 years ago Persia stole precious silkworms from China. Today such spying is called industrial espionage. Usually spies hope to steal the secret of some valuable invention or idea. Automobile plans and even cookie recipes have been stolen. High-tech companies, such as makers of airplane or computer chips (see below), are also targets.

Sometimes spies are sent to learn secrets to protect national security. Other times industrial secrets simply help businesses make money. Experts believe that stolen secrets may cost American companies billions of dollars each year. **What are some reasons a company or country might steal industrial secrets?**

★ A Slow Start for Manufacturing

Manufacturing in the United States grew slowly. In 1810 Secretary of the Treasury Albert Gallatin suggested reasons why the United States had few factories.

 History Makers Speak

❝[The reasons include] . . . the superior attractions of agricultural pursuits [farming], . . . the abundance of land compared with the population, the high price of labor, and the want [lack] of sufficient capital [investment].❞

—Albert Gallatin, quoted in *Who Built America,* edited by Bruce C. Levine et al.

Gallatin reasoned that few people would choose to work in a factory if they could own their own farm instead. In Great Britain, on the other hand, land was scarce and expensive. As a result, fewer people were able to buy farms. Only a few industries had found a place in the U.S. economy. These included cotton goods, flour milling, weapons, and the production of iron.

Because Britain had plenty of factory workers, British manufacturers were able to produce large amounts of goods at low cost. They could charge lower prices for the goods, which made it difficult for American manufacturers to compete. This situation discouraged Americans from investing money to build new factories and machinery.

✔ **Reading Check Finding the Main Idea** Why did Great Britain lead the United States in the growth of manufacturing in the early 1800s?

⭐ The War of 1812 and Manufacturing

Manufacturing began to change around the time of the War of 1812. Since the 1790s, wars in Europe had interfered with U.S. trade. American customers were no longer able to get all the manufactured goods they needed. During the war British ships also blockaded eastern seaports, preventing foreign ships from delivering goods. Americans began to buy the items they needed from American manufacturers. As profits grew, manufacturers spent more money expanding their factories. State banks and private investors began to lend money to manufacturers for their businesses.

At the same time, many Americans began to realize that the United States had been relying too much on foreign goods. Thomas Jefferson, who had once opposed manufacturing, began to change his mind. He, too, realized that the United States was too dependent on imports. Jefferson explained that "to be independent for the comforts of life we must fabricate [make] them ourselves. We must now place the manufacturer by the side of the agriculturalist [farmer]." If the United States could not meet its own needs, it would be weak and open to attack.

In February 1815, New Yorkers celebrated the end of the war and return of free trade. The streets were decorated and filled with representatives of ships loaded with goods. "With Peace and Commerce, American Prospers," declared one display. Eager New Yorkers prepared to lead the United States into a period of industrial growth. After the war, northern manufacturers used northern politicians to pass higher tariffs on foreign goods to protect U.S. companies.

✔ **Reading Check** **Analyzing Information** How did the War of 1812 aid the growth of American manufacturing and the free enterprise system?

This clock was made in a factory opened by Seth Thomas in 1812.

Section 1 Review

go. hrw .com **Homework Practice Online** keyword: SF3 HP13

1 Define and explain:
- textiles
- technology
- interchangeable parts
- mass production

2 Identify and explain:
- Industrial Revolution
- Richard Arkwright
- Samuel Slater
- Eli Whitney

3 Summarizing Copy the chart below. Use it to list the key events that led to the growth of factories and changes in daily life in the United States.

Invention	How the Invention Changed Manufacturing
Arkwright	
Slater	
Whitney	

4 Finding the Main Idea
a. Why were more factories built in New England than in the southern states?

b. In what ways did the War of 1812 lead to the growth of manufacturing in the United States?

5 Writing and Critical Thinking
Supporting a Point of View Imagine that you are an American manufacturer seeking a bank loan in order to expand your factory in 1814. Write your best argument to convince the bank to give you the money you need.

Consider the following:
- the benefits of mass production
- the need for American-made goods
- your entrepeneurship and profit potential

Changes in Working Life

Read to Discover

1. How were the Rhode Island system and the Lowell system different?
2. In what ways did the introduction of factories influence the daily life of workers in the northeastern United States?
3. How did Sarah G. Bagley and other reformers contribute to the early labor-union movement?

Define
- trade unions
- strikes

Identify
- Rhode Island system
- Francis Cabot Lowell
- Lowell system
- Sarah G. Bagley

WHY IT MATTERS TODAY

The U.S. government makes laws governing many working conditions. Use CNNfyi.com or other **current events** sources to learn about one of these laws. Record your findings in your journal.

The Story Continues

Smith Wilkinson was a boy in Pawtucket, Rhode Island, when Samuel Slater built his first textile mill there. After it opened, Wilkinson got a job at the mill. "I was then in my tenth year," remembered Wilkinson, "and went to work with him [Slater], and began attending the breaker [a machine]." In the early 1800s many children worked in the textile mills. Children even younger than Wilkinson might work as many as 12 hours a day. Wilkinson spent much of his life working in mills. Eventually he ran one himself.

Textile companies used cloth labels like this one.

⭐ Factory Families

Many mill owners in the United States could not find enough people to work in their factories. At first, Samuel Slater used apprentices—young men who worked for several years to learn the trade. However, these young men often did only simple work. Their jobs included feeding cotton into the machines and cleaning the mill equipment. Apprentices like James Horton ran away from Slater's mill because "Mr. Slater . . . keep me always at one thing. I might have stayed there until this time and never knew nothing."

Eventually Slater began to hire entire families who would move to Pawtucket and work in the mills. This practice allowed Slater to fill his labor needs at a low cost. Children as well as adults worked in the mills. On many farms children already worked to help their families. Therefore, few people complained about them working in factories instead. H. Humphrey, an author of books on raising children, told parents that children needed to be useful. Humphrey wrote, "If he [a child] will not study, put him on to a farm, or send him into the shop, or in some other way provide regular employment for him."

The machines made many tasks in the mill simple enough for children to perform. Mill owners paid children very low wages. Adults usually earned as much in a day as most children did in a week.

Slater's practice of hiring families and dividing factory work into simple tasks became known as the **Rhode Island system**. Mill owners throughout the Northeast adopted Slater's methods. Owners advertised for "Men with growing families wanted." They also sent recruiters to poor communities to find new workers.

✔ **Reading Check: Summarizing** What problem did Slater have in his mills, and how did he solve it?

Interpreting the Visual Record

New opportunities *Some people left farm life to go to work in textile factories. How would you describe the mix of workers shown in this picture?*

★ The Lowell System

Not all mill owners followed Samuel Slater's system. **Francis Cabot Lowell**, a businessman from New England, developed a very different approach. His ideas completely changed the textile industry in the Northeast. First, Lowell decided to build a water-powered loom based on one he had seen in Great Britain. This loom could both spin thread and weave cloth in the same mill. Lowell's other idea was to hire young unmarried women from local farms instead of entire families. These practices became known as the **Lowell system**.

Lowell received financial help from the investors of the Boston Manufacturing Company. They finished building the first textile mill to use the Lowell system in 1814. It was located in Waltham, Massachusetts. "From the first starting of the first power loom there was not . . . doubt about the success," wrote one investor. In 1822 the company built a larger mill in a town later named Lowell, Massachusetts. Visitors to Lowell were amazed by the machinery. The clean factories and the neatly kept boardinghouses for the workers also impressed them.

Research on the ROM

Free Find:
Francis Cabot Lowell
After reading about Francis Cabot Lowell on the **Holt Researcher CD–ROM**, create an advertisement for jobs in one of Lowell's factories. Include descriptions of the work and the benefits that are offered.

The *Lowell Offering*

The Lowell Offering *began publication in 1840. This monthly magazine featured editorials, poems, and stories about the lives of mill workers. In many ways the* Lowell Offering *gave an unrealistic view of mill life. The December 1845 cover, for example, showed a setting that looked more like a garden than a factory mill. The artist who created the cover apparently followed magazine policy by ignoring the harsh realities of mill life. In 1845 Harriet Farley, the editor of the* Offering, *defended the image of Lowell shown in the magazine.*

We have been accused of representing unfairly the relative advantages and disadvantages of factory life. . . . Are we guilty? . . . We have never published anything which our own experience had convinced us was unfair. But, if in our sketches, there is too much light, and too little shade, let our excuse be found in the circumstances which have brought us before the public. We have not thought it necessary to state . . . that our life was a **toilsome**[1] one—for we supposed that would be universally understood, after we had stated how many hours in a day we **tended**[2] our machines. We have not thought a constant repetition of the fact necessary, that our life was one of confinement; when it was known that we work in one spot of one room. These facts have always been so generally understood that the worth, happiness and intelligence, which really exists, have been undervalued.

[1]**toilsome:** difficult   [2]**tended:** watched

Understanding What You Read

1. **Literature and History** Why does Harriet Farley say the *Lowell Offering* describes factory life as it does?

2. **Literature and You** What kind of description would you write of the Lowell factory if you worked there?

The young female mill workers soon became known as Lowell girls. The mills paid them between $2 and $4 each week. The workers paid $1.25 for room and board. These wages were much better than women could earn teaching or doing domestic work. Many young women from across New England came to Lowell. They wanted the chance to earn money instead of working on the family farm and earning nothing. The typical Lowell girl stayed at the mills for about four years.

Unlike other factory workers, the Lowell girls were encouraged to use their free time to take classes and form women's clubs. They even wrote their own magazine, the *Lowell Offering*. Lucy Larcom, who started working in Lowell at age 11, later praised her fellow workers.

Analyzing Primary Sources

Drawing Inferences and Conclusions How do you think Larcom's background influenced her opinion of the Lowell girls?

 History Makers Speak

❝I regard it as one of the privileges [advantages] of my youth that I was permitted to grow up among those active, interesting girls, whose lives . . . had principle [ideals] and purpose distinctly their own.❞

—Lucy Larcom, *A New England Girlhood*

For many women, however, the disadvantages of mill work outweighed the good points. The workday was between 12 and 14 hours long, and daily life was carefully controlled. Ringing bells ordered workers to breakfast or lunch. Throughout the 1800s, mill owners steadily increased the size and speed of their machines. They forced employees to work harder and faster to keep up with the equipment. According to an 1846 newspaper, each Lowell girl usually had to look after three looms. "Doing so requires constant attention," said the article. In addition, the spinning rooms were also filled with cotton dust, which caused health problems for workers.

✔ **Reading Check: Contrasting** In what ways were the Lowell system and the Rhode Island system different?

⭐ Workers Organize

Factories continued to spread in the 1800s, and craftspeople—people who made goods by hand—felt threatened. Factories produced low-priced goods quickly. To compete with factories, shop owners had to hire more workers and pay them less money. Shoemaker William Frazier complained about this situation in the mid-1840s. "We have to sit on our seats from twelve to sixteen hours per day, to earn one dollar."

The wages of factory workers also stayed the same or even went down as people competed for jobs. A wave of immigration in the 1840s brought in new people willing to work for low pay. More immigrants

Interpreting the Visual Record

Factory work *This scene from an early New England textile mill shows the growing use of machinery in industry.* **How do you think factory work in this scene was different from farm work?**

Interpreting the Visual Record

The Panic of 1837 *This cartoon shows bill collectors paying a visit to a family with its starving children.* **How does this image reflect the hard times that people faced during the Panic of 1837?**

came to the Northeast, where the mills were located, than to the South. At the Lowell mills, pay decreased and working conditions worsened. Some Lowell girls refused to keep working. Eventually, immigrants replaced the Lowell girls. Competition also came from people who had become unemployed during the Panic of 1837. Some 50,000 workers in New York City alone had lost their jobs.

Skilled workers thus faced low wages, long hours, and the fear of losing their jobs. These concerns led many skilled workers to form groups called **trade unions**. Trade unions tried to improve pay and working conditions for their members. In time, factory workers also formed trade unions. Most employers and factory owners did not want their workers to join unions. Employers often refused to hire union workers. In 1836 a group of New York employers expressed a typical business owner's opinion.

Analyzing Primary Sources

Identifying Points of View How does the quotation reflect manufacturers' concerns that trade unions hurt free enterprise?

 History Makers Speak ❝We consider such associations [unions] illegal because they are harmful to trade and prevent us from competing successfully with manufacturers of similar goods in our neighboring towns and cities.❞

—New York employers group, from *Voices of America*, edited by Thomas R. Frazier

Union members wanted to get business owners to listen to them. Sometimes they staged protests called **strikes**. Workers on strike refuse to work until their employers meet their demands. Most early strikes were not very successful, however. Courts and police usually supported companies rather than striking union members. Union members wanted new laws that would protect workers. Many decided to become more politically active. One union warned its members not to vote for "proud members of the upper class who cannot subscribe to [believe in] the . . . principles [ideals] of the workers." The group asked workers to vote instead for candidates who supported working people.

✔ **Reading Check: Analyzing Information** What issues concerned workers in the mid-1800s, and how did they respond?

★ Labor Reform Efforts

One of the strongest voices in the union movement belonged to mill worker **Sarah G. Bagley**, who founded the Lowell Female Labor Reform Association in 1844. The association made public the struggles of factory laborers. One of Bagley's causes was to fight for shorter working hours. In 1840 President Martin Van Buren had granted a 10-hour workday to many federal employees. Bagley wanted this rule to also apply to employees of private businesses. At the time, these men and women often worked 12 to 14 hours, typically six days a week. Huldah Stone, a reformer, attacked this practice. She wrote, "Call ye this *life*—to labor, eat, drink and die?"

Many working men and women supported the 10-hour workday campaign, despite the opposition of business owners. In 1845 Sarah G. Bagley was elected vice president of the New England Workingmen's Association. She was also put in charge of the 10-hour-day reform. This election made her the first woman to hold such a high-ranking position in the American labor movement.

The unions achieved some legal victories. Connecticut, Maine, New Hampshire, Ohio, Pennsylvania, and a few other states passed 10-hour-workday laws. However, companies could often avoid these new laws by making workers sign special contracts agreeing to work longer hours. For factory workers in other states, long hours remained common. Union supporters continued to fight for work reforms during the 1800s.

This union banner was created by the New York chapter of the United Brotherhood of Carpenters and Joiners.

✔ **Reading Check: Finding the Main Idea** What were the main goals of union reformers such as Sarah G. Bagley, and what did they achieve?

Section 2 Review

go.hrw.com Homework Practice Online
keyword: SF3 HP13

1 **Define** and explain:
• trade unions
• strikes

2 **Identify** and explain:
• Rhode Island system
• Francis Cabot Lowell
• Lowell system
• Sarah G. Bagley

3 **Categorizing** Copy the web diagram below. Use it to fill in information about how each person or group of people contributed to changes in workers' daily lives.

Business Leaders

Changes in Lives of Workers

Lowell & Slater

Bagley & Trade Unions

4 **Finding the Main Idea**
a. Imagine that you are a mill owner. Decide whether you will use the Rhode Island system or the Lowell system. Explain your choice.

b. How effective were Sarah G. Bagley and other reformers in helping industrial workers? Explain your answer.

5 **Writing and Critical Thinking**
Analyzing Information Imagine that you are a factory worker who also writes for a workers' magazine. Write a short column called "Factory Life" describing how factories have changed daily life for workers in the Northeast.

Consider the following:
• the effects of factories on farm families
• the effects of factories on craftspeople
• the disadvantages and advantages of mill work

The Transportation Revolution

Read to Discover

1. How did the Transportation Revolution change life in the United States?
2. What was the effect of the Supreme Court case *Gibbons* v. *Ogden*?
3. How did the growth of railroads benefit the nation?

WHY IT MATTERS TODAY

Today inventors are working to improve transportation. Use **CNNfyi.com** or other **current events** sources to identify a new advance in or idea for transportation. Record your findings in your journal.

Identify

- Transportation Revolution
- Robert Fulton
- *Clermont*
- *Gibbons* v. *Ogden*
- Peter Cooper

This picture shows an early design for a steam engine.

The Story Continues

In 1806 inventor Robert Fulton returned to America from Europe. Neither the French nor the British wanted to give him money to build his steam-powered ships. Still, Fulton continued his work. In August 1807 he took his boat, which doubters called Fulton's Folly, out on the Hudson River. He traveled up the river, passing sailboats along the way. Instead of being a disaster, Fulton's Folly was a success. The steamboat was faster than sailboats and did not rely on the wind for power. Fulton's boat revolutionized water transportation.

★ New Ways to Travel

In addition to the Industrial Revolution, during the 1800s the United States experienced a **Transportation Revolution**—a period of rapid growth in the speed and convenience of travel. Americans expanded roads and built thousands of miles of canals in the Northeast. Two important new forms of transportation were also invented: the steamboat and the railroad. Both relied on steam engines to supply power.

The Transportation Revolution helped the expansion of free enterprise by opening up new markets across the country. Shipping times were greatly reduced. In 1817 shipping cargo from Cincinnati, Ohio, to New York City took almost two months. By the early 1850s that same trip took only one week. Shipping costs also fell. For example, a merchant might pay $100 to ship a load of goods by land across New York State. It would cost that merchant only $5 to ship the same goods by canal. Along with goods, people and information moved more easily and quickly.

The growth in communication, trade, and travel also encouraged the development of new towns. In 1835 one foreign visitor commented on the rapid spread of transportation networks in America.

 History Makers Speak 66The Americans . . . have already changed the whole order of nature for their own advantage. They have joined the Hudson to the Mississippi, and made the Atlantic Ocean communicate with the Gulf of Mexico, across a continent.99

—Alexis de Tocqueville, *Democracy in America*

✔ **Reading Check: Comparing** List the key benefits the Transportation Revolution brought to free enterprise and daily life.

Analyzing Primary Sources
Drawing Inferences and Conclusions How is Tocqueville suggesting that the growth of transportation has changed the United States?

★ The Steamboat

One of the first breakthroughs of the Transportation Revolution occurred with water transportation. American and European inventors had developed steam-powered boats in the late 1700s. American **Robert Fulton** tested a model steamboat design in 1803 in France.

Interpreting the Visual Record

Steamboats *Because they made it cheaper and faster to travel upstream, steamboats were used for a variety of purposes.* **What are the steamboats in the picture being used for?**

Several years passed before Fulton could test a full-sized commercial steamboat in the United States. Fulton's ship was called the *Clermont*. On August 9, 1807, the *Clermont* traveled up the Hudson River without any trouble. A demand for a steamboat ferry service soon arose. Within a few months Fulton and his partners had earned back all the money they had spent building the ship.

The steamboat was well suited to river travel. It could move quickly against the current and did not rely on wind power. Steamboats cut months off the time it had taken to travel from New Orleans to Pittsburgh, Pennsylvania. Before the steamboat was invented, people rarely traveled upstream by boat. However, the steamboat made such trips easier and cheaper. The price of a trip upriver fell by some 90 percent from 1815 to 1860. Westerners found it easier to send goods, such as grain and lumber, to eastern markets. Steamboats also made it easier for eastern companies to ship their goods to western buyers. Increased trade and cheaper transportation encouraged more settlers to move to the Midwest.

CONNECTING TO
SCIENCE AND TECHNOLOGY

The Age of Steam

Before the Industrial Revolution began, people used natural sources of energy to do work. These sources included animals, waterpower, and wind power. Steam power provided a new source of energy. The first steam engines were built in the early 1700s in Europe. In the 1800s American Oliver Evans helped develop a smaller and more powerful steam engine. This engine was ideal for steamboats running on the Mississippi River or trains racing across the American countryside. Engineers continued to use and improve steam engines throughout the 1800s. **How do you think steam engines changed the way people lived and worked?**

Throttle lever

Steam room

Steam dome

Water

Firebox

Steam flow

Steam control valve

Piston

Steamboat travel was dangerous. The engines could build up too much pressure and explode. But these risks did not stop steamboats from becoming common on the Mississippi River. More than 500 of them were in use by 1840. By the 1850s steamboats were also being used to carry people and goods across the ocean.

✔ **Reading Check: Finding the Main Idea** How did steamboat travel benefit Americans?

⭐ *Gibbons v. Ogden*

The growth of the steamboat shipping industry led to the first Supreme Court ruling on commerce between states. Thomas Gibbons was operating his steamboats between New Jersey and Manhattan using a federal license. However, he did not have a state license to travel in New York waters. New York had already given Aaron Ogden a monopoly on the steamboat business. When Ogden sued Gibbons and won, Gibbons appealed.

The case of ***Gibbons v. Ogden*** reached the Supreme Court in 1824. The Court ruled that Gibbons had the right to operate in New York. Chief Justice John Marshall spoke for the Court and explained that the federal law overruled the state law. Thus Gibbons's federal license had priority over Ogden's state license.

The Marshall Court's ruling reinforced the federal government's authority over the states. In doing so he also expanded the definition of commerce to include the transportation of people. *Gibbons* v. *Ogden* was one of Marshall's most important decisions. Over time, the interpretation of commerce has even come to include the use of new communications technology. The decision also tore down a barrier to free enterprise by eliminating Ogden's state monopoly.

✔ **Reading Check: Summarizing** Explain the events surrounding *Gibbons* v. *Ogden* and how the ruling affected the power of the federal government.

⭐ American Railroads

What the steamboat did for water travel, the train did for travel on land. Steam-powered trains had first been developed in Britain in the early 1800s, but they did not become popular in the United States until the 1830s. About 1830 **Peter Cooper** built the *Tom Thumb*. Although this locomotive was small, it had great power and speed. Railroad fever spread throughout the United States, particularly in the North. By 1840, railroad companies had laid about 2,800 miles of track. French economist Michel Chevalier described Americans as having "a perfect passion for railroads."

Engineers and mechanics had to overcome physical obstacles such as steep mountains, swift rivers, and tight curves. To meet these challenges,

CONNECTING TO
MATH

Just the Facts

The Railroad Boom, 1830–1860

Year	Miles of Railroad Operated
1830	23
1835	1,098
1840	2,818
1845	4,633
1850	9,021
1855	18,374
1860	30,626

Using Mathematical Skills

1. How much more track was in operation in 1840 than in 1830?

2. Create a line graph that illustrates changes in the total amount of railroad track operated from 1830 to 1860.

3. Imagine that you are a business leader in 1860. Using the figures above, prepare a speech to give to a group of investors. Explain why you think starting a new railroad company is or is not a good idea.

Transportation Methods of the Mid-1800s

TYPE OF TRANSPORTATION	AVERAGE SPEED	SHIPPING COSTS
Roads	2 miles per hour by wagon 6–8 miles per hour by stagecoach	$0.12 per ton per mile
Canals	1.5–5 miles per hour	$0.045 per ton per mile
Steamboats	around 20 miles per hour	$0.007 per ton per mile
Clipper Ships (Ocean Travel)	11.5–17 miles per hour (depending on weather)	$10.00 per ton for trans-Atlantic shipment
Railroads	around 20 miles per hour (including stops)	$0.06 per ton per mile

Source: George Rodger Taylor, *The Transportation Revolution, 1815 to 1860*

they built faster and more powerful steam locomotives.

Trains were the fastest form of transportation most people had ever experienced. Train wrecks were common, however, whenever engineers trying to stay on schedule traveled too fast. Englishman Charles Richard Weld was on a railroad car that flew off the tracks. To his amazement, the other passengers praised the engineer for trying to keep on schedule.

The free enterprise system helped the railroad system grow. Railroad companies knew they could earn a great deal of money transporting factory goods, freight, and people. By 1860 about 30,000 miles of railroad had been laid, and railroads linked most major cities in the eastern United States. Railroad companies became some of the most powerful businesses in the nation. As the railroad system grew, manufacturers and farmers were able to send their goods to distant markets. Thus, they could look for markets with the best prices. Competition in national markets also lowered prices for consumers.

Railroads contributed to the nation's physical growth as well. They helped cities grow because trains brought new residents as well as raw materials for industry and construction.

✔ **Reading Check: Analyzing Information** In what ways did the railroads affect the economy of the United States?

Section 3 Review

 keyword: SF3 HP13 — Homework Practice Online

1 Identify and explain:
- Transportation Revolution
- Robert Fulton
- *Clermont*
- *Gibbons* v. *Ogden*
- Peter Cooper

2 Sequencing Copy the time line below. Use it to create a flowchart listing the key events that led to the emergence of the steamboat and the railway locomotive in the United States.

The Emergence of the Steamboat and Locomotive

	1807	1840	
1790s Steam-powered boats developed	**Early 1800s** Steam trains	1830	1860

3 Finding the Main Idea
a. What were the results of the Supreme Court case *Gibbons* v. *Ogden*?

b. In what ways did railroads in the United States benefit from the free enterprise system?

4 Writing and Critical Thinking
Summarizing Write a dialogue between an American and a visitor from another country discussing how the Transportation Revolution has affected the nation's development.

Consider the following:
- the invention of steamboats and railroads
- the benefits for free enterprise
- the growth of cities

More Technological Advances

Read to Discover

1. What ideas did Samuel Morse draw upon in order to invent the telegraph?
2. How did new developments benefit factory and farm work?
3. What new inventions did Cyrus McCormick and Isaac Singer develop?

WHY IT MATTERS TODAY

New technology continues to dramatically change the daily lives of people around the world. Use CNNfyi.com or other **current events** sources to learn about inventions for the home that have made life easier for people. Record your findings in your journal.

Define

- telegraph

Identify

- Samuel Morse
- Morse code
- John Deere
- Cyrus McCormick
- Isaac Singer

The Story Continues

On May 24, 1844, Samuel Morse sat down in the Capitol Building in Washington. He was about to conduct the first public test of his new device. His friend Annie Elsworth wrote down a message on a slip of paper. Morse read the message. He then used his invention to send Elsworth's message instantly to Baltimore, Maryland, about 40 miles away. His associate in Baltimore quickly sent the message—"What hath God wrought?"—back to Morse. This exchange had taken place in only a minute.

The telegraph marked the beginning of a new age of communications.

★ Messages by Wire

In 1832 **Samuel F. B. Morse** invented the **telegraph**, which could send information over wires across great distances. To develop the telegraph, Morse studied electricity and magnetism. Around 1800 Italian scientist Alessandro Volta had built the first battery, which provided a steady supply of electricity. About 20 years later, André-Marie Ampère of

THE GRANGER COLLECTION, NEW YORK

BIOGRAPHY

Samuel F. B. Morse

(1791–1872)

Like steamboat creator Robert Fulton, American Samuel Morse began his career as a painter rather than an inventor. In 1832 Morse was a widower struggling to raise his three children alone. He became interested in the idea of sending messages electrically. Morse hoped he could invent a device that would earn him enough money to support his family. In time, earnings from the telegraph made Morse extremely wealthy. **What motivated Samuel Morse to invent the telegraph?**

France determined some of the rules governing the relationship between electricity and magnetism. Morse was the first person to put the work of these scientists together in a practical machine. He spent years trying to achieve his goal of creating the telegraph.

The telegraph sent pulses of electric current through a wire. The telegraph operator tapped a bar, called a telegraph key, that controlled the length of each pulse. At the other end of the wire, these pulses were changed into clicking sounds. A short click was called a dot, while a long click was called a dash. Morse's assistant, Alfred Lewis Vail, developed a system known as **Morse code**. In Morse code, different combinations of dots and dashes are used to stand for letters of the alphabet. For example, *dot dot dot, dash dash dash, dot dot dot* is the distress call SOS. Skilled telegraph operators could send and receive many words every minute.

Several years passed before Morse could connect two locations with telegraph wires. Even then, people doubted that he was actually reading messages sent from miles away. They claimed that he was making lucky guesses. Morse's break came during the 1844 Democratic National Convention in Baltimore, Maryland. A telegraph wired news of a presidential candidate's nomination to politicians in Washington. The politicians responded, "Three cheers for the telegraph!" Telegraphs were soon sending and receiving information for businesses, the government, newspapers, and private citizens.

The telegraph grew with the railroad. Telegraph companies strung telegraph lines on poles alongside railroads across the country. They established telegraph offices in many train stations. Thousands more miles of telegraph were added every year in the 1850s. The first transcontinental line was finished in 1861. By the time he died in 1872, Morse was famous across the United States.

✔ **Reading Check: Evaluating** How did scientific discoveries help make Morse's invention of the telegraph possible?

Interpreting the Visual Record

Communication revolution *Several new inventions greatly increased the speed of communication in the 1800s. What do you see in the picture that might have improved communication?*

★ New Factories

At the start of the Industrial Revolution, most factories ran on waterpower. Over time, however, factory owners began using steam power to run their machines. This shift brought major changes to the nation's industrial growth. While water-wheels remained popular in many areas, water-powered factories had to be built near fast-flowing streams or waterfalls. The use of steam engines allowed business owners to build their factories almost anywhere. Yet the Northeast was still home to most of the nation's industry. By 1860 New England alone had as many factories as the entire South.

Some companies decided to build their factories closer to cities and transportation centers. This location gave them easier access to workers, allowing them to lower the cost of labor. Being closer to cities also reduced shipping costs. As factories moved, so did the nation's population. Cities soon became the center of industrial growth. People from rural areas as well as foreign countries flocked to the cities to take factory jobs.

Americans also improved the designs of many kinds of machines. Mechanics invented tools that could cut and shape metal, stone, and wood with great precision. Englishman Joseph Whitworth wrote a report on American manufacturing in 1854. He noted how much Americans used their new inventions.

This pin-making machine was one of the technological advances developed during the early 1800s.

History Makers Speak

❝[Americans] call in the aid of machinery in almost every department [area] of industry. Wherever it can be introduced as a substitute for manual labor, it is universally [widely] and willingly resorted [turned] to.❞

—Joseph Whitworth, quoted in *From the American System to Mass Production*, by David A. Hounshell

Analyzing Primary Sources

Identifying Points of View What does Whitworth's opinion of American industry seem to be?

By the 1840s this new machinery was able to produce interchangeable parts. Gunmakers at the federal Springfield Armory in Massachusetts finally achieved Eli Whitney's dream. They built weapons using interchangeable parts and mass production. Within a short period of time, the growing machine-tool industry was even making customized equipment. By 1859 the value of the products of American industry was greater than the value of crops. Inventions also spread quickly in America. For example, just 15 years after the sewing machine was invented, America had 15 times as many sewing machines as England.

✔ **Reading Check: Finding the Main Idea** How did new technology change the way goods were manufactured?

★ Better Farm Equipment

During the 1830s technology began transforming the farm as well as the factory. In 1837 blacksmith **John Deere** saw that his farming friends in Illinois had problems plowing the thick soil because the dirt stuck to their iron plows. Deere thought that a steel blade like one he had seen in a sawmill, might slice through the earth. His steel plow design was a success. By 1846 Deere was selling 1,000 plows per year. His business continued to prosper as more farmers moved west.

While Deere's plow made planting wheat easier, harvesting it was still time-consuming and difficult. About the same time Deere developed his plow, **Cyrus McCormick** was developing a new harvesting machine. He later recalled, "I was often advised by my father and family to abandon [my work]." Despite this advice, he went on to create the mechanical reaper, which cut down wheat quickly and efficiently.

McCormick continued to improve his design, and in the 1840s he sold his first machines. He later entered the device in international competitions, where it achieved great success. McCormick soon began mass-producing his reapers in a large factory in Chicago. His factory was one of the first to use steam-engine technology to run its saws and other machines. McCormick overcame competition from other inventors and became a millionaire. McCormick's business talents and marketing ideas contributed to his great success. His company advertised, gave demonstrations, and provided a repair and spare-parts department. The company also allowed customers to buy on credit.

The combination of Deere's plow and McCormick's reaper allowed midwestern farmers to plant and harvest huge fields of wheat. The process was both fast and cheap. In 1830 harvesting an acre of wheat took 20 hours. McCormick's farm machinery eventually reduced that time to an hour per acre. By 1860 farmers in the United States were producing more than 170 million bushels of wheat and more than 800 million bushels of corn a year.

✔ **Reading Check: Analyzing Information** What marketing methods did McCormick use to help sell his farm equipment?

New advertisements helped sell farm machinery, such as the McCormick reaper shown below, to farmers.

★ Changing Life at Home

Some inventions of the Industrial Revolution simply made life easier. When Alexis de Tocqueville of France visited the United States, he identified what he called a very American quality.

History Makers Speak

"[Americans want] to be always making life more comfortable and convenient, to avoid trouble, and to satisfy the smallest wants [desires] without effort and almost without cost."

Alexis de Tocqueville, *Democracy in America*

The sewing machine was one of these many conveniences. Elias Howe, a factory apprentice in Lowell, Massachusetts, first invented the sewing machine. However, **Isaac Singer** made improvements to this design. His Singer sewing machine grew increasingly popular in the 1850s. It had a clever design and was easy to use. Early advertisements claimed, "Even a child can run it." Singer worked very hard to promote his product. Like McCormick, he also allowed customers to buy goods on credit and provided service with sales. Singer's strategies worked well. Many women bought sewing machines to try to earn a living at home by making clothing for large companies. In some homes, fancy sewing machines became signs of wealth. By 1860 Singer's company was the world's largest maker of sewing machines.

By the late 1800s many American homes had sewing machines.

Other advances improved on everyday items. In the 1830s iceboxes cooled by large blocks of fresh ice became available, allowing people to store fresh food safely. Iron cookstoves began replacing cooking fires and stone hearths. Companies also began to mass-produce old inventions cheaply. This method allowed many families to afford household items such as clocks.

More cities also built public water systems. Some wealthy families had water pumps installed inside their houses. However, very few homes had plumbing above the first floor. Hotels were often the first buildings in a city to have such advances. Other useful items were developed during this period. For example, matches were introduced in the 1830s, and the safety pin was invented in 1849. All of these inventions helped make life at home more convenient for an increasing number of Americans.

✔ **Reading Check** **Comparing** How did the different labor-saving inventions affect daily life?

Section 4 Review

go.hrw.com
Homework Practice Online
keyword: SF3 HP13

1 **Define** and explain:
• telegraph

2 **Identify** and explain:
• Samuel F. B. Morse
• Morse code
• John Deere
• Cyrus McCormick
• Isaac Singer

3 **Summarizing** Copy the graphic organizer below. Use it to show the significant technological developments of the 1800s and who created them. Then briefly explain each development's significance.

Farm Equipment

Household Items

Inventions of the Early 1800s

4 **Finding the Main Idea**
a. What are the key factors that contributed to Samuel Morse's invention of the telegraph and its success?

b. How did the introduction of steam power affect manufacturing and the U.S. population?

5 **Writing and Critical Thinking**
Identifying Cause and Effect Imagine that you are a reporter in the mid-1800s. Write an article explaining to your readers how the new inventions are improving life at home and at work.

Consider the following:
• improved production methods
• the usefulness of new household conveniences
• the marketing methods used to sell goods

Chapter 13 Review

The Chapter at a Glance

Examine the visual summary of the chapter below. Make a chart listing the inventions you think were most important and explain why. Share your chart with another student. Place each invention in the appropriate category.

INDUSTRIAL REVOLUTION
• Mass production
• Interchangeable parts
• The Lowell and Rhode Island systems

TRANSPORTATION REVOLUTION

Telegraph

Factories

Water and Steam Power

Railroad and Steamboat

New Farm Machinery

To Growing Cities →

Identifying People and Ideas

Use the following terms or people in historically significant sentences.

1. Industrial Revolution
2. interchangeable parts
3. mass production
4. Lowell system
5. Sarah G. Bagley
6. Transportation Revolution
7. Robert Fulton
8. *Gibbons* v. *Ogden*
9. telegraph
10. Cyrus McCormick

Understanding Main Ideas

Section 1 *(Pages 398–403)*

1. How did the innovations of Samuel Slater and Eli Whitney contribute to the growth of American manufacturing?

Section 2 *(Pages 404–409)*

2. What were the characteristics of the two main factory systems that developed in New England?
3. Why did workers organize trade unions?

Section 3 *(Pages 410–414)*

4. How did the steamboat and the railroad affect the growth of cities?

Section 4 *(Pages 415–419)*

5. Compare the contributions made by John Deere and Cyrus McCormick to American farming.

6. How did the different types of home appliances make daily life easier?

You Be the Historian— Reviewing Themes

1. **Government** What did the Supreme Court rule in *Gibbons* v. *Ogden*, and what was significant about the case?
2. **Science, Technology & Society** How did the growth of factories change American life?
3. **Economics** How did the Transportation Revolution benefit the U.S. economy and free enterprise?

Thinking Critically

1. **Drawing Inferences and Conclusions** How do you think the U.S. free enterprise system helped make the Industrial Revolution and Transportation Revolution possible?
2. **Supporting a Point of View** Do you think Cyrus McCormick and Isaac Singer would have been so successful without using new sales methods? Explain your answer.
3. **Analyzing Information** Explain the influence of key inventors and their inventions on the industrial growth of the United States during the 1800s.

Interpreting Charts

Study the chart below. Then use the information on the chart to help you answer the questions that follow.

Causes and Effects of the Industrial Revolution in America, 1790–1860

Long-Term Causes

Industrial Revolution in Britain

Transportation Revolution (canals, improved roads, railroads, steamboats)

Introduction of steam power

Growing cities

Rise in immigration

Immediate Causes

Technological innovations by individuals such as Samuel Slater and Eli Whitney in early 1800s

War of 1812

Founding of Lowell mills, 1822

Tariffs on foreign manufactured goods

The Industrial Revolution in America, 1790–1860

Effects

Economic growth

More manufactured goods produced at lower prices

Factory jobs change working habits and conditions

Women and children become wage-earners

1. Which of the following was not an immediate cause of the Industrial Revolution in America?
   a. the War of 1812
   b. the Lowell mills
   c. tariffs on foreign goods
   d. a rise in immigration

2. Based on your knowledge of the period, how do you think the long-term causes listed on the chart contributed to the Industrial Revolution in the United States?

Analyzing Primary Sources

Read the following quote by John H. B. Latrobe, a railroad developer, and then answer the questions that follow.

> "In the beginning, no one dreamed of steam upon the [rail]road. Horses were to do the work . . . ; relays of horses trotted the cars from place to place. . . . There was this difficulty about introducing an English [steam] engine on an American road. An English road was virtually a straight road. An American road had curves. . . . For a brief season it was believed that this feature of the early American roads would prevent the use of locomotive engines."

3. Which of the following statements best describes the problem with using steam engines on early American railroads?
   a. Americans wanted to use horses to pull railcars.
   b. American railroads had too many curves in them.
   c. All the steam engines were built in England.
   d. People were afraid of steam locomotives.

4. Based on your knowledge of the period, what are some ways in which Americans could have made railroads work in the American environment?

Alternative Assessment

Building Your Portfolio

American History

Cooperative Learning

Complete the following activity in small groups. Each group should come up with an idea for a new invention that would make daily life easier. Draw a diagram or create a model of the proposed invention and create an advertisement for the invention that explains its benefits. Then share your invention idea with the class.

internet connect

Internet Activity: go.hrw.com
keyword: SF3 CF13

Choose an activity on Industrial Growth in the North to:
- Create a database and graph of the economic and social impact of the McCormick reaper.
- Create an annotated map of the Erie Canal.
- Write a biography of Samuel Slater.

14 Agricultural Changes in the South

(1790–1860)

Eli Whitney's cotton gin had a simple design but made a tremendous impact on the southern economy.

In addition to being an inventor, Jean Étienne Boré served as the first mayor of New Orleans under American rule.

UNITED STATES

1793 Eli Whitney invents the cotton gin, which enables southern farmers to grow more cotton.

1795 Jean Étienne Boré invents a new sugar-processing system.

1808 A congressional ban on the importing of slaves into the United States takes effect.

1790	1800	1810	1820

WORLD

1794 France ends slavery in its colonies.

1806 The British cotton industry employs more than 250,000 workers.

1807 Parliament bans the slave trade in the British Empire.

1825 A revolt against the Russian czar is crushed.

After Britain banned the slave trade, British warships tried to stop slave ships on the high seas.

Build on What You Know

While industrial growth was changing the society of the North, a distinct southern culture emerged. The South's agricultural economy relied on the labor of enslaved African Americans. Southern society was led by planters and also included yeomen, poor whites, and free African Americans.

Southern cotton plantations depended upon the labor of enslaved African Americans.

Slaves produced crafts, such as this quilt below showing stories from the Bible, that reflected their cultural and spiritual beliefs.

1831 Nat Turner's Rebellion leads to fears of further slave revolts in the South.

1845 The U.S. Naval Academy opens in Annapolis, Maryland.

1848 Joseph R. Anderson becomes owner of the Tredegar Iron Works, the South's only large iron factory.

1860 The South grows two thirds of all cotton in the United States.

1830 **1840** **1850** **1860**

1835 Alexis de Tocqueville publishes *Democracy in America.*

1837 Victoria is crowned queen of Great Britain.

1854 The disease cholera spreads through London.

If you were there . . .
What type of business would you start in the South?

You Be the Historian

Themes Journal

What's Your Opinion? Do you **agree** or **disagree** with the following statements? Support your point of view in your journal.

- **Science, Technology & Society** New technology does not always lead to the growth of manufacturing.
- **Economics** Concentrating on making one product will lead to economic success.
- **Culture** Each region of the country has only one distinct culture.

The Growth of Cotton

Read to Discover

1. What happened to agriculture and slavery in the South immediately after the American Revolution?
2. What effect did the cotton gin have on the South and slavery?
3. How did the cotton boom affect the South's economy?

Define
- cotton gin
- cotton belt

Identify
- Eli Whitney

WHY IT MATTERS TODAY

After 1800 the southern economy came to depend more and more on the production of cotton. Use CNNfyi.com or other **current events** sources to find a region or a country whose economy today depends on one major product. Record your findings in your journal.

This fan was owned by a wealthy southerner.

The Story Continues

On an August day in 1770, slaveholder Landon Carter rode out to view his tobacco crops. He was pleased by the thick healthy plants he saw. Carter was a successful plantation owner in Virginia. He and his neighbors believed that the ability to produce good crops reflected a person's good character. "I know in this neighborhood people are very fond of speaking meanly of their neighbor's Crops," he noted. "However, when I ride out, I declare I do not see any so good [as mine]."

★ The South's Agricultural Economy

Successful plantation owners like Landon Carter saw farming as an art to be passed down from generation to generation. Southerners prided themselves on their ties to the land. Many believed that the future of the United States rested on agriculture. Thomas Jefferson expressed this view.

Analyzing Primary Sources
Identifying Points of View
What was Jefferson's attitude toward independent farmers?

History Makers Speak

❝Those [independent white farmers] who labor in the earth are the chosen people of God. . . . Corruption of morals in the mass of cultivators [farmers] is a phenomenon [event] of which no age nor nation has furnished an example.❞

—Thomas Jefferson, quoted in *The Annals of America*

However, southern agriculture began to decline after the American Revolution. Prices for major cash crops such as indigo, rice, and tobacco all fell. With prices falling, landowners cut production or began switching to crops that needed less labor, like wheat. With less demand for farm workers in the Upper South, the value of slaves began to drop.

Some slaveholders freed their slaves for moral or political reasons. Certain Revolutionary leaders believed that a nation founded on liberty could not support slavery. Northern states gradually began to abolish slavery completely. In the South there were some planters, such as Richard Randolph, who freed their slaves in their wills. Randolph had come to view slavery as "the most lawless and monstrous tyranny [injustice]." As more slaves gained their freedom, some leaders predicted that slavery would eventually die out.

✔ **Reading Check: Summarizing** Why did slavery decline in the Upper South at the end of the 1700s?

In 1781 the slave Mum Bett successfully sued for her freedom in a Massachusetts court.

★ Whitney and the Cotton Gin

Some southerners saw cotton as a cash crop that would help the economy. The expanding British and American textile industries used cotton to make cloth. However, farmers had difficulty keeping up with the demand for raw cotton because it was difficult to grow and process.

Southerners had been growing small amounts of cotton since Jamestown was founded in 1607. Long-staple, or black-seed, cotton was the easiest to process. Workers could easily remove the seeds from its long fibers. But long-staple cotton only grew well in a few places in the South.

CONNECTING TO
SCIENCE AND TECHNOLOGY

The Cotton Gin

Early cotton gins, or engines, could not remove the seeds from the type of cotton that would grow most easily in the South. Eli Whitney's cotton gin consisted of rollers with wire teeth set inside a box. As the rollers turned they pulled the cotton from the box but left the seeds behind. Another roller brushed away the cotton lint from the wire-teeth rollers to keep them from being clogged. Many southerners made copies of Whitney's cotton gin. Soon other inventors had improved on his original design. **What was the advantage of Whitney's design?**

Comb

Teeth

Cotton hopper

Cleaned cotton

Crank handle

★ ★ ★ ★ ★ ★ ★ ★ ★ ★ ★ ★
That's Interesting!
★ ★ ★ ★ ★ ★ ★ ★ ★ ★ ★ ★

All Glory, No Gain Did you know that the inventor of the cotton gin made practically no money from his machine? It's true! After perfecting the cotton gin, Eli Whitney was given the sole right to make the machine in 1794. But others could easily make the gins, and planters did not need Whitney's help. Whitney sued planters for violating his rights, but he gained next to nothing from his legal battles. "[A]n invention can be so valuable," Whitney concluded, "as to be worthless to the inventor."

Although short-staple, or green-seed, cotton grew well across the South, removing its seeds was very hard. A worker might take an entire day to remove the seeds from just one pound of green-seed cotton. Cotton growers needed a machine that could more easily do this job.

Northerner **Eli Whitney** finally built such a machine in 1793. In 1792 Whitney had visited a Georgia plantation owned by Catherine Greene. Workers were using a machine to remove seeds from long-staple cotton. Greene asked Whitney to help improve the machine. By the following spring, Whitney had perfected a machine for removing short-staple seeds from cotton fibers.

A simple device, the **cotton gin** used a hand-cranked cylinder with wire teeth to pull cotton fibers apart from the seeds. Whitney described how his invention would improve the cotton business.

History Makers Speak

❝One man will clean ten times as much cotton as he can in any other way before known and also clean it much better than in the usual mode [method]. This machine may be turned by water or with a horse, with the greatest ease, and one man and a horse will do more than fifty men with the old machines.❞

—Eli Whitney, quoted in *Eli Whitney and the Birth of American Technology*, by Constance McLaughlin Green

Whitney's gin revolutionized the cotton industry and gave new life to southern agriculture. Planters—large-scale farmers who held more than 20 slaves—built gins that could process tons of cotton quickly. Other southerners, like William McCreight of South Carolina, established successful businesses making gins for cotton growers.

✔ **Reading Check: Finding the Main Idea** Why was the way the cotton gin worked important?

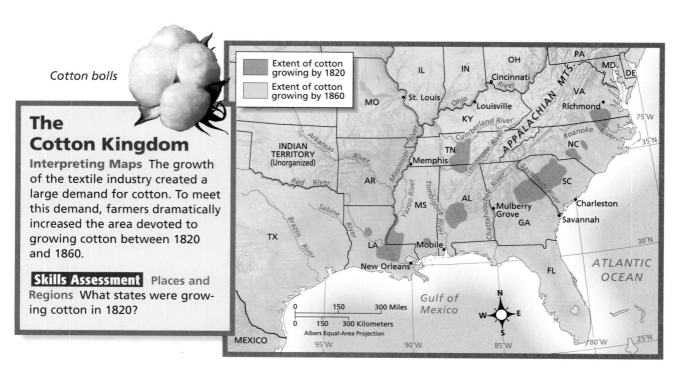

Cotton bolls

The Cotton Kingdom

Interpreting Maps The growth of the textile industry created a large demand for cotton. To meet this demand, farmers dramatically increased the area devoted to growing cotton between 1820 and 1860.

Skills Assessment Places and Regions What states were growing cotton in 1820?

★ The Cotton Boom

Whitney's gin began a cotton boom. Short-staple cotton grew easily almost everywhere in the South. In theory, a farmer needed only land and labor to raise a cotton crop. By 1860 the southern states east of the Mississippi produced two thirds of all U.S. cotton. Cotton accounted for more than half of all American exports. Farmers eager to profit from the cotton boom headed west to find land. The new Cotton Kingdom included land stretching from South Carolina to Texas. This area became known as the **cotton belt**, the region that grew most of the country's cotton crop.

As the cotton belt expanded, farmers continued trying to improve the crop. In the 1830s, disease wiped out short-staple cotton in many areas. Agricultural scientists like Dr. Rush Nutt worked at breeding stronger types of cotton that were soon grown across the cotton belt.

Cotton had many advantages as a cash crop. Besides being easy to grow, it cost little to market. Unlike food staples, harvested cotton could be stored for a long time. Because cotton was lighter than other staple crops, it also cost less to transport.

Growing and harvesting cotton required many field hands. So did other southern crops, such as Louisiana sugarcane. Rather than pay wages to free workers, planters began to use more slave labor than ever before. Congress made the importation of slaves into the United States illegal in 1808. However, the growing demand for slaves led to an increase in the domestic slave trade. Many slaveholders from states like Virginia and Maryland profited by selling slaves to cotton or sugar planters from states farther south.

The cotton boom led to an increased dependence on slave labor in the South.

✔ **Reading Check: Identifying Cause and Effect** What caused the cotton boom, and how did it affect slavery and the southern economy?

Section 1 Review

go.
hrw
.com
Homework Practice Online
keyword: SF3 HP14

1 **Define** and explain:
• cotton gin
• cotton belt

2 **Identify** and explain:
• Eli Whitney

3 **Identifying Cause and Effect** Copy the graphic organizer below. Use it to show what led to the cotton boom and what effects increased cotton production had on slavery and the southern economy.

Cause: → Cotton Boom → Economy / Slavery

4 **Finding the Main Idea**
a. What happened to the Upper South's economy and to slavery in the late 1700s?

b. How did the cotton gin affect the agricultural system in the South?

5 **Writing and Critical Thinking**
Analyzing Information Imagine that you are a southern planter in the cotton belt in the early 1800s. Write an advertisement for cotton seeds that explains cotton's advantages as a cash crop.

Consider the following:
• the demand for cotton
• where cotton can be grown
• cotton's storage qualities

Agricultural Changes in the South **427**

The Southern Economy

Read to Discover

1. How did trade affect the southern economy?
2. Why were crops other than cotton important to the southern economy?
3. What kinds of factories were located in the South?

WHY IT MATTERS TODAY

Southerners tried to use science to grow better crops. Use **CNNfyi.com** or other **current events** sources to find out how scientists work to improve farming today. Record your findings in your journal.

Define

- factors
- scientific agriculture

Identify

- Jean Étienne Boré
- Joseph R. Anderson
- Tredegar Iron Works

The Story Continues

In an 1858 speech before the U.S. Senate, South Carolina politician James Henry Hammond declared, "Cotton is King!" Southern senators listened closely. Like many of them, Hammond was a planter who believed that the cotton trade had turned the South into a global power. Without cotton, Hammond claimed, the world economy would fail. "No power on earth dares to make war upon it," he declared. "Who can doubt . . . that cotton is supreme?"

Cotton was typically shipped in large 400-pound bales.

★ The Cotton Trade

Many southerners shared James Henry Hammond's view about cotton and the cotton trade. Southerner David Christy declared, "*king cotton* is a profound [learned] statesman, and knows what measures will best sustain his throne." Great Britain became the South's most valued foreign trading partner. Southerners also sold tons of cotton to the growing textile industry in the northeastern states. This increased trade led to the growth of major port cities in the South. These cities included Charleston, South Carolina; Savannah, Georgia; and New Orleans, Louisiana.

In these port cities, crop brokers called **factors** managed the cotton trade. Farmers sold their cotton to merchants who then made deals with factors. Merchants and factors also arranged loans to farmers who needed to buy supplies. In addition, they often advised farmers on how to invest their profits. Once farmers got their cotton to the port cities, factors arranged transport aboard trading ships.

Getting crops to the ports was a major challenge for farmers. Most southern farmers relied on the region's many rivers to ship their goods. On the Ohio and Mississippi Rivers, flatboats carried cotton and other products to port. With the invention of the steam engine, steamboats became the main method of transportation. Hundreds of steamboats soon traveled up and down the mighty Mississippi. As a result, New Orleans became a major port city.

Shipping cotton by land was very difficult in the South. The few major road projects were limited to the Southeast. Southern states were also slow to build canals. By 1850 the South had only about 14 percent of the country's total canal mileage. In addition, the South had fewer miles of railroad. Thus, the Transportation Revolution had a wider impact in the North than in the South.

✔ **Reading Check: Summarizing** How did farmers transport and sell their cotton?

Daily Life

King Cotton The cotton boom involved much more than growing and harvesting cotton. Harvested cotton had to be ginned, pressed into bales, and then shipped to market or to warehouses. Special agents helped do everything from marketing cotton to customers to insuring crops against loss or damage. Factories were built to produce items needed by cotton farmers, such as ropes to bale cotton. As a result, cotton was part of the lives of many people beyond those who produced it. **What were some of the different tasks required to produce and sell cotton?**

Agricultural Changes in the South **429**

GLOBAL CONNECTIONS

The Cotton Trade

By the mid-1820s the South was known as the Cotton Kingdom. The region was the largest supplier of cotton in the world. During the late 1840s the South exported more than 900 million pounds of cotton per year. To supply its textile mills, Great Britain bought more than half of all cotton grown in the South. Other European countries, particularly France, also bought thousands of bales of cotton.

The success of the cotton trade made the South confident of its important position in the global economy. But cotton-growing countries such as Brazil, China, Egypt, India, and Russia were becoming significant competitors. **How did the cotton gin contribute to the increase in the South's foreign trade?**

Textile mills produced fabric sample books such as this one to show off their patterns and colors.

★ Agricultural Diversity

Some southern farmers supported **scientific agriculture**—the use of scientific methods to improve farming. One goal was to increase crop production. Scientists also wanted to protect the land used to grow cotton. Planting cotton over and over again on the same piece of land wore out the soil. Virginia farmer Edmund Ruffin wrote many articles on better ways to use fertilizers. Others told farmers to regularly change the kinds of crops that they grew on a piece of land. This practice, called crop rotation, would help keep the soil healthy. These scientific practices helped farmers protect their soil.

Some southern leaders worried that farmers relied too much on cotton. Editor James D. B. De Bow and others wanted southerners to try a variety of crops and investments. In 1847 De Bow wrote an article describing the South's problem.

 History Makers Speak ❝This is the great evil under which the southwest labors. She is yearly wearing out her soil in the production of one great staple, which has become ruinously [severely] low in price by reason of its great supply: she parts with this staple at prime cost, and purchases almost all her necessary appliances of comfort from abroad, not at prime cost.❞

—James D. B. De Bow, *Commercial Review of the South and West,* March 1847

Some farmers were already growing other crops. Corn remained the most important southern food crop. By the late 1830s, the top three corn-growing states in the nation were all in the South. Tennessee, the leader, produced some 45 million bushels of corn in 1839. Kentucky and Virginia ran close behind. The South's other common food crops included rice, sweet potatoes, sugarcane, and wheat. High demand for flour in Great Britain increased the value of southern wheat. London bakers particularly liked the type of flour made from Alabama wheat.

The French introduced sugarcane to Louisiana about 1700. However, the crop never became popular until **Jean Étienne Boré** (ay-tyen bohr-AY) invented a new system for processing sugar in 1795. Using Caribbean techniques, Boré perfected a way of processing Louisiana sugarcane into granulated sugar. Louisiana became the center of the sugar industry in the United States. So important was sugar to the state's economy that many planters described Boré as the "savior of Louisiana."

Some southern farmers also produced cash crops other than cotton. Production of tobacco, the South's first major cash crop, was particularly time-consuming. Many farmers prepared their harvested tobacco for market by curing, or drying, it in small barns. In 1839 a slave discovered a way to improve the drying process. By using heat from burning

Interpreting the Visual Record

A long day *These slave laborers on a sugar plantation are returning home after a long day working in the fields.* **What does this image suggest about the types of work done by enslaved men and women?**

charcoal, workers could cure tobacco more quickly. This discovery boosted tobacco farming, but tobacco still took much longer to process than most crops.

Partly as a result of the cotton boom, hemp and flax became major cash crops. Their fibers were used to make rope and sackcloth. Farmers across the cotton belt used rope produced in Kentucky, Missouri, and Tennessee to bundle cotton into bales.

✔ **Reading Check: Comparing** How did southerners use scientific agriculture and new technology to improve crop production in the South?

★ Southern Factories

Southern industries sprang up to serve the needs of farmers. The rope industry was one example. Some, such as the lumber industry, benefited from new technology. In 1803 the nation's first steam-powered sawmill was built in Donaldsonville, Louisiana. Factories were not as common in the South as they were in the Northeast, however. Many of the first factories in the South were built to process crops.

Turning sugarcane into sugar, for example, required many machines. Writer Mark Twain once described the interior of a southern sugar-processing factory. "[It was] a wilderness of tubs and tanks and vats and filters, pumps, pipes, and machinery." Some southerners, such as Hinton Rowan Helper, believed that the South needed even more industries.

History Makers Speak
"We should . . . keep pace with the progress of the age. We must expand our energies, and acquire habits of enterprise and industry; we should arouse ourselves from the couch of lassitude [laziness], and inure [set] our minds to thought and our bodies to action."

—Hinton Rowan Helper, *The Impending Crisis of the South: How to Meet It*

Research on the ROM

Free Find: Agriculture and Slavery After reading about agriculture and slavery on the **Holt Researcher CD–ROM**, imagine that you are a farmer trying to get financial backing to produce a crop. Write a brief proposal explaining the crop you have chosen and why you think it will sell.

Analyzing Primary Sources
Identifying Points of View What did Helper think the South's economy needed?

Working at the mill *This textile mill in Columbus, Georgia, was one of the relatively few factories in the South during the early 1800s.* **Does this mill appear to be located in the countryside or in a city?**

Joseph R. Anderson, a graduate of the military academy at West Point, followed Helper's advice. In 1848, he became the owner of the **Tredegar Iron Works** in Richmond. His company had the only large southern factory that made iron products. By 1860 Anderson had turned his factory into one of the most productive iron works in the nation. Tredegar produced boilers, bridge materials, cannons, locomotives, steam engines, and other products.

The South's industrial growth lagged behind that of the North. Cash crops, like tobacco and cotton, seemed to promise great wealth. As a result, most farmers and planters invested in more land and slaves in order to grow more cotton. They poured their profits into the developing plantation system, not into southern industry.

✔ **Reading Check: Summarizing** What kinds of factories were most common in the South, and why did the South build fewer factories than the North?

Section 2 Review

go. hrw .com **Homework Practice Online**

keyword: SF3 HP14

1. **Define** and explain:
   • factors
   • scientific agriculture

2. **Identify** and explain:
   • Jean Étienne Boré
   • Joseph R. Anderson
   • Tredegar Iron Works

3. **Summarizing** Copy the graphic organizer below. Use it to show the reasons that James D. B. De Bow and others advised southerners to grow a variety of crops and why Helper and others advised southerners to expand industry.

Reasons to Diversify ←→ Reasons to Expand Industry

4. **Finding the Main Idea**
   a. How did international trade affect the South's economy?

   b. What were typical factories in the South designed to manufacture?

5. **Writing and Critical Thinking**
   Supporting a Point of View Imagine that you are a southern farmer. Write a letter to your relatives explaining what crops you have decided to grow. Be sure to explain your choices.

   Consider the following:
   • the markets for southern crops
   • the most common southern crops
   • the effect of crops on the soil

Southern Society

Read to Discover

1. What was life like for southern planters and owners of small farms?
2. What was the urban South like?
3. What challenges did free African Americans face in the South?

Define
• yeomen

Identify
• Mark Twain

WHY IT MATTERS TODAY

The lifestyles of rural and urban southerners varied in important ways. Use CNNfyi.com or other **current events** sources to learn about issues affecting the lives of city residents and rural Americans in one area of the United States today. Record your findings in your journal.

The Story Continues

Many writers romanticized southern life. They wrote about what they saw as its unique characteristics. In 1832 Baltimore writer John Pendleton Kennedy, one of the first novelists to write about plantations, wrote *Swallow Barn*. The story glorifies the lives of planter families. In one scene, the narrator described his ideal of southern life. It was "a thousand acres of good land, an old manor-house, . . . a hundred [slaves], a large library, a host of friends, . . . and . . . a house full of pretty, intelligent, and docile [obedient] children." A booming market in plantation novels followed the publication of Kennedy's book. In reality, however, plantation life was very different from the scenes in Kennedy's writing.

THE GRANGER COLLECTION, NEW YORK

A wealthy southern family might own finely crafted furniture such as this chair.

⭐ The Planters

Popular fiction often made it seem that all white southerners had many slaves and lived on large plantations. This was hardly the case. In the first half of the 1800s, about one third of white southern families had slaves. Fewer families had plantations. Despite their small numbers, these planters had a powerful influence over the South. Many served as

THE GRANGER COLLECTION, NEW YORK

The children of planters often received a privileged upbringing.

political leaders. As the wealthiest members of southern society, planters also greatly influenced the economy. Some showed off their wealth by living in beautiful mansions. Many others chose to live more simply. A visitor described wealthy planter Alexander Stephens's estate as "an old wooden house" surrounded by weeds. Some planters saved all their money to buy more land and slaves.

Male planters were primarily concerned with raising crops and supervising slave laborers. They left the running of the plantation household to their wives. The planter's wife oversaw the raising of their children and supervised the work of all slaves within the household. Slave women typically cooked, cleaned, and helped care for the planter's children. Wives also took on the important social duties of the family. For example, many southern leaders discussed political issues at the dances and dinners hosted by their wives.

Planters often arranged their children's marriages based on business interests. Lucy Breckinridge, the daughter of a wealthy Virginia planter, was married by arrangement in 1865. Three years earlier, she had described in her journal how she dreaded the very thought of marriage. "A woman's life after she is married, unless there is an immense amount of love, is nothing but suffering and hard work." How Breckinridge's life in her own arranged marriage would have turned out cannot be known. She died of typhoid fever just months after her wedding.

✔ **Reading Check: Finding the Main Idea** How did planters maintain their influence in southern society?

★ Southern Society and Culture

Most southern white women married **yeomen**, or owners of small farms. Yeomen made up the majority of southern farmers. Typically they held few slaves or none at all. By 1860 about 80 percent of all southern farmers owned their own land. The typical yeoman farm averaged about 100 acres. Yeomen took great pride in their work. In 1849 a young Georgia man wrote that "I desire above all things to be a 'Farmer.' It is the most honest, upright, and sure way of securing all the comforts of life." In fact, most yeomen families had few material comforts. They worked long days at many tasks. "My life is one of toil," wrote yeoman Ferdinand Steel in 1839, "but blessed be God that it is as well with me as it is." Many yeomen farmers hoped one day to become planters themselves.

Some yeomen earned enough money to buy a few slaves. Yet, unlike the planters, yeomen generally worked side by side with slaves. Many planters believed they should maintain their control over slaves by treating them harshly.

Planters and yeomen alike often looked down on the poorest of white southerners. These landless people made up less than 10 percent

Corn was the most common food crop grown in the South, and many yeomen produced it.

The Southern Population, 1860

Total Population

- ■ Nonslaveholding whites
- ■ Slaves
- ■ Slaveholding whites
- ■ Free African Americans
- ■ Other

1%
2%
16%
47%
34%

Slaveholding Households

- ■ Fewer than 10 slaves
- ■ 10–49 slaves
- ■ 50–99 slaves
- ■ 100 or more slaves

1%
2%
25%
72%

Sources: *Historical Statistics of the United States; The Black American Reference Book; Slavery and the Southern Economy*

Interpreting Graphs Despite the importance of slavery to the South's agricultural economy, most southerners held no slaves.

Skills Assessment

1. Which group made up the largest percentage of the southern population?
2. What percent of slaveholding households had 100 or more slaves?

of the white southern population. Most of them lived on lands that were not suited to growing cash crops. They survived by hunting, fishing, raising a few animals, tending small gardens, and doing odd jobs for money.

White southerners did share a common culture in many ways. For example, religion was central to southern social life. Farm families were often isolated from one another. They might see their neighbors only at church events, such as revivals or socials. Although they were not allowed to become ministers, rural women often played volunteer roles in their churches.

Other wealthy white southerners used religion to justify their position in society and the institution of slavery. They argued that God created some people, like themselves, to rule over African Americans. This belief set them against those northern Christians who believed that God opposed slavery.

Some southern writers tried to increase national awareness of southern culture. Charleston, South Carolina, attracted many writers who gathered to discuss their poems, short stories, and essays. Most southern writers, such as John Pendleton Kennedy, greatly romanticized southern culture—particularly life on plantations. Some later writers provided a more even-handed look at southern society during the mid-1800s. Among these writers was Samuel Clemens, better known by his pen name, **Mark Twain**. He based this pen name on river slang for shallow water only two fathoms deep. Several of Twain's most popular works, such as *The Adventures of Huckleberry Finn* and *The Adventures of Tom Sawyer*, are set in the South.

Caroline Howard Gilman began a successful career as a southern writer in the 1830s.

✔ **Reading Check: Comparing and Contrasting** How were planters, yeomen, and poor whites similar to and different from each other?

Interpreting the Visual Record

Busy port *Many of the larger southern cities, such as Charleston, South Carolina, and New Orleans, Louisiana, were also busy seaports.* **What goods can you see being prepared for shipment on the dock?**

⭐ The Urban South

Influenced by the products of the plantations, the urban economy was also an important part of the South. But cities had many different businesses, people, and social organizations. City residents often took on many key roles in their communities. James A. Cowardin of Richmond, Virginia, was a typical urban business leader who also edited a small newspaper and served in the state legislature.

In many ways, southern cities were like those in the North. City governments built public water systems and provided well-maintained streets. Public education was available in some places. Sometimes wealthy residents gave large sums of money to charities—from orphanages to public libraries. Southern urban leaders wanted their cities to appear as modern as possible. They hoped to impress foreign visitors who came to the South to do business.

As on plantations, slaves did much of the work in southern cities. Slaves worked as domestic servants, in mills, in shipyards, and at skilled jobs. Compared with rural white southerners, urban whites were more likely to hold slaves. Many business leaders held slaves or hired them from nearby plantations.

✔ **Reading Check: Finding the Main Idea** What were public services and slavery like in southern cities?

Research on the R🔘M

Free Find:
South Carolina
After looking at the population figures for South Carolina on the **Holt Researcher CD–ROM**, imagine that you are a member of the Census Bureau. Create a line graph showing the changes in the population of South Carolina from 1800 to 1850.

⭐ Free African Americans

Some free African Americans also found work in southern cities. In 1860 more than half of all free African Americans were living in the South. Some were the descendants of slaves who had been freed after the American Revolution. Still others had won their freedom, often by running away.

Free African Americans who lived in southern cities worked in a variety of jobs, mostly as skilled artisans. A small number became fairly successful in their businesses. Free African Americans in rural areas often hired out their services to plantations. A few of them were quite financially successful. Churches often served as the center of social life for free southern African Americans. In the early 1800s free and enslaved African Americans in Charleston, South Carolina, started a rare independent-church movement.

Free African Americans faced constant discrimination. White southerners feared that free African Americans would try to encourage slave rebellions. Many cities and states passed laws limiting the rights of free African Americans. Most could not vote, travel freely, or hold certain types of jobs. In some places, laws forced them to have a white person represent them in their business dealings.

An 1806 Virginia law banned former slaves from living in the state without special permission. Jemima Hunt, a free African American woman, was able to buy the freedom of Stephen, her husband. She asked the Virginia legislature to grant him permission to stay in the state.

Some African Americans had to wear badges such as this one to prove that they were free.

 History Makers Speak **"**Your petitioner [Hunt] farther states that she has a numerous family of Children by the said Stephen, who are dependent upon the daily labor of herself & husband for a support, & without the assistance of her husband Stephen they must suffer.**"**

—Jemima Hunt, quoted in *Enduring Voices, Volume I: To 1877*, edited by James J. Lorence

Analyzing Primary Sources
Identifying Points of View
Why was it important for Jemima Hunt to have her husband with her?

Many white southerners felt that free African Americans could not take care of themselves. "The status of slavery is the only one for which the African is adapted," wrote one white Mississippian. But free African Americans proved that they could survive outside the slave system. As a result, many white southerners viewed them as a threat to the institution of slavery.

✔ **Reading Check: Summarizing** What economic, legal, and social challenges did free African Americans face in southern society?

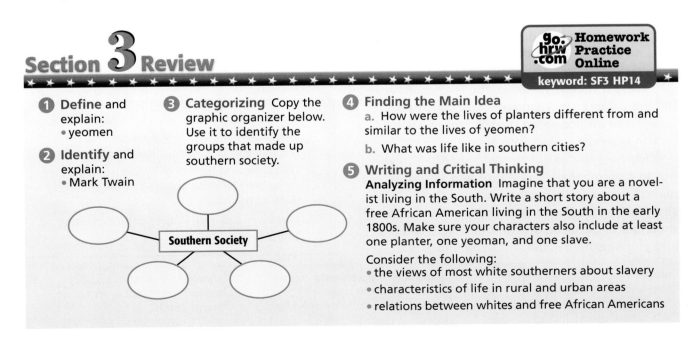

Section 3 Review

go.hrw.com **Homework Practice Online** keyword: SF3 HP14

1 **Define** and explain:
• yeomen

2 **Identify** and explain:
• Mark Twain

3 **Categorizing** Copy the graphic organizer below. Use it to identify the groups that made up southern society.

Southern Society

4 **Finding the Main Idea**
a. How were the lives of planters different from and similar to the lives of yeomen?

b. What was life like in southern cities?

5 **Writing and Critical Thinking**
Analyzing Information Imagine that you are a novelist living in the South. Write a short story about a free African American living in the South in the early 1800s. Make sure your characters also include at least one planter, one yeoman, and one slave.

Consider the following:
• the views of most white southerners about slavery
• characteristics of life in rural and urban areas
• relations between whites and free African Americans

Literature

Life on the Mississippi
Mark Twain

Mark Twain wrote several books
about life on and around the
Mississippi River.

Samuel Langhorne Clemens, better known as Mark Twain, was born in 1835 in Missouri. One of America's most humorous writers, Twain enriched his works by using local color—writing that expresses the culture and language of a particular region. In the following passage from Twain's book Life on the Mississippi, *he recalls a lesson from Mr. Bixby, a steamboat pilot who taught him to pilot a riverboat on the Mississippi River.*

Nothing ever had the same shape when I was coming downstream as it had **borne**[1] when I went up. I mentioned these little difficulties to Mr. Bixby. . . . It was plain that I had got to learn the shape of the river in all the different ways that could be thought of—upside down, wrong end first, inside out, **fore-and-aft**,[2] and **"thort-ships"**[3]—and then know what to do on gray nights when it hadn't any shape at all. So I set about it. In the course of time I began to get the best of this knotty lesson, and my **self-complacency**[4] moved to the front once more. Mr. Bixby was all fixed, and ready to start it to the rear again. He opened on me after this fashion—

"How much water did we have in the idle crossing at Hole-in-the-Wall, trip before last?"

I considered this an outrage. I said—

"Every trip, down and up, the **leadsmen**[5] are singing through that tangled place for three quarters of an hour on a stretch. How do you reckon I can remember such a mess as that?"

"My boy, you've got to remember it. You've got to remember the exact spot and the exact **marks**[6] the boat lay in when we had the **shoalest**[7] water, in every one of the five hundred shoal places between St. Louis and New Orleans; and you mustn't get the shoal soundings and

marks of one trip mixed up with the shoal soundings and marks of another, either, for they're not often twice alike. You must keep them separate."

When I came to myself again, I said—

"When I get so that I can do that, I'll be able to raise the dead, and then I won't have to pilot a steamboat to make a living. I want to retire from this business. I want a slush-bucket and a brush; I'm only fit for a **roustabout**.[8] I haven't got brains enough to be a pilot; and if I had I wouldn't have strength enough to carry them around, unless I went on crutches."

"Now drop that! When I say I'll **learn**[9] a man the river, I mean it. And you can depend on it, I'll learn him or kill him."

Understanding What You Read

1. **Literature and History** Why is remembering the shape of the river difficult?
2. **Literature and History** Why is it important for steamboat pilots to know all of the changing parts of the river?
3. **Literature and You** Why might this passage be funny to some readers?

---

[1]**borne:** held
[2]**fore-and-aft:** front and back
[3]**"thort-ships":** shore to shore
[4]**self-complacency:** lack of concern

[5]**leadsmen:** workers who measure the water's depth
[6]**marks:** measurements of water depth

[7]**shoalest:** most shallow
[8]**roustabout:** laborer on a boat
[9]**learn:** teach

The Slave System

Read to Discover

1. What were work and daily life like for most slaves?
2. How did slaves' family, religion, and other aspects of their culture help them cope with the slave system?
3. How did enslaved African Americans challenge the slave system?

Define
- folktales
- spirituals

Identify
- Nat Turner
- Nat Turner's Rebellion

WHY IT MATTERS TODAY

Spirituals were one aspect of slave culture. Use CNNfyi.com or other **current events** sources to find out how art, literature, or music serves as part of a group's culture today. Record your findings in your journal.

The Story Continues

Harriet Jacobs was born into slavery in 1813. Jacobs worked for many years in a doctor's household. Determined that her children would not live as slaves, Jacobs ran away. "I had . . . a mother's love for my children," she explained. "I resolved that out of the darkness . . . a brighter dawn should rise for them." Jacobs knew that it would be hard to survive as a runaway slave, but she was hopeful. "My master had power and law on his side . . . ," Jacob noted. "I had a determined will."

This slave auction poster identifies and describes the people that the company planned to sell.

⭐ Slaves and Work

Although treatment of enslaved African Americans varied, most slaveholders tried to get as much work as they could out of slaves. Enslaved people living on small farms usually did a wide variety of jobs. On large plantations most slaves were assigned to specific tasks. The majority of slaves worked in the fields. Drivers, who were sometimes slaves themselves, made sure that slaves followed orders. Drivers also carried out punishments.

DETAIL OF JOHN ANTROBUS, PLANTATION BURIAL, (1860) OIL ON CANVAS, THE HISTORICAL NEW ORLEANS COLLECTION

Interpreting the Visual Record

Funeral *Slaves often tried to practice their religious beliefs and ceremonies out of sight of slaveholders. Here a group of slaves conducts a funeral at night in the woods.* **Why do you think slaves might have wanted privacy for a ceremony like this one?**

Most plantation owners used the gang labor system. In this system all hands worked on the same task at the same time. They usually worked from sunup to sundown. Former slave Harry McMillan had worked on a plantation in South Carolina. He recalled that the field hands usually did not even get a break to eat lunch. "You had to get your victuals [food] standing at your hoe," he remembered.

Men, women, and even children older than about 10 usually did the same work. Hardly anything, even sickness and poor weather, stopped the work. "The times I hated most was picking cotton when the frost was on the bolls [seed pods]," recalled former Louisiana slave Mary Reynolds. "My hands git sore and crack open and bleed."

Some slaves worked as butlers, cooks, or nurses in the planter's home. These slaves often had better food and clothing than field hands. But they often worked longer hours. They had to serve the planter's family 24 hours a day. House servants could also be sent to work in the fields. On larger plantations, some slaves worked at skilled jobs such as blacksmithing or carpentry. Sometimes planters let these slaves hire out their services to other people. In this way, some skilled slaves earned enough money to buy their freedom. For example, William Ellison earned his freedom by working for wages as a cotton gin maker. For years he worked late at night and on Sundays. He bought his freedom with the money he earned. Eventually, he was also able to buy the freedom of his wife and daughter.

✔ **Reading Check: Categorizing** What were some of the different types of work that slaves did on plantations?

Slaveholders used shackles like this metal collar and these leg irons to punish slaves.

⭐ Life under Slavery

Generally, slaveholders tended to view slaves as property, not as people. Some slaves were bought, worked, and sold to make a profit. Slave traders even kidnapped free African Americans and then sold them into slavery. For example, Solomon Northup was kidnapped in Washington. He spent 12 years as a slave, "shut out from the sweet light of liberty." He finally proved his identity and gained his release.

Most slaves received very poor clothing and shelter. They lived in small cabins with dirt floors, leaky roofs, and few furnishings. Field hands like Delia Garlic recalled that her slave clothing "was made out of the cheapest cloth that could be bought." Some slaves tried to brighten up their clothes by using old scraps of cloth to sew designs on the fabric. In this way, they individualized the clothing given to them by the planters. Likewise, many slaves did what they could to improve their food rations. Some planters allowed slaves to keep their own vegetable gardens, and chickens for eggs. If they had time, slaves might catch fish or pick berries.

Some planters offered more food or better living conditions to encourage slaves' obedience. However, many slaveholders used punishment instead. Some would punish one slave in front of others as a warning to them all. Harry McMillan recalled some of the punishments he witnessed.

History Makers Speak

66The punishments were whipping, putting you in the stocks [wooden frames to lock people in] and making you wear irons and a chain at work. Then they had a collar to put round your neck with two horns, like cows' horns, so that you could not lie down. . . . This also kept you from running away for the horns would catch in the bushes. Sometimes they dug a hole like a well with a door on top. This they called a dungeon keeping you in it two or three weeks or a month, or sometimes till you died in there.99

—Harry McMillan, quoted in *Major Problems in the History of the American South, Volume I,* edited by Paul D. Escott and David R. Goldfield

Analyzing Primary Sources

Making Generalizations and Predictions What effect do you think the treatment Harry McMillan describes would have on slave workers?

To further control slaves' actions, many states had strict slave codes that limited what slaves could do. Some laws prohibited slaves from traveling far from their homes. Teaching slaves to read or write was usually illegal. Slaves thus did not have freedom of movement and the benefits of simple education.

✔ **Reading Check: Analyzing Information** How did slaveholders try to keep slaves under control?

Interpreting the Visual Record

Auction *Families of enslaved African Americans were often broken up at auctions.* **Why might an auction like this one frighten an enslaved person?**

441

Research on the ROM

Free Find:
Nat Turner's Confessions
After reading Nat Turner's Confession on the **Holt Researcher CD–ROM,** imagine that you are a journalist from the North. Write a brief article summarizing Nat Turner's views.

COLLECTION OF THE NEW-YORK HISTORICAL SOCIETY

BIOGRAPHY

Nat Turner

(1800–1831)

Nat Turner grew up believing he was called by God to do something important. As a child on a Virginia plantation, he gained a reputation among the other slaves for his religious beliefs and intelligence. Turner became a well-respected minister in the local slave community. In 1827 he even baptized a white overseer. When a solar eclipse took place in 1831, Turner interpreted it as a sign that the time had come to start a revolt. **What event led Nat Turner to believe that he should start a slave revolt?**

★ Slave Culture

Despite the harsh realities of daily life, many slaves took comfort in their community and culture. They worked hard to maintain strong ties to one another and to their heritage. The most important unit of slave communities was the family. Most slaves feared being separated from their families more than physical punishment. Josiah Henson never forgot the day that he and his family were sold at a slave auction. His mother begged the slaveholder who bought her to buy Josiah also. If he did, then she would have at least one of her children with her. The slaveholder refused, and Henson's entire family was separated. "I must have been then between five or six years old," he recalled years later. "I seem to see and hear my poor weeping mother now."

Enslaved parents made sure that children never forgot their heritage. They passed down family histories, as well as African customs and traditions. They also told **folktales,** or stories with a moral, to teach lessons about how to survive under slavery. Folktales often warned slaves not to trust slaveholders, who were often represented in the stories by powerful animals. Clever characters called tricksters were used to show slaves how to survive by outsmarting slaveholders.

Religion was also an important part of slave culture. By the early 1800s many slaves were Christians. White ministers often tried to use religion to control slaves. They preached that God wanted slaves to obey slaveholders. However, enslaved African Americans noted that the Bible suggested that all people are equal in God's eyes. They came to see themselves as God's chosen people. Much like the Hebrew slaves in ancient Egypt, slaves in the South had faith that they would someday live in freedom.

Some slaves used **spirituals,** emotional Christian songs that blended African and European music, to express their religious beliefs. For example, "The Heavenly Road" reflected slaves' belief in their equality in the eyes of God.

Primary Sources

❝Come, my brother, if you never did pray,
I hope you may pray tonight;
For I really believe I'm a child of God
As I walk in the heavenly road.❞

—Anonymous, quoted in *Afro-American Religious History,* edited by Milton C. Sernett

Slaves blended aspects of traditional African religions with those of Christianity. For example, spirituals developed in part out of a dance called the ring shout, which was based on African ceremonial dances performed in a ring. Slaves worshipped in secret, out of sight of the slaveholder. Some historians have called slave religion the invisible institution.

✔ **Reading Check: Summarizing** What did slaves use to keep a sense of community among themselves?

⭐ Challenging Slavery

Slaves rebelled in small ways against the slave system on a daily basis. Sometimes this meant working slower to protest long hours in the fields. Other times it meant running away for a few days. Some slaves tried to escape, but most left only for short periods, usually to see relatives. However, thousands of enslaved people did manage to escape to the North.

Although violent slave revolts were rare, white southerners lived in fear that they would occur. Denmark Vesey planned a rebellion in Charleston, South Carolina, in 1822, but he was found out and stopped before it could be carried out. Authorities executed most of those involved. The most violent slave revolt in the United States occurred in 1831. **Nat Turner**, a slave from Virginia, believed that God had called on him to end slavery. **Nat Turner's Rebellion** began on an August night in 1831. Turner led a group of slaves that set out to kill slaveholders and their families. The rebels killed about 60 white people in the area.

More than 100 slaves were killed in an attempt to put down the rebellion. Turner himself was caught within weeks and executed on November 11, 1831. After the rebellion, many states strengthened their slave codes. The codes were meant to place stricter controls on the slave population. Despite the resistance of enslaved people, slavery continued to spread.

THE GRANGER COLLECTION, NEW YORK

Interpreting the Visual Record

Nat Turner's Rebellion *Nat Turner believed that his revolt was justified. "I am willing to suffer the fate that awaits me," he said.* **Why do you think Turner and his fellow rebels are in the swamp?**

✔ **Reading Check: Finding the Main Idea** What was Nat Turner's Rebellion, and what happened as a result?

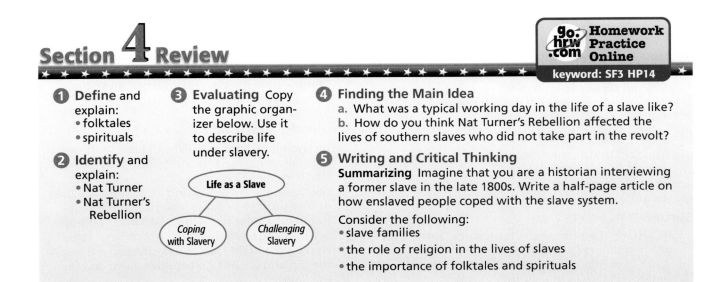

Section 4 Review

go.hrw.com **Homework Practice Online** keyword: SF3 HP14

1 Define and explain:
• folktales
• spirituals

2 Identify and explain:
• Nat Turner
• Nat Turner's Rebellion

3 Evaluating Copy the graphic organizer below. Use it to describe life under slavery.

Life as a Slave
— Coping with Slavery
— Challenging Slavery

4 Finding the Main Idea
a. What was a typical working day in the life of a slave like?
b. How do you think Nat Turner's Rebellion affected the lives of southern slaves who did not take part in the revolt?

5 Writing and Critical Thinking
Summarizing Imagine that you are a historian interviewing a former slave in the late 1800s. Write a half-page article on how enslaved people coped with the slave system.

Consider the following:
• slave families
• the role of religion in the lives of slaves
• the importance of folktales and spirituals

Chapter **14** Review

The Chapter at a Glance

Examine the visual summary of the chapter below. Create a five-question quiz on how the main ideas in each section are related to each other to exchange with a classmate.

Southern Economy

Cotton Gin

Cotton + = Cotton Boom

In addition to cotton, southern farmers grew cash crops like sugar and tobacco and staple crops like corn.

The Urban South

Factories **Cities**

The South had fewer factories and large cities than the North. Most free African Americans lived in urban areas.

Southern Society

Planters were at the top of southern society, which also included yeoman farmers, poor whites, and enslaved and free African Americans. Planters were the largest slaveholders.

Understanding People and Ideas

Use the following terms or people in historically significant sentences.

1. Eli Whitney
2. cotton gin
3. cotton belt
4. factors
5. Jean Étienne Boré
6. Tredegar Iron Works
7. yeomen
8. folktales
9. spirituals
10. Nat Turner's Rebellion

Understanding Main Ideas

Section 1 *(Pages 424–427)*

1. Why did cotton production increase in the 1800s?
2. Why did slavery seem to decline after the American Revolution, and why did it increase again in the 1800s?

Section 2 *(Pages 428–432)*

3. What did southerners mean when they proclaimed that "Cotton is King"?
4. What kinds of factories existed in the South in the 1800s?

Section 3 *(Pages 433–438)*

5. How were the economic interests of planters and yeomen similar?
6. What kind of discrimination did free African Americans face in the South?

Section 4 *(Pages 439–443)*

7. What role did family and religion play in the lives of enslaved African Americans?

You Be the Historian— Reviewing Themes

1. **Science, Technology & Society** How did the invention of the cotton gin by Eli Whitney lead to an increased demand for slave labor in the South?
2. **Economics** How did the cotton boom affect the economy and society of the South?
3. **Culture** How did slavery influence southern African American culture in the 1800s?

Thinking Critically

1. **Analyzing Information** Why did the southern economy develop differently from that of the North in the 1800s?
2. **Comparing and Contrasting** How were the lives of free southern African Americans different from and similar to the lives of slaves? Consider political and social factors.
3. **Finding the Main Idea** What effects did the cotton gin and scientific agriculture have on life in the South?

Interpreting Graphs

Study the graph below. Then use the information on the graph to help you answer the questions that follow.

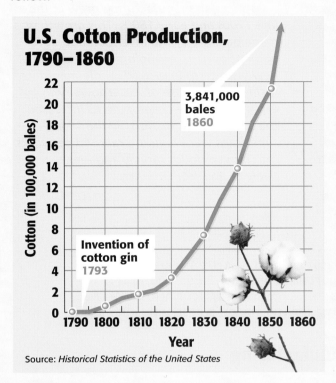

U.S. Cotton Production, 1790–1860

3,841,000 bales
1860

Invention of cotton gin
1793

Cotton (in 100,000 bales)

Year

Source: *Historical Statistics of the United States*

1. At about what year did the production of cotton rise beyond 1 million bales?
   a. 1840
   b. 1835
   c. 1830
   d. 1825

2. Based on the graph and your knowledge of the period, what event contributed to the increase in cotton production in the South?

Analyzing Primary Sources

Read the following quote by planter Bennet H. Barrow, and then answer the questions that follow.

"If I employ a laborer to perform a certain quantum [amount] of work per day, and I agree to pay him a certain amount for the performance of said work when he has accomplished it, I of course have no further claim on him for his time or services [when he is done]—but how different is it with a slave. . . . If I furnish my [slave] with every necessary of life, . . . am I not entitled to an exclusive right to his time? . . . A plantation might be considered as a piece of machinery; to operate successfully, all of its parts should be uniform [the same]."

3. Which of the following best describes Barrow's attitude toward slaves?
   a. A planter should treat slaves like parts of a machine and have control over all their time.
   b. Slavery is actually more expensive than paying people's wages.
   c. Once they have finished their work, slaves should have free time to themselves.
   d. Plantations should make use of modern machinery as well as slaves.

4. According to his own words, how would Barrow expect to treat free workers whom he paid wages?
   a. They would have to work for him whenever he wanted.
   b. He would pay them only when he was satisfied with their work.
   c. When they finished a job, their free time would be their own.
   d. He would expect to provide for all of their needs in addition to paying wages.

Alternative Assessment

Building Your Portfolio

American History

Interdisciplinary Connection to Literature
Create a folktale that enslaved African American parents might have told their children. Use animals to represent the main characters. Have one of the characters play the trickster's role—to outwit a stronger creature. The folktale should try to teach a moral lesson about how to survive in slavery. Present your folktale to the class, and have students discuss the story's lesson.

🖅 **internet** connect

Internet Activity: go.hrw.com
keyword: SF3 CF14

Choose a topic on Agricultural Changes in the South to:
● Learn about slave revolts in Haiti and the abolition of slavery in France.
● Understand sugar production and make a flow chart.
● Research and report on the Tredegar Iron Works.

Agricultural Changes in the South **445**

A Growing Economy

From 1790 to 1860, the economy of each region of the United States grew and developed in very different ways. The economies of the South and the West were based largely on farming. The economy of the North was increasingly focused on industry.

In some ways these differences worked together to help the nation grow. For example, the South provided some raw materials, such as cotton, to northern factories. The Midwest provided large supplies of food, which helped feed the growing population of northern cities.

American manufacturing grew in the late 1700s and early 1800s. This growth was made possible by the invention and development of new technologies. For example, new inventions improved textile manufacturing, and the use of waterpower was expanded. These developments increased the speed of production. By the 1830s, Americans were building railroad networks that moved goods rapidly and inexpensively to and from market.

The North

The North developed an industrial economy partly because of its geography and superior transportation system. Farmland in the North was not generally suited for large-scale agriculture. Industrial development was thus necessary for the region's economic growth.

Distribution of U.S. Manufacturing Establishments, 1860

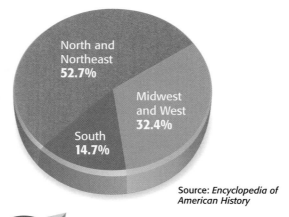

North and Northeast 52.7%

Midwest and West 32.4%

South 14.7%

Source: *Encyclopedia of American History*

History Note 1

By 1860 only about one in seven U.S. factories and other manufacturing establishments were located in the South. As industry increased in the North, so did the region's urban population. Cities, particularly those in the Northeast and Midwest, grew larger as factories provided more and more jobs. In the South, which had fewer factories, urban growth was much slower.

Geography **Skills**

Interpreting Pie Graphs

1. What region had the largest percentage of the nation's manufacturing establishments in 1860?
2. **Comparing** How much greater was the percentage of manufacturing establishments in the Midwest and West than in the South in 1860?

Industry in the North, 1860

Railroad

Canal

Canalized river

Industries

- Clothing accessories
- Food products
- Iron or steel
- Machinery or equipment
- Paper
- Textiles
- Weaponry
- Diverse industries
- Clocks, watches
- Other

Geography Skills

Interpreting Thematic Maps

1. Have a fellow student look at this map. Then ask him or her to create a bar graph comparing the number of iron, steel, and textile industries in the North.

2. **Environment and Society** How do you think the construction of so many railroads and canals helped northern industry?

3. **Analyzing Information** What geographic features made New England more suitable for early industries?

History Note 2

Improved transportation networks in the North encouraged industrial expansion. Businesses shipped goods on rivers, the Great Lakes, and the growing networks of canals and railroads. The benefits of expanded transportation networks on industrial growth could be clearly seen in New England in the first half of the 1800s. Connecticut, Massachusetts, and Rhode Island provide good examples of this important relationship.

The South

While industry in the North grew, agriculture in the South boomed. The invention of the cotton gin in 1793 encouraged growth in southern cotton production. However, as that region's economy grew, so did disapproval in the North and the West of the South's use of slave labor.

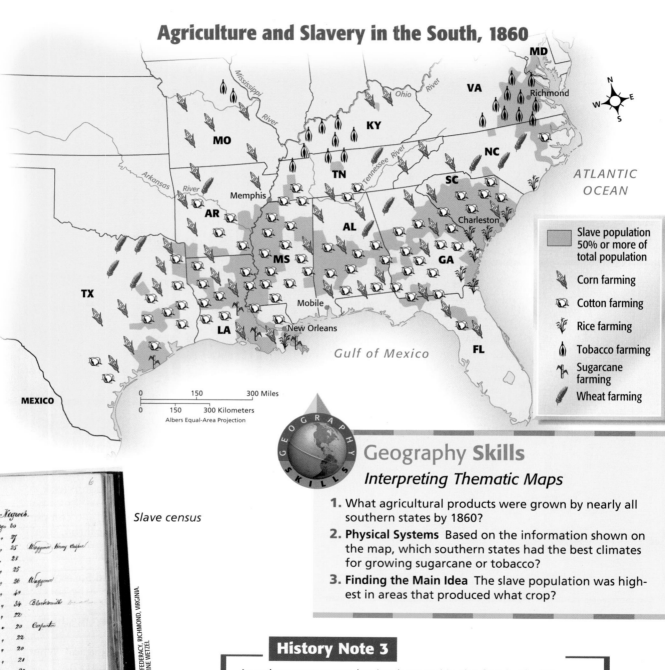

Agriculture and Slavery in the South, 1860

Legend:
- Slave population 50% or more of total population
- Corn farming
- Cotton farming
- Rice farming
- Tobacco farming
- Sugarcane farming
- Wheat farming

Slave census

Geography Skills
Interpreting Thematic Maps

1. What agricultural products were grown by nearly all southern states by 1860?

2. **Physical Systems** Based on the information shown on the map, which southern states had the best climates for growing sugarcane or tobacco?

3. **Finding the Main Idea** The slave population was highest in areas that produced what crop?

History Note 3

American cotton production boomed in the first half of the 1800s. Cotton production was concentrated within a region called the cotton belt, which ran from South Carolina to eastern Texas. In 1860 the United States exported more than $190 million worth of cotton, most of it grown in the cotton belt.

THE MUSEUM OF THE CONFEDERACY, RICHMOND, VIRGINIA. PHOTOGRAPHY BY KATHERINE WETZEL.

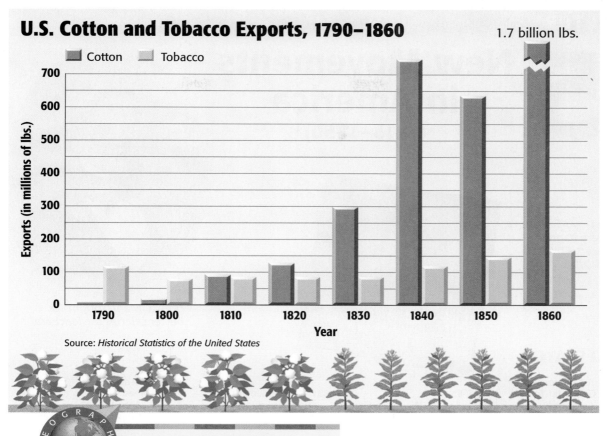

U.S. Cotton and Tobacco Exports, 1790–1860

1.7 billion lbs.

■ Cotton   ■ Tobacco

Exports (in millions of lbs.)

700
600
500
400
300
200
100
0

1790 1800 1810 1820 1830 1840 1850 1860

Year

Source: *Historical Statistics of the United States*

Geography **Skills**

Interpreting Bar Graphs

1. By what year had the amount of cotton exports overtaken the amount of tobacco exports?

2. **Summarizing** Show this bar graph to a classmate. Have this person write a paragraph describing the general trends in tobacco and cotton exports from 1790 to 1860.

History Note 4

Together Alabama, Georgia, Louisiana, and Mississippi produced about two thirds of the cotton in the United States in 1860. States that produced smaller amounts of cotton often produced larger amounts of other agricultural products. For example, in 1860 Virginia produced relatively little cotton. However, it produced nearly 30 percent of the nation's tobacco. South Carolina produced nearly two thirds of the nation's rice in that year.

Slaves returning from a hard day of laboring in the fields

NEW YOR

CHAPTER

15 New Movements in America
(1815–1850)

William Lloyd Garrison's antislavery banner announced, "I WILL BE HEARD."

THE LIBERATOR
COMMENCED JANUARY 1st 1831.

W.L.G.

"I am in earnest! I will not equivocate! I will not excuse! I will not retreat a single inch. And *I WILL BE HEARD!*"

THE GRANGER COLLECTION, NEW YORK

Horace Mann fought for better salaries for teachers.

UNITED STATES

1817 Thomas Gallaudet founds a school for people who are hearing impaired.

1821 Emma Willard starts the Troy Female Seminary.

1831 William Lloyd Garrison begins publishing the abolitionist newspaper *The Liberator*.

1837 Horace Mann becomes the first secretary of education in Massachusetts.

1815	**1820**	**1825**	**1830**	**1835**

WORLD

1822 The American Colonization Society founds the city of Monrovia on Africa's west coast.

1829 French educator Louis Braille creates a system of writing that uses raised dots for people who are blind.

Slavery is banned in Mexico.

1834 A law abolishing slavery in the British Empire goes into effect.

THE GRANGER COLLECTION, NEW YORK

Monrovia became the capital of the African nation Liberia.

Build on What You Know

The North and South developed very different economies during the early 1800s. Rising immigration led to population growth, especially in the North. As the country faced new challenges, social reform movements emerged in response. Many people joined groups to fight alcohol abuse, end slavery, or improve education.

Organizers of the Seneca Falls Convention based the Declaration of Sentiments in part on the Declaration of Independence.

During the mid-1800s, large numbers of German and Irish immigrants came to the United States.

1848 The first meeting for women's rights—the Seneca Falls Convention—is held in New York.

1850 Nathaniel Hawthorne publishes *The Scarlet Letter.*

1855 Boston lets African American children attend white schools.

1860 About 13 percent of the American population is foreign born.

1840   1845   1850   1855   1860

1840 The World's Anti-Slavery Convention is held in London.

1845 A potato famine in Ireland causes more Irish to move to the United States.

1860 In England Florence Nightingale founds the first school for training nurses.

In 1907 Florence Nightingale became the first woman to receive Britain's Order of Merit.

You Be the Historian

Themes Journal

What's Your Opinion? Do you **agree** or **disagree** with the following statements? Support your point of view in your journal.

- **Culture** People should try to improve the lives of the less fortunate.
- **Economics** Immigration makes a country's economy grow.
- **Citizenship** Citizens should try to change laws that they feel are unjust.

If you were there . . .
What social issues would you choose to work on?

America's Spiritual Awakening

Read to Discover

1. How did religion affect Americans during the Second Great Awakening?
2. What were the transcendentalists' views of American society?
3. What were some ideas of the romantic movement?

WHY IT MATTERS TODAY

Art is a way to learn more about a culture or a community. Use **CNNfyi.com** or other **current events** sources to learn more about an American writer who is alive today. Record your findings in your journal.

Define

- transcendentalism
- utopian communities

Identify

- Second Great Awakening
- Charles Grandison Finney
- Ralph Waldo Emerson
- Margaret Fuller
- Henry David Thoreau
- Thomas Cole
- Nathaniel Hawthorne
- Edgar Allan Poe
- Emily Dickinson
- Walt Whitman

Traveling ministers were key to the success of the Second Great Awakening.

The Story Continues

In her early teens, New Yorker Huldah Baldwin began thinking seriously about her spiritual life. When she became deathly ill, she asked relatives and friends to come to her bedside. She was concerned about the state of their souls. She pleaded with her family members as death grew near. "O live for him [God] that we may meet hereafter and enjoy a blessed eternity together." Such deep religious beliefs were increasingly common in the early 1800s in New York.

★ The Second Great Awakening

Beginning in the 1790s some Americans took part in a movement of Christian renewal called the **Second Great Awakening**. It swept through towns across upstate New York and through the frontier regions of Kentucky, Ohio, Tennessee, and South Carolina. By the 1820s and 1830s this new interest in religion had spread to New England, the Appalachians, and the South.

Charles Grandison Finney was one of the most important leaders of the Second Great Awakening. After experiencing a dramatic religious conversion in 1821, Finney left his career as a lawyer and began preaching. Speaking in a forceful and direct style, Finney challenged some traditional Protestant beliefs. He told congregations that each individual was responsible for his or her own salvation. He also believed that sin was avoidable. Finney held prayer meetings that would last for days. Many people converted to Christianity during these revivals. Finney told these converts to demonstrate their faith by doing good deeds.

Finney's preaching angered some traditional ministers like Lyman Beecher of Boston. Beecher wanted to prevent Finney from holding revivals in the city. "You mean to carry a streak of fire to Boston. If you attempt it, as the Lord liveth, I'll meet you . . . and fight every inch of the way." However, the First Amendment guarantee of freedom of religion prevented local or state governments from passing laws banning the new religious practices. Ministers were thus free to spread their message of faith and salvation to whomever wished to listen.

As a result of their efforts, church membership across the country grew a great deal during the Second Great Awakening. Many of these new church members were women. African Americans were among those drawn to the new religious movement. Some became Baptist, Methodist, or Presbyterian ministers. The African Methodist Episcopal Church spread across the Middle Atlantic states. Although the movement had begun in the Northeast and on the frontier, the Second Great Awakening renewed Americans' religious faith throughout the country.

✔ **Reading Check: Finding the Main Idea** How did the Second Great Awakening affect Americans?

In 1794 Richard Allen founded the Bethel African Methodist Episcopal Church in Philadelphia.

Daily Life

Revival Meetings Religious revivals swept the United States in the early 1800s. Some meetings drew up to 20,000 people at a time to huge outdoor camps. James Finley, who later became a Methodist preacher, described one revival as a "vast sea of human beings [that] seemed to be agitated as if by a storm." Preachers traveled from town to town, urging sinners to seek salvation. **How does this image portray the emotional qualities of a revival meeting?**

THE GRANGER COLLECTION, NEW YORK

Utopian communities *Brook Farm, a utopian community in Massachusetts, attracted a number of famous writers.* **What do you see in this picture that might attract people to live there?**

Analyzing Primary Sources

Drawing Inferences and Conclusions Why did Thoreau live in a cabin in the woods?

★ Transcendentalism and Utopian Communities

Some New England writers and thinkers found spiritual inspiration in **transcendentalism**. Transcendentalism was the belief that people could transcend, or rise above, the material things in life, such as money and personal belongings. Transcendentalists believed that people should depend on themselves instead of upon outside authority. Some important figures who believed in this philosophy were **Ralph Waldo Emerson**, **Margaret Fuller**, and **Henry David Thoreau**.

Emerson wrote an essay titled "Self-Reliance" in 1841. In this essay, he said that Americans depended too much on institutions and traditions. Emerson wanted people to follow their personal beliefs and use their own judgment. "What I must do is all that concerns me, not what the people think," he wrote. Fuller edited the transcendentalist publication *The Dial*. In 1845 she wrote a book called *Woman in the Nineteenth Century*. In it, she said that women had the right to choose their own paths in life. Some people saw her as a champion of women's rights.

Thoreau also believed in self-reliance and did not trust institutions. He expressed many of his ideas in *Walden, or Life in the Woods*, published in 1854. For two years, Thoreau lived alone in a small cabin in Massachusetts. He wrote about his experiences living near Walden Pond.

 Primary Sources

❝I went to the woods because I wished to live deliberately [with a purpose], to front [experience] only the essential facts of life, and see if I could learn what it had to teach, and not, when I came to die, discover that I had not lived.❞

—Henry David Thoreau, *Walden*

In the 1840s some transcendentalists formed a community at Brook Farm, Massachusetts. Brook Farm did not last very long, however. It was one of many experiments with **utopian communities** that took place in America. These communities tried to form a perfect society on Earth. Some Americans founded utopian communities as places to practice their religious beliefs. In 1774 Ann Lee started a community of Shakers—so named because their bodies would often shake during worship. By the 1830s this group had about 6,000 members living in various communities. The Shakers did not believe in private ownership of property and lived a very plain lifestyle. The furniture they made reflected their simple approach to life.

Other utopian communities were based on social philosophies. Many groups wanted men and women to be equal. Mary Paul, a member of a group in Red Bank, New Jersey, explained this view. She said that in the community "both men and women have the *same pay* for the *same* work." Such utopian communities allowed people to pursue spiritual and cooperative lifestyles. However, only a few of these communities lasted very long. Most groups failed to get their members to work together well enough for the community to survive.

✔ **Reading Check: Identifying Points of View** How did transcendentalists believe people should live?

⭐ The American Romantics

Ideas about spirituality, the simple life, and nature also shaped painters and writers in the early 1800s. Some artists became part of the romantic movement, which began in Europe and drew upon the idea that each person brings a unique view to the world. Romantic artists such as **Thomas Cole** painted the American landscape. These images of nature and the wilderness contrasted with the large cities and the corruption that many Americans saw in Europe.

During this time the number of notable American authors grew. Many female authors, such as Ann Sophia Stephens, wrote historical fiction. These works became very popular during the mid-1800s. One of the best-known examples of romantic literature is *The Scarlet Letter*. This novel by New England writer **Nathaniel Hawthorne** describes Puritan life in the 1600s. Hawthorne's friend Herman Melville was a writer and a former sailor who wrote tales of the sea. *Moby-Dick* and *Billy Budd* are some of his more famous works.

Along with novels, American romantic authors also wrote many famous short stories and poems. **Edgar Allan Poe**, for example, is best known for his short stories and poetry. A verse from Poe's haunting poem, "The Raven," follows.

"Once upon a midnight dreary,[1]
  while I pondered,[2] weak and weary,
Over many a quaint[3] and curious
  volume of forgotten lore[4] —
While I nodded, nearly napping,
  suddenly there came a tapping,
As of some one gently rapping,
  rapping at my chamber door—
''Tis some visiter,' I muttered,
  'tapping at my chamber door—
Only this and nothing more.'"

—Edgar Allan Poe, "The Raven," from *Anthology of American Literature*, edited by George McMichael

This illustration shows a scene from Edgar Allan Poe's poem "The Raven."

---

[1]**dreary:** gloomy   [2]**pondered:** thought   [3]**quaint:** odd   [4]**lore:** legends

CONNECTING TO *Literature*

"This Is My Letter to the World"

Emily Dickinson

Born in 1830, Emily Dickinson led a quiet life in Amherst, Massachusetts. Her first published collection of poetry included the following selection.

This is my letter to the World
 That never wrote to Me—
The simple News that Nature told—
With tender Majesty

Her Message is committed
To Hands I cannot see—
For love of Her—Sweet—countrymen
Judge tenderly—of Me.

Understanding What You Read
Literature and History What does Dickinson mean by her "Letter to the World"?

The United States produced several other gifted American poets during this period. These writers included **Emily Dickinson**, Henry Wadsworth Longfellow, John Greenleaf Whittier, and **Walt Whitman**. Only two of Dickinson's poems were published during her lifetime, both anonymously. After her death in 1886, her family discovered hundreds of her poems, some written on loose scraps of paper. Longfellow was the best-known poet of the mid-1800s. His long story-poems, such as *Hiawatha*, the *Courtship of Miles Standish*, and *Tales of a Wayside Inn* became favorites in many American households. Whittier spoke out against slavery in works such as *Poems Written during the Progress of the Abolition Question*.

Walt Whitman praised both American individualism and democracy in his simple, unrhymed poetry. His work *Leaves of Grass*, published in 1855, is noted for its distinct style. Whitman expressed his view of America's poetic gifts in the preface to *Leaves of Grass*. "Americans of all nations at any time upon the earth have probably the fullest poetical nature," he wrote. "The United States themselves are essentially the greatest poem."

✔ **Reading Check: Analyzing Information** What was the romantic movement, and who were some of the major American artists and writers of this movement?

Section 1 Review

go.hrw.com Homework Practice Online
keyword: SF3 HP15

❶ **Define** and explain:
• transcendentalism
• utopian communities

❷ **Identify** and explain:
• Second Great Awakening
• Charles Grandison Finney
• Ralph Waldo Emerson
• Margaret Fuller
• Henry David Thoreau
• Thomas Cole
• Nathaniel Hawthorne
• Edgar Allan Poe
• Emily Dickinson
• Walt Whitman

❸ **Summarizing** Copy the graphic organizer below. Use it to identify the new ideas that emerged from religion, philosophy, art, and literature during the early 1800s.

```
Religion          Philosophy
        ↘        ↙
       New Ideas
        ↗        ↖
  Art              Literature
```

❹ **Finding the Main Idea**
a. What was the Second Great Awakening, and what effect did it have on religious life in America?

b. How did the transcendentalists describe American society?

❺ **Writing and Critical Thinking**
Analyzing Information Imagine that you are an American poet in the early 1800s. Write a poem on a subject of your choice based on the style of the romantics.

Consider the following:
• the work of other romantic poets and writers
• your personal perspective on life
• an appeal to your readers' emotions

Immigrants and Cities

Read to Discover

1. Why did so many Irish and German immigrants come to the United States in the 1840s and 1850s?
2. How did some Americans react to immigrants?
3. What caused U.S. cities to grow, and what benefits and problems did this growth create?

WHY IT MATTERS TODAY

Many immigrants are still drawn to the United States today. Use CNNfyi.com or other **current events** sources to learn why people immigrate to the United States. Record your findings in your journal.

Define

- nativists
- middle class
- tenements

Identify

- Know-Nothing Party

The Story Continues

Irish immigrants to the United States traveled in tightly packed sections of ships. They received little fresh air or light on their long journey. Dozens of immigrants suffered and died from fever and disease. In Herman Melville's story *Redburn*, a cabin boy describes one such journey in which fever had a terrible effect on the passengers. "By their own countrymen, they were torn from the clasp [embrace] of their wives . . . and with hurried rites [ceremonies], were dropped into the ocean." Of the millions of immigrants who left their homes in the mid-1800s, not all made it safely across the Atlantic.

Advertisements like this one encouraged people to immigrate to the United States.

Waves of Immigrants

In the mid-1800s large numbers of immigrants crossed the Atlantic Ocean to begin new lives in the United States. More than 4 million immigrants settled in the United States between 1840 and 1860, most of them from Europe. More than 3 million of these immigrants were German or Irish. Many immigrants were fleeing economic or political troubles in their native countries.

Just the Facts

Some Occupations of Immigrants in New York, 1855

Occupation	Total Number of Workers	Foreign-Born Workers
Bakers	3,692	3,323
Blacksmiths	2,642	2,159
Leather workers	1,386	980
Jewelers	1,705	1,037
Carpenters	7,531	4,863
Clerks	13,929	5,921
Dressmakers/ seamstresses	9,819	6,606
Shoemakers/ tailors	19,354	18,600
Domestic servants	31,749	29,470
Merchants	6,299	1,705
Physicians	1,469	566

Using Mathematical Skills

1. Which occupation had the highest number of immigrant workers in 1855?
2. Create a bar graph that compares the total number of workers to the number of foreign-born workers.
3. Imagine that you are an immigrant. Write a letter to family members overseas, using the statistics in this chart to persuade them to immigrate to New York City.

Most immigrants from the British Isles during this period were Irish. In the mid-1840s potato blight, a disease that causes rot, left many families in Ireland with little food. Thomas Francis Meagher, an Irish leader, sadly commented, "One business survives! . . . That fortunate business . . . is the Irish coffin-maker's." More than 1 million Irish people died of starvation and disease. Even more fled to the United States. Most Irish immigrants were very poor. Many settled in towns and cities in Massachusetts, New Jersey, New York, and Pennsylvania. Those who did not live in cities commonly worked on building canals and railroads. Irish women often worked as domestic servants for wealthy families, laboring 16 hours or more a day. Irish men in the cities could usually find only unskilled work. As an 1849 Boston health committee reported, low wages forced most Irish immigrants to live in poor housing.

Nevertheless, some immigrants enjoyed a new feeling of equality. Patrick Dunny wrote home to his family about this situation.

History Makers Speak

"People that cuts a great dash [style] at home . . . think it strange [in the United States] for the humble class of people to get as much respect as themselves."

—Patrick Dunny, quoted in *Who Built America?*, by Bruce Levine et al.

Many Germans also came to the United States during this time. In 1848, numbers of German people had revolted against harsh rule. Some educated Germans came to the United States to escape persecution during this time. However, most of them came for economic reasons. Working-class Germans began to leave as well. These immigrants came in search of new economic opportunity and freedom from government control. While most Irish immigrants were Catholics, German immigrant groups included Protestants, Catholics, and Jews.

Many German immigrants arrived in the United States with money in hand. Germans were more likely than the Irish to become farmers and to live in rural areas. They moved particularly to midwestern states such as Michigan, Ohio, and Wisconsin where more land was available than in the eastern United States. German immigrants—like the Irish—often had to take low-paying jobs, despite their skills. The *Chicago Daily Tribune* declared that the German immigrant population was "fitted to do the cheap . . . labor of the country."

✔ **Reading Check: Comparing and Contrasting** What factors—both similar and different—led Irish and German people to immigrate to the United States in the mid-1800s?

★ The Nativist Response

Industrialization and the waves of people from Europe greatly changed the American labor force. The chance of getting farmland in the Midwest drew many immigrants to this area. Industrial jobs in the Northeast drew many immigrants who filled the need for cheap labor in many towns and cities. These new workers fueled the local economies, which led to the creation of new jobs for clerks, merchants, supervisors, and professional workers.

Yet many native-born citizens feared losing their jobs to immigrants who might work for lower wages. Many native-born Americans also felt threatened by the different cultures and religions of immigrant groups. Before Catholic immigrants arrived, most people living in the United States were Protestants. American Protestants did not always trust Catholic immigrants because of long-standing conflicts between Catholics and Protestants in Europe. Americans who held such views and who opposed immigration were called **nativists**.

In the 1840s and 1850s some of these people became politically active. One of their main goals was to try to stir up anti-immigrant feeling. An 1844 election flyer gave Americans a warning.

❝Look at the . . . thieves and vagabonds [tramps], roaming about our streets . . . monopolizing [taking] the business which properly belongs to our own native and true-born citizens.❞

—Election flyer, quoted in *Who Built America?*, by Bruce Levine et al.

In 1849, nativists founded a secret society that became a political organization known as the **Know-Nothing Party**. The party was so named because when asked questions by outsiders, its members usually answered, "I know nothing." The Know-Nothings wanted to keep Catholics and immigrants out of public office. They also wanted immigrants to have to live in the United States for at least 21 years before they could become citizens. Party politicians had some success, winning several state elections during the 1850s. They also controlled the Massachusetts legislature for a short time.

✔ **Reading Check: Analyzing Information** How did anti-Catholicism contribute to the views of nativists and the creation of the Know-Nothing Party?

Analyzing Primary Sources

Identifying Bias Why might a reader think that the author of this quotation is a nativist?

A protest by a nativist group led to this riot in Philadelphia in 1844. Similar riots took place elsewhere in the country.

THE GRANGER COLLECTION, NEW YORK

Urban Growth

American cities in the Northeast began to grow rapidly in the mid-1800s.

Rural Migration

Immigration from Europe

City Growth

Transportation Revolution (helped business and travel)

Industrial Revolution (provided jobs)

Visualizing History

1. **Geography** What factors contributed to the growth of American cities?
2. **Connecting to Today** How do you think these factors influence urban growth today?

★ ★ ★ ★ ★ ★ ★ ★ ★ ★ ★ ★
That's Interesting!
★ ★ ★ ★ ★ ★ ★ ★ ★ ★ ★ ★

Where are the police?
Can you imagine a city of more than 500,000 people without a permanent police force? Well, that's just what New York City was like before 1853. Before permanent forces were created, a volunteer night watch patrolled the city. During the daytime, an officer called a constable was on duty. He was paid a fee for each crime that he and his assistants helped stop. Private citizens were also asked to catch criminals. As cities grew larger, crime often grew out of hand. Many constables took bribes to ignore crimes. So the people of New York City created a paid police force.

★ The Growth of Cities

The Industrial Revolution led to the creation of many new jobs in U.S. cities. These city jobs drew immigrants as well as migrants from rural areas. The Transportation Revolution helped connect cities and made it easier for people to move to them. As a result of these two trends, U.S. cities grew rapidly during the mid-1800s. Cities in the northeastern and Middle Atlantic states grew the most. By the mid-1800s three quarters of the country's manufacturing jobs were in these areas.

The rise of industry and the growth of cities changed American life. Those who owned their own businesses or worked in skilled jobs benefited most from the changes. The families of these merchants, manufacturers, professionals, and master craftspeople made up a growing social class. This new **middle class** was a social and economic level between the wealthy and the poor.

In the growing cities, people found entertainment and an enriched cultural life. Many enjoyed visiting places such as libraries and clubs. In the early 1800s people also attended urban theaters. Favorite pastimes, such as bowling and playing cards, also provided recreation for urban residents.

Cities during this time were compact and crowded. Many people walked to work. Wagons carried goods down streets paved with stones, making a noisy, busy scene. One person noted that the professionals in New York City always had "a hurried walk."

✔ **Reading Check: Summarizing** How did the Industrial Revolution and the Transportation Revolution affect life in American cities?

★ Urban Problems

American cities in the early and mid-1800s faced many challenges as a result of their rapid growth. Because public and private transportation was limited, many city residents lived within a short distance of their workplaces. The crowded conditions meant that poor wage workers, members of the rising middle class, and the wealthy often lived near each other. Poor city dwellers often felt that they were treated unfairly by the rich—who in turn often accused the poor of being rude and violent. Disagreements between these social classes led to increasing conflict and sometimes even led to riots.

Other major problems in most large cities were the lack of safe housing and public services. Many people, particularly immigrants, could afford to live only in dirty, overcrowded buildings called **tenements**. Many cities did not have clean water, public health regulations, or clean ways to get rid of garbage and human waste. Diseases spread easily in these unhealthy conditions. In 1832 and 1849, for example, New York City suffered cholera epidemics that killed thousands of people.

Urban areas also became centers of criminal activity. Most cities—including New York City, Boston, and Philadelphia—had no permanent police force to fight crime. Instead, they used volunteer night watches, which offered little protection. Fire protection was often poor as well. Most cities were served by volunteer fire companies. Firefighters had to use hand pumps and buckets to put out fires. All of these conditions combined to make life difficult for many city residents.

During the 1800s poor city residents often lived in overcrowded tenement neighborhoods like this one.

✔ **Reading Check: Analyzing Information** What were some of the problems caused by urbanization?

Section 2 Review

go.hrw.com **Homework Practice Online** keyword: SF3 HP15

1 **Define** and explain:
- nativists
- middle class
- tenements

2 **Identify** and explain:
- Know-Nothing Party

3 **Identifying Cause and Effect** Copy the graphic organizer below. Use it to identify the causes and effects of immigration and of urban growth.

Immigration

Causes → Effects

Urban Growth

Causes → Effects

4 **Finding the Main Idea**
a. Why did many German and Irish people immigrate to the United States between 1840 and 1860?

b. Why did nativists oppose immigration in the mid-1800s?

5 **Writing and Critical Thinking**
Evaluating Imagine that you are visiting a northeastern American city in the mid-1800s. Create a postcard showing a city street scene. On the back of the card, write a short letter to a friend back home that describes the scene.

Consider the following:
- the benefits of city growth
- the problems caused by city growth
- immigration to cities

Reforming Society

Read to Discover

1. How did reformers improve prisons in the early and mid-1800s?
2. Why did reformers start the temperance movement?
3. How did Americans' educational opportunities change during the early and mid-1800s?

WHY IT MATTERS TODAY

Many Americans today take part in reform efforts. Use CNN**fyi**.com or other **current events** sources to learn about current campaigns for efforts such as education reform. Record your findings in your journal.

Define

- temperance movement
- common-school movement

Identify

- Dorothea Dix
- Lyman Beecher
- Horace Mann
- Catharine Beecher
- Emma Willard
- Mary Lyon
- Samuel Gridley Howe
- Thomas Hopkins Gallaudet

The Story Continues

THE GRANGER COLLECTION, NEW YORK

Dorothea Dix helped improve the prison system in the United States.

In 1841 Dorothea Dix visited a jail in Cambridge, Massachusetts, to teach a Sunday school class. What she saw there shocked her. Mentally ill women were jailed beside common criminals in dirty cells. Dix became angry at the conditions she found there and in other Massachusetts jails. As a result, she began to work to improve the care of mentally ill people across the country. She joined many other women reformers in the early and mid-1800s.

Prison Reform

The teachings of the Second Great Awakening had inspired many people to try to improve society. The growth of cities had caused social problems that many Americans wanted to correct. Often members of the growing middle class, particularly women, led these reform efforts. Many of these women did not work outside the home. Some hired domestic servants to help care for their households, which gave them more time to take part in reform groups.

Dorothea Dix was a middle-class reformer who helped change the prison system in the United States. After visiting prisons throughout

Massachusetts, Dix reported the terrible conditions. Mentally ill people were often jailed with criminals. Dix told the state legislature of her findings in this speech.

"I come to present the strong claims of suffering humanity . . . the miserable, the desolate [deserted], the outcast . . . to call your attention to the present state of insane persons confined within this Commonwealth, in cages, closets, cellars, stalls, pens! Chained, naked, beaten with rods, and lashed into obedience."

—Dorothea Dix, from *Memorial to the Legislature of Massachusetts*

Dorothea Dix opposed the use of cages like this one to confine mentally ill people.

In response, the government of Massachusetts created special, separate facilities for mentally ill people. The influence of Dix's work spread across the country. Eventually more than 100 state hospitals where mentally ill people received more professional care were built.

Other reformers protested the treatment of young offenders. Children who committed crimes such as begging or stealing were treated the same as adult criminals. Boston mayor Josiah Quincy asked that these young people be given different punishments than adults. In the 1820s several state and local governments founded reform schools for children who were once housed in prisons. In these schools children lived under strict rules. While living there, they received vocational training—learning useful skills through work.

Some reformers also tried to end the overcrowding and cruel conditions in prisons. Their efforts led to the creation of houses of correction. These institutions did not use punishment alone. Instead, they tried to change prisoners' behavior through education.

✔ **Reading Check: Summarizing** How did reformers try to change prisons in the early 1800s?

Reformers wanted to help prison inmates become productive citizens. These inmates are learning to make hats.

Temperance *Posters like this one urged people to stop drinking and thus help their families.* **How do the scenes in this picture encourage people to give up drinking?**

⭐ Campaigning against Alcohol Abuse

A number of reformers also worked to prevent alcohol abuse. Many people believed that Americans were drinking liquor at an alarming rate in the early and mid-1800s. During the 1830s the average alcohol consumption per person was seven gallons a year. Abraham Lincoln recalled that in his youth liquor was an "angel of death." Many reformers believed alcohol abuse caused social problems such as family violence, poverty, and criminal behavior.

Americans' worries about the effects of alcohol led to the growth of a **temperance movement.** This social reform effort urged people to stop drinking hard liquor and limit drinking of beer and wine to small amounts. Various groups such as the American Temperance Society and the American Temperance Union helped spread this message. Minister **Lyman Beecher** spoke widely about the evils of alcohol. He said that people who drank alcohol were "neglecting the education of their families—and corrupting their morals."

Many people across the country were in favor of the temperance movement. However, some people believed that temperance alone would not fix social problems caused by alcohol abuse. People such as Neal Dow of Maine wanted to outlaw the sale of alcohol. Dow's efforts resulted in the Maine Law of 1846, which made selling alcohol illegal in the state. Banning the sale of alcohol became a major goal of reformers. By 1855 a dozen other states had passed laws like the one in Maine.

✔ **Reading Check: Finding the Main Idea** What were the goals of the temperance movement?

⭐ Education in America

Another problem facing America in the early 1800s was poor public education. As immigration increased, reformers argued that education would help Americans become good workers and citizens. Most families in the United States believed education was important. However, they did not expect their children to receive a great deal of formal schooling. Many children worked in factories or on farms to help support their families. Parents generally wanted their children to be able to read the Bible, write, and do simple math.

The availability of education varied a great deal throughout the United States. New England had the most schoolhouses, while the South and the West had the fewest. Most schoolteachers were untrained young men. They often taught for a short time before becoming farmers or practicing another trade. Teachers usually worked in small, poorly built schoolhouses, teaching students of many ages and abilities. As reformer Horace Mann wrote, students ranged from "infants just out of their cradles" to "men . . . enrolled in the militia."

Mary reciting her Lesson.

Mary had learned to read and spell from the "Pictorial Primer" well. Could sew and knit a little too, and many other things could do, while her mother ever kind, would study to improve her mind, and in hymns of praise and love taught her to lift her heart above.

THE GRANGER COLLECTION, NEW YORK

ADDISON GALLERY OF AMERICAN ART, PHILLIPS ACADEMY

The textbooks most often used in public schools in the mid-1800s were the McGuffey's *Readers*. William Holmes McGuffey, an educator and Presbyterian minister, put together these textbooks. They were made up mostly of selections from British and American literature. McGuffey's *Readers* were used to teach students about moral and social values as well as literature and reading.

People from different backgrounds received very different educations in the United States. Rich people could send their children to private schools or hire private tutors. However, poor children could only attend public school. Girls could attend school, but parents kept them home more often than boys. The result was that fewer girls learned to read.

Interpreting the Visual Record

Early schools *Many children attended one-room schoolhouses in their local communities. Primers such as the one shown above were the most common textbooks.* **How is the school shown here similar to or different from yours?**

⭐ The Common-School Movement

To teach children the necessary values and skills, reformers called for better schools. People in the **common-school movement** wanted all children educated in a common place, regardless of class or background. <u>Horace Mann</u> was the leading voice for education reform in the mid-1800s. He explained the idea of the common school.

History Makers Speak

"It is on this common platform that a general acquaintance-ship [friendship] should be formed between the children of the same neighborhood. It is here that the affinities [bonds] of a common nature should unite them together."

—Horace Mann, quoted in *The Age of the Common School, 1830–1865,* by Frederick M. Binder

Analyzing Primary Sources

Supporting a Point of View Do you agree with Horace Mann's idea? Why or why not?

Mann became the first secretary of education for Massachusetts in 1837. The former lawyer and state legislator worked very hard—speaking, traveling, and writing—to help improve children's education. He doubled the state school budget and helped teachers earn better salaries. He also made the school year longer and founded the first school for teacher training.

ANDOVER, MA   GIFT OF MAXIM KAROLIK, COURTESY, MUSEUM OF FINE ARTS   BOSTON

Beyond grade school, classes for women were usually separated from classes for men.

Mann's ideas on education spread throughout the United States, and to Latin America and Europe as well. Mann won over many other educators by saying that "the common school, improved and energized, may become the most effective . . . of all the forces of civilization." Mann's work set the standard for education reform throughout the country.

✔ **Reading Check: Summarizing** Why did Horace Mann want to improve schools, and what did he accomplish?

★ Women's Education

The education reform movement also created greater opportunities for women. Before the 1820s few women in the United States could attend classes beyond grade school. **Catharine Beecher**, daughter of Lyman Beecher, grew up in a family committed to social reform. She became one of the most effective reformers of women's education in the early 1800s.

Catharine Beecher believed that women were better at teaching the moral lessons that made good citizens. "Let every woman become so . . . refined in intellect that her taste and judgment will be respected," she wrote. Beecher started an all-female academy in Hartford, Connecticut. She also wrote several important essays, including *On the Education of Female Teachers.*

In 1821 the citizens of Troy, New York, called on educator **Emma Willard** to found a college-level institution for women. Willard's Troy Female Seminary was the first school of its kind in the United States. At this school women studied many different subjects, ranging from mathematics to philosophy. Between 1821 and 1872, more than 12,000 women attended the school.

Several women's colleges opened in the 1830s. One of these colleges was Mount Holyoke Seminary in Massachusetts, founded by educator **Mary Lyon** in 1837. Lyon answered critics of her work by saying, "I am doing a great work, I cannot come down." In 1837 Oberlin College, located in Ohio, became the first co-educational college in the United States. This meant that both men and women were allowed to study there.

THE GRANGER COLLECTION, NEW YORK

African American Schools

Free African Americans also enjoyed some benefits of education reform. Although African Americans found more educational opportunities, they almost always went to separate schools from white students. The New York African Free School, which had opened in New York City in 1787, produced some notable scholars and leaders, such as Henry Highland Garnet.

The people of Philadelphia also supported the development of African American education. By 1800 the city had seven schools for black students. In 1820 Boston opened a separate elementary school for African American children. Also, in 1855 the city began allowing African Americans to attend white schools. However, James Thomas, a free African American in Tennessee, described the unequal education that many received in the 1830s.

Mount Holyoke Seminary was one of the country's best schools for women.

 History Makers Speak

"School was kept occasionally. It was regarded a great favor to have it allowed at any time. Each pupil or scholar paid one dollar per month. Often there was no school because there was no teacher."

—James Thomas, quoted in *From Slavery to Freedom,*
by John Hope Franklin and Alfred A. Moss Jr.

African Americans rarely attended college because only a few institutions of higher education would accept them. In 1835 Oberlin became the first to do so. Harvard later joined Oberlin in accepting African Americans. Black colleges also began to be founded in the 1840s. For example, in 1842 the Institute for Colored Youth and in 1849 Avery College were opened in Philadelphia.

As the examples above show, free African Americans did have some opportunities to attend school in the Midwest and the North. In the South, however, fewer free African Americans were able to obtain an education. Laws in the South prevented most slaves from receiving any education, in part due to southern whites' fears of potential slave rebellions.

✔ **Reading Check: Comparing** What educational challenges did women and African Americans face in the 1800s?

Analyzing Primary Sources

Making Generalizations and Predictions How might citizens solve the problem with schooling that Thomas describes?

This typewriter produced raised dots representing the alphabet created by Louis Braille for visually impaired people.

⭐ Teaching People with Disabilities

Efforts to improve education also helped people with special needs. **Samuel Gridley Howe** worked to improve the education of visually impaired Americans. Howe also worked for education reform, prison reform, and care for mentally ill people. In 1831 Howe opened a school called the Perkins Institution in Massachusetts for people with visual impairments. He trained the school's workers to address the particular needs of the students. He also traveled to 17 other states to talk about teaching visually impaired people. Howe ran the Perkins Institution for 45 years. During this time he showed that people with visual impairments could lead economically and socially productive lives.

After graduating from Yale College, **Thomas Hopkins Gallaudet** worked to improve the education and lives of people who were hearing impaired. He went to Europe for two years to study ways to teach such students. In 1817, after he returned to the United States, Gallaudet founded the first free American school for people with hearing impairments in Hartford, Connecticut. He served as the school's principal until 1830. After he retired from the school, Gallaudet became a professor of philosophy of education at New York University. He called for special schools to train teachers and wrote textbooks for children and people with hearing impairments. Gallaudet University in Washington, D.C., was named in his honor. Thus, school reformers helped people in many parts of American society during the early and mid-1800s.

✔ **Reading Check: Summarizing** What kinds of schools were founded for people with disabilities?

Section 3 Review

go.hrw.com **Homework Practice Online** keyword: SF3 HP15

1 **Define** and explain:
• temperance movement
• common-school movement

2 **Identify** and explain:
• Dorothea Dix
• Lyman Beecher
• Horace Mann
• Catharine Beecher
• Emma Willard
• Mary Lyon
• Samuel Gridley Howe
• Thomas Hopkins Gallaudet

3 **Categorizing** Copy the chart below. Use it to match reform leaders with their respective movements and the accomplishments of each movement.

Movement	Leaders	Accomplishments
Prison & Mental Health Reform		
Temperance		
Education		

4 **Finding the Main Idea**
a. Describe the ways that reformers changed prisons and the treatment of the mentally ill.

b. What did members of the temperance movement try to achieve?

5 **Writing and Critical Thinking**
Summarizing Imagine that you are Horace Mann visiting a foreign country. Write a speech that describes the ways in which many more Americans gained the opportunity to receive an education in the early and mid-1800s.

Consider the following:
• education for women
• education for African Americans
• educating people with disabilities

The Movement to End Slavery

Read to Discover

1. Why did some Americans become abolitionists?
2. How did abolitionists spread the movement's message?
3. Why were some Americans against abolition?

WHY IT MATTERS TODAY

Citizens still organize to seek changes in laws. Use **CNNfyi.com** or other **current events** sources to learn more about a group trying to change a law. Record your findings in your journal.

Define
- abolition
- emancipation

Identify
- Robert Finley
- American Colonization Society
- David Walker
- William Lloyd Garrison
- *The Liberator*
- American Anti-Slavery Society
- Angelina and Sarah Grimké
- Frederick Douglass
- Underground Railroad
- Harriet Tubman

The Story Continues

During the mid-1800s John Fairfield helped enslaved African Americans escape to freedom in the North. Fairfield traveled throughout the South under different disguises. Sometimes he posed as a slaveholder. Other times he dressed as a trader, or a peddler. Once he led 28 slaves to freedom by disguising them as part of a funeral procession. Most antislavery activists did not take such risks. However, they all helped a movement that grew much stronger in the mid-1800s.

Newspapers often published advertisements for the capture of runaway slaves.

⭐ Abolition

During the 1830s Americans who had been against slavery for years began to take organized action. They formed a movement to support **abolition**, or a complete end to slavery, in the United States. Some of these people wanted immediate **emancipation**. Through emancipation, all enslaved African Americans would be freed from slavery.

British Abolitionists

Many American abolitionists looked to Great Britain for examples of how to fight slavery. Britain had outlawed the slave trade in 1807. In 1834 a law abolishing slavery in the British Empire went into effect. However, British antislavery work did not stop there. In 1840 the British and Foreign Anti-Slavery Society held the World's Anti-Slavery Convention in London. Convention members asked the British government to pressure other countries to end slavery as well. In the mid-1800s British warships began stopping slave ships in the Atlantic and Indian Oceans and freeing the slaves they found. **How did British abolitionists try to end slavery outside of Britain?**

Analyzing Primary Sources
Identifying Points of View
Why was Walker against colonization?

This antislavery medallion was first used by an antislavery society in London.

Abolitionists were in the minority in the United States, but they were very vocal. They came from many different backgrounds and wanted to ban slavery for different reasons. The Quakers were among the first groups to challenge slavery on religious grounds. The Quakers had begun working for abolition during colonial times. Some ministers of the Second Great Awakening also believed that slavery was morally wrong. People such as Charles Grandison Finney and Theodore Weld moved many others to take up the cause of abolition. Other abolitionists pointed to the ideals of the Declaration of Independence. They reminded people that the American Revolution supported equality.

Abolitionists disagreed about what ending slavery should mean for African Americans. Some abolitionists thought that African Americans should be treated the same as white Americans. Many others, however, opposed full social and political equality for African Americans.

Some antislavery reformers wanted to send freed African Americans to Africa to start new colonies there. They thought that this would prevent conflicts between different races in the United States. Many Americans supported this view. J. C. Galloway of North Carolina described this idea. "It is impossible for us [whites] to be happy, if . . . they [freed African Americans] are to remain among us," he wrote.

In 1817 a minister named **Robert Finley** started the **American Colonization Society**. Five years later the society founded the colony of Liberia on the west coast of Africa. About 12,000 African Americans eventually settled in Liberia. However, many who were once in favor of colonization later turned against it. Some African Americans also opposed the colonization movement. **David Walker** was one such person. In an 1829 essay, *Appeal to the Colored Citizens of the World*, Walker explained why he was against colonization.

History Makers Speak

❝The greatest riches in all America have arisen from our blood and tears: And they [whites] will drive us from our property and homes, which we have earned with our blood.❞

—David Walker, quoted in *From Slavery to Freedom*, by John Hope Franklin and Alfred A. Moss Jr.

✔ **Reading Check: Contrasting** How did some abolitionists' goals differ?

⭐ Spreading the Abolitionist Message

Abolitionists found many ways to further their cause. Some abolitionists went on speaking tours or wrote newspaper articles and pamphlets. Editor Horace Greeley became a strong voice in the movement through the *New York Tribune*. Others, like John Greenleaf Whittier, spread the abolitionist message through their poetry and literature. **William Lloyd Garrison** published an abolitionist newspaper. This newspaper, ***The Liberator***, first appeared in 1831. Garrison became one of the most outspoken and controversial leaders of the movement. In 1833 Garrison helped found the **American Anti-Slavery Society**. This group wanted immediate emancipation and racial equality for African Americans. Garrison later became the group's president.

Both *The Liberator* and the Anti-Slavery Society relied on the support of free African Americans. Members of the society spread antislavery literature throughout the North and Midwest. They also sent petitions to Congress. In these petitions, they asked for an end to all federal support of slavery. Then in 1840 the American Anti-Slavery Society split. One group wanted immediate freedom for enslaved African Americans. This group also believed women should take part in the abolition movement on an equal basis with men. The other group wanted slower emancipation and a limited role for women.

Angelina and Sarah Grimké, two white southern women, became well-known antislavery activists of the 1830s. The sisters were members of a slaveholding family in South Carolina. They did not share their parents' support of slavery, however. Instead, they moved to Philadelphia and joined the abolition movement. Angelina Grimké tried to bring other white southern women to the cause. She wrote a pamphlet titled *Appeal to the Christian Women of the South* in 1836.

 History Makers Speak 	❝I know you do not make the laws, but . . . if you really suppose you can do nothing to overthrow slavery, you are greatly mistaken. . . . Try to persuade your husband, father, brothers and sons that slavery is a crime against God and man.❞

—Angelina Grimké, quoted in *The Grimké Sisters from South Carolina*, edited by Gerda Lerner

Analyzing Primary Sources
Evaluating Sources How did Grimké believe women could help bring an end to slavery?

This essay was quite popular in the North. As a result, the Grimké sisters became the first women to speak before male and female audiences of the Anti-Slavery Society. The sisters gave lectures and formed dozens of female antislavery societies. In 1839 they wrote *American Slavery As It Is* with Angelina's husband, abolitionist leader Theodore Weld. This book was one of the most important antislavery writings of the time.

✔ **Reading Check: Finding the Main Idea** How did the members of the Anti-Slavery Society fight slavery?

THE GRANGER COLLECTION, NEW YORK

William Lloyd Garrison's The Liberator *became one of the most widely read abolitionist newspapers in the North.*

CONNECTING TO Literature

Narrative of the Life of Frederick Douglass

In 1845 Frederick Douglass published the first of three autobiographies describing his life as a slave and his abolitionist efforts once he gained his freedom. In the following excerpt he explains the purpose of his autobiography.

Sincerely and earnestly hoping that this little book may do something toward throwing light on the American slave system, and **hastening**[1] the glad day of deliverance to the millions of my **brethren**[2] in bonds—faithfully relying on the power of truth, love, and justice, for success in my humble efforts—and solemnly pledging myself anew to the sacred cause,—I **subscribe**[3] myself, Frederick Douglass.

[1]**hastening:** quickening [3]**subscribe:** pledge
[2]**brethren:** brothers and sisters

Understanding What You Read
Literature and History Why did Frederick Douglass write his narrative?

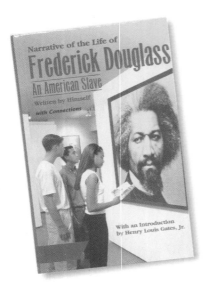

★ African Americans Fight against Slavery

Many former slaves were very active in the antislavery movement. **Frederick Douglass**, who escaped from slavery at age 20, became one of the most important African American leaders of the 1800s. Douglass had secretly learned to read and write as a boy. In addition, his public-speaking skills greatly impressed the members of the Anti-Slavery Society. In 1841 they asked Douglass to give regular lectures. Speaking at a Fourth of July celebration in 1852, he captured the audience's attention with his powerful voice.

 History Makers Speak

❝The blessings in which you, this day, rejoice, are not enjoyed in common. . . . This Fourth of July is *yours*, not *mine*. You may rejoice, I must mourn.❞

—Frederick Douglass, quoted in *From Slavery to Freedom,* by John Hope Franklin and Alfred A. Moss Jr.

Douglass went on many speaking tours in the United States and Europe. He also published a pro-abolition newspaper called *North Star* and wrote several autobiographies.

African Americans such as Charles Remond and Sojourner Truth also helped the abolitionist cause. Truth became famous in the antislavery movement for her dramatic and fiery speeches. In 1842 Remond asked the Massachusetts legislature to end racial discrimination in the state. "It is JUSTICE I stand here to claim, and not FAVOR for either complexion [skin color]," he declared.

Other African Americans wrote slave narratives about their experiences. In 1861 abolitionists helped publish *Incidents in the Life of a Slave Girl* by Harriet Jacobs, one of the few slave narratives written by a woman. William Wells Brown wrote an antislavery play and an antislavery novel called *Clotel.* These writers and many other African Americans contributed significantly to the abolitionist cause.

★ The Underground Railroad

By the 1830s a loosely organized group had begun helping slaves escape from the South. Free African Americans, former slaves, and a few white abolitionists worked together to create the **Underground Railroad**. This network of people arranged transportation and hiding places for fugitives, or escaped slaves. Often wearing disguises, fugitives moved along the "railroad" at night, guided by the North Star. They stopped to rest during the day at various "stations." These stations were the homes of abolitionists known as conductors. The conductors hid the fugitives in barns, attics, and other secret locations. They would then send word to the next station farther north that they were on the way.

The most famous and daring conductor on the Underground Railroad was **Harriet Tubman**. When Tubman herself escaped in 1849, she left behind her husband, parents, sisters, and brothers. She returned to the South 19 times. Tubman successfully led her family and more than 300 other slaves to freedom. She never lost a fugitive. At one time the reward for Tubman's capture climbed to $40,000. Historians estimate that 40,000 slaves used the Underground Railroad to reach freedom between 1810 and 1850.

✔ **Reading Check: Analyzing Information** How did free African Americans and former slaves try to end slavery?

Harriet Tubman

Percentage of Slaves in Total Population in 1860

- Slave population 50% or more
- Slave population 10%–50%
- Slave population 10% or less
- Slave population 0% or no data
- → Escape route

The Underground Railroad

Interpreting Maps The Underground Railroad helped thousands of slaves escape to freedom.

Skills Assessment

1. **Places and Regions** Through which states might slaves pass if they were escaping from Alabama to Ohio?

2. **Analyzing Information** To what destinations besides the northern states did slaves escape?

SLAVERY AS IT EXISTS IN AMERICA.

SLAVERY AS IT EXISTS IN ENGLAND.

THE GRANGER COLLECTION, NEW YORK

Southern defenders of slavery used images like this one to argue that American slaves enjoyed a better life than British factory workers.

⭐ Opposition to Abolition

Many white northerners did not believe in equal treatment for African Americans. Newspaper editors and politicians often warned that freed slaves would move north and take jobs from white workers. Leaders of the abolitionist movement received threats. Some northerners joined violent mobs that attacked African Americans and burned antislavery literature.

The federal government also stood in the way of the abolitionist movement. Between 1836 and 1844 the U.S. House of Representatives used a Gag Rule to prevent discussion of the thousands of antislavery petitions it received. This rule effectively violated the First Amendment right of citizens to petition the government. But southern congressmen were against any debate about slavery, and many northern congressmen just wanted to avoid the issue.

Many white southerners thought slavery was a vital part of the South's economy and culture. White southerners also generally believed that outsiders had no business interfering with their way of life. After Nat Turner's Rebellion in 1831, open talk of the slavery question disappeared in the South. Abolitionists like the Grimké sisters chose to leave.

Some white southerners said slavery protected African Americans. Virginia lawyer George Fitzhugh said that freed slaves would "freeze or starve" in the North. Racism, fear, and the South's economic dependence on slavery made the idea of emancipation unpopular in the South.

✔ **Reading Check: Identifying Points of View** Why did some Americans oppose emancipation?

Section 4 Review

go.hrw.com **Homework Practice Online**
keyword: SF3 HP15

1 Define and explain:
- abolition
- emancipation

2 Identify and explain:
- Robert Finley
- American Colonization Society
- David Walker
- William Lloyd Garrison
- *The Liberator*
- American Anti-Slavery Society
- Angelina and Sarah Grimké
- Frederick Douglass
- Underground Railroad
- Harriet Tubman

3 Analyzing Information
Copy the graphic organizer below. Use it to explain why some Americans joined the abolitionist movement and the methods they used to fight slavery.

Reasons for Abolition   Methods

4 Finding the Main Idea
a. For what reasons did many Americans in the North and the South oppose abolition?

b. How might the issue of slavery lead to conflict as the United States expanded?

5 Writing and Critical Thinking
Supporting a Point of View Imagine that you are a member of one of the antislavery societies in 1840. Create a poster announcing your group's next meeting.

Consider the following:
- the goals of the abolitionist movement
- why Americans should become active in the movement
- ways or methods to persuade other Americans to join the cause

Women's Rights

Read to Discover

1. How did the abolitionist movement affect the women's rights movement?
2. What were some goals of the women's rights movement?
3. What was the purpose of the Seneca Falls Convention, and why was it significant?

WHY IT MATTERS TODAY

The women's rights movement is still active in the United States today. Use CNNfyi.com or other **current events** sources to learn about the important roles women play in America today. These roles include positions in business, government, and society in general. Record your findings in your journal.

Identify

- Elizabeth Cady Stanton
- Lucretia Mott
- Seneca Falls Convention
- Declaration of Sentiments
- Lucy Stone
- Susan B. Anthony

The Story Continues

In February 1838 Angelina Grimké nervously prepared to speak before the Massachusetts legislature. "I never was so near fainting under the tremendous pressure of feeling," she wrote her future husband. "My heart almost died within me." Grimké planned to present antislavery petitions to the 1,500 people gathered. However, she felt a great responsibility. She was the first woman to speak before a legislature in the United States. As she spoke, Grimké bravely addressed both the issue of abolition and the question of women's rights.

Angelina Grimké was one of the first women to speak on behalf of the American Anti-Slavery Society.

⭐ The Influence of Abolition

Many female abolitionists, such as the Grimké sisters and Sojourner Truth, later became part of the women's rights movement of the mid-1800s. These women found that they had to defend their right to speak in public, particularly when a woman addressed both men and women. For example, members of the press, the clergy, and even some male abolitionists criticized the Grimké sisters for speaking in public. These critics believed that women should not give public speeches, and they did not want women to leave their traditional female roles. However, the Grimkés had a different view. They told their critics that women had a moral duty to lead the antislavery movement.

In 1838 Sarah Grimké published a pamphlet arguing for equal rights for women. She titled the essay "Letters on the Equality of the Sexes and the Condition of Women."

 History Makers Speak

66 I ask no favors for my sex. . . . All I ask our brethren [brothers] is, that they will take their feet from off our necks, and permit us to stand upright on that ground which God designed us to occupy. 99

—Sarah Grimké, quoted in *The Grimké Sisters from South Carolina*, edited by Gerda Lerner

Sarah Grimké also argued for equal educational opportunities. She pointed out laws that negatively affected women and called for equal pay for equal work.

Sojourner Truth was another powerful speaker for both abolition and women's rights. Writer Harriet Beecher Stowe said that she had never spoken "with anyone who had more . . . personal presence than this woman." Truth stood six feet tall and was a confident speaker. She often recalled her experiences as a slave. In 1851 she gave a speech at a women's rights convention. In her speech, she challenged the audience members not to think of women as the "weaker sex."

 History Makers Speak

66 That man over there says that women need to be helped into carriages and lifted over ditches, and to have the best place everywhere. Nobody ever helps me into carriages or over mud puddles, or gives me any best place. . . . Look at me! I have ploughed and planted and . . . no man could head [outwork] me. And ain't I a woman? 99

—Sojourner Truth, quoted in *A History of Women in America*, by Carol Hymowitz and Michaele Weissman

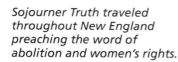
Sojourner Truth traveled throughout New England preaching the word of abolition and women's rights.

Truth and other supporters of the women's rights movement were determined to be heard.

✔ **Reading Check: Identifying Cause and Effect** Why did some people oppose women's efforts in the abolitionist movement, and how did this opposition affect the women's rights movement?

★ Women's Rights

Publications about women's rights first appeared in the United States shortly after the American Revolution. However, women's concerns did not become a national movement for many more years. This change took place when women took part in reform and abolition efforts. Other social changes also led to the rise of the movement. Women took advantage of better educational opportunities. They also learned how to organize more effectively by working together in reform groups. Some men also took part in the struggle for women's rights. Many activists were upset that women could not vote. In addition, married women in many states had little or no control over their own property.

Many people, both men and women, did not agree with some of the goals of the women's rights movement. Many women believed that they did not need any new rights. They said that women were not unequal to men, only different. Some critics believed that women should not try to work for social changes in public. In other words, they should work for change at home from within their families. "Let her not look away from her own little family circle for the means of producing moral and social reforms," wrote T. S. Arthur. His advice appeared in a popular women's magazine called *The Lady at Home*.

Some people also thought that women did not have the physical or mental strength to survive without men's protection. Such people believed that a woman needed to be under a man's authority. They also believed that her husband should control her property. Despite this strong opposition, women still pursued their goal of greater rights.

✔ **Reading Check: Summarizing** Why were some people against the goals of the women's movement?

★ The Seneca Falls Convention

In 1840 **Elizabeth Cady Stanton** attended the World's Anti-Slavery Convention in London, England, while on her honeymoon. Stanton had to watch the meeting separately from her husband, however, because women could not participate. Women in attendance had to sit in a separate gallery of the convention hall, hidden from the men's view by a curtain. In protest, William Lloyd Garrison sat with them, refusing to join a proceeding that did not allow women's equal participation.

This treatment of women abolitionists angered Stanton and her new friend, **Lucretia Mott**. Stanton later wrote that they "resolved to hold a convention as soon as we returned home." Mott and Stanton planned to "form a society to advance the rights of women." Eight years passed, however, before Stanton and Mott sent out a notice announcing the **Seneca Falls Convention**. The meeting, which began on July 19, 1848, in Seneca Falls, New York, launched an organized women's rights movement. This convention was the first public meeting about women's rights to be held in the United States.

To present their case, the convention organizers wrote a **Declaration of Sentiments** based on the language of the Declaration of Independence. The document detailed their beliefs about social injustice toward women. Some 100 people signed the Declaration of Sentiments.

Some 240 people attended the Seneca Falls Convention, including some men such as Frederick Douglass. Most of these reformers also worked in the temperance or antislavery movements. In addition,

BIOGRAPHY

Elizabeth Cady Stanton
(1815–1902)

Elizabeth Cady grew up in a wealthy family near Albany, New York. Her father, a judge, had a strong influence on her life. When Cady asked her father's opinion of her accomplishments, he replied sadly, "My daughter, you should have been a boy." Yet Cady did enjoy a happy childhood in which boys and girls played together. Cady did very well in school and attended a female seminary. In 1840 Cady married antislavery activist Henry Stanton, and they had seven children. She went on to become one of the most important leaders of the women's rights movement. She was a primary author of the Declaration of Sentiments. **What was significant about Stanton's childhood?**

several women who worked in nearby factories participated in the convention as well. For example, 19-year-old Charlotte Woodward signed the Declaration of Sentiments because she was tired of making gloves for low wages. Woodward earned pennies that she then had to turn over to her father.

Women had spoken out for their rights earlier. However, the Seneca Falls Convention marked the first time that women in the United States organized as a group to promote their rights.

✔ **Reading Check: Finding the Main Idea** Why was the Seneca Falls Convention important?

1848 SENECA FALLS DECLARATION OF SENTIMENTS

THE GRANGER COLLECTION, NEW YORK

A woman speaking before the Seneca Falls Convention

On July 19 and 20, 1848, people gathered in Seneca Falls, New York, to discuss women's rights. Elizabeth Cady Stanton and Lucretia Mott had organized the event. They also helped write the Declaration of Sentiments. Signed by some 100 people, this document helped shape the future of the women's rights movement.

We hold these truths to be **self-evident:**[1] that all men and women are created equal; that they are **endowed**[2] by their Creator with certain **inalienable**[3] rights; that among these are life, liberty, and the pursuit of happiness. . . .

The history of mankind is a history of repeated injuries and **usurpations**[4] on the part of man toward woman, having in direct object the establishment of an absolute **tyranny**[5] over her. To prove this, let facts be submitted to a **candid**[6] world.

He has never permitted her to exercise her inalienable right to . . . [the vote]. . . .

He has taken from her all right in property, even to the wages she earns. . . .

He has **monopolized**[7] nearly all the profitable employments, and from those she is permitted to follow, she receives but a scanty **remuneration**.[8] He closes against her all the avenues to wealth and distinction which he considers most honorable to himself. . . .

He has denied her the **facilities**[9] for obtaining a thorough education, all colleges being closed against her. . . .

He has endeavored, in every way that he could, to destroy her confidence in her own powers, to lessen her self-respect, and to make her willing to lead a dependent and **abject**[10] life. . . .

Resolved, That woman is man's equal—was intended to be so by the Creator, and the highest good of the race demands that she should be recognized as such.

---

[1]**self-evident:** obvious
[2]**endowed:** provided
[3]**inalienable:** permanent
[4]**usurpations:** seizures

[5]**tyranny:** unjust rule
[6]**candid:** fair
[7]**monopolized:** taken control of

[8]**remuneration:** payment
[9]**facilities:** means
[10]**abject:** hopeless

Analyzing Primary Sources

1. What are some of the injustices that the declaration describes?
2. How is the Declaration of Sentiments modeled after the Declaration of Independence?
3. Are the rights demanded in the declaration granted to women in the United States today? Explain your answer.

★ The Continuing Struggle

Although women's rights activists encountered many difficulties, they continued working together after the Seneca Falls Convention. **Lucy Stone** and Susan B. Anthony, along with Elizabeth Cady Stanton, became the most important leaders. Lucy Stone was a well-known member of the Anti-Slavery Society. She soon took on the cause of women's rights as well. During the early years of the women's rights movement, Stone became known as a gifted speaker.

Susan B. Anthony brought strong organizational skills to the women's rights movement. Anthony was largely responsible for turning the fight for women's rights into a political movement. As a single woman who supported herself, women's economic struggles were of particular importance to her. Anthony argued that women and men should receive equal pay for equal work and that women should be allowed to enter traditionally male professions such as law.

Anthony led a campaign to change laws regarding women's property rights. She wrote in her diary that no woman could be free without "a purse of her own." Anthony organized a network to cover every area of New York State. She collected more than 6,000 signatures to petition for a new property rights law. In 1860 New York finally gave married women ownership of their wages and property. Other states in the Northeast and Midwest followed with similar laws. Other major reforms, such as the right to vote, were not achieved at this time. However, more American women than ever before became actively involved in efforts to attain equal rights.

In 1979 Susan B. Anthony became the first American woman to be depicted on U.S. currency.

✔ **Reading Check: Comparing** What were some of the contributions of women's rights leaders Lucy Stone and Susan B. Anthony?

Section 5 Review

go.hrw.com **Homework Practice Online** keyword: SF3 HP15

1 **Identify and explain:**
   • Elizabeth Cady Stanton
   • Lucretia Mott
   • Seneca Falls Convention
   • Declaration of Sentiments
   • Lucy Stone
   • Susan B. Anthony

2 **Summarizing** Copy the graphic organizer below. Use it to explain how the women's rights movement grew out of the abolitionist movement.

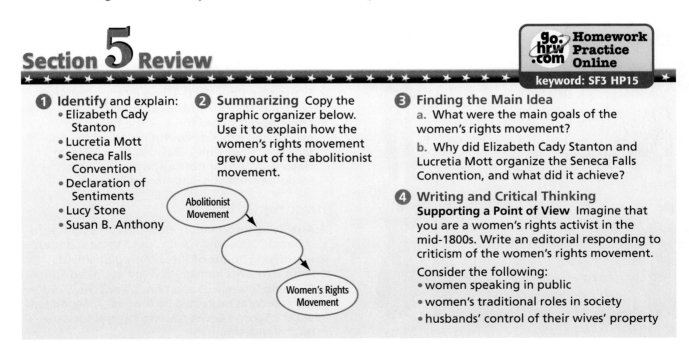

Abolitionist Movement

Women's Rights Movement

3 **Finding the Main Idea**
   a. What were the main goals of the women's rights movement?

   b. Why did Elizabeth Cady Stanton and Lucretia Mott organize the Seneca Falls Convention, and what did it achieve?

4 **Writing and Critical Thinking**
   Supporting a Point of View Imagine that you are a women's rights activist in the mid-1800s. Write an editorial responding to criticism of the women's rights movement.

   Consider the following:
   • women speaking in public
   • women's traditional roles in society
   • husbands' control of their wives' property

Chapter 15 Review

The Chapter at a Glance

Examine the visual summary of the chapter below. Then create a set of flash cards listing the key leaders of each reform movement on one side of the card and one key accomplishment on the other side. Use the flash cards to review the chapter material with a classmate.

PRISON REFORM
- Better treatment for criminals, orphans, and people with mental illnesses

TEMPERANCE
- Limit alcohol consumption
- Ban the sale of alcohol

EDUCATION
- Common schools for all children
- Colleges for women
- Schools for African Americans and the disabled

ABOLITION
- End slavery in the United States
- Full social and political equality for African Americans wanted by some abolitionists

WOMEN'S RIGHTS
- Right to vote
- Equal property rights

Identifying People and Ideas

Use the following terms or people in historically significant sentences.

1. Second Great Awakening
2. Henry David Thoreau
3. nativists
4. tenements
5. Horace Mann
6. abolition
7. Angelina Grimké
8. Frederick Douglass
9. Elizabeth Cady Stanton
10. Seneca Falls Convention

Understanding Main Ideas

Section 1 *(Pages 452–456)*
1. What did the transcendentalists and members of utopian communities believe?
2. Who were some of the most important artists and authors of the romantic movement?

Section 2 *(Pages 457–461)*
3. What caused the increase in immigration to the United States during the mid-1800s?

Section 3 *(Pages 462–468)*
4. What social issues did reformers address in the early to mid-1800s?

Section 4 *(Pages 469–474)*
5. Why did people join the abolitionist movement, and what were their goals?

Section 5 *(Pages 475–479)*
6. What were the major goals of the women's rights movement?

You Be the Historian— Reviewing Themes

1. **Culture** How did the Second Great Awakening affect the reform movements of the mid-1800s?
2. **Economics** How did U.S. immigration between 1840 and 1860 affect the economy?
3. **Citizenship** Choose three of the following people and explain how they worked to end slavery: Robert Finley, David Walker, William Lloyd Garrison, Angelina and Sarah Grimké, Frederick Douglass, and Harriet Tubman.

Thinking Critically

1. **Analyzing Information** How did cities change in the mid-1800s, and what caused these changes?
2. **Identifying Points of View** Why did nativists want to restrict immigration to the United States?
3. **Drawing Inferences and Conclusions** How did the freedoms protected by the First Amendment aid the Second Great Awakening and social reform movements?

Interpreting Graphs

Study the graph below. Then use the information on the graph to help you answer the questions that follow.

Immigration to the United States, 1840 and 1850

Immigrants (in thousands)

Year

- ▮ British
- ▮ German
- ▮ Irish
- ▮ Other

Source: *Historical Statistics of the United States*

1. Based on your knowledge of the period, what events could have led to the increase in the number of German and Irish immigrants to the United States between 1840 and 1850?

2. Which of the following statements was not true for 1850?
   a. The Irish were the largest group of immigrants to the United States.
   b. The number of German immigrants rose greatly from 1840.
   c. There were fewer immigrants from Britain than in 1840.
   d. There were nearly 80,000 immigrants from "Other" countries in 1850.

Analyzing Primary Sources

Read the following quote by abolitionist William Lloyd Garrison, then answer the questions that follow.

> **❝I will be as harsh as truth, and as uncompromising as justice. On this subject, I do not wish to think, to speak, or write, with moderation. . . . I am in earnest—I will not equivocate [lie]—I will not excuse—I will not retreat a single inch—AND I WILL BE HEARD.❞**

3. What is the best interpretation for what Garrison means by, "I will be as harsh as truth, and as uncompromising as justice"?
   a. He will treat everyone equally.
   b. He will be truthful and fair in what he writes about slavery.
   c. He will pursue abolition no matter how long it takes or whom he offends.
   d. He will punish slaveholders for their crimes.

4. Based on your knowledge of the period, why do you think Garrison felt he needed to state his determination so forcefully?

5. Whom do you think Garrison was addressing when he made the statement above?

Alternative Assessment

Building Your Portfolio

American History

Linking to Community

As a group, select an issue that you think is important to your community today. Plan a campaign to educate the public about this issue. Assign each group member one of the following roles—artist, speechwriter, or presenter. The artists should design a poster explaining the issue. The speechwriters should write a script for a speech about the issue. Finally, the presenters should formally deliver the speech and artwork to the class.

◪ internet connect

Internet Activity: go.hrw.com
keyword: SF3 CF15

Access the Internet through the HRW Go site to learn about the Astor Place riot of 1849 and how the riot reflected developments in drama and urban society in the 1800s. Then imagine that radio had been invented during this time and conduct a radio broadcast with one of the actors or witnesses of the riot. Include direct references to your research in our broadcast.

Social Studies Skills
WORKSHOP

Study Skills

Taking notes and summarizing are key study skills. The following activities will help you develop and practice these skills.

Taking Notes

Taking notes helps you identify the main points of whatever you are studying, whether it is a book or a lecture. You should write your notes in your own words to help you understand them. Try to use the following steps when taking notes:

1. Identify the subject or main topic.
2. Identify the main ideas.
3. Note interesting and important details.
4. Identify key vocabulary terms.
5. Review your notes shortly after you write them.

Summarizing

Taking good notes can be very helpful when creating a summary—a brief statement of the important ideas in what you are studying. Summaries are a good tool to use when doing research for a report or presentation. The following strategies will help you write a summary:

- Write the summary in paragraph form, using as few words as possible without being inaccurate or too brief.

- Include key words and facts.
- Review your summary when you are finished.

Example

The underlined words in the following passage represent key facts and ideas that you would record when taking notes. Notice how they are used in the summary that follows the passage.

Waves of Immigrants

In the mid-1800s many immigrants crossed the Atlantic Ocean. <u>More than 4 million immigrants from Europe</u> settled in the United States <u>between 1840 and 1860</u>. <u>More than 3 million</u> of these immigrants arrived <u>from Ireland and Germany</u>. <u>Many immigrants were fleeing from economic or political troubles</u> in their native countries.

Summary More than 3 million Irish and German immigrants came to the United States between 1840 and 1860. Many immigrants came because of economic or political problems at home.

Practicing the Skills

1. Look at Chapter 15: Section 4, The Movement to End Slavery. Read the subsection titled The Underground Railroad. On your own paper, take notes by writing down the key words and phrases from each paragraph.

2. Now look at the notes that you have taken. Using only these notes and the strategies outlined above, write a short summary of the subsection. Show your summary to another student to see if he or she can understand the subject based on your summary.

History in Action

UNIT 6 SIMULATION

You Make the Decision . . .

What Should Immigrants Bring with Them to the United States?

Complete the following activity in small cooperative groups. It is the mid-1800s and America is the land of opportunity. Many people are coming to the United States from other countries to start new lives. Usually traveling in tightly packed sections of ships, immigrants are limited in what they can bring with them to America. Your community has asked you to serve on a committee to develop a flyer that will identify for immigrants what items to bring with them to make the successful transition to life in the United States. Follow these steps to reach your decision.

1. Gather Information. Use your textbook and other resources to find information that might help you decide which items immigrants need to bring to America to start their new lives. Be sure to use what you learned from this unit's Skills Workshop on Summarizing and Taking Notes to help you record the information that you gather. You may want to divide different parts of the research among group members.

2. Identify Options. After reviewing the information you have gathered, consider the options for items to recommend. Your final decision may be easier to reach if you consider as many options as possible. Be sure to record your possible options for the preparation of your flyer.

3. Predict Consequences. Now consider what might be the outcome if immigrants decide to bring or not to bring each of these items. Ask yourselves questions like: "Will the immigrants have enough room to bring these items on the ship?" Once you have predicted the consequences, record them as notes for the preparation of your flyer.

4. Take Action to Implement Your Decision. After you have considered your options, you should plan and create your flyer to present to the community board. Be sure to make your decision on which items immigrants should bring to the United States very clear. You will need to support your decisions by including information you gathered and by explaining why you rejected other options. Your flyer needs to be visually appealing to the community board. When you are ready, decide which committee members will present each part of the flyer, and then take your flyer to the community board (the rest of the class). Good Luck!

UNIT 7 The Nation Expands West

(1790–1860)

Young People
IN HISTORY
Young Pioneers

The young pioneers who set out for the West with their families in the 1840s and 1850s showed great courage. They knew that hardship and perhaps death lay ahead on the western trails. Young Martha Gay traveled to Oregon in the 1850s. She remembered, "We often saw human skulls bleached by sun and storms lying scattered around" along the trail.

Many teenagers were willing to push ahead, regardless of the conditions. Young Nancy Kelsey was one of the first group of pioneers to head for California in 1841. When the group's horses began to tire, Kelsey and the others had to leave their wagons at the Great Salt Lake. She recalled their struggles.

Young pioneers travel across the western frontier in the 1800s.

> **"We had a difficult time to find a way down the [Sierra Nevada] mountains. . . . We were then out of provisions [supplies], having killed and eaten all our cattle. I walked barefeeted until my feet were blistered and lived on roasted acorns for two days."**

Kelsey arrived in California soon afterward.

Young pioneers worked hard every day to keep their families healthy and safe. Older boys watched the livestock. Even boys as young as 12 took turns standing watch around the wagon train at night. Teenage girls took care of their younger brothers and sisters and helped with chores.

Teenagers still found ways to have fun during the trip. They played music and danced during the evenings. Fifteen-year-old Mary Margaret Hezlep stitched patch blocks for a quilt during her trip to California. The blocks tell the story of her journey. Other young pioneers brought along books like *The Life of Daniel Boone*, *Pilgrim's Progress*, and *Robinson Crusoe* to read. Some teenagers kept diaries.

If You Were There *What would you do for fun while traveling along the pioneer trails?*

LEFT PAGE: *In the mid-1800s, Emanuel Gottlieb Leutze painted this scene of the frontier, titled* Westward the Course of Empire Takes Its Way.

16 Expanding West

(1790–1850)

By the 1810s fur trappers were already crossing the Rocky Mountains in search of wild game and new trading partners.

Moses Austin played an important role in bringing U.S. settlers to Texas.

UNITED STATES

1811 John Jacob Astor founds the fur-trading post Astoria on the Columbia River.

1821 Moses Austin becomes the first American to receive a contract to bring settlers to Texas.

1800	**1805**	**1810**	**1815**	**1820**

WORLD

1810 The Mexican war for independence begins.

1821 Mexico wins its independence from Spain.

1824 Mexico creates a republican constitution.

The national flag of Mexico features an eagle at its center.

This mural celebrates the efforts of Father José María Morelos y Pavón to win independence for Mexico.

Build on What You Know

By the mid-1800s there were many different reform movements changing American society. Some Americans saw the West as a place for a fresh start and a way to avoid overcrowding in the East. These settlers' quest for land brought them into conflict with Mexican citizens and the many different American Indian groups living in the region.

ALBERT BIERSTADT, "EMIGRANTS CROSSING THE PLAINS," 1867, OIL ON CANVAS, A.011.1T: NATIONAL COWBOY HALL OF FAME, OKLAHOMA CITY, OK

After the Battle of San Jacinto, Texan leader Sam Houston accepted the surrender of Mexican general Santa Anna.

Albert Bierstadt's painting Emigrants Crossing the Plains *shows settlers moving west to Oregon Country in the mid-1800s.*

1827 The United States and Great Britain agree to continue joint occupation of Oregon Country.

1835 The Texas Revolution begins.

1836 Mexican troops defeat the Texan forces at the Alamo in San Antonio on March 6.

On April 21 Sam Houston leads Texans to victory over Mexican troops at San Jacinto.

1843 A territorial government is set up in Oregon Country.

1844 Texas president Sam Houston signs a peace agreement with Mexico.

| 1825 | 1830 | 1835 | 1840 | 1845 |

1833 General Antonio López de Santa Anna becomes president of Mexico.

1837 Reformers in Canada rebel against the government.

THE GRANGER COLLECTION, NEW YORK

Santa Anna was one of Mexico's most influential military and political leaders from the 1820s to the 1840s.

If you were there . . .
Why would you settle in the West?

You Be the Historian

Themes Journal

What's Your Opinion? Do you **agree** or **disagree** with the following statements? Support your point of view in your journal.

- **Citizenship** A group of people have the right to declare independence from their country.

- **Culture** Immigration always brings positive change to a region.

- **Geography** People seek to settle only certain types of land.

487

The Spanish West and Southwest

Read to Discover

1. How was society structured in Spanish California, New Mexico, and Texas?
2. What events led to the establishment of the republic of Mexico?
3. How did the Mexican war for independence affect California and Texas?

Identify

- Californios
- Tejanos
- Father Miguel Hidalgo y Costilla
- Agustín de Iturbide

WHY IT MATTERS TODAY

Missions are just one example of the Hispanic heritage of the United States. Use or other **current events** sources to find out about other ways our nation is influenced by its Hispanic heritage. Record your findings in your journal.

The style of the San Miguel Chapel was common to many colonial churches in northern New Spain.

The Story Continues

Bishop Pedro Tamarón y Romeral toured northern New Spain in 1760. When visiting Santa Fe, Tamarón was particularly interested in the town's churches, which were all built from adobe. This building style, adopted from the Pueblo Indians, was just one example of how Spanish towns on the frontier combined European and American Indian ways of life.

⭐ Life in Northern New Spain

New Spain's northern frontier was made up of California, New Mexico, and Texas. New Mexico was the oldest and most important of these provinces, with its capital at Santa Fe. By the mid-1800s settlers lived in small villages scattered across New Mexico. These Spanish colonists were influenced greatly by the Pueblo Indians of the region. In turn, the Spanish changed many aspects of Pueblo life, bringing new tools and new foods, such as peaches, to the region. The Pueblo introduced the Spanish to southwestern foods such as beans and corn. The Spanish also began to build with adobe, as the Pueblo did.

Life in California was very different from life in New Mexico. Missions were the center of California's colonial life. Between 1769 and 1823 the Spanish built 21 missions in California along the coast from San Diego to San Francisco. Each California mission was one day's travel from the next. Spanish military forts called presidios protected the missions from attack. New Spain's leaders also hoped this military presence would keep the British and Russians out of the region.

The missions held a great deal of land, which was used for farming and ranching. American Indians who lived on mission lands and were supervised by Catholic priests performed most of this labor. The crowded living conditions in the California missions led to outbreaks of disease that killed tens of thousands of mission Indians over the years.

The missions supported themselves into the 1800s. Often they sold their goods to local communities. Colonist Guadalupe Vallejo remembered the early days of Spanish California.

 History Makers Speak

"We were the pioneers of the Pacific coast, building towns and Missions while General [George] Washington was carrying on the war of the Revolution."

—Guadalupe Vallejo, quoted in *Sketches of Early California*, edited by Donald DeNevi

Spanish colonists in California were known as **Californios**. They were basically cut off from the rest of New Spain because of the great distance. This isolation was one reason that only some 3,200 Spanish people lived in California by 1821.

✔ **Reading Check: Contrasting** How was life for Spanish settlers in New Mexico and California different?

Analyzing Primary Sources
Making Generalizations and Predictions How do you think Vallejo would say that the Spanish and English colonists were similar?

THE GRANGER COLLECTION, NEW YORK

Interpreting the Visual Record

Mission life *Missions such as San Diego de Alcala, shown here, controlled much of the land in early Spanish California.* **Does the setting shown in this picture appear to be agricultural or industrial? Explain your answer.**

Expanding West **489**

⭐ Early Texas

The Spanish built up to 40 missions in Texas, but the mission system in Texas was weaker than the one in California. One reason was that the Texas missions were located far apart from each other. In addition, the Spanish often fought local American Indians, such as the Comanche and the Apache. Because of this fighting, fewer Spanish settlers moved to Texas during the early 1700s.

The Spanish government responded by offering land grants to settlers. By the mid-1700s only a few thousand Spanish settlers, called **Tejanos** (tay-HAH-nohs), were living in what is now Texas. They introduced new breeds of cattle and soon created a cattle-ranching society on the huge Texas grasslands.

The Comanche and the Apache still controlled much of Texas, however, limiting Spanish expansion. Viceroy Bernardo de Gálvez commented on the situation in the late 1700s. According to Gálvez, "A bad peace with all the [Indian] tribes which ask for it would be more fruitful [helpful] than the gains of a successful war."

⭐ Mexico Gains Independence

Father Miguel Hidalgo y Costilla led a rebellion against Spain.

In September 1810 about 80,000 poor American Indians and mestizos in Mexico joined in revolt against Spanish rule. **Father Miguel Hidalgo y Costilla**, a Mexican priest from the town of Dolores, led this rebellion. The rebels hoped that independence would improve their living conditions. Their rallying call was the Grito de Dolores, or "Cry of Dolores." The cry went, "Long live our Lady of Guadalupe, down with bad government, death to the Spaniards!"

Support for Father Hidalgo grew. As his army marched across the countryside, he began reforms, such as ending the enslavement and unfair taxation of American Indians. But Father Hidalgo could not unite all of Mexico's villages. In 1811 the Spanish defeated the rebels and killed the priest.

Father José María Morelos y Pavón continued the revolution and Hidalgo's reforms. Morelos fought bravely until his capture in 1815. Finally, in 1821 under **Agustín de Iturbide** (ee-toor-BEE-day), the rebels defeated the Spanish. Mexico had won its independence. Although he did not have great political support, Iturbide made himself Mexico's emperor. After only two and a half years the army made him step down. A new congress created the Constitution of 1824, which made Mexico a republic. The country included what is now Arizona, California, Nevada, New Mexico, Texas, and Utah. It also contained parts of Colorado, Kansas, Oklahoma, and Wyoming.

✔ **Reading Check: Sequencing** Describe in the order that they took place the events that led to the creation of the republic of Mexico.

⭐ Changes in California and Texas

In 1833 Mexico ended the Spanish mission system in California, and officials gave the mission lands to Californios. A group of about 500 families created large ranchos, or ranches. The largest ranchos had up to 90,000 acres of land and huge herds of cattle. American Indians did much of the hard physical labor on ranches and farms. For most American Indians, life did not improve greatly with the end of the mission system.

In his novel *Two Years before the Mast,* American Richard Henry Dana Jr. wrote about his many encounters with Californio culture. In one small town, a local man served a feast to Dana and his friend.

Primary Sources

❝We took out some money and asked him how much we were to pay. He shook his head and crossed himself, saying that it was charity—that the Lord gave it to us.❞

—Richard Henry Dana Jr., *Two Years before the Mast*

After Mexico's war for independence, Texas merged with the Mexican province of Coahuila (koh-ah-WEE-lah) to form a single state called Coahuila y Texas. Fighting during the war had killed or chased away many Tejanos. By 1821 only about 2,500 of them were left, mostly on scattered ranches and in a few towns, such as San Antonio. Mexican officials worried that so few people could not protect all of Texas. The government decided to recruit more settlers to help protect the northern frontier from American Indian attacks or possible invasion by another nation.

✔ **Reading Check: Summarizing** What changes did the new Mexican government make in California and Texas?

Interpreting the Visual Record

Californios *The Californios developed a reputation as skilled horse riders. They were also known for their generosity to guests.* **What characteristics of this horseman suggest his wealth?**

Section 1 Review

go.hrw.com Homework Practice Online
keyword: SF3 HP16

① Identify and explain:
- Californios
- Tejanos
- Father Miguel Hidalgo y Costilla
- Agustín de Iturbide

② Comparing and Contrasting Copy the chart below. Use it to compare and contrast the key characteristics of Texas and California before and after Mexico gained its independence.

	Spanish Rule	Mexican Rule
Texas		
California		

③ Finding the Main Idea

a. Why did American Indians and mestizos join forces to revolt against their Spanish rulers, and what effect did this have on Mexico?

b. How much of an effect do you think American Indians had on Spanish settlement in California, New Mexico, and Texas?

④ Writing and Critical Thinking

Summarizing Imagine that you are a trader traveling through the Spanish territories of California, New Mexico, and Texas. Write a journal entry that lists how society was structured in each of these regions.

Consider the following:
- settlement patterns
- the role of American Indians
- the population in each region

Texas Gains Independence

Read to Discover

1. Why did many U.S. settlers in Texas rebel against the Mexican government?
2. What were the most important events of the Texas Revolution?
3. What was the result of the Texas Revolution?

WHY IT MATTERS TODAY

Throughout the world many groups are struggling for political independence. Use **CNNfyi.com** or other **current events** sources to find out about one of these groups. Record your findings in your journal.

Define

• *empresarios*

Identify

• Stephen F. Austin
• Antonio López de Santa Anna
• Alamo
• Battle of Goliad
• Sam Houston
• Battle of San Jacinto

The Story Continues

In 1819 James Long led a group of Mississippi traders into Spanish Texas. The group built a fort by Galveston Bay, but Long and others were arrested in 1822 by Mexican troops. His wife, Jane, pregnant with their second child, stayed at the fort with their daughter. She survived the winter but left for Louisiana after learning of her husband's death. However, she was determined to return to Texas someday.

Jane Long had to protect herself and her children from American Indian attacks at Galveston Bay.

★ American Settlers in Texas

The new Mexican republic wanted to attract more people to Texas. Mexico hired **empresarios**, or agents, to bring settlers to Texas. In exchange, these *empresarios* received land—as much as 67,000 acres for every 200 families. American Moses Austin was an early *empresario* who died before he could bring anyone to Texas. However, in 1821 his son **Stephen F. Austin** selected a colony site on the lower Colorado River. Then he began carefully choosing settlers, including Jane Long. These first 300 families became known as the Old Three Hundred.

Austin worked to keep the peace between the Mexican government and the American settlers. His devotion to Texas helped make the colony a success. Other American and Mexican *empresarios,* such as John McMullen and Martín de León, brought more settlers. By 1834 more than 20,000 Americans had moved to Texas.

Most American settlers came from the southern states. In some parts of the South, the letters *GTT*—"Gone To Texas"—commonly appeared on empty houses. The promise of cheap or free land attracted most of these families. Each man could receive 640 acres, with additional land for his wife and each child. Other grants offered about 4,600 acres of free land to every married man.

✔ **Reading Check: Finding the Main Idea** Why did Americans move to Texas?

★ Trouble in Texas

By 1821 Mexico had set requirements for all foreign immigrants. They had to become Mexican citizens, obey Mexican laws, and support the Roman Catholic Church. However, most U.S. settlers were not interested in adapting to Mexican culture or becoming Mexican citizens.

By 1830 there were many more American settlers than Tejanos in Texas. These settlers often ignored Mexican laws, acting as if they were still in the United States and not on Mexican soil. Many American settlers came to Texas illegally and felt little loyalty to Mexico. Mexican officials

ALAMO COLLECTION, PHOTOGRAPH COURTESY THE DAUGHTERS OF THE REPUBLIC OF TEXAS LIBRARY, CT9723

Interpreting the Visual Record

Rebellion *Stephen F. Austin pursued peaceful relations with the Mexican government, but was ultimately unsuccessful.* ***What does Austin seem prepared to do in this painting?***

The Texas War for Independence

Interpreting Maps After defeats at Goliad and the Alamo, Texans rallied behind their leader, Sam Houston, and won a decisive victory at San Jacinto.

Skills Assessment

1. **The World in Spatial Terms** What battle took place within the boundaries of Austin's Colony?
2. **Drawing Inferences and Conclusions** In terms of geography, what advantage did the Texans have over the Mexican forces?

complained about this lack of respect for their government. One Mexican warned the country's minister of war and navy, "Either the [Mexican] government occupies Texas now, or it is lost forever." For their part, some Texans—Americans and Tejanos alike—argued that they were not fairly represented in Mexico's government. These Texans thought Mexico's central government was too powerful. They called for the Mexican Constitution of 1824 to be more strictly followed.

Mexico responded by enforcing its laws more strictly. For example, the Mexican government limited American immigration in 1830. Officials worked to keep settlers from bringing slaves, which concerned settlers who were slaveholders. Tariffs on goods from the United States were raised, and Mexico sent more soldiers to Texas.

While these actions angered many Texans, Stephen F. Austin tried to keep the peace. In 1833 Austin went to Mexico with a petition asking for more self-government, but he was thrown in jail. That same year General **Antonio López de Santa Anna** was elected president of Mexico. Santa Anna suspended Mexico's republican constitution in 1834. Austin was released from jail after a year and a half. Soon he called for all Texans to rebel against Mexico.

Analyzing Primary Sources

Supporting a Point of View
How does this statement show Austin's feelings about the Mexican government?

History Makers Speak

"War is our only resource [option]. There is no other remedy [solution]. We must defend our rights, ourselves, and our country by force of arms."

—Stephen F. Austin, quoted in *Lone Star*, by T. R. Fehrenbach

✔ **Reading Check: Summarizing** What policies of the Mexican government caused Texans to rebel?

The outnumbered Texan defenders at the Alamo could only hope to keep the Mexican army outside the walls.

★ The Texas Revolution Begins

The Texas Revolution started in the town of Gonzales in October 1835, when the Mexican army tried to remove a cannon located there. A group of rebels stood next to the gun with a flag reading "Come and take it." In a brief battle, Texans defeated the Mexican soldiers.

In November 1835 a group of Texans formed a temporary government with the goals of defeating Santa Anna and restoring Mexico's republican constitution. Texas volunteers soon captured the towns of Goliad and San Antonio. Led by William Travis and Jim Bowie, Texans occupied the **Alamo**, an old mission in San Antonio. Santa Anna was determined to put down the rebellion and led an army of about 1,800 troops to San Antonio. Travis, however, refused to retreat. Volunteers including Juan Seguín and frontiersman Davy Crockett joined the Alamo defenders. When Santa Anna arrived on February 23, 1836, Travis had only 189 troops. For 13 days the Mexican troops surrounded the Alamo. Travis sent Seguín on a daring mission through enemy lines to try to get reinforcements. Despite the terrible odds, Travis also wrote a bold letter. It was addressed "To the People of Texas and All Americans in the World."

"I shall never surrender or retreat. . . . I call on you in the name of Liberty, of patriotism, and everything dear to the American character, to come to our aid with all dispatch [speed]. . . . If this call is neglected I am determined to sustain [keep] myself as long as possible and die like a soldier who never forgets what is due his honor and that of his country. VICTORY OR DEATH."

—William Travis, from *Documents of Texas History,*
edited by Ernest Wallace and David M. Vigness

Before dawn on March 6, 1836, the Mexican army attacked. Although the Mexicans suffered heavy losses, they soon overpowered the Texans. All the defenders of the Alamo were killed. Santa Anna spared the lives of a few people not involved in the fighting, including Susanna Dickinson. Along with others, she spread the story of the fall of the Alamo throughout Texas. The news increased support for the revolution. "Remember the Alamo!" became a rallying cry in Texas and the United States.

Following the victory at the Alamo, Mexican forces attacked the Texas troops near the town of Goliad. The Texans were greatly outnumbered. At the **Battle of Goliad** Texas commander James Fannin chose to surrender. Santa Anna ordered the execution of Fannin and almost all of his soldiers. This act outraged many Texans and shocked some of the Mexican troops. Francita Alavez, a nurse, hid several of Fannin's men. Because of her, they escaped the firing squads, and she became known as the Angel of Goliad for this act of mercy.

✔ **Reading Check: Supporting a Point of View** Do you think that the early battles of the Texas Revolution were a success or a failure for the Texans? Explain your answer.

Interpreting the Visual Record

Independence *The delegates to the Convention of 1836 are shown here listening to the Texas Declaration of Independence.* **How do the delegates appear to be responding to the declaration?**

Susanna Dickinson was one of the few survivors of the Alamo.

Despite some criticism of his leadership, Sam Houston led the Texas army to victory over Mexico.

⭐ Texas Becomes a Republic

Four days before the Battle of the Alamo, Texas delegates had met to declare independence from Mexico. Within two weeks they had written a constitution. Both the Texas Declaration of Independence and Constitution were modeled on those of the United States. However, there were some differences between the Texan and U.S. documents. For example, the Texas Constitution specifically made slavery legal. The delegates elected politician David Burnet as temporary president. They chose *empresario* Lorenzo de Zavala as vice president.

Sam Houston became the commander in chief of the new Texas army. Outnumbered and untrained, Houston's soldiers had to retreat east. The Texans finally made a stand at San Jacinto, near the present-day city of Houston. Santa Anna was confident of victory and had chosen his campsite carelessly. As a result, the Mexican army had poor defenses. On the afternoon of April 21, 1836, many of the Mexican soldiers were resting. They awoke to the sounds of Houston's forces attacking the camp and shouting "Remember the Alamo! Remember Goliad!" The **Battle of San Jacinto** had begun. Caught by surprise, Santa Anna's troops were driven back and trapped in the nearby woods. One Mexican officer later recalled the scene. "The enemy's cavalry surrounded the grove [woods], while his infantry . . . [pursued] us with fierce and bloodthirsty feelings."

The defeat destroyed Santa Anna's army. Texans captured the Mexican leader and forced him to sign a treaty giving Texas its independence. Santa Anna was thrown out of power when he returned home. Although the fighting was over, many Mexican officials did not truly accept that Texas was now independent.

✔ **Reading Check: Finding the Main Idea** What was the importance of the Battle of San Jacinto?

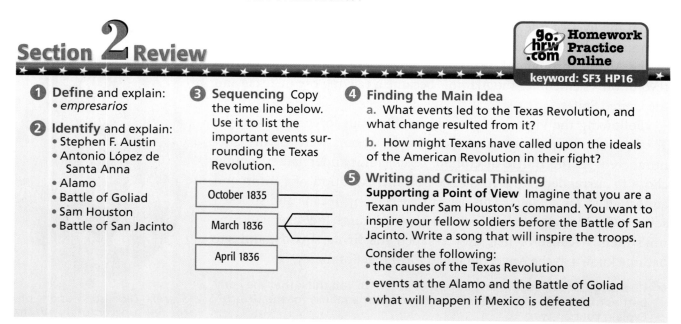

Section 2 Review

go.hrw.com **Homework Practice Online**
keyword: SF3 HP16

1. **Define** and explain:
   • *empresarios*

2. **Identify** and explain:
   • Stephen F. Austin
   • Antonio López de Santa Anna
   • Alamo
   • Battle of Goliad
   • Sam Houston
   • Battle of San Jacinto

3. **Sequencing** Copy the time line below. Use it to list the important events surrounding the Texas Revolution.

   | October 1835 |
   | March 1836 |
   | April 1836 |

4. **Finding the Main Idea**
   a. What events led to the Texas Revolution, and what change resulted from it?

   b. How might Texans have called upon the ideals of the American Revolution in their fight?

5. **Writing and Critical Thinking**
   Supporting a Point of View Imagine that you are a Texan under Sam Houston's command. You want to inspire your fellow soldiers before the Battle of San Jacinto. Write a song that will inspire the troops.

   Consider the following:
   • the causes of the Texas Revolution
   • events at the Alamo and the Battle of Goliad
   • what will happen if Mexico is defeated

The Lone Star Republic

Read to Discover

1. What difficulties did American Indians and Tejanos face in the Republic of Texas?
2. What drew new immigrants to Texas?
3. What economic and foreign challenges faced the Texas government?

Define

- annex

Identify

- Republic of Texas
- Mirabeau Lamar

WHY IT MATTERS TODAY

In recent years, different regions of the world have become independent nations. Use **CNNfyi.com** or other **current events** sources to find out about the problems facing new nations' governments. Record your findings in your journal.

The Story Continues

In December 1836 President Andrew Jackson faced a difficult decision. Texas had declared its independence from Mexico earlier that year. Congress had asked Jackson to recognize, or formally accept, the new Texas government. However, Mexico still considered Texas a part of its territory. In a speech to Congress, Jackson described his problem. He said that the people of Texas "are bound to many of our citizens by ties of friendship and kindred [family] blood." Yet in his view it was too soon to take sides in the fight between Texas and Mexico.

This was the flag adopted by the Republic of Texas.

★ Texas Faces the World

The independent nation of Texas was called the **Republic of Texas**. Its capital was the new town of Houston. Voters elected Sam Houston, victor at San Jacinto and a former governor of Tennessee, as president. **Mirabeau Lamar** was chosen as vice president.

In 1837 the new government asked the United States to **annex**, or take control of, Texas. The vast majority of Texans hoped that Texas

BIOGRAPHY

Juan Seguín
(1806–1890)

Born to an important San Antonio family in 1806, Juan Seguín became a well-known Tejano politician. Seguín led a troop of Tejano cavalry in the victory at San Jacinto.

After the war, Seguín served in the Texas Senate and later became mayor of San Antonio. In 1842 Seguín moved his family to Mexico because of rising tensions between Anglos and Tejanos. **What role did Seguín play in the winning of Texas independence?**

Analyzing Primary Sources
Identifying Points of View How do you think Seguín feels about attacks against Tejanos?

would eventually become a U.S. state. Most Texas leaders, including Houston, supported this decision. In contrast, Lamar wanted to expand the republic to the west and increase its power.

Members of the U.S. Congress wanted to annex Texas, but President Andrew Jackson was concerned because Texas supported slavery. Adding Texas to the Union would upset the balance between free states and slave states. Jackson also did not want to go to war with Mexico over Texas. He recognized Texas as an independent nation, but he would not annex it. Martin Van Buren, the next U.S. president, did the same. France recognized the Texas government in 1839, and Great Britain did so the next year. However, Mexico still refused to agree that its former province had become an independent country.

✔ **Reading Check: Finding the Main Idea** Why did Texas not immediately become part of the United States?

★ American Indians and Tejanos

As a young man, Sam Houston had lived with the Cherokee in Tennessee. His experience led him, as president of Texas, to support a peaceful relationship with American Indians. However, Texas's Indian policy changed in 1838 when Mirabeau Lamar became president. Lamar demanded that American Indians leave their homelands and follow all Texas laws. He threatened military action if they refused.

Fighting soon broke out with American Indian groups such as the Cherokee and the Comanche. Comanche raids on Texan settlements increased. Many Texans believed that the Cherokee were plotting with Mexico to overthrow the republic. After Houston was elected to a second term as president in 1841, the fighting slowed. By then, however, Texans had forced most American Indians from their eastern lands.

Relations between Tejanos and American settlers also suffered under the new republic. Tejanos often faced unfair treatment. Tejanos lost land, political power, and property. This situation angered many Tejanos who had taken part in Texas's war for independence. Juan Seguín, a hero of the revolution and the mayor of San Antonio, described some of the problems faced by Tejanos.

 History Makers Speak 66At every hour of the day and night, my countrymen [Tejanos] ran to me for protection against the assaults [attacks] . . . of these [American] adventurers. . . . Were not the victims my own countrymen, friends, and associates?99

—Juan Seguín, quoted in *Anglos and Mexicans in the Making of Texas, 1836–1986,* by David Montejano

Despite such treatment, many Tejanos chose to remain in Texas.

✔ **Reading Check: Summarizing** What problems did American Indians and Tejanos face in the new nation of Texas?

⭐ New Immigrants

In 1836 the population of Texas was approximately 52,700, including some 22,700 American Indians, African Americans, and Tejanos. To increase the republic's population, Texas leaders decided to offer land grants to American and European settlers. In the years 1840 and 1841 alone, the government gave out nearly 37 million acres. The Texas population grew by about 100,000 from 1836 to 1847. By 1845 so many immigrants were arriving daily that they had to wait for hours at ferry crossings. As more people came, settlements expanded to the north and west.

The largest group of immigrants to Texas was from the United States. They came in search of land and economic opportunities, particularly after the economic depression caused by the Panic of 1837. One Texan reported to a New Orleans newspaper about the rush of U.S. settlers to Texas. "All are land-hunting, seeking sugar, cotton, and stock farm lands."

The majority of these settlers came from southern states. Most were small farmers who did not own slaves. However, because the Constitution of 1836 made slavery legal, many slaveholders were also attracted to the republic. As a result, the population of enslaved African Americans in Texas increased from some 5,000 in 1836 to almost 70,000 by 1845.

Life for slaves was difficult. Long days of hard labor and the threat of harsh punishments were common. The laws of the republic also made life difficult for free African Americans. In 1840 the Texas Congress passed a

Daily Life

Austin, Texas As more settlers came to Texas, the population began to spread to the west. Leaders such as Mirabeau Lamar worried that the republic's capital, Houston, was too far from such settlements. In 1839 the Congress selected the tiny settlement of Waterloo in central Texas to be the site of the new capital. Officials renamed the town Austin in honor of Stephen F. Austin. **Looking at the picture, what challenges do you think officials faced in preparing Austin to be the republic's capital?**

THE GRANGER COLLECTION, NEW YORK

law that banned free African Americans from immigrating to Texas. The law stated that free African Americans living in Texas would have to leave within two years or be sold into slavery. Although this legal deadline was later postponed, by 1850 there were fewer than 400 free African Americans reported as living in Texas.

Germans made up the largest group of European immigrants to Texas. In 1843 the Congress required laws to be published in German as well as English. Germans established farming communities. They also founded towns such as New Braunfels and Fredericksburg, both in central Texas. German immigrant Gustav Dresel described the rapid growth in the 1840s.

 History Makers Speak

66There was land in abundance. . . . The lawyers . . . accepted payment in land. The innkeepers received so and so many hundreds of thousands of acres of land for board [food] and lodging from the army officers or big estate owners.99

—Gustav Dresel, quoted in *Gustav Dresel's Houston Journal,* translated and edited by Max Freund

German customs had a strong influence on the culture of many towns in central Texas. Other European immigrants came to Texas from France, Ireland, and Poland. Czech immigrants from central Europe also settled in Texas. Each of these groups brought with it different traditions in areas such as architecture, food, and music.

✔ **Reading Check: Analyzing Information** What attracted settlers to the Republic of Texas, and what was life like for African Americans there?

⭐ Struggles of the Republic

With its small, scattered population, Texas faced many challenges as an independent country. During the years of the republic, only four Texas towns—Galveston, Houston, New Braunfels, and San Antonio—had more than 1,000 residents. Travel between the newer settlements was slow, difficult, and often dangerous.

Texas also had significant economic problems. Its economy was based largely on farming and ranching with very little industry. Although the republic was rich in resources, particularly in land, it had little cash. Taxes on imports and property failed to bring in much revenue. As a result the new nation was almost bankrupt. Texas's debt rose dramatically, while the value of its paper currency dropped sharply.

The government's lack of funds made it difficult for Texas to defend its vast territory. Due to problems with discipline among some of the soldiers, President Houston was forced to disband most of the Texas army. For defense and frontier protection, he relied instead on militia companies and the Texas Rangers. Formed in 1835, the Rangers were a frontier defense force that later acted as law officers as well. To make

LINKING PAST to PRESENT

Ethnic Traditions

In Texas a wide range of cultures influence everything from food to holidays. Holiday celebrations like Diez y Seis de Septiembre are among many Texas traditions that date back to the first Tejano settlers. Diez y Seis celebrates the call for Mexican independence on September 16, 1810.

Thousands of European immigrants moved to Texas in the 1840s, bringing their customs with them. For example, a modern festival in the city of New Braunfels features traditional German music and polka dancing.

Every year the Institute of Texan Cultures in San Antonio hosts the Folklife Festival. Texans from 70 counties representing different backgrounds participate. How do Texans currently honor their ethnic traditions?

Texas children participate in a German festival.

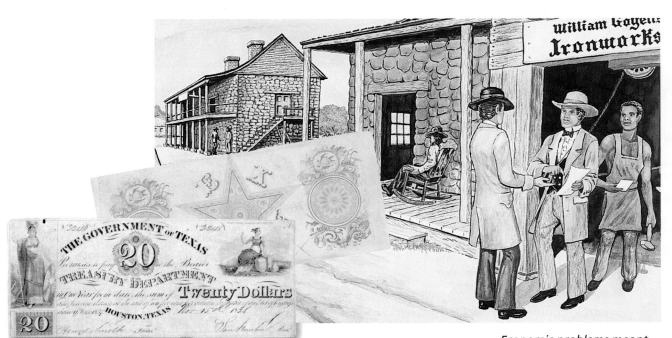

Economic problems meant that paper money issued by the Republic of Texas steadily decreased in value, making it harder to buy goods and services.

matters worse, Mexico still considered Texas to be its property. President Mirabeau Lamar vowed to fight Mexico if necessary. Upon taking office he declared, "If peace can only be obtained by the sword, let the sword do its work."

In 1841 Lamar authorized a military attack on Santa Fe in the Mexican territory of New Mexico. The invasion lacked the approval of the Texas Congress and failed miserably. Mexico responded by sending its troops into Texas. The Mexican army even took control of San Antonio on two occasions. After Sam Houston returned to the presidency in 1841, he worked hard to end the fighting. Finally, Texas and Mexico signed a peace treaty in 1844.

✔ **Reading Check: Finding the Main Idea** What problems did Texas have with its economy and its dealings with Mexico?

Section 3 Review

go.
hrw
.com
Homework Practice Online
keyword: SF3 HP16

1 Define and explain:
• annex

2 Identify and explain:
• Republic of Texas
• Mirabeau Lamar

3 Categorizing Copy the graphic organizer below. Use it to explain the major problems that challenged the Republic of Texas.

Challenges for the Republic of Texas

Economic Problems   Social Problems   Foreign Problems

4 Finding the Main Idea
a. Explain the problems American Indians, Tejanos, Mexicans, and African Americans experienced in the Republic of Texas.

b. Why do you think many Texans wanted Texas to become part of the United States?

5 Writing and Critical Thinking
Analyzing Information Imagine that you are a Texas official. Create an advertisement to encourage immigrants to move to Texas.

Consider the following:
• the availability of land
• economic opportunities
• the reasons that settlers are wanted

Oregon and the Far West

Read to Discover

1. Why did Americans first travel to the Rocky Mountains and farther west?
2. Why did Americans decide to settle in Oregon Country?
3. What was life like on the Oregon Trail?

WHY IT MATTERS TODAY

In the 1800s, Oregon was known as a place that offered the opportunity for a new life to Americans and immigrants. Use CNNfyi.com or other **current events** sources to find out why Oregon is in the news today. Record your findings in your journal.

Define
- mountain men
- rendezvous

Identify
- John Jacob Astor
- Marcus and Narcissa Whitman
- Oregon Trail

The Story Continues

Fur trapper Manuel Lisa was one of the earliest explorers of the Rocky Mountains. Lisa once wrote to the famous explorer William Clark. "I go a great distance while some are considering whether they will start today or tomorrow." In 1807 Lisa led an expedition up the Missouri River. The explorers braved deadly river rapids and freezing weather. In the winter, he stopped at the Little Bighorn River, in present-day Montana. Lisa's accomplishment helped blaze the westward trail for future generations.

The clothing of fur trappers was often influenced by American Indian styles.

⭐ The Fur Traders

Most of the first non–American Indians who traveled to the Rocky Mountains and the Pacific Northwest were fur traders and trappers. They were known as **mountain men.** In the early 1800s eastern companies wanted furs to make hats and clothing that were popular in the United States and Europe. They hired many mountain men to bring back the furs of beavers and other animals. One of the largest businesses that bought furs from trappers was the American Fur Company, owned by **John Jacob Astor**.

Mountain men lived lonely and often dangerous lives. They trapped animals on their own, far from towns and settlements. Mountain men such as Jedediah Smith, Manuel Lisa, and Jim Bridger survived many hardships during their search for wealth and adventure. To survive on the frontier, mountain men adopted American Indian customs and clothing. In addition, mountain men often married American Indian women. The Indian wives of trappers often worked hard to contribute to their success.

Pioneer William Ashley saw that bringing furs out of the Rocky Mountains was expensive. He asked his traders to stay in the mountains and meet once a year to trade and socialize. This practice helped make the fur trade more profitable. The yearly meeting was known as the **rendezvous**. At the rendezvous, mountain men and American Indian trappers sold their furs to fur company agents. It was thus important to bring as many furs as possible. One trapper described the people at a typical rendezvous in 1837. He saw Americans, Canadian French, some Europeans, and "Indians, of nearly every tribe in the Rocky Mountains."

The rendezvous was filled with celebrating and storytelling. At the same time, the meeting was also about conducting business. Western artist Alfred Jacob Miller described how trade was begun in the rendezvous camp.

This 1841 drawing of Fort Walla Walla in Oregon Country shows fur trappers and American Indians meeting to trade. Fur coats such as the one shown were commonly worn by fur trappers.

History Makers Speak

"The Fur Company's great tent is raised; the Indians erect their picturesque [beautiful] white lodges; the accumulated [collected] furs of the hunting season are brought forth and the Company's tent is a . . . busy place."

—Alfred Jacob Miller, quoted in *The Fur Trade of the American West*, by David J. Wishart

Analyzing Primary Sources

Summarizing According to Miller, what groups participated in the rendezvous?

The stories and rugged lives of the mountain men caught the American imagination. However, the era of American fur trading in the Pacific Northwest lasted only a short time. By the 1840s the demand for beaver furs had fallen because fashions changed. Too much trapping had also greatly lowered the number of beavers. Some mountain men gave up their work and moved back east. Others began guiding farmers, miners, and ranchers to the West. In the 1840s these new settlers replaced the mountain men on the frontier.

✔ **Reading Check: Analyzing Information** What economic and environmental conditions did mountain men have to face?

★★★★★★★★★★★★★★
That's Interesting!
★★★★★★★★★★★★★★

The Long Way Home
Can you imagine traveling to Oregon via Antarctica? That's what some pioneers did in the 1800s! Not everyone wanted to spend four months walking from the East Coast to Oregon. So they went by water around the tip of South America and along the edge of Antarctica. But this trip sometimes took a year! Some pioneers tried a short-cut by crossing what is now Panama and waiting for a boat. Sometimes they waited for months. Many of the ships that picked up these pioneers were not safe and sank before reaching the West Coast.

★ Oregon Country

In 1811 American merchant John Jacob Astor founded Astoria as a center for the fur trade. It was located at the mouth of the Columbia River in the Pacific Northwest. This small outpost was one of the earliest American settlements in the region later called Oregon Country.

At the beginning of the 1800s, Oregon Country was occupied by American Indians. These Indian groups included the Cayuse, the Flathead, the Nez Percé, and the Shoshone. Great Britain, Russia, Spain, and the United States also claimed this region. The United States based its claim on the exploration of merchant captain Robert Gray, who had reached the mouth of the Columbia River in 1792.

In 1819 Spain and the United States signed the Adams-Onís Treaty. Spain gave up all claims to land beyond the northern border of what is now California. In 1824 Russia also signed a treaty with the United States. Russia gave up its land claims up to the southern border of what is now Alaska. These treaties left American Indians, Britain, and the United States as rivals for the Pacific Northwest.

The United States and Britain had signed a treaty in 1818 that allowed both countries to occupy Oregon Country. In 1827 they decided to extend this treaty. The agreement did not state how long this shared ownership would last, however. Both sides wanted to maintain use of the Columbia River and its surrounding land. Still, neither country was willing to start a war over the territory.

The British were interested in the Pacific Northwest primarily for the fur trade. Only a few British or Canadians settled in the area. In contrast, many Americans had begun heading to Oregon Country.

✔ **Reading Check: Summarizing** What nations claimed Oregon Country, and how were their claims resolved?

★ The Missionary Spirit

Missionaries were among the first Americans to settle in Oregon Country. The Second Great Awakening had brought a new religious spirit to the United States. Some churches decided to bring Christianity to American Indians in the Far West. Oregon Country was one such destination. In 1836, missionaries **Marcus and Narcissa Whitman** went there to convert American Indians to Christianity.

The Whitmans settled in Walla Walla, in present-day Washington State. They founded a mission called Waiilatpu. However, the Whitmans had limited success bringing Christianity to the local Cayuse Indians. Narcissa Whitman found her new life difficult and lonely. She wrote to her sister in 1846, "My health has been so poor, and my family has increased so rapidly, that it [frontier life] has been impossible."

Narcissa Whitman and another missionary's wife were the first white women known to have crossed North America.

Despite the challenges the Whitmans faced, Marcus Whitman remained hopeful. He wrote letters encouraging more Americans to move out west. "I have no doubt our greatest work is . . . to aid the white settlement of this country," he wrote to his parents. He also made trips back east to recruit more settlers.

The Whitmans' efforts ended in tragedy. Settlers stopping at Waiilatpu brought diseases that led to an epidemic that killed many Cayuse children. In anger a group of Cayuse killed the Whitmans and at least 10 others.

✔ **Reading Check: Identifying Cause and Effect** Why did the Whitmans go to Oregon Country, and what were the effects of their efforts?

Interpreting the Visual Record

Mission in Oregon *The Whitmans provided rest and shelter at their Waiilatpu mission for many settlers arriving in Oregon Country.* **Why might settlers want to stop at a place like Waiilatpu?**

⭐ A New Life Out West

Missionaries were not the only early American settlers in the Pacific Northwest. Thousands of people from the Midwest also moved to Oregon Country. These families looked to the West as a place where they could improve their lives. They had learned that Oregon Country offered rich farmland, great forests, rivers full of fish, and a good climate. Newspapers encouraged people to move. Many settlers also decided to go west following the economic hardships of the Panic of 1837.

A new territorial government was set up in 1843. It started a system of land grants to attract even more settlers. After 1843 each married man who settled in Oregon could claim 640 acres of land. In May 1843 the *Ohio Statesman* reported, "The Oregon fever is raging in almost every part of the Union."

Most of the new settlers moved into the Willamette Valley. The majority stayed and prospered in what is now Oregon. Others settled in what is now the state of Washington. The population growth in the region led to increased conflict with American Indians. It also caused greater tension with Great Britain over control of Oregon Country.

✔ **Reading Check: Finding the Main Idea** What attractions did Oregon Country hold for American settlers?

Research on the R⊙M

Free Find:
Narcissa Whitman
After reading about Narcissa Whitman on the **Holt Researcher CD–ROM**, write a fictional journal entry describing her daily life as a missionary in the West.

★ The Oregon Trail

Many of the settlers moving to Oregon Country and other western areas followed the **Oregon Trail**. The Oregon Trail stretched more than 2,000 miles across the northern Great Plains and the Rocky Mountains. Traveling the trail challenged the strength and determination of pioneer families. Pioneers started their journey in Independence or St. Joseph, Missouri, or Council Bluffs, Iowa. The trail followed the Platte and Sweetwater Rivers over the Plains. After it crossed the Rockies, the trail split into two paths, one to Oregon Country and the other to California.

The pioneers' journey usually began after the rainy season ended in late spring. The trip lasted about six months. A family of four needed about $600 to buy the supplies necessary for making the trip—a lot of money at a time when laborers made around $1.50 per day. Young families

Major Overland Routes to the West

Interpreting Maps The rough terrain and a lack of constant water supply made many of the overland routes extremely difficult.

Skills Assessment The World in Spatial Terms What trails led between Fort Laramie and Fort Bridger, and what pass allowed settlers to cut through the Rocky Mountains?

made up most groups of settlers. They gathered in wagon trains for the trip. There could be as few as 10 wagons or as many as several dozen in a wagon train.

Shortages of food, supplies, and water were a constant problem for many wagon trains. Pioneers also faced rough weather and natural barriers, such as rivers and mountains. Travelers often got confused over the best route to take.

Pioneers often walked to save their animals' strength. They kept up a tiring pace, traveling from dawn until dusk. Settler Jesse Applegate recalled the advice he received from an experienced Oregon pioneer: "Travel, *travel,* TRAVEL. . . . Nothing is good that causes a moment's delay."

At the end of each day, much work remained to be done, such as unpacking, cooking, cleaning, and looking after children and livestock. Martha Ann Morrison recalled that when the men were busy, "the women helped pitch [set up] the tents, helped unload, and helped yokeing up [harnessing] the cattle." Children helped out their parents with the day-to-day work. One out of every five pioneers was a child.

American Indians from many different groups also helped the pioneers. Indians often acted as guides, carried messages between wagon trains, and traded food for goods. Although newspapers reported American Indian "massacres" of pioneers, few settlers died because of Indian attacks. The settlers who arrived safely in Oregon and California found generally healthy and pleasant climates. They also found fertile valleys for farming. By 1845 about 5,000 settlers occupied the Willamette Valley. Thousands more Americans chose to brave the dangers of the Oregon Trail to find new opportunities in the West.

Pioneers had to make room in their wagons to carry supplies, household goods, and sick people.

✔ **Reading Check: Supporting a Point of View** Do you think that life in the West was worth the risk for families who went there? Explain your answer.

Section 4 Review

go.hrw.com **Homework Practice Online**
keyword: SF3 HP16

1 **Define** and explain:
• mountain men
• rendezvous

2 **Identify** and explain:
• John Jacob Astor
• Marcus and Narcissa Whitman
• Oregon Trail

3 **Summarizing** Copy the web diagram below. Use it to explain why the following groups of people traveled to the Rocky Mountains and farther west and what challenges they faced.

4 **Finding the Main Idea**
a. What factors led to the rise and decline of the fur trade?

b. How did missionaries influence future settlement in Oregon?

5 **Writing and Critical Thinking**
Supporting a Point of View Imagine that you are a pioneer on your way to Oregon. Write a letter to a friend back east to tell him or her about life on the trail.

Consider the following:
• hardships and dangers
• activities and chores
• interactions with American Indians

California and the Southwest

Read to Discover

1. Why did Americans start traveling to California in the early 1800s?
2. Why did American merchants establish a new route to New Mexico?
3. What types of images did frontier artists paint?

Identify

- Donner party
- John Sutter
- Sutter's Fort
- George Catlin

WHY IT MATTERS TODAY

Today the U.S. wilderness is a place for recreation instead of survival. Use CNNfyi.com or other **current events** sources to find out about nature activities around the country. Record your findings in your journal.

This Mexican gold coin was used as currency in California.

The Story Continues

In 1835 American Richard Henry Dana Jr. arrived in San Francisco Bay on board a merchant ship. Dana and the crew spent a few days ashore. He admired the climate, calling it "as near to being perfect as any in the world." He also praised the nearby town of Yerba Buena. It supplied traders and whaling ships with food. Dana's crew then set sail for more destinations on the California coast. As they left the bay, Dana glanced up at the hills and made a prediction. "If California ever becomes a prosperous [rich] country, this bay will be the center of its prosperity."

⭐ Going to California

In the 1830s and 1840s California was still under Mexican rule. The main route to California started with the Oregon Trail. At the Snake River in present-day Idaho, the trail split. Settlers who wanted to go to California took the southern route, known as the California Trail. This route ran through a mountain range called the Sierra Nevada. American emigrants and traders on the California Trail tried to cross these mountains before the season's first snows.

The **Donner party** was a group of western travelers with bad luck and poor judgment. The party began its journey west in the spring of 1846. Trying to find a shortcut, the group left the main trail and got lost. When the Donner party reached the Sierra Nevada, they became trapped by heavy snows. Virginia Reed later wrote to her sister about the party's struggles to survive the winter.

The members of the Donner party found themselves trapped by high snows in the Sierra Nevada.

"There was 15 in the cabin we was in and half of us had to lay [in] a bed all the time. . . . there was 10 starved to death. . . . It snowed and would cover the cabin all over so we could not get out for 2 or 3 days.**"**

—Virginia Reed, quoted in *Ordeal by Hunger: The Story of the Donner Party,* by George R. Stewart

A rescue party found the starving and freezing group in February 1847. Of the original 87 travelers, 42 had died.

Although more Americans were traveling along the California Trail, few actually settled in California. Instead, California became a meeting ground for merchants from Mexico and the United States. American merchants traded manufactured goods for gold and silver coins, cowhides, and tallow (animal fat used to make soap and candles) from Mexico.

Mexicans and American Indians made up most of California's population. Mexican officials did not want many Americans to settle in the province. However, in 1839 they did give Swiss immigrant **John Sutter** permission to start a colony. **Sutter's Fort** was located near the Sacramento River and soon became a popular rest stop for many American immigrants. These new arrivals praised Sutter's generosity and helpfulness. By the mid-1840s some Anglo-Californians were publishing guidebooks encouraging other settlers to move west.

✔ **Reading Check: Finding the Main Idea** Why were most Americans interested in California?

COURTESY OF THE CALIFORNIA HISTORY ROOM, CALIFORNIA STATE LIBRARY, SACRAMENTO, CALIFORNIA

Interpreting the Visual Record

Sutter's Fort *Many Americans chose Sutter's Fort as their destination in California.* ***What parts of this drawing help explain why the colony was called a fort?***

THE GRANGER COLLECTION, NEW YORK

CONNECTING TO
THE ARTS

George Catlin Artists like George Catlin brought images of the West to the rest of the country. Catlin is best known for his paintings of American Indians. From 1830 to 1836 he traveled throughout the western Great Plains. He painted portraits and important events such as buffalo hunts and religious ceremonies. In the East, thousands of people viewed Catlin's paintings. Today his many paintings provide a valuable record of American Indian culture. Why do you think Catlin's paintings were so popular with people in the East?

Analyzing Primary Sources

Drawing Inferences and Conclusions What seems to be Magoffin's reaction to the wreck of the wagon?

 ## Other Southwestern Trails

Other major western trails at this time were mostly used as trade routes to the Southwest rather than as routes for settlers. Unlike the Spanish, the Mexican government agreed to allow American merchants to come to New Mexico. American traders seized this opportunity by starting the Santa Fe Trail.

The trail ran from Independence, Missouri, to Santa Fe, New Mexico. American merchants loaded their wagon trains with cloth and other manufactured goods. In Santa Fe they exchanged these products with Mexican merchants for horses, mules, and silver.

The long trip across the desert and mountains was difficult and dangerous. Yet traders took the risk because a successful journey could earn high profits. The U.S. government also offered these merchants protection by sending troops and providing money to ensure American Indian cooperation. By the mid-1800s the traders were even traveling to southern California by following the Old Spanish Trail, which began in Santa Fe.

In 1846 Susan Shelby Magoffin became one of the first white women to travel on the Santa Fe Trail. She made this dangerous journey with her husband and their load of trade goods. At one point their wagon plunged into a gully, or small valley, an event she later described.

 ❝To see the wreck of that carriage now with the top and sides entirely broken to pieces, [one] could never believe that people had come out of it alive.❞

—Susan Shelby Magoffin, from *Down the Santa Fe Trail and into Mexico*, edited by Stella M. Drumm

✔ **Reading Check: Summarizing** Why did American traders establish the Santa Fe Trail?

⭐ Frontier Artists

Stories of the people and scenery in the West inspired some artists to travel with explorers to the frontier. <u>George Catlin</u> gave up a career as a portrait painter in Philadelphia to go west. He painted more than 500 images of American Indians, including spiritual and military leaders. In 1840 he wrote, "I have visited forty-eight tribes . . . containing in all 400,000 souls." When Catlin returned to the East, thousands of people flocked to his art shows. His paintings were the only images many would ever see of the American West. Catlin made his shows more exciting by showing Indian clothing, giving talks, and telling tales about life in the West.

Artist Alfred Jacob Miller traveled through the Rocky Mountains, painting striking images of the landscape. He also created portraits of the mountain men who hunted and trapped in remote regions. Other artists such as John Mix Stanley and Seth Eastman also painted American Indians and the western environment. Not all of these artists had great talent, and their paintings often exaggerated the things that they saw. Together, however, the works of these artists became extremely popular in the East and in Europe. Their paintings captured people's imaginations and shaped their ideas about the West.

Interpreting the Visual Record

Western art *Frontier artist John Mix Stanley painted* Buffalo Hunt on the Southwestern Plains. *What does this painting suggest about the risks and skills involved in the buffalo hunt?*

✔ **Reading Check: Drawing Inferences and Conclusions** What did western artists depict, and why do you think their work was so popular?

Section 5 Review

go.hrw.com **Homework Practice Online** keyword: SF3 HP16

❶ Identify and explain:
- Donner party
- John Sutter
- Sutter's Fort
- George Catlin

❷ Comparing and Contrasting Copy the diagram below. Use it to compare and contrast the characteristics of the California Trail and the Santa Fe Trail.

California Trail   Santa Fe Trail

❸ Finding the Main Idea
a. Why did some Americans traveling west go to California or New Mexico?

b. Who established the early trails from the United States to the Southwest, and how did the trails benefit others?

❹ Writing and Critical Thinking
Analyzing Information Imagine that you are an art historian studying images of American Indian life in the American West. Write a review of a piece you might see and describe what it represents.

Consider the following:
- how western artists showed American Indian life and culture
- images of landscapes
- artists' personal interest in the West

Chapter 16 Review

The Chapter at a Glance

Examine the visual summary of the chapter below. Use standard grammar, spelling, sentence structure, and punctuation to write a sentence about each label attached to an image in the visual summary. In pairs, discuss the sentences that you write.

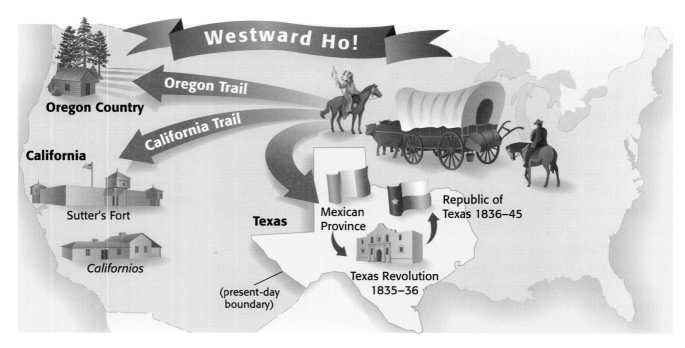

Westward Ho!

Oregon Trail

Oregon Country

California Trail

California

Sutter's Fort

Californios

Texas

Mexican Province

Republic of Texas 1836–45

Texas Revolution 1835–36

(present-day boundary)

Identifying People and Ideas

Use the following terms or people in historically significant sentences.

1. Tejanos
2. Father Miguel Hidalgo y Costilla
3. Stephen F. Austin
4. Sam Houston
5. Battle of San Jacinto
6. annex
7. mountain men
8. John Jacob Astor
9. Sutter's Fort
10. George Catlin

Understanding Main Ideas

Section 1 *(Pages 488–491)*

1. What changes took place in California and Texas soon after Mexico won its independence?

Section 2 *(Pages 492–496)*

2. List in the proper sequence the important events of the Texas Revolution.

Section 3 *(Pages 497–501)*

3. What problems did the Republic of Texas and some of its citizens face?

Section 4 *(Pages 502–507)*

4. Why did different groups of Americans journey west of the Rocky Mountains to Oregon Country?

Section 5 *(Pages 508–511)*

5. What new economic opportunities did California and New Mexico offer?

You Be the Historian— Reviewing Themes

1. **Citizenship** Describe the series of events that led Texans to declare their independence from Mexico.
2. **Culture** How did German immigrants affect the Republic of Texas?
3. **Geography** How was the geography of the Pacific Northwest different from that of the Southwest, and why do you think people settled in each region?

Thinking Critically

1. **Supporting a Point of View** Do you think that the United States should have annexed Texas immediately? Explain your answer.
2. **Analyzing Information** How did religion play a role in the settlement of Oregon Country?
3. **Comparing** What attracted American settlers to Oregon Country and Texas?

Interpreting Maps

Study the map below. Then use the information on the map to help you answer the following questions.

Settlements in Texas, 1850

German area of settlement

French area of settlement

NEW MEXICO TERRITORY

INDIAN TERR.

Disputed

Red River

AR

Ft. Worth

TX

LA

Colorado River

Brazos River

Pedernales R.

Fredericksburg

Austin

Houston

New Braunfels

Castroville

San Antonio

Rio Grande

San Antonio River

Nueces River

MEXICO

Gulf of Mexico

28°N

26°N

96°W   94°W

0   100   200 Miles

0   100   200 Kilometers

Albers Equal-Area Projection

1. What cities were located within the German area of settlement?
   a. Castroville and San Antonio
   b. Fort Worth and Castroville
   c. Fort Worth and Houston
   d. Fredericksburg and New Braunfels

2. Based on your knowledge of the period and the information shown on the map, why do you think Texans moved the capital from Houston to Austin?

Analyzing Primary Sources

Read the following quote by Mrs. W. W. Buck, a pioneer on the Oregon Trail, and then answer the questions that follow.

> **❝**Of course, we were all anxious to hear about the country we were bound for, and our captain said Doctor White, tell us about Oregon. He jumped upon the wagon tongue and all our eyes and ears were open to catch every word. He said: 'Friends, you are traveling to the garden of Eden, a land flowing with milk and honey. And just let me tell you, the clover grows wild all over Oregon, and when you wade [walk] through it, it reaches your chin.' We believed every word, and for days, I thought that not only our men, but our poor tired oxen, stepped lighter for having met Dr. White.**❞**

3. Which of the following statements best describes the reaction of the pioneers to Dr. White's speech?
   a. They were not interested in hearing stories about Oregon.
   b. Some people doubted what Dr. White told them.
   c. They wanted Dr. White to lead their wagon train.
   d. They were happy and encouraged by the news.

4. Based on your knowledge of the period, how do you think Dr. White's description of Oregon compares with the actual situation that settlers in Oregon Country encountered?

Alternative Assessment

Building Your Portfolio

American History

Interdisciplinary Connection to the Arts

Select an artist of the American West and write a critique of one or more of that person's works. Use the library to find information about the artist. Your critique should examine the artist's point of view, use of color, and choice of subject matter. Artists may include, but are not limited to, the following: Albert Bierstadt, George Caleb Bingham, Karl Bodmer, and George Catlin.

🖅 internet connect

Internet Activity: go.hrw.com
keyword: SF3 CF16

Access the Internet through the HRW Go site to locate databases, primary and secondary sources, and interviews about the causes of the Texas Revolution. Then write a report, using these sources to support your point of view. Make sure you evaluate the accuracy of your sources and use standard grammar, punctuation, sentence structure, and spelling in your report.

go.hrw.com

17 Manifest Destiny and War
(1840–1860)

John Gast's 1879 painting shows the spirit of manifest destiny leading settlers and modern technology westward across the continent.

UNITED STATES

1840 William Henry Harrison is elected president.

1845 John O'Sullivan coins the phrase *manifest destiny.* This term is used to promote westward expansion.

1846 The United States declares war on Mexico.

1848 Gold is discovered in California on January 24.

The Treaty of Guadalupe Hidalgo is signed on February 2, ending the Mexican War and granting the United States California and other western territories.

1840	1842	1844	1846	1848

WORLD

1842 China gives Great Britain control of the island of Hong Kong.

1844 The United States negotiates a trade treaty with China.

1847 Liberia, an African nation founded by former slaves from the United States, becomes an independent republic.

This Chinese punch bowl depicts trading centers at the port of Guangzhou (Canton).

China ceded Hong Kong to the British in the Treaty of Nanking.

Build on What You Know

By 1840 the United States was roughly twice its original size. Americans had been moving west ever since the country won its independence. Many Americans believed it was their country's destiny to extend to the Pacific Coast. While this idea encouraged the United States to acquire more territory, it also led to tensions with other nations.

Newly arrived gold-seekers in San Francisco were forced to live in tent communities on Telegraph Hill as the town struggled to keep up with its rapid growth.

Wooden rockers like this one were used for mining gold.

1853 Under the Gadsden Purchase the United States buys part of what is now Arizona and New Mexico from Mexico.

1850 The population of San Francisco exceeds 25,000.

1850	1852	1854	1856	1858

1851 A huge gold rush takes place in the colony of Victoria in Australia.

1852 The South African Republic is created.

1858 Great Britain assumes formal control of India.

The gold found in Victoria was often in the form of nuggets that were of great size and value.

If you were there . . .

How would you react to efforts to make the country even bigger?

You Be the Historian

What's Your Opinion? Do you **agree** or **disagree** with the following statements? Support your point of view in your journal.

- **Global Relations** Nations only grow through conquest.
- **Culture** When different groups first meet, conflict is bound to take place.
- **Geography** Settlers moving to new areas react to the environment just as they did in their old homes.

Manifest Destiny and Expansion

Read to Discover

1. How did Americans' belief in manifest destiny affect western expansion?
2. How did the United States acquire Oregon and Texas?
3. What events led to the Mexican War?

WHY IT MATTERS TODAY

The United States still has close relations with Canada and Mexico today. Use **CNN fyi.com** or other **current events** sources to learn about one policy of the United States today that affects either Canada or Mexico. Record your findings in your journal.

Define
- manifest destiny

Identify
- John O'Sullivan
- John Tyler
- Henry Clay
- James K. Polk
- Zachary Taylor

THE
UNITED STATES MAGAZINE,
AND
DEMOCRATIC REVIEW.

The Democratic Review was one of several magazines that supported western expansion.

The Story Continues

In 1843 South Carolina senator John C. Calhoun gave a speech to Congress. In it he described the great changes he had seen during his lifetime. "In the period of thirty-two years which have elapsed [passed] since I took my seat . . . [the] frontier has receded [moved] 1,000 miles to the west," he noted proudly. Then he talked about the future. "Our population is rolling toward the shores of the Pacific with an impetus [force] greater than what we realize." Calhoun believed that if the United States was patient and avoided unnecessary wars, it would become the strongest nation in the world.

★ The Roots of Manifest Destiny

By the 1840s many Americans shared Senator Calhoun's view. The United States, they thought, was sure to expand all the way to the Pacific Ocean. They believed that nothing could stop this growth from taking place. This expansionist view became known as **manifest destiny**. The term was first used by **John O'Sullivan**, a New York editor.

Interpreting the Visual Record

Heading west *In Emanuel Gottlieb Leutze's painting* Westward the Course of Empire Takes Its Way, *a scout points the way west for the eager settlers.* **Based on this image, do you think the artist has a positive view of westward expansion? Why or why not?**

History Makers Speak

❝The American claim is by the right of our manifest destiny to overspread and to possess the whole of the continent which Providence [God's blessing] has given us for the development of the great experiment of liberty. We are the nation of human progress, and who will, what can, set limits to our onward march?❞

—John O'Sullivan, quoted in *"It's Your Misfortune and None of My Own,"* by Richard White

Analyzing Primary Sources
Identifying Points of View
Why did O'Sullivan think that Americans were meant to rule the continent?

The roots of manifest destiny lay in Americans' economic, political, and social experiences. Many Puritan colonists had believed North America was a promised land that God had given to them so they could set up a new society. This society would then become a religious example to the rest of the world. Puritans hoped others would follow the Protestant teachings of the Reformation.

The American Revolution added to the idea that America was special. Patriots believed that the United States would prove to the rest of the world that democracy could work in a large and growing country. Thomas Jefferson and James Madison also believed that the American people needed new lands to settle to prevent increased social tensions as city populations grew larger.

After the United States became independent, there were strong economic reasons to expand. As the eastern population grew, people sought more room. Farmers wanted more land to grow crops, and industry needed more natural resources. Businesses wanted more markets for American goods. Soon business leaders, pioneers, and politicians were looking to the West and its millions of acres of land.

✔ **Reading Check: Summarizing** What were the social, political, and economic roots of the American belief in manifest destiny?

John O'Sullivan first used the phrase manifest destiny *in his magazine the* Democratic Review.

★ Gone West

By the 1840s many Americans had accepted the idea of manifest destiny. They thought that the United States had been chosen by God to spread its democratic, economic, and religious values. Americans would fulfill this destiny by spreading across the continent. In the process, Americans believed they would bring liberty, improve the land, and spread the Christian gospel. At the same time, this westward movement of people would reduce social tensions in the East, such as overcrowding in the cities. Expansion would allow the growing eastern population to find new opportunities on the frontier.

Belief in manifest destiny encouraged many Americans to build settlements beyond the boundaries of the United States. They moved to places such as California, Oregon, and Texas. Settlers in Oregon were attracted by the rich farmland. One woman, for example, recalled the stories told by an Oregon pioneer, who said, "Friends, you are traveling to the garden of Eden, a land flowing with milk and honey."

There were already thousands of American Indians and Mexicans living in the West. Yet most supporters of manifest destiny ignored this fact. As Americans saw it, the West was not being fully developed by the people living there. Politicians and settlers wanted to bring farms and industry to the region. They felt that by doing this Americans would be improving the West.

✔ **Reading Check: Identifying Points of View** How did believers in manifest destiny view the West?

Expanding Westward

Many Americans believed that the United States had a special destiny to expand across the continent.

Visualizing History

1. **Culture** How do you think people of other cultures and nations viewed the idea of manifest destiny?
2. **Connecting to Today** What special purpose in the world do you think the United States has today?

Social Factors
The desire to spread religious beliefs and ease overcrowding combined with a belief in American superiority

Manifest Destiny

Political Factors
The desire to spread democracy and American ideals of liberty

Economic Factors
The desire for more farmland, more natural resources, and more markets for economic growth

⭐ The Election of 1844

President **John Tyler** helped make western expansion an important subject in the election of 1844. Tyler had been elected as William Henry Harrison's vice president in 1840. He became president when Harrison died in April 1841. Tyler was a pro-slavery Whig from Virginia, who wanted to extend the political power of the southern slave states. Tyler believed that the annexation of Texas would help by adding another slave state to the country.

Tyler's ideas about Texas started a national debate. Many Whigs disagreed with his expansionist beliefs. As a result, he was too unpopular within his own party to win the 1844 presidential nomination. Instead, the Whigs chose Senator **Henry Clay** of Kentucky as their candidate. When Clay began his presidential campaign, he said he was against the annexation of Texas. After being pressured by southern voters, however, he decided halfheartedly to support annexation. Many of his original backers became angry when Clay changed his mind. The Democratic Party chose former Tennessee governor **James K. Polk** as its presidential candidate. Unlike Clay, Polk strongly favored acquiring both Texas and Oregon.

The idea of manifest destiny played an important part in the campaign. There were rumors that the Republic of Texas might end slavery, and southern politicians feared the loss of a potential slave state. It was also rumored that independent Texas might become an ally of Great Britain. If this were to happen, Americans would again be facing British power, this time at the Texas border.

When the votes had been counted, Polk had defeated Clay by a very narrow margin. Clay believed his defeat was caused by "a most extraordinary combination of adverse [bad] circumstances." Polk, on the other hand, insisted that the American people had voted for his views on westward expansion.

✔ **Reading Check: Finding the Main Idea** What were the major issues in the election of 1844, and how did the major political parties view them?

THE GRANGER COLLECTION, NEW YORK

James K. Polk

James K. Polk was born into a wealthy Tennessee farming family in 1795. After graduating from college, Polk practiced law before serving in the House of Representatives. He became Speaker of the House and later served as governor of Tennessee. However, Polk was not well known nationally when nominated by the Democratic Party as its presidential candidate. He did not let this discourage him during the campaign. He promised voters that as president he would make every effort to annex Texas and acquire Oregon. As president, Polk considered himself "the hardest working man in this country." **What were Polk's major goals as president?**

⭐ Acquiring New Territory

President Polk quickly set out to fulfill his campaign promises. He was sure that he could bring Oregon and Texas into the United States. In the 1810s and 1820s Russia and Spain had given up their claims to Oregon Country. Britain and the United States had agreed to occupy the area together. As more Americans settled there, they began to ask that Oregon become part of the United States. Polk wanted to protect these settlers' interests. Some politicians saw other opportunities. They thought that Oregon Country would offer a Pacific port for the growing U. S. trade with China.

Research on the R●M

Free Find:
Oregon
After reading about Oregon on the **Holt Researcher CD–ROM,** create a line graph showing the increase in Oregon's population after it became a U.S. territory.

Interpreting the Visual Record

New settlements *As more pioneers came to Oregon Country, they began founding settlements such as Oregon City, built in 1829 along the Willamette River.* **What environmental features do you see in the picture that might have made this a good place for settlers to live?**

Meanwhile, Britain and the United States disagreed over where in Oregon to draw the U.S.-Canada border. War between the two countries seemed possible. American expansionists cried, "Fifty-four forty or fight!" This slogan referred to the 54°40' parallel, the line to which Americans wanted their northern territory to extend. However, neither side truly wanted a war. Congressman Robert C. Winthrop expressed this wish. "This question, from its very nature, is . . . one for negotiation, compromise, and amicable [friendly] adjustment." In 1846 Britain and the United States signed a treaty that gave the United States all Oregon land south of the 49th parallel. This treaty drew the present-day border between Canada and the United States in the Pacific Northwest. Oregon became a U.S. territory in August 1848.

Polk and his supporters also wanted to acquire Texas. By March 1845 Congress had already approved annexation and needed only the support of the Republic of Texas. Many Americans continued to move to Texas, and Texas politicians hoped that joining the United States would help solve the republic's financial and military problems. Editor John O'Sullivan spoke for the expansionists. He wrote, "It is time . . . for common sense to give in to what is inevitable." The Texas Congress approved annexation in June, and Texas became the 28th state in December 1845. This action angered the Mexican government, which considered Texas a "stolen province."

✔ **Reading Check: Summarizing** How did compromise settle the dispute over Oregon?

THE GRANGER COLLECTION, NEW YORK

⭐ War Breaks Out

Mexico reacted to the annexation of Texas by cutting off all diplomatic ties with the United States. Mexico also ordered American settlers to leave California and banned further American immigration there. The Mexican government continued to reject the Texas and U.S. claim that the Rio Grande marked the southern border of Texas, arguing that the real southern border lay along the Nueces River farther north.

The artwork on this cigar case shows General Zachary Taylor leading his troops across the Rio Grande.

In June 1845 Polk ordered General **Zachary Taylor** to take U.S. troops into the disputed border region. Polk said that this force was intended to protect Texas from a possible Mexican attack. Meanwhile, Polk sent diplomat John Slidell to Mexico City to negotiate the Texas boundary dispute. The president also told Slidell to offer to buy California and New Mexico from the Mexican government for $30 million. However, when Slidell arrived in Mexico City, officials there refused to speak to him, making negotiations impossible.

In March 1846 General Taylor led his troops to the Rio Grande and made camp. In April the Mexican commander insisted that General Taylor remove the U.S. forces from the region, or else "arms and arms alone must decide the question." Taylor refused to move. Mexican soldiers then crossed the river and attacked a group of 63 U.S. soldiers. They killed 11 Americans, wounded 5 others, and captured the rest.

When the news reached Polk, he quickly prepared to inform Congress. On May 11, 1846, Polk declared, "Mexico has shed American blood upon the American soil." Polk's war message had its desired effect. Two days later Congress declared war on Mexico.

✔ **Reading Check: Identifying Cause and Effect** What problem arose from the annexation of Texas, and what happened as a result?

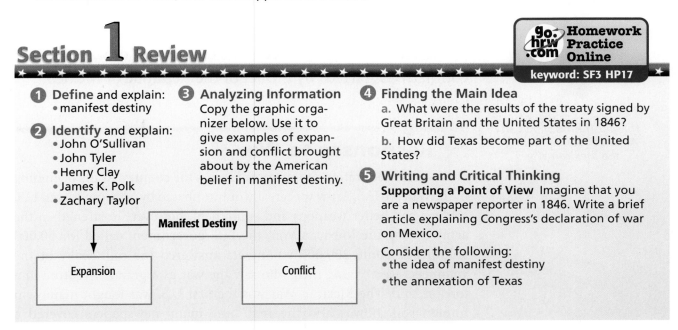

Section 1 Review

go.hrw.com **Homework Practice Online** keyword: SF3 HP17

1 **Define and explain:**
• manifest destiny

2 **Identify and explain:**
• John O'Sullivan
• John Tyler
• Henry Clay
• James K. Polk
• Zachary Taylor

3 **Analyzing Information** Copy the graphic organizer below. Use it to give examples of expansion and conflict brought about by the American belief in manifest destiny.

Manifest Destiny

→ Expansion

→ Conflict

4 **Finding the Main Idea**
a. What were the results of the treaty signed by Great Britain and the United States in 1846?

b. How did Texas become part of the United States?

5 **Writing and Critical Thinking**
Supporting a Point of View Imagine that you are a newspaper reporter in 1846. Write a brief article explaining Congress's declaration of war on Mexico.

Consider the following:
• the idea of manifest destiny
• the annexation of Texas

The Mexican War

Read to Discover

1. How did Americans react to the declaration of war against Mexico?
2. What were the major events and battles of the war?
3. What were the terms of the treaty that ended the Mexican War?

WHY IT MATTERS TODAY

Nations and groups continue to go to war with one another. Use CNN fyi.com or other **current events** sources to learn about an armed conflict somewhere in the world today. Record your findings in your journal.

Identify

- Henry David Thoreau
- Stephen Kearny
- Bear Flag Revolt
- John C. Frémont
- Winfield Scott
- Treaty of Guadalupe Hidalgo
- Mexican Cession
- Gadsden Purchase

This illustration shows an American soldier during the Mexican War.

The Story Continues

The days following Polk's war message to Congress were full of angry debate. Some members of the Whig Party believed that the president had intentionally started the conflict with Mexico. Congressman Garrett Davis of Kentucky spoke bitterly. "It is our own President who began this war." The House of Representatives, however, stood firmly by the president. The House stated in its declaration of war that the conflict was started "by the act of the Republic of Mexico."

★ Responses to War

News of the declaration of war spread across the country. At the beginning of the war, the U.S. Army was greatly outnumbered by Mexican forces. U.S. soldiers had better weapons and equipment, however. To strengthen the army during the Mexican War, the U.S. government called for 50,000 volunteers. Some 200,000 volunteers answered the call. Many of the volunteers were young men who saw the war as a grand adventure in a foreign land. The Mexican War was the first U.S. war fought mainly on foreign soil. It was also the first time many newspapers covered a

U.S. conflict. Reporters used horses to send articles back East quickly. In addition, the war was one of the first to be photographed.

On the home front, many men and women supported the soldiers. They collected supplies and wrote patriotic poems and songs. One popular war song urged soldiers to "Arm and strike for liberty!" For many Americans the war led to greater national pride. Many people who supported the war argued that it would spread republican values.

Not all Americans supported the war, however. Many members of the Whig Party thought that the conflict was unjustified and unnecessary. The conflict also upset people who were against expansion or war. Transcendentalist writer and philosopher **Henry David Thoreau** went to jail for refusing to pay taxes because he believed they would support the war in Mexico.

Northern abolitionists opposed the Mexican War, fearing that the United States might gain lands in the Southwest. If so, they reasoned, southern states would try to establish slavery in these new lands. But some pro-slavery southerners worried that new territories might choose to ban slavery. This concern led southern politicians such as John C. Calhoun to question the goals of the Mexican War. Thoreau's fellow transcendentalist Ralph Waldo Emerson predicted that these disagreements over the Mexican War would further divide Americans.

This painting shows Mexican cavalry charging U.S. Army cannons in the Battle of Palo Alto.

 History Makers Speak

"The United States will conquer Mexico, but it will be as the man swallows the arsenic [a poison], which brings him down in turn. Mexico will poison us.**"**

—Ralph Waldo Emerson, quoted in *Battle Cry of Freedom*, by James M. McPherson

✔ **Reading Check: Summarizing** What reasons did Americans such as Henry David Thoreau give for opposing the Mexican War?

Analyzing Primary Sources

Drawing Inferences and Conclusions What do you think Emerson meant when he said that "Mexico will poison us"?

★ American Victories

While supporters and opponents of the war argued, the fighting had already started. Even before the official declaration of war, General Zachary Taylor's soldiers fought and won battles south of the Nueces River. He defeated Mexican forces at Palo Alto and Resaca de la Palma on May 8 and 9, 1846. Taylor's victories drove the Mexican troops back into Mexico. Taylor then crossed the Rio Grande and occupied Matamoros. While Taylor waited for reinforcements, Polk ordered Brigadier General **Stephen Kearny** to attack New Mexico. Kearny took the city of Santa Fe without a fight. He claimed the entire territory of New Mexico for the United States. Then Kearny marched toward southern California in June 1846.

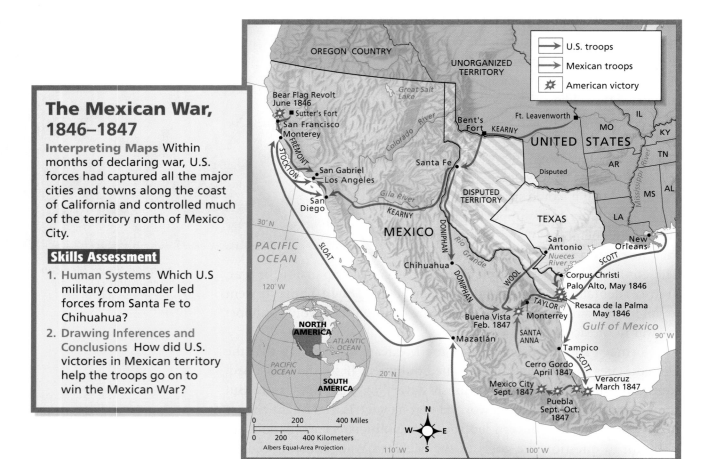

The Mexican War, 1846–1847

Interpreting Maps Within months of declaring war, U.S. forces had captured all the major cities and towns along the coast of California and controlled much of the territory north of Mexico City.

Skills Assessment

1. **Human Systems** Which U.S military commander led forces from Santa Fe to Chihuahua?

2. **Drawing Inferences and Conclusions** How did U.S. victories in Mexican territory help the troops go on to win the Mexican War?

California settlers raised this flag in 1846 to declare their independence from Mexico.

At the same time, a small group of American settlers near the town of Sonoma revolted against the Californios. These rebels declared that California was an independent republic. To represent this new nation, the rebels created a flag with a single star and a grizzly bear. As a result, the rebellion was called the **Bear Flag Revolt**. Army explorer **John C. Frémont** played an important part in the revolt. Frémont had been leading an expedition across the Sierra Nevada when he heard that the United States might go to war with Mexico. Frémont returned to the Sacramento Valley. Upon his arrival, he encouraged Americans to revolt and then joined them.

While the revolt was taking place, the U.S. Navy took Monterey, the capital of the Mexican province of California. Naval forces then planned another invasion of California, aided by the arrival of Kearny's army from New Mexico. The towns of San Diego, Los Angeles, and San Francisco soon fell to the Americans. In August 1846, Commodore Robert Stockton declared that California belonged to the United States. Some Californios continued to resist until early 1847, when they surrendered. General Kearny was appointed governor of California by President Polk.

✔ **Reading Check: Summarizing** How did the United States gain control of California during the Mexican War?

★ The War's End

In Mexico, Taylor finally got his reinforcements. His army soon drove the Mexican army deeper into Mexico. At the heavily fortified city of Monterrey, U.S. troops won a hard-fought battle. Both sides spent a few months trying to improve their positions. General Santa Anna then took over Mexico's government. He led his army north in February 1847, clashing with Taylor's forces at Buena Vista.

Santa Anna sent the outnumbered U.S. soldiers a note demanding their surrender, but General Taylor refused. After two days of hard fighting, Santa Anna's men retreated under the cover of darkness.

Taylor's success earned him popularity with his troops and back home. Soldiers called him Old Rough-and-Ready. Taylor's popularity troubled President Polk, who feared the general might run for president in 1848. Polk was also concerned that Taylor might not be able to win the war. For these reasons, Polk gave the command to General **Winfield Scott**, known as Old Fuss and Feathers.

Scott sailed down to the port of Veracruz, which was the strongest fortress in Mexico. On March 29, after an 88-hour artillery attack, Veracruz fell to Scott's army. The next part of the plan was to attack Mexico City.

Scott's men pushed some 200 miles inland to the heart of Mexico. Santa Anna tried to stop the U.S. forces at Cerro Gordo in mid-April. With a daring uphill attack on the Mexican position, U.S. soldiers won a key victory. By August 1847, U.S. troops were at the edge of Mexico City.

After a truce failed to end the war, Scott ordered a massive attack on Mexico City. Mexican soldiers and civilians fought fiercely. At a military school atop the steep and fortified hill of Chapultepec, young cadets bravely defended their position. Finally, on September 14, 1847, U.S. soldiers captured the Mexican capital.

✔ **Reading Check: Sequencing** List the major battles that brought an end to the Mexican War in their proper sequence.

Interpreting the Visual Record

The end of the war *U.S. soldiers entered Mexico City in September 1847. Santa Anna fled the country soon afterward.* **What does the painting suggest about the culture of Mexico?**

525

★★★★★★★★★★★★★★
That's Interesting!
★★★★★★★★★★★★★★

An Unpopular Peace Can you imagine being fired for negotiating a peace treaty? That's what happened to Nicholas Trist. President Polk had sent Trist, a State Department official, to help end the war with Mexico. Trist had little success for months, but he finally got his chance when Scott captured Mexico City. However, Polk had ordered Trist back to Washington to receive new instructions. Not wanting to lose his chance for a treaty, the diplomat ignored his orders. He stayed in Mexico and negotiated the Treaty of Guadalupe Hidalgo. When Polk first heard about the treaty, he was so angry that he fired Trist!

The Treaty of Guadalupe Hidalgo

★ More New Territories

The war ended after Scott took Mexico City. The **Treaty of Guadalupe Hidalgo** marked the new peace. Signed in February 1848, it ceded, or turned over, much of Mexico's northern territory to the United States. Known as the **Mexican Cession**, this land included the present-day states of California, Nevada, and Utah. It also included most of Arizona and New Mexico and parts of Colorado and Wyoming. The United States also got the area claimed by Texas north of the Rio Grande. The Mexican Cession totaled more than 500,000 square miles. It increased the size of the United States by almost 25 percent. The United States agreed to pay Mexico $15 million and to assume claims of more than $3 million held by American citizens against Mexico. The treaty also addressed the status of Mexicans in the Mexican Cession.

The treaty itself caused a controversy. Some Americans wanted to take all of Mexico. Antislavery and antiwar activists, people who thought that Mexicans would not make good republican citizens, and Whigs were all against the treaty. Polk answered them by pointing out the benefits the United States would gain from the treaty. The Senate ratified the treaty in March 1848. James Gadsden, U.S. minister to Mexico, negotiated the **Gadsden Purchase** in December 1853. Under the terms of the purchase, the U.S. government paid Mexico $10 million for the southern parts of what are now Arizona and New Mexico. With this purchase, the continental boundaries of the United States were finally fixed.

✔ **Reading Check: Finding the Main Idea** How did the American victory in the Mexican War affect the United States?

Section 2 Review

★★★

go.hrw.com **Homework Practice Online**
keyword: SF3 HP17

1 **Identify** and explain:
• Henry David Thoreau
• Stephen Kearny
• Bear Flag Revolt
• John C. Frémont
• Winfield Scott
• Treaty of Guadalupe Hidalgo
• Mexican Cession
• Gadsden Purchase

2 **Sequencing** Copy the graphic organizer below. Use it to show the sequence of major events leading to the end of the Mexican War.

Treaty of Guadalupe Hidalgo

Annexation of Texas

3 **Finding the Main Idea**
a. Why did some Americans support the Mexican War, and what reasons did other Americans give for opposing the war?

b. What did each side gain in the Treaty of Guadalupe Hidalgo?

4 **Writing and Critical Thinking**
Summarizing Imagine that you are a U.S. soldier in California during the Mexican War. Write a short report to your commanders describing how the United States gained control of California.

Consider the following:
• Polk's offer to buy California
• the Bear Flag Revolt
• actions by Kearny's and Stockton's forces

Literature

"Civil Disobedience"

Henry David Thoreau

Transcendentalist Henry David Thoreau was one of many Americans who protested the Mexican War. He even went to jail rather than pay taxes to help fight the war. His belief in peaceful resistance later inspired leaders around the world. Mohandas Gandhi of India and Martin Luther King Jr. of the United States followed his ideas. In his essay "Civil Disobedience," Thoreau discusses an individual's personal responsibility to society.

Henry David Thoreau argued for nonviolent opposition to the Mexican War.

I heartily accept the motto, "That government is best which governs least"; and I should like to see it acted up to more rapidly and **systematically**.[1] Carried out, it finally amounts to this, which also I believe—"That government is best which governs not at all"; and when men are prepared for it, that will be the kind of government which they will have. Government is at best but an **expedient**;[2] but most governments are usually, and all governments are sometimes, **inexpedient**[3]. . . . The government itself, which is only the **mode**[4] which the people have chosen to execute their will, is equally liable to be abused and **perverted**[5] before the people can act through it. Witness the present Mexican war, the work of . . . a few individuals using the standing government as their tool; for, in the outset, the people would not have consented to this measure. . . .

Unjust laws exist: shall we be content to obey them, or shall we **endeavor**[6] to amend them, and obey them until we have succeeded, or shall we **transgress**[7] them at once? Men generally, under such a government as this, think that they ought to wait until they have persuaded the majority to alter them [the laws]. They think that, if they should resist, the remedy would be worse than the evil. But it is the fault of the government

itself that the remedy is worse than the evil. It makes it worse. Why is it not more **apt**[8] to anticipate and provide for reform? Why does it not cherish its wise minority . . . ?

If the injustice is part of the necessary friction of the machine of government, let it go, let it go: **perchance**[9] it will wear smooth—certainly the machine will wear out. If the injustice has a spring, or a pulley, or a rope, or a crank, exclusively for itself, then perhaps you may consider whether the remedy will not be worse than the evil; but if it is of such a nature that it requires you to be the agent of injustice to another, then, I say, break the law.

Understanding What You Read

1. **Literature and History** Under what conditions does Thoreau support breaking the law?
2. **Literature and You** Do you agree with Thoreau that it is acceptable to peacefully break a law that has been passed by the government? Why or why not?

---

[1]**systematically:** regularly
[2]**expedient:** means to an end
[3]**inexpedient:** unwise
[4]**mode:** method
[5]**perverted:** twisted
[6]**endeavor:** try
[7]**transgress:** break
[8]**apt:** suitable
[9]**perchance:** maybe

More Settlers Head West

Read to Discover

1. What conflicts did new U.S. settlement cause in the Southwest?
2. How did various cultures interact in the Southwest?
3. Why did the Mormons move to the West, and what were their achievements there?

WHY IT MATTERS TODAY

California, Texas, and the Southwest continue to be areas of rapid growth today. Use **CNN fyi.com** or other **current events** sources to learn about a city or region in the West or Southwest that is experiencing growth due to immigration or migration. Record your findings in your journal.

Identify

- Joseph Smith
- Mormons
- Brigham Young
- Mormon Trail

THE SQUATTER

AND

THE DON.

A NOVEL DESCRIPTIVE OF CONTEMPORARY OCCURRENCES IN CALIFORNIA.

C. LOYAL.

SAN FRANCISCO
1885

COURTESY THE BANCROFT LIBRARY

The Squatter and the Don described the efforts of a Californio family to keep their land.

The Story Continues

In her novel *The Squatter and the Don,* María Amparo Ruiz de Burton described the struggles of the Californios. A Californio landowner herself, Ruiz de Burton put her family's anger and despair into the words of her characters. "Is it possible that there is no law to protect us; to protect our property?" asked Doña Josefa Alamar. "The treaty said that our rights would be the same as those enjoyed by all other American citizens," Don Mariano Alamar answered her. "[But] we have had no one to speak for us."

★ Conflicts over Land

After the Mexican War, a flood of traders, trappers, settlers, and speculators moved to the Southwest. Most Mexicans, Mexican Americans, and American Indians faced legal, economic, and social discrimination. American newcomers struggled against longtime residents to control the land. They also competed to control other valuable resources, such as water and minerals.

Interpreting the Visual Record

New customs *This image shows a Mexican family in the 1800s making tortillas at home. **What customs do you see in the image that American settlers might adopt from this family?***

The Treaty of Guadalupe Hidalgo promised to protect the property rights of residents of the Mexican Cession. However, the U.S. government often made Mexican American landowners go to court to prove that they had titles to their land. These legal battles often bankrupted landowners. In the 1850s magazine writer John S. Hittell described the situation faced by Californios.

History Makers Speak

"It was not their fault that the Mexican land system differed from the American. . . . It was severe hardship for owners of land under grants from Mexico, that they should be required to sue the government of the United States, or lose their land."

—John S. Hittell, from *A Documentary History of the Mexican Americans,* edited by Wayne Moquin with Charles Van Doren

Analyzing Primary Sources

Identifying Points of View Why does Hittell think that Mexican landowners were treated unfairly?

In other areas, new settlers usually ignored Mexican legal ideas such as community property or community water rights. Conflicts over the ownership of cattle and sheep were also common. Some rich Tejanos tried to protect their property by marrying into powerful Anglo families.

The steady arrival of new settlers and the policies of the U.S. government greatly affected American Indians in the Southwest. In some areas, new white settlers soon outnumbered Indians. These settlers often tried to take control of valuable water resources and grazing lands. Settlers rarely respected Indian holy places, such as mountain lakes and burial grounds. Sometimes Indian raiding parties took settlers' cattle and attacked settlements. In response, angry westerners fought the raiding parties. They also often attacked Indian peoples or villages that were not involved in the fighting, thus causing new conflicts.

✔ **Reading Check: Identifying Cause and Effect** What were the causes and results of conflict between Anglo settlers, Mexican Americans, and American Indians?

Interpreting the Visual Record

San Antonio *By 1860, San Antonio had become the largest city in Texas.* **What qualities of the city shown in this painting do you think would attract settlers?**

COURTESY OF THE WITTE MUSEUM, SAN ANTO-

★ Cultural Encounters

Despite conflicts, American Indian, Mexican, and Anglo cultures influenced one another in the Southwest. As American settlers made homes there, they adopted some of the customs and practices of the peoples they met.

In settlements with large Mexican American populations, laws were often printed in both English and Spanish. The Spanish language was also important in trade and daily life, especially in California, New Mexico, and Texas. Place-names such as San Antonio, San Diego, and Taos show the Mexican and American Indian heritage of the Southwest. Communities throughout the Southwest regularly celebrated both Mexican and American holidays. One example was Diez y Seis de Septiembre, which celebrates the declaration of the Grito de Dolores in Mexico in 1810. This holiday became popular in Texas. In addition, there were numbers of French and German immigrants in towns of Central Texas. In these towns, people kept many of their traditional customs.

Mexican and American Indian knowledge and traditions also shaped the local economies of many American communities in the Southwest. Mexican Americans taught Anglo settlers about mining in the rugged mountains. The ranching communities of the West were first started by Mexican settlers. These communities grew as new ranchers moved in and new markets opened. In addition, Mexican Americans introduced new types of saddles, clothing, and other equipment to American ranchers. Adobe, a building material originally developed by the Anasazi, was adopted from the Pueblo by the Spanish. It was commonly used in Arizona, California, and New Mexico. In addition, new settlers adopted Mexican and American Indian foods such as beans, tamales, and tortillas.

Trade also changed the Southwest and the people living there. Even small communities were pulled into the growing market economy. For example, the Navajo made more handwoven woolen blankets to sell to Americans. The Navajo also became known as skilled silversmiths. They had learned the metalworking craft from Mexican American settlers.

Americans, in turn, brought manufactured goods and money to the Southwest. They brought new firearms and other trade goods. Settlers and traders also brought new breeds of animals from elsewhere in the United States. As a result, the economies of many Mexican American and American Indian communities in the Southwest began to change.

✔ **Reading Check: Categorizing** What cultural and economic influences did American Indians and Mexican Americans have on Anglo settlers in the Mexican Cession?

This Navajo woman is using traditional methods to weave a woolen blanket.

⭐ The Mormons

One group of American settlers traveled to the West in search of religious freedom. In 1830 a young man named **Joseph Smith** founded the Church of Jesus Christ of Latter-Day Saints in western New York. The members of this church became known as **Mormons**. Smith told his followers that he had found and translated a set of golden tablets containing religious revelations. These writings became the Book of Mormon.

The Mormons stressed hard work and community, and their church membership grew rapidly. However, some Mormon beliefs and practices made them the target of persecution. For example, some Mormon men practiced polygamy—in which one man is married to several women at the same time.

In the early 1830s Smith and his growing number of converts left New York. They formed new communities, first in Ohio and then in Missouri. The Ohio settlement's bank went under during the Panic of 1837. Moving on to Missouri, Mormons left their settlement when they were chased away by a mob of local people. Their next settlement, at Nauvoo, Illinois, was quite successful. The city grew to some 20,000 converts. But an anti-Mormon mob murdered Smith in jail in 1844. "I can tell you it is a sorrowful time here at present," wrote Mormon Sarah Scott after Smith's death. Following Smith's murder, **Brigham Young** became the head of the Mormon Church. The Mormons decided to move west to build a new community. Young chose what is now Utah as the group's new home. At the time, Utah was still Mexican territory, outside the boundaries of the United States.

Young was a gifted leader who carefully planned the long trip west. An advance party arrived at a pass overlooking the Great Salt Lake in July 1847. Follower Erastus Snow recalled Young's words: "This is the place whereon we will plant our feet." These pioneers began preparing the area for other Mormon immigrants.

Tens of thousands of Mormons took to the **Mormon Trail**. Many pushed or pulled heavy handcarts along the rough ground. Mormons

Water Usage in the West

When the Mormons arrived at the Great Salt Lake in Utah, they saw a barren plain. Mormon leader Brigham Young created strict rules about water use. Young allowed individuals to build dams, but they had to use the water for beneficial purposes such as farming, mining, or manufacturing. In any dispute over water use, the good of the community outweighed the interests of individuals.

In 1902 the federal government created the Bureau of Reclamation. The bureau built dams, reservoirs, and canals to bring additional water to dry western regions. Today the bureau manages all the water in 17 states west of the Mississippi River. **How has the environment shaped federal water management in the West?**

Interpreting the Visual Record

The Mormon Trail *After Joseph Smith was murdered, Mormons moved west to Utah.* **What challenges does the illustration show the Mormons facing?**

fleeing persecution in the East and the Midwest were joined by converts immigrating to America from Great Britain and Scandinavia.

The Mormons selected a desert valley for their new home and established a very disciplined community. "Those that do not like our looks and customs are at liberty to go where they please," Brigham Young declared. The main Mormon settlement at Salt Lake City became a thriving community with broad roads and surrounding farms. After his arrival in 1847, Young chose the site for the Mormons' Great Temple. In December 1860 the Mormon population of Utah stood at about 40,000.

✔ **Reading Check:** **Finding the Main Idea** Why did Mormons move to the West?

Section 3 Review

go.hrw.com

Homework Practice Online

keyword: SF3 HP17

1 **Identify** and explain:
• Joseph Smith
• Mormons
• Brigham Young
• Mormon Trail

2 **Summarizing** Copy the chart below. Use it to show three factors that made interaction among new Anglo settlers, Mexican Americans, and American Indians difficult in the Mexican Cession.

Factors	Groups Affected

3 **Finding the Main Idea**
a. What conflicts arose among American settlers, American Indians, and Mexican Americans as more settlers moved into the West and the Southwest?

b. What caused the Mormons to move to the West, and what did they accomplish there?

4 **Writing and Critical Thinking**
Analyzing Information Imagine that you are a traveler to the Southwest in the mid-1800s. Write a journal entry describing how Mexican, American Indian, and Anglo cultures are mingling in the region.

Consider the following:
• characteristics of American Indian, Anglo, and Mexican cultures
• the idea of manifest destiny
• conflicts between the three cultures

The Gold Rush

Read to Discover

1. Why did many people head west to California in 1849?
2. What was life like in gold rush mining camps and towns?
3. How did the gold rush change California?

WHY IT MATTERS TODAY

Individuals, corporations, and nations still search for and use Earth's mineral wealth. Use CNNfyi.com or other **current events** sources to learn about discoveries of oil, precious metals, or other minerals in recent years. Record your findings in your journal.

Define

• forty-niners
• prospect

Identify

• California Gold Rush
• Biddy Mason

The Story Continues

In the early 1840s there were still relatively few Americans in California. On January 24, 1848, James W. Marshall made a discovery that suddenly changed this situation. Marshall recalled that he was working that day near Sutter's Mill in California when he glanced down. "My eye was caught with the glimpse of something shining in the bottom of the ditch. . . . I reached my hand down and picked it up; it made my heart thump, for I was certain it was gold. The piece was about half the size and of the shape of a pea."

Advertisements like this one encouraged travelers to move to California.

⭐ The Forty-Niners

John Sutter, the owner of Sutter's Mill, soon learned that gold had been discovered on his property. At first, according to Sutter, he could not believe it. "I thought something had touched Marshall's brain." When Sutter saw the gold, however, he "was fairly thunderstruck." Both men agreed to keep the discovery a secret. However, when they went to examine the work site the next day, they met a Spanish-speaking Indian worker holding a nugget and shouting, "Oro [gold]! Oro! Oro!" Sutter's workers soon quit to search for gold. Stories of the discovery spread across the country. President Polk added to the national excitement by

Map legend:
- Gold mining area
- Leading gold mine
- Trails to California
- Leading supply route

UTAH TERR.

Truckee R.

Lake Tahoe

Carson River

Sacramento River

SIERRA NEVADA

American R.

Sutter's Fort (Sacramento)

Sutter's Mill

CALIFORNIA

January 24, 1848: James Marshall discovers gold while building a sawmill.

San Joaquin R.

Stockton

San Francisco

By 1850, San Francisco grows to a booming port of more than 25,000 people.

PACIFIC OCEAN

0   20   40 Miles
0   20   40 Kilometers
Albers Equal-Area Projection

The California Gold Rush

Interpreting Maps California drew national attention after the discovery of gold at Sutter's Mill.

Skills Assessment Places and Regions What city is located at the junction of three trails and a supply route?

Mining tools

confirming the California gold strike in his farewell message to Congress in December 1848.

In 1849 the **California Gold Rush** caused a huge rise in California's population. That year about 80,000 gold-seekers came to California, hoping to strike it rich. These migrants were known as **forty-niners**. As one Iowa woman who left with her husband to find gold recalled, "At that time the 'gold fever' was contagious, and few, old, or young, escaped the malady [sickness]." Nearly 80 percent of the forty-niners were Americans, while the rest came from all over the world.

Most of the forty-niners braved long and often dangerous journeys to reach California. Many easterners and Europeans took one of two major sea routes. One route went down the Atlantic coast and up the Pacific coast of South America. The other combined ship and land travel across Nicaragua or the Isthmus of Panama. The trip around Cape Horn at the tip of South America took six to nine months but was fairly safe. The Central American route was much shorter, but travelers had to cross jungles. They risked catching deadly diseases such as malaria or yellow fever.

Midwestern gold-seekers usually traveled west in wagon trains along overland routes. Some of these forty-niners took a northern route from Missouri or Iowa through the South Pass of the Rocky Mountains. Others followed a southern trail that went through Santa Fe and the southwestern deserts. With luck, a wagon train could cover the roughly 2,000 miles to the gold fields in about three months. Overland travelers were commonly delayed by poor planning, bad weather, and rough ground, however. Many travelers did not bring enough water and other supplies to last through the hot Nevada deserts. Buying supplies along the way was very expensive.

Whatever their method of travel, most forty-niners arrived in San Francisco. The port town had a fine natural harbor and was located close to the newly discovered gold strikes. For these reasons, San Francisco became a convenient trade center and stopping point for travelers. As a result, San Francisco grew more rapidly than any other city in the world at the time. Its population jumped from about 800 in March 1848 to more than 25,000 by 1850.

✔ **Reading Check: Identifying Cause and Effect** Why did the forty-niners go to California, and what effect did they have on the area's population?

⭐ Gold Fever

Few of the forty-niners had any previous gold-mining experience. Some people had quick success. Most of the forty-niners, however, found the work to be difficult and time-consuming. The forty-niners would **prospect**, or search, for gold along the banks of streams or in shallow surface mines. The early forty-niners worked an area that ran for 70 miles in northern California. Later, the forty-niners began searching for gold in the Sierra Nevada mountain range.

Early miners frequently banded together to prospect for gold. The first person to arrive at a site would "stake a claim." The miners agreed that each would keep a share of whatever gold was discovered. When one group abandoned a claim, more recent arrivals often took it over, hoping for success. Sometimes two or more groups staked rival claims in the same area. In the early gold rush days, before courts were established, this competition led to conflicts—some of them violent.

CONNECTING TO
SCIENCE AND TECHNOLOGY

Early Mining Methods

Most gold miners in California searched for gold by using water to separate gold particles from lighter rock and dirt. Common tools included pans and larger wooden devices such as cradles, rockers, and sluice boxes. To get the steady flow of water they needed, miners often built small dams and directed the water to their claims. Sometimes the miners' digging and tree cutting caused soil erosion. Piles of dirt and rock washed downstream from mining camps, clogging rivers. **How did mining sometimes affect the environment?**

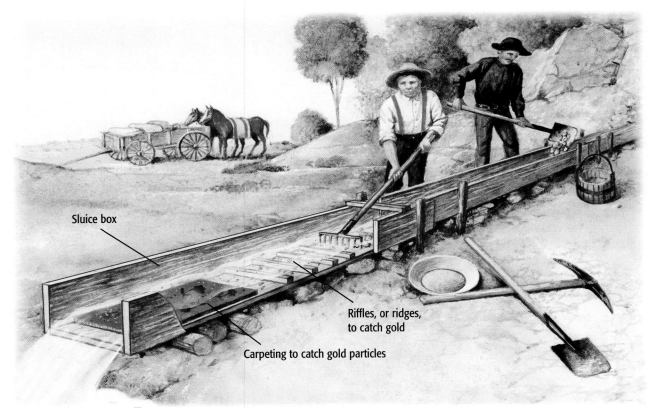

Sluice box

Riffles, or ridges, to catch gold

Carpeting to catch gold particles

In 1853 California's yearly gold production peaked at more than $60 million. Individual success stories inspired many miners. One lucky man got two and a half pounds of gold after only 15 minutes of work. Two African American miners found a rich gold deposit that became known as Negro Hill in honor of their discovery. But the vast majority of gold rush miners did not become rich. Forty-niner Alonzo Delano commented that the "lean, meager [thin], worn-out and woe-begone [sorrowful] miner . . . might daily be seen at almost every point in the upper mines." The good luck that made some miners wealthy never came to thousands of gold-seekers. Most of them found little but misery and debt.

✔ **Reading Check: Finding the Main Idea** How successful were most of the forty-niners?

★ Mining Camps and Towns

Mining camps sprang up wherever enough people gathered to look for gold. Mining camps often disappeared as quickly as they were built, as rich claims opened up and other claims dried out. Miners found themselves making money one day and broke the next. Under these circumstances, theft and miscommunication were common. There were rarely any local authorities to provide law and order. Some early miners tried to prevent violence and stealing, but others lived wild and often dangerous lives. William Perkins was concerned when he visited the Sonora mining camp in 1850. "It is surprising how indifferent [uncaring] people become to the sight of violence and bloodshed in this country."

Daily Life

Mining camps Some areas in California grew so fast that new arrivals had to live in tents. Most of the residents in these camps were young, unmarried men. Crime, drinking, fighting, and gambling were common problems in these temporary communities, which often had names like Hangtown or Poker Flat. The few women who migrated to California found towns like Columbia, shown below, to be very different from what they left behind. **What parts of this scene suggest that the town has grown rapidly?**

THE GRANGER COLLECTION, NEW YORK

Miners in the camps came from many cultural backgrounds. Most miners were young, unmarried men. Only around five percent of gold rush immigrants were women or children. Some married women did make the journey to California with their husbands, however. These hardworking wives generally made good money by cooking meals, washing clothes, and operating boardinghouses. Catherine Haun recalled her first home in California.

History Makers Speak 66We were glad to settle down and go housekeeping in a shed that was built in a day of lumber purchased with the first fee. . . . For neighbors, we had a real live saloon. I never have received more respectful attention than I did from these neighbors.99

—Catherine Haun, from *Ordinary Americans,* edited by Linda R. Monk

Haun's husband, who was a lawyer, concluded that practicing law was actually more profitable than panning for gold. He was one of many people who found that they could make a good living by supplying miners with food, clothing, equipment, or services. Miners paid high prices for basic necessities because the large amounts of gold in circulation caused severe inflation in California. A loaf of bread, for example, might cost five cents back East, but it would sell for 50 to 75 cents in San Francisco. Eggs sold for $1 apiece. Prices could rise even higher when goods had to be shipped to isolated mining camps. There was also a great demand for mining supplies such as clothes, shovels, nails, and mercury. Clipper ships, known for their speed, could not bring enough of these goods to meet the demand. People who found ways to supply needed goods or services could sell to the highest bidder.

Some settlers took full advantage of these free-enterprise conditions. **Biddy Mason** and her family arrived in California as slaves. They were brought there by a Georgia slaveholder during the gold rush years. He quickly discovered that most Californians opposed slavery. Mason and her family gained their liberty and moved to the small village of Los Angeles. By working as a nurse for $2.50 a week and doing domestic work, Mason saved enough money to buy some land. Over time, Mason's property increased in value from $250 to $200,000. She became one of the wealthiest landowners in California. Mason used one of her houses to help needy travelers. In addition, she used some of her money to support education for African American children. Mason found in California an even greater prize than gold—her freedom.

✔ **Reading Check: Summarizing** What role did free enterprise play in the economic life of the mining camps?

CONNECTING TO MATH

Just the Facts

Gold Production, 1847–1860
(in thousands of fine troy ounces)

Year	Amount	Year	Amount
1847	43	1854	2,902
1848	484	1855	2,661
1849	1,935	1856	2,661
1850	2,419	1857	2,661
1851	2,661	1858	2,419
1852	2,902	1859	2,419
1853	3,144	1860	2,225

Using Mathematical Skills
1. How much did gold production increase between 1848 and 1849? Why do you think this happened?
2. Create a graph that shows the annual production of gold and silver for this period.
3. Imagine that you are an economic adviser to the president of the United States. Prepare a written report in which you discuss how increased gold production might affect prices, especially in California.

Perhaps 1,000 of the prospectors in California were African Americans.

Research on the R⊙M

Free Find:
California
After reading about California on the **Holt Researcher CD–ROM,** imagine that you work for the state tourism board. Create a short pamphlet describing California's natural resources.

⭐ Immigrants to California

The lure of gold attracted miners from around the world to California. Many were from countries that had had few people move to the United States in the past. Famine and economic hardships in southeastern China encouraged many Chinese men to come to America. They looked for fortunes in the American West. These immigrants were known in Chinese as *gam saan haak,* or "travelers to Gold Mountain." Most of them hoped to find great wealth and then return home to China. Between 1849 and 1853 some 24,000 young Chinese men migrated to California. "From far and near we came and were pleased," wrote merchant Lai Chun-Chuen in 1855.

Chinese immigrants soon found that many Americans did not welcome them, however. In 1852 California placed a high monthly tax on all foreign miners. Chinese miners had no choice but to pay this tax if they wished to prospect for gold in California. Chinese workers were also the targets of violent attacks in the mining camps. The legal system offered little protection. It often favored Americans over Chinese and other immigrants.

Many Chinese immigrants continued working in the gold mines, despite such treatment. Some looked for different jobs, and many opened their own businesses. A California newspaper reported that Chinese worked as "ploughmen, laundrymen, placer miners, woolen spinners and weavers, domestic servants, cigar makers, [and] shoemakers."

Prospectors also came to California from Europe, Mexico, and South America. Some 20,000 immigrants had come to California in 1849 alone. Like most American gold-seekers, these new arrivals intended to return home after they had made their fortunes. However, even when they did not become rich, many decided to stay. Some who remained in California became successful business owners. Levi Strauss, a German immigrant, earned his fortune by making tough denim work pants to sell to miners.

✔ **Reading Check: Comparing and Contrasting** How were Chinese immigrants similar to and different from other immigrants who came to California?

Interpreting the Visual Record

Immigrant workers *Chinese miners faced steep taxes, harsh working conditions, and discrimination in the gold fields.* **What parts of this image suggest harsh working conditions?**

COURTESY OF THE CALIFORNIA HISTORY ROOM, CALIFORNIA STATE LIBRARY, SACRAMENTO, CALIFORNIA. IMAGE HAS BEEN ALTERED.

Growth in the West

During the Spanish and then Mexican periods of settlement, California's population had grown slowly. The arrival of the forty-niners changed this dramatically. Almost overnight, business growth, gold mining, and trade transformed California's economy. As the gold rush faded, frontier society became more stable. Great wealth became more difficult to achieve, but with luck and hard work, immigrants could build good lives for themselves in the West.

Fast population growth had negative consequences for many Californios and California Indians. One early observer of the gold rush described why.

Clipper ships provided transportation to California.

> **History Makers Speak** "The Yankee regarded every man but a native American [meaning a white U.S. citizen] as an interloper [trespasser], who had no right to come to California and pick up the gold of 'free and enlightened citizens.'"
>
> —W. Kelly, quoted in *The Other Californians,* by Robert F. Heizer and Alan F. Almquist

Californio Mariano Vallejo observed California's growing population. "The good ones were few and the wicked many," he concluded.

Without the gold rush, California would probably have continued to grow slowly. It would have become a U.S. territory and eventually a state. The California Gold Rush changed this, however. California's population explosion made it eligible for statehood only two years after being acquired by the United States. Along with the gold rush came an economic boom. This boom led to growth in agriculture and industry.

✔ **Reading Check: Finding the Main Idea** What political effect resulted from California's rapid population growth?

Section 4 Review

go.hrw.com Homework Practice Online
keyword: SF3 HP17

① **Define** and explain:
• forty-niners
• prospect

② **Identify** and explain:
• California Gold Rush
• Biddy Mason

③ **Evaluating** Copy the web diagram below. Use it to show how the gold rush changed California.

[diagram: Discovery of Gold]

④ **Finding the Main Idea**
a. What caused people to travel to California in 1849?
b. How were the mining camps an example of free enterprise?

⑤ **Writing and Critical Thinking**
Summarizing Imagine that you are a prospector looking for gold in California. Write a letter to your family back home telling them about life in the local mining town.

Consider the following:
• law and order in the town
• available goods and services
• the diversity of the population

Chapter 17 Review

The Chapter at a Glance

Examine the visual summary of the chapter below. Create five fill-in-the-blank statements that show the cause-and-effect relationship between two items in the visual summary. Give the questions to a classmate to answer.

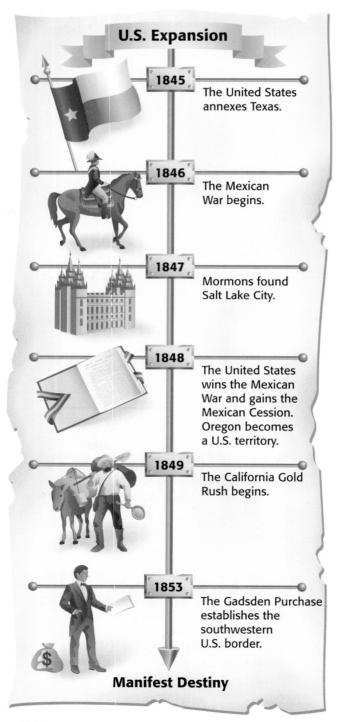

U.S. Expansion

1845 The United States annexes Texas.

1846 The Mexican War begins.

1847 Mormons found Salt Lake City.

1848 The United States wins the Mexican War and gains the Mexican Cession. Oregon becomes a U.S. territory.

1849 The California Gold Rush begins.

1853 The Gadsden Purchase establishes the southwestern U.S. border.

Manifest Destiny

Identifying People and Ideas

Use the following terms or people in historically significant sentences.
1. manifest destiny
2. James K. Polk
3. Henry David Thoreau
4. Bear Flag Revolt
5. Mexican Cession
6. Mormons
7. Brigham Young
8. California Gold Rush
9. forty-niners
10. prospect

Understanding Main Ideas

Section 1 *(Pages 516–21)*
1. What were the economic, political, and social origins of the idea of manifest destiny?
2. Why did the United States declare war against Mexico?

Section 2 *(Pages 522–27)*
3. What lands did the United States gain as a result of the Mexican War?

Section 3 *(Pages 528–32)*
4. Why did Mormons move west?

Section 4 *(Pages 533–39)*
5. How did the discovery of gold in California affect the region and the United States?
6. Why did Chinese immigrants come to California, and how were they treated?

You Be the Historian— Reviewing Themes

1. **Global Relations** How did Texas, Oregon, and California become parts of the United States?
2. **Culture** What conflicts arose as a result of the encounters among Mexican Americans, American Indians, and Anglos in the Mexican Cession?
3. **Geography** How did the Mormons adapt to their new environment?

Thinking Critically

1. **Analyzing Information** How did the idea of manifest destiny affect the growth of the United States?
2. **Supporting a Point of View** Several presidents— Washington, Jackson, and Taylor for example— were elected partly because of their popularity as military leaders. Do you think military experience is an important qualification for the presidency? Explain your answer.
3. **Evaluating** Do you think Mexico should have negotiated with the United States over the Texas border dispute instead of going to war? Explain your answer.

Interpreting Political Cartoons

Study the political cartoon on the Mexican War below. Then answer the questions that follow.

VOLUNTEERS FOR TEXAS

THE GRANGER COLLECTION, NEW YORK

1. What is the soldier nearest the front of the cartoon holding at his shoulder?
   a. a rifle
   b. a briefcase
   c. an umbrella
   d. a treaty

2. Based on your knowledge of the period and your understanding of the cartoon, what message do you think the artist is trying to convey about Mexican War volunteers and the war itself?

Analyzing Primary Sources

Read the following quote by John O'Sullivan, which discusses the annexation of Texas, and then answer the questions that follow.

> **It is time now for opposition to the annexation of Texas to cease [end], all further agitation of the waters of bitterness and strife [fighting], . . . even though it may perhaps be required of us as a necessary condition of the freedom of our institutions, that we must live on forever in a state of unpausing struggle and excitement upon some subject of party division or other. But, in regard to Texas, enough has now been given to party. It is time for the common duty of patriotism to the country to succeed; or . . . it is at least time for common sense to acquiesce [accept] with decent grace in the inevitable and the irrevocable.**

3. Which of the following statements best summarizes what the author is saying?
   a. With freedom comes responsibility.
   b. Americans should stop disagreeing about the future of Texas and accept annexation.
   c. American political parties spend too much time disagreeing about important issues.
   d. Patriotism is more important than any other responsibility that a U.S. citizen might have.

4. What does O'Sullivan mean when he says that disagreement and party divisions are "a necessary condition of the freedom of our institutions"?
   a. People will never get along.
   b. Americans enjoy arguing.
   c. People in a democracy will disagree because they have the freedom to express their views.
   d. Political parties are essential to democracy.

5. Based on what you know about the period, whom do you think O'Sullivan was addressing?

Alternative Assessment

American History

Building Your Portfolio

Interdisciplinary Connection to Economics

Complete the following activity in small groups. Imagine that you and your partners are planning to open a general store in a California mining camp. Create a poster showing the layout of your store and labeling the different items you will sell. Create advertisements to show your products. For each item, write one or two sentences explaining why you think it will be profitable.

🖸 internet connect

Internet Activity: go.hrw.com
keyword: SF3 CF17

Choose a topic about Manifest Destiny and War to:
- Research the causes and effects of the Mexican War.
- Conduct an interview with James K. Polk and Henry David Thoreau.
- Learn about the journey westward to California during the Gold Rush.

Westward Expansion

After the Louisiana Purchase of 1803, the boundaries of the United States stretched roughly from the Atlantic Ocean to the Rocky Mountains. Gradually, American pioneers moved across the Mississippi River, pushing the frontier of American farms and settlements farther west.

In 1846 Britain and the United States agreed to divide Oregon Country, using the 49th parallel as a boundary line. The land south of the 49th parallel became U.S. territory. In 1848, after a war with Mexico, the United States added California and the Southwest. The present southern boundary of the United States was set in 1853.

The Early West

The United States annexed Texas in 1845. After winning the war with Mexico, the United States added the lands of the Mexican Cession. This vast area extended west from Texas to the Pacific Ocean. Combined with Oregon Country and the Gadsden Purchase, these new lands added more than 1.2 million square miles to the United States.

The West, 1845

0   250   500 Miles
0   250   500 Kilometers
Albers Equal-Area Projection

Legend:
- United States
- Mexico
- UTE American Indian tribe
- Claimed by Britain and United States
- Claimed by Mexico and Texas

Geography **Skills**

Interpreting Thematic Maps

1. **Locate** Where did the Oregon and Santa Fe Trails begin?
2. **Comparing** Compare this map to the U.S. map on page 543. What current states occupy land that was Mexican territory in 1845?

U.S. Boundaries in 1853

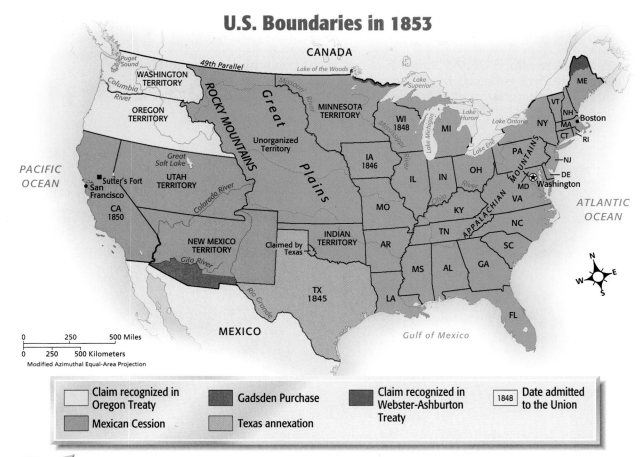

Legend:
- Claim recognized in Oregon Treaty
- Mexican Cession
- Gadsden Purchase
- Texas annexation
- Claim recognized in Webster-Ashburton Treaty
- 1848 Date admitted to the Union

0 250 500 Miles
0 250 500 Kilometers
Modified Azimuthal Equal-Area Projection

Geography Skills
Interpreting Thematic Maps

1. What states and territories were formed in the new U.S. lands?

2. **Places and Regions** What river became the boundary between Texas and Mexico?

3. **Summarizing** Compare this map to the current map of the United States on page 544. What two current states include territory from the Gadsden Purchase? What three states were formed from Oregon Country?

Many settlers heading to the West had to cross the Rocky Mountains.

History Note 1

The territory granted to the United States in the Mexican Cession had long belonged to Spain and then Mexico. Yet the Hispanic population there was outnumbered by settlers from the United States by 1850.

The West Today

The southwestern United States has historical ties with Spain and Mexico. These ties are reflected in the people and culture of the region. The largest concentration of Hispanic Americans is found in the Southwest.

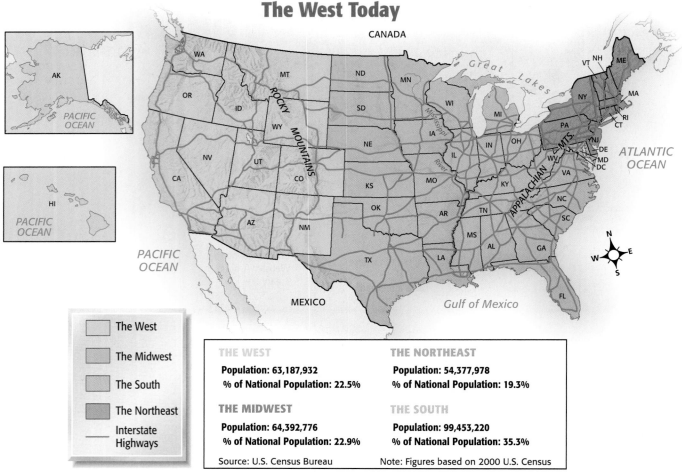

The West Today

Legend:
- The West
- The Midwest
- The South
- The Northeast
- Interstate Highways

THE WEST
Population: 63,187,932
% of National Population: 22.5%

THE NORTHEAST
Population: 54,377,978
% of National Population: 19.3%

THE MIDWEST
Population: 64,392,776
% of National Population: 22.9%

THE SOUTH
Population: 99,453,220
% of National Population: 35.3%

Source: U.S. Census Bureau   Note: Figures based on 2000 U.S. Census

Geography Skills

Interpreting Charts and Thematic Maps

1. **The World in Spatial Terms** Which region of the United States has the largest area?
2. **Human Systems** What region of the United States has the highest population?
3. **Drawing Inferences and Conclusions** What environmental conditions might have contributed to the large populations of the South and West?

History Note 2

According to the 2000 census, there were about 19.7 million Hispanic or Latino Americans living in California, Texas, Arizona, and New Mexico. This figure is more than half the total Hispanic population of the entire United States. California also has nearly 3.7 million Asian Americans and some 2.25 million African Americans, making it the most diverse state in the nation.

Sources of Immigration to the United States in 1850

Total number of immigrants in 1850: 369,980

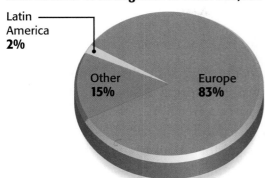

Latin America 2%

Other 15%

Europe 83%

Source: *Datapedia of the United States, 1790–2000: America Year by Year*

Geography **Skills**
Interpreting Pie Graphs

1. Create a bar graph showing the percentages of emigrants from the regions shown in 1850.
2. **Finding the Main Idea** Which part of the world provided most of the immigrants to the United States in 1850?

History Note 3

California has become a major entry point for immigrants to the United States. About one quarter of all immigrants to the United States in 1998 entered through California. In recent years, Latin America, particularly Mexico, has provided about half of all immigrants to the United States.

A Chinese American celebration

Foreign-Born U.S. Population in 2000 by Region of Origin

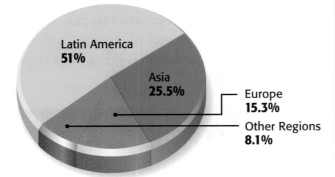

Latin America 51%

Asia 25.5%

Europe 15.3%

Other Regions 8.1%

Source: U.S. Census Bureau, *Current Population Survey*, March 2000

Geography **Skills**
Interpreting Pie Graphs

1. Which part of the world provided the highest percentage of the foreign-born population in the United States in 2000?
2. **Human Systems** Compare the pie graphs for the years 1850 and 2000. Then create a five-question quiz on the information contained in the graphs.
3. **Making Generalizations and Predictions** In what ways do you think the change in immigration from 1850 to today has changed or will change the nation? Explain your answer.

NEW YORK

Social Studies Skills

WORKSHOP

Using Primary and Secondary Sources

There are many sources of firsthand historical information. These sources include diaries, editorials, letters, and legal documents such as wills and titles. All of these are *primary sources*. Newspaper reports are also considered primary sources. However, they are typically written after an event has taken place. The same is true for personal memoirs and autobiographies. These works are usually written late in a person's life. The editorial cartoons, paintings, and photographs that make up history's visual record are also primary sources. Primary sources are valuable historical tools that allow a close-up look at the past.

Secondary sources are descriptions or interpretations of historical events written after the events have occurred by persons who did not take part in or witness the events. Biographies, encyclopedias, history books, and other reference works are examples of secondary sources. Writers of secondary sources have the advantage of knowing the long-range consequences of events. This knowledge helps shape their viewpoints.

How to Study Primary and Secondary Sources

1. **Study the material carefully.** Consider the nature of the material. Is it verbal or visual? Is it based on firsthand information or on the accounts of others? Note the major ideas and supporting details.

2. **Consider the audience.** Ask yourself: For whom was this message originally meant? Whether a message was intended for the general public or for a specific private audience may have influenced its style or content.

3. **Check for bias.** Watch for certain words or phrases that signal a one-sided view of a person or event.

4. **When possible, compare sources.** Study more than one source on a topic if you can. Comparing sources gives you a more complete and balanced account.

Practicing the Skill

1. How are secondary sources different from primary sources?

2. What advantages do secondary sources have over primary sources?

3. Select a topic from Unit 7. Write a brief report on this topic, using one primary source and one secondary source. Explain why each source is considered a primary or a secondary source.

History in Action

UNIT 7 SIMULATION

You Make the Decision . . .

Should Your Family Move Westward to the Great Plains?

Complete the following activity in small cooperative groups. It is early 1838. Your family has lived very comfortably in the East for generations. However, following the economic hardships of the Panic of 1837, the lure of moving west for adventure, riches, and land is very tempting. Your family includes your spouse and three children, all under the age of 15. You have to decide whether your family will move westward onto the Great Plains. You have to prepare a presentation that will convince the rest of your family that your decision is best for all of them. Follow these steps to reach your decision.

1. Gather Information. Use your textbook and other resources to find information that might help you decide whether to move your family westward. Be sure to use what you learned from this unit's Skills Workshop on Using Primary and Secondary Sources to help you make an informed decision. You may want to divide different parts of the research among group members.

2. Identify Options. After reviewing the information you have gathered, identify the different reasons you might consider for moving or not moving to the West. Your final decision may be easier to reach if you consider as many options as possible. Be sure to record your possible options for your presentation.

3. Predict Consequences. Now take each option your group came up with and consider what might be the outcome of each course of action. Ask yourselves questions like: "Will my family be safe on the frontier?" Once you have predicted the consequences, record them as notes for your presentation.

4. Take Action to Implement Your Decision. After you have considered your options, you should plan and create your presentation. Be sure to make your decision on moving westward very clear. You will need to support your decision by including information you gathered and by explaining why you rejected other options. Your presentation needs to be visually appealing to gain the support of your family. When you are ready, decide which group members will make each part of the presentation, and then take your decision to your family (the rest of the class). Good luck!

8 The Nation Breaks Apart

(1848–1877)

Young People

IN HISTORY

Young Soldiers

During the Civil War, 15-year-old Union soldier Thomas Galway described a fierce battle.

"Now we are close to the enemy. They rise up in the sunken lane and pour deadly fire into us. Our men drop. . . . We go forward on the run, heads downward as if under a pelting rain. . . . We are kneeling in the soft grass and I notice for a long time that almost every blade of grass is moving. For some time I supposed that this is caused by the merry crickets; and it is not until I made a remark to that effect to one of our boys near me and notice him laugh, that I know it is bullets that are falling thickly around us!"

Galway was one of the thousands of youths who fought in the Civil War.

Both the North and the South tried to keep boys out of their armies. However, many teenagers lied about their ages in order to join. Elisha Stockwell's father would not let his 15-year-old son enlist. So, Elisha told his parents that he was going to a dance in town. Instead, he joined the Union army. Although young Stockwell did not return home for two years, he thought of home often. One such time was during his first battle, kneeling on the ground in the middle of exploding shells. "I thought what a foolish boy I was to run away and get into such a mess as I was in."

Other boys joined the army as drummers. The beat of the drum was an important way to communicate orders to soldiers. Therefore, drummer boys often found themselves the target of enemy fire. Johnny Clem went from drummer boy to fighting soldier during the Battle of Shiloh. After his drum was shattered, 11-year-old Clem picked up a gun and began firing. Within two years, Clem was promoted to sergeant.

Young Union soldiers relax between battles.

If You Were There *How would you view the war?*

LEFT PAGE: *Members of the 54th Massachusetts Infantry attack Confederate soldiers at Fort Wagner.*

18 A Divided Nation
(1848–1860)

Martin Van Buren and Charles F. Adams were the first presidential and vice presidential candidates of the Free-Soil Party.

THE GRANGER COLLECTION, NEW YORK

Harriet Beecher Stowe was the daughter of Lyman Beecher, a prominent minister and reformer.

UNITED STATES

1848 The Free-Soil Party is formed on August 9.

Zachary Taylor is elected president on November 7.

1850 On September 9 California enters the Union as a free state.

Congress passes the Fugitive Slave Act on September 18.

1852 Harriet Beecher Stowe publishes *Uncle Tom's Cabin.*

1853 Franklin Pierce is inaugurated as president.

1848	1850	1852	1854

1848 Revolutionary movements sweep across Europe.

1850 Hundreds of thousands of peasants and workers in China join the Taiping Rebellion against the Manchu dynasty.

1852 Louis-Napoléon declares himself Emperor Napoléon III of France.

1853 The Crimean War begins.

WORLD

In 1848 German revolutionaries demanding a new republican government fought soldiers in the streets of Frankfurt.

Build on What You Know

After winning the Mexican War, the United States gained the Mexican Cession. Settlement of these lands renewed heated debate between northerners who opposed the expansion of slavery and southerners who supported it. Some southerners threatened to support secession if the government tried to block the westward expansion of slavery.

On February 4, 1861, delegates from the seceding states met in Alabama to form the Confederate States of America.

CHARLESTON MERCURY EXTRA:

THE UNION IS DISSOLVED!

The Granger Collection, New York

The Charleston Mercury *issued a special broadside to announce the secession of South Carolina.*

1856 In the Sack of Lawrence, pro-slavery forces attack the town of Lawrence, Kansas, on May 21.

On May 24 abolitionist John Brown and his followers kill five pro-slavery settlers in the Pottawatomie Massacre.

1858 The Lincoln-Douglas debates begin in Illinois.

1859 John Brown takes control of the federal arsenal at Harpers Ferry, Virginia.

1860 Abraham Lincoln is elected president on November 6.

On December 20 South Carolina votes to secede from the United States.

1856 1858 1860 1862

1856 British and French forces defeat Russia in the Crimean War.

1857 Indian soldiers in the British army begin the Sepoy Mutiny against British control of India.

If you were there . . .
How would you try to solve the country's conflicts?

You Be the Historian

Themes Journal

What's Your Opinion? Do you **agree** or **disagree** with the following statements? Support your point of view in your journal.

- **Geography** Expansion often leads to conflict within a country.
- **Citizenship** The Supreme Court must protect all individuals' rights.
- **Constitutional Heritage** States should be able to legally leave the Union.

551

The Debate over Slavery

Read to Discover

1. How did the outcome of the Mexican War affect the debate over the expansion of slavery?
2. What were the major provisions of the Compromise of 1850, and what reasons were given for supporting or opposing it?
3. Why was the Fugitive Slave Act controversial in the North?

WHY IT MATTERS TODAY

Congressional compromises are still an important part of the U.S. government. Use **CNNfyi.com** or other **current events** sources to learn about a recent issue that has led to compromise legislation in Congress. Record your findings in your journal.

Define

- sectionalism
- popular sovereignty

Identify

- Wilmot Proviso
- Free-Soil Party
- Henry Clay
- Daniel Webster
- Compromise of 1850
- Fugitive Slave Act
- Anthony Burns
- *Uncle Tom's Cabin*
- Harriet Beecher Stowe

The Story Continues

O n August 8, 1846, the members of the U.S. House of Representatives slowly returned from dinner. They resumed their talk of the ongoing war with Mexico. It was one of the hottest nights of the summer. Ice water and fans were in heavy demand. As the representatives began to talk about the possible outcomes of the war, a congressman from Pennsylvania asked to speak. David Wilmot held the floor for 10 minutes—and changed the course of history.

This illustration shows the U.S. Capitol as it looked in the 1800s.

★ The Expansion of Slavery

Victory in the Mexican War in 1848 added more than 500,000 square miles to the United States and renewed the bitter debate over the expansion of slavery. The Missouri Compromise of 1820 had let Missouri enter the Union as a slave state. The Compromise divided the rest of the Louisiana Purchase into free and slave territory. Slavery was not allowed north of latitude 36°30'. President James K. Polk and others now wanted to run the 36°30' line to the Pacific coast, dividing the Mexican Cession into free and slave territory.

Some northerners wanted to prohibit slavery in all parts of the Mexican Cession. During the war, Representative David Wilmot had proposed a plan known as the **Wilmot Proviso**. It stated that "neither slavery nor involuntary servitude shall ever exist in any part of [the] territory." The House of Representatives, which had a northern majority, passed the proviso, but it died in the Senate, where the South had more power. Although the Wilmot Proviso never became law, the debate over the plan showed the growing **sectionalism** of the country. Sectionalism happens when people favor the interests of one region over the interests of the country as a whole.

Senator Lewis Cass of Michigan hoped to solve the conflict over slavery in new territories. He pushed for **popular sovereignty**, which would allow voters in a territory to decide whether they wanted to ban or allow slavery. They would make their choice by electing antislavery or pro-slavery representatives to their territorial legislatures. Based on the will of the majority, these legislatures then would pass laws either to ban or to allow slavery.

CONGRESSIONAL SCALES,
A TRUE BALANCE.

The debate over slavery in the Mexican Cession dominated the presidential campaign of 1848. However, neither the Democrats nor the Whigs took a clear position on slavery in the West. For this reason, thousands of antislavery northerners formed a new political party. In August 1848 in Buffalo, New York, they formed the **Free-Soil Party**. The Free-Soilers supported the Wilmot Proviso. They chose former president Martin Van Buren of New York as their candidate. The new party won 10 percent of the popular vote. This helped Whig candidate Zachary Taylor, a Mexican War hero, win a narrow victory over Democratic opponent Lewis Cass.

The California Gold Rush caused a population boom that allowed California to skip the territorial stage and apply directly for admission into the Union. This raised the issue of whether California would join as a free state or a slave state. Most Californians did not want slavery and hoped to enter the Union as a free state. However, doing so would upset the balance between free and slave states.

To many southerners such a step was unacceptable. "We are about permanently to destroy the balance of power between the sections," warned Senator Jefferson Davis of Mississippi. He and many other southerners declared that they would oppose the admission of California to the Union as a free state.

✔ **Reading Check: Contrasting** How were the Wilmot Proviso and the principle of popular sovereignty different?

Interpreting Political Cartoons

Balancing act *The controversy over the Wilmot Proviso forced President Zachary Taylor to try to balance antislavery and pro-slavery interests.* **How does the cartoonist show Taylor's efforts to preserve peace?**

"General Taylor Never Surrenders" is the motto of this 1848 Zachary Taylor campaign button.

A Divided Nation **553**

★ The Compromise of 1850

<u>Henry Clay</u> had helped settle the Missouri crisis of 1819–20 and the nullification crisis of 1832–33. This senator from Kentucky, nicknamed "The Great Compromiser," now stepped forward with another plan. Clay's proposal had five main parts.

1. He urged Congress to let California enter the Union as a free state.

2. He called for the rest of the Mexican Cession to be organized as a federal territory. In this territory—already called New Mexico—popular sovereignty would decide the status of slavery.

3. He addressed a border dispute between Texas and New Mexico. He called on Texas to give up its claim to all land east of the upper Rio Grande. In exchange, the federal government would pay Texas's old debts. These debts remained from its days as an independent republic.

4. He called for an end to the slave trade—but not slavery—in the country's capital.

5. He called for a new, more effective fugitive slave law.

Almost immediately, Clay's plan came under fire. Senator William Seward of New York spoke for antislavery northerners. He demanded the admission of California "directly, without conditions, without qualifications, and without compromise." Senator John C. Calhoun of South Carolina spoke for many in the South. Near death, Calhoun was so weak that another senator had to read his speech. Calhoun argued that letting California enter as a free state would destroy the balance

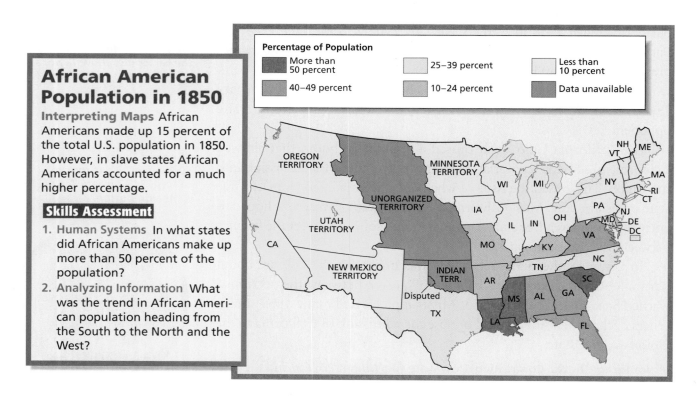

African American Population in 1850

Interpreting Maps African Americans made up 15 percent of the total U.S. population in 1850. However, in slave states African Americans accounted for a much higher percentage.

Skills Assessment

1. **Human Systems** In what states did African Americans make up more than 50 percent of the population?

2. **Analyzing Information** What was the trend in African American population heading from the South to the North and the West?

THE GRANGER COLLECTION, NEW YORK

Interpreting the Visual Record

Clay's compromise *In 1850 Senator Henry Clay once again urged Congress to compromise on the issue of slavery in the territories.* **How does the image indicate that Clay was a central figure in the debates over slavery?**

between the two sections of the country. The slave states could not "remain in the Union consistently with their honor and their safety," he said. Calhoun asked that they be allowed "to separate and part in peace."

Others, such as Senator **Daniel Webster** of Massachusetts, were in favor of Clay's plan. Although Webster himself was opposed to the expansion of slavery, he argued that preserving the Union was more important than any regional differences.

Analyzing Primary Sources
Drawing Inferences and Conclusions How did Senator Webster avoid sectionalism in his speech?

History Makers Speak

❝I wish to speak today, not as a Massachusetts man, nor as a Northern man, but as an American. . . . I speak today for the preservation of the Union. Hear me for my cause.❞

—Daniel Webster, quoted in *Battle Cry of Freedom*, by James M. McPherson

Webster criticized northern abolitionists and scolded southerners who spoke of breaking away from the Union. He also argued that fighting over slavery in the West was unnecessary. Because of the soil and climate in this region, he claimed, the kinds of crops for which slave labor was used would not grow.

The **Compromise of 1850** became law in September of that year. It accomplished most of what Clay had wanted. California entered the Union as a free state. The rest of the Mexican Cession was divided into two territories. In these territories—Utah and New Mexico—the status of slavery would be decided by popular sovereignty. Texas agreed to give up its land claims in New Mexico. In exchange, the federal government gave Texas the financial help it needed. Finally, the compromise outlawed the slave trade in the nation's capital and produced a new fugitive slave law that replaced the previous law of 1793.

Research on the R⊙M

Free Find:
John C. Calhoun
After reading about John C. Calhoun on the **Holt Researcher CD–ROM**, create a political profile of him. Be sure to give details of Calhoun's life and explain his positions on important political issues of the era.

✔ **Reading Check: Summarizing** How did the Compromise of 1850 attempt to resolve conflicts over the expansion of slavery?

BIOGRAPHY

Frederick Douglass

(1817–1895)

Frederick Douglass was born to an enslaved family in Maryland. At age 20, he escaped to freedom in the North. There he began speaking and writing for the abolition movement. In 1845 he published the *Narrative of the Life of Frederick Douglass*. The detail in this autobiography forced him to leave the country to avoid being arrested as a fugitive slave. He returned in 1847 and bought his freedom. He started an antislavery newspaper, which he named *North Star*. In the first issue, Douglass called on other former slaves to join his crusade for freedom. **Why did Douglass have to leave the country?**

Analyzing Primary Sources
Identifying Points of View
How did Delany react to the new fugitive slave law?

★ The Fugitive Slave Act

One part of the Compromise of 1850 kept slavery very much on the minds of Americans. The **Fugitive Slave Act** made it a federal crime to help runaway slaves. The act even let officials arrest runaways in areas where slavery was illegal. Under the new law, slaveholders and their agents could take suspected fugitive slaves before U.S. commissioners. They would then try to prove ownership through documents or through the testimony of white witnesses. In contrast, the accused fugitives could not testify in their own defense. Commissioners who rejected a slaveholder's claim received $5 for their services. Those who returned a suspected fugitive to the slaveholder in the South received $10. Anyone who hid or otherwise helped a runaway slave faced six months in jail and a $1,000 fine.

In the 10 years after Congress passed this law, 343 fugitive slave cases came under the commissioners' review in the North. The accused fugitive was declared free in only 11 of these cases. Such numbers worried many African Americans living in the North—free individuals as well as former slaves. Thousands of African Americans went to Canada to escape potential prosecution under the Fugitive Slave Act.

The Fugitive Slave Act upset many northerners. They did not agree with the lack of a trial by jury. These northerners also disliked the higher fee given to commissioners who returned fugitives. This apparent bribe encouraged commissioners to send a suspected fugitive slave back to the South. As expected, abolitionists led the protests against the new law. One abolitionist said it was every citizen's duty to make sure that the new law was "resisted, disobeyed at all hazards." Martin R. Delany, a doctor and a leading African American abolitionist, spoke publicly to the mayor of Pittsburgh, Pennsylvania.

 "If any man approaches that house in search of a slave—I care not who he may be . . . if he crosses the threshold of my door, and I do not lay him a lifeless corpse at my feet, I hope the grave may refuse my body a resting place, and righteous Heaven my spirit a home."

—Martin R. Delany, quoted in *The Negro Caravan*, edited by Sterling A. Brown, Arthur P. Davis, and Ulysses Lee

In general, northerners who resisted the Fugitive Slave Act did so without using violence. However, blood was spilled on several occasions. In 1854, for example, the case of **Anthony Burns** caught the nation's attention. Burns, a fugitive slave from Virginia, was arrested and jailed in Boston. A group of abolitionists in the city tried to rescue Burns by force. A deputy marshal was killed in the attempt, but Burns was eventually returned to slavery in Virginia.

✔ **Reading Check: Finding the Main Idea** How did many northerners respond to the Fugitive Slave Act?

★ Antislavery Literature

Abolitionists in the North used the stories of fugitive slaves such as Anthony Burns to help their cause. They also made use of slave narratives, which became popular around 1840. Among the best known were the narratives of Frederick Douglass and Sojourner Truth. Truth's narrative differed from most other slave narratives in two ways. First, its central character was a woman. Second, Truth had been a slave not in the South but in New York.

No other literary work, however, had the influence of **Uncle Tom's Cabin**. This powerful antislavery novel was written by **Harriet Beecher Stowe**. Stowe was born into a religious family in Connecticut and moved to Ohio at the age of 21. There she met with fugitive slaves and learned about the cruelty of slavery. The passage of the Fugitive Slave Act of 1850 greatly angered Stowe, so she decided to write a book that would show northerners what slavery was really like.

Uncle Tom's Cabin was published in 1852. The main character is a kindly old slave named Tom, who is separated from his wife and sold. Tom becomes the slave of a cruel cotton planter in Louisiana. The novel sparked outrage in the South and gained praise in the North. Within 10 years, more than 2 million copies of *Uncle Tom's Cabin* were sold in the United States. The book's popularity caused one northerner to remark that Stowe had created "two millions of abolitionists."

Abolitionists protested the arrest of suspected fugitive slaves, such as the capture shown above.

✔ **Reading Check: Analyzing Information** How did literature help the antislavery movement?

Section 1 Review

go.hrw.com Homework Practice Online
keyword: SF3 HP18

❶ **Define** and explain:
• sectionalism
• popular sovereignty

❷ **Identify** and explain:
• Wilmot Proviso
• Free-Soil Party
• Henry Clay
• Daniel Webster
• Compromise of 1850
• Fugitive Slave Act
• Anthony Burns
• *Uncle Tom's Cabin*
• Harriet Beecher Stowe

❸ **Contrasting** Copy the diagram below. Use it to explain how the Compromise of 1850, Fugitive Slave Act, and antislavery literature related to the debate over the expansion of slavery.

```
Compromise        Fugitive
of 1850          Slave Act
      \            /
     Slavery Debate
           ↑
     Antislavery
     Literature
```

❹ **Finding the Main Idea**
a. How did U.S. territory change after the Mexican War ended, and how did this change renew the debate over slavery?
b. What did the Compromise of 1850 propose? Why did Senator Daniel Webster support it, and why did Senator John C. Calhoun oppose it?

❺ **Writing and Critical Thinking**
Supporting a Point of View Imagine that you are a northerner who is opposed to the Fugitive Slave Act. Create a handbill that you would pass out at a town meeting to persuade members of your community to protest the law.

Consider the following:
• lack of trial by jury
• "bribes" given to commissioners
• examples of abolitionist protests

A Divided Nation **557**

Uncle Tom's Cabin

Harriet Beecher Stowe

Like Mark Twain, Harriet Beecher Stowe was a local-color writer, concentrating on describing regional culture and language. Stowe wrote mostly about New England. However, she is best remembered for Uncle Tom's Cabin, *a powerful novel about slavery. In the following passage, Simon Legree is a northerner who has moved south and become a cruel slaveholder. He has ordered Sambo, a slave driver, to whip Tom. Legree wants to learn what Tom knows about the disappearance of two slaves. Tom, a slave, is one of the main characters of the novel. He has maintained his religious faith despite the brutality he has witnessed and experienced. The scene shows the consequences of slavery—both to the suffering slave and to the soul of the slaveholder. The criticism of slavery in the first and last paragraphs is the author's voice.*

Uncle Tom's Cabin *helped convince many Americans of the moral wrongs of slavery.*

Scenes of blood and cruelty are shocking to our ear and heart. What man has nerve to do, man has not nerve to hear. What brother-man and brother-Christian must suffer, cannot be told us, even in our secret chamber, it so **harrows up**[1] the soul! And yet, oh my country; these things are done under the shadow of thy laws! O, Christ! thy church sees them, almost in silence! . . . "He's most **gone**,[2] **Mas'r**,[3]" said Sambo, touched, in spite of himself, by the patience of his victim.

"Pay away, till he give up! Give it to him!— give it to him!" shouted Legree. "I'll take every drop of blood he has, unless he confesses!"

Tom opened his eyes, and looked upon his master. "Ye poor miserable crittur!" he said, "there ain't no more ye can do! I forgive ye, with all my soul!" and he fainted entirely away.

"I b'lieve, my soul, he's done for, finally," said Legree, stepping forward, to look at him. "Yes, he is! Well, his mouth's shut up, at last,—that's one comfort!"

Yes, Legree; but who shall shut up that voice in thy soul? that soul, **past repentance**,[4] past prayer, past hope, in whom the fire that never shall be quenched is already burning!

Understanding What You Read

1. **Literature and History** In the opening paragraph, whom does Stowe criticize for allowing slavery to occur?
2. **Literature and You** What do you think Stowe is asking of the reader?

---

[1]**harrows up:** frightens or shocks
[2]**gone:** dead
[3]**Mas'r:** master

[4]**past repentance:** beyond the ability to turn away from sin; past regret

Trouble in Kansas

Read to Discover

1. How did different regions of the country react to the Kansas-Nebraska Act?
2. In what ways did people try to settle the conflict over slavery in Kansas?
3. What series of violent events showed growing division over slavery in the United States?

Identify

- Franklin Pierce
- Stephen Douglas
- Kansas-Nebraska Act
- Pottawatomie Massacre
- Charles Sumner
- Preston Brooks

WHY IT MATTERS TODAY

In the 1850s events in Kansas affected the entire nation. Use CNN**fyi**.com or other **current events** sources to learn about events in one part of the country that have affected the entire country. Record your findings in your journal.

The Story Continues

Franklin and Jane Pierce spent the morning taking a peaceful carriage ride just outside Boston, Massachusetts. On their way back to their hotel in the city, they saw a horseman racing toward them. When the rider reached the Pierces' carriage, he shouted the news. The Democratic convention in Baltimore, Maryland, had nominated Franklin Pierce for the presidency. The Pierces were stunned.

The Democratic Party nominated Franklin Pierce for president in 1852.

★ The Election of 1852

As the Democratic convention opened in 1852, there were four leading candidates for the presidential nomination. It soon became clear, however, that no one could win a majority of votes. After nearly 50 ballots, the frustrated delegates chose **Franklin Pierce**. Pierce was a little-known politician from New Hampshire. However, he and his party promised to honor the Compromise of 1850 and enforce the Fugitive Slave Act. Thus, many southerners saw Pierce "as reliable as Calhoun himself" on the slavery question.

The Whigs also held their convention in Baltimore in 1852. The divided party hoped to repeat earlier successes by nominating a well-known soldier for the presidency. They passed over Millard Fillmore, who had become president after Zachary Taylor's death. Instead, the Whigs chose Winfield Scott, a hero from the Mexican War. Although Scott was born in Virginia, many southerners did not trust him because he had not completely supported the Compromise of 1850.

The Democrats won the election by a large margin. Pierce won 27 of the 31 states. Even Scott's home state of Virginia voted for Pierce. Whig Representative Lewis Campbell of Ohio feared the worst after this painful defeat. "We are slayed," he cried. "The party is dead—dead—dead!"

✔ **Reading Check: Identifying Cause and Effect** Who won the 1852 presidential election, and how did the election affect the Whig Party?

★ The Kansas-Nebraska Act

Since entering Congress in the mid-1840s, **Stephen Douglas** had supported building a railroad to the Pacific. Douglas wanted a line running from Chicago, in his home state of Illinois. To build this railroad, however, the rest of the Louisiana Purchase had to be made into a federal territory. The Missouri Compromise banned slavery in this region, meaning that the land would eventually become free states.

Southerners in Congress did not support Douglas's plan. They wanted a line running from New Orleans across Texas. It would run through the already organized territory of New Mexico and into southern California. However, Douglas was determined to have the railroad start in Chicago. Thus, he asked a few key southern senators to support

Slave and Free Territory in 1850 and 1854

Interpreting Maps The Compromise of 1850 and the Kansas-Nebraska Act of 1854 gave new states and territories the right to vote on whether to allow slavery.

Skills Assessment Places and Regions How did the status and boundaries of the western territories change between 1850 and 1854?

Comparing the Compromises

As disagreements over the expansion of slavery divided the nation, congressional leaders tried to find a compromise that would end sectional disagreements.

Missouri Compromise

No slavery in new states north of 36° 30' line

Missouri joins the Union as a slave state

Maine joins the Union as a free state

Henry Clay

Compromise of 1850

California joins the Union as a free state

New Mexico and Utah Territories to use popular sovereignty to decide status of slavery

Stronger fugitive slave law passed

Slave trade ended in Washington, D.C.

Border dispute between New Mexico and Texas is resolved

Henry Clay

Daniel Webster

John C. Calhoun

Kansas-Nebraska Act

Kansas and Nebraska Territories are created

No more 36° 30' boundary for slave states

Kansas and Nebraska Territories will use popular sovereignty

Stephen Douglas

Visualizing History

1. **Government** What are the main similarities and differences among the three compromises?

2. **Connecting to Today** Do you think compromise is still an important political tool today? Why or why not?

his plan. They said they would give up their plans for a southern railroad route. In return, they wanted the new territory west of Missouri opened up to slavery.

In January 1854 Douglas introduced what became the **Kansas-Nebraska Act**. This plan would divide the rest of the Louisiana Purchase into two territories—Kansas and Nebraska. In each territory, popular sovereignty would decide the question of slavery. Douglas's plan would remove the Missouri Compromise's restriction on slavery north of the 36°30' line.

Antislavery northerners were outraged. Some called the proposal a "gross violation of a sacred pledge." They thought it was part of a southern plot to turn free territory into a "dreary region . . . inhabited by masters and slaves." All across the North, citizens attended protest meetings and sent anti-Nebraska petitions to Congress. However, the measure carried strong southern support. Douglas and President Pierce also tried to get their fellow Democrats to vote for it. The measure passed the Senate in March and the House two months later. The president signed the act into law on May 30, 1854. Lost in the controversy was Douglas's proposed railroad to the Pacific. Congress would not approve the construction of such a railroad until 1862.

Advertisements like this 1855 poster encouraged settlers to buy land in Kansas.

✔ **Reading Check: Finding the Main Idea** Why were antislavery northerners angry about the Kansas-Nebraska Act?

Antislavery activist Henry Ward Beecher helped raise money to send weapons to abolitionist settlers in Kansas.

 ## "Bleeding Kansas"

Both northern and southern politicians saw that a contest had begun. As a result, antislavery and pro-slavery groups rushed to get people to Kansas. Senator William Seward of New York spoke on the issue.

> **History Makers Speak** ❝Gentlemen of the Slave States, since there is no escaping your challenge, I accept it in behalf of the cause of freedom. We will engage in competition for . . . Kansas, and God give victory to the side which is stronger in numbers as it is in right.❞
>
> —William Henry Seward, quoted in *The Impending Crisis, 1848–1861,* by David M. Potter

Elections for the Kansas territorial legislature were held in March 1855. To ensure a pro-slavery victory, thousands of men crossed the border from Missouri, voted in Kansas, and then returned home. As a result, the territorial legislature, located at Lecompton, had a huge pro-slavery majority. The new legislature passed a series of strict pro-slavery laws. One law made it a crime to question anyone's right to hold slaves. Another law stated that anyone caught helping a fugitive slave could be punished by death. In protest, antislavery Kansans formed their own legislature 25 miles away in Topeka.

By early 1856 Kansas had two governments and an angry population divided into two armed camps. Many of the pro-slavery settlers had brought guns with them to the new territory. Meanwhile antislavery settlers had asked for shipments of weapons from their friends in the East. With both sides heavily armed, violence soon broke out. In May 1856 a pro-slavery grand jury charged the leaders of the antislavery government with treason. A posse of more than 700 men rode to Lawrence, where they destroyed buildings and printing presses.

Abolitionist John Brown decided that it was his duty to punish pro-slavery forces for the so-called Sack of Lawrence. He said it was time to

Interpreting the Visual Record

The Sack of Lawrence *A pro-slavery force came to the town of Lawrence seeking to arrest antislavery leaders. When they could not find these people, they attacked the rest of the town, killing one man.* **How does this image portray the violence of the pro-slavery settlers?**

"strike terror in the hearts of the pro-slavery people." Brown was a New Englander who moved to Kansas in 1855 with some of his sons. On the night of May 24, 1856, he led a group of seven men along Pottawatomie Creek in eastern Kansas. They killed five pro-slavery men in what became known as the **Pottawatomie Massacre**. Kansas collapsed into a state of civil war. About 200 people were killed in the months that followed. The events in "Bleeding Kansas" became front-page stories in many of the country's newspapers.

THE GRANGER COLLECTION, NEW YORK

Conflict also swept Congress, where Senator **Charles Sumner** of Massachusetts gave a speech called "The Crime Against Kansas." In it, he criticized pro-slavery efforts in Kansas and insulted Senator Andrew Pickens Butler of South Carolina. Representative **Preston Brooks**, a relative of Butler, was greatly upset. On May 22, 1856, Brooks approached Sumner in the Senate chamber and beat him unconscious with a walking cane. A newspaper editor in Virginia praised Brooks's actions.

Preston Brooks was fined $300 by a federal court for his attack on Charles Sumner, who was unable to return to the Senate until after a three-year absence.

History Makers Speak

66We consider the act good in conception [thought], better in execution. . . . These vulgar [rude] abolitionists in the Senate . . . must be lashed into submission [surrender]. Sumner, in particular, ought to have nine-and-thirty [lashes] early every morning.99

—*Richmond Enquirer,* June 2, 1856

Analyzing Primary Sources

Identifying Bias How can you tell that the speaker supports the spread of slavery?

Dozens of southerners sent Brooks new canes. In the North Sumner's beating outraged many people, who called the attacker Bully Brooks.

✔ **Reading Check: Comparing and Contrasting** How did northerners and southerners react to events involving Kansas?

Section 2 Review

go.hrw.com Homework Practice Online
keyword: SF3 HP18

1 **Identify** and explain:
• Franklin Pierce
• Stephen Douglas
• Kansas-Nebraska Act
• Pottawatomie Massacre
• Charles Sumner
• Preston Brooks

2 **Sequencing** Copy the graphic organizer below. Use it to describe the Kansas-Nebraska Act and the conflicts that followed in the order that they occurred.

Kansas-Nebraska Act

3 **Finding the Main Idea**
a. What did northerners and southerners think of the Kansas-Nebraska Act?

b. How did antislavery forces hope to prevent slavery in Kansas, and how did pro-slavery groups influence the Kansas territorial elections in 1855?

4 **Writing and Critical Thinking**
Summarizing Imagine that you are a historian writing about the beating of Charles Sumner by Preston Brooks. Write a half-page essay describing the events leading up to the beating and the public's reactions.

Consider the following:
• reasons for the attack
• northern reactions to the beating
• southern reactions to the beating

A Divided Nation **563**

Political Divisions

Read to Discover

1. How did the Kansas-Nebraska Act affect U.S. political parties?
2. Why did Dred Scott sue for his freedom, and how did the Supreme Court rule on his case?
3. How did Abraham Lincoln and Stephen Douglas differ in their views on slavery?

WHY IT MATTERS TODAY

Supreme Court decisions have a major impact on life in the United States. Use CNN**fyi**.com or other **current events** sources to learn about how a recent Supreme Court decision will affect the whole country. Record your findings in your journal.

Identify

- Republican Party
- James Buchanan
- John C. Frémont
- Dred Scott
- Roger B. Taney
- *Dred Scott* decision
- Abraham Lincoln
- Lincoln-Douglas debates
- Freeport Doctrine

The Story Continues

On July 5, 1854, hundreds of people met at the town of Jackson, Michigan, to form a new political party. "We will . . . be known as Republicans," they declared in their platform. They promised to uphold the principles of republican government. They also said they would fight the spread of slavery "until the contest be terminated."

THE GRANGER COLLECTION, NEW YORK

This crowd has gathered to hear a speaker at the first Republican National Convention.

★ New Divisions

Political unrest led Whigs, some Democrats, Free-Soilers, and abolitionists to join and form the **Republican Party** in 1854. These different groups united to oppose the spread of slavery in the West. The Kansas-Nebraska Act of 1854 had once again raised this issue and divided the Democratic and Whig Parties. Under pressure from Senator Stephen Douglas and President Franklin Pierce, nearly 60 northern Democrats had voted for the Kansas-Nebraska bill. They suffered politically for their support, however. In the next congressional elections, only seven of the northern Democrats who voted for the bill kept their seats in the House of Representatives.

The Kansas-Nebraska Act was even more damaging to the Whigs. Every northern Whig voted against Douglas's bill. Most southern Whigs, however, voted for it.

The presidential election of 1856 showed just how divided the country was becoming. Some longtime Whigs and Democrats joined the Know-Nothing Party, which quickly fell apart over the slavery issue. Northern delegates left the convention hall when southerners refused to support the repeal of the Kansas-Nebraska Act. Many northerners later supported the Republican Party. Those Know-Nothings who remained behind chose former president Millard Fillmore as their presidential candidate.

The Democrats knew that they could not nominate anyone closely associated with the Kansas-Nebraska Act, which ruled out President Pierce and Senator Douglas. They chose **James Buchanan** of Pennsylvania instead. Buchanan had served roughly 20 years in Congress and as Polk's secretary of state for 4 years. Most importantly, he had not been involved in the Kansas-Nebraska controversy.

At their first presidential nominating convention, the Republicans chose **John C. Frémont** as their candidate. Frémont had little political experience, but his opposition to the spread of slavery appealed to Republicans. Although the Republicans also favored issues such as protective tariffs, they generally were seen as a "single-issue party." Their antislavery platform meant the Republicans had almost no supporters outside of the free states.

Some white southerners even said that they would not accept a Republican victory in the election. A politician from Georgia made a prediction: "The election of Frémont would be the end of the Union." On election day, Buchanan won 14 of the 15 slave states and 5 of the free states, the rest of which went to Frémont. Fillmore, meanwhile, won only one state—Maryland. Buchanan won the election.

✔ **Reading Check: Summarizing** How did the Kansas-Nebraska Act affect political parties in the 1856 election?

★ ★ ★ ★ ★ ★ ★ ★ ★ ★ ★
That's Interesting!
★ ★ ★ ★ ★ ★ ★ ★ ★ ★ ★

Watching Every Dime Would you remember to correct the error if you underpaid a bill by three cents? It was everyday policy for James Buchanan to follow such precision in his accounting. Throughout his life, he kept books in which he carefully recorded every penny that he earned or spent. While serving as ambassador to Great Britain, Buchanan recorded such daily details as how much he spent on pins and suspender buttons. One time during his presidency he realized he had underpaid by three cents for some food. Even though the merchant ignored the error, the president made sure the owner received his three pennies.

THE GRANGER COLLECTION, NEW YORK

James Buchanan's inaugural parade stretched far down the streets of Washington, D.C.

Dred Scott argued that living on free soil had made him a free man.

⭐ The *Dred Scott* Decision

Just two days after Buchanan became president, the Supreme Court issued a ruling that threw the country back into crisis. This case involved **Dred Scott**, the slave of an army surgeon from St. Louis, Missouri. In the 1830s Scott had gone with the surgeon on tours of duty in Illinois and the northern part of the Louisiana Purchase. In 1846 Scott sued for his freedom after returning to Missouri. He argued that he had become free when he lived in free territory.

The case reached the U.S. Supreme Court in 1856. The justices—a majority of whom were from the South—had three key issues before them. First, the Court had to rule on whether Scott was a citizen of the United States. This ruling would determine if he was able to sue in federal court. Second, the Court had to decide if the time he had spent living on free soil made him free. Third, the Court had to decide whether the ban on slavery in parts of the Louisiana Purchase was constitutional. This last ruling would affect the Missouri Compromise.

The Chief Justice of the Supreme Court was **Roger B. Taney** (TAW-nee). Taney came from a slaveholding family in Maryland. He wrote the majority opinion in the ***Dred Scott* decision** in March 1857. Taney said the nation's founders believed that African Americans "had no rights which a white man was bound to respect." He therefore concluded that African Americans were not citizens under the U.S. Constitution. Thus, Dred Scott did not have the right to file suit in federal court.

Taney then said that living on free soil had not made Scott free. Thus, "his *status*, as free or slave, depended on the laws of Missouri." Finally, Taney said that the Missouri Compromise restriction on slavery north of 36°30' was unconstitutional. He used the Fifth Amendment as support. It said no one could "be deprived of life, liberty, or property without due process of law." Slaves were considered property, so Congress could not ban someone from taking slaves into a federal territory.

Most white southerners cheered the decision. It "covers every question regarding slavery and settles it in favor of the South," reported a Georgia newspaper. The ruling stunned many northerners. Republicans were particularly upset by the Court's ruling on the Missouri Compromise. Indeed, some northerners feared that the spread of slavery would not stop with the federal territories. Illinois lawyer **Abraham Lincoln** warned about the Court's future rulings.

Analyzing Primary Sources
Identifying Points of View What concerned Lincoln about the *Dred Scott* decision?

History Makers Speak

❝We shall *lie down* pleasantly dreaming that the people of *Missouri* are on the verge of [close to] making their state free; and we shall *awake* to the *reality*, instead, that the *Supreme* Court has made *Illinois* a *slave* state.❞

—Abraham Lincoln, from *The Collected Works of Abraham Lincoln*, edited by Roy P. Basler

✔ **Reading Check: Summarizing** What were the three key issues in the Supreme Court's ruling on the *Dred Scott* case?

The Lincoln-Douglas Debates

At the time of the *Dred Scott* decision, few people outside of Illinois knew Abraham Lincoln. A native of Kentucky, he had moved to the Midwest in 1816. Lincoln became involved in politics, serving four terms in the Illinois legislature and one term in Congress. A longtime Whig, he joined the Republican Party in 1856. He supported the party's efforts to halt the spread of slavery.

In 1858 Illinois Republicans nominated Lincoln for a U.S. Senate seat. His opponent was Democrat Stephen Douglas, who had represented Illinois in the Senate since 1847. Douglas was well known for the Kansas-Nebraska Act, so Lincoln tried to take advantage of his opponent's fame. He challenged Douglas to a series of debates throughout the state.

Thousands of people attended the **Lincoln-Douglas debates**. In each of the seven debates, Lincoln stressed that the central issue in the campaign involved slavery and its future in the West. Lincoln said that the Democrats wanted to spread slavery across the continent. As a Republican, Lincoln believed that slavery was wrong. Lincoln added that "one of the methods of treating it as a wrong is to make provision [ensure] that *it shall grow no larger.*" Lincoln also said that African Americans were "entitled to all the natural rights" listed in the Declaration of Independence. He specifically named "the right to life, liberty, and the pursuit of happiness."

Some voters asked Lincoln about his views on racial equality. He replied that African Americans were not necessarily the political or social equals of whites. However, "in the right to eat the bread . . . which his own hand earns, he [an African American] *is my equal and the equal of Judge Douglas.*" Douglas insisted that Lincoln "thinks that the Negro is his brother. . . . Those of you who believe that the Negro is your equal . . . of course will vote for Mr. Lincoln." Douglas hoped that these statements would shock many voters and cost Lincoln votes.

Research on the ROM

Free Find:
Stephen Douglas
After reading about Stephen Douglas on the **Holt Researcher CD–ROM**, imagine that you are hosting one of the Lincoln-Douglas debates. Write a speech that introduces Stephen Douglas to the crowd of spectators.

Interpreting the Visual Record

Political debate *The Lincoln-Douglas debates established the reputation of Abraham Lincoln as a gifted public speaker. In this painting of the fourth debate in the series, Lincoln is standing to speak and Stephen Douglas is seated to Lincoln's right.* **What is the mood of the politicians and audience members shown in this painting?**

A Divided Nation **567**

Supporters of Stephen Douglas made this wooden campaign doll.

Douglas also criticized Lincoln for saying that the country could not remain "half slave and half free." He said that the Republicans wanted to make every state a free state. If this happened, he warned, it would only lead to "a dissolution [destruction] of the Union" and "warfare between the North and the South."

The second debate was held in the northern Illinois town of Freeport. At this meeting, Lincoln pointed out the difference between the Democrats' belief in popular sovereignty and the terms of the *Dred Scott* decision. He asked Douglas to explain how Congress could allow the citizens of a federal territory to ban slavery if Congress itself could not ban it. Douglas's response became known as the **Freeport Doctrine**. "It matters not" what the Supreme Court decides about slavery, responded Douglas.

History Makers Speak

"The people have the lawful means [way] to introduce it or exclude it [shut it out] as they please, for the reason that slavery cannot exist a day or an hour anywhere, unless it is supported by local police regulations."

—Stephen Douglas, quoted in *Stephen A. Douglas*, by Robert W. Johannsen

The Freeport Doctrine would put control of the slavery question back in the hands of American citizens. The doctrine helped Douglas win the Senate seat. However, Lincoln had made a strong showing in the debates. As a result, he became one of the important leaders of the new Republican Party.

✔ **Reading Check: Contrasting** How did Douglas oppose Lincoln's views on slavery and African Americans?

Section 3 Review

go.hrw.com **Homework Practice Online** keyword: SF3 HP18

1 **Identify** and explain:
• Republican Party
• James Buchanan
• John C. Frémont
• Dred Scott
• Roger B. Taney
• *Dred Scott* decision
• Abraham Lincoln
• Lincoln-Douglas debates
• Freeport Doctrine

2 **Analyzing Information** Copy the chart below. Use it to identify examples of deepening political divisions caused by the slavery issue.

Event	Results
Election of 1856	
Dred Scott decision	
Lincoln-Douglas debates	

3 **Finding the Main Idea**
a. How did different political parties respond to the Kansas-Nebraska Act?

b. What did Dred Scott claim made him free, and how did the Supreme Court rule in his case?

4 **Writing and Critical Thinking**
Summarizing Imagine that you are an Illinois resident who attended the Lincoln-Douglas debates. Write a letter to a friend in another state explaining the candidates' views on the spread of slavery.

Consider the following:
• Lincoln's views on slavery and racial equality
• Douglas's response to Lincoln
• the Freeport Doctrine

Secession

Read to Discover

1. How did Americans react to John Brown's raid on Harpers Ferry?
2. What factors led to Lincoln's victory in the presidential election of 1860?
3. Why did some southern states decide to leave the Union?

WHY IT MATTERS TODAY

There is still diversity among the different regions of the United States. Use CNN**fyi**.com or other **current events** sources to identify issues or features that show these differences. Record your findings in your journal.

Define

• secession

Identify

• John Brown's raid
• John C. Breckinridge
• Constitutional Union Party
• John Bell
• John J. Crittenden
• Confederate States of America
• Jefferson Davis

The Story Continues

After the Pottawatomie Massacre, John Brown was a hunted man. He left Kansas and eventually returned to New England. There Brown was frustrated that most abolitionists wanted to end slavery without using violence. "Talk! talk! talk!" he said with disgust after attending a meeting of the New England Anti-Slavery Society. "That will never free the slaves. What is needed is action—action."

John Brown believed that violence was the only way to end slavery.

The Raid on Harpers Ferry

In 1858 John Brown worked to start a slave uprising. He wanted to attack the federal arsenal, or military storehouse, in Virginia and seize the weapons stored there. He then planned to arm the slaves in the surrounding area. Brown was prepared to take hostages or kill any white southerners who stood in the way. He urged his fellow abolitionists to give him enough money to recruit, train, and supply a small army. However, after nearly two years of preparation, Brown's band had about 20 men, including three of his sons and himself.

On the night of October 16, 1859, **John Brown's raid** began. Brown and his men entered Harpers Ferry, Virginia. The town lay next to the Potomac River, about 55 miles northwest of Washington, D.C. Brown first took over the federal arsenal. Then he sent several of his men into the countryside to get slaves to come to Harpers Ferry.

Brown hoped enslaved African Americans would join him. None did. They most likely knew they would be severely punished if they were caught taking part in an uprising. Instead, white southerners from Harpers Ferry and the surrounding area armed themselves and attacked Brown. Eight of his men and three local men were killed in the exchange of gunfire. Brown and some of his followers retreated to the safety of a firehouse.

Federal troops arrived in Harpers Ferry on the night of October 17. The following morning Colonel Robert E. Lee ordered a squad of marines to storm the firehouse. In a matter of seconds, the marines killed two more of Brown's men. They captured the rest—including Brown.

★ Judging John Brown

Brown was quickly charged and convicted of treason, murder, and conspiracy to stir up slave rebellion. Some of the men who took part in the raid received death sentences. On the way to his execution, John Copeland—a fugitive slave—defended his actions. "If I am dying for freedom, I could not die for a better cause—I had rather die than be a slave!" On November 2, convinced that he also would be sentenced to death by the state of Virginia. Brown delivered a memorable speech.

> **History Makers Speak**
>
> **"It is unjust that I should suffer such a penalty. . . . I believe that to have interfered . . . in behalf of His [God's] despised [hated] poor, is no wrong, but right. Now, if it is deemed [thought] necessary that I should forfeit [give up] my life for the furtherance of the ends of justice, and mingle [mix] my blood . . . with the blood of millions in this slave country whose rights are disregarded by wicked, cruel, and unjust enactments, I say, let it be done."**
>
> —John Brown, quoted in *John Brown, 1800–1859,* by Oswald Garrison Villard

As expected, the judge ordered Brown to be hanged. The sentence was carried out a month later, on December 2, 1859.

Many people in the North mourned the death of John Brown. Novelist Louisa May Alcott referred to him as "Saint John the Just." Not everyone who opposed slavery supported Brown's actions, however. Abraham Lincoln said Brown "agreed with us in thinking slavery wrong." He continued, "That cannot excuse violence, bloodshed, and treason." Most southern whites—including slaveholders and non-slaveholders—felt threatened. White southerners worried that a "John Brown the Second" might attack another southern target. One South Carolina newspaper wrote about these fears. "We are convinced the safety of the South lies only outside the present Union." Another journal from the same state was more blunt: "The sooner we get out of the Union, the better."

✔ **Reading Check: Summarizing** How did northerners differ in their reactions to John Brown's raid and execution?

GLOBAL CONNECTIONS

Reactions to John Brown's Raid

News of the raid on Harpers Ferry raised strong emotions across the Atlantic, particularly in Great Britain. British politician William Edward Forster expressed his views. "Whatever John Brown may have done toward freeing the slaves . . . he has exposed the utter [complete] weakness of the slave system." Other Europeans also praised Brown and the abolitionist cause.

In early 1860 the French writer Victor Hugo made a prediction. He thought that Brown's execution would lead to the breakup of the United States. "Between the North and the South stands the gallows of Brown," Hugo wrote. "Union is no longer possible: such a crime cannot be shared." **Why might Victor Hugo have said that Brown's raid would lead to the breakup of the Union?**

John Brown, shown here kissing an African American child, was led to his execution on December 2, 1859.

THE METROPOLITAN MUSEUM OF ART

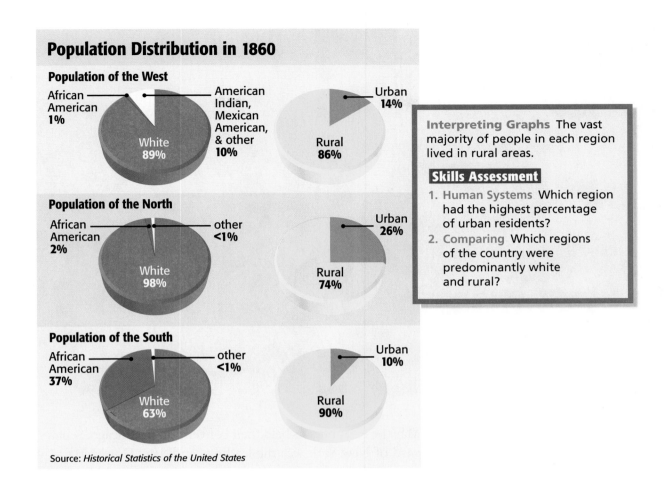

Population Distribution in 1860

Population of the West

African American 1%
White 89%
American Indian, Mexican American, & other 10%

Urban 14%
Rural 86%

Population of the North

African American 2%
White 98%
other <1%

Urban 26%
Rural 74%

Population of the South

African American 37%
White 63%
other <1%

Urban 10%
Rural 90%

Source: *Historical Statistics of the United States*

Interpreting Graphs The vast majority of people in each region lived in rural areas.

Skills Assessment

1. **Human Systems** Which region had the highest percentage of urban residents?
2. **Comparing** Which regions of the country were predominantly white and rural?

★ The Election of 1860

In this mood of distrust, Americans prepared for another presidential election. The Democrats were the first party to meet to nominate a presidential candidate in 1860. They met in Charleston, South Carolina, in late April. Yet the northern and southern members of the party could not agree on a candidate. When they could not agree, the party split in two. The Democrats met again six weeks later in Baltimore. Northern Democrats chose Senator Stephen Douglas. Southern Democrats backed the current vice president, **John C. Breckinridge** of Kentucky. Breckinridge strongly supported slavery in the territories. He did not believe, however, that a Republican victory in the election would give states the right to break up the Union.

Meanwhile, in early May some northerners and southerners—many of them former Whigs—decided to form a new political party. Called the **Constitutional Union Party**, its platform was simple. It recognized "no political principles other than the Constitution of the country, the Union of the states, and the enforcement of the laws." Members of this new party also met in Baltimore, Maryland. They selected **John Bell** of Tennessee as their presidential candidate. Bell was a slaveholder, but he had been against the Kansas-Nebraska Act in 1854.

THE GRANGER COLLECTION, NEW YORK

Daily Life

Political parties Crowds gathered at the 1860 Republican National Convention, the second time the Republicans had fielded a presidential candidate. The 1850s had seen the rise and fall of several political parties as Americans struggled to address the slavery issue. The Free-Soil, Know-Nothing, and Whig Parties had all collapsed or been greatly weakened during this period. Shortly before the Republican convention met, yet another political party—the Constitutional Union Party—had formed. Voters thus faced many choices but seemingly few solutions to the divisions that plagued the nation. **Why do you think women would have attended the Republican convention although they did not yet have the right to vote?**

In mid-May the Republicans held their convention in Chicago. Senator William Seward of New York was the leading candidate. However, many Republicans worried that his strong antislavery views made him a poor choice. Thus, Abraham Lincoln won the nomination on the third ballot. Lincoln was a moderate who was against the spread of slavery. He said, however, that he would not try to abolish slavery where it already existed.

The four-man election contest was really a pair of two-man contests. Lincoln challenged Douglas for the North's electoral votes. Bell and Breckinridge competed for those of the South. Douglas, Bell, and Breckinridge each knew he might not win the election. However, they hoped to win enough votes to prevent Lincoln from winning in the electoral college. Such an outcome would send the election to the House of Representatives.

In this they failed. Lincoln won the race. Although he gained less than 40 percent of the overall popular vote, he won 180 of the 183 electoral votes in the free states. Breckinridge and Bell split the electoral votes of slave states, with the exception of Missouri. Douglas had the second-highest number of overall popular votes. However, he won only one state—Missouri—outright. He finished with just 12 electoral votes. The election results angered many southerners. Lincoln did not carry a single southern state, yet he would be the next president. This election was a strong reminder of how the South was losing its political power on the national level.

✔ **Reading Check: Finding the Main Idea** How did Lincoln and the Republican Party win the presidential election of 1860?

★ Breaking with the Union

Many southern whites believed that once in power, Lincoln would move to abolish slavery in the South. They feared this action would destroy the South's economy and society. Lincoln insisted he would not change slavery in the southern states. He had said, however, that slavery had to end at some point in the future. That was enough to greatly concern many southerners. A man in Mississippi urged white southerners to act quickly to protect their interests. "Let us rally . . . before the enemy can make good his promise to overwhelm us."

Just four days after Lincoln's election, South Carolina's legislature called for a special convention. There delegates met to consider the question of **secession**, the act of formally withdrawing from the Union. The convention opened in Charleston on December 17, 1860. After three days of speeches, all of the delegates voted to secede. They wanted to dissolve "the union now subsisting [existing] between South Carolina and other States."

The Constitution does not directly address the issue of secession. Therefore, southerners who wanted to secede believed that there was no constitutional barrier to a state leaving the Union. They pointed out that each of the original states had voluntarily joined the Union. Each of these states had held a special state convention to ratify the Constitution. Surely, southerners reasoned, states could also leave the Union by the same process.

This banner supports Republican candidates Abraham Lincoln and Hannibal Hamlin.

Lincoln and Hamlin

The Election of 1860

Interpreting Maps The division between North and South was clearly reflected in the election of 1860. Lincoln's victory increased tensions between the regions, and secession soon followed.

Skills Assessment

1. **Places and Regions** Which state had the most electoral votes, and which candidate won this state?
2. **Analyzing Information** Which candidate finished second to Lincoln in the electoral and popular votes?

	Electoral Vote	Popular Vote	% of Pop. Vote
Lincoln	180	1,865,593	39.8
Douglas	12	1,382,713	29.5
Breckinridge	72	848,356	18.1
Bell	39	592,906	12.6

*New Jersey cast four electoral votes for Lincoln and three for Douglas.

Source: *Historical Statistics of the United States*

Electoral Winner by State
- Lincoln (Republican)
- Douglas (Northern Democrat)
- Breckinridge (Southern Democrat)
- Bell (Constitutional Union)
- 4 Electoral votes

Just the Facts

Slave and Free States in Congress

Number of Representatives

Year	Slave states	Free states
1820	90	113
1830	99	125
1840	88	114
1850	89	118
1860	84	123

Source: *Historical Statistics of the United States*

Using Mathematical Skills

1. What was the largest gap between representatives of free and slave states?

2. Create a line graph that illustrates the statistics in the chart above. Label the x-axis "Number of Representatives," and label the y-axis "Year."

3. Imagine that you are a southern politician in 1860. Write a speech describing the trend that has taken place in the House between 1820 and 1860 and what it means to southern politics.

Critics of secession flatly rejected this idea. President Buchanan said that the Union was not "a mere voluntary association of States, to be dissolved at pleasure by any one of the contracting parties." President-elect Abraham Lincoln agreed. He said, "No State, upon its own mere motion, can lawfully get out of the Union." Lincoln added, 'They can only do so against [the] law, and by revolution."

While South Carolina representatives were meeting, Congress reviewed a plan to preserve the Union. Senator **John J. Crittenden** of Kentucky proposed a series of constitutional amendments to satisfy the South. One would extend the line created by the Missouri Compromise to the Pacific coast. It would allow slavery in all territories "now held, or hereafter acquired" south of this line. Another would use federal money to pay slaveholders who could not recover their fugitive slaves in the North. Crittenden hoped his plan would address the chief fears of slaveholders. He also hoped that the country would avoid secession and a civil war.

President-elect Lincoln did not agree with this plan. To express his views, he sent many letters to Republicans in the Senate. In these letters he asked Congress to vote against Crittenden's plan. "Entertain [consider] no proposition for a compromise in regard to the extension of slavery," Lincoln wrote. "The tug has to come and better now than later." A Senate committee voted on the Crittenden Compromise. Every Republican on the committee rejected it, as Lincoln had requested.

✔ **Reading Check: Identifying Points of View** Why did South Carolina decide to leave the Union, and how did politicians react?

★ The Confederate States of America

By February 1, 1861, Mississippi, Florida, Alabama, Georgia, Louisiana, and Texas had seceded from the Union. Their actions did not mean that everyone in these states supported secession, however. Some public figures even tried to slow or stop the march toward secession. However, such individuals quickly suffered the consequences of opposing the public will. In Texas, for example, Governor Sam Houston was removed from office for standing in the way of secession.

On February 4, delegates from six of the seven seceding states met in the town of Montgomery, Alabama. They established a new nation—the **Confederate States of America**, also known as the Confederacy. The delegates passed their new constitution on February 8. The document closely resembled the U.S. Constitution in many ways. However, the constitution of the Confederacy guaranteed that its citizens could hold slaves.

Jefferson Davis of Mississippi was elected president of the Confederate States of America. Alexander H. Stephens of Georgia became vice president. Davis was a graduate of West Point and a veteran of the Mexican War. He had been secretary of war under President Pierce and had served in the Senate until Mississippi left the Union. Davis had opposed secession as late as 1860, although he believed that states had the right to secede. But his loyalty to the South outweighed his hopes for peace. With his military background, Davis hoped to be appointed general in command of Mississippi's troops. He did not seek the presidency of the Confederacy. He greeted the news of his election with silence. Davis's wife, Varina, wrote about his reaction.

THE GRANGER COLLECTION, NEW YORK

 History Makers Speak

❝He looked so grieved that I feared some evil had befallen [happened to] our family. After a few minutes' painful silence he told me [what the telegram contained], as a man might speak of a sentence of death.❞

—Varina Davis, *Jefferson Davis: A Memoir*

Davis was a highly intelligent and hardworking politician. He also was very loyal to his friends. However, he tended to involve himself in details that would have been better left to his staff. Furthermore, his devotion to his friends often clouded his judgment. These personal qualities would increase the difficulty of the challenges he would face as president of the Confederacy.

As an officer during the Mexican War, Jefferson Davis had led U.S. forces to victory in the Battle of Buena Vista.

✔ **Reading Check: Summarizing** What did the seceding states do in 1860 and 1861 after leaving the Union?

Section 4 Review

go.hrw.com **Homework Practice Online**
keyword: SF3 HP18

1 **Define and explain:**
• secession

2 **Identify and explain:**
• John Brown's raid
• John C. Breckinridge
• Constitutional Union Party
• John Bell
• John J. Crittenden
• Confederate States of America
• Jefferson Davis

3 **Summarizing** Copy the graphic organizer below. Use it to identify the causes of the secession of southern states in 1860 and 1861.

Causes

Secession

4 **Finding the Main Idea**
a. Describe the northern and southern reactions to John Brown's raid on Harpers Ferry.

b. How did the four-way race for president help Lincoln win the election of 1860?

5 **Writing and Critical Thinking**
Supporting a Point of View Imagine that you are a foreign ambassador witnessing the conflicts over slavery in the United States. Write a speech for your home country that responds to South Carolina's secession from the Union.

Consider the following:
• reasons for secession
• whether or not the Constitution mentions secession
• your support for or opposition to South Carolina's secession

Chapter 18 Review

The Chapter at a Glance

Examine the visual summary of the chapter below. Make notes about each topic listed in the image. Then use the notes to create a simple board game to be played with a partner. Each player must explain the topics he or she lands on to continue proceeding along the "pathway to secession."

The Balance Is Broken

Secession

Northern Complaints
- Fugitive Slave Act
- Kansas-Nebraska Act
- "Bleeding Kansas"
- Dred Scott decision
- Westward expansion of slavery

Southern Complaints
- Uncle Tom's Cabin
- "Bleeding Kansas"
- John Brown's raid
- Lincoln's election
- Growing power of the North

The United States of America

Compromise of 1850

Identifying People and Ideas

Use the following terms or people in historically significant sentences.

1. sectionalism
2. Free-Soil Party
3. Daniel Webster
4. Stephen Douglas
5. Republican Party
6. Dred Scott
7. John Brown's raid
8. secession
9. Confederate States of America
10. Jefferson Davis

Understanding Main Ideas

Section 1 *(Pages 552–558)*

1. What were the parts of the Compromise of 1850?
2. How did the Fugitive Slave Act affect free and enslaved African Americans?

Section 2 *(Pages 559–563)*

3. How did pro-slavery and antislavery forces oppose each other in Kansas?

Section 3 *(Pages 564–568)*

4. Why was the Republican Party created, and what goals did it promote?

Section 4 *(Pages 569–575)*

5. How did each of the four presidential candidates in 1860 view the slavery issue?

6. What led many of the southern states to leave the Union?

You Be the Historian— Reviewing Themes

1. **Geography** Why did the Mexican Cession renew tensions about slavery between northern and southern states?
2. **Citizenship** How did the *Dred Scott* decision affect African Americans, and what was the response to the decision?
3. **Constitutional Heritage** What legal argument did South Carolina's officials use to justify secession?

Thinking Critically

1. **Summarizing** What roles did the politicians John C. Calhoun, Henry Clay, and Daniel Webster play in the compromise efforts prior to the Civil War?
2. **Comparing and Contrasting** How were the Compromise of 1850 and the Missouri Compromise similar, and how were they different?
3. **Analyzing Information** How did both congressional conflicts and efforts to compromise contribute to greater divisions within the United States?

576 Chapter 18

Interpreting Maps

Study the map below. Then use the information on the map to help you answer the following questions.

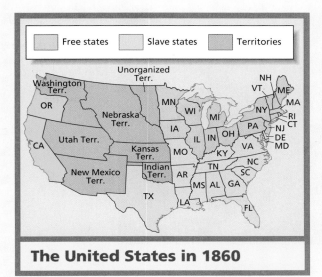

The United States in 1860

1. How many slave states and free states were there in 1860?
   a. 13 slave states, 20 free states
   b. 15 slave states, 16 free states
   c. 14 slave states, 18 free states
   d. 15 slave states, 18 free states

2. What would the total number of senators have been for the slave states and for the free states in 1860?
   a. 30 and 36
   b. 28 and 36
   c. 30 and 34
   d. 30 and 32

3. Based on the map and your knowledge of the period, where do you think southern politicians hoped to add additional slave states to the Union?

Analzying Primary Sources

Read the following quote by a reader of Harriet Beecher Stowe's *Uncle Tom's Cabin* and answer the questions that follow.

> ❝My Dear Mrs. Stowe,—I sat up last night until long after one o'clock, reading and finishing "Uncle Tom's Cabin." I *could not* leave it any more than I could have left a dying child. . . . I thought I was a thoroughgoing abolitionist before, but your book has awakened so strong a feeling of indignation and of compassion that I seem never to have had *any* feeling on this subject till now. But what can we do? Alas! Alas! what *can* we do?❞

4. Which of the following statements best describes the letter writer's feelings about *Uncle Tom's Cabin*?
   a. The criticism of slavery offended her greatly and made her angry.
   b. The book made her want to do even more to try to abolish slavery.
   c. The book changed her mind about slavery, which had not bothered her before.
   d. The book does not matter because nobody can do anything about slavery.

5. Based on your knowledge of the period, why would such reactions to *Uncle Tom's Cabin* have been important to the relationship between the North and the South?

Alternative Assessment

Building Your Portfolio

American History

Cooperative Learning

As a group, prepare a chart showing the political parties that were formed from 1848 to 1860. The chart should include information on the year the party was formed (and ended, if applicable), the party's platform, presidential candidates, and region of strongest support. Add appropriate images to your chart and write a paragraph to explain the importance of third parties in political elections.

⌨ internet connect

Internet Activity: go.hrw.com
keyword: SF3 CF18

Choose a topic on the Divided Nation to:
- Understand the causes and effects of the European revolutions of 1848.
- Create a newspaper on John Brown and resistance movements against slavery.
- Research Supreme Court decisions regarding slavery.

19

The Civil War
(1861–1865)

The fierce fighting at the First Battle of Bull Run surprised many Americans who had expected the war to be over swiftly.

THE GRANGER COLLECTION, NEW YORK

UNITED STATES

1861 Confederate guns open fire on Fort Sumter in South Carolina on April 12.

1861 Confederate forces win the first battle of the Civil War on July 21 at Bull Run Creek in Virginia.

1862 The *Monitor* fights the *Virginia* on March 9.

1862 On December 13 General Robert E. Lee wins a major victory at Fredericksburg, Virginia.

1863 The Emancipation Proclamation goes into effect on January 1.

1861 1862 1863

1861 On March 17 nationalist leader Giuseppe Garibaldi declares Victor Emmanuel II king of Italy.

1862 Jean-Henri Dunant of Switzerland proposes the creation of the International Red Cross.

This medal was used by the International Red Cross.

WORLD

Together, Giuseppe Garibaldi and Victor Emmanuel II helped unify Italy.

Build on What You Know

In the 1850s the North and the South were strongly divided over the issue of slavery. The election of Republican Abraham Lincoln as president in 1860 led 11 southern states to leave the Union. When the North refused to accept this secession, the opposing views of each side soon led to a terrible civil war between North and South.

When Lee surrendered to Grant, the Union commander agreed to treat the defeated Confederate troops with dignity.

This sword belonged to Robert E. Lee.

1863 Union forces capture Vicksburg, Mississippi, on July 4. That same day, General Lee's forces retreat after losing the Battle of Gettysburg in Pennsylvania.

1863 On November 19 President Lincoln delivers the Gettysburg Address.

1864 Union general William Techumseh Sherman takes Atlanta on September 2.

1865 General Lee surrenders to General Grant at Appomattox Courthouse on April 9.

1864

1865

1863 On June 7, French forces capture Mexico City.

1864 The Taiping Rebellion in China ends after the capture of Nanjing in July.

If you were there . . .
Would you support or oppose secession?

You Be the Historian

Themes Journal

What's Your Opinion? Do you **agree** or **disagree** with the following statements? Support your point of view in your journal.

- **Science, Technology & Society** New technology always makes wars easier to win.
- **Economics** Wars are bad for a nation's economy.
- **Citizenship** All citizens have a duty to support their government during a war.

The War Begins

Read to Discover

1. What led to the bombardment of Fort Sumter, and why was this event important?
2. Which side of the conflict did Arkansas and the Upper South join, and why?
3. Why did both the North and the South want to claim the border states?
4. What strategies did each side follow at the beginning of the war?

WHY IT MATTERS TODAY

Many countries around the world are currently experiencing civil wars. Use CNN**fyi**.com or other **current events** sources to find out about some of these places. Record your findings in your journal.

Define

- border states
- cotton diplomacy

Identify

- Fort Sumter
- Abraham Lincoln
- Elizabeth Blackwell
- Winfield Scott

The Spirit of '61 was used as a symbol of Union pride on recruiting posters.

The Story Continues

When Abraham Lincoln took office, seven states had already left the Union. He wanted to keep more southern states from seceding. Lincoln gave his inaugural address on March 4, 1861. He pledged that he would not try to end slavery in the South. He also promised the South that the federal "government will not assail [attack] you. You can have no conflict without being yourselves the aggressors." At the same time, however, Lincoln spoke of his intention to preserve the Union.

⭐ Lincoln Faces a Crisis

The South did not respond to these calls for unity. Confederate officials were already taking over many federal mints, arms storehouses, and forts. One important federal post was **Fort Sumter**, located near Charleston, South Carolina. The fort controlled the entrance to Charleston Harbor. By early March 1861 the federal troops at Fort Sumter were running low on supplies. Instead of ordering the troops to surrender, President **Abraham Lincoln** decided to resupply them.

LINCOLN'S FIRST INAUGURAL ADDRESS

In the following excerpt from Abraham Lincoln's first inaugural address, he discusses the disagreements that led to the nation's greatest crisis.

I hold that, in contemplation of universal law, and of the Constitution, the Union of these States is **perpetual.**[1] . . .

It follows from these views that no State, upon its own mere **motion,**[2] can lawfully get out of the Union, —that **resolves**[3] and **ordinances**[4] to that effect are legally void; and that acts of violence, within any State or States, against the authority of the United States, are **insurrectionary**[5] or revolutionary, according to circumstances.

I therefore consider that, in view of the Constitution and the laws, the Union is unbroken. . . . I trust this will not be regarded as a menace, but only as the declared purpose of the Union that it *will* constitutionally defend, and maintain itself. In doing this there needs to be no bloodshed or violence; and there shall be none, unless it be forced upon the national authority. . . .

One section of our country believes that slavery is *right*, and ought to be extended, while the other believes it is *wrong*, and ought not to be extended. This is the only **substantial**[6] dispute. . . .

My countrymen, one and all, think calmly and *well*, upon this whole subject. . . . In *your* hands, my dissatisfied fellow countrymen, and not in *mine*, is the momentous issue of civil war.

Analyzing Primary Sources

1. According to Lincoln, what do the Constitution of the United States and the laws of the government say about the Union?

2. What does Lincoln say is the main dispute between the states?

[1]**perpetual:** everlasting
[2]**motion:** action
[3]**resolves:** resolutions
[4]**ordinances:** laws
[5]**insurrectionary:** rebellious
[6]**substantial:** important

Before the supply ships arrived, however, South Carolina demanded that the Union troops leave the fort. The fort's commander, Major Robert Anderson, refused to do so. He told the southerners, "Gentlemen, I will await your fire."

Before sunrise on April 12, 1861, Confederate guns opened fire on Fort Sumter. The Civil War had begun. A witness wrote that the first shots brought "every man, woman, and child in the city of Charleston from their beds." The fort withstood 34 hours of Confederate bombardment. Then Anderson had no choice but to surrender.

The attack on Fort Sumter outraged the North. Lincoln declared that the South was in rebellion and asked the state governors to provide 75,000 militiamen to help put down the revolt. Mary Boykin Chesnut, whose husband became a Confederate general, wrote about the events in her diary.

April 12, 1861
The Confederacy attacks Fort Sumter, starting the Civil War.

 History Makers Speak **"**I did not know that one could live in such days of excitement. . . . Everybody tells you half of something, and then rushes off . . . to hear the last news.**"**

—Mary Boykin Chesnut, *Mary Chesnut's Civil War*, edited by C. Vann Woodward

Analyzing Primary Sources

Drawing Inferences and Conclusions How do Chesnut and the people around her regard the start of the Civil War?

✔ **Reading Check: Drawing Inferences and Conclusions** How do you think states' rights issues contributed to the attack on Fort Sumter?

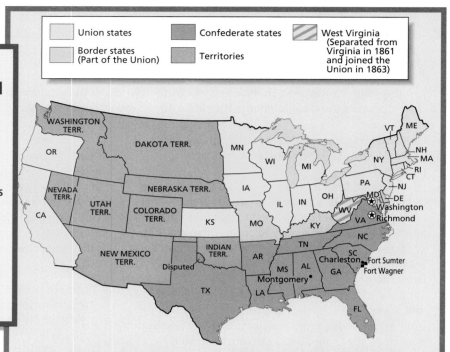

The Union and Confederacy in 1861

Interpreting Maps After the 1860 election many slave states left the Union to form the Confederacy.

Skills Assessment

1. **Places and Regions** What states made up the Confederacy, and what states made up the Union?
2. **Analyzing Information** How was the state of Maryland strategically important to the Union in relationship to Washington, D.C.?

Map legend: Union states; Border states (Part of the Union); Confederate states; Territories; West Virginia (Separated from Virginia in 1861 and joined the Union in 1863)

The Union printed recruitment posters such as this one to encourage volunteers for the war effort.

⭐ Choosing Sides

Democratic senator Stephen Douglas supported Lincoln's call for troops. He declared, "Every man must be for the United States or against it." The free northern states were solidly in the Union. Meanwhile, slave states that had not joined the Confederacy had to choose sides. The states of the Upper South—North Carolina, Tennessee, and Virginia—all joined the Confederacy soon after Lincoln's request for troops. So did Arkansas. "The South must go with the South," wrote a North Carolinian. The Upper South provided the Confederacy with soldiers and industrial resources. Richmond, Virginia, became the Confederacy's capital.

Four slave states—Delaware, Kentucky, Maryland, and Missouri—bordered the North. The position of these **border states** made them important to both the North and the South. Kentucky and Missouri controlled key stretches of the Ohio and Mississippi Rivers. The federal capital of Washington, D.C., was located within Maryland.

Slaveholders in Delaware supported secession, but they were few in number. In Kentucky, Missouri, and Maryland, however, people were deeply divided. Troops from Kentucky and Missouri served with each side in the war. There were riots against Union soldiers in Maryland. However, these three states eventually voted against secession. Lincoln sent federal troops into Maryland and into western Virginia, whose population was mostly loyal to the Union. People in the region set up their own state government. The new state of West Virginia joined the Union in 1863.

✔ **Reading Check: Comparing and Contrasting** Identify the similarities and differences between the Upper South and the border states.

The Volunteer Spirit

Neither side was prepared for war. Therefore, both sides depended on volunteers. At the start of the war, the Union army had only 16,000 troops. Thousands of volunteers quickly joined the army. One Union recruit from the Midwest explained why he signed up.

History Makers Speak

❝[It is] a duty I owe to my country and to my children to do what I can to preserve this government as I shudder to think what is ahead for them if this government should be overthrown.❞

—Union soldier, quoted in *Battle at Bull Run*, by William C. Davis

Virginian Thomas Webber also defended his way of life. He wanted to fight "against the invading foe [enemy] who now pollute the sacred soil of my beloved native state." Many southern volunteers shared his view. Early in the war, Union soldiers asked one southerner why he was fighting. He replied, "I'm fighting because you're down here."

In the border states, members of the same family often joined opposing sides in the war. The president's Kentucky-born wife, Mary Todd Lincoln, had four brothers who fought for the Confederacy. Disagreements over the war deeply divided many friends and families.

Civilians on both sides also helped the war effort. They raised money, provided aid for soldiers and their families, and ran emergency hospitals. Dr. **Elizabeth Blackwell**, the first woman to earn a medical license, helped convince President Lincoln to form the U.S. Sanitary Commission in June 1861. The Sanitary, as it was known, had tens of thousands of volunteers. They sent bandages, medicines, and food to Union army camps and hospitals. Staff and volunteers also worked to keep the Union troops healthy.

✔ **Reading Check: Analyzing Information** How did civilians help the war effort in both the North and the South?

The North versus the South

At the beginning of the war, the North had several key advantages over the South. The much larger population of the North provided more soldiers. The North had most of the nation's factories and more shipyards. It also had a better network of railways, which allowed for more efficient transportation. Finally, the Union was able to raise more money to spend on the war.

The Confederacy also had advantages. The South's military tradition provided it with many skilled officers. In addition, the South needed only to defend itself until the North grew tired of the war. In contrast, the North had to defeat southern forces and occupy large areas of enemy territory.

Both the Union and the Confederacy based their military strategies on their strengths. Union general **Winfield Scott** developed the Union's

THE GRANGER COLLECTION, NEW YORK

PRESIDENTIAL PROFILES

Abraham Lincoln

Abraham Lincoln was born on February 12, 1809, in Kentucky. He entered politics in 1834, serving four terms in the state legislature of Illinois and one in the U.S. House of Representatives. He helped spread the message of the new Republican Party in the 1850s and was elected president in 1860. Lincoln was a strong leader during the Civil War. With the Emancipation Proclamation, he began the process of freeing the slaves.

Today Lincoln is one of four presidents whose image is carved into the monument at Mount Rushmore, South Dakota. President's Day, a federal holiday, is held on the third Monday of every February near his birthday. **What were some of Lincoln's major accomplishments as a political leader?**

Many Confederate soldiers came from rural areas to fight for the South.

THE MUSEUM OF THE CONFEDERACY, RICHMOND, VIRGINIA
PHOTOGRAPHY BY KATHERINE WETZEL

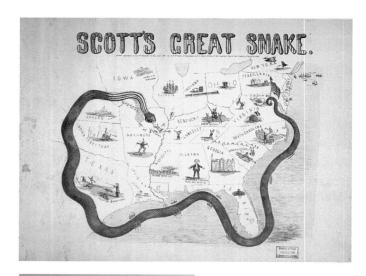

SCOTT'S GREAT SNAKE.

Interpreting Political Cartoons

Scott's Great Snake *This cartoon shows Union general Winfield Scott's plan to block-ade the Confederacy as a giant snake wrapped around the southern coastline.* **Why do you think the artist chose to represent the blockade plan as a snake squeezing the Confederacy?**

basic two-part strategy. He wanted to destroy the South's economy through a naval blockade of southern seaports. Scott also wanted to gain control of the Mississippi River to divide the Confederacy and cut its communications. Scott believed that this strategy would defeat the Confederacy "with less bloodshed than by any other plan." However, it would take time to succeed. Many northern leaders also called for a direct attack on Richmond, the Confederate capital.

The Confederacy's early strategy was to defend its territory and to wear down the Union's will to fight. Its offensive plan focused on taking Washington, D.C. Confederate president Jefferson Davis played a major role in the war. A demanding leader, Davis became so involved in war planning that he went through six secretaries of war in four years.

Davis and other Confederate leaders also tried to win foreign allies through **cotton diplomacy.** Cotton diplomacy was based on the southern belief that the British government would support them because cotton was important to Great Britain's textile industry. The British, however, had a large supply of cotton stockpiled when the war began. They were also able to get cotton from India and Egypt.

The strategies of the North and the South led to a war that was fought on land and at sea. As leaders made their plans, soldiers on both sides prepared to fight.

✔ **Reading Check: Supporting a Point of View** Which side do you think was best prepared for victory? Explain your answer.

Section 1 Review

go.hrw.com
Homework Practice Online
keyword: SF3 HP19

1 **Define** and explain:
• border states
• cotton diplomacy

2 **Identify** and explain:
• Fort Sumter
• Abraham Lincoln
• Elizabeth Blackwell
• Winfield Scott

3 **Summarizing** Copy the chart below. Use it to identify key characteristics of the North and the South at the start of the Civil War.

	The North	The South
Slave states that joined		
Advantages		
Disadvantages		
Strategies		

4 **Finding the Main Idea**
a. Why did the Confederates attack Fort Sumter, and what happened as a result?

b. What did Arkansas, North Carolina, Tennessee, and Virginia decide about the Confederacy, and why did they make this decision?

5 **Writing and Critical Thinking**
Analyzing Information Imagine that you are an adviser to President Lincoln. Write a plan that describes how the Union can keep the border states from seceding.

Consider the following:
• possible military actions
• the loyalty of the states' citizens

The War in the East

Read to Discover

1. What battles did the Confederates win in Virginia, and why were they important?
2. What stopped the northward advance of the Confederate army?
3. What was the significance of the *Monitor* and the *Virginia*?

WHY IT MATTERS TODAY

During the Civil War, powerful new types of warships were developed. Use CNNfyi.com or other **current events** sources to find out about the types of ships used by the U.S. Navy today. Record your findings in your journal.

Define
• ironclad
Identify
• Thomas "Stonewall" Jackson
• First Battle of Bull Run
• George B. McClellan
• Robert E. Lee
• Seven Days' Battles
• Second Battle of Bull Run
• Battle of Antietam

The Story Continues

After the fall of Fort Sumter, northerners demanded bold action. The Confederate Congress was supposed to meet in Richmond on July 20, 1861. Union troops gathered in Washington during the early summer. A northern newspaper headline urged, "Forward to Richmond! Forward to Richmond! The Rebel Congress Must Not Be Allowed to Meet There." President Lincoln decided to listen to public opinion. He ordered an attack on the Confederate capital.

This drum was used by the Union army.

★ Two Armies Meet

The first major clash of Union and Confederate armies took place in July 1861. President Lincoln had General Irvin McDowell lead about 35,000 troops from Washington toward Richmond. The soldiers were barely trained. McDowell complained that they "stopped every moment to pick blackberries or get water; they would not keep in the ranks."

The two armies met about 30 miles outside of Washington, near Manassas Junction, Virginia. Some 35,000 Confederates were lined along Bull Run Creek. At first the Union troops drove the left side of the

Confederate line back. However, a unit led by General **Thomas "Stonewall" Jackson** held firmly in place. Jackson's example inspired the other Confederate troops. "There is Jackson standing like a stone wall!" one southern officer cried out. "Rally behind the Virginians!" General "Stonewall" Jackson ordered his troops against the northern line. They charged forward, letting out the terrifying rebel yell.

Northern journalist Charles Coffin saw the battle. He described the confusion and shock of the fighting.

Analyzing Primary Sources

Drawing Inferences and Conclusions Based on Coffin's observation, what do you think the soldiers had expected war to be like?

History Makers Speak

“There is smoke, dust, wild talking, shouting; hissings, howlings, explosions. It is a new, strange, unanticipated [surprising] experience to the soldiers of both armies, far different from what they thought it would be.”

—Charles Coffin, quoted in *Voices of the Civil War*, by Richard Wheeler

Fresh southern troops soon arrived, driving the Union army back. Soon the northerners were retreating to Washington. The Confederates might have captured the Union capital if they had not been so tired and disorganized. In the **First Battle of Bull Run**, the Confederacy broke the Union's hopes of winning the war quickly and easily.

✔ **Reading Check:** **Analyzing Information** Why did the Confederates win the First Battle of Bull Run?

Civil War photographs such as this one showed civilians the horrors of the battlefield.

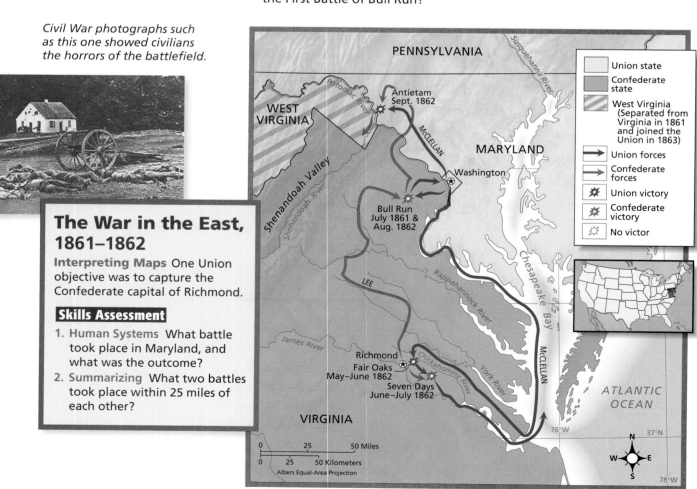

The War in the East, 1861–1862

Interpreting Maps One Union objective was to capture the Confederate capital of Richmond.

Skills Assessment

1. **Human Systems** What battle took place in Maryland, and what was the outcome?
2. **Summarizing** What two battles took place within 25 miles of each other?

★ More Battles in Virginia

Lincoln still wanted to capture Richmond. He sent his new commander, General **George B. McClellan**, back into Virginia. By early April 1862 McClellan and a huge force were camped near Yorktown, Virginia, southeast of Richmond. McClellan did not attack, however, because he thought his troops were outnumbered. This gave the Confederates time to strengthen Richmond's defenses. In early May, McClellan finally took Yorktown. The Union army forced the southern troops to retreat. At the end of the month, the two armies fought again near Richmond.

President Jefferson Davis put General **Robert E. Lee** in charge of the Confederate army in Virginia in June 1862. Lee was one of the most talented officers on either side. A graduate of the U.S. Military Academy at West Point, he had served in the Mexican War. Later, Lee was an engineer for the Army Corps of Engineers. He had also led the federal troops that captured John Brown at Harpers Ferry. Lincoln had even asked Lee in 1861 to command the Union forces. Although Lee was against slavery and secession, he was loyal to the South. As he told a northern friend, "I cannot raise my hand against my birthplace, my home, my children." When Virginia left the Union, Lee resigned from the U.S. Army and returned home.

During the summer of 1862, General Lee strengthened his positions. Then he began attacking, hoping to push McClellan's army away from Richmond. After scouting Union positions, Lee attacked on June 26, 1862. During the next week, the two armies fought five separate times. This fighting became known as the **Seven Days' Battles**. Confederate general D. H. Hill described one failed attack. "It was not war—it was murder." The Confederates suffered more than 20,000 casualties, and the Union suffered nearly 16,000. However, Lee forced McClellan to retreat from the area around Richmond.

Next, Lincoln ordered General John Pope to advance directly on Richmond from Washington. Pope told his soldiers, "Let us look before us and not behind. Success and glory are in the advance." To stop the Union forces, Lee sent Jackson's troops around Pope's right side. Then Lee's main force fell upon the Union's left side. This battle became known as the **Second Battle of Bull Run**. Caught off guard, Pope's army fell apart. By the end of August 1862, Lee had pushed most of the Union forces out of Virginia. He then decided to take the war into the North.

General Robert E. Lee was widely respected in both the North and the South for his leadership and daring strategies.

✔ **Reading Check: Summarizing** How did Lee's forces drive the Union army from Virginia?

⭐ The Battle of Antietam

Confederate leaders hoped a victory on northern soil might break the Union's spirit and convince European powers to aid the South. On September 4, 1862, some 40,000 Confederate soldiers entered Maryland. Union soldiers, however, found a copy of Lee's battle plan, which General McClellan used to plan a counterattack. On September 17, 1862, the armies met along Antietam Creek in Maryland. The **Battle of Antietam** lasted for hours. By the end of the day, the Union had suffered more than 12,000 casualties, and the Confederates more than 13,000. Antietam was the bloodiest single-day battle of the war, but the Union won a key victory.

Antietam cost Lee many of his troops and stopped his northward advance. However, McClellan allowed Lee to retreat to Virginia. Two months later, tired of McClellan's delays, Lincoln took the command in the East away from him.

✔ **Reading Check: Finding the Main Idea** How did the Battle of Antietam help the Union?

CONNECTING TO
SCIENCE AND TECHNOLOGY

Photography and the Civil War

In 1862 Mathew Brady shocked the people of New York with his photographs from the Battle of Antietam. Brady and other photographers followed the Union army to record events with their cameras. The early cameras were bulky and hard to set up quickly. They could only be used to take pictures of still objects. As a result, the photographs of the Civil War were mostly portraits of soldiers and scenes of camp life. Brady's pictures of battlefields were taken only after the fighting had stopped. Why did Brady not show images of battle?

The lens allows light to enter the camera and produces an image on a glass plate.

The glass plate was rushed to a nearby darkroom wagon to be developed.

Photographers carefully handled the glass plates, which were covered with dangerous chemicals.

⭐ The War at Sea

While the two armies fought for control of the land, the Union controlled the sea. The North had most of the U.S. Navy's small fleet and enough industry to build more ships. The Union navy blockaded the South, cutting off southern trade and hurting the economy. The blockade was hard to maintain because the Union navy had to patrol thousands of miles of coastline from Virginia to Texas. The South used small, fast ships called blockade runners to outrun the larger Union warships and reach trading ports. These ships, however, could not make up for the South's loss of trade.

The Confederacy turned to a new type of warship, the **ironclad**, which was heavily armored with iron. The Confederates had turned a captured Union ship into an ironclad, renamed the *Virginia*. One Union sailor described it as "a huge half-submerged crocodile." In early March 1862 the ironclad sailed north into Hampton Roads, Virginia. Union ships guarded access to this important waterway. Before nightfall, the *Virginia* easily sank two of the Union's wooden warships while suffering only minor damage.

However, the Union navy had already built its own ironclad. The *Monitor* had unusual new features such as a revolving gun turret. Although small, the *Monitor* carried powerful guns and had thick plating. When the *Virginia* returned to Hampton Roads on March 9, 1862, the *Monitor* was waiting. After several hours of fighting neither ship was seriously damaged, but the *Monitor* forced the *Virginia* to withdraw. This success saved the Union fleet and kept the blockade going.

✔ **Reading Check: Identifying Cause and Effect** Why did the Confederates send the *Virginia* to sea in 1862, and what was the result?

Interpreting the Visual Record

Ironclads *The duel of the* Virginia *and the* Monitor *was the first naval battle between ironclad ships.* **What features of these ships do you think made them more effective in combat?**

Section 2 Review

go.hrw.com **Homework Practice Online**
keyword: SF3 HP19

1 **Define** and explain:
- ironclad

2 **Identify** and explain:
- Thomas "Stonewall" Jackson
- First Battle of Bull Run
- George B. McClellan
- Robert E. Lee
- Seven Days' Battles
- Second Battle of Bull Run
- Battle of Antietam

3 **Summarizing** Copy the graphic organizer below. Use it to identify the battles of the Civil War that took place in 1861 and 1862, which side won each, and their significance.

Battle → Location
Battle → Winner
Battle → Significance

4 **Finding the Main Idea**
a. Of the Confederate victories in Virginia, which do you think was the most important? Explain your answer.

b. Why was the victory of the *Monitor* over the *Virginia* in 1862 important?

5 **Writing and Critical Thinking**
Identifying Points of View Imagine that you are a war correspondent. Write an imaginary interview with Robert E. Lee.

Consider the following:
- why Lee is fighting for the South
- Lee's training and experience
- the South's strategy

The War in the West

Read to Discover

1. What was General Ulysses S. Grant's strategy for the Union army in the West?
2. Why was the fall of Vicksburg, Mississippi, important?
3. What fighting took place in the Far West?

Identify

- Ulysses S. Grant
- Battle of Shiloh
- David Farragut
- John C. Pemberton
- Siege of Vicksburg
- Battle of Pea Ridge

WHY IT MATTERS TODAY

The brave actions of the soldiers and civilians who participated in the Civil War are remembered today. Use CNN fyi.com or other **current events** sources to find out about different ways that soldiers are honored. Record your findings in your journal.

Heavy mortars like this one were used to lob artillery shells onto forts.

The Story Continues

In February 1862 General Ulysses S. Grant led Union forces into Tennessee. Grant hoped to capture two important forts—Fort Henry and Fort Donelson. With help from Union gunboats, Grant took Fort Henry on February 6. He then attacked Fort Donelson six days later. The Confederate commander of Fort Donelson asked to discuss surrender terms. Grant replied, "No terms except an unconditional and immediate surrender can be accepted." The Confederate officer had no choice. Grant got his surrender and the fort.

⭐ Western Strategy

Union strategy in the West focused on controlling the Mississippi River. This strategy would allow the North to cut the eastern states of the Confederacy off from important sources of food production in the western states of Arkansas, Louisiana, and Texas. From bases on the Mississippi, the Union army would also be able to attack the South's communication and transportation network.

Ulysses S. Grant was the most important figure in the war in the West. A graduate of West Point, Grant had served in the Mexican War.

He later resigned from the army. When the Civil War broke out, Grant quickly volunteered to serve with the Union army. By September 1861, Lincoln had made him a general. Grant's strength in battle set him apart. *"I can't spare this man,"* Lincoln said of Grant. *"He fights."*

By late February 1862, Union forces had captured Nashville. They controlled Kentucky and much of Tennessee. By the spring the Union controlled key stretches of the Tennessee and Cumberland Rivers, as well as some important southern railroads. General Grant advanced south along the Tennessee River toward Mississippi. Following orders, he halted just north of the border. There, near a creek and a church named Shiloh, he waited for additional Union troops.

On April 6, 1862, the Confederates began the **Battle of Shiloh**. Catching Grant by surprise, they pushed his army back. Grant ordered his troops to hold their ground, whatever the cost. During the night, more Union soldiers arrived. On April 7, Grant began a counterattack. By evening's end, the Confederates were in retreat, and the Union had won greater control of the Mississippi River valley. The Battle of Shiloh was one of the first major battles of the war. Teenage Union soldier John Cockerill looked out in shock at the dead soldiers on the battlefield. "The blue and gray were mingled [mixed] together . . . as though they had bled to death while trying to aid each other," he wrote.

✔ **Reading Check: Analyzing Information** What role did the Battle of Shiloh play in Grant's western strategy?

Ulysses S. Grant was working as a businessman when the Civil War broke out.

⭐ Fighting for the Mississippi River

General Grant and other Union commanders wanted to capture key southern positions along the Mississippi River. The Union navy would first try to take the port of New Orleans, the largest city in the South. The Union could then send forces up the Mississippi to join Grant's army advancing from the north. However, two forts guarded the approach to New Orleans from the Gulf of Mexico.

The capture of New Orleans fell to Flag Officer **David Farragut**. He was a daring Union naval leader from Tennessee who had refused to serve in the Confederacy. Unable to destroy the forts guarding New Orleans, Farragut decided to sail boldly past them. Before dawn on April 24, 1862, Farragut ordered his warships to advance through a hail of Confederate fire. His ships arrived in New Orleans the next day, and the city surrendered on April 29. Farragut then sailed farther up the Mississippi River. Next he took Baton Rouge, Louisiana, and Natchez, Mississippi. After that, only the strong defenses at Vicksburg, Mississippi, stood in his way.

The southern defenders of Vicksburg had an important advantage—the city's high bluffs overlooking the river. These bluffs allowed the Confederates under General **John C. Pemberton** to cover the area with heavy guns. Previous attempts to take Vicksburg by land and sea had failed.

★★★★★★★★★★★★
That's Interesting!
★★★★★★★★★★★★

Cave Homes Would you believe that during the Siege of Vicksburg people lived in underground caves? It's true! To protect themselves from the Union cannons, many people moved into caves dug into the hillsides. Caves for a single family usually had one or two rooms. Some large caves could hold as many as 200 people. People furnished their caves with carpets, rocking chairs, and mirrors. They also built shelves into the walls to hold books, candles, flowers, and water jugs.

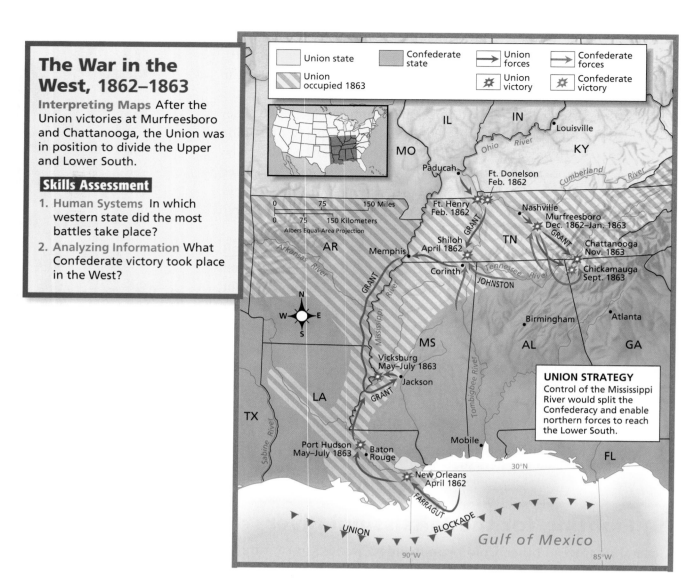

The War in the West, 1862–1863

Interpreting Maps After the Union victories at Murfreesboro and Chattanooga, the Union was in position to divide the Upper and Lower South.

Skills Assessment

1. **Human Systems** In which western state did the most battles take place?
2. **Analyzing Information** What Confederate victory took place in the West?

UNION STRATEGY
Control of the Mississippi River would split the Confederacy and enable northern forces to reach the Lower South.

July 4, 1863
General Grant's troops capture Vicksburg.

In the spring of 1863 General Grant blocked southern forces from aiding Vicksburg. He then surrounded the city with his troops. The **Siege of Vicksburg** lasted about six weeks. As supplies ran out, the residents and soldiers inside the city survived by eating horses, dogs, and rats. "We are utterly [completely] cut off from the world, surrounded by a circle of fire," wrote one woman. "People do nothing but eat what they can get, sleep when they can and dodge the shells." In late June a group of Confederate soldiers sent General Pemberton a warning letter.

Analyzing Primary Sources

Supporting a Point of View What reason do the soldiers give Pemberton for thinking that surrender is necessary?

 History Makers Speak

❝The army is now ripe for mutiny [rebellion], unless it can be fed. If you can't feed us, you'd better surrender us, horrible as the idea is.❞

—Confederate soldiers at Vicksburg, quoted in *The Civil War*, by Geoffrey C. Ward

There was no real hope of relief. Pemberton surrendered Vicksburg on July 4, 1863, giving the Union control of the Mississippi River.

✔ **Reading Check: Summarizing** What events led to the Union gaining control of the Mississippi River in 1863?

⭐ The Far West

Fighting also took place in Arkansas and Missouri, along the Texas coast, and in New Mexico. Little or no fighting occurred in California, which was strongly pro-Union. In August 1861, Confederate forces from Texas marched into New Mexico. Union forces advancing from Colorado defeated the Confederates at Glorieta Pass, near Santa Fe, New Mexico. The Union victory ended Confederate hopes of controlling the Southwest.

The Confederates also tried to take Missouri. Union forces turned the Confederates back in their attempt to seize the federal arsenal at St. Louis in the summer of 1861. In March 1862, Union forces and pro-Confederate Missourians met at the **Battle of Pea Ridge** in northwestern Arkansas. Some American Indians, mainly Cherokee, fought on the side of the Confederates. They hoped that Confederate leaders would give the Indian nations greater independence than the Union had. In addition, slavery was legal in Indian Territory, and some American Indians who were slaveholders supported the Confederacy. Despite being outnumbered, the Union forces won the Battle of Pea Ridge. This victory gave the Union the upper hand in Missouri, but its hold was far from complete. Pro-Confederate units remained active in the region throughout the war. They attacked Union forts and raided towns in Missouri and Kansas forcing Union commanders to keep valuable troops stationed in the area.

Much of the fighting in the West involved the struggle for control of the Mississippi River. Neither side had many troops to spare for the fighting in the Far West.

✔ **Reading Check: Summarizing** What was the significance of the Battle of Pea Ridge, and what fighting took place afterward?

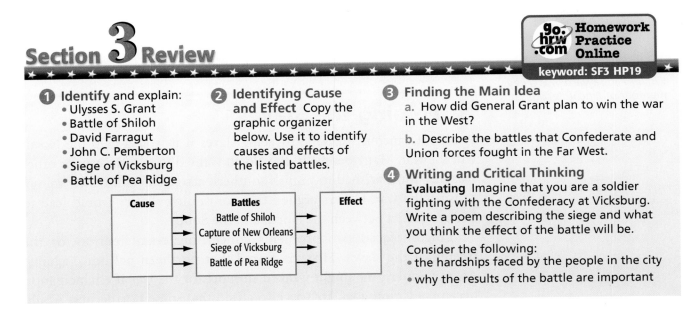

Section 3 Review

go.hrw.com Homework Practice Online
keyword: SF3 HP19

1 **Identify and explain:**
- Ulysses S. Grant
- Battle of Shiloh
- David Farragut
- John C. Pemberton
- Siege of Vicksburg
- Battle of Pea Ridge

2 **Identifying Cause and Effect** Copy the graphic organizer below. Use it to identify causes and effects of the listed battles.

Cause	Battles	Effect
	Battle of Shiloh	
	Capture of New Orleans	
	Siege of Vicksburg	
	Battle of Pea Ridge	

3 **Finding the Main Idea**
a. How did General Grant plan to win the war in the West?

b. Describe the battles that Confederate and Union forces fought in the Far West.

4 **Writing and Critical Thinking**
Evaluating Imagine that you are a soldier fighting with the Confederacy at Vicksburg. Write a poem describing the siege and what you think the effect of the battle will be.

Consider the following:
- the hardships faced by the people in the city
- why the results of the battle are important

Life during the War

Read to Discover

1. How did different groups in the North react to Abraham Lincoln's Emancipation Proclamation?
2. How did African Americans and women contribute to the war effort?
3. How did northerners and southerners respond to the new draft laws?

Define

- contrabands
- *habeas corpus*

Identify

- Emancipation Proclamation
- 54th Massachusetts Infantry
- Copperheads
- Clara Barton

WHY IT MATTERS TODAY

During the Civil War, President Lincoln faced opposition from many Democrats in Congress. Use or other **current events** sources to find out about a current conflict between the president and members of the opposing party in Congress. Record your findings in your journal.

The Story Continues

In July 1862 President Lincoln met privately with members of his cabinet, including William H. Seward, to discuss freeing the slaves in the South—a topic of great concern to him. Lincoln felt that slavery strengthened and supported the South. "We must free the slaves or be ourselves subdued [defeated]," he explained. Lincoln's cabinet members told him to wait for a better time to put his plan into action.

Secretary of State William H. Seward was a key member of Lincoln's cabinet.

★ Freeing the Slaves

President Lincoln supported freeing slaves if it would help the North win the war. Many people in the North wanted to end slavery for other reasons. Some wished to punish southern slaveholders for their role in causing the war. Others argued that continuing slavery would lead to future conflict between the North and the South.

Lincoln faced two problems concerning emancipation, or the freeing of the slaves. First, he feared that northern prejudice against African Americans might weaken support for the war if emancipation became a Union goal. He was also afraid that some northerners would

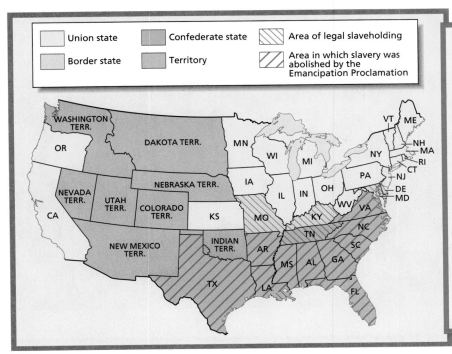

Map Legend:
- Union state
- Border state
- Confederate state
- Territory
- Area of legal slaveholding
- Area in which slavery was abolished by the Emancipation Proclamation

WASHINGTON TERR. · OR · DAKOTA TERR. · MN · WI · MI · VT · ME · NH · MA · NY · RI · CT · PA · NJ · NEVADA TERR. · UTAH TERR. · COLORADO TERR. · NEBRASKA TERR. · IA · IL · IN · OH · DE · MD · CA · KS · MO · KY · WV · VA · NEW MEXICO TERR. · INDIAN TERR. · AR · TN · NC · SC · TX · MS · AL · GA · LA · FL

Emancipation in 1863

Interpreting Maps The Emancipation Proclamation freed slaves in states that were in rebellion against the Union. The Proclamation did not, however, free slaves in Union states or in areas occupied by Union troops.

Skills Assessment

1. **Places and Regions** In which states were slaves granted freedom by the Emancipation Proclamation?
2. **Summarizing** What was the location of most of the states where slaveholding remained legal?

consider slaves to be property that southerners had the right to keep. In addition, the Constitution did not give the president the power to end slavery in the United States.

Lincoln decided to issue a military order freeing slaves only in areas controlled by the Confederacy. Lincoln felt that his authority to end slavery did not apply to the loyal, slaveholding border states. He also did not want to anger citizens in these states.

President Lincoln waited for a northern victory in the East before announcing his plans. The Battle of Antietam was the victory he needed. On September 22, 1862, Lincoln called for all slaves in Confederate-controlled areas to be freed. This **Emancipation Proclamation** went into effect on January 1, 1863. News of the order encouraged southern slaves to escape when they heard that Union troops were nearby. This loss of slave labor hurt the southern economy and the Confederate war effort. Many African Americans and northerners praised the Emancipation Proclamation. Abolitionist Frederick Douglass called January 1, 1863, "the great day which is to determine the destiny [fate] not only of the American Republic, but that of the American Continent." There was also popular support for the Proclamation in Great Britain and France.

Many northern Democrats, however, opposed the Emancipation Proclamation. They wanted only to restore the Union, not to end slavery. A few abolitionists, on the other hand, argued that Lincoln had not gone far enough. William Lloyd Garrison complained that the president had left "slavery, as a system . . . , still to exist in all the so-called loyal Slave States."

✔ **Reading Check: Contrasting** In what different ways did people in the North view the Emancipation Proclamation?

GLOBAL CONNECTIONS

Reactions to Emancipation

Abraham Lincoln's Emancipation Proclamation drew the attention of many people in Europe. Some workers from Manchester, England, wrote to the president. "We joyfully honor you . . . [for] your belief in the words of your great founders: 'All men are created free and equal.'" A British noble praised the Union's high moral purpose in the Civil War. Giuseppe Garibaldi, an Italian leader, hailed Lincoln as "the heir of the aspirations [dreams] of . . . [abolitionist] John Brown." **How did some Europeans react to the Emancipation Proclamation?**

Daily Life

African American soldiers Frederick Douglass encouraged African Americans to fight in the Union army, calling it their "golden opportunity." Many men responded to the call. Despite making up only 2 percent of the North's population, African Americans made up nearly 10 percent of the Union army by the end of the war. Although they faced discrimination, many soldiers celebrated the opportunity to fight for freedom. **What reasons do you think African Americans would have had for joining the Union army cause despite facing discrimination?**

Analyzing Primary Sources

Identifying Points of View According to Douglass, what will serving as soldiers accomplish for African Americans?

★ African Americans and the War

The question of whether to permit African Americans to serve in the military also troubled many northern leaders. The Union navy had already been accepting African American volunteers. Since the war began, abolitionists had called for the Union army to recruit African Americans as well. Frederick Douglass stated that military service would help African Americans earn equal rights.

 History Makers Speak

❝Once let the black man get upon his person the brass letters, U.S.; . . . and a musket on his shoulder and bullets in his pocket, and there is no power on earth which can deny that he has earned the right to citizenship.❞

—Frederick Douglass, quoted in *Battle Cry of Freedom*, by James McPherson

Northern leaders also saw a practical reason to enlist African Americans—the Union needed soldiers. Congress allowed the army to sign up African American volunteers as laborers in July 1862. The War Department also gave **contrabands,** or escaped slaves, the right to join the Union army in South Carolina. Free African Americans in Louisiana and Kansas also formed units in the Union army.

By the spring of 1863, African American units were fighting in the field with the Union army. They took part in a Union attack on Port Hudson, Louisiana, in May 1863. The **54th Massachusetts Infantry** consisted mostly of free African Americans. In July 1863 this regiment played a key role in the attack on South Carolina's Fort Wagner. Lewis Douglass, Frederick Douglass's son, fought in the battle. "My regiment [unit] has established its reputation as a fighting regiment—not a man flinched," he proudly wrote later. The 54th became the most famous African American unit of the war.

About 180,000 African Americans served with the Union army during the war. Despite discrimination, African American soldiers fought bravely. For most of the war, African Americans received less pay than white soldiers. They were usually led by white officers. They also faced greater danger from Confederate troops, who often killed African American prisoners of war or sold them into slavery. In 1864 President Lincoln suggested rewarding African American soldiers in Louisiana by giving them the right to vote. He also wrote a letter praising the contributions of African Americans to the military effort.

 History Makers Speak 66**Abandon all the posts now possessed by black men, surrender all these advantages to the enemy, and we would be compelled [forced] to abandon the war in three weeks.**99

—Abraham Lincoln, quoted in *Battle Cry of Freedom*, by James McPherson

Analyzing Primary Sources
Identifying Points of View
How does Lincoln view African American soldiers?

✔ **Reading Check: Finding the Main Idea** Why did African Americans serve in the Union army despite the problems they faced?

⭐ Problems in the North

The issue of ending slavery added to the problems already brewing in the North. Northerners were growing upset by the length of the war and the increasing number of casualties. A group of northern Democrats led by Clement L. Vallandigham of Ohio began to speak out against the war. War supporters compared these Democrats to a poisonous type of snake, calling them **Copperheads**. Many Copperheads were midwesterners who sympathized with the South, objected to abolition, and wanted the war to end. Vallandigham asked what the war had gained and then said, "Let the dead at Fredericksburg and Vicksburg answer."

Lincoln believed the Copperheads threatened the war effort. To stop them, he suspended the right of *habeas corpus*—the constitutional

THE GRANGER COLLECTION, NEW YORK

Interpreting Political Cartoons

The Copperheads *In this cartoon, northern Democrats who called for peace are shown as deadly copperhead snakes threatening the Union.* ***Why do you think the artist chose to depict these politicians in this way?***

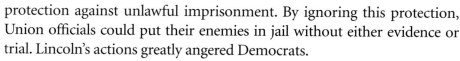

Research on the R⊙M

Free Find:
Mary Boykin Chesnut
After reading about Mary Boykin Chesnut on the **Holt Researcher CD–ROM,** imagine that you are writing an entry in her journal. Describe the situation faced by the Confederacy during a particular period of the Civil War.

protection against unlawful imprisonment. By ignoring this protection, Union officials could put their enemies in jail without either evidence or trial. Lincoln's actions greatly angered Democrats.

More debate arose in March 1863 when Congress passed a law allowing men to be drafted into military service. Critics noted that dishonesty in the draft was common. Wealthy people could legally buy their way out of military service. The Copperheads complained that it was unfair to force unwilling white men to fight for the freedom of southern slaves.

Other critics shared this belief. In July 1863, riots targeting African Americans and draft officials broke out in New York City. Many of the rioters were poor immigrants afraid of losing their jobs to freed African Americans. Rioters damaged a great deal of property and killed more than 100 people before Union troops could stop the violence.

✔ **Reading Check: Identifying Cause and Effect** Why were people unhappy with Lincoln's war policies, and how did Lincoln attempt to deal with them?

Southern Struggles

The South also faced many challenges. The North's naval blockade took a heavy toll on southerners. Soldiers did not have enough supplies. "Every day we grow weaker. . . . Already they [Confederate soldiers] begin to cry out for more ammunition, and already the blockade is beginning to shut it all out," wrote Mary Boykin Chesnut. The value of Confederate money fell as southern exports dropped. The price of food, clothing, and medicine shot up as supplies ran low. Basic items such as bread cost more than most people could afford.

The severe shortages caused unrest in the South. In the spring of 1863, food riots took place in several southern cities, including Richmond. Southern officials ordered local newspapers not to mention these riots. Confederate president Jefferson Davis feared that the news would embarrass the South and encourage the North to keep fighting.

The government of the Confederacy faced problems because its officials disagreed on many issues. There was also controversy among southerners over their new draft law, approved by Davis in 1862 despite much criticism. One problem was that the southern draft did not apply to men who held many slaves. This rule angered poor southerners, who generally held few, if any, slaves. Confederate private Sam Watkins wrote that the draft law "raised the howl of 'rich man's war, poor man's fight.'" The draft was very unpopular in rural areas such as western North Carolina. Hatred of the draft and some pro-Union feeling in this region led to protests. Some southerners even took up arms against Confederate officials.

✔ **Reading Check: Comparing** What problems did both northerners and southerners have with the new draft laws, and how did they show their feelings?

Southerner Mary Boykin Chesnut kept an extensive journal describing her experiences during the Civil War.

⭐ Life on the Home Front

In both the North and the South, the war effort involved people at all levels of society. People too young or too old for military service worked in factories, on farms, and in other areas. Southern women also ran farms and plantations after their husbands and sons went to war.

Women played an important role in providing medical care for soldiers. Dorothea Dix headed more than 3,000 women who served as paid nurses in the Union army. <u>Clara Barton</u> worked as a volunteer, organizing the collection of medicine and supplies for delivery to Union troops on the battlefield. Barton often remained at field hospitals to comfort the wounded. Her work formed the basis for what would become the American Red Cross. Women in the South also cared for sick and wounded soldiers. For example, Sally Louisa Tompkins established a hospital in Richmond.

The efforts of these women volunteers were very important. Soldiers faced great dangers in daily life as well as in battles. For every day of fighting, soldiers spent weeks living in uncomfortable and unhealthy camps. They faced bad weather, disease, and unsafe food. About twice as many Civil War soldiers died of disease than died in combat.

Military prisoners also suffered greatly during the Civil War. The worst conditions were at Andersonville, in southwestern Georgia. Thousands of Union soldiers were held there with no shelter and little food. Following her visit to the prison, southerner Eliza Andrews was told that "at one time the prisoners died at the rate of a hundred and fifty a day."

Interpreting the Visual Record

Camp life *Civil War soldiers on both sides often brought their families to camp with them.* **What do you think some of the advantages and disadvantages of soldiers having their families with them might be?**

✔ **Reading Check: Analyzing Information** How did southern and northern women affect the war efforts?

Section 4 Review

go.hrw.com **Homework Practice Online**
keyword: SF3 HP19

① **Define and explain:**
  • contrabands
  • *habeas corpus*

② **Identify and explain:**
  • Emancipation Proclamation
  • 54th Massachusetts Infantry
  • Copperheads
  • Clara Barton

③ **Categorizing** Copy the graphic organizer below. Use it to list the ways that people in different parts of society contributed to or reacted to the war.

④ **Finding the Main Idea**
  a. Describe how each of the following groups reacted to the Emancipation Proclamation: African Americans, abolitionists, and Copperheads.

  b. What actions did Lincoln take that angered Democrats in the North?

⑤ **Writing and Critical Thinking**
  Summarizing Imagine that you are a foreign journalist reporting on the war in the North and the South. Write a half-page newspaper article about life on the home front.

  Consider the following:
  • responses to new draft laws
  • the contributions of African Americans
  • the contributions of women

The Tide of the War Turns

Read to Discover

1. Why was the Battle of Gettysburg important?
2. What campaigns were launched in Virginia and the Lower South?
3. How and when did the war finally end?

WHY IT MATTERS TODAY

Many people participate in reenactments of Civil War battles or visit national parks located on Civil War battle sites. Use CNNfyi.com or other **current events** sources to find out about either a historical reenactment taking place today or a historical national park. Record your findings in your journal.

Define

• total war

Identify

• Battle of Gettysburg
• George G. Meade
• George Pickett
• Pickett's Charge
• Gettysburg Address
• Wilderness Campaign
• William Tecumseh Sherman
• Appomattox Courthouse

General Stonewall Jackson was shot during the Battle of Chancellorsville.

The Story Continues

In May 1863 General Lee's troops defeated a larger Union force near the town of Chancellorsville, Virginia. The fighting was heavy. While riding at the front lines, Lee's trusted general Stonewall Jackson was accidentally shot by his own troops. Doctors cut off Jackson's left arm in an effort to save his life. Still, his condition grew worse. When Lee found out that Jackson was hurt, he told an aide, "Tell him to . . . come back to me as soon as he can. He has lost his left arm, but I have lost my right." Jackson died just a few days after the battle ended.

★ The Battle of Gettysburg

In addition to the stunning victory at Chancellorsville, the Confederates also triumphed at Fredericksburg, Virginia. These successes encouraged General Lee to launch another offensive into Union territory. As before, his goals were to break the North's will to fight and to capture much-needed supplies for his army. Lee hoped that another victory would turn the tide of war in the Confederacy's favor.

Pickett's Charge *Confederate general George Pickett led thousands of troops in a costly charge against Union defenses.* **How does this image show the violence of the Civil War?**

In mid-June 1863 Lee cut across northern Maryland into southern Pennsylvania. Lee's forces gathered near a small town called Gettysburg. Lee was unaware that Union soldiers were just northwest of the town. When a Confederate raiding party went to Gettysburg for supplies, the troops came under fire. This event triggered the **Battle of Gettysburg**. Some 75,000 Confederate soldiers faced about 90,000 Union troops.

The battle began on July 1, 1863. The Confederates pushed the Union line back to Cemetery Ridge, just south of the town. The Confederate forces occupied nearby Seminary Ridge. On July 2 Lee ordered an attack on the left side of the Union line. The bold charge of Union colonel Joshua Chamberlain's troops at Little Round Top, however, helped turn back the Confederates. Then General **George G. Meade** placed more soldiers on the Union line.

Lee planned to rush the center of the Union line. This task fell to three divisions of Confederate soldiers. General **George Pickett** commanded the largest unit. In the late afternoon, about 14,000 men took part in **Pickett's Charge** up Cemetery Ridge. The attack was a disaster. Confederate lieutenant G. W. Finley was part of the charge. "Men were falling all around us, and cannon and muskets were raining death upon us," he wrote. Fewer than half of Pickett's troops reached the top of the ridge. All those who reached the Union wall were captured or killed. Only about 6,500 men returned to the Confederate rear. Lee ordered Pickett to organize his division for a possible counterattack. "General Lee, I *have* no division now," Pickett replied. "The battle was now over," wrote Union lieutenant Jesse Young, "but nobody knew it."

✔ **Reading Check: Identifying Cause and Effect** What led to the Battle of Gettysburg, and what was its outcome?

★ A Turning Point

Rain slowed Meade's troops, allowing Lee to retreat from Gettysburg on July 4 and return to Virginia. Nonetheless, Gettysburg was a turning point in the war. Lee's troops would never again launch an attack onto northern soil. The Union victory at Gettysburg took place on the same day as General Grant's capture of Vicksburg in Mississippi. These critical victories made northerners believe that the Confederacy could be defeated. The Union triumph at Gettysburg, however, had come at a high price. Union casualties numbered more than 23,000. The Confederacy suffered more than 28,000 casualties.

President Lincoln expressed the Union's new sense of confidence and commitment. He delivered the **Gettysburg Address** on November 19, 1863. This short, moving speech is one of the most famous in American history. Lincoln spoke of the importance of liberty, equality, and democratic ideals. He reminded listeners that the war was being fought to protect these cherished principles. Lincoln dedicated himself and the rest of the North to winning the war and preserving the Union. He knew that a difficult road still lay ahead.

✔ **Reading Check: Drawing Inferences and Conclusions** Why do you think Lincoln talked about liberty, equality, democratic ideals, and unity in the Gettysburg Address?

This painting shows Robert E. Lee with some of his generals at his side in 1863.

⭐ Grant's Drive to Richmond

Lincoln was impressed with General Grant's successes at Vicksburg and in the West. He brought Grant to the East and gave him command of the Union army. In early 1864 Grant forced Lee to fight a series of battles in Virginia that stretched Confederate soldiers and supplies to their limits.

From May through June, the opposing armies fought a series of battles in northern and central Virginia. Union troops launched the **Wilderness Campaign** with about 100,000 men against 70,000 Confederates. The first battle took place in early May about 50 miles northwest of Richmond. Grant then ordered General Meade southeast to Spotsylvania. There the fighting raged for 10 days. Over the next month, Union soldiers pressed the Confederate troops back to just north of Richmond. The Battle of Cold Harbor took place from June 1 to June 3, only 10 miles northeast of Richmond. It was Grant's worst defeat of the campaign. During one brief assault some 7,000 Union troops were killed or wounded. The battle ended Grant's plans to advance on the Confederate capital.

Union forces suffered incredible losses in the Wilderness Campaign, with twice as many casualties as their Confederate opponents. Even so, Grant continued his aggressive strategy. He knew he would be getting additional soldiers, but that Lee was running low on troops. Grant slowly but surely pressed forward. He told another officer, "I propose to fight it out along this line if it takes all summer."

After Cold Harbor, Grant moved south of Richmond. He had hoped to take the key railroad junction at Petersburg, Virginia. Lee's army, however, formed a solid defense. Grant called off his attack and prepared to lay siege to Petersburg. Grant was winning the war, but he had not captured Richmond. This failure was discouraging for Lincoln.

✔ **Reading Check: Analyzing Information** Why was Grant's 1864 campaign in Virginia successful despite the huge casualties?

Interpreting the Visual Record

Battles *During the Civil War, soldiers on each side were often ordered to charge well-defended positions, leading to very high casualties.* **Whose perspective is the artist trying to portray? Explain your answer.**

★★★★★★★★★★★★★
That's Interesting!
★★★★★★★★★★★★★

A Desperate Plan Did you know that near the end of the war the Confederacy considered having slaves serve in its army? It's true! As the South lost thousands of soldiers, some leaders suggested that slaves should serve in the army. They would then be freed after the war was over. Lee was in favor of this plan. Another general, however, was upset at the thought of drafting African Americans. He wrote, "If slaves will make good soldiers, our whole theory of slavery is wrong." In early 1865 the Confederate president Jefferson Davis had signed a "Negro Soldier Law." The war ended, however, before this law had much effect on Confederate forces.

Interpreting the Visual Record

Total war *General William Tecumseh Sherman, shown above, led his Union troops on a destructive March to the Sea.* **What evidence of Sherman's total-war strategy can you identify in the scene shown above?**

⭐ Sherman Strikes the South

Lincoln needed a victory to help him win re-election in 1864. The bold campaign of General **William Tecumseh Sherman** provided this key victory. Sherman carried out the Union plan to destroy southern railroads and industries. In the spring of 1864, Sherman marched south from Tennessee with 100,000 troops. His goal was to take Atlanta, Georgia. From May through August, Sherman's army moved steadily through the Appalachian Mountains toward Atlanta. Several times, Sherman avoided defenses set up by Confederate general Joseph Johnston.

In July Sherman was within sight of Atlanta. His troops drove back Confederate forces trying to protect the city. The Confederate troops retreated as Sherman held Atlanta under siege. Atlanta fell to Sherman on September 2, 1864. Much of the city was destroyed by artillery and fire. Sherman ordered the residents who still remained to leave. The loss of Atlanta cost the South an important railroad link and center of industry. The victory also showed northerners that progress was being made in defeating the South. This success helped convince Union voters to re-elect Lincoln in a landslide.

Shortly after the election, General Sherman began his next attack. His goal was the port city of Savannah, Georgia. In mid-November 1864 Sherman left Atlanta with a force of about 60,000 men. He said he would "make Georgia howl!"

On his March to the Sea, Sherman waged **total war**—destroying both civilian and military resources. Sherman felt that total war would ruin the South's economy and its ability to fight. He ordered his troops to destroy railways, bridges, crops, livestock, and other resources. They burned plantations and freed slaves. Sherman's army reached Savannah on December 10, 1864. They left behind them a wide path of destruction more than 250 miles long. Sherman believed his tactics would hasten the end of the war.

✔ **Reading Check: Sequencing** List the key events in Sherman's march through the South in 1864 in their proper sequence.

⭐ The South Surrenders

In early April Sherman closed in on the last Confederate defenders in North Carolina. Grant finally broke through the Confederate defenses at Petersburg. On April 2 Lee was forced to retreat from Richmond. As Union troops poured into the Confederate capital, the final days of the war began.

By the second week of April 1865, Grant had surrounded Lee's army and demanded its surrender. Lee hoped to join the remaining Confederates in North Carolina, but Grant cut off his escape just west of Richmond. Trapped in the small town of **Appomattox Courthouse**, Lee concluded that the situation was hopeless.

The Union and Confederate leaders met on Palm Sunday, April 9, 1865. There Lee signed the surrender documents, ending the long bloody war. Grant later wrote that he found the scene at Appomattox Courthouse more tragic than joyful.

General Robert E. Lee signs the surrender documents. "There is nothing left for me to do but go and see General Grant," Lee had said. "I would rather die a thousand deaths."

 History Makers Speak

❝I felt . . . sad and depressed at the downfall of a foe [enemy] who had fought so long and valiantly [bravely], and had suffered so much for a cause, though that cause was, I believe, one of the worst for which a people ever fought.❞

—Ulysses S. Grant, *Personal Memoirs*

The Civil War had deep and lasting effects. Almost 620,000 Americans lost their lives in the four years of fighting. It was the most costly conflict in American history. Bitterness over the war would linger in both the North and the South for many years as the nation tried to heal its wounds and rebuild.

April 9, 1865
General Lee surrenders to General Grant at Appomattox Courthouse.

✔ **Reading Check: Finding the Main Idea** Why did Lee surrender?

Section 5 Review

go.hrw.com Homework Practice Online
keyword: SF3 HP19

1. **Define** and explain:
   • total war

2. **Identify** and explain:
   • Battle of Gettysburg
   • George G. Meade
   • George Pickett
   • Pickett's Charge
   • Gettysburg Address
   • Wilderness Campaign
   • William Tecumseh Sherman
   • Appomattox Courthouse

3. **Sequencing** Copy the graphic organizer below. Use it to fill in and explain the events that led to the end of the Civil War.

July 1–3, 1863
May–June, 1864
September 2, 1864
December 10, 1864
April 2, 1865
April 9, 1865

4. **Finding the Main Idea**
   a. How might the war have been different if Confederate forces had won the Battle of Gettysburg in 1863?

   b. How did the Union win the war in the East and in the South?

5. **Writing and Critical Thinking**
   Evaluating Imagine that you are either a northern or southern soldier present at Appomattox Courthouse. Write an account of General Lee's surrender.

   Consider the following:
   • the campaign against Richmond
   • the relations between northerners and southerners

1863

THE EMANCIPATION PROCLAMATION

When the Union army won the Battle of Antietam, President Lincoln felt that the timing was right for a bold move. In late September 1862 he issued a preliminary Emancipation Proclamation. On January 1, 1863, the following official Proclamation went into effect.

A poster celebrating the Emancipation Proclamation

A Proclamation by the President of the United States of America

Whereas on the twenty-second day of September, A.D. 1862, a proclamation was issued by the President of the United States, containing, among other things, the following, **to wit**:[1]

"That on the first day of January, A.D. 1863, all persons held as slaves within any state or designated part of a state, the people whereof shall then be in rebellion against the United States, shall be then, **thenceforward**,[2] and forever free; and the executive government of the United States, including the military and naval authority thereof, will recognize and maintain the freedom of such persons and will do no act or acts to **repress**[3] such persons or any of them, in any efforts they may make for their actual freedom.

"That the Executive will on the 1st day of January aforesaid, by proclamation, **designate**[4] the states and parts of states, if any, in which the people thereof, . . . shall then be in rebellion against the United States; and the fact that any state or the people thereof shall on that day be in good faith represented in the Congress of the United States by members chosen thereto at elections wherein a majority of the qualified voters of such states shall have participated shall, in the absence of strong **countervailing**[5] testimony, be **deemed conclusive**[6] evidence that such state and

the people thereof are not then in rebellion against the United States."

Now, therefore, I, Abraham Lincoln, President of the United States, by virtue of the power in me **vested**[7] as Commander-in-Chief of the Army and Navy of the United States in time of actual armed rebellion against the authority and government of the United States, and as a fit and necessary war measure for suppressing said rebellion, do, on this first day of January, A.D. 1863, and in **accordance**[8] with my purpose so to do, publicly proclaimed for the full period of one hundred days from the first day above mentioned, order and designate as the states and parts of states wherein the people thereof, . . . are in this day in rebellion against the United States. . . .

And I hereby **enjoin upon**[9] the people so declared to be free to **abstain**[10] from all violence, unless in necessary self-defense; and I recommend to them that, in all cases when allowed, they labor faithfully for reasonable wages.

And I further declare and make known that such persons of suitable condition will be received into the armed service of the United States to **garrison**[11] forts, positions, stations, and other places, and to man vessels of all sorts in said service.

And upon this act, sincerely believed to be an act of justice, warranted by the Constitution upon military necessity, I **invoke**[12] the considerate judgment of mankind and the gracious favor of Almighty God.

Analyzing Primary Sources

1. What authority did Lincoln claim allowed him to issue the Emancipation Proclamation?
2. Why do you think Lincoln did not free all slaves?

[1]**to wit:** namely
[2]**thenceforward:** afterward
[3]**repress:** keep down
[4]**designate:** name

[5]**countervailing:** opposing
[6]**deemed conclusive:** considered certain
[7]**vested:** given
[8]**accordance:** agreement

[9]**enjoin upon:** order
[10]**abstain:** hold back
[11]**garrison:** defend
[12]**invoke:** call upon

1863

ABRAHAM LINCOLN'S GETTYSBURG ADDRESS

On November 19, 1863, Abraham Lincoln addressed a crowd gathered to dedicate a cemetery at the Gettysburg battlefield. His short speech reminded Americans of the ideals on which the Republic was founded.

Lincoln gives the Gettysburg Address.

Four score and seven years ago our fathers brought forth on this continent, a new nation, **conceived**[1] in Liberty, and dedicated to the **proposition**[2] that all men are created equal.

Now we are engaged in a great civil war, testing whether that nation, or any nation so conceived and so dedicated, can long endure. We are met on a great battlefield of that war. We have come to dedicate a portion of that field, as a final resting place for those who here gave their lives that that nation might live. It is altogether fitting and proper that we should do this.

But, in a larger sense, we can not dedicate—we can not **consecrate**[3]—we can not **hallow**[4]—this ground. The brave men, living and dead, who struggled here, have consecrated it, far above our poor power to add or **detract**.[5] The world will little note nor long remember what we say here, but it can never forget what they did here. It is for us the living, rather, to be dedicated here to the unfinished work which they who fought here have thus far so nobly advanced. It is rather for us to be here dedicated to the great task remaining before us—that from these honored dead we take increased devotion to that cause for which they gave the last full measure of devotion—that we here highly **resolve**[6] that these dead shall not have died in vain—that this nation, under God, shall have a new birth of freedom—and that government of the people, by the people, for the people shall not perish from the earth.

Analyzing Primary Sources

1. For what cause does Lincoln say the soldiers at Gettysburg died?
2. How does Lincoln value liberty, equality, and democracy?

[1]**conceived:** created
[2]**proposition:** idea

[3]**consecrate:** set apart
[4]**hallow:** make holy

[5]**detract:** take away from
[6]**resolve:** decide

Chapter 19 Review

The Chapter at a Glance

Examine the visual summary of the chapter below. Work with a classmate to create a time line that shows the key events of the war.

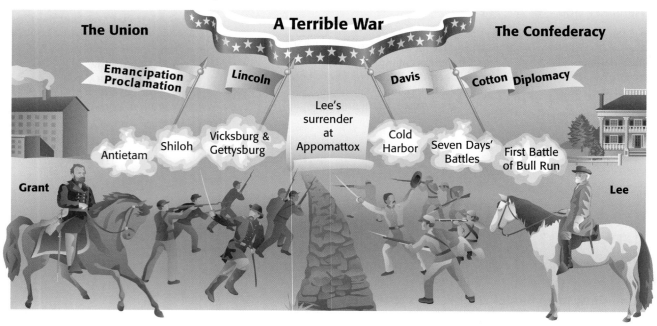

A Terrible War

The Union — The Confederacy

Emancipation Proclamation — Lincoln — Davis — Cotton Diplomacy

Antietam — Shiloh — Vicksburg & Gettysburg — Lee's surrender at Appomattox — Cold Harbor — Seven Days' Battles — First Battle of Bull Run

Grant — Lee

Identifying People and Ideas

Use the following terms or people in historically significant sentences.

1. Fort Sumter
2. border states
3. First Battle of Bull Run
4. Robert E. Lee
5. Ulysses S. Grant
6. Siege of Vicksburg
7. Emancipation Proclamation
8. *habeas corpus*
9. Battle of Gettysburg
10. Appomattox Courthouse

Understanding Main Ideas

Section 1 *(Pages 580–584)*

1. What advantages and disadvantages did the North and the South each have at the beginning of the Civil War?

Section 2 *(Pages 585–589)*

2. How did the First Battle of Bull Run in 1861 change many northerners' ideas about the war?
3. How did the South attempt to avoid the naval blockade?

Section 3 *(Pages 590–593)*

4. How did the Siege of Vicksburg help the Union gain control of the Mississippi River?

Section 4 *(Pages 594–599)*

5. How did African Americans help the war effort?

Section 5 *(Pages 600–605)*

6. What campaigns did Grant plan in Virginia and the Lower South?
7. How did the war end in 1865?

You Be the Historian— Reviewing Themes

1. **Science, Technology & Society** How did ironclads reflect the changes that new technology brought to the war?
2. **Economics** What effect did the war have on the South's economy?
3. **Citizenship** How did northerners and southerners oppose the war, and how did the Union and Confederate governments respond?

Thinking Critically

1. **Supporting a Point of View** Which key 1863 battle—Vicksburg or Gettysburg—do you think was the most important turning point in the war? Explain your answer.
2. **Comparing and Contrasting** In what ways were the beliefs of, and challenges faced by, Presidents Lincoln and Davis similar and different?
3. **Summarizing** What ideas about equality, government, liberty, and union did Lincoln present in his first inaugural address and the Gettysburg Address?

Interpreting Graphs

Study the graph below. Then use the information on the graph to help you answer the following questions.

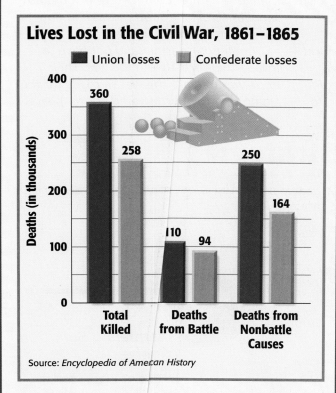

Lives Lost in the Civil War, 1861–1865

■ Union losses ■ Confederate losses

Deaths (in thousands)

Total Killed: 360, 258
Deaths from Battle: 110, 94
Deaths from Nonbattle Causes: 250, 164

Source: *Encyclopedia of American History*

1. About how many soldiers in total were killed during the war?
   a. 418,000
   b. 618,000
   c. 102,000
   d. more than 1 million

2. About what percentage of the total deaths from battle were Union soldiers?
   a. about 66 percent
   b. about 30 percent
   c. about 54 percent
   d. 50 percent

3. Based on your knowledge of the period, why do you think the number of deaths from nonbattle causes was higher than the number of deaths caused by battles?

Analyzing Primary Sources

Read the following excerpt about the Fugitive Slave Act from Abraham Lincoln's first inaugural address, then answer the questions that follow.

> **❝**Again, in any law upon this subject, ought not all the safeguards of liberty known in civilized and humane jurisprudence to be introduced, so that a free man be not, in any case, surrendered as a slave? And might it not be well, at the same time, to provide by a law for the enforcement of that clause in the Constitution which guarranties that 'The citizens of each State shall be entitled to all previleges and immunities of citizens in the several States?'**❞**

4. Which of the following statements best describes Lincoln's view of liberty?
   a. No matter what their race, no free person should ever be treated like a slave.
   b. Different laws on freedom should apply to people in different states.
   c. Slavery is wrong and should be abolished.
   d. The current Fugitive Slave Act is fair.

5. How do you think Lincoln views the government's role in preserving the equality of all citizens?

Alternative Assessment

Building Your Portfolio

American History

Cooperative Learning

Organize the class into small groups. Each group will write part of a chapter for a textbook on the consequences of the Civil War. Choose one of the following topics: the role of women during the war, the lives of soldiers, or the war's effect on former slaves and free African Americans. Each group should conduct research and then write its section. Be sure to create images, maps, or charts as needed to place in your group's section.

🖳 **internet** connect

Internet Activity: go.hrw.com
keyword: **SF3 CF19**

Choose a topic about the Civil War to:
● View photographs and write a poem describing the life of a soldier in the war.
● Research Civil War authors.
● Create a 3-D model of the battlefield at Gettysburg and then pose and answer questions with a partner about the events of the battle.

go.hrw.com

Theaters of War

Geography played an important role in the development of military strategies during the Civil War. The Confederacy occupied a large stretch of land from the Atlantic Ocean to west Texas. To achieve military victory, Union leaders had to capture key parts of this large region. Union leaders planned to gain control of key river routes, railroads, and seaports. The Union wanted to stop the movement of Confederate troops and supplies across the South, as well as Confederate trade with Europe.

Confederate armies did not have to invade the North to win the war. Their hope was to make the war so costly for the Union that the North would ask for peace.

Resources and Strategies

The North entered the war with many advantages over the South. The North had more people, industry, and money.

Farm Values by Region, 1860 and 1870

Value (in billions of dollars)

Northeast   Midwest   South   West   Total U.S.

■ 1860
□ 1870

Source: *Historical Statistics of the United States*

Geography Skills

Interpreting Bar Graphs

1. Which region's farms had the highest total value in 1860? in 1870?
2. **Analyzing Information** Where did farms have the greatest growth in value from 1860 to 1870?

Cotton plants

Comparing the North and the South, 1860

■ North ■ South

	Percent
Total population	North 61%, South 39%
Railroad tracks	North 72%, South 28%
Factories	North 86%, South 14%
Total farm value	North 72%, South 28%
Cotton production	North 0.1%, South 99.9%
Horses	North 72%, South 28%
Donkeys and mules	North 29%, South 71%

0 10 20 30 40 50 60 70 80 90 100
Percent

Source: *The Civil War Day by Day: An Almanac, 1861–1865*

Geography **Skills**

Interpreting Bar Graphs

1. What percentage of the nation's population lived in the North at the beginning of the war?
2. **Human Systems** What resources did the Union have more of than the Confederacy? What resources did the Confederacy have more of than the Union?
3. **Making Generalizations and Predictions** How do you think the resource advantages enjoyed by the Union affected the outcome of the Civil War?

History Note 2

The Union also had a great advantage in communications. The North controlled far more miles of telegraph line than the South. The telegraph made Union supply and reinforcement easier because field commanders could communicate quickly with officials in Washington. The South's expansion and repair of telegraph lines were hurt by a shortage of equipment and operators.

History Note 1

One of the North's major advantages was its greater population, which allowed Union generals to put more soldiers in the field. In late 1862, an estimated 300,000 Confederate soldiers faced nearly 700,000 Union soldiers. By the end of the war, the Union had about 1 million troops. Confederate soldiers probably numbered fewer than 160,000.

A telegraph key

Theaters of War

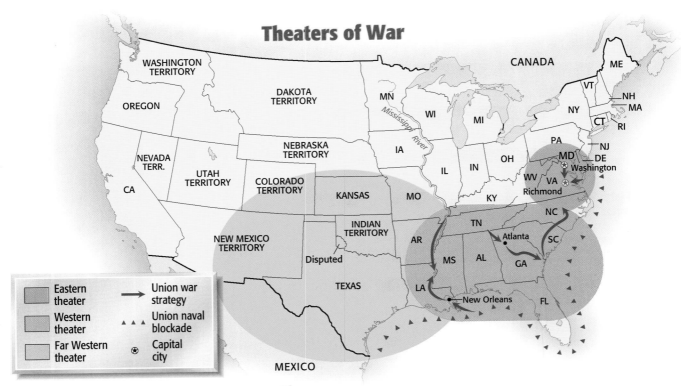

Legend:
- Eastern theater
- Western theater
- Far Western theater
- → Union war strategy
- ▲▲▲ Union naval blockade
- ⊛ Capital city

Geography Skills

Interpreting Thematic Maps

1. In what theater were the capitals of the Union and the Confederacy located?
2. What geographic feature of the Confederacy made the Union blockade difficult?
3. **The Uses of Geography** What river was a key to the Union strategy in the western theater? Why would controlling this river have been important?
4. **Drawing Inferences and Conclusions** Based on the map, why do you think the Union and the Confederacy concentrated little effort on the Far Western theater?

Union gunboat

History Note 3

Both the Union and the Confederacy concentrated their efforts in the eastern and western theaters of war. Battles took place on a smaller scale in the less-populated far western theater. For example, in 1862 a Confederate force of about 3,000 troops invaded the New Mexico Territory. They were eventually turned back. Part of the Union strategy when the war began was to split the Confederacy. Union commanders planned to cut off Arkansas, Louisiana, and Texas by taking control of the Mississippi River.

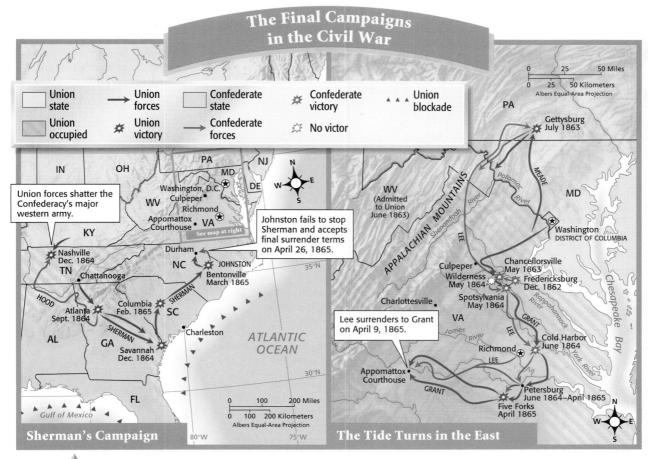

The Final Campaigns in the Civil War

Legend:
- Union state
- Union occupied
- Union forces →
- Union victory ✦
- Confederate state
- Confederate forces →
- Confederate victory ✦
- No victor ✧
- Union blockade ▲▲▲

Sherman's Campaign

Union forces shatter the Confederacy's major western army.

Johnston fails to stop Sherman and accepts final surrender terms on April 26, 1865.

IN · OH · PA · NJ · MD · DE

Washington, D.C. · Culpeper · Richmond · Appomattox Courthouse · VA · WV · KY

Nashville Dec. 1864 · TN · Chattanooga · Durham · NC · Bentonville March 1865

HOOD · Atlanta Sept. 1864 · Columbia Feb. 1865 · SC · SHERMAN · Charleston

AL · GA · Savannah Dec. 1864

FL · Gulf of Mexico

ATLANTIC OCEAN

0 100 200 Miles / 0 100 200 Kilometers / Albers Equal-Area Projection

35°N · 30°N · 80°W · 75°W

The Tide Turns in the East

0 25 50 Miles / 0 25 50 Kilometers / Albers Equal-Area Projection

PA · Gettysburg July 1863 · MEADE

WV (Admitted to Union June 1863) · APPALACHIAN MOUNTAINS · Potomac River · Shenandoah River · MD · Washington DISTRICT OF COLUMBIA · LEE

Culpeper · Chancellorsville May 1863 · Fredericksburg Dec. 1862 · Wilderness May 1864 · Rappahannock River · Chesapeake Bay

Charlottesville · Spotsylvania May 1864 · VA · GRANT

James River · Cold Harbor June 1864 · York River · Richmond · LEE

Lee surrenders to Grant on April 9, 1865.

Appomattox Courthouse · GRANT · Petersburg June 1864–April 1865 · Five Forks April 1865

Geography **Skills**

Interpreting Thematic Maps

1. Where did Sherman's army go after taking Savannah?

2. **Locate** Identify and list in the order that they occurred the battles fought during Sherman's campaign.

3. **Drawing Inferences and Conclusions** Why did so many eastern battles occur between the James and Potomac Rivers?

THE GRANGER COLLECTION, NEW YORK

Richmond, Virginia, after the war

History Note 4

Most of the major battles near the end of the war took place in Virginia or the Lower South. Union commanders hoped to cut off Virginia from the Lower South. To do so, General William Techumseh Sherman led an army from Tennessee through Georgia to the Atlantic coast. Union leaders then planned to defeat Robert E. Lee's army and capture the Confederate capital of Richmond, Virginia.

20 Reconstruction
(1865–1877)

The race riots in New Orleans led to the deaths of 34 African Americans.

THE GRANGER COLLECTION, NEW YORK

This ticket allowed a spectator to observe President Andrew Johnson's impeachment trial.

UNITED STATES

1865 The Thirteenth Amendment is ratified, abolishing slavery.

1866 Race riots break out in New Orleans.

1867 Congress passes the first federal Reconstruction Act.

1868 President Andrew Johnson is impeached on February 24.

On July 28 the Fourteenth Amendment is ratified by the states, granting African Americans citizenship.

On November 3 Union general Ulysses S. Grant is elected president.

1870 On February 25, Hiram Revels becomes the first African American in the U.S. Senate.

The Fifteenth Amendment is ratified on March 30, giving African Americans the right to vote.

1865	1866	1867	1868	1869	1870	1871

WORLD

1868 The Meiji dynasty returns to power in Japan.

1869 The Suez Canal opens, linking the Mediterranean and Red Seas.

1870 France and the German state of Prussia go to war against each other.

1871 France loses the Franco-Prussian War.

This image shows the opening-day procession of ships through the Suez Canal.

Build on What You Know

The Civil War left two major issues unresolved. First, the federal government had to decide the conditions by which the defeated southern states could rejoin the Union. Second, it had to define the rights of African Americans freed by the Emancipation Proclamation. As southerners tried to rebuild their lives, the nation attempted to heal its wounds.

This poster—which includes images of African American preachers, soldiers, and students—celebrated the passage of the Fifteenth Amendment.

1872 The General Amnesty Act of 1872 restores voting rights to most former Confederate officials.

1874 Republicans lose their majority in the House of Representatives.

1875 Congress passes the Civil Rights Act of 1875.

1877 The Compromise of 1877 ends Reconstruction.

1872   **1873**   **1874**   **1875**   **1876**   **1877**

1873 Spain becomes a republic.

1874 The Spanish republic collapses, and the monarchy is restored.

1876 Queen Victoria of Great Britain becomes empress of India.

If you were there . . .
How would you try to reunite the nation?

You Be the Historian

Themes Journal

What's Your Opinion? Do you **agree** or **disagree** with the following statements? Support your point of view in your journal.

- **Constitutional Heritage** Amending the Constitution is necessary to keep up with changes in government and society.
- **Government** New governments are necessary to rebuild a nation after a civil war.
- **Culture** Political changes bring about new forms of cultural expression.

Rebuilding the South

Read to Discover

1. What effect did the end of the Civil War have on African Americans in the South?
2. How did President Lincoln, Congress, and President Johnson differ in their views on Reconstruction?

WHY IT MATTERS TODAY

Nations today continue to rebuild after wars or natural disasters. Use **CNN fyi.com** or other **current events** sources to find a modern country or region that is rebuilding after a destructive event or period. Record your findings in your journal.

Define

- amnesty

Identify

- Reconstruction
- Ten Percent Plan
- Wade-Davis Bill
- Thirteenth Amendment
- Freedmen's Bureau
- John Wilkes Booth
- Andrew Johnson

The Story Continues

When the Civil War ended, much of the South lay in ruins. Union troops had destroyed many major southern cities and railroads, wrecking trade and commerce. In the countryside, farms had suffered a similar fate. Harvests of corn, cotton, rice, and other important crops were well below normal prewar levels. In South Carolina, Mary Boykin Chesnut wrote in her diary about another problem faced by southerners in many communities—isolation. "We are shut in here. . . . All RR's [railroads] destroyed—bridges gone. We are cut off from the world."

Much of Richmond, Virginia, burned in the last days of the war.

★ Planning Reconstruction

After the South's surrender, tired southern soldiers returned home to find that the world they had left behind was gone. Because of high food prices and widespread crop failures, many southerners faced starvation. The Confederate money most southerners held was now worthless. Banks failed and merchants went bankrupt because people could not repay their debts. Former Confederate general Braxton Bragg found that "*all, all* was lost, except my debts."

The U.S. government faced the question of how to deal with the defeated southern states. **Reconstruction** was the process of reuniting the nation and rebuilding the southern states without slavery. It lasted from 1865 to 1877.

President Lincoln wanted to reunite the nation as quickly and painlessly as possible. He had proposed a plan for readmitting the southern states even before the war ended. Lincoln wanted to offer southerners **amnesty**, or an official pardon, for all illegal acts supporting the rebellion. To receive amnesty, southerners had to swear an oath of loyalty to the United States and accept a ban on slavery. Once 10 percent of voters in a state made these pledges, they could form a new government. The state then could be readmitted to the Union. Louisiana quickly elected a new state legislature under this **Ten Percent Plan**. Other southern states that had been occupied by Union troops followed Louisiana back into the Union.

Some politicians pointed out that Congress had the power to admit new states. They argued that Congress, not the president, should control the southern states' return to the Union. Also, many Republican members of Congress simply disagreed with Lincoln's Ten Percent Plan. Two Republicans—Senator Benjamin Wade and Representative Henry Davis—had an alternative to Lincoln's plan. Under the **Wade-Davis Bill**, a state had to meet two conditions before it could rejoin the Union.

Historical Document

1865

LINCOLN'S SECOND INAUGURAL ADDRESS

On March 4, 1865, President Lincoln laid out his approach to Reconstruction in his second inaugural address. As this excerpt shows, Lincoln hoped to peacefully reunite the nation and its people.

"On the occasion corresponding to this four years ago, all thoughts were anxiously directed to an **impending**[1] civil war. . . . One eighth of the whole population were colored slaves, not **distributed**[2] generally over the Union, but localized in the southern part of it. These slaves **constituted**[3] a peculiar and powerful interest. All knew that this interest was somehow the cause of the war. To strengthen, **perpetuate**,[4] and extend this interest was the object for which the **insurgents**[5] would **rend**[6] the Union even by war, while the Government claimed no right to do more than to restrict the territorial enlargement of it. . . . With **malice**[7] toward none; with charity for all; with firmness in the right, as God gives us to see the right, let us strive on to finish the work we are in, to bind up the nation's wounds, to care for him who shall have borne the battle, and for his widow, and his orphan—to do all which may achieve and cherish a just, and a lasting peace."

---

[1]**impending:** coming
[2]**distributed:** spread
[3]**constituted:** formed
[4]**perpetuate:** continue
[5]**insurgents:** rebels
[6]**rend:** tear apart
[7]**malice:** hatred

Analyzing Primary Sources

1. What does Lincoln believe the spread of slavery was doing to the Union, and how does he believe the government had to respond?

2. How do you think Lincoln views the issue of freeing the slaves?

3. How does Lincoln's speech promote union and equal treatment?

First, it had to ban slavery. Second, a majority of adult males in the state had to take the loyalty oath. However, only southerners who swore that they had never supported the Confederacy could vote or hold office. Because of this rule, the Wade-Davis Bill made it much harder for southern states to rejoin the Union than did Lincoln's plan. President Lincoln refused to sign this bill into law. He thought that few southern states would agree to meet its requirements.

✔ **Reading Check: Contrasting** How did Lincoln's Ten Percent Plan and the Wade-Davis Bill treat southerners differently?

⭐ The Thirteenth Amendment

One issue Republicans agreed on was abolishing slavery. The Emancipation Proclamation had freed slaves only in the Confederate states that had not been occupied by Union forces. Slavery continued in the border states. In addition, many people feared that the federal courts might someday declare the Emancipation Proclamation unconstitutional.

On January 31, 1865, at Lincoln's urging, Congress proposed the **Thirteenth Amendment** to the Constitution. It made slavery illegal throughout the United States. The amendment was ratified and took effect on December 18, 1865. When abolitionist William Lloyd Garrison heard the news, he declared that his work was now finished. He called for

Many African American families bought family records like this one after the war.

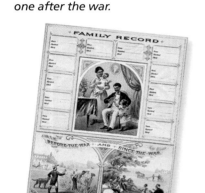

Aid for Freedpeople

Interpreting Maps In order to help African Americans, the Freedmen's Bureau and several private aid societies distributed food and clothing, set up hospitals, and operated schools.

Skills Assessment

1. **Places and Regions** According to the map, which states had major private aid projects?
2. **Drawing Inferences and Conclusions** Why do you think that most private aid societies had their headquarters in northern states?

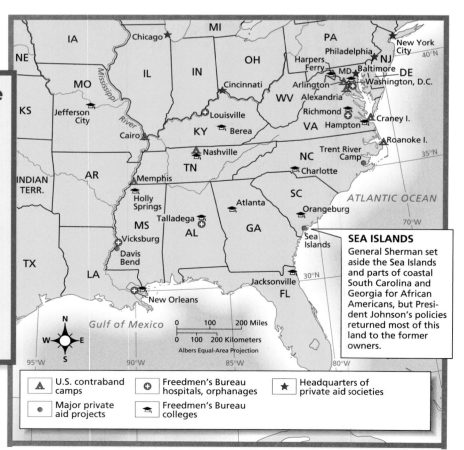

SEA ISLANDS
General Sherman set aside the Sea Islands and parts of coastal South Carolina and Georgia for African Americans, but President Johnson's policies returned most of this land to the former owners.

Interpreting the Visual Record

New schools *This school for freedpeople was established in Vicksburg, Mississippi.* **What does this image reveal about the ages of students in these early schools?**

the American Anti-Slavery Society to break up. Not all abolitionists agreed, however. Frederick Douglass insisted that "slavery is not abolished until the black man has the ballot [vote]."

Freedom did bring many changes to the lives of former slaves. Many couples held ceremonies to legalize marriages that had not been recognized under slavery. Many people searched for relatives who had been sold away from their families years earlier.

Some former slaves began to test their new freedom of movement. A South Carolina woman explained this need. "I must go, if I stay here I'll never know I'm free." Freedom to travel was just the first step on a long road toward equal rights and a new way of life. Adults took new last names. They insisted on being called Mr. or Mrs., rather than by their first name or by nicknames.

Across the South, freedpeople also demanded the same economic and political rights as white citizens. Henry Adams, a former slave, argued that "if I cannot do like a white man I am not free." Many former slaves wanted their own land to farm. Near the end of the Civil War, General William Tecumseh Sherman issued an order setting aside coastal lands in South Carolina, Georgia, and Florida for former slaves. However, the federal government soon returned these lands to the original owners. Many former slaves remained unsure about their future. They did not know where they would live, what kind of work they would do, and what rights they had.

✔ **Reading Check: Summarizing** What did the Thirteenth Amendment achieve, and how did this change the lives of enslaved African Americans?

LINKING
PAST to PRESENT

Historically Black Colleges and Universities

After the Civil War, colleges for African Americans were established in the South. These schools, now known as historically black colleges and universities, offered traditional education, training, and teaching degrees. At one time, laws in many states prohibited African Americans from attending white schools. Today, however, many students choose historically black colleges and universities for their emphasis on African American identity and history. According to United Negro College Fund president William H. Gray III, students receive valuable support from the faculty, administration, and fellow students. **What do historically black colleges and universities provide their students?**

African American students studying art

★ The Freedmen's Bureau

In 1865 Congress established the **Freedmen's Bureau**. Its purpose was to provide relief for all poor people—black and white—in the South. Under Oliver O. Howard, the Bureau distributed food to the poor and supervised labor contracts between freedpeople and their employers. The Bureau also assisted African American war veterans.

In addition, the Freedmen's Bureau helped promote education in the South. Laws against educating slaves had kept most of them from learning to read or write. The Bureau and other groups established schools and provided books and teachers. Some former slaves also organized their own education efforts. African Americans opened schools in abandoned buildings. Some white southerners, however, burned down schools and attacked teachers and students. But by 1869, more than 3,000 schools had been established. More than 150,000 students attended these schools. The Freedmen's Bureau helped establish several colleges for African Americans, including Howard University in Washington, D.C., and Fisk University in Nashville, Tennessee. Students quickly filled the new classrooms, and working adults attended classes in the evening.

✔ **Reading Check: Analyzing Information** How did the Freedmen's Bureau help to provide educational reform in the South?

★ A New President

On the evening of April 14, 1865, President Lincoln and his wife attended a performance of *Our American Cousin* at Ford's Theatre in Washington. During the play, **John Wilkes Booth** sneaked into the president's theater box and shot him. Booth was a southerner who opposed Lincoln's policies. Lincoln was rushed to a boardinghouse across the street, where he died at about 7:30 the next morning. Across the North people were stunned and saddened by the news of Lincoln's death. His body was sent home to Springfield, Illinois, for burial. Vice President **Andrew Johnson** was sworn into office that morning. Reconstruction was now his responsibility.

Republicans liked President Johnson because he seemed to favor a tougher approach to Reconstruction than Lincoln had. Johnson's plan for bringing southern states back into the Union was similar to Lincoln's plan. Johnson gave amnesty to all southerners who took an oath of loyalty and who agreed to support the abolition of slavery. However, wealthy southerners and former Confederate officials would need a presidential pardon to qualify for amnesty. In the end, this restriction was not as harsh as it might seem. Johnson shocked Republicans by eventually pardoning more than 7,000 people.

✔ **Reading Check: Finding the Main Idea** How did Lincoln's assassination affect the nation?

★ President Johnson's Reconstruction Plan

Lincoln's funeral procession was witnessed by thousands of mourners.

Johnson's plan for Reconstruction established a system for setting up new southern state governments. First, he appointed a temporary governor for each state. Then southerners who had taken the loyalty oath elected delegates to a convention that would revise their state's constitution. Next, voters elected new state officials and representatives to the U.S. Congress. Each new state government was required to declare that secession was illegal. It also had to refuse to pay Confederate debts. No state could rejoin the Union until it had met these requirements. Governments already set up under Lincoln's Ten Percent Plan—in Arkansas, Louisiana, Tennessee, and Virginia—were allowed to remain in place.

By the end of 1865 all the southern states except Texas had created new governments. Johnson approved them all and declared that the United States was restored. Newly elected representatives soon came to Washington, D.C., from each reconstructed southern state. But Congress refused to allow them to take their seats in the House and Senate.

Republicans complained that many of the new southern representatives had been military officers and political leaders of the Confederacy. For example, Alexander H. Stephens, the newly elected U.S. senator from Georgia, had been the vice president of the Confederacy. Many Republicans did not believe that people like Stephens were truly loyal to the United States. Congress therefore refused to readmit the reconstructed southern states into the Union. Clearly, the nation was still divided over who should control Reconstruction and what direction it should take.

✔ **Reading Check: Summarizing** What steps did Johnson require southern states to take in order to be readmitted into the Union?

Section 1 Review

go.hrw.com **Homework Practice Online** keyword: SF3 HP20

1 **Define** and explain:
amnesty

2 **Identify** and explain:
- Reconstruction
- Ten Percent Plan
- Wade-Davis Bill
- Thirteenth Amendment
- Freedmen's Bureau
- John Wilkes Booth
- Andrew Johnson

3 **Comparing and Contrasting** Copy the graphic organizer below. Use it to describe the three plans for Reconstruction that were developed over time.

Lincoln's Ten Percent Plan

Wade-Davis Bill

Johnson's Reconstruction Plan

4 **Finding the Main Idea**
a. How did life in the South begin to change for African Americans after the Civil War?

b. What effect did Lincoln's assassination have on Reconstruction?

5 **Writing and Critical Thinking**
Summarizing Imagine that you are a southern newspaper editor in 1865. Write a brief editorial that describes the condition of the South after the Civil War.

Consider the following:
- the economic condition of the South
- the political situation of the ex-Confederate states
- the effect of the Thirteenth Amendment

The Fight over Reconstruction

Read to Discover

1. How did Black Codes restrict African Americans' freedoms?
2. Why did Radical Republicans try to impeach President Johnson?
3. How did Republicans try to protect the civil rights of African Americans?

WHY IT MATTERS TODAY

In the 1860s the Radical Republicans used their control of Congress to pass major laws. Use CNN fyi.com or other **current events** sources to identify which political party controls each house of Congress today and one piece of legislation that party is trying to pass. Record your findings in your journal.

Identify

- Black Codes
- Radical Republicans
- Thaddeus Stevens
- Civil Rights Act of 1866
- Fourteenth Amendment
- Reconstruction Acts
- Fifteenth Amendment

A federal soldier protects an African American man from violence.

The Story Continues

To test his newfound freedom, in 1865 Henry Adams left the plantation where he had been a slave. A group of white men stopped Adams on the road, demanding to know who owned him. When Adams replied that he was a free man, the strangers beat him. Such violent attacks were not unusual in the South in the years following the Civil War. Many white southerners opposed and feared African Americans' freedom. This resentment also affected local authorities and state governments.

★ The Black Codes

In 1866 Congress continued to debate the rules for restoring the Union. Meanwhile, new state legislatures approved by President Johnson had already begun passing laws to deny African Americans' civil rights. "This is a white man's government, and intended for white men only," declared Governor Benjamin F. Perry of South Carolina. Soon every southern state passed **Black Codes**—laws that greatly limited the freedom of African Americans.

Black Codes required African Americans to sign work contracts. This arrangement created working conditions similar to those experienced under slavery. In most southern states, any African American who could not prove he or she had a job could be arrested. Their punishment might be one year of forced labor without pay. African Americans were also prevented from owning guns. In addition, African Americans were not allowed to rent property in cities.

The Black Codes alarmed African Americans. As one Civil War veteran asked, "If you call this Freedom, what do you call Slavery?" African Americans organized to oppose the codes. One group sent a petition to officials in South Carolina.

Under the Black Codes, white southerners could arrest unemployed African Americans and auction their labor to the highest bidder.

"We simply ask . . . that the same laws which govern *white men* shall govern *black men*; that we have the right of trial by a jury of our peers; that schools be established for the education of *colored children* as well as white . . . that, in short, we be dealt with as others are—in equity [equality] and justice."

—Petition by an African American convention, quoted in *There Is a River: The Black Struggle for Freedom in America*, by Vincent Harding

Analyzing Primary Sources

Identifying Points of View What rights did these African Americans want?

Such calls for equality had little effect on the new state governments, however.

✔ **Reading Check: Finding the Main Idea** How were southern African Americans treated after the Civil War, and why did they receive this treatment?

★ The Radical Republicans

The Black Codes angered many Republicans who felt the South was returning to its old ways. Most Republicans were moderates who wanted the South to have loyal state governments. They also believed that African Americans should have rights as citizens. Most moderates hoped that the national government would not have to force the South to follow federal laws.

Radical Republicans wanted the southern states to change much more than they already had before they could return to the Union. Like the moderates, they thought the Black Codes were cruel and unjust. Radicals, however, wanted the federal government to be much more involved in Reconstruction. They feared that too many southern leaders

Thaddeus Stevens was one of the most vocal Radical Republicans in Congress.

PRESIDENTIAL PROFILES

Andrew Johnson

Andrew Johnson had a long political career before becoming president. Born to a poor family in North Carolina, Johnson became a tailor's apprentice. Unhappy with this arrangement, the young Johnson ran away to Tennessee and started his own tailoring business. Eventually, he became a prosperous landowner and entered politics. However, he never forgot his humble beginnings and often criticized wealthy southern planters. Johnson served as governor of Tennessee and later as a U.S. senator from that state. When Tennessee seceded, Johnson remained loyal to the Union. The Republicans selected Johnson as Lincoln's running mate in the presidential campaign of 1864. They hoped that he would appeal to voters in the border states. He had been vice president for less than six weeks when Lincoln was assassinated. What parts of Andrew Johnson's experience prepared him for the presidency?

were still loyal to the former Confederacy. **Thaddeus Stevens** of Pennsylvania and Charles Sumner of Massachusetts were the leaders of the Radical Republicans.

A harsh critic of President Johnson, Stevens was known for his honesty and sharp tongue. He wanted economic and political justice for both African Americans and poor white southerners.

History Makers Speak

"Have not loyal blacks quite as good a right to choose rulers and make laws as rebel whites? Every man, no matter what his race or color . . . has an equal right to justice, honesty, and fair play with every other man; and the law should secure him those rights."

—Thaddeus Stevens, quoted in *Sources of the American Republic*

Sumner had been a strong opponent of slavery before the Civil War. He continued to argue for African Americans' civil rights, which included the right to vote and the right to fair treatment under the law. Both Stevens and Sumner felt that President Johnson's Reconstruction plan was a failure. Although the Radicals did not control Congress, they gained support among moderates when President Johnson ignored criticism of the Black Codes. "The same national authority that destroyed slavery must see that this other pretension [racial inequality] is not permitted to survive," said Sumner.

✔ **Reading Check: Comparing and Contrasting** How were Radical Republicans and moderate Republicans similar and different?

★ Johnson versus Congress

In early 1866 Congress proposed a bill to give the Freedmen's Bureau more powers. The law would allow the Freedmen's Bureau to use military courts to try people accused of violating African Americans' rights. The bill's supporters hoped that these courts would be fairer than local courts in the South. To the surprise of many members of Congress, Johnson vetoed the bill. He insisted that Congress could not pass any new laws until the southern states were represented in Congress. Johnson also argued that the Freedmen's Bureau was unconstitutional. He believed that African Americans did not need any special assistance.

Republicans responded with the **Civil Rights Act of 1866**. This act provided African Americans with the same legal rights as white Americans. President Johnson once again used his veto power. He argued that the law would give too much power to the federal government. He also rejected the principle of equal rights for African Americans. The president insisted that they did not understand "the nature and character of our institutions." Congress, however, overrode Johnson's veto.

✔ **Reading Check: Identifying Points of View** What Congressional laws did Johnson veto, and why?

★ The Fourteenth Amendment

Republicans feared the Civil Rights Act might be overturned. To protect civil rights laws from hostile presidents, courts, or future legislators, Republicans proposed a constitutional amendment in the summer of 1866. The **Fourteenth Amendment** included the following provisions.

1. It defined all people born or naturalized within the United States, except American Indians, as U.S. citizens.
2. It guaranteed to citizens the equal protection of the laws.
3. It said that states could not "deprive any person of life, liberty, or property, without due process of law."
4. It banned many former Confederate officials from holding state or federal offices.
5. It made state laws subject to review by federal courts.
6. It gave Congress the power to pass any laws needed to enforce any part of the amendment.

President Johnson and most Democrats opposed the Fourteenth Amendment. As a result, civil rights for African Americans became a key issue in the 1866 congressional elections. Republican candidates asked Americans to support civil rights by voting for the Republican Party. Johnson traveled around the country defending his Reconstruction plan, but his tour was of little help to Democratic Party candidates.

Two major riots in the South also hurt Johnson's campaign. On May 1, 1866, a dispute in Memphis, Tennessee, took place between local police and black Union soldiers. The dispute turned into a three-day wave of violence against African Americans. By the time the riots ended, 46 African Americans were dead. About three months later, another riot took place in New Orleans when African Americans attempted to hold a peaceful political demonstration. This time 34 African Americans and three white Republicans were killed. Federal troops had to restore order.

✔ **Reading Check: Summarizing** What issue did the Fourteenth Amendment address, and how did it affect the congressional elections of 1866?

THE GRANGER COLLECTION, NEW YORK

Research on the ROM

Free Find:
Civil Rights Act of 1866
After reading about the Civil Rights Act of 1866 on the **Holt Researcher CD–ROM**, create an illustrated diagram that shows what rights former slaves had before and after Congress passed the act.

Interpreting the Visual Record

Johnson's tour *President Andrew Johnson often got into arguments with audience members during his speaking tour in 1866. When someone cried out, "Hang Jeff Davis!" Johnson replied angrily, "Why not hang Thad Stevens?"* **What does this image tell you about how Johnson traveled on his tour?**

★ Congress Takes Charge

The 1866 elections gave the Republican Party a commanding two-thirds majority in both the House and the Senate. This majority gave the Republicans the power to override any presidential veto. In addition, the Republicans became united as the moderates joined with the Radicals. Together they called for a new form of Reconstruction.

In March 1867 Congress passed the first of several **Reconstruction Acts**. These laws divided the South into five districts, with a U.S. military commander in control of each district. The military would remain in the South until the southern states rejoined the Union. To be readmitted, a state had to write a new state constitution supporting the Fourteenth Amendment. Finally, the state had to give African American men the right to vote.

President Johnson disagreed strongly with the Reconstruction Acts. He argued that African Americans did not deserve the same treatment as white people. The Reconstruction Acts, he said, used "powers not granted to the federal government or any one of its branches." Republicans knew

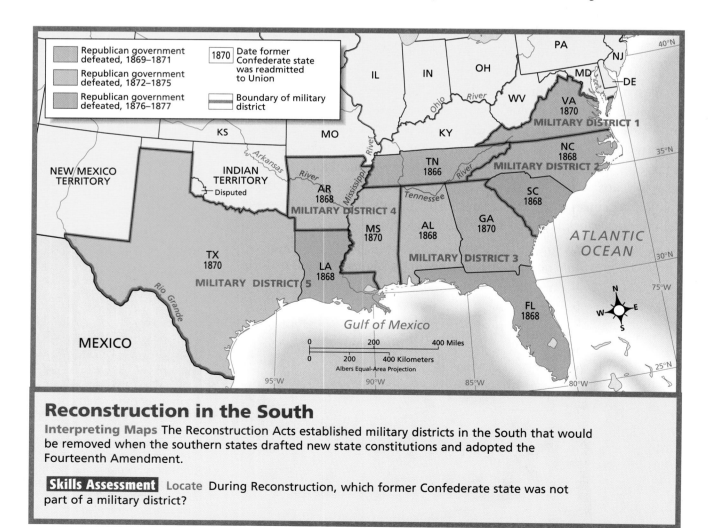

Reconstruction in the South

Interpreting Maps The Reconstruction Acts established military districts in the South that would be removed when the southern states drafted new state constitutions and adopted the Fourteenth Amendment.

Skills Assessment Locate During Reconstruction, which former Confederate state was not part of a military district?

that Johnson did not support their Reconstruction policies, so they passed a law to limit his power. This law prevented the president from removing cabinet officials without the U.S. Senate's approval. Johnson quickly broke the law by firing Edwin Stanton, the secretary of war.

The House of Representatives responded by voting to impeach the president. Impeachment is the process used by a legislative body to bring charges of wrongdoing against a public official. This was the first time in U.S. history that a president had been impeached. The next step, under Article I of the Constitution, was a trial in the Senate. If a two-thirds majority of the senators found Johnson guilty, he would be removed from office.

Although Johnson was unpopular with Republicans, some of them believed he was being judged unfairly. Others did not trust the president *pro tempore* of the Senate, Benjamin Wade, who would become president if Johnson were removed from office. By a single vote, Senate Republicans failed to convict Johnson. Even so, the trial broke his power.

THE GRANGER COLLECTION, NEW YORK

President Andrew Johnson's impeachment trial in the Senate attracted many onlookers.

✔ **Reading Check: Analyzing Information** What was the purpose of the Reconstruction Acts, and how did they affect the South?

★ The Election of 1868

The Democratic Party did not nominate Johnson for another term in 1868. Instead, the Democrats chose former New York governor Horatio Seymour as their presidential candidate. The Republicans selected Ulysses S. Grant. As a war hero, Grant appealed to many northern voters. He had no political experience but supported the congressional Reconstruction plan. He ran under the slogan "Let Us Have Peace."

Shortly after Grant was nominated, Congress readmitted seven southern states—Alabama, Arkansas, Florida, Georgia, Louisiana, North Carolina, and South Carolina. (Tennessee already had been readmitted in 1866.) Under the terms of readmission, these seven states approved the Fourteenth Amendment. They also agreed to let African American men have the vote. However, white southerners used violence to keep African Americans away from the polls during the presidential election.

Despite such tactics, hundreds of thousands of African Americans voted for Grant and the "party of Lincoln." The *New Orleans Tribune* reported that many former slaves "see clearly enough that the Republican party [is] their political life boat." African American votes helped Grant win a narrow victory.

✔ **Reading Check: Analyzing Information** What voters did Grant appeal to in the presidential election of 1868?

★★★★★★★★★★★★
That's Interesting!
★★★★★★★★★★★★

A Good Show Can you imagine a trial becoming a social event? That's just what happened when Andrew Johnson was impeached. People had to have tickets to attend the trial, and only 1,000 were printed. William H. Crook, President Johnson's bodyguard, described the scene. "Everyone who by any possible means could get a ticket . . . [showed] it early that morning at the Capitol. The floor and galleries were crowded." Washingtonians attended in their finest clothes and hoped for a good show. However, they were soon disappointed. Few were interested in the long speeches, and President Johnson did not even appear at his trial.

Interpreting the Visual Record

Gaining the vote *This illustration shows African Americans voting after the passage of the Fifteenth Amendment. **What types of individuals are shown in the voting line?***

⭐ The Fifteenth Amendment

Congressional Republicans wanted to protect their Reconstruction plan from any major changes. They believed that most African American voters would support Republican policies. In addition, some Radical Republicans argued that it was not fair that many northern states had laws that prevented African Americans from voting. After all, every southern state was now required to grant suffrage to African American men under the Republican plan.

These were some of the reasons why Congress proposed the **Fifteenth Amendment** in 1869. The amendment gave African American men throughout the United States the right to vote. Abolitionist William Lloyd Garrison praised "this wonderful, quiet, sudden transformation of four millions of human beings from . . . the auction block to the ballot-box." The amendment went into effect in 1870, and it was one of the last important Reconstruction measures passed at the federal level.

The Fifteenth Amendment did not please every reformer, however. Writer and editor Henry Adams commented that the Fifteenth Amendment was "more remarkable for what it does not than for what it does contain." For example, the act did not guarantee African Americans the right to hold public office. It also did not extend the right to vote to all Americans. This particularly upset women's rights activists, many of whom believed it was unfair to grant African American men the vote while still denying suffrage to all American women. Many women's rights activists opposed the amendment for this reason.

✔ **Reading Check: Finding the Main Idea** What did the Fifteenth Amendment achieve?

Section 2 Review

go. hrw .com Homework Practice Online
keyword: SF3 HP20

★ ★ ★ ★ ★ ★ ★ ★ ★ ★ ★ ★ ★ ★ ★ ★ ★ ★ ★ ★

1 **Identify** and explain:
• Black Codes
• Radical Republicans
• Thaddeus Stevens
• Civil Rights Act of 1866
• Fourteenth Amendment
• Reconstruction Acts
• Fifteenth Amendment

2 **Sequencing** Copy the time line below. Use it to list, in order, the reform legislation Congress proposed or passed as part of Reconstruction. Include the significance of each law or amendment.

Congressional Reconstruction

1866   1867   1870

3 **Finding the Main Idea**
a. In what ways did the Black Codes restrict the freedom of African Americans?

b. Why did Radical Republicans want to remove President Johnson from office?

4 **Writing and Critical Thinking**
Identifying Points of View Imagine that you are a member of the Republican Party. Write a slogan that might have been used by the Republican Party to appeal to voters in either the 1866 congressional elections or the 1868 presidential election.

Consider the following:
• how the party tried to protect the rights of African Americans
• new amendments and congressional laws
• differences between moderate and Radical Republicans

Reconstruction in the South

Read to Discover

1. What reforms did Reconstruction governments carry out?
2. What factors led to the end of Reconstruction?
3. How did southern laws and governments change after Reconstruction ended?

WHY IT MATTERS TODAY

During Reconstruction, there were many Republican governments in the South. As Reconstruction ended, Democrats gained power. Use CNN**fyi**.com or other **current events** sources to learn which political party is leading a southern state today. Record your findings in your journal.

Define

- carpetbaggers
- scalawags
- poll tax
- segregation

Identify

- Hiram Revels
- Blanche K. Bruce
- Ku Klux Klan
- General Amnesty Act of 1872
- Panic of 1873
- Civil Rights Act of 1875
- Compromise of 1877
- Redeemers
- Jim Crow laws
- *Plessy* v. *Ferguson*

The Story Continues

Governments elected with the support of African American voters took control of most southern states. Planter Henry William Ravenel expressed concerns about the future in his daily journal. "The experiment [Reconstruction] is now to be tried. . . . It produces a financial, political, and social revolution [in] the South." Ravenel worried about how the actions of the new governments would affect southern society.

Henry William Ravenel hoped that Reconstruction would be successful.

Reconstruction Governments

The Republican Party controlled most southern governments, partly because the Fourteenth Amendment banned many former Confederates, who were Democrats, from holding office. Most of the Republican officeholders were unpopular with the majority of white southerners.

Some northern-born Republicans had moved south after the war. Many white southerners called these Republicans **carpetbaggers**. Supposedly the northerners carried all their possessions in bags made from

This is an example of the type of carpetbag from which the nickname carpetbaggers developed.

carpeting. Many southerners resented these northerners, believing that they had moved south to profit from Reconstruction. Some of the newcomers wanted to help former slaves. Others hoped to make money while rebuilding the southern economy.

Southern Democrats cared even less for white southern Republicans. They referred to them as **scalawags,** or "mean fellows." Democrats believed that these southerners had betrayed the South by voting for the Republican Party. Many southern Republicans were small farmers who had supported the Union during the war. Others, like Mississippi governor James Alcorn, were former members of the Whig Party. They preferred to become Republicans rather than join the Democrats.

African Americans were the largest group of southern Republican voters. During Reconstruction, more than 600 African Americans were elected as representatives to state legislatures. Of these politicians, 16 were elected to Congress. Other African Americans held important state offices such as lieutenant governor, treasurer, and secretary of state. Many more held local offices in counties throughout the southern states. Apart from their regular duties, African American politicians helped enforce laws that white officials ignored. In Georgia, for example, Justice of the Peace Tunis Campbell protected African Americans from attack by angry whites. One African American called Campbell "the champion of their rights and the bearer of their burden."

African American politicians came from many different backgrounds. **Hiram Revels** was born free in North Carolina and went to college in Illinois. He became a Methodist minister and served as a chaplain in the Union army. In 1870 Revels became the first African American in the U.S. Senate. He took over the seat previously held by Jefferson Davis in Mississippi. Unlike Revels, **Blanche K. Bruce** grew up in slavery in Virginia. He became an important Republican in Mississippi and served one term as a U.S. senator.

Reconstruction governments provided money for many new programs and organizations. They helped to establish some of the first state-funded public school systems in the South. They also built new hospitals, prisons, and orphanages and passed laws prohibiting discrimination against African Americans. Southern states under Republican control spent large amounts of money. They aided the construction or repair of railroads, bridges, and public buildings. These improvements were intended to help the southern economy recover from the war. To get the money for these projects, the Reconstruction governments raised taxes and issued bonds.

✔ **Reading Check: Summarizing** What reforms did Reconstruction state governments carry out?

THE GRANGER COLLECTION, NEW YORK

Interpreting the Visual Record

Representatives *The first African American members of Congress included, from left to right, Hiram Revels, Benjamin Turner, Robert DeLarge, Josiah Walls, Jefferson Long, Joseph Rainey, and Robert Elliott.* **What was significant about the election of these politicians?**

⭐ Opposition to Reconstruction

Despite these efforts to rebuild the South, most white southerners opposed Reconstruction. Democrats claimed that the Reconstruction governments were corrupt and illegal. They also disliked having federal soldiers stationed in their states. Many white southerners disapproved of African American officeholders.

In 1866 a group of white southerners in Tennessee created the **Ku Klux Klan**. This secret society opposed civil rights, particularly suffrage, for African Americans. Klan members wore robes and disguises to hide their identities. The Klan used violence and terror against African Americans, white Republican voters, and public officials. The Klan's membership grew rapidly as it spread throughout the South. In response, Congress passed laws that made it a federal crime to interfere with elections or to deny citizens equal protection under the law. Within a few years the Klan was no longer an organized threat, but violence against African Americans and Republicans continued throughout the 1870s.

✔ **Reading Check: Finding the Main Idea** What was the purpose of the Ku Klux Klan?

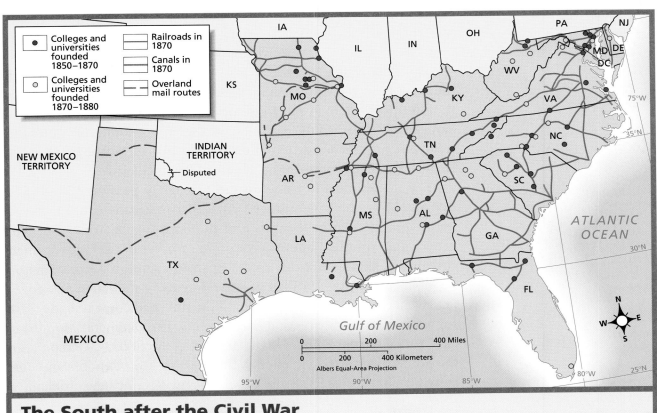

The South after the Civil War

Interpreting Maps After the Civil War many Reconstruction programs contributed to the rapid growth in transportation and education in the South.

Skills Assessment Places and Regions How many colleges and universities were founded in Alabama from 1850 to 1870?

Interpreting the Visual Record

Disputed votes *A special Election Commission heard testimony on disputed returns from the presidential election of 1876.* **Why do you think so many people gathered to watch these proceedings?**

★ The End of Reconstruction

The violence of the Ku Klux Klan was not the only challenge to Reconstruction. The **General Amnesty Act of 1872** allowed former Confederates, except those who had held high ranks, to hold public office. Many of these former Confederates were soon elected to southern governments. Most were Democrats who opposed Reconstruction.

The Republican Party also began losing its power in the North. Although President Grant was re-elected in 1872, scandals in his administration upset voters. A poor economy also hurt the Republicans. The **Panic of 1873** marked the beginning of a severe economic downturn that soon put an estimated 2 million people out of work. In 1874 the Democrats gained control of the House of Representatives.

The Republicans in Congress did manage to pass the **Civil Rights Act of 1875**, which guaranteed African Americans equal rights in public places such as theaters and public transportation. But with Americans worried about economic problems and government corruption, the Republican Party began to abandon Reconstruction. Republicans selected for their 1876 presidential candidate Ohio governor Rutherford B. Hayes. He believed the time had come to end federal support of the Reconstruction governments. The Democrats nominated New York governor Samuel J. Tilden. During the election, Democrats in the South again used violence at the polls to keep Republican voters away. Senator Blanche K. Bruce of Mississippi described the problem.

Analyzing Primary Sources

Summarizing How did Democrats act to ensure that Republicans were defeated at the polls?

History Makers Speak

“In many parts of the State corrupt and violent influences were brought to bear [used] . . . changing the number of votes cast; . . . threats and violence were practiced directly upon the masses of voters . . . to deter [prevent] them from [voting].”

—Blanche K. Bruce, quoted in *Crossing the Danger Water*, edited by Deirdre Mullane

The election between Hayes and Tilden was very close. Tilden appeared to have won. Republicans, however, challenged the electoral votes in Oregon and three southern states. A special Election Commission of 10 members of Congress and five Supreme Court justices settled the issue. The commission narrowly decided to give all the disputed votes to Hayes, who thus won the election by one electoral vote. In the **Compromise of 1877**, the Democrats agreed to accept Hayes's victory. In return, they wanted all remaining federal troops removed from the South. They also asked for funding for internal improvements in the South and the appointment of a southern Democrat to the president's cabinet. Shortly after he took office in 1877, President Hayes removed the last of the federal troops from the South.

✔ **Reading Check: Sequencing** What issues led up to the Compromise of 1877, and how did it affect Reconstruction?

Interpreting Political Cartoons

Compromise of 1877 *Some saw the Compromise of 1877 as the only way to avoid violence in the South after the disputed election results.* **Why do you think the artist chose to show a hand grasping at a pistol?**

⭐ Jim Crow and *Plessy* v. *Ferguson*

Gradually, Democrats regained control of state governments in the South. These Democrats were called **Redeemers**. They came from a variety of backgrounds. Texas governor Richard Coke, like many other Redeemers, was a former officer in the Confederate army. Some Redeemers came from business backgrounds. In general, Redeemers wanted to reduce the size of state government and limit the rights of African Americans. They lowered state budgets and got rid of social programs. The Redeemers cut property taxes and reduced public funding for schools.

Redeemers set up the **poll tax** in an effort to deny the vote to African Americans. The poll tax was a special tax people had to pay before they could vote. Some states also targeted African American voters by requiring them to pass a literacy test. A so-called grandfather clause written into law affected men whose fathers or grandfathers could vote before 1867. In those cases, a voter did not have to pay a poll tax or pass a literacy test. As a result, almost every white man could escape the voting restrictions, while few black men could.

Redeemer governments also introduced legal **segregation**, the forced separation of whites and African Americans in public places. **Jim Crow laws**—laws that required segregation—were common in southern states in the 1880s. African Americans had to stay in different hotels than whites. They had to sit in separate theater sections and ride in separate railcars. One white southerner described the segregated areas that African Americans were forced to use as "the most uncomfortable, uncleanest, and unsafest place[s]."

African Americans challenged Jim Crow laws in court. In 1883, however, the U.S. Supreme Court ruled that the Civil Rights Act of 1875 was unconstitutional. The Court also ruled that the Fourteenth

This African American man is being ordered to leave a whites-only railroad car.

Research on the ROM

Free Find:
Plessy v. *Ferguson*
After reading about *Plessy* v. *Ferguson* on the **Holt Researcher CD–ROM**, imagine that you are a newspaper reporter working at the time of the Supreme Court decision. Write a newspaper article about the case and the Court's decision.

Analyzing Primary Sources
Identifying Points of View
What does it mean to say that the Constitution is "color-blind"?

Amendment applied only to the actions of state governments. This ruling allowed private individuals and businesses to practice segregation.

In 1896 the U.S. Supreme Court returned to the issue of segregation in the case ***Plessy v. Ferguson***. Homer Plessy, an African American, had purchased a ticket on a Louisiana train. When he refused to leave the whites-only section of the train car, he was arrested. Louisiana's Jim Crow laws did not allow African Americans to ride in cars with whites. Plessy's lawyers argued that the law violated his right to equal treatment under the Fourteenth Amendment.

The Court ruled that segregation was allowed if "separate-but-equal" facilities were provided for African Americans. Among the justices, only John Marshall Harlan disagreed with the Court's decision. He explained his disagreement in a dissenting opinion.

History Makers Speak
"In the eye of the law, there is in this country no superior, dominant [controlling], ruling class of citizens. . . . Our Constitution is color-blind, and neither knows nor tolerates classes among citizens. In respect of civil rights, all citizens are equal before the law."

—John Marshall Harlan, quoted in *American Issues*

Despite Harlan's view, segregation became widespread across the country. African Americans were forced to use separate public schools, libraries, and parks. When they existed, these facilities were usually of poorer quality than those created for whites. In practice, these so-called separate-but-equal facilities were separate and unequal.

✔ **Reading Check: Making Generalizations and Predictions** Why might the *Plessy* v. *Ferguson* decision make it hard to establish racial equality?

Section 3 Review

go.hrw.com **Homework Practice Online**
keyword: SF3 HP20

1 **Define** and explain:
• carpetbaggers
• scalawags
• poll tax
• segregation

2 **Identify** and explain:
• Hiram Revels
• Blanche K. Bruce
• Ku Klux Klan
• General Amnesty Act of 1872
• Panic of 1873
• Civil Rights Act of 1875
• Compromise of 1877
• Redeemers
• Jim Crow laws
• *Plessy* v. *Ferguson*

3 **Evaluating** Copy the graphic organizer below. Use it to identify the factors leading to the end of Reconstruction.

Factors Leading to the End of Reconstruction

4 **Finding the Main Idea**
a. What reforms took place under the Reconstruction state governments?

b. Describe laws passed by the new southern state governments after Reconstruction ended.

5 **Writing and Critical Thinking**
Supporting a Point of View Imagine that you are a Republican who opposes the *Plessy* v. *Ferguson* ruling. Write a letter to a friend in the North that expresses your views on the ruling.

Consider the following:
• the Fourteenth Amendment
• the actions of Redeemer governments in the South
• Jim Crow laws

The New South

Read to Discover

1. How did southern agriculture change after the Civil War?
2. Why did some business leaders hope to create a "New South"?
3. What were some popular forms of southern culture during and after Reconstruction?

WHY IT MATTERS TODAY

Many large corporations today try to diversify, or produce a variety of goods and services, rather than relying on one product. Use CNN**fyi**.com or other **current events** sources to find a modern company that makes many different products. Record your findings in your journal.

Define
• sharecropping

Identify
• Henry W. Grady
• Mary Noailles Murfree
• Joel Chandler Harris
• Charles W. Chesnutt

The Story Continues

After farming for years, Charley White and his wife, Lucille, had saved enough money to buy their own farm in Texas. White later reflected on the purchase. "The house wasn't much more than a shack." But that it belonged to them made all the difference. "It just set us on fire. We didn't seem to get half as tired, or if we did we didn't notice it." Lucille White told her husband that "even the rocks look pretty." For many African American farmers, however, owning their own farms remained just a dream.

Sharecroppers and other poor farmers often planted gardens to help provide food for their families.

⭐ Sharecropping

Few African Americans in the South could afford to buy or even rent farms. Moving west also was costly. Many African Americans, therefore, remained on plantations. Others tried to make a living in the cities.

African Americans who stayed on plantations often became part of a system known as **sharecropping**, or sharing the crop. Landowners provided the land, tools, and supplies, while sharecroppers provided the labor. At harvest time the sharecropper often had to give most of the

The Sharecropping Cycle

The sharecropping system trapped many black and white farmers in a cycle of poverty.

The landowner provides land and tools to the sharecropper in exchange for part of the crop.

The sharecropper buys goods from merchants on credit during the growing season.

The cycle begins again.

A poor harvest or unfair merchant or landowner often leaves the sharecropper in debt or with little to show.

Visualizing History

1. **Economics** What economic disadvantages did sharecroppers face?
2. **Connecting to Today** What policies or programs might help poor farmers today?

crop to the owner. Whatever remained belonged to the sharecropper. Many sharecroppers hoped to save enough money from selling their share of the crops to one day be able to buy a farm. Unfortunately, only a few ever achieved this dream.

Most sharecroppers instead lived in a cycle of debt. When they needed food, clothing, or supplies, most families had to buy goods on credit because they had little cash. When sharecroppers sold their crops, they hoped to pay off these debts. However, bad weather, poor harvests, or low crop prices often made this impossible. Merchants sometimes cheated sharecroppers by charging them for items they did not buy. Some landowners also cheated sharecroppers by taking more than their fair share of the crops. Abolitionist Frederick Douglass complained about this poor treatment of sharecroppers.

Analyzing Primary Sources

Identifying Points of View According to Douglass, how did merchants keep sharecroppers in debt?

 History Makers Speak

❝The merchant puts him [the sharecropper] off with his poorest commodities [goods] at highest prices, and can say to him take these or nothing. . . . By this means the laborer is brought into debt, and hence is kept always in the power of the landowner.❞

—Frederick Douglass, quoted in *Enduring Voices*

As a result of such practices, most sharecroppers found themselves ever deeper in debt. They owed more at the end of the harvest than they had when they planted their crops.

Most sharecroppers grew cotton, one of the South's most important cash crops. When too many farmers planted cotton, however, the supply became too great. As a result, the price per bale dropped. One man wrote his father about a drop in the price of cotton. "It nearly ruined us. . . . But getting ready to plant cotton again."

Many farmers understood the drawbacks of planting cotton. However, they felt too much pressure from banks or landlords to change their ways. "Cotton raising has grown to be a necessity more than a choice," a farmer in Alabama said. A southern farmer explained why so many sharecroppers depended on cotton.

 History Makers Speak

❝Cotton is the thing to get credit on in this country. . . . You can always sell cotton. You leave home with a wagon load of cotton and you will go home that night with money in your pocket; you load up your wagon with wheat or corn . . . and I doubt some days whether you could sell it.❞

—Anonymous farmer, quoted in *The Promise of the New South*, by Edward L. Ayers

✔ **Reading Check: Finding the Main Idea** How did the sharecropping system limit the economic freedom of southern farmers?

Southern Industry

The southern economy suffered through cycles of good and bad years as cotton prices went up and down. Some business leaders hoped industry would strengthen the southern economy. They wanted to create a "New South." **Henry W. Grady**, an Atlanta newspaper editor, was a leader of the New South movement. Grady and his supporters wanted to take advantage of the South's resources. With its cotton production and cheap and abundant labor, the South could build textile mills and other factories.

The most successful industrial development in the South involved textile production. Businesspeople built textile mills in many small towns to produce cotton fabric. Hundreds of people from rural areas came to work in the mills. However, few cotton mills hired African Americans.

Work in the cotton mills appealed to farm families who had trouble making ends meet. As one mill worker explained, "It was a necessity to move and get a job, rather than depend on the farm." Recruiters sent out by the mills promised good wages and steady work. Entire families often worked in the same mill. Mills employed large numbers of women and children. Many children started working at about the age of 12. Women did most of the spinning and were valued workers. However, few women had the opportunity to advance within the company.

Mill work was often unpleasant. One unhappy worker described it as "the same thing over and over again. . . . The more you do, the more they want done." Workers often labored 12 hours a day, six days a week. Cotton dust and lint filled the air. This unhealthy air caused asthma and an illness known as brown-lung disease. Fast-moving machinery caused injuries and even some deaths. Despite the long hours and dangerous working conditions, wages were low. But mill work did offer an alternative to farming.

✔ **Reading Check: Comparing and Contrasting** How was work in the cotton mills similar to and different from sharecropping?

CONNECTING TO

MATH

Just the Facts

Cotton Production and Price

Year	Bales produced	Price per pound
1876	4,474,000	9.71¢
1877	4,773,000	8.53¢
1878	5,074,000	8.16¢
1879	5,756,000	10.28¢
1880	6,606,000	9.83¢
1881	5,456,000	10.66¢
1882	6,949,000	9.12¢
1883	5,713,000	9.13¢
1884	5,682,000	9.19¢
1885	6,576,000	8.39¢

Using Mathematical Skills

1. In how many of the years shown on the chart did the price of cotton go up?

2. Use these figures to create two line graphs, one showing cotton production from 1876 to 1885 and the other showing cotton prices during the same period.

3. What happened to cotton production each time the price rose to over 10 cents a pound? Why do you think this was the case?

THE GRANGER COLLECTION, NEW YORK

A young African American girl working in the cotton fields

⭐ Southern Literature

The New South movement sought to modernize the South. Many southerners looked to the arts to keep their longstanding traditions alive, however. Southern literature gained national popularity in the late 1800s. Part of the reason for this was that many southern stories involved people and places in the South that seemed exciting and even exotic to northerners.

Mark Twain wrote many stories about the South, including *The Adventures of Tom Sawyer*. He was considered to be the most famous writer about the South at the end of Reconstruction. **Mary Noailles Murfree** wrote popular short stories and novels about the mountain people of eastern Tennessee. George Washington Cable wrote novels about the African American community in New Orleans. Cable used his writing to protest racial prejudice in the South. **Joel Chandler Harris** wrote short stories about fictional plantation life. His main character was a slave named Uncle Remus, who taught lessons by reciting folktales. Harris based his work on stories he was first told by enslaved African Americans.

Many white southern writers set their stories in a pre–Civil War South full of beautiful plantations and happy slaves. **Charles W. Chesnutt**, an African American, did not share this romantic image. Born in Ohio but raised in North Carolina, his plantation stories showed the greed and cruelty of slaveholders. Many of his short stories are collected in a book called *The Conjure Woman.*

✔ **Reading Check: Analyzing Information** What were the most common topics of southern literature in the late 1800s?

CONNECTING TO
THE ARTS

The Fisk Jubilee Singers
During Reconstruction, students from Fisk University in Nashville, Tennessee, formed the Fisk Jubilee Singers. They traveled widely, touring the North in 1871 and 1872. They later performed in Europe. As they brought African American music, such as spirituals, to a wider audience, they made Fisk University famous. They also raised enough money to help the university build its first permanent building. Other African American colleges, such as Hampton Institute in Virginia, formed similar singing groups. As a result, the popularity of spirituals increased. What is notable about the Fisk Jubilee Singers?

JUBILEE SINGERS, COURTESY OF FISK UNIVERSITY

⭐ Southern Music

Southern music also grew in popularity after the Civil War. Some of the musical instruments popular in the South were the fiddle, the banjo, and the guitar. Fiddle players provided the music for square dancing, a favorite pastime.

One of the most important types of songs in the South was the spiritual. Spirituals were based on Christian hymns and African music sung in the days of slavery. The lead singer often called out a verse that the rest of the singers would repeat. Sometimes the lead singer might change the words slightly to reflect current events. The lyrics usually described the sorrows of slavery and the hope for freedom. One of the best-known spirituals was "Swing Low, Sweet Chariot." It expressed a longing for the promised land, where African Americans would be free from slavery.

Dancing parties were a common pastime in many parts of the South.

Primary Sources

“Swing low, sweet chariot,
Comin' for to carry me home,
Swing low, sweet chariot,
Comin' for to carry me home,
I look'd over Jordan, an' what did I see,
Comin' for to carry me home,
A band of angels comin' after me,
Comin' for to carry me home,
If you get-a there befo' I do,
Tell all my friends I'm comin' too.”

—From *Crossing the Danger Water,* edited by Deirdre Mullane

Analyzing Primary Sources

Drawing Inferences and Conclusions What does "home" represent in "Swing Low, Sweet Chariot"?

✔ **Reading Check: Making Generalizations and Predictions** How might the universal themes of spirituals have helped them become popular in the late 1800s?

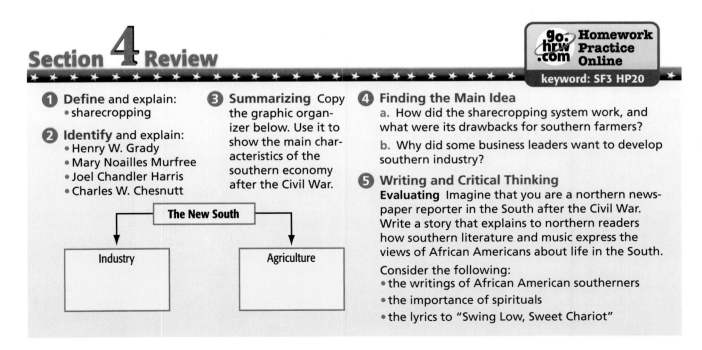

Section 4 Review

go. hrw .com **Homework Practice Online**

keyword: SF3 HP20

❶ **Define** and explain:
• sharecropping

❷ **Identify** and explain:
• Henry W. Grady
• Mary Noailles Murfree
• Joel Chandler Harris
• Charles W. Chesnutt

❸ **Summarizing** Copy the graphic organizer below. Use it to show the main characteristics of the southern economy after the Civil War.

The New South
Industry   Agriculture

❹ **Finding the Main Idea**
a. How did the sharecropping system work, and what were its drawbacks for southern farmers?

b. Why did some business leaders want to develop southern industry?

❺ **Writing and Critical Thinking**
Evaluating Imagine that you are a northern newspaper reporter in the South after the Civil War. Write a story that explains to northern readers how southern literature and music express the views of African Americans about life in the South.

Consider the following:
• the writings of African American southerners
• the importance of spirituals
• the lyrics to "Swing Low, Sweet Chariot"

Chapter 20 Review

The Chapter at a Glance

Examine the visual summary of the chapter below. Use it to write a five-question quiz for a classmate.

Reuniting the Nation

The Thirteenth, Fourteenth, and Fifteenth Amendments are ratified, ending slavery, granting equal protection to all citizens, and giving African Americans the vote. Other civil rights laws are also passed.

The Reconstruction Acts divide the South into military districts and install new governments. The changes lead to conflict between African Americans and white southerners and Republicans and Democrats.

The Compromise of 1877 ends Reconstruction. Legal segregation is upheld in the South by Jim Crow laws and by the Supreme Court ruling in *Plessy* v. *Ferguson*.

Identifying People and Ideas

Use the following terms or people in historically significant sentences.

1. Thirteenth Amendment
2. Freedmen's Bureau
3. Andrew Johnson
4. Black Codes
5. Fourteenth Amendment
6. Fifteenth Amendment
7. Hiram Revels
8. Compromise of 1877
9. *Plessy* v. *Ferguson*
10. sharecropping

Understanding Main Ideas

Section 1 *(Pages 616–621)*
1. How did the Reconstruction plans of Lincoln, the Radical Republicans, and Johnson differ?

Section 2 *(Pages 622–628)*
2. List the major parts of Congress's plan for Reconstruction.
3. Why did the Radical Republicans impeach President Johnson?

Section 3 *(Pages 629–634)*
4. How did Reconstruction state governments try to change and help rebuild the South?
5. What events helped bring about the end of Reconstruction?

Section 4 *(Pages 635–639)*
6. How did African American literature and music contrast with the romantic image of the South painted by many white southern writers?

You Be the Historian— Reviewing Themes

1. **Constitutional Heritage** How did the Thirteenth, Fourteenth, and Fifteenth Amendments protect the rights of African Americans?
2. **Government** How did Reconstruction affect governments in the South?
3. **Culture** What contributions did African Americans make to southern society, government, and culture after the Civil War?

Thinking Critically

1. **Analyzing Information** What economic problems did the South face during Reconstruction?
2. **Drawing Inferences and Conclusions** How do you think Abraham Lincoln would have viewed Reconstruction had he lived to see it?
3. **Evaluating** Do you think that Reconstruction was a success or a failure? Explain your answer, considering the perspectives of all groups involved.

Interpreting Political Cartoons

Study the political cartoon of Reconstruction below. Then answer the questions that follow.

THE GRANGER COLLECTION, NEW YORK

THE "STRONG" GOVERNMENT 1869–1877.

1. Which of the following best describes the message that the artist is trying to present?
   a. Poor people in the South are forced to work on behalf of the rich.
   b. The South is being unfairly punished by the harsh military rule of the federal government.
   c. Military forces have taken control of President Grant and the federal government.
   d. The South is helping carry the burdens of the rest of the nation.

2. Based on your knowledge of the period and the imagery in this cartoon, do you think the artist would have been pleased by the Compromise of 1877? Explain your answer.

3. Based on your knowledge of the period, what do you think the carpetbag in the cartoon is supposed to represent?
   a. the military power of the federal government
   b. the corrupt politics of Grant's administration
   c. northern Republicans who have moved south to take part in Reconstruction
   d. the desire of southerners to move away from the Reconstruction South

Analyzing Primary Sources

Read the following excerpt from a southern African American newspaper in 1866, then answer the questions that follow.

❝The future looks dark, and we predict, that we are entering upon the greatest political contest that has ever agitated the people of the country—a contest, in which, we of the South must be for the most part spectators [observers]; not indifferent [unconcerned] spectators, for it is about us that the political battle is fought. The issue is fairly joined [begun].❞

4. Which of the following statements best describes the viewpoint of the author?
   a. Reconstruction will unite the country peacefully and smoothly.
   b. Reconstruction will divide the nation, and the South can do little to control it.
   c. Few people in the South care one way or the other about Reconstruction.
   d. Southerners will play a major role in determining Reconstruction policies.

5. Based on your knowledge of the period, do you think these predictions were accurate? Explain your answer.

Alternative Assessment

American History

Building Your Portfolio

Interdisciplinary Connection to the Arts

Write a poem or song describing how an African American who was set free at the end of the Civil War might have felt. If you create a poem, find an image to illustrate it. If you write a song, select a musical style in which you want it to be performed.

📶 internet connect

Internet Activity: go.hrw.com
keyword: SF3 CF20

Access the Internet through the HRW Go site to locate and use primary and secondary sources to acquire information on the differing points of view of Reconstruction. Then assume the point of view of someone living during the time and create a newspaper that reflects the historical context of Reconstruction and the frame of reference which influenced its participants.

Social Studies Skills

WORKSHOP

Distinguishing Fact from Opinion and Identifying Bias

Historical sources may contain both facts and opinions. Sources such as diaries, letters, and speeches usually express personal views. The ability to distinguish facts from opinions is very important. It allows you to judge the accuracy of an argument or a historical account.

When reading historical sources, try to identify a writer's bias—prejudices or strong feelings. Many famous historical people had strong opinions that appear in their writings and speeches. Remember that just because a person is famous does not mean that you must agree with his or her opinions.

How to Distinguish Fact from Opinion

1. **Identify the facts.** Ask yourself: Can the statement be proven? Determine whether the idea can be checked for accuracy in a source such as an almanac or encyclopedia. If so, the statement probably concerns a matter of fact. If not, it probably contains an opinion.

2. **Identify the opinions.** Look for clues that indicate a statement of opinion. These clues include phrases such as "I think" and "I

believe," comparative words like *greatest* and *more important,* and value-filled words like *extremely* and *ridiculous.* All of these words imply a judgment and, thus, an opinion.

How to Identify Bias

1. **Evaluate the information presented.** What are the sources of information? How reliable are they? Why might a historical figure have supported one view over another? Be sure to distinguish between provable facts and someone's opinions.

2. **Make your own judgment.** Remember that many of the historical documents you read are created by people who have their own opinions and points of view. It is up to you to read each document critically and to draw your own conclusions.

Practicing the Skills

Read the excerpt below, in which a southern newspaper editor defends Representative Preston Brooks's beating of Senator Charles Sumner. Then answer the questions that follow.

    ❝We consider the act good in conception [thought], better in execution. . . . These vulgar abolitionists . . . must be lashed into submission. Sumner, in particular, ought to have nine-and-thirty [lashes] early every morning.❞

1. Is this excerpt an example of a fact or an opinion? Which words let you know?

2. What bias, if any, does the author express? If you found bias, how did you identify it?

History in Action

UNIT 8 SIMULATION

You Make the Decision . . .

Should Your Border State Support the Union or the Confederacy?

Complete the following activity in small cooperative groups. It is April 12, 1861. The Confederates have opened fire on Fort Sumter. You live in one of the four border states in which slavery is legal—Delaware, Kentucky, Maryland, or Missouri. The people in your state have strong feelings for both sides in the conflict. Your state legislature has asked a special committee to make a recommendation about which side your state should support—the Union or the Confederacy. Follow these steps to reach your decision.

1. Gather Information. Use your textbook and other resources to find information that might help you decide whether to support the North or the South in this conflict. Be sure to use what you learned from this unit's Skills Workshop on Distinguishing Fact from Opinion and Identifying Bias to help you make an informed decision. You may want to divide different parts of the research among group members.

2. Identify Options. After reviewing the information you have gathered, identify the options you might consider for which side to support in the Civil War. Your final solution to the problem may be easier to reach if you consider as many options as possible. Be sure to record your possible options for your presentation.

3. Predict Consequences. Now take each option your group came up with and consider what might be the outcome if you followed each course of action. Ask yourselves questions like: "Is it possible for our state to remain neutral during this conflict?" Once you have predicted the consequences, record them as notes for your presentation.

4. Take Action to Implement Your Decision. After you have considered your options, you should plan and create your presentation. Be sure to make your decision on whether to support the North or the South very clear. You will need to support your committee's recommendation by including information you gathered and by explaining why you rejected other options. Your presentation needs to be visually appealing to gain the support of the state legislature. When you are ready, decide which group members will make each part of the presentation, and then take your decision to the state legislature (the rest of the class). Good luck!

UNIT 9
A Growing America
(1850–1920)

Young People

IN HISTORY

Young Cowhands

Cowhands herded Texas longhorn cattle northward across the Great Plains to be sold in Kansas railroad towns. A cattle drive of this distance required working long hours in all kinds of weather. Sometimes cowhands would run into problems with cattle thieves known as rustlers. The greatest danger, however, was a stampede.

Many cowhands began working cattle when they were children. A rancher paid young Cliff Newland 50 cents a day to haul supplies to cattle drivers 75 miles away. From this job, Newland turned to wrangling—the work of herding and caring for livestock. To help him learn to stay in the saddle while training horses, Newland's father tied him onto the seat. By age 13, Newland had already been on three cattle drives and had a job training young horses.

Not all the young cowhands were boys. At age 13, Agnes Morley and her younger brother traveled across 130 miles of harsh New Mexico landscape to sell some cattle.

Many cowhands left home to work the cattle drives while they were still children. E. C. Abbott, also known as "Teddy Blue," went on his first cattle drive when he was 11 years old. He recalled his trip up the Western Trail in 1879.

Many young cowhands like this female broncobuster gained recognition for their unique skills.

> **That trip up the trail in '79 was my second, but in a way it was the first that counted, because I was only a button [youngster] the other time. I wasn't nineteen years old when I come up the trail with the Olive herd, but don't let that fool you. I was a man in my own estimation and a man in fact.**

Teddy Blue recalled a story he had once heard about a schoolteacher. She wanted a Texas cowhand to tell her about life on the trail. She asked, "Oh, Mister So-and-So, didn't the boys used to have a lot of fun riding their ponies?" He replied, "Madam, there wasn't any boys or ponies. They was all horses and men."

If You Were There *Would the life of a cowhand be appealing to you?*

LEFT PAGE: *In many western families, like this one, all family members had to work hard.*

21 The West
(1850–1890)

Fort Laramie was a fur-trading post built in 1834.

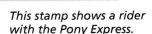

This stamp shows a rider with the Pony Express.

UNITED STATES

1851 The Treaty of Fort Laramie is signed.

1860 The Pony Express begins delivering mail between the East and West.

1862 Congress passes the Homestead Act.

1869 The first transcontinental railroad is completed.

1874 Gold is discovered in the Black Hills of the Dakota Territory.

| 1850 | 1855 | 1860 | 1865 | 1870 |

WORLD

1855 Paris holds a world's fair.

1864 French scientist Louis Pasteur invents the process of pasteurization.

Cans like this one were used to store meat.

People flocked to the 1855 World's Fair in Paris, shown below.

Build on What You Know

After the Civil War, the U.S. population grew rapidly. Settlements spread throughout the West. A flood of miners, ranchers, and farmers transformed the western landscape and adapted to their new environment. Often, however, these new settlers came into conflict with American Indians already living in the region.

Golden spike that joined the Central Pacific and Union Pacific Railroads

This painting shows cowboys herding cattle.

1876 The Sioux defeat the U.S. Army in the Battle of the Little Bighorn.

1879 Thousands of African Americans migrate from the South to Kansas.

1886 Ranchers lose most of their cattle during a severe winter.

1889 President Benjamin Harrison opens the Oklahoma District to settlers.

1890 The Massacre at Wounded Knee occurs.

1875   **1880**   **1885**   **1890**

1880 Australian merchants send meat to Great Britain for the first time by using refrigerated ships.

1883 The Orient Express makes its first run from Paris to Istanbul.

1888 Brazil abolishes slavery.

The Orient Express traveled across southeastern Europe.

You Be the Historian

 Themes Journal

What's Your Opinion? Do you **agree** or **disagree** with the following statements? Support your point of view in your journal.

- **Economics** The federal government should promote economic development in underdeveloped regions.

- **Culture** Cultural conflict will result when two different groups come into contact.

- **Geography** People will endure harsh environmental conditions in order to have new opportunities.

If you were there . . .
What kind of work would you do in the West, and why?

The Wars for the West

Read to Discover

1. What animals did the Plains Indians use, and why were they important?
2. What caused conflicts between American Indians and American settlers in the West, and what were the results of these conflicts?
3. How did the reservation system and the Dawes Act affect American Indians?

WHY IT MATTERS TODAY

Many American Indians continue to live on reservations. Use CNNfyi.com or other **current events** sources to find out about American Indians living on reservations today. Record your findings in your journal.

Define

• reservations

Identify

• Treaty of Fort Laramie
• Crazy Horse
• Treaty of Medicine Lodge
• George Armstrong Custer
• Sitting Bull
• Battle of the Little Bighorn
• Ghost Dance
• Massacre at Wounded Knee
• Geronimo
• Sarah Winnemucca
• Dawes General Allotment Act

THE GRANGER COLLECTION, NEW YORK

The Cheyenne used shields like this one in battle.

The Story Continues

Like many Sioux before him, Standing Bear was eager for his first buffalo hunt. "Watch the buffalo closely. . . . They are very quick and powerful," warned his father. When he got close to the buffalo herd, Standing Bear recalled, "I realized how small I was." He brought down a buffalo and rode proudly back to camp to give his mother the animal's skin. Buffalo hunts were important to American Indians' ways of life on the Great Plains.

⭐ The Plains Indians

The Great Plains lie roughly between the 98th meridian and the Rocky Mountains. They stretch north into Canada and south into Texas. Despite their sometimes harsh conditions, the region was home to the Plains Indians. Groups such as the Apache and the Comanche lived in Texas and what is now Oklahoma. The Cheyenne and the Arapaho lived in different parts of the central Plains. The Pawnee lived in Nebraska. To the north were the Sioux, who spread from Minnesota to Montana.

For survival, Plains Indians depended on two animals—the horse and the buffalo. The Spanish brought horses to America in the 1500s. Plains Indians learned to ride horses and used them to follow the buffalo herds. They used the buffalo for food, shelter, and tools. The Plains Indians prospered and by 1850 some 75,000 American Indians were living on the Plains.

Miners and settlers began crossing the Great Plains in the mid-1800s. To protect these travelers, U.S. officials sent agents to negotiate treaties with the Plains Indians. The first major agreement was the **Treaty of Fort Laramie**, signed with northern Plains nations in Wyoming in 1851. Two years later, several southern Plains nations signed a treaty at Fort Atkinson in Nebraska. These treaties accepted Indian claims to much of the Great Plains. They also allowed Americans to build forts and roads and to travel across Indian homelands. The U.S. government promised to pay for any damages to Indian lands.

Sioux moccasins

✔ **Reading Check: Analyzing Information** What compromise did the United States and American Indians reach to allow miners and settlers to cross Indian lands?

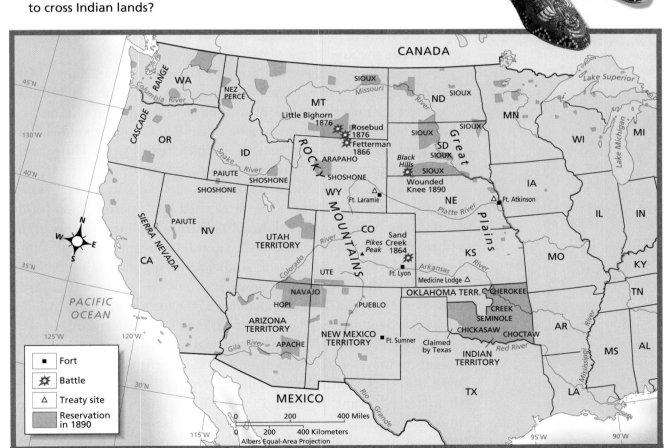

Indian Reservations and Battles to 1890

Interpreting Maps As more and more settlers moved to the West, American Indians were forced to accept treaties that placed them on reservations.

Skills Assessment Human Systems Which present-day state contained the most reservation lands?

Several African American cavalry regiments served in the western U.S. Army. American Indians nicknamed these African American troops, who were known for their courage and discipline, "buffalo soldiers."

⭐ War on the Plains

The treaties did not keep the peace for long. Gold was discovered in what is now Colorado in 1858. The news brought thousands of miners to the West, where they soon clashed with the Cheyenne and the Arapaho. In 1861 the U.S. government negotiated a new treaty with these Indians. The treaty created **reservations**, areas of federal land set aside for American Indians. The government expected Indians to stay on the reservations, which made hunting buffalo almost impossible.

Many American Indians refused to live on reservations. Some continued to fight, while others shared the view of Cheyenne chief Black Kettle. "It is not my intention or wish to fight the whites," he declared. He did not get his wish. In November 1864, U.S. Army troops attacked Black Kettle's camp on Sand Creek in southeastern Colorado. The soldiers killed about 200 men, women, and children. Black Kettle was among the Cheyenne who escaped the Sand Creek Massacre.

Pioneers and miners continued to cross the Great Plains. Many miners used the Bozeman Trail, which ran from Wyoming to Montana. To protect the miners, the U.S. Army built forts along the trail, which ran through Sioux hunting grounds. Sioux chief Red Cloud responded to the army's actions with war. In late 1866 a chief named **Crazy Horse** and a group of Sioux ambushed 81 cavalry troops, killing them all.

William Tecumseh Sherman, the famous Civil War general, was in charge of the western armies. He threatened the "extermination [of the Sioux] men, women, and children." The army had little success in this effort, however, and asked Red Cloud to negotiate. Red Cloud responded, "When we see the soldiers moving away and the forts abandoned, then I will come down and talk." In 1868 the U.S. Army closed the Bozeman Trail and abandoned the forts along it. Many Sioux then moved to the Black Hills Reservation in Dakota Territory.

Meanwhile, the U.S. government was also asking southern Plains Indians to move off their lands. In the 1867 **Treaty of Medicine Lodge**, most of these peoples agreed to live on reservations. However, many of them did not want to give up their hunting grounds. Fighting soon broke out between the Comanche and the Texans. The U.S. Army and the Texas Rangers were unable to defeat the Comanche forces in battle. So U.S. forces cut off the Comanche's access to food. The Comanche could not survive under these conditions. In 1875 Quanah Parker, the last of the Comanche war leaders, surrendered.

✔ **Reading Check: Summarizing** What was the federal policy toward Plains Indians in the 1860s and 1870s?

⭐ The U.S. War with the Sioux

As fighting on the southern Plains ended, new trouble was starting to the north. In 1874 Lieutenant Colonel **George Armstrong Custer**'s soldiers found gold in the Black Hills of the Dakota Territory. The U.S. government responded by insisting that the Sioux sell their reservation land in the Black Hills. **Sitting Bull**, a Sioux leader, protested these new demands.

 History Makers Speak

❝What treaty that the whites have kept has the red man broken? Not one. What treaty that the white man ever made with us have they kept? Not one.❞

—Sitting Bull, quoted in *Touch the Earth,* by T. C. McLuhan

Other Sioux leaders listened to Sitting Bull and refused to give up the Black Hills. Fighting soon broke out between the U.S. Army and the Sioux.

Custer, a Civil War veteran, was in command of the U.S. Army 7th Cavalry. On June 25, 1876, his scouts found a Sioux camp along the Little Bighorn River in Montana. Leading 264 of his soldiers, Custer raced ahead without waiting for any backup forces. The Battle of the Little Bighorn followed. Sioux forces, led by Crazy Horse and Sitting Bull, surrounded Custer and his troops. Sitting Bull's cousin Pte-San-Waste-Win described the fighting. "The soldiers fired many shots, but the Sioux shot straight and the soldiers fell dead. When we came to the hill . . . Long Hair [Custer] lay dead among the rest." Newspapers called the battle "Custer's Last Stand."

The **Battle of the Little Bighorn** was the worst defeat the U.S. Army had suffered in the West. It was also the Sioux's last major victory. In late 1877 Crazy Horse was killed in prison after surrendering to the U.S. Army.

Analyzing Primary Sources
Identifying Points of View
Why did Sitting Bull not trust the U.S. government?

Interpreting the Visual Record

The Battle of the Little Bighorn *The 7th Cavalry suffered a devastating defeat at the hands of Sioux forces at the Battle of the Little Bighorn.* **What advantages does the illustration show each side having?**

THE GRANGER COLLECTION, NEW YORK

"I Will Fight No More Forever"

Chief Joseph

Chief Joseph led the Nez Percé from 1871 to 1877. He gave the following speech to the U.S. Army officers who took him prisoner on October 5, 1877. Chief Joseph died in 1904.

Tell General Howard I know his heart. What he told me before, I have in my heart. I am tired of fighting. Our chiefs are killed. . . . The old men are all dead. It is the young men who say yes and no. **He who led on the young men**[1] is dead. It is cold and we have no blankets. The little children are freezing to death. My people, some of them, have run away to the hills, and have no blankets, no food; no one knows where they are—perhaps freezing to death. I want to have time to look for my children and see how many I can find. Maybe I shall find them among the dead. Hear me, my chiefs. I am tired; my heart is sick and sad. From where the sun now stands I will fight no more forever.

---

[1]**He who led on the young men:** Joseph's brother, Alokut

Understanding What You Read

Literature and History Why has Chief Joseph chosen to "fight no more forever"?

Ghost Dance shirt

Sitting Bull fled to Canada with a few of his followers. With two of their most important leaders gone, the northern Plains Indians soon surrendered.

In 1881 Sitting Bull and his Sioux followers returned from Canada. They had run out of food during the hard winter. "I wish it to be remembered," Sitting Bull said, "that I was the last man of my tribe to surrender my rifle." He joined most of the Sioux on Standing Rock Reservation in Dakota Territory.

Wovoka, a Paiute Indian, began a religious movement known as the **Ghost Dance**. He predicted the arrival of a paradise for American Indians. Indians who performed the dance believed that it would lead to a new life free from suffering. In this paradise, the buffalo herds would return, and the settlers would disappear. When the Ghost Dance spread across the Plains, U.S. officials feared it would lead to a Sioux uprising. While following orders to arrest Sitting Bull, reservation police killed the Sioux leader in 1890. In response, many Sioux left the reservations. Later that year, the U.S. Army found a camp of Sioux near Wounded Knee Creek in South Dakota. When the two groups faced one another, a shot rang out. The U.S. troops began firing and killed about 150 Indians. Known as the **Massacre at Wounded Knee**, this attack was the last major event of more than 25 years of war on the Great Plains.

✔ **Reading Check: Sequencing** List the conflicts between the Great Plains Indians and U.S. forces in the order that they occurred.

★ Indians in the Southwest and Far West

Far from the Great Plains, other American Indians resisted being moved to reservations. The Navajo lived in what became Arizona and New Mexico. In 1863 when the U.S. government ordered them to settle on a reservation, the Navajo refused. In response, Kit Carson, a former scout, led U.S. troops in raids on the Navajo's fields, homes, and livestock.

When the Navajo ran out of food and shelter, they started surrendering to the U.S. Army. In 1864 the army led Navajo captives on the Long Walk. This 300-mile march took the Navajo across the desert to a reservation at Bosque Redondo, New Mexico. Along the way, hundreds of Navajo died. At Bosque Redondo the Navajo suffered harsh conditions. In 1868 they negotiated for a new reservation located in Arizona and New Mexico.

The U.S. government had promised to let the peaceful Nez Percé keep their homelands in northeastern Oregon. Within a few years, however, settlers asked the government to remove them. The government ordered the Nez Percé to a reservation in what is now Idaho. Nez Percé leader Chief Joseph reluctantly agreed to move. Before leaving, a few angry Nez Percé killed some local settlers. Fearing that U.S. forces would fight back, the Nez Percé fled. The U.S. Army chased this band of about 700 Indians across what are now Idaho, Wyoming, and Montana. Although outnumbered, the band defeated or avoided the army for weeks before trying to escape to Canada. Less than 40 miles from the border, U.S. troops overtook and surrounded the Nez Percé. Chief Joseph surrendered on October 5, 1877. The U.S. government sent the Nez Percé to a reservation in what is now Oklahoma.

By the 1880s most American Indians had stopped fighting. The Apache of the Southwest, however, continued to battle the U.S. Army. The Apache were raiders, known for their ability to survive in the desert. In the 1870s the U.S. Army gathered some Apache on a reservation in San Carlos, Arizona. One Apache called the reservation "nothing but cactus, rattlesnakes, heat, rocks, and insects."

A Chiricahua Apache named **Geronimo** and his small band of raiders left the reservation and avoided capture until 1884. The following year Geronimo escaped again. When the U.S. Army caught him, he broke free once more on the way to the reservation. "I feared treachery [dishonesty]," he said. This time the army sent 5,000 soldiers and 500 Apache scouts to capture Geronimo and 24 of his followers. Finally, in September 1886, he surrendered, ending the Apache armed resistance. The U.S. government sent Geronimo and many Chiricahua Apache to Florida as prisoners of war.

✔ **Reading Check: Identifying Cause and Effect** What led to some of the conflicts that took place between American settlers and American Indians in the 1800s, and what were the results of these conflicts?

★ Policy and Protest

By the 1870s many American Indian peoples were living on reservations. Indian leaders spoke out against the reservation system. They complained that government agents stole food and money meant for Indians. In addition, reservation land was usually not useful for farming or buffalo hunting. As a result, many Indians were starving.

BIOGRAPHY

Geronimo
(1829–1909)

Many Apache found it difficult to get along with Geronimo. He had grown bitter after Mexican soldiers killed his mother, wife, and children. Despite this bitterness, other Apache admired Geronimo for his intelligence and his ability to handle difficult situations.

Geronimo led his own band of troops. He was captured several times, but usually managed to escape. Geronimo finally surrendered to U.S. troops in 1886. His courage and determination to remain free made Geronimo a legend. **Why was Geronimo admired by other Apache?**

In the late 1870s a Paiute Indian named **Sarah Winnemucca** became one of the first American Indians to call for reforms. She gave lectures on the problems of the reservation system and eventually pleaded her case in Washington, D.C. After listening to her, "many people were moved to tears," according to one spectator. Writer Helen Hunt Jackson also pushed for reform. In 1881 she published *A Century of Dishonor*. This book criticized the federal government's treatment of Indians. Jackson wrote that "it makes little difference where one opens the record of the history of the Indians; every page and every year has its dark stain." The popularity of her writings helped spread the reform message.

Many reformers believed that American Indians would be better off if they adopted the ways of white people. The **Dawes General Allotment Act**, passed by Congress in 1887, reflected this view. It tried to lessen the traditional influences on Indian society by making land ownership private rather than shared. Reservation lands were to be divided into 160-acre plots for families and 80 acres for single adults. The act also promised U.S. citizenship to American Indians.

After breaking up reservation land, the government sold the acreage that remained. As a result, Indians lost much of the land that they occupied before the Dawes Act. Reformers had hoped the Dawes Act would help American Indians. Instead, it resulted in the loss of about two thirds of their land. As enforced, the Dawes Act also did not lead to citizenship for many American Indians. Overall, the new policy failed to improve Indians' lives.

Sarah Winnemucca went to Washington, D.C., to ask for reforms for American Indians.

✔ **Reading Check: Drawing Inferences and Conclusions** How did reformers who fought for American Indian rights influence Indians' lives?

Section 1 Review

go.hrw.com **Homework Practice Online**
keyword: SF3 HP21

① **Define** and explain:
• reservations

② **Identify** and explain:
• Treaty of Fort Laramie
• Crazy Horse
• Treaty of Medicine Lodge
• George Armstrong Custer
• Sitting Bull
• Battle of the Little Bighorn
• Ghost Dance
• Massacre at Wounded Knee
• Geronimo
• Sarah Winnemucca
• Dawes General Allotment Act

③ **Identifying Cause and Effect** Copy the graphic organizer below. Use it to list the causes and effects of conflicts between the United States and American Indians in the West.

Causes → Conflicts → Effects

④ **Finding the Main Idea**
a. Why were the horse and the buffalo important to the lives of Plains Indians?

b. Why do you think the Ghost Dance was important to American Indians on the Great Plains?

⑤ **Writing and Critical Thinking**
Comparing and Contrasting Imagine that you are an American Indian who has been affected by the Dawes Act. Write a letter to a member of Congress describing how your life has changed.

Consider the following:
• life on reservations
• the positive and negative aspects of land ownership
• the value of citizenship

Section 2

Miners and Railroads

Read to Discover

1. What were some of the challenges of mining in the West?
2. What obstacles did the builders of the transcontinental railroad face?
3. How did the transcontinental railroad affect the settlement and development of the West?

WHY IT MATTERS TODAY

Railroads are still an important means of transportation in the United States. Use CNNfyi.com or other **current events** sources to learn about the role of railroads in the U.S. transportation system today. Record your findings in your journal.

Define

- bonanza
- boomtowns
- transcontinental railroad

Identify

- Comstock Lode
- Pony Express
- Pacific Railway Acts
- Leland Stanford

The Story Continues

In 1858 gold was discovered in Colorado. After traveling west to see the new mine, *New York Tribune* editor Horace Greeley announced that the "discovery is . . . the richest and greatest [gold mine] in America." Thousands of prospectors raced west to the mining region around Pikes Peak. Many labeled their wagons "Pikes Peak or Bust." Most of them soon learned that Greeley had been fooled about the richness of the strike. The early prospectors had started the rush by filling part of the mine with extra gold.

The dream of finding pieces of gold ore like this one drew miners to the West.

⭐ The Mining Booms

The following year miners found gold and silver in western Nevada. The strike became known as the **Comstock Lode**, named after miner Henry Comstock. This time the wealth was real. The Comstock Lode was a **bonanza**— a large deposit of precious ore. Over the next 20 years, the Comstock Lode produced over $500 million worth of gold and silver. It took expensive equipment to remove the silver and gold trapped within the quartz rock. Large companies bought up claims from miners who

THE GRANGER COLLECTION, NEW YORK

Interpreting the Visual Record

Prospectors *This image shows prospectors at the entrance of a mineshaft.* ***What challenges do you think these miners faced?***

could not afford such equipment. As a result, mining became a big business in the West, dominated by corporations.

As companies dug bigger and deeper mines, the work became more dangerous. Miners had to use unsafe equipment such as wall-less elevator platforms. Many of the poorly lit tunnels had so little oxygen that candles would not burn. Dust from drilling also caused serious lung problems. Unexpected explosions killed or injured many miners. When there were cave-ins or floods from underground springs, miners were sometimes killed or trapped below ground. The threat of fire in the mines was also a great concern. In deeper tunnels, temperatures sometimes rose above 130° F. With all these hazards, mining was probably the most dangerous job in the country. In the West, worries about safety and pay led miners to form several labor unions in the 1860s.

Some miners came from the eastern United States. Others emigrated from Europe, Central and South America, Australia, and Asia. Some Mexican immigrants and Mexican Americans were skilled in assaying, or testing, the contents of valuable ore. Despite their skill, they were often denied the better-paying mining jobs. Chinese immigrants faced similar job discrimination.

✔ **Reading Check: Summarizing** How did mining affect the western economy, and what were its risks?

★ Mining Towns

Mining booms also produced **boomtowns**. These towns were communities that sprang up when a mine opened. They often disappeared just as quickly when the mine closed down. Most boomtowns had general stores, saloons, and boardinghouses. However, they were also dangerous places that lacked basic law and order. In his autobiographical work *Roughing It*, Mark Twain described Virginia City during its boom years.

Analyzing Primary Sources

Supporting a Point of View Judging from Twain's description, would you have chosen to live in a boomtown? Why or why not?

❝[It] had grown to be the 'livest' town . . . that America had ever produced. The sidewalks swarmed with people. . . . The streets themselves were just as crowded. . . . Money-getting schemes . . . were . . . in every brain.❞

—Mark Twain, *Roughing It*

There were few women or families in most boomtowns. In 1860, for example, there were more than 75 men to each woman in Virginia City. Most women who lived in mining towns faced lives of hard work and few friends. "I was never so lonely and homesick in all my life," wrote one young woman. Women contributed to the local economy by washing, cooking, making clothes, and chopping wood. They also raised families, taught in schools, and wrote for local newspapers. Their work helped turn some mining camps into successful permanent towns.

✔ **Reading Check: Finding the Main Idea** Why were boomtowns created, and what was life like there?

⭐ Linking East and West

As more Americans began moving west, the need to send goods and information between the East and West increased. In 1860 the **Pony Express** was formed to meet this need. This company used a system of messengers on horseback to carry mail between relay stations on a route about 2,000 miles long. Telegraph lines, which sent messages faster, soon put the Pony Express out of business, however.

Americans thought of other ways to improve communication and travel across the United States. Some Americans wanted to build a **transcontinental railroad** to connect the East to the West. As a result, the federal government passed the **Pacific Railway Acts** of 1862 and 1864. These acts gave railroad companies loans and large land grants, which could be sold to pay for construction costs. Congress had granted tens of millions of acres of public land to railroad companies. In exchange, the government asked the railroads to carry U.S. mail and troops at lower rates. The railway acts inspired many companies to begin laying tracks.

✔ **Reading Check: Analyzing Information** What innovations helped link the East and the West?

GLOBAL CONNECTIONS

The Railroads of India

As the United States was completing the world's first transcontinental railroad, Great Britain was building a huge railroad system in India to transport goods to and from remote regions. Between 1859 and 1869, Indian workers laid more than 5,000 miles of track. Workers had to build 81 bridges and 38 tunnels just to get through one mountain range. By 1900 the Indian rail network was the second largest in Asia after Russia's. The railroad carried mail, freight, and passengers. **What benefits did the railroad system in India have in common with the transcontinental railroad in the United States?**

Railroad building in the West involved overcoming many physical obstacles and dangers. Here Chinese workers celebrate the completion of a tunnel in the Sierra Nevada.

Interpreting the Visual Record

Celebration *The Central Pacific and Union Pacific connected their tracks at Promontory in Utah Territory.* **Why would the completion of the transcontinental railroad have been a cause for celebration?**

This advertisement for the Union Pacific Railroad praised the speed and comfort of railroad travel to the West.

⭐ The Great Race

Two companies, the Central Pacific and the Union Pacific, led the race to complete the transcontinental railroad. In February 1863 the Central Pacific began building east from Sacramento, California. At the end of the year, the Union Pacific started building west from Omaha, Nebraska.

The Union Pacific hired thousands of railroad workers, including Irish immigrants and Civil War veterans. The Central Pacific hired many Chinese immigrants. The railroad's part-owner **Leland Stanford** praised these Chinese workers, but he paid them less than white laborers. Chinese crews were also given the most dangerous tasks and longer hours. However, Chinese workers could earn much more money working for the Central Pacific than in China.

Railroad companies faced many geographic challenges. The Central Pacific workers struggled to cross the Sierra Nevada range in California. Large amounts of explosives were used to blast a way through the mountains. In the winter of 1866, snowdrifts more than 60 feet high trapped and killed many workers. Meanwhile, the Union Pacific's workers faced harsh weather on the Great Plains.

For both lines, providing food and supplies for their workers was vital. To feed their workers, the railroad companies often relied on local resources. Professional hunters such as William "Buffalo Bill" Cody shot thousands of buffalo to feed workers for the Union Pacific.

Congress required the two railroads to connect at Promontory, Utah. On May 10, 1869, workers and reporters watched the two lines finally meet. In a dramatic ceremony, a golden spike was used to connect the railroad tie joining the two tracks. The transcontinental railroad had united the East and the West.

✔ **Reading Check: Summarizing** What difficulties did the builders of the transcontinental railroad face?

The Effects of the Railroads

The transcontinental railroad increased both economic and population growth in the West. Railroad companies provided better transportation for people and goods. They also sold land to settlers, encouraging people to move west. In addition, railroads saved time. The Union Pacific advertised that a trip from Omaha, Nebraska, to San Francisco, California, would take four days. By wagon the trip took about a month.

In addition, the new railroads helped businesses. Western timber and mining companies shipped wood and metals east by railroad. In exchange, eastern factories shipped manufactured goods to the West.

Railroad companies encouraged investors to put their money into the railroad business, which they did—sometimes unwisely. Railroad speculation and the collapse of railroad owner Jay Cooke's banking firm helped start the Panic of 1873. A depression soon followed. By the 1880s many of the smaller western railroads were deep in debt. Despite such setbacks, Americans remained interested in railroad investments. In 1865 only about 35,000 miles of railroad track existed, but by 1890 about 199,000 miles were in operation. Railroads had become the biggest industry in the United States.

✔ **Reading Check: Finding the Main Idea** How did the railroad affect the settlement and development of the West?

Population of Omaha

102,555

1,833

1860   1900

Sources: Bureau of the Census; U.S. Department of Commerce

Interpreting Graphs In 1863 the Union Pacific Railroad laid its tracks through the city of Omaha, Nebraska, causing the population to soar.

Skills Assessment Analyzing Information How much did Omaha's population increase between 1860 and 1900?

Section 2 Review

go. hrw .com **Homework Practice Online** keyword: SF3 HP21

1 **Define** and explain:
• bonanza
• boomtowns
• transcontinental railroad

2 **Identify** and explain:
• Comstock Lode
• Pony Express
• Pacific Railway Acts
• Leland Stanford

3 **Comparing** Copy the graphic organizer below. Use it to compare how mining and railroads led to the settlement and development of the West.

4 **Finding the Main Idea**
a. Where did miners come from, and why was their job one of the most dangerous in the West?

b. What were some of the difficulties faced in building a transcontinental railroad?

5 **Writing and Critical Thinking**
Summarizing Imagine that you are a railroad worker. Write a short song that might have been sung in your community after the connection of the Union Pacific and the Central Pacific Railroads.

Consider the following:
• the challenges of building the railroad
• how the railroad will change life in the West
• improved communication between family members

The West **659**

The Cattle Kingdom

Read to Discover

1. What led to the cattle boom?
2. What was life like for cowboys?
3. What caused the decline of the Cattle Kingdom?

WHY IT MATTERS TODAY

Cattle ranching continues to be important to the economy of many western states. Use **CNNfyi**.com or other **current events** sources to learn about cattle ranching today. Record your findings in your journal.

Define

- Texas longhorn
- open range
- range rights
- vaqueros
- roundup
- cattle drive
- range wars

Identify

- Joseph McCoy
- Cattle Kingdom
- Elizabeth Collins
- Nat Love
- Chisholm Trail

The Story Continues

The Texas longhorn was well suited to living on the Plains.

In the mid-1800s Texas ranchers began gathering huge herds of wild cattle. One rancher described how ranchers let their herds roam. "Cattle are permitted to range . . . over a large surface of country, thirty, forty, and even fifty miles in extent [size]." Keeping track of these roaming cattle required great skill. The ranch hands who did this work faced many hardships. However, one rancher believed that ranch hands liked their work. "The young men that follow this 'Cow-Boy' life . . . generally become attached to it," he wrote. These cowboys and ranchers helped start the cattle-ranching industry in the West.

⭐ The Cattle Boom

Spanish settlers brought their cattle to California and Texas in the 1700s. These cattle later mixed with English breeds to create the **Texas longhorn.** This breed spread quickly throughout western Texas. Longhorn cattle were lean and tough, with horns up to five feet across. Many butchers said the longhorn had too little meat. They called it "8 pounds of hamburger on 800 pounds of bone and horn." Nonetheless, settlers preferred to raise longhorns. Because the animals needed very little water and could survive harsh weather, they were more suitable for the environment.

Following the Civil War, the demand for beef increased in the East. The expanding economy and growing population created the higher demand. A steer worth $3 to $6 in Texas could be sold for $38 in Kansas. In New York it could be sold for $80. Nobody drove the longhorns to eastern markets, however. In addition to the problem of distance, people feared the western cattle would infect eastern farm animals with a disease called Texas fever.

In 1867 businessman **Joseph McCoy** had an idea. He decided "to establish a market whereat the southern . . . [rancher] and the northern buyer would meet." McCoy built pens for cattle in the small town of Abilene, Kansas. The Kansas Pacific Railroad line went through Abilene. As a result, cattle could be shipped by rail from there. Soon many Texas ranchers were making the trip north to sell their herds of cattle.

Around the same time, cattle ranching began to expand onto the Great Plains. The tough longhorns did well on the Plains. Ranchers began taking their cattle north to Colorado, Wyoming, Nebraska, and Montana. They built many ranches in the region stretching from Texas north to Canada. Eventually, this area became known as the **Cattle Kingdom**. Throughout the area, ranchers grazed their huge herds on public land called the **open range**. This land had once been occupied by Plains Indians and buffalo herds.

✔ **Reading Check: Finding the Main Idea** What factors led to the cattle boom?

Daily Life

Cattle Towns Long cattle drives ended at a town located along a railroad. In these towns, brokers bought cattle to ship east on railroad cars. Early cattle towns consisted of little more than a general store, a hotel or boardinghouse, a railroad depot, and a stockyard. Towns that drew enough business grew larger. They bustled with activity from spring to fall when the long drives took place. Prosperous cattle towns attracted businesspeople, doctors, lawyers, and their families. Once families arrived, the cattle towns built schools, hired teachers, and established police forces to maintain order. **How did the railroad contribute to the growth of western towns and businesses?**

⭐ The Ranches

One person who saw the profits to be made in ranching was **Elizabeth Collins**. She and her husband had had trouble mining gold, so they decided "to discontinue the business of mining and engage in that of cattle raising." She moved to the Teton Valley in Montana and started ranching. She was so successful that she earned the name Cattle Queen of Montana.

Collins was just one of many ranchers who became wealthy during the cattle boom. Charles Goodnight started the first ranch in the Texas Panhandle. It was more than 250 miles from any town or railroad.

Elizabeth Collins became a successful cattle rancher in Montana.

The West **661**

Speculators in the East and in Europe invested money in ranches the same way that they did in railroads. Some of the resulting ranches were huge. For example, the XIT Ranch covered more than 3 million acres. Few ranchers owned this much land, however. Instead, they concentrated on buying the **range rights**, or water rights, to ponds and rivers. Buying the range rights let them use the scarce water as well as the land around it. In this way, ranchers could cut out their competition by stopping farmers and other ranchers from using the water.

Because of the remote locations of many ranches, some ranchers served as the local authorities. Joseph McCoy described the view of a cattle rancher. He saw himself as "an independent sovereign [ruler] . . . capable of conducting his affairs in his own way." Mary Jaques, who lived on a Texas ranch for two years, noted ranchers' many different skills.

Analyzing Primary Sources
Drawing Inferences and Conclusions Why do you think it was necessary for ranchers to have so many skills?

History Makers Speak 66The ideal ranchman must be butcher, baker, carpenter, . . . blacksmith, plain cook, milker. . . . It is a fact that each of these trades will have to be practiced to some extent sooner or later.99

—Mary Jaques, *Texan Ranch Life: With Three Months through Mexico in a "Prairie Schooner"*

✔ **Reading Check: Analyzing Information** How did ranchers influence western life?

⭐ The Cowboys

The workers who took care of ranchers' cattle were known as cowhands or cowboys. Cowboys borrowed many of their techniques from Mexican **vaqueros** (vah-KER-ohs), ranch hands who cared for cattle and horses. From the vaqueros came the western saddle, the lariat—a rope used for lassoing cattle—and the leather chaps cowboys wore over their pants for protection against the thorny brush. The cowboys borrowed the vaqueros' broad felt hat. However, they changed it into the familiar high-peaked cowboy hat. Cowboys also adopted the bandanna, a cloth that covered the face to protect it from dust. Sometimes it served as a handkerchief or bandage as well. Many cowboys were Mexican Americans or African Americans, like **Nat Love**, who wrote an autobiography about his life as a cowboy. Although most cowhands were men, some women worked alongside cowboys.

Gathering the cattle together was known as a **roundup**. During spring roundups, cowboys branded young calves and horses with a ranch's unique mark to prevent thieves from selling stolen horses and cattle.

Cowboys faced the danger of cattle thieves, bad weather, and unpredictable livestock. Although they worked hard, wages were low, and few were able to make enough money to start their own ranches. Despite these factors, many cowboys like Nat Love enjoyed their days on the range.

Nat Love

Cowboys borrowed many types of clothes, equipment, and cattle-driving methods from the vaqueros.

Cattle drives *Towns like Dodge City could be suddenly filled with cowboys driving the longhorns to market.* **What does the image suggest about how cattle drives affected a town?**

⭐ Cattle Drives and Cattle Towns

One of the cowboy's most important and dangerous duties was the **cattle drive**. On these long journeys, cowboys herded cattle to the market or to the northern Plains for grazing. These trips usually lasted several months and covered hundreds of miles. The **Chisholm Trail** was one of the earliest and most popular routes for cattle drives. It was blazed, or marked, by Texas cowboy Jesse Chisholm in the late 1860s. This trail ran from San Antonio, Texas, to the cattle town of Abilene, Kansas. Charles Goodnight blazed a trail leading from Texas to New Mexico Territory, which became known as the Goodnight-Loving Trail. One of the most heavily used routes, the Western Trail, headed north from San Antonio to Dodge City, Kansas.

Cowboys herded their cattle through harsh country. They lived for months with "no tents or shelter of any sort other than [their] blankets," as cowboy James H. Cook recalled. The cattle could be difficult to handle, and they might stampede during storms. Then cowboys would have to track down the strays and round them up again. At night, cowboys had to stand watch over the cattle herds. Most cowboys were happy to reach the end of a cattle drive.

A large cattle town such as Dodge City or Abilene usually lay at the end of the trail. Small businesses sprang up as more cowboys passed through these towns. Some of these businesses were owned or operated by women. For example, Malinda Jenkins became a successful businesswoman who ran several boardinghouses.

Boardinghouses, hotels, saloons, and restaurants depended on tired cowboys spending money when they were in town. Cowboys spent their pay on food, hot baths, and comfortable beds after weeks on the trail. At times, rowdy cowboys could make life in cattle towns rough and violent. There were rarely shoot-outs in the streets, but disorderly behavior was common. Law officials such as Wyatt Earp became famous for keeping the peace in cattle towns.

✔ **Reading Check: Analyzing Information** How did the railroad affect the location and development of cattle trails and cattle towns?

Cattle Trails and Western Railroads to 1890

Interpreting Maps The development of railroads and cattle trails allowed for the transportation of livestock and other goods between eastern and western states.

Skills Assessment Physical Systems What mountain range did every railroad that reached the Pacific coast have to cross?

★ The End of the Open Range

In the early 1880s the introduction of the refrigerator railroad car made it possible to carry meat from packing plants to eastern cities. As the national demand for beef grew, cities such as Chicago, Illinois, became famous for their meatpacking plants.

While the cattle business boomed, ranchers faced more competition for use of the open range. Farmers began to buy range land on the Great Plains where cattle had once grazed. Smaller ranchers also began competing with the large ranchers for land. Then in 1874 Joseph Glidden patented barbed wire, which allowed westerners to fence off large areas of land at a low cost.

As barbed wire came into wider use, large ranchers moved quickly to fence in the open range and valuable water sources, keeping out farmers and smaller ranchers. Some farmers and small ranchers cut the fences and moved onto the land or stole cattle in response. This competition led to **range wars** between large ranchers, small ranchers, and farmers. Large ranchers often won these battles, but few could let their cattle roam free on public land.

Cattle ranchers also fought with sheep owners. As the number of sheep grew even greater in the 1880s, so did the competition for grasslands. Sheep chewed the grass down so far that there was nothing left for the cattle. Despite threats and violence against them, sheep ranchers still usually did well in the West.

By the 1880s some 7.5 million cattle roamed the Great Plains. With the U.S. economy in a depression, cattle prices dropped in 1885. To improve prices, ranchers began to bring eastern cattle to the western range. These cattle produced more beef than the Texas longhorns but were not well adapted to the conditions on the Plains.

In 1885 and 1886 disaster struck the Cattle Kingdom. The huge cattle herds on the Plains had eaten much of the prairie grass that ranchers depended on for feed. Unusually severe winters in both years made the ranching situation even worse. Thousands of cattle died, and most ranchers lost at least 30 percent of their herds. Many ranchers were ruined financially. Cattle towns were also hit hard. While cattle ranching continued, it became more costly. Ranchers were forced to buy winter feed for their cattle and to reduce the size of their herds. Low prices, harsh weather, and greater competition for grazing land brought an end to the reign of the Cattle Kingdom.

Before Joseph Glidden invented barbed wire, westerners had not built fences because traditional fencing materials, such as stone and lumber, were scarce in the Great Plains.

✔ **Reading Check: Finding the Main Idea** Why did the Cattle Kingdom come to an end?

Section 3 Review

go.hrw.com **Homework Practice Online**
keyword: SF3 HP21

1 **Define** and explain:
• Texas longhorn
• open range
• range rights
• vaqueros
• roundup
• cattle drive
• range wars

2 **Identify** and explain:
• Joseph McCoy
• Cattle Kingdom
• Elizabeth Collins
• Nat Love
• Chisholm Trail

3 **Analyzing Information** Copy the graphic organizer below. Use it to describe the factors that caused the boom and then the bust of the Cattle Kingdom.

Boom	Bust
1.	1.
2.	2.
3.	3.

4 **Finding the Main Idea**
a. What was cowboy life like?

b. In what ways did the cattle boom show the benefits of free enterprise in the West?

5 **Writing and Critical Thinking**
Summarizing Imagine that you are a cowboy during the late 1800s. Write a diary entry explaining what your daily life is like.

Consider the following:
• salary
• work on ranches and cattle drives
• freedom on the open range

Farming the Great Plains

Read to Discover

1. What groups settled the Great Plains, and what were their reasons for moving there?
2. How did the environment of the Great Plains affect settlers' farming methods?
3. What was life on the Great Plains like for settlers, and how did they adapt to the conditions?

WHY IT MATTERS TODAY

Farming is still central to the economy of the Great Plains states, as well as much of the world. Use **CNNfyi**.com or other **current events** sources to learn about new farming methods being developed today. Record your findings in your journal.

Define

• sodbusters
• dry farming

Identify

• Homestead Act
• Morrill Act
• Exodusters
• Cyrus McCormick

A pioneer's rail ticket

The Story Continues

In 1879 Scottish writer Robert Louis Stevenson took the transcontinental railroad across the United States. Most of the other passengers were settlers moving to the West. When a passenger began to play the song "Home Sweet Home," all conversation stopped. "The faces began to lengthen," noted Stevenson. Then "an elderly, hard-looking man . . . [asked] the performer [to] stop. 'I've heard about enough of that,' he [said]. 'Give us something about the good country we're going to.'" The passengers agreed, and the performer began to play music for dancing. Despite being homesick, most settlers hoped to build a better life in the West.

⭐ New Lands for Settlement

In 1862 Congress passed two important land-grant acts that helped open the West to settlers. The **Homestead Act** gave government-owned land to small farmers. Any adult who was a U.S. citizen or planned to become one could receive 160 acres of land. In exchange, homesteaders paid a small registration fee. They also promised to live on the land for five years. The **Morrill Act** granted more than 17 million acres of federal land to the states. The act required each state to sell this land and use the money to build colleges, such as Texas A&M, to teach agriculture and engineering.

The federal government also offered land in what is now Oklahoma. Some of this land had belonged to Creek and Seminole Indians. In April 1889, officials opened these lands to homesteaders. Within a month of the government's announcement, more than 50,000 people rushed to Oklahoma to stake their claims. In all, the settlers claimed more than 11 million acres of former Indian land in the Oklahoma land rush.

✔ **Reading Check: Contrasting** List the different land acts that the federal government passed, and explain how they were different.

Interpreting the Visual Record

Westward expansion *The thousands of settlers who moved west formed many new communities. **How does this picture show settlers modifying their physical environment?***

⭐ Settling the Plains

People from all over the country chose to move west. Settlers who had already moved to the Great Plains often chose to move again after a few years. All of these settlers hoped to find success on the Plains, often by starting their own farms. Many farming families moved from areas where farmland was becoming too scarce or expensive, such as New England. Others were the descendants of earlier pioneers to the Midwest. To encourage the presence of families and settlements in the West, the Homestead Act granted land to unmarried women.

The promise of land also drew a large group of Southern African Americans west. These settlers became known as **Exodusters** because of their exodus, or mass departure, from the South. Many Exodusters were sharecroppers such as John Solomon Lewis. He explained his reasons for moving his family.

History Makers Speak

"I one day said to the man I rented [land] from: 'It's no use, I works hard and raises big crops and you sells it and keeps the money, and brings me more and more in debt, so I will go somewhere else.'"

—John Solomon Lewis, quoted in *Exodusters: Black Migration to Kansas after Reconstruction,* by Nell Irvin Painter

Soon black communities such as Nicodemus, Kansas, developed. They drew many African Americans west by land advertisements. Exodusters wanted more economic opportunity as well as equal rights that they were being denied in the South after Reconstruction.

Research on the R◉M

Free Find:
Homestead Act
After reading about the Homestead Act on the **Holt Researcher CD–ROM**, create a newspaper ad that advertises the land available through this act.

Many African American families, such as the Shores family shown here, moved to the Great Plains.

Western homesteads also were attractive to immigrants. Like Americans, they could get land grants under the Homestead Act if they planned to become citizens and promised to stay on the land for five years. Norwegian, Swedish, Danish, German, and Czech immigrants looking for economic opportunity formed many small communities on the Great Plains. Usually, a relative made the journey to America first. Then this person wrote letters home telling other family members to come. In addition, a number of Mennonites, members of a Protestant religious group, moved to the Great Plains from Russia. They were among the first to begin large-scale farming in the region.

✔ **Reading Check: Summarizing** Who moved to the Great Plains, and why did they choose to move there?

⭐ Farming on the Plains

The inexpensive land of the Great Plains drew settlers. Yet the Plains had many unique challenges. Plains settlers found a mostly flat landscape covered with grass. Settlers also encountered extreme seasons. In the winter, temperatures on the northern Plains could fall to −40° F. Hot summer temperatures in the southern Plains could reach 110° F. The climate of the Plains was much drier than in the East. Settlers also faced the threat of blizzards and tornadoes. All of these factors meant that farmers could not raise the same crops that they had grown in the East.

Farmers survived the challenges of the Great Plains by developing new farming equipment and methods. The root-filled sod, or dirt, of the Plains was so tough that it actually broke the plows of many farmers. Manufacturer John Deere's deep steel plow broke through the tough sod and enabled farmers to plant crops. This hard work of breaking up the sod earned farmers on the Plains the nickname **sodbusters**.

In the 1890s farmers on the western Plains began to learn a new method called **dry farming**. This method shifted the focus from water-dependent crops such as corn to hardier crops like a type of red wheat introduced by Mennonite farmers to the Plains. In addition, farmers left part of their fields unplanted each year to preserve water in the soil. Even on the eastern Plains, which got more rain, farmers found that the soil needed special care. These dry-farming methods helped farmers make it through drought years.

By the 1880s mechanical farming was becoming increasingly common. **Cyrus McCormick** made his fortune designing, building, and

★★★★★★★★★★★★
That's Interesting!
★★★★★★★★★★★★

Attack of the Grasshoppers
Can you imagine the fields of the Great Plains covered in grasshoppers four inches deep? Well, that's exactly what happened in the summer of 1874. The grasshoppers appeared without warning. Within a few minutes, swarms had blocked out the Sun. These bugs liked to eat plants the best, but they didn't stop there. They ate curtains, old boots, and even straw hats. One settler said that he saw grasshoppers eating the wool off of a live sheep! One couple managed to save enough wheat for seed by swinging a clothesline in the air when the grasshoppers attacked. Other people were not so lucky.

Populating the West

Interpreting Maps By 1890, settlements stretched across the western United States, which was experiencing rapid population growth.

Skills Assessment Human Systems What man-made features typically correspond with the populated areas on the map?

selling farm equipment. Horse-drawn machines such as McCormick reapers collected wheat stalks. Threshing machines separated the grain from the husk. By using machinery, farmers could harvest large fields more quickly and with fewer workers. Wealthy farmers could afford the land and machinery needed to create huge farms that employed hundreds of workers. Once they harvested their crops, farmers shipped the grain east by train. Some of it was then shipped to customers overseas. As farming technology improved, the Great Plains became known as the breadbasket of the world because of the grain that the region's farms produced.

A poster intending to persuade people to move west

✔ **Reading Check: Identifying Cause and Effect** What was the environment of the Great Plains like, and how did farmers change the region into a breadbasket?

Causes and Effects of Increased Western Settlement

Long-Term Causes
Desire for new farm and ranch land
Search for natural resources
Growth of national and foreign markets

Immediate Causes
Homestead Act, 1862
Completion of the transcontinental railroad in 1869 and the building of other western railroads

Increased Western Settlement Mid-1800s to 1900

Effects
Increased conflict with American Indian cultures in the West
Immigrants and migrants come to the West in search of a new life
Great expansion of the western economy
Creation of new states

⭐ Daily Life on the Plains

Settler Gro Svendsen described the challenges of Plains life. "When one begins to farm, it takes a great deal to get started—especially when one must begin with nothing." Building a house was one of the first challenges that settlers faced. With very little wood available, many families built houses from bricks of sod cut out of the ground. Although cheap to build, these sod homes were often very small and uncomfortable. Pioneer May Avery explained a few of the common problems. "The roof leaked something awful [and inside] we killed a snake or two . . . and several centipedes." For all their faults, however, the small homes did provide necessary shelter.

Once a home was built, daily chores kept pioneer families busy. For example, settlers had to make and mend their own clothes. They had no washing machines, so washing clothes was a big chore that filled the entire day. Pioneers usually made their wash soap from lye, a liquid made from wood ashes and animal fat. One pioneer woman listed 11 washday chores. She started with "build fire in back yard to heat kettle of rain water." The list ended with "brew cup of tea, set and rest and rock a spell and count blessings." Women prepared meals and often grew vegetables. They also raised chickens or made butter to earn money for the family.

Farming families raised livestock and worked hard in the fields, plowing and planting. Pioneers often had to build most of their farm buildings and repair their machinery. Children helped with many tasks around the farms. Farm families were often large, and everyone had chores.

✔ **Reading Check: Categorizing** What different types of work did Great Plains farmers do?

Windmills were used to pump water in the West.

☆ Communities on the Great Plains

This group of pioneer students posed with their teacher in October 1893.

Communities were an important part of life on the Plains. Many early settlers found life on their remote farms to be extremely difficult. Esther Clark explained her mother's life as a pioneer. "It took [courage] to live twenty-four hours at a time, month in and out, on the lonely and lovely prairie." Farmers formed communities so that they could assist one another in times of need.

One of the first things that many pioneer communities did was establish a local church and a school. Churches offered a place for pioneer families to meet. Even small communities made efforts to get schools started. Many towns raised money by putting on plays or dinners. In many cases, townspeople even helped build the schools and ran them themselves. One woman recalled proudly, "They [the school board] and the pupils and I built that school house with our own hands."

Pioneer schools were usually small one-room buildings. A stove in the middle of the room provided heat, while the sunlight gave reading light. In these schools, children of all ages learned together in one class. Few children had schoolbooks. Many children went to school only part of the year because they had to help with farm work. Most teachers in these pioneer schools were young women who made little money. Frontier families worked very hard to provide communities for themselves and for their children. Through these efforts, more people found the West an appealing place to live and raise a family.

✔ **Reading Check: Summarizing** What roles did communities play in life on the Great Plains?

Section 4 Review

go.hrw.com **Homework Practice Online**
keyword: SF3 HP21

1 **Define** and explain:
- sodbusters
- dry farming

2 **Identify** and explain:
- Homestead Act
- Morrill Act
- Exodusters
- Cyrus McCormick

3 **Categorizing** Copy the graphic organizer below. Use it to identify the groups that settled on the Great Plains and what made them choose to move there.

Groups

Motivation → Plains Settlement

4 **Finding the Main Idea**
a. How did the environment of the Plains affect farming methods, and how did settlers cope with these conditions?

b. What was life on the Great Plains like, and how did pioneers adapt to this life?

5 **Writing and Critical Thinking**
Supporting a Point of View Imagine that you are a pioneer on the Plains in the late 1800s. Write a newspaper advertisement encouraging other people to settle the region.
Consider the following:
- availability of land and economic opportunity
- technological and scientific advances that have made Plains farming easier
- growth of churches and schools

The West **671**

Chapter **21** Review

The Chapter at a Glance

Examine the visual summary of the chapter below. Use it to create a chart listing five major events discussed in this chapter. Then give your list to a classmate and ask him or her to write the results or descriptions of these events.

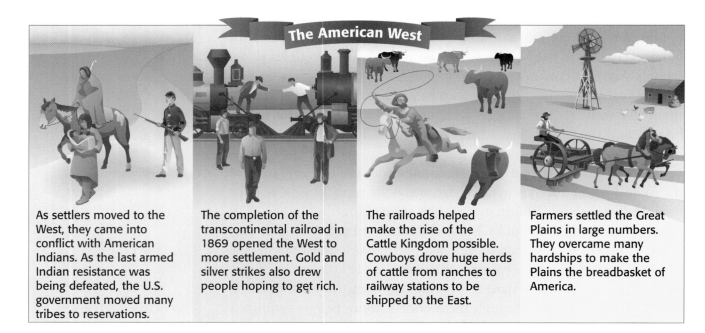

The American West

As settlers moved to the West, they came into conflict with American Indians. As the last armed Indian resistance was being defeated, the U.S. government moved many tribes to reservations.

The completion of the transcontinental railroad in 1869 opened the West to more settlement. Gold and silver strikes also drew people hoping to get rich.

The railroads helped make the rise of the Cattle Kingdom possible. Cowboys drove huge herds of cattle from ranches to railway stations to be shipped to the East.

Farmers settled the Great Plains in large numbers. They overcame many hardships to make the Plains the breadbasket of America.

Identifying People and Ideas

Use the following terms or people in historically significant sentences.

1. reservations
2. George Armstrong Custer
3. Sitting Bull
4. Comstock Lode
5. Pacific Railway Acts
6. Joseph McCoy
7. Elizabeth Collins
8. Chisholm Trail
9. Homestead Act
10. Exodusters

Understanding Main Ideas

Section 1 *(Pages 648–654)*

1. What caused some of the conflicts between the United States and American Indians, and what were the results of these conflicts?
2. How did reformers change the U.S. government's Indian policy in the late 1800s?

Section 2 *(Pages 655–659)*

3. What factors made mining in the West such a dangerous job?
4. What effect did the transcontinental railroad have on western settlement?

Section 3 *(Pages 660–665)*

5. Why was there a cattle boom in the 1870s?

Section 4 *(Pages 666–671)*

6. Why did many immigrants move to the West?
7. How did settlers use new scientific methods and technology to farm on the Great Plains?

You Be the Historian— Reviewing Themes

1. **Economics** What factors led to the expansion of the economy in the West in the late 1800s?
2. **Culture** How did U.S. settlement of the West affect American Indians?
3. **Geography** In what ways did the environment of the Great Plains affect the crops that farmers planted and the farming methods they used?

Thinking Critically

1. **Summarizing** What types of economic and social contributions did women make in the West?
2. **Evaluating** List two positive and two negative results of economic development in the West.
3. **Analyzing Information** What were some of the different ways in which immigrant groups interacted with and changed the environment of the West?

Interpreting Graphs

Study the graph below. Then use the information on the graph to help you answer the questions that follow.

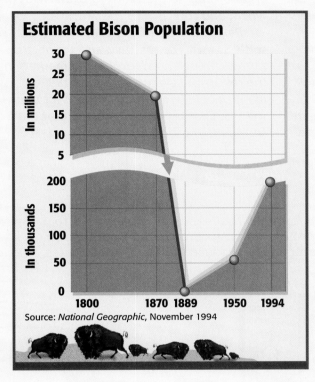

Estimated Bison Population

In millions
30
25
20
15
10
5

In thousands
200
150
100
50
0

1800   1870   1889   1950   1994

Source: *National Geographic*, November 1994

1. How many buffalo (bison) were there in the United States in 1800?
   a. 30
   b. 50 million
   c. 75 million
   d. 30 million

2. How many buffalo were there in the United States in 1889?

3. Based on your knowledge of the period and of current events, what factors do you think might have accounted for the increase in the buffalo population since 1889?

Analyzing Primary Sources

Read the following quotation about cattle drives from an American cowboy song, then answer the questions.

“It's whooping and yelling and driving the dogies;
   Oh how I wish you would go on;
It's whooping and punching and go on little dogies,
   For you know Wyoming will be your new home.

Some boys go up the trail for pleasure
   But that's where you get it most awfully wrong;
For you haven't any idea of the trouble they give us
   While we go driving them along.”

4. Which of the following statements best describes the author's point of view?
   a. A cowboy's life is easy.
   b. Some people mistakenly believe that a cowboy's life is easy.
   c. More people should become cowboys.
   d. Cowboys do not get enough respect.

5. Based on the material that you have read about cattle drives, what problems on the trail might have led to the creation of this song? Give specific examples.

6. What do you think the lines, "It's whooping and yelling and driving the dogies" tells about cattle drives?

Alternative Assessment

Building Your Portfolio

American History

Linking to Community
Mining, ranching, and farming continue to be important to the U.S. economy. Identify a person from your community who works in one of these fields. Then make a list of questions to use while interviewing this person. Conduct an interview to find out what his or her job is like today. When you finish the interview, share your results with the class.

internet connect

Internet Activity: go.hrw.com
keyword: SF3 CF21

Choose a topic on the West to:

● Learn the facts and mythology surrounding the Pony Express.

● Research Geronimo and other American Indian leaders and write biographies of their lives.

● Analyze the myths and realities of the West and the ways in which it shaped the United States.

The Economy of the West

In the last half of the 1800s, great numbers of settlers followed the trails of earlier pioneers to the West. People moved west for new economic opportunities in farming, mining, and ranching.

Prospectors and miners came to California during the gold rush of 1849. Many of these settlers continued pursuing the dream of striking it rich. Cattle drives brought the ranching industry from Texas to the northern Great Plains. Growing numbers of farmers also came to the Plains to plant fields of wheat and corn.

Railroads helped bring many of these settlers west. The railroads also connected farmers, miners, and ranchers to markets in the rest of the United States. By 1890 so many people had settled in the West that the U.S. Census Bureau reported that the frontier had officially closed.

Western Mining

A mining boom in the late 1800s brought thousands of prospectors to the West. Successful strikes in western mining contributed to a huge increase in the amount of gold and silver produced in the United States.

The Mining Boom

Gold mining region

Silver mining region

▲ Major lode

Geography Skills
Interpreting Thematic Maps

1. What types of mines surrounded Deadwood and Carson City?
2. **Environment and Society** What U.S. cities developed near gold-mining regions in the West?
3. **Comparing** In what type of terrain did most of the gold and silver strikes take place?

Mining tools

Connecting to Geography

U.S. Gold Production, 1840–1910

Amount Produced (in thousands of fine troy ounces)

Year	Amount
1840	24
1850	2,419
1860	2,225
1870	2,419
1880	1,742
1890	1,589
1900	3,830
1910	4,585

Source: *Historical Statistics of the United States*

History Note 1

Individual prospectors found many of the richest gold and silver deposits in the West. Some prospectors became wealthy from their discoveries. However, the majority of the gold and silver produced was mined by corporations. Most of the profits from western mining were made by investors. They provided the money for heavy steam-powered machinery and equipment used in the mines.

U.S. Silver Production, 1860–1910

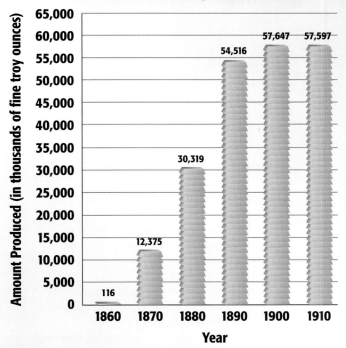

Amount Produced (in thousands of fine troy ounces)

Year	Amount
1860	116
1870	12,375
1880	30,319
1890	54,516
1900	57,647
1910	57,597

Source: *Historical Statistics of the United States*

Geography **Skills**
Interpreting Bar Graphs

1. In what year shown on the graph was gold production the highest in the United States? Silver production?

2. Combine the information on these two bar graphs for the year 1860 into a pie graph comparing the amount of gold and silver produced that year.

3. **Drawing Inferences and Conclusions** What discovery would account for the dramatic increase in U.S. gold production between 1840 and 1850?

History Note 2

Gold and silver have been made into coins since around 700 B.C. These precious metals continue to be used as currency and to create jewelry and art. In addition, gold and silver are used in electronics and manufacturing. Most gold and silver mined in the United States today still comes from western states.

The Changing West

In the 1860s the U.S. government passed laws to encourage western settlement. The Homestead Act sold government-owned western lands at very low cost. The Pacific Railway Acts encouraged railroad construction. The acts gave railroad companies land for every mile of track they laid. By 1900 a network of railroad lines crossed the mountains and farmlands of the West.

The West around 1870

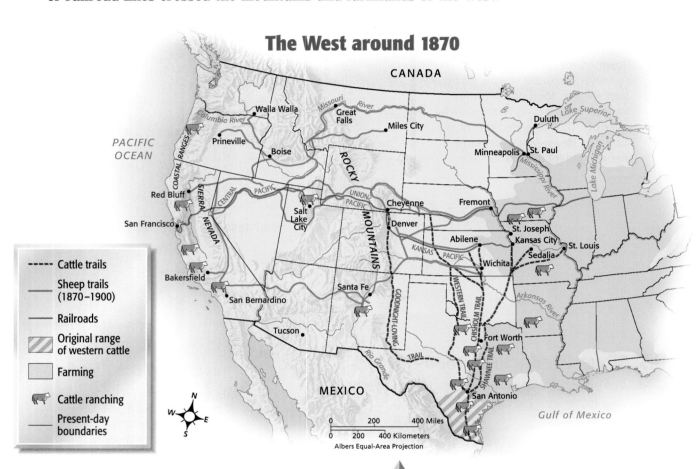

Legend:
- Cattle trails (dashed line)
- Sheep trails (1870–1900)
- Railroads
- Original range of western cattle
- Farming
- Cattle ranching
- Present-day boundaries

Albers Equal-Area Projection

History Note 3

Many of our images of the West are of cowboys and cattle drives. However, sheepherders also moved millions of sheep along a network of western trails. These experienced sheepherders were often immigrants from places like France, Mexico, and Spain. They helped move large western herds that sometimes numbered more than 10,000 sheep. One of the first great sheep drives in the West provided food for miners during the California Gold Rush.

Geography Skills
Interpreting Thematic Maps

1. What directions did cattle trails run? What about sheep trails?
2. **Human Systems** What areas of the West were focused on farming by around 1870? What regions were focused on ranching?
3. **Drawing Inferences and Conclusions** Why do you think cattle trails ended at towns along railroad lines?

The West around 1900

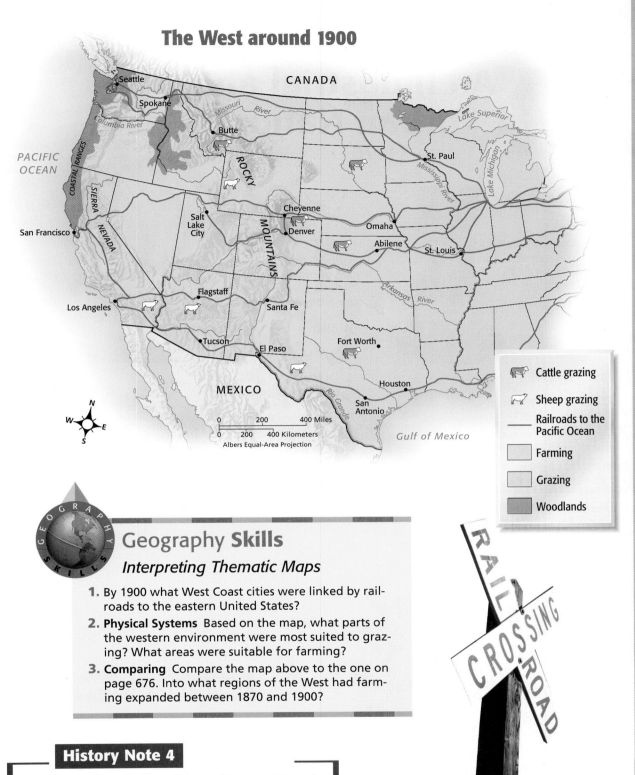

**Map labels:**

CANADA

Seattle
Spokane
Missouri River
Columbia River
Butte
Lake Superior

PACIFIC OCEAN

ROCKY

St. Paul
Mississippi River
Lake Michigan

SIERRA NEVADA
COASTAL RANGES

Salt Lake City
Cheyenne
Denver
MOUNTAINS
Omaha
Abilene
St. Louis

San Francisco

Los Angeles
Flagstaff
Santa Fe
Arkansas River

Tucson
El Paso
Fort Worth

MEXICO
Rio Grande
San Antonio
Houston

Gulf of Mexico

0 200 400 Miles
0 200 400 Kilometers
Albers Equal-Area Projection

N W E S

Legend:
- Cattle grazing
- Sheep grazing
- Railroads to the Pacific Ocean
- Farming
- Grazing
- Woodlands

Geography Skills

Interpreting Thematic Maps

1. By 1900 what West Coast cities were linked by railroads to the eastern United States?

2. **Physical Systems** Based on the map, what parts of the western environment were most suited to grazing? What areas were suitable for farming?

3. **Comparing** Compare the map above to the one on page 676. Into what regions of the West had farming expanded between 1870 and 1900?

History Note 4

The construction of railroads in the West contributed much to the settlement of the region. It also helped the industrialization of the U.S. economy. In 1880 there were more than 93,000 miles of steel track in the United States. By 1900 there were almost 259,000 more miles. Much of the new mileage was located in the rapidly growing West.

RAILROAD CROSSING

NEW YO[RK]

CHAPTER

22 An Industrial and Urban Nation
(1876–1900)

An early version of Alexander Graham Bell's telephone

Thomas Edison's team of inventors at Menlo Park, New Jersey, works on creating a lightbulb.

UNITED STATES

1876 Alexander Graham Bell patents the telephone.

1879 Thomas Alva Edison invents the first lightbulb.

1880 Philanthropist Andrew Carnegie begins creating the Carnegie libraries.

1882 Congress passes the Chinese Exclusion Act, banning Chinese immigrants from entering the United States for 10 years.

1884 Telephone wires are strung between New York and Boston.

1886 More than 70 police officers are injured or killed during the Haymarket Riot.

| **1876** | **1878** | **1880** | **1882** | **1884** | **1886** |

1876 British inventors introduce the high-wheel bicycle to the United States at the Centennial Exhibition.

1878 Electric streetlights are introduced in London.

1880 The public is granted full admission to the British Museum.

1884 The first subway opens in London.

1885 The Canadian Pacific Railway is finished.

WORLD

High-wheel bicycles were difficult and often dangerous to ride.

Build on What You Know

Even as many settlers were heading west to start new lives, the Second Industrial Revolution was bringing great changes to the nation. New industries boomed, and immigrants seeking a better life came to the United States in record numbers. Workers and farmers also sought to improve their lives using political influence.

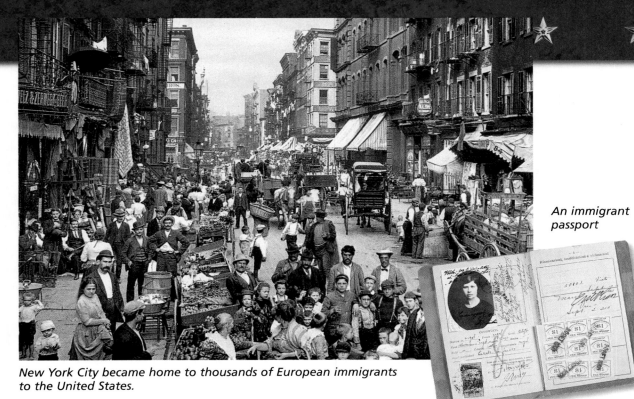

An immigrant passport

New York City became home to thousands of European immigrants to the United States.

1888 Benjamin Harrison is elected president.

1890 Congress passes the Sherman Antitrust Act, which makes monopolies illegal.

1892 The federal government opens the Ellis Island station in New York Harbor to receive immigrants to the United States.

1896 William McKinley is elected president.

1897 Eugene V. Debs helps form the Social Democratic Party.

1888   1890   1892   1894   1896   1898

1889 The Eiffel Tower is built in Paris.

1890 Japan holds its first general election.

1894 Rudolph Diesel invents the diesel engine.

1896 The first modern Olympics are held in Athens, Greece.

1898 French scientists Pierre and Marie Curie discover radium.

Marie Curie won a Nobel Prize for her research.

If you were there . . .
Would you seek your fortune in the country or in the city?

You Be the Historian

Themes Journal

What's Your Opinion? Do you **agree** or **disagree** with the following statements? Support your point of view in your journal.

- **Science, Technology & Society** New forms of technology always boost a country's economy.

- **Government** The government should keep careful control over economic and industrial growth.

- **Citizenship** Private citizens cannot shape the way the national economy develops and changes.

The Second Industrial Revolution

Read to Discover

1. What developments occurred in the steel, oil, and electric-power industries during the Second Industrial Revolution?
2. What changes occurred in the way that businesses were organized?
3. Why did some Americans oppose monopolies, and what actions did they take against them?

WHY IT MATTERS TODAY

Entrepreneurs continue to start new businesses today. Many of these companies ask for funding from outside sources. Use **CNNfyi.com** or other **current events** sources to learn about organizations that offer financial backing and other opportunities for entrepreneurs. Record your findings in your journal.

Define

- patents
- free enterprise
- entrepreneurs
- corporations
- vertical integration
- horizontal integration
- trust

Identify

- Second Industrial Revolution
- Bessemer process
- Orville and Wilbur Wright
- Thomas Alva Edison
- Andrew Carnegie
- John D. Rockefeller
- Sherman Antitrust Act

The Corliss steam engine weighed some 700 tons and stood about 40 feet high. Many people were awed by its size and power.

The Story Continues

The most popular exhibit at the 1876 Centennial Exhibition in Philadelphia was the huge Corliss steam engine, which helped power the equipment in Machinery Hall. Millions of people came to see what author William Dean Howells called "an athlete of steel and iron." For many, the Corliss engine symbolized the ever-improving future that modern machines seemed to promise.

⭐ An Age of Steel

Technological advances, such as the Corliss steam engine, were important to the **Second Industrial Revolution**. The Second Industrial Revolution was a period of rapid growth in U.S. manufacturing in the late 1800s. By the mid-1890s, the United States had become the industrial leader of the world.

Some of the most important advances in technology took place in the steel industry. Steel is iron that has been made stronger by heating it and adding other metals. Skilled workers once made steel in small batches, but the process was difficult and expensive. In the 1850s Henry Bessemer found a quick, cheap way to make steel by blasting hot air through melted iron to quickly remove waste material. Before Bessemer developed this method, it took a day or more to turn several tons of iron into steel. The **Bessemer process** took only 10 to 20 minutes.

Using the Bessemer process, U.S. steel production rose from 77,000 tons in 1870 to more than 1 million tons in 1879. At first the need for steel rails for railroads fueled this growth. However, steel mills were also soon making parts for tall buildings and bridges. As mills made more steel, steel prices dropped. People could afford to use steel for items such as nails, wire, and pipes.

Railroad companies took advantage of lower construction costs to build thousands of miles of new steel track. Railroad mileage increased from some 30,000 miles in 1860 to 193,000 miles by 1900. These stronger, longer-lasting rails could carry heavier loads. A network of rail lines soon carried heavy cargo across the nation.

New technology also made railroad travel safer. Inventor George Westinghouse's improved air brakes made travel on these heavier, faster trains safer. Passenger service also improved. George Pullman designed elegant passenger and sleeping cars that made long-distance trips more comfortable. Cornelius Vanderbilt and other railroad owners began buying smaller companies to form larger companies. This process improved efficiency and made rail travel faster. In 1860 it had taken two days and 17 line changes to go from New York City to Chicago. By 1870 the trip took one day and did not require changing trains.

Daily Life

Railroads Improvements in safety and comfort made railroad travel more appealing to Americans. Railroads also became faster and more efficient, helping businesses run more smoothly. Railroads thus helped drive the economy while connecting the nation. This image shows the Illinois Central Railroad connecting rural people to the rest of the world in the 1800s. **What do the various images in the cartoon represent?**

CONNECTING TO
SCIENCE AND TECHNOLOGY

The Wizard of Menlo Park

In 1876 Thomas Alva Edison built himself a new laboratory in Menlo Park, New Jersey. His plan was to create an "invention factory" where he and his team of skilled specialists would create all sorts of useful technologies. The idea proved to be a great success. In fewer than six years at Menlo Park, Edison patented more than 400 devices or processes, including the phonograph and the electric lightbulb. Such achievements gained Edison the nickname The Wizard of Menlo Park. **What was the purpose of the laboratory at Menlo Park?**

An early model of an electric lightbulb

Analyzing Primary Sources

Identifying Points of View
Why did Edison not consider himself a pure scientist?

The railroads had a major impact on the development of the country's economy. Manufacturers and farmers could get their products to market faster. Cities where major rail lines crossed, such as Chicago and Kansas City, grew rapidly. Railroads also spurred western growth by offering free tickets to settlers. As rail travel and shipping increased, railroads and their related industries employed more and more people.

✔ **Reading Check:** **Identifying Cause and Effect** How did steel processing change in the 1850s, and what effects did this change have on the population and economy of the United States?

★ New Sources of Power

Another important technological breakthrough in the late 1800s was the use of petroleum, or oil, as a power source. In the 1850s Dr. Benjamin Silliman Jr. discovered how to change crude, or unprocessed, oil into a fuel called kerosene. Kerosene could be used for cooking, heating, and home lighting. Suddenly the demand for oil increased. In 1859 Edwin L. Drake proved that it was possible to pump crude oil from the ground. Oil became a big business. States such as Ohio, Pennsylvania, and West Virginia began producing millions of barrels of oil a year.

In the late 1800s people found another use for oil—powering machinery. In 1876 German engineer Nikolaus A. Otto invented an engine powered by gasoline, another fuel made from oil. In 1893 Charles and J. Frank Duryea used a gasoline engine to build the first practical motorcar in the United States. By the early 1900s American manufacturers were building thousands of cars. Most of these early cars were too expensive for anyone but the wealthy to afford.

New engine technology also helped make another transportation breakthrough possible—flight. **Orville and Wilbur Wright** were bicycle makers. Fascinated by the possibility of flying, the brothers built a lightweight airplane with a small gas-powered engine. In Kitty Hawk, North Carolina, Orville Wright made the first piloted flight in a gas-powered plane on December 17, 1903. The Wright brothers patented their airplane in 1906.

Electricity became another source of power during the Second Industrial Revolution. Inventors such as **Thomas Alva Edison** investigated the practical uses of electricity, as he explained.

History Makers Speak

❝I do not regard myself as a pure scientist, as so many persons have insisted that I am. I do not search for the laws of nature . . . for the purpose of learning truth. I am only a professional inventor.❞

—Thomas Edison, quoted in *American Made*, by Harold C. Livesay

Edison went on to be awarded more than 1,000 **patents**. A patent is an exclusive right to make or sell an invention. This right encourages inventors to develop new technologies.

In 1878, after viewing an experimental electric light source, Edison announced that he would soon invent a practical electric light. By the end of 1879 Edison and his team of inventors had created the electric lightbulb. Edison began supplying electricity to some buildings in New York City in September 1882. In the late 1880s Edison and George Westinghouse competed to provide communities with electric power. As a result, electric use spread rapidly, and electricity soon lit homes and businesses across the country. Streetcars in cities also ran on electrical power.

Electricity also played a part in communications advances. By 1861, telegraph wires connected the East and West Coasts. Five years later, a cable was laid on the floor of the Atlantic Ocean to connect the United States and Great Britain. Alexander Graham Bell invented the "talking telegraph," or telephone, in 1876. By the mid-1890s major cities such as Boston, Chicago, and New York were linked by telephone lines. The number of telephones in U.S. homes and businesses increased rapidly.

✔ **Reading Check: Comparing** What new sources of power became available in the late 1800s, and how were they used?

⭐ Free Enterprise and Big Business

As the U.S. economy grew during the Second Industrial Revolution, the federal government favored **free enterprise**, a term that means the government usually does not interfere with business. In the late 1800s this policy continued in the form of laissez-faire capitalism, with little government regulation of the market economy. Laissez-faire means "allow to do" in French. However, the government took some actions to help business. Protective tariffs aided manufacturers and land grants helped railroad companies. As a result, **entrepreneurs**—people who start new businesses—had a lot of freedom and many opportunities.

Many entrepreneurs formed their businesses as **corporations.** Corporations are formed by selling shares of ownership, called stock, to a number of individuals known as stockholders. Stockholders in a corporation typically get a share of company profits, based on how much stock they own. Corporations must be approved and chartered by state governments. Although the stockholders actually own the corporation, they do not run its day-to-day operations. Instead, they elect a board of directors. The board then chooses the main leaders of the corporation.

Corporations provide several important advantages over earlier ways of organizing companies. Unlike business partners or members of joint-stock companies, the stockholders in a corporation are not personally responsible for the debts of the business. As a result, if a corporation fails, the stockholders lose only the money that they invested. Stockholders are also usually free to sell their shares to whomever they want, whenever they want. These benefits encouraged investment. By 1900 more than 100 million shares a year were being traded on the New York Stock Exchange.

★ ★ ★ ★ ★ ★ ★ ★ ★ ★ ★
That's Interesting!
★ ★ ★ ★ ★ ★ ★ ★ ★ ★ ★

Why "Wall Street"? Did you know that the New York Stock Exchange (NYSE) began in 1792 as a group of stock-brokers meeting to trade stocks under a buttonwood tree? It's true! The tree has long since vanished, but it is believed to have stood somewhere near what is now 11 Wall Street, the current location of the NYSE. And by the way, Wall Street was named for the boundary stockade, or wall, that Dutch colonists built in 1653 for protection from English colonists and American Indians.

A stock certificate

BIOGRAPHY

Andrew Carnegie
(1835–1919)

Andrew Carnegie was born in Scotland. He immigrated to Pennsylvania at age 12. Carnegie constantly impressed his employers because he worked hard and learned quickly. One employer loaned Carnegie $600 to make his first investment in a company. He soon became wealthy by making wise investment and business choices. Unlike many other successful businesspeople of his era, Carnegie still lived very simply. He did not believe in showing off wealth. After retiring, Carnegie devoted his time to charitable efforts. **In what ways was Andrew Carnegie different from other successful businesspeople of his time?**

★ Business Leaders

Entrepreneurs and business leaders were some of the most widely respected members of American society in the late 1800s. Many Americans looked up to these self-made, wealthy individuals. Political leaders often praised prosperous businessmen as examples of American hard work, talent, and success.

Andrew Carnegie was one of the most admired business leaders of the late 1800s. While working for the Pennsylvania Railroad as a young man, Carnegie borrowed money and invested it in iron mills and bridge-building businesses. His investments did so well that Carnegie left the railroad company in 1865. "I was no longer merely an official working for others . . . ," he wrote, "but a full-fledged business man."

In 1873 Carnegie focused his efforts on steel production. He expanded his business by buying out his competitors when steel prices were low. Carnegie never held a monopoly on steel production in the United States. However, by 1901 Carnegie's mills were producing more steel than all of Great Britain's steel mills combined. He used a method called **vertical integration**—owning the businesses involved in each step of a manufacturing process. To lower his production costs, Carnegie bought the iron ore mines, the coal fields, and the railroads needed to supply and support his steel mills.

Another powerful businessman, **John D. Rockefeller**, started out as a bookkeeper. By age 21 he was a partner in a wholesale business, and he soon decided to start an oil-refining company. By 1870 Rockefeller's Standard Oil Company was the country's largest oil refiner. Like Carnegie, Rockefeller used vertical integration to improve production and profits. Standard Oil made its own barrels and controlled most of the pipelines, tank cars, and storage buildings it used. Many railroads offered lower rates to Standard Oil to attract its valuable shipping business. At times Rockefeller even got railroads to agree not to provide service to his competitors.

Rockefeller's company also used **horizontal integration**—owning all the businesses in a certain field. By 1880 he controlled some 90 percent of the oil-refining businesses in the United States. This level of control gave Rockefeller's companies a monopoly on the American oil-refining industry. Rockefeller used consolidation to cut his costs. He also formed a **trust**—a grouping together of a number of companies under one board of directors. To earn higher profits, trusts often tried to get rid of competition in their industry and to control production. These practices resulted in higher prices for buyers. Rockefeller explained, "The day of combination [trusts] is here to stay. Individualism has gone, never to return."

✔ **Reading Check: Summarizing** Describe the economic situation in the United States during the late 1800s.

Vertical and Horizontal Integration

Business methods such as horizontal and vertical integration helped corporations make huge profits.

Vertical Integration
Companies owned by U.S. Steel

Steel Mills

Railroads and Ships

Coal Mines

Iron Mines

Horizontal Integration
Competitors bought by Standard Oil Company

Standard Oil Company

Oil-Refining Companies

Visualizing History

1. **Economics** Why would horizontal or vertical integration help a company?

2. **Connecting to Today** Would such business practices be allowed today? Explain your answer.

★ Social Darwinism and Philanthropy

Many people who favored free enterprise also believed in social Darwinism. This view of society was based loosely on scientist Charles Darwin's theory of natural selection. Darwin thought that species evolved by adapting to their environments over long periods of time. Social Darwinists said that "survival of the fittest" also determined who would succeed in human society. Sociologist Herbert Spencer even argued that government regulation of businesses hurt the "natural" economic order.

Many business leaders agreed. John D. Rockefeller declared, "The growth of large business is merely a survival of the fittest." Some wealthy business leaders argued that it was the poor person's responsibility to work hard for a better life. However, others claimed that the wealthy had a duty to aid the poor. These leaders practiced philanthropy—giving money to the needy. For example, during his lifetime Andrew Carnegie donated more than $350 million to charity. By the late 1800s, charities had received millions of dollars from philanthropists.

✔ **Reading Check: Analyzing Information** Did all business leaders become philanthropists? Explain your answer.

Interpreting Political Cartoons

Powerful trusts Some cartoonists portrayed trusts as oversized bullies taking advantage of consumers. *What actions are the trusts taking in this cartoon?*

★ The Antitrust Movement

Critics of big business said that unfair business practices were responsible for the successes of many large companies. For example, big corporations often used their size and power to eliminate competition by driving smaller competitors out of business. Some trusts also gained monopolies on certain products or services. Members of the trust would then agree to match one another's prices on goods to avoid competition.

Many citizens and small-business owners wanted the government to control monopolies and trusts. People who favored trusts responded that trusts were more efficient and gave the consumer dependable products and services. One newspaper editor declared that "the right to cooperate is as unquestionable as the right to compete."

Many in Congress were sympathetic to the interests of big business. However, they could not ignore the voters' concerns. As Senator John Sherman explained, "You must heed [pay attention to] their appeal [request]. . . . Society is now disturbed by forces never felt before." In July 1890 Congress passed the **Sherman Antitrust Act**, which outlawed monopolies and trusts that restrained trade. However, the act did not clearly define what a trust was in legal terms. The antitrust laws were thus difficult to enforce, and corporations and trusts continued to grow in power.

✔ **Reading Check: Sequencing** How did antitrust feelings lead to the Sherman Antitrust Act?

Section 1 Review

go.hrw.com **Homework Practice Online** keyword: SF3 HP22

1 **Define** and explain:
• patents
• free enterprise
• entrepreneurs
• corporations
• vertical integration
• horizontal integration
• trust

2 **Identify** and explain:
• Second Industrial Revolution
• Bessemer process
• Orville and Wilbur Wright
• Thomas Alva Edison
• Andrew Carnegie
• John D. Rockefeller
• Sherman Antitrust Act

3 **Summarizing** Copy the chart below. Use it to list the developments that took place in the steel, oil, and electric-power industries during the Second Industrial Revolution.

Industry	Developments
steel	
oil	
electricity	

4 **Finding the Main Idea**
a. What are vertical integration and horizontal integration, and how did business leaders use these methods to organize their corporations?

b. Why did some people oppose business monopolies, and what did these people do to control them?

5 **Writing and Critical Thinking**
Supporting a Point of View Imagine that you are an editor of a magazine in the 1880s. Write a short editorial explaining what you think the key business innovation of the time is and why.

Consider the following:
• uses of steel, oil, and electricity
• free enterprise and entrepreneurs
• vertical and horizontal integration, monopolies, and trusts

Industrial Workers

Read to Discover

1. How did the Second Industrial Revolution affect American workers?
2. Why did workers form labor unions, and how were they organized?
3. How did major labor strikes affect workers?

WHY IT MATTERS TODAY

Workers around the world use unions to fight for their rights. Use **CNNfyi.com** or other **current events** sources to learn about labor unions in another country. Record your findings in your journal.

Define

- collective bargaining
- anarchists

Identify

- Frederick W. Taylor
- Knights of Labor
- Terence V. Powderly
- Mary Harris Jones
- American Federation of Labor
- Samuel Gompers
- Haymarket Riot
- Homestead strike
- Pullman strike

The Story Continues

At the beginning of the Second Industrial Revolution, skilled workers called puddlers turned hot liquid iron into steel. Puddlers' skills made them valuable employees. However, as new technologies were developed, puddlers found themselves being replaced by machines. Like many other skilled workers, puddlers began searching for ways to increase their bargaining power with employers.

This announcement for a union meeting was written in both English and German.

⭐ The New Workplace

During the Second Industrial Revolution, machines run by unskilled workers took the places of many skilled craftspeople. These low-paid workers needed little training and could easily be replaced. As a result, untrained workers feared that complaining about pay or working conditions would cost them their jobs.

As machines became more widely used in industry, factories moved toward specialization. Specialization is having workers perform a single step in the production process again and again. This approach lowered costs and raised production. Such results encouraged managers to seek even more efficient production methods.

In the early 1880s **Frederick W. Taylor**, an engineer with a steel company, worked to find ways to increase production and lower costs. In 1911 he published *The Principles of Scientific Management* and established efficiency studies as a basic part of American industry. Taylor's idea of scientific management defined workers more as parts of the production process than as people. This approach led many factory managers to ignore unhealthy working conditions. More workers got hurt as they used more machines and were pushed to work faster. Companies rarely took responsibility for work-related injuries. As conditions grew worse, workers looked for ways to bring about change.

✔ **Reading Check: Identifying Cause and Effect** Why did companies begin to use scientific management, and how did it affect workers?

Interpreting the Visual Record

Knights of Labor The Knights of Labor was one of the few unions to accept African Americans. Here union member Frank J. Farrell (left) is shown introducing union president Terence V. Powderly (center). *How might accepting members of different races be beneficial to the union?*

Research on the ROM

Free Find:
Mother Jones
After reading about Mary Harris Jones on the **Holt Researcher CD–ROM**, write a short speech she might have given to workers that draws upon her life experiences.

★ Labor Unions

To improve working conditions, workers formed labor unions. Union leaders tried to win better wages and labor conditions for all workers in a factory or industry. When workers acted collectively, or together, they had a much greater chance of winning labor disputes with employers. This method is called **collective bargaining**. Most employers opposed collective bargaining. One company president said, "I shall never give in. I would rather go out of business."

Founded by Uriah Stephens, the **Knights of Labor** was a union originally set up like a secret society. During an economic downturn in the early 1870s, the union built a network of local groups. Stephens said the goal of the Knights was to "include men and women of every creed and color." In 1879 **Terence V. Powderly** became the leader of the Knights. He ended the organization's secrecy, making it the first truly national labor union in the United States. Under Powderly's leadership, the Knights worked for improvements for workers. The union's goals included an eight-hour workday, equal pay for equal work for men and women, and an end to child labor. It also wanted the government to regulate trusts. Unlike most unions at the time, the Knights had both skilled and unskilled workers.

Many women joined the Knights of Labor and took active roles in it. Union organizer **Mary Harris Jones** was called Mother Jones by the workers whose rights she fought to protect. She organized many strikes among workers, such as one group of poorly paid Virginia miners whose lives were very difficult. Jones described their living conditions.

History Makers Speak

❝In some of these [company] camps the miners are forced to pay as much as $9 a barrel for sugar, 18 cents a pound for fat pork, and $8 to $10 a month rent for a company shack, the roof of which is so poor that when it rains the bed is moved from place to place in the attempt to find a dry spot. Many a miner works his whole life and never handles a cent of money.❞

—Mary Harris Jones, *The Speeches and Writings of Mother Jones*

Analyzing Primary Sources

Drawing Inferences and Conclusions Why do you think some miners never got to handle any money?

The **American Federation of Labor** (AFL), led by **Samuel Gompers**, took a different approach. Unlike the Knights, the AFL organized individual national unions such as the mineworkers' and the steelworkers' unions. In addition, the AFL limited its membership to skilled workers. This practice gave the union great bargaining power but left out most workers. Gompers said that the AFL tried to "accomplish the best results in improving the conditions of the working people . . . today and tomorrow." The AFL tried to get better wages, hours, and working conditions for its members. By 1890 the AFL had more members than the Knights did.

✔ **Reading Check: Summarizing** How were the national unions organized?

★ The Haymarket Riot

By 1886, other unions were gaining strength as well. In May, thousands of union members in Chicago went on strike for an eight-hour workday. Two strikers were killed in a fight with police. The next night workers met at Haymarket Square to protest the killings. When police came to break up the crowd, someone threw a dynamite bomb. Seven officers and one civilian were killed, and some 60 other officers were wounded. The police responded by firing into the crowd. Several people were killed, and about 100 others were injured. The terrible event became known as the **Haymarket Riot**.

An investigation led to the arrest and conviction of eight **anarchists**—people who oppose all forms of government—on charges of conspiracy. One of them had a Knights of Labor membership card. Powderly and the other Knights' leaders never supported the strike or the Haymarket protest. However, several local chapters of the Knights had. Public opinion soon linked the Knights to the Haymarket Riot and its violence. News of the incident caused the membership in the Knights to fall quickly.

✔ **Reading Check: Identifying Cause and Effect** What led to the Haymarket Riot, and how did it affect labor unions?

Interpreting the Visual Record

A deadly riot The bombing at Haymarket Square stunned both police and demonstrators and caused many injuries and deaths. *How does this scene depict the violence and confusion of the riot?*

⭐ The Homestead and Pullman Strikes

Unions continued to use strikes to try to improve working conditions. However, business owners sometimes pushed unions into striking in the hope of getting government support to break up a union. One such conflict happened at one of Andrew Carnegie's steel plants.

Workers had always gotten along well with managers at the Carnegie Steel Company in Homestead, Pennsylvania. This situation changed in 1889 when Henry Frick became company chairman. In 1892, union members protested Frick's plan to add new machinery that would replace workers. When an agreement could not be reached, Frick set out to break the union and cut costs. He announced that the company would try to work out labor contracts with individual workers, not the union.

On June 29 the **Homestead strike** began. Frick locked workers out of the plant. He refused to bargain with the union or allow union members back to work. The workers responded by seizing control of the town of Homestead. Frick then hired private detectives from the Pinkerton agency to break the power of the union by force.

On July 6, the Pinkerton detectives tried to enter the steelworks. Gunfire broke out and nine workers and seven detectives died as a result of the battle that followed. After a long standoff, the outnumbered and

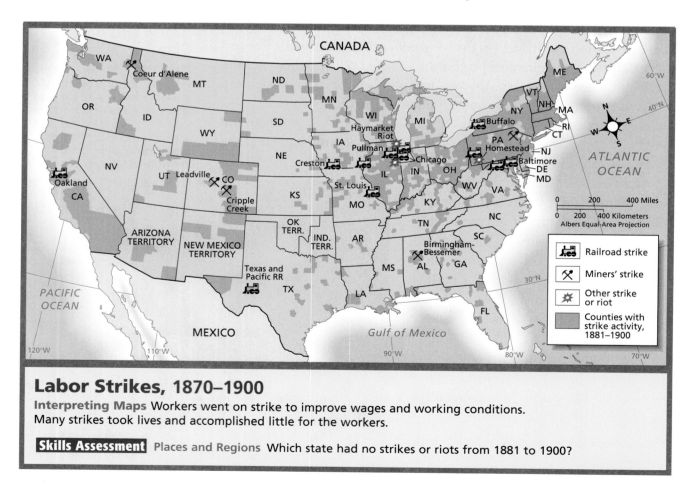

Labor Strikes, 1870–1900

Interpreting Maps Workers went on strike to improve wages and working conditions. Many strikes took lives and accomplished little for the workers.

Skills Assessment Places and Regions Which state had no strikes or riots from 1881 to 1900?

trapped detectives surrendered. They were then marched through the streets and insulted by crowds. Pennsylvania's governor called out the state militia to restore order. The strike continued for four more months. However, the union was eventually defeated. Frick sent a message to Carnegie, "Our victory is now complete."

Another major strike took place at George Pullman's Palace Car Company. Most of the company's workers lived in the company town of Pullman, Illinois. These workers had to pay higher rents and utility costs than people in nearby towns.

During the economic depression that began in 1893, Pullman laid off about half of the company's workers. He then cut the wages of those who were left. In May 1894, workers protesting the wage cuts began the **Pullman strike**. Support for the strike quickly spread throughout the railroad industry. The American Railway Union, headed by Eugene V. Debs, refused to work on trains carrying Pullman cars. By July, this strike had stopped traffic on most midwestern rail lines.

Railroad officials then ordered the Pullman cars to be attached to U.S. mail cars. Workers who stopped Pullman cars could then be charged with the federal crime of interfering with the U.S. mail. The federal government backed the railroad companies in this move. Despite the protest of Illinois's governor, President Grover Cleveland sent federal troops to Chicago.

The U.S. attorney general then used the Sherman Antitrust Act to stop the strikers. He obtained a court order stating that the strike was interfering with interstate trade. Debs was arrested for violating the court order. Government support for big business and defeats like that suffered in the Pullman strike set the labor movement back for several years.

The majority of trains in the United States carried Pullman cars. The strike against George Pullman's company thus proved crippling for railroad traffic.

✔ **Reading Check: Evaluating** What were the effects of early major strikes on workers and companies?

Section 2 Review

go.
hrw
.com **Homework Practice Online**
keyword: SF3 HP22

1 **Define** and explain:
• collective bargaining
• anarchists

2 **Identify** and explain:
• Frederick W. Taylor
• Knights of Labor
• Terence V. Powderly
• Mary Harris Jones
• American Federation of Labor
• Samuel Gompers
• Haymarket Riot
• Homestead strike
• Pullman strike

3 **Analyzing Information** Copy the diagram below. Use it to show the effects that the Second Industrial Revolution had on businesses, workers, and the labor movement.

4 **Finding the Main Idea**
a. Why were the Knights of Labor and the American Federation of Labor formed, and how did they operate?

b. How did the major strikes of the late 1800s affect American workers?

5 **Writing and Critical Thinking**
Analyzing Information Imagine that you are a newspaper journalist during the Haymarket Riot. Write a short article describing the events and outcome of the riot.

Consider the following:
• events that took place during the riot
• connection to the Knights of Labor
• public reaction to the riot

Immigrants and the Cities

Read to Discover

1. Why did immigrants come to the United States, and what countries did they emigrate from during the late 1800s?
2. How did some Americans try to limit immigration?
3. How did city residents try to deal with the challenges of urban life?

WHY IT MATTERS TODAY

People still immigrate to the United States today. Use CNNfyi.com or other **current events** sources to learn about today's immigration trends. Record your findings in your journal.

Define

- old immigrants
- new immigrants
- steerage
- benevolent societies
- suburbs
- settlement houses

Identify

- Chinese Exclusion Act
- Immigration Restriction League
- Hull House
- Jane Addams
- Ellen Gates Starr

Asian immigrants in the United States in the 1800s

The Story Continues

Lee Chew lived in China. He was a poor peasant working on his father's farm with little hope of ever owning his own land. When a man from his village "returned with unlimited wealth, which he had obtained in the country of the American wizards," Lee decided to leave China. Like millions of other immigrants to the United States, he left behind everything and everyone he knew. He traveled to a strange new land, carrying little but his dream of success.

⭐ Increased Immigration

During the late 1800s immigrants like Lee continued to come to the United States by the millions. However, immigration patterns began to change. Immigrants who had come to the United States before the 1880s were mostly from Britain, Germany, Ireland, and Scandinavia. Most were Protestants, except for the Irish and some Germans who were Catholic. Many of them spoke English. These people, often called **old immigrants**, frequently settled outside cities and became farmers.

During the 1880s the number of immigrants to the United States increased dramatically. Many of these so-called **new immigrants** came from southern and eastern Europe. The jobs created by the Second Industrial Revolution attracted many people.

Other groups, including Armenians and Jews, were escaping political and religious persecution. New immigrants brought cultural practices with them that were unfamiliar to many native-born Americans. They also held diverse religious beliefs, such as Eastern Orthodox Christianity, Roman Catholicism, and Judaism.

Immigrants usually faced a difficult journey to America. Most of them bought the cheapest tickets available. They traveled in **steerage**, an area below deck on a ship's lower levels near where the steering mechanisms for the ship were located. In these cramped conditions, passengers often experienced overcrowding and seasickness. Some passengers even died from disease.

When immigrants reached the United States, they had to go first to immigration processing centers. In 1890 the federal government began assuming control of these immigration centers. One of the largest centers opened in 1892 on Ellis Island in New York Harbor. At these centers, officials interviewed immigrants to decide whether to let them enter the country. Officials also conducted physical examinations, deporting any person who carried a disease such as tuberculosis.

Ellis Island became so well known that songs were written about it.

✔ **Reading Check: Contrasting** How did immigration patterns change in the late 1800s?

★ Immigrant Life

Immigrants drawn to the United States by stories of wealth and quick success often found that the reality was more difficult. One girl described her adjustment to her new home.

History Makers Speak

❝[I dreamed] of the golden stairs leading to the top of the American palace where father was supposed to live. [I] went 'home' to . . . an ugly old tenement in the heart of the Lower East Side. There were stairs to climb but they were not golden.❞

—Miriam Shomer Zunser, *Yesterday: A Memoir of a Russian Jewish Family*

Most immigrants settled in cities, where unskilled industrial jobs were plentiful but low paying. With little money or knowledge of English, these unskilled jobs were the only work most immigrants could get at first. Entire families often worked to survive. Despite such challenges, many immigrants found opportunities in the United States that they never had at home.

Many immigrants worked hard to build communities by moving into neighborhoods with others who shared their nationality. There they could hear their native languages, eat familiar foods, and keep their customs. Some immigrant communities formed **benevolent societies**, which offered help in cases of death, sickness, and unemployment. At that time, there were few national government agencies to provide such aid.

★★★★★★★★★★★★

That's Interesting!

★★★★★★★★★★★★

The People's Statue The Statue of Liberty was a gift from France to the United States. To make the trip to America the huge 151-foot-tall statue had to be separated into 350 pieces. For four months after reaching its new home, the statue stayed in pieces. There were parts of the statue throughout New York. The torch lay in Madison Square. Visitors even climbed inside it! Some people wanted to keep the statue in pieces. Others, such as publisher Joseph Pulitzer, set about raising funds to build the pedestal on which the statue would be built. Pulitzer asked his readers to give any money they could. Although many people donated less than a dollar, the funds were raised. The statue was put back together and raised again in 1886.

Immigrant families such as this one often worked together in sweatshops making clothing.

Many immigrant groups published newspapers in their own languages. They also founded schools, clubs, and places of worship to preserve their beliefs and customs. New immigrants also eagerly embraced American culture. They wanted their children to learn English and adopt American customs. While immigrants' lives were often difficult, they were usually able to build a better future for their families.

✔ **Reading Check: Summarizing** What steps did new immigrants take to help themselves and others?

⭐ Opposition to Immigration

Anti-immigrant feelings grew along with the increase in immigration in the late 1800s. People opposed to immigration believed that the new immigrants' poverty and lack of education would harm American society. Nativism—the favoring of native-born residents over the foreign-born—had started in the 1840s and 1850s with opposition to Irish Catholic newcomers. Many nativists held racial and religious prejudices against immigrants from Asia and southern and eastern Europe in particular.

Some labor unions also opposed immigration. They feared that immigrants willing to work for low wages would take jobs away from union members. Some business leaders favored immigration because the supply of new low-wage workers kept labor costs down. One businessman described the benefits of immigration. "Their home countries have borne [paid] the expense of rearing them . . . and then America . . . reaps whatever profits there are" from their work.

In some places nativists rioted violently against immigrants. Other nativists called for laws to stop or limit immigration. In 1882 Congress passed the **Chinese Exclusion Act**. This law banned Chinese people from coming to the United States for 10 years. The law marked the first time people of a specific nationality were banned from entering the country. Congress later extended the ban into the 1900s.

To further decrease the flow of immigrants, nativists formed the **Immigration Restriction League** in 1894. The league wanted all immigrants to prove that they could read and write in some language before being allowed into the country. Congress passed a law requiring a literacy test for immigrants in 1897. However, President Cleveland vetoed the bill, calling it "narrow, and un-American."

Despite opposition, the new immigrants played a key role in industrial growth in the late 1800s. They did much of the low-paying work on U.S. buildings, highways, and railroads that drove rapid growth.

✔ **Reading Check: Analyzing Information** Why did nativists oppose immigration, and what steps did they take against it?

Research on the R⊙M

Free Find:
Immigrant Voices
After reading the selection of immigrant stories on the **Holt Researcher CD–ROM**, write your own story about what you might have experienced as an immigrant coming to the United States.

★ The Growth of Urban Communities

During the late 1800s immigrants and native-born Americans moved to cities in record numbers. In 1850 only six cities in the United States had populations greater than 100,000. By 1900 there were more than 35 such cities. In midwestern cities, in particular, the population grew rapidly during those years. Chicago's population, for example, rose from 30,000 in 1850 to 1.7 million in 1900. By 1900 about 40 percent of Americans lived in urban areas. This percentage continued to climb in the early 1900s.

Some city residents were businesspeople and skilled workers. But many more were poor laborers. Farming troubles drove large numbers of people to the cities looking for work. Author Henry Blake Fuller said Chicago's new residents had "come for the common avowed object [declared goal] of making money."

City residents often started organizations to improve their communities and bring their neighborhoods together. For example, African American religious groups organized and aided urban communities. African American ministers often served as both political and spiritual leaders in black neighborhoods. One report from a Baptist group described the ministers as "a class of men who . . . have won the confidence, love, and respect of their people."

✔ **Reading Check: Finding the Main Idea** Why did cities grow so quickly in the late 1800s, and how did people respond to the problems that resulted from this growth?

Interpreting the Visual Record

Urban crowding *Cities such as Chicago grew rapidly in the late 1800s, thanks to immigration, migration, and industrial development.* **What aspects of this scene show the size of the city?**

The Sail Boat Pond, Central Park, New York City.

CONNECTING TO
THE ARTS

Central Park In 1857 Frederick Law Olmsted was appointed superintendent of New York City's Central Park, the first major public park in the United States. Olmsted wanted the park to be a place where city-dwellers could relax surrounded by nature. The park's design contained many trees and several bodies of water. In addition, Central Park offered activities such as horseback riding, ice-skating, boating, and baseball. Central Park proved to be very popular, drawing an average of 30,000 visitors a day for a total of 10 million in 1871. It remains a popular destination today for New York City's residents as well as its tourists. **Why do you think Central Park is so popular?**

Analyzing Primary Sources
Drawing Inferences and Conclusions What do you think was difficult about the living conditions described?

⭐ Urban Changes and Problems

Organizations such as churches and social groups helped make life easier for many city residents. New technologies also brought improvements to urban centers. Engineers built taller buildings by using steel-beam frames for support. Elisha Otis's steam-powered elevators carried people up and down the floors of these so-called skyscrapers. Small local stores gave way to department stores, which offered a wider variety of goods in one place.

Cities sometimes grew too fast. Overcrowding and lack of sanitation resulted, leading to disease and poor health. Poor people, who often lived in run-down housing, suffered the most, as Jacob Riis described.

 History Makers Speak
❝Nine lived in two rooms, one about ten feet square that served as parlor, bedroom, and eating room, the other a small hall room made into a kitchen. The rent was . . . more than a week's wages for the husband.❞

—Jacob Riis, *How the Other Half Lives*

Many cities began building parks to preserve green spaces for recreation. Cities also offered libraries, museums, theaters, and the best schools and hospitals. However, some people wanted private space. Many middle-class Americans chose to live in quieter areas where they could own homes. They moved to **suburbs**—neighborhoods outside of downtown areas. Mass transit networks of streetcars, subways, and commuter trains made living in the suburbs and working in the cities possible.

✔ **Reading Check: Summarizing** What developments eased the problems that arose from the rapid growth of cities?

★ Settlement Houses

Few government programs existed to help the urban poor in the late 1800s. However, many private aid organizations assisted poor people. In addition, **settlement houses**—neighborhood centers in poor areas staffed by professionals and volunteers—offered education, recreation, and social activities.

Settlement houses began in Great Britain and then became common in the United States. Janie Porter Barrett established an African American settlement house in Hampton, Virginia. The most famous settlement house was Chicago's **Hull House**, founded by **Jane Addams** and **Ellen Gates Starr** in 1889. Like many upper-class women of their era, they had received a college education. However, they found few job opportunities open to them. Addams wanted to help the poor. To reach this goal, she and Starr opened Hull House in a run-down building in a poor Chicago neighborhood. The work at Hull House focused most on the needs of families, especially immigrant families. Hull House served as a model for other settlement houses.

Addams and her staff took part in a variety of activities. They started the first kindergarten and public playground in Chicago. They also taught classes in English and U.S. government to help immigrants become citizens. In addition, the staff worked for reform of child-labor laws and the adoption of an eight-hour workday for women. Many of the women involved in running Hull House later became active in a variety of national reform movements.

Jane Addams, who remained active in reform movements her entire life, won the Nobel Peace Prize in 1931.

Research on the ROM

Free Find:
Jane Addams
After reading about Jane Addams on the **Holt Researcher CD–ROM**, create a list of community services you would provide if you worked in a settlement house.

✔ **Reading Check: Drawing Inferences and Conclusions** How might working at Hull House have prepared women to seek national reform?

Section 3 Review

Homework Practice Online
keyword: SF3 HP22

❶ **Define** and explain:
- old immigrants
- new immigrants
- steerage
- benevolent societies
- suburbs
- settlement houses

❷ **Identify** and explain:
- Chinese Exclusion Act
- Immigration Restriction League
- Hull House
- Jane Addams
- Ellen Gates Starr

❸ **Summarizing** Copy the diagram below. Use it to show how city residents organized to deal with the challenges of urban life.

Facing the challenges of urban life

❹ **Finding the Main Idea**
a. What led immigrants to come to the United States, and what regions did they come from in the late 1800s?

b. What were the nativists' attitudes toward new immigrants, and what actions arose from their bias?

❺ **Writing and Critical Thinking**
Supporting a Point of View Imagine that you are an immigrant to the United States in 1885. Write a letter to your family back home, telling them about your good and bad experiences. Try to persuade them to join you.

Consider the following:
- the journey to the United States
- adjusting to a new country
- support systems

Populism

Read to Discover

1. What effects did industrialization have on farmers, and what actions did farmers take to bring about change?
2. Why did farmers want changes in the money supply?
3. What were the political and economic goals of the National Grange and the Populist Party?

WHY IT MATTERS TODAY

The United States has been off the gold standard since 1971. The Federal Reserve, founded in 1913, currently maintains the stability of the country's monetary system. Use CNNfyi.com or other **current events** sources to learn how "The Fed" works. Record your findings in your journal.

Define

- free coinage
- gold standard

Identify

- Oliver Hudson Kelley
- National Grange
- Interstate Commerce Act
- Interstate Commerce Commission
- William Jennings Bryan
- Benjamin Harrison
- Sherman Silver Purchase Act
- Farmers' Alliances
- Populist Party
- James B. Weaver

The Story Continues

In the late 1800s many farmers blamed their economic hardships on the railroads. Frank Norris's 1901 novel *The Octopus* offers the farmers' point of view. In the story, high railroad rates threaten to leave Farmer Dyke with no profit from his harvest. He had borrowed money to raise his crops. Unless he pays it back, the bank will foreclose. Dyke realizes that "not only would the Railroad devour every morsel of his profits, but also it would take from him his home."

Many farm families faced hard times in the late 1800s.

⭐ Rural Unrest and the National Grange

From 1860 to 1900 the U.S. population more than doubled. During this same time, the number of farms tripled. Many farmers borrowed money to buy land and machinery. With new machines, farmers in 1900 could produce a bushel of wheat almost 20 times faster than in 1830. However, the combination of more farms and greater productivity led to overproduction, which in turn led to lower prices for crops. Many farmers responded by increasing crop production, causing even lower prices.

Agricultural Regions, 1900

Interpreting Maps The diverse climates and soils of the United States enabled farmers to grow a wide variety of crops.

Skills Assessment Human Systems What types of agricultural products did people raise along the western coast of the United States?

Corn was a major American crop.

As their incomes decreased, many farmers found it more difficult to pay their bills, which the cost of new machinery had often increased. Farmers who could not make their mortgage payments lost their farms and homes due to bank foreclosures. Many of these hard-hit families became tenant farmers, while others could not even afford to rent land and thus became farm workers. By 1880 one fourth of all farms were rented by tenants, and the number kept growing.

Many farmers blamed businesspeople—wholesalers, brokers, grain buyers, and particularly railroad owners—for profiting at their expense. An editor of a North Carolina farm journal expressed this view.

History Makers Speak

❝There is something radically wrong. . . . The railroads have never been so prosperous. . . . The banks have never done a better . . . business. . . . Manufacturing enterprises have never made more money. . . . Towns and cities flourish and 'boom,' . . . and yet agriculture languishes [declines].❞

—Leonidas Polk, quoted in *The Shaping of Modern America, 1877–1916,* by Vincent P. DeSantis

Analyzing Primary Sources

Drawing Inferences and Conclusions What does Polk seem to say about the way that railroads, banks, and manufacturers deal with farmers?

As economic conditions for farmers grew worse, they began to organize associations as workers had done. In 1866 government official

An Industrial and Urban Nation **699**

The Grangers formed farm cooperatives to overcome lower crop prices and the cost of maintaining expensive new farm machinery such as this tractor.

Oliver Hudson Kelley toured the South for the U.S. Department of Agriculture. Kelley saw firsthand how the country's farmers suffered. After that tour, Kelley and several government clerks founded the National Grange of the Patrons of Husbandry in 1867. The **National Grange** was a social and educational organization dedicated to improving farmers' lives. Membership grew rapidly as local chapters were quickly started.

Granges formed organizations called cooperatives to buy goods in bulk, or large quantities, at lower prices. Farmers also formed cooperative groups to sell their crops at higher prices. Unfortunately, these cooperatives were often run by people who were not experienced in business. In addition, banks, merchants, and railroads often united to work against these cooperatives. As a result, most of the cooperatives did poorly.

✔ **Reading Check: Finding the Main Idea** How did new agricultural technologies affect farmers?

★ Fighting the Railroads

The National Grange soon changed its focus from economics to politics. Members campaigned for political candidates who supported farmers' interests. The Grange also called for laws to regulate rates for the use of railroads and grain elevators. In a few states, the Grange backed laws regulating railroads, which benefited farmers when shipping their crops.

The issue of railroad regulation by individual states came before the U.S. Supreme Court in 1877. The Court ruled in *Munn* v. *Illinois* that state governments could regulate the railroads and other businesses that affect the public interest. However, the Supreme Court modified this position in 1886. In *Wabash* v. *Illinois,* the Court said that state governments could not regulate traffic that crossed state boundaries. Only the federal government could regulate interstate traffic.

In February 1887 Congress passed the **Interstate Commerce Act**, which provided some consistent national regulations on trade between states. It also created the **Interstate Commerce Commission** (ICC) to ensure that railroads charged fair rates and did not favor big shippers. However, the commission lacked the power to enforce its regulations. In addition, the courts gave the agency little help when it appealed to them for assistance.

✔ **Reading Check: Analyzing Information** How did the government regulate railroads, and how successful were these efforts?

⭐ The Free Silver Debate

Railroad rates were not the only concern that farmers faced. Their problems usually involved money issues, such as credit, debt, and low crop prices. Many farmers thought that help would come only from national legislation that would affect the money supply.

Since 1792 the United States had allowed **free coinage**, meaning that both gold and silver were made into coins. Paper money was worth a specific amount of gold or silver. The Coinage Act of 1873 placed the United States on a strict **gold standard**, under which only gold could back U.S. currency. Tied to the gold standard, the money supply tended to grow more slowly than the country's population. This situation led to deflation—a drop in the money supply combined with falling prices.

Farmers favored coining silver to create inflation—an increase in the money supply and a rise in prices. They hoped that rising crop prices would then increase their income. During the late 1870s many farmers began backing political candidates who wanted free silver coinage. One such politician was **William Jennings Bryan** of Nebraska. In 1878 Congress passed the Bland-Allison Act, allowing limited silver coinage.

A new political party, the Greenback Party, favored inflating the money supply with paper dollars not backed by gold or silver. However, the two major parties largely ignored the money issue in the 1880 and 1884 presidential elections. In 1880 Republican James A. Garfield won the presidency over Democrat Winfield Scott Hancock in a close election. In 1884 Democrat Grover Cleveland defeated Republican James G. Blaine in another close contest. The Republicans finally made continued coinage of silver an issue in the 1888 elections. President Cleveland lost his bid for re-election that year to Republican **Benjamin Harrison**. After the election, the Republican-controlled Congress passed the **Sherman Silver Purchase Act.** The act increased the amount of silver the government bought for coinage, but the money supply did not increase enough to satisfy silver supporters.

✔ **Reading Check: Finding the Main Idea** Why did farmers want free coinage of silver?

Some Americans wanted paper money based on a silver standard, such as the silver-dollar bill shown at left, while others favored a gold standard.

Mary Elizabeth Lease published her views on populism in an influential book, The Problem of Civilization Solved.

⭐ The Populist Party

Many farmers formed their own political organizations to increase their power. These groups became known as the **Farmers' Alliances**. The Texas alliance started in 1877 and quickly grew to become the Grand State Alliance in 1879. Membership soared. The Colored Farmers' Alliance had more than 1 million members of its own. The Farmers' Alliances were more politically active than the Grange had been. They focused their efforts on getting legislation passed to help farmers by regulating railroads and lowering interest rates.

In the 1890 elections, the Alliances were a strong political force. Alliance-backed candidates won the governorships of Texas and Georgia. In addition, many candidates for Congress who had expressed support for the Alliances were elected to office. At a conference in Cincinnati, Ohio, in 1891, Alliance leaders met with labor and reform organizations. At a convention in St. Louis in February 1892, they formed a new national political party, the People's Party. This organization, better known as the **Populist Party**, was the high point of farmers' political activity.

The Populist Party held its first national convention in 1892. The group adopted a platform of far-reaching reforms. The Populists' goal was to end the power that big business had over government. Populist speaker Mary Elizabeth Lease called for greater democracy and a voice in the government for all Americans. The Populist platform called for government ownership of railroads and telephone and telegraph systems. It also backed the "free and unlimited coinage of silver." To win votes from laborers, the Populists supported the eight-hour workday and immigration restrictions.

In the 1892 presidential election Democrat Grover Cleveland beat Republican Benjamin Harrison. The chief issue of the campaign was the Republicans' support for high tariffs. **James B. Weaver**, the Populist candidate, won about 8.5 percent of the total popular vote.

✔ **Reading Check: Analyzing Information** Why did farmers and laborers form the Populist Party?

The Colored Farmers' Alliance fought for the rights of African American farmers such as this family in Virginia.

⭐ The Election of 1896

The Panic of 1893 led more people to join the Populists in calling for economic reforms. The depression had many causes, but some Americans blamed the money system. Many people sold their investments in exchange for gold, which in turn caused a shortage in U.S. gold reserves.

In 1896 the Republicans nominated William McKinley for president. McKinley was firmly against free coinage of silver. Many Democrats saw this opposition as an opportunity to win Populist and some Republican votes. At the Democratic Party's national convention, their nominee, William Jennings Bryan, swept the crowd with an emotional speech. He said, "You shall not press down upon the brow of labor this crown of thorns. You shall not crucify mankind upon this cross of gold!"

The Democrats had put the Populists in a difficult position by adopting their strongest issue. The Populists had to decide between running their own candidate and thus splitting the silver vote, or supporting Bryan. Supporting Bryan might put them in danger of being absorbed by the Democrats. The Populists decided to nominate Bryan, but they chose their own vice president.

The Democrats won the South and the West. However, the Republicans won the election. The heavily populated Midwest and Northeast provided strong Republican support. The party's well-financed campaign had convinced many workers that free coinage would cause unemployment to rise. This election marked the end of the Populist Party, and organized political action by farmers declined.

Interpreting Political Cartoons

"Cross of Gold" Judge *magazine published this cartoon on its cover after William Jennings Bryan gave his famous "Cross of Gold" speech.* **Do you think the cartoon is intended to support or make fun of Bryan's speech? Explain your answer.**

✔ **Reading Check: Finding the Main Idea** Why did McKinley's victory in 1896 mark the end of the Populist Party?

Section 4 Review

go.hrw.com **Homework Practice Online**
keyword: SF3 HP22

① **Define** and explain:
- free coinage
- gold standard

② **Identify** and explain:
- Oliver Hudson Kelley
- National Grange
- Interstate Commerce Act
- Interstate Commerce Commission
- William Jennings Bryan
- Benjamin Harrison
- Sherman Silver Purchase Act
- Farmers' Alliances
- Populist Party
- James B. Weaver

③ **Identifying Cause and Effect** Copy the graphic organizer below. Use it to identify in order the problems that farmers faced as a result of industrialization, how they responded, and the eventual outcome of their actions.

④ **Finding the Main Idea**
a. What problems did farmers face during the late 1800s?
b. Why did many farmers support the free coinage of silver?

⑤ **Writing and Critical Thinking**
Evaluating Imagine that you are a member of the Populist Party. Write a journal entry explaining the goals of the Populist Party and why it did not win the 1896 presidential election.

Consider the following:
- the depression of 1893
- Democratic adoption of free-coinage issue
- well-funded Republican campaign

Chapter 22 Review

The Chapter at a Glance

Examine the visual summary of the chapter below. Create a five-question, fill-in-the-blank quiz covering the chapter's main ideas that you might give to a classmate.

Inventions and Big Business

- Bessemer process
- Lightbulb
- Telephone
- Automobile
- Airplane
- Growth of corporations
- Rise of stock markets
- Carnegie and Rockefeller
- Sherman Antitrust Act

Immigration

- New immigrants from eastern and southern Europe
- Nativism
- Benevolent societies
- Chinese Exclusion Act

Labor Movement

- Knights of Labor
- American Federation of Labor
- Haymarket Riot
- Homestead strike
- Pullman strike

Populism

- National Grange
- Free coinage of silver
- Farmers' Alliances
- Populist Party

Identifying People and Ideas

Use the following terms or people in historically significant sentences.

1. Bessemer process
2. Thomas Alva Edison
3. free enterprise
4. Andrew Carnegie
5. Terence V. Powderly
6. Pullman strike
7. benevolent societies
8. suburbs
9. Jane Addams
10. gold standard

Understanding Main Ideas

Section 1 *(Pages 680–686)*

1. Explain the methods of vertical and horizontal integration used by business leaders to organize their corporations.
2. Why did some people oppose trusts, and what actions did they take?

Section 2 *(Pages 687–691)*

3. How did the Second Industrial Revolution affect workers?
4. What was the overall outcome of the major labor strikes in the late 1800s?

Section 3 *(Pages 692–697)*

5. Where did immigrants to the United States in the late 1800s come from, and why did they come?

Section 4 *(Pages 698–703)*

6. What problems did farmers face in the late 1800s, and how did they respond?

You Be the Historian— Reviewing Themes

1. **Science, Technology & Society** How did technological breakthroughs help bring about the Second Industrial Revolution?
2. **Government** What actions did government take to assist and control big business?
3. **Citizenship** Why was the Populist Party formed?

Thinking Critically

1. **Analyzing Information** Why do you think old immigrants were able to become a part of American society more quickly than new immigrants?
2. **Comparing and Contrasting** How was the Knights of Labor different from and similar to the American Federation of Labor?
3. **Evaluating** Although the Populist Party lost the presidential election of 1892, several reforms listed in the party's platform were later put into effect. Which reform do you think was the most important? Explain your answer.

Interpreting Charts

Study the charts below. Then use the information on the charts to answer the questions that follow.

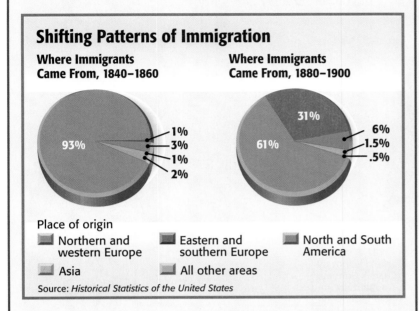

Shifting Patterns of Immigration

Where Immigrants Came From, 1840–1860

93%
1%
3%
1%
2%

Where Immigrants Came From, 1880–1900

31%
61%
6%
1.5%
.5%

Place of origin
- Northern and western Europe
- Eastern and southern Europe
- North and South America
- Asia
- All other areas

Source: *Historical Statistics of the United States*

1. What regions had the smallest percentage of immigrants to the United States from 1840 to 1860?
   a. North and South America
   b. Asia and eastern and southern Europe
   c. northern and western Europe
   d. Asia and Africa

2. What regions showed the greatest percentage increase in immigration to the United States between 1840 and 1860 and 1880 and 1900?

3. Based on your knowledge of the period, how do you think the changes in immigration shown on these charts affected the United States?

Analyzing Primary Sources

Read the following quotation by Mary Elizabeth Lease, who supported the Farmer' Alliances, then answer the questions that follow.

"The great common people of this country are slaves, and monopoly is the master. . . . The politicians said we suffered from overproduction. Overproduction, when 10,000 little children, so statistics tell us, starve to death every year in the United States. . . . We will stand by our homes and stay by our fireside by force if necessary, and we will not pay our debts to the loan-shark companies until the government pays its debt to us."

4. Which of the following statements best describes Lease's point of view?
   a. The government owes farmers money and should pay them back immediately.
   b. Farmers would be more powerful if they united and formed a monopoly.
   c. The fact that American children starve to death proves that American farmers are not producing too much food.
   d. The loan sharks are treating farmers unfairly and driving them out of business.

5. Based on what you know about farming in the late 1800s, how might Lease suggest that farmers try to improve their situation?

Alternative Assessment

Building Your Portfolio

American History

Linking to Community

Many immigrant communities established during the 1800s still thrive in U.S. cities today. Use the library and local historical societies to research an immigrant community today. Create a tourist brochure to attract visitors to that community. Your brochure should include some historical information about the community as well as descriptions and images of current attractions.

🖅 **internet** connect

Internet Activity: go.hrw.com
keyword: SF3 CF22

Choose a topic on the Industrial and Urban Nation to:
- Write a report on the effect of technology on daily life.
- Research the lives of steelworkers.
- Write a biography of Mother Jones and her work in the organized labor movement.

23

The Spirit of Reform
(1868–1920)

This "Tammany Bank" reflects the political corruption of the 1870s. Place a coin in the politician's hand, and he puts it in his pocket.

Corrupt officials are shown weighing down President Grant's administration.

UNITED STATES

1868 Ulysses S. Grant is elected president.

1872 The Crédit Mobilier scandal reveals corruption in Grant's administration.

1873 The first public kindergarten in the United States opens in St. Louis, Missouri.

1881 President Garfield is shot by Charles Guiteau, a mentally unstable federal-job seeker, and later dies from the wounds.

1865	1870	1875	1880	1885	1890

1871 The British Parliament makes labor unions legal.

1873 Slave markets and the exporting of slaves are abolished on the African island of Zanzibar.

1888 Brazil officially outlaws slavery.

1894 Alfred Dreyfus is arrested on questionable treason charges, leading to political upheaval in France.

WORLD

French army captain Alfred Dreyfus had his sword broken as part of a ceremony intended to humiliate him.

Build on What You Know

After the Civil War ended, increased immigration caused American cities to grow. As cities grew, however, new problems arose. Reformers swung into action in areas such as city government, politics, public schools, and the workplace. African Americans, American Indians, immigrants, and women also called for reforms.

Theodore Roosevelt hit the campaign trail for the Progressive Party in 1912.

Booker T. Washington established the Tuskegee Institute in Alabama.

1895 Booker T. Washington gives his Atlanta Compromise speech, which calls for economic independence for African Americans.

1901 President William McKinley is killed and Vice President Theodore Roosevelt becomes president.

1905 The Industrial Workers of the World labor union is founded.

1911 The Triangle Shirtwaist Fire leads to calls for building-safety reforms.

1912 Theodore Roosevelt runs for president as the candidate of the Progressive Party but loses to Democrat Woodrow Wilson.

1916 Montana representative Jeannette Rankin is the first woman elected to Congress.

1920 The Nineteenth Amendment, which gives women the vote, is ratified.

1895   1900   1905   1910   1915   1920

1901 The first Nobel Prizes are awarded.

1903 Emmeline Pankhurst forms the Women's Social and Political Union to fight for women's suffrage in Great Britain.

1912 The British luxury liner *Titanic* sinks after hitting an iceberg during its first voyage.

1913 Norway gives women the right to vote.

1917 Mexico adopts a new constitution.

The Nobel Prize bears the image of Swedish inventor Alfred Nobel, who created a fund for the awards.

If you were there . . .
Which reform would you support?

You Be the Historian

Themes Journal

What's Your Opinion? Do you **agree** or **disagree** with the following statements? Support your point of view in your journal.

- **Citizenship** Citizens should accept the government they have.

- **Constitutional Heritage** The rights of workers can only be determined by the Supreme Court.

- **Economics** The government should not regulate the economy.

707

The Gilded Age

Read to Discover

1. In what ways did bosses control city politics?
2. How did scandals affect national politics during the Gilded Age?
3. How did the appointment of federal officials change during the late 1800s?

WHY IT MATTERS TODAY

Politicians today still try to solve problems by passing new laws. Use CNN fyi.com or other **current events** sources to learn about a problem that the U.S. government is trying to solve today. Record your findings in your journal.

Define
- political machines
- bosses
- mugwumps

Identify
- William Marcy Tweed
- Rutherford B. Hayes
- James A. Garfield
- Chester A. Arthur
- Grover Cleveland
- Benjamin Harrison
- William McKinley
- Pendleton Civil Service Act

In the best-selling novel The Gilded Age, *Mark Twain argued that the United States lived by the motto "Get rich; dishonestly if we can, honestly if we must."*

The Story Continues

In 1873 Mark Twain and Charles Dudley Warner published the best-selling novel *The Gilded Age*. Twain believed that American society looked golden from a distance but was merely gilded, or coated with cheap gold paint. According to Twain, despite its positive outward appearance, society was ugly and corrupt on the inside.

★ Corruption in Politics

Politics at all levels experienced corruption during the Gilded Age. Powerful organizations called **political machines** influenced city and county politics. These groups used both legal and illegal means to get candidates elected to public office. For example, members of a political machine often printed election ballots listing only candidates from their party. They sometimes paid people for votes. If bribing voters did not work, the political machines might hire the people who counted the votes. Through such actions, a political party could control local government. During the late 1800s, Tammany Hall, the Democratic political machine in New York City, became widely known throughout the country for its power and corruption.

Political machines were run by powerful leaders known as **bosses**. The boss traded favors for votes. For example, a boss might need a certain number of votes to elect a candidate to office. In exchange for the votes he received, the boss might offer city jobs, order neighborhood improvements, or allow an illegal business to continue to operate.

The bosses drew much of their support from immigrants, who relied on them for jobs and social mobility. After winning city elections in 1888, Tammany Hall members rewarded supporters with some 12,000 jobs. Many jobs went to Irish immigrants. Some politicians saw nothing wrong with machines that exchanged money and jobs for working-class votes. However, once in power, bosses might use their control of the government to get rich. For example, Tammany Hall boss **William Marcy Tweed** may have stolen as much as $200 million from the city treasury. He was later convicted, however, and died in jail.

Corruption was also common in the federal government at this time. Many people saw the administration of Republican Ulysses S. Grant—who was elected president in 1868 and re-elected in 1872—as corrupt. During Grant's second term, for example, several government revenue officials were jailed for their part in the "Whiskey Ring." These officials took bribes from whiskey distillers who wanted to avoid paying taxes.

In 1872 the *New York Sun* printed a story about corruption in the U.S. Congress. The owners of the Union Pacific Railroad had started a construction company called Crédit Mobilier of America. The owners gave or sold shares in Crédit Mobilier to members of Congress. In return, these congressmembers approved large federal land grants to Crédit Mobilier. Scandals like these led many Americans to question the honesty of national leaders.

✔ **Reading Check: Comparing** How was political corruption at the city level like corruption at the federal level of government during the Gilded Age?

Interpreting Political Cartoons

The Tweed Ring *Cartoonist Thomas Nast portrayed the political and business associates of Boss Tweed as crooks trying to blame each other for gaining money in questionable ways.* **Why do you think Nast chose to show the Tammany Hall politicians standing in a circle?**

Republican reformers, known as mugwumps, supported Democratic presidential candidate Grover Cleveland instead of Republican James Blaine in the 1884 election.

Analyzing Primary Sources

Drawing Inferences and Conclusions What did the crowds supporting Cleveland think would happen if he were elected?

⭐ Gilded Age Presidents

During the 1876 presidential campaign, Democrats called for government reform. Their candidate, Samuel J. Tilden, promised to run an honest administration. The Republicans chose **Rutherford B. Hayes**, a Civil War hero they believed to be honest. Hayes promised to reform the civil service. In the disputed election that followed, a special electoral commission chose Hayes over Tilden by one vote.

Republicans won another close presidential race in 1880 when **James A. Garfield** and his vice president, **Chester A. Arthur**, were elected. On July 2, 1881, Charles Guiteau, an angry and mentally unstable federal-job seeker, confronted President Garfield at a Washington railroad station. He shouted, "Arthur [is] President now," and shot Garfield twice. The president died from his wounds in September, and Arthur became president.

In the 1884 election, Republicans chose James G. Blaine instead of another reform candidate. Many Republican reformers linked Blaine with corruption and did not want to back him. These Republican reformers came to be known as **mugwumps** (the Algonquian word for "big chiefs"). The dissatisfied mugwumps left the Republican Party and supported Democratic nominee **Grover Cleveland**. Unlike Blaine, Cleveland was known for his honesty. In a presidential race full of personal attacks, American voters chose Cleveland over Blaine. As president, Cleveland hired and fired government workers based on their merit, not on their party ties.

Four years later Cleveland again won the popular vote. This time, however, he lost the electoral vote to Republican **Benjamin Harrison**. Harrison supported passage of the Sherman Antitrust Act, which regulated monopolies. In addition, Harrison's support helped in the passage of a pension act and passage of the McKinley Tariff. However, Cleveland remained popular, and in 1892 crowds sang their support for him.

 Primary Sources "Grover, Grover, four more years of Grover— Out they go and in we come and we'll be in the clover."

—Grover Cleveland supporters, quoted in *The Gilded Age*, by Mark Wahlgren Summers

Cleveland won the presidential election of 1892, but the country's economy entered a depression. Cleveland angered many fellow Democrats by opposing free coinage of silver and supporting a gold standard. In 1896 the Democrats chose William Jennings Bryan to run for president. He lost the election to Republican **William McKinley**. Practical and friendly, McKinley worked well with Congress and was re-elected in 1900.

✔ **Reading Check: Sequencing** List the winners of presidential elections between 1876 and 1900 in the order that the elections took place.

★ Civil Service Reform

Reacting to the corruption of the Gilded Age, many Americans called for changes in the civil service, or government jobs. Both major parties took advantage of the so-called spoils system when in power. Under the spoils system, government jobs were given to loyal party supporters, even if they were not qualified. Every time a new party took power, it fired many government employees to replace them with party members. Henry Adams, author and grandson of former president John Quincy Adams, remarked on this custom in 1870. "All my friends have been or are on the point of being driven out of the government."

A fellow official congratulates Senator George Pendleton on his plan for civil service reform.

Reformers wanted those seeking government jobs to take examinations. It was believed that such a system would reward merit rather than political connections. Reformers believed that an examination system would help prevent people who were unfit or corrupt from getting government jobs. Some Americans also believed that the spoils system was to blame for President Garfield's assassination. The *Nation*, a weekly newspaper, noted that "the crime seems to have acted on public opinion . . . like a spark on a powder-magazine [gunpowder storage]."

After Garfield was killed, President Chester A. Arthur addressed problems caused by the spoils system by supporting the **Pendleton Civil Service Act**. This law, passed in 1883, set up a merit system controlled by the Civil Service Commission. At first, the act affected only about 14,000 of 130,000 federal jobs. The act has since been expanded so that more than 90 percent of government jobs are covered by the Civil Service Commission.

✔ **Reading Check: Finding the Main Idea** How did the Pendleton Civil Service Act reform government?

Section 1 Review

go.hrw.com **Homework Practice Online**
keyword: SF3 HP23

① **Define** and explain:
- political machines
- bosses
- mugwumps

② **Identify** and explain:
- William Marcy Tweed
- Rutherford B. Hayes
- James A. Garfield
- Chester A. Arthur
- Grover Cleveland
- Benjamin Harrison
- William McKinley
- Pendleton Civil Service Act

③ **Categorizing** Copy the graphic organizer below. Use it to identify the impact of government corruption at the local and federal levels during the Gilded Age, and the results of this corruption.

Gilded Age Corruption

Federal level:

Local level:

Results:

④ **Finding the Main Idea**
a. How did bosses and political machines control city governments?

b. What led to civil service reform, and how did the reform affect the appointment of federal officials?

⑤ **Writing and Critical Thinking**
Supporting a Point of View Imagine that you are a political adviser to President Arthur in 1883. Prepare a memorandum urging the president either to sign or veto the recently passed Pendleton Civil Service Act.

Consider the following:
- examples of political corruption in the Gilded Age
- the assassination of President Garfield
- the terms of the Pendleton Civil Service Act

The Progressive Movement

Read to Discover

1. What roles did middle-class reformers and muckrakers play in the progressive movement?
2. How did progressives change government?
3. How did progressives address the country's social problems?

WHY IT MATTERS TODAY

Reformers still seek to change the world today. Use CNNfyi.com or other **current events** sources to find out about one reform campaign going on in the United States. Record your findings in your journal.

Define

- progressives
- muckrakers
- direct primary
- recall
- initiative
- referendum

Identify

- Ida Tarbell
- Seventeenth Amendment
- Robert M. La Follette
- Wisconsin Idea
- John Dewey
- Joseph McCormack

Hull House, a settlement house in Chicago, gained a national reputation for its social work.

The Story Continues

One cold snowy morning in late December 1891, Florence Kelley and her three children arrived on the front steps of Hull House in Chicago. When she knocked on the door, Jane Addams answered. "We were welcomed as though we had been invited," Kelley later wrote. At Hull House, Kelley not only found refuge but also joined the growing movement for reform. She went on to become one of the country's leading social reformers.

⭐ The Progressive Movement

In the late 1800s reformers, who became known as **progressives**, began working to solve problems caused by rapid industrial and urban growth. Many progressives fought crime, disease, and poverty by trying to change the conditions that caused these problems. A large number of progressives were part of the growing middle class, which included professionals and small-business owners. These people were educated and often had the free time and training needed to start reform movements. Some working-class and wealthy Americans also worked for reforms.

Progressives did not always agree on which social problems were the most important. Even when they did agree, they might disagree on how to solve these problems. As a result, progressives worked for reforms in several areas. Some wanted health and education programs in poor neighborhoods as well as government reforms, while others fought for better working conditions. Many progressives did agree, however, that to reach these goals the federal government needed to step in. These progressives wanted the government and the public to solve social problems together.

Journalists moved progressives to action by writing about corruption in business and politics. Many journalists hoped their articles would lead to greater public awareness of problems. Eventually, reforms might follow. These journalists were soon nicknamed **muckrakers** because they "raked up" and exposed the muck, or filth, of society. Some muckrakers became well known for articles about the unfair business practices that accompanied the rise of corporations. <u>Ida Tarbell</u> wrote articles attacking John D. Rockefeller's Standard Oil Company.

 History Makers Speak 66**Very often people who admit the facts, who are willing to see that Mr. Rockefeller has employed force and fraud to secure his ends, justify him by declaring, 'It's business'. That is, 'it's business' has come to be a legitimate [acceptable] excuse for hard dealing, sly tricks, [and] special privileges.**99

—Ida Tarbell, *The History of the Standard Oil Company*

Muckrakers also wrote about child labor, racial discrimination, and slum housing. Their articles angered many politicians and business leaders, but they helped unite progressives. Muckrakers influenced voters to question corrupt practices, and politicians to call for reforms.

 Reading Check: Comparing and Contrasting How were progressives and muckrakers alike, and how were they different?

⭐ Expanding Democracy

Worries about political corruption caused some progressives to work to change state and local governments and reduce the power of political machines. In many places, reformers replaced multiple ballots that political parties distributed with government-prepared ballots listing all candidates. Under pressure from reformers, many states adopted secret ballots that gave every voter a private vote.

Reformers also tried to give voters more power. For example, they fought for the **direct primary**. The direct primary let voters choose candidates for public office instead of allowing party leaders to select them. Progressives also favored the <u>Seventeenth Amendment</u>. Passed in 1913, the amendment allowed Americans to vote directly for U.S. senators. In the past, senators had been selected by state legislatures.

Analyzing Primary Sources
Identifying Points of View
What is Tarbell's opinion of Rockefeller's defenders?

Ida Tarbell wrote many muck-raking articles for McClure's *Magazine.*

Other reform measures allowed voters to call for action on political issues. Some states and cities created a procedure known as the **recall**. This process allows voters to sign a petition asking for a special vote. The purpose is to recall, or remove, an elected official before the end of his or her term. If enough voters sign the petition, the vote takes place. If the majority votes to recall the official, then he or she is removed from office.

Progressives also pushed for reforms to give voters a direct voice in new legislation. The **initiative** allows voters to propose a new law by getting signatures on a petition. If enough people sign the petition, the proposed law is voted on at the next election. The **referendum** allows voters to approve or disapprove a law that has already been proposed or passed by state or local governments. This procedure gives voters a chance to overrule laws with which they disagree.

✔ **Reading Check: Summarizing** What types of reforms did progressives favor to change the ways that people took part in the political process?

★ Reforming City and State Governments

In addition to increasing political participation, progressives worked to change the structure of local government. Businesspeople and professionals wanted to make government more efficient and responsive to citizens' needs. Some reformers wanted city government to be run more like a business. Several cities changed to a council-manager system where voters elect a city council, which then chooses a professional manager to run the city. Progressives also started the commission form of government. Under this system, a group of elected leaders run city government. Each official runs a major city agency, such as housing, sanitation, or transportation. These new forms of government were most popular in small to medium-sized cities.

State governments faced some of the same problems as cities. City bosses and other corrupt urban officials were often part of a statewide political machine. Progressive Republican **Robert M. La Follette** took on the power of the party bosses in Wisconsin. La Follette favored the direct primary, tax reform, and new state commissions that relied on professionals to manage social problems.

La Follette failed to win his party's nomination for governor in 1896 and in 1898. He finally won the governor's race in 1900. As governor, La Follette developed the **Wisconsin Idea**, a program of reforms. The program set out to reduce the influence of political machines and to make state government more efficient in meeting the people's needs. This idea became a model for progressive reformers in other states.

✔ **Reading Check: Analyzing Information** What reforms did progressives back to reduce the power of political machines and make governments more responsive to the needs of the people?

Progressive leader Robert M. La Follette served as governor of Wisconsin from 1900 to 1906 and as U.S. senator from 1906 to 1925.

★ City Planning

Many native-born Americans and immigrants moved to U.S. cities looking for work. As cities grew, many people crowded into tenements, or poorly built, overcrowded apartments. The tenement owners often failed to make needed repairs to improve living conditions. As a result, thousands of poor families lived in dirty and dangerous buildings. Progressive Lawrence Veiller described the way tenement living hurt children and society.

 History Makers Speak ❝A child living its early years in dark rooms, without sunlight or fresh air, does not grow up to be a normal, healthy person. . . . It is not of such material that strong nations are made.❞

—Lawrence Veiller, quoted in *Readings in American History,* edited by Robert C. Cotner et al.

Analyzing Primary sources
Identifying Points of View According to Veiller, what happens to children who grow up in poor living conditions?

Progressives called on state and local governments to address these problems. Veiller helped get the New York State Tenement House Act passed in 1901. This act made it illegal to build poorly lit and airless tenements. The law also required new buildings to have better ventilation, running water, and toilets. New York's law became a model for housing reform in other states. Many progressives also started settlement houses like Jane Addams's Hull House in Chicago. These organizations worked to improve education, housing, and sanitation in immigrant and poor communities.

Urban reforms led to new professions such as city planning and civil engineering. City planners worked with local officials to control city growth. They passed zoning laws, created building-safety codes, and developed public parks. Civil engineers planned street-paving and bridge-building projects. Sanitation engineers tried to solve the problems of water supply, waste disposal, and pollution. Where these problems were attacked, death rates dropped dramatically. Many of these improvements gave urban Americans some of the best public services in the world.

✔ **Reading Check: Identifying Cause and Effect** What led to the rise of new professions such as city planning and civil engineering, and how did they change life in urban America?

Causes and Effects of the Progressive Movement

Long-Term Causes
Urbanization
Growth of the middle class
Industrial working conditions

Immediate Causes
Scandals about political corruption
Rise of powerful corporations
Changes in immigration

Progressive Movement

Effects
Expanded democracy
Antitrust legislation
Business reforms
Social reforms
Urban reforms

★ ★ ★ ★ ★ ★ ★ ★ ★ ★ ★ ★
That's Interesting!
★ ★ ★ ★ ★ ★ ★ ★ ★ ★ ★ ★

Learning to Play Did you know that the progressive movement led to some of the first playgrounds in the United States? It's true! In the early 1900s some progressives noticed that many urban children played in parking lots and other vacant areas. As a result, they formed the Playground Association of America (PAA) in 1906. The PAA built playgrounds with safe equipment in U.S. cities. The group even published a magazine called *Playground*. The PAA later merged with other playground groups to form the National Recreation and Park Association (NRPA). The NRPA continues to support park and recreation efforts today.

★ Social Reforms

Progressives also worked to improve education. School enrollment increased greatly in the late 1800s as states passed laws requiring children to attend school. Reformers pushed for new public high schools with courses in citizenship, health, and job training. Many progressives also opened kindergartens to teach basic social skills to poor children between the ages of three and seven. In 1873 reformer Susan Blow opened the first American public kindergarten in St. Louis, Missouri. By 1898, more than 4,000 kindergartens had opened in the United States. **John Dewey** was an important philosopher and educator who changed American education. His goal was to help children learn critical-thinking skills to aid them in everyday life. Dewey wanted children to learn problem-solving skills, not just to memorize their lessons. His teaching methods became the model for progressive education across the country.

Progressives also tried to improve the education of medical professionals. In the late 1800s the United States had few well-trained and professionally organized doctors. Researchers knew the causes of diseases such as malaria, pneumonia, tuberculosis, and yellow fever. However, there were few medical organizations to help spread this knowledge. Under the leadership of **Joseph McCormack**, the American Medical Association (AMA) was reorganized in 1901. The AMA brought local medical organizations together and supported laws protecting public health. The group's work showed how progressives could unite professionals to help improve society.

✔ **Reading Check: Summarizing** What educational reforms did progressives favor?

Section 2 Review

go.hrw.com **Homework Practice Online**
keyword: SF3 HP23

① **Define** and explain:
• progressives
• muckrakers
• direct primary
• recall
• initiative
• referendum

② **Identify** and explain:
• Ida Tarbell
• Seventeenth Amendment
• Robert M. La Follette
• Wisconsin Idea
• John Dewey
• Joseph McCormack

③ **Categorizing** Copy the diagram below. Use it to identify ways that progressives supported each type of reform.

The Progressive Movement

Government:

Education:

Urban Health:

④ **Finding the Main Idea**
a. What contributions did middle-class reformers and muckrakers make to the progressive movement?

b. What caused progressives to fight corruption in local and state governments, and what effects did their efforts have?

⑤ **Writing and Critical Thinking**
Analyzing Information Imagine that you are a muckraker for *McClure's Magazine*. Write a short article explaining how progressives have addressed social and political problems in U.S. cities in the early 1900s.

Consider the following:
• urban problems
• the work of other muckrakers
• new professions related to urban planning

Reforming the Workplace

Read to Discover
1. What laws did progressives want to pass to protect workers?
2. How did the courts react to labor legislation?
3. How did labor organize to help improve working conditions?

WHY IT MATTERS TODAY

Women still seek full equality around the world today. Use CNNfyi.com or other **current events** sources to find out about a situation or country in which women face inequality. Record your findings in your journal.

Define
- socialism

Identify
- Florence Kelley
- Triangle Shirtwaist Fire
- Industrial Workers of the World
- William "Big Bill" Haywood

The Story Continues

Sadie Frowne was 15 years old. She worked in a garment factory in Brooklyn, New York. Every day at 7:00 A.M. she sat down at her machine. "The machines go like mad all day, because the faster you work the more money you get," she explained. "Sometimes in my haste I get my finger caught and the needle goes right through it." One of the progressives' main goals was to establish better working conditions for people like Sadie.

Many children, such as these young textile workers, labored in potentially dangerous jobs.

★ Child Labor Reform

Low wages for unskilled workers in the late 1800s meant that a growing number of children had to work to help support their families. Boys and some girls sold newspapers or shined shoes on the streets. Girls often cooked and cleaned for boarders staying with their families. Some girls worked at home, sewing garments with their mothers.

In addition, more than 1.75 million children, age 15 and under, worked in mines, mills, and factories by 1900. One wealthy reformer, Marie Van Vorst, posed as a poor woman so that she could investigate child labor conditions. She saw children as young as five years old working in a South Carolina textile mill.

Daily Life

Child factory workers In the early 1900s, many children labored in textile factories. Among their tasks was the responsibility of watching the bobbins, or cylinders that held thread. When the thread broke, children had to quickly tie the two ends together. Other children replaced bobbins that were full of thread with empty ones. Such jobs forced children to stand all day and risk injury by climbing on equipment. One little girl earned 4 cents for every 36 buttons she sewed. Many of the children who worked in factories did not go to school. One reformer noted that children who did attend school often fell asleep in class because they had been up late working. **How does the image show the difficult working conditions that these children faced?**

As more progressives learned about child labor, they began to take action. **Florence Kelley**, who had raised her three children at Chicago's Hull House, led the progressive fight against child labor. Kelley's plan was to "investigate, educate, legislate, and enforce." She was also a board member of the National Consumers' League, a group that spoke out on labor issues involving women and children. Kelley started about 60 local consumer leagues throughout the United States. The National Child Labor Committee worked for laws against child labor in many states. Congress passed federal child labor laws in 1916 and 1919. The Supreme Court, however, ruled that they were unconstitutional. A later attempt to pass a constitutional amendment limiting child labor failed.

✔ **Reading Check: Finding the Main Idea** How did reformers try to improve child labor conditions?

⭐ Safety in the Workplace

Child labor reform was only part of the progressive effort to help workers. Many progressives worked with labor unions to fight for the eight-hour workday. The National Consumers' League favored legislation for higher wages and fewer working hours. As a result, many states passed minimum-wage laws and maximum-hour laws for women.

Tragic accidents in the workplace led reformers to call for laws protecting workers from dangerous conditions. In 1900 some 35,000 people were killed by industrial accidents. About 500,000 others were hurt. One shocking incident took place in 1911 at the Triangle Shirtwaist Company in New York City. As some 500 workers, most of whom were immigrant women, prepared to leave the clothing factory, a fire broke out. They tried to escape through exit doors of the 10-story building but found the doors locked. By the time firefighters brought the **Triangle Shirtwaist Fire** under control, 146 workers had died. At a memorial service for the fire victims, union leader Rose Schneiderman called for action.

History Makers Speak

❝This is not the first time girls have been burned alive in the city. Each week I must learn of the untimely death of one of my sister workers. . . . The life of men and women is so cheap and property is so sacred. . . . It is up to the working people to save themselves.❞

—Rose Schneiderman, *All for One*

Analyzing Primary Sources

Identifying Points of View
Why does Schneiderman say that life had become so cheap?

Incidents such as the Triangle Shirtwaist Fire led to laws that improved factory safety standards and working conditions.

Labor leaders and progressives also fought for laws to pay workers injured on the job. In 1902, Maryland became the first state to adopt a workers' compensation law. But because workplace laws were not strictly enforced, working conditions remained poor in many places.

✔ **Reading Check: Summarizing** What types of laws did progressives and labor leaders support in order to improve working conditions?

★ The Courts and the Workplace

Some business leaders opposed workforce regulations, arguing that the government should not interfere with the economy. State and federal courts often upheld this view and ruled against progressive reform laws. Courts ruled that the Fourteenth Amendment protected businesses against laws that would take their property without due process of law.

In 1898 the Supreme Court ruled that states could limit workers' hours in dangerous jobs. The state of New York later passed a law that limited bakers to a 10-hour workday because of the unhealthy working conditions. But a bakery owner, Joseph Lochner, challenged the law. He claimed that this law interfered with his right to run his business. The case made its way to the Supreme Court. In *Lochner* v. *New York* the Supreme Court ruled that states could not restrict the rights of employers and workers to sign any type of labor agreement that they wished. The Court ruled that the New York law was unconstitutional. According to the Court, workers should be free to accept any conditions of employment that business owners required—even if that meant working 14 to 16 hours a day.

The Supreme Court did uphold some laws limiting the working hours of women and children. In *Muller* v. *Oregon* (1908) the Court upheld laws limiting women's working hours. According to the Court, the differences between women and men made the health and safety of women a matter of public interest. The Court then ruled that these differences meant laws regulating working conditions for women were constitutional. For the progressives, this was a key decision. It was the first case successfully argued from social evidence rather than precedent, or prior legal principle. Progressives continued to work to extend legal protections in the workplace to men.

✔ **Reading Check: Analyzing Information** How did the Supreme Court address labor laws in the late 1800s and early 1900s?

GLOBAL CONNECTIONS

Worker Reforms

Like American laborers, European workers also formed unions. The labor movement was strongest in Great Britain, where there were about 4 million union members in 1913. As their standard of living dropped during the early 1900s, British workers staged several protests. Transportation strikes paralyzed the country in 1911.

In the early 1900s, British workers won retirement pensions and miners gained an eight-hour workday. In 1911 Parliament passed the British National Insurance Act, which gave some workers unemployment insurance. **What gains did British workers make?**

This pamphlet contained labor songs for members of the Industrial Workers of the World.

⭐ Labor Organizations

Unions fought for better working conditions and higher pay by bargaining with employers. Union membership rose from more than 800,000 in 1900 to about 5 million in 1920. Because most unions discouraged women from joining, some female workers formed their own unions. Reformers started the national Women's Trade Union League in 1903.

The American Federation of Labor (AFL) remained one of the most powerful labor unions, organizing workers in skilled trades. The goals of the AFL were better working conditions, higher pay, and union recognition. AFL president Samuel Gompers and others like him favored the economic system called capitalism. In this system, privately owned businesses run most industries, and competition determines prices and wages.

More radical unions claimed that capitalism itself was unfair. They supported **socialism**—an economic system in which the government owns and operates a country's means of production. Socialists hoped that the government would be more responsive to workers' needs. Some socialists and union leaders started the **Industrial Workers of the World** (IWW) in 1905. The IWW brought together many workers who were not welcome in the AFL. The union took in African Americans, immigrants, migrant workers, unskilled laborers, and women.

Led by **William "Big Bill" Haywood**, the IWW's goal was to organize all workers into one large union that eventually would try to overthrow capitalism. The IWW organized strikes across the country, but business leaders and many other Americans were alarmed by the IWW. Arrests of union leaders, government investigations, and political opposition weakened the IWW, and by 1920 the union had almost disappeared.

✔ **Reading Check: Comparing and Contrasting** How were the goals of the AFL and the IWW similar, and how were they different?

Section 3 Review

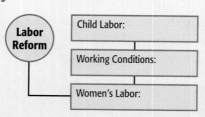

go.hrw.com **Homework Practice Online**
keyword: SF3 HP23

1 **Define** and explain:
• socialism

2 **Identify** and explain:
• Florence Kelley
• Triangle Shirtwaist Fire
• Industrial Workers of the World
• William "Big Bill" Haywood

3 **Analyzing Information** Copy the diagram below. Use it to identify how progressives tried to reform child labor, working conditions, and women's labor.

Labor Reform
Child Labor:
Working Conditions:
Women's Labor:

4 **Finding the Main Idea**
a. What working conditions led unions and progressives to call for laws to protect laborers?
b. What were the major goals of most unions?

5 **Writing and Critical Thinking**
Summarizing Imagine that you are a news reporter covering the Supreme Court in the early 1900s. Write a feature article about cases in which the Court has made rulings about laws involving workers' hours.

Consider the following:
• working conditions for women and children
• the case of *Lochner* v. *New York*
• the case of *Muller* v. *Oregon*

The Rights of Women and Minorities

Read to Discover

1. Why did many women participate in the progressive movement, and what were their goals?
2. How did African American leaders try to improve conditions for African Americans?
3. What groups did not benefit from the progressive movement?

WHY IT MATTERS TODAY

Women are much more active in political life than they were before gaining the right to vote. Use **CNNfyi**.com or other **current events** sources to find out about the number of women who voted in recent elections and the number elected to office. Record your findings in your journal.

Identify

- Woman's Christian Temperance Union
- Frances Willard
- Eighteenth Amendment
- National American Woman Suffrage Association
- Carrie Chapman Catt
- Alice Paul
- National Woman's Party
- Nineteenth Amendment
- Booker T. Washington
- Atlanta Compromise
- Ida B. Wells
- W. E. B. Du Bois
- National Association for the Advancement of Colored People

The Story Continues

During the summer of 1910, a campaign tour for women's right to vote stopped in Warren, Illinois. Tour participants told the local crowd that greeted them that their state representative had opposed the woman suffrage bill. The crowd brought the representative forward. They demanded to know if he would support the bill the next time. "It looks as if I would have to," he responded. To the delight of the crowd, he shouted, "I can't fight against a woman's campaign. I'm for you."

This women's suffrage supporter marched in front of the White House.

⭐ Progressive Women

New educational opportunities drew more women into the progressive movement. In the late 1800s, women began attending colleges like Smith, Vassar, and Wellesley in record numbers. Their goal was "to develop as fully as may be the powers of womanhood," said Sophia Smith, founder of Smith College. New state universities also began to admit women. Educators like Professor Edward Clarke of Harvard Medical School opposed the admission of women, however. In 1872, Clarke argued that the physical and mental strain of too much thinking would harm a woman's health.

Despite such views, women seized the opportunities to improve their educations. In 1870 only some 20 percent of college students were women. By 1910 that number had doubled. However, many female graduates found few jobs open to them. Jane Addams explained that she could "not understand this apparent waste of herself, this elaborate [complex] preparation, if no work is provided for her." Many female graduates did enter fields such as teaching, social work, and library management. Yet they found it much harder to enter professions such as law and medicine, which were dominated by men. Denied such careers, women found that they could play active roles in reform movements. Women's clubs campaigned for dozens of causes, including child welfare, political reform, temperance, and women's suffrage.

✔ **Reading Check: Finding the Main Idea** What problem did college-trained women face after graduation?

Interpreting Political Cartoons

Carry Nation *Cartoons often showed temperance leader Carry Nation as a warrior attacking alcohol.* **How does this cartoon illustrate women's role in the temperance movement?**

⭐ The Temperance Movement

Progressive women played a vital role in the temperance movement. Since the 1840s temperance reformers had blamed alcohol for many of society's problems. By the 1870s the movement had spread to hundreds of small towns. More than 1,000 saloons were forced to shut down by these reformers. Some temperance activists followed the example of Carry Nation. In the 1890s Nation would storm into saloons with an ax, chopping bars and smashing liquor bottles and glasses.

In 1874, reformers formed the **Woman's Christian Temperance Union** (WCTU). Women from many different backgrounds united in the fight against alcohol abuse. **Frances Willard** served as president of the organization from 1879 to 1898. Under her leadership, the WCTU started 10,000 local branches that represented every state, territory, and major city in the United States. As a result of such pressure, many state and local governments passed laws restricting the sale of alcohol. Temperance efforts eventually led to the passage of the **Eighteenth Amendment** in 1919. This amendment outlawed the production and sale of alcoholic beverages in the United States.

✔ **Reading Check: Identifying Cause and Effect** Why did the WCTU fight for prohibition, and what effects did their crusade have?

Susan B. Anthony

WOMEN'S RIGHT TO THE SUFFRAGE

After women's rights activist Susan B. Anthony was arrested for voting, she defended herself before a U.S. district court in New York in 1873. The following is an excerpt from a speech she gave to her supporters.

"Friends and fellow citizens: I stand before you to-night under indictment for the alleged crime [accusation] of having voted at the last presidential election, without having a lawful right to vote. It shall be my work this evening to prove to you that in thus voting, I not only committed no crime, but, instead, simply exercised my citizen's rights, guaranteed to me and all United States citizens by the National Constitution. . . . It was we, the people, not we, the white male citizens; nor yet we, the male citizens; but we, the whole people, who formed the Union. And we formed it, not to give the blessings of liberty, but to secure them; not to the half of ourselves and the half of our posterity, but to the whole people—women as well as men."

Susan B. Anthony

Analyzing Primary Sources
1. What crime was Susan B. Anthony accused of committing?
2. Why does Anthony believe that women should have the vote?

⭐ Women's Suffrage

The WCTU also started to fight for women's suffrage, but this movement had many opponents. Some people worried about what women might do if they had the vote. Political bosses were troubled by the anticorruption efforts of women. Many businesspeople believed that women voters would support child labor laws and minimum-wage laws. Some people simply believed that women belonged in the home, not in politics.

Elizabeth Cady Stanton and Susan B. Anthony began the **National American Woman Suffrage Association** (NAWSA) in 1890 to help get the vote for women. That same year, women gained the right to vote in Wyoming. Colorado, Idaho, and Utah followed in the 1890s.

Carrie Chapman Catt had fought successfully for women's suffrage in the West. After becoming president of the NAWSA in 1900, Catt mobilized more than 1 million volunteers. She argued that female voters were needed to help bring about progressive reforms. Catt insisted that women should have a voice in creating the laws that affected them.

However, some women believed that the efforts of the NAWSA did not go far enough. In 1913 NAWSA member **Alice Paul** left the organization and founded what would become the **National Woman's Party** (NWP). The NWP used parades, public demonstrations, and more controversial methods to draw attention to its cause. The party used hunger strikes,

Suffrage marchers *These women are marching in a suffragette parade in New York City in 1912.* **How do you think the public would react to such a parade?**

pickets, and various forms of civil disobedience to build support. Paul and other NWP leaders were jailed several times for their actions.

The efforts of the NAWSA and the NWP helped lead to success. In 1919, 26 state legislatures asked Congress to pass a women's suffrage amendment. In 1920 the **Nineteenth Amendment** gave the vote to women in the United States.

✔ **Reading Check: Comparing and Contrasting** How were the NAWSA and the NWP alike, and how were they different?

⭐ African Americans Fight for Change

White progressive reformers often ignored issues such as discrimination and segregation. Some African American leaders like **Booker T. Washington** tried to improve the conditions of African Americans. Born into slavery, Washington became a respected educator while in his twenties. In 1881 he founded the Tuskegee Institute in Alabama for African Americans. He encouraged African Americans to improve their own educational and economic well-being rather than fight discrimination and segregation. Washington explained his philosophy in his **Atlanta Compromise** speech of 1895.

Analyzing Primary Sources

Drawing Inferences and Conclusions What social relationship between African Americans and whites does Washington seem to support?

History Makers Speak

❝In all things that are purely social we [whites and African Americans] can be as separate as the fingers, yet one as the hand in all things essential to mutual [shared] progress.❞

—Booker T. Washington, Atlanta Compromise speech

Other African Americans, such as journalist **Ida B. Wells**, (later Wells-Barnett) were more outspoken about discrimination. Editorials in her Memphis newspaper, *Free Speech*, drew attention to the mob lynching, or violent killing, of black men. Her work gained her many enemies. Eventually, she had to move to the North because of death threats. In 1895 she published *Red Record*, which reported lynching statistics for a three-year period. Wells-Barnett later helped start an international crusade against lynching.

<u>W. E. B. Du Bois</u> also took a direct approach to fighting racial injustice. Born in Massachusetts, Du Bois attended Fisk University. He later went on to earn a doctoral degree from Harvard. Du Bois disagreed with Washington's focus on job training and downplaying of liberal arts education. Du Bois publicized cases of racial prejudice and wrote dozens of articles and speeches.

In 1905 Du Bois and other African Americans who wanted faster change met at Niagara Falls, Canada. Calling themselves the Niagara Movement, the group called for economic and educational equality, as well as an end to segregation and discrimination. The movement's Declaration of Principles said that "to ignore, overlook, or apologize for these wrongs is to prove ourselves unworthy of freedom."

Du Bois and other reformers founded the <u>**National Association for the Advancement of Colored People**</u> (NAACP) in 1909. Among the new organization's members were many well-known progressives such as Jane Addams and John Dewey. Du Bois acted as the director of publications and research and edited the NAACP journal, *The Crisis*. Opposing Washington's views, the NAACP worked to bring racial inequality to the attention of white Americans. The organization also attacked racial discrimination through the court system. In 1915 the NAACP won the important case of *Guinn* v. *United States*, which outlawed the grandfather clause. This type of law had been widely used in the South to keep African Americans from voting. It imposed qualifications on voters, unless the voters' grandfathers had been allowed to vote.

Another important organization, the National Urban League, was formed in 1911. This organization aided many African Americans moving from the South to northern cities. It helped them find jobs and housing and get used to life in the city.

✔ **Reading Check: Comparing and Contrasting** How were the views of Washington like and unlike those of Du Bois?

⭐ The Limits of Progressive Reform

The progressive movement left behind members of other minority groups. In the 1890s the American Indian population in the United States had declined to less than 250,000, its lowest point ever. To deal with poverty among American Indians, the Society of American Indians was started in 1911. Society members wanted Indians to obey the Dawes Act and adopt the ways of white society. The Society believed this would help solve the problems of poverty and unemployment, but most of its members did not understand the views of American Indians who lived

Research on the R⊙M

Free Find:
Booker T. Washington and W. E. B. Du Bois
After reading about Booker T. Washington and W. E. B. Du Bois on the **Holt Researcher CD–ROM**, imagine that you are hosting the two leaders on a talk show. Write a short transcript of a conversation that the two leaders might have.

W. E. B. Du Bois wrote many influential essays on race relations.

Interpreting the Visual Record

Immigrant communities *As Chinese immigrants arrived in the United States, they established communities, like this one in San Francisco, to maintain their culture.* **How do you think immigrant communities changed the makeup of U.S. cities?**

on the reservations. Many of these American Indians wanted to preserve their traditional culture. They thought the breakup of reservations under the Dawes Act would bring an end to their way of life. Despite their poverty, some 2,000 Cherokee by 1912 had refused to accept lands granted to them by the government. Other Indians wanted to slow down the allotment process and allow people to stay on reservations. Eventually, new laws let Indians stay on reservations if they wanted to.

Some immigrant groups were also ignored by white progressives. Many Chinese immigrants who came to the United States to mine gold and build railroads had hard lives. Chinese immigration slowed sharply because of the Chinese Exclusion Act of 1882, which prohibited Chinese people from immigrating to the United States for 10 years. Congress later extended the ban, attempting to make immigration from China permanently illegal. Chinese immigrants also faced violence as well as discrimination. Anti-Chinese riots took place in several western states and territories during the late 1800s. As a result, many Chinese Americans formed their own communities in cities such as San Francisco.

While Chinese immigration dropped, Mexican immigration rose between 1901 and 1930. During this time, immigrants could move fairly easily across the U.S. borders with Mexico and Canada. Most Mexican immigrants moved to areas that had once been part of Mexico. Immigrants then invited their family and friends to move to the United States. Although Mexican immigrants were a key part of the Southwest economy, they faced discrimination and harsh labor conditions.

✔ **Reading Check: Summarizing** What groups received few benefits from the efforts of progressive reformers?

Section 4 Review

go. hrw .com **Homework Practice Online** keyword: SF3 HP23

1 **Identify** and explain:
• Woman's Christian Temperance Union
• Frances Willard
• Eighteenth Amendment
• National American Woman Suffrage Association
• Carrie Chapman Catt
• Alice Paul
• National Woman's Party
• Nineteenth Amendment
• Booker T. Washington
• Atlanta Compromise
• Ida B. Wells
• W. E. B. Du Bois
• National Association for the Advancement of Colored People

2 **Sequencing** Copy the graphic organizer below. Use it to list the events that led to the passage of the Nineteenth Amendment in the order that they occurred.

| Nineteenth Amendment |

3 **Finding the Main Idea**
a. What caused women to join the progressive movement, and what did they hope to achieve?

b. What groups in the United States were not helped by progressive reformers?

4 **Writing and Critical Thinking**
Analyzing Information Imagine that you are a muckraking magazine writer. Write an article that compares and contrasts the ways African Americans and women tried to reach their goals during the Progressive Era.

Consider the following:
• discrimination against African Americans and women
• the similarities and differences between Booker T. Washington and W. E. B. Du Bois
• the similarities and differences between the NAWSA and the NWP

Section 5

The Progressive Presidents

Read to Discover

1. What were the major points of President Roosevelt's progressive policy?
2. Why did progressives turn against President Taft?
3. What reforms did Woodrow Wilson accomplish during his presidency?

WHY IT MATTERS TODAY

The relationship between government and business is still changing. Use CNNfyi.com or other **current events** sources to find out one way in which government tries to control business today. Record your findings in your journal.

Define

- arbitration
- conservation

Identify

- Theodore Roosevelt
- Pure Food and Drug Act
- William Howard Taft
- Bull Moose Party
- Woodrow Wilson
- Underwood Tariff Act
- Sixteenth Amendment
- Federal Reserve Act
- Clayton Antitrust Act
- Federal Trade Commission
- Louis Brandeis

The Story Continues

On the tour following his second inauguration in 1901, President William McKinley was met by friendly people eager to shake his hand. As McKinley greeted a crowd in Buffalo, New York, however, anarchist Leon Czolgosz pulled out a pistol and shot the president at point-blank range. As he lay mortally wounded, the president whispered, "My wife, be careful how you tell her—oh be careful!" Just eight days later, McKinley was dead.

President William McKinley was assassinated in 1901.

★ President Theodore Roosevelt

After the assassination of McKinley in 1901, Vice President **Theodore Roosevelt** took office. Most Gilded Age presidents had seen themselves as administrators. However Roosevelt believed the president should be an active leader. He believed the interests of businesspeople, laborers, and consumers should be balanced for the public good. Roosevelt used this policy—known as the Square Deal—in the coal miners' strike in 1902. The strike lasted several months, causing coal shortages and rising coal prices. The country was in danger of having no heating fuel for the winter. Roosevelt declared that the coal shortages had "become a matter of vital concern to the whole nation." Roosevelt threatened to take over the mines unless managers agreed to **arbitration**, a formal process to settle disputes, with the strikers. Unlike previous presidents, Roosevelt helped labor to bargain with management. In 1903 he gave a promise.

History Makers Speak

"The labor unions shall have a square deal, and the corporations shall have a square deal, and in addition all private citizens shall have a square deal."

—President Theodore Roosevelt, quoted in *The Presidency of Theodore Roosevelt*, by Lewis L. Gould

Analyzing Primary Sources

Drawing Inferences and Conclusions What does Roosevelt mean by the word *square*?

Roosevelt used the Square Deal as a slogan in his successful presidential campaign in 1904.

President Roosevelt made regulating trusts the top goal of his first administration. He thought there were "good" trusts, which helped society, and "bad" trusts, which hurt the public. Roosevelt took on the Northern Securities Company, a big railroad trust in the Northwest. In 1904 the Supreme Court found that the Northern Securities Company had violated the Sherman Antitrust Act. The Court's ruling sent a warning to large corporations. The public was pleased, and Roosevelt gained a public reputation as a trustbuster. Business leaders, on the other hand, were outraged. They feared growing government interference in the country's economy and thus in their businesses.

In some cases, public pressure forced President Roosevelt to seek reform. Muckrakers helped build popular support for a larger government role in addressing problems. The American Medical Association also called for better food standards and proper labeling. Yet Congress would not pass reforms. Then Upton Sinclair's account of the meat-processing industry in his 1906 novel, *The Jungle*, shocked the public. Roosevelt responded by opening an investigation.

Roosevelt persuaded Congress to pass the **Pure Food and Drug Act** in 1906. The new law stopped the manufacture, sale, or transportation of mislabeled or contaminated food and drugs sold in interstate commerce. Congress also passed the Meat Inspection Act, which required inspections of meatpacking plants. Finally, Roosevelt got Congress to regulate railroad shipping rates. The public supported this expansion of federal regulatory powers. Roosevelt's activism set a standard for later progressive presidents.

Because of his love of the outdoors, Roosevelt became the first president to strongly favor **conservation**, or protection of nature and its resources. There were two different points of view among supporters of conservation. Preservationists believed that nature should be preserved because of its beauty. Many preservationists, such as John Muir, wanted to protect the remaining ancient forests of the West from logging. Other members of the conservation movement were known as conservationists.

PRESIDENTIAL PROFILES

Theodore Roosevelt

Theodore Roosevelt was born into a wealthy family in New York City in 1858. Despite his privileged upbringing, Roosevelt believed that his success came as a result of his hard work.

As a boy, he suffered from severe asthma and poor eyesight. At the age of 11, however, he began improving his health through exercise and outdoor activities. His asthma got better, and he became a strong and confident young man.

Reporter Lincoln Steffens once wrote about Roosevelt, "He took joy in everything he did, in hunting, camping, in ranching, in politics, in reforming the police or the civil service." What qualities made Roosevelt a strong leader?

These people wanted to save the natural resources of the United States. For example, Chief Forester Gifford Pinchot (PIN-shoh) valued forests because they produced the materials needed to build "prosperous homes."

By 1870, tens of millions of acres of federal land had been sold or given to private mining, logging, and railroad companies. These companies were against efforts to conserve federal land. Yet, while Roosevelt was in office, the forest service gained control of nearly 150 million acres of public land. Roosevelt doubled the number of national parks, created 16 national monuments, and started 51 wildlife refuges.

✔ **Reading Check: Analyzing Information** What reforms did President Roosevelt introduce when he was in office?

⭐ Taft Angers the Progressives

Theodore Roosevelt hoped that his secretary of war, **William Howard Taft**, would succeed him as president in 1908. Like Roosevelt, Taft opposed socialism and favored business regulation. With Roosevelt's help, Taft beat William Jennings Bryan in the election of 1908. However, despite their friendship, Roosevelt and Taft held different ideas about how a president should act. Taft thought Roosevelt had claimed more power than the executive branch was constitutionally allowed. Therefore, Taft chose to move more cautiously toward reform and regulation, which upset many progressives. Although he started twice as many antitrust suits as Roosevelt had, this was not enough to please progressives like Bryan and Robert M. La Follette, who wanted to destroy the trusts entirely. Taft angered progressives further when he signed the Payne-Aldrich Tariff of 1909. Although the Payne-Aldrich Tariff did reduce some rates, it raised others. The result was that tariffs were not reduced as much as many progressives wanted.

Taft's battle with Roosevelt's close friend and ally Gifford Pinchot also proved politically costly. In 1909 Pinchot accused Secretary of the Interior Richard Ballinger of hurting conservation efforts by leasing public lands to big business. Taft decided to fire Pinchot, which upset conservationists and many other progressives, including Roosevelt. Taft actually transferred more land into government reserves than Roosevelt had. However, he could not win back progressive support.

✔ **Reading Check: Summarizing** What actions did Taft take that angered Roosevelt and other progressives?

Interpreting Political Cartoons

Trustbusting *Roosevelt responds to public concerns by trying to break up trusts.* **What roles are Roosevelt and the trusts assigned in this 1904 cartoon entitled "Jack the Giant Killer"?**

Research on the ROM

Free Find:
Pure Food and Drug Act
After reading about the Pure Food and Drug Act on the **Holt Researcher CD–ROM**, write a short essay that explains the role of this law in protecting public health.

The First Automobile at the White House Did you know that William Howard Taft was the first president to keep a car at the White House? It's true! In fact, Taft had four cars. When the Roosevelts left the White House in their horse-drawn carriage on inauguration day, the rest of the White House carriages were put in storage. An exception was made for Mrs. Jaffray, the White House housekeeper. She was afraid of cars and preferred to do her errands by carriage. The Taft family loved taking afternoon automobile rides.

★ The Election of 1912

Roosevelt was among the many progressives who believed that Taft was not running the government effectively. Explaining that "the bulk of the people wanted a given job done, and . . . wanted me to do that job," Roosevelt decided to run for president again. When he lost the Republican nomination to Taft, Roosevelt and his followers formed the Progressive Party. The party was nicknamed the **Bull Moose Party** after Roosevelt said he was "as strong as a bull moose." The party's platform was based on Roosevelt's progressive plan, the New Nationalism, which he proposed in August 1910. Roosevelt's plan called for more active regulation, increased social welfare measures, and a stronger executive.

The Democratic Party chose **Woodrow Wilson**. Born in Virginia, Wilson earned a doctoral degree in history, became a professor, and served as president of Princeton University. In 1910 he was elected governor of New Jersey. Wilson based his presidential campaign on a program called the New Freedom, which called for government action against monopolies as well as lower tariffs.

Wilson, Roosevelt, Taft, and Eugene V. Debs, the candidate of the Socialist Party, all were reformers in some fashion. Taft, however, represented more conservative views. All of the candidates disagreed on specific reforms and on how to achieve them. The split between Taft and Roosevelt divided the Republican Party and the Republican vote. Although no one received a majority of the popular vote, Wilson won the electoral vote by a wide margin and became the next president.

✔ **Reading Check: Summarizing** In 1912 who were the four candidates for the presidency, and what parties did each represent?

Interpreting Political Cartoons

Taft's presidency *Many Americans thought that President Taft struggled with issues that Theodore Roosevelt had handled with ease.* **Whom do you think the man looking in the window represents, and what do you think he is doing?**

Woodrow Wilson's Reforms

In his inaugural address, Wilson spoke of the terrible social conditions under which many working-class Americans lived.

 History Makers Speak
"We have been proud of our industrial achievements, but we have not hitherto [yet] stopped thoughtfully enough to count the human cost, . . . the fearful physical and spiritual cost to the men and women and children upon whom the . . . burden of it all has fallen."

—Woodrow Wilson, First Inaugural Address

Reform legislation was Wilson's top goal, and he pushed for two measures soon after taking office: tariff revision and banking reform. Wilson backed the **Underwood Tariff Act** of 1913, which brought the lowest tariff rates in many years. The act also introduced a version of the modern income tax on personal earnings. This new tax on earnings was made possible when the **Sixteenth Amendment** was ratified in February 1913. This amendment allows the federal government to impose direct taxes on people's incomes.

President Wilson knew that banking reform would be much more difficult to pass than the tariff legislation. Some legislators favored a centralized banking system, while others wanted a decentralized system. The result was a compromise called the **Federal Reserve Act**. Passed in December 1913, the act created a national banking system called the Federal Reserve. This system is made up of 12 regional Federal Reserve

Analyzing Primary Sources
Making Generalizations and Predictions What policy would you expect Wilson to follow during his presidency?

A button and bull moose pendant from Roosevelt's 1912 presidential campaign

Map: The Election of 1912

States and electoral votes:

WA 7, MT 4, ND 5, MN 12, OR 5, ID 4, WY 3, SD 5, WI 13, MI 15, NV 3, UT 4, CO 6, NE 8, IA 13, IL 29, IN 15, OH 24, CA 13*, AZ 3, NM 3, KS 10, MO 18, KY 13, WV 8, VA 12, NC 12, OK 10, AR 9, TN 12, SC 9, MS 10, AL 12, GA 14, TX 20, LA 10, FL 6, NH 4, VT 4, ME 6, NY 45, MA 18, RI 5, CT 7, NJ 14, PA 38, DE 3, MD 8

	Electoral Vote	Popular Vote	% of Pop. Vote
Wilson	435*	6,296,547	41.9
T. Roosevelt	88	4,118,571	27.4
Taft	8	3,486,720	23.2
Debs (Socialist)		900,672	6.0
Other parties		235,025	1.5

*Two electors in California voted for Wilson.
Source: *Historical Statistics of the United States*

Electoral Winner by State
- Wilson (Democratic)
- T. Roosevelt (Progressive)
- Taft (Republican)
- 4 Electoral votes

The Election of 1912
Interpreting Maps Wilson's strength was in the South. Although he won the electoral vote by a landslide, the only states outside the former Confederacy where he won at least half the popular votes were Kentucky, Maryland, and Oklahoma.

Skills Assessment
Places and Regions Which state split its electoral vote?

This 1913 cartoon depicts President Wilson's antitrust legislation as a fence protecting small businesses.

banks as well as many privately owned banks. An independent decision-making board oversees the Federal Reserve. This new banking system enabled the government to try to prevent sudden changes between boom and bust in the economy. Wilson also pushed for laws to regulate big business. The **Clayton Antitrust Act** of 1914 strengthened earlier federal laws against monopolies. The new **Federal Trade Commission**, created in 1914, had the power to stop unfair trade practices by investigating corporations and issuing restraining orders.

As Wilson ran for re-election in 1916, he began to give more attention to farmers, businesspeople, and workers. He appointed **Louis Brandeis**, a progressive lawyer with a reputation for helping people, to the Supreme Court. Brandeis was the first Jewish Supreme Court justice. Wilson also helped pass the Keating-Owen Child Labor Act. In addition, he backed a law providing workers' compensation for federal employees. He also supported the Adamson Act, which limited the workday for railroad workers to eight hours. Wilson's actions helped him win a higher percentage of the vote in the 1916 election.

President Wilson showed great skill and determination in guiding his reform programs through Congress. He told a friend in 1913 that legislators followed his lead because "I do know how to put my mind at the service of others for the accomplishment of a common purpose."

✔ **Reading Check: Summarizing** What major reforms were carried out under President Wilson?

Section 5 Review

go.hrw.com **Homework Practice Online** keyword: SF3 HP23

1 **Define** and explain:
• arbitration
• conservation

2 **Identify** and explain:
• Theodore Roosevelt
• Pure Food and Drug Act
• William Howard Taft
• Bull Moose Party
• Woodrow Wilson
• Underwood Tariff Act
• Sixteenth Amendment
• Federal Reserve Act
• Clayton Antitrust Act
• Federal Trade Commission
• Louis Brandeis

3 **Identifying Cause and Effect** Copy the graphic organizer below. Use it to show what caused Roosevelt and other progressives to turn against Taft and the effects this change had on the Republican Party in 1912.

Causes

↓

Roosevelt turns on Taft

↓

Effects

4 **Finding the Main Idea**
a. What progressive actions did President Roosevelt take against large corporations and railroads?

b. What reforms did President Wilson guide through Congress?

5 **Writing and Critical Thinking**
Analyzing Information Imagine that you are a political adviser working for Theodore Roosevelt during the 1912 presidential campaign. Prepare a brochure that explains to the people why they should vote for Roosevelt, instead of the other candidates.

Consider the following:
• Roosevelt's record as president from 1901 to 1909
• Roosevelt's conflict with Taft and the Republican Party
• Roosevelt's New Nationalism program

CONNECTING TO *Literature*

The Jungle
Upton Sinclair

Upton Sinclair wrote The Jungle *to create sympathy for immigrants, who lived and worked under difficult conditions. Readers were shocked by his descriptions of the unsanitary practices in the meatpacking industry. Sinclair later said about Americans' reaction, "I aimed at the public's heart, and by accident I hit it in the stomach." In the following excerpt from* The Jungle, *Jurgis Rudkus describes conditions at a Chicago meatpacking plant.*

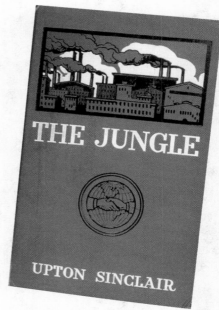

Meat sales dropped after The Jungle *was published.*

The family had a first-hand knowledge of the great majority of Packingtown swindles. For it was the custom, as they found, whenever meat was so spoiled that it could not be used for any-thing else, either to can it or else to chop it up into sausage. With what had been told them by Jonas, who had worked in the **pickle**[1] rooms, they could now study the whole of the spoiled-meat industry on the inside, and read a new and grim meaning into that old Packingtown jest—that they use everything of the pig except the squeal.

Jonas had told them how the meat that was taken out of pickle would often be found sour, and how they would rub it up with soda to take away the smell, and sell it to be eaten on free-lunch counters; also of all the miracles of chem-istry which they performed, giving to any sort of meat, fresh or salted, whole or chopped, any color and any flavor and any odor they chose. . . .

It was only when the whole ham was spoiled that it came into the department of Elzbieta. . . . Mixed with half a ton of other meat, no odor that ever was in a ham could make any differ-ence. There was never the least attention paid to what was cut up for sausage; there would come all the way back from Europe old sausage that had been rejected. . . . There would be meat that had tumbled out on the floor, in the dirt and sawdust, where the workers had tramped and

spit uncounted billions of . . . germs. There would be meat stored in great piles in rooms; and the water from leaky roofs would drip over it, and thousands of rats would race about on it. . . . These rats were nuisances, and the packers would put poisoned bread out for them, they would die, and then rats, bread, and meat would go into the **hoppers**[2] together. This is no fairy story and no joke.

---

[1]pickle: vinegar solution
[2]hoppers: containers for the temporary storage of material

Understanding What You Read

1. **Literature and History** Why do you think the descriptions in *The Jungle* led to new health laws? Use examples from the excerpt to support your answer.
2. **Literature and You** Conduct research to find out how consumers today can tell that their meats are safe to eat.

Chapter 23 Review

The Chapter at a Glance

Examine the visual summary of the chapter below. Create an outline of the major parts of the chapter, and compare your outline to a classmate's.

Progressive Reforms

Gilded Age

Political machines contributed to widespread political corruption, leading to civil service reform.

Progressive Era

Progressives supported democratic reforms such as the initiative, recall, and referendum. They also tried to improve government efficiency and workplace safety and worked to end child labor.

Progressive Presidents

Presidents Theodore Roosevelt, William Howard Taft, and Woodrow Wilson regulated trusts. Progressive presidents also concentrated on banking reform and conservation and called for new laws regulating food and drugs.

Women's and Minorities' Rights

Women's rights groups won the right to vote for women and addressed other social issues. Organizations such as the NAACP fought for fairer treatment for minorities.

Identifying People and Ideas

Use the following terms or people in historically significant sentences.

1. political machines
2. John Dewey
3. Industrial Workers of the World
4. Frances Willard
5. Carrie Chapman Catt
6. Nineteenth Amendment
7. Booker T. Washington
8. Atlanta Compromise
9. Theodore Roosevelt
10. Underwood Tariff Act

Understanding Main Ideas

Section 1 *(Pages 708–711)*

1. How did bosses use political machines to control local and city governments?

Section 2 *(Pages 712–716)*

2. Why did progressives want to reform local and state governments, and what did they achieve?

Section 3 *(Pages 717–720)*

3. What were working conditions like for children and other factory workers in the late 1800s, and what changes did reformers try to make?

Section 4 *(Pages 721–726)*

4. What caused some women to form the Woman's Christian Temperance Union?

Section 5 *(Pages 727–732)*

5. What was President Roosevelt's attitude toward trusts?
6. What reforms did President Wilson pass during his presidency?

You Be the Historian—Reviewing Themes

1. **Citizenship** Why did women form the National American Woman Suffrage Association?
2. **Constitutional Heritage** What was the significance of the Supreme Court's ruling in *Lochner* v. *New York*, and how did its decision in *Muller* v. *Oregon* partially reverse the earlier ruling?
3. **Economics** What role did Roosevelt believe government should play in the economy?

Thinking Critically

1. **Comparing and Contrasting** How were progressives and earlier reformers alike and different?
2. **Evaluating** Which of the progressive presidents do you think was most successful in reforming American society? Explain your answer.
3. **Identifying Cause and Effect** What led to the growth of the conservation movement, and what effects did it have on natural resources in the United States?

Interpreting Graphs

Study the graphs below. Then use the information on the graphs to help you answer the questions that follow.

Labor and Wages, 1900–1910

Source: *Historical Statistics of the United States*

1. About how long was the average workday, and about how much was the average hourly wage in 1900?
   a. 15 hours per day and 10 cents per hour
   b. 10 hours per day and 15 cents per hour
   c. 8 hours per day and 20 cents per hour
   d. 9.5 hours per day and 20 cents per hour

2. What was the general trend in the length of the workday and the hourly wage between 1900 and 1910?

Analyzing Primary Sources

Read the following quotation by reformer Jacob Riis, from his book *How the Other Half Lives*. Then answer the following questions.

66Suppose we look into [a tenement on] Cherry Street. Be a little careful, please! The hall is dark and you might stumble. . . . A flight of stairs. You can feel your way, if you cannot see it. . . . all the fresh air that ever enters these stairs comes from the hall door. . . . Here is a door. Listen! That short hacking cough, that tiny, helpless wail—what do they mean? . . . Oh! a sadly familiar story—before the day is at an end. The child is dying with measles. With half a chance it might have lived; but it had none. That dark bedroom killed it.99

3. Which of the following best expresses Riis's view of tenement conditions?
   a. Landlords should lower tenement rents to help people with families.
   b. The lack of light and air is unhealthy, particularly for children.
   c. Mostly poor people live in tenements.
   d. There should be better medical care for people living in tenements.

4. Why do you think Riis uses the language he does to describe the tenement?
   a. He could not see things very clearly on his visit.
   b. He wants to create sympathy by helping the reader feel what the conditions are really like.
   c. He was frightened while in the tenement.
   d. He wants to reassure people that the tenements are not that bad.

5. Based on your knowledge of this period, how do you think people might have responded to Riis's description of tenement life?

Alternative Assessment

American History

Building Your Portfolio

Cooperative Learning

Complete the following activity in small groups. If muckrakers were investigating problems in American society today, what do you think would be the top five problems they would address? Find newspaper and magazine articles and images related to these topics. Use this information to create a bulletin board display titled Important Issues Today.

internet connect

Internet Activity: go.hrw.com
keyword: SF3 CF23

Choose an activity on the Spirit of Reform to:
● Learn about the role of the Tammany Hall political machine in the lives of citizens of New York City.
● Write a report on city planning in the early 1900s.
● Learn how the Federal Reserve system works today.

24 America as a World Power
(1865–1914)

This eagle represents the United States stretching its wings across the Pacific.

THE GRANGER COLLECTION, NEW YORK

Alaska's beautiful scenery and natural resources made it a valuable addition to the United States.

UNITED STATES

1867 The United States buys Alaska.

1887 Planters in Hawaii force King Kalakaua to sign a new constitution reducing his power.

1890 Congress passes the McKinley Tariff, which gives a subsidy to U.S. sugar producers.

| 1865 | 1870 | 1875 | 1880 | 1885 | 1890 |

WORLD

1868 Japan begins a period of modernization known as the Meiji Restoration.

1881 A French company begins building a canal across the Isthmus of Panama.

1885 The Indian National Congress is formed in British-controlled India.

1894 China and Japan fight a war for control of Korea.

An international army storms into Beijing to free foreign diplomats trapped by the Boxer Rebellion in China.

Build on What You Know

While progressive reformers tried to solve political and social problems that went with the nation's rapid growth, the United States also began to expand overseas and play a greater role in world affairs. The Spanish-American War and the Mexican Revolution made Americans think about what role the United States should play in the politics of neighboring countries.

The Rough Riders and the 9th and 10th Cavalries fight to help secure the town of Santiago de Cuba during the Spanish-American War.

1898 The United States wins the Spanish-American War, gaining the Philippine Islands and Puerto Rico.

1904 President Theodore Roosevelt presents his corollary to the Monroe Doctrine. Construction of the Panama Canal begins.

1914 The Panama Canal opens.

1895   1900   1905   1910   1915

1895 Cuba revolts against Spain.

1900 The Boxer Rebellion occurs in China.

1903 Panama declares itself an independent nation.

1904 The Russo-Japanese War begins.

1910 The Mexican Revolution begins.

José Martí was a leader in the struggle for Cuban independence.

If you were there . . .
Would you favor U.S. expansion overseas?

You Be the Historian

What's Your Opinion? Do you **agree** or **disagree** with the following statements? Support your point of view in your journal.

- **Geography** Distant lands have little value as colonies or territories.
- **Economics** A country's economic issues always affect its foreign policy.
- **Global Relations** A powerful nation should take part in the political affairs of its neighbors.

The United States Gains Overseas Territories

Read to Discover

1. Why did some people favor expansion over isolationism?
2. What events led to the U.S. annexation of Hawaii?
3. What was the goal of U.S. foreign policy in Japan and China?

WHY IT MATTERS TODAY

The United States still has military bases overseas. Use **CNNfyi.com** or other **current events** sources to find information about one U.S. military base located overseas. Record your findings in your journal.

Define

- imperialism
- isolationism
- subsidy
- spheres of influence

Identify

- William H. Seward
- McKinley Tariff
- Liliuokalani
- Matthew Perry
- Open Door Policy
- Boxer Rebellion

The Story Continues

On March 16, 1889, one British, three German, and three U.S. warships prepared to fight for control of Samoa. Before any fighting could begin, however, a sudden storm blew in and destroyed all the ships except the British vessel. The storm prevented a battle that day, but it did not end Western countries' race to expand around the world.

In this cartoon, nations fight over a woman who symbolizes Samoa. In 1899 the United States and Germany agreed to divide Samoa between them.

⭐ Imperialism and Expansion

Europeans were willing to risk war in such far-off places as Samoa because they wanted to build naval bases and protect shipping routes in the Pacific. This effort was part of **imperialism**—the practice of building an empire by founding colonies or conquering other nations. Between 1870 and 1914, powerful Western nations built large colonial empires. They took control of most of Africa and much of Southeast Asia.

Several forces drove this wave of imperialism. Countries wanted raw materials—such as copper, rubber, and tin—to help their industrial growth. At the same time, businesspeople needed new markets to sell their goods. Many people also saw colonies as a source of power and national pride.

In 1867 the lure of land and resources encouraged Secretary of State **William H. Seward** to arrange the purchase of Alaska from Russia. At $7.2 million, the cost was less than two cents per acre. People laughed at the purchase, calling it "Seward's Folly" and the "Alaskan Icebox." However, Alaska added some 600,000 square miles to the United States and had valuable natural resources such as furs, minerals, and timber.

The United States did not begin expanding overseas until the late 1800s. Previously, Americans had followed a policy of **isolationism**—avoiding involvement in the affairs of other countries. Long before, President George Washington had warned Americans "to steer clear of permanent alliances" with other countries—particularly those in Europe. U.S. leaders had tried to follow this advice by staying out of overseas conflicts.

Not everyone favored isolationism. Some Americans thought the United States needed to expand to keep the country's economy strong. Alfred Thayer Mahan, in *The Influence of Sea Power upon History*, wrote that the United States needed a strong navy. Published in 1890, Mahan's book argued that the navy could protect U.S. economic interests abroad. This economic growth would in turn increase American military power. Senator Henry Cabot Lodge repeated Mahan's call for economic expansion through naval power.

Analyzing Primary Sources
Drawing Inferences and Conclusions What does Lodge mean when he says that "commerce follows the flag"?

History Makers Speak **"**Commerce follows the flag, and we should build up a navy strong enough to give protection to Americans in every quarter of the globe.**"**

—Henry Cabot Lodge, quoted in *The Annals of America*

Interpreting the Visual Record

A mighty fleet *A modern navy helped the United States compete against other global powers.* **How might such a fleet help the United States expand overseas?**

✔ **Reading Check: Contrasting** How do imperialism and isolationism differ?

BIOGRAPHY

Queen Liliuokalani

(1838–1917)

Liliuokalani was born in Honolulu and was educated by American missionaries. In 1887 she toured the United States. Liliuokalani became queen of Hawaii in 1891. After the revolt that ended her short reign, she worked to reclaim her throne. In her autobiography, *Hawaii's Story by Hawaii's Queen*, she questioned whether overseas expansion was a proper goal for the United States. Throughout her life, Liliuokalani remained a symbol of Hawaiian pride and history. **What contact did Liliuokalani have with the United States?**

Research on the ROM

Free Find: Liliuokalani
After reading about Liliuokalani on the **Holt Researcher CD–ROM**, write a song that honors her efforts on behalf of the Hawaiian people.

★ Hawaii

Another Pacific island nation—Hawaii—also interested imperial powers. The Hawaiian Islands had a tropical climate and fertile soil. The Hawaiian people had first contact with Europeans in 1778 when British explorer Captain James Cook arrived. Trading and whaling ships in the Pacific then began stopping in Hawaii for supplies. Later, American missionaries came to convert the Hawaiians to Christianity. These missionaries opened businesses and raised crops such as sugarcane. Some missionary families became rich sugar planters.

By the 1840s most shops and shipyards in Hawaii were owned by Americans. Sugar had become a leading export of the Hawaiian economy. An 1875 treaty allowed Hawaiian sugar to be shipped duty-free to the United States. In return, Hawaii agreed not to give territory or special privileges to any other country.

Hawaiian sugar production boomed, and the power of the planters grew. In 1887 they forced King Kalakaua (kah-LAH-KAH-ooh-ah) to sign a new constitution. This constitution granted more political power to the Hawaiian parliament, which the planters controlled. Many Hawaiians worried that foreigners were becoming too powerful.

Hawaiian sugar planters suffered a major economic setback in 1890 when Congress passed the **McKinley Tariff**. This law allowed all countries to ship sugar duty-free to the United States. However, the tariff also gave U.S. sugar producers a **subsidy**, or bonus payment by the government, of two cents per pound. The prices of Hawaiian sugar dropped, and the islands' economy collapsed.

In 1893 Queen **Liliuokalani** (li-lee-uh-woh-kuh-LAHN-ee) presented a new constitution that returned power to the monarchy. In response, the planters revolted. John L. Stevens, U.S. minister to Hawaii, called 150 U.S. Marines ashore to support the revolt. The rebellion succeeded without a shot being fired. The planters then formed a new government with lawyer Sanford B. Dole serving as president. Acting without authority from the U.S. State Department, Stevens recognized, or formally acknowledged, the new government. He declared Hawaii to be under U.S. control on February 1, 1893. "The Hawaiian pear is now fully ripe," wrote Stevens, "and this is the golden hour for the United States to pluck it."

President Grover Cleveland, who had met Hawaii's Queen Liliuokalani when she was a princess, disapproved of the revolt and refused to annex Hawaii. However, he took little effective action to help restore the monarchy. The islands remained an independent republic until July 7, 1898, when Congress annexed them. Hawaii became a U.S. territory in 1900 and the 50th state in 1959.

✔ **Reading Check: Finding the Main Idea** What effects did the McKinley Tariff have on Hawaii?

⭐ The Opening of Japan

By the mid-1800s some European powers had formed strong trade ties with much of East Asia. But the island nation of Japan had isolated itself from the rest of the world for hundreds of years. Japan's leaders had also banned travel to other countries.

The United States wanted to open Japan's trade before Europeans got there. President Millard Fillmore sent Commodore **Matthew Perry** to secure "friendship, commerce, a supply of coal and provisions." On July 8, 1853, a crowd of astonished Japanese watched a fleet of four U.S. warships enter Edo (now called Tokyo) Harbor. Perry delivered a letter to the Japanese government from President Fillmore suggesting peaceful trade ties. Perry returned to Japan in February 1854 with seven warships. He brought gifts showing some of the technological benefits the United States could offer. This effort—and the presence of American military power—persuaded Japanese leaders to sign a treaty opening trade with the United States. In 1856 Townsend Harris arrived in Japan as the first U.S. consul general, or chief diplomat. Despite some opposition in Japan, he negotiated a trade treaty in 1858.

Japanese leaders who believed their country needed to industrialize wanted trade with the United States. In 1868, those favoring industrialization came to power in Japan, beginning a time of modernization known as the Meiji (MAY-jee) Restoration. During the next 40 years, Japanese leaders invested heavily in industry and in making the country's military stronger. The government sent Japanese students to Western schools to study science, technology, and Western government. One such student explained his goal.

 History Makers Speak

❝The final purpose of all my work was to create in Japan a civilized nation as well equipped in the arts of war and peace as those of the Western world.❞

—Yukichi Fukuzawa, *The Autobiography of Yukichi Fukuzawa*

By the 1890s, Japan was becoming a major imperial power. Japan invaded China in 1894. After defeating China's military, Japan gained the same trade privileges in China as European countries enjoyed, in addition to winning new territory. In 1904, Japan and Russia went to war. President Theodore Roosevelt helped negotiate a peace treaty to end the war a year later. The Japanese had won the respect they desired. Japan gained Korea, a lease on Port Arthur in China, and other rights. In just 50 years, Japan had changed from an isolated nonindustrial country to a major world power. Hilary Herbert, U.S. secretary of the navy, said, "Japan has leaped, almost at one bound, to a place among the great nations of the earth."

✔ **Reading Check: Sequencing** List the steps Japan took after the arrival of Matthew Perry to become a world power.

CONNECTIONS

Japan and Hawaii

In the 1860s the first Japanese immigrants began arriving in Hawaii. By 1923 they made up almost 43 percent of the population. Many Japanese went to work on the islands' sugar plantations. Workers had a difficult life raising and harvesting the sugarcane.

Many Japanese immigrants remained in Hawaii after their work contracts ended. Today people of Japanese descent make up about one fourth of Hawaii's population. They live on all the major islands and work in all types of fields, including education, government, and law. **How have Japanese immigrants contributed to Hawaiian society?**

⭐ Foreign Powers in China

Economic interests drew the United States not only to Hawaii and Japan but also to China. There the United States and many European nations engaged in profitable trade. After Japan defeated China in 1895, other countries quickly took further advantage of China's weakness. These nations seized **spheres of influence**—areas where foreign nations could control trade and natural resources. Many nations joined in what was called "the carving up of the Chinese melon." Germany took control of a harbor in Shandong Province in November 1897. Other nations did likewise. France and Japan occupied land in China's southern provinces, Russia moved into northern China, and Great Britain took over territory on the coast opposite Hong Kong Island. The United States, however, lacked the naval power to establish its own sphere of influence.

Fearing that the United States would be closed out of Chinese markets, U.S. Secretary of State John Hay announced the **Open Door Policy**. Hay sent a series of notes to Japan and some European countries in 1899. The main argument of the Open Door Policy was that all nations should have equal access to trade in China. When the European powers and Japan neither accepted nor rejected the policy, Hay announced that it had been accepted.

Within China there was strong resentment of the power and control held by foreign nations. In 1900 this antiforeign hostility grew until it erupted in the **Boxer Rebellion**. The Boxers were Chinese nationalists who were members of a group called the Fists of Righteous Harmony. Boxers got their name from foreigners who called the group this

Asian goods such as this decorated fan became popular trade items in the United States in the late 1800s.

PEABODY ESSEX MUSEUM, SALEM, MASSACHUSETTS

U.S. Territories in the Pacific

Interpreting Maps Between 1856 and 1900 Alaska and many Pacific islands, including Hawaii, became U.S. territories.

Skills Assessment

1. **Places and Regions** What U.S. territory was located below the equator?
2. **Analyzing Information** In what year did the United States acquire the most territories?

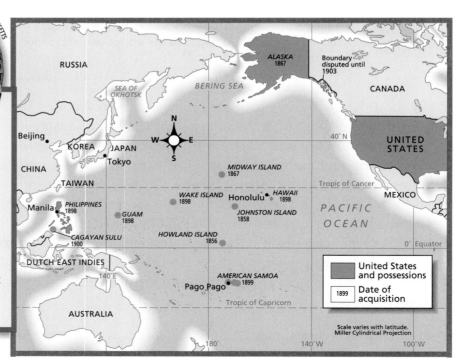

because of the boxing rituals that the members practiced. The Boxers were angered by foreign involvement in China's affairs and by the Chinese government's poor management. They were also frustrated by the hunger and homelessness caused by a series of natural disasters. In June the Boxers took to the streets of Beijing, China's capital, and laid siege to the walled settlement in which foreigners lived. They killed more than 200 people during the attack. Seeing that the attack was doomed, the Chinese government did not support the Boxers.

For two months the siege continued as military forces that included U.S. Marines fought their way from the port of Tianjin to Beijing. The Boxers were soon defeated, and China was forced to accept a harsh settlement. The Chinese had to make a $333 million cash payment to foreign governments, $25 million of which went to the United States.

Secretary of State Hay then sent another Open Door note to Japan and the European nations. He restated the U.S. position that all nations should have equal access to Chinese markets. Hay wanted to prevent any European colonization of China that would limit U.S. influence. The Open Door Policy remained in effect long after the Boxer Rebellion.

Boxers attack the foreigners' compound in Beijing.

✔ **Reading Check: Identifying Cause and Effect** What factors led to the Boxer Rebellion in China, and what was the result?

Section 1 Review

go.hrw.com **Homework Practice Online** keyword: SF3 HP24

1 **Define** and explain:
• imperialism
• isolationism
• subsidy
• spheres of influence

2 **Identify** and explain:
• William H. Seward
• McKinley Tariff
• Liliuokalani
• Matthew Perry
• Open Door Policy
• Boxer Rebellion

3 **Summarizing** Copy the graphic organizer below. Use it to describe the territories in the Pacific acquired by the United States and to show U.S. influence.

American Expansion

| Areas Gained: | Trade and Other Involvements with Asian Nations: |

4 **Finding the Main Idea**
a. What arguments did supporters of American expansionism make in the 1890s?

b. How did Hawaii become a U.S. territory?

5 **Writing and Critical Thinking**
Supporting a Point of View Imagine that you are a member of Congress around 1900. Write a short speech that you might give to Congress about U.S. policy toward China and Japan. You may either support or oppose U.S. policy.

Consider the following:
• reasons the United States should expand
• China's attitude toward foreign nations
• Japan's attitude toward foreign nations

America as a World Power **743**

The Spanish-American War

Read to Discover

1. How did the press affect U.S. involvement in the conflict between Spain and Cuba?
2. What enabled the United States to win the war against Spain?
3. How did the Spanish-American War affect the Philippines, Cuba, and Puerto Rico?

WHY IT MATTERS TODAY

America's relations with Cuba have changed significantly since the Spanish-American War. Use CNNfyi.com or other **current events** sources to find out about one aspect of the relationship between the United States and Cuba today. Record your findings in your journal.

Define

- yellow journalism

Identify

- Joseph Pulitzer
- William Randolph Hearst
- Teller Amendment
- Emilio Aguinaldo
- Anti-Imperialist League
- Platt Amendment

President McKinley was sympathetic to the cause of Cuba's rebels.

THE GRANGER COLLECTION, NEW YORK

The Story Continues

In 1895, Cubans revolted against Spanish colonial rule. In response, the Spanish army gathered several hundred thousand Cubans into *reconcentrados,* or reconcentration camps. Some 200,000 Cubans died in the camps because of poor food and sanitation. Such harsh measures led many Americans to support the Cuban rebels in their struggle for independence from Spain.

★ The Road to War

Many Americans believed Cuba's battle with Spain resembled America's Revolutionary War. The Cuban conflict was widely reported, even exaggerated, in the American press, further increasing American support for the Cubans.

The *New York World,* published by **Joseph Pulitzer**, was very critical of the Spanish, as was **William Randolph Hearst's** *New York Journal.* In their competition for more readers, both men printed sensational, often exaggerated stories. This exaggeration of news stories in order to sell newspapers became known as **yellow journalism**.

Pulitzer was first to engage in yellow journalism, but Hearst quickly responded and proved better at it. To sell papers and to get support for U.S. military action in Cuba, Hearst hired artist and illustrator Frederic Remington to provide pictures of conditions on the island. Remington supposedly sent Hearst a telegram from Cuba that read, "Everything is quiet. There is no trouble here. There will be no war." Hearst is said to have answered, "You furnish [provide] the pictures and I'll furnish the war."

Despite growing public support for military action, President Grover Cleveland remained strongly opposed to U.S. involvement in Cuba. However, in 1896, William McKinley, a supporter of Cuban independence, was elected president.

On January 25, 1898, the U.S. battleship *Maine* arrived in Havana Harbor to protect U.S. citizens and economic interests. On February 9 Hearst published a letter written by the Spanish minister to the United States that called President McKinley a weak leader. The letter outraged many Americans and embarrassed the Spanish government. Six days after Hearst published the letter, 260 American sailors were killed when the *Maine* exploded. Although the cause of the explosion was unclear, many Americans immediately blamed Spain.

Congress approved $50 million that McKinley requested to prepare for war. Spain offered to negotiate but would not consider Cuban independence. Congress then passed a resolution on April 20 declaring the island independent and giving Spain three days to leave the island. Attached to the resolution was the **Teller Amendment**, which stated that the United States had no interest in taking control of Cuba. In response to the U.S. declaration that Spain had to leave Cuba, the Spanish government declared war on the United States on April 24. The next day Congress passed and McKinley signed a declaration of war against Spain.

✔ **Reading Check: Sequencing** List the events in order that resulted in the Spanish-American War.

⭐ War with Spain

While attention was focused on Cuba, the U.S. Navy won a quick and spectacular victory nearly halfway around the world. Commodore George Dewey led the American Asiatic squadron at Hong Kong. When the war began, Dewey set out to attack the Spanish Philippines. On May 1 Dewey's ships boldly sailed into Manila Bay and destroyed Spain's Pacific fleet. While the Spanish lost 381 lives, none of Dewey's men were killed.

Interpreting the Visual Record

Manila Bay *On May 1, 1898, Commodore George Dewey's fleet destroyed Spain's Pacific fleet in a decisive battle.* **How does this image represent the success of the U.S. ships?**

April 25, 1898

The United States declares war on Spain.

Research on the R◉M

Free Find:
William Randolph Hearst
After reading about William Randolph Hearst on the **Holt Researcher CD–ROM**, create a front page for a newspaper with current news stories that reflect Hearst's style of journalism.

★ ★ ★ ★ ★ ★ ★ ★ ★ ★ ★
That's Interesting!
★ ★ ★ ★ ★ ★ ★ ★ ★ ★ ★

Cuban Baseball Did you know that baseball played a part in the Cuban struggle for independence? It's true! Cubans had been playing professional baseball since 1878. They learned the game from American college students and from sailors. One of the founders of Cuban baseball, Emilio Sabourín, was also a supporter of Cuban independence. He gave money to Cuban patriot José Martí to support a revolution against Spain. After the war, baseball remained hugely popular in Cuba, and many American baseball players and teams toured Cuba to play against the local stars.

Interpreting the Visual Record

The Rough Riders *The diverse members of the Rough Riders included American Indians, college athletes, cowboys, and miners. Together, their heroic actions gained national attention.* **How does this painting depict the dangers faced by the Rough Riders and their heroism?**

Dewey had defeated the Spanish, but he lacked the forces necessary to occupy the islands. He decided to wait, and reinforcements eventually arrived. On August 13, U.S. troops helped take control of the Philippine capital, Manila. They were joined by Filipino rebels led by **Emilio Aguinaldo** (ahg-ee-NAHL-doh).

Training and supplying thousands of volunteer troops took longer than getting the navy under way. When the war began, only about 28,000 soldiers were serving in the U.S. Army. The army was unprepared to train and supply the 280,000 marines, sailors, and soldiers who would eventually see active duty. The army was at first unprepared to train and support them. There were shortages of bullets and rifles. Soldiers received warm woolen uniforms to wear in the tropical heat. Once in Cuba, many soldiers were struck by yellow fever and other deadly diseases. Of the few thousand members of the U.S. forces who died during the war, only a small percentage died in battle. The rest died from disease, food poisoning, and other causes unrelated to fighting.

The most colorful group of soldiers in the war was the First Volunteer Cavalry, or the Rough Riders. Organized by Lieutenant Colonel Theodore Roosevelt and led by General Leonard Wood, the volunteers came from many walks of life. Newspaper accounts of Roosevelt's charm and the Rough Riders' heroism earned the group the admiration of the American public. Many other U.S. soldiers also served bravely. Four privates of the African American 10th Cavalry received the Congressional Medal of Honor for their actions.

The U.S. Navy trapped the Spanish Caribbean fleet in the harbor of Santiago de Cuba in June 1898. U.S. troops landed on Cuba and moved to capture the hills around the Spanish forces. At the village of El Caney on

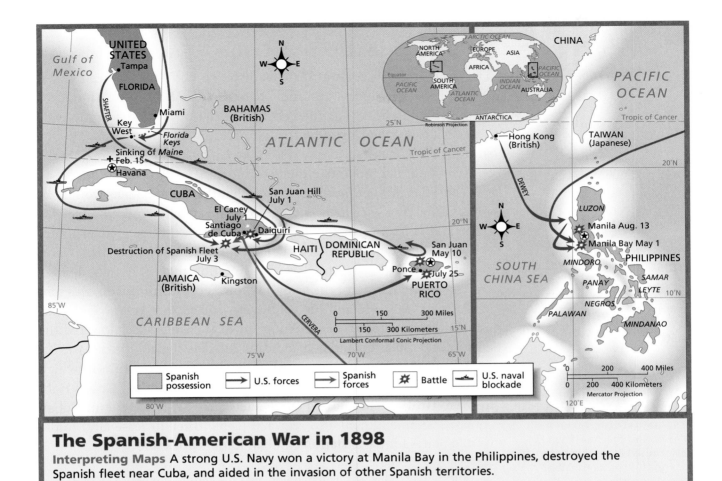

The Spanish-American War in 1898

Interpreting Maps A strong U.S. Navy won a victory at Manila Bay in the Philippines, destroyed the Spanish fleet near Cuba, and aided in the invasion of other Spanish territories.

Skills Assessment Places and Regions Near what Cuban cities did the Battle of San Juan Hill take place?

July 1, some 7,000 U.S. soldiers overwhelmed about 600 Spanish defenders. The main U.S. force under General Hamilton Hawkins then attacked and captured San Juan Hill. The Rough Riders and the African American 9th and 10th Cavalries captured nearby Kettle Hill. A journalist on the scene described their charge.

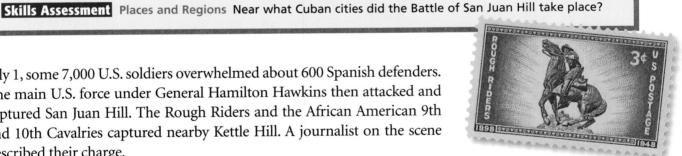

A postage stamp commemorating the Rough Riders

History Makers Speak

"It was a miracle of self-sacrifice, a triumph of bulldog courage. . . . The fire of the Spanish riflemen . . . doubled and trebled [tripled] in fierceness, the crests of the hills crackled and burst in amazed roars and rippled with waves of tiny flame. But the blue line [of U.S. soldiers] crept steadily up and on."

—Richard Harding Davis, quoted in *The American Reader*, edited by Paul M. Angle

On July 3 the Spanish fleet tried to break through the U.S. blockade. Every Spanish ship was destroyed in the battle, with 474 Spaniards killed and 1,750 others captured. U.S. forces suffered only two casualties. Santiago surrendered on July 17. U.S. troops soon captured Puerto Rico as well. Spain asked for peace and signed a cease-fire on August 12, 1898.

Analyzing Primary Sources

Identifying Bias Do you think this reporter supported the war? Explain your answer.

✔ **Reading Check: Summarizing** How did the Spanish-American War progress for the United States in the Philippines, Cuba, and Puerto Rico?

U.S. Trade with Cuba

Year	Imports from Cuba*	Exports to Cuba*
1890	54	13
1891	62	12
1892	78	18
1893	79	24
1894	76	20
1895	53	13
1896	40	8
1897	18	8
1898	15	10
1899	25	19
1900	31	26

*in millions of dollars
Source: *Historical Statistics of the United States*

Using Mathematical Skills

1. In what year shown on the chart did the United States have the most exports to Cuba? the least?

2. Imagine that you are a member of the presidential cabinet. Use these figures to create a bar graph comparing exports to and imports from Cuba from 1890 to 1900.

3. Then write a memo explaining whether you think the value of U.S. trade with Cuba was a factor in leading the United States into war with Spain.

★ The Question of Cuba

The peace treaty between Spain and the United States placed Cuba, Puerto Rico, the Philippines, and Guam under U.S. control. Americans who opposed the treaty formed the **Anti-Imperialist League**. The League accused the United States of building a colonial empire. Despite such protests, the peace treaty was approved by a vote of 57 to 27 in the Senate—one vote more than the two-thirds majority needed.

The Teller Amendment had stated that the United States would not annex Cuba. But McKinley wanted to create stability and increase U.S. trade and influence in the area, so he set up a military government there. He appointed General Leonard Wood governor, and Wood quickly began building schools and a sanitation system. To fight disease, Dr. Walter Reed, head of the army's Yellow Fever Commission, was sent to Cuba in 1900. He and his volunteers proved that yellow fever was transmitted by mosquitoes. Getting rid of standing water lowered the mosquito population and helped health officials control the disease.

Wood also oversaw the drafting of a Cuban constitution, which included the **Platt Amendment**. This amendment limited Cuba's right to make treaties and allowed the United States to intervene in Cuban affairs. The amendment also required Cuba to sell or lease land to the United States for naval stations. Cuban leaders protested.

History Makers Speak

❝[This was like] handing over the keys to our house so that they [the Americans] can enter it at any time, whenever the desire seizes them, day or night, whether with good or evil design [intentions].❞

—A committee report on the Constitutional Convention, quoted in *The Twentieth Century: A People's History,* by Howard Zinn

The Cubans reluctantly accepted the Platt Amendment, and U.S. troops withdrew. The amendment remained in force until 1934.

✔ **Reading Check: Evaluating** How did the Platt Amendment restrict Cuba's freedom?

★ New U.S. Lands

Spain had surrendered the Philippines in return for a $20 million payment from the United States. Many Americans wondered why their country wanted the islands. Some believed that it would be wrong to annex the islands without the consent of the Filipinos. Other people agreed with President McKinley, who said that the United States would benefit from the islands' naval and commercial value. He also argued that annexing the islands would keep Europeans from seizing them.

Filipino rebels had helped U.S. forces capture Manila. Now they expected to gain their independence. When the United States decided to keep the islands, the rebels began a guerrilla war against U.S. forces. Some 70,000 U.S. soldiers fought in the Philippines. Hundreds of thousands of Filipinos died before the conflict ended more than three years later, in 1902. The Philippine Government Act, passed in 1902 by the U.S. Congress, allowed Filipinos some governing control. The act provided that the Philippines would be ruled by an appointed governor and a two-house legislature. The lower house was to be elected. In 1946 the United States granted full independence to the Philippines.

Like Cubans and Filipinos, Puerto Ricans had hoped for independence after the war. Instead, the U.S. government made Puerto Rico a territory. On April 12, 1900, the Foraker Act established a civil government headed by a governor and including a two-house legislature.

After the United States acquired Puerto Rico, the government built many new schools.

A debate about the citizenship of the people in the new territories soon arose. Residents of Puerto Rico were considered citizens of the island but not of the United States. In 1916 the Jones Act granted Puerto Ricans U.S. citizenship and made both houses of the Puerto Rican legislature elective. However, another 30 years passed before Puerto Ricans could elect their own governor. In 1952 Puerto Rico became a U.S. commonwealth. This unique status means that the island has its own constitution and elected officials. As with the 50 states, Puerto Rico can change its constitution as long as it does not conflict with the U.S. Constitution.

✔ **Reading Check: Comparing and Contrasting** How was U.S. treatment of the Philippines similar to and different from its treatment of Puerto Rico?

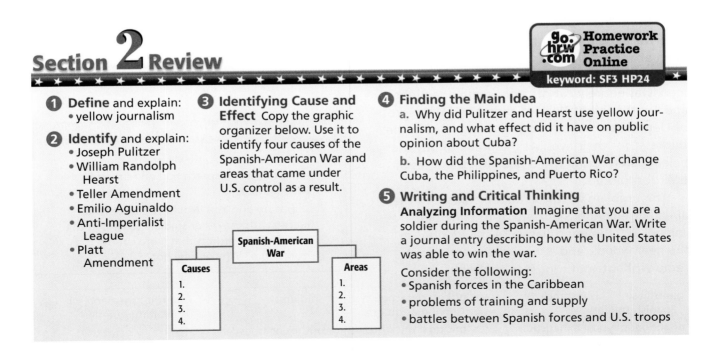

Section 2 Review

go.hrw.com **Homework Practice Online** keyword: SF3 HP24

❶ **Define** and explain:
• yellow journalism

❷ **Identify** and explain:
• Joseph Pulitzer
• William Randolph Hearst
• Teller Amendment
• Emilio Aguinaldo
• Anti-Imperialist League
• Platt Amendment

❸ **Identifying Cause and Effect** Copy the graphic organizer below. Use it to identify four causes of the Spanish-American War and areas that came under U.S. control as a result.

Spanish-American War

Causes	Areas
1.	1.
2.	2.
3.	3.
4.	4.

❹ **Finding the Main Idea**
a. Why did Pulitzer and Hearst use yellow journalism, and what effect did it have on public opinion about Cuba?

b. How did the Spanish-American War change Cuba, the Philippines, and Puerto Rico?

❺ **Writing and Critical Thinking**
Analyzing Information Imagine that you are a soldier during the Spanish-American War. Write a journal entry describing how the United States was able to win the war.

Consider the following:
• Spanish forces in the Caribbean
• problems of training and supply
• battles between Spanish forces and U.S. troops

The War Dispatches of Stephen Crane

THE GRANGER COLLECTION, NEW YORK

Most readers know of Stephen Crane for his novel The Red Badge of Courage. *He also worked as a journalist during the Spanish-American War, publishing many gripping war reports. While in his twenties, Crane was already so popular that his editors made a point of putting his name in their front-page headlines to attract more readers. The following war dispatch, "Night Attacks on the Marines and a Brave Rescue," describing fighting between U.S. Marines and Spanish soldiers, appeared in the* New York World *on July 16, 1898.*

Stephen Crane

Guantanamo, July 4. —

Once upon a time there was a great deal of fighting between the marines and the **guerrillas**[1] here, and during that space things occurred.

The night attacks were heart-breaking affairs, from which the men emerged in the morning exhausted to a final degree, like people who had been swimming for miles. From colonel to smallest trumpeter went a great thrill when the dawn broke slowly in the eastern sky, and the weary band quite cheerfully ate breakfast. . . . Afterward the men slept, sunk upon the ground in an **abandon**[2] that was almost a **stupor**.[3]

Lieut. Neville, with his **picket**[4] of about twenty men, was entirely cut off from camp one night, and another night Neville's picket and the picket of Lieut. Shaw were cut off, fighting hard in the **thickets**[5] for their lives. At the break of day the **beleaguered**[6] camp could hear still the rifles of their lost pickets.

The problem of rescue added anxiety to the already tremendous anxiety of the fine old colonel. . . . the guerrillas were still **lurking**[7] in the near woods, and it was unsafe enough in camp without venturing into the bush.

Volunteers from Company C were called for, and these seventeen privates volunteered: Boniface, Conway, Fitzgerald, Heilner, Harmson, Hemerle, Lewin, Mann, Mills, Monahan, Nolan, O'Donnell, Ryan, Riddle, Sinclair, Sullivan, W.A., and Smith, J.H.

They went out under Lieut. Lucas. They arrived in Neville's vicinity just as he and his men, together with Shaw and his men, were being finally surrounded at close range. Lucas and his seventeen men broke through the guerrillas and saved the pickets, and the whole body then fell back to Crest Hill. That is all there is to it.

Understanding What You Read

1. **Literature and History** What effect do you think this war dispatch had on readers in the United States?

2. **Literature and You** Would you have volunteered with the other soldiers to help in the rescue of the pickets that were cut off from camp? Why or why not?

---

[1]**guerrillas:** in this instance, Spanish soldiers

[2]**abandon:** physical exhaustion

[3]**stupor:** daze

[4]**picket:** detached body of soldiers serving as guards

[5]**thickets:** thick growth of bushes or trees

[6]**beleaguered:** surrounded

[7]**lurking:** sneaking, or waiting quietly

The United States and Latin America

Read to Discover

1. What steps did the United States take to build a canal across Panama?
2. How did U.S. involvement in Latin America change under President Theodore Roosevelt?
3. How did Presidents Taft and Wilson enforce the Monroe Doctrine?

WHY IT MATTERS TODAY

Businesses in the United States continue to have economic interests in other countries. Use **CNN fyi.com** or other **current events** sources to find out something about U.S. businesses that have manufacturing plants or major offices in other nations. Record your findings in your journal.

Define
- dollar diplomacy

Identify
- John Hay
- Hay-Herrán Treaty
- Philippe Bunau-Varilla
- Hay–Bunau-Varilla Treaty
- Panama Canal
- Roosevelt Corollary

The Story Continues

When the Spanish-American War began in 1898, the U.S. battleship *Oregon* was stationed at Puget Sound in Washington State. After receiving orders, the *Oregon* set out at top speed on a 12,000-mile voyage. It traveled around the southern tip of South America to join the fighting near Cuba. Newspapers charted the *Oregon*'s daily progress while the American public "breathlessly pushed her along." The trip lasted from March 19 to May 24—67 days!

The U.S. battleship Oregon *took more than two months to join the fighting in the Caribbean.*

⭐ The Panama Canal

The *Oregon* barely arrived in time to take part in the major battles around Cuba because travel around the southern tip of South America took weeks. This delay concerned many people. In the late 1800s some U.S. leaders began to explore ways to dig a canal across the narrow neck of Central America. Such a canal would link the Atlantic and Pacific

This poster celebrates the growing strength of the U.S. Navy under President Roosevelt.

★ ★ ★ ★ ★ ★ ★ ★ ★ ★ ★ ★

That's Interesting!

★ ★ ★ ★ ★ ★ ★ ★ ★ ★ ★ ★

A Visit to Panama Did you know that the first president to leave the United States while in office was Theodore Roosevelt? It's true! No president from George Washington through William McKinley had done that, despite all the foreign policy decisions and despite the major treaties that had been signed. When Roosevelt left the country in 1906, it wasn't because of politics. He wanted to see firsthand the construction of the Panama Canal. A famous picture of Roosevelt's trip shows the president sitting at the controls of a huge steam shovel. It almost seems as if Roosevelt is digging the canal himself!

Oceans and cut 8,000 miles off the voyage. It would also allow the U.S. Navy to link the Atlantic and Pacific naval fleets quickly.

In 1850 the United States and Great Britain had signed the Clayton-Bulwer Treaty. This agreement called for the two countries to jointly build and maintain a canal. Despite the treaty, they never built a canal. In 1881 France began work on a canal in Central America. After spending nearly $300 million and losing some 20,000 lives, the company became financially ruined in 1887. Less than one third of the planned 51-mile canal had been dug.

No one was a stronger supporter of a Central American canal than Theodore Roosevelt. Roosevelt had become president after the assassination of William McKinley in 1901. Influenced by the ideas of Alfred Thayer Mahan, Roosevelt believed that a canal was important to U.S. naval power, security, and strength. Earlier, Roosevelt had written to Mahan, "I believe we should build the [Central American] canal at once." Secretary of State **John Hay** negotiated the Hay-Pauncefote Treaty with Britain in 1901. The British gave up their interest in a Central American canal. In return, the United States agreed to keep the canal open to all vessels at all times.

Hay then began negotiations with Colombia, because the Isthmus of Panama was part of that country. Hay and the Colombian minister Thomas Herrán soon reached an agreement. The United States would pay $10 million plus $250,000 a year for a 99-year lease on a strip of land across the isthmus. The U.S. Senate approved the **Hay-Herrán Treaty** in 1903. However, the Colombian senate, hoping for better terms, rejected the treaty. President Roosevelt refused to pay more to Colombia. He considered other ways of gaining the Isthmus of Panama, such as seizing it by force.

Philippe Bunau-Varilla, chief engineer of the French Canal Company, offered an alternative plan. He met with Hay and Roosevelt and told them of a possible revolt in the Colombian province of Panama. Bunau-Varilla knew about the effort because he was organizing the plot. Bunau-Varilla left the meeting believing that the United States would not oppose or might even support the Panamanian revolt.

On November 2, 1903, a U.S. warship arrived in Colón, Panama. The next day a revolt began. Colombian forces tried to stop the rebellion but could not get to Panama. Dense jungles blocked land routes, and the U.S. warship blocked travel in the Atlantic Ocean. Panama then declared itself an independent country. The United States recognized the new nation on November 6. On November 13, Bunau-Varilla arrived in the United States as Panama's new foreign minister. Five days later he signed the **Hay–Bunau-Varilla Treaty**. This agreement closely resembled the Hay-Herrán Treaty. One exception was that the canal zone was widened to 10 miles.

✔ **Reading Check: Making Generalizations and Predictions** Do you think the United States would have given up its goal of building a canal if Panama had not gained independence? Explain your answer.

Building the Canal

Building the canal proved to be very difficult. The first obstacle to overcome was tropical disease. The canal route ran through jungles and swamps filled with mosquitoes, many of which carried malaria and yellow fever. Dr. William C. Gorgas, who had helped Dr. Walter Reed in Cuba, organized a successful effort to rid the canal route of disease-carrying mosquitoes. If Gorgas had not been successful, the canal's construction would have taken much longer. It also would have cost much more in terms of both lives and money.

Even with the reduced risk of disease, the work was very dangerous. The high mountain range of central Panama created a major obstacle. Much of the canal had to be blasted out of solid rock. Engineers directed workers to use dozens of steam shovels to cut a narrow, eight-mile-long channel through the mountains.

CONNECTING TO
SCIENCE AND TECHNOLOGY

The Panama Canal

Completed in 1914, the Panama Canal remains one of the greatest engineering accomplishments in the world. To travel from the Atlantic to the Pacific Ocean, a ship enters the Panama Canal near the town of Colón. The ship travels through the Gatun Locks, where the water level, and therefore the ship, is raised 85 feet. Then the ship travels down a long channel in Gatun Lake until it passes through the Gaillard Cut in the mountains. There the vessel is lowered 31 feet. The ship eventually descends to sea level by another series of locks, after which it follows another channel out into the ocean. The entire Panama Canal is about 51 miles long. A typical trip takes about nine hours. The canal reduces the distance a ship has to travel from one coast of the United States to the other by about 8,000 miles. **How do ships travel through the Panama Canal?**

Gaillard Cut

Gatun Locks

Culebra Mountain

Canal

Gatun Lake

To Pacific

To Atlantic

Locks

Sea level

Locks

THE GRANGER COLLECTION, NEW YORK

Daily Life

Digging the Canal Excavating the huge amounts of rock necessary to build the Panama Canal was extremely dangerous, requiring workers to handle powerful explosives. Workers sometimes died when their shovels struck the caps of unexploded charges. On one occasion, a bolt of lightning struck a 12-ton explosive charge, killing seven workers. Landslides were also a danger. **What about this image shows the scale of the effort needed to build the canal?**

August 15, 1914
The Panama Canal opens.

Some 6,000 lives were lost building the **Panama Canal**, which was finally opened to traffic on August 15, 1914. The cost was $375 million on top of the nearly $300 million spent in the failed French effort. In the end, however, the world had its "highway between the oceans."

✔ **Reading Check: Finding the Main Idea** Why did construction of the canal cost so many lives?

⭐ Roosevelt and Latin America

The Panama Canal allowed the United States to become more involved in Latin America. In 1823 President James Monroe had warned European nations not to interfere in the Western Hemisphere. In what became known as the Monroe Doctrine, he outlined his views. "The American continents . . . are henceforth not to be considered as subjects for future colonization by any European powers." The United States would view any such actions as a threat to its security.

The Monroe Doctrine had become a major principle of U.S. foreign policy. When Monroe presented the doctrine, however, the United States did not have the military power to enforce it. Instead, the United States had to rely on Britain's large navy. Britain had an interest in keeping other European countries out of the Americas. As the United States grew stronger and expanded its influence, particularly after the Spanish-American War, it became less dependent upon British naval power.

During the late 1800s many European investors had made loans to a number of Latin American countries. Venezuela, under the rule of dictator Cipriano Castro, fell deeply in debt to British and German investors. In 1902 the Venezuelan government refused to repay these debts or to have the claims settled by a neutral third party.

European leaders wanted to act but were worried about the Monroe Doctrine. In 1901, however, President Roosevelt had stated that the United States did "not guarantee any State against punishment if it misconducts itself." The European countries interpreted this to mean that they could collect their debts—by force if necessary. Britain and Germany sent ships to blockade Venezuela. Castro then asked Roosevelt to propose having the matter settled by a third party, which the Europeans accepted.

THE GRANGER COLLECTION, NEW YORK

Interpreting Political Cartoons

Roosevelt's big stick *In this cartoon President Roosevelt carries a big stick and leads a string of gunboats through the Caribbean Sea.* **Why do you think the artist chose to portray Roosevelt wading through the Caribbean?**

A similar situation arose in the Caribbean country of the Dominican Republic in 1904. Again, European countries considered using force to collect debts. This time Roosevelt worried that foreign forces might not leave once they had collected their debts. The presence of European forces in the Caribbean would violate the Monroe Doctrine. Furthermore, their presence could threaten U.S. power in the region and control of the Panama Canal.

But what if the United States kept European creditors from collecting debts owed them? Roosevelt knew that U.S. officials would then have to force debtor nations to repay their loans. In December 1904 the president explained his thinking in what became known as the **Roosevelt Corollary** to the Monroe Doctrine.

History Makers Speak

"Chronic wrongdoing . . . may in America, as elsewhere, ultimately require intervention [involvement] by some civilized nation, and in the Western Hemisphere the adherence [observance] of the United States to the Monroe Doctrine may force the United States, however reluctantly [unwillingly], in flagrant [extreme] cases of such wrongdoing . . . to the exercise of an international police power."

—Theodore Roosevelt, quoted in *A Diplomatic History of the American People,* by Thomas A. Bailey

Analyzing Primary Sources
Identifying Points of View
How did Roosevelt view the other nations of the Western Hemisphere?

This new role of the United States as the "police officer" of the Western Hemisphere suited Roosevelt's style. In 1900 he had said, "I have always been fond of the West African proverb: 'Speak softly and carry a big stick, you will go far.'" Roosevelt actively enforced the corollary throughout the rest of his presidency.

✔ **Reading Check: Finding the Main Idea** What responsibility did the United States take on as a result of the Roosevelt Corollary?

★ Taft and Wilson

When William Taft became president in 1909, he also acted to protect U.S. interests in Latin America. However, instead of Roosevelt's "big stick," Taft used a policy known as **dollar diplomacy**. Taft tried to influence Latin American governments through economic, not military, intervention. He wanted to encourage stability in Latin America by expanding American business interests there.

Analyzing Primary Sources

Identifying Points of View
According to Taft, how would dollar diplomacy help the United States control Latin America?

 History Makers Speak

❝[Dollar diplomacy] has been characterized as substituting dollars for bullets. It is . . . directed to the increase of American trade . . . [and] the substitution of arbitration [negotiation] and reason for war in the settlement of international disputes.❞

—William Howard Taft, quoted in *The Annals of America*

Taft tried to replace European investments in Latin America with U.S. investments. For example, in June 1911 the United States agreed to help obtain private loans from American banks to pay Nicaragua's national debt. In return, Nicaraguan leaders would allow U.S. troops in Nicaragua. The United States also signed a similar agreement with Honduras. Although the U.S. Senate rejected both agreements, the Taft administration followed the treaty terms anyway. In July, Nicaragua failed to repay a large loan from British investors. American bankers gave Nicaragua a $1.5 billion loan in exchange for control of the

U.S. Foreign Policy

Following the example of James Monroe, the progressive presidents each developed their own diplomatic policy toward Latin America.

Monroe Doctrine
The United States will defend its interests in the Western Hemisphere and keep European powers out.

Roosevelt Corollary
The United States will police wrongdoing by nations in the Western Hemisphere.

Wilson and Democracy
The United States will promote and protect democracy in the Western Hemisphere.

Taft's Dollar Diplomacy
The United States will aid its business interests in the Western Hemisphere.

Visualizing History

1. **Government** Compare and contrast the main goal of each president's foreign policy.

2. **Connecting to Today** How would you characterize current U.S. relations with Latin America?

National Bank of Nicaragua and the national railway. Local anger over this agreement soon led to a revolt in Nicaragua. Taft sent in U.S. Marines to protect American interests. The marines remained until 1925, returned the next year, and finally left in 1933.

When President Woodrow Wilson took office in 1913, he rejected Taft's dollar diplomacy. Wilson did not like the role of big business in foreign affairs. Instead, he believed the United States had a moral obligation to promote democracy in Latin America. He wanted to protect U.S. interests in the area by backing democratic government.

Wilson often opposed imperialism. Yet he sent more troops into Latin America than any president before him. For example, the Caribbean country of Haiti had long suffered economic and political problems. In 1915 another revolt took place in Haiti. Previously, Germany and France had sent troops to Haiti for short times to protect their interests. Wilson feared that those countries might try to take control of Haiti during the unrest. To keep this from taking place, U.S. Marines landed in Haiti on July 29, 1915, and quickly restored peace.

Similar events took place in the Dominican Republic. The customs policies set up by Roosevelt in 1905 had brought a stable government to this country. In 1911, however, the Dominican president was killed, and troubles returned. By threatening to withhold customs revenue, Secretary of State Philander Knox forced the Dominicans to accept a U.S.-backed government. Fearing more political unrest, President Wilson declared martial law on the island and set up a government run by the U.S. Navy in 1916. Wilson, like Roosevelt and Taft, would not allow unrest in Latin America to threaten U.S. interests there.

These U.S. Marines were among the many that President Wilson sent to restore order in Haiti.

✔ **Reading Check: Contrasting** How were the foreign policies of Roosevelt, Taft, and Wilson different?

Section 3 Review

go.
hrw
.com
Homework Practice Online
keyword: SF3 HP24

1. **Define** and explain:
   • dollar diplomacy

2. **Identify** and explain:
   • John Hay
   • Hay-Herrán Treaty
   • Philippe Bunau-Varilla
   • Hay–Bunau-Varilla Treaty
   • Panama Canal
   • Roosevelt Corollary

3. **Sequencing** Copy the diagram below. Use it to identify the four treaties signed by the United States to gain land and build the Panama Canal.

   Panama Canal Treaties

1850
1901
1903
1903

4. **Finding the Main Idea**
   a. How did Roosevelt change U.S. policy in the Western Hemisphere?

   b. In what ways did Presidents Taft and Wilson differ from Roosevelt in their handling of the Monroe Doctrine?

5. **Writing and Critical Thinking**
   Summarizing Imagine that you are a worker helping to build the Panama Canal. Write a letter home to your family, describing the difficulties you have encountered during your time in Panama.

   Consider the following:
   • the geography
   • new technology
   • disease

The United States and Mexico

Read to Discover

1. Why did the Mexican people revolt against their government in 1910?
2. What caused Mexican immigration to the United States to increase in the early 1900s?
3. Why did President Woodrow Wilson intervene in the Mexican Revolution?

WHY IT MATTERS TODAY

Relations between the United States and Mexico continue to change. Use CNNfyi.com or other **current events** sources to find out about current economic, political, or social issues involving these two countries. Record your findings in your journal.

Identify

- Porfirio Díaz
- Francisco Madero
- Mexican Revolution
- Victoriano Huerta
- Venustiano Carranza
- Francisco "Pancho" Villa
- Emiliano Zapata
- ABC Powers
- John J. Pershing

The Story Continues

In 1910 Mexico celebrated the 100th anniversary of the Grito de Dolores, Father Miguel Hidalgo y Costilla's call for revolution against Spain. Mexican president Porfirio Díaz treated international guests to entertainment and fine food. They toasted Mexico's independence, but little did Díaz realize that he would soon face a revolution against his own rule.

Porfirio Díaz refused to resign and allow free elections.

⭐ The Mexican Revolution

<u>Porfirio Díaz</u> was president of Mexico from 1877 to 1880 and 1884 to 1911, a total of 30 years. During his rule he eagerly welcomed foreign investment. The United States became the biggest investor in Mexico. By 1913, Americans had invested more than $1 billion in Mexican land, mining, oil, railways, and manufacturing. More than 50,000 U.S. citizens lived and worked in Mexico. Díaz ruled the Mexican people harshly. He imprisoned his opponents and rewarded his supporters. Most of Mexico's 15 million people were landless and poor.

The revolutionaries *Followers of Emiliano Zapata, known as* zapatistas, *march in August 1914.* **What does the photograph reveal about the forces that fought in the Mexican Revolution?**

Many Mexicans found a new leader in democratic reformer **Francisco Madero**, who began the **Mexican Revolution** in 1910. Madero gained support throughout Mexico, violently forcing Díaz to resign in May. The Taft administration wanted a stable government in Mexico and quickly recognized the Madero administration.

The revolution to end the Díaz dictatorship caused a civil war. Many Mexicans came to the United States to escape the violence and to avoid political persecution. These immigrants came from all levels of Mexican society. Many hoped to find industrial jobs in the United States. Between 1905 and 1909, 28,000 Mexicans came to the United States. Between 1910 and 1915, that number rose to more than 100,000. Many Mexican citizens fled to South Texas, and cities such as San Antonio became important refugee centers.

However, the struggle for power continued. In February 1913 General **Victoriano Huerta** took power and had Madero killed. The violence angered President-elect Woodrow Wilson. Once in office, Wilson refused to recognize the Huerta government.

A revolt led by **Venustiano Carranza** against Huerta began to gain support in Mexico. Wilson wanted the two sides to stop fighting and agree to hold a free election. If they agreed, Wilson said he would help the newly elected Mexican government obtain loans from U.S. banks. However, Wilson said that Huerta could not be a candidate. Not surprisingly, Huerta refused Wilson's urging.

Wilson then lifted U.S. restrictions against selling arms to Mexico so that weapons could be supplied to the forces opposing Huerta. Wilson also stationed U.S. warships in the Gulf of Mexico to block any foreign aid to Huerta. In addition to Carranza, two other major revolutionaries led movements to overthrow Huerta. **Francisco "Pancho" Villa** led rebels in the north, and **Emiliano Zapata** led rebels in the south. Like Carranza, both Villa and Zapata had supported Madero against Díaz. Both were heroes to Mexico's poor.

Carranza, Villa, and Zapata had a common goal in hoping to overthrow Huerta. However, they were not close allies.

✔ **Reading Check: Identifying Cause and Effect** What caused the Mexican Revolution, and what were its immediate effects on Mexico?

Pancho Villa (left) and Emiliano Zapata (right) led revolutionaries against Victoriano Huerta's government.

THE GRANGER COLLECTION, NEW YORK

America as a World Power **759**

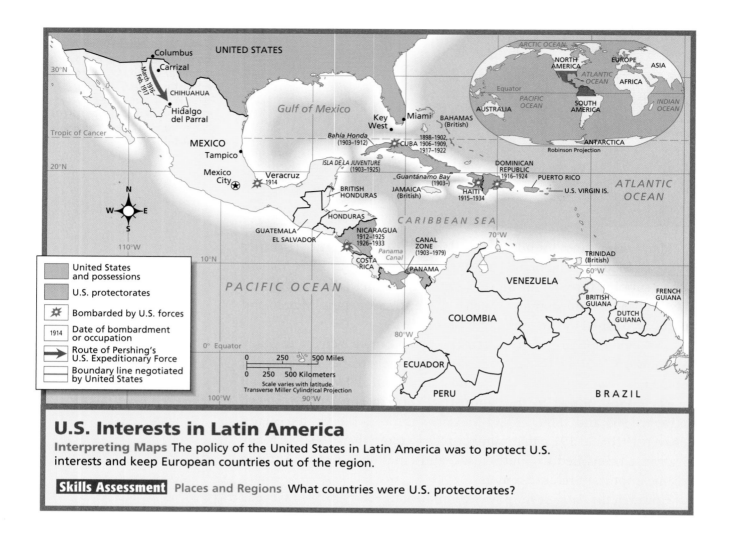

U.S. Interests in Latin America

Interpreting Maps The policy of the United States in Latin America was to protect U.S. interests and keep European countries out of the region.

Skills Assessment Places and Regions What countries were U.S. protectorates?

Wilson's Reaction

A number of American business leaders feared they would lose investments in Mexico. They wanted Huerta out of office, by force if necessary. President Wilson, however, refused to intervene, despite added pressure from Congress and the press. He explained his reasoning.

Analyzing Primary Sources

Identifying Points of View Why does Wilson have to remind himself that he does not have vested interests in Mexico?

> **History Makers Speak** ❝I have to pause and remind myself that I am President of the United States and not of a small group of Americans with vested interests [investments] in Mexico.❞
>
> —Woodrow Wilson, quoted in *A Diplomatic History of the American People*, by Thomas A. Bailey

Wilson adopted a policy of "watchful waiting" toward the unrest in Mexico. At the same time, he looked for a chance to act against Huerta.

In 1914 Wilson finally found a reason to act. In April, a group of U.S. sailors from the cruiser *Dolphin* landed in a restricted area of Tampico, Mexico. They were arrested but were soon released with an apology. However, Huerta refused the commander of the *Dolphin*'s demands for severe punishment of the responsible Mexican officer and for a 21-gun salute to the American flag. With tensions running high, Wilson learned that a German ship carrying a large supply of arms was headed to the port of Veracruz. To keep the weapons from Huerta, Wilson ordered the U.S. Navy to seize Veracruz. In late April 1914, U.S. forces captured the city.

The quick assault on Veracruz united Mexicans against the United States, and the two countries stood on the edge of war. Then the **ABC Powers**, Argentina, Brazil, and Chile, offered to negotiate the dispute. Wilson accepted the proposed settlement, but Huerta and Carranza did not. In July, fighting in Mexico forced Huerta to flee. In August 1914, Carranza and his forces took Mexico City and set up a new government a year later. The United States recognized Carranza as president of Mexico in October 1915, and U.S. troops withdrew from Veracruz six months later.

Although Huerta was no longer in power, Pancho Villa and Emiliano Zapata continued their revolts. Villa hoped to destroy the Carranza government and to win the support of the Mexican people by attacking the United States. In January, Villa and his troops stopped a train at Santa Ysabel, Mexico, killing 18 American mining engineers on board. On March 9, 1916, Villa and his troops attacked Columbus, New Mexico, burning the town and killing 17 U.S. citizens.

In response, President Wilson sent General **John J. Pershing** and 15,000 soldiers into Mexico. Pershing's forces chased Villa more than 300 miles but failed to capture him. Wilson eventually agreed to recall the troops. In 1917 Carranza approved a new constitution to bring orderly rule to Mexico. However, in 1920 the forces of Álvaro Obregón, a trusted aide to Carranza, revolted and killed the Mexican leader. After 1920 peace gradually returned to Mexico.

General John J. "Black Jack" Pershing led the failed effort to capture Pancho Villa.

✔ **Reading Check: Summarizing** How did Wilson respond to events in Mexico?

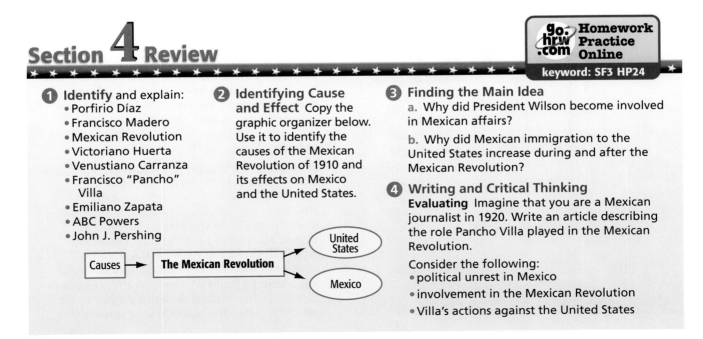

Section 4 Review

go.hrw.com
Homework Practice Online
keyword: SF3 HP24

1 **Identify** and explain:
• Porfirio Díaz
• Francisco Madero
• Mexican Revolution
• Victoriano Huerta
• Venustiano Carranza
• Francisco "Pancho" Villa
• Emiliano Zapata
• ABC Powers
• John J. Pershing

2 **Identifying Cause and Effect** Copy the graphic organizer below. Use it to identify the causes of the Mexican Revolution of 1910 and its effects on Mexico and the United States.

Causes → The Mexican Revolution → United States / Mexico

3 **Finding the Main Idea**
a. Why did President Wilson become involved in Mexican affairs?

b. Why did Mexican immigration to the United States increase during and after the Mexican Revolution?

4 **Writing and Critical Thinking**
Evaluating Imagine that you are a Mexican journalist in 1920. Write an article describing the role Pancho Villa played in the Mexican Revolution.

Consider the following:
• political unrest in Mexico
• involvement in the Mexican Revolution
• Villa's actions against the United States

Chapter 24 Review

The Chapter at a Glance

Examine the visual summary of the chapter below. Use the visual summary to write five multiple-choice questions to ask a classmate about when, where, and why the United States intervened in foreign affairs.

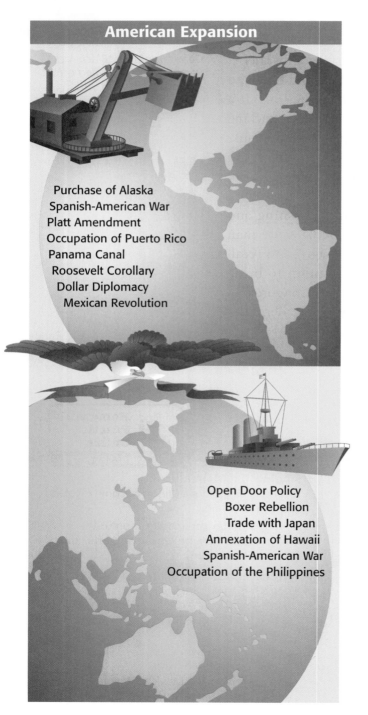

American Expansion

Purchase of Alaska
Spanish-American War
Platt Amendment
Occupation of Puerto Rico
Panama Canal
Roosevelt Corollary
Dollar Diplomacy
Mexican Revolution

Open Door Policy
Boxer Rebellion
Trade with Japan
Annexation of Hawaii
Spanish-American War
Occupation of the Philippines

Identifying People and Ideas

Use the following terms or people in historically significant sentences.

1. imperialism
2. Liliuokalani
3. Boxer Rebellion
4. Teller Amendment
5. Panama Canal
6. Roosevelt Corollary
7. dollar diplomacy
8. Francisco "Pancho" Villa
9. ABC Powers
10. John J. Pershing

Understanding Main Ideas

Section 1 *(Pages 738–743)*

1. Why did the United States propose the Open Door Policy, and how was it received?

Section 2 *(Pages 744–749)*

2. How did the press help spark U.S. involvement in the conflict in Cuba?
3. How did the outcome of the Spanish-American War affect the United States, Spain, and Cuba?

Section 3 *(Pages 751–757)*

4. Explain the steps that the United States took to build and control the Panama Canal.
5. What policies did Roosevelt, Taft, and Wilson use to expand U.S. power in the Western Hemisphere?

Section 4 *(Pages 758–761)*

6. What were the causes of the Mexican Revolution, and what effects did the Mexican Revolution have on Mexico and the United States?

You Be the Historian— Reviewing Themes

1. **Geography** Why did the United States want to control certain Pacific islands?
2. **Economics** How did U.S. business interests affect U.S. foreign policy in Asia and Latin America?
3. **Global Relations** Why did the United States support Cuba against Spain?

Thinking Critically

1. **Evaluating** Do you think the Spanish-American War helped or hurt the people of Cuba, the Philippines, and Puerto Rico? Explain your answer.
2. **Identifying Cause and Effect** Why did the United States build the Panama Canal, and what effect did this have on U.S. foreign policies in the Western Hemisphere?
3. **Supporting a Point of View** Which president's foreign policy in Latin America do you think was most effective? Explain your answer.

Interpreting Political Cartoons
Study the political cartoon shown below. Then answer the following questions.

PATIENT WAITERS ARE NO LOSERS.
UNCLE SAM.—I ain't in a hurry;—it 'll drop into my basket when it gets ripe!

THE GRANGER COLLECTION, NEW YORK

1. Which of the following answers best describes what the pieces of fruit on the tree and in the basket represent?
   a. nations with which the United States is at war
   b. foreign allies of the United States
   c. territories that the United States claims or wants to claim
   d. overseas colonies of the United States

2. Based on the political cartoon, do you think the artist was in favor of imperialism or isolationism? Explain your answer.

Analyzing Primary Sources
Read the following statement by President William McKinley and answer the questions that follow.

"We have the right as conquerors to hold the Philippines. . . . This policy may be characterized as unjust to Spain; but it is the result of the fortunes of war. All nations recognize that the conqueror may dictate the terms of peace. . . . The Philippines are a foothold for us in the Far East. Their possession gives us standing and influence. It gives us also valuable trade both in exports and imports."

3. Which of the following statements best explains McKinley's view on why the United States should keep the Philippines?
   a. Holding the Philippines will gain the United States respect and valuable trade in Asia.
   b. Spain should be punished for losing the war.
   c. Under international law the United States is required to keep the Philippines.
   d. Keeping the Philippines will pay for the U.S. war expenses.

4. What justification does McKinley give for keeping the Philippines?
   a. The United States won the war.
   b. The Philippines have asked for U.S. control.
   c. The Philippines are not ready for independence.
   d. Spain no longer wants the Philippines.

5. Do you think that most Americans would agree with McKinley's statement? Explain your answer.

Alternative Assessment

Building Your Portfolio

American History

Interdisciplinary Connection to Science
Use the library and the HRW Web site to research the construction of the Panama Canal. Then create a poster in which you outline the steps in the canal's construction. Your display should include illustrations, graphics, and at least 10 statistics about the canal.

internet connect

Internet Activity: go.hrw.com
keyword: SF3 CF24

Choose a topic on America as a World Power to:
- Research Stephen Crane's life and career as a novelist and journalist.
- Create a public service advertisement on the effort to stop yellow fever.
- Create a brochure on the Panama Canal.

Social Studies Skills

WORKSHOP

Using the Internet and Creating a Database

There is a wealth of information on the Internet. However, it takes a careful approach to find accurate and useful information.

Using the Internet. There are many Web sites that concentrate on specific topics. Government sites such as the Library of Congress and the U.S. Census Bureau provide economic, historical, and political information. Other sites such as CNNfyi.com allow you to access up-to-the-minute news and information. If you are not sure which Web site might have the data you want, directories and search engines can help you search the Internet. Many Internet browsers include lists of such search tools. Whatever tool you use, reading its search tips files can help you search more efficiently.

Once you have found a Web site, you should determine whether the information it contains is reliable. Ask yourself the following questions:

- Is a well-respected organization sponsoring the site?

- Does the text contain any obvious mistakes?

- Has the Web site been updated recently, and are most of the page links active?

- Does the information appear biased?

Creating a Database. Much of the information available on the Internet is presented in database form. A database is a collection of information that is organized so that you can find the facts you need efficiently. You can also use the Internet to gather facts for creating your own database on a research topic.

Whatever information sources you use, you should follow some guidelines when creating a database.

- Give your database a clear title and use headings to identify the types of data it includes, such as dates, locations, or quantities. It is often useful to identify the source of your information as well.

- Make sure the information included under each heading follows a consistent format. For example, if your heading is STATES, it should not include data for a city.

Example

Most Populous States, 2000*		
State	**Population**	**Rank**
California	33,930,798	1
Florida	16,028,890	3
New York	19,004,973	4
Texas	20,903,994	2
*Based on Census 2000 figures		

Practicing the Skills

Search the Internet to find information on the U.S. economy. This could include information on employment, inflation, new jobs, or U.S. trade with foreign countries. Use this information to create a database that clearly displays the facts and figures about the economy that you have found.

History in Action

UNIT 9 SIMULATION

Lincoln Charter School

You Solve the Problem . . .

How Can the Progressives Reform American Politics?

Complete the following activity in small cooperative groups. The year is 1900. Your city is going to be hosting a large conference of progressives from all around the country. Your group will be giving a presentation to these men and women on reforming the political process in the United States to make it more democratic. Follow these steps to solve your problem.

 1. Gather Information. Use your textbook and other resources to find information that might influence the arguments you will make in your presentation. Be sure to use what you learned from this unit's Skills Workshop on Using the Internet and Creating a Database to help you find a solution. You may want to divide up different parts of the research among group members.

2. List and Consider Options. Based on the information you have gathered, list and consider the options you might recommend for making the American political process more democratic. Your final solution to the problem may be easier to reach if you consider as many options as possible. Be sure to record your possible options to help you prepare your presentation.

3. Consider Advantages and Disadvantages. Now consider the advantages and disadvantages of taking each option. Ask yourselves questions like: "How will this reform help more people participate in the political process?" Once you have considered the advantages and disadvantages, record them as notes for use in your presentation.

4. Choose, Implement, and Evaluate a Solution. After considering the advantages and disadvantages, you should plan and create your presentation. Be sure to make your proposal politics very clear. You will need to support your plan for reforming American politics by including information you gathered and by explaining why you rejected other options. Your presentation needs to be visually appealing to gain the interest of others attending the conference. When you are ready, decide who in your group will make which part of the presentation and take your solution to the other progressives at the convention (the rest of the class). Good luck!

EPILOGUE Modern America
(1914–Present)

A 1929 political cartoon warns of an upcoming economic downturn.

President Franklin D. Roosevelt became well liked as a result of his weekly radio address to the nation in the 1930s.

UNITED STATES

1929 The New York stock market crashes.

1933 President Franklin D. Roosevelt's administration begins the New Deal.

1941 Japanese attack a naval base at Pearl Harbor, Hawaii, on December 7, drawing the United States into World War II.

1954 The U.S. Supreme Court declares segregated schools unconstitutional in *Brown* v. *Board of Education*.

1900	**1910**	**1920**	**1930**	**1940**	**1950**

1914 Austrian archduke Franz Ferdinand and his wife are assassinated, which leads to the beginning of World War I.

1917 The first U.S. troops arrive in Europe to fight in World War I.

1944 The Allies, led by U.S. General Dwight D. Eisenhower, begin the D-Day invasion of France during World War II.

1949 The United States, Great Britain, and 10 other countries form the North Atlantic Treaty Organization (NATO).

WORLD

During World War I, soldiers wore gas masks to protect themselves from the poisonous gases that were used.

Allied flags from World War I

Build on What You Know

In the first part of the 1900s the United States took a leadership role in global affairs and became one of the most powerful countries in the world. At the same time, economic and social changes brought new opportunities for women, minorities, and younger Americans. Americans have helped shape many of the most important events of modern times.

Alan Shepard, a crew member of Apollo 14, *holding the American flag*

President George W. Bush greets firefighters while touring the rubble of the World Trade Center after the September 11 attack.

1969 American astronaut Neil Armstrong becomes the first person to walk on the Moon.

1987 The United States and the Soviet Union sign the Intermediate-Range Nuclear Forces Treaty.

2000 Weeks after election day, George W. Bush wins the presidency in a presidential race unlike any other.

2001 On September 11, terrorists attack the World Trade Center and the Pentagon.

1960   1970   1980   1990   2000

1961 The Berlin Wall is built.

1968 The Tet Offensive is launched in Vietnam but is driven back by U.S. troops.

1979 U.S. president Jimmy Carter negotiates a peace treaty between Israel and Egypt.

1989 Germans tear down the Berlin Wall.

1994 The North American Free Trade Agreement (NAFTA), a plan for free trade among Canada, Mexico, and the United States, takes effect.

If you were there . . .
How would you react to the changes sweeping the nation?

You Be the Historian

Themes Journal

What's Your Opinion? Do you **agree** or **disagree** with the following statements? Support your point of view in your journal.

- **Global Relations** War is the only way to resolve a conflict between two countries.

- **Citizenship** Citizens have a right to disagree with their government.

- **Economics** All countries must work together to promote economic development.

World War I and the 1920s

Read to Discover

1. Why did the United States get involved in World War I, and what role did it play in the war?
2. What changes took place in the U.S. economy during and after World War I?
3. What was American society like during the Roaring Twenties?

WHY IT MATTERS TODAY

The United States is still involved in global organizations. Use **CNNfyi.com** or other **current events** sources to find out about some of the ties that the United States keeps with other nations and why. Record your findings in your journal.

Define

- militarism
- armistice
- prohibition

Identify

- Woodrow Wilson
- Selective Service Act
- Treaty of Versailles
- Communists
- Red Scare
- Twenty-first Amendment
- Jazz Age
- Harlem Renaissance
- Lost Generation

The Story Continues

World War I artillery

Ever since Austria-Hungary annexed the province of Bosnia and Herzegovina in 1908, the Balkans region had been a source of conflict. As problems grew worse, many people began to refer to the region as a "powder keg" ready to explode. On June 28, 1914, Archduke Franz Ferdinand, the heir to the throne of Austria-Hungary, and his wife, Sophie, visited Bosnia. As Ferdinand and Sophie rode through Sarajevo, a Serb assassin stepped out and killed the couple. This event sparked a war that soon spread throughout the world.

☆ The World at War

World War I resulted from years of growing tensions in Europe. Excessive nationalism—a feeling of pride in one's nation, language, or culture above all others—helped cause this tension. Tensions also grew as countries tried to gain territories and build overseas empires. Some nations built up their armed forces and developed new weapons to be ready for war. This policy, along with the strong influence of military institutions and values on a society, is known as **militarism**.

This military buildup had Europe on the brink of war when Franz Ferdinand and his wife were assassinated. Believing that the Serbian government was behind the murder, Austria-Hungary declared war on Serbia in July 1914. A system of alliances drew most of the major European nations into the fight within a few days. Austria-Hungary and Germany, and later Bulgaria and the Ottoman Empire, formed the Central Powers. The Allied Powers, or Allies—which included France, Great Britain, Russia, and later Italy—fought against them.

World War I was unlike any other war that had been fought. New weapons such as machine guns and poison gas made traditional ways of fighting almost useless. The opposing armies dug hundreds of miles of trenches, or ditches, for protection. The result was that neither side could overcome the other's defenses.

Most Americans wanted to stay out of the war. President **Woodrow Wilson** continued to work for a lasting peace, but neither side would negotiate. Then German submarines attacked American ships, and Wilson broke off diplomatic relations in February 1917. One month later Wilson learned that German foreign minister Arthur Zimmermann had sent a telegram to the German minister in Mexico. Known as the Zimmermann Note, the telegram suggested that Germany and Mexico form an alliance against the United States. In response, Wilson asked Congress to declare war on Germany on April 2, 1917.

To raise troops, Congress quickly passed the **Selective Service Act**. This act required men between the ages of 18 and 45 to sign up for the draft. More than 4.5 million Americans served in World War I. The more than 350,000 African Americans who enlisted served in segregated units. Thousands of women also served in the army or in the Red Cross, many as nurses, secretaries, clerks, or ambulance drivers. One driver recalled the dangers she faced on duty during an air raid.

Daily Life

Trench warfare Life in the trenches along the western front varied a great deal. In quieter areas, troops suffered from boredom. In areas with more fighting, soldiers faced danger and anxiety. During the night, troops often completed construction and repair work. These jobs might include laying cable or barbed wire. Most attacks began in the early morning. At daybreak, soldiers on both sides usually waited with their rifles loaded. If there was no enemy attack, they would eat their breakfast and prepare for a day of listening to mortar fire. **What challenges did soldiers face in the trenches?**

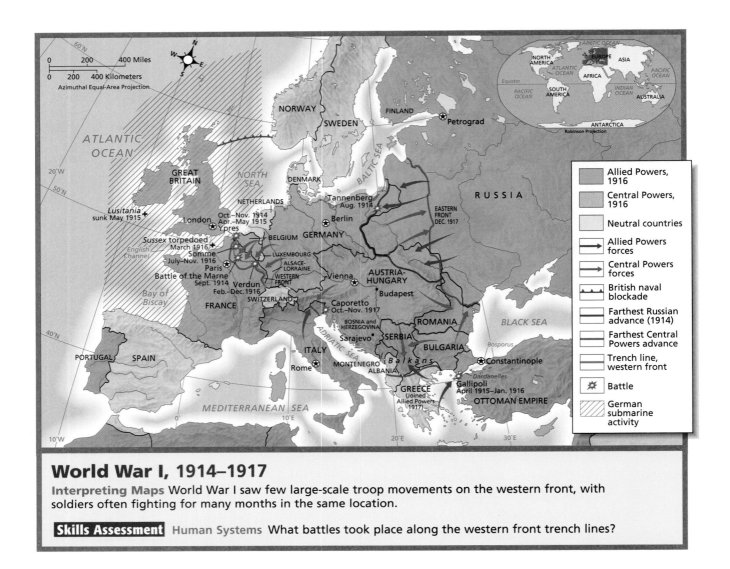

World War I, 1914–1917

Interpreting Maps World War I saw few large-scale troop movements on the western front, with soldiers often fighting for many months in the same location.

Skills Assessment Human Systems What battles took place along the western front trench lines?

Analyzing Primary Sources

Drawing Inferences and Conclusions How does this woman react to the potential dangers of war?

❝I had just stopped my engine . . . when shrapnel [shell fragments] whizzed past my head and there was a tremendous crash close beside. . . . Then an ambulance call came and I tore off.❞

—Mrs. Guy Napier-Martin, quoted in *Into the Breach,* by Dorothy and Carl J. Schneider

To fund the war, Congress raised taxes and sold war bonds. About 9.4 million Americans spent nearly $4 billion on bonds. The federal government also took greater control of the country's resources. The new War Industries Board looked after the production and distribution of manufactured goods. The Food Administration increased farm production and controlled food prices. Some Americans volunteered to eat less by taking part in "wheatless Mondays" and "meatless Tuesdays."

Some people benefited from greater employment opportunities as departing soldiers left jobs to be filled at home. Some 1 million women filled positions in the labor force, and thousands of Hispanics and African Americans moved north to find factory work.

✔ **Reading Check: Identifying Cause and Effect** Why did the United States join World War I, and how did the war effort change the country?

★ The Push for Peace

U.S. forces began arriving in France in June 1917 and joined the Allied forces. In the spring of 1918, the Germans launched a brutal attack on the western front. With the help of U.S. soldiers, the Allies held the German army back.

By the fall of 1918, the Allies were on the offensive. On November 11, 1918, Germany signed an **armistice**, or truce, with the Allies. World War I had finally ended. More than 8.5 million soldiers had been killed. Industry and agriculture in many parts of Europe had been destroyed. After the war ended, President Wilson created a plan, called the Fourteen Points, to avoid future wars. Among other things, Wilson's plan called for the creation of the League of Nations, an international organization dedicated to preventing future conflicts.

In January 1919, leaders of 27 nations attended the peace conference held at the palace of Versailles in France. They signed the final peace treaty of World War I, the **Treaty of Versailles**. The treaty punished Germany by making the country pay billions of dollars for the costs and damages of the war. The treaty also created the League of Nations. However, some Americans, including a number of senators, believed that membership in the organization would force the United States into more international conflicts. Therefore, Congress refused to join the League of Nations and rejected the Treaty of Versailles.

✔ **Reading Check: Analyzing Information** What were some of the results of World War I?

Seated from left to right are Italian prime minister Vittorio Orlando, British prime minister David Lloyd George, French premier Georges Clemenceau, and U.S. president Woodrow Wilson.

November 11, 1918
Germany and the Allied Powers sign an armistice that ends World War I.

★ A Changing Nation

After the war, American industries boomed, and more Americans moved to the growing cities. However, with the return of military personnel, there were soon too many workers and not enough jobs. Many women were forced out of their wartime jobs. Prices and unemployment continued to rise while wages fell or stayed about the same, causing a severe recession. In 1919 more than 4 million workers went on strike to demand higher pay. Many Americans saw the strikes as a sign that **Communists**—people who favor the equal distribution of wealth and the end of all forms of private property—were trying to take over the country. A successful communist revolt in Russia in 1917 touched off in the United States a wave of anticommunist fear called the **Red Scare**. The Red Scare gradually died down, but a general fear and hatred of foreigners remained.

The 1920s brought better times for many people in the United States. In 1920, women had won the right to vote. The first election in which they cast their ballots also began a new era of Republican leadership.

The Model T Ford was also called the Tin Lizzie.

President Warren Harding's administration worked to strengthen the economy but was weakened by scandal. When Harding died unexpectedly in 1923, his vice president, Calvin Coolidge, became president. Declaring that "the business of America is business," Coolidge promised continued prosperity and economic growth. As with Harding, most of Coolidge's policies benefited the wealthy. Although the gap between the rich and the poor grew, overall the economy went through a period of growth.

Automobile manufacturer Henry Ford helped the economy by introducing the Model T in 1908. Over time Ford made his factories more efficient by introducing the moving assembly line. This production system cut the Model T's assembly time and, as a result, lowered its price. By 1927, Americans had bought some 15 million of his Model Ts. The automobile industry had become the biggest business in the country and caused related industries to grow.

The popularity of the car changed the landscape of the United States. Roadside diners, service stations, and motels—or "motor hotels"—sprang up. More people moved to the suburbs and drove to their jobs in the cities. Many businesses moved to the edges of towns where real estate was cheaper. The car industry also changed the way business was done. Other industries used the car industry's production and advertising techniques to sell their products. Demand for new goods kept business booming.

The 1920s were also a time of clashing ideals. In 1919 Congress passed the Eighteenth Amendment calling for **prohibition**—the banning of the manufacture, distribution, and sale of alcohol. However, many Americans still drank at home and in clubs that illegally served liquor. Organized crime increased as gangsters fought for control of the illegal alcohol business. Such problems later led to passage of the **Twenty-first Amendment** in 1933, ending prohibition. Refusing to obey prohibition was only one of the many ways that young people rebelled against society in the 1920s. Young women called flappers rejected traditional ideas about proper behavior and styles for women. Flappers wore makeup and cut their hair short to show their independence.

Popular magazines reflected the changing fashions and music of the 1920s.

While many Protestant groups had joined together to push for prohibition, other issues divided them. Some people were against Charles Darwin's theory of evolution because it disagreed with the Bible's story of creation. In 1925 Tennessee outlawed the teaching of evolution, but a schoolteacher in that state, John Scopes, broke the law. That year, people around the world followed his trial. Although Scopes was convicted, this decision was overturned two years later.

Nativism, or strong anti-immigrant feelings, also increased in the 1920s. In response to these views, the U.S. government greatly limited immigration from all countries except Mexico. The growing dislike of immigrants also helped bring about the rebirth of the Ku Klux Klan. Members targeted African Americans, Catholics, Jews, and foreigners, often using violence.

✔ **Reading Check:** **Summarizing** What conflicts arose in the United States in the 1920s?

★ The Roaring Twenties

For many Americans, however, the 1920s brought good times. Many people had more money to spend and more time for fun. They listened to music and sports on radios and went to the movies. In 1927 the first talkie—a movie with sound—appeared.

The 1920s are often known as the **Jazz Age** because of the popularity of jazz. The roots of this musical style are found in African American culture. As African Americans moved to northern cities, they brought jazz to white audiences. Harlem, a neighborhood in New York City, became the center of African American cultural life. Writer and artist Elton Fax explained why the neighborhood attracted African Americans. "Harlem epitomized [symbolized] a kind of freedom that we did not know: 'Once I get to Harlem, I won't need to worry about anything. Nobody's gonna bother me in Harlem.'" This period of African American artistic achievement was called the **Harlem Renaissance**. Harlem Renaissance artists often showed the pride that they felt for their cultural heritage in their work.

Other writers, known as the **Lost Generation**, took part in another literary movement. Writers such as Ernest Hemingway responded to the death and destruction of World War I. Hemingway called the war "the most colossal [huge], murderous, mismanaged butchery that has ever taken place on earth." Overall, however, the Roaring Twenties showed that most Americans felt positive about the future.

Louis Armstrong was nick-named Satchmo, and Bessie Smith was known as the Empress of Blues.

✔ Reading Check: **Supporting a Point of View** Do you think that the 1920s should be better known for the problems or the good times? Explain your answer.

Section 1 Review

go.hrw.com **Homework Practice Online**
keyword: SF3 HPE

1 **Define** and explain:
• militarism
• armistice
• prohibition

2 **Identify** and explain:
• Woodrow Wilson
• Selective Service Act
• Treaty of Versailles
• Communists
• Red Scare
• Twenty-first Amendment
• Jazz Age
• Harlem Renaissance
• Lost Generation

3 **Sequencing** Copy the time line below. Use it to list what you consider to be the five most important events that took place in either the United States or the world between 1914 and 1928.

1914 1916 1918 1920 1922 1924 1926 1928

4 **Finding the Main Idea**
a. What caused the United States to join World War I, and how did it contribute to an Allied victory?

b. Describe the economic, social, and cultural changes that took place in the United States after World War I.

5 **Writing and Critical Thinking**
Summarizing Imagine that you are preparing a museum exhibit on American life during the Roaring Twenties. Write a proposal explaining what your exhibit will include.

Consider the following:
• the popularity of the car
• jazz music and the Harlem Renaissance
• the ways society changed during the years following World War I

The Great Depression and World War II

Read to Discover

1. How did the Great Depression affect American society?
2. What did President Roosevelt's administration do to try to help Americans get through the depression?
3. In what ways did the United States contribute to the Allied war effort in World War II?

WHY IT MATTERS TODAY

The U.S. stock market still experiences ups and downs. Use **CNNfyi.com** or other **current events** sources to find out about recent changes in the stock market. Record your findings in your journal.

Define

- public works
- fascism

Identify

- Great Depression
- Herbert Hoover
- Franklin D. Roosevelt
- New Deal
- Federal Deposit Insurance Corporation
- Social Security Act
- Nazis
- Lend-Lease Act
- D-Day
- Holocaust

A newspaper headline announces the crash of the stock market.

The Story Continues

On October 29, 1929, the U.S. stock market had its single worst day in history. As stock prices plunged, investors desperately tried to sell their increasingly worthless stock. Fistfights broke out on the floor of the New York Stock Exchange. People reportedly lost shoes, glasses, and false teeth. Journalist Jonathan Leonard was on Wall Street the day of the crash. "This was real panic," he recalled. "When the closing bell rang, the great bull market [stock market with rising prices] was dead and buried."

★ The Dawn of the Depression

Despite the economic good times of the 1920s, there had been signs of trouble ahead. Industries such as lumber, mining, and agriculture had never recovered from the financial setbacks brought by the end of World War I. The gap between wealthy and poor Americans meant that few people had the money to buy goods. As a result, there was not enough demand to support businesses. Still, the U.S. stock market seemed to be on a constant rise. Americans everywhere were investing in stocks in hopes of making money. In September 1929 stock prices rose to an all-time high. However, prices soon began to slide downward. On October 29, 1929, nervous investors rushed to sell their stock, causing prices to drop even lower. Losses for that day—known as Black Tuesday—totaled around $15 billion. Many investors who had bought their stock on credit lost everything they had.

In the months after the stock market crash, businesses slowed down or closed, and laid off workers. By 1933 about 25 percent of Americans were unemployed. Banks also failed, partly because investors could not repay their loans. People across the country lost their savings. Around the world, people were hurt by the **Great Depression**—the severe economic downturn that had begun with the U.S. stock market crash.

To help Americans, President **Herbert Hoover** cut taxes and bought farmers' extra crops, hoping to raise prices. He tried to provide jobs by putting government money in **public works**—construction projects for the public good. Hoover, however, did not believe that the government should provide direct aid such as food, clothing, shelter, and money. Most suffering Americans saw his viewpoint as a sign that he did not care about their difficulties.

✔ **Reading Check: Identifying Cause and Effect** What caused the Great Depression, and how did it affect Americans?

⭐ Roosevelt Takes Charge

In 1932, voters elected Democrat **Franklin D. Roosevelt** to the presidency. "This great nation will . . . revive [recover] and will prosper [succeed] . . . ," he promised at his inauguration in 1933. "The only thing we have to fear is fear itself." Roosevelt's plan for improving the economy was called the **New Deal**. In his first three months in office, Congress passed many New Deal programs. One of Roosevelt's first steps, however, was to close the nation's banks and only allow financially secure banks to reopen. Congress also created the **Federal Deposit Insurance Corporation** (FDIC), which insured a person's bank deposits up to $5,000. Roosevelt's administration also gave aid to states and municipalities through the Federal Emergency Relief Administration (FERA). The states and municipalities then distributed aid to poor Americans. Many people, however, wanted jobs instead of government aid. Job programs that hired people to work on federal projects helped many Americans reclaim their self-respect. New Deal legislation also brought some relief to farmers.

In 1935 Roosevelt suggested a new series of reforms to help American businesses, as well as the millions of citizens who were still out of work. Congress created a relief agency known as the Works Progress

PRESIDENTIAL PROFILES

Franklin D. Roosevelt

Franklin D. Roosevelt was born into a wealthy New York family. Roosevelt served in the New York legislature and as assistant secretary of the navy. In 1920 he was the Democratic vice presidential candidate. Although he was popular and intelligent, Roosevelt was not considered a strong leader.

His life changed dramatically in 1921 when he suffered an attack of polio. This disease left him paralyzed in both legs. He learned to move again with the help of leg braces, though he often used a wheelchair. He reentered politics and enjoyed great success. Roosevelt's private battle with polio made him more compassionate. It also gave him the strength to lead the nation during the depression crisis. **What event changed Roosevelt's life?**

Research on the R◉M

Free Find:
Social Security Act
After reading about the Social Security Act on the **Holt Researcher CD–ROM**, imagine that you are a senior citizen. Write a letter to President Roosevelt explaining how the Social Security Act has helped you.

Analyzing Primary Sources
Drawing Inferences and Conclusions Why do you think Armstrong was so shocked by this scene?

Interpreting the Visual Record

Documenting the depression *Photographer Dorothea Lange was hired by a New Deal program to create a record of rural life during the depression.* **What mood is expressed in the photograph?**

Administration (WPA). Between 1935 and 1943, the WPA employed millions of Americans. WPA workers built public buildings, taught classes, and produced art. Also in 1935 Roosevelt signed perhaps the most far-reaching legislation of his presidency—the **Social Security Act**. The act gave pensions to retired workers and unemployment insurance to workers who lost their jobs.

✔ **Reading Check: Contrasting** Contrast President Roosevelt's work to help poor Americans with President Hoover's.

⭐ Hard Times Everywhere

During the depression people relied on the help of family, community, and even soup kitchens for help. Some 20 percent of children did not have enough to eat. Writer Louise V. Armstrong described a city scene.

History Makers Speak

❝One vivid [distinct], gruesome moment of those dark days we shall never forget. We saw a crowd of some fifty men fighting over a barrel of garbage which had been set outside the back door of a restaurant. American citizens fighting for scraps of food like animals!❞

—Louise V. Armstrong, *We, Too, Are the People*

Some people who lost their houses were forced to live on the streets.

As crop prices fell, many farmers had no money to pay their mortgages, so they lost their land. A severe drought in the Great Plains made the situation even worse. As winds blew away the dry topsoil in huge clouds of dust, the area became known as the Dust Bowl. Unable to grow crops, many farmers headed west to find a better life. However, once in California, many of these farmers found jobs only as migrant workers.

African Americans and Mexican Americans were also hit hard by the depression. They were often the last employees to be hired and the first to be fired. Many Mexican immigrants were sent back to Mexico. African Americans, however, still made some advances. President Roosevelt placed several African Americans in his administration. Along with First Lady Eleanor Roosevelt, these leaders fought for greater civil rights.

Depression-era programs also brought some welcomed changes for American Indians. Congress had granted U.S. citizenship to American Indians in 1924, but many Indians still lived in substandard conditions. The Indian Reorganization Act of 1934 returned tribal rule and some tribal lands to American Indians.

In addition, New Deal legislation supported the rights of workers and helped them form unions. Employers were encouraged to meet the demands of striking workers. The New Deal programs slowly improved the economy, but the nation stayed in a slump until the 1940s.

✔ **Reading Check: Contrasting** What were some of the negative and positive outcomes of the depression?

⭐ World War II

The Great Depression affected countries throughout the world in the 1930s. As a result of these hard times, many countries turned to new forms of government that promised relief. In the end, however, many of these new governments led their people into war. Some countries were also unhappy with the terms of the Treaty of Versailles. For example, Italians felt that they should have been given more territory after World

Legend:
- Axis controlled, June 1944
- Allied controlled, June 1944
- Neutral country
- Farthest Axis advance, 1942
- → Allied advance
- ✹ Major battle
- ✹ Allied air attack

World War II in Europe, 1942–1945

Interpreting Maps In 1939 Germany began an aggressive attack, conquering most of Europe by 1942.

Skills Assessment Places and Regions Which European countries remained neutral?

Interpreting the Visual Record

Pearl Harbor *The Japanese surprise attack on Pearl Harbor stunned Americans.* **Why do you think the nation was shocked by the attack?**

War I. Italy's dictator, Benito Mussolini, pledged to make his country a world power through **fascism.** Fascism is a political movement that favors a dictatorial government and believes nation and race are more important than the individual.

The Treaty of Versailles had also made Germany pay $33 billion to the countries it had attacked. Then the Great Depression increased Germany's economic difficulties. A new leader, Adolf Hitler, appealed to many Germans. Members of his National Socialist Party, the **Nazis**, blamed Jews, intellectuals, and Communists for Germany's problems. Hitler took over Austria and part of Czechoslovakia. At first, European leaders gave in to Hitler to avoid war with Germany. Then on September 1, 1939, Germany invaded Poland. Great Britain and France—the Allied Powers—declared war on Germany.

German forces quickly overran much of Europe and then invaded the Soviet Union in 1941. As a result, the Soviets joined the Allied Powers. In 1936, Germany and Italy had joined together to form the Axis Powers, and Japan joined the alliance in 1940. Japan had invaded China in the 1930s and hoped to gain more power in Asia.

Although the United States stayed out of the war at first, it helped the Allies. In 1941 Congress passed the **Lend-Lease Act**, which let the United States lend or lease weapons and supplies to Great Britain and, later, the Soviet Union. The government also refused to sell airline fuel to Japan and froze Japanese funds in the United States.

On December 7, 1941, Japan responded with a surprise attack on the U.S. naval base at Pearl Harbor, Hawaii. Congress declared war on Japan the next day. Germany and Italy, the other major Axis Powers, soon declared war on the United States in support of Japan.

✔ **Reading Check: Identifying Cause and Effect** What German actions led to World War II, and what effect did they have on Europe?

★ The Home Front

Americans quickly geared up for the war effort. Many people went to work in factories to produce war materials. Unemployment dropped to an all-time low of slightly more than 1 percent in 1944. The federal government also became more involved in industry. Officials limited the sale of many goods, such as tires, meat, and gasoline, to the public. The Office of War Information reminded citizens that their actions affected U.S. forces overseas. Americans responded to the call of duty by buying billions of dollars in bonds.

Americans used government-issued books of ration stamps to buy scarce goods during World War II.

Millions of men and about 300,000 women enlisted for military service. About 1 million African Americans and some 300,000 Mexican Americans served in the military as well. Some 33,000 Japanese Americans also volunteered. They served even though the U.S. government sent more than 110,000 Japanese Americans to detention camps because some officials believed they threatened national security. In addition, many Japanese Americans lost their homes and businesses.

✔ **Reading Check: Analyzing Information** How did the lives of Americans change after the United States entered World War II?

World War II in the Pacific, 1941–1945

Interpreting Maps By 1942 Japan's area of control stretched far into the Pacific and across much of eastern Asia.

Skills Assessment The World in Spatial Terms What islands did the Allies attack after taking the Marshall Islands?

Interpreting the Visual Record

The Holocaust *Prisoners at this concentration camp in Evensee, Austria, were liberated by U.S. troops in 1945.* **How does the condition of these prisoners show the harsh conditions of the concentration camp?**

★ Allied Victory

In 1942 the Allies began to turn back the Axis Powers in Europe. On June 6, 1944, the Allies launched the **D-Day** invasion of Nazi-occupied France and then began fighting east toward Germany. Soviet forces were also pushing west toward the German capital of Berlin. With its capital as well as many other cities in ruins, Germany surrendered to the Allies on May 7, 1945.

Despite Germany's defeat, brutal fighting raged on in the Pacific. To end the war and prevent further casualties, President Harry S Truman, who took office after Roosevelt's death in April 1945, approved using a powerful new weapon, the atomic bomb, on Japan. On August 6, 1945, a U.S. plane dropped an atomic bomb on Hiroshima, destroying the city. Three days later, a more powerful atomic bomb was dropped on Nagasaki. Japan surrendered on August 14, 1945.

World War II was finally over but with great costs. Some 50 million civilians and soldiers had died, including about 400,000 Americans. From London to Tokyo, cities lay in ruins. Millions of people had lost their homes. During the war Hitler and the Nazis had systematically killed about 6 million Jews and 3 million members of other groups in concentration camps. This tragic ordeal became known as the **Holocaust**.

✔ **Reading Check: Summarizing** Explain the role that the United States played in the Allied victories over Germany and Japan.

Section 2 Review

go.hrw.com
Homework Practice Online
keyword: SF3 HPE

1 **Define** and explain:
• public works
• fascism

2 **Identify** and explain:
• Great Depression
• Herbert Hoover
• Franklin D. Roosevelt
• New Deal
• Federal Deposit Insurance Corporation
• Social Security Act
• Nazis
• Lend-Lease Act
• D-Day
• Holocaust

3 **Summarizing** Copy the graphic organizer below. Use it to identify some of the depression-era programs and policies of the Roosevelt Administration.

Programs and Policies	
1933–34	1935–40

4 **Finding the Main Idea**
a. How did the depression affect Americans, and how did the government try to help?

b. How did the United States contribute to victory over the Axis Powers, both before and after joining the fighting in World War II?

5 **Writing and Critical Thinking**
Comparing and Contrasting Imagine that you are a teacher preparing a lesson about World War II. Write an explanation of how the war in Europe and the war in the Pacific were alike and different to use in a class discussion.

Consider the following:
• U.S. actions against Germany and Japan before entry into the war
• the entry of the United States into the war
• the progress and eventual victory of the Allies

Postwar America

Read to Discover

1. How did the Cold War influence U.S. foreign and domestic policies?
2. What changes took place in American society in the 1950s?
3. How did African Americans work to gain civil rights in the 1950s?

WHY IT MATTERS TODAY

The United Nations continues to take an active role in worldwide peace efforts. Use **CNNfyi.com** or other **current events** sources to learn how the United Nations is helping the world today. Record your findings in your journal.

Identify

- Yalta Conference
- United Nations
- Cold War
- Truman Doctrine
- Marshall Plan
- North Atlantic Treaty Organization
- House Un-American Activities Committee
- Dwight D. Eisenhower
- *Brown* v. *Board of Education*
- Montgomery Bus Boycott
- Martin Luther King Jr.

The Story Continues

One day in the spring of 1945, U.S. and Soviet troops met at the Elbe River in Germany. The Soviets waited on the eastern shore, and the Americans on the western shore. Through translators, the two groups spoke. "There were tears in the eyes of most of us. . . ," remembered Private Joseph Polowsky. The soldiers pointed to the ruins around them, embraced, and "swore never to forget." Despite their shared relief at the end of the war, Polowsky felt "a sense of foreboding [uneasiness] that things might not be as perfect in the future as we anticipated [expected]."

This commemorative stamp was issued to celebrate the meeting of Soviet and U.S. troops along the Elbe River.

⭐ Postwar Peace

Even before the end of World War II, the Allies began working to maintain peace after the war. In February 1945 President Roosevelt, British prime minister Winston Churchill, and Soviet leader Joseph Stalin met at the **Yalta Conference** to plan how to end the war. The leaders also agreed to form the **United Nations** (UN). This new organization would settle disagreements between countries.

Clement Attlee, Harry S Truman, and Joseph Stalin are seated left to right at the Potsdam Conference. Attlee had become British Prime Minister and replaced Churchill during the conference.

After Germany's surrender, the four primary Allies—Great Britain, France, the Soviet Union, and the United States—divided Germany into four occupation zones. France, Britain, and the United States each took control of an area in what became known as West Germany, the more industrialized region. The Soviets took control of the poorer, more rural eastern part of Germany. Berlin, Germany's capital, was located within the Soviet section, but the Allies also divided it into four zones of occupation.

The Allies, however, disagreed sharply over the future status of Poland. Stalin wanted a Soviet-friendly government in neighboring Poland, but the Western nations wanted a democratic government there. Stalin's installation of a pro-Soviet government in Poland and his refusal to allow free elections there contributed to the growing tensions between the Soviet Union and the West.

✔ **Reading Check: Summarizing** In what ways did the Allies work together to bring about a postwar peace?

★ The Truman Years

These tensions between the United States and the Soviet Union grew as the Soviets became very powerful in Eastern Europe. As a result, the United States and the Soviet Union became involved in a **Cold War**—a long struggle for global power. Europe was divided between the democratic nations of the West and the communist nations of the East.

In 1947 President Truman announced the **Truman Doctrine**, which stated that the United States would help any country fighting against communism. The following year, the United States started the **Marshall Plan** to help postwar economic recovery. The United States offered about

Research on the ROM

Free Find:
Marshall Plan
After reading about the Marshall Plan on the **Holt Researcher CD–ROM**, write a press release that outlines the plan's objectives.

$12.5 billion in relief aid to keep Europeans from turning to communism. Secretary of State George Marshall said that U.S. policy was not directed against any country or belief. However, the Soviet Union and its allies in Eastern Europe refused U.S. aid.

The Western Allies also decided to make the western part of Germany an independent country. In response to this action and the Marshall Plan, the Soviets began a blockade to halt all ground traffic to West Berlin in 1948. The United States and Great Britain responded by running the Berlin Airlift for 321 days. Pilots flew more than 7,000 tons of food and supplies to the people of West Berlin each day. The Soviets eventually gave up their blockade in May 1949.

The same year the blockade ended, the United States, Great Britain, and 10 other countries formed the **North Atlantic Treaty Organization** (NATO). The member countries promised to defend each other from enemy attack. Later the Soviet Union and other Eastern European countries signed their own military alliance called the Warsaw Pact.

The United States worried that communism would spread across Asia after Communists came to power in China in 1949. Events in North and South Korea made such fears stronger. Following World War II, Korea had been temporarily divided between the United States and the Soviet Union. A communist, Soviet-backed government took power in North Korea, while a more democratic, U.S.-backed government formed in South Korea. Each side wanted to unite the country under its own government. In June 1950 North Korea invaded South Korea. Within days, the United Nations voted to send troops—mostly American—to defend South Korea. North Korea was winning the Korean War until UN forces landed behind enemy lines. They pushed the North Koreans back toward the Chinese border. China then sent troops to help North Korean forces. Eventually, the two sides stopped near the original dividing line of the two Koreas. In 1953 the final cease-fire left Korea divided into two countries.

✔ **Reading Check: Identifying Cause and Effect** What caused the Cold War to deepen in the 1940s and 1950s, and what was the result of this change?

A cargo of sugar is on its way to Europe as part of the Marshall Plan.

⭐ The Cold War at Home

Cold War tensions also sparked fears of communism at home. In May 1938 Congress had created the **House Un-American Activities Committee** (HUAC) to look into disloyalty and harmful foreign influences in the United States. In 1945 the House of Representatives voted to make HUAC permanent. Then in 1947, the government launched new investigations into possible communist ties among federal employees, who had to sign loyalty oaths. HUAC also gave out anticommunist materials. Pamphlets gave warnings such as "Where can Communists be found? Everywhere."

During the 1950s, many films and magazines warned that Communists were plotting to destroy the United States.

★★★★★★★★★★★★★★
That's Interesting!
★★★★★★★★★★★★★★

First "Man" in Space Did you know that Ivan Ivanovich actually beat Yuri Gagarin into space by more than three weeks? It's true! In March 1961 the Soviets launched Ivan Ivanovich—a lifelike human model—into space as a test. He appeared so real that technicians wrote "model" on his forehead so that anyone who found him would not be confused! Ivanovich orbited for a while and then reentered Earth's atmosphere where he was ejected from the spacecraft, parachuting safely into the snowy Ural Mountains. Ivanovich has remained on display in his spacesuit for more than 40 years.

Analyzing Primary Sources

Drawing Inferences and Conclusions Do you think Dulles would favor negotiating with the Soviet Union?

During this time, Senator Joseph McCarthy of Wisconsin took advantage of Cold War fears. In 1950 he said that he had a list of hundreds of Communists who worked in the U.S. government. McCarthy's accusations led to public hearings that were aired on television. It became clear to some 20 million viewers that McCarthy had little proof to back up his accusations. The public turned against him. However, he had already destroyed the reputations of many innocent people.

✔ **Reading Check: Analyzing Information** What actions were taken against communism in the United States?

★ Eisenhower and the Cold War

The Cold War was one of the reasons that Americans elected **Dwight D. Eisenhower** president in 1952. Eisenhower had led the Allied invasion of Europe in World War II, and he helped end the Korean War. The Eisenhower administration also pledged to help any Middle Eastern nation threatened by communism. The Eisenhower Doctrine greatly increased U.S. involvement in the Middle East.

During Eisenhower's administration, the United States built growing numbers of nuclear weapons. Rather than relying on a larger army, the U.S. military planned to be ready to launch a massive nuclear attack on the country's enemies, particularly the Soviet Union. This policy was known as massive retaliation. Meanwhile, the Soviets had begun building their own nuclear weapons. These new weapons—hydrogen bombs—were much more powerful than earlier atomic bombs. People around the world grew frightened of the great destruction these weapons could cause.

Eisenhower based his foreign policy mostly on brinkmanship—the willingness to go to the brink, or edge, of war to fight communism. Secretary of State John Foster Dulles explained brinkmanship in an article in *Life* magazine.

History Makers Speak ❝You have to take chances for peace, just as . . . in war. . . . The ability to get to the verge [edge] without getting into war is the necessary art . . . . If you try to run away from it, if you are scared to go to the brink [edge], you are lost.❞

—John Foster Dulles, quoted in *Life*, January 1956

The United States and the Soviet Union also competed in a space race. The Soviets sent *Sputnik,* the first artificial satellite, into space in October 1957. Americans were shocked to find themselves falling behind the Soviets in the space race. In January 1958 the United States launched its first satellite. Later that year, Congress created the National Aeronautics and Space Administration (NASA) to advance U.S. space exploration.

✔ **Reading Check: Finding the Main Idea** What efforts did President Eisenhower take to stop the spread of communism?

★ A Changing America

The economic growth of the United States helped fuel its efforts to win the Cold War. President Truman had approved a series of reforms to strengthen the economy, which continued to improve under Eisenhower. Incomes rose as unemployment remained low, and a new era of prosperity was born in postwar America. After World War II the birthrate also rose dramatically. To find larger houses, many middle-class Americans moved to the suburbs. Although popular culture idealized women who stayed at home, many women also held jobs outside the home.

Television greatly shaped American culture in the 1950s. By the mid-1950s, more than 65 percent of all American homes had television sets. Americans enjoyed watching many types of shows, including comedies, dramas, game shows, soap operas, and westerns. Television advertisements—some featuring stars of television shows—urged viewers to buy all the latest products.

Some argued that the suburbs and television encouraged a consumer culture and pressured Americans, especially teenagers, to conform to social expectations. However, many teenagers rebelled by reading books and watching movies that echoed their dissatisfaction with suburban life. They also listened to rock 'n' roll music, which drew heavily on African American rhythm and blues. Although many adults argued that this music sounded awful and contributed to antisocial behavior, rock 'n' roll became increasingly popular.

 Reading Check: Supporting a Point of View Do you think changes that took place in the 1950s improved life for the average American? Explain your answer.

★ The Civil Rights Movement Begins

Other groups also challenged 1950s society in different ways. After World War II many African Americans resolved to win their civil rights and fight discrimination. President Truman desegregated the U.S. armed forces in 1948, but many African Americans thought he moved too slowly. The NAACP began to address segregation in public education. The Supreme Court had long upheld this practice based on the "separate-but-equal" principle. However, black schools were rarely able to offer equal facilities or opportunities for African American children.

In 1954, Linda Brown, an African American girl living in Topeka, Kansas, went with her father to enroll in their all-white neighborhood school. However, she was not allowed to enroll. Instead, the principal told her that she had to attend the all-black school that was a half-hour bus ride away. Brown's parents and the NAACP sued the Topeka school board. In 1954 the Supreme Court ruled in ***Brown v. Board of Education*** that segregated public schools were unconstitutional.

Interpreting the Visual Record

Starting school *Elizabeth Eckford tries to make her way into Little Rock's Central High School.* **What dangers does Eckford face?**

Martin Luther King Jr. with his wife, Coretta, and his children

Still, by 1957 only four southern states had begun to integrate their schools. That year the school board of Little Rock, Arkansas, selected nine outstanding African American students to attend the all-white Central High School. The so-called Little Rock Nine tried to start school in the fall. However, Arkansas governor Orval Faubus ordered the National Guard to keep the students from entering the school. Eventually, President Eisenhower sent federal troops to uphold the Supreme Court's ruling and enforce desegregation.

African Americans also fought segregation of public transportation. In 1955 Rosa Parks of Montgomery, Alabama, refused to give up her bus seat to a white passenger. Parks was arrested, and her actions inspired other African Americans to protest segregation. The Montgomery Improvement Association and local NAACP leaders organized the **Montgomery Bus Boycott**. African Americans made up more than 75 percent of Montgomery's bus riders, and almost all of them joined the boycott. To get to work, they formed car pools or walked. The boycott lasted for nearly a year. In November 1956 the Supreme Court ruled that Montgomery's segregated bus system was illegal.

This boycott led African Americans in other communities to carry out boycotts. It also introduced the country to an outstanding African American leader, **Martin Luther King Jr.** A young minister and exciting speaker, King would become one of the most important figures in the civil rights movement.

✔ **Reading Check: Analyzing Information** What was the importance of the civil rights movement in the 1950s?

Section 3 Review

go.hrw.com **Homework Practice Online** keyword: SF3 HPE

1 Identify and explain:
- Yalta Conference
- United Nations
- Cold War
- Truman Doctrine
- Marshall Plan
- North Atlantic Treaty Organization
- House Un-American Activities Committee
- Dwight D. Eisenhower
- *Brown* v. *Board of Education*
- Montgomery Bus Boycott
- Martin Luther King Jr.

2 Summarizing Copy the chart below. Use it to list some of the Cold War's main events and policies as well as their outcomes.

Events/Policies	Outcomes

3 Finding the Main Idea
a. What U.S. foreign policies and programs arose from Cold War fears?

b. How did African Americans fight segregation in public schools and city buses, and how successful were their efforts?

4 Writing and Critical Thinking
Analyzing Information Imagine that you are a journalist living in the 1950s. Write an article on how life in America has changed since the end of World War II.

Consider the following:
- increased television viewing
- the rise of the suburbs
- teenagers and rock 'n' roll

Searching for Solutions

Read to Discover

1. What were the foreign policies of Presidents Kennedy and Johnson?
2. What were the strategies and achievements of the 1960s civil rights movement?
3. What domestic problems faced the United States in the 1970s?

WHY IT MATTERS TODAY

The cost of fuel is still an important issue for Americans today. Use **CNNfyi**.com or other **current events** sources to find out about how Americans are trying to conserve energy today. Record your findings in your journal.

Define
- energy crisis

Identify
- John F. Kennedy
- Cuban missile crisis
- Lyndon B. Johnson
- Great Society
- Freedom Rides
- Civil Rights Act of 1964
- Voting Rights Act of 1965
- National Organization for Women
- Gulf of Tonkin Resolution
- Tet Offensive
- Richard Nixon
- Watergate
- Jimmy Carter

The Story Continues

During President John F. Kennedy's inaugural address, he urged Americans to work for a better country. "The energy, the faith, the devotion which we bring to this endeavor [effort] will light our country . . . ," the president said. "And so, my fellow Americans—ask not what your country can do for you—ask what you can do for your country."

John F. Kennedy promised to "get the country moving again" if he was elected president in 1960.

⭐ Kennedy and Johnson

When **John F. Kennedy** took office, he faced several major international crises. Kennedy supported an invasion of Cuba by 1,500 Cubans living in the United States. These exiles wanted to overthrow Soviet-backed communist dictator Fidel Castro. This invasion attempt failed and caused a major embarrassment for the United States. U.S.-Soviet relations worsened even more when Soviet leader Nikita Khrushchev had the Berlin Wall built later that year. The wall divided East and West Berlin to keep East Germans from fleeing to Western Europe.

Interpreting the Visual Record

A new president *Lyndon B. Johnson was sworn in as president on Air Force One just hours after Kennedy's assassination.* **How was Johnson's swearing in different from the way most presidents take office?**

The most serious crisis took place in October 1962, when U.S. spy planes discovered Soviet missiles in Cuba. President Kennedy demanded that the Soviets remove these weapons. For the next week, the world nervously waited for the outcome of the **Cuban missile crisis**. Finally, the Soviets agreed to remove the missiles.

On November 22, 1963, President Kennedy was assassinated in Dallas, Texas. Within hours, Vice President **Lyndon B. Johnson** became the new president. President Johnson launched the War on Poverty to improve job opportunities and provide better education for poor Americans. After winning the presidential election in 1964, Johnson began the **Great Society**, a series of programs that gave more people health insurance and more schools federal money.

During the 1960s the United States reached other important goals. On July 20, 1969, the world watched as U.S. astronaut Neil Armstrong stepped onto the Moon's surface. However, other challenges remained. For example, the country went through a great deal of social conflict in the late 1960s. Young people began to disagree with many of the views and ideals of the older generation. Some young people rejected society entirely. They "dropped out" and formed a new culture, called the counterculture.

 Reading Check: Summarizing What challenges did Presidents Kennedy and Johnson face?

⭐ The Civil Rights Movement

One important movement in the 1960s was the continuing fight for civil rights. Beginning in 1960, African American students led sit-ins, refusing to leave segregated restaurants until they were served. In 1961 African American and white riders took part in **Freedom Rides**, riding buses through several southern states to protest bus-segregation policies. Angry white mobs met the first bus with clubs and firebombs, but the riders kept coming. Transportation companies and other businesses across the South gradually ended their segregation policies.

These successes gave greater hope to the movement, as did a new civil rights bill presented by President Kennedy in 1963. To show their support for this bill, civil rights leaders planned the March on Washington. On the steps of the Lincoln Memorial, Martin Luther King Jr. described his hopes for racial harmony in his "I Have a Dream" speech.

Interpreting the Visual Record

Demonstrations *During the March on Washington, more than 200,000 people—both African American and white—gathered to listen to speakers.* **What kind of message do you think such a large gathering would send to other Americans?**

History Makers Speak

"I have a dream that my four little children will one day live in a nation where they will not be judged by the color of their skin but by the content of their character."

—Martin Luther King Jr., "I Have a Dream"

Analyzing Primary Sources
Drawing Inferences and Conclusions In your own words, what is King's dream?

Congress later passed the **Civil Rights Act of 1964**. This act banned racial discrimination by administrators of public services and by employers who contract with the federal government.

Despite these successes, African Americans in the South still faced challenges. Threats and unfair laws, such as poll taxes and literacy tests, kept many of them from voting. During the "Freedom Summer" of 1964, hundreds of college students traveled to Mississippi to register African American voters. Volunteers worked hard, even after they received threats of violence, and some workers disappeared and were later found murdered. Protest marches in Alabama added support to a voting rights bill. Soon afterward, President Johnson signed the **Voting Rights Act of 1965**, which ensured every U.S. citizen's right to vote.

The search for the three missing Freedom Summer volunteers focused national attention on civil rights.

★ Other Paths

Some African Americans did not follow the path taken by King and other peaceful civil rights organizers. Leaders like Malcolm X and groups like the Black Panthers questioned the success of nonviolence. These leaders focused on the fact that African Americans still faced economic inequality and discrimination. Believing that progress was too slow, these leaders favored the use of force, when necessary, to gain their civil rights and economic independence. Continued discrimination fueled deepening anger, which later caused riots in cities around the country in the late 1960s. Severe rioting also followed the assassination of Martin Luther King

Civil rights activist César Chávez used boycotts to draw attention to the suffering of migrant workers.

Jr. in April 1968. With a leading figure in the civil rights movement gone, many others vowed to continue the struggle.

The successes of the civil rights movement inspired other groups of Americans to fight for their rights. The Chicano movement worked to end discrimination and to increase cultural pride among Mexican Americans. César Chávez led the fight for greater rights for Hispanic migrant workers. The American Indian Movement (AIM) held protests to protect American Indians' rights and raise awareness of American Indian issues. Some Indian nations successfully sued the U.S. government over broken treaties, winning land or cash awards.

Women's rights activists formed the **National Organization for Women** in 1966 to increase women's political power. In 1972 Congress passed the Equal Rights Amendment to guarantee women equal protection under the law, but the necessary number of states failed to ratify it. However, women did become more involved in politics and increasingly entered traditionally male-dominated professions.

 Reading Check: Supporting a Point of View How successful were civil rights activists of the 1960s in achieving their goals?

★ The Vietnam War

In the early 1960s the United States became increasingly involved in a conflict in the Southeast Asian nation of Vietnam. The Vietnamese had won their freedom from French rule in 1954. The peace agreement that followed divided Vietnam into two countries but called for elections to reunite these two countries in 1956.

North Vietnam had a communist government, while South Vietnam had a U.S.-backed government led by Ngo Dinh Diem (NGOH DIN de-EM). An ineffective and unpopular ruler, Diem refused to allow elections to take place in 1956 because he feared that he would lose. As his rule became more brutal, some pro-communist South Vietnamese, known as the Vietcong, began to fight against his government. By the late 1950s South Vietnam was in the middle of a civil war.

In 1963 South Vietnamese military leaders overthrew Diem. The new government wanted to work out a peace agreement with North Vietnam. The United States, however, feared that if Vietnam fell to communism, other countries would follow. In August 1964 there were reports that North Vietnamese boats had attacked U.S. ships in the Gulf of Tonkin. In response, Congress passed the **Gulf of Tonkin Resolution**. This resolution gave President Johnson the power to "take all necessary measures [steps] to repel [turn back] any armed attack against forces of the United States" and to secure peace in Southeast Asia. By 1968 more than 500,000 U.S. soldiers were serving in Vietnam.

The fighting was difficult. The Vietcong and North Vietnamese troops began hit-and-run attacks and knew the thick jungle better than U.S.

The purple heart medal is given to those who are injured or killed while serving their country.

forces did. Still, U.S. military leaders told the American public that victory was near. Public faith in such claims was shattered in late January 1968. Enemy soldiers began a major series of attacks, called the **Tet Offensive**, that reached into the heart of U.S. defenses. U.S. troops eventually drove back the attacks. However, the Tet Offensive showed that the North Vietnamese still had military strength and would not give up fighting.

After the Tet Offensive, some 49 percent of U.S. citizens said that the United States should never have sent troops to Vietnam. Many Americans protested U.S. involvement in the war. Students took part in numerous demonstrations and even closed down some college campuses across the country.

As the antiwar feelings of the American public grew, President Johnson announced that he would not run for re-election. Voters elected Republican **Richard Nixon**, who promised to bring about "peace with honor." Nixon began a process of Vietnamization, or letting the South Vietnamese army take charge of the fighting. He called back U.S. troops, but he also increased bombing raids on the Vietcong's supply lines. Finally, on January 27, 1973, U.S. officials reached a peace agreement and pulled all U.S. forces out. Fighting went on until 1975, when North Vietnamese forces took over South Vietnam and placed the reunited country under a communist government.

The war took the lives of more than 1.5 million Vietnamese. In the following years, more than 1.5 million refugees fled Vietnam, many coming to the United States. Some 58,000 Americans died in the war, while returning veterans faced an often bitter public. Some Americans also lost faith in their leaders. Since the Vietnam War, U.S. leaders have been more cautious about sending troops to foreign wars.

✔ **Reading Check: Identifying Cause and Effect** What led to U.S. involvement in Vietnam, and what was the result?

The Vietnam War

Interpreting Maps North Vietnam used the Ho Chi Minh Trail to supply communist forces in the South.

Skills Assessment Places and Regions Through which countries did the Ho Chi Minh Trail pass?

A button calling for the end of U.S. involvement in Vietnam

⭐ The 1970s

In the 1970s Americans faced economic problems. For the first time, the country suffered from stagflation—rising inflation and unemployment during a period of little economic growth. Although President Nixon enforced wage and price controls, the economy did not recover. The economy got worse when Middle Eastern countries raised their oil prices. The cost of gasoline and heating oil rose, leading to the **energy crisis**.

In foreign affairs, Nixon improved ties with China by meeting with Chinese leader Mao Zedong in 1972. He was the first U.S. president to visit China. That same year, Nixon visited Soviet leaders in Moscow. The peace talks that followed led to the signing of a treaty to limit nuclear missiles. U.S. and Soviet leaders also called for a policy of détente, or a lessening of military and diplomatic tensions.

A scandal called **Watergate** soon overshadowed President Nixon's successes, however. In June 1972 five men were caught breaking into the Democratic National Committee headquarters at the Watergate apartment-hotel complex in Washington, D.C. When Congress looked into the incident, members of Nixon's administration were arrested for taking part in the break-in. These men said the president tried to cover up the incident, but Nixon said he was not involved. Tape-recorded conversations showed that he had been part of the cover-up. To avoid possible impeachment, Nixon resigned on August 8, 1974.

Vice President Gerald Ford took office and quickly pardoned Nixon for his role in Watergate. Ford faced domestic problems, such as continued inflation. In foreign policy, he continued the policy of détente and worked on improving ties with Middle Eastern countries.

✔ **Reading Check: Categorizing** What were some of the successes and failures of Nixon's and Ford's presidencies?

Interpreting the Visual Record

Nixon's resignation *As President Nixon boarded a helicopter to leave the White House, the* Washington Post *announced his resignation.* **Does Nixon's expression seem appropriate for the occasion? Explain your answer.**

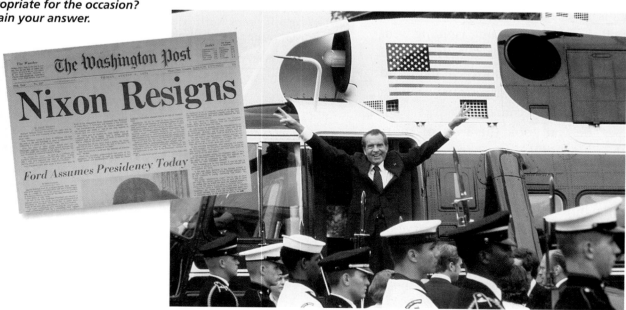

⭐ Jimmy Carter's Presidency

By the mid-1970s the country was ready for new leadership. Former Georgia governor **Jimmy Carter**, a Democrat, was elected to the White House in 1976. As the energy crisis and economic problems dragged on, however, President Carter seemed to have few solutions.

Carter did offer a new type of foreign policy, supporting human rights and the freedom of peoples in Latin America and Africa. However, U.S.-Soviet relations grew worse after the Soviets invaded the Asian country of Afghanistan in 1979. After the invasion, Congress would not pass a new arms treaty between the United States and the Soviet Union. In addition, President Carter called for a U.S. boycott of the 1980 Summer Olympics in Moscow. Although many Americans disapproved of the Soviet invasion, the boycott hurt many U.S. athletes.

Carter had his greatest success and his worst failure in the Middle East. In 1979 he negotiated the Camp David Accords, a peace treaty between longtime enemies Israel and Egypt. However, in November 1979, anti-American events shook Iran. Angry about Carter's aid to their former leader, some Iranians took more than 50 Americans hostage in the U.S. Embassy in Iran's capital, Tehran. Carter kept working to free the hostages. However, the crisis dragged on for more than a year, and the president received most of the blame for the 444-day imprisonment.

Interpreting the Visual Record

Carter's inauguration *Jimmy Carter tried to show that he was a president for all people, rich and poor, when he and his family walked to his inauguration instead of riding in a limousine.* **How do you think Carter's actions might change the tone of American politics?**

✔ **Reading Check: Comparing** How were the policies of Presidents Nixon and Carter, and the challenges they faced, similar?

Section 4 Review

go.hrw.com **Homework Practice Online**

keyword: SF3 HPE

① **Define** and explain:
- energy crisis

② **Identify** and explain:
- John F. Kennedy
- Cuban missile crisis
- Lyndon B. Johnson
- Great Society
- Freedom Rides
- Civil Rights Act of 1964
- Voting Rights Act of 1965
- National Organization for Women
- Gulf of Tonkin Resolution
- Tet Offensive
- Richard Nixon
- Watergate
- Jimmy Carter

③ **Comparing and Contrasting** Copy the diagram below. Use it to compare and contrast U.S. foreign policy under Presidents Kennedy and Johnson.

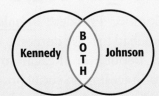

Kennedy | BOTH | Johnson

④ **Finding the Main Idea**
a. What strategies did African Americans use to gain their civil rights in the 1960s, and how successful were they?

b. What domestic problems did Presidents Nixon, Ford, and Carter face?

⑤ **Writing and Critical Thinking**
Supporting a Point of View Imagine that you are a teenager living in the United States in the 1970s. Write a letter that describes your life to a teenager living in another country.

Consider the following:
- involvement with foreign countries
- domestic affairs
- the Watergate scandal

The Modern Era

Read to Discover

1. How did the Cold War progress in the 1980s?
2. What domestic issues did the Clinton administration address?
3. How did the United States take part in world affairs in the 1990s?

WHY IT MATTERS TODAY

One part of the federal government's job is to spend taxpayers' money wisely. Use **CNNfyi.com** or other **current events** sources to learn about the federal budget and issues involving the budget today. Record your findings in your journal.

Define

- supply-side economics

Identify

- Ronald Reagan
- Iran-Contra affair
- George Bush
- War on Drugs
- Operation Desert Storm
- Bill Clinton
- Contract with America
- North American Free Trade Agreement
- Al Gore
- George W. Bush

Ronald and Nancy Reagan

The Story Continues

Inauguration Day 1981 was like no other in American history. Although he was about to step down, President Jimmy Carter was working frantically to get Iran to free the American hostages. Before he could do so, Ronald Reagan was sworn in as president. Just moments later, the news came that the hostages were indeed free. Americans cheered this announcement by their new leader. At that moment, it was clear that a new spirit of hope was emerging in the country.

The Reagan Years

When he took office, President **Ronald Reagan** insisted that people, not the government, had to solve domestic difficulties facing the United States. A conservative Republican, Reagan lowered taxes, reduced government activity, and cut spending on social programs. He based his policies on the theory of **supply-side economics**, which held that lowering taxes would cause people to invest their savings in business. These investments would then boost the economy. By 1984 the economy was thriving. Yuppies, or young urban professionals, did particularly well. On the other hand, critics doubted that the economic boom was helping poor Americans. However, Reagan's policies and optimism made him very popular, and he was easily re-elected in 1984.

In foreign matters, Reagan took a strong stand against communism. He believed that the Cold War was a moral struggle of "good versus evil, right against wrong." Reagan's administration spent hundreds of billions of dollars on the military and on new weapons, and the defense budget increased greatly from 1981 to 1985. This spending added to the huge amount of money that the U.S. government borrows each year, which makes up the federal deficit.

The Reagan administration also gave military aid to some countries that were trying to defeat communist movements. However, Congress voted to cut off aid to Nicaragua's anticommunist forces, known as the Contras. Despite this ban, some top White House officials kept funding the Contras. To get the money, they illegally sold weapons to Iran. The **Iran-Contra affair** was the biggest scandal of the Reagan years.

Over time, U.S.-Soviet relations began to improve. New Soviet leaders allowed greater political and economic openness in their country. In 1987 Reagan met with Soviet leader Mikhail Gorbachev (gawr-buh-chawf). They signed the Intermediate-Range Nuclear Forces Treaty, which reduced the nuclear weapons of both countries.

✔ **Reading Check: Contrasting** How did President Reagan's attitude toward the Soviet Union change while he was in office?

Not all Americans benefited from Ronald Reagan's economic policies. Bumper stickers like this one encouraged Americans to support U.S. manufacturers.

⭐ George Bush's Presidency

Ronald Reagan's vice president, **George Bush**, won the presidency in 1988. President Bush followed many of Reagan's policies. For example, in 1989 he increased support for the **War on Drugs**, a large-scale effort to stop illegal drugs from entering the United States. President Bush also tried to improve public education for children.

Many changes took place around the world while Bush was in office. Several Eastern European countries broke free from Soviet influence. The Berlin Wall was torn down in 1989, and a year later East and West Germany reunited. In November 1990 the United States, the Soviet Union, and many European countries signed a treaty of security and cooperation, signaling that the Cold War was over. Then in 1991 the Soviet Union broke apart.

The United States also became involved in the Middle East again. In the summer of 1990 Iraq invaded the small, oil-rich country of Kuwait. Despite international outrage, Iraq refused to withdraw. U.S.-led forces launched **Operation Desert Storm**, an offensive to force Iraq to withdraw from Kuwait, in

Interpreting the Visual Record

The Gulf War *In Operation Desert Storm, U.S. and UN troops defeated Iraq quickly by moving around and behind enemy lines.* **What environmental conditions might make these soldiers' duties more challenging?**

Analyzing Primary Sources

Drawing Inferences and Conclusions How do you think Powell feels about U.S. involvement in Operation Desert Storm?

January 1991. U.S. Army general Colin Powell later explained how he had been sure of a U.S. victory.

History Makers Speak

❝I had no doubt we would be successful. We had the troops, the weapons, and the plan. What I did not know was how long it would take, and how many of our troops would not be coming home.❞

—Colin Powell, *My American Journey*

The U.S.-led forces began a fierce, six-week bombing campaign. The ground assault that followed drove the Iraqi army from Kuwait, and soon Bush ordered an end to the fighting.

✔ **Reading Check: Summarizing** What were some of the important Cold War events that occurred in the 1980s?

★ The Clinton Administration

By 1992 a recession had many Americans worried. President Bush faced two opponents in the 1992 election. He ran against Arkansas governor **Bill Clinton**, a Democrat, and Texas billionaire Ross Perot, an independent candidate. Many voters felt that Bush was ignoring the recession that had hit the U.S. economy. As a result, Clinton won the election with 43 percent of the popular vote. Perot, however, still won 19 percent of the popular vote.

Affordable health care was one of the many programs that President Clinton wanted to start. His plan, which sparked much debate, never came to a vote in Congress. Some people believed that Clinton's health care plan would be too expensive. Others felt the plan would limit people's ability to make their own decisions on health care.

In 1994, voters elected a Republican-controlled Congress for the first time in 42 years. Many of these Republicans had signed the **Contract with America**, a 10-point plan with a balanced budget among its key points. The Republicans were able to push only some of these reforms through Congress.

Despite Republicans' congressional success, voters re-elected President Clinton in 1996. By the end of Clinton's second term, the United States had gone through the longest economic boom in its history. The stock market had made major gains as well. Many Americans benefited from greater job opportunities and a low unemployment rate.

Despite the strong economy, questions about Clinton's personal and official conduct arose. A special prosecutor's report charged that, among other things, Clinton had lied under oath before a grand jury. The House of Representatives impeached Clinton and put him on trial. The Senate, however, found Clinton not guilty, and he remained in office.

✔ **Reading Check: Supporting a Point of View** Based on what you have read, what do you think were the high and low points of the Clinton administration? Explain your answer.

Third Political Parties

E ver since the 1790s, the United States has had a two-party political system. However, at times Americans have formed third political parties, such as the Populist Party.

Some Americans were not satisfied with the Democratic and Republican presidential candidates for the 1992 and 1996 elections. Ross Perot ran as an independent candidate in 1992, winning 19 percent of the popular vote. Perot then founded the Reform Party and ran as its candidate in 1996. Both times he campaigned on a platform of government reform.

Although a third-party candidate has yet to win a presidential election, third parties remain an important part of the democratic process. What roles do you think third parties play in the democratic process?

Ralph Nader ran for president in 1996 and 2000 as the Green Party's candidate.

Global Affairs

Since the Cold War had ended, the United States was the world's only superpower and took a broader role in world affairs. During Clinton's administration, U.S. troops aided many countries around the world. The United States helped Somalia, an African country torn by famine and civil war. In the Caribbean country of Haiti, U.S. troops helped return the elected leader to power. U.S. diplomats worked hard for peace in the Eastern European nation of Bosnia. This country had been torn apart by civil war. The United States also worked with NATO on a peacekeeping mission in Kosovo, Yugoslavia.

Economic interactions between countries increased in the 1990s. Congress passed the **North American Free Trade Agreement** (NAFTA) with Canada and Mexico in 1993, and the agreement took effect on January 1, 1994. NAFTA allowed goods, people, and services to move freely among the three countries. Many other nations expanded existing trade agreements. In January 1995 the World Trade Organization (WTO) was formed to settle economic disputes between trading partners.

The end of the Cold War led to greater U.S.-Russian cooperation. The two countries made plans to build a new space station. U.S. astronauts worked aboard the Russian space station *Mir*. On its own, the United States sent a crewless mission to Mars. Other technological advances included the development of faster, less expensive computers and the continued growth of the global Internet. This new technology changed the way Americans lived. More people began to use their computers to do research, share ideas, shop, and even work from home.

✔ **Reading Check: Analyzing Information** How did the end of the Cold War change U.S. foreign involvement in the 1990s?

Free Find:
Bill Clinton
After reading about Bill Clinton on the **Holt Researcher CD-ROM,** write a short essay that explains how his goals as president may have reflected the experiences he had growing up in Arkansas.

UN troops in Bosnia try to maintain the peace.

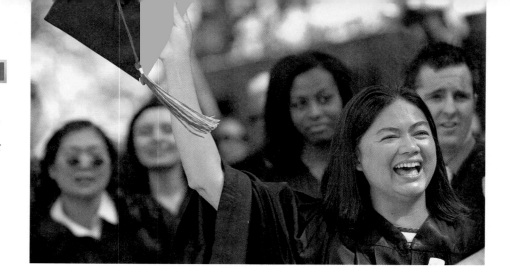

Graduation day *A college education remains an important goal for many Americans. Here a student celebrates her graduation.* **Why do you think a college education is still important?**

★ ★ ★ ★ ★ ★ ★ ★ ★ ★ ★
That's Interesting!
★ ★ ★ ★ ★ ★ ★ ★ ★ ★ ★

And the Winner Is... Can you imagine being told you were president... and then finding out you weren't? On November 7, 2000, all major television networks first predicted the state of Florida's 25 electoral votes would go to Al Gore. Many people believed the vice president was well on his way to victory. By about 2:00 A.M. EST, however, most networks changed their position and announced that George W. Bush had won Florida! As a result, Gore called Governor Bush to concede the election. As results from Florida continued to come in, the networks declared that Florida was now too close to call. Gore called Bush again—this time to take back his concession. It would be another five weeks before George W. Bush was declared the winner.

★ America in the 1990s and Beyond

Despite the economic boom, challenges still faced the country. Terrorist attacks posed threats to U.S. security. Terrorists are people who use violence to try to achieve their goals. In 1993 Arab terrorists bombed the World Trade Center in New York City. Then in 1995 a federal office building in Oklahoma City, Oklahoma, was bombed. The explosion killed 168 people and hurt hundreds of others. Two U.S. Army veterans were later convicted of this crime. In response to such violence, the Clinton administration passed an antiterrorism bill in 1996. It helped victims of terrorism by starting a crime victims' fund.

Civil rights and race relations were still important issues in the 1990s. Some political leaders debated the passage of different laws to address racially motivated crimes. Both President Clinton and Attorney General Janet Reno spoke of the need for new, broader federal laws.

Many Americans worried about the increasing costs of educational and social services. The competitive job market made it more important for people looking for jobs to have a college degree. At the same time, the cost of a college education rose steadily. Many Americans also worried that by the time they retired government programs such as Social Security would be bankrupt. Many Americans, therefore, invested their own money for retirement.

✔ **Reading Check: Summarizing** What national and international issues did Americans face in the 1990s and beyond?

★ The 2000 Presidential Election

In 2000 the Democrats nominated Vice President **Al Gore** as their presidential candidate. Gore chose Senator Joe Lieberman of Connecticut to be his running mate. Lieberman became the first Orthodox Jew to run on a major party ticket in the United States. Gore and Lieberman ran on a promise to keep paying down the national debt. They also wanted to use the government surplus for programs such as education and health care.

Republicans chose as their candidate **George W. Bush**, the governor of Texas and the son of former president George Bush. Bush chose former defense secretary Dick Cheney as his running mate. Bush ran on the promise to use most of the government surplus for tax cuts and to bring people from both parties together to work for change.

The presidential election of 2000 was unlike any race most Americans had ever seen. The vote was so close that several states could not declare a winner. The results of Florida's first tally were so close that recounts were called for. Court challenges over manual recounts, ballot designs, and absentee ballots held the country in suspense for five weeks. Eventually, the issue went all the way to the Supreme Court. The Court ruled that hand recounts in several Florida counties were not valid. Florida's 25 electoral votes were awarded to Bush, who became the first president in more than 100 years to win the electoral vote but not the popular vote.

President Bush took steps to unite Americans by choosing a diverse cabinet, including General Colin Powell, who became the first African American to serve as secretary of state. The newly seated Congress was almost equally divided between Republicans and Democrats. The Senate was split 50-50, with Vice President Cheney holding the tie-breaking vote. However, the balance of power shifted again when Jim Jeffords, a senator from Vermont, left the Republican Party to become an independent in 2001. In the House of Representatives, the Republicans kept a narrow lead. This close division showed the need for Republicans and Democrats to work together for the good of all Americans.

George W. Bush (at top) and Al Gore (at bottom) ran an extremely close presidential contest.

✔ **Reading Check: Making Generalizations and Predictions** What steps do you think President Bush might take to unite all Americans?

Section 5 Review

go.hrw.com **Homework Practice Online** keyword: SF3 HPE

1 **Define** and explain:
• supply-side economics

2 **Identify** and explain:
• Ronald Reagan
• Iran-Contra affair
• George Bush
• War on Drugs
• Operation Desert Storm
• Bill Clinton
• Contract with America
• North American Free Trade Agreement
• Al Gore
• George W. Bush

3 **Summarizing** Copy the graphic organizer below. Use it to describe the progress of the Cold War in the 1980s.

End of Cold War

5.
4.
3.
2.
1.

4 **Finding the Main Idea**
a. What were some of the main challenges that the government faced while President Clinton was in office?

b. How has the United States taken part in world affairs in the 1990s, and where?

5 **Writing and Critical Thinking**
Supporting a Point of View Imagine that you are a foreign-policy adviser to the president of the United States. Based on the events of the 1990s, write a statement telling the president how to prepare for the future.

Consider the following:
• the end of the Cold War
• the increase of trade agreements such as NAFTA
• peacekeeping missions

September 11, 2001:
A Day That Changed the World

Read to Discover

1. How was the United States attacked on September 11, 2001, and how did Americans respond?
2. How did the events of September 11 affect the economy?
3. What immediate steps did U.S. leaders take to find those responsible and bring them to justice?

WHY IT MATTERS TODAY

The terrorist attacks of September 11, 2001, continue to affect American life and U.S. foreign policy. Use CNNfyi.com or other **current events** sources to learn about the latest issues and events stemming from this national tragedy.

Identify

- World Trade Center
- Pentagon
- Rudolph Giuliani
- George W. Bush
- Tom Ridge
- Donald Rumsfeld
- Colin Powell

The Story Continues

On Tuesday morning, September 11, 2001, it was business as usual in the downtown financial district of New York City. In the World Trade Center complex, an estimated 10,000 employees were starting their workday. Most of them were within the Twin Towers that dominated the Manhattan skyline. On Fifth Avenue a group of pedestrians noticed a large airplane passing overhead. "We all thought it would be unusual for a plane to be flying so low over the city," recalled one man. Moments later they witnessed a terrible disaster.

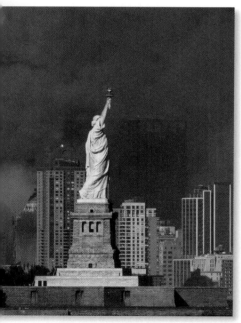

As seen from New York Harbor, smoke, ash, and debris obscure downtown Manhattan after the terrorist attacks.

⭐ The Attack

At 8:48 A.M., an American Airlines passenger jet crashed into the north tower of the **World Trade Center**. The impact was devastating, as though a bomb had struck the 110-story building. Stunned men and women began evacuating the building as emergency crews rushed to the scene. Then at 9:03 A.M. a second plane slammed into the south tower and exploded.

Many Americans saw the second crash broadcast live on television and realized that this was not a tragic accident but a deliberate attack. It was also soon clear that New York was not the terrorists' only target. At approximately 9:40 A.M. a third plane hit the west side of the **Pentagon**. Located just outside Washington, D.C., the Pentagon is the headquarters of the U.S. military. The impact of the crash caused massive damage and started fires deep within the huge five-sided building.

At the World Trade Center complex, hundreds of rescue workers struggled to aid victims and firefighters tried to control the raging fires. Then, further disaster struck. Just before 10:00 A.M. the south tower suddenly collapsed, followed half an hour later by the fall of the north tower. The collapse of the massive buildings killed or trapped thousands of people still inside or near the towers, including hundreds of firefighters, police officers, and other rescuers.

A fourth plane was also hijacked and still in the air over southern Pennsylvania. Passengers aboard the plane made cell phone calls indicating that they learned of the other attacks and decided to stop the terrorists on board from hitting their next target. Flight 93 crashed southeast of Pittsburgh at 10:10 A.M., between the times the World Trade Center's Twin Towers collapsed.

In downtown New York City, clouds of smoke, dust, and ash drifted through the streets. Meanwhile, emergency teams battling fires in the Pentagon were unable to search for survivors. All 265 passengers and crew aboard the four hijacked flights had been killed. Americans everywhere were shocked, wondering what was to come next.

✔ **Reading Check: Sequencing** In what order did the events on the morning of September 11, 2001, take place?

★ The Nation Responds

Government officials raced to increase rescue efforts and placed the U.S. military on full alert. The Federal Aviation Administration temporarily grounded air traffic nationwide and closed airports. Key government centers, such as the White House and the Capitol, were evacuated.

Firefighters and other rescue workers from across the nation came to New York. There they joined state and city emergency personnel searching the rubble for survivors. Their efforts were blocked by the intense heat from underground fires. New York hospitals mobilized hundreds of doctors but found, tragically, that there were relatively few survivors to treat. New York mayor **Rudolph Giuliani** said of the final death toll, "It will be more than we can bear." More than 5,500 people were killed by the attack on the World Trade Center. This number included more than 300 firefighters and many other rescue workers who were on the scene. At the Pentagon, 189 military and civilian personnel, including those on the hijacked plane, were killed.

©2001 *The Record* (Bergen, NJ) by Thomas E. Franklin, Staff Photographer

Firefighters raise an American flag over the rubble of the World Trade Center towers.

GLOBAL CONNECTIONS

The World Reaches Out

The tragic events of September 11, 2001, drew sympathy and support from around the world. Citizens of more than 40 countries were among the missing. The European Union declared September 14 a day of mourning. British prime minister Tony Blair called the terrorist acts "an attack on the free and democratic world everywhere." The French newspaper *Le Monde* ran a headline saying, "WE ARE ALL AMERICANS." Russian and Chinese leaders gave their condolences. Even traditional opponents of the United States, such as Cuba and Iran, expressed their sympathy and regret. U.S. leaders gave thanks for these gestures and worked to form an active coalition against terrorism. **Why might global support be important to the United States?**

BIOGRAPHY

Rudolph Giuliani

(1944–)

As mayor of New York City, Rudolph Giuliani played a key role during the early weeks of the crisis. Coordinating relief efforts, consoling victims, and calling for resolve and renewed confidence, he served as an important symbol of strength to the city and the nation as a whole. A national poll conducted following the attacks found a 95 percent approval rating for how the mayor performed his duties. **Why do you think Giuliani's popularity increased after the attacks?**

Analyzing Primary Sources

Drawing Inferences and Conclusions What do you think James Earl Jones means when he says what Americans share is greater than what divides them?

Congress swiftly approved a $40 billion relief package to fund emergency assistance and national security measures. The government also passed legislation that provided financial support to the families of victims. Democrats and Republicans displayed an unusual degree of cooperation in pushing through these measures.

Political leaders also tried to rally Americans' spirit on the day of the attack. Mayor Giuliani assured fellow New Yorkers, "We're going to rebuild and rebuild stronger." President **George W. Bush**, who had been in Florida visiting an elementary school, was moved to a safer location. From there, he gave a brief speech to the nation and told Americans that "we [the United States] will do whatever is necessary to protect America and Americans." Republican and Democratic members of Congress issued a joint declaration to the country from the Capitol steps. They said that the United States would not be intimidated by terrorism. The members then sang a chorus of "God Bless America."

Perhaps the greatest show of unity came from the American people themselves. Many were inspired to displays of charity and patriotism. Within two days Wal-Mart, the nation's largest retail chain, had sold its entire stock of half a million American flags. Charitable groups across the country moved swiftly to raise funds for relief efforts. Thousands of people went to Red Cross centers to donate blood.

People also came together in public to heal their wounds and show their strength. When professional sports leagues resumed their schedules, stadiums were filled with patriotic tributes and fans waving flags. Actor James Earl Jones drew cheers as he opened a mass prayer service held in New York City's Yankee Stadium.

 History Makers Speak

"Our spirit is unbroken. In fact, it is stronger than ever. Today we reaffirm our faith in the essential dignity of every individual. What we share as Americans and as human beings is far greater than what divides us."

—James Earl Jones, prayer service, September 23, 2001

Religious leaders representing many faiths led prayers for the victims and called for unity as a nation. The Boys and Girls Choir of Harlem sang a stirring version of "We Shall Overcome."

✔ **Reading Check: Summarizing** In what ways did Americans first respond to the terrorist attacks?

★ The Investigation

Immediately after the attacks, the largest criminal investigation in U.S. history began. Within 48 hours the Federal Bureau of Investigation (FBI) placed more than 4,000 special agents on the case. The FBI soon released the names of 19 suspected hijackers from several nations in the Middle East. Investigators gathered evidence suggesting that each group of hijackers included trained pilots. Some of these men had been living and training in the United States for months. Even more crucial was the identity of those who had planned these acts of terror.

A prime suspect surfaced almost immediately—Osama bin Laden. This wealthy Saudi Arabian exile was already wanted for his suspected role in earlier terrorist attacks against U.S. forces overseas. A supporter of an extreme form of Islamic fundamentalism, bin Laden had publicly called for attacks on the United States. He claimed that the United States had corrupted and oppressed Muslims. Bin Laden's global terrorism network is known as al Qaeda, or "the Base." U.S. officials believe that it is one of the few terrorist groups with the resources and organizational structure to have carried out the attacks.

Historical Document

PRESIDENT BUSH'S ADDRESS TO THE NATION

On September 20, 2001, President George W. Bush addressed the joint houses of Congress and the American people. The following is an excerpt from his speech.

Tonight we are a country awakened to danger and called to defend freedom. Our grief has turned to anger, and anger to resolution. . . .

Every nation, in every region, now has a decision to make. Either you are with us, or you are with the terrorists. From this day forward, any nation that continues to harbor or support terrorism will be regarded by the United States as a hostile regime. . . .

Great harm has been done to us. We have suffered great loss. And in our grief and anger we have found our mission and our moment. Freedom and fear are at war. The advance of human freedom . . . now depends on us. . . . We will not tire, . . . and we will not fail.

Analyzing Primary Sources

1. What did President Bush call on other nations to do?
2. How did the president say the United States would react to terrorist acts?

Experts also agreed that the attacks of September 11 likely involved the cooperation of more than one terrorist group. Investigators from a broad range of federal agencies began a global manhunt with assistance from other nations. Investigators sifted through debris at the crash sites to find physical evidence. They also attempted to track airline, telephone, credit card, and other financial records to trace terrorists' movements. The Bush administration pledged to release conclusive evidence about the attacks as soon as it was possible to do so.

✔ **Reading Check: Analyzing Information** What early conclusions did investigators draw about who carried out the attacks, and how did they investigate them?

 ## The Economic Impact

The terrorist strikes on the World Trade Center also had a high cost in economic terms. The costs related to the immediate physical damage were estimated at $25 billion. In addition, the New York Stock Exchange (NYSE) had to shut down operations for four days, the longest period of time since it closed at the beginning of World War I in 1914. When the NYSE reopened, it had one of the worst weeks in its history.

One area of particular concern was the airline industry. Major airlines were forced to shut down operations for days and faced greatly

Interpreting the Visual Record

The stock market *Concerns about a potential war and poor economic indicators caused prices on the NASDAQ stock exchange to fall dramatically after the market reopened following the terrorist attacks. European and Asian stock markets also suffered heavy losses.* **How does this photograph reflect that decline?**

increased security expenses. In addition, many people were reluctant to fly. Major airlines took heavy financial losses and laid off thousands of workers. Tourism declined severely around the nation, and companies relying on supplies shipped by air continued to have shortages. The president and Congress rushed to pass a $15 billion bail-out package to help keep the nation's airlines operating.

One of the most difficult economic problems for the government to address was falling consumer confidence. Many Americans had been concerned about the economy before the terrorist attacks. The events of September 11 raised feelings of uncertainty and made many Americans believe the country was headed for a recession. Government officials responded by emphasizing that the long-term health of the economy was strong, even if difficult times lay ahead.

✔ **Reading Check: Finding the Main Idea** What immediate effects did the terrorist attacks have on the U.S. economy?

⭐ A Call to Action

In a national address on September 20, President George W. Bush called the attacks on the World Trade Center and the Pentagon "an act of war." He promised that the United States would bring those responsible to justice and wage war on terrorism itself. President Bush emphasized that the efforts of the United States would be aimed not only against terrorist organizations but also against national governments that supported and protected terrorists.

In his speech the president singled out one government—the ruling Taliban of Afghanistan—as a key sponsor of terror. The Taliban emerged in the mid-1990s as a splinter group of fundamentalist Muslims. Many members had fought against the Soviets during their occupation of Afghanistan. The Taliban's leaders had developed ties to Osama bin Laden, whom they later sheltered. Bush demanded that the Taliban turn Osama bin Laden over to the U.S. government.

The campaign against terrorism involved defensive and offensive measures. President Bush appointed Pennsylvania governor **Tom Ridge** to head the Office of Homeland Security, a new cabinet-level position. This office was created to coordinate the domestic national security efforts of various government agencies. Key goals included improving airport security and protecting vital systems such as transportation and power networks from attack. Political leaders such as U.S. Attorney General John Ashcroft also called for expanded law-enforcement powers to combat terrorism. This led to debate over how best to protect Americans' civil liberties while increasing domestic security.

Administration officials, including Secretary of Defense **Donald Rumsfeld**, agreed that locating and striking at terrorists outside the United States would be a lengthy and difficult task.

The Bush administration sought to fight terrorism using economic, diplomatic, and military means. The president froze the assets of individuals, groups, and companies with suspected terrorist ties. Secretary of State **Colin Powell** led U.S. efforts to build an international coalition against terrorism and to isolate the Taliban regime.

The United States also began mobilizing military forces. Aircraft carrier groups and ground troops were assembled in preparation for possible attacks on terrorist targets. On October 7, the United States and Great Britain began air strikes against Afghanistan. The strikes targeted al Qaeda and Taliban training camps, air-defense systems, and airfields, as well as Kabul, the country's capital. President Bush explained that the Taliban regime had been warned to meet American demands to surrender Osama bin Laden.

Meanwhile, as the military action continued, Americans and the military remained on alert for other possible terrorist actions. Several letters containing dried anthrax spores were sent to locations in Florida, New York City, and Washington, D.C., including Senator Tom Daschle's office. Some who handled these letters, including postal workers, became infected and died. Anthrax is a potentially deadly disease caused by spore-form bacterium. It was used in World War I as a means of biological warfare.

As U.S. leaders responded to the attacks, it was evident that a new era in global relations had begun. The events of September 11 had exposed both the vulnerability and the strength of the United States. Americans faced the uncertain future with hope and determination.

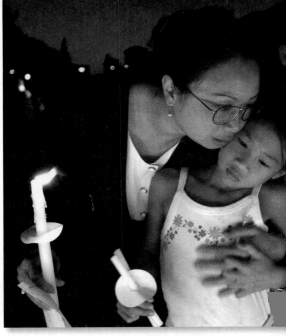

This mother and her daughter joined many Americans who attended an interfaith memorial service for the victims of the September 11 attacks.

internet connect

GO TO: go.hrw.com
KEYWORD: SS Attack
FOR: Web sites about the events of September 11, 2001, and the aftermath

✔ **Reading Check: Summarizing** What early steps did U.S. leaders take to respond to the terrorist attacks on the United States?

Section 6 Review

go.hrw.com **Homework Practice Online**

keyword: SF3 HPE

1 Identify and explain:
- World Trade Center
- Pentagon
- Rudolph Giuliani
- George W. Bush
- Tom Ridge
- Donald Rumsfeld
- Colin Powell

2 Analyzing Information
Copy the graphic organizer below. Use it to explain some of the ways in which the government responded to protect Americans and bring terrorists to justice.

Security		Diplomatic
	Government Actions	
Economic		Military

3 Finding the Main Idea
a. Whom did investigators suspect of carrying out the terrorist attacks of September 11, 2001, and how did they pursue the investigation?
b. How did the attacks affect the economy?

4 Writing and Critical Thinking
Evaluating Imagine that you are first learning of the attacks on September 11, 2001, and want to help however you can. Write a paragraph describing possible actions you could take to assist those in need.

Consider the following:
- the efforts of relief agencies to help victims
- the need for national unity
- the importance of tolerance

EPILOGUE Review

The Chapter at a Glance
Examine the visual summary of the chapter below. Use it to brainstorm what you think are the most important changes that took place in the 1900s. Compare your list with a classmate's list, and then discuss how your lists are similar and different.

Modern America

World War I • **1914–1918**

Stock Market Crash • **1929**

Great Depression • **1930s**

World War II • **1941–1945**

Cold War • **1947–1990**

Korean War • **1950–1953**

Civil Rights Movement **1950s** and **1960s**

Vietnam War **1960s–1975**

Energy Crisis **1970s**

Watergate • **1972–74**

Iran-Contra Affair • **1980s**

Operation Desert Storm • **1991**

Development of the Internet • **1990s**

Presidential Election • **2000**

Identifying People and Ideas
Use the following terms or people in historically significant sentences.
1. Woodrow Wilson
2. Harlem Renaissance
3. Great Depression
4. Holocaust
5. Marshall Plan
6. Martin Luther King Jr.
7. John F. Kennedy
8. energy crisis
9. supply-side economics
10. Bill Clinton

Understanding Main Ideas
Section 1 *(Pages 768–773)*
1. How did life in the United States change after World War I?

Section 2 *(Pages 774–780)*
2. How did President Roosevelt's administration help Americans get through the depression?

Section 3 *(Pages 781–786)*
3. How did the Cold War influence U.S. foreign and domestic policy?

Section 4 *(Pages 787–793)*
4. How did African Americans gain greater civil rights in the 1960s, and what were these rights?
5. What domestic and international concerns faced the United States in the 1970s?

Section 5 *(Pages 794–799)*
6. How was the United States involved with other countries in the 1980s and 1990s?

Section 6 *(Pages 800–805)*
7. How did Americans try to help after the terrorist attacks of September 11, 2001?

You Be the Historian— Reviewing Themes
1. **Global Relations** Why did the United States enter the fighting in World Wars I and II?
2. **Citizenship** What strategies did civil rights workers use in the 1950s and 1960s?
3. **Economics** How did some nations strengthen their global economic ties in the 1990s?

Thinking Critically
1. **Contrasting** How did American life in the 1930s differ from American life in the 1920s?
2. **Drawing Inferences and Conclusions** What do you think are the three most important reasons that the United States chose to take military action in the 1990s?
3. **Making Generalizations and Predictions** Based on trends you have observed in your study of the past 100 years, what do you think the next 100 years will be like?

Interpreting Political Cartoons

Study the cartoon below. Then use the cartoon to help you answer the questions that follow.

"You've got to admit we're getting Watergate behind us."

THE PARDON
COVER-UP
TRIAL
"TRANSITIONAL" EXPENSES
NIXON SUIT TAPES

1. What is the cartoon's message?
   a. Watergate continued to trouble President Ford and the nation even after Nixon resigned.
   b. Nixon abused his powers as president.
   c. Ford was not prepared for the new responsibilities that he assumed as president.
   d. Nixon was a stronger leader than Ford.

2. What is President Ford doing and why?

Analyzing Primary Sources

Read the following quotation by Justice Sandra Day O'Connor, the first woman ever to serve on the U.S. Supreme Court, then answer the questions.

❝Judges are supposed to be objective; they're supposed to study and look at the law and apply the law to the particular case in an objective way, not from any particular point of view. So does being a woman make a difference in what answer is given? I tend to think that probably at the end of the day, a wise old woman and a wise old man are going to reach the same answer.❞

3. What point of view does Justice O'Connor express about the qualifications of women to be judges?
   a. Men make better judgments than women.
   b. Women make better judgments than men.
   c. Men and women make the same judgments.
   d. Men and women come to different conclusions.

4. What information does Justice O'Connor use to help support her conclusion?
   a. Judges are supposed to apply the law in an objective way.
   b. Justice O'Connor is well educated.
   c. Judges have many different points of view.
   d. It is important that both men and women serve on the Supreme Court.

5. Do you agree or disagree with Justice O'Connor's statement? Explain your answer.

Alternative Assessment

Building Your Portfolio

American History

Linking to Community
Go to a local public library or historical society, and study old copies of your local community's newspaper to learn how its residents experienced World War I. Answer the following questions in a brief written report. Who enlisted? Who was drafted? Did anyone protest U.S. involvement? What role did women and African Americans play? How did the community support troops overseas? Present your written report to the class.

✔ internet connect

Internet Activity: go.hrw.com
keyword: SF3 CFEP

Choose an activity on Modern America to:
● Research changes in submarine technology and the impact of submarine warfare.
● Write a biography of Louis Armstrong.
● Create an example of Berlin Wall art that portrays the breakup of the Soviet Union.

American pocket watch

Early American flag

Cotton, an important southern product

The Granger Collection, New York

One of the first American locomotives, c. 1830

James Madison's quill pen

Native American totem pole

HOLT
CALL TO FREEDOM
Beginnings to 1914

REFERENCE

The Statue of Liberty

Colonial pottery
Colonial Williamsburg Foundation

Advertisement for the Pony Express

Collection of the American Numismatic Society

U.S. coins celebrating Thomas Jefferson's inauguration

Presidents
of the
United States

The Official Portraits

1 GEORGE WASHINGTON
Born: 1732   Died: 1799
Years in Office: 1789–97
Political Party: None
Home State: Virginia
Vice President: John Adams

2 JOHN ADAMS
Born: 1735   Died: 1826
Years in Office: 1797–1801
Political Party: Federalist
Home State: Massachusetts
Vice President: Thomas Jefferson

3 THOMAS JEFFERSON
Born: 1743   Died: 1826
Years in Office: 1801–09
Political Party: Republican*
Home State: Virginia
Vice Presidents: Aaron Burr,
George Clinton

4 JAMES MADISON
Born: 1751   Died: 1836
Years in Office: 1809–17
Political Party: Republican
Home State: Virginia
Vice Presidents: George Clinton,
Elbridge Gerry

5 JAMES MONROE
Born: 1758   Died: 1831
Years in Office: 1817–25
Political Party: Republican
Home State: Virginia
Vice President: Daniel D. Tompkins

6 JOHN QUINCY ADAMS
Born: 1767   Died: 1848
Years in Office: 1825–29
Political Party: Republican
Home State: Massachusetts
Vice President: John C. Calhoun

7 ANDREW JACKSON
Born: 1767   Died: 1845
Years in Office: 1829–37
Political Party: Democratic
Home State: Tennessee
Vice Presidents: John C. Calhoun,
Martin Van Buren

* The Republican Party of the third through sixth presidents is not the party of Abraham Lincoln, which was founded in 1854.

8 MARTIN VAN BUREN
Born: 1782   Died: 1862
Years in Office: 1837–41
Political Party: Democratic
Home State: New York
Vice President: Richard M. Johnson

9 WILLIAM HENRY HARRISON
Born: 1773   Died: 1841
Years in Office: 1841
Political Party: Whig
Home State: Ohio
Vice President: John Tyler

10 JOHN TYLER
Born: 1790   Died: 1862
Years in Office: 1841–45
Political Party: Whig
Home State: Virginia
Vice President: None

11 JAMES K. POLK
Born: 1795   Died: 1849
Years in Office: 1845–49
Political Party: Democratic
Home State: Tennessee
Vice President: George M. Dallas

12 ZACHARY TAYLOR
Born: 1784   Died: 1850
Years in Office: 1849–50
Political Party: Whig
Home State: Louisiana
Vice President: Millard Fillmore

13 MILLARD FILLMORE
Born: 1800   Died: 1874
Years in Office: 1850–53
Political Party: Whig
Home State: New York
Vice President: None

14 FRANKLIN PIERCE
Born: 1804   Died: 1869
Years in Office: 1853–57
Political Party: Democratic
Home State: New Hampshire
Vice President: William R. King

15 JAMES BUCHANAN
Born: 1791   Died: 1868
Years in Office: 1857–61
Political Party: Democratic
Home State: Pennsylvania
Vice President: John C. Breckinridge

16 ABRAHAM LINCOLN
Born: 1809   Died: 1865
Years in Office: 1861–65
Political Party: Republican
Home State: Illinois
Vice Presidents: Hannibal Hamlin,
Andrew Johnson

PRESIDENTS OF THE UNITED STATES

17 ANDREW JOHNSON
Born: 1808 **Died:** 1875
Years in Office: 1865–69
Political Party: Republican
Home State: Tennessee
Vice President: None

18 ULYSSES S. GRANT
Born: 1822 **Died:** 1885
Years in Office: 1869–77
Political Party: Republican
Home State: Illinois
Vice Presidents: Schuyler Colfax,
Henry Wilson

19 RUTHERFORD B. HAYES
Born: 1822 **Died:** 1893
Years in Office: 1877–81
Political Party: Republican
Home State: Ohio
Vice President: William A. Wheeler

20 JAMES A. GARFIELD
Born: 1831 **Died:** 1881
Years in Office: 1881
Political Party: Republican
Home State: Ohio
Vice President: Chester A. Arthur

21 CHESTER A. ARTHUR
Born: 1829 **Died:** 1886
Years in Office: 1881–85
Political Party: Republican
Home State: New York
Vice President: None

22 GROVER CLEVELAND
Born: 1837 **Died:** 1908
Years in Office: 1885–89
Political Party: Democratic
Home State: New York
Vice President: Thomas A. Hendricks

23 BENJAMIN HARRISON
Born: 1833 **Died:** 1901
Years in Office: 1889–93
Political Party: Republican
Home State: Indiana
Vice President: Levi P. Morton

24 GROVER CLEVELAND
Born: 1837 **Died:** 1908
Years in Office: 1893–97
Political Party: Democratic
Home State: New York
Vice President: Adlai E. Stevenson

25 WILLIAM MCKINLEY
Born: 1843 **Died:** 1901
Years in Office: 1897–1901
Political Party: Republican
Home State: Ohio
Vice Presidents: Garret A. Hobart,
Theodore Roosevelt

26 THEODORE ROOSEVELT
Born: 1858　**Died:** 1919
Years in Office: 1901–09
Political Party: Republican
Home State: New York
Vice President: Charles W. Fairbanks

27 WILLIAM HOWARD TAFT
Born: 1857　**Died:** 1930
Years in Office: 1909–13
Political Party: Republican
Home State: Ohio
Vice President: James S. Sherman

28 WOODROW WILSON
Born: 1856　**Died:** 1924
Years in Office: 1913–21
Political Party: Democratic
Home State: New Jersey
Vice President: Thomas R. Marshall

29 WARREN G. HARDING
Born: 1865　**Died:** 1923
Years in Office: 1921–23
Political Party: Republican
Home State: Ohio
Vice President: Calvin Coolidge

30 CALVIN COOLIDGE
Born: 1872　**Died:** 1933
Years in Office: 1923–29
Political Party: Republican
Home State: Massachusetts
Vice President: Charles G. Dawes

31 HERBERT HOOVER
Born: 1874　**Died:** 1964
Years in Office: 1929–33
Political Party: Republican
Home State: California
Vice President: Charles Curtis

32 FRANKLIN D. ROOSEVELT
Born: 1882　**Died:** 1945
Years in Office: 1933–45
Political Party: Democratic
Home State: New York
Vice Presidents: John Nance Garner,
　Henry Wallace, Harry S Truman

33 HARRY S TRUMAN
Born: 1884　**Died:** 1972
Years in Office: 1945–53
Political Party: Democratic
Home State: Missouri
Vice President: Alben W. Barkley

34 DWIGHT D. EISENHOWER
Born: 1890　**Died:** 1969
Years in Office: 1953–61
Political Party: Republican
Home State: Kansas
Vice President: Richard M. Nixon

35 JOHN F. KENNEDY
Born: 1917   Died: 1963
Years in Office: 1961–63
Political Party: Democratic
Home State: Massachusetts
Vice President: Lyndon B. Johnson

36 LYNDON B. JOHNSON
Born: 1908   Died: 1973
Years in Office: 1963–69
Political Party: Democratic
Home State: Texas
Vice President: Hubert H. Humphrey

37 RICHARD M. NIXON
Born: 1913   Died: 1994
Years in Office: 1969–74
Political Party: Republican
Home State: California
Vice Presidents: Spiro T. Agnew,
    Gerald R. Ford

38 GERALD R. FORD
Born: 1913
Years in Office: 1974–77
Political Party: Republican
Home State: Michigan
Vice President: Nelson A. Rockefeller

39 JIMMY CARTER
Born: 1924
Years in Office: 1977–81
Political Party: Democratic
Home State: Georgia
Vice President: Walter F. Mondale

40 RONALD REAGAN
Born: 1911
Years in Office: 1981–89
Political Party: Republican
Home State: California
Vice President: George Bush

41 GEORGE BUSH
Born: 1924
Years in Office: 1989–93
Political Party: Republican
Home State: Texas
Vice President: J. Danforth Quayle

42 BILL CLINTON
Born: 1946
Years in Office: 1993–2001
Political Party: Democratic
Home State: Arkansas
Vice President: Albert Gore Jr.

43 GEORGE W. BUSH
Born: 1946
Years in Office: 2001–
Political Party: Republican
Home State: Texas
Vice President: Richard B. Cheney

Facts About the States

STATE	YEAR OF STATEHOOD	2000 POPULATION	REPS. IN CONGRESS	AREA (SQ. MI.)	POPULATION DENSITY (SQ. MI.)	CAPITAL
Alabama	1819	4,461,130	7	51,705	86.3	Montgomery
Alaska	1959	628,933	1	591,004	1.1	Juneau
Arizona	1912	5,140,683	8	114,000	45.1	Phoenix
Arkansas	1836	2,679,733	4	53,187	50.4	Little Rock
California	1850	33,930,798	53	158,706	213.8	Sacramento
Colorado	1876	4,311,882	7	104,247	41.4	Denver
Connecticut	1788	3,409,535	5	5,018	679.5	Hartford
Delaware	1787	785,068	1	2,057	381.7	Dover
District of Columbia	—	572,059	—	69	8,290.7	—
Florida	1845	16,028,890	25	58,664	273.2	Tallahassee
Georgia	1788	8,206,975	13	58,910	139.3	Atlanta
Hawaii	1959	1,216,642	2	6,471	188.0	Honolulu
Idaho	1890	1,297,274	2	83,557	15.5	Boise
Illinois	1818	12,439,042	19	56,400	220.6	Springfield
Indiana	1816	6,090,782	9	36,291	167.8	Indianapolis
Iowa	1846	2,931,923	5	56,275	52.1	Des Moines
Kansas	1861	2,693,824	4	82,277	32.7	Topeka
Kentucky	1792	4,049,431	6	40,395	100.2	Frankfort
Louisiana	1812	4,480,271	7	48,523	92.3	Baton Rouge
Maine	1820	1,277,731	2	33,265	38.4	Augusta
Maryland	1788	5,307,886	8	10,460	507.4	Annapolis
Massachusetts	1788	6,355,568	10	8,284	767.2	Boston
Michigan	1837	9,955,829	15	58,527	170.1	Lansing
Minnesota	1858	4,925,670	8	84,068	58.6	St. Paul
Mississippi	1817	2,852,927	4	47,689	59.8	Jackson
Missouri	1821	5,606,260	9	69,697	80.4	Jefferson City
Montana	1889	905,316	1	147,046	6.2	Helena
Nebraska	1867	1,715,369	3	77,355	22.2	Lincoln
Nevada	1864	2,002,032	3	110,561	18.1	Carson City
New Hampshire	1788	1,238,415	2	9,279	133.5	Concord
New Jersey	1787	8,424,354	13	7,787	1,081.8	Trenton
New Mexico	1912	1,823,821	3	121,593	15.0	Santa Fe
New York	1788	19,004,973	29	49,576	383.4	Albany
North Carolina	1789	8,067,673	13	52,669	153.2	Raleigh
North Dakota	1889	643,756	1	70,655	9.1	Bismarck
Ohio	1803	11,374,540	18	41,222	275.9	Columbus
Oklahoma	1907	3,458,819	5	69,956	49.4	Oklahoma City
Oregon	1859	3,428,543	5	97,073	35.3	Salem
Pennsylvania	1787	12,300,670	19	45,333	271.3	Harrisburg
Rhode Island	1790	1,049,662	2	1,212	866.1	Providence
South Carolina	1788	4,025,061	6	31,113	129.4	Columbia
South Dakota	1889	756,874	1	77,116	9.8	Pierre
Tennessee	1796	5,700,037	9	42,144	135.3	Nashville
Texas	1845	20,903,994	32	266,807	78.3	Austin
Utah	1896	2,236,714	3	84,899	26.3	Salt Lake City
Vermont	1791	609,890	1	9,609	63.5	Montpelier
Virginia	1788	7,100,702	11	40,767	174.2	Richmond
Washington	1889	5,908,684	9	68,192	86.6	Olympia
West Virginia	1863	1,813,077	3	24,181	75.0	Charleston
Wisconsin	1848	5,371,210	8	56,154	95.7	Madison
Wyoming	1890	495,304	1	97,914	5.1	Cheyenne

The American Flag

The American flag is a symbol of the nation. It is recognized instantly, whether as a big banner waving in the wind or a tiny emblem worn on a lapel. The flag is so important that it is a major theme of the national anthem, "The Star-Spangled Banner." One of the most popular names for the flag is the Stars and Stripes. It is also known as Old Glory.

THE MEANING OF THE FLAG

The American flag has 13 stripes—7 red and 6 white. In the upper-left corner of the flag is the union—50 white five-pointed stars against a blue background.

The 13 stripes stand for the original 13 American states, and the 50 stars represent the states of the nation today. According to the U.S. Department of State, the colors of the flag also are symbolic:

Red stands for courage.

White symbolizes purity.

Blue is the color of vigilance, perseverance, and justice.

DISPLAYING THE FLAG

It is customary not to display the American flag in bad weather. It is also customary for the flag to be displayed outdoors only from sunrise to sunset, except on certain occasions. In a few special places, however, the flag is always flown day and night. When flown at night, the flag should be illuminated.

Near a speaker's platform, the flag should occupy the place of honor at the speaker's right. When carried in a parade with other flags, the American flag should be on the marching right or in front at the center. When flying with the flags of the 50 states, the national flag must be at the center and the highest point. In a group of national flags, all should be of equal size and all should be flown from staffs, or flagpoles, of equal height.

The flag should never touch the ground or the floor. It should not be marked with any insignia, pictures, or words. Nor should it be used in any disrespectful way—as an advertising decoration, for instance. The flag should never be dipped to honor any person or thing.

SALUTING THE FLAG

The United States, like other countries, has a flag code, or rules for displaying and honoring the flag. For example, all those present should stand at attention facing the flag and salute it when it is being raised or lowered or when it is carried past them in a parade or procession. A man wearing a hat should take it off and hold it with his right hand over his heart. All women and hatless men should stand with their right hands over their hearts to show respect. The flag should also receive these honors during the playing of the national anthem and the reciting of the Pledge of Allegiance.

THE PLEDGE OF ALLEGIANCE

The Pledge of Allegiance was written in 1892 by Massachusetts magazine (*Youth's Companion*) editor Francis Bellamy. (Congress added the words "under God" in 1954.)

I pledge allegiance to the flag of the United States of America and to the republic for which it stands, one nation under God, indivisible, with liberty and justice for all.

Civilians should say the Pledge of Allegiance with their right hands over their hearts. People in the armed forces give the military salute. By saying the Pledge of Allegiance, we promise loyalty ("pledge allegiance") to the United States and its ideals.

"THE STAR-SPANGLED BANNER"

"The Star-Spangled Banner" is the national anthem of the United States. It was written by Francis Scott Key during the War of 1812. While being detained by the British aboard a ship on September 13-14, 1814, Key watched the British bombardment of Fort McHenry at Baltimore. The attack lasted 25 hours. The smoke was so thick that Key could not tell who had won. When the air cleared, Key saw the American flag that was still flying over the fort. "The Star-Spangled Banner" is sung to music written by British composer John Stafford Smith. In 1931 Congress designated "The Star-Spangled Banner" as the national anthem.

I

Oh, say, can you see, by the dawn's early light,
What so proudly we hailed at the twilight's last gleaming,
Whose broad stripes and bright stars through the perilous fight,
O'er the ramparts we watched were so gallantly streaming?
And the rockets' red glare, the bombs bursting in air,
Gave proof through the night that our flag was still there.
Oh, say, does that star-spangled banner yet wave
O'er the land of the free, and the home of the brave?

II

On the shore, dimly seen through the mists of the deep,
Where the foe's haughty host in dread silence reposes,
What is that which the breeze, o'er the towering steep,
As it fitfully blows, half conceals, half discloses?
Now it catches the gleam of the morning's first beam,
In full glory reflected, now shines on the stream.
'Tis the star-spangled banner; oh, long may it wave
O'er the land of the free, and the home of the brave!

III

And where is that band who so vauntingly swore
That the havoc of war and the battle's confusion
A home and a country should leave us no more?
Their blood has washed out their foul footsteps' pollution.
No refuge could save the hireling and slave
From the terror of flight, or the gloom of the grave:
And the star-spangled banner in triumph doth wave
O'er the land of the free, and the home of the brave!

IV

Oh! thus be it ever when freemen shall stand
Between their loved homes and the war's desolation!
Blest with victory and peace, may the heaven-rescued land
Praise the Power that hath made and preserved us a nation!
Then conquer we must, for our cause it is just,
And this be our motto: "In God is our trust!"
And the star-spangled banner in triumph shall wave,
O'er the land of the free, and the home of the brave!

Sheet music to the national anthem

"AMERICA, THE BEAUTIFUL"

One of the most beloved songs celebrating our nation is "America, the Beautiful." Katharine Lee Bates first wrote the lyrics to the song in 1893 after visiting Colorado. The version of the song we know today is set to music by Samuel A. Ward. The first and last stanzas of "America, the Beautiful" are shown below.

O beautiful for spacious skies,
For amber waves of grain,
For purple mountain majesties
Above the fruited plain!
America! America!
God shed his grace on thee
And crown thy good with brotherhood
From sea to shining sea!

• •

O beautiful for patriot dream
That sees beyond the years
Thine alabaster cities gleam
Undimmed by human tears!
America! America!
God shed his grace on thee
And crown thy good with brotherhood
From sea to shining sea!

Important Supreme Court Cases

MARBURY v. MADISON, 1 CRANCH (5 U.S.) 137 (1803)

Significance: This ruling established the Supreme Court's power of judicial review, by which the Court decides whether laws passed by Congress are constitutional. This decision greatly increased the prestige of the Court and gave the judiciary branch a powerful check against the legislative and executive branches.

Background: William Marbury and several others were commissioned as judges by Federalist president John Adams during his last days in office. This act angered the new Democratic-Republican president, Thomas Jefferson. Jefferson ordered his secretary of state, James Madison, not to deliver the commissions. Marbury took advantage of a section in the Judiciary Act of 1789 that allowed him to take his case directly to the Supreme Court. He sued Madison, demanding the commission and the judgeship.

Decision: This case was decided on February 24, 1803, by a vote of 5 to 0. Chief Justice John Marshall spoke for the Court, which decided against Marbury. The court ruled that although Marbury's commission had been unfairly withheld, he could not lawfully take his case to the Supreme Court without first trying it in a lower court. Marshall said that the section of the Judiciary Act that Marbury had used was actually unconstitutional, and that the Constitution must take priority over laws passed by Congress.

MCCULLOCH v. MARYLAND, 4 WHEAT. (17 U.S.) 316 (1819)

Significance: This ruling established that Congress had the constitutional power to charter a national bank. The case also established the principle of national supremacy, which states that the Constitution and other laws of the federal government take priority over state laws. In addition, the ruling reinforced the loose construction interpretation of the Constitution favored by many Federalists.

Background: In 1816 the federal government set up the Second Bank of the United States to stabilize the economy following the War of 1812. Many states were opposed to the competition provided by the new national bank. Some of these states passed heavy taxes on the Bank. The national bank refused to pay the taxes. This led the state of Maryland to sue James McCulloch, the cashier of the Baltimore, Maryland, branch of the national bank.

Decision: This case was decided on March 6, 1819, by a vote of 7 to 0. Chief Justice John Marshall spoke for the unanimous Court, which ruled that the national bank was constitutional because it helped the federal government carry out other powers granted to it by the Constitution. The Court declared that any attempt by the states to interfere with the duties of the federal government could not be permitted.

GIBBONS v. OGDEN, 9 WHEAT. (22 U.S.) 1 (1824)

Significance: This ruling was the first case to deal with the clause of the Constitution that allows Congress to regulate interstate and foreign commerce. This case was important because it reinforced both the authority of the federal government over the states and the division of powers between the federal government and the state governments.

Background: Steamboat operators who wanted to travel on New York waters had to obtain a state license. Thomas Gibbons had a federal license to travel along the coast, but not a state license for New York. He wanted the freedom to compete with state-licensed Aaron Ogden for steam travel between New Jersey and the New York island of Manhattan.

Decision: This case was decided on March 2, 1824, by a vote of 6 to 0. Chief Justice John Marshall spoke for the Court, which ruled in favor of Gibbons. The Court stated that the congressional statute (Gibbons's federal license) took priority over the state statute (Ogden's state-monopoly license). The ruling also defined commerce as more than simply the exchange of goods, broadening it to include the transportation of people and the use of new inventions (such as the steamboat).

WORCESTER v. GEORGIA, 6 PET. (31 U.S.) 515 (1832)

Significance: This ruling made Georgia's removal of the Cherokee illegal. However, Georgia, with President Andrew Jackson's support, defied the Court's decision. By not enforcing the Court's ruling, Jackson violated his constitutional oath as president. As a result, the Cherokee and other American Indian tribes continued to be forced off of lands protected by treaties.

Background: The state of Georgia wanted to remove Cherokee Indians from lands they held by treaty. Samuel Worcester, a missionary who worked with the Cherokee Nation, was arrested for failing to take an oath of allegiance to the state and to obey a Georgia militia order to leave the Cherokee's lands. Worcester sued, charging that Georgia had no legal authority on Cherokee lands.

Decision: This case was decided on March 3, 1832, by a vote of 5 to 1 in favor of Worcester. Chief Justice John Marshall spoke for the Supreme Court, which ruled that the Cherokee were an independent political community. The Court decided that only the federal government, not the state of Georgia, had authority over legal matters involving the Cherokee people.

SCOTT v. SANDFORD, 19 HOW. (60 U.S.) 393 (1857)

Significance: This ruling denied enslaved African Americans U.S. citizenship and the right to sue in federal court. The decision also invalidated the Missouri Compromise, which had prevented slavery in territories north of the 36° 30' line of latitude. The ruling increased the controversy over the expansion of slavery in new states and territories.

Background: John Emerson, an army doctor, took his slave Dred Scott with him to live in Illinois and then Wisconsin Territory, both of which had banned slavery. In 1842 the two moved to Missouri, a slave state. Four years later, Scott sued for his freedom according to a Missouri legal principle of "once free, always free." The principle meant that a slave was entitled to freedom if he or she had once lived in a free state or territory.

Decision: This case was decided March 6–7, 1857, by a vote of 7 to 2. Chief Justice Roger B. Taney spoke for the Court, which ruled that slaves did not have the right to sue in federal courts because they were considered property, not citizens. In addition, the Court ruled that Congress did not have the power to abolish slavery in territories because that power was not strictly defined in the Constitution. Furthermore, the Court overturned the once-free, always-free principle.

PLESSY v. FERGUSON, 163 U.S. 537 (1896)

Significance: This case upheld the constitutionality of racial segregation by ruling that separate facilities for different races were legal as long as those facilities were equal to one another. This case provided a legal justification for racial segregation for nearly 60 years until it was overturned by *Brown* v. *Board of Education* in 1954.

Background: An 1890 Louisiana law required that all railway companies in the state use "separate-but-equal" railcars for white and

African American passengers. A group of citizens in New Orleans banded together to challenge the law and chose Homer Plessy to test the law in 1892. Plessy took a seat in a whites-only coach, and when he refused to move, he was arrested. Plessy eventually sought review by the U.S. Supreme Court, claiming that the Louisiana law violated his Fourteenth Amendment right to equal protection.

Decision: This case was decided on May 18, 1896, by a vote of 7 to 1. Justice Henry Billings Brown spoke for the Court, which upheld the constitutionality of the Louisiana law that segregated railcars. Justice John M. Harlan dissented, arguing that the Constitution should not be interpreted in ways that recognize class or racial distinctions.

LOCHNER v. NEW YORK, 198 U.S. 45 (1905)

Significance: This decision established the Supreme Court's role in overseeing state regulations. For more than 30 years *Lochner* was often used as a precedent in striking down state laws such as minimum-wage laws, child labor laws, and regulations placed on the banking and transportation industries.

Background: In 1895 the state of New York passed a labor law limiting bakers to working no more than 10 hours per day or 60 hours per week. The purpose of the law was to protect the health of bakers, who worked in hot and damp conditions and breathed in large quantities of flour dust. In 1902 Joseph Lochner, the owner of a small bakery in New York, claimed that the state law violated his Fourteenth Amendment rights by unfairly depriving him of the liberty to make contracts with employees. This case went to the U.S. Supreme Court.

Decision: This case was decided on April 17, 1905, by a vote of 5 to 4 in favor of Lochner. The Supreme Court judged that the Fourteenth Amendment protected the right to sell and buy labor, and that any state law restricting that right was unconstitutional. The Court rejected the argument that the limited workday and workweek were necessary to protect the health of bakery workers.

MULLER v. OREGON, 208 U.S. 412 (1908)

Significance: A landmark for cases involving social reform, this decision established the Court's recognition of social and economic conditions (in this case, women's health) as a factor in making laws.

Background: In 1903 Oregon passed a law limiting workdays to 10 hours for female workers in laundries and factories. In 1905 Curt Muller's Grand Laundry was found guilty of breaking this law. Muller appealed, claiming that the state law violated his freedom of contract (the Supreme Court had upheld a similar claim that year in *Lochner* v. *New York*). When this case came to the Court, the National Consumers' League hired lawyer Louis D. Brandeis to present Oregon's argument. Brandeis argued that the Court had already defended the state's police power to protect its citizens' health, safety, and welfare.

Decision: This case was decided on February 24, 1908, by a vote of 9 to 0 upholding the Oregon law. The Court agreed that women's well-being was in the state's public interest and that the 10-hour law was a valid way to protect their well-being.

BROWN v. BOARD OF EDUCATION, 347 U.S. 483 (1954)

Significance: This ruling reversed the Supreme Court's earlier position on segregation set by *Plessy* v. *Ferguson* (1896). The decision also inspired Congress and the federal courts to help carry out further civil rights reforms for African Americans.

Background: Beginning in the 1930s, the National Association for the Advancement of Colored People (NAACP) began using the courts to challenge racial segregation in public education. In 1952 the NAACP took a number of school segregation cases to the Supreme Court. These included the Brown family's suit against the school board of Topeka, Kansas, over its "separate-but-equal" policy.

Decision: This case was decided on May 17, 1954, by a vote of 9 to 0. Chief Justice Earl Warren spoke for the unanimous Court, which ruled that segregation in public education created inequality. The Court held that racial segregation in public schools was by nature unequal, even if the school facilities were equal. The Court noted that such segregation created feelings of inferiority that could not be undone. Therefore, enforced separation of the races in public education is unconstitutional.

GIDEON v. WAINWRIGHT, 372 U.S. 335 (1963)

Significance: This ruling was one of several key Supreme Court decisions establishing free legal help for those who cannot otherwise afford representation in court.

Background: Clarence Earl Gideon was accused of robbery in Florida. Gideon could not afford a lawyer for his trial, and the judge refused to supply him with one for free. Gideon tried to defend himself and was found guilty. He eventually appealed to the U.S. Supreme Court, claiming that the lower court's denial of a court-appointed lawyer violated his Sixth and Fourteenth Amendment rights.

Decision: This case was decided on March 18, 1963, by a vote of 9 to 0 in favor of Gideon. The Court agreed that the Sixth Amendment (which protects a citizen's right to have a lawyer for his or her defense) applied to the states because it fell under the due process clause of the Fourteenth Amendment. Thus, the states are required to provide legal aid to those defendants in criminal cases who cannot afford to pay for legal representation.

MIRANDA v. ARIZONA, 384 U.S. 436 (1966)

Significance: This decision ruled that an accused person's Fifth Amendment rights begin at the time of arrest. The ruling caused controversy because it made questioning suspects and collecting evidence more difficult for law enforcement officers.

Background: In 1963 Ernesto Miranda was arrested in Arizona for a kidnapping. Miranda signed a confession and was later found guilty of the crime. The arresting police officers, however, admitted that they had not told Miranda of his right to talk with an attorney before his confession. Miranda appealed his conviction on the grounds that by not informing him of his legal rights the police had violated his Fifth Amendment right against self-incrimination.

Decision: This case was decided on June 13, 1966, by a vote of 5 to 4. Chief Justice Earl Warren spoke for the Court, which ruled in Miranda's favor. The Court decided that an accused person must be given four warnings after being taken into police custody: (1) the suspect has the right to remain silent, (2) anything the suspect says can and will be used against him or her, (3) the suspect has the right to consult with an attorney and to have an attorney present during questioning, and (4) if the suspect cannot afford a lawyer, one will be provided before questioning begins.

REED v. REED, 404 U.S. 71 (1971)

Significance: This ruling was the first in a century of Fourteenth Amendment decisions to say that gender discrimination violated the equal protection clause. This case was later used to strike down other statutes that discriminated against women.

Background: Cecil and Sally Reed were separated. When their son died without a will, the law gave preference to Cecil to be appointed the administrator of the son's estate. Sally sued Cecil for the right to administer the estate, challenging the gender preference in the law.

Decision: This case was decided on November 22, 1971, by a vote of 7 to 0. Chief Justice Warren Burger spoke for the unanimous Supreme Court. Although the Court had upheld laws based on gender preference in the past, in this case it reversed its position. The Court declared that gender discrimination violated the equal protection clause of the Fourteenth Amendment and therefore could not be the basis for a law.

Gazetteer

Africa Second-largest continent. Lies in both the Northern and the Southern Hemispheres. **A10**

Alabama (AL) State in the southern United States. Admitted as a state in 1819. Capital: Montgomery. (33°N 87°W) **A1**

Alaska (AK) U.S. state in northwestern North America. Purchased from Russia in 1867. Organized as a territory in 1912. Admitted as a state in 1959. Capital: Juneau. (64°N 150°W) **A1**

Albany Capital of New York State. (42°N 74°W) **A1**

Alsace-Lorraine Region between Belgium, France, Germany, and Switzerland. **770**

Andes Mountain range that extends along almost the entire western coast of South America. **68**

Antarctica Continent that surrounds the South Pole. **A4**

Antietam Creek Creek in northern Maryland. Site of an important Union army victory during the Civil War. **586**

Appalachian Mountains Mountain system in eastern North America that extends from Canada to central Alabama. **161**

Appomattox Courthouse Town in central Virginia where Robert E. Lee surrendered to Ulysses S. Grant, ending the Civil War. **613**

Arctic Ocean Ocean north of the Arctic Circle. **A4**

Argentina Republic located in the south-central and southern part of South America. Capital: Buenos Aires. (34°S 64°W) **A7**

Arizona (AZ) State in the southwestern United States. Organized as a territory in 1863. Admitted as a state in 1912. Capital: Phoenix. (34°N 113°W). **A1**

Arkansas (AR) State in the south-central United States. Admitted as a state in 1836. Capital: Little Rock. (35°N 93°W) **A1**

Asia Largest continent. Occupies the same landmass as Europe. **A9**

Atlanta Capital of Georgia. (33°N 84°W) **A1**

Atlantic Ocean Body of water separating North and South America from Europe and Africa. **A4**

Austin Capital of Texas. (30°N 98°W) **A1**

Australia Island, continent, and country located between the Indian and the Pacific Oceans. Capital: Canberra. (25°S 1 35°E) **A11**

Austria-Hungary Monarchy in central Europe from 1867 to 1918. Consisted of Austria, Bohemia, Hungary, and parts of Italy, Poland, Romania, and Yugoslavia. **770**

Bahamas Country in the Atlantic Ocean consisting of hundreds of islands. Captal: Nassau. **A6**

Baltimore Maryland city northeast of Washington, D.C., on the Chesapeake Bay. (39°N 76°W) **351**

Berlin Capital of Germany. Divided into East Berlin and West Berlin in 1945. Reunited in 1990. (52°N 13°E) **A8**

Bosnia and Herzegovina Country annexed to Austria-Hungary in 1908; after World War I became part of what would become Yugoslavia; declared independence in 1992. Capital: Sarajevo. (44°N 17°E) **A8**

Boston Capital of Massachusetts. (42°N 71°W) **187**

Brazil Republic in eastern South America. Capital: Brasília. (9°S 53°W) **A7**

Bunker Hill Hill in Boston, Massachusetts. Site of an early Revolutionary War battle. **187**

California (CA) State in the western United States. Admitted as a state in 1850. Capital: Sacramento. (38°N 121°W) **A1**

Cambodia Republic in southeastern Asia. Capital: Phnom Penh. (11°N 105°E) **791**

Canada Country in northern North America. Capital: Ottawa. (50°N 100°W) **A6**

Cape of Good Hope Southern tip of Africa. **36**

Caribbean Sea Arm of the Atlantic Ocean between North and South America. **A4**

Central America The southern portion of North America, beginning south of Mexico. **A6**

Charleston Port city in southeastern South Carolina. Originally called Charles Town. (33°N 80°W) **A1**

Chesapeake Bay Inlet of the Atlantic Ocean in Virginia and Maryland. **95**

Chicago City in northeastern Illinois on Lake Michigan. Major port and large U.S. city. (42°N 88°W) **A1**

China Country in East Asia with the world's largest population. Capital: Beijing. (Official name: People's Republic of China) **A9**

Chile Country in southwestern South America. Capital: Santiago. (35°S 72°W) **A7**

Colorado (CO) State in the west-central United States. Admitted as a state in 1876. Capital: Denver. (39°N 107°W) **A1**

Concord One of two northeastern Massachusetts towns (along with Lexington) where the first fighting of the Revolutionary War took place in 1775. (42°N 71°W) **187**

Connecticut (CT) State in the northeastern United States. One of the original thirteen colonies. Admitted as a state in 1788. Capital: Hartford. (41°N 73°W) **A1**

Cuba Country in the Caribbean about 90 miles south of Florida. Capital: Havana. (22°N 79°W) **A6**

Delaware (DE) State in the eastern United States. One of the original thirteen colonies. Capital: Dover. (38°N 75°W) **A1**

Denmark Kingdom in northwestern Europe. Capital: Copenhagen. (56°N 10°E) **A8**

District of Columbia Federal district between Maryland and Virginia where the capital of the United States is located. (39°N 77°W) **A1**

Dominican Republic Country in the Caribbean Sea. Located on the eastern part of the island of Hispaniola. Capital: Santo Domingo. (19°N 70°W) **760**

El Paso City in western Texas. (32°N 106°W) **A1**

England Country of the United Kingdom that makes up most of the southern part of the island of Great Britain. Capital: London. (51°N 1°W) **A8**

English Channel Strait between southern England and northern France that connects the Atlantic Ocean with the North Sea. **A8**

Europe Continent occupying the same landmass as Asia. **A8**

Florida (FL) State in the southeastern United States. Organized as a territory in 1822. Admitted as a state in 1845. Capital: Tallahassee. (30°N 84°W) **A1**

Fort Detroit Political and trading center of the Great Lakes region located along the Detroit River. Site of what is now Detroit, Michigan. **205**

Fort McHenry U.S. fort that guarded Baltimore, Maryland, in the War of 1812. **351**

Fort Necessity Site where the French defeated British colonists in 1754, in what was the first battle of the French and Indian War. **161**

Fort Sumter Fort on Charleston Harbor, South Carolina. Attack by Confederate forces here began the Civil War. **582**

Fort Ticonderoga Fort in northern New York captured by Patriots during the American Revolution. **205**

France Country in western Europe. Capital: Paris. (46°N 1°E) **A8**

Georgia (GA) State in the southeastern United States. Admitted as a state in 1788. One of the original thirteen colonies. Capital: Atlanta. (32°N 84°W) **A1**

Germany Country in central Europe. Capital: Berlin. (51°N 8°E) **A8**

Gettysburg Town in southern Pennsylvania. (40°N 77°W) **613**

Grand Canyon Enormous gorge in northwest Arizona. **A2**

Great Basin Region including Nevada and parts of California, Idaho, Oregon, Utah, and Wyoming that was home to some American Indian nations. **11**

Great Britain Kingdom in Western Europe. Consists of England, Scotland, and Wales. Capital: London. (54°N 4°W) **A8**

Great Lakes Chain of lakes located in central North America that extends across the U.S.-Canada border. Includes Lake Superior, Lake Michigan, Lake Huron, Lake Erie, and Lake Ontario. **86**

Great Plains Region of central North America that lies between the Mississippi River and the Rocky Mountains, stretching north into Canada and south into Texas. **A2**

Great Salt Lake Salty lake in northern Utah. **506**

Guam Pacific island that became a U.S. territory after the Spanish-American War. Capital: Agana. (14°N 143°E) **742**

Guatemala Republic in Central America. Capital: Guatemala City. (15°N 91°W) **A6**

Gulf of Mexico Gulf on the southeastern coast of North America, bordered by the United States, Mexico, and Cuba. **A6**

Haiti Country in the Caribbean Sea located on the western part of the island of Hispaniola. Capital: Port-au-Prince. (19°N 72°W) **742**

Hanoi Capital of Vietnam. (21°N 106°E) **A9**

Havana Capital and seaport of Cuba located on the northwest coast. (23°N 82°W) **747**

Hawaii (HI) U.S. state in the central Pacific Ocean that is made up of the Hawaiian Islands. Organized as a territory in 1900. Admitted as a state in 1959. Capital: Honolulu. (20°N 157°W) **A1**

Hispaniola Island that includes the countries of Haiti and the Dominican Republic. **41**

Hiroshima Japanese city bombed by a U.S. atomic weapon in August 1945. (34°N 132°F) **779**

Honduras Republic in Central America. Capital: Tegucigalpa. (15°N 86°W) **A6**

Houston City in southeastern Texas. (30°N 95°W) **A1**

Hudson Bay Inland sea in east-central Canada. Explored by Henry Hudson in 1610. **86**

Hudson River River flowing from northeastern to southern New York. **86**

Iceland Island republic located between the Arctic and North Atlantic Oceans. Capital: Reykjavik (65°N 18°W) **A8**

Idaho (ID) State in the northwestern United States. Admitted as a state in 1890. Capital: Boise. (44°N 115°W) **A1**

Illinois (IL) State in the north-central United States. Admitted as a state in 1818. Capital: Springfield. (40°N 90°W) **A1**

India Large republic in southern Asia. Capital: New Delhi. (28°N 77°E) **A9**

Indiana (IN) State in the north-central United States. Admitted as a state in 1816 Capital: Indianapolis. (40°N 86°W) **A1**

Indiana Territory Former territory created from the division of the Northwest Territory in 1800. Iincluded Illinois, Indiana, Wisconsin, much of Michigan, and part of Minnesota. **340**

Indian Ocean Body of water east of Africa, south of Asia, west of Australia, and north of Antarctica. **A4**

Indian Territory Former territory in the south-central United States. Set aside in 1820 as a home for forcibly displaced American Indians. **381**

Iowa (IA) State in the north-central United States. Admitted as a state in 1846. Capital: Des Moines. (42°N 94°W) **A1**

Iran Country in southwestern Asia. Capital: Tehran. (31°N 53°E) **A9**

Iraq Country in southwestern Asia. Capital: Baghdad. (32°N 43°E) **A9**

Ireland Island in the British Isles. Divided into Northern Ireland (Capital: Belfast), which is part of Great Britain, and the independent Republic of Ireland (Capital: Dublin). (54°N 8°W) **A8**

Israel Country in Southwest Asia on the eastern Mediterranean coast. Capital: Jerusalem. (32°N 34°E) **A9**

Isthmus of Panama Thin landmass that links North America to South America and separates the Atlantic and Pacific Oceans. Forms the Republic of Panama. **A6**

Italy Country in southern Europe. Capital: Rome. (44°N 11 °E) **A8**

Jamaica Island-nation in the Caribbean Sea. Capital: Kingston. (18°N 78°W) **A6**

James River River in Virginia that flows into Chesapeake Bay. **95**

Jamestown First successful English colony in America. Established in eastern Virginia in 1607. **95**

Japan Country in the western Pacific Ocean. Made up of a chain of islands. Capital: Tokyo. (37°N 134°E) **A9**

Jerusalem Capital of Israel. **A9**

Kansas (KS) State in the central United States. Organized as a territory in 1854. Admitted as a state in 1861. Capital: Topeka. (38°N 99°W) **A1**

Kentucky (KY) State in the east-central United States. Admitted as a state in 1792. Capital: Frankfort. (37°N 87°W) **A1**

Kuwait Country on the northeast Arabian Peninsula at the northern end of the Persian Gulf. Capital: Kuwait City. (29°N 48°E) **A9**

Lake Erie One of the Great Lakes, located in the United States and Canada. Site of battle in War of 1812. **351**

Laos Country in southeastern Asia. Capital: Vientiane. (18°N 102°E) **791**

Lebanon Country at the eastern end of the Mediterranean Sea. Capital: Beirut. (34°N 36°F) **A9**

Lexington One of two northeastern Massachusetts towns (along with Concord) where the first fighting of the American Revolution took place in 1775. (42°N 71°W) **187**

Liberia Country on the west coast of Africa, founded in 1822 as a colony for freed American slaves. (6°N 10°W) **A10**

London Capital of the United Kingdom. Located in England. (51°N 0°W) **A8**

Los Angeles Large city in southern California. (34°N 118°W) **A1**

Louisiana (LA) State in the southeastern United States carved out of the Louisiana Territory. Admitted as a state in 1812. Capital: Baton Rouge. (31°N 92°W) **A1**

Louisiana Territory Organized in 1805, extended from the Mississippi River to the Rocky Mountains and from the Gulf of Mexico to Canada, except for the Orleans Territory. **340**

Lowell Massachusetts city on the Merrimack River, northwest of Boston. (42°N 71°W) **447**

Maine (ME) State in the northeastern United States. Admitted as a state in 1820. Capital: Augusta. (45°N 70°W) **A1**

Maryland (MD) State in the east-central United States. One of the original thirteen colonies. Admitted as a state in 1788. Capital: Annapolis. (39°N 76°W) **A1**

Massachusetts (MA) State in the northeastern United States. One of the original thirteen colonies. Admitted as a state in 1788. Capital: Boston. (42°N 72°W) **A1**

Mediterranean Sea Large sea bordered by southern Europe, Southwest Asia, and northern Africa. **A8**

Mexico Country in southern North America. Capital: Mexico City. (23°N 104°W) **A6**

Michigan (MI) State in the north-central United States. Admitted as a state in 1837. Capital: Lansing. (46°N 87°W) **A1**

Middle East Vast region made up of countries in southwestern Asia and northeastern Africa. **A9**

Minnesota (MN) State in the north-central United States. Admitted as a state in 1858. Capital: St. Paul. (46°N 90°W) **A1**

Mississippi (MS) State in the southeastern United States. Admitted as a state in 1817. Capital: Jackson. (32°N 90°W) **A1**

Mississippi River River that flows from Minnesota south to the Gulf of Mexico. **A3**

Missouri (MO) State in the central United States. Admitted as a state in 1821. Capital: Jefferson City. (38°N 93°W) **A1**

Missouri River River that flows from southern Montana and joins the Mississippi River north of St. Louis, Missouri. **A3**

Montana (MT) State in the northwestern United States. Admitted as a state in 1889. Capital: Helena. (47°N 112°W) **A1**

Montgomery Capital of Alabama. (32°N 86°W) **A1**

Montreal City in southeastern Canada founded by the French in 1642. (46°N 74°W) **86**

Moscow Capital of Russia. (61°N 60°E) **A8**

Nagasaki Second Japanese city bombed by a U.S. atomic weapon in August 1945. (32°N 130°E) **779**

Nebraska (NE) State in the central United States. Admitted as a state in 1867. Capital: Lincoln. (41°N 101°W) **A1**

Netherlands Country in northwestern Europe. Capital: Amsterdam. (52°N 5°E) **A8**

Nevada (NV) State in the western United States. Organized as a territory in 1861. Admitted as a state in 1864. Capital: Carson City. (39°N 117°W) **A1**

New Amsterdam Dutch settlement on the island of Manhattan. Founded in 1620s. **89**

New England Northeastern section of the United States. Made up of Connecticut, Maine, Massachusetts, New Hampshire, Rhode Island, and Vermont. **106**

Newfoundland Island off the eastern coast of Canada. **86**

New France Former French territory in North America that included eastern Canada and the Mississippi Valley. **86**

New Hampshire (NH) State in the northeastern United States. One of the original thirteen colonies. Admitted as a state in 1788. Capital: Concord. (44°N 71°W) **A1**

New Jersey (NJ) State in the northeastern United States. One of the original thirteen colonies. Admitted as a state in 1787. Capital: Trenton. (40°N 75°W) **A1**

New Mexico (NM) State in the southwestern United States. Organized as a territory that included Arizona and part of Colorado in 1850. Admitted as a state in 1912. Capital: Santa Fe. (34°N 107°W) **A1**

New Netherland Dutch colony in North America that included parts of what are now Connecticut, Delaware, New Jersey, and New York. **89**

New Orleans Port city in southeastern Louisiana. (30°N 90°W) **A1**

New Spain Vast area of North America controlled by Spain. It extended from Mexico to California and Florida and included some Caribbean islands and also the Philippines. **75**

New Sweden Swedish colony in North America that was located along the Delaware River. **89**

New York (NY) State in the northeastern United States. One of the original thirteen colonies. Admitted as a state in 1788. Capital: Albany. (42°N 78°W) **A1**

New York City Largest city in the United States. (41°N 74°W) **A1**

Nicaragua Central American country on the Caribbean Sea and the Pacific Ocean. Capital: Managua. (12°N 86°W) **760**

Normandy Historic region in northern France that was the site of the D-Day invasion during World War II. **777**

North America Continent in the northern Western Hemisphere. **A6**

North Carolina (NC) State in the southeastern United States. One of the original thirteen colonies. Admitted as a state in 1789. Capital: Raleigh. (35°N 81°W) **A1**

North Dakota (ND) State in the north-central United States. Organized as part of the Dakota Territory in 1861. Admitted as a state in 1889. Capital: Bismarck. (47°N 102°W) **A1**

Northwest Territory Region of the north-central United States that extended from the Ohio and Mississippi Rivers to the Great Lakes. Later divided into what are now Illinois, Indiana, Michigan, Ohio, Wisconsin, and part of Minnesota. **225**

Nova Scotia Province of eastern Canada. **161**

Norway Kingdom in northwestern Europe. Capital: Oslo. (62°N 10°E) **A8**

Ohio (OH) State in the north-central United States. Originally part of the Northwest Territory. Admitted as a state in 1803. Capital: Columbus. (40°N 83°W) **A1**

Ohio River River that flows through Pennsylvania, Ohio, Indiana, and Illinois and empties into the Mississippi. **A3**

Oklahoma (OK) State in the south-central United States. Organized as a territory in 1890. Admitted as a state in 1907. Capital: Oklahoma City. (36°N 98°W) **A1**

Oklahoma City Capital of Oklahoma. (35°N 98°W) **A1**

Omaha City in Nebraska. (41°N 96°W) **669**

Oregon (OR) State in the northwestern United States. Admitted as a state in 1859. Capital: Salem. (43°N 1 22°W) **A1**

Oregon Country Region in northwestern North America that extended from the Pacific coast to the Rocky Mountains and from the northern border of California to Alaska. **542**

Pacific Ocean Body of water extending from the Arctic Circle to Antarctica and from western North and South America to Australia, the Malay Archipelago, and East Asia. **A4**

Panama Country in southern Central America that occupies the Isthmus of Panama. Location of the Panama Canal. Capital: Panama City. (8°N 81°W) **A6**

Paris Capital of France. (49°N 2°E) **A8**

Pearl Harbor Harbor on the Hawaiian island of Oahu the Japanese launched a surprise attack against U.S. Pacific Fleet in 1941. (21°N 158°W) **799**

Pennsylvania (PA) State in the eastern United States. One of the original thirteen colonies. Admitted as a state in 1787. Capital: Harrisburg. (41°N 78°W) **A1**

Persian Gulf Arm of the Arabian Sea between the Arabian Sea between the Arabian peninsula and southwestern Iran in southwestern Asia. **A9**

Peru Country in western South America. Capital: Lima. (10°S 75°W) **A7**

Philadelphia City in southeastern Pennsylvania. Capital of the United States from 1790 to 1800. (40°N 75°W) **A1**

Philippines Country in the western Pacific Ocean. Made up of an archipelago of about 7,100 islands lying approximately 500 miles off the southeast coast of Asia. Capital: Manila. (14°N 125°E) **A9**

Pikes Peak Mountain in east-central Colorado that was part of an important mining region in the mid- to late 1800s. **340**

Pittsburgh City in southwestern Pennsylvania. (40°N 80°W) **A1**

Plymouth Site in Massachusetts where the Pilgrims first landed in North America in 1620. (42°N 71°W) **106**

Poland Country in central Europe bordering on the Baltic Sea. Capital: Warsaw. (52°N 17°E) **A8**

Portugal Country in southwestern Europe on the western Iberian Peninsula. (38°N 8°W) **A8**

Potomac River River that flows through West Virginia, Virginia, and Maryland and empties into Chesapeake Bay. **A3**

Princeton Town in west-central New Jersey. (40°N 75°W) **205**

Providence Capital of Rhode Island. (42°N 71°W) **106**

Puerto Rico Island east of Cuba and southeast of Florida. A U.S. territory acquired in the Spanish-American War. Capital: San Juan. (18°N 67°W) **A6**

Red River River that flows from eastern New Mexico through Texas, Arkansas, and Louisiana, where it empties into the Mississippi River. **340**

Red Sea Inland sea between the Arabian Peninsula and northeastern Africa. **A9**

Rhode Island (RI) State in the northeastern United States. One of the original thirteen colonies. Admitted as a state in 1790. Capital: Providence. (41°N 71°W) **A1**

Richmond Capital of Virginia. Capital of the Confederate States of America during the Civil War. (37°N 77°W) **586**

Rio Grande Spanish for Great River. Forms the border between Texas and Mexico. **340**

Roanoke Island Island off the coast of North Carolina. Site of early English attempt at settlement. **86**

Rocky Mountains Mountain range in western North America that extends from Alaska south to Mexico. **A2**

Rome Capital of Italy. (42°N 12°E) **A8**

Russia Vast country that extends from eastern Europe through northern Asia. Capital: Moscow. (61°N 60°E) **A9**

Sacramento Capital of California. (38°N 121°W) **534**

Sahara Vast desert in northern Africa. **26**

Saigon City in South Vietnam that is now known as Ho Chi Minh City. (11°N 106°F) **791**

Saudi Arabia Kingdom on the Arabian Peninsula in southwest Asia. Capital: Riyadh. (22°N 46°E) **A9**

St. Augustine City in northeastern Florida on the Atlantic coast. **75**

St. Lawrence River River in southeastern Canada. **86**

Salt Lake City Capital of Utah. (41°N 1 12°W) **A1**

San Antonio City in southern Texas. Site of the Mexican victory over Texas forces at the Alamo during the Texas Revolution. (29°N 99°W) **493**

San Diego City in southern California. Located on San Diego Bay, an inlet of the Pacific Ocean near the Mexican border. (33°N 1 17°W) **A1**

San Francisco City in western California on a peninsula between the Pacific Ocean and San Francisco Bay. (38°N 122°W) **534**

Santa Fe Capital of New Mexico. (35°N 106°W) **75**

Saratoga Site in eastern New York of a key battle of the Revolutionary War. **205**

Savannah Port city in southeastern Georgia. Founded by James Oglethorpe in 1733. (32°N 81°W) **117**

Scandinavia Region of northern Europe that includes Denmark, Norway, and Sweden. **A8**

Sierra Nevada Mountain range in eastern California. **A2**

South America Continent in the southern Western Hemisphere. **A7**

South Carolina (SC) State in the southeastern United States. One of the original thirteen colonies. Admitted as a state in 1788. Capital: Columbia. (34°N 81°W) **A1**

South Dakota (SD) State in the north-central United States. Organized as part of the Dakota Territory in 1861. Admitted as a state in 1889. Capital: Pierre. (44°N 102°W) **A1**

South Korea Country in southeastern Asia. Established in 1948. Capital: Seoul. (40°N 127°F) **A9**

Soviet Union Former communist country in Eastern Europe and Asia. **777**

Spain Country in southwestern Europe that occupies the greater part of the Iberian Peninsula and includes the Balearic and Canary Islands. Capital: Madrid. (40°N 4°W) **A8**

Strait of Magellan Strait at the southern tip of South America that connects the southern Atlantic Ocean with the southern Pacific Ocean. **47**

Sweden Kingdom in northwestern Europe. Capital: Stockholm. (62°N 15°E) **A8**

Switzerland Country in central Europe. Capital: Bern. (47°N 7°E) **A8**

Tennessee (TN) State in the southeast-central United States. Admitted as a state in 1796. Capital: Nashville. (36°N 88°W) **A1**

Tenochtitlán Aztec island-city that was located on the site of what is now Mexico City. **68**

Texas (TX) State in the south-central United States. Independent republic from 1836 to 1845. Admitted as a state in 1845. Capital: Austin. (31°N 101°W) **A1**

Tonkin, Gulf of Arm extending from the South China Sea, east of North Vietnam. **791**

Trenton Capital of New Jersey. (40°N 75°W) **205**

Turkey Country in southwestern Asia and southeastern Europe between the Mediterranean and the Black Seas. Capital: Ankara. (38°N 32°W) **A9**

United States of America Country in central North America. Capital: Washington, D.C. (38°N 110°W) **A1**

Utah (UT) State in the western United States. Admitted as a state in 1896. Capital: Salt Lake City. (39°N 112°W) **A1**

Valley Forge Site in southeastern Pennsylvania where General George Washington and his troops spent the harsh winter of 1777–78 during the Revolutionary War. **205**

Venezuela Country in northern South America on the Caribbean Sea. Capital: Caracas. (8°N 65°W) **A7**

Vermont (VT) State in the northeastern United States. Admitted as a state in 1791. Capital: Montpelier. (44°N 73°W) **A1**

Vicksburg City in western Mississippi on the bluffs above the Mississippi River. (32°N 91°W) **592**

Vietnam Country in southeastern Asia. Capital: Hanoi. (18°N 107°E) **A9**

Virginia (VA) State in the eastern United States. One of the original thirteen colonies. Admitted as a state in 1788. Capital: Richmond. (37°N 78°W) **A1**

Washington (WA) State in the northwestern United States. Bounded by British Columbia, Canada, to the north and by the Pacific Ocean to the west. Admitted as a state in 1889. Capital: Olympia. (47°N 121°W) **A1**

Washington, D.C. Capital of the United States. Located on the Potomac River between Virginia and Maryland. (39°N 77°W) **A1**

West Virginia (WV) State in the east-central United States. Part of Virginia until the area refused to join the Confederacy in 1861. Admitted as a state in 1863. Capital: Charleston. (39°N 81°W) **A1**

Wisconsin (WI) State in the north-central United States. Became part of the Northwest Territory in 1787. Admitted as a state in 1848. Capital: Madison. (44°N 91 °W) **A1**

Wyoming (WY) State in the western United States. Admitted as a state in 1890. Capital: Cheyenne. (43°N 108°W) **A1**

Yorktown Town in southeastern Virginia. Site of the last battle of the Revolutionary War. (37°N 76°W **205**

Yugoslavia Country in southeastern Europe that was formed as the Kingdom of the Serbs, Croats, and Slovenes after the collapse of Austria-Hungary in 1918; renamed Yugoslavia in 1929; Serbia and Montenegro formed new Federal Republic of Yugoslavia in 1992. Capital: Belgrade. **A8**

Glossary

This Glossary contains terms you need to understand as you study American history. After each key term there is a brief definition or explanation of the meaning of the term as it is used in *Call to Freedom*. The page number refers to the page on which the term is introduced in the textbook.

Phonetic Respelling and Pronunciation Guide

Many of the key terms in this textbook have been respelled to help you pronounce them. The letter combinations used in the respelling throughout the narrative are explained in the following phonetic respelling and pronunciation guide. The guide is adapted from *Webster's Tenth New College Dictionary, Merriam-Webster's New Geographical Dictionary,* and *Merriam-Webster's New Biographical Dictionary.*

MARK	AS IN	RESPELLING	EXAMPLE
a	alphabet	a	*AL-fuh-bet
ā	Asia	ay	AY-zhuh
ä	cart, top	ah	KAHRT, TAHP
e	let, ten	e	LET, TEN
ē	even, leaf	ee	EE-vuhn, LEEF
i	it, tip, British	i	IT, TIP, BRIT-ish
ī	site, buy, Ohio	y	SYT, BY, oh-HY-oh
	iris	eye	EYE-ris
k	card	k	KAHRD
ō	over, rainbow	oh	OH-vuhr, RAYN-boh
ù	book, wood	ooh	BOOHK, WOOHD
ò	all, orchid	aw	AWL, AWR-kid
òi	foil, coin	oy	FOYL, KOYN
aù	out	ow	OWT
ə	cup, butter	uh	KUHP, BUHT-uhr
ü	rule, food	oo	ROOL, FOOD
yü	few	yoo	FYOO
zh	vision	zh	VIZH-uhn

*A syllable printed in small capital letters receives heavier emphasis than the other syllable(s) in a word.

ABC Powers Argentina, Brazil, and Chile. **761**

abolition An end to slavery. **469**

Adams-Onís Treaty (1819) Agreement in which Spain gave up all of Florida to the United States. **366**

Alamo Spanish mission in San Antonio, Texas, that was the site of a famous battle of the Texas Revolution in 1836; the Mexican army's victory resulted in the deaths of all the Texans defending the building. **494**

Albany Plan of Union (1754) Plan written by Benjamin Franklin and other colonial delegates that called for the colonies to unite under a common governing body. **160**

Alien and Sedition Acts (1798) Laws passed by a Federalist-dominated Congress aimed at protecting the government from treasonous ideas, actions, and people; used against members of the Democratic-Republican party. **322**

amendments Official changes, corrections, or additions to a law or constitution. **246**

American Anti-Slavery Society Group founded in 1833 by William Lloyd Garrison and others to work for immediate abolition and racial equality for African Americans. **471**

American Colonization Society Society organized in 1817 that established the colony of Liberia in West Africa as a home for free African Americans. **470**

American Federation of Labor (AFL) One of the first large unions in the United States; organized in the 1880s by Samuel Gompers to include only skilled workers. **689**

American System Henry Clay's plan for raising tariffs to pay for internal improvements such as better roads and canals. **370**

amnesty An official pardon issued by the government for an illegal act. **617**

anarchists People who oppose all forms of government. **689**

annex To take control of land and incorporate into a country, state, etc. **497**

Antifederalists People who opposed ratification of the Constitution. **242**

Anti-Imperialist League American organization that opposed the creation of a U.S. colonial empire. **748**

Appomattox Courthouse Virginia town where General Robert E. Lee was forced to surrender, thus ending the Civil War. **605**

apportionment The use of population to determine how many legislative representatives an area will have. **258**

apprentices People who learn skilled trades from a master craftsperson. **133**

archaeology Scientific study of the unwritten past. **5**

arbitration Formal process of settling disputes using a third party. **728**

armistice A truce between warring groups. **771**

Articles of Confederation (1777) Document that created the first central government for the United States; was replaced by the Constitution in 1789. **225**

artifacts Remains of objects that have been made by humans. **5**

astrolabe A tool once used by navigators to determine a ship's position at sea by charting the position of the stars. **35**

Atlanta Compromise Speech by Booker T. Washington stating that African Americans should focus on improving their economic and educational status rather than fighting discrimination and segregation. **724**

backcountry Frontier region in Virginia and the Carolinas between coastal settlements and the Appalachian Mountains. **163**

Bacon's Rebellion (1676) Attack led by Nathaniel Bacon against American Indians and the colonial government in Virginia. **97**

balance of trade Relationship between what goods a country purchases from other countries and what goods it sells to other countries. **126**

Bank of the United States National bank chartered by Congress in 1791 to provide security for the U.S. economy. **309**

Battle of Antietam (1862) Union victory in the Civil War that marked the bloodiest single-day battle in U.S. military history. **588**

Battle of Brandywine Creek (1777) Revolutionary War battle in which British forces overwhelmed the Patriots in Pennsylvania. **204**

Battle of Bunker Hill (1775) Revolutionary War battle in Boston that demonstrated that the colonists could fight well against the British army. **188**

Battle of Fallen Timbers (1794) Battle between U.S. troops and an American Indian confederation resisting white settlement in the Northwest Territory; led to Treaty of Greenville. **316**

Battle of Gettysburg (1863) Union Civil War victory that turned the tide against the Confederates at Gettysburg, Pennsylvania; resulted in the loss of more than 50,000 soldiers. **601**

Battle of Goliad (1836) Mexican victory during the Texas Revolution in which Mexican leader Antonio López de Santa Anna ordered the execution of Texas soldiers after their surrender. **495**

Battle of Horseshoe Bend (1814) U.S. victory in the War of 1812 in which Andrew Jackson's troops forced Creek Indians to give up much of their land in the South. **353**

Battle of Lake Erie (1813) U.S. victory in the War of 1812, led by Oliver Hazard Perry; broke Britain's control of Lake Erie. **352**

Battle of New Orleans (1815) Greatest U.S. victory in the War of 1812; actually took place two weeks after a peace treaty had been signed ending the war. **354**

Battle of Pea Ridge (1862) Civil War battle in which Confederate forces from Missouri, joined by some American Indians, were defeated in Northwestern Arkansas. **593**

Battle of Princeton (1777) Revolutionary War battle in which the Patriots drove back British forces in New Jersey. **203**

Battle of San Jacinto (1836) Final battle of the Texas Revolution; resulted in the defeat of the Mexican army and independence for Texas. **496**

Battle of Saratoga (1777) Revolutionary War battle in New York that resulted in a major defeat of British troops; marked the Patriots' greatest victory up to that point in the war. **204**

Battle of Shiloh (1862) Civil War battle in Tennessee in which the Union army gained greater control over the Mississippi River valley. **591**

Battle of the Little Bighorn (1876) "Custer's Last Stand"; battle between U.S. soldiers, led by George Armstrong Custer, and Sioux forces, led by Crazy Horse and Sitting Bull, that resulted in the worst defeat for the U.S. Army in the West. **651**

Battle of the Thames (1813) U.S. victory in the War of 1812, led by William Henry Harrison, that ended the Indian-British alliance in the Great Lakes. **352**

Battle of Tippecanoe (1811) U.S. victory over an Indian confederation that wanted to stop white settlement in the Northwest Territory; increased tensions between Great Britain and the United States. **347**

Battle of Trenton (1776) Revolutionary War battle in New Jersey in which Patriot forces captured more than 900 Hessian troops. **203**

Battle of Vincennes (1779) Revolutionary War battle in the West in which Patriots retook Vincennes, a mostly French town along the Wabash River, from the British. **210**

Battle of Yorktown (1781) Last major battle of the Revolutionary War; site of British general Charles Cornwallis's surrender to the Patriots in Virginia. **212**

Bear Flag Revolt (1846) Revolt against Mexico by American settlers in California who declared the territory an independent republic. **524**

benevolent societies Organizations that helped immigrants in case of sickness, unemployment, and death. **693**

Bessemer process A quick and inexpensive method of producing steel by blasting hot air through melted iron; developed by Henry Bessemer in the 1850s. **681**

bicameral legislature A lawmaking body made up of two houses. **121**

Bill of Rights First 10 amendments to the Constitution; ratified in 1791. **247**

Black Codes Laws passed in the southern states during Reconstruction that greatly limited the freedom and rights of African Americans. **623**

Black Death An epidemic that spread through Europe from 1348 to about 1350 that killed as many as 30 million people. **32**

bonanza A large deposit of precious ore. **655**

bonds Certificates that represent money the government has borrowed from private citizens. **305**

boomtowns Western communities that grew quickly because of the mining boom and often disappeared when the boom ended. **656**

borderlands Region of Spanish America where few Europeans lived; included northern Mexico, Florida, and parts of present-day Arizona, California, New Mexico, and Texas. **75**

border states Delaware, Kentucky, Maryland, and Missouri; slave states that lay between the North and the South and did not join the Confederacy during the Civil War. **582**

bosses Powerful leaders who controlled political machines by trading favors, such as jobs, for votes. **709**

Boston Massacre (1770) Incident in which British soldiers fired into a crowd of angry colonists, killing five people. **172**

Boston Tea Party (1773) Protest against the Tea Act in which a group of colonists boarded British tea ships and dumped some 340 chests of tea into Boston Harbor. **174**

Boxer Rebellion Revolt by Chinese nationalists in 1900 against foreign involvement in Chinese affairs and poor management by the Chinese government. **742**

boycott To refuse to buy certain goods; method often used in protest movements. **169**

Brown* v. *Board of Education (1954) Supreme Court ruling that segregated public schools were unconstitutional. **785**

Bull Moose Party Nickname for the Progressive Party, which was formed by Theodore Roosevelt and his supporters in 1912. **730**

Bureau of Indian Affairs Government agency created in the 1800s to oversee federal policy toward American Indians. **382**

cabinet Group made up of the heads of the executive departments that advises the U.S. president. **260**

California Gold Rush Migration of thousands of people to California in 1849 after gold was discovered there. **534**

Californios Spanish colonists in California. **489**

capital Money or property that is used to earn more money. **33**

caravel A fast, maneuverable ship originally designed by the Portuguese. **36**

carpetbaggers Name given to northerners who moved to the South during Reconstruction. **629**

cash crops Agricultural products grown primarily to be sold for profits, not for personal use. **131**

casualties People who are killed, wounded, captured, or missing in a war. **161**

cattle drive Long journeys on which cowboys herded cattle to northern markets or grazing lands. **663**

Cattle Kingdom Area of the Great Plains, stretching from Texas to Canada, on which many ranchers raised cattle in the late 1800s. **661**

charter Official document that gives a person the right to establish a colony. **87**

checks and balances A system established by the Constitution that prevents any branch of government from becoming too powerful. **241**

Chinese Exclusion Act (1882) Law banning Chinese people from coming to the United States for 10 years. **694**

Chisholm Trail Trail from San Antonio, Texas, to Abilene, Kansas, established by Jesse Chisholm in 1867 for cattle drives. **663**

circumnavigate To sail completely around. **49**

Civil Rights Act of 1866 Law that gave African Americans legal rights equal to those of white Americans. **624**

Civil Rights Act of 1875 Law guaranteeing African Americans equal rights in public places such as theaters and public transportation. **632**

Civil Rights Act of 1964 Law banning racial discrimination by administrators of public services and federal contractors. **789**

Clayton Antitrust Act (1914) Law that strengthened existing antitrust legislation. **732**

Clermont First full-sized U.S. commercial steamboat; developed by Robert Fulton and tested in 1807. **412**

Cold War The struggle for global power between the United States and the Soviet Union that began following World War II. **782**

collective bargaining Process in which employee representatives, often union leaders, negotiate with employers to gain improved wages and labor conditions for all workers in a factory or industry. **688**

Columbian Exchange Transfer of plants, animals, and diseases between the Americas and Europe, Asia, and Africa. **51**

Commercial Revolution Period of economic development that began in Europe in the 1200s and greatly expanded trade. **33**

Committees of Correspondence Committees created in Massachusetts in the 1760s to help towns and colonies share information about resisting the new British laws. **169**

common-school movement Social reform efforts begun in the mid-1800s that promoted the idea of having all children educated in a common place regardless of social class or background. **465**

Common Sense (1776) Pamphlet written by Thomas Paine that criticized monarchies and convinced many American colonists of the need to break away from Britain. **190**

Communists People who favor the equal distribution of wealth and the end of private property. **771**

Compromise of 1850 Henry Clay's proposed agreement that allowed California to enter the Union as a free state and divided the rest of the Mexican Cession into two territories where slavery would be decided by popular sovereignty; also settled land claims between Texas and New Mexico, abolished the slave trade in Washington, and produced a new Fugitive Slave Act. **555**

Compromise of 1877 Agreement to settle the disputed presidential election of 1876; Democrats agreed to accept Republican Rutherford B. Hayes as president in return for the removal of federal troops from the South. **633**

Comstock Lode Nevada gold and silver deposit discovered by Henry Comstock in 1859. **655**

concurrent powers Powers that are shared by the federal and state governments. **257**

Confederate States of America Nation formed by the southern states on February 4, 1861; also known as the Confederacy. **574**

conquistadores Spanish soldiers and explorers who led military expeditions in the Americas and captured land for Spain. **66**

conservation Movement to preserve nature and its resources. **728**

constitution A set of basic principles that determines the powers and duties of a government. **224**

Constitutional Convention (1787) Meeting in Philadelphia at which delegates from the states wrote the Constitution. **237**

Constitutional Union Party Political party formed in 1860 by a group of northerners and southerners who supported the Union, its laws, and the Constitution. **571**

Continental Army Army created by the Second Continental Congress in 1775 to defend the American colonies from Britain. **186**

contrabands Escaped or captured slaves taken in by the Union army during the Civil War. **596**

Contract with America Ten-point Republican reform plan introduced in 1994, including a balanced budget amendment; not all proposals were passed. **796**

Convention of 1818 Agreement between the United States and Great Britain that settled fishing rights and established new North American borders. **365**

convert To change beliefs. **42**

Copperheads Northern Democrats who opposed abolition and sympathized with the South during the Civil War. **597**

corporations Companies that sell shares of ownership, called stocks, to help raise investment money; investors in a corporation are not liable for its debts. **683**

cotton belt Region stretching from Georgia to east Texas where most U.S. cotton was produced during the mid-1800s. **427**

cotton diplomacy Confederate efforts to use the importance of southern cotton to Britain's textile industry to persuade the British to support the Confederacy in the Civil War. **584**

cotton gin Device invented by Eli Whitney in 1793 to separate cotton plants' fibers from the seeds; revolutionized the cotton industry. **426**

Council of the Indies Group of royal officials established in 1524 that oversaw the government and enforced laws in Spanish America. **72**

covenant Sacred agreement. **104**

creditors People who lend money. **233**

Crusades (1096–1221) Series of wars launched by European Christians to gain possession of the Holy Land. **25**

Cuban missile crisis (1962) Confrontation between the United States and the Soviet Union over the placement of Soviet missiles in Cuba. **788**

culture Common values and traditions of a society, such as language, government, and family relationships. **6**

Cumberland Road First federal road project, construction of which began in 1815; ran from Cumberland, Maryland, to present-day Wheeling, West Virginia. **371**

D-Day June 6, 1944; Allied invasion of France during World War II. **780**

Daughters of Liberty Women's groups that used boycotts and other measures to support the colonies' resistance to the British. **171**

Dawes General Allotment Act (1887) Legislation passed by Congress that split up Indian reservation lands among individual Indians and promised them citizenship. **654**

debtors People who owe money. **233**

Declaration of Independence (1776) Statement of the Second Continental Congress that defined the colonists' rights, outlined their complaints against Great Britain, and declared the colonies' independence. **191**

Declaration of Sentiments (1848) Statement written and signed by women's rights supporters at the Seneca Falls Convention; detailed their complaints about social injustice against women. **477**

delegated powers Powers that are specifically granted to the federal government by the Constitution. **256**

Democratic Party Political party formed by supporters of

Andrew Jackson after the presidential election of 1824. **375**

Democratic-Republican Party Political party founded in the 1790s that sought to preserve the power of the state governments and promote agriculture. **320**

deport To send an immigrant back to his or her country of origin. **291**

depression A steep drop in economic activity combined with rising unemployment. **233**

direct primary Method of allowing voters to choose their own candidates for office. **713**

dissenters People who disagree with official religious or political opinions. **103**

dollar diplomacy President William Taft's policy of influencing Latin American governments through economic rather than military intervention. **756**

domestication Process of breeding plants and animals for use by humans. **6**

Dominion of New England Union of northeastern American colonies created by King James II in 1686; lasted until 1689. **123**

Donner party Group of western travelers who were stranded in the Sierra Nevada during the winter of 1846-47; only 40 of the party's 87 members survived. **509**

double jeopardy Illegal act of trying a person twice for the same crime. **289**

draft A system of required service in the armed forces. **293**

Dred Scott **decision** (1857) U.S. Supreme Court ruling that declared African Americans were not U.S. citizens, that the Missouri Compromise's restriction on slavery was unconstitutional, and that Congress did not have the right to ban slavery in any federal territory. **566**

dry farming Method of farming used by Plains farmers in the 1890s that allowed them to grow certain crops with less water. **668**

due process Fair application of the law. **289**

duties Taxes on imported goods. **127**

Eighteenth Amendment (1919) Amendment that outlawed the production and sale of alcoholic beverages in the United States. **722**

elastic clause Article I, Section 8, of the Constitution that has been interpreted as giving Congress authority to stretch its delegated powers to address issues not otherwise specified in the document; also known as the "necessary and proper" clause. **257**

El Camino Real "The King's Road"; built by Spanish settlers to link communities in New Spain. **76**

electoral college Group selected from each of the states to cast votes in presidential elections. The number of each state's electors is equal to the number of its representatives and senators in Congress. The electors are expected to vote for the candidate chosen by popular vote in their states. **301**

emancipation Freedom from slavery. **469**

Emancipation Proclamation (1862) Order issued by President Abraham Lincoln freeing the slaves in areas rebelling against the Union; took effect January 1, 1863. **595**

embargo Banning of trade with a country. **345**

Embargo Act (1807) Law that prohibited American merchants from trading with other countries. **345**

eminent domain The government's power to take personal property to further the public good. **287**

empresarios Agents who were contracted by the Mexican republic to bring settlers to Texas in the early l800s. **492**

encomienda **system** System in Spanish America that gave settlers the right to tax local Indians or to demand their labor in exchange for protecting them and teaching them skills. **74**

energy crisis Economic shock during the 1970s caused by rising oil prices. **792**

Enlightenment Age of Reason; movement that began in Europe in the 1700s as people began examining the natural world, society, and government. **141**

English Bill of Rights (1689) Shifted political power from the British monarchy to Parliament. **125**

entrepreneurs People who start new businesses. **683**

environments Climates and landscapes that surround living things. **6**

Erie Canal Canal that ran from Albany to Buffalo, New York; completed in 1825. **371**

executive branch Division of the federal government that includes the president and the administrative departments; enforces the nation's laws. **240**

executive order Nonlegislative directive issued by the U.S. president in certain circumstances; an executive order has the force of congressional law. **259**

Exodusters A large group of southern African Americans who settled western lands in the late 1800s. **667**

exports Items that a country sells to other countries. **126**

factors Crop brokers who managed the trade between southern planters and their customers. **429**

Farmers' Alliances Political groups formed by various farmers' organizations in the late 1800s that called for more railroad regulation and lower interest rates. **702**

fascism A political movement that favors a dictatorial government and the superiority of the government to individual rights. **778**

Federal Deposit Insurance Corporation (FDIC) Organization created by Congress in the 1930s to insure bank deposits. **775**

federalism System of government in which power is distributed between a central authority and individual states. **240**

Federalist Papers Series of essays that defended the Constitution and tried to reassure Americans that the states would not be overpowered by the proposed national government. **244**

Federalist Party Political party created in the 1790s that wanted to strengthen the federal government and promote industry and trade. **320**

Federalists People who supported ratification of the Constitution. **243**

feudalism System of government that arose during the Middle Ages in which people gave their loyalty to a lord in exchange for land or protection. **19**

Federal Reserve Act (1913) Law that created the national banking system known as the Federal Reserve. **731**

Federal Trade Commission Commission created in 1914 to investigate and prevent unfair business practices. **732**

Fifteenth Amendment (1870) Constitutional amendment that gave African American men the right to vote. **628**

54th Massachusetts Infantry African American Civil War regiment that played a key role in the attack on Fort Wagner in South Carolina. **596**

First Battle of Bull Run (1861) First major battle of the Civil War, resulting in a Confederate victory; showed that the Civil War would not be won easily. **586**

First Continental Congress (1774) Meeting of colonial delegates in Philadelphia to decide how to respond to increased taxes and abuses of authority by the British government; delegates petitioned King George III, listing the freedoms they believed colonists should enjoy. **184**

folktales Oral stories that often provide a moral lesson. **442**

Fort Sumter Federal outpost in Charleston, South Carolina, that was attacked by the Confederates in April 1861, sparking the Civil War. **580**

forty-niners Gold-seekers who moved to California during the gold rush. **534**

Fourteenth Amendment (1866) Constitutional amendment that, among other provisions, gave full rights of citizenship to all people born or naturalized in the United States, except for American Indians. **625**

free coinage Monetary system in which both gold and silver are coined. **701**

Freedmen's Bureau Agency established by Congress in 1865 to help poor people throughout the South. **620**

Freedom Rides (1961) Bus trips taken by civil rights workers through several southern states to challenge the segregated bus system. **788**

free enterprise Economic system in which there is competition between businesses with little government control. **127, 683**

Freeport Doctrine (1858) Argument made by Stephen Douglas during the Lincoln-Douglas debates that popular sovereignty would determine whether a state or territory could permit slavery. **568**

Free-Soil Party Political party formed in 1848 by antislavery northerners who left the Whig and Democratic Parties because neither addressed the slavery issue. **553**

French Revolution French rebellion begun in 1789 in which the French people overthrew the monarchy and made their country a republic. **310**

Fugitive Slave Act (1850) Law that made it a crime to help runaway slaves; allowed for the arrest of escaped slaves in areas where slavery was illegal and required their return to slaveholders. **556**

Fundamental Orders of Connecticut (1639) A written set of principles that made Connecticut's colonial government more democratic. **105**

Gadsden Purchase (1853) U.S. purchase of land from Mexico that included the southern parts of present-day Arizona and New Mexico. **526**

General Amnesty Act of 1872 Law repealing Section III of the Fourteenth Amendment, which forbade former Confederates from holding public office. **632**

Gettysburg Address (1863) Speech given by Abraham Lincoln in which he praised the bravery of Union soldiers and renewed his commitment to winning the Civil War. **602**

Ghost Dance A religious movement among Plains Indians in the 1880s. **652**

Gibbons v. Ogden (1824) Supreme Court ruling that federal law has priority over equivalent state law; expanded definition of interstate commerce. **413**

Glorious Revolution (1688) A revolt in England against Catholic king James II that led to his overthrow and put Protestants Mary and William of Orange on the throne. **124**

glyphs Symbols or images, particularly when cut into a surface or carved in relief. **6**

gold standard Monetary system in which only gold can be coined. **701**

Great Awakening A Christian movement that became widespread in the American colonies in the 1730s and 1740s. **137**

Great Compromise (1787) Agreement worked out at the Constitutional Convention establishing that a state's population would determine representation in the lower house of the legislature, while each state would have equal representation in the upper house of the legislature. **238**

Great Depression The severe global economic downturn that followed the U.S. stock market crash in 1929. **775**

Great Migration Mass migration of thousands of English people to the Americas that took place between 1630 and 1640. **104**

Great Society A series of social programs established by President Lyndon Johnson in the 1960s. **788**

guerrilla warfare Type of fighting in which soldiers use swift hit-and-run attacks against the enemy, usually behind the battle lines. **211**

Gulf of Tonkin Resolution (1964) Resolution passed by Congress giving President Johnson authority to use military force against the Vietnamese. **790**

habeas corpus Constitutional protection against unlawful imprisonment. **597**

Harlem Renaissance A period of African American artistic and cultural achievement taking place in the 1920s and named after the Harlem neighborhood of New York City. **773**

Hartford Convention (1815) Meeting of Federalists at Hartford, Connecticut, to protest the War of 1812. **355**

Hay-Bunau-Varilla Treaty (1903) Agreement between the United States and Panama that gave the United States a 99-year lease to build a canal on a 10-mile-wide strip of land across the Isthmus of Panama. **752**

Hay-Herrán Treaty (1903) Proposed agreement between Colombia and the United States to allow the United States to build a transatlantic canal in Colombia. **752**

Haymarket Riot (1886) Incident in which a bomb exploded during a union demonstration held at Haymarket Square, Chicago; led to the deaths of several police officers and union members. **689**

headright System set up by the London Company that gave 50 acres of land to colonists who paid their own way to Virginia. **95**

Holocaust The systematic murder of 6 million Jews and some 3 million members of other groups by the Nazis during World War II. **780**

Homestead Act (1862) Law passed by Congress to encourage settlement in the West by giving government-owned land to small farmers. **666**

Homestead strike (1892) Strike at Andrew Carnegie's Homestead steel factory in Pennsylvania that erupted into violence between strikers and private detectives. **690**

horizontal integration Ownership of all the businesses in a particular field of business or industry. **684**

House of Burgesses Colonial Virginia's elected assembly. **122**

House Un-American Activities Committee (HUAC) Congressional committee created in 1938 to investigate disloyalty and harmful foreign influences in the United States. **783**

Hudson River school Group of American artists in the mid-1800s whose pictures focused on the American landscape. **388**

Hull House A Chicago settlement house founded by Jane Addams and Ellen Gates in 1889. **697**

hunter-gatherers People who hunt animals and gather wild plants to provide for their needs. **5**

igloos Houses that were built out of blocks of ice or other materials by the Inuit and Aleut peoples in what are now Canada and Alaska. **12**

immigrants People who move to another country after leaving their homeland. **99**

Immigration Restriction League Group formed in 1894 that wanted to require all prospective immigrants to pass a literacy test. **694**

impeach To vote to bring charges against. **259**

imperialism The practice of building an empire by founding colonies or conquering other nations. **738**

imports Items that a country purchases from other countries. **126**

impressment British practice of forcing people, including U.S. citizens, to serve in the British army or navy; led to increasing tensions between Great Britain and the United States in the early 1800s. **345**

indentured servants Colonists who received free passage to North America in exchange for working without pay for a certain number of years. **96**

Indian Removal Act (1830) Congressional act that authorized the removal of American Indians who lived east of the Mississippi River. **381**

Indian Territory Area covering most of present-day Oklahoma to which most American Indians in the Southeast were forced to move in the 1830s. **381**

indict To formally accuse. **287**

Industrial Revolution Period of rapid growth in the use of machines in manufacturing and production that began in the mid-1700s. **399**

Industrial Workers of the World A union formed in 1905 that sought to combine all workers into one union that would challenge capitalism. **720**

inflation Increased prices for goods and services combined with the reduced value of money. **82, 232**

initiative Method that allows voters to propose new laws by collecting a certain number of signatures on a petition. **714**

interchangeable parts Process developed by Eli Whitney in the 1790s that called for making each vital part of a machine exactly the same. **401**

interstate commerce Trade that is conducted between states. **232**

Interstate Commerce Act (1887) A law which provided more consistent national regulations on interstate trade. **700**

Interstate Commerce Commission Commission created to ensure that railroads treated all shipping customers fairly. **700**

Intolerable Acts (1774) A set of laws, also called the Coercive Acts, passed by Parliament to punish the colonists for the Boston Tea Party and to tighten government control of the colonies. **175**

Iran-Contra affair Scandal involving illegal aid given by U.S. government officials in the 1980s to Contra rebels in Nicaragua; the money was raised by illegally selling weapons to Iran. **795**

ironclads Warships heavily armored with iron. **589**

Iroquois League A political confederation of five northeastern American Indian nations—the Seneca, Oneida, Mohawk, Cayuga, and Onondaga—that made decisions concerning war and peace. **16**

Islam A faith that arose in the Middle East in the A.D. 600s under the guidance of Muhammad; its holy book is the Qur'an. **23**

isolationism Policy of avoiding involvement in the affairs of other countries. **739**

Jay's Treaty (1794) Agreement negotiated by John Jay to work out problems between Britain and the United States over the western frontier trade in the Caribbean, British seizure of U.S. ships, and debts owed to British merchants. **313**

Jazz Age Nickname given to the 1920s because of the popularity of jazz music. **773**

Jim Crow laws Laws that enforced segregation in the southern states. **633**

John Brown's raid (1859) Incident in which abolitionist John Brown and 21 other men captured a federal arsenal in Harpers Ferry, Virginia, in hopes of starting a slave rebellion. **569**

joint-stock companies Businesses formed by a group of people who jointly make an investment and share in the profits and losses. **33**

judicial branch Division of the federal government that is made up of the national courts; interprets laws, punishes criminals, and settles disputes between states. **240**

judicial review The Supreme Court's power to declare acts of Congress unconstitutional. **337**

Judiciary Act of 1789 Legislation passed by Congress that created the federal court system. **303**

Kansas-Nebraska Act (1854) Law that allowed voters in the Kansas and Nebraska territories to choose whether to allow slavery. **561**

kayaks One-person canoes almost completely enclosed by animal skins. **12**

Kentucky and Virginia Resolutions (1798–1799) Republican documents that argued the Alien and Sedition Acts were unconstitutional. **322**

kitchen cabinet President Andrew Jackson's group of informal advisers; so called because they sometimes met in the White House kitchen. **376**

kivas Circular ceremonial rooms used for religious activities by Native American peoples of the American Southwest. **14**

Knights of Labor The first truly national labor union in the United States; organized in 1869 to include African Americans, women, and skilled and unskilled workers. **688**

Know-Nothing Party Political organization founded in 1849 by nativists who supported measures making it difficult for foreigners to become citizens and to hold office. **459**

Ku Klux Klan Secret society created by white southerners in 1866 that used terror and violence to keep African Americans from obtaining their civil rights. **631**

Land Ordinance of 1785 Legislation passed by Congress authorizing surveys and the division of public lands in the western region of the country. **226**

legislative branch Division of the government that proposes bills and passes them into laws. **240**

Lend-Lease Act (1941) Law which allowed the United States to lend or lease weapons to Great Britain and the Soviet Union. **778**

Lewis and Clark expedition Expedition led by Meriwether Lewis and William Clark that began in 1804 to explore the lands bought from France by the United States in the Louisiana Purchase. **342**

libel A false statement, usually published, that damages a person's reputation. **122**

Liberator, The Antislavery newspaper first published by William Lloyd Garrison in 1831. **470**

limited government A political principle which holds that government should be bound by laws that limit its power. **224**

Lincoln-Douglas debates Series of seven debates between Republican Abraham Lincoln and Democrat Stephen Douglas during the 1858 U.S. Senate campaign in Illinois. **567**

Line of Demarcation Boundary established by Pope Alexander VI in 1493 about 300 miles west and south of the Azores; gave unclaimed land west of the line to Spain, and east of the line to Portugal. **42**

longhouses Rectangular dwellings built by the Iroquois that were shared by several families. **16**

loose construction Way of interpreting the Constitution that allows the federal government to take actions that the Constitution does not specifically forbid it from taking. **308**

Lord Dunmore's Proclamation (1775) Statement issued by Virginia's royal governor promising freedom to any slave who fought for the British in the American Revolution. **199**

Lost Generation A group of American writers, disillusioned by World War I, who criticized postwar society. **773**

Louisiana Purchase (1803) Purchase of French land between the Mississippi River and the Rocky Mountains that nearly doubled the size of the United States. **340**

Lowell system The use of water powered textile mills that employed young unmarried women in the 1800s. **405**

Loyalists Colonists who sided with Britain in the American Revolution. **192**

Magna Carta (1215) Great Charter; agreed to by King John of England, it gave nobles and other individuals greater rights and made it clear that the nobility and monarchs must obey the law. **22**

maize Corn, the most important crop grown by Native Americans in North America and Mesoamerica. **6**

manifest destiny Belief shared by many Americans in the mid-1800s that the United States was meant to expand across the continent to the Pacific Ocean. **516**

manors Large estates held by monarchs and nobles in the Middle Ages. **19**

Marbury v. *Madison* (1803) U.S. Supreme Court case that established the principle of judicial review. **336**

Marshall Plan (1948) U.S. plan to give money to European countries to help them rebuilt their economies after World War II. **782**

Massacre at Wounded Knee (1890) U.S. Army's killing of approximately 150 Sioux at Wounded Knee Creek in South Dakota; ended U.S-Indian wars on the Plains. **652**

mass production Efficient production of large numbers of identical goods. **402**

Mayflower Compact (1620) Document written by the Pilgrims that established general guidelines for self government. **99**

McCulloch v. *Maryland* (1819) U.S. Supreme Court case that declared the Second Bank of the United States was constitutional and that because it was a federal institution Maryland could not interfere with the bank's operations. **377**

McKinley Tariff (1890) Law allowing all nations to ship sugar duty-free to the United States but also subsidizing U.S. sugar producers. **740**

mercantilism Practice of creating and maintaining wealth by carefully controlling trade. **126**

mercenaries Hired foreign soldiers. **199**

Mexican Cession (1848) Land that Mexico gave to the United States after the Mexican War through the Treaty of Guadalupe Hidalgo; included in what is now California, Nevada, and Utah; most of Arizona and New Mexico; and parts of Colorado, Texas, and Wyoming. **526**

Mexican Revolution Revolution against Mexican dictator Porfirio Díaz begun in 1910 by reformer Francisco Madero. **759**

Middle Ages Period of European history that lasted from about A.D. 500 to 1500. **19**

middle class Social and economic level between the wealthy and the poor. **460**

Middle Passage Voyage that brought enslaved Africans across the Atlantic Ocean to North America and the West Indies. **129**

migration Movement of people from one region to another. **5**

militia An army made up of civilians serving temporarily as soldiers. **158**

militarism A policy of building up armed forces combined with the strong influence of military institutions and values on a society. **768**

minutemen American colonial militia members who were supposed to be ready to fight at a minute's notice. **185**

missions Settlements established by priests in Spanish America to convert local Indians to Catholicism. **73**

Missouri Compromise (1820) Agreement proposed by Henry Clay that allowed Missouri to enter the Union as a slave state and Maine to enter as a free state; also outlawed slavery in any territories or states north of the 36°30′ line. **369**

monopoly Sole economic control of a business or product. **35**

Monroe Doctrine (1823) President James Monroe's statement forbidding further colonization in the Americas and declaring that the United States would view any attempt by a foreign country to colonize as a hostile act. **367**

Montgomery Bus Boycott Boycott of the Montgomery, Alabama segregated bus system by the NAACP and local African American groups. **786**

Mormon Trail Route by which Mormons traveled west to Utah. **531**

Mormons Members of the Church of Jesus Christ of Latter-Day Saints. **531**

Morrill Act (1862) Federal law passed by Congress that gave land to western states to encourage them to build colleges. **667**

Morse code System developed by Samuel Morse's assistant that represented each letter of the alphabet by a certain combination of dots and dashes; used with the telegraph. **416**

mountain men Men who trapped animals for fur in the Rocky Mountains and other western regions of the United States. **502**

muckrakers Journalists who wrote about corruption in business and politics, hoping to bring about reform. **713**

mugwumps Republican reformers who left the party to support Democrat Grover Cleveland during the 1884 presidential election. **710**

National American Woman Suffrage Association (NAWSA) Organization formed in 1890 to get the vote for women. **723**

National Association for the Advancement of Colored People (NAACP) Organization formed in 1909 to attack racial discrimination. **725**

national debt Total amount of money owed by a country to its lenders. **305**

National Grange An educational and social organization formed in 1867 to improve farmers lives. **700**

National Organization for Women (NOW) Organization formed in 1966 to increase women's political power. **790**

National Woman's Party (NWP) Organization formed in 1914 to use more aggressive methods to demand the vote for women. **723**

nativists U.S. citizens who opposed immigration because they were suspicious of immigrants and feared losing jobs to them. **459**

Nat Turner's Rebellion (1831) Rebellion in which Nat Turner led a group of slaves in Virginia in an unsuccessful attempt to overthrow and kill planter families. **443**

naturalized citizen A person born in another country who has been granted citizenship. **291**

Navigation Acts (1650–96) A series of English laws that required the American colonies to trade primarily with England; set duties on some goods. **127**

Nazis The National Socialist Party; led by Adolf Hitler, it rose to power in Germany in the 1930s. **778**

Neutrality Proclamation (1793) Statement made by President George Washington that the United States would not side with any of the nations at war in Europe following the French Revolution. **312**

New Deal President Franklin D. Roosevelt's plan for improving the national economy during the Great Depression. **775**

new immigrants Immigrants who came to the United States during and after the 1880s, mostly from southern and eastern Europe. **692**

New Jersey Plan Proposal to create a unicameral government with representation by state rather than by population; rejected at the Constitutional Convention. **238**

Nineteenth Amendment (1920) Amendment that gave the vote to women in the United States. **724**

nominating conventions Meetings where a political party selects its presidential and vice presidential candidates; first held in the 1820s. **374**

Non-Intercourse Act (1809) Law that replaced the Embargo Act and restored trade with all nations except Britain and France. **346**

North American Free Trade Agreement (NAFTA) Agreement between the United States, Canada, and Mexico in 1994 that allowed goods, people, and services to move more freely between the three nations. **797**

North Atlantic Treaty Organization Military alliance formed by the United States and 11 other nations in 1949. **783**

Northwest Ordinance of 1787 Legislation passed by Congress to establish a political structure for the lands in the Northwest Territory and create a system for the admission of new states. **226**

Northwest Passage A nonexistent path through North America that early explorers searched for, which would allow ships to sail from the Atlantic to the Pacific Ocean. **52**

Northwest Territory Lands including present-day Illinois, Indiana, Michigan, Ohio, Wisconsin, and part of Minnesota; organized by the Northwest Ordinance of 1787. **226**

nullification crisis A dispute between South Carolina and the federal government in the late 1820s over the state's right to nullify, or cancel, an unpopular tariff. **377**

old immigrants Immigrants who came to the United States before the 1880s, mostly from northern Europe. **692**

Olive Branch Petition (1775) Peace request sent by the Second Continental Congress to Britain's King George III, who rejected it. **186**

Open Door Policy U.S. policy of preserving equal access for all nations to trade in China. **742**

open range Public land used by ranchers who were part of the Cattle Kingdom. **661**

Operation Desert Storm (1991) Invasion by U.S.-led UN forces to force Iraq to withdraw from Kuwait. **795**

Oregon Trail A 2,000-mile trail stretching through the Great Plains from western Missouri to Oregon Country. **506**

Pacific Railway Acts (1862, 1864) Two laws passed by the federal government that gave loans and land grants to railroad companies to encourage them to build a transcontinental railroad. **657**

Paleo-Indians The first Americans who crossed from Asia into North America sometime between 10,000 and 3,800 B.C. **5**

Panama Canal Canal across the Isthmus of Panama completed by the United States in 1914. **754**

Panic of 1837 A financial crisis in the United States that led to an economic depression. **378**

Panic of 1873 A financial crisis in the United States that led to an economic depression and weakened the Republican Party. **632**

pardon Freedom from punishment. **259**

Parliament The British national legislature. **121**

Patriots American colonists who fought for independence from Great Britain during the Revolutionary War. **192**

patents Exclusive rights to make or sell inventions. **682**

Pendleton Civil Service Act (1883) Law that reformed the Civil Service by setting up a merit system for awarding federal jobs. **711**

petition A formal request. **285**

Pickett's Charge (1863) Failed Confederate attack, led by General George Pickett, at the Battle of Gettysburg. **601**

Pilgrims Members of a Puritan Separatist sect that left England in the early 1600s to settle in the Americas. **99**

Pinckney's Treaty (1795) Agreement between the United States and Spain that changed Florida's border and made it easier for American ships to use the port of New Orleans. **314**

pioneers People who first settle an area. **163**

plantations Large farms that usually specialize in growing one kind of crop. **74**

planters Wealthy farmers with large plantations. **97**

Platt Amendment (1902) Section of the Cuban constitution granting the United States the right to intervene in Cuban affairs. **748**

Plessy v. Ferguson (1896) U.S. Supreme Court case that established the separate-but-equal doctrine for public facilities. **634**

political action committees (PACs) Organizations that collect money to distribute to candidates who support the same issues as the contributors. **294**

political machines Organizations that help elect government officials and influence government policies. **708**

political parties Groups of people who organize to help elect government officials and influence government policies. **319**

poll tax A special tax that a person had to pay in order to vote. **633**

Pontiac's Rebellion (1763) Unsuccessful effort by Ottawa chief Pontiac and his allies to drive out British settlers on the frontier. **165**

Pony Express A system of messengers that carried mail between relay stations on a route from St. Joseph, Missouri, to San Francisco, California, in 1860 and 1861. **657**

popular sovereignty The idea that political authority belongs to the people; also a principle that would allow voters in a particular territory to decide whether to ban or permit slavery. **240, 553**

Populist Party Political party formed in 1891 that supported free coinage, government ownership of railroad, telegraph, and telephone systems, and immigration restrictions. **702**

potlatches Ceremonial events held by Indian peoples of the American Northwest at which hosts gave away most of their goods to gain respect. **12**

Pottawatomie Massacre (1856) Incident in which abolitionist John Brown and seven other men murdered pro-slavery Kansans. **563**

Powhatan Confederacy Powerful alliance of Algonquian Indians under the leadership of Wahunsonacock. **94**

precedent An action or decision that later serves as an example. **302**

presidios Spanish military bases located in the Americas. **73**

privateers Private ships authorized by a nation to attack its enemies. **312**

Privy Council Group of royal advisers who set policies for Britain's American colonies. **120**

Proclamation of 1763 British proclamation banning colonial settlement west of the Appalachian Mountains. **166**

progressives Reformers who supported social and political reform in the late 1800s. **712**

prohibition The banning of the manufacture, distribution, and sale of alcohol. **772**

propaganda Stories and images designed to support a particular point of view. **172**

proprietors Owners. **110**

prospect To search for gold. **535**

protective tariff A tax on imported goods that raises the price of imports so people will buy domestic goods. **307**

Protestant Reformation Religious movement begun by Martin Luther and others in 1517 to reform the Catholic Church. **78**

Protestants Reformers who protested certain practices of the Catholic Church. **78**

public works Construction projects for the public good. **775**

pueblos Spanish towns in the Americas. **73**

Pullman Strike (1894) Railroad strike against the Pullman Palace Car Company that shut down many rail lines until federal courts ordered strikers to return to work. **691**

Pure Food and Drug Act (1906) Law stopping the manufacture, sale, or transportation of mislabeled or contaminated food used in interstate commerce. **728**

Puritans Protestants who wanted to reform the Church of England. **98**

Quakers Society of Friends; Protestant sect founded in 1640s in England whose members believed that salvation was available to all people. **113**

Radical Republicans Republican members of Congress who felt that southern states needed to make great social changes before they could be readmitted to the Union. **623**

range rights Rights to water on the Plains that smaller ranchers bought from larger ranchers. **662**

range wars Competition among large ranchers, small ranchers, and farmers on the Plains for the use of the open range. **665**

ratification Formal approval. **226**

recall Procedure in which voters can remove an official from office before the end of his or her term. **714**

Reconquista Centuries-long struggle to drive the Moors from Spain; ended in 1492 with the surrender of the kingdom of Granada. **39**

Reconstruction (1865–77) Period following the Civil War during which the U.S. government worked to reunite the nation and to rebuild the southern states. **617**

Reconstruction Acts (1867–68) Laws that put the southern states under U.S. military control and required them to draft new constitutions upholding the Fourteenth Amendment. **626**

Redcoats British soldiers who fought against the colonists in the American Revolution; so called because of their bright red uniforms. **186**

Redeemers Group of southerners who helped return the Democrats to political power in the South during Reconstruction and tried to limit the civil rights of African Americans. **633**

Red Scare A wave of anticommunist fear that swept through the United States after the Bolshevik Revolution in Russia in 1917. **771**

referendum A process that allows voters to overrule laws already proposed or passed by the government. **714**

Renaissance Rebirth of interest in the arts and learning in Europe that began in Italy in the mid-1300s and lasted until the 1600s. **34**

rendezvous Annual event held by mountain men to trade furs and socialize. **503**

repeal To abolish. **170**

representative democracy A government that is composed of representatives of the people. **256**

Republic of Texas Independent nation of Texas, which lasted from 1836 until 1848, when Texas was annexed to the United States. **497**

republicanism Support for a system of representative government known as a republic. **224**

Republican Party Political party formed in the 1850s to stop the spread of slavery in the West. **564**

reservations Federal lands set aside for American Indians. **650**

reserved powers Powers retained by the state governments or by citizens. **257**

revivals Public church gatherings at which ministers preach to a large number of people. **136**

Rhode Island System System developed by Samuel Slater in the mid-1800s, in which families were hired as textile workers. **405**

right of deposit Right to transfer goods at a destination without having to pay fees for the cargo. **313**

Roosevelt Corollary (1904) President Theodore Roosevelt's addition to the Monroe Doctrine, stating the intention of the United States to police the Western Hemisphere. **755**

roundup Act of driving cattle together and collecting them into a herd. **662**

Rush-Bagot Agreement (1817) Agreement that limited naval power on the Great Lakes to the United States and British Canada. **364**

scalawags Name given to white southerners who supported Reconstruction for private gain; roughly defined as mean fellows. **630**

scientific agriculture Use of scientific techniques to improve crop production. **430**

scientific method Observation of and experimentation with natural events in order to form theories that could predict other events or behaviors. **141**

Scientific Revolution Period of great learning that began in the 1600s as European scientists, mathematicians, and astronomers looked for explanations about how the universe worked. **140**

sea dogs English sailors encouraged by Queen Elizabeth I to raid Spanish treasure ships in the late 1500s. **80**

search warrant A judge's order authorizing the search of a person's home or property to look for evidence of a crime. **286**

secession Act of formally withdrawing from an organization, such as a country. **573**

Second Battle of Bull Run (1862) Civil War battle in which the Confederate army forced most of the Union army out of Virginia. **587**

Second Continental Congress (1775) Meeting of colonial delegates in Philadelphia to decide how to react to fighting at Lexington and Concord. **186**

Second Great Awakening A period of religious evangelism that began in the 1790s and became widespread in the United States by the 1830s. **452**

Second Industrial Revolution A period of rapid growth in U.S. manufacturing in the late 1800s. **680**

sect A religious group. **98**

sectionalism A devotion to the interests of one geographic region rather than those of the country as a whole. **553**

segregation Forced separation of people of different races in public places. **633**

Selective Service Act (1917) Law that required men between the ages of 18 and 45 to register for the draft. **769**

Seneca Falls Convention (1848) First national women's rights convention, at which the Declaration of Sentiments was written. **477**

separation of powers The division of governmental power into distinct areas with different branches of government exercising different powers; prevents one branch from becoming too powerful. **257**

Separatists Radical group of Puritans who wanted to cut all ties with the Church of England. **98**

settlement houses Neighborhood centers in poor areas that offered education, recreation, and social activities. **697**

Seven Days' Battles (1862) Series of Civil War battles in which Confederate army successes forced the Union army to retreat from near Richmond, Virginia, the Confederate capital. **587**

Seventeenth Amendment (1913) Amendment that allows Americans to vote directly for U.S. senators. **713**

sharecropping System used on southern farms after the Civil War in which farmers worked land owned by someone else in return for a small portion of the crops. **635**

Shays's Rebellion (1786–87) Uprising of Massachusetts farmers, led by Daniel Shays, to protest high taxes, heavy debt, and farm foreclosures. **234**

Sherman Antitrust Act (1890) Legislation outlawing monopolies and trusts that restrained trade; proved difficult to enforce. **686**

Sherman Silver Purchase Act (1890) Law that increased the amount of silver purchased by the United States for coinage. **701**

siege Military blockade of a city or fort. **187**

Siege of Vicksburg (1863) Union army's six-week blockade of Vicksburg that led the city to surrender during the Civil War. **592**

Silk Road Overland trade route that linked China with other Asian markets as far west as the Black Sea. **25**

Sixteenth Amendment (1913) Amendment allowing the federal government to impose direct taxes on people's incomes. **731**

slave codes Laws passed in the colonies to control slaves. **132**

socialism An economic system in which the government owns and operates a country's means of production. **720**

Social Security Act (1935) Law that provided pensions for retired workers and unemployment benefits to workers who lose their jobs. **776**

societies Groups of people who live together and share a culture. **6**

sodbusters Name given to both the Plains farmers and the plows they used to break up the region's tough sod. **668**

Sons of Liberty Secret societies formed in the mid-1700s by colonists to protest new taxes and to frighten tax collectors. **169**

Spanish Armada Large Spanish fleet defeated by England in 1588. **80**

speculators Investors who buy items at low prices in hopes that their value will rise. **305**

spheres of influence Areas of a country where foreign nations control trade and natural resources. **742**

spirituals Emotional Christian songs sung by slaves in the South that mixed African and European elements and usually expressed slaves' religious beliefs. **442**

spoils system Politicians' practice of giving government jobs to their supporters. **376**

Stamp Act (1765) Law passed by Parliament that raised tax money by requiring colonists to pay for an official stamp whenever they bought paper items such as newspapers, licenses, and legal documents. **169**

staple crops Crops that are continuously in demand. **134**

states' rights Belief that the power of the federal government regarding the states is strictly limited. **379**

steerage Cramped area below deck on a ship; many immigrants to the United States traveled on this level. **693**

strait Narrow, winding sea passage. **48**

strict construction Way of interpreting the Constitution that allows the federal government to take only those actions the Constitution specifically says it can take. **308**

strikes Refusals of workers to perform their jobs until employers meet their demands. **408**

subsidy Bonus payment by the government to the producer of some good. **740**

suburbs Residential areas outside of a central city. **696**

suffrage Voting rights. **224**

Sugar Act (1764) Law passed by the British Parliament setting taxes on molasses and sugar imported by the colonies. **167**

supply-side economics Economic theory that supports lowering taxes in order to boost business investments and the economy. **794**

Sutter's Fort Northern California colony founded by Swiss immigrant John Sutter in 1839 that became a popular destination for American immigrants. **509**

Tariff of Abominations (1828) Nickname given to a new tariff by southerners who opposed it. **376**

tariffs Taxes on imports or exports. **232**

Tea Act (1773) Law passed by Parliament allowing the British East India Company to sell its low-cost tea directly to the colonies, undermining colonial tea merchants; led to the Boston Tea Party. **173**

technology Tools used to produce goods or to do work. **401**

Tejanos Spanish settlers who lived in what is now southern Texas. **490**

telegraph Machine invented by Samuel Morse in 1837 that uses pulses of electric current to send messages across long distances through wires. **415**

Teller Amendment (1898) A pledge by the United States not to take control of Cuba. **745**

temperance movement A social reform effort begun in the mid-1800s to encourage people to drink less alcohol. **464**

Ten Percent Plan President Abraham Lincoln's plan for Reconstruction; once 10 percent of voters in a former Confederate state took a U.S. loyalty oath, they could form a new state government and be readmitted to the Union. **617**

tenements Poorly built, overcrowded housing where many immigrants lived. **461**

Tet Offensive (1968) Massive attack by North Vietnamese and Vietcong forces against U.S. troops in Vietnam. **791**

Texas longhorn Hearty breed of cattle raised by ranchers throughout western Texas. **660**

textiles Cloth. **399**

Thirteenth Amendment (1865) Constitutional amendment that outlawed slavery. **618**

Three-Fifths Compromise (1787) Agreement worked out at the Constitutional Convention stating that three fifths of the slaves in each state should be counted as part of the state's population for determining representation in the lower house of Congress. **239**

Toleration Act of 1649 Maryland law that made restricting the religious rights of Christians a crime; one of the first laws protecting religious tolerance to be passed in the English colonies. **110**

total war Type of war in which an army destroys its opponent's ability to fight by targeting civilian and economic as well as military resources. **604**

totems Images of ancestors or animal spirits; often carved onto tall poles by Native American peoples of the Pacific Northwest. **12**

town meeting Political meeting at which people make decisions on local issues; used primarily in New England. **122**

Townshend Acts (1767) Laws passed by Parliament placing duties on certain items imported by the colonists. **171**

trade unions Workers' organizations that try to improve pay and working conditions. **408**

Trail of Tears (1838–39) An 800-mile forced march made by the Cherokee from their homeland in Georgia to Indian Territory; resulted in the deaths of thousands of Cherokee. **383**

transcendentalism Idea that people could rise above the material things in life; philosophy shared by some New England writers in the mid-1800s. **454**

transcontinental railroad Railroad that crossed the continental United States; construction began in 1863 and was completed in 1869. **657**

Transportation Revolution Rapid growth in the speed and convenience of transportation; in the United States this began in the early 1800s. **410**

Treaty of Dancing Rabbit Creek (1830) Agreement in which the Choctaw gave up more than 10 million acres of land in Mississippi and accepted removal to Indian Territory. **382**

Treaty of Fort Laramie (1851) The first major treaty between the U.S. government and Plains Indians; allowed U.S. citizens to travel across Indian homelands. **649**

Treaty of Ghent (1814) Treaty signed by the United States and Britain ending the War of 1812. **355**

Treaty of Greenville (1795) Agreement between American Indian confederation leaders and the U.S. government that gave the United States Indian lands in the southeastern part of the Northwest Territory and guaranteed that U.S. citizens could safely travel through the region. **316**

Treaty of Guadalupe Hidalgo (1848) Treaty that ended the Mexican War and gave the United States much of Mexico's northern territory. **526**

Treaty of Medicine Lodge (1867) Agreement between the U.S. government and southern Plains Indians in which the Indians agreed to move onto reservations. **650**

Treaty of Paris (1763) Peace agreement that ended the French and Indian War. **162**

Treaty of Paris of 1783 Peace agreement that officially ended the Revolutionary War and established British recognition of the United States. **213**

Treaty of Tordesillas (1494) Treaty signed by Spain and Portugal in which both countries agreed to move the Line of Demarcation 800 miles farther west. **42**

Treaty of Versailles (1919) Treaty ending World War I, requiring Germany to pay billions of dollars in war costs and establishing the League of Nations. **771**

Tredegar Iron Works Large iron factory that operated in Richmond, Virginia, in the early to mid-1800s. **432**

Triangle Shirtwaist Fire A factory fire in New York City that killed some 146 workers in 1911. **718**

triangular trade Trading networks in which goods and slaves moved among England, the American colonies, the West Indies and West Africa. **128**

Truman Doctrine (1947) President Truman's policy of providing U.S. aid to any nation fighting communism. **782**

trust A legal arrangement that groups several companies under one board of directors to eliminate competition and regulation production. **684**

Twelfth Amendment (1804) Constitutional amendment that created a separate ballot for president and vice president. **324**

Twenty-first Amendment (1933) Amendment that repealed the Eighteenth Amendment and ended prohibition. **772**

unalienable rights Basic human rights such as life, liberty, and the pursuit of happiness. **191**

Uncle Tom's Cabin (1852) Antislavery novel written by Harriet Beecher Stowe that showed northerners the violent reality of slavery and drew many people to the abolitionists' cause. **557**

Underground Railroad Network of people who helped thousands of slaves escape to the North by providing transportation and hiding places. **472**

Underwood Tariff Act (1913) Law that reduced tariffs and introduced a personal income tax. **731**

United Nations (UN) International organization formed in 1945 to resolve international disputes. **781**

utopian community Place where people worked to establish a perfect society; such communities were popular in the United States during the late 1700s and early to mid-1800s. **454**

vaqueros Mexican cowboys in the West who tended cattle and horses. **662**

vertical integration Ownership of businesses involved in each step of a manufacturing process. **684**

veto To cancel. **259**

viceroy A royal governor in Spanish America. **39**

Virginia Plan (1787) Plan for government proposed at the Constitutional Convention in which the national government would have three branches—executive, judicial, and legislative; representation in the legislature would be determined by state population. **237**

Virginia Statute for Religious Freedom (1786) Legislation that gave people in Virginia freedom of worship and freedom to speak their opinions about religion. **224**

Voting Rights Act of 1965 Law ensuring every U.S. citizen's right to vote. **789**

Wade-Davis Bill Reconstruction plan that imposed two conditions for a former Confederate state to rejoin the United States—it had to outlaw slavery, and majority of adult males had to take a loyalty oath; those who had supported the Confederacy could not vote or hold office. **617**

War Hawks Members of Congress who wanted to declare war against Britain in the early 1800s. **348**

War on Drugs A large-scale effort to stop illegal drugs from entering the United States. **795**

Watergate Scandal involving a break-in at the Democratic National Committee headquarters; resulted in the resignation of President Richard Nixon in 1974. **792**

Whig Party Political party formed by opponents of Andrew Jackson in 1834 who supported a strong legislature. **378**

Whiskey Rebellion (1794) Protests by small farmers in Pennsylvania against new taxes on whiskey and other alcohol. **316**

wigwams Small circular huts in which some northeastern Native American peoples lived. **16**

Wilderness Campaign (May–June 1864) A series of battles between Union and Confederate forces in northern and central Virginia that stretched Confederate resources to their limit. **603**

Wilmot Proviso (1846) Proposal to outlaw slavery in the territory added to the United States by the Mexican Cession; passed in the House of Representatives but was defeated in the Senate. **553**

Wisconsin Idea A program of progressive reforms created by Wisconsin governor Robert La Follette. **714**

Woman's Christian Temperance Union (WCTU) Temperance organization created in 1874 to fight against alcohol abuse. **722**

Worcester v. Georgia (1832) Supreme Court ruling that the Cherokee Nation was a distinct territory over which only the federal government had authority; ignored by both President Andrew Jackson and the state of Georgia. **383**

writs of assistance Special search warrants that allowed tax collectors to search for smuggled goods. **171**

XYZ affair (1797) Incident in which French agents attempted to get a bribe and loans from U.S. diplomats in exchange for an agreement that French privateers would no longer attack American ships; it led to an undeclared naval war between the two countries. **321**

Yalta Conference (1945) World War II meeting between Franklin D. Roosevelt, Winston Churchill, and Joseph Stalin to discuss the postwar future of the world. **781**

yellow journalism The exaggeration of news stories in order to boost sales. **744**

yeomen Small landowning farmers. **434**

Glossary/Glosario

This Glossary contains terms you need to understand as you study American history. After each key term there is a brief definition or explanation of the meaning of the term as it is used in *Call to Freedom*. The page number refers to the page on which the term is introduced in the textbook.

ABC Powers/potencias ABC Argentina, Brasil y Chile. **761**

abolition/abolición Poner fin a la esclavitud. **469**

Adams-Onís Treaty/Tratado Adams-Onís (1819) Acuerdo en el que España cede el territorio de Florida a Estados Unidos. **366**

Alamo/Álamo Misión española en San Antonio, Texas. Sitio de una famosa batalla durante la Revolución texana de 1836. La victoria del ejército mexicano dio como resultado la muerte de todos los texanos defensores del edificio. **494**

Albany Plan of Union/Plan de Unión Albany (1754) Plan redactado por Benjamín Franklin y otros delegados para pedir a las colonias que se unieran bajo un gobierno común. **160**

Alien and Sedition Acts/Leyes de sedición y extranjería (1798) Leyes aprobadas por un congreso mayoritariamente federal con la finalidad de proteger al gobierno de la influencia de ideas, acciones y personas; fue usado en contra de miembros del partido Demócrata Republicano. **322**

amendments/enmiendas Cambios, correcciones o agregados hechos de manera oficial a una ley o constitución. **246**

American Anti-Slavery Society/Sociedad Estadounidense contra la Esclavitud Grupo fundado en 1833 por William Lloyd Garrison y otras personas para la abolición inmediata de la esclavitud y la igualdad racial de los afroestadounidenses. **471**

American Colonization Society/Sociedad Estadounidense de Colonización Sociedad organizada en 1817 para establecer en África Occidental una colonia llamada Liberia como hogar para los afroestadounidenses libres. **470**

American Federation of Labor/Federación Estadounidense del Trabajo (AFL, por sus siglas en inglés) Uno de los primeros sindicatos del trabajo en Estados Unidos; fundado en la década de 1880 por Samuel Gompers para agrupar varios sindicatos de obreros calificados. **689**

American System/Sistema estadounidense Plan de alza de impuestos creado por Henry Clay para realizar mejoras internas como la reparación de caminos y canales. **370**

amnesty/amnistía Perdón oficial otorgado por el gobierno ante un acto ilegal. **617**

anarchists/anarquistas Personas que se oponen a cualquier forma de gobierno. **689**

annex/anexar Tomar control de un territorio para incorporarlo a un estado, país, etc. **497**

Antifederalists/Antifederalistas Personas que se oponían a la ratificación de la Constitución. **242**

Anti-Imperialist League/Liga Antiimperialista Grupo de estadounidenses que se oponía al tratado que daba por terminada la guerra entre Estados Unidos y España porque creían que Estados Unidos tenía intenciones de crear un imperio colonial. **738**

Appomattox Courthouse/Appomattox Courthouse Poblado de Virginia donde el general Robert E. Lee fue obligado a rendirse, dando fin a la Guerra Civil. **605**

apportionment/adjudicamiento Uso de la población para determinar cuántos representantes legislativos debe tener un área determinada. **258**

apprentices/aprendices Personas que aprenden un oficio de un experto en la materia. **133**

arbitration/arbitraje Encuentros formales para analizar y solucionar desacuerdos. **728**

archaeology/arqueología Estudio científico del pasado no escrito. **5**

armistice/armisticio Tregua entre grupos o países en guerra. **769**

Articles of Confederation/Artículos de la Confederación (1777) Documento que creó el primer gobierno central en Estados Unido; fue reemplazado por la Constitución en 1789. **225**

artifacts/artefactos Restos de objetos hechos por el hombre. **5**

astrolabe/astrolabio Instrumento usado por los navegantes en algún tiempo para determinar la posición de una embarcación con base en la posición de las estrellas.

Atlanta Compromise/Compromiso de Atlanta (1895) Discurso en el que Booker T. Washington criticó a los afroestadounidenses enfatizando que deberían mejorar su educación y situación económica en lugar de crear revueltas en contra de la discriminación y segregación racial. **724**

backcountry/*backcountry* Región fronteriza de Virginia y las Carolinas, localizada entre la costa y los montes Apalaches. **163**

Bacon's Rebellion/Rebelión de Bacon (1676) Ataque encabezado por Nathaniel Bacon contra los indígenas estadounidenses y el gobierno colonial en Virginia. **97**

balance of trade/balanza de intercambio Relación entre los bienes que un país adquiere de otros países y los que les vende. **126**

Bank of the United States/Banco de Estados Unidos Banco nacional rentado por el Congreso en 1791 para ofrecer seguridad a la economía de Estados Unidos. **309**

Battle of Antietam/Batalla de Antietam (1862) Victoria del ejército de la Unión en la batalla de un solo día más sangrienta en la historia de Estados Unidos. **588**

Battle of Brandywine Creek/Batalla de Brandywine Creek (1777) batalla de la Revolución en la que las fuerzas británicas arrasaron con los patriotas en Pennsylvania. **204**

Battle of Bunker Hill/Batalla de Bunker Hill (1775) Batalla de la Revolución que tuvo lugar en Boston y que demostró que los colonos podían luchar contra el ejército británico. **188**

Battle of Fallen Timbers/Batalla de Fallen Timbers (1794) Batalla entre las tropas estadounidenses y una confederación indígena estadounidense resistiéndose al establecimiento de personas de raza blanca en el noroeste de Estados Unidos; esta batalla condujo al Tratado de Greenville. **316**

Battle of Gettysburg/Batalla de Gettysburg (1863) Victoria del ejército de la Unión que revirtió las condiciones de lucha en contra de los Confederados en Gettysburg, Pennsylvania. En esta batalla perdieron la vida más de 50,000 soldados. **601**

Battle of Goliad/Batalla de Goliad (1836) Victoria del ejército mexicano durante la Revolución de Texas en la que el general Antonio López de Santa Anna ordenó la ejecución de soldados texanos después de su rendición. **495**

Battle of Horseshoe Bend/Batalla de Horsehoe Bend (1814) Victoria del ejército estadounidense durante la Guerra de 1812 en la que las tropas de Andrew Jackson obligaron a los indios Creek a ceder gran parte de su territorio en el sur del país. **353**

Battle of Lake Erie/Batalla del Lago Erie (1813) Victoria en la que, comandado por Oliver Hazard Perry, el ejército estadounidense puso fin al control británico del Lago Erie. **352**

Battle of New Orleans/Batalla de Nueva Orleáns (1815) Aunque ésta fue la mayor victoria del ejército estadounidense en la Guerra de 1812, tuvo lugar dos semanas después de la firma de un tratado de paz en el que se declaraba la terminación de la guerra. **354**

Battle of Pea Ridge/Batalla de Pea Ridge (1862) Batalla de la Guerra Civil en la que el ejército Confederado establecido en Missouri y al que se habían unido algunos indígenas estadounidenses, fue derrotado en el noroeste de Arkansas. **593**

Battle of Princeton/Batalla de Princeton (1777) Batalla de la Revolución en la que los Patriotas hicieron retroceder a las fuerzas británicas en Nueva Jersey. **203**

Battle of San Jacinto/Batalla de San Jacinto (1836) Batalla final de la Revolución en la que el ejército estadounidense derrotó al ejército mexicano, obteniendo la independencia de Texas. **496**

Battle of Saratoga/Batalla de Saratoga (1777) Batalla de la Revolución que tuvo lugar en Nueva York y en la que las fuerzas británicas sufrieron una de sus mayores derrotas y los Patriotas su mayor victoria hasta ese momento. **204**

Battle of Shiloh/Batalla de Shiloh (1862) Batalla de la Guerra Civil realizada en Tennessee en la que el ejército de la Unión adquirió mayor control sobre el Valle del Mississippi. **591**

Battle of the Little Bighorn/Batalla de Little Bighorn (1876) Última batalla del general Custer. Esta batalla entre las tropas de George Armstrong Custer y los guerreros sioux al mando de los jefes Caballo Loco y Toro Sentado produjo la mayor derrota del ejército estadounidense en el oeste. **651**

Battle of the Thames/Batalla del Támesis (1813) Victoria del ejército estadounidense al mando de William Henry Harrison que puso fin a la alianza de indígenas y británicos durante la Guerra de 1812. **352**

Battle of Tippecanoe/Batalla de Tippecanoe (1811) Victoria del ejército estadounidense sobre la confederación indígena que intentaba evitar el establecimiento de poblaciones de blancos en el noroeste. Esta batalla aumentó las hostilidades entre Gran Bretaña y Estados Unidos. **347**

Battle of Trenton/Batalla de Trenton (1776) Batalla de la Revolución que tuvo lugar en Nueva Jersey y en la que las fuerzas de los patriotas capturaron a más de 900 soldados hesianos. **203**

Battle of Vincennes/Batalla de Vincennes (1779) Batalla de la Revolución librada en el oeste, en la que los patriotas retomaron de manos de los británicos el poblado de Vincennes, de población mayoritariamente francesa y localizado en la ribera del río Wabash. **210**

Battle of Yorktown/Batalla de Yorktown (1871) La mayor batalla de la Revolución. Sitio de rendición del general británico Charles Cornwallis ante las tropas de los patriotas establecidas en Virginia. **212**

Bear Flag Revolt/Revuelta de Bear Flag (1846) Revuelta iniciada por colonos estadounidenses en contra del gobierno de México para declarar al territorio de California como una república independiente. **524**

benevolent societies/sociedades de beneficencia Organizaciones que brindaban ayuda a los inmigrantes en caso de enfermedad, desempleo y muerte. **639**

Bessemer process/Proceso de Bessemer Proceso más económico de producción de acero, desarrollado en la década de 1850. **681**

bicameral legislature/legislatura de cámara dual Cuerpo de legisladores compuesto por las dos Cámaras. **121**

Bill of Rights/Declaración de Derechos Primeras 10 enmiendas hechas a la Constitución. Fue ratificada en 1791. **247**

Black Codes/códigos negros Decretos aprobados en los estados sureños en la época de la Reconstrucción con la finalidad de limitar al máximo la libertad y los derechos de los afroestadounidenses. **623**

Black Death/muerte negra Epidemia que se extendió por toda Europa de 1348 a 1350 y causó la muerte a 30 millones de personas. **32**

bonanza/bonanza Gran yacimiento de mineral precioso. **655**

bonds/bonos Certificados que representan el dinero de los ciudadanos tomado en préstamo por el gobierno. **305**

boomtowns/pueblos en explosión Comunidades del Oeste que se desarrollaron con gran rapidez debido a la fiebre del oro, pero que desaparecieron cuando los yacimientos se agotaron. **656**

borderlands/territorio fronterizo Región dominada por España que abarcaba el norte de México, Florida y partes de los actuales estados de Arizona, Nuevo México y Texas donde vivían algunos europeos. **75**

border states/estados fronterizos Delaware, Kentucky, Maryland y Missouri. Estados ubicados entre el norte y el sur en los que se practicaba la esclavitud y que no se adhirieron a la Confederación durante la Guerra Civil. **582**

bosses/caciques Líderes políticos corruptos que usaban sobornos y favores especiales para ganar votos en las elecciones. **709**

Boston Massacre/matanza de Boston (1770) Incidente en el que los soldados británicos abrieron fuego entre una multitud de colonizadores, ocasionando la muerte a cinco personas. **172**

Boston Tea Party/Motín del Té (1773) Protesta en contra de la ley del té en la que un grupo de colonos abordó los barcos británicos que transportaban té y echaron al mar alrededor de 340 cofres con este producto. **174**

Boxer Rebellion/rebelión de los Boxers (1900) Ataque de un grupo de nacionalistas chinos conocidos como Boxers a un grupo de extranjeros que dio por terminada la participación de China en asuntos externos; la revuelta fue controlada por las tropas navales de Estados Unidos después de dos meses. **743**

boycott/boicot Rechazo a la compra de bienes específicos. Método usado con frecuencia como protesta contra determinados movimientos. **169**

Brown* v. *Board of Education/Consejo de Educación* versus *Brown (1954) Decreto de la Suprema Corte que declaraba ilegales a las escuelas públicas en las que se practicaba la segregación racial. Puso fin a la doctrina *Plessy-Ferguson* de separatismo, establecida en 1896. **783**

Bull Moose Party/Partido del Alce sobrenombre dado al Partido Progresista formado por Theodore Roosevelt y sus simpatizantes en 1912. **730**

Bureau of Indian Affairs/Oficina de Asuntos Indígenas Agencia creada por el gobierno en el siglo XIX con la finalidad de hacer llegar las políticas federales a territorios habitados por tribus indígenas. **382**

cabinet/gabinete Grupo conformado por los jefes de los departamentos ejecutivos para brindar asesoría al presidente de Estados Unidos. **260**

California Gold Rush/fiebre del oro en California Migración masiva de personas a California en 1849, luego del descubrimiento de yacimientos de oro en la zona. **534**

Californios/californios Colonos españoles que habitaron en California. **489**

capital/capital Dinero o propiedades usadas para obtener más dinero. **33**

caravel/carabela Barco rápido y fácil de maniobrar diseñado por los portugueses. **36**

carpetbaggers/*carpetbaggers* Nombre dado a los norteños que emigraron al sur durante la Reconstrucción. **629**

cash crops/cultivo para la venta Nombre dado a los productos cosechados con la finalidad de obtener ganancias económicas y no para consumo personal. **131**

casualties/bajas Personas asesinadas, heridas, capturadas o extraviadas durante una guerra. **161**

cattle drive/travesía de ganado Viajes largos en los que un grupo de vaqueros arreaba ganado para llevarlo a los mercados del norte o a mejores pastizales. **663**

Cattle Kingdom/Cattle Kingdom Área de las Grandes Planicies que se extiende de Texas a Canadá en la que muchos rancheros se establecieron como productores de ganado a finales del siglo XIX. **661**

charter/carta Documento legal que da a una persona el derecho de establecer una colonia. **87**

checks and balances/revisión y balance Sistema establecido por la Constitución para evitar que cualquier rama del gobierno adquiera demasiado poder en relación con las demás. **241**

Chinese Exclusion Act/Ley de exclusión de Chinos (1882) Ley que prohibió la inmigración de los chinos a Estados Unidos por un periodo de 10 años. **694**

Chisholm Trail/Camino de Chisholm Camino creado por Jesse Chisholm en 1867 de San Antonio, Texas, hasta Abilene, Kansas, para realizar travesías de ganado. **663**

circumnavigate/circunnavegar Hacer una navegación completa alrededor de algo. **49**

Civil Rights Act of 1866/Ley de derechos civiles de 1866 Ley que daba a los afroestadounidenses derechos legales similares a los que tenían los ciudadanos de raza blanca. **624**

Civil Rights Act of 1875/Ley de derechos civiles de 1875 Ley que garantizaba a los afroestadounidenses igualdad de derechos en lugares públicos como teatros y medios públicos de transporte. **632**

Civil Rights Act of 1964/Ley de derechos civiles de 1964 Ley que prohibía la segregación racial en lugares públicos y el rechazo de patrones, sindicatos y universidades a cualquier persona por su color, nacionalidad, religión o sexo. **787**

Clayton Antitrust Act/Ley Clayton antimonopolios
(1914) Ley que fortaleció las leyes federales antimonopolio. **732**

Clermont/Clermont Primer barco comercial de vapor de grandes dimensiones, diseñado por Robert Fulton y probado en 1807. **412**

Cold War/guerra fría Periodo de lucha de poderes entre Estados Unidos y la Unión Soviética que se extendió de 1945 a 1991. **780**

collective bargaining/negociación de contrato colectivo Proceso en el que los líderes de un sindicato negocian con los dueños de las industrias, con la finalidad de obtener mejores salarios y condiciones de trabajo para los obreros. **688**

Columbian Exchange/intercambio colombino Intercambio de plantas, animales y enfermedades entre Estados Unidos y Europa, Asia y África. **51**

Commercial Revolution/Revolución Comercial Periodo de auge económico iniciado en Europa en el siglo trece con una gran expansión comercial. **33**

Committees of Correspondence/comités de correspondencia Comités creados por la Cámara de Representantes de Massachusetts en la década de 1760 para que poblados y colonias compartieran información que los ayudara a enfrentar las leyes británicas vigentes. **169**

common-school movement/Movimiento de Escuelas Comunes Reforma social iniciada a mediados del siglo XIX para fomentar la idea de que todos los niños recibieran educación en un mismo lugar sin importar su origen o clase social. **465**

Common Sense/Common Sense (1776) Folleto escrito por Thomas Paine en el que criticaba a las monarquías con la finalidad de convencer a los colonos estadounidenses de la necesidad de independizarse de Gran Bretaña. **190**

Communists/comunistas Personas que buscan la distribución igualitaria de la riqueza y el fin de cualquier forma de propiedad privada. **769**

Compromise of 1850/Compromiso de 1850 Acuerdo redactado por Henry Clay en que se permitía a California ingresar a la Unión como estado libre, se proponía la división del resto del territorio cedido por México en dos partes donde el tema de la esclavitud sería reglamentado por soberanía popular, se aclaraban los reclamos de tierras entre Texas y Nuevo México, se abolía el intercambio de esclavos con Washington y se fortalecía el Ley de esclavos fugitivos. **555**

Compromise of 1877/Compromiso de 1877 Acuerdo en el que se definió la situación de las elecciones presidenciales de 1876. Los demócratas aceptaron al republicano Rutherford B. Hayes como presidente a cambio del retiro de las tropas federales del sur. **633**

Comstock Lode/veta de Comstock Yacimiento de oro y plata descubierto en Nevada por Henry Comstock en 1859. **655**

concurrent powers/poderes concurrentes Poderes compartidos por el gobierno federal y los gobiernos estatales. **257**

Confederate States of America/Estados Confederados Nación formada por los estados del sur el 4 de febrero de 1861, también conocida como Confederación. **574**

conquistadores/conquistadores Soldados y exploradores españoles que encabezaron las expediciones militares en Estados Unidos y reclamaron territorios en nombre de España. **66**

conservation/conservación Protección de la naturaleza y sus recursos. **729**

Constitution/Constitución Conjunto de principios básicos que determina los poderes y las obligaciones de un gobierno. **224**

Constitutional Convention/Convención Constitucional de Filadelfia (1787) Encuentro realizado en Filadelfia en el que delegados de los estados redactaron la Constitución. **237**

Constitutional Union Party/Partido Unido de la Constitución Partido político formado en 1860 por habitantes del norte y del sur en apoyo de la Unión, sus leyes y la Constitución. **571**

Continental Army/Ejército Continental Ejército creado por el Segundo Congreso Continental en 1775 para defender las colonias estadounidenses del dominio británico. **186**

contrabands/contrabando Esclavos que escapaban o eran capturados por el ejército de la Unión durante la Guerra Civil. **596**

Contract with America/Contrato con Estados Unidos Reforma republicana de diez puntos creada a mediados de la década de 1990. **794**

Convention of 1818/Convención de 1818 Acuerdo entre Estados Unidos y Gran Bretaña para definir los derechos de pesca y establecer las nuevas fronteras al norte. **365**

convert/convertir Cambio de creencias religiosas. **42**

Copperheads/copperheads Demócratas del norte que se oponían a la abolición de la esclavitud y simpatizaban con las creencias sureñas durante la Guerra Civil. **597**

corporations/corporaciones Compañías que venden parte de las mismas en forma de acciones del mercado de valores para recaudar fondos. **684**

cotton belt/región algodonera Región que se extendía de Georgia al este de Texas en la que se producía la mayor parte del algodón cosechado en Estados Unidos a mediados del siglo XIX. **427**

cotton diplomacy/Diplomacia del algodón Esfuerzos de la Confederación por aprovechar la influencia de la industria textil británica del sur para convencer a Gran Bretaña de apoyar su causa durante la Guerra Civil. **584**

cotton gin/desmotadora de algodón Dispositivo inventado por Eli Whitney en 1793 para separar las fibras de algodón de las semillas. Este invento revolucionó la industria del algodón. **426**

Council of the Indies/Consejo de Indias Grupo de funcionarios de la realeza establecido en 1524 para vigilar las acciones del gobierno y la aplicación de las leyes españolas en América. **72**

covenant/pacto Acuerdo sagrado. **104**

creditors/acreedores Personas que prestan dinero. **233**

Crusades/Cruzadas (1096-1221) Serie de guerras emprendidas por los cristianos europeos para tomar posesión de las Tierras Santas. **25**

Cuban missile crisis /crisis de los misiles de Cuba (1962) Crisis militar que estuvo a punto de ocasionar una guerra nuclear. Finalmente, la Unión Soviética aceptó retirar sus misiles nucleares de Cuba a cambio de que Estados Unidos prometiera no invadir la isla y retirara algunos de sus misiles de Europa. **786**

culture/cultura Valores y tradiciones comunes de una sociedad, como el lenguaje, forma de gobierno y relaciones familiares. **6**

Cumberland Road/Camino Cumberland Primer proyecto federal de construcción de carreteras, iniciado en 1815 para crear caminos entre Cumberland, Maryland y el poblado que actualmente lleva el nombre de Wheeling, West Virginia. **371**

D-Day/Día D 6 de junio de 1944. Invasión del Ejército Aliado a la ocupación Nazi en territorio francés durante la Segunda Guerra Mundial. **778**

Daughters of Liberty/Hijas de la Libertad Grupos de mujeres que realizaron boicots y adoptaron otras medidas para apoyar la resistencia de las colonias al dominio británico. **171**

Dawes General Allotment Act/Ley Dawes de lotificación (1887) Ley aprobada por el Congreso para dividir las reservaciones de terreno indígenas en partes individuales con la promesa de otorgarles la ciudadanía estadounidense. **654**

debtors/deudores Personas que deben dinero. **233**

Declaration of Independence/Declaración de Independencia (1776) Declaración redactada por el Segundo Congreso Continental para definir los derechos de los colonos, expresar sus quejas contra Gran Bretaña y declarar la independencia de las colonias. **191**

Declaration of Sentiments/Declaración de sentimientos (1848) Declaración redactada y firmada por varias personas en apoyo de los derechos de las mujeres durante la Convención de Seneca Falls en la que se describía con detalle su punto de vista sobre las injusticias sociales en su contra. **477**

delegated powers/poderes delegados Poderes otorgados de manera específica por la Constitución al gobierno federal. **256**

Democratic Party/Partido Demócrata Asociación política formada por partidarios de Andrew Jackson después de las elecciones presidenciales de 1824. **375**

Democratic-Republican Party/Partido Demócrata-Republicano Asociación política formada en la década de 1790 con la finalidad de preservar el poder de los gobiernos estatales y promover la agricultura. **320**

deport/deportar Enviar a un inmigrante de regreso a su país de origen. **291**

depression/depresión Descenso considerable en la actividad económica, combinado con un alza del desempleo. **233**

direct primary/elecciones primarias Método de elección en el que los votantes eligen a sus candidatos a los cargos públicos. **713**

dissenters/opositores Personas que están en contra de las opiniones oficiales, sean religiosas o políticas. **103**

dollar diplomacy/Diplomacia del dólar Política creada por el presidente William Howard Taft para influir en los gobiernos de América Latina mediante la intervención económica y no militar. **756**

domestication/domesticación Proceso de reproducción de plantas y animales para consumo humano. **6**

Dominion of New England/Dominio de Nueva Inglaterra Unión de algunas colonias del noreste, organizada por el rey James II en 1686, que duró hasta 1689. **123**

Donner party/partida Donner Grupo de viajeros del oeste extraviados en la Sierra Nevada durante el invierno de 1846-1847. Sólo 40 de los 98 viajeros sobrevivieron. **509**

double jeopardy/doble riesgo Imposibilidad legal de juzgar a una persona dos veces por el mismo crimen. **289**

draft/reclutamiento Sistema de aceptación de personal de las fuerzas armadas. **293**

Dred Scott **decision/Decisión** *Dred Scott* (1857) Decreto aprobado por la Suprema Corte en el que se declaraba que los afroestadounidenses no podían ser ciudadanos de Estados Unidos, que la restricción de la esclavitud presentada en el Compromiso de Missouri era anticonstitucional y que el Congreso no tenía derecho de abolir la esclavitud en ninguna parte del territorio federal. **566**

dry farming/cultivo de sequía Método de cultivo que usaban los agricultores de las Planicies en la década de 1890 para cosechar determinados productos con menos agua. **665**

due process/proceso debido Aplicación justa de la ley. **289**

duties/aranceles Impuestos pagados por la importación de bienes. **127**

Eighteenth Amendment/Decimoctava enmienda (1919) Enmienda constitucional que prohibía la producción, venta y transporte de bebidas alcohólicas en Estados Unidos. Esta enmienda fue rechazada en 1933. **722**

elastic clause/cláusula elástica Artículo I, Sección 8 de la Constitución en la que se otorga al Congreso autoridad para ampliar sus poderes delegados en asuntos no especificados en la Carta Magna. **257**

El Camino Real/El camino real o "Camino del rey", construido por los colonizadores españoles para comunicar las comunidades de la Nueva España. **76**

electoral college/Colegio Electoral Grupo elegido en cada estado para reunir votos en las elecciones presidenciales. El número de electores inscritos en cada estado debe ser proporcional al número de representantes y senadores en el Congreso. En cada estado, los electores deben votar por el candidato elegido por su partido. **301**

emancipation/emancipación Liberación de la esclavitud. **469**

Emancipation Proclamation/Proclamación de Emancipación (1862) decreto emitido por el presidente Abraham Lincoln para liberar a los esclavos en las áreas adheridas a la lucha contra la Unión. Tomó efecto el primero de enero de 1863. **595**

embargo/embargo Prohibición de los tratados de comercio con un país. **345**

Embargo Act/Ley de embargo (1807) Ley que prohibía a los comerciantes estadounidenses realizar intercambios con otros países. **345**

eminent domain/expropiación Poder otorgado al gobierno para tomar propiedades particulares con la finalidad de aumentar su patrimonio. **287**

empresarios/empresarios Personas contratadas por la República mexicana para establecer poblaciones en Texas a principios del siglo XIX. **492**

encomienda **system/Sistema de** *encomienda* Sistema adoptado en Hispanoamérica para que los colonos tuvieran derecho de cobrar impuestos a los indígenas o exigirles trabajo a cambio de protección o la enseñanza de oficios específicos. **74**

energy crisis/crisis energética Situación creada a principios de la década de 1970 por el alza de los precios de los combustibles y la escasez de los mismos. **790**

Enlightenment/Ilustración Era de la razón. Movimiento iniciado en Europa en el siglo dieciocho cuando las personas empezaron a adquirir más conocimientos sobre la naturaleza, la sociedad y el gobierno. **141**

English Bill of Rights/Cesión Inglesa de Derechos (1689) Cambio del poder político de la monarquía británica al parlamento inglés. **125**

entrepreneurs/emprendedores Personas que inician nuevos negocios. **683**

environments/medio ambiente Clima y paisaje donde habitan seres vivos. **6**

Erie Canal/canal de Erie Canal que corre de Albany a Búfalo, en el estado de Nueva York. Su construcción se completó en 1825. **371**

executive branch/poder Ejecutivo División del gobierno federal que incluye al presidente y los departamentos administrativos. Su labor es vigilar la aplicación de las leyes de la nación. **240**

executive order/acción ejecutiva Orden no legislativa emitida por el presidente en circunstancias específicas. Una acción ejecutiva tiene la validez de las leyes del Congreso. **259**

Exodusters/Éxodo Migración de afroestadounidenses del sur al oeste a finales del siglo XIX. **667**

exports/exportaciones Productos que un país vende a otros países. **126**

factors/comisionados Intermediarios que administraron el intercambio entre las plantaciones del sur y sus clientes. **429**

Farmers' Alliances/Alianzas de Agricultores Grupos políticos formados por agricultores a finales del siglo XIX para elegir candidatos a cargos públicos que favorecieran sus intereses **702**

fascism/fascismo Sistema de dictadura militar que glorifica a la nación. **776**

Federal Deposit Insurance Corporation/Corporación de Seguros para Depósitos Financieros (FDIC, por sus siglas en inglés) Organización creada por el Congreso durante el periodo de los Cien Días para proteger los ahorros bancarios mediante depósitos de seguridad. **773**

federalism/federalismo Sistema de gobierno en el que el poder es distribuido entre una autoridad centralizada y varios estados. **240**

Federalist Papers/Federalist papers Conjunto de documentos que defienden y explican la Constitución con la finalidad de que los ciudadanos sepan que las leyes federales no deben sobreponerse a las de los estados. **244**

Federalist Party/Partido Federalista Asociación política creada en la década de 1790 siguiendo las ideas de Alexander Hamilton con la finalidad de fortalecer al gobierno federal y fomentar la industria y el intercambio comercial. **320**

Federalists/federales Personas que apoyaban la ratificación de la Constitución. **243**

Federal Reserve Act/Ley de la reserva federal (1913) Ley que creó el sistema bancario nacional para ayudar al gobierno a regular la economía del país. **731**

Federal Trade Commission/Comisión Federal de Comercio Comisión que se creó en 1914 para investigar y prevenir las actividades comerciales y de negocios injustas y desleales. **732**

feudalism/feudalismo Sistema de gobierno creado en la Edad Media en que los habitantes ofrecían lealtad absoluta a un señor feudal a cambio de protección. **19**

Fifteenth Amendment/Decimoquinta enmienda (1870) Enmienda constitucional que otorgaba a los afroestadounidenses el derecho al voto. **628**

54th Massachusetts Infantry/54ᵃᵛᵒ Batallón de Infantería de Massachusetts Regimiento de la Guerra Civil formado por soldados afroestadounidenses que tuvo un papel determinante en el ataque al Fuerte Wagner en Carolina del Sur. **596**

First Battle of Bull Run/Primera Batalla de Bull Run (1861) Primera batalla importante de la Guerra Civil. El ejército confederado obtuvo la victoria. En esta batalla se demostró que ninguno de los bandos ganaría la guerra con facilidad. **586**

First Continental Congress/Primer Congreso Continental (1774) Encuentro de delegados de las colonias en Filadelfia para decidir cómo responderían al cierre del Puerto de Boston, al alza de impuestos y a los abusos de las autoridades británicas. Los delegados hicieron una serie de peticiones al rey George III, incluyendo los derechos que consideraban justos para los colonos. **184**

folktales/cuentos populares Narraciones orales que con frecuencia ofrecen una moraleja. **442**

Fort Sumter/Fuerte Summer Base federal de Charleston, Carolina del Sur, cuyo ataque por los federales en abril de 1861 dio origen a la Guerra Civil. **580**

forty-niners/gambusinos Buscadores de oro que emigraron a California durante la fiebre del oro. **534**

Fourteenth Amendment/Decimocuarta enmienda (1866) Enmienda constitucional que otorgaba derechos completos de ciudadanía a todas las personas nacidas en Estados Unidos o naturalizadas estadounidenses, con excepción de los indígenas. **625**

free coinage/acuñación libre Sistema monetario en el que se acuñaban monedas de oro y plata, y papel moneda cuyo valor estaba respaldado por una cantidad específica de oro o plata. **701**

Freedmen's Bureau/Oficina de liberados Departamento creado por el Congreso en 1865 para ayudar a los pobres del sur del país. **620**

Freedom Rides/Viajes de la libertad (1961) Viajes en autobús de Washington, D.C. a varios estados del sur con los que los partidarios de los derechos civiles desafiaban la segregación ilegal en los autobuses. **786**

free enterprise/libre empresa Sistema económico en el que varios negocios compiten con poca intervención del gobierno. **683**

Freeport Doctrine/Doctrina de la libertad (1858) Declaración hecha por Stephen Douglas durante los debates Lincoln-Douglas en la que fomenta el uso de la soberanía popular para aprobar o rechazar la esclavitud. **568**

Free-Soil Party/Partido de la libertad de suelo Asociación política formada en 1848 por habitantes de los estados del norte que apoyaban la abolición de la esclavitud y que habían abandonado al Partido de Whig y al Partido Demócrata porque ninguno de los dos apoyaba esta causa. **553**

French Revolution/Revolución francesa Rebelión francesa iniciada en 1789 en que la población francesa se rebeló ante la monarquía y tomó el país para convertirlo en una república. **310**

Fugitive Slave Act/Ley de esclavos fugitivos (1850) Ley que calificaba como un crimen ayudar a un esclavo a escapar de su amo, además de permitir la captura de esclavos fugitivos incluso en zonas donde la esclavitud era ilegal para devolverlos a sus dueños. **556**

Fundamental Orders of Connecticut/Decretos Fundamentales de Connecticut (1639) Primeros principios del recién creado gobierno de Estados Unidos presentados por escrito. **108**

Compra de Gadsen/Gadsden Purchase (1853) Compra por parte del gobierno de Estados Unidos de territorio mexicano que incluía la región ocupada actualmente por Arizona y Nuevo México. **526**

General Amnesty Act of 1872/Ley general de amnistía de 1872 Ley que rechazaba la Sección III de la decimocuarta enmienda en la que se prohibía a los confederados ejercer cualquier cargo público. **632**

Gettysburg Address/Discurso de Gettysburg (1863) Discurso presentado por Abraham Lincoln en el que alababa la valentía de las tropas de la Unión y renovaba su compromiso de triunfo en la Guerra Civil. **602**

Ghost Dance/Danza de los Espíritus Movimiento religioso de los indígenas estadounidenses que se extendió en la región de las Planicies en la década de 1880. **652**

Gibbons v. *Ogden/Gibbons* versus *Ogden* (1824) Decreto de la Suprema Corte que establece que la ley federal tiene prioridad sobre las leyes estatales equivalentes; definición ampliada del comercio interestatal. **413**

Glorious Revolution/Revolución gloriosa (1688) Revuelta ocurrida en Inglaterra contra el rey católico James II que condujo a su destitución y al levantamiento de los protestantes Mary y William de Orange como nuevos monarcas. **124**

glyphs/glifos Símbolos o imágenes, especialmente aquellos tallados en una superficie o grabados en relieve. **6**

gold standard/estándar del oro Sistema monetario en el que el valor de una moneda está respaldado por una reserva de oro. **701**

Great Awakening/Gran Despertar Movimiento cristiano que se extendió a todas las colonias estadounidenses en las décadas de 1730 y 1740. **137**

Great Compromise/El Gran Compromiso (1787) Acuerdo redactado durante la Convención Constitucional de Filadelfia en el que se establece que la población de un estado debe determinar su representación en la cámara baja y que cada estado debe tener igual representación en la cámara alta. **238**

Great Depression/Gran Depresión Seria disminución de la actividad económica mundial producida por la caída del mercado de valores estadounidense en 1929. **773**

Great Migration/Gran Migración masiva de habitantes de Inglaterra a tierras americanas de 1630 a 1640. **104**

Great Society/Gran Sociedad Serie de programas sociales presentados por el presidente Lyndon B. Johnson para terminar con la pobreza y el racismo. **786**

guerrilla warfare/guerrilla Tipo de guerra en la que los soldados realizan ataques y escapes rápidos contra el enemigo, por lo general detrás de la trinchera. **211**

Gulf of Tonkin Resolution/Resolución del Golfo de Tonkin (1964) Medida constitucional que dio al presidente Lyndon B. Johnson autoridad para declarar la guerra a Vietnam. **788**

habeas corpus/habeas corpus Protección constitucional contra los arrestos ilegales. **597**

Harlem Renaissance/Renacimiento de Harlem Periodo de realización artística que inició en la década de 1920; lleva el nombre del vecindario de Harlem de la ciudad de Nueva York. **771**

Hartford Convention/Convención de Hartford (1815) Encuentro de federales en Hartford, Connecticut, para protestar por la Guerra de 1812. **355**

Hay-Bunau-Varilla Treaty/Tratado Hay-Bunau-Varilla (1903) Acuerdo entre Estados Unidos y Panamá que dio a Estados Unidos una concesión de 99 años para operar un canal de 10 millas de largo que cruzara el istmo de Panamá. **752**

Hay-Herrán Treaty/Tratado Hay-Terrán (1903) Acuerdo entre Colombia y Estados Unidos que proponía dar a Estados Unidos una concesión de 99 años para operar el canal construido en el istmo de Panamá; este acuerdo fue rechazado por el senado colombiano. **752**

Haymarket Riot/Revuelta de Haymarket (1886) Incidente en el que murieron varios oficiales de policía al explotar una bomba durante una protesta laboral realizada en la Plaza Haymarket de Chicago. **689**

headright/concesión Sistema creado por la London Company en el que se otorgaban 50 acres de tierra a los colonos que pagaran el viaje para establecerse en Virginia. **95**

Holocaust/Holocausto Matanza sistemática con que los nazis eliminaron a casi de 6 millones de judíos y 3 millones de personas de otras religiones durante la Segunda Guerra Mundial. **778**

Homestead Act/Ley Homestead (1862) Ley aprobada por el Congreso para fomentar la colonización del oeste mediante el otorgamiento de tierras a los agricultores. **690**

Homestead strike/Ataque de Homestead (1892) Ataque a la fábrica de acero de Andrew Carnegie en Homestead, Pennsylvania, que originó brotes de violencia entre atacantes y detectives privados. **684**

horizontal integration/integración horizontal Posesión de todos los negocios de una rama particular del comercio. **684**

House of Burgesses/Casa de los burgueses Asamblea electa en Virginia durante la época de la Colonia. **122**

House Un-American Activities Committee/Comité de Actividades Externas (HUAC, por sus siglas en inglés) Comité creado por el Congreso en 1938 para investigar a los ciudadanos acusados de realizar actividades comunistas. **781**

Hudson River school/Escuela del Río Hudson Grupo de artistas creado a mediados del siglo XIX cuya obra muestra diversos paisajes del territorio estadounidense. **388**

Hull House/Hull House Casa de acuerdos fundada por Jane Adams y Ellen Gates Starr en Chicago en el año de 1889. **697**

hunter-gatherers/cazadores recolectores Personas que cazaban animales y recolectaban plantas para satisfacer sus necesidades. **5**

igloos/iglúes Casas construidas con bloques de hielo por los habitantes de las tribus inuit y aleut en el territorio que actualmente ocupan Alaska y Canadá. **12**

immigrants/inmigrantes Personas que abandonan su país para establecerse en un país diferente. **99**

Immigration Restriction League/Liga de Restricción de Inmigración Organización formada en 1894 por nativos con la finalidad de reducir la inmigración; esta ley exigía a los inmigrantes que demostraran que sabían leer y escribir antes de entrar a Estados Unidos. **694**

impeach/inculpar Votar para hacer cargos en contra. **259**

imperialism/imperialismo Práctica en la que una nación extiende su poder mediante la adquisición de territorios para un imperio colonial. **738**

imports/importaciones Productos que un país compra a otras naciones. **126**

impressment/leva Práctica británica que obligaba a los colonos, incluidos los ciudadanos estadounidenses, a servir en las fuerzas armadas británicas, lo cual aumentó las fricciones entre Gran Bretaña y Estados Unidos a principios del siglo XIX. **345**

indentured servants/sirvientes por contrato Colonos que recibían pasajes gratuitos a América del Norte a cambio de trabajo sin salario por varios años. **96**

Indian Removal Act/Ley de expulsión de indígenas (1830) Ley redactada por el Congreso que autorizaba la remoción de indígenas que habitaban al este del río Mississippi. **381**

Indian Territory/territorio indígena Área que abarcaba la mayor parte del actual estado de Oklahoma en la que muchas tribus indígenas del sureste fueron obligadas a establecerse durante la década de 1830. **381**

indict/procesar Acusar formalmente. **287**

Industrial Revolution/Revolución Industrial Periodo de rápido desarrollo debido al uso de maquinaria en la fabricación de productos iniciado a mediados del siglo XVIII. **399**

Industrial Workers of the World/Trabajadores Industriales del Mundo (IWW, por sus siglas en inglés) Organización socialista formada en 1905 para agrupar a los obreros en un gran sindicato. **720**

inflation/inflación Alza de los precios de los bienes y servicios en combinación con la disminución del valor del dinero. 82, **232**

initiative/iniciativa Ley que permite a los votantes proponer nuevas leyes mediante la reunión de firmas en una petición colectiva. **714**

interchangeable parts/partes intercambiables Proceso desarrollado por Eli Whitney en la década de 1790 para que las partes fundamentales de todas las máquinas similares fueran exactamente iguales.

Internet/Internet Extensa red internacional por computadora que conecta negocios, gobiernos, escuelas y personas. **709**

interstate commerce/comercio interestatal Intercambio comercial entre estados. **237**

Interstate Commerce Act/Ley de comercio interestatal (1887) Ley que ofrece reglamentos uniformes de comercio entre estados. **700**

Interstate Commerce Commission/Comisión de Comercio Interestatal (ICC, por sus siglas en inglés, 1887) Comisión creada por la ley de comercio interestatal para que las compañías ferrocarrileras cobraran el precio justo por sus servicios. **700**

Intolerable Acts /Leyes intolerables (1774) Serie de decretos aprobados por el parlamento para castigar a los colonos que participaron en el Motín del Té y mantener su control sobre las colonias. **175**

Iran-Contra affair/Asunto Irán–Contras Escándalo en el que funcionarios de la administración de Ronald Reagan patrocinaron ilegalmente a los rebeldes o contras de Nicaragua con fondos obtenidos mediante la venta secreta de armas a Irán. **793**

ironclads/acorazados buques de guerra fuertemente armados con elementos de hierro. **589**

Iroquois League/Liga de iroqueses Confederación política formada por cinco naciones indígenas del noreste de Estados Unidos (Seneca, Oneida, Mohawk, Cayuga y Onondaga) para tomar decisiones relacionadas con asuntos de guerra y de paz. **16**

isolationism/aislamiento Política en que una nación evita involucrarse en los asuntos de otras naciones. **739**

Jay's Treaty/Tratado de Jay (1794) Acuerdo negociado por John Jay para resolver los problemas entre Gran Bretaña y Estados Unidos en relación con los tratados del oeste, la incautación de barcos estadounidenses por las autoridades británicas y las deudas con los comerciantes británicos. **313**

Jazz Age/época del jazz Término popular para designar la década de 1920. Llamada así por la gran popularidad de la música de jazz entre la población. **771**

Jim Crow laws/Leyes de Jim Crow Leyes que fomentaban la segregación en los estados del sur. **633**

John Brown's raid/Ataque de John Brown (1859) Incidente en el que el abolicionista John Brown y 21 hombres más se apropiaron de un arsenal federal en Harpers Ferry, Virginia, con la esperanza de iniciar una rebelión de esclavos. **569**

joint-stock companies/compañías de acciones combinadas Negocios formados por grupos de personas que realizan inversiones, compartiendo las ganancias y las pérdidas. **33**

judicial branch/poder Judicial División del gobierno federal conformada por las cortes de justicia para interpretar las leyes, castigar los actos criminales y resolver disputas entre estados. **240**

judicial review/revisión judicial Poder de la Suprema Corte para declarar anticonstitucionales las acciones del Congreso. **337**

Judiciary Act of 1789/Ley judicial de 1789 Decreto aprobado por el Congreso para crear el sistema federal de aplicación de justicia. **303**

Kansas-Nebraska Act/Ley de Kansas-Nebraska (1854) Ley que permitía a los votantes de los territorios de Kansas y Nebraska decidir la aprobación o abolición de la esclavitud. **561**

kayaks/kayaks Canoas casi completamente cerradas, con capacidad para una persona, fabricadas con pieles de animales. **12**

Kentucky and Virginia Resolutions/Resoluciones de Kentucky y Virginia (1798-1799) Documentos republicanos que argumentaban el carácter anti-constitucional de las leyes de extranjería y sedición. **322**

kitchen cabinet/gabinete de cocina Grupo informal de consejeros del presidente Andrew Jackson. Fue llamado así porque en ocasiones se reunían en la cocina de la Casa Blanca. **376**

kivas/kivas Cámaras ceremoniales circulares usadas en las actividades religiosas de los indígenas estadounidenses del suroeste. **14**

Knights of Labor/Knights of Labor Primer sindicato del trabajo en Estados Unidos; fundado en 1869 para agrupar a trabajadores de distintas razas, géneros y capacidades. **688**

Know-Nothing Party/Partido "no sé nada" Organización política fundada en 1849 con la finalidad de dificultar a los inmigrantes de otros países la adquisición de la ciudadanía estadounidense y su nombramiento en cargos públicos. **459**

Ku Klux Klan/Ku Klux Klan Sociedad secreta creada en 1866 por habitantes de raza blanca del sur que usaba el terror y la violencia para evitar que los afroestadounidenses obtuvieran derechos civiles. **631**

Land Ordinance of 1785/Ordenanza de territorios de 1785 Decreto aprobado por el Congreso en el que se autorizaba el uso de encuestas y la división de territorios públicos del oeste del país. **226**

legislative branch /poder Legislativo División del gobierno federal que propone iniciativas legales y las somete a aprobación para convertirlas en leyes. **240**

Lend-Lease Act/Ley de préstamos del Gobierno (1941) Ley que permitía a Estados Unidos prestar armas y otros suministros de guerra a la Gran Bretaña y más tarde a la Unión Soviética para combatir a las potencias del eje durante la Segunda Guerra Mundial. **776**

Lewis and Clark expedition/expedición de Lewis y Clark Expedición encabezada por Meriwether Lewis y William Clark que partió en 1804 con la finalidad de explorar el territorio comprado por Estados Unidos a Francia en la región de Louisiana. **342**

libel/libelo declaración falsa, generalmente impresa, que daña la reputación de una persona. **122**

Liberator, The/Liberator, The Periódico abolicionista publicado por William Lloyd Garrison a partir de 1831. **470**

limited government/gobierno limitado Principio político que establece que el gobierno debe estar confinado por leyes que limiten su poder. **224**

Lincoln-Douglas debates/debates Lincoln–Douglas Serie de siete debates entre el republicano Abraham Lincoln y el demócrata Stephen Douglas durante la campaña de 1858 para el senado por Illinois. **567**

Line of Demarcation/Línea de demarcación Límite establecido por el papa Alejandro VI en 1493 a aproximadamente 300 millas de las Islas Azores. Según el documento, los territorios no reclamados al oeste del límite pertenecían a España y los del oeste a Portugal. **42**

longhouses/grandes viviendas comunes Edificaciones rectangulares construidas en Irak, en las que habitan varias familias. **16**

loose construction/construcción suelta Interpretación de la Constitución que permite al gobierno federal tomar acciones que la misma carta magna no prohíbe de manera específica. **308**

Lord Dunmore's Proclamation/Proclamación de Lord Dunmore (1775) Declaración emitida por el gobernador real de Virginia con la promesa de otorgar su libertad a los esclavos que participaran en la lucha contra el ejército británico durante la Revolución de Independencia. **199**

Lost Generation/generación perdida Grupo de escritores estadounidenses cuya obra criticaba severamente a la sociedad de la posguerra en rechazo de la destrucción y la muerte provocadas por la Primera Guerra Mundial. **771**

Louisiana Purchase/Compra de Louisiana (1803) Adquisición del territorio localizado entre el río Mississippi y las montañas Rocosas, perteneciente al gobierno francés, que duplicó el tamaño del territorio de Estados Unidos. **340**

Lowell system/sistema Lowell Aprovechamiento de los molinos de agua en la industria textil, medida que dio empleo a muchas mujeres jóvenes solteras en el siglo diecinueve. **405**

Loyalists/leales Colonos que siempre apoyaron la causa británica durante la Revolución de Independencia. **192**

Magna Carta /Carta Magna (1215) Carta real. Acuerdo firmado por el rey John de Inglaterra en el que se otorgaba mayores derechos a los individuos, estableciendo que incluso la nobleza y el rey debían obedecer la ley. **22**

maize/maíz El cultivo más importante de los indígenas estadounidenses en América del Norte y América Central. **6**

manifest destiny/destino manifiesto Creencia de muchos ciudadanos estadounidenses a mediados del siglo XIX que hablaba sobre la expansión de Estados Unidos hacia el océano Pacífico. **516**

manors/feudos Estados de mayor tamaño gobernados por reyes y nobles en la Edad Media. **19**

Marbury* v. *Madison/Marbury versus Madison (1803) Caso de la Suprema Corte que dio origen a las revisiones judiciales. **336**

Marshall Plan/Plan Marshall (1948) Plan estadounidense que ofrecía a los países europeos ayuda económica para reconstruir su economía después de la Segunda Guerra Mundial. **780**

Massacre at Wounded Knee/Matanza de Wounded Knee (1890) Matanza de aproximadamente 150 indios Sioux en Wounded Knee, Dakota del Sur, por parte del ejército de Estados Unidos. Este episodio dio por terminados los enfrentamientos con los indios en las Planicies. **652**

mass production/producción en masa Producción eficiente de grandes cantidades de productos idénticos. **402**

Mayflower Compact/Síntesis del Mayflower (1620) Documento redactado por los colonizadores británicos que establecía los principios para gobernarse a sí mismos. **99**

McCulloch* v. *Maryland/McCulloch versus Maryland (1819) Caso de la Suprema Corte que declaraba que el Segundo Banco de la Nación era una empresa constitucional y que al ser una institución federal Maryland no podía intervenir en sus operaciones. **377**

McKinley Tariff/Arancel McKinley (1890) Ley que permitía a cualquier país vender azúcar a Estados Unidos sin pagar aranceles. **740**

mercantilism/mercantilismo Creación y conservación de riquezas mediante un control minucioso de intercambios comerciales. **126**

mercenaries/mercenarios Soldados extranjeros contratados por un salario. **201**

Mexican Cession/cesión mexicana (1848) Tierras que México cedió Estados Unidos mediante el Tratado de Guadalupe Hidalgo, después de la guerra entre ambos. La cesión incluía la actual California, Nevada y Utah y la mayor parte de Arizona y Nuevo México, así como parte de Colorado, Texas y Wyoming. **526**

Mexican Revolution/Revolución Mexicana Revolución iniciada en 1910 por Francisco Madero para derrocar al dictador mexicano Porfirio Díaz. **759**

Middle Ages/Edad Media Periodo de la historia europea entre los años 500 y 1500 d. C. **19**

middle class/clase media Estrato social y económico ubicado entre la clase rica y la clase pobre. **460**

Middle Passage/Travesía media Viaje a través del Atlántico para llevar esclavos africanos a América del Norte y a las Indias Occidentales. **129**

migration/migración Desplazamiento de personas de una región a otra. **5**

militarism/militarismo Política de control militar del gobierno. **766**

militia/milicia Fuerzas armadas formadas por civiles que sirven de manera temporal como soldados. **158**

Minutemen/milicianos Miembros de la milicia en la época de la Colonia que estaban preparados para combatir en cualquier momento si la situación lo requería. 185

missions/misiones Poblaciones establecidas por sacerdotes en Hispano América con la finalidad de convertir a los indígenas al catolicismo. 73

Missouri Compromise/Compromiso de Missouri (1820) Acuerdo redactado por Henry Clay en el que se aceptaba a Missouri en la Unión como un estado en el que se permitía la esclavitud y a Maine como estado independiente, además de prohibir la esclavitud en los territorios localizados al norte del meridiano 36°30'. 369

monopoly/monopolio Control económico exclusivo de un negocio o venta de un producto. 35

Monroe Doctrine/Doctrina Monroe (1823) Declaración hecha por el presidente James Monroe en la que se prohibía la colonización de Estados Unidos a partir de entonces, considerando cualquier intento como inicio de hostilidades. 367

Montgomery bus boycott/boicot de autobuses de Montgomery (1955-1956) Boicot realizado por afroestadounidenses a los autobuses que condujo a la creación de leyes contra la discriminación racial en este medio de transporte. 784

Mormon Trail/Camino Mormón Ruta que siguieron los mormones del oeste hasta Utah. 531

Mormons/mormones Miembros de la Iglesia de Jesucristo de los Santos de los Últimos Días. 531

Morrill Act/Ley de Morril (1862) Decreto federal aprobado por el Congreso para dar tierras a los estados del oeste con la finalidad de fomentar la construcción de universidades. 667

Morse code/clave Morse Sistema desarrollado por un asistente de Samuel Morse en el que las letras del alfabeto son representadas por combinaciones de puntos y rayas para transmitir mensajes telegráficos. 416

mountain men/montañeses Hombres contratados por compañías occidentales para atrapar animales y obtener pieles en las montañas Rocosas y otras regiones del oeste de Estados Unidos. 502

muckrakers/muckrackers Periodistas que escribían artículos acerca de la corrupción en los negocios y la política para originar una reforma. 713

mugwumps/mugwumps Reformadores republicanos que abandonaron al partido para apoyar al candidato demócrata Grover Cleveland en las elecciones presidenciales de 1884. 710

national debt/deuda pública Cantidad de dinero que un país debe a sus acreedores. 305

National American Woman Suffrage Association/ Asociación Nacional Estadounidense para el Sufragio Femenino (NAWSA, por sus siglas en inglés) Grupo formado en 1890 por Elizabeth Cady Stanton y Susan B. Anthony para luchar por el derecho al voto de las mujeres. 723

National Association for the Advancement of Colored People/Asociación Nacional para el Progreso de la Gente de Color (NAACP, por sus siglas en inglés) Grupo formado en 1909 por W. E. B. Du Bois y algunos simpatizantes con la finalidad de ofrecer a los afroestadounidenses igualdad económica, educativa y social tomando como inspiración el movimiento del Niagara. 725

National Grange/National Grange Organización social y educativa fundada en 1867 para dar a los agricultores mayor representación política y así mejorar su calidad de vida. 700

nationalism/nacionalismo Creencia de que una nación, idioma o cultura específica es superior a las demás. 690

National Organization for Women/Organización Nacional de Mujeres (National Organization for Women, NOW) Grupo partidario de los derechos femeninos formado en 1966. 788

National Woman's Party/Partido Nacional de la Mujer (NWP, por sus siglas en inglés) Organización fundada por Alice Paul en 1913 que usó métodos controvertidos para obtener el derecho al voto femenino. 723

nativists/nativos Ciudadanos estadounidenses que se oponen a la aceptación de inmigrantes porque sospechaban de ellos y temían perder sus empleos. 459

Nat Turner's Rebellion/Rebelión de Nat Turner (1831) Rebelión de un grupo de esclavos encabezados por Nat Turner en Virginia en un frustrado intento de derrocar y asesinar a los dueños de las plantaciones. 443

naturalized citizen/ciudadano naturalizado Persona nacida en otro país que ha recibido la ciudadanía estadounidense. 291

natural rights/derecho natural Derecho fundamental de una persona, como la libertad de prácticas religiosas e igualdad ante la ley. 224

Navigation Acts/Leyes de navegación (1650-1696) Serie de leyes británicas que regulaban el intercambio comercial entre las colonias con la finalidad de recibir mayores beneficios económicos. 127

Nazis/Nazi Partido Nacional Socialista. Asociación política comandada por Adolf Hitler que asumió el poder de Alemania en la década de 1930. 776

Neutrality Proclamation/Proclamación de neutralidad (1793) Declaración en la que el presidente George Washington anuncia que Estados Unidos no será aliado de ninguna de las naciones europeas en guerra durante la Revolución Francesa. 312

New Deal/New Deal Plan de ayuda económica de Franklin D. Roosevelt para restablecer la economía estadounidense luego de la Gran Depresión. 773

new immigrants/nuevos inmigrantes Inmigrantes que llegaron a Estados Unidos durante y después de la década de 1880; en su mayoría eran del sur y occidente de Europa. 692

New Jersey Plan/Plan Nueva Jersey Propuesta de creación de un gobierno con una sola cámara con representación de cada estado, pero no de la población. La propuesta fue rechazada en la Convención Constitucional de Filadelfia. **238**

Nineteenth Amendment/Decimonovena enmienda (1920) Enmienda constitucional que otorga a la mujer el derecho al voto. **724**

nominating conventions/convenciones de nominación Encuentros en los que los partidos políticos eligen a sus candidatos a la presidencia y la vicepresidencia. Se realizaron por primera vez en la década de 1820. **374**

Non-Intercourse Act/Ley de no interacción (1809) Ley que reemplazaba al ley de embargo, restableciendo el intercambio comercial con todas las naciones, excepto Gran Bretaña y Francia. **346**

North American Free Trade Agreement/Tratado de Libre Comercio de América del Norte (North American Free Agreement, NAFTA) Acuerdo de intercambio comercial entre Estados Unidos, Canadá y México, firmado a principios de la década de 1990. **795**

North Atlantic Treaty Organization/Organización del Tratado del Atlántico Norte, OTAN (North Atlantic Treaty Organization, NATO) Alianza formada en 1949 por Estados Unidos, Inglaterra y 10 países más para defenderse entre sí en caso de sufrir algún ataque. **781**

Northwest Ordinance of 1787/Ordenanza del Noroeste de 1877 Decreto aprobado por el Congreso para establecer una estructura política en el territorio del noroeste y crear un sistema de admisión de nuevos estados. **226**

Northwest Passage/Pasaje del Noroeste Camino inexistente buscado por muchos exploradores a lo largo de América del Norte para cruzar en barco del océano Atlántico al océano Pacífico. **52**

Northwest Territory/territorio del Noroeste Organización del territorio que incluía los actuales estados de Illinois, Indiana, Michigan, Ohio, Wisconsin y parte de Minnesota. Creado por la Ordenanza del Noroeste en 1787. **229**

nullification crisis/crisis de anulación Disputa entre Carolina del Sur y el gobierno federal, a finales de la década de 1820, por el derecho del estado para anular o cancelar un arancel impopular. **377**

old immigrants/primeros inmigrantes Inmigrantes que llegaron a Estados Unidos antes de la década de 1880; en su mayoría eran del norte de Europa. **692**

Olive Branch Petition/Petición de la rama de olivo (1775) Paz solicitada por el Segundo Congreso Continental al rey George III de Gran Bretaña, quien decidió rechazarla. **186**

Open Door Policy/Política de puertas abiertas (1899) Declaración del secretario de estado John Hay de que todas las naciones deben tener el mismo acceso al intercambio comercial con China. **742**

open range/campo abierto Tierras públicas aprovechadas por los rancheros que formaban parte del Cattle Kingdom. **661**

Operation Desert Storm/Operación Tormenta del Desierto (1991) Invasión de Estados Unidos al territorio iraquí con la finalidad de obligar a las tropas iraquíes a retirarse de Kuwait. **793**

Oregon Trail/Camino de Oregón Ruta de 2,000 millas que cruzaba las Grandes Planicies desde Missouri occidental hasta la región de Oregón. **506**

Pacific Railway Acts/Leyes de ferrocarriles del Pacífico (1862, 1864) Par de decretos aprobados por el gobierno federal con la finalidad de otorgar préstamos a las compañías ferroviarias para fomentar la construcción de líneas transcontinentales de ferrocarril. **657**

Paleo-Indians/paleoindígenas Los primeros habitantes de América que llegaron de Asia cruzando el Estrecho de Bering entre el 10,000 y el 3,800 a. C. **5**

Panama Canal/Canal de Panamá Canal de cruce localizado en el istmo de Panamá. Su construcción fue patrocinada por Estados Unidos y se completó en 1914. **754**

Panic of 1837/Pánico de 1837 Crisis financiera de Estados Unidos que provocó una importante depresión económica. **378**

Panic of 1873/Pánico de 1873 Crisis financiera de Estados Unidos que provocó una importante depresión económica y debilitó al Partido Republicano. **632**

pardon/indulto Liberación de un castigo. **259**

Parliament/parlamento Legislatura británica. **121**

patents/patentes Derechos de exclusividad para la fabricación o venta de un invento. **683**

Patriots/Patriotas Colonos estadounidenses que lucharon para independizarse de Gran Bretaña durante la Revolución. **192**

Pendleton Civil Service Act/Ley Pendleton de servicio civil (1833) Ley que estableció un sistema de méritos para otorgar empleos en el gobierno federal. **711**

petition/petición Solicitud formal. 285

Pickett's Charge/Ataque de Pickett (1863) Ataque fallido del ejército confederado, al mando del general George Pickett, durante la Batalla de Gettysburg. **601**

Pilgrims/peregrinos Miembros de una secta separatista puritana que emigró de Inglaterra a principios del siglo XVII para establecerse en América. **99**

Pinckney's Treaty/Tratado de Pinckney (1795) Acuerdo entre Estados Unidos y España que modificó los límites de Florida y facilitó a los barcos estadounidenses el uso del puerto de Nueva Orleáns. **314**

pioneers/pioneros Primeras personas que llegan a poblar una región. **163**

plantations/plantaciones Grandes granjas que por lo general se especializan en un cultivo específico. **74**

planters/hacendados Agricultores acaudalados dueños de grandes plantaciones. **97**

Platt Amendment/Enmienda Platt (1902) Enmienda de la constitución cubana que daba a Estados Unidos el derecho de involucrarse en los asuntos internos y externos de Cuba; esta ley perdió efecto en 1934. **748**

Plessy v. Ferguson/Plesy versus *Ferguson* (1896) Caso en el que la Suprema Corte estableció la doctrina iguales-pero-separados en los lugares públicos. **634**

political action committees/comités de acciones políticas (political action commitees, PACs) Organizaciones que recolectan dinero para distribuirlo entre los candidatos que apoyan los mismos asuntos que los contribuyentes. **294**

political machines/maquinaria política Organizaciones políticas que usaban métodos legales e ilegales para asegurar la victoria de sus candidatos en las elecciones. **708**

political parties/partidos políticos Organizaciones que ayudan a elegir funcionarios para el gobierno e influyen en las políticas gubernamentales. **319**

poll tax/impuesto de voto de boleta Impuesto que las personas pagaban en el pasado para tener derecho al voto. **633**

Pontiac's Rebellion/Rebelión de Pontiac (1763) Ataque frustrado del jefe de la tribu ottawa, Pontiac, y sus aliados, contra los fuertes británicos de la frontera, en un intento por lograr que los colonizadores europeos abandonaran el país. **165**

Pony Express/*Pony Express* Sistema de mensajeros que transportaba el correo entre estaciones de relevo de St. Joseph, Missouri, a San Francisco, California, de 1860 a 1861. **657**

popular sovereignty/soberanía popular Idea de que la autoridad política pertenecía al pueblo. Principio que en una época permitió a los votantes de una región aceptar o rechazar la esclavitud. **240, 553**

Populist Party/Partido Populista Asociación política formada en 1891 para apoyar la libre producción de monedas de plata, reformas laborales y restricciones migratorias, además de asignar al gobierno la propiedad de los sistemas ferroviario, telegráfico y telefónico. **702**

potlatches/ofrendas Ritos ceremoniales en que los invitados de los indígenas del noroeste del país entregaban sus posesiones de valor para ganar respeto. **12**

Pottawatomie Massacre/Matanza de Pottawatomie (1856) Incidente en el que el abolicionista John Brown y siete hombres más asesinaron a los habitantes de Kansas que apoyaban la esclavitud. **563**

Powhatan Confederacy/Confederación de Powhatan Poderosa alianza de indígenas algonquinos al mando de Wahunsonacock. **94**

precedent/precedente Acción o decisión que más tarde sirve como ejemplo. **302**

presidios/presidios Bases militares españolas localizadas en América. **73**

privateers/corsarios Barcos privados autorizados por una nación para atacar a sus enemigos. **312**

Privy Council/Consejo Privado Grupo de consejeros reales que definían las políticas de las colonias de Gran Bretaña en América. **120**

Proclamation of 1763/Proclamación de 1763 Proclamación británica que prohibía el establecimiento en el futuro de colonias al oeste de los montes Apalaches y ordenaba a las colonias ya establecidas en ese lugar que se establecieran en otro lugar. **166**

progressives/progresistas Grupo de reformistas que trabajaban a favor del mejoramiento social y para resolver los problemas políticos a finales del siglo XIX. **712**

prohibition/prohibición Restricción absoluta en la fabricación, distribución y venta de bebidas alcohólicas como decreto federal en la decimoctava enmienda. Esta medida fue rechazada en la vigesimoprimera enmienda. **770**

propaganda/propaganda Historias e imágenes diseñadas para apoyar un punto de vista particular. **172**

proprietors/propietarios Dueños. **110**

prospect/prospector Buscador de oro. **535**

protective tariff/arancel de protección Impuesto sobre artículos importados que eleva su precio con la finalidad de que los habitantes prefieran los productos locales. **307**

Protestant Reformation/Reforma Protestante Movimiento religioso encabezado por Martín Lutero y otros en 1517, con la finalidad de reformar la Iglesia Católica. **78**

Protestants/protestantes Reformistas que protestaban por la realización de ciertas prácticas de la Iglesia Católica. **78**

public works/obras públicas Proyectos de construcción de hospitales, caminos y escuelas realizados con fondos federales. **773**

pueblos/pueblos Poblaciones españolas establecidas en América. **73**

Pullman strike/huelga de Pullman (1894) Paro de labores de los trabajadores de las compañías ferroviarias que impidió la operación de los ferrocarriles hasta que las cortes federales les ordenaron que volvieran a sus empleos. **691**

Pure Food and Drug Act/Ley de alimentos y drogas puros (1906) Ley que prohibía la fabricación, venta y transportación interestatal de alimentos y medicamentos contaminados o mal envasados. **728**

Puritans/puritanos Protestantes que querían reformar la Iglesia Británica. **98**

Quakers/cuáqueros Sociedad de amigos. Secta protestante fundada en la década de 1640 en Inglaterra. Sus integrantes creían que la salvación estaba al alcance de cualquier persona. **113**

Radical Republicans/republicanos radicales Integrantes del Congreso convencidos de que los estados del sur necesitaban realizar grandes cambios antes de ser admitidos en la Unión. **623**

range rights/derechos de pradera Derechos que los ganaderos menores adquirían de los ganaderos mayores sobre el uso del agua en las Planicies. **662**

range wars/guerra de pradera Competencia entre ganaderos grandes y pequeños, y agricultores de las Planicies por el uso del agua en campo abierto. **665**

ratification/ratificación Aprobación formal. **226**

recall/recordatorio Medida que, de ser necesario, permitía a los votantes destituir a un funcionario de su cargo antes de que su periodo de funciones terminara. **714**

Reconquista/Reconquista Lucha de varios siglos para expulsar a los moros de España. La guerra terminó en 1492 con la rendición del reino de Granada. **39**

Reconstruction/Reconstrucción (1865-67) Periodo posterior a la Guerra Civil en el que el gobierno de Estados Unidos trabajó por lograr la unificación de la nación y la reconstrucción de los estados del sur. **617**

Reconstruction Acts /Leyes de reconstrucción (1867-1868) Leyes que declaraban a los estados del sur territorio sujeto a control militar y los obligaba a reformar sus constituciones, aboliendo la decimocuarta enmienda. **626**

Redcoats/casacas rojas Soldados británicos que lucharon contra los colonos en la Revolución Estadounidense. Llamados así por el color rojo brillante de sus uniformes. **186**

Redeemers/redentores Grupo de sureños que ayudaron a los demócratas a recuperar el poder político en el sur durante la Reconstrucción, al tiempo que trataban de limitar los derechos civiles de los afroestadounidenses. **633**

Red Scare/Temor rojo Racha de temor anticomunista que invadió a Estados Unidos después de la Primera Guerra Mundial. **769**

referendum/referéndum Medida que permite a los ciudadanos votar por propuestas de ley. **714**

Renaissance/Renacimiento Resurgimiento del interés por las artes y el aprendizaje en Europa que inició en Italia a mediados del siglo XIV y continuó hasta el siglo XVII. **34**

rendezvous/*rendevouz* Reunión anual realizada por personas que habitaban en las montañas para intercambiar pieles y socializar. **503**

repeal/rechazar Abolir. **170**

representative democracy/democracia representativa Gobierno compuesto por representantes del pueblo. **256**

Republic of Texas/República de Texas Nación independiente de Texas que duró de 1836 a 1848, cuando la región se adhirió a Estados Unidos. **497**

republicanism/republicanismo Apoyo a un sistema de gobierno representativo. **224**

Republican Party/Partido Republicano Asociación política creada en la década de 1850 para detener la expansión de la esclavitud en el oeste. **564**

reservations/reservaciones Territorios federales exclusivos para los indígenas estadounidenses. **650**

reserved powers/poderes reservados Poderes otorgados al gobierno o a ciertos ciudadanos. **257**

revivals/restauraciones Reuniones públicas eclesiásticas en las que los ministros daban sermones ante grandes cantidades de personas. **136**

Rhode Island System/Sistema de Rhode Island Sistema desarrollado por Samuel Slater a mediados del siglo XIX con la finalidad de contratar a familias completas para laborar en la industria textil. **405**

right of deposit/derecho de depósito Derecho de transferir bienes a otro destino sin pagar cuota alguna. **313**

Roosevelt Corollary/corolario Roosevelt (1904) Agregado del presidente Theodore Roosevelt a la Doctrina Monroe; declaraba que Estados Unidos vigilaría los asuntos del hemisferio occidental para evitar que los países europeos intervinieran en la región. **755**

roundup/rodear Arreo del ganado formando un círculo para formar una sola manada. **662**

Rush-Bagot Agreement/Acuerdo de Rush-Bargo (1817) Acuerdo que limitaba el poder naval en los Grandes Lagos a embarcaciones de Estados Unidos y Canadá. **364**

scalawags/*scalawags* Nombre dado a los sureños de raza blanca que apoyaban la Reconstrucción en busca de ganancias económicas. Significa "pícaro", "bribón". **630**

scientific agriculture/agricultura científica Uso de técnicas científicas para mejorar la producción agrícola. **430**

scientific method/método científico Observación y experimentación con sucesos naturales que permiten elaborar teorías con el propósito de predecir otros sucesos o comportamientos. **141**

Scientific Revolution/Revolución científica Periodo de gran aprendizaje iniciado en el siglo XVII, en el que científicos, matemáticos y astrónomos europeos trataron de obtener explicaciones acerca de los misterios del universo. **140**

sea dogs/sabuesos de mar Marineros ingleses patrocinados por la reina Elizabeth I para robar los tesoros de los navíos españoles a finales del siglo XVI. **80**

search warrant/orden de cateo Orden de un juez que permite buscar en el hogar y posesiones de una persona posibles evidencias de un crimen. **286**

secession/secesión Retiro formal de una organización (un país, por ejemplo). **573**

Second Battle of Bull Run/Segunda Batalla de Bull Run (1862) Batalla de la Guerra Civil en la que el ejército Confederado obligó a gran parte de las tropas de la Unión a abandonar el territorio de Virginia. **587**

Second Continental Congress/Segundo Congreso Continental (1775) Reunión de delegados de la colonia realizada en Filadelfia para tomar decisiones acerca de la lucha en Lexington y Concord. **186**

Second Great Awakening/Segundo gran despertar Periodo de evangelización religiosa iniciado en la década de 1790 que se extendió por Estados Unidos en la década de 1830. **452**

Second Industrial Revolution/Segunda Revolución Industrial Periodo de gran crecimiento en la manufactura y en la industria, iniciado a fines del siglo XIX. **680**

sect/secta Grupo religioso. **98**

sectionalism/regionalismo Dedicación a los intereses de una región geográfica y no a los de un país. **553**

segregation/segregación Separación obligada de personas de diferentes razas en lugares públicos. **633**

Selective Service Act/Ley de Servicio Selectivo (1917) Ley que obligaba a los hombres entre 21 y 30 años de edad a registrarse en la lista de disponibilidad de las fuerzas armadas. **767**

Seneca Falls Convention/Convención de Seneca Falls (1848) Primera convención nacional a favor de los derechos de la mujer en la cual se redactó la Declaración de sentimientos. **447**

separation of powers/separación de poderes División de los poderes del gobierno en varias ramas con el propósito de evitar que cualquiera de ellas adopte poderes en exceso. **257**

Separatists/separatistas Grupo radical de puritanos que tenía como propósito eliminar cualquier relación con la Iglesia Británica. **98**

settlement houses/casas de recreo Centros comunitarios creados en la década de 1890 para ofrecer educación, recreación y actividades sociales a inmigrantes y personas de escasos recursos. **697**

Seven Days' Battles/Batallas de los Siete Días (1862) Serie de batallas de la Guerra Civil en las que el ejército Confederado obliga a las tropas de la Unión a retirarse de Richmond, Virginia, la capital confederada. **587**

Seventeenth Amendment/Decimoséptima enmienda (1913) Enmienda constitucional que permite a los votantes estadounidenses elegir directamente a sus senadores. **713**

sharecropping/agricultura compartida Sistema usado en los campos agrícolas después de la Guerra Civil en el que los agricultores trabajaban las tierras de alguien más a cambio de una pequeña porción de la cosecha. **635**

Shays's Rebellion/Rebelión de Shay (1786-87) Levantamiento de los agricultores de Massachusetts, encabezados por Daniel Shay, para protestar por los altos impuestos, el aumento de sus deudas y el cierre de las granjas. **234**

Sherman Antitrust Act/Ley Sherman antimonopolio (1890) Ley que prohibía la creación de monopolios o firmas que restringieran el libre comercio. **686**

Sherman Silver Purchase Act/Ley Sherman de adquisición de plata (1890) Ley que incrementó la cantidad de plata adquirida por el gobierno de Estados Unidos para acuñar monedas. **701**

siege/sitio Bloqueo militar de una ciudad o fuerte. **187**

Siege of Vicksburg/Sitio de Vicksburg (1863) Bloqueo de seis semanas realizado por el ejército de la Unión en Vicksburg para forzar la rendición de esa ciudad durante la Guerra Civil. **592**

Silk Road/ruta de la seda Ruta de intercambio comercial que comunicaba a China con otros mercados asiáticos hasta el Mar Negro. **25**

Sixteenth Amendment/Decimosexta enmienda (1913) Enmienda constitucional que permite al gobierno federal aprobar impuestos directos como el impuesto sobre el trabajo. **731**

slave codes/códigos de esclavos Leyes aprobadas por las colonias para el control de los esclavos. **132**

socialism/socialismo Sistema económico en el que el gobierno o los trabajadores son propietarios de los medios de producción. **720**

Social Security Act/Ley de seguridad social (1935) Ley que ofrecía pensiones y seguro de desempleo a los trabajadores estadounidenses jubilados. **774**

societies/sociedades Grupos de personas que viven juntas y comparten la misma cultura. **6**

sodbusters/cortadores de césped Nombre dado a los agricultores de las Planicies y a las herramientas usadas para cortar los altos pastos de la región. **668**

Sons of Liberty/Hijos de la libertad Sociedades secretas formadas a mediados del siglo XVIII por los colonos para protestar por la creación de nuevos impuestos y para atemorizar a los recaudadores. **169**

Spanish Armada/Armada española Enorme ejército que fue derrotado por las tropas de Inglaterra en 1588. **80**

speculators/especuladores Inversionistas que compran artículos a precios bajos con la esperanza de que aumente su valor. **305**

spheres of influence/esferas de influencia Áreas de un país, especialmente de China, cuyos recursos naturales y comercio eran controlados por otras naciones; práctica común a finales del siglo XIX. **742**

spirituals/espirituales Canciones religiosas cantadas con gran emotividad por los esclavos del sur que combinaban elementos de origen africano y europeo para expresar sus creencias religiosas. **442**

spoils system/sistema de mimos Práctica política de ofrecer empleos a los partidarios de una causa. **376**

Stamp Act/Ley del timbre (1765) Ley aprobada por el Parlamento en la que se obligaba a los colonos a pagar un impuesto de estampilla cada vez que compraran artículos de papel, como periódicos, licencias y documentos legales. **169**

staple crops/cultivos básicos Productos de demanda constante. **134**

states' rights/derechos estatales Creencia de que queda estrictamente limitado el poder del gobierno federal en lo que a los estados se refiere. **379**

steerage/tercera clase Área inferior del casco de un barco en la que muchos inmigrantes viajaban a Estados Unidos para ahorrar dinero. **693**

strait/estrecho Paso angosto y serpenteante en el mar. **48**

strict construction/construcción estricta Interpretación de la Constitución que sólo permite al gobierno federal realizar las acciones expresadas de manera específica en ella. **308**

strike/huelga Negativa de un grupo de empleados a laborar hasta que sus empleadores satisfagan sus demandas. **408**

subsidy/subsidio Pago de una bonificación. **740**

suburbs/suburbios Vecindarios residenciales en las afueras de una ciudad. **696**

suffrage/sufragio Derecho al voto. **224**

Sugar Act/Ley del azúcar (1764) Ley aprobada por el Parlamento británico que establece el pago de impuestos sobre la remolacha y el azúcar importada por las colonias. **167**

supply-side economics/economía lateral Teoría económica que sugiere la disminución de los impuestos para mejorar la economía. **792**

Sutter's Fort/Fuerte Sutter Colonia del norte de California fundada por el inmigrante suizo John Sutter en 1839, que se convirtió en un popular destino para los inmigrantes. **509**

Tariff of Abominations/arancel de abominaciones (1828) Sobrenombre dado a cada nueva tarifa de impuestos rechazada por los habitantes del sur. **376**

tariffs/aranceles Impuestos pagados por los bienes importados o exportados. **233**

Tea Act/Ley del té (1773) Ley aprobada por el Parlamento británico que permitía a la compañía British East India vender té a bajo costo a las colonias sin intermediarios, afectando a los comerciantes locales de té. Esta decisión dio origen al Motín del Té de Boston. **173**

technology/tecnología Herramientas usadas para producir bienes o realizar un trabajo. **401**

Tejanos/tejanos Colonizadores españoles que habitaban en la región que actualmente es el norte de Texas. **490**

telegraph/telégrafo Máquina inventada por Samuel Morse en 1837 para enviar mensajes a grandes distancias mediante impulsos eléctricos transmitidos por cables. **415**

Teller Amendment/Enmienda Teller (1898) Enmienda de la resolución en la que Estados Unidos declaraba que no tenía la intención de invadir y apropiarse de Cuba. **735**

temperance movement/movimiento de abstinencia Reforma social iniciada a mediados del siglo diecinueve apara fomentar la disminución en el consumo de bebidas alcohólicas. **464**

Ten Percent Plan/Plan de diez por ciento Plan de reconstrucción del presidente Abraham Lincoln. Si 10 por ciento de los votantes de un estado que había sido parte de la Confederación tomaba un voto de lealtad a la nación, tenían derecho a formar un nuevo gobierno y ser admitidos en la Unión. **617**

tenements/barracas Casas mal construidas donde vivían en hacinamiento una gran cantidad de inmigrantes. **461**

Tet Offensive/Ofensiva del Tet (1968) Ataque de las tropas de Vietnam del Norte y del Vietcong contra Vietnam del Sur que demostró el interés de éstas por permanecer en la lucha. **789**

Texas longhorn/cuernos largos Raza de ganado vacuno de gran tamaño criada por los ganaderos del oeste de Texas. **660**

textiles/textiles Ropa. **399**

Thirteenth Amendment/Decimotercera enmienda (1865) Enmienda constitucional que abolió la esclavitud. **618**

Three-Fifths Compromise/Compromiso de las tres quintas partes (1787) Acuerdo realizado durante la Convención Constitucional en el que se estableció que tres quintas partes de los esclavos de cada estado serían contados como parte de la población para determinar la representación de ese estado en el Congreso. **239**

Toleration Act of 1649/Ley de tolerancia de 1649 Ley de Maryland que calificaba como crimen la restricción de los derechos religiosos de los cristianos; fue una de las primeras leyes en proteger la libertad de credo religioso que se aprobó en las colonias inglesas. **110**

total war/guerra total Tipo de guerra en la que un ejército destruye la capacidad de lucha su oponente mediante ataques a la población civil, la economía y los recursos militares. **604**

totems/tótems Imágenes de antepasados o animales talladas en troncos de árboles cortados por los indígenas del noroeste de la costa del Pacífico. **12**

town meeting/reunión del pueblo Reunión política en la que los habitantes de una población toman decisiones sobre temas locales. Las primeras reuniones de este tipo se realizaron en Nueva Inglaterra. **122**

Townshend Acts/Leyes Townshend (1767) Leyes aprobadas por el Parlamento para asignar aranceles a algunos de los artículos que importaban los colonos. **171**

trade unions/sindicatos de intercambio comercial Organizaciones formadas por los trabajadores para mejorar su salario y sus condiciones laborales. **408**

Trail of Tears/Sendero de las lágrimas (1838-1839) Marcha de 800 millas que realizó de manera obligada la tribu cheroquí de su territorio natal en Georgia al nuevo territorio, en la que perdieron la vida miles de estos indígenas. **383**

transcendentalism/trascendentalismo Creencia de que las personas podían elevarse sobre los objetos materiales en vida. Movimiento popular entre los escritores y pensadores de Nueva Inglaterra a mediados del siglo XIX. **454**

transcontinental railroad/ferrocarril transcontinental Línea de ferrocarril que cruzaba Estados Unidos de un extremo a otro. Su construcción inició en 1863. **657**

Transportation Revolution/revolución del transporte Rápido crecimiento de la velocidad y comodidad ofrecida por los medios de transporte que en Estados Unidos inició a principios del siglo XIX. **410**

Treaty of Dancing Rabbit Creek/Tratado de Dancing Rabbit Creek (1830) Acuerdo en el que la tribu choctaw cedió más de 10 millones de acres de su territorio a Mississippi y aceptó reubicarse en el nuevo territorio indígena. **382**

Treaty of Fort Laramie/Tratado del Fuerte Laramie (1851) Acuerdo entre el gobierno de Estados Unidos y los indígenas de las Planicies del norte que permitía la creación de poblaciones de blancos con la promesa de proteger el territorio indígena. **644**

Treaty of Ghent/Tratado de Ghent (1814) Acuerdo firmado por Estados Unidos y Gran Bretaña para dar fin a la Guerra de 1812. **355**

Treaty of Greenville/Tratado de Greenville (1795) Acuerdo entre la Confederación Indígena Estadounidense y el gobierno de Estados Unidos que otorgó a la nación la parte sudeste del territorio indígena ubicado al noroeste del país y garantizó la seguridad a los ciudadanos estadounidenses que viajaran por esas tierras. **316**

Treaty of Guadalupe Hidalgo/Tratado de Guadalupe-Hidalgo (1848) Acuerdo que daba por terminada la guerra contra México y daba posesión a Estados Unidos de gran parte del norte del territorio mexicano. **526**

Treaty of Medicine Lodge/Tratado de Medicine Lodge (1867) Acuerdo del gobierno de Estados Unidos y los indígenas de las Planicies en el que éstos aceptaban reubicarse en las nuevas reservaciones. **650**

Treaty of Paris/Tratado de París (1763) Acuerdo de paz que dio por terminada la guerra de los franceses contra los indígenas estadounidenses. **162**

Treaty of Paris of 1783/Tratado de París de 1783 Acuerdo de paz que oficialmente daba por terminada la Guerra Revolucionaria y en el que Gran Bretaña reconocía la soberanía de Estados Unidos. **213**

Treaty of Tordesillas/Tratado de Tordesillas (1494) Acuerdo firmado por España y Portugal en el que ambos países se comprometían a desplazar la línea de demarcación 800 millas al oeste de su posición original en relación con las Islas Azores. **42**

Treaty of Versailles/Tratado de Versalles (1919) Tratado con el que finaliza la Primera Guerra Mundial y en el que se exige a Alemania el pago de varios miles de millones de dólares como gastos de guerra, además de establecer la Liga de las Naciones. **769**

Tredegar Iron Works/Tradegar Iron Works Gran fábrica de acero que operaba a mediados del siglo XIX en Richmond, Virginia. **432**

triangular trade/acuerdo triangular Redes de intercambio de esclavos entre Inglaterra, las colonias estadounidenses y África Occidental. **128**

Triangle Shirtwaist Fire/Incendio de la camisas Accidente ocurrido en una fabrica de la ciudad de Nueva York en el que murieron 146 trabajadores al incendiarse el edificio; este suceso obligó al Congreso a crear nuevos estándares de seguridad en las fábricas. **718**

Truman Doctrine/Doctrina Truman (1947) Política del presidente Harry S. Truman en la que Estados Unidos ofrecía ayuda a cualquier país que decidiera combatir el comunismo y evitar su expansión. **780**

trust/monopolio Acuerdo legal que agrupa a varias compañías bajo el mando de un solo consejo directivo para eliminar la competencia y reglamentar la producción. **684**

Twelfth Amendment/Décimosegunda enmienda (1804) Enmienda constitucional que decretó la creación de casillas separadas para la elección de presidente y vicepresidente. **324**

Twenty-first Amendment/Vigesimoprimera enmienda (1933) Enmienda constitucional que dio por terminada la prohibición mediante la anulación de la Decimoctava enmienda. **770**

unalienable rights/derechos inalienables Derechos básicos de la humanidad, como el derecho a la vida, a la libertad y a la búsqueda de la felicidad. **191**

Uncle Tom's Cabin/La cabaña del tío Tom (1852) Novela abolicionista escrita por Harriet Beecher Stowe que mostró a los habitantes del norte del país la cruda realidad de a esclavitud e hizo que muchos de ellos se adhirieran a la causa del abolicionismo. **557**

Underground Railroad/ferrocarril clandestino Red de personas que ayudó a miles de esclavos a escapar al norte ofreciéndoles transporte y lugares para ocultarse. **472**

Underwood Tariff Act/Ley de reducción de aranceles (1913) Ley que redujo de manera significativa los aranceles e introdujo la primera reforma moderna de impuestos personales. **731**

United Nations/Organización de las Naciones Unidas (ONU) Organización internacional establecida en la Conferencia de Yalta con el propósito de resolver conflictos entre las naciones. **779**

utopian community/comunidad utópica Lugar en el que un grupo de personas trabaja para establecer una comunidad perfecta, como las que se popularizaron en Estados Unidos a finales del siglo XVIII y de principios a mediados del XIX. 454

vaqueros/vaqueros Arrieros mexicanos que vivían en el oeste y se ganaban la vida arreando ganado y caballos. 662

vertical integration/integración vertical Propiedad de los medios implícita en cada paso de un proceso de manufactura. 684

veto/veto Cancelación. 259

viceroy/virrey Gobernador real de Hispanoamérica. 39

Virginia Plan/Plan de Virginia (1787) Plan del gobierno propuesto en la Convención Constitucional para dividir al gobierno en tres ramas: El poder Ejecutivo, el poder Legislativo y el poder Judicial. También establecía que la representación de cada estado en la legislatura debía ser determinada por la población de ese estado. 237

Virginia Statute for Religious Freedom/Estatuto de Virginia para la libertad religiosa (1786) Ley que otorgaba a los habitantes de Virginia la libertad de elegir y practicar cualquier religión, además de expresar sus opiniones religiosas. 224

Voting Rights Act of 1965/Ley de derecho al voto de 1965 Ley que otorgó a todo ciudadano elegible de Estados Unidos el derecho al voto. 787

Wade-Davis Bill/Plan Wade-Davis Plan de reconstrucción que imponía dos condiciones a los estados que habían pertenecido a la Confederación para adherirse a los Estados Unidos: abolir la esclavitud y pedir a los hombres adultos un juramento de lealtad a la nación. Sin embargo, quienes apoyaban a la Confederación no tenían derecho al voto ni podían aceptar cargos públicos. 617

War Hawks/halcones de guerra Integrantes del Congreso que tenían la intención de declarar la guerra a Gran Bretaña a principios del siglo XIX. 348

War on Drugs/guerra contra las drogas Esfuerzo del gobierno para terminar con la venta y consumo ilegal de drogas tanto en Estados Unidos como en el extranjero. 793

Watergate/Watergate Escándalo en el que el presidente Richard M. Nixon autorizó la desintegración del cuartel general del Comité Nacional Demócrata y lo obligó a renunciar a su cargo en 1974. 790

Whig Party/Partido Whig Asociación política formada por oponentes de Andrew Jackson en 1834 para demandar una legislatura más fuerte. 378

Whiskey Rebellion/Rebelión del Whisky (1794) Protesta de pequeños agricultores de Pennsylvania contra los nuevos impuestos cobrados a la producción de whisky y otras bebidas alcohólicas. 316

wigwams/wigwams Pequeñas habitaciones circulares en las que vivían los indígenas estadounidenses del noreste del país. 16

Wilderness Campaign/Campaña en despoblado (mayo-junio de 1864) Serie de batallas entre la Unión y los Confederados al norte y al centro de Virginia que estuvo a punto de agotar los recursos del ejército Confederado. 603

Wilmot Proviso/Propuesta Wilmot (1846) Propuesta de abolición de la esclavitud en el territorio adherido a los Estados Unidos por la cesión mexicana. Fue aprobada por la Cámara de representantes, pero rechazada por el Senado. 553

Wisconsin Idea/Idea de Wisconsin Programa de reformas creado por el gobernador de Wisconsin Robert La Follete a principios del siglo XX que se convirtió en modelo a seguir para otros estados. 714

Woman's Christian Temperance Union/Unión de Mujeres Cristianas por la Abstinencia Organización de mujeres reformistas fundada en 1874 para luchar contra el abuso en el consumo del alcohol. 722

Worcester v. Georgia/Worcester versus Georgia (1832) Caso en que la Suprema Corte declaró a la nación cheroquí como un territorio distinto sobre el que sólo el gobierno federal tenía autoridad. Fue ignorado por el presidente Andrew Jackson y por el estado de Georgia. 383

writs of assistance/mandato de asistencia Garantías que permitían a los recaudadores de impuestos buscar bienes ocultos por los contribuyentes. 171

XYZ affair/asunto XYZ (1797) Incidente en el que funcionarios franceses intentaron obtener sobornos y préstamos de diplomáticos estadounidenses a cambio de que sus barcos no atacaran más a los navíos de Estados Unidos, con lo cual se originó una batalla naval no declarada entre ambos países. 321

Yalta Conference/Conferencia de Yalta (1945) Reunión entre el presidente Frankiln D. Roosevelt, el primer ministro de Gran Bretaña Winston Churchill y el líder soviético Joseph Stalin para planear el futuro al término de la Segunda Guerra Mundial. 779

yellow journalism/amarillismo Publicación de historias sensacionalistas y con frecuencia exageradas en los periódicos para atraer la atención de los lectores. 744

yeomen/pequeños terratenientes pequeños agricultores. 434

Index

Acknowledgments

For permission to reprint copyrighted material, grateful acknowledgment is made to the following sources:

Harvard University Press, Cambridge, Mass.: "World, in "Hounding Me" by Sor Juana Inés de la Cruz from *A Sor Juana Anthology,* translated by A. S. Trueblood. Copyright © 1988 by the President and Fellows of Harvard College.

Harvard University Press and the Trustees of Amherst College: From "This is my Letter to the World" from *The Poems of Emily Dickinson,* edited by Thomas H. Johnson. Copyright © 1951, 1955, 1979, 1983 by the President and Fellows of Harvard College. Published by the Belknap Press of Harvard University Press, Cambridge, Mass.

Simon & Schuster Books for Young Readers, an imprint of Simon & Schuster Children's Division: From *My Brother Sam is Dead* by James Lincoln Collier and Christopher Collier. Copyright © 1974 by James Lincoln Collier and Christopher Collier.

Sources Cited:

Quote by an Aztec messenger and from an Aztec poem from *The Broken Spears: The Aztec Account of the Conquest of Mexico,* Expanded and Updated Edition, edited by Miguel León-Portilla. Published by Beacon Press, Boston, 1992.

Quote by Bernal Díaz from *Cortés and the Downfall of the Aztec Empire* by Jon Manchip White. Published by Carroll & Graff Publishers, Inc., New York, 1971.

From "Across the Plains in a Prairie Schooner" by Catherine Haun from *Ordinary Americans,* edited by Linda R. Monk. Published by Close Up Publishing, 1994.

Quote by 'Abd al-Latif from *The Rise of Colleges: Institutions of Learning in Islam and the West,* translated by G. Makdisi. Published by Edinburgh University Press, 1981.

Quote by Elton Fax from *You Must Remember This: An Oral History of Manhattan from the 1890s to World War II* by Jeff Kisseloff. Published by Harcourt Brace & Company, San Diego, 1989.

From "A Comparison Between Ancient and Modern Ingenuity" by Alessandro Tassoni from *Philosophy, Technology and the Arts in the Early Modern Era* by Paolo Rossi, translated by Salvator Attanasio. Published by HarperCollins Publishers, New York, 1970.

Quote by Bartolomé Las Casas from *The Conquest of America: The Question of the Other* by Tzvetan Todorov, translated by Richard Howard. Published by HarperCollins Publishers, Inc., New York, 1984.

From *Yesterday: A Memoir of a Russian Jewish Family* by Miram Shomer Zunser, edited by Emily Wortis Leider. Published by HarperCollins Publishers, New York, 1978.

From "Recantation of the women of Andover, 1692" from *The History of the Colony and Province of Massachusetts Bay* by Thomas Hutchinson, edited by Lawrence Shaw Mayo. Published by Harvard University Press, Cambridge, 1936.

Quote by Agnolo di Tura from *The Black Death, A Turning Point in History?* edited by William Bowsky. Published by Holt, Rinehart and Winston.

Quote by Shawnee chief Tecumseh from *Indian Wars* by Robert M. Utley and Wilcomb E. Washburn. Published by Houghton Mifflin Company, Boston, 1977.

From *My People the Sioux* by Luther Standing Bear. Published by Houghton Mifflin Company, 1928.

Quotes by Joseph Brant and Little Turtle from *The Ohio Frontier: Crucible of the Old Northwest, 1720-1830* by R. Douglas Hurt. Published by Indiana University Press, Bloomington, 1996.

Quote by Karlsevni from *Voyages To Vinland: The First American Saga,* translated and interpreted by Einar Haugen. Published by Alfred A. Knopf, Inc., New York, 1942.

From "Newsletters Find Haven Online" by Sreenath Sreenivasan from *The New York Times,* July 7, 1997. Published by The New York Times Company, New York, 1997.

From *The Book of the Courtier* by Baldassare Castiglione, translated by George Bull. Published by Penguin Classics, London, 1967.

Quote by Alvise da Cadamosto and Bartholomeu Dias from *The Discoverers* by Daniel J. Boorstin. Published by Random House, Inc., New York, 1983.

Quote by Esther Clark from *Pioneer Women: Voices from the Kansas Frontier* by Joanna L. Stratton. Published by Simon & Schuster, Inc., New York, 1981.

From "The Narrative of the Expedition of Hernando de Soto" by the Gentleman of Elvas, edited by Theodore H. Lewis from *Spanish Explorers: In the Southern United States 1528-1543.* Published by the Texas State Historical Association, Austin, 1990.

From *Ancient North America: The Archaeology of a Continent* by Brian M. Fagan. Published by Thames and Hudson Inc., New York, 1991, 1995.

Quote by Gentleman of Elvas from *The De Soto Chronicles: The Expedition of Hernando de Soto to North America 1539-1543,* vol. 1, translated by James Alexander Robertson, edited by Lawrence A. Clayton, et al. Published by the University of Alabama Press, Tuscaloosa, 1993.

Quote by a Victorio follower from *In the Days of Victorio: Recollections of a Warm Springs Apache* by Eve Ball. Published by University of Arizona Press, Tucson, 1970.

From Castaways: The Narrative of Alvar Núñez Cabeza de Vaca, edited by Enrique Pupo-Walker, translated by Frances M. López-Morillas. Published by the University of California Press, Berkeley, 1993.

From Castaways: The Narrative of Alvar Núñez Cabeza de Vaca, edited by Enrique Pupo-Walker, translated by Frances M. López-Morillas. Published by the University of California Press, Berkeley, 1993.

Quote by Chester Copeland and from interview with Paul and Pauline Griffith from *Like a Family: The Making of a Southern Cotton Mill World* by Jacquelyn Dowd Hall, et al. Published by the University of North Carolina Press, 1987.

From interview with Madge Alford from *Indian-Pioneer Papers,* University of Oklahoma, Norman, OK.

From an Aztec poem from *Aztec Thought and Culture: A Study of the Ancient Nahuatl Mind* by Miguel León-Portilla, translated by Jack Emory Davis. Published by the University of Oklahoma Press, Norman, 1963.

From "Life and Activities in Houston" from *Gustav Dresel's Houston Journal: Adventures in North America and Texas 1837-1841,* translated and edited by Max Freund. Published by the University of Texas Press, Austin, 1954.

Quote by Hernán Cortés from *Hernán Cortés: Letters from Mexico,* translated and edited by Anthony Pagden. Published by Yale University Press, New Haven, 1986.

Photography Credits:

Abbreviated as follows: (t) top, (b) bottom, (l) left, (r) right, (c) center.

Cover and Title Page: Wells Fargo Historical Services.

Table of Contents and Front Matter: Page iv, Jerry Jacka/Courtesy Dennis Lyon Collection; v (tr), The Granger Collection, New York; (b), Musee des Beaux-Arts, Orleans, France/Bridgeman Art Library, London/New York; vi North Wind Picture Archives; vii, The Granger Collection, New York; viii(t, bl), The Granger Collection, New York; viii(bc), The Museum of American Political Life, University of Hartford, West Hartford, CT;), ix(bl), Carl Socolon/The Landis Valley Museum; ix(bc), Library of Congress/PRC Archive; x Illinois Secretary of State; xi(tc), Werner Forman Archive, Pohrt Collection, Plains Indian Museum, BBHC, Cody Wyoming, USA/Art Resource, NY; xiii (t), Independence National Historical Park Collection; xi(tl), Alfred Jacob Miller, Fort Laramie. Beinecke Rare Book and Manuscript Library, Yale University; (b), Culver Pictures; xiv, The Field Museum, Neg #A93851.1c, Chicago; xv, Library of Congress; xvi, Jeffrey Brown/Liaison Agency; xvii (tl), Paul Conklin; (tc), Independence National Historical Park Collection; xix, Sandra Baker/Liaison Agency; xx (cl) Image Copyright © 2003 PhotoDisc, Inc./HRW Photo; (b), Sam Dudgeon/HRW Photo; xxi, Sam Dudgeon/HRW Photo; xxii, The Granger Collection, New York; xxv (br), HRW Photo; xxvi, from THE CIVIL WAR:FORWARD TO RICHMOND, Photograph by Al Freni, ©1983 Time-Life Books, Inc. Courtesy, Troiani Collection; xxviii, Courtesy CNNfyi.com; xxix (tl), Annie Griffiths Belt/CORBIS; (br), Ruth Fremson/AP/Wide World Photos; xxx (bl), ©Image Ideas, Inc.; (tl), Derek P. Redfearn/The Image Bank; (r), The Granger Collection, New York; xxxi (tr), COMEX/DRASSM/Xavier Desmier/Rapho Agency/Liaison Agency; (br), HRW Photo; xxxii (l), Bob Daemmrich/Stock Boston; (tr), The Granger Collection, New York; (br), Ken Cobb/Library of Congress; xxxiii, Laurence Parent; S0(bl, cl), Annie Griffits Belt/CORBIS; (tl), Courtesy the Bostonian Society, The Old State House; (b), The Granger Collection, New York; S1(bl), The Granger Collection, New York; (cr), Library of Congress; (br), National Archives (NARA) negative 30.60.E.082; S2(l), National Geographic Image Collection; (cr), Library of Congress; S2(br), HRW Photo, S3(tl), The Granger Collection, New York; S3(b), S4, S5, S6, S8(c), HRW Photos; S8(br), Peter Newark's Western Americana; S9, S12, S14, S17 HRW Photo.

Unit One: Page 0 The Granger Collection, New York; 1 Tate Gallery, London/Art Resource, NY.

Chapter One: Page 2(tl), Sam Dudgeon/HRW Photo; 2(tr), Werner Forman Archive, British Museum, London/Art Resource, NY; 2(bl), Roger Ressmeyer/CORBIS; 2(bc), Adrian Neal/Stone; 3(tr), Michael Holford; 3(tl), ©Robert Frerck/Woodfin Camp & Associates; 4 George Lepp/Stone; 6 Dean Conger/CORBIS; 7(t), Bodleian Library, Oxford, image MS Arch. Sheldon A.1 folio 37R; 7(b), Alain Keler/Art Resource, NY; 8 Laurence Parent; 9 Superstock; 10 Jerry Jacka/Courtesy Dennis Lyon Collection; 12(t), National Museum of Natural History, Smithsonian Institution, Washington, D.C./Peter Harholdt/SuperStock; 12(tc), Peter Newark's American Pictures; 13 Lawrence Migdale/Photo Researchers, Inc.; 14(tr), Werner Forman/Art Resource, NY; 14(tl), Ray Manley/SuperStock; 15 National Museum of American Art, Washington DC/Art Resource, NY; 16 Library of Congress; 17 Viking ship: The Gokstad Ship, Science Museum, London, UK/Bridgeman Art Library, London/New York; 18 *Vikings attacking a Greenland Eskimo camp,* Nationalmuseet, Copenhagen, Denmark/Bridgeman Art Library, London/New York; 19(br), Greenwich suit of armor, C. 1550, Christie's Images/Bridgeman Art Library, London, UK/New York; 19(bl), Musee Conde, Chantilly/Giraudon; 20 Michael Holford; 21(t), Portrait of William the Conqueror (1027-87)/Philip Mould, Historical Portraits Ltd, London, UK/Bridgeman Art Library, London/New York; 21(b), Nik Wheeler/CORBIS; 23 AKG Photo, London; 24 Ancient Art & Architecture Collection Ltd.; 25 Art Archive; 27 CORBIS.

Chapter Two: Page 30(cl), *Gambling Patoli and the god, Xochipilli* from Codex Maghabecciano, Aztec manuscript, Private Collection/Bridgeman Art Library, London/New York; 30(b), Saint Bride Printing Library; 30(tr), Stock Montage/SuperStock; 31(t), Henry E. Huntington Library & Art Gallery/SuperStock; 32

Ancient Art & Architecture Collection; 33(t), Ancient Art & Architecture Collection; 33(b), British Library/Art Archive; 34(cl), Ancient Art & Architecture Collection Ltd.; 34(b), Scala/Art Resource, NY; 35 The Granger Collection, New York; 37 Boltin Picture Library; 38 The Metropolitan Museum of Art, Gift of J.Pierpont Morgan, 1900. (00.18.2) Photograph copyright 1979 The Metropolitan Museum of Art; 39 Superstock; 40 Robert Frerck/Odyssey/Chicago; 42(l), Bettmann/CORBIS; 42(t), The Granger Collection, New York; 43 The Granger Collection, New York; 44 Victoria & Albert Museum, London/Art Resource, NY; 45 Bettmann/CORBIS; 46 AKG Photo; 47 AKG Photo, London; 48 The Granger Collection, New York; 49 Michael Holford; 50 AKG Photo; 51 Grant Heilman Photography; 52 C.Chesek/J.Becket/Negatives/ Transparencies #4051, Courtesy Department of Library Services, American Museum of Natural History; 53 North Wind Picture Archives; 55(t), Paul Dupuy Museum, Toulouse, France/Lauros-Giraudon, Paris/SuperStock; 55(b), Image Copyright © 2003 PhotoDisc, Inc./HRW Photo.; 56(tl), National Maritime Museum/E.T. Archive; 56(cr), Image Copyright © 2003 PhotoDisc, Inc./HRW Photo.; 57 Richard Weiss/Peter Arnold, Inc.; 58 Image Copyright © 2003 PhotoDisc, Inc./HRW Photo.; 59 ©Scott Camazine/Photo Researchers, Inc.; 61 Sam Dudgeon/HRW Photo.

Unit Two: Page 62 The Granger Collection, New York; 63 *Sioux ball player Ah-No-Je-Nange,* "He who stands on both sides," 19th century litho, Private Collection/Bridgeman Art Library, London/New York. **Chapter Three:** Page 64(tl), Stock Montage/SuperStock; 64(tr), Archivo General de Indias, Sevilla/SuperStock; 64(bl), Mireille Vautier/Picture Quest; 65(tl), The Granger Collection, New York; 65(cr), James Stevenson/National Maritime Museum; 66 Bettmann/CORBIS; 67(b), "The Taking of Tenochtitlan by Cortes," 1521, British Embassy, Mexico City/Bridgeman Art Library, London/New York; 67(r), Piti Palace, Florence/Art Archive; 69 Bettmann/CORBIS; 70 Private Collection/Bridgeman Art Library, London/New York; 71 The Granger Collection, New York; 72 Scala/Art Resource, NY; 73 Bob Daemmrich Photo, Inc.; 74 AKG Photo, London; 75 Mark Nohl/New Mexico Magazine; 76 Art Resource, NY; 77 North Wind Picture Archives; 78 Scala/Art Resource, NY; 79 The Granger Collection, New York; 80 Bettmann/CORBIS; 81 The Granger Collection, New York; 82(coin), Michael Holford; 82(cup), Boltin Picture Library; 84 American Museum of Natural History/Photo by Lynton Gardiner; 85, 87 Bettmann/CORBIS; 85 The Granger Collection, New York. **Chapter Four:** Page 90(tr), The Granger Collection, New York; 90(tc), The Granger Collection, New York; 90(bl), American Bible Society; 91(t), *Penn's Treaty with the Indians* (1771-72) by Benjamin West, oil on canvas, Courtesy of the Museum of American Art of the Pennsylvania Academy of the Fine Arts Philadelphia. Gift of Mrs. Sarah Harrison (The Joseph Harrison, Jr. Collection); 91(tr), Layne Kennedy/CORBIS; 92 The Granger Collection, New York; 93 Colonial Williamsburg Foundation; 95 Detail from the National Portrait Gallery, Smithsonian Institution, Washington, DC/Art Resource, NY; 96(cl), Archive Photos; 96(bl), Colonial Williamsburg Foundation; 97 North Wind Picture Archives; 98 Detail, *Portrait of King James I and VI of Scotland* by John Whitehead Walton, (1831-85), (after Paul van Somer), The Crown Estate/Institute of Directors, London, UK/Bridgeman Art Library, London/New York; 99 Detail, Courtesy of the Pilgrim Society, Plymouth, Massachusetts; 100 The Granger Collection, New York; 101 Private Collection/Bridgeman Art Library, London/New York; 102, 103 The Granger Collection, New York; 104 North Wind Picture Archives; 107 The Granger Collection, New York; 108 CORBIS; 109 Courtesy St. Ignatius Church; 110 Enoch Pratt Free Library; 111, 112, 113 The Granger Collection, New York; 114 Stock Montage, Inc.; 115 The Granger Collection, New York. **Chapter Five:** Page 118(tr), Peter Newark's American Pictures; 118(bl), Fitzwilliam Museum, University of Cambridge, UK/ Bridgeman Art Library, London/New York; 118(tl), Library of Congress; 119(tl), Stock Montage, Inc.; 119(tr), Science & Society Picture Library; 120 David Muench/CORBIS; 121 State Capitol, Commonwealth of Virginia, Courtesy Library of Virginia, image altered.; 122 ©Daniel MacDonald/Stock Boston; 123, 124, 125 The Granger Collection, New York; 126 Royal Albert Memorial Museum, Exeter, Devon, UK/ Bridgeman Art Library, London/New York; 128 Courtesy of the John Carter Brown Library at Brown University; 130 Hulton Deutsch Collection Ltd./Stone; 131 Maryland Commission on Artistic Property of the Maryland State Archives. MSA SC 1545-1106; 132(tl), The Granger Collection, New York; 132(t), Bettmann/CORBIS; 133 The Granger Collection, New York; 134 Rare Book Department, The Free Library Of Philadelphia; 135 Maryland Historical Society, Baltimore; 137 *George Whitefield Preaching* by Collett/National Portrait Library, London/Bridgeman Art Library, London/New York; 138 The Granger Collection, New York; 139 Culver Pictures; 140 Scala/Art Resource, NY; 141 Culver Pictures; 142(t, b), The Granger Collection, New York; 143 Musee des Beaux-Arts, Orleans, France/Bridgeman Art Library, London/New York; 144 Detail from The Pierpont Morgan Library/Art Resource, NY; 145 Private Collection/Bridgeman Art Library, London/New York; 148(tl), Image Copyright © 2003 PhotoDisc, Inc./HRW Photog.; 148(c), Image Copyright © 2003 PhotoDisc, Inc./HRW Photo; 149 Jas. Townsend & Son, Inc.; 151(b), *The Slave Market* by Amadeo Preziosi, (1816-82), Victoria & Albert Museum/Bridgeman Art Library, London, UK/New York; 151(t), Image Copyright © 2003 PhotoDisc, Inc./HRW Photo; 153 Sam Dudgeon/HRW Photo.

Unit Three: 154 *Patrick Henry Before the Virginia House of Burgesses* (1851) by Peter F. Rothermel. Red Hill, The Patrick Henry National Memorial, Brookneal, Virginia; 155(c), Bettmann/CORBIS. **Chapter Six:** Page 156(tl), Bettmann/CORBIS; 156(tr), The Granger Collection, New York; 156(bl), CORBIS; 157(tl), North Wind Picture Archives; 157(tr), Courtesy the Bostonian Society, The Old State House; 158 Archive Photos; 159 North Wind Picture Archives; 160 *The American Revolution: A Picture Sourcebook,* Dover Publications, Inc.; 161 Medal commemorating the British capture of Quebec, 1759, Private Collection/Bridgeman Art Library, London/New York; 163 The Granger Collection, New York; 164(t), Courtesy of the Hunt Institute for Botanical Documentation, Carnegie Mellon University, Pittsburgh, PA; 164(b), *Chief Pontiac,* attributed to John Mix Stanley, Detroit Historical Society; 165, 166 The Granger Collection, New York; 167 Archive Photos; 168 Deposited by the City of Boston,

Courtesy, Museum of Fine Arts, Boston; 169 Colonial Williamsburg Foundation; 170 Courtesy of the John Carter Brown Library at Brown University; 171 Jas. Townsend & Son, Inc.; 172 CORBIS; 173 Peter Newark's American Pictures; 175 Bequest of Winslow Warren, Courtesy Museum of Fine Arts, Boston MA. Reproduced with Permission. © 2000 Museum of Fine Arts, Boston. All Rights Reserved; 176 Colonial Williamsburg Foundation; 178(t), [neg. 1920.166] ©Collection of The New-York Historical Society; 178(c), HRW Photo Research Library; 179 Archive Photos; 180 Image Copyright © 2003 PhotoDisc, Inc./HRW Photo; 181 Bettmann/CORBIS. **Chapter Seven:** Page 182(tl), Peter Newark's American Pictures; 182(tr), Independence National Historical Park Collection; 182(bl), North Wind Picture Archives; 182(c), Larry Stevens/Nawrocki Stock Photo; 183(tl), SuperStock; 183(tr), Colonial Williamsburg Foundation; 183 Sam Dudgeon/HRW Photo; 184 The Granger Collection, New York; 185(t), Gift of Joseph W. Revere, William B. Revere, and Edward H.R. Revere, Courtesy, Museum of Fine Arts, Boston; 185(b), The Granger Collection, New York; 186 CORBIS; 187 Photograph courtesy of the Concord Museum, Concord, Massachusetts and the Lexington Historical Society, Inc., Lexington, Massachusetts. Photograph by David Bohl; 188 The Granger Collection, New York; 189 Victoria Smith/HRW Photo, Courtesy, Scholastic Inc.; 190(cl), The Granger Collection, New York; 190(bl), Library of Congress/HRW; 191 Archive Photos; 192 Peter Newark's American Pictures; 193 Culver Pictures; 194 Larry Lee/CORBIS; 198 Mount Vernon Ladies' Association; 199(tr), Christie's Images; 199(b), Benninghoff Collection of the American Revolution; 200 The Granger Collection, New York; 201(l, r), Collection of The New-York Historical Society; 202 Anne S.K. Brown Military Collection, Brown University Library; 203 Art Resource, NY; 204 The Granger Collection, New York; 206(tl), Bettmann/CORBIS; 206(cl), The Historic New Orleans Collection, Museum/Research Center, color added; 207 The Granger Collection, New York; 208(tr), Peter Newark's American Pictures; 208(tl), The Granger Collection, New York; 209 Courtesy of The Library of Virginia; 210(b), The Granger Collection, New York; 210(tl), William James Warren/CORBIS; 212 *The Battle of Yorktown* from Janice Meredith by Paul Leicester, Ford, Dodd, Mead & Co., 1899./Delaware Art Museum, Howard Pyle Collection; 213 CORBIS.

Unit Four: 218 Library of Congress; 219 The Granger Collection, New York. **Chapter Eight:** Page 220(tr), SuperStock; 220(c), Johns Hopkins University, Larry Stevens/Nawrocki Stock Photo Inc.; 220(bl), Prado, Madrid/Bridgeman Art Library, London/New York; 221(t), Virginia Museum of Fine Arts, Richmond, VA. Detail of Washington as Statesman at the Constitutional Convention by Junius Brutus Stearns. Gift of Edgar William and Bernice Chrysler Garbisch. Photo: Ron Jennings ©2000 Virginia Museum of Fine Arts; 221(t), Joseph Sohm/Chromosohm Inc./CORBIS; 222 Independence National Historical Park Collection; 223(t), Art Archive, London/SuperStock; 223(cr), Stock Montage, Inc.; 224 The Granger Collection, New York; 225 Rare Books and Manuscripts Division, The New York Public Library, Astor, Lenox and Tilden Foundations; 226 Ted Spiegel; 227 North Wind Picture Archives; 228(t), CORBIS; 228(b), British Library/The Art Archive; 230 Jas. Townsend & Son, Inc.; 231 Courtesy, Winterthur Museum; 232 Eileen Tweedy/The Art Archive; 233(c), The Granger Collection, New York; 233(t), Courtesy of the Massachusetts Historical Society; 234(t), The Granger Collection, New York; 234(l), North Wind Picture Archives; 235 Stock Montage, Inc.; 236 The Granger Collection, New York; 237(b), The Granger Collection, New York; 237(t), Joseph Sohm/Stock, Boston; 238(b), Nebraska State Historical Society; 238(t), Courtesy Winterthur Museum; 239 The Library Company of Philadelphia; 241 National Archives (NARA); 242 Library of Congress; 243 PRC Archive; 244 The Granger Collection, New York; 246, 247 The Granger Collection, New York; 250(t, c), Image Copyright © 2003 PhotoDisc, Inc./HRW Photo; 251 H. Abernathy/H. Armstrong Roberts; 252(t), Image Copyright © 2003 PhotoDisc, Inc./HRW Photog.; 252(bl), Reuters NewMedia Inc./CORBIS; 253(all), Lance Schriner/HRW Photo. **Chapter Nine:** Page 254(tr, tl), The Granger Collection, New York; 254(b), ©Hulton Getty/Liaison Agency; 254(br), Wally McNamee/CORBIS-Sygma; 255(tr), Bob Daemmrich/Stock Boston; 255(tl), Lisa Quinones/Black Star; 255(bl), Woodfin Camp & Associates; 256 Bernard Boutrit/Woodfin Camp & Associates; 257(br), Paul S. Conklin; 257(t), PICTOR; 258 Stock Montage, Inc.; 259(b), Abby Aldrich Rockefeller Folk Art Museum; 260 Collection, the Supreme Court of the United States, courtesy The Supreme Court Historical Society; 261 Paul Conklin; 262 The Granger Collection, New York; 263 H. Armstrong Roberts; 264, 284 Independence National Historical Park Collection; 285 The Granger Collection, New York; 286 Jeffrey Brown/Liaison Agency; 287 Bob Daemmrich Photo, Inc.; 289 Louie Psihoyos/Woodfin Camp & Associates, Inc.; 290 Sandra Baker/Liaison Agency; 291 Paul Sakuma/AP/Wide World Photos; 292 Spencer Grant/PhotoEdit; 293 Jeff Greenberg/PhotoEdit; 294(tl), Joe Marquette/AP/Wide World Photos; 294(bl), Richard B. Levine; 295 Bob Daemmrich/Stock, Boston. **Chapter Ten:** Page 298(tl), The Granger Collection, New York; 298(b), Gianni Dagli Orti/CORBIS; 298(tr), Bettmann/CORBIS; 299(tl), Daniel Huntington 1816-1906, *The Republican Court* 1861, Oil on Canvas, 167.6 x 277.0(66 x 109), The Brooklyn Museum 39.536.1, Gift of the Crescent-Hamilton Athletic Club; 299(t), The Art Archive/Yale University New Haven/Album/Joseph Martin; 300 Courtesy of the John Carter Brown Library at Brown University; 301 The Granger Collection, New York; 302 Bettmann/CORBIS; 303 The Granger Collection, New York; 304 National Portrait Gallery, Smithsonian Institution, Washington, DC, Gift of Henry Cabot Lodge/Art Resource, NY; 305 Museum of American Financial History; 306(tl), The Granger Collection, New York; 306(tr), R. Foulds / Washington Stock Photo; 307 Library of Congress; 308 ©Laurie Platt Winfrey Inc./Woodfin Camp & Associates; 309(tr), Larry Stevens/Nawrocki Stock Photo; 309(tl), The Granger Collection, New York; 310 Mansell Collection/TimePix; 311(cr), Giraudon/Art Resource, NY; 311(t), Giraudon/Art Resource, NY; 312 Michael Nicholson/CORBIS; 313 The Granger Collection, New York; 314 The Historic New Orleans Collection; 315 New York State Historical Association, Cooperstown, New York; 316 The Metropolitan Museum of Art, Gift of

Association, Cooperstown, New York; 316 The Metropolitan Museum of Art, Gift of Edgar William and Bernice Chrysler Garbisch, 1963. (63.201.2); 317 HRW Photo Research Library; 318 ©Laurie Platt Winfrey Inc./Woodfin Camp & Associates; 319 The Granger Collection, New York; 320(b), Sally Anderson-Bruce/The Museum of American Political Life, University of Hartford, West Hartford,CT; 320(t), McAlphin Collection, Miriam and Ira D. Wallach Division of Art, Prints and Photographs, The New York Public Library, Astor, Lenox and Tilden Foundations; 322, 324, 325, 327(t), The Granger Collection, New York; 329 Sam Dudgeon/HRW.

Unit Five: 330 Christie's Images; 331 Courtesy Oregon State Archives, Mural located in Oregon State Capitol by Frank H. Schwartz c. 1938. **Chapter Eleven:** Page 332(tl), North Wind Picture Archives; 332(bl), Giraudon/Art Resource; 332(tr), The Granger Collection, New York; 333(tl), Peter Newark's American Pictures; 333(tr), CORBIS; 334(c), Collection of the American Numismatic Society; 335 *View of the West Front of Monticello and Garden* (1825) by Jane Braddick Peticolas (1791-1852) watercolor on paper, courtesy of the Thomas Jefferson Memorial Foundation, Inc., Photographer: Edward Owen; 336(b), Stock Montage, Inc.; 336(tl), National Archives negative 68-2488-2 G1945-22; 337, 338 North Wind Picture Archives; 339 The Granger Collection, New York; 340 Fred J. Maroon; 341 Charles M. Russel, *Lewis and Clark Expedition*, oil on canvas, 1918, 0137.2267, From the Collection of Gilcrease Museum, Tulsa; 342 North Wind Picture Archives; 343 The Granger Collection, New York; 344 Courtesy of The Mariners' Museum, Newport News, VA; 345 North Wind Picture Archives; 346 ©The Field Museum, Neg #A93851.1c, Chicago; 347(t), The Granger Collection, New York; 347(br), National Portrait Gallery, Smithsonian Institution; gift of Mrs. Herbert Lee Pratt, Jr.; 348 National Portrait Gallery, Smithsonian Institution/Art Resource, NY; 349 HRW Photo Research Library; 350 Courtesy of The Mariners' Museum, Newport News, VA; 351(c), North Wind Picture Archives; 351(cr),Mickey Osterreicher/Black Star; 352 The Granger Collection, New York; 353(br), ©Laurie Platt Winfrey Inc./Woodfin Camp & Associates, Inc.; 353(bl), 354, 355, 359(bl), The Granger Collection, New York; 359(tr, tl), Christie's Images; 359(ad), HRW Photo Research Library; 360 Image Copyright © 2003 PhotoDisc, Inc./HRW Photo. **Chapter Twelve:** Page 362(tr), (Detail) Collection of the New-York Historical Society, neg #34684; 362(br), North Wind Picture Archives; 362(tl), Larry Stevens/Nawrocki Stock Photo; 362(bl), Victoria & Albert Museum, London/Art Resource, NY; 363(t), HRW Photo Research Library; 363(tl), The Granger Collection, New York; 363(tr), The Museum of American Political Life, University of Hartford, West Hartford,CT; 363 Sam Dudgeon/HRW Photo; 364 National Portrait Gallery, Smithsonian Institution, Washington, DC/Art Resource, NY; 365 Historical Society of Pennsylvania, *Fourth of July Celebration in Center Square* by John Lewis Krimmel (Bc 882 K897); 366 National Archives (NARA); 367 ©Laurie Platt Winfrey Inc./Woodfin Camp & Associates, Inc.; 368 © Shelburne Museum, Shelburne, Vermont, detail of the painting *Conestoga Wagon* by Thomas Birch; 369 The Granger Collection, New York; 371 Maryland Historical Society, Baltimore, Maryland; 373 ©Laurie Platt Winfrey Inc./Woodfin Camp & Associates, Inc.; 374 Woodfin Camp & Associates; 375 National Portrait Gallery, Smithsonian Institution, Gift of the Swedish Colonial Society through Mrs. William Hacker/Art Resource, NY; 376 Karen Blier/AFP/CORBIS; 377 [neg. #42459] ©Collection of The New-York Historical Society; 378, 379 The Granger Collection, New York; 380 Bettmann/CORBIS; 381 Peabody Museum-Harvard University/Photograph by Hillel Burger; 382(b), The Granger Collection, New York; 382(cl), Robert D. Rubic/Rare Books and Manuscripts Division, the New York Public Library, Astor, Lenox and Tilden Foundations; 383 WOOLAROC MUSEUM, BARTLESVILLE, OKLAHOMA; 384 North Wind Picture Archives; 385 Patrick Henry, (1736-99), pictured on a decorative pendant, Carnegie Institute, Pittsburgh, PA, USA/Bridgeman Art Library, London/New York; 386 Detail of *The Headless Horseman Pursuing Ichabod Crane*, by John Quidor, 1858, Smithsonian American Art Museum, Washington DC/Art Resource, NY; 387, 388 The Granger Collection, New York; 389 Courtesy Barnes & Noble Publishing; 391 The Granger Collection, New York.

Unit Six: 394, 395 The Granger Collection, New York. **Chapter Thirteen:** Page 396(tl), Culver Pictures; 396(tr), SuperStock; 396(b, c), The Granger Collection, New York; 397(tl), Library of Congress, Washington DC/SuperStock; 397(tr), National Museum of American History, Smithsonian Institution, Washington, D.C.; 398, 399 The Granger Collection, New York; 400, 401 Bettmann/CORBIS; 402 FPG International; 403 *Columned clock* by Seth Thomas (1785-1859), c. 1855/Strike One, London, UK/Bridgeman Art Library, London/New York; 404 American Textile History Museum; 405, 406 The Granger Collection, New York; 407 Bettmann/CORBIS; 408 Library of Congress; 409 Bettmann/CORBIS; 410 Archive Photos; 411 Scala/Art Resource, NY; 414 Peter Newark's American Pictures; 415 Science & Society Picture Library; 416(t), The Granger Collection, New York; 416(b), Bettmann/CORBIS; 417 Smithsonian Institution, Washington, DC; 418(c), Bettmann/CORBIS; 418(b), National Museum of American History 1999/Smithsonian Institution; 419 Bettmann/CORBIS. **Chapter Fourteen:** Page 422(tr), Louisiana State Museum; 422(tl), Kim Neilsen/Smithsonian Institution, Washington, DC/PRC Archive; 422(bl), North Wind Picture Archives; 423(tr), Smithsonian Institution neg. #75-2984; 423(tl), Christie's Images/SuperStock; 424 Colonial Williamsburg Foundation; 425 Courtesy of the Massachusetts Historical Society ; 426 Richard Hamilton Smith/CORBIS; 427 The Granger Collection, New York; 428 PRC Archive; 429 Library of Congress/PRC Archive; 430 Courtesy, The Winterthur Museum: Joseph Downs Collection of Manuscripts and Printed Ephemera; 431 North Wind Picture Archives; 432 New York Public Library; 433, 434(t), The Granger Collection, New York; 434(b), Culver Pictures, Inc.; 436 Private Collection/Bridgeman Art Library, London/SuperStock; 437 Courtesy of the Charleston Museum, Charleston, South Carolina; 438 CORBIS; 439 Stock Montage, Inc.; 440(t), Detail of John Antrobus, *Plantation Burial* (1860), oil on canvas, The Historic New Orleans Collection; 440(bc), Chicago Historical Society, X.1354; 440(b), Louisiana State Museum; 441 Private Collection, Photograph Courtesy of Kennedy Galleries, NY; 442 North Wind Picture Archives; 443 The Granger Collection, New

York; 446(t, c), Image Copyright © 2003 PhotoDisc, Inc./HRW Photo; 448(b), The Museum of the Confederacy, Richmond, Virginia, Photograph by Katherine Wetzel; 448(t), Culver Pictures; 449 Stock Montage, Inc. **Chapter Fifteen:** page 450(b, tr), The Granger Collection, New York; 450(tl), Courtesy of the Massachusetts Historical Society; 451(tr), HRW Photo by Maria Paraskevas, courtesy Historical Documents; 451(tl), Peter Newark's American Pictures; 451(cl), National Army Museum, Chelsea, UK; 452 Bettmann/CORBIS; 453 The Granger Collection, New York; 453(t), George Goodwin/United Methodist Church; 454 Courtesy of Massachusetts Historical Society; 455 Bettmann/CORBIS; 456 Brown Brothers; 457 Courtesy of the Bostonian Society/Old State House, photo by Mark Sexton; 459 The Granger Collection, New York; 461 North Wind Picture Archives; 462 The Granger Collection, New York; 463(b), Culver Pictures; 463(t), National Library of Medicine / PRC Archive; 464 Archive Photos; 465(tr), The Granger Collection, New York; 465(tl), Winslow Homer, *Country School* (1873), oil on canvas, 1928.56, gift of anonymous donor, Addison Gallery of American Art, Phillips Academy, Andover, MA; 466 Anonymous, *Girls Evening School*, American. Pencil and watercolor, 13 1/2 x 18 1/8 in. Gift of Maxim Karolik for the M. & M. Karolik Collection of American Drawings and Watercolors, 1800-1875. Courtesy, Museum of Fine Arts, Boston.; 467(t), The Granger Collection, New York; 467(c), The Mount Holyoke College Archives and Special Collections; 468 ©Roger-Viollet; 469 Courtesy of the Illinois State Historical Library; 470 Photographs and Prints Division, Schomburg Center for Research in Black Culture, The New York Public Library, Astor, Lenox and Tilden Foundations; 471 The Granger Collection, New York; 472 Victoria Smith/HRW Photo; 473(cr), North Wind Picture Archives; 474, 475 The Granger Collection, New York; 476 Archive Photos; 477 Bettmann/CORBIS; 478 The Granger Collection, New York; 479 HRW Photo; 483 Sam Dudgeon/HRW Photo.

Unit Seven: 484 Emanuel Gottlieb Leutze, *Westward the Course of Empire Takes Its Way*, ca. 1861, oil on canvas, 0126.1615, From the Collection of Gilcrease Museum, Tulsa; 485 Bettmann/CORBIS. **Chapter Sixteen:** Page 486(bl), The Art Archive/National History Museum Mexico City/Dagli Orti; 486(tl), Missouri Historical Society, St. Louis; 486(tr), Joslyn Art Museum, Omaha, Nebraska; 486(c), United Nations; 487(tl), Albert Bierstadt, *Emigrants Crossing the Plains* 1867, Oil on Canvas, A.011.1T: National Cowboy Hall of Fame, Oklahoma City, OK.; 487(cl), The Granger Collection, New York; 487(tr), Texas State Library and Archives Commission; 488 Bettmann/CORBIS; 489 The Granger Collection, New York; 490 Bettmann/CORBIS; 491 Peter Newark's Western Americana; 492 From the Collections of the Fort Bend County Museum Association, Richmond, Texas; 493(br), Daughters of the Republic of Texas Library; 493(t), ©Laurie Platt Winfrey Inc./Woodfin Camp & Associates, Inc.; 494 Bettmann/CORBIS; 495(br), ©Laurie Platt Winfrey Inc./Woodfin Camp & Associates, Inc.; 495(t), *Reading of the Texas Declaration of Independence* by Charles and Fanny Normann, Collection of the Joe Fultz estate, Navasota, Texas/Courtesy of the Star of the Republic Museum; 496 The San Jacinto Museum of History, Houston; 497 The Granger Collection, New York; 498 Texas State Library and Archives Commission; 499 The Granger Collection, New York; 500 Bob Daemmrich Photography; 501(tr), No. 75-576, The UT Institute of Texan Cultures at San Antonio; 501(tl, tc), Texas State Library and Archives Commission; 502 Harcourt Brace Photo; 503(cr), Colorado Historical Society; 503(tr), Joseph Drayton, *Indians and Trappers at Fort Walla Walla, Oregon Territory*, 1841, Oregon Historical Society, Negative number OrHi 959; 504 Culver Pictures; 507 Carl Socolon/The Landis Valley Museum; 508 Collection of the American Numismatic Society; 509(b), The Granger Collection, New York; 509(t), Courtesy of the California History Room, California State Library, Sacramento, California; 510(t), Stock Montage, Inc.; 511 National Museum of American Art, Washington DC/Art Resource, NY. **Chapter Seventeen:** Page 514(t), Library of Congress/PRC Archive; 514(b), Mary Evans Photo Library, England; 514(c), The Metropolitan Museum of Art, The Helena Woolworth McCaan Collection, Winfield Foundation Gift, 1958. (58.52); 515(t), Wells Fargo Bank; 515(cr), Courtesy of the Oakland Museum of California; 515(c), Larry Stevens/Nawrocki Stock Photo; 516 Courtesy Cornell University Library, Ithaca, New York; 517(t), National Museum of American Art, Washington DC/Art Resource, NY; 517(b), Library of Congress; 519, 520 The Granger Collection, New York; 521 Collection of David J. and Janice L. Frent / PRC Archive; 522 Culver Pictures, Inc.; 523 Stock Montage, Inc.; 524 Society of California Pioneers; 525 Texas State Library and Archives Commission; 526 National Archives; 527 National Portrait Gallery, Smithsonian Institution, Washington, DC/Art Resource, NY; 528 Courtesy The Bancroft Library, University of California, Berkeley, F855.1 B974s; 529 North Wind Picture Archives; 530 Courtesy of the Witte Museum, San Antonio, Texas; 531 Bettmann/CORBIS; 532(tl), Bettmann/CORBIS; 532(tr), *Handcart Pioneers* by C.C.A. Christensen, © by Intellectual Reserve, Inc. Courtesy of Museum of Church History and Art, Used by Permission.; 533 Courtesy of The Bostonian Society, Old State House; 534 Colorado Historical Society; 536 The Granger Collection, New York; 537, 538 Courtesy of the California History Room, California State Library, Sacramento, California; 539 Peter Newark's American Pictures; 541 The Granger Collection, New York; 542(t), Image Club Graphics ©1997 Adobe Systems; 542(cr), Courtesy *Texas Highways* Magazine; 543 Christie's Images; 544 Image Copyright © 2003 PhotoDisc, Inc./HRW Photog.; 545 Vickie Silbert/PhotoEdit; 546 Llewellyn/Pictor Uniphoto; 547 Sam Dudgeon/HRW Photo.

Unit Eight: 548 The Granger Collection, New York; 549 Library of Congress. **Chapter Eighteen:** Page 550(tl, tr), The Granger Collection, New York; 550(bl), AKG London; 551 The Granger Collection, New York; 552 Bettmann/CORBIS; 553(b), Steven Laschever/Museum of American Political Life, University of Hartford, West Hartford, CT; 553(t), Library of Congress; 555 The Granger Collection, New York; 556 Natinonal Archives (NARA); 557(c, t), The Granger Collection, New York; 558 Nancy Gewitz/ Antique Textile Resources; 559 Collection of Janice L. and David J. Frent/ PRC Archive; 561 Kansas State Historical Society; 562(t, b), 563, 564, 565, 566 The Granger Collection, New York; 567 Illinois Secretary of State; 568 National Portrait Gallery, Smithsonian Institution, Art Resource, NY; 569 Library of

Congress; 570 The Metropolitan Museum of Art, Gift of Mr. and Mrs. Carl Stoeckel, 1897. (97.5) ©1982 by The Metropolitan Museum of Art; 572 The Granger Collection, New York; 573 Library of Congress; 575 The Granger Collection, New York. **Chapter Nineteen:** Page 578(tl), The Granger Collection, New York; 578(bl), The Art Archive/Palazzo Pubblico Siena/Dagli Orti; 578(c), Ken Cobb/Library of Congress; 579(tl), National Geographic Image Collection; 579(tr), The Museum of the Confederacy, Richmond, VA. Photography by Katherine Wetzel; 580 Library of Congress; 582 Bettmann/CORBIS; 583(br), The Museum of the Confederacy, Richmond, VA, Photography by Katherine Wetzel; 583(t), The Granger Collection, New York; 584 Library of Congress; 585 from THE CIVIL WAR: FORWARD TO RICHMOND, Photograph by Al Freni, ©1983 Time-Life Books, Inc. Courtesy, Troiani Collection; 586 Bettmann/CORBIS; 587 Virginia Historic Society; 589 Bettmann/CORBIS; 590 U.S. War Dept. General Staff photo/National Archives (NARA) negative 165SB75/LCB81841055; 591 Bettmann/CORBIS; 593 Woodfin Camp & Associates; 594 North Wind Picture Archives; 596 The Historical Society of Pennsylvania; 597 The Granger Collection, New York; 598 National Portrait Gallery, Smithsonian Institution, Washington DC/Art Resource, NY; 599 Bettmann/CORBIS; 600 Anne S. Brown Military Collection, Brown University; 601 State Museum of Pennsylvania; 602 Virginia Historical Society; 603 Collection of the Mercer Museum of The Bucks County Historical Society; 604(tl), Lloyd Ostendorf Collection; 604(t), Atlanta History Center; 605 Tom Lovell/National Geographic Image Collection (detail); 606 Library of Congress; 607 North Wind Picture Archives; 610(tl), National Archives (NARA), negative 615.00A.004; 610(tr), Image Copyright © 2003 PhotoDisc, Inc./HRW Photo; 610(bl), SuperStock; 611 Stock Montage, Inc.; 612 Library of Congress, Manuscripts Division; 613 The Granger Collection, New York. **Chapter Twenty:** Page 614(tl), The Granger Collection, New York; 614(tr), Louisiana Collection, Howard Tilton Memorial Library, New Orleans, LA 70118; 614(bl), The Granger Collection, New York; 615(tl), Library of Congress; 615(tr), H. Armstrong Roberts; 616 The Valentine Museum; 618 Library of Congress; 619 North Wind Picture Archives; 620 © William Taufic/The Stock Market; 621 Peter Newark's Pictures; 622 Stock Montage, Inc.; 623(t), The Granger Collection, New York; 623(b), Bettmann/CORBIS; 624 SuperStock; 625, 627 The Granger Collection, New York; 628 North Wind Picture Archives; 629 Courtesy of South Caroliniana Library, University of South Carolina, Columbia; 630(b), The Granger Collection, New York; 630(t), Private Collection/PRC Archive; 632 U.S. Senate Collection; 633(b), The Granger Collection, New York; 633(t), Bettmann/CORBIS; 635 The Metropolitan Museum of Art , Morris K. Jesup Fund, 1940. (40.40). Photograph © 1985 The Metropolitan Museum of Art; 637 The Granger Collection, New York; 638 Jubilee Singers, Courtesy of Fisk University Library, Special Collections; 639 North Wind Picture Archives; 641 The Granger Collection, New York., 642 © 1995 Jeffery Titcomb/Liaison International; 643 Sam Dudgeon/HRW Photo.

Unit Nine: 644 Denver Public Library Western History Collection; 645 Buffalo Bill Historical Center, Cody, Wyoming. **Chapter twenty-one:** Page 646(tl), Alfred Jacob Miller, Fort Laramie. Beinecke Rare Book and Manuscript Library, Yale University; 646(tr), Courtesy Wells Fargo Bank; 646(bl), AKG Photo, London; 646(c), Michael Freeman/CORBIS; 647(tr), Iris & B. Gerald Cantor Center for Visual Arts at Stanford University; 1998.115/Gift of David Hewes; 647(bl), Mary Evans Photo Library, England; 647(tl), Christie's Images; 648 The Granger Collection, New York; 649 Werner Forman Archive, Pohrt Collection, Plains Indian Museum, BBHC, Cody Wyoming, USA/Art Resource, NY; 650, 651 The Granger Collection, New York; 652 The Field Museum, #A111822-2c; 653 Bettmann/CORBIS; 654 The Granger Collection, New York; 655 E.R. Degginger/Color-Pic, Inc.; 656 The Granger Collection, New York; 657 Peter Newark's Western Americana; 658(b), Peter Newark's Western Americana; 658(t), Union Pacific Historical Collection; 659 Union Pacific Historical Collection; 660 ©Laurence Parent; 661(t), Peter Newark's Western Americana; 661(b), Montana Historical Society, Helena; 662(bl), Peter Newark's Western Americana; 662(cl), Solomon D. Butcher Collection, Library of Congress; 664 ©2003 PhotoDisc; 665 The Granger Collection, New York; 666, 667 Peter Newark's Western Americana; 668 Nebraska State Historical Society; 669 ©Collection of the New-York Historical Society, negative #41800; 670(t-bkgd) ©PI/Photo © David Hardwood/Panoramic Images, Chicago 1998; 670(t), Peter Newark's Western Americana; 670(tr), The Granger Collection, New York; 670 Batavia Depot Museum, Batavia, Illinois/Courtesy, Chicago Historical Society; 671 Library of Congress; 674(b), Colorado Historical Society; 674(t, cr), Image Copyright © 2003 PhotoDisc, Inc./HRW Photo; 676 National Archives (NARA) negative 30.20.E.079; 677 Image Copyright © 2003 PhotoDisc, Inc./HRW. **Chapter Twenty-two:** 678(tl), Property of AT&T Archives. Printed with permission of AT&T; 678(bl), © Collection of the New-York Hisorical Society, negative #51392; 678(bc), Leonard de Selva/CORBIS; 678(tl), The Granger Collection, New York; 679(tl), Library of Congress #LCUSZC4-4637 DLC Detroit Publishing Co. Photo Collection; 679(cr), Chermayeff and Geismar, Inc./MetaForm, Inc.; 679(cl), Bettmann/CORBIS; 680 Archive Photos; 681 The Granger Collection, New York; 682 Science Museum, London, UK/Bridgeman Art Library, London/New York; 683 Culver Pictures, Inc.; 685 National Portrait Gallery, Smithsonian Institution, Washington D.C./Art Resource, NY; 686 Culver Pictures, Inc.; 687 Bettmann/CORBIS; 688 The Granger Collection, New York; 689 Bettmann/CORBIS; 691(tc), Chicago Historical Society, neg. no. IChi-30421; 691(t), Bettmann/CORBIS; 693 Frank Driggs Collection; 694, 695 The Granger Collection, New York; 696 Lake County (IL) Museum/Curt Teich Postcard Archives/Museum/PRC Arcive; 697 National Gallery of Art, Washington, D.C./SuperStock; 698 Kansas State Historical Society; 699 C Squared Studios/Photodisc/Picture Quest; 700(tl), Randy Leffingwell; 700(tl), The Granger Collection, New York; 701(tr), Courtesy of the Museum of the American Numismatic Association; 701(b), Library of Congress; 702 HRW; 703 Bettmann/CORBIS; **Chapter Twenty-three:** 706(tr), The Granger Collection, New York; 706(tl), Collection of Janice L. and David J. Frent/ PRC Archive; 706(b), Ann Ronan / Image Select, Inc.; 707(tr), Bettmann/CORBIS; 707(tl), The Granger Collection, New York; 707(cl), Knudsens Fotosenter, Oslo; 707(br), Sam Dudgeon/HRW; 708 Photo Courtesy of The Newberry Library, Chicago; 709 The Granger Collection, New York; 710 Collection of Janice L. and David J. Frent / PRC Archive; 711 The Granger Collection, New York; 712 Brown Brothers; 713(b), Bettmann/CORBIS; 713(bc), Culver Pictures, Inc.; 714 Library of Congress; 715(bc), Everett/CSU Archives; 715(br), CORBIS; 715(bkgd), SuperStock; 717 Bettmann/CORBIS; 718 The Granger Collection, New York; 719 Brown Brothers; 720 The Granger Collection, New York; 721 Library of Congress; 722, 723 Bettmann/CORBIS; 724 The Granger Collection, New York; 725(cr), Library of Congress; 725(tr), Courtesy of the Crisis Publishing Co., Inc., the publisher of the magazine of the National Association for the Advancement of Colored People. General Research and Reference Division; Schomburg Center for Research in Black Culture; The New York Public Library; Astor, Lenox and Tilden Foundations; 726 Private Collection/PRC Archive; 727 Library of Congress; 728 Theodore Roosevelt Collection, Harvard College Library; 729 Library of Congress/PRC Archive; 730 The Granger Collection, New York; 731 Bettmann/CORBIS; 732 Stock Montage, Inc.; 733 Laurie Platt Winfrey/Woodfin Camp & Associates. **Chapter Twenty-four:** 736(tl), Anchorage Museum of History and Art, Gift of Mr. and Mrs. John M. Sorenson; 736(tr), The Granger Collection, New York; 736(bl), Library of Congress; 737(cl), Brown Brothers; 737(t), Library of Congress; 738 Stock Montage, Inc.; 739 Courtesy of the U. S. Naval Academy Museum/PRC Archive; 740 UPI/Bettmann/CORBIS; 741 Bishop Museum, The State Museum of Natural and Cultural History; 742 Peabody Essex Museum, Salem, Massachusetts; 743 Trustees of the British Museum; 744 The Granger Collection, New York; 745 Library of Congress; 746 National Guard Bureau/PRC Archive; 747 USPS; 749 Keystone-Mast Collection #X6637, UCR/University of California at Riverside/California Museum of Photography; 750 The Granger Collection, New York; 751 U.S. Naval Institute Photo Archives; 752 Courtesy of The Mariners' Museum, Newport News, VA; 754, 755 The Granger Collection, New York; 757 Bettmann/CORBIS; 758, 759(b), The Granger Collection, New York; 759(t), UPI/Bettmann/CORBIS; 761, 763, The Granger Collection, New York; 765 Sam Dudgeon/HRW Photo. **Epilogue:** 766(tl, tr), The Granger Collection, New York; 766(bl), Rykoff Collection/CORBIS; 766(bc), Collection of Colonel Stuart S. Corning. © Rob Huntley/Lightstream/Courtesy of PRC Archive; 767(tl), NASA; 767(tr), Doug Mills/AP/Wide World Photos; 767(br), Sam Dudgeon/HRW; 768 Culver Pictures, Inc.; 769 Culver Pictures, Inc.; 771 The Granger Collection, New York; 772(b), John Held Jr., LIFE Magazine, © TIME Inc./Courtesy of the general libraries, The University of Texas at Austin/HRW photo by Victoria Smith; 772(t), The Granger Collection, New York; 773(tr), Archive Photos; 773(tl), SuperStock; 774 The Granger Collection, New York; 775 National Portrait Gallery, Smithsonian Institution/Art Resource, NY; 776 Library of Congress; 778(tl), The Granger Collection, New York; 778(cl), HRW Photo by Sam Dudgeon, stamps courtesy Kristen Darby; 780 Bettmann/CORBIS; 781 USPS; 782 UPI/Bettmann/CORBIS; 783(b), Archive Photos; 783(t), Woodfin Camp & Associates, Inc.; 784 Smithsonian Institute, neg #9716252; 785 UPI/Bettmann/CORBIS Newsphotos; 786 Brown Brothers; 787 Owen/Black Star; 788 AP/Wide World Photos; 789(t, b), UPI/Bettmann/CORBIS; 790(t), Archive Photos; 790(b), CORBIS/Nathan Benn; 791 Sara Matthews/Swarthmore College Peace Collection; 792(br), UPI/Bettmann/CORBIS; 792(bl), Photri; 793 Wally McNamee/Woodfin Camp & Associates, Inc.; 794 Lester Sloan/Woodfin Camp & Associates, Inc.; 795(t), Michael J. Okonlewski/Liaison Agency; 795(b), Bill Gentile/SIPA Press; 796 Victoria Smith/HRW; 797 CORBIS/Peter Turnley; 798 Ben Margot/AP/Wide World Photos; 799(cr), Doug Mills/AP/Wide World Photos; 799(tl), Eric Gay/AP/Wide World Photos; 800 Daniel Hulshizer/AP/Wide World Photos; 801 Thomas E. Franklin/The Record (Bergen County, NJ)/Corbis SABA; 802 Shannon Stapleton/REUTERS/TimePix; 803 Mark Wilson/Getty Images; 804 Spencer Platt/Getty Images; 805 Lucy Nicholson/AFP/CORBIS; 807 Draper Hill/ © 1974 The Commercial Appeal, Memphis.

Back Matter: Page R0-R1(bkgd), Maps Division, The New York Public Library, Astor, Lenox and Tilden Foundations; R0(tl), Image Copyright © 2003 PhotoDisc, Inc./HRW; R0(tc), Sam Dudgeon/HRW Photo, courtesy Fred Hay; R0(cr), The Granger Collection, New York; R0(b), Independence National Historical Park Collection; R0(l), F. Stuart Westmorland/Allstock/Picture Quest; R0(tr), Image Copyright © 2003 PhotoDisc, Inc./HRW; R1(r), Sandra Baker/Liaison Agency; R1(cl), Colonial Williamsburg Foundation; R1(bcr, bcl), Collection of the American Numismatic Society; R1(bl), Peter Newark's Western Americana; R1(tl), Image Copyright © 2003 PhotoDisc, Inc./HRW; R2-R5(all), R6(all except bc, br), White House Collection, copyright White House Historical Association; (bc, br), The White House; R8 Image copyright ©2003 PhotoDisc Inc.; R9 The Granger Collection, New York; R10-R13(border), Jay Mallin Photos.

Feature Borders:

Young People in History: Pages 1, 63, 155, 219, 331, 395, 485, 549, 645, (cap, marbles, thread, soldier), Images copyright ©2003 PhotoDisc/HRW; (cameo, buttons, umbrella), Sam Dudgeon/HRW.

Connecting To Geography: Pages 56, 59, 148, 151, 178, 181, 250, 253, 358, 361, 446, 449, 542, 545, 610, 613, 674, 677, Victoria Smith/HRW/Courtesy National Geographic/MapQuest.

Illustrator Credits

All maps created by MapQuest.com, Inc.

Unit One: Chapter One: Page 5 (b), Nenad Jakesevic; 28 (t), Kenneth Batelman. **Chapter Two:** Page 54 (t), Kenneth Batelman.

Unit Two: Page 149 (tl), Dave Merrill/Steven Edsey & Sons; 152 (cr), Greathead Studios, Inc. **Chapter Three:** 82 (tl), Dave Merrill/Steven Edsey & Sons; 88 (t), Kenneth Batelman. **Chapter Four:** Page 116 (l), Kenneth Batelman. **Chapter Five:** Page 127 (b), Argosy; 127 (b), Argosy; 146 (l), Kenneth Batelman; 147 (tl), Greathead Studios Inc.

Unit Three: Page 178 (c), Steven Stankiewicz. **Chapter Six:** Page 168 (t), Argosy; 174 (t), Leslie Kell; 176 (t), Kenneth Batelman; 177 (tl), Charles Apple. **Chapter Seven:** Page 214 (l), Kenneth Batelman; 215 (tl), Karen Minot.

Unit Four: Page 252 (t), Karen Minot; 253 (t), Charles Apple. **Chapter Eight:** Page 245 (b), Leslie Kell; 248 (t), Kenneth Batelman. **Chapter Nine:** Page 283 (b), Karen Minot; 288 (t), Karen Minot; 292 (b), Argosy; 296 (t), Kenneth Batelman. **Chapter Ten:** Page 305 (tr), Saul Rosenbaum/Deborah Wolfe Ltd.; 325 (b), Nenad Jakesevic; 326 (l), Kenneth Batelman.

Unit Five: Page 359 (tr), Dave Merrill/Steven Edsey & Sons. **Chapter Eleven:** Page 356 (l), Kenneth Batelman. **Chapter Twelve:** Page 370 (b), Argosy; 372 (t), Nenad Jakesevic; 390 (t), Kenneth Batelman.

Unit Six: Page 449 (t), Karen Minot. **Chapter Thirteen:** Page 412 (b), Nenad Jakesevic; 414 (tl), Leslie Kell; 420 (t), Kenneth Batelman. **Chapter Fourteen:** Page 425 (br), Craig Attebery/Jeff Lavaty Artist Agent; 435 (t), Charles Apple; 444 (t), Kenneth Batelman. **Chapter Fifteen:** Page 460 (t), Argosy; 480 (l), Kenneth Batelman; 481 (tl), Dave Merrill/Steven Edsey & Sons.

Unit Seven: Page 545 (tl), Charles Apple. **Chapter Sixteen:** Page 512 (t), Kenneth Batelman; 513 (tl), MapQuest.com, Inc. **Chapter Seventeen:** Page 518 (b), Argosy; 540 (l), Kenneth Batelman; 535 (b), Nenad Jakesevic.

Unit Eight: Chapter Eighteen: Page 561 (t), Argosy; 571 (t), Saul Rosenbaum/Deborah Wolfe Ltd.; 576 (t), Kenneth Batelman. **Chapter Nineteen:** Page 588 (b), Nenad Jakesevic; 608 (t), Kenneth Batelman; 609 (tl), Charles Apple. **Chapter Twenty:** 640 (t), Argosy; 644 (l), Kenneth Batelman.

Unit Nine: Page 646 (c), Charles Apple; 649 (cl), Charles Apple. **Chapter Twenty-one:** Page 659 (tr), Saul Rosenbaum/Deborah Wolfe Ltd.; 670 (t), Charles Apple; 672 (t), Kenneth Batelman; 673 (tl), Charles Apple. **Chapter Twenty-two:** Page 684 (b), Argosy; 704 (t), Kenneth Batelman; 705 (tl), Charles Apple. **Chapter Twenty-**